# THE GREAT DUNE TRILOGY

*Dune*
*Dune Messiah*
*Children of Dune*

## FRANK HERBERT

GOLLANCZ
LONDON

The right of Frank Herbert to be identified as the author of
this work has been asserted by him in accordance with the
Copyright, Designs and Patents Act 1988.

First published in Great Britain in 1979 by
Gollancz
An imprint of the Orion Publishing Group
Orion House, 5 Upper St Martin's Lane, London WC2H 9EA
An Hachette Livre UK Company

13  15  17  19  20  18  16  14

A CIP catalogue record for this book is available
from the British Library

ISBN 978-0-575-07070-7

Printed in Great Britain by
Clays Ltd, St Ives plc

The Orion Publishing Group's policy is to use papers that
are natural, renewable and recyclable products and
made from wood grown in sustainable forests. The logging
and manufacturing processes are expected to conform to
the environmental regulations of the country of origin.

www.orionbooks.co.uk

# Contents

DUNE 7

DUNE MESSIAH 407

CHILDREN OF DUNE 567

Appendix I 871

Appendix II 879

Appendix III 887

Appendix IV 891

Terminology of the Imperium 895

Cartographic Notes for Map 911

# DUNE

To the people whose labors go beyond ideas into the realm of "real materials"—to the dry-land ecologists, wherever they may be, in whatever time they work, this effort at prediction is dedicated in humility and admiration.

# DUNE

*A beginning is the time for taking the most delicate care that the balances are correct. This every sister of the Bene Gesserit knows. To begin your study of the life of Muad'Dib, then, take care that you first place him in his time: born in the 57th year of the Padishah Emperor, Shaddam IV. And take the most special care that you locate Muad'Dib in his place: the planet Arrakis. Do not be deceived by the fact that he was born on Caladan and lived his first fifteen years there. Arrakis, the planet known as Dune, is forever his place.*

**—from "Manual of Muad'Dib" by the Princess Irulan**

In the week before their departure to Arrakis, when all the final scurrying about had reached a nearly unbearable frenzy, an old crone came to visit the mother of the boy, Paul.

It was a warm night at Castle Caladan, and the ancient pile of stone that had served the Atreides family as home for twenty-six generations bore that cooled-sweat feeling it acquired before a change in the weather.

The old woman was let in by the side door down the vaulted passage by Paul's room and she was allowed a moment to peer in at him where he lay in his bed.

By the half-light of a suspensor lamp, dimmed and hanging near the floor, the awakened boy could see a bulky female shape at his door, standing one step ahead of his mother. The old woman was a witch shadow—hair like matted spiderwebs, hooded 'round darkness of features, eyes like glittering jewels.

"Is he not small for his age, Jessica?" the old woman asked. Her voice wheezed and twanged like an untuned baliset.

Paul's mother answered in her soft contralto: "The Atreides are known to start late getting their growth, Your Reverence."

"So I've heard, so I've heard," wheezed the old woman. "Yet he's already fifteen."

"Yes, Your Reverence."

"He's awake and listening to us," said the old woman. "Sly little rascal." She chuckled. "But royalty has need of slyness. And if he's really the Kwisatz Haderach . . . well . . . ."

Within the shadows of his bed, Paul held his eyes open to mere slits. Two bird-bright ovals—the eyes of the old woman—seemed to expand and glow as they stared into his.

"Sleep well, you sly little rascal," said the old woman. "Tomorrow you'll need all your faculties to meet my gom jabbar."

And she was gone, pushing his mother out, closing the door with a solid thump.

Paul lay awake wondering: *What's a gom jabbar?*

In all the upset during this time of change, the old woman was the strangest thing he had seen.

*Your Reverence.*

And the way she called his mother Jessica like a common serving wench instead of what she was—a Bene Gesserit Lady, a duke's concubine and mother of the ducal heir.

*Is a gom jabbar something of Arrakis I must know before we go there?* he wondered.

He mouthed her strange words: *Gom jabbar . . . Kwisatz Haderach.*

There had been so many things to learn. Arrakis would be a place so different from Caladan that Paul's mind whirled with the new knowledge. *Arrakis—Dune—Desert Planet.*

Thufir Hawat, his father's Master of Assassins, had explained it: their mortal enemies, the Harkonnens, had been on Arrakis eighty years, holding the planet in quasi-fief under a CHOAM Company contract to mine the geriatric spice, melange. Now the Harkonnens were leaving to be replaced by the House of Atreides in fief-complete—an apparent victory for the Duke Leto. Yet, Hawat had said, this appearance contained the deadliest peril, for the Duke Leto was popular among the Great Houses of the Landsraad.

"A popular man arouses the jealousy of the powerful," Hawat had said. *Arrakis—Dune—Desert Planet.*

Paul fell asleep to dream of an Arrakeen cavern, silent people all around him moving in the dim light of glowglobes. It was solemn there and like a cathedral as he listened to a faint sound—the drip-drip-drip of water. Even while he remained in the dream, Paul knew he would remember it upon awakening. He always remembered the dreams that were predictions.

The dream faded.

Paul half awoke to feel himself in the warmth of his bed—thinking . . . thinking. This world of Castle Caladan, without play or companions his own age, perhaps did not deserve sadness in farewell. Dr. Yueh, his teacher, had hinted that the faufreluches class system was not rigidly guarded on Arrakis. The planet sheltered people who lived at the desert edge without caid or bashar to command them: will-o'-the-sand people called Fremen, marked down on no census of the Imperial Regate.

*Arrakis—Dune—Desert Planet.*

Paul sensed his own tensions, decided to practice one of the mind-body lessons his mother had taught him. Three quick breaths triggered the responses: he fell into the floating awareness . . . focusing the consciousness . . . aortal dilation . . . avoiding the unfocused mechanism of consciousness . . . to be conscious by choice . . . blood enriched and swift-flooding the overload regions . . . *one does not obtain food-safety-freedom by instinct alone* . . . animal consciousness does not extend beyond the given moment nor into the idea that its victims may become extinct . . . the animal destroys and does not produce . . .

animal pleasures remain close to sensation levels and avoid the perceptual . . . the human requires a background grid through which to see his universe . . . focused consciousness by choice, this forms your grid . . . bodily integrity follows nerve-blood flow according to the deepest awareness of cell needs . . . all things/cells/beings are impermanent . . . strive for flow-permanence within . . . .

Over and over and over within Paul's floating awareness the lesson rolled.

When dawn touched Paul's window sill with yellow light, he sensed it through closed eyelids, opened them, hearing then the renewed bustle and hurry in the castle, seeing the familiar patterned beams of his bedroom ceiling.

The hall door opened and his mother peered in, hair like shaded bronze held with a black ribbon at the crown, her oval face emotionless and green eyes staring solemnly.

"You're awake," she said. "Did you sleep well?"

"Yes."

He studied the tallness of her, saw the hint of tension in her shoulders as she chose clothing for him from the closet racks. Another might have missed the tension, but she had trained him in the Bene Gesserit Way—in the minutiae of observation. She turned, holding a semiformal jacket for him. It carried the red Atreides hawk crest above the breast pocket.

"Hurry and dress," she said. "Reverend Mother is waiting."

"I dreamed of her once," Paul said. "Who is she?"

"She was my teacher at the Bene Gesserit school. Now, she's the Emperor's Truthsayer. And Paul . . . ." She hesitated. "You must tell her about your dreams."

"I will. Is she the reason we got Arrakis?"

"We did not *get* Arrakis." Jessica flicked dust from a pair of trousers, hung them with the jacket on the dressing stand beside his bed. "Don't keep Reverend Mother waiting."

Paul sat up, hugged his knees. "What's a gom jabbar?"

Again, the training she had given him exposed her almost invisible hesitation, a nervous betrayal he felt as fear.

Jessica crossed to the window, flung wide the draperies, stared across the river orchards toward Mount Syubi. "You'll learn about . . . the gom jabbar soon enough," she said.

He heard the fear in her voice and wondered at it.

Jessica spoke without turning. "Reverend Mother is waiting in my morning room. Please hurry."

The Reverend Mother Gaius Helen Mohiam sat in a tapestried chair watching mother and son approach. Windows on each side of her overlooked the curving southern bend of the river and the green farmlands of the Atreides family holding, but the Reverend Mother ignored the view. She was feeling her age this morning, more than a little petulant. She blamed it on space travel and association with that abominable Spacing Guild and its secretive ways. But here was a mission that required personal attention from a Bene Gesserit-with-the-Sight. Even the Padishah Emperor's Truthsayer couldn't evade that responsibility when the duty call came.

*Damn that Jessica!* the Reverend Mother thought. *If only she'd borne us a girl as she was ordered to do!*

Jessica stopped three paces from the chair, dropped a small curtsy, a gentle flick of left hand along the line of her skirt. Paul gave the short bow his dancing master had taught—the one used "when in doubt of another's station."

The nuances of Paul's greeting were not lost on the Reverend Mother. She said: "He's a cautious one, Jessica."

Jessica's hand went to Paul's shoulder, tightened there. For a heartbeat, fear pulsed through her palm. Then she had herself under control. "Thus he has been taught, Your Reverence."

*What does she fear?* Paul wondered.

The old woman studied Paul in one gestalten flicker: face oval like Jessica's, but strong bones . . . hair: the Duke's black-black but with browline of the maternal grandfather who cannot be named, and that thin, disdainful nose; shape of directly staring green eyes: like the old Duke, the paternal grandfather who is dead.

*Now, there was a man who appreciated the power of bravura—even in death,* the Reverend Mother thought.

"Teaching is one thing," she said, "the basic ingredient is another. We shall see." The old eyes darted a hard glance at Jessica. "Leave us. I enjoin you to practice the meditation of peace."

Jessica took her hand from Paul's shoulder. "Your Reverence, I—"

"Jessica, you know it must be done."

Paul looked up at his mother, puzzled.

Jessica straightened. "Yes . . . of course."

Paul looked back at the Reverend Mother. Politeness and his mother's obvious awe of this old woman argued caution. Yet he felt an angry apprehension at the fear he sensed radiating from his mother.

"Paul. . . ." Jessica took a deep breath. ". . . this test you're about to receive . . . it's important to me."

"Test?" He looked up at her.

"Remember that you're a duke's son," Jessica said. She whirled and strode from the room in a dry swishing of skirt. The door closed solidly behind her.

Paul faced the old woman, holding anger in check. "Does one dismiss the Lady Jessica as though she were a serving wench?"

A smile flicked the corners of the wrinkled old mouth. "The Lady Jessica *was* my serving wench, lad, for fourteen years at school." She nodded. "And a good one, too. Now, *you* come here!"

The command whipped out at him. Paul found himself obeying before he could think about it. *Using the Voice on me,* he thought. He stopped at her gesture, standing beside her knees.

"See this?" she asked. From the folds of her gown, she lifted a green metal cube about fifteen centimeters on a side. She turned it and Paul saw that one side was open—black and oddly frightening. No light penetrated that open blackness.

"Put your right hand in the box," she said.

Fear shot through Paul. He started to back away, but the old woman said: "Is this how you obey your mother?"

He looked up into bird-bright eyes.

Slowly, feeling the compulsions and unable to inhibit them, Paul put his hand into the box. He felt first a sense of cold as the blackness closed around his hand, then slick metal against his fingers and a prickling as though his hand were asleep.

A predatory look filled the old woman's features. She lifted her right hand away from the box and poised the hand close to the side of Paul's neck. He saw a glint of metal there and started to turn toward it.

"Stop!" she snapped.

*Using the Voice again!* He swung his attention back to her face.

"I hold at your neck the gom jabbar," she said. "The gom jabbar, the high-handed enemy. It's a needle with a drop of poison on its tip. Ah-ah! Don't pull away or you'll feel that poison."

Paul tried to swallow in a dry throat. He could not take his attention from the seamed old face, the glistening eyes, the pale gums around silvery metal teeth that flashed as she spoke.

"A duke's son *must* know about poisons," she said. "It's the way of our times, eh? Musky, to be poisoned in your drink. Aumas, to be poisoned in your food. The quick ones and the slow ones and the ones in between. Here's a new one for you: the gom jabbar. It kills only animals."

Pride overcame Paul's fear. "You dare suggest a duke's son is an animal?" he demanded.

"Let us say I suggest you may be human," she said. "Steady! I warn you not to try jerking away. I am old, but my hand can drive this needle into your neck before you escape me."

"Who are you?" he whispered. "How did you trick my mother into leaving me alone with you? Are you from the Harkonnens?"

"The Harkonnens? Bless us, no! Now, be silent." A dry finger touched his neck and he stilled the involuntary urge to leap away.

"Good," she said. "You pass the first test. Now, here's the way of the rest of it: If you withdraw your hand from the box you die. This is the only rule. Keep your hand in the box and live. Withdraw it and die."

Paul took a deep breath to still his trembling. "If I call out there'll be servants on you in seconds and *you'll* die."

"Servants will not pass your mother who stands guard outside that door. Depend on it. Your mother survived this test. Now it's your turn. Be honored. We seldom administer this to men-children."

Curiosity reduced Paul's fear to a manageable level. He heard truth in the old woman's voice, no denying it. If his mother stood guard out there . . . if this were truly a test . . . . And whatever it was, he knew himself caught in it, trapped by that hand at his neck: the gom jabbar. He recalled the response from the Litany against Fear as his mother had taught him out of the Bene Gesserit rite.

"*I must not fear. Fear is the mind-killer. Fear is the little-death that brings total obliteration. I will face my fear. I will permit it to pass over me and through me. And when it has gone past I will turn the inner eye to see its path. Where the fear has gone there will be nothing. Only I will remain.*"

He felt calmness return, said: "Get on with it, old woman."

"Old woman!" she snapped. "You've courage, and that can't be denied. Well, we shall see, sirra." She bent close, lowered her voice almost to a whisper. "You will feel pain in this hand within the box. Pain. But! Withdraw the hand and I'll touch your neck with my gom jabbar—the death so swift it's like the fall of the headsman's axe. Withdraw your hand and the gom jabbar takes you. Understand?"

"What's in the box?"

"Pain."

He felt increased tingling in his hand, pressed his lips tightly together. *How could this be a test?* he wondered. The tingling became an itch.

The old woman said: "You've heard of animals chewing off a leg to escape a trap? There's an animal kind of trick. A human would remain in the trap, endure the pain, feigning death that he might kill the trapper and remove a threat to his kind."

The itch became the faintest burning. "Why are you doing this?" he demanded.

"To determine if you're human. Be silent."

Paul clenched his left hand into a fist as the burning sensation increased in the other hand. It mounted slowly: heat upon heat upon heat . . . upon heat. He felt the fingernails of his free hand biting the palm. He tried to flex the fingers of the burning hand, but couldn't move them.

"It burns," he whispered.

"Silence!"

Pain throbbed up his arm. Sweat stood out on his forehead. Every fiber cried out to withdraw the hand from the burning pit . . . but . . . the gom jabbar. Without turning his head, he tried to move his eyes to see that terrible needle poised beside his neck. He sensed that he was breathing in gasps, tried to slow his breaths and couldn't.

Pain!

His world emptied of everything except that hand immersed in agony, the ancient face inches away staring at him.

His lips were so dry he had difficulty separating them.

*The burning! The burning!*

He thought he could feel skin curling black on that agonized hand, the flesh crisping and dropping away until only charred bones remained.

It stopped!

As though a switch had been turned off, the pain stopped.

Paul felt his right arm trembling, felt sweat bathing his body.

"Enough," the old woman muttered. "Kull wahad! No woman child ever withstood that much. I must've wanted you to fail." She leaned back, with-drawing the gom jabbar from the side of his neck. "Take your hand from the box, young human, and look at it."

He fought down an aching shiver, stared at the lightless void where his hand seemed to remain of its own volition. Memory of pain inhibited every move-ment. Reason told him he would withdraw a blackened stump from that box.

"Do it!" she snapped.

He jerked his hand from the box, stared at it astonished. Not a mark. No sign of agony on the flesh. He held up the hand, turned it, flexed the fingers.

"Pain by nerve induction," she said. "Can't go around maiming potential humans. There're those who'd give a pretty for the secret of this box, though." She slipped it into the folds of her gown.

"But the pain—" he said.

"Pain," she sniffed. "A human can override any nerve in the body."

Paul felt his left hand aching, uncurled the clenched fingers, looked at four bloody marks where fingernails had bitten his palm. He dropped the hand to his side, looked at the old woman. "You did that to my mother once?"

"Ever sift sand through a screen?" she asked.

The tangential slash of her question shocked his mind into a higher aware-ness: *Sand through a screen.* He nodded.

"We Bene Gesserit sift people to find the humans."

He lifted his right hand, willing the memory of the pain. "And that's all there is to it—pain?"

"I observed you in pain, lad. Pain's merely the axis of the test. Your mother's told you about our ways of observing. I see the signs of her teaching in you. Our test is crisis and observation."

He heard the confirmation in her voice, said: "It's truth!"

She stared at him. *He senses truth! Could he be the one? Could he truly be the one?* She extinguished the excitement, reminding herself: *"Hope clouds observation."*

"You know when people believe what they say," she said.

"I know it."

The harmonics of ability confirmed by repeated test were in his voice. She heard them, said: "Perhaps you are the Kwisatz Haderach. Sit down, little brother, here at my feet."

"I prefer to stand."

"Your mother sat at my feet once."

"I'm not my mother."

"You hate us a little, eh?" She looked toward the door, called out: "Jessica!"

The door flew open and Jessica stood there staring hard-eyed into the room. Hardness melted from her as she saw Paul. She managed a faint smile.

"Jessica, have you ever stopped hating me?" the old woman asked.

"I both love and hate you," Jessica said. "The hate—that's from pains I must never forget. The love—that's . . . ."

"Just the basic fact," the old woman said, but her voice was gentle. "You may come in now, but remain silent. Close the door and mind it that no one interrupts us."

Jessica stepped into the room, closed the door and stood with her back to it. *My son lives,* she thought. *My son lives and is . . . human. I knew he was . . . but . . . he lives. Now, I can go on living.* The door felt hard and real against her back. Everything in the room was immediate and pressing against her senses.

*My son lives.*

Paul looked at his mother. *She told the truth.* He wanted to get away alone and think this experience through, but knew he could not leave until he was dismissed. The old woman had gained a power over him. *They spoke truth.* His mother had undergone this test. There must be terrible purpose in it . . . the pain and fear had been terrible. He understood terrible purposes. They drove against all odds. They were their own necessity. Paul felt that he had been infected with terrible purpose. He did not know yet what the terrible purpose was.

"Some day, lad," the old woman said, "you, too, may have to stand outside a door like that. It takes a measure of doing."

Paul looked down at the hand that had known pain, then up to the Reverend Mother. The sound of her voice had contained a difference then from any other voice in his experience. The words were outlined in brilliance. There was an edge to them. He felt that any question he might ask her would bring an answer that could lift him out of his flesh-world into something greater.

"Why do you test for humans?" he asked.

"To set you free."

"Free?"

"Once men turned their thinking over to machines in the hope that this would set them free. But that only permitted other men with machines to enslave them."

"'Thou shalt not make a machine in the likeness of a man's mind,'" Paul quoted.

"Right out of the Butlerian Jihad and the Orange Catholic Bible," she said. "But what the O.C. Bible should've said is: 'Thou shalt not make a machine to counterfeit a *human* mind.' Have you studied the Mentat in your service?"

"I've studied *with* Thufir Hawat."

"The Great Revolt took away a crutch," she said. "It forced *human* minds to develop. Schools were started to train *human* talents."

"Bene Gesserit schools?"

She nodded. "We have two chief survivors of those ancient schools: the Bene Gesserit and the Spacing Guild. The Guild, so we think, emphasizes almost pure mathematics. Bene Gesserit performs another function."

"Politics," he said.

"Kull wahad!" the old woman said. She sent a hard glance at Jessica.

"I've not told him, Your Reverence," Jessica said.

The Reverend Mother returned her attention to Paul. "You did that on remarkably few clues," she said. "Politics indeed. The original Bene Gesserit school was directed by those who saw the need of a thread of continuity in human affairs. They saw there could be no such continuity without separating human stock from animal stock—for breeding purposes."

The old woman's words abruptly lost their special sharpness for Paul. He felt an offense against what his mother called his *instinct for rightness*. It wasn't that the Reverend Mother lied to him. She obviously believed what she said. It was something deeper, something tied to his terrible purpose.

He said: "But my mother tells me many Bene Gesserit of the schools don't know their ancestry."

"The genetic lines are always in our records," she said. "Your mother knows that either she's of Bene Gesserit descent or her stock was acceptable in itself."

"Then why couldn't she know who her parents are?"

"Some do . . . . Many don't. We might, for example, have wanted to breed her to a close relative to set up a dominant in some genetic trait. We have many reasons."

Again, Paul felt the offense against rightness. He said: "You take a lot on yourselves."

The Reverend Mother stared at him, wondering: *Did I hear criticism in his voice?* "We carry a heavy burden," she said.

Paul felt himself coming more and more out of the shock of the test. He leveled a measuring stare at her, said: "You say maybe I'm the . . . Kwisatz Haderach. What's that, a human gom jabbar?"

"Paul," Jessica said. "You mustn't take that tone with—"

"I'll handle this, Jessica," the old woman said. "Now, lad, do you know about the Truthsayer drug?"

"You take it to improve your ability to detect falsehood," he said. "My mother's told me."

"Have you ever seen truthtrance?"

He shook his head. "No."

"The drug's dangerous," she said, "but it gives insight. When a Truthsayer's gifted by the drug, she can look many places in her memory—in her body's memory. We look down so many avenues of the past . . . but only feminine avenues." Her voice took on a note of sadness. "Yet, there's a place where no Truthsayer can see. We are repelled by it, terrorized. It is said a man will come one day and find in the gift of the drug his inward eye. He will look where we cannot—into both feminine and masculine pasts."

"Your Kwisatz Haderach?"

"Yes, the one who can be many places at once: the Kwisatz Haderach. Many men have tried the drug . . . so many, but none has succeeded."

"They tried and failed, all of them?"

"Oh, no." She shook her head. "They tried and died."

---

*To attempt an understanding of Muad'Dib without understanding his mortal enemies, the Harkonnens, is to attempt seeing Truth without knowing Falsehood. It is the attempt to see the Light without knowing Darkness. It cannot be.*

**—from "Manual of Muad'Dib" by the Princess Irulan**

It was a relief globe of a world, partly in shadows, spinning under the impetus of a fat hand that glittered with rings. The globe sat on a freeform stand at one wall of a windowless room whose other walls presented a patchwork of multicolored scrolls, filmbooks, tapes and reels. Light glowed in the room from golden balls hanging in mobile suspensor fields.

An ellipsoid desk with a top of jade-pink petrified elacca wood stood at the center of the room. Veriform suspensor chairs ringed it, two of them occupied. In one sat a dark-haired youth of about sixteen years, round of face and with sullen eyes. The other held a slender, short man with effeminate face.

Both youth and man stared at the globe and the man half-hidden in shadows spinning it.

A chuckle sounded beside the globe. A basso voice rumbled out of the chuckle: "There it is, Piter—the biggest mantrap in all history. And the Duke's headed into its jaws. Is it not a magnificent thing that I, the Baron Vladimir Harkonnen, do?"

"Assuredly, Baron," said the man. His voice came out tenor with a sweet musical quality.

The fat hand descended onto the globe, stopped the spinning. Now, all eyes in the room could focus on the motionless surface and see that it was the kind of globe made for wealthy collectors or planetary governors of the Empire. It had the stamp of Imperial handicraft about it. Latitude and longitude lines were laid in with hair-fine platinum wire. The polar caps were insets of finest cloud-milk diamonds.

The fat hand moved, tracing details on the surface. "I invite you to observe," the basso voice rumbled. "Observe closely, Piter, and you, too, Feyd-Rautha, my darling: from sixty degrees north to seventy degrees south—these exquisite ripples. Their coloring: does it not remind you of sweet caramels? And nowhere do you see blue of lakes or rivers or seas. And these lovely polar caps—so small. Could anyone mistake this place? Arrakis! Truly unique. A superb setting for a unique victory."

A smile touched Piter's lips. "And to think, Baron: the Padishah Emperor believes he's given the Duke your spice planet. How poignant."

"That's a nonsensical statement," the Baron rumbled. "You say this to confuse young Feyd-Rautha, but it is not necessary to confuse my nephew."

The sullen-faced youth stirred in his chair, smoothed a wrinkle in the black leotards he wore. He sat upright as a discreet tapping sounded at the door in the wall behind him.

Piter unfolded from his chair, crossed to the door, cracked it wide enough to accept a message cylinder. He closed the door, unrolled the cylinder and scanned it. A chuckle sounded from him. Another.

"Well?" the Baron demanded.

"The fool answered us, Baron!"

"Whenever did an Atreides refuse the opportunity for a gesture?" the Baron asked. "Well, what does he say?"

"He's most uncouth, Baron. Addresses you as 'Harkonnen'—no 'Sire et Cher Cousin,' no title, nothing."

"It's a good name," the Baron growled, and his voice betrayed his impatience. "What does dear Leto say?"

"He says: 'Your offer of a meeting is refused. I have ofttimes met your treachery and this all men know.'"

"And?" the Baron asked.

"He says: 'The art of kanly still has admirers in the Empire.' He signs it: 'Duke Leto of Arrakis.'" Piter began to laugh. "Of Arrakis! Oh, my! This is almost too rich!"

"Be silent, Piter," the Baron said, and the laughter stopped as though shut off with a switch. "Kanly, is it?" the Baron asked. "Vendetta, heh? And he uses the nice old word so rich in tradition to be sure I know he means it."

"You made the peace gesture," Piter said. "The forms have been obeyed."

"For a Mentat, you talk too much, Piter," the Baron said. And he thought: *I must do away with that one soon. He has almost outlived his usefulness.* The Baron stared across the room at his Mentat assassin, seeing the feature about him that most people noticed first: the eyes, the shaded slits of blue within blue, the eyes without any white in them at all.

A grin flashed across Piter's face. It was like a mask grimace beneath those eyes like holes. "But, Baron! Never has revenge been more beautiful. It is to see a plan of the most exquisite treachery: to *make* Leto exchange Caladan for Dune—and without alternative because the Emperor orders it. How waggish of you!"

In a cold voice, the Baron said: "You have a flux of the mouth, Piter."

"But I am happy, my Baron. Whereas you . . . you are touched by jealousy."

"Piter!"

"Ah-ah, Baron! Is it not regrettable you were unable to devise this delicious scheme by yourself?"

"Someday I will have you strangled, Piter."

"Of a certainty, Baron. Enfin! But a kind act is never lost, eh?"

"Have you been chewing verite or semuta, Piter?"

"Truth without fear surprises the Baron," Piter said. His face drew down into a caricature of a frowning mask. "Ah, hah! But you see, Baron, I know as a Mentat when you will send the executioner. You will hold back just so long as I am useful. To move sooner would be wasteful and I'm yet of much use. I know what it is you learned from that lovely Dune planet—waste not. True, Baron?"

The Baron continued to stare at Piter.

Feyd-Rautha squirmed in his chair. *These wrangling fools!* he thought. *My uncle cannot talk to his Mentat without arguing. Do they think I've nothing to do except listen to their arguments?*

"Feyd," the Baron said. "I told you to listen and learn when I invited you in here. Are you learning?"

"Yes, Uncle." The voice was carefully subservient.

"Sometimes I wonder about Piter," the Baron said. "I cause pain out of necessity, but he . . . I swear he takes a positive delight in it. For myself, I can feel pity toward the poor Duke Leto. Dr. Yueh will move against him soon, and that'll be the end of all the Atreides. But surely Leto will know whose hand directed the pliant doctor . . . and knowing that will be a terrible thing."

"Then why haven't you directed the doctor to slip a kindjal between his ribs quietly and efficiently?" Piter asked. "You talk of pity, but—"

"The Duke *must* know when I encompass his doom," the Baron said. "And the other Great Houses must learn of it. The knowledge will give them pause. I'll gain a bit more room to maneuver. The necessity is obvious, but I don't have to like it."

"Room to maneuver," Piter sneered. "Already you have the Emperor's eyes on you, Baron. You move too boldly. One day the Emperor will send a legion or two of his Sardaukar down here onto Giedi Prime and that'll be an end to the Baron Vladimir Harkonnen."

"You'd like to see that, wouldn't you, Piter?" the Baron asked. "You'd enjoy seeing the Corps of Sardaukar pillage through my cities and sack this castle. You'd truly enjoy that."

"Does the Baron need to ask?" Piter whispered.

"You should've been a Bashar of the Corps," the Baron said. "You're too interested in blood and pain. Perhaps I was too quick with my promise of the spoils of Arrakis."

Piter took five curiously mincing steps into the room, stopped directly behind Feyd-Rautha. There was a tight air of tension in the room, and the youth looked up at Piter with a worried frown.

"Do not toy with Piter, Baron," Piter said. "You promised me the Lady Jessica. You promised her to me."

"For what, Piter?" the Baron asked. "For pain?"

Piter stared at him, dragging out the silence.

Freyd-Rautha moved his suspensor chair to one side, said: "Uncle, do I have to stay? You said you'd—"

"My darling Feyd-Rautha grows impatient," the Baron said. He moved within the shadows beside the globe. "Patience, Feyd." And he turned his attention back to the Mentat. "What of the Dukeling, the child Paul, my dear Piter?"

"The trap will bring him to you, Baron," Piter muttered.

"That's not my question," the Baron said. "You'll recall that you predicted the Bene Gesserit witch would bear a daughter to the Duke. You were wrong, eh, Mentat?"

"I'm not often wrong, Baron," Piter said, and for the first time there was fear in his voice. "Give me that: I'm not often wrong. And you know yourself these Bene Gesserit bear mostly daughters. Even the Emperor's consort has produced only females."

"Uncle," said Feyd-Rautha, "you said there'd be something important here for me to—"

"Listen to my nephew," the Baron said. "He aspires to rule my Barony, yet he cannot rule himself." The Baron stirred beside the globe, a shadow among shadows. "Well then, Feyd-Rautha Harkonnen, I summoned you here hoping to teach you a bit of wisdom. Have you observed our good Mentat? You should've learned something from this exchange."

"But, Uncle—"

"A most efficient Mentat, Piter, wouldn't you say, Feyd?"

"Yes, but—"

"Ah! Indeed *but!* But he consumes too much spice, eats it like candy. Look at his eyes! He might've come directly from the Arrakeen labor pool. Efficient, Piter, *but* he's still emotional and prone to passionate outbursts. Efficient, Piter, *but* he still can err."

Piter spoke in a low, sullen tone: "Did you call me in here to impair my efficiency with criticism, Baron?"

"Impair your efficiency? You know me better, Piter. I wish only for my nephew to understand the limitations of a Mentat."

"Are you already training my replacement?" Piter demanded.

"Replace *you?* Why, Piter, where could I find another Mentat with your cunning and venom?"

"The same place you found me, Baron."

"Perhaps I should at that," the Baron mused. "You do seem a bit unstable lately. And the spice you eat!"

"Are my pleasures too expensive, Baron? Do you object to them?"

"My dear Piter, your pleasures are what tie you to me. How could I object to that? I merely wish my nephew to observe this about you."

"Then I'm on display," Piter said. "Shall I dance? Shall I perform my various functions for the eminent Feyd-Rau—"

"Precisely," the Baron said. "You are on display. Now, be silent." He glanced at Feyd-Rautha, noting his nephew's lips, the full and pouting look of them, the Harkonnen genetic marker, now twisted slightly in amusement. "This is a Mentat, Feyd. It has been trained and conditioned to perform certain duties. The fact that it's encased in a human body, however, must not be overlooked. A serious drawback, that. I sometimes think the ancients with their thinking machines had the right idea."

"They were toys compared to me," Piter snarled. "You yourself, Baron, could outperform those *machines*."

"Perhaps," the Baron said. "Ah, well . . . ." He took a deep breath, belched. "Now, Piter, outline for my nephew the salient features of our campaign against the House of Atreides. Function as a Mentat for us, if you please."

"Baron, I've warned you not to trust one so young with this information. My observations of—"

"I'll be the judge of this," the Baron said. "I give you an order, Mentat. Perform one of your various functions."

"So be it," Piter said. He straightened, assuming an odd attitude of dignity—as though it were another mask, but this time clothing his entire body. "In a few days Standard, the entire household of the Duke Leto will embark on a Spacing Guild liner for Arrakis. The Guild will deposit them at the city of Arrakeen rather than at our city of Carthag. The Duke's Mentat, Thufir Hawat, will have concluded rightly that Arrakeen is easier to defend."

"Listen carefully, Feyd," the Baron said. "Observe the plans within plans within plans."

Feyd-Rautha nodded, thinking: *This is more like it. The old monster is letting me in on secret things at last. He must really mean for me to be his heir.*

"There are several tangential possibilities," Piter said. "I indicate that House Atreides will go to Arrakis. We must not, however, ignore the possibility the Duke has contracted with the Guild to remove him to a place of safety outside the System. Others in like circumstances have become renegade Houses, taking family atomics and shields and fleeing beyond the Imperium."

"The Duke's too proud a man for that," the Baron said.

"It is a possibility," Piter said. "The ultimate effect for us would be the same, however."

"No, it would not!" the Baron growled. "I must have him dead and his line ended."

"That's the high probability," Piter said. "There are certain preparations that indicate when a House is going renegade. The Duke appears to be doing none of these things."

"So," the Baron sighed. "Get on with it, Piter."

"At Arrakeen," Piter said, "the Duke and his family will occupy the Residency, lately the home of Count and Lady Fenring."

"The Ambassador to the Smugglers," the Baron chuckled.

"Ambassador to what?" Feyd-Rautha asked.

"Your uncle makes a joke," Piter said. "He calls Count Fenring Ambassador to the Smugglers, indicating the Emperor's interest in smuggling operations on Arrakis."

Feyd-Rautha turned a puzzled stare on his uncle. "Why?"

"Don't be dense, Feyd," the Baron snapped. "As long as the Guild remains effectively outside Imperial control, how could it be otherwise? How else could spies and assassins move about?"

Freyd-Rautha's mouth made a soundless "Oh-h-h-h."

"We've arranged diversions at the Residency," Piter said. "There'll be an attempt on the life of the Atreides heir—an attempt which could succeed."

"Piter," the Baron rumbled, "you indicated—"

"I indicated accidents can happen," Piter said. "And the attempt must appear valid."

"Ah, but the lad has such a sweet young body," the Baron said. "Of course, he's potentially more dangerous than the father . . . with that witch mother training him. Accursed woman! Ah, well, please continue, Piter."

"Hawat will have divined that we have an agent planted on him," Piter said. "The obvious suspect is Dr. Yueh, who is indeed our agent. But Hawat has investigated and found that our doctor is a Suk School graduate with Imperial Conditioning—supposedly safe enough to minister even to the Emperor. Great store is set on Imperial Conditioning. It's assumed that ultimate conditioning cannot be removed without killing the subject. However, as someone once observed, given the right lever you can move a planet. We found the lever that moved the doctor."

"How?" Feyd-Rautha asked. He found this a fascinating subject. *Everyone* knew you couldn't subvert Imperial Conditioning!

"Another time," the Baron said. "Continue, Piter."

"In place of Yueh," Piter said, "we'll drag a most interesting suspect across

Hawat's path. The very audacity of this suspect will recommend her to Hawat's attention."

"Her?" Feyd-Rautha asked.

"The Lady Jessica herself," the Baron said.

"Is it not sublime?" Piter asked. "Hawat's mind will be so filled with this prospect it'll impair his function as a Mentat. He may even try to kill her." Piter frowned, then: "But I don't think he'll be able to carry it off."

"You don't want him to, eh?" the Baron asked.

"Don't distract me," Piter said. "While Hawat's occupied with the Lady Jessica, we'll divert him further with uprisings in a few garrison towns and the like. These will be put down. The Duke must believe he's gaining a measure of security. Then, when the moment is ripe, we'll signal Yueh and move in with our major force . . . ah . . . ."

"Go ahead, tell him all of it," the Baron said.

"We'll move in strengthened by two legions of Sardaukar disguised in Harkonnen livery."

"Sardaukar!" Feyd-Rautha breathed. His mind focused on the dread Imperial troops, the killers without mercy, the soldier-fanatics of the Padishah Emperor.

"You see how I trust you, Feyd," the Baron said. "No hint of this must ever reach another Great House, else the Landsraad might unite against the Imperial House and there'd be chaos."

"The main point," Piter said, "is this: since House Harkonnen is being used to do the Imperial dirty work, we've gained a true advantage. It's a dangerous advantage, to be sure, but if used cautiously, will bring House Harkonnen greater wealth than that of any other House in the Imperium."

"You have no idea how much wealth is involved, Feyd," the Baron said. "Not in your wildest imaginings. To begin, we'll have an irrevocable director-ship in the CHOAM Company."

Feyd-Rautha nodded. Wealth was the thing. CHOAM was the key to wealth, each noble House dipping from the company's coffers whatever it could under the power of the directorships. Those CHOAM directorships—they were the real evidence of political power in the Imperium, passing with the shifts of voting strength within the Landsraad as it balanced itself against the Emperor and *his* supporters.

"The Duke Leto," Piter said, "may attempt to flee to the few Fremen scum along the desert's edge. Or he may try to send his family into that imagined security. But that path is blocked by one of His Majesty's agents—the planetary ecologist. You may remember him—Kynes."

"Feyd remembers him," the Baron said. "Get on with it."

"You do not drool very prettily, Baron," Piter said.

"Get on with it, I command you!" the Baron roared.

Piter shrugged. "If matters go as planned," he said, "House Harkonnen will have a subfief on Arrakis within a Standard year. Your uncle will have dispensation of that fief. His own *personal* agent will rule on Arrakis."

"More profits," Feyd-Rautha said.

"Indeed," the Baron said. And he thought: *It's only just. We're the ones who tamed Arrakis . . . except for the few mongrel Fremen hiding in the skirts of the desert . . . and some tame smugglers bound to the planet almost as tightly as the native labor pool.*

"And the Great Houses will know that the Baron has destroyed the Atreides," Piter said. "They will know."

"They will know," the Baron breathed.

"Loveliest of all," Piter said, "is that the Duke will know, too. He knows now. He can already feel the trap."

"It's true the Duke knows," the Baron said, and his voice held a note of sadness. "He could not help but know . . . more's the pity."

The Baron moved out and away from the globe of Arrakis. As he emerged from the shadows, his figure took on dimension—grossly and immensely fat. And with subtle bulges beneath folds of his dark robes to reveal that all this fat was sustained partly by portable suspensors harnessed to his flesh. He might weigh two hundred Standard kilos in actuality, but his feet would carry no more than fifty of them.

"I am hungry," the Baron rumbled, and he rubbed his protruding lips with a beringed hand, stared down at Feyd-Rautha through fat-enfolded eyes. "Send for food, my darling. We will eat before we retire."

> *Thus spoke St. Alia-of-the-Knife: "The Reverend Mother must combine the seductive wiles of a courtesan with the untouchable majesty of a virgin goddess, holding these attributes in tension so long as the powers of her youth endure. For when youth and beauty have gone, she will find that the place-between, once occupied by tension, has become a wellspring of cunning and resourcefulness."*

### —from "Muad'Dib, Family Commentaries" by the Princess Irulan

"Well, Jessica, what have you to say for yourself?" asked the Reverend Mother.

It was near sunset at Castle Caladan on the day of Paul's ordeal. The two women were alone in Jessica's morning room while Paul waited in the adjoining soundproofed Meditation Chamber.

Jessica stood facing the south windows. She saw and yet did not see the evening's banked colors across meadow and river. She heard and yet did not hear the Reverend Mother's question.

There had been another ordeal once—so many years ago. A skinny girl with hair the color of bronze, her body tortured by the winds of puberty, had entered the study of the Reverend Mother Gaius Helen Mohiam, Proctor Superior of the Bene Gesserit school on Wallach IX. Jessica looked down at her right hand, flexed the fingers, remembering the pain, the terror, the anger.

"Poor Paul," she whispered.

"I asked you a question, Jessica!" The old woman's voice was snappish, demanding.

"What? Oh . . . ." Jessica tore her attention away from the past, faced the Reverend Mother, who sat with back to the stone wall between the two west windows. "What do you want me to say?"

"What do I want you to say? What do I want you to say?" The old voice carried a tone of cruel mimicry.

"So I had a son!" Jessica flared. And she knew she was being goaded into this anger deliberately.

"You were told to bear only daughters to the Atreides."

"It meant so much to him," Jessica pleaded.

"And you in your pride thought you could produce the Kwisatz Haderach!" Jessica lifted her chin. "I sensed the possibility."

"You thought only of your Duke's desire for a son," the old woman snapped. "And his desires don't figure in this. An Atreides daughter could've been wed to a Harkonnen heir and sealed the breach. You've hopelessly complicated matters. We may lose both bloodlines now."

"You're not infallible," Jessica said. She braved the steady stare from the old eyes.

Presently, the old woman muttered: "What's done is done."

"I vowed never to regret my decision," Jessica said.

"How noble," the Reverend Mother sneered. "No regrets. We shall see when you're a fugitive with a price on your head and every man's hand turned against you to seek your life and the life of your son."

Jessica paled. "Is there no alternative?"

"Alternative? A Bene Gesserit should ask that?"

"I ask only what you see in the future with your superior abilities."

"I see in the future what I've seen in the past. You well know the pattern of our affairs, Jessica. The race knows its own mortality and fears stagnation of its heredity. It's in the bloodstream—the urge to mingle genetic strains without plan. The Imperium, the CHOAM Company, all the Great Houses, they are but bits of flotsam in the path of the flood."

"CHOAM," Jessica muttered. "I suppose it's already decided how they'll redivide the spoils of Arrakis."

"What is CHOAM but the weather vane of our times," the old woman said. "The Emperor and his friends now command fifty-nine point six-five per cent of the CHOAM directorship's votes. Certainly they smell profits, and likely as others smell those same profits his voting strength will increase. This is the pattern of history, girl."

"That's certainly what I need right now," Jessica said. "A review of history."

"Don't be facetious, girl! You know as well as I do what forces surround us. We've a three-point civilization: the Imperial Household balanced against the Federated Great Houses of the Landsraad, and between them, the Guild with its damnable monopoly on interstellar transport. In politics, the tripod is the most unstable of all structures. It'd be bad enough without the complication of a feudal trade culture which turns its back on most science."

Jessica spoke bitterly: "Chips in the path of the flood—and this chip here, this is the Duke Leto, and this one's his son, and this one's—"

"Oh, shut up, girl. You entered this with full knowledge of the delicate edge you walked."

" 'I am Bene Gesserit: I exist only to serve,' " Jessica quoted.

"Truth," the old woman said. "And all we can hope for now is to prevent this from erupting into general conflagration, to salvage what we can of the key bloodlines."

Jessica closed her eyes, feeling tears press out beneath the lids. She fought down the inner trembling, the outer trembling, the uneven breathing, the ragged pulse, the sweating of the palms. Presently, she said, "I'll pay for my own mistake."

"And your son will pay with you."

"I'll shield him as well as I'm able."

"Shield!" the old woman snapped. "You well know the weakness there! Shield your son too much, Jessica, and he'll not grow strong enough to fulfill *any* destiny."

Jessica turned away, looked out the window at the gathering darkness. "Is it really that terrible, this planet of Arrakis?"

"Bad enough, but not all bad. The Missionaria Protectiva has been in there and softened it up somewhat." The Reverend Mother heaved herself to her feet, straightened a fold in her gown. "Call the boy in here. I must be leaving soon."

"Must you?"

The old woman's voice softened. "Jessica, girl, I wish I could stand in your place and take your sufferings. But each of us must make her own path."

"I know."

"You're as dear to me as any of my own daughters, but I cannot let that interfere with duty."

"I understand . . . the necessity."

"What you did, Jessica, and why you did it—we both know. But kindness forces me to tell you there's little chance your lad will be the Bene Gesserit Totality. You mustn't let yourself hope too much."

Jessica shook tears from the corners of her eyes. It was an angry gesture. "You make me feel like a little girl again—reciting my first lesson." She forced the words out: " 'Humans must never submit to animals.' " A dry sob shook her. In a low voice, she said: "I've been so lonely."

"It should be one of the tests," the old woman said. "Humans are almost always lonely. Now summon the boy. He's had a long, frightening day. But he's had time to think and remember, and I must ask the other questions about these dreams of his."

Jessica nodded, went to the door of the Meditation Chamber, opened it. "Paul, come in now, please."

Paul emerged with a stubborn slowness. He stared at his mother as though she were a stranger. Wariness veiled his eyes when he glanced at the Reverend Mother, but this time he nodded to her, the nod one gives an equal. He heard his mother close the door behind him.

"Young man," the old woman said, "let's return to this dream business."

"What do you want?" he asked.

"Do you dream every night?"

"Not dreams worth remembering. I can remember every dream, but some are worth remembering and some aren't."

"How do you know the difference?"

"I just know it."

The old woman glanced at Jessica, back to Paul. "What did you dream last night? Was it worth remembering?"

"Yes." Paul closed his eyes. "I dreamed a cavern . . . and water . . . and a girl there—very skinny with big eyes. Her eyes are all blue, no whites in them. I talk to her and tell her about you, about seeing the Reverend Mother on Caladan." Paul opened his eyes.

"And the thing you tell this strange girl about seeing me, did it happen today?"

Paul thought about this, then: "Yes. I tell the girl you came and put a stamp of strangeness on me."

"Stamp of strangeness," the old woman breathed, and again she shot a glance at Jessica, returned her attention to Paul. "Tell me truly now, Paul, do you often have dreams of things that happen afterward exactly as you dreamed them?"

"Yes. And I've dreamed about that girl before."

"Oh? You know her?"

"I will know her."

Tell me about her."

Again, Paul closed his eyes. "We're in a little place in some rocks where it's sheltered. It's almost night, but it's hot and I can see patches of sand out of an opening in the rocks. We're . . . waiting for something . . . for me to go meet some people. And she's frightened but trying to hide it from me, and I'm excited. And she says: 'Tell me about the waters of your homeworld, Usul.'" Paul opened his eyes. "Isn't that strange? My homeworld's Caladan. I've never even heard of a planet called Usul."

"Is there more to this dream?" Jessica prompted.

"Yes. But maybe she was calling *me* Usul," Paul said. "I just thought of that." Again, he closed his eyes. "She asks me to tell her about the waters. And I take her hand. And I say I'll tell her a poem. And I tell her the poem, but I have to explain some of the words—like beach and surf and seaweed and seagulls."

"What poem?" the Reverend Mother asked.

Paul opened his eyes. "It's just one of Gurney Halleck's tone poems for sad times."

Behind Paul, Jessica began to recite:

"I remember salt smoke from a beach fire
And shadows under the pines—
Solid, clean . . . fixed—
Seagulls perched at the tip of land,
White upon green . . .
And a wind comes through the pines

To sway the shadows;
The seagulls spread their wings,
Lift
And fill the sky with screeches.
And I hear the wind
Blowing across our beach,
And the surf,
And I see that our fire
Has scorched the seaweed."

"That's the one," Paul said.

The old woman stared at Paul, then: "Young man, as a Proctor of the Bene Gesserit, I seek the Kwisatz Haderach, the male who truly can become one of us. Your mother sees this possibility in you, but she sees with the eyes of a mother. Possibility I see, too, but no more."

She fell silent and Paul saw that she wanted him to speak. He waited her out.

Presently, she said: "As you will, then. You've depths in you; that I'll grant."

"May I go now?" he asked.

"Don't you want to hear what the Reverend Mother can tell you about the Kwisatz Haderach?" Jessica asked.

"She said those who tried for it died."

"But I can help you with a few hints at why they failed," the Reverend Mother said.

*She talks of hints,* Paul thought. *She doesn't really know anything.* And he said: "Hint then."

"And be damned to me?" She smiled wryly, a criscross of wrinkles in the old face. "Very well: 'That which submits rules.'"

He felt astonishment; she was talking about such elementary things as tension within meaning. Did she think his mother had taught him nothing at all?

"That's a hint?" he asked.

"We're not here to bandy words or quibble over their meaning," the old woman said. "The willow submits to the wind and prospers until one day it is many willows—a wall against the wind. This is the willow's purpose."

Paul stared at her. She said *purpose* and he felt the word buffet him, reinfecting him with terrible purpose. He experienced a sudden anger at her: fatuous old witch with her mouth full of platitudes.

"You think I could be this Kwisatz Haderach," he said. "You talk about me but you haven't said one thing about what we can do to help my father. I've heard you talking to my mother. You talk as though my father were dead. Well, he isn't!"

"If there were a thing to be done for him, we'd have done it," the old woman growled. "We may be able to salvage you. Doubtful, but possible. But for your father, nothing. When you've learned to accept that as a fact, you've learned a *real* Bene Gesserit lesson."

Paul saw how the words shook his mother. He glared at the old woman. How could she say such a thing about his father? What made her so sure? His mind seethed with resentment.

The Reverend Mother looked at Jessica. "You've been training him in the Way—I've seen the signs of it. I'd have done the same in your shoes and devil take the Rules."

Jessica nodded.

"Now, I caution you," said the old woman, "to ignore the regular order of training. His own safety requires the Voice. He already has a good start in it, but we both know how much more he needs . . . and that desperately." She stepped close to Paul, stared down at him. "Goodbye, young human. I hope you make it. But if you don't—well, we shall yet succeed."

Once more she looked at Jessica. A flicker sign of understanding passed between them. Then the old woman swept from the room, her robes hissing, with not another backward glance. The room and its occupants already were shut from her thoughts.

But Jessica had caught one glimpse of the Reverend Mother's face as she turned away. There had been tears on the seamed cheeks. The tears were more unnerving than any other word or sign that had passed between them this day.

*You have read that Muad'Dib had no playmates his own age on Caladan. The dangers were too great. But Muad'Dib did have wonderful companion-teachers. There was Gurney Halleck, the troubadour-warrior. You will sing some of Gurney's songs as you read along in this book. There was Thufir Hawat, the old Mentat Master of Assassins, who struck fear even into the heart of the Padishah Emperor. There were Duncan Idaho, the Swordmaster of the Ginaz; Dr. Wellington Yueh, a name black in treachery but bright in knowledge; the Lady Jessica, who guided her son in the Bene Gesserit Way, and—of course—the Duke Leto, whose qualities as a father have long been overlooked.*

**—from "A Child's History of Muad'Dib"**
**by the Princess Irulan**

Thufir Hawat slipped into the training room of Castle Caladan, closed the door softly. He stood there a moment, feeling old and tired and storm-leathered. His left leg ached where it had been slashed once in the service of the Old Duke.

*Three generations of them now,* he thought.

He stared across the big room bright with the light of noon pouring through the skylights, saw the boy seated with back to the door, intent on papers and charts spread across an ell table.

*How many times must I tell that lad never to settle himself with his back to a door?* Hawat cleared his throat.

Paul remained bent over his studies.

A cloud shadow passed over the skylights. Again, Hawat cleared his throat.

Paul straightened, spoke without turning: "I know. I'm sitting with my back to a door."

Hawat suppressed a smile, strode across the room.

Paul looked up at the grizzled old man who stopped at a corner of the table. Hawat's eyes were two pools of alertness in a dark and deeply seamed face.

"I heard you coming down the hall," Paul said. "And I heard you open the door."

"The sounds I make could be imitated."

"I'd know the difference."

*He might at that,* Hawat thought. *That witch-mother of his is giving him the deep training, certainly. I wonder what her precious school thinks of that? Maybe that's why they sent the old Proctor here—to whip our dear Lady Jessica into line.*

Hawat pulled up a chair across from Paul, sat down facing the door. He did it pointedly, leaned back and studied the room. It struck him as an odd place suddenly, a stranger-place with most of its hardware already gone off to Arrakis. A training table remained, and a fencing mirror with its crystal prisms quiescent, the target dummy beside it patched and padded, looking like an ancient foot soldier maimed and battered in the wars.

*There stand I,* Hawat thought.

"Thufir, what're you thinking?" Paul asked.

Hawat looked at the boy. "I was thinking we'll all be out of here soon and likely never see the place again."

"Does that make you sad?"

"Sad? Nonsense! Parting with friends is a sadness. A place is only a place." He glanced at the charts on the table. "And Arrakis is just another place."

"Did my father send you up to test me?"

Hawat scowled—the boy had such observing ways about him. He nodded. "You're thinking it'd have been nicer if he'd come up himself, but you must know how busy he is. He'll be along later."

"I've been studying about the storms on Arrakis."

"The storms. I see."

"They sound pretty bad."

"That's too cautious a word: *bad.* Those storms build up across six or seven thousand kilometers of flatlands, feed on anything that can give them a push—coriolis force, other storms, anything that has an ounce of energy in it. They can blow up to seven hundred kilometers an hour, loaded with everything loose that's in their way—sand, dust, everything. They can eat flesh off bones and etch the bones to slivers."

"Why don't they have weather control?"

"Arrakis has special problems, costs are higher, and there'd be maintenance and the like. The Guild wants a dreadful high price for satellite control and your father's House isn't one of the big rich ones, lad. You know that."

"Have you ever seen the Fremen?"

*The lad's mind is darting all over today,* Hawat thought.

"Like as not I have seen them," he said. "There's little to tell them from the folk of the graben and sink. They all wear those great flowing robes. And they stink to heaven in any closed space. It's from those suits they wear—call them 'stillsuits'—that reclaim the body's own water."

Paul swallowed, suddenly aware of the moisture in his mouth, remembering a dream of thirst. That people could want so for water they had to recycle their body moisture struck him with a feeling of desolation. "Water's precious there," he said.

Hawat nodded, thinking: *Perhaps I'm doing it, getting across to him the importance of this planet as an enemy. It's madness to go in there without that caution in our minds.*

Paul looked up at the skylight, aware that it had begun to rain. He saw the spreading wetness on the gray meta-glass. "Water," he said.

"You'll learn a great concern for water," Hawat said. "As the Duke's son you'll never want for it, but you'll see the pressures of thirst all around you."

Paul wet his lips with his tongue, thinking back to the day a week ago and the ordeal with the Reverend Mother. She, too, had said something about water starvation.

"You'll learn about the funeral plains," she'd said, "about the wilderness that is empty, the wasteland where nothing lives except the spice and the sandworms. You'll stain your eyepits to reduce the sun glare. Shelter will mean a hollow out of the wind and hidden from view. You'll ride upon your own two feet without 'thopter or groundcar or mount."

And Paul had been caught more by her tone—singsong and wavering—than by her words.

"When you live upon Arrakis," she had said, "khala, the land is empty. The moons will be your friends, the sun your enemy."

Paul had sensed his mother come up beside him away from her post guarding the door. She had looked at the Reverend Mother and asked: "Do you see no hope, Your Reverence?"

"Not for the father." And the old woman had waved Jessica to silence, looked down at Paul. "Grave this on your memory, lad: A world is supported by four things . . . ." She held up four big-knuckled fingers. ". . . the learning of the wise, the justice of the great, the prayers of the righteous and the valor of the brave. But all of these are as nothing . . . ." She closed her fingers into a fist. ". . . without a ruler who knows the art of ruling. Make *that* the science of your tradition!"

A week had passed since that day with the Reverend Mother. Her words were only now beginning to come into full register. Now, sitting in the training room with Thufir Hawat, Paul felt a sharp pang of fear. He looked across at the Mentat's puzzled frown.

"Where were you woolgathering that time?" Hawat asked.

"Did you meet the Reverend Mother?"

"That Truthsayer witch from the Imperium?" Hawat's eyes quickened with interest. "I met her."

"She . . . ." Paul hesitated, found that he couldn't tell Hawat about the ordeal. The inhibitions went deep.

"Yes? What did she?"

Paul took two deep breaths. "She said a thing." He closed his eyes, calling up the words, and when he spoke his voice unconsciously took on some of the old woman's tone: " 'You, Paul Atreides, descendant of kings, son of a Duke, you must learn to rule. It's something none of your ancestors learned.' " Paul opened his eyes, said: "That made me angry and I said my father rules an entire planet. And she said, 'He's losing it.' And I said my father was getting a richer planet. And she said, 'He'll lose that one, too.' And I wanted to run and warn my father, but she said he'd already been warned—by you, by Mother, by many people."

"True enough," Hawat muttered.

"Then why're we going?" Paul demanded.

"Because the Emperor ordered it. And because there's hope in spite of what that witch-spy said. What else spouted from this ancient fountain of wisdom?"

Paul looked down at his right hand clenched into a fist beneath the table. Slowly, he willed the muscles to relax. *She put some kind of hold on me,* he thought. *How?*

"She asked me to tell her what it is to rule," Paul said. "And I said that one commands. And she said I had some unlearning to do."

*She hit a mark there right enough,* Hawat thought. He nodded for Paul to continue.

"She said a ruler must learn to persuade and not to compel. She said he must lay the best coffee hearth to attract the finest men."

"How'd she figure your father attracted men like Duncan and Gurney?" Hawat asked.

Paul shrugged. "Then she said a good ruler has to learn his world's language, that it's different for every world. And I thought she meant they didn't speak Galach on Arrakis, but she said that wasn't it at all. She said she meant the language of the rocks and growing things, the language you don't hear just with your ears. And I said that's what Dr. Yueh calls the Mystery of Life."

Hawat chuckled. "How'd that sit with her?"

"I think she got mad. She said the mystery of life isn't a problem to solve, but a reality to experience. So I quoted the First Law of Mentat at her: 'A process cannot be understood by stopping it. Understanding must move with the flow of the process, must join it and flow with it.' That seemed to satisfy her."

*He seems to be getting over it,* Hawat thought, *but that old witch frightened him. Why did she do it?*

"Thufir," Paul said, "will Arrakis be as bad as she said?"

"Nothing could be that bad," Hawat said and forced a smile. "Take those Fremen, for example, the renegade people of the desert. By first-approximation analysis, I can tell you there're many, many more of them than the Imperium suspects. People live there, lad: a great many people, and . . . ." Hawat put a sinewy finger beside his eye. ". . . they hate Harkonnens with a bloody passion. You must not breathe a word of this, lad. I tell you only as your father's helper."

"My father has told me of Salusa Secundus," Paul said. "Do you know, Thufir, it sounds much like Arrakis . . . perhaps not quite as bad, but much like it."

"We do not really know of Salusa Secundus today," Hawat said. "Only what it was like long ago . . . mostly. But what is known—you're right on that score."

"Will the Fremen help us?"

"It's a possibility." Hawat stood up. "I leave today for Arrakis. Meanwhile, you take care of yourself for an old man who's fond of you, heh? Come around here like the good lad and sit facing the door. It's not that I think there's any danger in the castle; it's just a habit I want you to form."

Paul got to his feet, moved around the table. "You're going today?"

"Today it is, and you'll be following tomorrow. Next time we meet it'll be on the soil of your new world." He gripped Paul's right arm at the bicep. "Keep your knife arm free, heh? And your shield at full charge." He released the arm, patted Paul's shoulder, whirled and strode quickly to the door.

"Thufir!" Paul called.

Hawat turned, standing in the open doorway.

"Don't sit with your back to any doors," Paul said.

A grin spread across the seamed old face. "That I won't, lad. Depend on it." And he was gone, shutting the door softly behind.

Paul sat down where Hawat had been, straightened the papers. *One more day here*, he thought. He looked around the room. *We're leaving.* The idea of departure was suddenly more real to him than it had ever been before. He recalled another thing the old woman had said about a world being the sum of many things—the people, the dirt, the growing things, the moons, the tides, the suns—the unknown sum called *nature*, a vague summation without any sense of the *now*. And he wondered: *What is the now?*

The door across from Paul banged open and an ugly lump of a man lurched through it preceded by a handful of weapons.

"Well, Gurney Halleck," Paul called, "are you the new weapons master?"

Halleck kicked the door shut with one heel. "You'd rather I came to play games, I know," he said. He glanced around the room, noting that Hawat's men already had been over it, checking, making it safe for a duke's heir. The subtle code signs were all around.

Paul watched the rolling, ugly man set himself back in motion, veer toward the training table with the load of weapons, saw the nine-string baliset slung over Gurney's shoulder with the multipick woven through the strings near the head of the fingerboard.

Halleck dropped the weapons on the exercise table, lined them up—the rapiers, the bodkins, the kindjals, the slow-pellet stunners, the shield belts. The inkvine scar along his jawline writhed as he turned, casting a smile across the room.

"So you don't even have a good morning for me, you young imp," Halleck said. "And what barb did you sink in old Hawat? He passed me in the hall like a man running to his enemy's funeral."

Paul grinned. Of all his father's men, he liked Gurney Halleck best, knew the man's moods and deviltry, his *humors*, and thought of him more as a friend than as a hired sword.

Halleck swung the baliset off his shoulder, began tuning it. "If y' won't talk, y' won't," he said.

Paul stood, advanced across the room, calling out: "Well, Gurney, do we come prepared for music when it's fighting time?"

"So it's sass for our elders today," Halleck said. He tried a chord on the instrument, nodded.

"Where's Duncan Idaho?" Paul asked. "Isn't he supposed to be teaching me weaponry?"

"Duncan's gone to lead the second wave onto Arrakis," Halleck said. "All you have left is poor Gurney who's fresh out of fight and spoiling for music." He struck another chord, listened to it, smiled. "And it was decided in council that you being such a poor fighter we'd best teach you the music trade so's you won't waste your life entire."

"Maybe you'd better sing me a lay then," Paul said. "I want to be sure how *not* to do it."

"Ah-h-h, hah!" Gurney laughed, and he swung into Galacian Girls, his multipick a blur over the strings as he sang:

"Oh-h-h, the Galacian girls
Will do it for pearls,
And the Arrakeen for water!
But if you desire dames
Like consuming flames,
Try a Caladanin daughter!"

"Not bad for such a poor hand with the pick," Paul said, "but if my mother heard you singing a bawdy like that in the castle, she'd have your ears on the outer wall for decoration."

Gurney pulled at his left ear. "Poor decoration, too, they having been bruised so much listening at keyholes while a young lad I know practiced some strange ditties on his baliset."

"So you've forgotten what it's like to find sand in your bed," Paul said. He pulled a shield belt from the table, buckled it fast around his waist. "Then, let's fight!"

Halleck's eyes went wide in mock surprise. "So! It was your wicked hand did that deed! Guard yourself today, young master—guard yourself." He grabbed up a rapier, laced the air with it. "I'm a hellfiend out for revenge!"

Paul lifted the companion rapier, bent it in his hands, stood in the *aguile*, one foot forward. He let his manner go solemn in a comic imitation of Dr. Yueh.

"What a dolt my father sends me for weaponry," Paul intoned. "This doltish Gurney Halleck has forgotten the first lesson for a fighting man armed and shielded." Paul snapped the force button at his waist, felt the crinkled-skin tingling of the defensive field at his forehead and down his back, heard external sounds take on characteristic shield-filtered flatness. "In shield fighting, one moves fast on defense, slow on attack," Paul said. "Attack has the sole purpose of tricking the opponent into a misstep, setting him up for the attack sinister. The shield turns the fast blow, admits the slow kindjal!" Paul snapped up the rapier, feinted fast and whipped it back for a slow thrust timed to enter a shield's mindless defenses.

Halleck watched the action, turned at the last minute to let the blunted blade pass his chest. "Speed, excellent," he said. "But you were wide open for an underhanded counter with a slip-tip."

Paul stepped back, chagrined.

"I should whap your backside for such carelessness," Halleck said. He lifted a naked kindjal from the table and held it up. "This in the hand of an enemy can let out your life's blood! You're an apt pupil, none better, but I've warned you that not even in play do you let a man inside your guard with death in his hand."

"I guess I'm not in the mood for it today," Paul said.

"Mood?" Halleck's voice betrayed his outrage even through the shield's filtering. "What has *mood* to do with it? You fight when the necessity arises—no matter the mood! Mood's a thing for cattle or making love or playing the baliset. It's not for fighting."

"I'm sorry, Gurney."

"You're not sorry enough!"

Halleck activated his own shield, crouched with kindjal outthrust in left hand, the rapier poised high in his right. "Now I say guard yourself for true!" He leaped high to one side, then forward, pressing a furious attack.

Paul fell back, parrying. He felt the field crackling as shield edges touched and repelled each other, sensed the electric tingling of the contact along his skin. *What's gotten into Gurney?* he asked himself. *He's not faking this!* Paul moved his left hand, dropped his bodkin into his palm from its wrist sheath.

"You see a need for an extra blade, eh?" Halleck grunted.

*Is this betrayal?* Paul wondered. *Surely not Gurney!*

Around the room they fought—thrust and parry, feint and counterfeint. The air within their shield bubbles grew stale from the demands on it that the slow interchange along barrier edges could not replenish. With each new shield contact, the smell of ozone grew stronger.

Paul continued to back, but now he directed his retreat toward the exercise table. *If I can turn him beside the table, I'll show him a trick,* Paul thought. *One more step, Gurney.*

Halleck took the step.

Paul directed a parry downward, turned, saw Halleck's rapier catch against the table's edge. Paul flung himself aside, thrust high with rapier and came in across Halleck's neckline with the bodkin. He stopped the blade an inch from the jugular.

"Is this what you seek?" Paul whispered.

"Look down, lad," Gurney panted.

Paul obeyed, saw Halleck's kindjal thrust under the table's edge, the tip almost touching Paul's groin.

"We'd have joined each other in death," Halleck said. "But I'll admit you fought some better when pressed to it. You seemed to get the *mood*." And he grinned wolfishly, the inkvine scar rippling along his jaw.

"The way you came at me," Paul said. "Would you really have drawn my blood?"

Halleck withdrew the kindjal, straightened. "If you'd fought one whit beneath your abilities, I'd have scratched you a good one, a scar you'd remember. I'll not have my favorite pupil fall to the first Harkonnen tramp who happens along."

Paul deactivated his shield, leaned on the table to catch his breath. "I deserved that, Gurney. But it would've angered my father if you'd hurt me. I'll not have you punished for my failing."

"As to that," Halleck said, "it was my failing, too. And you needn't worry about a training scar or two. You're lucky you have so few. As to your father—the Duke'd punish me only if I failed to make a first-class fighting man out of you. And I'd have been failing there if I hadn't explained the fallacy in this *mood* thing you've suddenly developed."

Paul straightened, slipped his bodkin back into its wrist sheath.

"It's not exactly play we do here," Halleck said.

Paul nodded. He felt a sense of wonder at the uncharacteristic seriousness in Halleck's manner, the sobering intensity. He looked at the beet-colored inkvine scar on the man's jaw, remembering the story of how it had been put there by Beast Rabban in a Harkonnen slave pit on Giedi Prime. And Paul felt a sudden shame that he had doubted Halleck even for an instant. It occurred to Paul, then, that the making of Halleck's scar had been accompanied by pain—a pain as intense, perhaps, as that inflicted by a Reverend Mother. He thrust this thought aside; it chilled their world.

"I guess I did hope for some play today," Paul said. "Things are so serious around here lately."

Halleck turned away to hide his emotions. Something burned in his eyes. There was pain in him—like a blister, all that was left of some lost yesterday that Time had pruned off him.

*How soon this child must assume his manhood,* Halleck thought. *How soon he must read that form within his mind, that contract of brutal caution, to enter the necessary fact on the necessary line: "Please list your next of kin."*

Halleck spoke without turning: "I sensed the play in you, lad, and I'd like nothing better than to join in it. But this no longer can be play. Tomorrow we go to Arrakis. Arrakis is real. The Harkonnens are real."

Paul touched his forehead with his rapier blade held vertical.

Halleck turned, saw the salute and acknowledged it with a nod. He gestured to the practice dummy. "Now, we'll work on your timing. Let me see you catch that thing sinister. I'll control it from over here where I can have a full view of the action. And I warn you I'll be trying new counters today. There's a warning you'd not get from a real enemy."

Paul stretched up on his toes to relieve his muscles. He felt solemn with the sudden realization that his life had become filled with swift changes. He crossed to the dummy, slapped the switch on its chest with his rapier tip and felt the defensive field forcing his blade away.

"En garde!" Halleck called, and the dummy pressed the attack.

Paul activated his shield, parried and countered.

Halleck watched as he manipulated the controls. His mind seemed to be in two parts: one alert to the needs of the training fight, and the other wandering in fly-buzz.

*I'm the well-trained fruit tree,* he thought. *Full of well-trained feelings and abilities and all of them grafted onto me—all bearing for someone else to pick.*

For some reason, he recalled his younger sister, her elfin face so clear in his mind. But she was dead now—in a pleasure house for Harkonnen troops. She had loved pansies . . . or was it daisies? He couldn't remember. It bothered him that he couldn't remember.

Paul countered a slow swing of the dummy, brought up his left hand *entretisser.*

*That clever little devil!* Halleck thought, intent now on Paul's interweaving hand motions. *He's been practicing and studying on his own. That's not Duncan's style, and it's certainly nothing I've taught him.*

This thought only added to Halleck's sadness. *I'm infected by mood,* he thought. And he began to wonder about Paul, if the boy ever listened fearfully to his pillow throbbing in the night.

"If wishes were fishes we'd all cast nets," he murmured.

It was his mother's expression and he always used it when he felt the blackness of tomorrow on him. Then he thought what an odd expression that was to be taking to a planet that had never known seas or fishes.

YUEH (yü'ē), Wellington (wĕl'ĭng-tŭn), Stdrd 10,082–10,191; medical doctor of the Suk School (grd Stdrd 10,112); md: Wanna Marcus, B.G. (Stdrd 10,092–10,186?); chiefly noted as betrayer of Duke Leto Atreides. (Cf: Bibliography, Appendix VII [Imperial Conditioning] and Betrayal, The.)

**—from "Dictionary of Muad'Dib" by the Princess Irulan**

Although he heard Dr. Yueh enter the training room, noting the stiff deliberation of the man's pace, Paul remained stretched out face down on the exercise table where the masseuse had left him. He felt deliciously relaxed after the workout with Gurney Halleck.

"You do look comfortable," said Yueh in his calm, high-pitched voice.

Paul raised his head, saw the man's stick figure standing several paces away, took in at a glance the wrinkled black clothing, the square block of a head with purple lips and drooping mustache, the diamond tattoo of Imperial Conditioning on his forehead, the long black hair caught in the Suk School's silver ring at the left shoulder.

"You'll be happy to hear we haven't time for regular lessons today," Yueh said. "Your father will be along presently."

Paul sat up.

"However, I've arranged for you to have a filmbook viewer and several lessons during the crossing to Arrakis."

"Oh."

Paul began pulling on his clothes. He felt excitement that his father would be coming. They had spent so little time together since the Emperor's command to take over the fief of Arrakis.

Yueh crossed to the ell table, thinking: *How the boy has filled out these past few months. Such a waste! Oh, such a sad waste.* And he reminded himself: *I must not falter. What I do is done to be certain my Wanna no longer can be hurt by the Harkonnen beasts.*

Paul joined him at the table, buttoning his jacket. "What'll I be studying on the way across?"

"Ah-h-h-h, the terranic life forms of Arrakis. The planet seems to have opened its arms to certain terranic life forms. It's not clear how. I must seek out the planetary ecologist when we arrive—a Dr. Keynes—and offer my help in the investigation."

And Yueh thought: *What am I saying? I play the hypocrite even with myself.*

"Will there be something on the Fremen?" Paul asked.

"The Fremen?" Yueh drummed his fingers on the table, caught Paul staring at the nervous motion, withdrew his hand.

"Maybe you have something on the whole Arrakeen population," Paul said.

"Yes, to be sure," Yueh said. "There are two general separations of the people—Fremen, they are one group, and the others are the people of the graben, the sink, and the pan. There's some intermarriage, I'm told. The women of pan and sink villages prefer Fremen husbands; their men prefer Fremen wives. They have a saying: 'Polish comes from the cities; wisdom from the desert.'"

"Do you have pictures of them?"

"I'll see what I can get you. The most interesting feature, of course, is their eyes—totally blue, no whites in them."

"Mutation?"

"No; it's linked to saturation of the blood with melange."

"The Fremen must be brave to live at the edge of that desert."

"By all acounts," Yueh said. "They compose poems to their knives. Their women are as fierce as the men. Even Fremen children are violent and dangerous. You'll not be permitted to mingle with them, I daresay."

Paul stared at Yueh, finding in these few glimpses of the Fremen a power of words that caught his entire attention. *What a people to win as allies!*

"And the worms?" Paul asked.

"What?"

"I'd like to study more about the sandworms."

"Ah-h-h-h, to be sure. I've a filmbook on a small specimen, only one hundred and ten meters long and twenty-two meters in diameter. It was taken in the northern latitudes. Worms of more than four hundred meters in length have been recorded by reliable witnesses, and there's reason to believe even larger ones exist."

Paul glanced down at a conical projection chart of the northern Arrakeen latitudes spread on the table. "The desert belt and south polar regions are marked uninhabitable. Is it the worms?"

"And the storms."

"But any place can be made habitable."

"If it's economically feasible," Yueh said. "Arrakis has many costly perils." He smoothed his drooping mustache. "Your father will be here soon. Before I go, I've a gift for you, something I came across in packing." He put an object on the table between them—black, oblong, no larger than the end of Paul's thumb.

Paul looked at it. Yueh noted how the boy did not reach for it, and thought: *How cautious he is.*

"It's a very old Orange Catholic Bible made for space travelers. Not a filmbook, but actually printed on filament paper. It has its own magnifier and electrostatic charge systen." He picked it up, demonstrated. "The book is held closed by the charge, which forces against spring-locked covers. You press the edge—thus, and the pages you've selected repel each other and the book opens."

"It's so small."

"But it has eighteen hundred pages. You press the edge—thus, and so . . . and the charge moves ahead one page at a time as you read. Never touch the actual pages with your fingers. The filament tissue is too delicate." He closed the book, handed it to Paul. "Try it."

Yueh watched Paul work the page adjustment, thought: *I salve my own conscience. I give him the surcease of religion before betraying him. Thus may I say to myself that he has gone where I cannot go.*

"This must've been made before filmbooks," Paul said.

"It's quite old. Let it be our secret, eh? Your parents might think it too valuable for one so young."

And Yueh thought: *His mother would surely wonder at my motives.*

"Well . . . ." Paul closed the book, held it in his hand. "If it's so valuable . . . ."

"Indulge an old man's whim," Yueh said. "It was given to me when I was very young." And he thought: *I must catch his mind as well as his cupidity.* "Open it to four-sixty-seven Kalima—where it says: 'From water does all life begin.' There's a slight notch on the edge of the cover to mark the place."

Paul felt the cover, detected two notches, one shallower than the other. He pressed the shallower one and the book spread open on his palm, its magnifier sliding into place.

"Read it aloud," Yueh said.

Paul wet his lips with his tongue, read: " 'Think you of the fact that a deaf person cannot hear. Then, what deafness may we not all possess? What senses do we lack that we cannot see and cannot hear another world all around us? What is there around us that we cannot—' "

"Stop it!" Yueh barked.

Paul broke off, stared at him.

Yueh closed his eyes, fought to regain composure. *What perversity caused the book to open at my Wanna's favorite passage?* He opened his eyes, saw Paul staring at him.

"Is something wrong?" Paul asked.

"I'm sorry," Yueh said. "That was . . . my . . . dead wife's favorite passage. It's not the one I intended you to read. It brings up memories that are . . . painful."

"There are two notches," Paul said.

*Of course,* Yueh thought. *Wanna marked her passage. His fingers are more sensitive than mine and found her mark. It was an accident, no more.*

"You may find the book interesting," Yueh said. "It has much historical truth in it as well as good ethical philosophy."

Paul looked down at the tiny book in his palm—such a small thing. Yet, it contained a mystery . . . something had happened while he read from it. He had felt something stir his terrible purpose.

"Your father will be here any minute," Yueh said. "Put the book away and read it at your leisure."

Paul touched the edge of it as Yueh had shown him. The book sealed itself. He slipped it into his tunic. For a moment there when Yueh had barked at him, Paul had feared the man would demand the book's return.

"I thank you for the gift, Dr. Yueh," Paul said, speaking formally. "It will be our secret. If there is a gift or favor you wish from me, please do not hesitate to ask."

"I . . . need for nothing," Yueh said.

And he thought: *Why do I stand here torturing myself? And torturing this poor lad . . . though he does not yet know it. Oeyh! Damn those Harkonnen beasts! Why did they choose me for their abomination?*

> *How do we approach the study of Muad'Dib's father? A man of surpassing warmth and surprising coldness was the Duke Leto Atreides. Yet, many facts open the way to this Duke: his abiding love for his Bene Gesserit lady; the dreams he held for his son; the devotion with which men served him. You see him there—a man snared by Destiny, a lonely figure with his light dimmed behind the glory of his son. Still, one must ask: What is the son but an extension of the father?*

> **—from "Muad'Dib, Family Commentaries"**
> **by the Princess Irulan**

Paul watched his father enter the training room, saw the guards take up stations outside. One of them closed the door. As always, Paul experienced a sense of *presence* in his father, someone totally *here.*

The Duke was tall, olive-skinned. His thin face held harsh angles warmed only by deep gray eyes. He wore a black working uniform with red armorial hawk crest at the breast. A silvered shield belt with the patina of much use girded his narrow waist.

The Duke said: "Hard at work, Son?"

He crossed to the ell table, glanced at the papers on it, swept his gaze around the room and back to Paul. He felt tired, filled with the ache of not showing his fatigue. *I must use every opportunity to rest during the crossing to Arrakis,* he thought. *There'll be no rest on Arrakis.*

"Not very hard," Paul said. "Everything's so . . . ." He shrugged.

"Yes. Well, tomorrow we leave. It'll be good to get settled in our new home, put all this upset behind."

Paul nodded, suddenly overcome by memory of the Reverend Mother's words: "*. . . for the father, nothing.*"

"Father," Paul said, "will Arrakis be as dangerous as everyone says?"

The Duke forced himself to the casual gesture, sat down on a corner of the table, smiled. A whole pattern of conversation welled up in his mind—the kind of thing he might use to dispel the vapors in his men before a battle. The pattern froze before it could be vocalized, confronted by the single thought:

*This is my son.*

"It'll be dangerous," he admitted.

"Hawat tells me we have a plan for the Fremen," Paul said. And he wondered: *Why don't I tell him what that old woman said? How did she seal my tongue?*

The Duke noted his son's distress, said: "As always, Hawat sees the main chance. But there's much more. I see also the Combine Honnete Ober Advancer Mercantiles—the CHOAM Company. By giving me Arrakis, His Majesty is forced to give us a CHOAM directorship . . . a subtle gain."

"CHOAM controls the spice," Paul said.

"And Arrakis with its spice is our avenue into CHOAM," the Duke said. "There's more to CHOAM than melange."

"Did the Reverend Mother warn you?" Paul blurted. He clenched his fists, feeling his palms slippery with perspiration. The *effort* it had taken to ask that question.

"Hawat tells me she frightened you with warnings about Arrakis," the Duke said. "Don't let a woman's fears cloud your mind. No woman wants her loved ones endangered. The hand behind those warnings was your mother's. Take this as a sign of her love for us."

"Does she know about the Fremen?"

"Yes, and about much more."

"What?"

And the Duke thought: *The truth could be worse than he imagines, but even dangerous facts are valuable if you've been trained to deal with them. And there's one place where nothing has been spared for my son—dealing with dangerous facts. This must be leavened, though; he is young.*

"Few products escape the CHOAM touch," the Duke said. "Logs, donkeys, horses, cows, lumber, dung, sharks, whale fur—the most prosaic and the most exotic . . . even our poor pundi rice from Caladan. Anything the Guild will transport, the art forms of Ecaz, the machines of Richesse and Ix. But all fades before melange. A handful of spice will buy a home on Tupile. It cannot be manufactured, it must be mined on Arrakis. It is unique and it has true geriatric properties."

"And now we control it?"

"To a certain degree. But the important thing is to consider all the Houses that depend on CHOAM profits. And think of the enormous proportion of those profits dependent upon a single product—the spice. Imagine what would happen if something should reduce spice production."

"Whoever had stockpiled melange could make a killing," Paul said. "Others would be out in the cold."

The Duke permitted himself a moment of grim satisfaction, looking at his son and thinking how penetrating, how truly *educated* that observation had been. He nodded. "The Harkonnens have been stockpiling for more than twenty years."

"They mean spice production to fail and you to be blamed."

"They wish the Atreides name to become unpopular," the Duke said. "Think of the Landsraad Houses that look to me for a certain amount of leadership—their unofficial spokesman. Think how they'd react if I were responsible for a serious reduction in their income. After all, one's own profits come first. The Great Convention be damned! You can't let someone pauperize you!" A harsh smile twisted the Duke's mouth. "They'd look the other way no matter *what* was done to me."

"Even if we were attacked with atomics?"

"Nothing that flagrant. No *open* defiance of the Convention. But almost anything else short of that . . . perhaps even dusting and a bit of soil poisoning."

"Then why are we walking into this?"

"Paul!" The Duke frowned at his son. "Knowing where the trap is—that's the first step in evading it. This is like single combat, Son, only on a larger scale—a feint within a feint within a feint . . . seemingly without end. The task is to unravel it. Knowing that the Harkonnens stockpile melange, we ask another question: Who else is stockpiling? That's the list of our enemies."

"Who?"

"Certain Houses we knew were unfriendly and some we'd thought friendly. We need not consider them for the moment because there is one other much more important: our beloved Padishah Emperor."

Paul tried to swallow in a throat suddenly dry. "Couldn't you convene the Landsraad, expose—"

"Make our enemy aware we know which hand holds the knife? Ah, now, Paul—we *see* the knife now. Who knows where it might be shifted next? If we put this before the Landsraad it'd only create a great cloud of confusion. The Emperor would deny it. Who could gainsay him? All we'd gain is a little time while risking chaos. And where would the next attack come from?"

"All the Houses might start stockpiling spice."

"Our enemies have a head start—too much of a lead to overcome."

"The Emperor," Paul said. "That means the Sardaukar."

"Disguised in Harkonnen livery, no doubt," the Duke said. "But the soldier fanatics nonetheless."

"How can Fremen help us against Sardaukar?"

"Did Hawat talk to you about Salusa Secundus?"

"The Emperor's prison planet? No."

"What if it were more than a prison planet, Paul? There's a question you never hear asked about the Imperial Corps of Sardaukar: Where do they come from?"

"From the prison planet?"

"They come from somewhere."

"But the supporting levies the Emperor demands from—"

"That's what we're led to believe: they're just the Emperor's levies trained young and superbly. You hear an occasional muttering about the Emperor's training cadres, but the balance of our civilization remains the same: the military forces of the Landsraad Great Houses on one side, the Sardaukar and their supporting levies on the other. *And* their supporting levies, Paul. The Sardaukar remain the Sardaukar."

"But every report on Salusa Secundus says S.S. is a hell world!"

"Undoubtedly. But if you were going to raise tough, strong, ferocious men, what environmental conditions would you impose on them?"

"Hou could you win the loyalty of such men?"

"There are proven ways: play on the certain knowledge of their superiority, the mystique of secret covenant, the esprit of shared suffering. It can be done. It has been done on many worlds in many times."

Paul nodded, holding his attention on his father's face. He felt some revelation impending.

"Consider Arrakis," the Duke said. "When you get outside the towns and garrison villages, it's every bit as terrible a place as Salusa Secundus."

Paul's eyes went wide. "The Fremen!"

"We have there the potential of a corps as strong and deadly as the Sardaukar. It'll require patience to exploit them secretly and wealth to equip them properly. But the Fremen are there . . . and the spice wealth is there. You see now why we walk into Arrakis, knowing the trap is there."

"Don't the Harkonnens know about the Fremen?"

"The Harkonnens sneered at the Fremen, hunted them for sport, never even bothered trying to count them. We know the Harkonnen policy with planetary populations—spend as little as possible to maintain them."

The metallic threads in the hawk symbol above his father's breast glistened as the Duke shifted his position. "You see?"

"We're negotiating with the Fremen right now," Paul said.

"I sent a mission headed by Duncan Idaho," the Duke said. "A proud and ruthless man, Duncan, but fond of the truth. I think the Fremen will admire him. If we're lucky, they may judge us by him: Duncan, the moral."

"Duncan, the moral," Paul said, "and Gurney the valorous."

"You name them well," the Duke said.

And Paul thought: *Gurney's one of those the Reverend Mother meant, a supporter of worlds—". . . the valor of the brave."*

"Gurney tells me you did well in weapons today," the Duke said.

"That isn't what he told me."

The Duke laughed aloud. "I figured Gurney to be sparse with his praise. He says you have a nicety of awareness—his own words—of the difference between a blade's edge and its tip."

"Gurney says there's no artistry in killing with the tip, that it should be done with the edge."

"Gurney's a romantic," the Duke growled. This talk of killing suddenly disturbed him, coming from his son. "I'd sooner you never had to kill . . . but if the need arises, you do it however you can—tip or edge." He looked up at the skylight, on which the rain was drumming.

Seeing the direction of his father's stare, Paul thought of the wet skies out there—a thing never to be seen on Arrakis from all accounts—and this thought of skies put him in mind of the space beyond. "Are the Guild ships really big?" he asked.

The Duke looked at him. "This *will* be your first time off planet," he said. "Yes, they're big. We'll be riding a Heighliner because it's a long trip. A Heighliner is truly big. Its hold will tuck all our frigates and transports into a little corner—we'll be just a small part of the ship's manifest."

"And we won't be able to leave our frigates?"

"That's part of the price you pay for Guild Security. There could be Harkonnen ships right alongside us and we'd have nothing to fear from them. The Harkonnens know better than to endanger their shipping privileges."

"I'm going to watch our screens and try to see a Guildsman."

"You won't. Not even their agents ever see a Guildsman. The Guild's as jealous of its privacy as it is of its monopoly. Don't do anything to endanger our shipping privileges, Paul."

"Do you think they hide because they've mutated and don't look . . . *human* anymore?"

"Who knows?" The Duke shrugged. "It's a mystery we're not likely to solve. We've more immediate problems—among them: you."

"Me?"

"Your mother wanted me to be the one to tell you, Son. You see, you may have Mentat capabilities."

Paul stared at his father, unable to speak for a moment, then: "A Mentat? Me? But I . . . ."

"Hawat agrees, Son. It's true."

"But I thought Mentat training had to start during infancy and the subject couldn't be told because it might inhibit the early . . . ." He broke off, all his past circumstances coming to focus in one flashing computation. "I see," he said.

"A day comes," the Duke said, "when the potential Mentat must learn what's being done. It may no longer be done *to* him. The Mentat has to share in the choice of whether to continue or abandon the training. Some can continue; some are incapable of it. Only the potential Mentat can tell this for sure about himself."

Paul rubbed his chin. All the special training from Hawat and his mother—the mnemonics, the focusing of awareness, the muscle control and sharpening of sensitivities, the study of languages and nuances of voices—all of it clicked into a new kind of understanding in his mind.

"You'll be the Duke someday, Son," his father said. "A Mentat Duke would be formidable indeed. Can you decide now . . . or do you need more time?"

There was no hesitation in his answer. "I'll go on with the training."

"Formidable indeed," the Duke murmured, and Paul saw the proud smile on his father's face. The smile shocked Paul: it had a skull look on the Duke's narrow features. Paul closed his eyes, feeling the terrible purpose reawaken within him. *Perhaps being a Mentat is a terrible purpose*, he thought.

But even as he focused on this thought, his new awareness denied it.

*With the Lady Jessica and Arrakis, the Bene Gesserit system of sowing implant-legends through the Missionaria Protectiva came to its full fruition. The wisdom of seeding the known universe with a prophecy pattern for the protection of B. G. personnel has long been appreciated, but never have we seen a condition-ut-extremis with more ideal mating of person and preparation. The prophetic legends had taken on Arrakis even to the extent of adopted labels (including Reverend Mother, canto and respondu, and most of the Shari-a panoplia propheticus). And it is generally accepted now that the Lady Jessica's latent abilities were grossly underestimated.*

**—from "Analysis: The Arrakeen Crisis"**
**by the Princess Irulan**
**[private circulation: B.G. file number AR-81088587]**

All around the Lady Jessica—piled in corners of the Arrakeen great hall, mounded in the open spaces—stood the packaged freight of their lives: boxes, trunks, cartons, cases—some partly unpacked. She could hear the cargo handlers from the Guild shuttle depositing another load in the entry.

Jessica stood in the center of the hall. She moved in a slow turn, looking up and around at shadowed carvings, crannies and deeply recessed windows. This giant anachronism of a room reminded her of the Sisters' Hall at her Bene Gesserit school. But at the school the effect had been of warmth. Here, all was bleak stone.

Some architect had reached far back into history for these buttressed walls and dark hangings, she thought. The arched ceiling stood two stories above her with great crossbeams she felt sure had been shipped here to Arrakis across space at monstrous cost. No planet of this system grew trees to make such beams—unless the beams were imitation wood.

She thought not.

This had been the government mansion in the days of the Old Empire. Costs had been of less importance then. It had been before the Harkonnens and their new megalopolis of Carthag—a cheap and brassy place some two hundred kilometers northeast across the Broken Land. Leto had been wise to choose this place for his seat of government. The name, Arrakeen, had a good sound, filled with tradition. And this was a smaller city, easier to sterilize and defend.

Again there came the clatter of boxes being unloaded in the entry. Jessica sighed.

Against a carton to her right stood the painting of the Duke's father. Wrapping twine hung from it like a frayed decoration. A piece of the twine was still clutched in Jessica's left hand. Beside the painting lay a black bull's head mounted on a polished board. The head was a dark island in a sea of wadded paper. Its plaque lay flat on the floor, and the bull's shiny muzzle pointed at the ceiling as though the beast were ready to bellow a challenge into this echoing room.

Jessica wondered what compulsion had brought her to uncover those two things first—the head and the painting. She knew there was something symbolic in this action. Not since the day when the Duke's buyers had taken her from the school had she felt this frightened and unsure of herself.

The head and the picture.

They heightened her feelings of confusion. She shuddered, glanced at the slit windows high overhead. It was still early afternoon here, and in these latitudes the sky looked black and cold—so much darker than the warm blue of Caladan. A pang of homesickness throbbed through her.

*So far away, Caladan.*

"Here we are!"

The voice was Duke Leto's.

She whirled, saw him striding from the arched passage to the dining hall. His black working uniform with red armorial hawk crest at the breast looked dusty and rumpled.

"I thought you might have lost yourself in this hideous place," he said.

"It is a cold house," she said. She looked at his tallness, at the dark skin that made her think of olive groves and golden sun on blue waters. There was woodsmoke in the gray of his eyes, but the face was predatory: thin, full of sharp angles and panes.

A sudden fear of him tightened her breast. He had become such a savage, driving person since the decision to bow to the Emperor's command.

"The whole city feels cold," she said.

"It's a dirty, dusty little garrison town," he agreed. "But we'll change that." He looked around the hall. "These are public rooms for state occasions. I've just glanced at some of the family apartments in the south wing. They're much nicer." He stepped closer, touched her arm, admiring her stateliness.

And again, he wondered at her unknown ancestry—a renegade House, perhaps? Some black-barred royalty? She looked more regal than the Emperor's own blood.

Under the pressure of his stare, she turned half away, exposing her profile. And he realized there was no single and precise thing that brought her beauty to focus. The face was oval under a cap of hair the color of polished bronze. Her eyes were set wide, as green and clear as the morning skies of Caladan. The nose was small, the mouth wide and generous. Her figure was good but scant: tall and with its curves gone to slimness.

He remembered that the lay sisters at the school had called her skinny, so his buyers had told him. But that description was oversimplified. She had brought a regal beauty back into the Atreides line. He was glad that Paul favored her.

"Where's Paul?" he asked.

"Someplace around the house taking his lessons with Yueh."

"Probably in the south wing," he said. "I though I heard Yueh's voice, but I couldn't take time to look." He glanced down at her, hesitating. "I came here only to hang the key of Caladan Castle in the dining hall."

She caught her breath, stopped the impulse to reach out to him. Hanging the key—there was finality in that action. But this was not the time or place for comforting. "I saw our banner over the house as we came in," she said.

He glanced at the painting of his father. "Where were you going to hang that?"

"Somewhere in here."

"No." The word rang flat and final, telling her she could use trickery to persuade, but open argument was useless. Still, she had to try, even if the gesture served only to remind herself that she would not trick him.

"My Lord," she said, "If you'd only . . . ."

"The answer remains no. I indulge you shamefully in most things, not in this. I've just come from the dining hall where there are—"

"My Lord! Please."

"The choice is between your digestion and my ancestral dignity, my dear," he said. "They will hang in the dining hall."

She sighed. "Yes, my Lord."

"You may resume your custom of dining in your rooms whenever possible. I shall expect you at your proper position only on formal occasions."

"Thank you, my Lord."

"And don't go all cold and formal on me! Be thankful that I never married you, my dear. Then it'd be your *duty* to join me at table for every meal."

She held her face immobile, nodded.

"Hawat already has our own poison snooper over the dining table," he said. "There's a portable in your room."

"You anticipated this . . . disagreement," she said.

"My dear, I think also of your comfort. I've engaged servants. They're locals, but Hawat has cleared them—they're Fremen all. They'll do until our own people can be released from their other duties."

"Can anyone from this place be truly safe?"

"Anyone who hates Harkonnens. You may even want to keep the head housekeeper: the Shadout Mapes."

"Shadout," Jessica said. "A Fremen title?"

"I'm told it means 'well-dipper,' a meaning with rather important overtones here. She may not strike you as a servant type, although Hawat speaks highly of her on the basis of Duncan's report. They're convinced she wants to serve—specifically that she wants to serve you."

"Me?"

"The Fremen have learned that you're Bene Gesserit," he said. "There are legends here about the Bene Gesserit."

*The Missionaria Protectiva,* Jessica thought. *No place escapes them.*

"Does this mean Duncan was successful?" she asked. "Will the Fremen be our allies?"

"There's nothing definite," he said. "They wish to observe us for a while, Duncan believes. They did, however, promise to stop raiding our outlying villages during a truce period. That's a more important gain than it might seem. Hawat tells me the Fremen were a deep thorn in the Harkonnen side, that the extent of their ravages was a carefully guarded secret. It wouldn't have helped for the Emperor to learn the ineffectiveness of the Harkonnen military."

"A Fremen housekeeper," Jessica mused, returning to the subject of the Shadout Mapes. "She'll have the all-blue eyes."

"Don't let the appearance of these people deceive you," he said. "There's a deep strength and healthy vitality in them. I think they'll be everything we need."

"It's a dangerous gamble," she said.

"Let's not go into that again," he said.

She forced a smile. "We *are* committed, no doubt of that." She went through the quick regimen of calmness—the two deep breaths, the ritual thought, then: "When I assign rooms, is there anything special I should reserve for you?"

"You must teach me someday how you do that," he said, "the way you thrust your worries aside and turn to practical matters. It must be a Bene Gesserit thing."

"It's a female thing," she said.

He smiled. "Well, assignment of rooms: make certain I have large office space next to my sleeping quarters. There'll be more paper work here than on Caladan. A guard room, of course. That should cover it. Don't worry about security of the house. Hawat's men have been over it in depth."

"I'm sure they have."

He glanced at his wristwatch. "And you might see that all our timepieces are adjusted for Arrakeen local. I've assigned a tech to take care of it. He'll be along presently." He brushed a strand of her hair back from her forehead. "I must return to the landing field now. The second shuttle's due any minute with my staff reserves."

"Couldn't Hawat meet them, my Lord? You look so tired."

"The good Thufir is even busier than I am. You know this planet's infested with Harkonnen intrigues. Besides, I must try persuading some of the trained spice hunters against leaving. They have the option, you know, with the change of fief—and this planetologist the Emperor and the Landsraad installed as Judge of the Change cannot be bought. He's allowing the opt. About eight hundred trained hands expect to go out on the spice shuttle and there's a Guild cargo ship standing by."

"My Lord . . . ." She broke off, hesitating.

"Yes?"

*He will not be persuaded against trying to make this planet secure for us,* she thought. *And I cannot use my tricks on him.*

"At what time will you be expecting dinner?" she asked.

*That's not what she was going to ask,* he thought. *Ah-h-h-h, my Jessica, would that we were somewhere else, anywhere away from this terrible place—alone, the two of us, without a care.*

"I'll eat in the officers' mess at the field," he said. "Don't expect me until very late. And . . . ah, I'll be sending a guardcar for Paul. I want him to attend our strategy conference."

He cleared his throat as though to say something else, then, without warning, turned and strode out, headed for the entry where she could hear more boxes being deposited. His voice sounded once from there, commanding and disdainful, the way he always spoke to servants when he was in a hurry: "The Lady Jessica's in the Great Hall. Join her there immediately."

The outer door slammed.

Jessica turned away, faced the painting of Leto's father. It had been done by the famed artist, Albe, during the Old Duke's middle years. He was portrayed in matador costume with a magenta cape flung over his left arm. The face looked young, hardly older than Leto's now, and with the same hawk features, the same gray stare. She clenched her fists at her sides, glared at the painting.

"Damn you! Damn you! Damn you!" she whispered.

"What are your orders, Noble Born?"

It was a woman's voice, thin and stringy.

Jessica whirled, stared down at a knobby, gray-haired woman in a shapeless sack dress of bondsman brown. The woman looked as wrinkled and desiccated as any member of the mob that had greeted them along the way from the landing field that morning. Every native she had seen on this planet, Jessica thought, looked prune dry and undernourished. Yet, Leto had said they were strong and vital. And there were the eyes, of course—that wash of deepest, darkest blue without any white—secretive, mysterious. Jessica forced herself not to stare.

The woman gave a stiff-necked nod, said: "I am called the Shadout Mapes, Noble Born. What are your orders?"

"You may refer to me as 'my Lady,' " Jessica said. "I'm not noble born. I'm the bound concubine of the Duke Leto."

Again that strange nod, and the woman peered upward at Jessica with a sly questioning. "There's a wife, then?"

"There is not, nor has there ever been. I am the Duke's only . . . companion, the mother of his heir-designate."

Even as she spoke, Jessica laughed inwardly at the pride behind her words. *What was it St. Augustine said?* she asked herself. *"The mind commands the body and it obeys. The mind orders itself and meets resistance."* Yes—I am meeting more resistance lately. I could use a quiet retreat by myself.

A weird cry sounded from the road outside the house. It was repeated: "Soo-soo-Sook! Soo-soo-Sook!" Then: "Ikhut-eigh! Ikhut-eigh!" And again: "Soo-soo-Sook!"

"What *is* that?" Jessica asked. "I heard it several times as we drove through the streets this morning."

"Only a water-seller, my Lady. But you've no need to interest yourself in such as they. The cistern here holds fifty thousand liters and it's always kept full." She glanced down at her dress "Why, you know, my Lady, I don't even have to wear my stillsuit here!" She cackled. "And me not even dead!"

Jessica hesitated, wanting to question this Fremen woman, needing data to guide her. But bringing order of the confusion in the castle was more imperative. Still, she found the thought unsettling that water was a major mark of wealth here.

"My husband told me of your title, Shadout," Jessica said. "I recognized the word. It's a very ancient word."

"You know the ancient tongues then?" Mapes asked, and she waited with an odd intensity.

"Tongues are the Bene Gesserit's first learning," Jessica said. "I know the Bhotani Jib and the Chakobsa, all the hunting languages."

Mapes nodded. "Just as the legend says."

And Jessica wondered: *Why do I play out this sham?* But the Bene Gesserit ways were devious and compelling.

"I know the Dark Things and the ways of the Great Mother," Jessica said. She read the more obvious signs in Mapes' action and appearance, the petit betrayals. "Miseces prejia," she said in the Chakobsa tongue. "Andral t're pera! Trada cik buscakri miseces perakri—"

Mapes took a backward step, appeared poised to flee.

"I know many things," Jessica said. "I know that you have born children, that you have lost loved ones, that you have hidden in fear and that you have done violence and will yet do more violence. I know many things."

In a low voice, Mapes said: "I meant no offense, my Lady."

"You speak of the legend and seek answers," Jessica said. "Beware the answers you may find. I know you came prepared for violence with a weapon in your bodice."

"My Lady, I . . . ."

"There's a remote possibility you could draw my life's blood," Jessica said, "but in so doing you'd bring down more ruin than your wildest fears could imagine. There are worse things than dying, you know—even for an entire people."

"My Lady!" Mapes pleaded. She appeared about to fall to her knees. "The weapon was sent as a gift to *you* should you prove to be the One."

"And as the means of my death should I prove otherwise," Jessica said. She waited in the seeming relaxation that made the Bene Gesserit-trained so terrifying in combat.

*Now we see which way the decision tips,* she thought.

Slowly, Mapes reached into the neck of her dress, brought out a dark sheath. A black handle with deep finger ridges protruded from it. She took sheath in one hand and handle in the other, withdrew a milk-white blade, held it up. The blade seemed to shine and glitter with a light of its own. It was double-edged like a kindjal and the blade was perhaps twenty centimeters long.

"Do you know this, my Lady?" Mapes asked.

It could only be one thing, Jessica knew, the fabled crysknife of Arrakis, the blade that had never been taken off the planet, and was known only by rumor and wild gossip.

"It's a crysknife," she said.

"Say it not lightly," Mapes said. "Do you know its meaning?"

And Jessica thought: *There was an edge to that question. Here's the reason this Fremen has taken service with me, to ask that one question. My answer could precipitate violence or . . . what? She seeks an answer from me: the meaning of a knife. She's called the Shadout in the Chakobsa tongue. Knife, that's "Death Maker" in Chakobsa. She's getting restive. I must answer now. Delay is as dangerous as the wrong answer.*

Jessica said: "It's a maker—"

"Eighe-e-e-e-e!" Mapes wailed. It was a sound of grief and elation. She trembled so hard the knife blade sent glittering shards of reflection shooting around the room.

Jessica waited, poised. She had intended to say the knife was a *maker of death* and then add the ancient word, but every sense warned her now, all the deep training of alertness that exposed meaning in the most casual muscle twitch.

The key word was . . . *maker.*

*Maker? Maker.*

Still, Mapes held the knife as though ready to use it.

Jessica said: "Did you think that I, knowing the mysteries of the Great Mother, would not know the Maker?"

Mapes lowered the knife. "My Lady, when one has lived with prophecy for so long, the moment of revelation is a shock."

Jessica thought about the prophecy—the Shari-a and all the panoplia propheticus, a Bene Gesserit of the Missionaria Protectiva dropped here long centuries ago—long dead, no doubt, but her purpose accomplished: the protective legends implanted in these people against the day of a Bene Gesserit's need.

Well, that day had come.

Mapes returned knife to sheath, said: "This is an unfixed blade, my Lady. Keep it near you. More than a week away from flesh and it begins to disintegrate. It's yours, a tooth of shai-hulud, for as long as you live."

Jessica reached out her right hand, risked a gamble: "Mapes, you've sheathed that blade unblooded."

With a gasp, Mapes dropped the sheathed knife into Jessica's hand, tore open the brown bodice, wailing: "Take the water of my life!"

Jessica withdrew the blade from its sheath. How it glittered! She directed the point toward Mapes, saw a fear greater than death-panic come over the woman.

*Poison in the point?* Jessica wondered. She tipped up the point, drew a delicate scratch with the blade's edge above Mapes' left breast. There was a thick welling of blood that stopped almost immediately. *Ultrafast coagulation,* Jessica thought. *A moisture-conserving mutation?*

She sheathed the blade, said: "Button your dress, Mapes."

Mapes obeyed, trembling. The eyes without whites stared at Jessica. "You are ours," she muttered. "You are the One."

There came another sound of unloading in the entry. Swiftly, Mapes grabbed the sheathed knife, concealed it in Jessica's bodice. "Who sees that knife must be cleansed or slain!" she snarled. "You *know* that, my Lady!"

*I know it now,* Jessica thought.

The cargo handlers left without intruding on the Great Hall.

Mapes composed herself, said: "The uncleansed who have seen a crysknife may not leave Arrakis alive. Never forget that, my Lady. You've been entrusted with a crysknife." She took a deep breath. "Now the thing must take its course. It cannot be hurried." She glanced at the stacked boxes and piled goods around them. "And there's work aplenty to while the time for us here."

Jessica hesitated. *"The thing must take its course."* That was a specific catchphrase from the Missionaria Protectiva's stock of incantations—*The coming of the Reverend Mother to free you.*

*But I'm not a Reverend Mother,* Jessica thought. And then: *Great Mother! They planted that one here! This must be a hideous place!*

In matter-of-fact tones, Mapes said: "What'll you be wanting me to do first, my Lady?"

Instinct warned Jessica to match that casual tone. She said: "The painting of the Old Duke over there, it must be hung on one side of the dining hall. The bull's head must go on the wall opposite the painting."

Mapes crossed to the bull's head. "What a great beast it must have been to carry such a head," she said. She stooped. "I'll have to be cleaning this first, won't I, my Lady?"

"No."

"But there's dirt caked on its horns."

"That's not dirt, Mapes. That's the blood of our Duke's father. Those horns were sprayed with a transparent fixative within hours after this beast killed the Old Duke."

Mapes stood up. "Ah, now!" she said.

"It's just blood," Jessica said. "Old blood at that. Get some help hanging these now. The beastly things are heavy."

"Did you think the blood bothered me?" Mapes asked. "I'm of the desert and I've seen blood aplenty."

"I . . . see that you have," Jessica said.

"And some of it my own," Mapes said. "More'n you drew with your puny scratch."

"You'd rather I'd cut deeper?"

"Ah, no! The body's water is scant enough 'thout gushing a wasteful lot of it into the air. You did the thing right."

And Jessica, noting the words and manner, caught the deeper implications in the phrase, "the body's water." Again she felt a sense of oppression at the importance of water on Arrakis.

"On which side of the dining hall shall I hang which one of these pretties, my Lady?" Mapes asked.

*Ever the practical one, this Mapes,* Jessica thought. She said: "Use your own judgment, Mapes. It makes no real difference."

"As you say, my Lady." Mapes stooped, began clearing wrappings and twine from the head. "Killed an old duke, did you?" she crooned.

"Shall I summon a handler to help you?" Jessica asked.

"I'll manage, my Lady."

*Yes, she'll manage,* Jessica thought. *There's that about this Fremen creature: the drive to manage.*

Jessica felt the cold sheath of the crysknife beneath her bodice, thought of the long chain of Bene Gesserit scheming that had forged another link here. Because of that scheming, she had survived a deadly crisis. "It cannot be hurried," Mapes had said. Yet there was a tempo of headlong rushing to this place that filled Jessica with foreboding. And not all the preparations of the Missionaria Protectiva nor Hawat's suspicious inspection of this castellated pile of rocks could dispel the feeling.

"When you've finished hanging those, start unpacking the boxes," Jessica said. "One of the cargo men at the entry has all the keys and knows where things should go. Get the keys and the list from him. If there are any questions I'll be in the south wing."

"As you will, my Lady," Mapes said.

Jessica turned away, thinking: *Hawat may have passed this residency as safe, but there's something wrong about the place. I can feel it.*

An urgent need to see her son gripped Jessica. She began walking toward the arched doorway that led into the passage to the dining hall and the family wings. Faster and faster she walked until she was almost running.

Behind her, Mapes paused in clearing the wrappings from the bull's head, looked at the retreating back. "She's the One all right," she muttered. "Poor thing."

> *"Yueh! Yueh! Yueh!" goes the refrain. "A million deaths were not enough for Yueh!"*

> **—from "A Child's History of Muad'Dib"**
> **by the Princess Irulan**

The door stood ajar, and Jessica stepped through it into a room with yellow walls. To her left stretched a low settee of black hide and two empty bookcases, a hanging waterflask with dust on its bulging sides. To her right, bracketing another door, stood more empty bookcases, a desk from Caladan and three chairs. At the windows directly ahead of her stood Dr. Yueh, his back to her, his attention fixed upon the outside world.

Jessica took another silent step into the room.

She saw that Yueh's coat was wrinkled, a white smudge near the left elbow as though he had leaned against chalk. He looked, from behind, like a fleshless stick figure in overlarge black clothing, a caricature poised for stringy movement at the direction of a puppet master. Only the squarish block of head with long ebony hair caught in its silver Suk School ring at the shoulder seemed alive—turning slightly to follow some movement outside.

Again, she glanced around the room, seeing no sign of her son, but the closed door on her right, she knew, let into a small bedroom for which Paul had expressed a liking.

"Good afternoon, Dr. Yueh," she said. "Where's Paul?"

He nodded as though to something out the window, spoke in an absent manner without turning: "Your son grew tired, Jessica. I sent him into the next room to rest."

Abruptly, he stiffened, whirled with mustache flopping over his purpled lips. "Forgive me, my Lady! My thoughts were far away . . . I . . . did not mean to be familiar."

She smiled, held out her right hand. For a moment, she was afraid he might kneel. "Wellington, please."

"To use your name like that . . . I . . . ."

"We've known each other six years," she said. "It's long past time formalities should've been dropped between us—in private."

Yueh ventured a thin smile, thinking: *I believe it has worked. Now, she'll think anything unusual in my manner is due to embarrassment. She'll not look for deeper reasons when she believes she already knows the answer.*

"I'm afraid I was woolgathering," he said. "Whenever I . . . feel especially sorry for you, I'm afraid I think of you as . . . well, Jessica."

"Sorry for me? Whatever for?"

Yueh shrugged. Long ago, he had realized Jessica was not gifted with the full Truthsay as his Wanna had been. Still, he always used the truth with Jessica whenever possible. It was safest.

"You've seen this place, my . . . Jessica." He stumbled over the name, plunged ahead: "So barren after Caladan. And the people! Those townswomen we passed on the way here wailing beneath their veils. The way they looked at us."

She folded her arms across her breast, hugging herself, feeling the crysknife there, a blade ground from a sandworm's tooth, if the reports were right. "It's just that we're strange to them—different people, different customs. They've known only the Harkonnens." She looked past him out the windows. "What were you staring at out there?"

He turned back to the window. "The people."

Jessica crossed to his side, looked to the left toward the front of the house where Yueh's attention was focused. A line of twenty palm trees grew there, the ground beneath them swept clean, barren. A screen fence separated them from the road upon which robed people were passing. Jessica detected a faint shimmering in the air between her and the people—a house shield—and went on to study the passing throng, wondering why Yueh found them so absorbing.

The pattern emerged and she put a hand to her cheek. The way the passing people looked at the palm trees! She saw envy, some hate . . . even a sense of hope. Each person raked those trees with a fixity of expression.

"Do you know what they're thinking?" Yueh asked.

"You profess to read minds?" she asked.

"Those minds," he said. "They look at those trees and they think: 'There are one hundred of us.' That's what they think."

She turned a puzzled frown on him. "Why?"

"Those are date palms," he said. "One date palm requires forty liters of water a day. A man requires but eight liters. A palm, then, equals five men. There are twenty palms out there—one hundred men."

"But some of those people look at the trees hopefully."

"They but hope some dates will fall, except it's the wrong season."

"We look at this place with too critical an eye," she said. "There's hope as well as danger here. The spice *could* make us rich. With a fat treasury, we can make this world into whatever we wish."

And she laughed silently at herself: *Who am I trying to convince?* The laugh broke through her restraints, emerging brittle, without humor. "But you can't buy security," she said.

Yueh turned away to hide his face from her. *If only it were possible to hate these people instead of love them!* In her manner, in many ways, Jessica was like his Wanna. Yet that thought carried its own rigors, hardening him to his purpose. The ways of the Harkonnen cruelty were devious. Wanna might not be dead. He had to be certain.

"Do not worry for us, Wellington," Jessica said. "The problem's ours, not yours."

*She thinks I worry for her!* He blinked back tears. *And I do, of course. But I must stand before that black Baron with his deed accomplished, and take my one chance to strike him then where he is weakest—in his gloating moment!*

He sighed.

"Would it disturb Paul if I looked in on him?" she asked.

"Not at all. I gave him a sedative."

"He's taking the change well?" she asked.

"Except for getting a bit overtired. He's excited, but what fifteen-year-old wouldn't be under these circumstances?" He crossed to the door, opened it. "He's in here."

Jessica followed, peered into a shadowy room.

Paul lay on a narrow cot, one arm beneath a light cover, the other thrown back over his head. Slatted blinds at a window beside the bed wove a loom of shadows across face and blanket.

Jessica stared at her son, seeing the oval shape of face so like her own. But the hair was the Duke's—coal-colored and tousled. Long lashes concealed the lime-toned eyes. Jessica smiled, feeling her tears retreat. She was suddenly caught by the idea of genetic traces in her son's features—her lines in eyes and facial outline, but sharp touches of the father peering through that outline like maturity emerging from childhood.

She thought of the boy's features as an exquisite distillation out of random patterns—endless queues of happenstance meeting at this nexus. The thought made her want to kneel beside the bed and take her son in her arms, but she was inhibited by Yueh's presence. She stepped back, closed the door softly.

Yueh had returned to the window, unable to bear watching the way Jessica stared at her son. *Why did Wanna never give me children?* he asked himself. *I know as a doctor there was no physical reason against it. Was there some Bene Gesserit reason? Was she, perhaps, instructed to serve a different purpose? What could it have been? She loved me, certainly.*

For the first time, he was caught up in the thought that he might be part of a pattern more involuted and complicated than his mind could grasp.

Jessica stopped beside him, said: "What delicious abandon in the sleep of a child."

He spoke mechanically: "If only adults could relax like that."

"Yes."

"Where do we lose it?" he murmured.

She glanced at him, catching the odd tone, but her mind was still on Paul, thinking of the new rigors in his training here, thinking of the differences in his life now—so very different from the life they once had planned for him.

"We do, indeed, lose something," she said.

She glanced out to the right at a slope humped with a wind-troubled gray-green of bushes—dusty leaves and dry claw branches. The too-dark sky hung over the slope like a blot, and the milky light of the Arrakeen sun gave the scene a silver cast—light like the crysknife concealed in her bodice.

"The sky's so dark," she said.

"That's partly the lack of moisture," he said.

"Water!" she snapped. "Everywhere you turn here, you're involved with the lack of water!"

"It's the precious mystery of Arrakis," he said.

"Why is there so little of it? There're volcanic rock here. There're a dozen power sources I could name. There's polar ice. They say you can't drill in the desert—storms and sandtides destroy equipment faster than it can be installed, if the worms don't get you first. They've never found water traces there, anyway. But the mystery, Wellington, the real mystery is the wells that've been drilled up here in the sinks and basins. Have you read about those?"

"First a trickle, then nothing," he said.

"But, Wellington, that's the mystery. The water was there. It dries up. And never again is there water. Yet another hole nearby produces the same result: a trickle that stops. Has no one ever been curious about this?"

"It is curious," he said. "You suspect some living agency? Wouldn't that have shown in core samples?"

"What would have shown? Alien plant matter . . . or animal? Who could recognize it?" She turned back to the slope. "The water is stopped. Something plugs it. That's my suspicion."

"Perhaps the reason's known," he said. "The Harkonnens sealed off many sources of information about Arrakis. Perhaps there was reason to suppress this."

"What reason?" she asked. "And then there's the atmospheric moisture. Little enough of it, certainly, but there's some. It's the major source of water here, caught in windtraps and precipitators. Where does that come from?"

"The polar caps?"

"Cold air takes up little moisture, Wellington. There are things here behind the Harkonnen veil that bear close investigation, and not all of those things are directly involved with the spice."

"We are indeed behind the Harkonnen veil," he said. "Perhaps we'll . . . ." He broke off, noting the sudden intense way she was looking at him. "Is something wrong?"

"The way you say 'Harkonnen,'" she said. "Even my Duke's voice doesn't carry that weight of venom when he uses the hated name. I didn't know you had personal reasons to hate them, Wellington."

*Great Mother!* he thought. *I've aroused her suspicions! Now I must use every trick my Wanna taught me. There's only one solution: tell the truth as far as I can.*

He said: "You didn't know that my wife, my Wanna . . . ." He shrugged, unable to speak past a sudden constriction in his throat. Then: "They . . . ." The words would not come out. He felt panic, closed his eyes tightly, experiencing the agony in his chest and little else until a hand touched his arm gently.

"Forgive me," Jessica said. "I did not mean to open an old wound." And she thought: *Those animals! His wife was Bene Gesserit—the signs are all over him. And it's obvious the Harkonnens killed her. Here's another poor victim bound to the Atreides by a cherem of hate.*

"I am sorry," he said. "I'm unable to talk about it." He opened his eyes, giving himself up to the internal awareness of grief. That, at least, was truth.

Jessica studied him, seeing the up-angled cheeks, the dark sequins of almond eyes, the butter complexion, and stringy mustache hanging like a curved frame around purpled lips and narrow chin. The creases of his cheeks and forehead, she saw, were as much lines of sorrow as of age. A deep affection for him came over her.

"Wellington, I'm sorry we brought you into this dangerous place," she said.

"I came willingly," he said. And that, too, was true.

"But this whole planet's a Harkonnen trap. You must know that."

"It will take more than a trap to catch the Duke Leto," he said. And that, too, was true.

"Perhaps I should be more confident of him," she said. "He is a brilliant tactician."

"We've been uprooted," he said. "That's why we're uneasy."

"And how easy it is to kill the uprooted plant," she said. "Especially when you put it down in hostile soil."

"Are we certain the soil's hostile?"

"There were water riots when it was learned how many people the Duke was adding to the population," she said. "They stopped only when the people learned we were installing new windtraps and condensers to take care of the load."

"There is only so much water to support human life here," he said. "The people know if more come to drink a limited amount of water, the price goes up and the very poor die. But the Duke has solved this. It doesn't follow that the riots mean permanent hostility toward him."

"And guards," she said. "Guards everywhere. And shields. You see the blurring of them everywhere you look. We did not live this way on Caladan."

"Give this planet a chance," he said.

But Jessica continued to stare hard-eyed out the window. "I can smell death in this place," she said. "Hawat sent advance agents in here by the battalion. Those guards outside are his men. The cargo handlers are his men. There've been unexplained withdrawals of large sums from the treasury. The amounts mean only one thing: bribes in high places." She shook her head. "Where Thufir Hawat goes, death and deceit follow."

"You malign him."

"Malign? I praise him. Death and deceit are our only hopes now. I just do not fool myself about Thufir's methods."

"You should . . . keep busy," he said. "Give yourself no time for such morbid—"

"Busy! What is it that takes most of my time, Wellington? I am the Duke's secretary—so busy that each day I learn new things to fear . . . things even he doesn't suspect I know." She compressed her lips, spoke thinly: "Sometimes I wonder how much my Bene Gesserit business training figured in his choice of me."

"What do you mean?" He found himself caught by the cynical tone, the bitterness that he had never seen her expose.

"Don't you think, Wellington," she asked, "that a secretary bound to one by love is so much safer?"

"That is not a worthy thought, Jessica."

The rebuke came naturally to his lips. There was no doubt how the Duke felt about his concubine. One had only to watch him as he followed her with his eyes.

She sighed. "You're right. It's not worthy."

Again, she hugged herself, pressing the sheathed crysknife against her flesh and thinking of the unfinished business it represented.

"There'll be much bloodshed soon," she said. "The Harkonnens won't rest until they're dead or my Duke destroyed. The Baron cannot forget that Leto is a cousin of the royal blood—no matter what the distance—while the Harkonnen titles came out of the CHOAM pocketbook. But the poison in him, deep in his mind, is the knowledge that an Atreides had a Harkonnen banished for cowardice after the Battle of Corrin."

"The old feud," Yueh muttered. And for a moment he felt an acid touch of hate. The old feud had trapped him in its web, killed his Wanna or—worse— left her for Harkonnen tortures until her husband did their bidding. The old feud had trapped him and these people were part of that poisonous thing. The irony was that such deadliness should come to flower here on Arrakis, the one source in the universe of melange, the prolonger of life, the giver of health.

"What are you thinking?" she asked.

"I am thinking that the spice brings six hundred and twenty thousand solaris the decagram on the open market right now. That is wealth to buy many things."

"Does greed touch even you, Wellington?"

"Not greed."

"What then?"

He shrugged. "Futility." He glanced at her. "Can you remember your first taste of spice?"

"It tasted like cinnamon."

"But never twice the same," he said. "It's like life—it presents a different face each time you take it. Some hold that the spice produces a learned-flavor reaction. The body, learning a thing is good for it, interprets the flavor as pleasurable—slightly euphoric. And, like life, never to be truly synthesized."

"I think it would've been wiser for us to go renegade, to take ourselves beyond the Imperial reach," she said.

He saw that she hadn't been listening to him, focused on her words, wondering: *Yes—why didn't she make him do this? She could make him do virtually anything.*

He spoke quickly because here was truth and a change of subject: "Would you think it bold of me . . . Jessica, if I asked a personal question?"

She pressed against the window ledge in an unexplainable pang of disquiet. "Of course not. You're . . . my friend."

"Why haven't you made the Duke marry you?"

She whirled, head up, glaring. "Made him marry me? But—"

"I should not have asked," he said.

"No." She shrugged. "There's good political reason—as long as my Duke remains unmarried some of the Great Houses can still hope for alliance. And . . . ." She sighed. ". . . motivating people, forcing them to your will, gives you a cynical attitude toward humanity. It degrades everything it touches. If I made him do . . . this, then it would not be his doing."

"It's a thing my Wanna might have said," he murmured. And this, too, was truth. He put a hand to his mouth, swallowing convulsively. He had never been closer to speaking out, confessing his secret role.

Jessica spoke, shattering the moment. "Besides, Wellington, the Duke is really two men. One of them I love very much. He's charming, witty, considerate . . . tender—everything a woman could desire. But the other man is . . . cold, callous, demanding, selfish—as harsh and cruel as a winter wind. That's the man shaped by the father." Her face contorted. "If only that old man had died when my Duke was born!"

In the silence that came between them, a breeze from a ventilator could be heard fingering the blinds.

Presently, she took a deep breath, said, "Leto's right—these rooms are nicer than the ones in the other sections of the house." She turned, sweeping the room with her gaze. "If you'll excuse me, Wellington, I want another look through this wing before I assign quarters."

He nodded. "Of course." And he thought: *If only there were some way not to do this thing that I must do.*

Jessica dropped her arms, crossed to the hall door and stood there a moment, hesitating, then let herself out. *All the time we talked he was hiding something, holding something back,* she thought. *To save my feelings, no doubt. He's a good man.* Again, she hesitated, almost turned back to confront Yueh and drag the hidden thing from him. *But that would only shame him, frighten him to learn he's so easily read. I should place more trust in my friends.*

*Many have marked the speed with which Muad'Dib learned the necessities of Arrakis. The Bene Gesserit, of course, know the basis of this speed. For the others, we can say that Muad'Dib learned rapidly because his first training was in how to learn. And the first lesson of all was the basic trust that he could learn. It is shocking to find how many people do not believe they can learn, and how many more believe learning to be difficult. Muad'Dib knew that every experience carries its lesson.*

**—from "The Humanity of Muad'Dib"
by the Princess Irulan**

Paul lay on the bed feigning sleep. It had been easy to palm Dr. Yueh's sleeping tablet, to pretend to swallow it. Paul suppressed a laugh. Even his mother had believed him asleep. He had wanted to jump up and ask her permission to go exploring the house, but had realized she wouldn't approve. Things were too unsettled yet. No. This way was best.

*If I slip out without asking I haven't disobeyed orders. And I will stay in the house where it's safe.*

He heard his mother and Yueh talking in the other room. Their words were indistinct—something about the spice . . . the Harkonnens. The conversation rose and fell.

Paul's attention went to the carved headboard of his bed—a false headboard attached to the wall and concealing the controls for this room's functions. A leaping fish had been shaped on the wood with thick brown waves beneath it. He knew if he pushed the fish's one visible eye that would turn on the room's suspensor lamps. One of the waves, when twisted, controlled ventilation. Another changed the temperature.

Quietly, Paul sat up in bed. A tall bookcase stood against the wall to his left. It could be swung aside to reveal a closet with drawers along one side. The handle on the door into the hall was patterned on an ornithopter thrust bar.

It was as though the room had been designed to entice him.

The room and this planet.

He thought of the filmbook Yueh had shown him—"Arrakis: His Imperial Majesty's Desert Botanical Testing Station." It was an old filmbook from before discovery of the spice. Names flitted through Paul's mind, each with its picture imprinted by the book's mnemonic pulse: *saguaro, burro bush, date palm, sand verbena, evening primrose, barrel cactus, incense bush, smoke tree, creosote bush . . . kit fox, desert hawk, kangaroo mouse . . . .*

Names and pictures, names and pictures from man's terranic past—and many to be found now nowhere else in the universe except here on Arrakis.

So many new things to learn about—the spice.

And the sandworms.

A door closed in the other room. Paul heard his mother's footsteps retreating down the hall. Dr. Yueh, he knew, would find something to read and remain in the other room.

Now was the moment to go exploring.

Paul slipped out of the bed, headed for the bookcase door that opened into the closet. He stopped at a sound behind him, turned. The carved headboard of the bed was folding down onto the spot where he had been sleeping. Paul froze, and immobility saved his life.

From behind the headboard slipped a tiny hunter-seeker no more than five centimeters long. Paul recognized it at once—a common assassination weapon that every child of royal blood learned about at an early age. It was a ravening sliver of metal guided by some near-by hand and eye. It could burrow into moving flesh and chew its way up nerve channels to the nearest vital organ.

The seeker lifted, swung sideways across the room and back.

Through Paul's mind flashed the related knowledge, the hunter-seeker's limitations: Its compressed suspensor field distorted the vision of its transmitter eye. With nothing but the dim light of the room to reflect his target, the operator would be relying on motion—anything that moved. A shield could slow a hunter, give time to destroy it, but Paul had put aside his shield on the bed. Lasguns would knock them down, but lasguns were expensive and notoriously cranky of maintenance—and there was always the peril of explosive pyrotechnics if the laser beam intersected a hot shield. The Atreides relied on their body shields and their wits.

Now, Paul held himself in near catatonic immobility, knowing he had only his wits to meet this threat.

The hunter-seeker lifted another half meter. It rippled through the slatted light from the window blinds, back and forth, quartering the room.

*I must try to grab it,* he thought. *The suspensor field will make it slippery on the bottom. I must grip tightly.*

The thing dropped a half meter, quartered to the left, circled back around the bed. A faint humming could be heard from it.

*Who is operating that thing?* Paul wondered. *It has to be someone near. I could shout for Yueh, but it would take him the instant the door opened.*

The hall door behind Paul creaked. A rap sounded there. The door opened. The hunter-seeker arrowed past his head toward the motion.

Paul's right hand shot out and down, gripping the deadly thing. It hummed and twisted in his hand, but his muscles were locked on it in desperation. With a violent turn and thrust, he slammed the thing's nose against the metal doorplate. He felt the crunch of it as the nose eye smashed and the seeker went dead in his hand.

Still, he held it—to be certain.

Paul's eyes came up, met the open stare of total blue from the Shadout Mapes.

"Your father has sent for you," she said. "There are men in the hall to escort you."

Paul nodded, his eyes and awareness focusing on this odd woman in a sacklike dress of bondsman brown. She was looking now at the thing clutched in his hand.

"I've heard of suchlike," she said. "It would've killed me, not so?"

He had to swallow before he could speak. "I . . . was its target."

"But it was coming for me."

"Because you were moving." And he wondered: *Who is this creature?*

"Then you saved my life," she said.

"I saved both our lives."

"Seems like you could've let it have me and made your own escape," she said.

"Who are you?" he asked.

"The Shadout Mapes, housekeeper."

"How did you know where to find me?"

"Your mother told me. I met her at the stairs to the weirding room down the hall." She pointed to her right. "Your father's men are still waiting."

*Those will be Hawat's men,* he thought. *We must find the operator of this thing.*

"Go to my father's men," he said. "Tell them I've caught a hunter-seeker in the house and they're to spread out and find the operator. Tell them to seal off the house and its grounds immediately. They'll know how to go about it. The operator's sure to be a stranger among us."

And he wondered: *Could it be this creature?* But he knew it wasn't. The seeker had been under control when she entered.

"Before I do your bidding, manling," Mapes said, "I must cleanse the way between us. You've put a water burden on me that I'm not sure I care to support. But we Fremen pay our debts—be they black debts or white debts. And it's known to us that you've a traitor in your midst. Who it is, we cannot say, but we're certain sure of it. Mayhap there's the hand guided that flesh-cutter."

Paul absorbed this in silence: *a traitor.* Before he could speak, the odd woman whirled away and ran back toward the entry.

He thought to call her back, but there was an air about her that told him she would resent it. She'd told him what she knew and now she was going to do his *bidding.* The house would be swarming with Hawat's men in a minute.

His mind went to other parts of that strange conversation: *weirding room.* He looked to his left where she had pointed. *We Fremen.* So that was a Fremen. He paused for the mnemonic blink that would store the pattern of her face in his memory—prune-wrinkled features darkly browned, blue-on-blue eyes without any white in them. He attached the label: *The Shadout Mapes.*

Still gripping the shattered seeker, Paul turned back into his room, scooped up his shield belt from the bed with his left hand, swung it around his waist and buckled it as he ran back out and down the hall to the left.

She'd said his mother was someplace down here—stairs . . . a *weirding room.*

*What had the Lady Jessica to sustain her in her time of trial? Think you carefully on this Bene Gesserit proverb and perhaps you will see: "Any road followed precisely to its end leads precisely nowhere. Climb the mountain just a little bit to test that it's a mountain. From the top of the mountain, you cannot see the mountain."*

**—from "Muad'Dib: Family Commentaries"**
**by the Princess Irulan**

At the end of the south wing, Jessica found a metal stair spiraling up to an oval door. She glanced back down the hall, again up at the door.

*Oval?* she wondered. *What an odd shape for a door in a house.*

Through the windows beneath the spiral stair she could see the great white sun of Arrakis moving on toward evening. Long shadows stabbed down the hall. She returned her attention to the stairs. Harsh sidelighting picked out bits of dried earth on the open metalwork of the steps.

Jessica put a hand on the rail, began to climb. The rail felt cold under her sliding palm. She stopped at the door, saw it had no handle, but there was a faint depression on the surface of it where a handle should have been.

*Surely not a palm lock,* she told herself. *A palm lock must be keyed to one individual's hand shape and palm lines.* But it looked like a palm lock. And there were ways to open any palm lock—as she had learned at school.

Jessica glanced back to make certain she was unobserved, placed her palm against the depression in the door. The most gentle of pressures to distort the lines—a turn of the wrist, another turn, a sliding twist of the palm across the surface.

She felt the click.

But there were hurrying footsteps in the hall beneath her. Jessica lifted her hand from the door, turned, saw Mapes come to the foot of the stairs.

"There are men in the great hall say they've been sent by the Duke to get young master Paul," Mapes said. "They've the ducal signet and the guard has identified them." She glanced at the door, back to Jessica.

*A cautious one, this Mapes,* Jessica thought. *That's a good sign.*

"He's in the fifth room from this end of the hall, the small bedroom," Jessica said. "If you have trouble waking him, call on Dr. Yueh in the next room. Paul may require a wakeshot."

Again, Mapes cast a piercing stare at the oval door, and Jessica thought she detected loathing in the expression. Before Jessica could ask about the door and what it concealed, Mapes had turned away, hurrying back down the hall.

*Hawat certified this place,* Jessica thought. *There can't be anything too terrible in here.*

She pushed the door. It swung inward onto a small room with another oval door opposite. The other door had a wheel handle.

*An air lock!* Jessica thought. She glanced down, saw a door prop fallen to the floor of the little room. The prop carried Hawat's personal mark. *The door was left propped open,* she thought. *Someone probably knocked the prop down accidentally, not realizing the outer door would close on a palm lock.*

She stepped over the lip into the little room.

*Why an airlock in a house?* she asked herself. And she thought suddenly of exotic creatures sealed off in special climates.

*Special climate!*

That would make sense on Arrakis where even the driest of off-planet growing things had to be irrigated.

The door behind her began swinging closed. She caught it and propped it open securely with the stick Hawat had left. Again, she faced the wheel-locked inner door, seeing now a faint inscription etched in the metal above the handle. She recognized Galach words, read:

"O, Man! Here is a lovely portion of God's Creation; then, stand before it and learn to love the perfection of Thy Supreme Friend."

Jessica put her weight on the wheel. It turned left and the inner door opened. A gentle draft feathered her cheek, stirred her hair. She felt change in the air, a richer taste. She swung the door wide, looked through into massed greenery with yellow sunlight pouring across it.

*A yellow sun?* she asked herself. Then: *Filter glass!*

She stepped over the sill and the door swung closed behind.

"A wet-planet conservatory," she breathed.

Potted plants and low-pruned trees stood all about. She recognized a mimosa, a flowering quince, a sondagi, green-blossomed pleniscenta, green and white striped akarso . . . roses . . . .

*Even roses!*

She bent to breathe the fragrance of a giant pink blossom, straightened to peer around the room.

Rhythmic noise invaded her senses.

She parted a jungle overlapping of leaves, looked through to the center of the room. A low fountain stood there, small with fluted lips. The rhythmic noise was a peeling, spooling arc of water falling thud-a-gallop onto the metal bowl.

Jessica sent herself through the quick sense-clearing regimen, began a methodical inspection of the room's perimeter. It appeared to be about ten meters square. From its placement above the end of the hall and from subtle differences in construction, she guessed it had been added onto the roof of this wing long after the original building's completion.

She stopped at the south limits of the room in front of the wide reach of filter glass, stared around. Every available space in the room was crowded with exotic wet-climate plants. Something rustled in the greenery. She tensed, then glimpsed a simple clock-set servok with pipe and hose arms. An arm lifted, sent out a fine spray of dampness that misted her cheeks. The arm retracted and she looked at what it had watered: a fern tree.

Water everywhere in this room—on a planet where water was the most precious juice of life. Water being wasted so conspicuously that it shocked her to inner stillness.

She glanced out at the filter-yellowed sun. It hung low on a jagged horizon above cliffs that formed part of the immense rock uplifting known as the Shield Wall.

*Filter glass,* she thought. *To turn a white sun into something softer and more familiar. Who could have built such a place? Leto? It would be like him to surprise me with such a gift, but there hasn't been time. And he's been busy with more serious problems.*

She recalled the report that many Arrakeen houses were sealed by airlock doors and windows to conserve and reclaim interior moisture. Leto had said it was a deliberate statement of power and wealth for this house to ignore such precautions, its doors and windows being sealed only against the omnipresent dust.

But this room embodied a statement far more significant than the lack of waterseals on outer doors. She estimated that this pleasure room used water enough to support a thousand persons on Arrakis—possibly more.

Jessica moved along the window, continuing to stare into the room. The move brought into view a metallic surface at table height beside the fountain and she glimpsed a white notepad and stylus there partly concealed by an overhanging fan leaf. She crossed to the table, noted Hawat's daysigns on it, studied a message written on the pad:

> "To the Lady Jessica—
> May this place give you as much pleasure as it has given me. Please permit the room to convey a lesson we learned from the same teachers: the proximity of a desirable thing tempts one to overindulgence. On that path lies danger.
>
>> My kindest wishes,
>> Margot Lady Fenring"

Jessica nodded, remembering that Leto had referred to the Emperor's former proxy here as Count Fenring. But the hidden message of the note demanded immediate attention, couched as it was in a way to inform her the writer was another Bene Gesserit. A bitter thought touched Jessica in passing: *The Count married his Lady.*

Even as this thought flicked through her mind, she was bending to seek out the hidden message. It had to be there. The visible note contained the code phrase every Bene Gesserit not bound by a School Injunction was required to give another Bene Gesserit when conditions demanded it: "On that path lies danger."

Jessica felt the back of the note, rubbed the surface for coded dots. Nothing. The edge of the pad came under her seeking fingers. Nothing. She replaced the pad where she had found it, feeling a sense of urgency.

*Something in the position of the pad?* she wondered.

But Hawat had been over this room, doubtless had moved the pad. She looked at the leaf above the pad. The leaf! She brushed a finger along the under surface, along the edge, along the stem. It was there! Her fingers detected the subtle coded dots, scanned them in a single passage:

"Your son and Duke are in immediate danger. A bedroom has been designed to attract your son. The H loaded it with death traps to be discovered, leaving one that may escape detection." Jessica put down the urge to run back to Paul; the full message had to be learned. Her fingers sped over the dots: "I do not know the exact nature of the menace, but it has something to do with a bed. The threat to your Duke involves defection of a trusted companion or lieutenant. The H plan to give you as gift to a minion. To the best of my knowledge, this conservatory is safe. Forgive that I cannot tell more. My sources are few as my Count is not in the pay of the H. In haste, MF."

Jessica thrust the leaf aside, whirled to dash back to Paul. In that instant the airlock door slammed open. Paul jumped through it, holding something in his right hand, slammed the door behind him. He saw his mother, pushed through the leaves to her, glanced at the fountain, thrust his hand and the thing it clutched under the falling water.

"Paul!" She grabbed his shoulder, staring at the hand. "What is that?"

He spoke casually, but she caught the effort behind the tone: "Hunter-seeker. Caught it in my room and smashed its nose, but I want to be sure. Water should short it out."

"Immerse it!" she commanded.

He obeyed.

Presently, she said: "Withdraw your hand. Leave the thing in the water."

He brought out his hand, shook water from it, staring at the quiescent metal in the fountain. Jessica broke off a plant stem, prodded the deadly sliver.

It was dead.

She dropped the stem into the water, looked at Paul. His eyes studied the room with a searching intensity that she recognized—the B.G. Way.

"This place could conceal anything," he said.

"I've reason to believe it's safe," she said.

"My room was supposed to be safe, too. Hawat said—"

"It was a hunter-seeker," she reminded him. "That means someone inside the house to operate it. Seeker control beams have limited range. The thing could've been spirited in here after Hawat's investigation."

But she thought of the message of the leaf: ". . . *defection of a trusted companion or lieutenant.*" *Not Hawat, surely. Oh, surely not Hawat.*

"Hawat's men are searching the house right now," he said. "That seeker almost got the old woman who came to wake me."

"The Shadout Mapes," Jessica said, remembering the encounter at the stairs. "A summons from your father to—"

"That can wait," Paul said. "Why do you think this room's safe?"

She pointed to the note, explained about it.

He relaxed slightly.

But Jessica remained inwardly tense, thinking: *A hunter-seeker! Merciful Mother!* It took all her training to prevent a fit of hysterical trembling.

Paul spoke matter of factly: "It's the Harkonnens, of course. We shall have to destroy them."

A rapping sounded at the airlock door—the code knock of one of Hawat's corps.

"Come in," Paul called.

The door swung wide and a tall man in Atreides uniform with a Hawat insignia on his cap leaned into the rom. "There you are, sir," he said. "The housekeeper said you'd be here." He glanced around the room. "We found a cairn in the cellar and caught a man in it. He had a seeker console."

"I'll want to take part in the interrogation," Jessica said.

"Sorry, my Lady. We messed him up catching him. He died."

"Nothing to identify him?" she asked.

"We've found nothing yet, my Lady."

"Was he an Arrakeen native?" Paul asked.

Jessica nodded at the astuteness of the question.

"He has the native look," the man said. "Put into that cairn more'n a month ago, by the look, and left there to await our coming. Stone and mortar where he came through into the cellar were untouched when we inspected the place yesterday. I'll stake my reputation on it."

"No one questions your thoroughness," Jessica said.

"I question it, my Lady. We should've used sonic probes down there."

"I presume that's what you're doing now," Paul said.

"Yes, sir."

"Send word to my father that we'll be delayed."

"At once, sir." He glanced at Jessica. "It's Hawat's order that under such circumstances as these the young master be guarded in a safe place." Again his eyes swept the room. "What of this place?"

"I've reason to believe it safe," she said. "Both Hawat and I have inspected it."

"Then I'll mount guard outside here, m'Lady, until we've been over the house once more." He bowed, touched his cap to Paul, backed out and swung the door closed behind him.

Paul broke the sudden silence, saying: "Had we better go over the house later ourselves? Your eyes might see things others would miss."

"This wing was the only place I hadn't examined," she said. "I put it off to last because . . . ."

"Because Hawat gave it his personal attention," he said.

She darted a quick look at his face, questioning.

"Do you distrust Hawat?" she asked.

"No, but he's getting old . . . he's overworked. We could take some of the load from him."

"That'd only shame him and impair his efficiency," she said. "A stray insect won't be able to wander into this wing after he hears about this. He'll be shamed that . . . ."

"We must take our own measures," he said.

"Hawat has served three generations of Atreides with honor," she said. "He deserves every respect and trust we can pay him . . . many times over."

Paul said: "When my father is bothered by something you've done he says *'Bene Gesserit!'* like a swear word."

"And what is it about me that bothers your father?"

"When you argue with him."

"You are not your father, Paul."

And Paul thought: *It'll worry her, but I must tell her what that Mapes woman said about a traitor among us.*

"What're you holding back?" Jessica asked. "This isn't like you, Paul."

He shrugged, recounted the exchange with Mapes.

And Jessica thought of the message of the leaf. She came to a sudden decision, showed Paul the leaf, told him its message.

"My father must learn of this at once," he said. "I'll radiograph it in code and get it off."

"No," she said. "You will wait until you can see him alone. As few as possible must learn about it."

"Do you mean we should trust no one?"

"There's another possibility," she said. "This message may have been meant to get to us. The people who gave it to us may believe it's true, but it may be that the only purpose was to get this message to us."

Paul's face remained sturdily somber. "To sow distrust and suspicion in our ranks, to weaken us that way," he said.

"You must tell your father privately and caution him about this aspect of it," she said.

"I understand."

She turned to the tall reach of filter glass, stared out to the southwest where the sun of Arrakis was sinking—a yellowed ball low above the cliffs.

Paul turned with her, said: "I don't think it's Hawat, either. Is it possible it's Yueh?"

"He's not a lieutenant or companion," she said. "And I can assure you he hates the Harkonnens as bitterly as we do."

Paul directed his attention to the cliffs, thinking: *And it couldn't be Gurney . . . or Duncan. Could it be one of the sub-lieutenants? Impossible. They're all from families that've been loyal to us for generations—for good reason.*

Jessica rubbed her forehead, sensing her own fatigue. *So much peril here!* She looked out at the filter-yellowed landscape, studying it. Beyond the ducal grounds stretched a high-fenced storage yard—lines of spice silos in it with stilt-legged watchtowers standing around it like so many startled spiders. She could see at least twenty storage yards of silos reaching out to the cliffs of the Shield Wall—silos repeated, stuttering across the basin.

Slowly, the filtered sun buried itself beneath the horizon. Stars leaped out. She saw one bright star so low on the horizon that it twinkled with a clear, precise rhythm—a trembling of light: blink-blink-blink-blink-blink . . .

Paul stirred beside her in the dusky room.

But Jessica concentrated on that single bright star, realizing that it was *too* low, that it must come from the Shield Wall cliffs.

*Someone signaling!*

She tried to read the message, but it was in no code she had ever learned.

Other lights had come on down on the plain beneath the cliffs: little yellows spaced out against blue darkness. And one light off to their left grew brighter, began to wink back at the cliff—very fast: blinksquirt, glimmer, blink!

And it was gone.

The false star in the cliff winked out immediately.

Signals . . . and they filled her with premonition.

*Why were lights used to signal across the basin?* she asked herself. *Why couldn't they use the communications network?*

The answer was obvious: the communinet was certain to be tapped now by agents of the Duke Leto. Light signals could only mean that messages were being sent between his enemies—between Harkonnen agents.

There came a tapping at the door behind them and the voice of Hawat's man: "All clear, sir . . . m'Lady. Time to be getting the young master to his father."

> *It is said that the Duke Leto blinded himself to the perils of Arrakis, that he walked heedlessly into the pit. Would it not be more likely to suggest he had lived so long in the presence of extreme danger he misjudged a change in its intensity? Or is it possible he deliberately sacrificed himself that his son might find a better life? All evidence indicates the Duke was a man not easily hoodwinked.*

**—from "Muad'Dib: Family Commentaries"**
**by the Princes Irulan**

The Duke Leto Atreides leaned against a parapet of the landing control tower outside Arrakeen. The night's first moon, an oblate silver coin, hung well above the southern horizon. Beneath it, the jagged cliffs of the Shield Wall shone like parched icing through a dust haze. To his left, the lights of Arrakeen glowed in the haze—yellow . . . white . . . blue.

He thought of the notices posted now above his signature all through the populous places of the planet: "Our Sublime Padishah Emperor has charged me to take possession of this planet and end all dispute."

The ritualistic formality of it touched him with a feeling of loneliness. *Who was fooled by that fatuous legalism? Not the Fremen, certainly. Nor the Houses Minor who controlled the interior trade of Arrakis . . . and were Harkonnen creatures almost to a man.*

*They have tried to take the life of my son!*

The rage was difficult to suppress.

He saw lights of a moving vehicle coming toward the landing field from Arrakeen. He hoped it was the guard and troop carrier bringing Paul. The delay was galling even though he knew it was prompted by caution on the part of Hawat's lieutenant.

*They have tried to take the life of my son!*

He shook his head to drive out the angry thoughts, glanced back at the field where five of his own frigates were posted around the rim like monolithic sentries.

*Better a cautious delay than . . . .*

The lieutenant was a good one, he reminded himself. A man marked for advancement, completely loyal.

*"Our Sublime Padishah Emperor . . . ."*

If the people of this decadent garrison city could only see the Emperor's private note to his "Noble Duke"—the disdainful allusions to veiled men and women: ". . . but what else is one to expect of barbarians whose dearest dream is to live outside the ordered security of the faufreluches?"

The Duke felt in this moment that his own dearest dream was to end all class distinctions and never again think of deadly order. He looked up and out of the dust at the unwinking stars, thought: *Around one of those little lights circles Caladan . . . but I'll never again see my home.* The longing for Caladan was a sudden pain in his breast. He felt that it did not come from within himself, but that it reached out to him from Caladan. He could not bring himself to call this dry wasteland of Arrakis his home, and he doubted he ever would.

*I must mask my feelings,* he thought. *For the boy's sake. If ever he's to have a home, this must be it. I may think of Arrakis as a hell I've reached before death, but he must find here that which will inspire him. There must be something.*

A wave of self-pity, immediately despised and rejected, swept through him, and for some reason he found himself recalling two lines from a poem Gurney Halleck often repeated—

> "My lungs taste the air of Time
> Blown past falling sands . . . ."

Well, Gurney would find plenty of falling sands here, the Duke thought. The central wastelands beyond those moon-frosted cliffs were desert—barren rock, dunes, and blowing dust, an uncharted dry wilderness with here and there along its rim and perhaps scattered through it, knots of Fremen. If anything could buy a future for the Atreides line, the Fremen just might do it.

Provided the Harkonnens hadn't managed to infect even the Fremen with their poisonous schemes.

*They have tried to take the life of my son!*

A scraping metal racket vibrated through the tower, shook the parapet beneath his arms. Blast shutters dropped in front of him, blocking the view.

*Shuttle's coming in,* he thought. *Time to go down and get to work.* He turned to the stairs behind him, headed down to the big assembly room, trying to remain calm as he descended, to prepare his face for the coming encounter.

*They have tried to take the life of my son!*

The men were already boiling in from the field when he reached the yellow-domed room. They carried their spacebags over their shoulders, shouting and roistering like students returning from vacation.

"Hey! Feel that under your dogs? That's gravity, man!" "How many G's does this place pull? Feels heavy." "Nine-tenths of a G by the book."

The crossfire of thrown words filled the big room.

"Did you get a good look at this hole on the way down? Where's all the loot this place's supposed to have?" "The Harkonnens took it with 'em!" "Me for a hot shower and a soft bed!" "Haven't you heard, stupid? No showers down here. You scrub your ass with sand!" "Hey! Can it! The Duke!"

The Duke stepped out of the stair entry into a suddenly silent room.

Gurney Halleck strode along at the point of the crowd, bag over one shoulder, the neck of his nine-string baliset clutched in the other hand. They were long-fingered hands with big thumbs, full of tiny movements that drew such delicate music from the baliset.

The Duke watched Halleck, admiring the ugly lump of a man, noting the glass-splinter eyes with their gleam of savage understanding. Here was a man who lived outside the faufreluches while obeying their every precept. What was it Paul called him? *"Gurney, the valorous."*

Halleck's wispy blond hair trailed across barren spots on his head. His wide mouth was twisted into a pleasant sneer, and the scar of the inkvine whip slashed across his jawline seemed to move with a life of its own. His whole air was of casual, shoulder-set capability. He came up to the Duke, bowed.

"Gurney," Leto said.

"My Lord." He gestured with the baliset toward the men in the room. "This is the last of them. I'd have preferred coming in with the first wave, but . . . ."

"There are still some Harkonnens for you," the Duke said. "Step aside with me, Gurney, where we may talk."

"Yours to command, my Lord."

They moved into an alcove beside a coin-slot water machine while the men stirred restlessly in the big room. Halleck dropped his bag into a corner, kept his grip on the baliset.

"How many men can you let Hawat have?" the Duke asked.

"Is Thufir in trouble, Sire?"

"He's lost only two agents, but his advance men gave us an excellent line on the entire Harkonnen setup here. If we move fast we may gain a measure of security, the breathing space we require. He wants as many men as you can spare—men who won't balk at a little knife work."

"I can let him have three hundred of my best," Halleck said. "Where shall I send them?"

"To the main gate. Hawat has an agent there waiting to take them."

"Shall I get about it at once, Sire?"

"In a moment. We have another problem. The field commandant will hold the shuttle here until dawn on a pretext. The Guild Heighliner that brought us is going on about its business, and the shuttle's supposed to make contact with a cargo ship taking up a load of spice."

"Our spice, m'Lord?"

"Our spice. But the shuttle also will carry some of the spice hunters from the old regime. They've opted to leave with the change of fief and the Judge of the Change is allowing it. These are valuable workers, Gurney, about eight hundred of them. Before the shuttle leaves, you must persuade some of those men to enlist with us."

"How strong a persuasion, Sire?"

"I want their willing cooperation, Gurney. Those men have experience and skills we need. The fact that they're leaving suggests they're not part of the Harkonnen machine. Hawat believes there could be some bad ones planted in the group, but he sees assassins in every shadow."

"Thufir has found some very productive shadows in his time, m'Lord."

"And there are some he hasn't found. But I think planting sleepers in this outgoing crowd would show too much imagination for the Harkonnens."

"Possibly, Sire. Where are these men?"

"Down on the lower level, in a waiting room. I suggest you go down and play a tune or two to soften their minds, then turn on the pressure. You may offer positions of authority to those who qualify. Offer twenty per cent higher wages than they received under the Harkonnens."

"No more than that, Sire? I know the Harkonnen pay scales. And to men with their termination pay in their pockets and the wanderlust on them . . . well, Sire, twenty per cent would hardly seem proper inducement to stay."

Leto spoke impatiently: "Then use your own discretion in particular cases. Just remember that the treasury isn't bottomless. Hold it to twenty per cent whenever you can. We particularly need spice drivers, weather scanners, dune men—any with open sand experience."

"I understand, Sire. 'They shall come all for violence: their faces shall sup up as the east wind, and they shall gather the captivity of the sand.' "

"A very moving quotation," the Duke said. "Turn your crew over to a lieutenant. Have him give a short drill on water discipline, then bed the men down for the night in the barracks adjoining the field. Field personnel will direct them. And don't forget the men for Hawat."

"Three hundred of the best, Sire." He took up his spacebag. "Where shall I report to you when I've completed my chores?"

"I've taken over a council room topside here. We'll hold staff there. I want to arrange a new planetary dispersal order with armored squads going out first."

Halleck stopped in the act of turning away, caught Leto's eye. "Are you anticipating *that* kind of trouble, Sire? I thought there was a Judge of the Change here."

"Both open battle and secret," the Duke said. "There'll be blood aplenty spilled here before we're through."

" 'And the water which thou takest out of the river shall become blood upon the dry land,' " Halleck quoted.

The Duke sighed. "Hurry back, Gurney."

"Very good, m'Lord." The whipscar rippled to his grin. " 'Behold, as a wild ass in the desert, go I forth to my work.' " He turned, strode to the center of the room, paused to relay his orders, hurried on through the men.

Leto shook his head at the retreating back. Halleck was a continual amazement—a head full of songs, quotations, and flowery phrases . . . and the heart of an assassin when it came to dealing with the Harkonnens.

Presently, Leto took a leisurely diagonal course across to the lift, acknowledging salutes with a casual hand wave. He recognized a propaganda corpsman, stopped to give him a message that could be relayed to the men through channels: those who had brought their women would want to know the women were safe and where they could be found. The others would wish to know that the population here appeared to boast more women than men.

The Duke slapped the propaganda man on the arm, a signal that the message had top priority to be put out immediately, then continued across the room. He nodded to the men, smiled, traded pleasantries with a subaltern.

*Command must always look confident,* he thought. *All that faith riding on your shoulders while you sit in the critical seat and never show it.*

He breathed a sigh of relief when the lift swallowed him and he could turn and face the impersonal doors.

*They have tried to take the life of my son!*

> *Over the exit of the Arrakeen landing field, crudely carved as though with a poor instrument, there was an inscription that Muad'Dib was to repeat many times. He saw it that first night on Arrakis, having been brought to the ducal command post to participate in his father's first full staff conference. The words of the inscription were a plea to those leaving Arrakis, but they fell with dark import on the eyes of a boy who had just escaped a close brush with death. They said: "O you who know what we suffer here, do not forget us in your prayers."*

**—from "Manual of Muad'Dib" by the Princess Irulan**

"The whole theory of warfare is calculated risk," the Duke said, "but when it comes to risking your own family, the element of *calculation* gets submerged in . . . other things."

He knew he wasn't holding in his anger as well as he should, and he turned, strode down the length of the long table and back.

The Duke and Paul were alone in the conference room at the landing field. It was an empty-sounding room, furnished only with the long table, old-fashioned three-legged chairs around it, and a map board and projector at one end. Paul sat at the table near the map board. He had told his father the experience with the hunter-seeker and given the reports that a traitor threatened him.

The Duke stopped across from Paul, pounded the table: "Hawat told me that house was secure!"

Paul spoke hesitantly: "I was angry, too—at first. And I blamed Hawat. But the threat came from outside the house. It was simple, clever, and direct. And it would've succeeded were it not for the training given me by you and many others—including Hawat."

"Are you defending him?" the Duke demanded.

"Yes."

"He's getting old. That's it. He should be—"

"He's wise with much experience," Paul said. "How many of Hawat's mistakes can you recall?"

"I should be the one defending him," the Duke said. "Not you."

Paul smiled.

Leto sat down at the head of the table, put a hand over his son's. "You've . . . matured lately, Son." He lifted his hand. "It gladdens me." He matched his son's smile. "Hawat will punish himself. He'll direct more anger against himself over this than both of us together could pour on him."

Paul glanced toward the darkened windows beyond the map board, looked at the night's blackness. Room lights reflected from a balcony railing out there. He saw movement and recognized the shape of a guard in Atreides uniform. Paul looked back at the white wall behind his father, then down to the shiny surface of the table, seeing his own hands clenched into fists there.

The door opposite the Duke banged open. Thufir Hawat strode through it looking older and more leathery than ever. He paced down the length of the table, stopped at attention facing Leto.

"My Lord," he said, speaking to a point over Leto's head, "I have just learned how I failed you. It becomes necessary that I tender my resig—"

"Oh, sit down and stop acting the fool," the Duke said. He waved to the chair across from Paul. "If you made a mistake, it was in *over*estimating the Harkonnens. Their simple minds came up with a simple trick. We didn't count on simple tricks. And my son has been at great pains to point out to me that he came through this largely because of your training. You didn't fail there!" He tapped the back of the empty chair. "Sit down, I say!"

Hawat sank into the chair. "But—"

"I'll hear no more of it," the Duke said. "The incident is past. We have more pressing business. Where are the others?"

"I asked them to wait outside while I—"

"Call them in."

Hawat looked into Leto's eyes. "Sire, I—"

"I know who my true friends are, Thufir," the Duke said. "Call in the men."

Hawat swallowed. "At once, my Lord." He swiveled in the chair, called to the open door: "Gurney, bring them in."

Halleck led the file of men into the room, the staff officers looking grimly serious followed by the younger aides and specialists, an air of eagerness among them. Brief scuffing sounds echoed around the room as the men took seats. A faint smell of rachag stimulant wafted down the table.

"There's coffee for those who want it," the Duke said.

He looked over his men, thinking: *They're a good crew. A man could do far worse for this kind of war.* He waited while coffee was brought in from the adjoining room and served, noting the tiredness in some of the faces.

Presently, he put on his mask of quiet efficiency, stood up and commanded their attention with a knuckle rap against the table.

"Well, gentlemen," he said, "our civilization appears to've fallen so deeply into the habit of invasion that we cannot even obey a simple order of the Imperium without the old ways cropping up."

Dry chuckles sounded around the table, and Paul realized that his father had said the precisely correct thing in precisely the correct tone to lift the mood here. Even the hint of fatigue in his voice was right.

"I think first we'd better learn if Thufir has anything to add to his report on the Fremen," the Duke said. "Thufir?"

Hawat glanced up. "I've some economic matters to go into after my general report, Sire, but I can say now that the Fremen appear more and more to be the allies we need. They're waiting now to see if they can trust us, but they appear to be dealing openly. They've sent us a gift—stillsuits of their own manufacture . . . maps of certain desert areas surrounding strongpoints the Harkonnens left behind . . . ." He glanced down the table. "Their intelligence reports have proved completely reliable and have helped us considerably in our dealings with the Judge of the Change. They've also sent some incidental things— jewelry for the Lady Jessica, spice liquor, candy, medicinals. My men are processing the lot right now. There appears to be no trickery."

"You like these people, Thufir?" asked a man down the table.

Hawat turned to face his questioner. "Duncan Idaho says they're to be admired."

Paul glanced at his father, back to Hawat, ventured a question: "Have you any new information on how many Fremen there are?"

Hawat looked at Paul. "From food processing and other evidence, Idaho estimates the cave complex he visited consisted of some ten thousand people, all told. Their leader said he ruled a sietch of two thousand hearths. We've reason to believe there are a great many such sietch communities. All seem to give their allegiance to someone called Liet."

"That's something new," Leto said.

"It could be an error on my part, Sire. There are things to suggest this Liet may be a local deity."

Another man down the table cleared his throat, asked: "Is it certain they deal with the smugglers?"

"A smuggler caravan left this sietch while Idaho was there, carrying a heavy load of spice. They used pack beasts and indicated they faced an eighteen-day journey."

"It appears," the Duke said, "that the smugglers have redoubled their operations during this period of unrest. This deserves some careful thought. We shouldn't worry too much about unlicenced frigates working off our planet—it's always done. But to have them completely outside our observation—that's not good."

"You have a plan, Sire?" Hawat asked.

The Duke looked at Halleck. "Gurney, I want you to head a delegation, an embassy if you will, to contact these romantic businessmen. Tell them I'll ignore their operations as long as they give me a ducal tithe. Hawat here estimates that graft and extra fighting men heretofore required in their operations have been costing them four times that amount."

"What if the Emperor gets wind of this?" Halleck asked. "He's very jealous of his CHOAM profits, m'Lord."

Leto smiled. "We'll bank the entire tithe openly in the name of Shaddam IV and deduct it legally from our levy support costs. Let the Harkonnens fight that! And we'll be ruining a few more of the locals who grew fat under the Harkonnen system. No more graft!"

A grin twisted Halleck's face. "Ahh, m'Lord, a beautiful low blow. Would that I could see the Baron's face when he learns of this."

The Duke turned to Hawat. "Thufir, did you get those account books you said you could buy?"

"Yes, my Lord. They're being examined in detail even now. I've skimmed them, though, and can give a first approximation."

"Give it, then."

"The Harkonnens took ten billion solaris out of here every three hundred and thirty Standard days."

A muted gasp ran around the table. Even the younger aides, who had been betraying some boredom, sat up straighter and exchanged wide-eyed looks.

Halleck murmured: " 'For they shall suck of the abundance of the seas and of the treasure hid in the sand.' "

"You see, gentlemen," Leto said. "Is there anyone here so naive he believes the Harkonnens have quietly packed up and walked away from all this merely because the Emperor ordered it?"

There was a general shaking of heads, murmurous agreement.

"We will have to take it at the point of the sword," Leto said. He turned to Hawat. "This'd be a good point to report on equipment. How many sand-crawlers, harvesters, spice factories, and supporting equipment have they left us?"

"A full complement, as it says in the Imperial inventory audited by the Judge of the Change, my Lord," Hawat said. He gestured for an aide to pass him a folder, opened the folder on the table in front of him. "They neglect to mention that less than half the crawlers are operable, that only about a third have carryalls to fly them to spice sands—that everything the Harkonnens left us is ready to break down and fall apart. We'll be lucky to get half the equipment into operation and luckier yet if a fourth of it's still working six months from now."

"Pretty much as we expected," Leto said. "What's the firm estimate on basic equipment?"

Hawat glanced at his folder. "About nine hundred and thirty havester-factories that can be sent out in a few days. About sixty-two hundred and fifty ornithopters for survey, scouting, and weather observation . . . carryalls, a little under a thousand."

Halleck said: "Wouldn't it be cheaper to reopen negotiations with the Guild for permission to orbit a frigate as a weather satellite?"

The Duke looked at Hawat. "Nothing new there, eh, Thufir?"

"We must pursue other avenues for now," Hawat said. "The Guild agent wasn't really negotiating with us. He was merely making it plain—one Mentat to another—that the price was out of our reach and would remain so no matter how long a reach we develop. Our task is to find out why before we approach him again."

One of Halleck's aides down the table swiveled in his chair, snapped: "There's no justice in this!"

"Justice?" The Duke looked at the man. "Who asks for justice? We make our own justice. We make it here on Arrakis—win or die. Do you regret casting your lot with us, sir?"

The man stared at the Duke, then: "No, Sire. You couldn't turn down the richest planetary source of income in our universe . . . and I could do nought but follow you. Forgive the outburst, but . . . ." He shrugged. ". . . we must all feel bitter at times."

"Bitterness I can understand," the Duke said. "But let us not rail about justice as long as we have arms and the freedom to use them. Do any of the rest of you harbor bitterness? If so, let it out. This is friendly council where any man may speak his mind."

Halleck stirred, said: "I think what rankles, Sire, is that we've had no volunteers from the other Great Houses. They address you as 'Leto the Just' and promise eternal friendship, but only as long as it doesn't cost them anything."

"They don't know yet who's going to win this exchange," the Duke said. "Most of the Houses have grown fat by taking few risks. One cannot truly blame them for this; one can only despise them." He looked at Hawat. "We were discussing equipment. Would you care to project a few examples to familiarize the men with this machinery?"

Hawat nodded, gestured to an aide at the projector.

A solido tri-D projection appeared on the table surface about a third of the way down from the Duke. Some of the men farther along the table stood up to get a better look at it.

Paul leaned forward, staring at the machine.

Scaled against the tiny projected human figures around it, the thing was about one hundred and twenty meters long and about forty meters wide. It was basically a long, buglike body moving on independent sets of wide tracks.

"This is a harvester factory," Hawat said. "We chose one in good repair for this projection. There's one dragline outfit that came in with the first team of Imperial ecologists, though, and it's still running . . . although I don't know how . . . or why."

"If that's the one they call 'Old Maria,' it belongs in a museum," an aide said. "I think the Harkonnens kept it as a punishment job, a threat hanging over their workers' heads. Be good or you'll be assigned to Old Maria."

Chuckles sounded around the table.

Paul held himself apart from the humor, his attention focused on the projection and the question that filled his mind. He pointed to the image on the table, said: "Thufir, are there sandworms big enough to swallow that whole?"

Quick silence settled on the table. The Duke cursed under his breath, then thought: *No—they have to face the realities here.*

"There're worms in the deep desert could take this entire factory in one gulp," Hawat said. "Up here closer to the Shield Wall where most of the spicing's done there are plenty of worms that could cripple this factory and devour it at their leisure."

"Why don't we shield them?" Paul asked.

"According to Idaho's report," Hawat said, "shields are dangerous in the desert. A body-size shield will call every worm for hundreds of meters around. It appears to drive them into a killing frenzy. We've the Fremen word on this and no reason to doubt it. Idaho saw no evidence of shield equipment at the sietch."

"None at all?" Paul asked.

"It'd be pretty hard to conceal that kind of thing among several thousand people," Hawat said. "Idaho had free access to every part of the sietch. He saw no shields or any indication of their use."

"It's a puzzle," the Duke said.

"The Harkonnens certainly used plenty of shields here," Hawat said. "They had repair depots in every garrison village, and their accounts show a heavy expenditure for shield replacements and parts."

"Could the Fremen have a way of nullifying shields?" Paul asked.

"It doesn't seem likely," Hawat said. "It's theoretically possible, of course— a shire-sized static counter charge is supposed to do the trick, but no one's ever been able to put it to the test."

"We'd have heard about it before now," Halleck said. "The smugglers have close contact with the Fremen and would've acquired such a device if it were available. And they'd have had no inhibitions against marketing it off planet."

"I don't like an unanswered question of this importance," Leto said. "Thufir, I want you to give top priority to solution of this problem."

"We're already working on it, my Lord." He cleared his throat. "Ah-h, Idaho did say one thing: he said you couldn't mistake the Fremen attitude toward shields. He said they were mostly amused by them."

The Duke frowned, then: "The subject under discussion is spicing equipment."

Hawat gestured to his aide at the projector.

The solido-image of the harvester-factory was replaced by a projection of a winged device that dwarfed the images of human figures around it. "This is a carryall," Hawat said. "It's essentially a large 'thopter, whose sole function is to deliver a factory to spice-rich sands, then to rescue the factory when a sandworm appears. They always appear. Harvesting the spice is a process of getting in and getting out with as much as possible."

"Admirably suited to Harkonnen morality," the Duke said.

Laughter was abrupt and too loud.

An ornithopter replaced the carryall in the projection focus.

"These 'thopters are fairly conventional," Hawat said. "Major modifications give them extended range. Extra care has been used in sealing essential areas against sand and dust. Only about one in thirty is shielded—possibly discarding the shield generator's weight for greater range."

"I don't like this de-emphasis on shields," the Duke muttered. And he thought: *Is this the Harkonnen secret? Does it mean we won't even be able to escape on shielded frigates if all goes against us?* He shook his head sharply to drive out such thoughts, said: "Let's get to the working estimate. What'll our profit figure be?"

Hawat turned two pages in his notebook. "After assessing the repairs and operable equipment, we've worked out a first estimate on operating costs. It's based naturally on a depreciated figure for a clear safety margin." He closed his eyes in Mentat semitrance, said: "Under the Harkonnens, maintenance and salaries were held to fourteen per cent. We'll be lucky to make it at thirty per cent at first. With reinvestment and growth factors accounted for, including the CHOAM percentage and military costs, our profit margin will be reduced to a very narrow six or seven per cent until we can replace worn-out equipment. We then should be able to boost it up to twelve or fifteen per cent where it belongs." He opened his eyes. "Unless my Lord wishes to adopt Harkonnen methods."

"We're working for a solid and permanent planetary base," the Duke said. "We have to keep a large percentage of the people happy—especially the Fremen."

"Most especially the Fremen," Hawat agreed.

"Our supremacy on Caladan," the Duke said, "depended on sea and air power. Here, we must develop something I choose to call *desert* power. This may include air power, but it's possible it may not. I call your attention to the lack of 'thopter shields." He shook his head. "The Harkonnens relied on turnover from off planet for some of their key personnel. We don't dare. Each new lot would have its quota of provocateurs."

"Then we'll have to be content with far less profit and a reduced harvest," Hawat said. "Our output the first two seasons should be down a third from the Harkonnen average."

"There it is," the Duke said, "exactly as we expected. We'll have to move fast with the Fremen. I'd like five full battalions of Fremen troops before the first CHOAM audit."

"That's not much time, Sire," Hawat said.

"We don't have much time, as you well know. They'll be in here with Sardaukar disguised as Harkonnens at the first opportunity. How many do you think they'll ship in, Thufir?"

"Four or five battalions all told, Sire. No more, Guild troop-transport costs being what they are."

"Then five battalions of Fremen plus our own forces ought to do it. Let us have a few captive Sardaukar to parade in front of the Landsraad Council and matters will be much different—profits or no profits."

"We'll do our best, Sire."

Paul looked at his father, back to Hawat, suddenly conscious of the Mentat's great age, aware that the old man had served three generations of Atreides. *Aged.* It showed in the rheumy shine of the brown eyes, in the cheeks cracked and burned by exotic weathers, in the rounded curve of shoulders and the thin set of the lips with the cranberry-colored stain of sapho juice.

*So much depends on one aged man,* Paul thought.

"We're presently in a war of assassins," the Duke said, "but it has not achieved full scale. Thufir, what's the condition of the Harkonnen machine here?"

"We've eliminated two hundred and fifty-nine of their key people, my Lord. No more than three Harkonnen cells remain—perhaps a hundred people in all."

"These Harkonnen creatures you eliminated," the Duke said, "were they propertied?"

"Most were well situated, my Lord—in the entrepreneur class."

"I want you to forge certificates of allegiance over the signatures of each of them," the Duke said. "File copies with the Judge of the Change. We'll take the legal position that they stayed under false allegiance. Confiscate their property, take everything, turn out their families, strip them. And make sure the Crown gets its ten per cent. It must be entirely legal."

Thufir smiled, revealing red-stained teeth beneath the carmine lips. "A move worthy of your grandsire, my Lord. It shames me I didn't think of it first."

Halleck frowned across the table, surprised a deep scowl on Paul's face. The others were smiling and nodding.

*It's wrong*, Paul thought. *This'll only make the others fight all the harder. They've nothing to gain by surrendering.*

He knew the actual no-holds-barred convention that ruled in kanly, but this was the sort of move that could destroy them even as it gave them victory.

" 'I have been a stranger in a strange land,' " Halleck quoted.

Paul stared at him, recognizing the quotation from the O.C. Bible, wondering: *Does Gurney, too, wish an end to devious plots?*

The Duke glanced at the darkness out the windows, looked back at Halleck. "Gurney, how many of those sandworkers did you persuade to stay with us?"

"Two hundred eighty-six in all, Sire. I think we should take them and consider ourselves lucky. They're all in useful categories."

"No more?" The Duke pursed his lips, then: "Well, pass the word along to—"

A disturbance at the door interrupted him. Duncan Idaho came through the guard there, hurried down the length of the table and bent over the Duke's ear.

Leto waved him back, said: "Speak out, Duncan. You can see this is strategy staff."

Paul studied Idaho, marking the feline movements, the swiftness of reflex that made him such a difficult weapons teacher to emulate. Idaho's dark round face turned toward Paul, the cave-sitter eyes giving no hint of recognition, but Paul recognized the mask of serenity over excitement.

Idaho looked down the length of the table, said: "We've taken a force of Harkonnen mercenaries disguised as Fremen. The Fremen themselves sent us a courier to warn of the false band. In the attack, however, we found the Harkonnens had waylaid the Fremen courier—badly wounded him. We were bringing him here for treatment by our medics when he died. I'd seen how badly off the man was and stopped to do what I could. I surprised him in the attempt to throw something away." Idaho glanced down at Leto. "A knife, m'Lord, a knife the like of which you've never seen."

"Crysknife?" someone asked.

"No doubt of it," Idaho said. "Milky white and glowing with a light of its own like." He reached into his tunic, brought out a sheath with a black-ridged handle protruding from it.

"Keep that blade in its sheath!"

The voice came from the open door at the end of the room, a vibrant and penetrating voice that brought them all up, staring.

A tall, robed figure stood in the door, barred by the crossed swords of the guard. A light tan robe completely enveloped the man except for a gap in the hood and black veil that exposed eyes of total blue—no white in them at all.

"Let him enter," Idaho whispered.

"Pass that man," the Duke said.

The guards hesitated, then lowered their swords.

The man swept into the room, stood across from the Duke.

"This is Stilgar, chief of the sietch I visited, leader of those who warned us of the false band," Idaho said.

"Welcome, sir," Leto said. "And why shouldn't we unsheath this blade?"

Stilgar glanced at Idaho, said: "You observed the customs of cleanliness and honor among us. I would permit you to see the blade of the man you befriended." His gaze swept the others in the room. "But I do not know these others. Would you have them defile an honorable weapon?"

"I am the Duke Leto," the Duke said. "Would you permit me to see this blade?"

"I'll permit you to earn the right to unsheath it," Stilgar said, and, as a mutter of protest sounded around the table, he raised a thin, darkly veined hand. "I remind you this is the blade of one who befriended you."

In the waiting silence, Paul studied the man, sensing the aura of power that radiated from him. He was a leader—a *Fremen* leader.

A man near the center of the table across from Paul muttered: "Who's he to tell us what rights we have on Arrakis?"

"It is said that the Duke Leto Atreides rules with the consent of the governed," the Fremen said. "Thus I must tell you the way it is with us: a certain responsibility falls on those who have seen a crysknife." He passed a dark glance across Idaho. "They are ours. They may never leave Arrakis without our consent."

Halleck and several of the others started to rise, angry expressions on their faces. Halleck said: "The Duke Leto determines whether—"

"One moment, please," Leto said, and the very mildness of his voice held them. *This must not get out of hand,* he thought. He addressed himself to the Fremen: "Sir, I honor and respect the personal dignity of any man who respects my dignity. I am indeed indebted to you. And I *always* pay my debts. If it is your custom that this knife remain sheathed here, then it is so ordered—by *me.* And if there is any other way we may honor the man who died in our service, you have but to name it."

The Fremen stared at the Duke, then slowly pulled aside his veil, revealing a thin nose and full-lipped mouth in a glistening black beard. Deliberately he bent over the end of the table, spat on its polished surface.

As the men around the table started to surge to their feet, Idaho's voice boomed across the room: "Hold!"

Into the sudden charged stillness, Idaho said: "We thank you, Stilgar, for the gift of your body's moisture. We accept it in the spirit with which it is given." And Idaho spat on the table in front of the Duke.

Aside to the Duke, he said: "Remember how precious water is here, Sire. That was a token of respect."

Leto sank back into his chair, caught Paul's eye, a rueful grin on his son's face, sensed the slow relaxation of tension around the table as understanding came to his men.

The Fremen looked at Idaho, said: "You measured well in my sietch, Duncan Idaho. Is there a bond on your allegiance to your Duke?"

"He's asking me to enlist with him, Sire," Idaho said.

"Would he accept a dual allegiance?" Leto asked.

"You wish me to go with him, Sire?"

"I wish you to make your own decision in the matter," Leto said, and he could not keep the urgency out of his voice.

Idaho studied the Fremen. "Would you have me under these conditions, Stilgar? There'd be times when I'd have to return to serve my Duke."

"You fight well and you did your best for our friend," Stilgar said. He looked at Leto. "Let it be thus: the man Idaho keeps the crysknife he holds as a mark of allegiance to us. He must be cleansed, of course, and the rites observed, but this can be done. He will be Fremen and soldier of the Atreides. There is precedent for this: Liet serves two masters."

"Duncan?" Leto asked.

"I understand, Sire," Idaho said.

"It is agreed, then," Leto said.

"Your water is ours, Duncan Idaho," Stilgar said. "The body of our friend remains with your Duke. His water is Atreides water. It is a bond between us."

Leto sighed, glanced at Hawat, catching the old Mentat's eye. Hawat nodded, his expression pleased.

"I will await below," Stilgar said, "while Idaho makes farewell with his friends. Turok was the name of our dead friend. Remember that when it comes time to release his spirit. You are friends of Turok."

Stilgar started to turn away.

"Will you not stay a while?" Leto asked.

The Fremen turned back, whipping his veil into place with a casual gesture, adjusting something beneath it. Paul glimpsed what looked like a thin tube before the veil settled into place.

"Is there reason to stay?" the Fremen asked.

"We would honor you," the Duke said.

"Honor requires that I be elsewhere soon," the Fremen said. He shot another glance at Idaho, whirled, and strode out past the door guards.

"If the other Fremen match him, we'll serve each other well," Leto said.

Idaho spoke in a dry voice: "He's a fair sample, Sire."

"You understand what you're to do, Duncan?"

"I'm your ambassador to the Fremen, Sire."

"Much depends on you, Duncan. We're going to need at least five battalions of those people before the Sardaukar descend on us."

"This is going to take some doing, Sire. The Fremen are a pretty independent bunch." Idaho hesitated, then: "And, Sire, there's one other thing. One of the mercenaries we knocked over was trying to get this blade from our dead Fremen friend. The mercenary says there's a Harkonnen reward of a million solaris for anyone who'll bring in a single crysknife."

Leto's chin came up in a movement of obvious surprise. "Why do they want one of those blades so badly?"

"The knife is ground from a sandworm's tooth; it's the mark of the Fremen, Sire. With it, a blue-eyed man could penetrate any sietch in the land. They'd question me unless I were known. I don't look Fremen. But . . . ."

"Piter de Vried," the Duke said.

"A man of devilish cunning, my Lord," Hawat said.

Idaho slipped the sheathed knife beneath his tunic.

"Guard that knife," the Duke said.

"I understand, m'Lord." He patted the transceiver on his belt kit. "I'll report soon as possible. Thufir has my call code. Use battle language." He saluted, spun about, and hurried after the Fremen.

They heard his footsteps drumming down the corridor.

A look of understanding passed between Leto and Hawat. They smiled.

"We've much to do, Sire," Halleck said.

"And I keep you from your work," Leto said.

"I have the report on the advance bases," Hawat said. "Shall I give it another time, Sire?"

"Will it take long?"

"Not for a briefing. It's said among the Fremen that there were more than two hundred of these advance bases built here on Arrakis during the Desert Botanical Testing Station period. All supposedly have been abandoned, but there are reports they were sealed off before being abandoned."

"Equipment in them?" the Duke asked.

"According to the reports I have from Duncan."

"Where are they located?" Halleck said.

"The answer to that question," Hawat said, "is invariably: 'Liet knows.'"

"God knows," Leto muttered.

"Perhaps not, Sire," Hawat said. "You heard this Stilgar use the name. Could he have been referring to a real person?"

"Serving two masters," Halleck said. "It sounds like a religious quotation."

"And you should know," the Duke said.

Halleck smiled.

"This Judge of the Change," Leto said, "the Imperial ecologist—Kynes . . . . Wouldn't he know where those bases are?"

"Sire," Hawat cautioned, "this Kynes is an Imperial servant."

"And he's a long way from the Emperor," Leto said. "I want those bases. They'd be loaded with materials we could salvage and use for repair of our working equipment."

"Sire!" Hawat said. "Those bases are still legally His Majesty's fief."

"The weather here's savage enough to destroy anything," the Duke said. "We can always blame the weather. Get this Kynes and at least find out if the bases exist."

" 'Twere dangerous to commandeer them," Hawat said. "Duncan was clear on one thing: those bases or the idea of them hold some deep significance for the Fremen. We might alienate the Fremen if we took those bases."

Paul looked at the faces of the men around them, saw the intensity of the way they followed every word. They appeared deeply disturbed by his father's attitude.

"Listen to him, Father," Paul said in a low voice. "He speaks truth."

"Sire," Hawat said, "those bases could give us material to repair every piece of equipment left us, yet be beyond reach for strategic reasons. It'd be rash to move without greater knowledge. This Kynes has arbiter authority from the Imperium. We mustn't forget that. And the Fremen defer to him."

"Do it gently, then," the Duke said. "I wish to know only if those bases exist."

"As you will, Sire." Hawat sat back, lowered his eyes.

"All right, then," the Duke said. "We know what we have ahead of us—work. We've been trained for it. We've some experience in it. We know what the rewards are and the alternatives are clear enough. You all have your assignments." He looked at Halleck. "Gurney, take care of that smuggler situation first."

" 'I shall go unto the rebellious that dwell in the dry land,' " Halleck intoned.

"Someday I'll catch that man without a quotation and he'll look undressed," the Duke said.

Chuckles echoed around the table, but Paul heard the effort in them.

The Duke turned to Hawat. "Set up another command post for intelligence and communications on this floor, Thufir. When you have them ready, I'll want to see you."

Hawat arose, glanced around the room as though seeking support. He turned away, led the procession out of the room. The others moved hurriedly, scraping their chairs on the floor, balling up in little knots of confusion.

*It ended in confusion,* Paul thought, staring at the backs of the last men to leave. Always before, Staff had ended on an incisive air. This meeting had just seemed to trickle out, worn down by its own inadequacies, and with an argument to top it off.

For the first time, Paul allowed himself to think about the real possibility of defeat—not thinking about it out of fear or because of warnings such as that of the old Reverend Mother, but facing up to it because of his own assessment of the situation.

*My father is desperate,* he thought. *Things aren't going well for us at all.*

And Hawat—Paul recalled how the old Mentat had acted during the conference—subtle hesitations, signs of unrest.

Hawat was deeply troubled by something.

"Best you remain here the rest of the night, Son," the Duke said. "It'll be dawn soon, anyway. I'll inform your mother." He got to his feet, slowly, stiffly. "Why don't you pull a few of these chairs together and stretch out on them for some rest."

"I'm not very tired, sir."

"As you will."

The Duke folded his hands behind him, began pacing up and down the length of the table.

*Like a caged animal,* Paul thought.

"Are you going to discuss the traitor possibility with Hawat?" Paul asked.

The Duke stopped across from his son, spoke to the dark windows. "We've discussed the possibility many times."

"The old woman seemed so sure of herself," Paul said. "And the message Mother—"

"Precautions have been taken," the Duke said. He looked around the room, and Paul marked the hunted wildness in his father's eyes. "Remain here. There are some things about the command posts I want to discuss with Thufir." He turned, strode out of the room, nodding shortly to the door guards.

Paul stared at the place where his father had stood. The space had been empty even before the Duke left the room. And he recalled the old woman's warning: ". . . for the father, nothing."

> *On that first day when Muad'Dib rode through the streets of Arrakeen with his family, some of the people along the way recalled the legends and the prophecy and they ventured to shout: "Mahdi!" But their shout was more a question than a statement, for as yet they could only hope he was the one foretold as the Lisan al-Gaib, the Voice from the Outer World. Their attention was focused, too, on the mother, because they had heard she was a Bene Gesserit and it was obvious to them that she was like the other Lisan al-Gaib.*

**—from "Manual of Muad'Dib" by the Princess Irulan**

The Duke found Thufir Hawat alone in the corner room to which a guard directed him. There was the sound of men setting up communications equipment in an adjoining room, but this place was fairly quiet. The Duke glanced around as Hawat arose from a paper-cluttered table. It was a green-walled enclosure with, in addition to the table, three suspensor chairs from which the Harkonnen "*H*" had been hastily removed, leaving an imperfect color patch.

"The chairs are liberated but quite safe," Hawat said. "Where is Paul, Sire?"

"I left him in the conference room. I'm hoping he'll get some rest without me there to distract him."

Hawat nodded, crossed to the door to the adjoining room, closed it, shutting off the noise of static and electronic sparking.

"Thufir," Leto said, "the Imperial and Harkonnen stockpiles of spice attract my attention."

"M'Lord?"

The Duke pursed his lips. "Storehouses are susceptible to destruction." He raised a hand as Hawat started to speak. "Ignore the Emperor's hoard. He'd secretly enjoy it if the Harkonnens were embarrassed. And can the Baron object if something is destroyed which he cannot openly admit that he has?"

Hawat shook his head. "We've few men to spare, Sire."

"Use some of Idaho's men. And perhaps some of the Fremen would enjoy a trip off planet. A raid on Giedi Prime—there are tactical advantages to such a diversion, Thufir."

"As you say, my Lord." Hawat turned away, and the Duke saw evidence of nervousness in the old man, thought: *Perhaps he suspects I distrust him. He must know I've private reports of traitors. Well—best quiet his fears immediately.*

"Thufir," he said, "since you're one of the few I can trust completely, there's another matter bears discussion. We both know how constant a watch we must keep to prevent traitors from infiltrating our forces . . . but I have two new reports."

Hawat turned, stared at him.

And Leto repeated the stories Paul had brought.

Instead of bringing on the intense Mentat concentration, the reports only increased Hawat's agitation.

Leto studied the old man and, presently, said: "You've been holding something back, old friend. I should've suspected when you were so nervous during Staff. What is it that was too hot to dump in front of the full conference?"

Hawat's sapho-stained lips were pulled into a prim, straight line with tiny wrinkles radiating into them. They maintained their wrinkled stiffness as he said: "My Lord, I don't quite know how to broach this."

"We've suffered many a scar for each other, Thufir," the Duke said. "You know you can broach *any* subject with me."

Hawat continued to stare at him, thinking: *This is how I like him best. This is the man of honor who deserves every bit of my loyalty and service. Why must I hurt him?*

"Well?" Leto demanded.

Hawat shrugged. "It's a scrap of a note. We took it from a Harkonnen courier. The note was intended for an agent named Pardee. We've good reason to believe Pardee was top man in the Harkonnen underground here. The note—it's a thing that could have great consequence or no consequence. It's susceptible to various interpretations."

"What's the delicate content of this note?"

"Scrap of a note, my Lord. Incomplete. It was on minimic film with the usual destruction capsule attached. We stopped the acid action just short of full erasure, leaving only a fragment. The fragment, however, is extremely suggestive."

"Yes?"

Hawat rubbed at his lips. "It says: '. . . eto will never suspect, and when the blow falls on him from a beloved hand, its source alone should be enough to destroy him.' The note was under the Baron's own seal and I've authenticated the seal."

"Your suspicion is obvious," the Duke said and his voice was suddenly cold.

"I'd sooner cut off my arms than hurt you," Hawat said. "My Lord, what if . . ."

"The Lady Jessica," Leto said, and he felt anger consuming him. "Couldn't you wring the facts out of this Pardee?"

"Unfortunately, Pardee no longer was among the living when we intercepted the courier. The courier, I'm certain, did not know what he carried."

"I see."

Leto shook his head, thinking: *What a slimy piece of business. There can't be anything in it. I know my woman.*

"My Lord, if—"

"No!" the Duke barked. "There's a mistake here that—"

"We cannot ignore it, my Lord."

"She's been with me for sixteen years! There've been countless opportunities for—You yourself investigated the school and the woman!"

Hawat spoke bitterly: "Things have been known to escape me."

"It's impossible, I tell you! The Harkonnens want to destroy the Atreides *line*—meaning Paul, too. They've already tried once. Could a woman conspire against her own son?"

"Perhaps she doesn't conspire against her son. And yesterday's attempt could've been a clever sham."

"It couldn't have been sham."

"Sire, she isn't supposed to know her parentage, but what if she does know? What if she were an orphan, say, orphaned by an Atreides?"

"She'd have moved long before now. Poison in my drink . . . a stiletto at night. Who has had better opportunity?"

"The Harkonnens mean to *destroy* you, my Lord. Their intent is not just to kill. There's a range of fine distinctions in kanly. This could be a work of art among vendettas."

The Duke's shoulders slumped. He closed his eyes, looking old and tired. *It cannot be,* he thought. *The woman has opened her heart to me.*

"What better way to destroy me than to sow suspicion of the woman I love?" he asked.

"An interpretation I've considered," Hawat said. "Still . . . ."

The Duke opened his eyes, stared at Hawat, thinking: *Let him be suspicious. Suspicion is his trade, not mine. Perhaps if I appear to believe this, that will make another man careless.*

"What do you suggest?" the Duke whispered.

"For now, constant surveillance, my Lord. She should be watched at all times. I will see it's done unobtrusively. Idaho would be the ideal choice for the job. Perhaps in a week or so we can bring him back. There's a young man we've been training in Idaho's troop who might be ideal to send to the Fremen as a replacement. He's gifted in diplomacy."

"Don't jeopardize our foothold with the Fremen."

"Of course not, Sire."

"And what about Paul?"

"Perhaps we could alert Dr. Yueh."

Leto turned his back on Hawat. " I leave it in your hands."

"I shall use discretion, my Lord."

*At least I can count on that*, Leto thought. And he said: "I will take a walk. If you need me, I'll be within the perimeter. The guard can—"

"My Lord, before you go, I've a filmclip you should read. It's a first-approximation analysis on the Fremen religion. You'll recall you asked me to report on it."

The Duke paused, spoke without turning. "Will it not wait?"

"Of course, my Lord. You asked what they were shouting, though. It was 'Mahdi!' They directed the term at the young master. When they—"

"At Paul?"

"Yes, my Lord. They've a legend here, a prophecy, that a leader will come to them, child of a Bene Gesserit, to lead them to true freedom. It follows the familiar messiah pattern."

"They think Paul is this . . . this . . . ."

"They only hope, my Lord." Hawat extended a filmclip capsule.

The Duke accepted it, thrust it into a pocket. "I'll look at it later."

"Certainly, my Lord."

"Right now, I need time to . . . think."

"Yes, my Lord."

The Duke took a deep, sighing breath, strode out the door. He turned to his right down the hall, began walking, hands behind his back, paying little attention to where he was. There were corridors and stairs and balconies and halls . . . people who saluted and stood aside for him.

In time he came back to the conference room, found it dark and Paul asleep on the table with a guard's robe thrown over him and a ditty pack for a pillow. The Duke walked softly down the length of the room and onto the balcony overlooking the landing field. A guard at the corner of the balcony, recognizing the Duke by the dim reflection of lights from the field, snapped to attention.

"At ease," the Duke murmured. He leaned against the cold metal of the balcony rail.

A predawn hush had come over the desert basin. He looked up. Straight overhead, the stars were a sequin shawl flung over blue-black. Low on the southern horizon, the night's second moon peered through a thin dust haze—an unbelieving moon that looked at him with a cynical light.

As the Duke watched, the moon dipped beneath the Shield Wall cliffs, frosting them, and in the sudden intensity of darkness, he experienced a chill. He shivered.

Anger shot through him.

*The Harkonnens have hindered and hounded and hunted me for the last time,* he thought. *They are dung heaps with village provost minds! Here I make my stand!* And he thought with a touch of sadness: *I must rule with eye and claw—as the hawk among lesser birds.* Unconsciously, his hand brushed the hawk emblem on his tunic.

To the east, the night grew a faggot of luminous gray, then seashell opalescence that dimmed the stars. There came the long, bell-tolling movement of dawn striking across a broken horizon.

It was a scene of such beauty it caught all his attention.

*Some things beggar likeness,* he thought.

He had never imagined anything here could be as beautiful as that shattered red horizon and the purple and ochre cliffs. Beyond the landing field where the night's faint dew had touched life into the hurried seeds of Arrakis, he saw great puddles of red blooms and, running through them, an articulate tread of violet . . . like giant footsteps.

"It's a beautiful morning, Sire," the guard said.

"Yes, it is."

The Duke nodded, thinking: *Perhaps this planet could grow on one. Perhaps it could become a good home for my son.*

Then he saw the human figures moving into the flower fields, sweeping them with strange scythe-like devices—dew gatherers. Water so precious here that even the dew must be collected.

*And it could be a hideous place,* the Duke thought.

*"There is probably no more terrible instant of enlightenment than the one in which you discover your father is a man—with human flesh."*

**—from "Collected Sayings of Muad'Dib"
by the Princess Irulan**

The Duke said: "Paul, I'm doing a hateful thing, but I must."

He stood beside the portable poison snooper that had been brought into the conference room for their breakfast. The thing's sensor arms hung limply over the table, reminding Paul of some weird insect newly dead.

The Duke's attention was directed out the windows at the landing field and its roiling of dust against the morning sky.

Paul had a viewer in front of him containing a short filmclip on Fremen religious practices. The clip had been compiled by one of Hawat's experts and Paul found himself disturbed by the references to himself.

*"Mahdi!"*

*"Lisan al-Gaib!"*

He could close his eyes and recall the shouts of the crowds. *So that is what they hope,* he thought. And he remembered what the old Reverend Mother had said: Kwisatz Haderach. The memories touched his feelings of terrible purpose, shading this strange world with sensations of familiarity that he could not understand.

"A hateful thing," the Duke said.

"What do you mean, sir?"

Leto turned, looked down at his son. "Because the Harkonnens think to trick me by making me distrust your mother. They don't know that I'd sooner distrust myself."

"I don't understand, sir."

Again, Leto looked out the windows. The white sun was well up into its morning quadrant. Milky light picked out a boiling of dust clouds that spilled over into the blind canyons interfingering the Shield Wall.

Slowly, speaking in a low voice to contain his anger, the Duke explained to Paul about the mysterious note.

"You might just as well mistrust me," Paul said.

"They have to think they've succeeded," the Duke said. "They must think me this much of a fool. It must look real. Even your mother may not know the sham."

"But, sir! Why?"

"Your mother's response must not be an act. Oh, she's capable of a supreme act . . . but too much rides on this. I hope to smoke out a traitor. It must seem that I've been completely cozened. She must be hurt this way that she does not suffer greater hurt."

"Why do you tell me, Father! Maybe I'll give it away."

"They'll not watch you in this thing," the Duke said. "You'll keep the secret. You must." He walked to the windows, spoke without turning. "This way, if anything should happen to me, you can tell her the truth—that I never doubted her, not for the smallest instant. I should want her to know this."

Paul recognized the death thoughts in his father's words, spoke quickly: "Nothing's going to happen to you, sir. The—

"Be silent, Son."

Paul stared at his father's back, seeing the fatigue in the angle of the neck, in the line of the shoulders, in the slow movements.

"You're just tired, Father."

"I am tired," the Duke agreed. "I'm morally tired. The melancholy degeneration of the Great Houses has afflicted me at last, perhaps. And we were such strong people once."

Paul spoke in quick anger: "Our House hasn't degenerated!"

"Hasn't it?"

The Duke turned, faced his son, revealing dark circles beneath hard eyes, a cynical twist of mouth. "I should wed your mother, make her my Duchess. Yet . . . my unwedded state gives some Houses hope they may yet ally with me through their marriageable daughters." He shrugged. "So, I . . . ."

"Mother has explained this to me."

"Nothing wins more loyalty for a leader than an air of bravura," the Duke said. "I, therefore, cultivate an air of bravura."

"You lead well," Paul protested. "You govern well. Men follow you willingly and love you."

"My propaganda corps is one of the finest," the Duke said. Again, he turned to stare out at the basin. "There's greater possibility for us here on Arrakis than the Imperium could ever suspect. Yet sometimes I think it'd have been better if we'd run for it, gone renegade. Sometimes I wish we could sink back into anonymity among the people, become less exposed to . . . ."

"Father!"

"Yes, I *am* tired," the Duke said. "Did you know we're using spice residue as raw material and already have our own factory to manufacture filmbase?"

"Sir?"

"We mustn't run short of filmbase," the Duke said. "Else, how could we flood village and city with our information? The people must learn how well I govern them. How would they know if we didn't tell them?"

"You should get some rest," Paul said.

Again, the Duke faced his son. "Arrakis has another advantage I almost forgot to mention. Spice is in everything here. You breathe it and eat it in almost everything. And I find that this imparts a certain natural immunity to some of the most common poisons of the Assassins' Handbook. And the need to watch every drop of water puts all food production—yeast culture, hydroponics, chemavit, everything—under the strictest surveillance. We cannot kill off large segments of our population with poison—and we cannot be attacked this way, either. Arrakis makes us moral and ethical."

Paul started to speak, but the Duke cut him off, saying: "I have to have someone I can say these things to, Son." He sighed, glanced back at the dry landscape where even the flowers were gone now—trampled by the dew gatherers, wilted under the early sun.

"On Caladan, we ruled with sea and air power," the Duke said. "Here, we must scrabble for desert power. This is your inheritance, Paul. What is to become of you if anything happens to me? You'll not be a renegade House, but a guerrilla House—running, hunted."

Paul groped for words, could find nothing to say. He had never seen his father this despondent.

"To hold Arrakis," the Duke said, "one is faced with decisions that may cost one his self-respect." He pointed out the window to the Atreides green and black banner hanging limply from a staff at the edge of the landing field. "That honorable banner could come to mean many evil things."

Paul swallowed in a dry throat. His father's words carried futility, a sense of fatalism that left the boy with an empty feeling in his chest.

The Duke took an antifatigue tablet from a pocket, gulped it dry. "Power and fear," he said. "The tools of statecraft. I must order new emphasis on guerrilla training for you. That filmclip there—they call you 'Mahdi'—'Lisan al-Gaib'—as a last resort, you might capitalize on that."

Paul stared at his father, watching the shoulders straighten as the tablet did its work, but remembering the words of fear and doubt.

"What's keeping that ecologist?" the Duke muttered. "I told Thufir to have him here early."

*My father, the Padishah Emperor, took me by the hand one day and I sensed in the ways my mother had taught me that he was disturbed. He led me down the Hall of Portraits to the ego-likeness of the Duke Leto Atreides. I marked the strong resemblance between them—my father and this man in the portrait—both with thin, elegant faces and sharp features dominated by cold eyes. "Princess-daughter," my father said, "I would that you'd been older when it came time for this man to choose a woman." My father was 71 at the time and looking no older than the man in the portrait, and I was but 14, yet I remember deducing in that instant that my father secretly wished the Duke had been his son, and disliked the political necessities that made them enemies.*

—**"In My Father's House" by the Princess Irulan**

His first encounter with the people he had been ordered to betray left Dr. Kynes shaken. He prided himself on being a scientist to whom legends were merely interesting clues, pointing toward cultural roots. Yet the boy fitted the ancient prophecy so precisely. He had "the questing eyes," and the air of "reserved candor."

Of course, the prophecy left certain latitude as to whether the Mother Goddess would bring the Messiah with her or produce Him on the scene. Still, there was this odd correspondence between prediction and persons.

They met in midmorning outside the Arrakeen landing field's administration building. An unmarked ornithopter squatted nearby, humming softly on standby like a somnolent insect. An Atreides guard stood beside it with bared sword and the faint air-distortion of a shield around him.

Kynes sneered at the shield pattern, thinking: *Arrakis has a surprise for them there!*

The planetologist raised a hand, signaled for his Fremen guard to fall back. He strode on ahead toward the building's entrance—the dark hole in plastic-coated rock. So exposed, that monolithic building, he thought. So much less suitable than a cave.

Movement within the entrance caught his attention. He stopped, taking the moment to adjust his robe and the set of his stillsuit at the left shoulder.

The entrance doors swung wide. Atreides guards emerged swiftly, all of them heavily armed—slow pellet stunners, swords and shields. Behind them came a tall man, hawk-faced, dark of skin and hair. He wore a jubba cloak with Atreides crest at the breast, and wore it in a way that betrayed his unfamiliarity with the garment. It clung to the legs of his stillsuit on one side. It lacked a free-swinging, striding rhythm.

Beside the man walked a youth with the same dark hair, but rounder in the face. The youth seemed small for the fifteen years Kynes knew him to have. But the young body carried a sense of command, a poised assurance, as though he saw and knew things all around him that were not visible to others. And he wore the same style cloak as his father, yet with casual ease that made one think the boy had always worn such clothing.

*"The Mahdi will be aware of things others cannot see,"* went the prophecy.

Kynes shook his head, telling himself: *They're just people.*

With the two, garbed like them for the desert, came a man Kynes recognized—Gurney Halleck. Kynes took a deep breath to still his resentment against Halleck, who had briefed him on how to *behave* with the Duke and ducal heir.

*"You may call the Duke 'my Lord' or 'Sire.' 'Noble Born' also is correct, but usually reserved for more formal occasions. The son may be addressed as 'young Master' or 'my Lord.' The Duke is a man of much leniency, but brooks little familiarity."*

And Kynes thought as he watched the group approach: *They'll learn soon enough who's master on Arrakis. Order me questioned half the night by that Mentat, will they? Expect me to guide them on an inspection of spice mining, do they?*

The import of Hawat's questions had not escaped Kynes. They wanted the Imperial bases. And it was obvious they'd learned of the bases from Idaho.

*I will have Stilgar send Idaho's head to this Duke,* Kynes told himself.

The ducal party was only a few paces away now, their feet in desert boots crunching the sand.

Kynes bowed. "My Lord, Duke."

As he had approached the solitary figure standing near the ornithopter, Leto had studied him: tall, thin, dressed for the desert in loose robe, stillsuit, and low boots. The man's hood was thrown back, its veil hanging to one side, revealing long sandy hair, a sparse beard. The eyes were that fathomless blue-within-blue under thick brows. Remains of dark stains smudged his eye sockets.

"You're the ecologist," the Duke said.

"We prefer the old title here, my Lord," Kynes said. "Planetologist."

"As you wish," the Duke said. He glanced down at Paul. "Son, this is the Judge of the Change, the arbiter of dispute, the man set here to see that the forms are obeyed in our assumption of power over this fief." He glanced at Kynes. "And this is my son."

"My Lord," Kynes said.

"Are you a Fremen?" Paul asked.

Kynes smiled. "I am accepted in both sietch and village, young Master. But I am in His Majesty's service, the Imperial Planetologist."

Paul nodded, impressed by the man's air of strength. Halleck had pointed Kynes out to Paul from an upper window of the administration building: "The man standing there with the Fremen escort—the one moving now toward the ornithopter."

Paul had inspected Kynes briefly with binoculars, noting the prim, straight mouth, the high forehead. Halleck had spoken in Paul's ear: "Odd sort of fellow. Has a precise way of speaking—clipped off, no fuzzy edges—razor-apt."

And the Duke, behind them, had said: "Scientist type."

Now, only a few feet from the man, Paul sensed the power in Kynes, the impact of personality, as though he were blood royal, born to command.

"I understand we have you to thank for our stillsuits and these cloaks," the Duke said.

"I hope they fit well, my Lord," Kynes said. "They're of Fremen make and as near as possible the dimensions given me by your man Halleck here."

"I was concerned that you said you couldn't take us into the desert unless we wore these garments," the Duke said. "We can carry plenty of water. We don't intend to be out long and we'll have air cover—the escort you see overhead right now. It isn't likely we'd be forced down."

Kynes stared at him, seeing the water-fat flesh. He spoke coldly: "You never talk of likelihoods on Arrakis. You speak only of possibilities."

Halleck stiffened. "The Duke is to be addressed as my Lord or Sire!"

Leto gave Halleck their private handsignal to desist, said: "Our ways are new here, Gurney. We must make allowances."

"As you wish, Sire."

"We are indebted to you, Dr. Kynes," Leto said. "These suits and the consideration for our welfare will be remembered."

On impulse, Paul called to mind a quotation from the O.C. Bible, said: " 'The gift is the blessing of the giver.' "

The words rang out overloud in the still air. The Fremen escort Kynes had left in the shade of the administration building leaped up from their squatting repose, muttering in open agitation. One cried out: "Lisan al-Gaib!"

Kynes whirled, gave a curt, chopping signal with a hand, waved the guard away. They fell back, grumbling among themselves, trailed away around the building.

"Most interesting," Leto said.

Kynes passed a hard glare over the Duke and Paul, said: "Most of the desert natives here are a superstitious lot. Pay no attention to them. They mean no harm." But he thought of the words of the legend: *They will greet you with Holy Words and your gifts will be a blessing.*

Leto's assessment of Kynes—based partly on Hawat's brief verbal report (guarded and full of suspicions)—suddenly crystallized: the man *was* Fremen. Kynes had come with a Fremen escort, which could mean simply that the Fremen were testing their new freedom to enter urban areas—but it had seemed an honor guard. And by his manner, Kynes was a proud man, accustomed to freedom, his tongue and his manner guarded only by his own suspicions. Paul's question had been direct and pertinent.

Kynes had gone native.

"Shouldn't we be going, Sire?" Halleck asked.

The Duke nodded. "I'll fly my own 'thopter. Kynes can sit up front with me to direct me. You and Paul take the rear seats."

"One moment, please," Kynes said. "With your permission, Sire, I must check the security of your suits."

The Duke started to speak, but Kynes pressed on: "I have concern for my own flesh as well as yours . . . my Lord. I'm well aware of whose throat would be slit should harm befall you two while you're in my care."

The Duke frowned, thinking: *How delicate this moment! If I refuse, it may offend him. And this could be a man whose value to me is beyond measure. Yet . . . to let him inside my shield, touching my person when I know so little about him?*

The thoughts flicked through his mind with decision hard on their heels. "We're in your hands," the Duke said. He stepped forward, opening his robe, saw Halleck come up on the balls of his feet, poised and alert, but remaining where he was. "And, if you'd be so kind," the Duke said, "I'd appreciate an explanation of the suit from one who lives so intimately with it."

"Certainly," Kynes said. He felt up under the robe for the shoulder seals, speaking as he examined the suit. "It's basically a micro-sandwich—a high-efficiency filter and heat-exchange system." He adjusted the shoulder seals. "The skin-contact layer's porous. Perspiration passes through it, having cooled the body . . . near-normal evaporation process. The next two layers . . ." Kynes tightened the chest fit. ". . . include heat exchange filaments and salt precipitators. Salt's reclaimed."

The Duke lifted his arms at a gesture, said: "Most interesting."

"Breathe deeply," Kynes said.

The Duke obeyed.

Keynes studied the underarm seals, adjusted one. "Motions of the body, especially breathing," he said, "and some osmotic action provide the pumping force." He loosened the chest fit slightly. "Reclaimed water circulates to catch-pockets from which you draw it through this tube in the clip at your neck."

The Duke twisted his chin in and down to look at the end of the tube. "Efficient and convenient," he said. "Good engineering."

Kynes knelt, examined the leg seals. "Urine and feces are processed in the thigh pads," he said, and stood up, felt the neck fitting, lifted a sectioned flap there. "In the open desert, you wear this filter across your face, this tube in the nostrils with these plugs to insure a tight fit. Breathe in through the mouth filter, out through the nose tube. With a Fremen suit in good working order, you won't lose more than a thimbleful of moisture a day—even if you're caught in the Great Erg."

"A thimbleful a day," the Duke said.

Kynes pressed a finger against the suit's forehead pad, said: "This may rub a little. If it irritates you, please tell me. I could slip-patch it a bit tighter."

"My thanks," the Duke said. He moved his shoulders in the suit as Kynes stepped back, realizing that it did feel better now—tighter and less irritating.

Kynes turned to Paul. "Now, let's have a look at you, lad."

*A good man but he'll have to learn to address us properly,* the Duke thought.

Paul stood passively as Kynes inspected the suit. It had been an odd sensation putting on the crinkling, slick-surfaced garment. In his force-consciousness had been the absolute knowledge that he had never before worn a stillsuit. Yet, each motion of adjusting the adhesion tabs under Gurney's inexpert guidance had seemed natural, instinctive. When he had tightened the chest to gain maximum pumping action from the motion of breathing, he had known what he did and why. When he had fitted the neck and forehead tabs tightly, he had known it was to prevent friction blisters.

Kynes straightened, stepped back with a puzzled expression. "You've worn a stillsuit before?" he asked.

"This is the first time."

"Then someone adjusted it for you?"

"No."

"Your desert boots are fitted slip-fashion at the ankles. Who told you to do that?"

"It . . . seemed the right way."

"That it most certainly is."

And Kynes rubbed his cheek, thinking of the legend: *"He shall know your ways as though born to them."*

"We waste time," the Duke said. He gestured to the waiting 'thopter, led the way, accepting the guard's salute with a nod. He climbed in, fastened his safety harness, checked controls and instruments. The craft creaked as the others clambered aboard.

Kynes fastened his harness, focused on the padded comfort of the air-craft—soft luxury of gray-green upholstery, gleaming instruments, the sensa-tion of filtered and washed air in his lungs as doors slammed and vent fans whirred alive.

*So soft!* he thought.

"All secure, Sire," Halleck said.

Leto fed power to the wings, felt them cup and dip—once, twice. They were airborne in ten meters, wings feathered tightly and afterjets thrusting them upward in a steep, hissing climb.

"Southeast over the Shield Wall," Kynes said. "That's where I told your sandmaster to concentrate his equipment."

"Right."

The Duke banked into his air cover, the other craft taking up their guard positions as they headed southeast.

"The design and manufacture of these stillsuits bespeaks a high degree of sophistication," the Duke said.

"Someday I may show you a sietch factory," Kynes said.

"I would find that interesting," the Duke said. "I note that suits are manufactured also in some of the garrison cities."

"Inferior copies," Kynes said. "Any Dune man who values his skin wears a Fremen suit."

"And it'll hold your water loss to a thimbleful a day?"

"Properly suited, your forehead cap tight, all seals in order, your major water loss is through the palms of your hands," Kynes said. "You can wear suit gloves if you're not using your hands for critical work, but most Fremen in the open desert rub their hands with juice from the leaves of the creosote bush. It inhibits perspiration."

The Duke glanced down to the left at the broken landscape of the Shield Wall—chasms of tortured rock, patches of yellow-brown crossed by black lines of fault shattering. It was as though someone had dropped this ground from space and left it where it smashed.

They crossed a shallow basin with the clear outline of gray sand spreading across it from a canyon opening to the south. The sand fingers ran out into the basin—a dry delta outlined against darker rock.

Kynes sat back, thinking about the water-fat flesh he had felt beneath the stillsuits. They wore shield belts over their robes, slow pellet stunners at the waist, coin-sized emergency transmitters on cords around their necks. Both the Duke and his son carried knives in wrist sheathes and the sheathes appeared well worn. These people struck Kynes as a strange combination of softness and armed strength. There was a poise to them totally unlike the Harkonnens.

"When you report to the Emperor on the change of government here, will you say we observed the rules?" Leto asked. He glanced at Kynes, back to their course.

"The Harkonnens left; you came," Kynes said.

"And is everything as it should be?" Leto asked.

Momentary tension showed in the tightening of a muscle along Kynes' jaw. "As Planetologist and Judge of the Change, I am a direct subject of the Imperium . . . my Lord."

The Duke smiled grimly. "But we both know the realities."

"I remind you that His Majesty supports my work."

"Indeed? And what is your work?"

In the brief silence, Paul thought: *He's pushing this Kynes too hard.* Paul glanced at Halleck, but the minstrel-warrior was staring out at the barren landscape.

Kynes spoke stiffly: "You, of course, refer to my duties as planetologist."

"Of course."

"It is mostly dry land biology and botany . . . some geological work—core drilling and testing. You never really exhaust the possibilities of an entire planet."

"Do you also investigate the spice?"

Kynes turned, and Paul noted the hard line of the man's cheek. "A curious question, my Lord."

"Bear in mind, Kynes, that this is now my fief. My methods differ from those of the Harkonnens. I don't care if you study the spice as long as I share what you discover." He glanced at the planetologist. "The Harkonnens discouraged investigation of the spice, didn't they?"

Kynes stared back without answering.

"You may speak plainly," the Duke said, "without fear for your skin."

"The Imperial Court is, indeed, a long way off," Kynes muttered. And he thought: *What does this water-soft invader expect? Does he think me fool enough to enlist with him?*

The Duke chuckled, keeping his attention on their course. "I detect a sour note in your voice, sir. We've waded in here with our mob of tame killers, eh? And we expect you to realize immediately that we're different from the Harkonnens?"

"I've read the propaganda you've flooded into sietch and village," Kynes said. "'Love the good Duke!' Your corps of—"

"Here now!" Halleck barked. He snapped his attention away from the window, leaned forward.

Paul put a hand on Halleck's arm.

"Gurney!" the Duke said. He glanced back. "This man's been long under the Harkonnens."

Halleck sat back. "Ayah."

"Your man Hawat's subtle," Kynes said, "but his object's plain enough."

"Will you open those bases to us, then?" the Duke asked.

Kynes spoke curtly: "They're His Majesty's property."

"They're not being used."

"They could be used."

"Does His Majesty concur?"

Kynes darted a hard stare at the Duke. "Arrakis could be an Eden if its rulers would look up from grubbing for spice!"

*He didn't answer my question,* the Duke thought. And he said: "How is a planet to become an Eden without money?"

"What is money," Kynes asked, "if it won't buy the services you need?"

*Ah now!* the Duke thought. And he said: "We'll discuss this another time. Right now, I believe we're coming to the edge of the Shield Wall. Do I hold the same course?"

"The same course," Kynes muttered.

Paul looked out his window. Beneath them, the broken ground began to drop away in tumbled creases toward a barren rock plain and a knife-edged shelf. Beyond the shelf, fingernail crescents of dunes marched toward the horizon with here and there in the distance a dull smudge, a darker blotch to tell of something not sand. Rock outcroppings, perhaps. In the heat-addled air, Paul couldn't be sure.

"Are there any plants down there?" Paul asked.

"Some," Kynes said. "This latitude's life-zone has mostly what we call minor water stealers—adapted to raiding each other for moisture, gobbling up the trace-dew. Some parts of the desert teem with life. But all of it has learned how to survive under these rigors. If *you* get caught down there, you imitate that life or you die."

"You mean steal water from each other?" Paul asked. The idea outraged him, and his voice betrayed his emotion.

"It's done," Kynes said, "but that wasn't precisely my meaning. You see, my climate demands a special attitude toward water. You are aware of water at all times. You waste nothing that contains moisture."

And the Duke thought: ". . . *my climate!*"

"Come around two degrees more southerly, my Lord," Kynes said. "There's a blow coming up from the west."

The Duke nodded. He had seen the billowing of tan dust there. He banked the 'thopter around, noting the way the escort's wings reflected milky orange from the dust-refracted light as they turned to keep pace with him.

"This should clear the storm's edge," Kynes said.

"That sand must be dangerous if you fly into it," Paul said. "Will it really cut the strongest metals?"

"At this altitude, it's not sand but dust," Kynes said. "The danger is lack of visibility, turbulence, clogged intakes."

"We'll see actual spice mining today?" Paul asked.

"Very likely," Kynes said.

Paul sat back. He had used the questions and hyperawareness to do what his mother called "registering" the person. He had Kynes now—tune of voice, each detail of face and gesture. An unnatural folding of the left sleeve on the man's robe told of a knife in an arm sheath. The waist bulged strangely. It was said that desert men wore a belted sash into which they tucked small necessities. Perhaps the bulges came from such a sash—certainly not from a concealed shield belt. A copper pin engraved with the likeness of a hare clasped the neck of Kynes' robe. Another smaller pin with similar likeness hung at the corner of the hood which was thrown back over his shoulders.

Halleck twisted in the seat beside Paul, reached back into the rear compartment and brought out his baliset. Kynes looked around as Halleck tuned the instrument then returned his attention to their course.

"What would you like to hear, young Master?" Halleck asked.

"You choose, Gurney," Paul said.

Halleck bent his ear close to the sounding board, strummed a chord and sang softly:

> "Our fathers ate manna in the desert,
> In the burning places where whirlwinds came.
> Lord, save us from that horrible land!
> Save us . . . oh-h-h-h, save us
> From the dry and thirsty land."

Kynes glanced at the Duke, said: "You *do* travel with a light complement of guards, my Lord. Are all of them such men of many talents?"

"Gurney?" The Duke chuckled. "Gurney's one of a kind. I like him with me for his eyes. His eyes miss very little."

The planetologist frowned.

Without missing a beat in his tune, Halleck interposed:

> "For I am like an owl of the desert, o!
> Aiyah! am like an owl of the des-ert!"

The Duke reached down, brought up a microphone from the instrument panel, thumbed it to life, said: "Leader to Escort Gemma. Flying object at nine o'clock, Sector B. Do you identify it?"

"It's merely a bird," Kynes said, and added: "You have sharp eyes."

The panel speaker crackled, then: "Escort Gemma. Object examined under full amplification. It's a large bird."

Paul looked in the indicated direction, saw the distant speck: a dot of intermittent motion, and realized how keyed up his father must be. Every sense was at full alert.

"I'd not realized there were birds that large this far into the desert," the Duke said.

"That's likely an eagle," Kybes said. "Many creatures have adapted to this place."

The ornithopter swept over a bare rock plain. Paul looked down from their two thousand meters' altitude, saw the wrinkled shadow of their craft and escort. The land beneath seemed flat, but shadow wrinkles said otherwise.

"Has anyone ever walked out of the desert?" the Duke asked.

Halleck's music stopped. He leaned forward to catch the answer.

"Not from the deep desert," Kynes said. "Men have walked out of the second zone several times. They've survived by crossing the rock areas where worms seldom go."

The timbre of Kynes' voice held Paul's attention. He felt his senses come alert the way they were trained to do.

"Ah-h, the worms," the Duke said. "I must see one sometime."

"You may see one today," Kynes said. "Wherever there is spice, there are worms."

"Always?" Halleck asked.

"Always."

"Is there relationship between worm and spice?" the Duke asked.

Kynes turned and Paul saw the pursed lips as the man spoke. "They defend spice *sands*. Each worm has a—territory. As to the spice . . . who knows? Worm specimens we've examined lead us to suspect complicated chemical interchanges within them. We find traces of hydrochloric acid in the ducts, more complicated acid forms elsewhere. I'll give you my monograph on the subject."

"And a shield's no defense?" the Duke asked.

"Shields!" Kynes sneered. "Activate a shield within the worm zone and you seal your fate. Worms ignore territory lines, come from far around to attack a shield. No man wearing a shield has ever survived such attack."

"How are worms taken, then?"

"High voltage electrical shock applied separately to each ring segment is the only known way of killing and preserving an entire worm," Kynes said. "They can be stunned and shattered by explosives, but each ring segment has a life of its own. Barring atomics, I know of no explosive powerful enough to destroy a large worm entirely. They're incredibly tough."

"Why hasn't an effort been made to wipe them out?" Paul asked.

"Too expensive," Kynes said. "Too much area to cover."

Paul leaned back in his corner. His truthsense, awareness of tone shadings, told him that Kynes was lying and telling half-truths, And he thought: *If there's a relationship between spice and worms, killing the worms would destroy the spice.*

"No one will have to walk out of the desert soon," the Duke said. "Trip these little transmitters at our necks and rescue is on its way. All our workers will be wearing them before long. We're setting up a special rescue service."

"Very commendable," Kynes said.

"Your tone says you don't agree," the Duke said.

"Agree? Of course I agree, but it won't be much use. Static electricity from sandstorms masks out many signals. Transmitters short out. They've been tried here before, you know. Arrakis is tough on equipment. And if a worm's hunting you there's not much time. Frequently, you have no more than fifteen or twenty minutes."

"What would you advise?" the Duke asked.

"You ask my advice?"

"As planetologist, yes."

"You'd follow my advice?"

"If I found it sensible."

"Very well, my Lord. Never travel alone."

The Duke turned his attention from the controls. "That's all?"

"That's all. Never travel alone."

"What if you're separated by a storm and forced down?" Halleck asked. "Isn't there anything you could do?"

"*Anything* covers much territory," Kynes said.

"What would *you* do?" Paul asked.

Kynes turned a hard stare at the boy, brought his attention back to the Duke. "I'd remember to protect the integrity of my stillsuit. If I were outside the worm zone or in rock, I'd stay with the ship. If I were down in open sand, I'd get away from the ship as fast as I could. About a thousand meters would be far enough. Then I'd hide beneath my robe. A worm would get the ship, but it might miss me."

"Then what?" Halleck asked.

Kynes shrugged. "Wait for the worm to leave."

"That's all?" Paul asked.

"When the worm has gone, one may try to walk out," Kynes said. "You must walk softly, avoid drum sands, tidal dust basins—head for the nearest rock zone. There are many such zones. You might make it."

"Drum sand?" Halleck asked.

"A condition of sand compaction," Kynes said. "The slightest step sets it drumming. Worms always come to that."

"And a tidal dust basin?" the Duke asked.

"Certain depressions in the desert have filled with dust over the centuries. Some are so vast they have currents and tides. All will swallow the unwary who step into them."

Halleck sat back, resumed strumming the baliset. Presently, he sang:

"Wild beasts of the desert do hunt there,
Waiting for the innocents to pass.
Oh-h-h, tempt not the gods of the desert,
Lest you seek a lonely epitaph.
The perils of the—"

He broke off, leaned forward. "Dust cloud ahead, Sire."

"I see it, Gurney."

"That's what we seek," Kynes said.

Paul stretched up in the seat to peer ahead, saw a rolling yellow cloud low on the desert surface some thirty kilometers ahead.

"One of your factory crawlers," Kynes said. "It's on the surface and that means it's on spice. The cloud is vented sand being expelled after the spice has been centrifugally removed. There's no other cloud quite like it."

"Aircraft over it," the Duke said.

"I see two . . . three . . . four spotters," Kynes said. "They're watching for wormsign."

"Wormsign?" the Duke asked.

"A sandwave moving toward the crawler. They'll have seismic probes on the surface, too. Worms sometimes travel too deep for the wave to show." Kynes swung his gaze around the sky. "Should be a carryall wing around, but I don't see it."

"The worm always comes, eh?" Halleck asked.

"Always."

Paul leaned forward, touched Kynes' shoulder. "How big an area does each worm stake out?"

Kynes frowned. The child kept asking adult questions.

"That depends on the size of the worm."

"What's the variation?" the Duke asked.

"Big ones may control three or four hundred square kilometers. Small ones—" He broke off as the Duke kicked on the jet brakes. The ship bucked as its tail pods whispered to silence. Stub wings elongated, cupped the air. The craft became a full 'thopter as the Duke banked it, holding the wings to a gentle beat, pointing with his left hand off to the east beyond the factory crawler.

"Is that wormsign?"

Kynes leaned across the Duke to peer into the distance.

Paul and Halleck were crowded together, looking in the same direction, and Paul noted that their escort, caught by the sudden maneuver, had surged ahead, but now was curving back. The factory crawler lay ahead of them, still some three kilometers away.

Where the Duke pointed, crescent dune tracks spread shadow ripples toward the horizon and, running through them as a level line stretching into the distance, came an elongated mount-in-motion—a cresting of sand. It reminded Paul of the way a big fish disturbed the water when swimming just under the surface.

"Worm," Kynes said. "Big one." He leaned back, grabbed the microphone from the panel, punched out a new frequency selection. Glancing at the grid chart on rollers over their heads, he spoke into the microphone: "Calling crawler at Delta Ajax niner. Wormsign warning. Crawler at Delta Ajax niner. Wormsign warning. Acknowledge, please." He waited.

The panel speaker emitted static crackles, then a voice: "Who calls Delta Ajax niner? Over."

"They seem pretty calm about it," Halleck said.

Kynes spoke into the microphone: "Unlisted flight—north and east of you about three kilometers. Wormsign is on intercept course, your position, estimated contact twenty-five minutes."

Another voice rumbled from the speaker: "This is Spotter Control. Sighting confirmed. Stand by for contact fix." There was a pause, then: "Contact in twenty-six minutes minus. That was a sharp estimate. Who's on that unlisted flight? Over."

Halleck had his harness off and surged forward between Kynes and the Duke. "Is this the regular working frequency, Kynes?"

"Yes. Why?"

"Who'd be listening?"

"Just the work crews in this area. Cuts down interference."

Again, the speaker crackled, then: "This is Delta Ajax niner. Who gets bonus credit for that spot? Over."

Halleck glanced at the Duke.

Kynes said: "There's a bonus based on spice load for whoever gives first worm warning. They want to know—"

"Tell them who had first sight of that worm," Halleck said.

The Duke nodded.

Kynes hesitated, then lifted the microphone: "Spotter credit to the Duke Leto Atreides. The Duke Leto Atreides. Over."

The voice from the speaker was flat and partly distorted by a burst of static: "We read and thank you."

"Now, tell them to divide the bonus among themselves," Halleck ordered. "Tell them it's the Duke's wish."

Kynes took a deep breath, then: "It's the Duke's wish that you divide the bonus among your crew. Do you read? Over."

"Acknowledged and thank you," the speaker said.

The Duke said: "I forgot to mention that Gurney is also very talented in public relations."

Kynes turned a puzzled frown on Halleck.

"This lets the men know their Duke is concerned for their safety," Halleck said. "Word will get around. It was on an area working frequency—not likely Harkonnen agents heard." He glanced out at their air cover. "And we're a pretty strong force. It was a good risk."

The Duke banked their craft toward the sandcloud erupting from the factory crawler. "What happens now?"

"There's a carryall wing somewhere close," Kynes said. "It'll come in and lift off the crawler."

"What if the carryall's wrecked?" Halleck asked.

"Some equipment *is* lost," Kynes said. "Get in close over the crawler, my Lord; you'll find this interesting."

The Duke scowled, busied himself with the controls as they came into turbulent air over the crawler.

Paul looked down, saw sand still spewing out of the metal and plastic monster beneath them. It looked like a great tan and blue beetle with many wide tracks extending on arms around it. He saw a giant inverted funnel snout poked into dark sand in front of it.

"Rich spice bed by the color," Kynes said. "They'll continue working until the last minute."

The Duke fed more power to the wings, stiffened them for a steeper descent as he settled lower in a circling glide above the crawler. A glance left and right showed his cover holding altitude and circling overhead.

Paul studied the yellow cloud belching from the crawler's pipe vents, looked out over the desert at the approaching worm track.

"Shouldn't we be hearing them call in the carryall?" Halleck asked.

"They usually have the wing on a different frequency," Kynes said.

"Shouldn't they have two carryalls standing by for every crawler?" the Duke asked. "There should be twenty-six men on that machine down there, not to mention cost of equipment."

Kynes said: "You don't have enough ex—"

He broke off as the speaker erupted with an angry voice: "Any of you see the wing? He isn't answering."

A garble of noise crackled from the speaker, drowned in an abrupt override signal, then silence and the first voice: "Report by the numbers! Over."

"This is Spotter Control. Last I saw, the wing was pretty high and circling off northwest. I don't see him now. Over."

"Spotter one: negative. Over."

"Spotter two: negative. Over."

"Spotter three: negative. Over."

Silence.

The Duke looked down. His own craft's shadow was just passing over the crawler. "Only four spotters, is that right?"

"Correct," Kynes said.

"There are five in our party," the Duke said. "Our ships are larger. We can crowd in three extra each. Their spotters ought to be able to lift off two each."

Paul did the mental arithmetic, said: "That's three short."

"Why don't they have two carryalls to each crawler?" barked the Duke.

"You don't have enough extra equipment," Kynes said.

"All the more reason we should protect what we have!"

"Where could that carryall go?" Halleck asked.

"Could've been forced down somewhere out of sight," Kynes said.

The Duke grabbed the microphone, hesitated with thumb poised over its switch. "How could they lose sight of a carryall?"

"They keep their attention on the ground looking for wormsign," Kynes said.

The Duke thumbed the switch, spoke into the microphone. "This is your Duke. We are coming down to take off Delta Ajax niner's crew. All spotters are ordered to comply. Spotters will land on the east side. We will take the west. Over." He reached down, punched out his own command frequency, repeated the order for his own air cover, handed the microphone back to Kynes.

Kynes returned to the working frequency and a voice blasted from the speaker: ". . . almost a full load of spice! We have almost a full load! We can't leave that for a damned worm! Over."

"Damn the spice!" the Duke barked. He grabbed back the microphone, said: "We can always get more spice. There are seats in our ships for all but three of you. Draw straws or decide any way you like who's to go. But you're going, and that's an order!" He slammed the microphone back into Kynes' hands, muttered: "Sorry," as Kynes shook an injured finger.

"How much time?" Paul asked.

"Nine minutes," Kynes said.

The Duke said: "The ship has more power than the others. If we took off under jet with three-quarter wings, we could crowd in an additional man."

"That sand's soft," Kynes said.

"With four extra men aboard on a jet takeoff, we could snap the wings, Sire," Halleck said.

"Not on this ship," the Duke said. He hauled back on the controls as the 'thopter glided in beside the crawler. The wings tipped up, braked the 'thopter to a skidding stop within twenty meters of the factory.

The crawler was silent now, no sand spouting from its vents. Only a faint mechanical rumble issued from it, becoming more audible as the Duke opened his door.

Immediately, their nostrils were assailed by the odor of cinnamon—heavy and pungent.

With a loud flapping, the spotter aircraft glided down to the sand on the other side of the crawler. The Duke's own escort swooped in to land in line with him.

Paul, looking out at the factory, saw how all the 'thopters were dwarfed by it—gnats beside a warrior beetle.

"Gurney, you and Paul toss out that rear seat," the Duke said. He manually cranked the wings out to three-quarters, set their angle, checked the jet pod controls. "Why the devil aren't they coming out of that machine?"

"They're hoping the carryall will show up," Kynes said. "They still have a few minutes." He glanced off to the east.

All turned to look the same direction, seeing no sign of the worm, but there was a heavy, charged feeling of anxiety in the air.

The Duke took the microphone, punched for his command frequency, said: "Two of you toss out your shield generators. By the numbers. You can carry one more man that way. We're not leaving any men for that monster." He keyed back to the working frequency, barked: "All right, you in Delta Ajax niner! Out! Now! This is a command from your Duke! On the double or I'll cut that crawler apart with a lasgun!"

A hatch snapped open near the front of the factory, another at the rear, another at the top. Men came tumbling out, sliding and scrambling down to the sand. A tall man in a patched working robe was the last to emerge. He jumped down to a track and then to the sand.

The Duke hung the microphone on the panel, swung out onto the wing step, shouted: "Two men each into your spotters."

The man in the patched robe began tolling off pairs of his crew, pushing them toward the craft waiting on the other side.

"Four over here!" the Duke shouted. "Four into that ship back there!" He jabbed a finger at an escort 'thopter directly behind him. The guards were just wrestling the shield generator out of it. "And four into that ship over there!" He pointed to the other escort that had shed its shield generator. "Three each into the others! Run, you sand dogs!"

The tall man finished counting off his crew, came slogging across the sand followed by three of his companions.

"I hear the worm, but I can't see it," Kynes said.

The others heard it then—an abrasive slithering, distant and growing louder.

"Damn sloppy way to operate," the Duke muttered.

Aircraft began flapping off the sand around them. It reminded the Duke of a time in his home planet's jungles, a sudden emergence into a clearing, and carrion birds lifting away from the carcass of a wild ox.

The spice workers slogged up to the side of the 'thopter, started climbing in behind the Duke. Halleck helped, dragging them into the rear.

"In you go, boys!" he snapped. "On the double!"

Paul, crowded into a corner by sweating men, smelled the perspiration of fear, saw that two of the men had poor neck adjustments on their stillsuits. He filed the information in his memory for future action. His father would have to order tighter stillsuit discipline. Men tended to become sloppy if you didn't watch such things.

The last man came gasping into the rear, said: "The worm! It's almost on us! Blast off!"

The Duke slid into his seat, frowning, said: "We still have almost three minutes on the original contact estimate. Is that right, Kynes?" He shut his door, checked it.

"Almost exactly, my Lord," Kynes said, and he thought: *A cool one, this duke.*

"All secure here, Sire," Halleck said.

The Duke nodded, watched the last of his escort take off. He adjusted the igniter, glanced once more at wings and instruments, punched the jet sequence.

The take-off pressed the Duke and Kynes deep into their seats, compressed the people in the rear. Kynes watched the way the Duke handled the controls—gently, surely. The 'thopter was fully airborne now, and the Duke studied his instruments, glanced left and right at his wings.

"She's very heavy, Sire," Halleck said.

"Well within the tolerances of this ship," the Duke said. "You didn't really think I'd risk this cargo, did you Gurney?"

Halleck grinned, said: "Not a bit of it, Sire."

The Duke banked his craft in a long easy curve—climbing over the crawler.

Paul, crushed into a corner beside a window, stared down at the silent machine on the sand. The wormsign had broken off about four hundred meters from the crawler. And now, there appeared to be turbulence in the sand around the factory.

"The worm is now beneath the crawler," Kynes said. "You are about to witness a thing few have seen."

Flecks of dust shadowed the sand around the crawler now. The big machine began to tip down to the right. A gigantic sand whirlpool began forming there to the right of the crawler. It moved faster and faster. Sand and dust filled the air now for hundreds of meters around.

Then they saw it!

A wide hole emerged from the sand. Sunlight flashed from glistening white spokes within it. The hole's diameter was at least twice the length of the crawler, Paul estimated. He watched as the machine slid into that opening in a billow of dust and sand. The hole pulled back.

"Gods, what a monster!" muttered a man beside Paul.

"Got all our floggin' spice!" growled another.

"Someone is going to pay for this," the Duke said. "I promise you that."

By the very flatness of his father's voice, Paul sensed the deep anger. He found that he shared it. This was criminal waste!

In the silence that followed, they heard Kynes.

"Bless the Maker and His water," Kynes murmured. "Bless the coming and going of Him. May His passage cleanse the world. May He keep the world for His people."

"What's that you're saying?" the Duke asked.

But Kynes remained silent.

Paul glanced at the men crowded around him. They were staring fearfully at the back of Kynes' head. One of them whispered: "Liet."

Kynes turned, scowling. The man sank back, abashed.

Another of the rescued men began coughing—dry and rasping. Presently, he gasped: "Curse this hell hole!"

The tall Dune man who had come last out of the crawler said: "Be you still, Coss. You but worsen your cough." He stirred among the men until he could look through them at the back of the Duke's head. "You be the Duke Leto, I warrant," he said. "It's to you we give thanks for our lives. We were ready to end it there until you came along."

"Quiet, man, and let the Duke fly his ship," Halleck muttered.

Paul glanced at Halleck. He, too, had seen the tension wrinkles at the corner of his father's jaw. One walked softly when the Duke was in a rage.

Leto began easing his 'thopter out of its great banking circle, stopped at a new sign of movement on the sand. The worm had withdrawn into the depths and now, near where the crawler had been, two figures could be seen moving north away from the sand depression. They appeared to glide over the surface with hardly a lifting of dust to mark their passage.

"Who's that down there?" the Duke barked.

"Two Johnnies who came along for the ride, Soor," said the tall Dune man.

"Why wasn't something said about them?"

"It was the chance they took, Soor," the Dune man said.

"My Lord," said Kynes, "these men know it's of little use to do anything about men trapped on the desert in worm country."

"We'll send a ship from base for them!" the Duke snapped.

"As you wish, my Lord," Kynes said. "But likely when the ship gets here there'll be no one to rescue."

"We'll send a ship anyway," the Duke said.

"They were right beside where the worm came up," Paul said. "How'd they escape?"

"The sides of the hole cave in and make the distances deceptive," Kynes said.

"You waste fuel here, Sire," Halleck ventured.

"Aye, Gurney."

The Duke brought his craft toward the Shield Wall. His escort came down from circling stations, took up positions above and on both sides.

Paul thought about what the Dune man and Kynes had said. He sensed half-truths, outright lies. The men on the sand had glided across the surface so surely, moving in a way obviously calculated to keep from luring the worm back out of its depths.

*Fremen!* Paul thought. *Who else would be so sure on the sand? Who else might be left out of your worries as a matter of course—because* they *are in no danger?* They *know how to live here!* They *know how to outwit the worm!*

"What were Fremen doing on that crawler?" Paul asked.

Kynes whirled.

The tall Dune man turned wide eyes on Paul—blue within blue within blue. "Who be this lad?" he asked.

Halleck moved to place himself between the man and Paul, said: "This is Paul Atreides, the ducal heir."

"Why says he there were Fremen on our rumbler?" the man asked.

"They fit the description," Paul said.

Kynes snorted. "You can't tell Fremen just by looking at them!" He looked at the Dune man. "You. Who were those men?"

"Friends of one of the others," the Dune man said. "Just friends from a village who wanted to see the spice sands."

Kynes turned away. "Fremen!"

But he was remembering the words of the legend: "*The Lisan al-Gaib shall see through all subterfuge.*"

"They be dead now, most likely, young Soor," the Dune man said. "We should not speak unkindly on them."

But Paul heard the falsehood in their voices, felt the menace that had brought Halleck instinctively into guarding position.

Paul spoke dryly: "A terrible place for them to die."

Without turning, Kynes said: "When God hath ordained a creature to die in a particular place, He causeth that creature's wants to direct him to that place."

Leto turned a hard stare at Kynes.

And Kynes, returning the stare, found himself troubled by a fact he had observed here: *This Duke was concerned more over the men than he was over the spice. He risked his own life and that of his son to save the men. He passed off the loss of a spice crawler with a gesture. The threat to men's lives had him in a rage. A leader such as that would command fanatic loyalty. He would be difficult to defeat.*

Against his own will and all previous judgments, Kynes admitted to himself: *I like this duke.*

> *Greatness is a transitory experience. It is never consistent. It depends in part upon the myth-making imagination of humankind. The person who experiences greatness must have a feeling for the myth he is in. He must reflect what is projected upon him. And he must have a strong sense of the sardonic. This is what uncouples him from belief in his own pretensions. The sardonic is all that permits him to move within himself. Without this quality, even occasional greatness will destroy a man.*
>
> **—from "Collected Sayings of Muad'Dib"**
> **by the Princess Irulan**

In the dining hall of the Arrakeen great house, suspensor lamps had been lighted against the early dark. They cast their yellow glows upward onto the black bull's head with its bloody horns, and onto the darkly glistening oil painting of the Old Duke.

Beneath these talismans, white linen shone around the burnished reflections of the Atreides silver, which had been placed in precise arrangements along the great table—little archipelagos of service waiting beside crystal glasses, each setting squared off before a heavy wooden chair. The classic central chandelier remained unlighted, and its chain twisted upward into shadows where the mechanism of the poison-snooper had been concealed.

Pausing in the doorway to inspect the arrangements, the Duke thought about the poison-snooper and what it signified in his society.

*All of a pattern,* he thought. *You can plumb us by our language—the precise and delicate delineations for ways to administer treacherous death. Will someone try chaumurky tonight—poison in the drink? Or will it be chaumas—poison in the food?*

He shook his head.

Beside each plate on the long table stood a flagon of water. There was enough water along the table, the Duke estimated, to keep a poor Arrakeen family for more than a year.

Flanking the doorway in which he stood were broad laving basins of ornate yellow and green tile. Each basin had its rack of towels. It was the custom, the housekeeper had explained, for guests as they entered to dip their hands ceremoniously into a basin, slop several cups of water onto the floor, dry their hands on a towel and fling the towel into the growing puddle at the door. After the dinner, beggars gathered outside to get the water squeezings from the towels.

*How typical of a Harkonnen fief,* the Duke thought. *Every degradation of the spirit that can be conceived.* He took a deep breath, feeling rage tighten his stomach.

"The custom stops here!" he muttered.

He saw a serving woman—one of the old and gnarled ones the housekeeper had recommended—hovering at the doorway from the kitchen across from him. The Duke signaled with upraised hand. She moved out of the shadows, scurried around the table toward him, and he noted the leathery face, the blue-within-blue eyes.

"My Lord wishes?" She kept her head bowed, eyes shielded.

He gestured. "Have these basins and towels removed."

"But . . . Noble Born . . . ." She looked up, mouth gaping.

"I know the custom!" he barked. "Take these basins to the front door. While we're eating and until we've finished, each begger who calls may have a full cup of water. Understood?"

Her leathery face displayed a twisting of emotions: dismay, anger . . . .

With sudden insight, Leto realized she must have planned to sell the water squeezings from the foot-trampled towels, wringing a few coppers from the wretches who came to the door. Perhaps that also was a custom.

His face clouded, and he growled: "I'm posting a guard to see that my orders are carried out to the letter."

He whirled, strode back down the passage to the Great Hall. Memories rolled in his mind like the toothless mutterings of old women. He remembered open water and waves—days of grass instead of sand—dazed summers that had whipped past him like windstorm leaves.

All gone.

*I'm getting old,* he thought. *I've felt the cold hand of my mortality. And in what? An old woman's greed.*

In the Great Hall, the Lady Jessica was the center of a mixed group standing in front of the fireplace. An open blaze crackled there, casting flickers of orange light onto jewels and laces and costly fabrics. He recognized in the group a stillsuit manufacturer down from Carthag, an electronics equipment importer, a water-shipper whose summer mansion was near his polar-cap factory, a representative of the Guild Bank (lean and remote, that one), a dealer in replacement parts for spice mining equipment, a thin and hard-faced woman whose escort service for off-planet visitors reputedly operated as cover for various smuggling, spying, and blackmail operations.

Most of the women in the hall seemed cast from a specific type—decorative, precisely turned out, an odd mingling of untouchable sensousness.

Even without her position as hostess, Jessica would have dominated the group, he thought. She wore no jewelry and had chosen warm colors—a long dress almost the shade of the open blaze, and an earth-brown band around her bronzed hair.

He realized she had done this to taunt him subtly, a reproof against his recent pose of coldness. She was well aware that he liked her best in these shades—that he saw her as a rustling of warm colors.

Nearby, more an outflanker than a member of the group, stood Duncan Idaho in glitterng dress uniform, flat face unreadable, the curling black hair neatly combed. He had been summoned back from the Fremen and had his orders from Hawat—"*Under pretext of guarding her, you will keep the Lady Jessica under constant surveillance.*"

The Duke glanced around the room.

There was Paul in the corner surrounded by a fawning group of the younger Arrakeen richece, and, aloof among them, three officers of the House Troop. The Duke took particular note of the young women. What a catch a ducal heir would make. But Paul was treating all equally with an air of reserved nobility.

*He'll wear the title well,* the Duke thought, and realized with a sudden chill that this was another death thought.

Paul saw his father in the doorway, avoided his eyes. He looked around at the clusterings of guests, the jeweled hands clutching drinks (and the unobtrusive inspections with tiny remote-cast snoopers). Seeing all the chattering faces, Paul was suddenly repelled by them. They were cheap masks locked on festering thoughts—voices gabbling to drown out the loud silence in every breast.

*I'm in a sour mood,* he thought, and wondered what Gurney would say to that.

He knew his mood's source. He hadn't wanted to attend this function, but his father had been firm. "You have a place—a position to uphold. You're old enough to do this. You're almost a man."

Paul saw his father emerge from the doorway, inspect the room, then cross to the group around the Lady Jessica.

As Leto approached Jessica's group, the water-shipper was asking: "Is it true the Duke will put in weather control?"

From behind the man, the Duke said: "We haven't gone that far in our thinking, sir."

The man turned, exposing a bland round face, darkly tanned. "Ah-h, the Duke," he said. "We missed you."

Leto glanced at Jessica. "A thing needed doing." He returned his attention to the water-shipper, explained what he had ordered for the laving basins, adding: "As far as I'm concerned, the old custom ends now."

"Is this a ducal order, m'Lord?" the man asked.

"I leave that to your own . . . ah . . . conscience," the Duke said. He turned, noting Kynes come up to the group.

One of the women said: "I think it's a very generous gesture—giving water to the—" Someone shushed her.

The Duke looked at Kynes, noting that the planetologist wore an old-style dark brown uniform with epaulets of the Imperial Civil Servant and a tiny gold teardrop of rank at his collar.

The water-shipper asked in an angry voice: "Does the Duke imply criticism of our custom?"

"This custom has been changed," Leto said. He nodded to Kynes, marked the frown on Jessica's face, thought: *A frown does not become her, but it'll increase rumors of friction between us.*

"With the Duke's permission," the water-shipper said, "I'd like to inquire further about customs."

Leto heard the sudden oily tone in the man's voice, noted the watchful silence in this group, the way heads were beginning to turn toward them around the room.

"Isn't it almost time for dinner?" Jessica asked.

"But our guest has some questions," Leto said. And he looked at the water-shipper, seeing a round-faced man with large eyes and thick lips, recalling Hawat's memorandum: " . . . *and this water-shipper is a man to watch—Lingar Bewt, remember the name. The Harkonnens used him but never fully controlled him.* "

"Water customs are so interesting," Bewt said, and there was a smile on his face. "I'm curious what you intend about the conservatory attached to this house. Do you intend to continue flaunting it in the people's faces . . . m'Lord?"

Leto held anger in check, staring at the man. Thoughts raced through his mind. It had taken bravery to challenge him in his own ducal castle, especially since they now had Bewt's signature over a contract of allegiance. The action had taken, also, a knowledge of personal power. Water was, indeed, power here. If water facilities were mined, for instance, ready to be destroyed at a signal . . . . The man looked capable of such a thing. Destruction of water facilities might well destroy Arrakis. That could well have been the club this Bewt held over the Harkonnens.

"My Lord, the Duke, and I have other plans for our conservatory," Jessica said. She smiled at Leto. "We intend to keep it, certainly, but only to hold it in trust for the people of Arrakis. It is our dream that someday the climate of Arrakis may be changed sufficiently to grow such plants anywhere in the open."

*Bless her!* Leto thought. *Let our water-shipper chew on that.*

"Your interest in water and weather control is obvious," the Duke said. "I'd advise you to diversify your holdings. One day, water will not be a precious commodity on Arrakis."

And he thought: *Hawat must redouble his efforts at infiltrating this Bewt's organization. And we must start on stand-by water facilities at once. No man is going to hold a club over my head!*

Bewt nodded, the smile still on his face. "A commendable dream, my Lord." He withdrew a pace.

Leto's attention was caught by the expression on Kynes' face. The man was staring at Jessica. He appeared transfigured—like a man in love . . . or caught in a religious trance.

Kynes' thoughts were overwhelmed at last by the words of prophecy: "*And they shall share your most precious dream.*" He spoke directly to Jessica: "Do you bring the shortening of the way?"

"Ah, Dr. Kynes," the water-shipper said. "You've come in from tramping around with your mobs of Fremen. How gracious of you."

Kynes passed an unreadable glance across Bewt, said: "It is said in the desert that possession of water in great amount can inflict a man with fatal carelessness."

"They have many strange sayings in the desert," Bewt said, but his voice betrayed uneasiness.

Jessica crossed to Leto, slipped her hand under his arm to gain a moment in which to calm herself. Kynes had said: ". . . the shortening of the way." In the old tongue, the phrase translated as "Kwisatz Haderach." The planetologist's odd question seemed to have gone unnoticed by the others, and now Kynes was bending over one of the consort women, listening to a low-voiced coquetry.

*Kwisatz Haderach,* Jessica thought. *Did our Missionaria Protectiva plant that legend here, too?* The thought fanned her secret hope for Paul. *He could be the Kwisatz Haderach. He could be.*

The Guild Bank representative had fallen into conversation with the water-shipper, and Bewt's voice lifted above the renewed hum of conversations: "Many people have sought to change Arrakis."

The Duke saw how the words seemed to pierce Kynes, jerking the planet-ologist upright and away from the flirting woman.

Into the sudden silence, a house trooper in uniform of a footman cleared his throat behind Leto, said: "Dinner is served, my Lord."

The Duke directed a questioning glance down at Jessica.

"The custom here is for host and hostess to follow their guests to table," she said, and smiled: "Shall we change that one, too, my Lord?"

He spoke coldly: "That seems a goodly custom. We shall let it stand for now."

*The illusion that I suspect her of treachery must be maintained,* he thought. He glanced at the guests filing past them. *Who among you believes this lie?*

Jessica, sensing his remoteness, wondered at it as she had done frequently the past week. *He acts like a man struggling with himself,* she thought. *Is it because I moved so swiftly setting up this dinner party? Yet, he knows how important it is that we begin to mix our officers and men with the locals on a social plane. We are father and mother surrogate to them all. Nothing impresses that fact more firmly than this sort of social sharing.*

Leto, watching the guests file past, recalled what Thufir Hawat had said when informed of the affair: "*Sire! I forbid it!*"

A grim smile touched the Duke's mouth. What a scene that had been. And when the Duke had remained adamant about attending the dinner, Hawat had shaken his head. "I have bad feelings about this, my Lord," he'd said. "Things move too swiftly on Arrakis. That's not like the Harkonnens. Not like them at all."

Paul passed his father escorting a young woman half a head taller than himself. He shot a sour glance at his father, nodded at something the young woman said.

"Her father manufactures stillsuits," Jessica said. "I'm told that only a fool would be caught in the deep desert wearing one of the man's suits."

"Who's the man with the scarred face ahead of Paul?" the Duke asked. "I don't place him."

"A late addition to the list," she whispered. "Gurney arranged the invitation. Smuggler."

"Gurney arranged?"

"At my request. It was cleared with Hawat, although I thought Hawat was a little stiff about it. The smuggler's called Tuek, Esmar Tuek. He's a power among his kind. They all know him here. He's dined at many of the houses."

"Why is he here?"

"Everyone here will ask that question," she said. "Tuek will sow doubt and suspicion just by his presence. He'll also serve notice that you're prepared to back up your orders against graft—by enforcement from the smugglers' end as well. This was the point Hawat appeared to like."

"I'm not sure *I* like it." He nodded to a passing couple, saw only a few of their guests remained to precede them. "Why didn't you invite some Fremen?"

"There's Kynes," she said.

"Yes, there's Kynes," he said. " Have you arranged any other little surprises for me?" He led her into step behind the procession.

"All else is most conventional," she said.

And she thought: *My darling, can't you see that this smuggler controls fast ships, that he can be bribed? We must have a way out, a door of escape from Arrakis if all else fails us here.*

As they emerged into the dining hall, she disengaged her arm, allowed Leto to seat her. He strode to his end of the table. A footman held his chair for him. The others settled with a swishing of fabrics, a scraping of chairs, but the Duke remained standing. He gave a hand signal, and the house troopers in footman uniform around the table stepped back, standing at attention.

Uneasy silence settled over the room.

Jessica, looking down the length of the table, saw a faint trembling at the corners of Leto's mouth, noted the dark flush of anger on his cheeks. *What has angered him?* she asked herself. *Surely not my invitation to the smuggler.*

"Some question my changing of the laving basin custom," Leto said. "This is my way of telling you that many things will change."

Embarrassed silence settled over the table.

*They think him drunk,* Jessica thought.

Leto lifted his water flagon, held it aloft where the suspensor lights shot beams of reflection off it. "As a Chevalier of the Imperium, then," he said, "I give you a toast."

The others grasped their flagons, all eyes focused on the Duke. In the sudden stillness, a suspensor light drifted slightly in an errant breeze from the serving kitchen hallway. Shadows played across the Duke's hawk features.

"Here I am and here I remain!" he barked.

There was an abortive movement of flagons toward mouths—stopped as the Duke remained with arm upraised. "My toast is one of those maxims so dear to our hearts: 'Business makes progress! Fortune passes everywhere!'"

He sipped his water.

The others joined him. Questioning glances passed among them.

"Gurney!" the Duke called.

From an alcove at Leto's end of the room came Halleck's voice. "Here, my Lord."

· "Give us a tune, Gurney."

A minor chord from the baliset floated out of the alcove. Servants began putting plates of food on the table at the Duke's gesture releasing them—roast desert hare in sauce cepeda, aplomage sirian, chukka under glass, coffee with melange (a rich cinnamon odor from the spice wafted across the table), a true pot-a-oie served with sparkling Caladan wine.

Still, the Duke remained standing.

As the guests waited, their attention torn between the dishes placed before them and the standing Duke, Leto said: "In olden times, it was the duty of the host to entertain his guests with his own talents." His knuckles turned white, so fiercely did he grip his water flagon. "I cannot sing, but I give you the words of Gurney's song. Consider it another toast—a toast to all who've died bringing us to this station."

An uncomfortable stirring sounded around the table.

Jessica lowered her gaze, glanced at the people seated nearest her—there was the round-faced water-shipper and his woman, the pale and austere Guild Bank representative (he seemed a whistle-faced scarecrow with his eyes fixed on Leto), the rugged and scar-faced Tuek, his blue-within-blue eyes downcast.

"Review, friends—troops long past review," the Duke intoned. "All to fate a weight of pains and dollars. Their spirits wear our silver collars. Review, friends—troops long past review. Each a dot of time without pretense or guile. With them passes the lure of fortune. Review, friends—troops long past review. When our time ends on its rictus smile, we'll pass the lure of fortune."

The Duke allowed his voice to trail off on the last line, took a deep drink from his water flagon, slammed it back onto the table. Water slopped over the brim onto the linen.

The others drank in embarrassed silence.

Again, the Duke lifted his water flagon, and this time emptied its remaining half onto the floor, knowing that the others around the table must do the same.

Jessica was first to follow his example.

There was a frozen moment before the others began emptying their flagons. Jessica saw how Paul, seated near his father, was studying the reactions around him. She found herself also fascinated by what her guests' actions revealed—especially among the women. This was clean, potable water, not something already cast away in a sopping towel. Reluctance to just discard it exposed itself in trembling hands, delayed reactions, nervous laughter . . . and violent obedience to the necessity. One woman dropped her flagon, looked the other way as her male companion recovered it.

Kynes, though, caught her attention most sharply. The planetologist hesitated, then emptied his flagon into a container beneath his jacket. He smiled at Jessica as he caught her watching him, raised the empty flagon to her in a silent toast. He appeared completely unembarrassed by his action.

Halleck's music still wafted over the room, but it had come out of its minor key, lilting and lively now as though he were trying to lift the mood.

"Let the dinner commence," the Duke said, and sank into his chair.

*He's angry and uncertain,* Jessica thought. *The loss of that factory crawler hit him more deeply than it should have. It must be something more than that loss. He acts like a desperate man.* She lifted her fork, hoping in the motion to hide her own sudden bitterness. *Why not? He is desperate.*

Slowly at first, then with increasing animation, the dinner got under way. The stillsuit manufacturer complimented Jessica on her chef and wine.

"We brought both from Caladan," she said.

"Superb!" he said, tasting the chukka. "Simply superb! And not a hint of melange in it. One gets so tired of the spice in everything."

The Guild Bank representative looked across at Kynes. "I understand, Doctor Kynes, that another factory crawler has been lost to a worm."

"News travels fast," the Duke said.

"Then it's true?" the banker asked, shifting his attention to Leto.

"Of course, it's true!" the Duke snapped. "The blasted carryall disappeared. It shouldn't be possible for anything that big to disappear!"

"When the worm came, there was nothing to recover the crawler," Kynes said.

"It should *not* be possible!" the Duke repeated.

"No one saw the carryall leave?" the banker asked.

"Spotters customarily keep their eyes on the sand," Kynes said. "They're primarily interested in wormsign. A carryall's complement usually is four men—two pilots and two journeymen attachers. If one—or even two of this crew were in the pay of the Duke's foes—"

"A-h-h, I see," the banker said. "And you, as Judge of the Change, do you challenge this?"

"I shall have to consider my position carefully," Kynes said, "and I certainly will not discuss it at table." And he thought: *That pale skeleton of a man! He knows this is the kind of infraction I was instructed to ignore.*

The banker smiled, returned his attention to his food.

Jessica sat remembering a lecture from her Bene Gesserit schooldays. The subject had been espionage and counter-espionage. A plump, happy-faced Reverend Mother had been the lecturer, her jolly voice contrasting weirdly with the subject matter.

*"A thing to note about any espionage and/or counter-espionage school is the similar basic reaction pattern of all its graduates. Any enclosed discipline sets its stamp, its pattern, upon its students. That pattern is susceptible to analysis and prediction.*

*"Now, motivational patterns are going to be similar among all espionage agents. That is to say: there will be certain types of motivation that are similar despite differing schools or opposed aims. You will study first how to separate this element for your analysis—in the beginning, through interrogation patterns that betray the inner orientation of the interrogators; secondly, by close observation of language-thought orientation of those under analysis. You will find it fairly simple to determine the root languages of your subjects, of course, both through voice inflection and speech pattern."*

Now, sitting at table with her son and her Duke and their guests, hearing the Guild Bank representative, Jessica felt a chill of realization: the man was a Harkonnen agent. He had the Giedi Prime speech pattern—subtly masked, but exposed to her trained awareness as though he had announced himself.

*Does this mean the Guild itself has taken sides against House Atreides?* she asked herself. The thought shocked her, and she masked her emotion by calling for a new dish, all the while listening for the man to betray his purpose. *He will shift the conversation next to something innocent, but with ominous overtones,* she told herself. *It's his pattern.*

The banker swallowed, took a sip of wine, smiled at something said to him by the woman on his right. He seemed to listen for a moment to a man down the table who was explaining to the Duke that native Arrakeen plants had no thorns.

"I enjoy watching the flights of birds on Arrakis," the banker said, directing his words at Jessica. "All of our birds, of course, are carrion-eaters, and many exist without water, having become blood-drinkers."

The stillsuit manufacturer's daughter, seated between Paul and his father at the other end of the table, twisted her pretty face into a frown, said: "Oh, Soo-Soo, you say the most disgusting things."

The banker smiled. "They call me Soo-Soo because I'm financial adviser to the Water Peddlers' Union." And, as Jessica continued to look at him without comment, he added: "Because of the water-sellers' cry—'Soo-Soo Sook!'" And he imitated the call with such accuracy that many around the table laughed.

Jessica heard the boastful tone of voice, but noted most that the young woman had spoken on cue—a set piece. She had produced the excuse for the banker to say what he had said. She glanced at Lingar Bewt. The water magnate was scowling, concentrating on his dinner. It came to Jessica that the banker had said: "*I, too, control that ultimate source of power on Arrakis—water.*"

Paul had marked the falseness in his dinner companion's voice, saw that his mother was following the conversation with Bene Gesserit intensity. On impulse, he decided to play the foil, draw the exchange out. He addressed himself to the banker.

"Do you mean, sir, that these birds are cannibals?"

"That's an odd question, young Master," the banker said. "I merely said the birds drink blood. It doesn't have to be the blood of their own kind, does it?"

"It was *not* an odd question," Paul said, and Jessica noted the brittle riposte quality of her training exposed in his voice. "Most educated people know that the worst potential competition for any young organism can come from its own kind." He deliberately forked a bite of food from his companion's plate, ate it. "They are eating from the same bowl. They have the same basic requirements."

The banker stiffened, scowled at the Duke.

"Do not make the error of considering my son a child," the Duke said. And he smiled.

Jessica glanced around the table, noted that Bewt had brightened, that both Kynes and the smuggler, Tuek, were grinning.

"It's a rule of ecology," Kynes said, "that the young Master appears to understand quite well. The struggle between life elements is the struggle for the free energy of a system. Blood's an efficient energy source."

The banker put down his fork, spoke in an angry voice: "It's said that the Fremen scum drink the blood of their dead."

Kynes shook his head, spoke in a lecturing tone: "Not the blood, sir. But all of a man's water, ultimately, belongs to his people—to his tribe. It's a necessity when you live near the Great Flat. All water's precious there, and the human body is composed of some seventy per cent water by weight. A dead man, surely, no longer requires that water."

The banker put both hands against the table beside his plate, and Jessica thought he was going to push himself back, leave in a rage.

Kynes looked at Jessica. "Forgive me, my Lady, for elaborating on such an ugly subject at table, but you were being told falsehood and it needed clarifying."

"You've associated so long with Fremen that you've lost all sensibilities," the banker rasped.

Kynes looked at him calmly, studied the pale, trembling face. "Are you challenging me, sir?"

The banker froze. He swallowed, spoke stiffly: "Of course not. I'd not so insult our host and hostess."

Jessica heard the fear in the man's voice, saw it in his face, in his breathing, in the pulse of a vein at his temple. The man was terrified of Kynes!

"Our host and hostess are quite capable of deciding for themselves when they've been insulted," Kynes said. "They're brave people who understand defense of honor. We all may attest to their courage by the fact that they are here . . . now . . . on Arrakis."

Jessica saw that Leto was enjoying this. Most of the others were not. People all around the table sat poised for flight, hands out of sight under the table. Two notable exceptions were Bewt, who was openly smiling at the banker's discomfiture, and the smuggler, Tuek, who appeared to be watching Kynes for a cue. Jessica saw that Paul was looking at Kynes in admiration.

"Well?" Kynes said.

"I meant no offense," the banker muttered. "If offense was taken, please accept my apologies."

"Freely given, freely accepted," Kynes said. He smiled at Jessica, resumed eating as though nothing had happened.

Jessica saw that the smuggler, too, had relaxed. She marked this: the man had shown every aspect of an aide ready to leap to Kynes' assistance. There existed an accord of some sort between Kynes and Tuek.

Leto toyed with a fork, looked speculatively at Kynes. The ecologist's manner indicated a change in attitude toward the House of Atreides. Kynes had seemed colder on their trip over the desert.

Jessica signaled for another course of food and drink. Servants appeared with *langues de lapins de garenne*—red wine and a sauce of mushroom-yeast on the side.

Slowly, the dinner conversation resumed, but Jessica heard the agitation in it, the brittle quality, saw that the banker ate in sullen silence. *Kynes would have killed him without hesitating,* she thought. And she realized that there was an offhand attitude toward killing in Kynes' manner. He was a casual killer, and she guessed that this was a Fremen quality.

Jessica turned to the stillsuit manufacturer on her left, said: "I find myself continually amazed by the importance of water on Arrakis."

"Very important," he agreed. "What is this dish? It's delicious."

"Tongues of wild rabbit in a special sauce," she said. "A very old recipe."

"I must have that recipe," the man said.

She nodded. "I'll see that you get it."

Kynes looked at Jessica, said: "The newcomer to Arrakis frequently underestimates the importance of water here. You are dealing, you see, with the Law of the Minimum."

She heard the testing quality in his voice, said, "Growth is limited by that necessity which is present in the least amount. And, naturally, the least favorable condition controls the growth rate."

"It's rare to find members of a Great House aware of planetological problems," Kynes said. "Water is the least favorable condition for life on Arrakis. And remember that *growth* itself can produce unfavorable conditions unless treated with extreme care."

Jessica sensed a hidden message in Kynes' words, but knew she was missing it. "Growth," she said. "Do you mean Arrakis can have an orderly cycle of water to sustain human life under more favorable conditions?"

"Impossible!" The water magnate barked.

Jessica turned her attention to Bewt. "Impossible?"

"Impossible on Arrakis," he said. "Don't listen to this dreamer. All the laboratory evidence is against him."

Kynes looked at Bewt, and Jessica noted that the other conversations around the table had stopped while people concentrated on this new interchange.

"Laboratory evidence tends to blind us to a very simple fact," Kynes said. "That fact is this: we are dealing here with matters that originated and exist out-of-doors where plants and animals carry on their normal existence."

"Normal!" Bewt snorted. "Nothing about Arrakis is normal!"

"Quite the contrary," Kynes said. "Certain harmonies could be set up here along self-sustaining lines. You merely have to understand the limits of the planet and the pressures upon it."

"It'll never be done," Bewt said.

The Duke came to a sudden realization, placing the point where Kynes' attitude had changed—it had been when Jessica had spoken of holding the conservatory plants in trust for Arrakis.

"What would it take to set up the self-sustaining system, Doctor Kynes?" Leto asked.

"If we can get three per cent of the green plant element on Arrakis involved in forming carbon compounds as foodstuffs, we've started the cyclic system," Kynes said.

"Water's the only problem?" the Duke asked. He sensed Kynes' excitement, felt himself caught up in it.

"Water overshadows the other problems," Kynes said. "This planet has much oxygen without its usual concomitants—wide-spread plant life and large sources of free carbon dioxide from such phenomena as volcanoes. There are unusual chemical interchanges over large surface areas here."

"Do you have pilot projects?" the Duke asked.

"We've had a long time in which to build up the Tansley Effect—small-unit experiments on an amateur basis from which my science may now draw its working facts," Kynes said.

"There isn't enough water," Bewt said. "There just isn't enough water."

"Master Bewt is an expert on water," Kynes said. He smiled, turned back to his dinner.

The Duke gestured sharply down with his right hand, barked: "No, I want an answer! Is there enough water, Doctor Kynes?"

Kynes stared at his plate.

Jessica watched the play of emotion on his face. *He masks himself well,* she thought, but she had him registered now and read that he regretted his words.

"Is there enough water?" the Duke demanded.

"There . . . may be," Kynes said.

*He's faking uncertainty!* Jessica thought.

With his deeper truthsense, Paul caught the underlying motive, had to use every ounce of his training to mask his excitement. *There is enough water! But Kynes doesn't wish it to be known.*

"Our planetologist has many interesting dreams," Bewt said. "He dreams with the Fremen—of prophecies and messiahs."

Chuckles sounded at odd places around the table. Jessica marked them—the smuggler, the stillsuit manufacturer's daughter, Duncan Idaho, the woman with the mysterious escort service.

*Tensions are oddly distributed here tonight,* Jessica thought. *There's too much going on of which I'm not aware. I'll have to develop new information sources.*

The Duke passed his gaze from Kynes to Bewt to Jessica. He felt oddly let down, as though something vital had passed him here. "*May* be," he muttered.

Kynes spoke quickly: "Perhaps we should discuss this another time, my Lord. There are so many—"

The planetologist broke off as a uniformed Atreides trooper hurried in through the service door, was passed by the guard and rushed to the Duke's side. The man bent, whispering into Leto's ear.

Jessica recognized the capsign of Hawat's corps, fought down uneasiness. She addressed herself to the stillsuit manufacturer's feminine companion—a tiny, dark-haired woman with a doll face, a touch of epicanthic fold to the eyes.

"You've hardly touched your dinner, my dear," Jessica said. "May I order you something?"

The woman looked at the stillsuit manufacturer before answering, then: "I'm not very hungry."

Abruptly, the Duke stood up beside his trooper, spoke in a harsh tone of command: "Stay seated, everyone. You will have to forgive me, but a matter has arisen that requires my personal attention." He stepped aside. "Paul, take over as host for me, if you please."

Paul stood, wanting to ask why his father had to leave, knowing he had to play this with the grand manner. He moved around to his father's chair, sat down at it.

The Duke turned to the alcove where Halleck sat, said: "Gurney, please take Paul's place at table. We mustn't have an odd number here. When the dinner's over, I may want you to bring Paul to the field C.P. Wait for my call."

Halleck emerged from the alcove in dress uniform, his lumpy ugliness seeming out of place in the glittering finery. He leaned his baliset against the wall, crossed to the chair Paul had occupied, sat down.

"There's no need for alarm," the Duke said, "but I must ask that no one leave until our house guard says its safe. You will be perfectly secure as long as you remain here, and we'll have this little trouble cleared up very shortly."

Paul caught the code words in his father's message—*guard-safe-secure-shortly*. The problem was security, not violence. He saw that his mother had read the same message. They both relaxed.

The Duke gave a short nod, wheeled and strode through the service door followed by his trooper.

Paul said: "Please go on with your dinner. I believe Doctor Kynes was discussing water."

"May we discuss it another time?" Kynes asked.

"By all means," Paul said.

And Jessica noted with pride her son's dignity, the mature sense of assurance.

The banker picked up his water flagon, gestured with it at Bewt. "None of us here can surpass Master Lingar Bewt in flowery phrases. One might almost assume he aspired to Great House status. Come, Master Bewt, lead us in a toast. Perhaps you've a dollop of wisdom for the boy who must be treated like a man."

Jessica clenched her right hand into a fist beneath the table. She saw a hand signal pass from Halleck to Idaho, saw the house troopers along the walls move into positions of maximum guard.

Bewt cast a venomous glare at the banker.

Paul glanced at Halleck, took in the defensive positions of his guards, looked at the banker until the man lowered the water flagon. He said: "Once, on Caladan, I saw the body of a drowned fisherman recovered. He—"

"Drowned?" It was the stillsuit manufacturer's daughter.

Paul hesitated, then: "Yes. Immersed in water until dead. Drowned."

"What an interesting way to die," she murmured.

Paul's smile became brittle. He returned his attention to the banker. "The interesting thing about this man was the wounds on his shoulders—made by another fisherman's claw-boots. This fisherman was one of several in a boat—a craft for travelling on water—that foundered . . . sank beneath the water. Another fisherman helping recover the body said he'd seen marks like this man's wounds several times. They meant another drowning fisherman had tried to stand on this poor fellow's shoulders in the attempt to reach up to the surface—to reach air."

"Why is this interesting?" the banker asked.

"Because of an observation made by my father at the time. He said the drowning man who climbs on your shoulders to save himself is understandable—except when you see it happen in the drawing room." Paul hesitated just long enough for the banker to see the point coming, then: "And, I should add, except when you see it at the dinner table."

A sudden stillness enfolded the room.

*That was rash,* Jessica thought. *This banker might have enough rank to call my son out.* She saw that Idaho was poised for instant action. The House troopers were alert. Gurney Halleck had his eyes on the men opposite him.

"Ho-ho-ho-o-o-o!" It was the smuggler, Tuek, head thrown back, laughing with complete abandon.

Nervous smiles appeared around the table.

Bewt was grinning.

The banker had pushed his chair back, was glaring at Paul.

Kynes said: "One baits an Atreides at his own risk."

"Is it Atreides custom to insult their guests?" the banker demanded.

Before Paul could answer, Jessica leaned forward, said: "Sir!" And she thought: *We must learn this Harkonnen creature's game. Is he here to try for Paul? Does he have help?*

"My son displays a general garment and you claim it's cut to your fit?" Jessica asked. "What a fascinating revelation." She slid a hand down her leg to the crysknife she had fastened in a calf-sheath.

The banker turned his glare at Jessica. Eyes shifted away from Paul and she saw him ease himself back from the table, freeing himself for action. He had focused on the code word: *garment. "Prepare for violence."*

Kynes directed a speculative look at Jessica, gave a subtle hand signal to Tuek.

The smuggler lurched to his feet, lifted his flagon. "I'll give you a toast," he said. "To young Paul Atreides, still a lad by his looks, but a man by his actions."

*Why do they intrude?* Jessica asked herself.

The banker stared now at Kynes, and Jessica saw terror return to the agent's face.

People began responding all around the table.

*Where Kynes leads, people follow,* Jessica thought. *He has told us he sides with Paul. What's the secret of his power? It can't be because he's Judge of the Change. That's temporary. And certainly not because he's a civil servant.*

She removed her hand from the crysknife hilt, lifted her flagon to Kynes, who responded in kind.

Only Paul and the banker—(*Soo-Soo! What an idiotic nickname!* Jessica thought.)—remained empty-handed. The banker's attention stayed fixed on Kynes. Paul stared at his plate.

*I was handling it correctly,* Paul thought. *Why do they interfere?* He glanced covertly at the male guests nearest him. *Prepare for violence? From whom? Certainly not from that banker fellow.*

Halleck stirred, spoke as though to no one in particular, directing his words over the heads of the guests across from him: "In our society, people shouldn't be quick to take offense. It's frequently suicidal." He looked at the stillsuit manufacturer's daughter beside him. "Don't you think so, miss?"

"Oh, yes. Yes. Indeed I do," she said. "There's too much violence. It makes me sick. And lots of times no offense is meant, but people die anyway. It doesn't make sense."

"Indeed it doesn't," Halleck said.

Jessica saw the near perfection of the girl's act, realized: *That empty-headed little female is not an empty-headed little female.* She saw then the pattern of the threat and understood that Halleck, too, had detected it. They had planned to lure Paul with sex. Jessica relaxed. Her son had probably been first to see it—his training hadn't overlooked the obvious gambit.

Kynes spoke to the banker: "Isn't another apology in order?"

The banker turned a sickly grin toward Jessica, said: "My Lady, I fear I've overindulged in your wines. You serve potent drink at table, and I'm not accustomed to it."

Jessica heard the venom beneath his tone, spoke sweetly: "When strangers meet, great allowance should be made for differences of custom and training."

"Thank you, my Lady," he said.

The dark-haired companion of the stillsuit manufacturer leaned toward Jessica, said: "The Duke spoke of our being secure here. I do hope that doesn't mean more fighting."

*She was directed to lead the conversation this way,* Jessica thought.

"Likely this will prove unimportant," Jessica said. "But there's so much detail requiring the Duke's personal attention in these times. As long as enmity continues between Atreides and Harkonnen we cannot be too careful. The Duke has sworn kanly. He will leave no Harkonnen agent alive on Arrakis, of course." She glanced at the Guild Bank agent. "And the Conventions, naturally, support him in this." She shifted her attention to Kynes. "Is this not so, Dr. Kynes?"

"Indeed it is," Kynes said.

The stillsuit manufacturer pulled his companion back. She looked at him, said: "I do believe I'll eat something now. I'd like some of that bird dish you served earlier."

Jessica signaled a servant, turned to the banker: "And you, sir, were speaking of birds earlier and of their habits. I find so many interesting things about Arrakis. Tell me, where is the spice found? Do the hunters go deep into the desert?"

"Oh, no, my Lady," he said. "Very little's known of the deep desert. And almost nothing of the southern regions."

"There's a tale that a great Mother Lode of spice is to be found in the southern reaches," Kynes said, "but I suspect it was an imaginative invention made solely for purposes of a song. Some daring spice hunters do, on occasion, penetrate into the edge of the central belt, but that's extremely dangerous— navigation is uncertain, storms are frequent. Casualties increase dramatically the farther you operate from Shield Wall bases. It hasn't been found profitable to venture too far south. Perhaps if we had a weather satellite . . . ."

Bewt looked up, spoke around a mouthful of food: "It's said the Fremen travel there, that they go anywhere and have hunted out soaks and sip-wells even in the southern latitudes."

"Soaks and sip-wells?" Jessica asked.

Kynes spoke quickly: "Wild rumors, my Lady. These are known on other planets, not on Arrakis. A soak is a place where water seeps to the surface or near enough to the surface to be found by digging according to certain signs. A sip-well is a form of soak where a person draws water through a straw . . . so it is said."

*There's deception in his words,* Jessica thought.

*Why is he lying?* Paul wondered.

"How very interesting," Jessica said. And she thought: "*It is said . . . .*" *What a curious speech mannerism they have here. If they only knew what it reveals about their dependence on superstitions.*

"I've heard you have a saying," Paul said, "that polish comes from the cities; wisdom from the desert."

"There are many sayings on Arrakis," Kynes said.

Before Jessica could frame a new question, a servant bent over her with a note. She opened it, saw the Duke's handwriting and code signs, scanned it.

"You'll all be delighted to know," she said, "that our Duke sends his reassurances. The matter which called him away has been settled. The missing carryall has been found. A Harkonnen agent in the crew overpowered the others and flew the machine to a smugglers' base, hoping to sell it there. Both man and machine were turned over to our forces." She nodded to Tuek.

The smuggler nodded back.

Jessica refolded the note, tucked it into her sleeve.

"I'm glad it didn't come to open battle," the banker said. "The people have such hopes the Atreides will bring peace and prosperity."

"Especially prosperity," Bewt said.

"Shall we have our dessert now?" Jessica asked. "I've had our chef prepare a Caladan sweet: pongi rice in sauce dolsa."

"It sounds wonderful," the stillsuit manufacturer said. "Would it be possible to get the recipe?"

"Any recipe you desire," Jessica said, *registering* the man for later mention to Hawat. The stillsuit manufacturer was a fearful little climber and could be bought.

Small talk resumed around her: "Such a lovely fabric . . . ." "He is having a setting made to match the jewel . . . ." "We might try for a production increase next quarter . . . ."

Jessica stared down at her plate, thinking of the coded part of Leto's message: "*The Harkonnens tried to get a shipment of lasguns. We captured them. This may mean they've succeeded with other shipments. It certainly means they don't place much store in shields. Take appropriate precautions.*"

Jessica focused her mind on lasguns, wondering. The white-hot beams of disruptive light could cut through any known substance, provided that substance was not shielded. The fact that feedback from a shield would explode both lasgun and shield did not bother the Harkonnens. Why? A lasgun-shield explosion was a dangerous variable, could be more powerful than atomics, could kill only the gunner and his shielded target.

The unknowns here filled her with uneasiness.

Paul said: "I never doubted we'd find the carryall. Once my father moves to solve a problem, he solves it. This is a fact the Harkonnens are beginning to discover."

*He's boasting,* Jessica thought. *He shouldn't boast. No person who'll be sleeping far below ground level this night as a precaution against lasguns has the right to boast.*

*"There is no escape—we pay for the violence of our ancestors."*

**—from "The Collected Sayings of Muad'Dib"
by the Princess Irulan**

Jessica heard the disturbance in the great hall, turned on the light beside her bed. The clock there had not been properly adjusted to local time, and she had to subtract twenty-one minutes to determine that it was about 2 A.M.

The disturbance was loud and incoherent.

*Is this the Harkonnen attack?* she wondered.

She slipped out of bed, checked the screen monitors to see where her family was. The screen showed Paul asleep in the deep cellar room they'd hastily converted to a bedroom for him. The noise obviously wasn't penetrating to his quarters. There was no one in the Duke's room, his bed was unrumpled. Was he still at the field C.P.?

There were no screens yet to the front of the house.

Jessica stood in the middle of her room, listening.

There was one shouting, incoherent voice. She heard someone call for Dr. Yueh. Jessica found a robe, pulled it over her shoulders, pushed her feet into slippers, strapped the crysknife to her leg.

Again, a voice called out for Yueh.

Jessica belted the robe around her, stepped into the hallway. Then the thought struck her: *What if Leto's hurt?*

The hall seemed to stretch out forever under her running feet. She turned through the arch at the end, dashed past the dining hall and down the passage to the Great Hall, finding the place brightly lighted, all the wall suspensors glowing at maximum.

To her right near the front entry, she saw two house guards holding Duncan Idaho between them. His head lolled forward, and there was an abrupt, panting silence to the scene.

One of the house guards spoke accusingly to Idaho: "You see what you did? You woke the Lady Jessica."

The great draperies billowed behind the men, showing that the front door remained open. There was no sign of the Duke or Yueh. Mapes stood to one side staring coldly at Idaho. She wore a long brown robe with serpentine design at the hem. Her feet were pushed into unlaced desert boots.

"So I woke the Lady Jessica," Idaho muttered. He lifted his face toward the ceiling, bellowed: "My sword was firs' blooded on Grumman!"

*Great Mother! He's drunk!* Jessica thought.

Idaho's dark, round face was drawn into a frown. His hair, curling like the fur of a black goat, was plastered with dirt. A jagged rent in his tunic exposed an expanse of the dress shirt he had worn at the dinner party earlier.

Jessica crossed to him.

One of the guards nodded to her without releasing his hold on Idaho. "We didn't know what to do with him, my Lady. He was creating a disturbance out front, refusing to come inside. We were afraid locals might come along and see him. That wouldn't do at all. Give us a bad name here."

"Where has he been?" Jessica asked.

"He escorted one of the young ladies home from the dinner, my Lady. Hawat's orders."

"Which young lady?"

"One of the escort wenches. You understand, my Lady?" He glanced at Mapes, lowered his voice. "They're always calling on Idaho for special surveillance of the ladies."

And Jessica thought: *So they are. But why is he drunk?*

She frowned, turned to Mapes. "Mapes, bring a stimulant. I'd suggest caffeine. Perhaps there's some of the spice coffee left."

Mapes shrugged, headed for the kitchen. Her unlaced desert boots slap-slapped against the stone floor.

Idaho swung his unsteady head around to peer at an angle toward Jessica. "Killed more'n three hunner' men f'r the Duke," he muttered. "Whadduh wanna know is why'm 'mere? Can't live unner th' groun' here. Can't live onna groun' here. Wha' kinna place is 'iss, huh?"

A sound from the side hall entry caught Jessica's attention. She turned, saw Yueh crossing to them, his medical kit swinging in his left hand. He was fully dressed, looked pale, exhausted. The diamond tattoo stood out sharply on his forehead.

"Th' good docker!" Idaho shouted. "Whad're you, Doc? Splint 'n' pill man?" He turned blearily toward Jessica. "Makin' uh damn fool uh m'self, huh?"

Jessica frowned, remained silent, wondering: *Why would Idaho get drunk? Was he drugged?*

"Too much spice beer," Idaho said, attempting to straighten.

Mapes returned with a steaming cup in her hands, stopped uncertainly behind Yueh. She looked at Jessica, who shook her head.

Yueh put his kit on the floor, nodded greeting to Jessica, said: "Spice beer, eh?"

"Bes' damn stuff ever tas'ed," Idaho said. He tried to pull himself to attention. "My sword was firs' blooded on Grumman! Killed a Harkon . . . Harkon . . . killed 'im f'r th' Duke."

Yueh turned, looked at the cup in Mapes' hand. "What is that?"

"Caffeine," Jessica said.

Yueh took the cup, held it toward Idaho. "Drink this, lad."

"Don' wan' any more t' drink."

"Drink it, I say!"

Idaho's head wobbled toward Yueh, and he stumbled one step ahead, dragging the guards with him. "I'm almighdy fed up with pleasin' th' 'Mperial Universe, Doc. Jus' once, we're gonna do th' thing my way."

"After you drink this," Yueh said. "It's just caffeine."

" 'Sprolly like all res' uh this place! Damn' sun 'stoo brighd. Nothin' has uh righd color. Ever'thing's wrong or . . . ."

"Well, it's nighttime now," Yueh said. He spoke reasonably. "Drink this like a good lad. It'll make you feel better."

"Don' wanna feel bedder!"

"We can't argue with him all night," Jessica said. And she thought: *This calls for shock treatment.*

"There's no reason for you to stay, my Lady," Yueh said. "I can take care of this."

Jessica shook her head. She stepped forward, slapped Idaho sharply across the cheek.

He stumbled back with his guards, glaring at her.

"This is no way to act in your Duke's home," she said. She snatched the cup from Yueh's hands, spilling part of it, thrust the cup toward Idaho. "Now drink this! That's an order!"

Idaho jerked himself upright, scowling down at her. He spoke slowly, with careful and precise enunciation: "I do not take orders from a damn' Harkonnen spy."

Yueh stiffened, whirled to face Jessica.

Her face had gone pale, but she was nodding. It all became clear to her—the broken stems of meaning she had seen in words and actions around her these past few days could now be translated. She found herself in the grip of anger almost too great to contain. It took the most profound of her Bene Gesserit training to quiet her pulse and smooth her breathing. Even then she could feel the blaze flickering.

*They were always calling on Idaho for surveillance of the ladies!*

She shot a glance at Yueh. The doctor lowered his eyes.

"You knew this?" she demanded.

"I . . . heard rumors, my Lady. But I didn't want to add to your burdens."

"Hawat!" she snapped. "I want Thufir Hawat brought to me immediately!"

"But, my Lady . . . ."

"Immediately!"

*It has to be Hawat,* she thought. *Suspicion such as this could come from no other source without being discarded immediately.*

Idaho shook his head, mumbled: "Chuck th' whole damn thing."

Jessica looked down at the cup in her hand, abruptly dashed its contents across Idaho's face. "Lock him in one of the guest rooms of the east wing," she ordered. "Let him *sleep* it off."

The two guards stared at her unhappily. One ventured: "Perhaps we should take him someplace else, m'Lady. We could . . . ."

"He's supposed to be here!" Jessica snapped. "He has a job to do here." Her voice dripped bitterness. "He's so good at watching the ladies."

The guard swallowed.

"Do you know where the Duke is?" she demanded.

"He's at the command post, my Lady."

"Is Hawat with him?"

"Hawat's in the city, my Lady."

"You will bring Hawat to me at once," Jessica said. "I will be in my sitting room when he arrives."

"But, my Lady . . . ."

"If necessary, I will call the Duke," she said. "I hope it will not be necessary. I would not want to disturb him with this."

"Yes, my Lady."

Jessica thrust the empty cup into Mapes' hands, met the questioning stare of the blue-within-blue eyes. "You may return to bed, Mapes."

"You're sure you'll not need me?"

Jessica smiled grimly. "I'm sure."

"Perhaps this could wait until tomorrow," Yueh said. "I could give you a sedative and . . . ."

"You will return to your quarters and leave me to handle this my way," she said. She patted his arm to take the sting out of her command. "This is the only way."

Abruptly, head high, she turned and stalked off through the house to her rooms. Cold walls . . . passages . . . a familiar door . . . . She jerked the door open, strode in, and slammed it behind her. Jessica stood there glaring at the shield-blanked windows of her sitting room. *Hawat! Could he be the one the Harkonnens bought? We shall see.*

Jessica crossed to the deep, old-fashioned armchair with an embroidered cover of schlag skin, moved the chair into position to command the door. She was suddenly very conscious of the crysknife in its sheath on her leg. She removed the sheath and strapped it to her arm, tested the drop of it. Once more, she glanced around the room, placing everything precisely in her mind against any emergency: the chaise near the corner, the straight chairs along the wall, the two low tables, her stand-mounted zither beside the door to her bedroom.

Pale rose light glowed from the suspensor lamps. She dimmed them, sat down in the armchair, patting the upholstery, appreciating the chair's regal heaviness for this occasion.

*Now, let him come,* she thought. *We shall see what we shall see.* And she prepared herself in the Bene Gesserit fashion for the wait, accumulating patience, saving her strength.

Sooner than she had expected, a rap sounded at the door and Hawat entered at her command.

She watched him without moving from the chair, seeing the crackling sense of drug-induced energy in his movements, seeing the fatigue beneath. Hawat's rheumy old eyes glittered. His leathery skin appeared faintly yellow in the room's light, and there was a wide, wet stain on the sleeve of his knife arm.

She smelled blood there.

Jessica gestured to one of the straight-backed chairs, said: "Bring that chair and sit facing me."

Hawat bowed, obeyed. *That drunken fool of an Idaho!* he thought. He studied Jessica's face, wondering how he could save this situation.

"It's long past time to clear the air between us," Jessica said.

"What troubles my Lady?" He sat down, placed hands on knees.

"Don't play coy with me!" she snapped. "If Yueh didn't tell you why I summoned you, then one of your spies in my household did. Shall we be at least that honest with each other?"

"As you wish, my Lady."

"First, you will answer me one question," she said. "Are you now a Harkonnen agent?"

Hawat surged half out of his chair, his face dark with fury, demanding: "You dare insult me so?"

"Sit down," she said. "You insulted me so."

Slowly, he sank back into the chair.

And Jessica, reading the signs on this face that she knew so well, allowed herself a deep breath. *It isn't Hawat.*

"Now I know you remain loyal to my Duke," she said. "I'm prepared, therefore, to forgive your affront to me."

"Is there something to forgive?"

Jessica scowled, wondering: *Shall I play my trump? Shall I tell him of the Duke's daughter I've carried within me these few weeks? No . . . Leto himself doesn't know. This would only complicate his life, divert him in a time when he must concentrate on our survival. There is yet time to use this.*

"A Truthsayer would solve this," she said, "but we have no Truthsayer qualified by the High Board."

"As you say. We've no Truthsayer."

"Is there a traitor among us?" she asked. "I've studied our people with great care. Who could it be? Not Gurney. Certainly not Duncan. *Their* lieutenants are not strategically enough placed to consider. It's not you, Thufir. It cannot be Paul. I *know* it's not me. Dr. Yueh, then? Shall I call him in and put him to the test?"

"You know that's an empty gesture," Hawat said. "He's conditioned by the High College. *That* I know for certain."

"Not to mention that his wife was a Bene Gesserit slain by the Harkonnens," Jessica said.

"So that's what happened to her," Hawat said.

"Haven't you heard the hate in his voice when he speaks the Harkonnen name?"

"You know I don't have the ear," Hawat said.

"What brought this base suspicion on me?" she asked.

Hawat frowned. "My Lady puts her servant in an impossible position. My first loyalty is to the Duke."

"I'm prepared to forgive much because of that loyalty," she said.

"And again I must ask: Is there something to forgive?"

"Stalemate?" she asked.

He shrugged.

"Let us discuss something else for a minute, then," she said. "Duncan Idaho, the admirable fighting man whose abilities at guarding and surveillance are so esteemed. Tonight, he overindulged in something called spice beer. I hear reports that others among our people have been stupefied by this concoction. Is that true?"

"You have your reports, my Lady."

"So I do. Don't you see this drinking as a symptom, Thufir?"

"My Lady speaks riddles."

"Apply your Mentat abilities to it!" she snapped. "What's the problem with Duncan and the others? I can tell you in four words—they have no home."

He jabbed a finger at the floor. "Arrakis, that's their home."

"Arrakis is an unknown! Caladan was their home, but we've uprooted them. They have no home. And they fear the Duke's failing them."

He stiffened. "Such talk from one of the men would be cause for—"

"Oh, stop that, Thufir. Is it defeatist or treacherous for a doctor to diagnose a disease correctly? My only intention is to cure the disease."

"The Duke gives me charge over such matters."

"But you understand I have a certain natural concern over the progress of this disease," she said. "And perhaps you'll grant I have certain abilities along these lines."

*Will I have to shock him severely?* she wondered. *He needs shaking up— something to break him from routine.*

"There could be many interpretations for your concern," Hawat said. He shrugged.

"Then you've already convicted me?"

"Of course not, my Lady. But I cannot afford to take *any* chances, the situation being what it is."

"A threat to my son got past you right here in this house," she said. "Who took that chance?"

His face darkened. "I offered my resignation to the Duke."

"Did you offer your resignation to me . . . or to Paul?"

Now he was openly angry, betraying it in quickness of breathing, in dilation of nostrils, a steady stare. She saw a pulse beating at his temple.

"I'm the Duke's man," he said, biting off the words.

"There is no traitor," she said. "The threat's something else. Perhaps it has to do with the lasguns. Perhaps they'll risk secreting a few lasguns with timing mechanisms aimed at house shields. Perhaps they'll . . . ."

"And who could tell after the blast if the explosion wasn't atomic?" he asked. "No, my Lady. They'll not risk anything *that* illegal. Radiation lingers. The evidence is hard to erase. No. They'll observe *most* of the forms. It has to be a traitor."

"You're the Duke's man," she sneered. "Would you destroy him in the effort to save him?"

He took a deep breath, then: "If you're innocent, you'll have my most abject apologies."

"Look at you now, Thufir," she said. "Humans live best when each has his own place, when each knows where he belongs in the scheme of things. Destroy the place and destroy the person. You and I, Thufir, of all those who love the Duke, are most ideally situated to destroy the other's place. Could I not whisper suspicions about you into the Duke's ear at night? When would he be most susceptible to such whispering, Thufir? Must I draw it for you more clearly?"

"You threaten me?" he growled.

"Indeed not. I merely point out to you that someone is attacking us through the basic arrangement of our lives. It's clever, diabolical. I propose to negate this attack by so ordering our lives that there'll be no chinks for such barbs to enter."

"You accuse me of whispering baseless suspicions?"

"Baseless, yes."

"You'd meet this with your own whispers?"

"*Your* life is compounded of whispers, not mine, Thufir."

"Then you question my abilities?"

She sighed. "Thufir, I want you to examine your own emotional involvement in this. The *natural* human's an animal without logic. Your projection of logic onto all affairs is *un*natural, but suffered to continue for its usefulness. You're the embodiment of logic—a Mentat. Yet, your problem solutions are concepts that, in a very real sense, are projected outside yourself, there to be studied and rolled around, examined from all sides."

"You think now to teach me my trade?" he asked, and he did not try to hide the disdain in his voice.

"Anything outside yourself, this you can see and apply your logic to it," she said. "But it's a human trait that when we encounter personal problems, those things most deeply personal are the most difficult to bring out for our logic to scan. We tend to flounder around, blaming everything but the actual, deep-seated thing that's really chewing on us."

"You're deliberately attempting to undermine my faith in my abilities as a Mentat," he rasped. "Were I to find one of our people attempting thus to sabotage any other weapon in our arsenal, I should not hesitate to denounce and destroy him."

"The finest Mentats have a healthy respect for the error factor in their computations," she said.

"I've never said otherwise!"

"Then apply yourself to these symptoms we've both seen: drunkenness among the men, quarrels—they gossip and exchange wild rumors about Arrakis; they ignore the most simple—"

"Idleness, no more," he said. "Don't try to divert my attention by trying to make a simple matter appear mysterious."

She stared at him, thinking of the Duke's men rubbing their woes together in the barracks until you could almost smell the charge there, like burnt insulation. *They're becoming like the men of the pre-Guild legend,* she thought: *Like the men of the lost star-searcher, Ampoliros—sick at their guns—forever seeking, forever prepared and forever unready.*

"Why have you never made full use of my abilities in your service to the Duke?" she asked. "Do you fear a rival for *your* position?"

He glared at her, the old eyes blazing. "I know some of the training they give you Bene Gesserit . . . ." He broke off, scowling.

"Go ahead, say it," she said. "Bene Gesserit *witches*."

"I know something of the *real* training they give you," he said. "I've seen it come out in Paul. I'm not fooled by what your schools tell the public: you exist only to serve."

*The shock must be severe and he's almost ready for it,* she thought.

"You listen respectfully to me in Council," she said, "yet you seldom heed my advice. Why?"

"I don't trust your Bene Gesserit motives," he said. "You may think you can look through a man; you may *think* you can make a man do exactly what you—"

"You poor *fool*, Thufir!" she raged.

He scowled, pushing himself back in the chair.

"Whatever rumors you've heard about our schools," she said, "the truth is far greater. If I wished to destroy the Duke . . . or you, or any other person within my reach, you could not stop me."

And she thought: *Why do I let pride drive such words out of me? This is not the way I was trained. This is not how I must shock him.*

Hawat slipped a hand beneath his tunic where he kept a tiny projector of poison darts. *She wears no shield,* he thought. *Is this just a brag she makes? I could slay her now . . . but, ah-h-h-h, the consequences if I'm wrong.*

Jessica saw the gesture toward his pocket, said: "Let us pray violence shall never be necessary between us."

"A worthy prayer," he agreed.

"Meanwhile, the sickness spreads among us," she said. "I must ask you again: Isn't it more reasonable to suppose the Harkonnens have planted this suspicion to pit the two of us against each other?"

"We appear to've returned to stalemate," he said.

She sighed, thinking: *He's almost ready for it.*

"The Duke and I are father and mother surrogates to our people," she said. "The position—"

"He hasn't married you," Hawat said.

She forced herself to calmness, thinking: *A good riposte, that.*

"But he'll not marry anyone else," she said. "Not as long as I live. And we are surrogates, as I've said. To break up this natural order in our affairs, to disturb, disrupt, and confuse us—which target offers itself most enticingly to the Harkonnens?"

He sensed the direction she was taking, and his brows drew down in a lowering scowl.

"The Duke?" she asked. "Attractive target, yes, but no one with the possible exception of Paul is better guarded. Me? I tempt them, surely, but they must know the Bene Gesserit make difficult targets. And there's a better target, one whose duties create, necessarily, a monstrous blind spot. One to whom suspicion is as natural as breathing. One who builds his entire life on innuendo and mystery." She darted her right hand toward him. "You!"

Hawat started to leap from his chair.

"I have not dismissed you, Thufir!" she flared.

The old Mentat almost fell back into the chair, so quickly did his muscles betray him.

She smiled without mirth.

"Now you know something of the *real* training they give us," she said.

Hawat tried to swallow in a dry throat. Her command had been regal, peremptory—uttered in a tone and manner he had found completely irresistible. His body had obeyed her before he could think about it. Nothing could have prevented his response—not logic, not passionate anger . . . nothing. To do what she had done spoke of a sensitive, intimate knowledge of the person thus commanded, a depth of control he had not dreamed possible.

"I have said to you before that we should understand each other," she said. "I meant *you* should understand *me*. I already understand you. And I tell you now that your loyalty to the Duke is all that guarantees your safety with me."

He stared at her, wet his lips with his tongue.

"If I desired a puppet, the Duke would marry me," she said. "He might even think he did it of his own free will."

Hawat lowered his head, looked upward through his sparse lashes. Only the most rigid control kept him from calling the guard. Control . . . and the suspicion now that the woman might not permit it. His skin crawled with the memory of how she had controlled him. In the moment of hesitation, she could have drawn a weapon and killed him!

*Does every human have this blind spot?* he wondered. *Can any of us be ordered into action before he can resist?* The idea staggered him. *Who could stop a person with such power?*

"You've glimpsed the fist within the Bene Gesserit glove," she said. "Few glimpse it and live. And what I did was a relatively simple thing for us. You've not seen my entire arsenal. Think on that."

"Why aren't you out destroying the Duke's enemies?" he asked.

"What would you have me destroy?" she asked. "Would you have me make a weakling of our Duke, have him forever leaning on me?"

"But, with such power . . . ."

"Power's a two-edged sword, Thufir," she said. "You think: 'How easy for her to shape a human tool to thrust into an enemy's vitals.' True, Thufir; even into your vitals. Yet, what would I accomplish? If enough of us Bene Gesserit did this, wouldn't it make all Bene Gesserit suspect? We don't want that, Thufir. We do not wish to destroy ourselves." She nodded. "We truly exist only to serve."

"I cannot answer you," he said. "You know I cannot answer."

"You'll say nothing about what has happened here to anyone," she said. "I know you, Thufir."

"My Lady . . . ." Again the old man tried to swallow in a dry throat.

And he thought: *She has great powers, yes. But would these not make her an even more formidable tool for the Harkonnens?*

"The Duke could be destroyed as quickly by his friends as by his enemies," she said. "I trust now you'll get to the bottom of this suspicion and remove it."

"If it proves baseless," he said.

"*If,*" she sneered.

"If," he said.

"You *are* tenacious," she said.

"Cautious," he said, "and aware of the error factor."

"Then I'll pose another question for you: What does it mean to you that you stand before another human, that you are bound and helpless and the other human holds a knife at your throat—yet this other human refrains from killing you, frees you from your bonds and gives you the knife to use as you will?"

She lifted herself out of the chair, turned her back on him. "You may go now, Thufir."

The old Mentat arose, hesitated, hand creeping toward the deadly weapon beneath his tunic. He was reminded of the bull ring and of the Duke's father (who'd been brave, no matter what his other failings) and one day of the *corrida* long ago: The fierce black beast had stood there, head bowed, immobilized and confused. The Old Duke had turned his back on the horns, cape thrown flamboyantly over one arm, while cheers rained down from the stands.

*I am the bull and she the matador,* Hawat thought. He withdrew his hand from the weapon, glanced at the sweat glistening in his empty palm.

And he knew that whatever the facts proved to be in the end, he would never forget this moment nor lose this sense of supreme admiration for the Lady Jessica.

Quietly, he turned and left the room.

Jessica lowered her gaze from the reflection in the windows, turned, and stared at the closed door.

"Now we'll see some proper action," she whispered.

*Do you wrestle with dreams?*
*Do you contend with shadows?*
*Do you move in a kind of sleep?*
*Time has slipped away.*
*Your life is stolen.*
*You tarried with trifles,*
*Victim of your folly.*

**—Dirge for Jamis on the Funeral Plain,**
**from "Songs of Muad'Dib" by the Princess Irulan**

Leto stood in the foyer of his house, studying a note by the light of a single suspensor lamp. Dawn was yet a few hours away, and he felt his tiredness. A Fremen messenger had brought the note to the outer guard just now as the Duke arrived from his command post.

The note read: "A column of smoke by day, a pillar of fire by night."

There was no signature.

*What does it mean?* he wondered.

The messenger had gone without waiting for an answer and before he could be questioned. He had slipped into the night like some smoky shadow.

Leto pushed the paper into a tunic pocket, thinking to show it to Hawat later. He brushed a lock of hair from his forehead, took a sighing breath. The antifatigue pills were beginning to wear thin. It had been a long two days since the dinner party and longer than that since he had slept.

On top of all the military problems, there'd been the disquieting session with Hawat, the report on his meeting with Jessica.

*Should I waken Jessica?* he wondered. *There's no reason to play the secrecy game with her any longer. Or is there?*

*Blast and damn that Duncan Idaho!*

He shook his head. *No, not Duncan. I was wrong not to take Jessica into my confidence from the first. I must do it now, before more damage is done.*

The decision made him feel better, and he hurried from the foyer through the Great Hall and down the passages toward the family wing.

At the turn where the passages split to the service area, he paused. A strange mewling came from somewhere down the service passage. Leto put his left hand to the switch on his shield belt, slipped his kindjal into his right hand. The knife conveyed a sense of reassurance. That strange sound had sent a chill through him.

Softly, the Duke moved down the service passage, cursing the inadequate illumination. The smallest of suspensors had been spaced about eight meters apart along here and tuned to their dimmest level. The dark stone walls swallowed the light.

A dull blob stretching across the floor appeared out of the gloom ahead.

Leto hesitated, almost activated his shield, but refrained because that would limit his movements, his hearing . . . and because the captured shipment of lasguns had left him filled with doubts.

Silently, he moved toward the gray blob, saw that it was a human figure, a man face down on the stone. Leto turned him over with a foot, knife poised, bent close in the dim light to see the face. It was the smuggler, Tuek, a wet stain down his chest. The dead eyes stared with empty darkness. Leto touched the stain—warm.

*How could this man be dead here?* Leto asked himself. *Who killed him?*

The mewling sound was louder here. It came from ahead and down the side passage to the central room where they had installed the main shield generator for the house.

Hand on belt switch, kindjal poised, the Duke skirted the body, slipped down the passage and peered around the corner toward the shield generator room.

Another gray blob lay stretched on the floor a few paces away, and he saw at once this was the source of the noise. The shape crawled toward him with painful slowness, gasping, mumbling.

Leto stilled his sudden constriction of fear, darted down the passage, crouched beside the crawling figure. It was Mapes, the Fremen housekeeper, her hair tumbled around her face, clothing disarrayed. A dull shininess of dark stain spread from her back along her side. He touched her shoulder and she lifted herself on her elbows, head tipped up to peer at him, the eyes black-shadowed emptiness.

"S'you," she gasped. "Killed . . . guard . . . sent . . . get . . . Tuek . . . escape . . . m'Lady . . . you . . . you . . . here . . . no . . . ." She flopped forward, her head thumping against the stone.

Leto felt for pulse at the temples. There was none. He looked at the stain: she'd been stabbed in the back. Who? His mind raced. Did she mean someone had killed a guard? And Tuek—had Jessica sent for him? Why?

He started to stand up. A sixth sense warned him. He flashed a hand toward the shield switch—too late. A numbing shock slammed his arm aside. He felt pain there, saw a dart protruding from the sleeve, sensed paralysis spreading from it up his arm. It took an agonizing effort to lift his head and look down the passage.

Yueh stood in the open door of the generator room. His face reflected yellow from the light of a single, brighter suspensor above the door. There was stillness from the room behind him—no sound of generators.

*Yueh!* Leto thought. *He's sabotaged the house generators! We're wide open!*

Yueh began walking toward him, pocketing a dartgun.

Leto found he could still speak, gasped: "Yueh! How?" Then the paralysis reached his legs and he slid to the floor with his back propped against the stone wall.

Yueh's face carried a look of sadness as he bent over, touched Leto's forehead. The Duke found he could feel the touch, but it was remote . . . dull.

"The drug on the dart is selective," Yueh said. "You can speak, but I'd advise against it." He glanced down the hall, and again bent over Leto, pulled out the dart, tossed it aside. The sound of the dart clattering on the stones was faint and distant to the Duke's ears.

*It can't be Yueh,* Leto thought. *He's conditioned.*

"How?" Leto whispered.

"I'm sorry, my dear Duke, but there *are* things which will make greater demands than this." He touched the diamond tattoo on his forehead. "I find it very strange, myself—an override on my pyretic conscience—but I wish to kill a man. Yes, I actually wish it. I will stop at nothing to do it."

He looked down at the Duke. "Oh, not you, my dear Duke. The Baron Harkonnen. I wish to kill the Baron."

"Bar . . . on Har . . . ."

"Be quiet, please, my poor Duke. You haven't much time. That peg tooth I put in your mouth after the tumble at Narcal—that tooth must be replaced. In a moment, I'll render you unconscious and replace that tooth." He opened his hand, stared at something in it. "An exact duplicate, its core shaped most exquisitely like a nerve. It'll escape the usual detectors, even a fast scanning. But if you bite down hard on it, the cover crushes. Then, when you expel your breath sharply, you fill the air around you with a poison gas—most deadly."

Leto stared up at Yueh, seeing madness in the man's eyes, the perspiration along brow and chin.

"You were dead anyway, my poor Duke," Yueh said. "But you will get close to the Baron before you die. He'll believe you're stupefied by drugs beyond any dying effort to attack him. And you will be drugged—and tied. But attack can take strange forms. And *you* will remember the tooth. The *tooth,* Duke Leto Atreides. You will remember the tooth."

The old doctor leaned closer and closer until his face and drooping mustache dominated Leto's narrowing vision.

"The tooth," Yueh muttered.

"Why?" Leto whispered.

Yueh lowered himself to one knee beside the Duke. "I made a shaitan's bargain with the Baron. And I must be certain he has fulfilled his half of it. When I see him, I'll know. When I look at the Baron, then I *will* know. But I'll never enter his presence without the price. You're the price, my poor Duke. And I'll know when I see him. My poor Wanna taught me many things, and one is to see certainty of truth when the stress is great. I cannot do it always, but when I see the Baron—then, I *will* know."

Leto tried to look down at the tooth in Yueh's hand. He felt this was happening in a nightmare—it could not be.

Yueh's purple lips turned up in a grimace. "I'll not get close enough to the Baron, or I'd do this myself. No. I'll be detained at a safe distance. But you . . . ah, now! You, my lovely weapon! He'll want you close to him—to gloat over you, to boast a little."

Leto found himself almost hypnotized by a muscle on the left side of Yueh's jaw. The muscle twisted when the man spoke.

Yueh leaned closer. "And you, my good Duke, my precious Duke, you must remember this tooth." He held it up between thumb and forefinger. "It will be all that remains to you."

Leto's mouth moved without sound, then: "Refuse."

"Ah-h, no! You mustn't refuse. Because, in return for this small service, I'm doing a thing for you. I will save your son and your woman. No other can do it. They can be removed to a place where no Harkonnen can reach them."

"How . . . save . . . them?" Leto whispered.

"By making it appear they're dead, by secreting them among people who draw knife at hearing the Harkonnen name, who hate the Harkonnens so much they'll burn a chair in which a Harkonnen has sat, salt the ground over which a Harkonnen has walked." He touched Leto's jaw. "Can you feel anything in your jaw?"

The Duke found that he could not answer. He sensed distant tugging, saw Yueh's hand come up with the ducal signet ring.

"For Paul," Yueh said. "You'll be unconscious presently. Good-by, my poor Duke. When we next meet we'll have no time for conversation."

Cool remoteness spread upward from Leto's jaw, across his cheeks. The shadowy hall narrowed to a pinpoint with Yueh's purple lips centered in it.

"Remember the tooth!" Yueh hissed. "The tooth!"

*There should be a science of discontent. People need hard times and oppression to develop psychic muscles.*

**—from "Collected Sayings of Muad'Dib"
by the Princess Irulan**

Jessica awoke in the dark, feeling premonition in the stillness around her. She could not understand why her mind and body felt so sluggish. Skin raspings of fear ran along her nerves. She thought of sitting up and turning on a light, but something stayed the decision. Her mouth felt . . . strange.

*Lump-lump-lump-lump!*

It was a dull sound, directionless in the dark. Somewhere.

The waiting moment was packed with time, with rustling needle-stick movements.

She began to feel her body, grew aware of bindings on wrists and ankles, a gag in her mouth. She was on her side, hands tied behind her. She tested the bindings, realized they were krimskell fiber, would only claw tighter as she pulled.

And now, she remembered.

There had been movement in the darkness of her bedroom, something wet and pungent slapped against her face, filling her mouth, hands grasping for her. She had gasped—one indrawn breath—sensing the narcotic in the wetness. Consciousness had receded, sinking her into a black bin of terror.

*It has come,* she thought. *How simple it was to subdue the Bene Gesserit. All it took was treachery. Hawat was right.*

She forced herself not to pull on her bindings.

*This is not my bedroom,* she thought. *They've taken me someplace else.*

Slowly, she marshaled the inner calmness.

She grew aware of the smell of her own stale sweat with its chemical infusion of fear.

*Where is Paul?* she asked herself. *My son—what have they done to him? Calmness.*

She forced herself to it, using the ancient routines.

But terror remained so near.

*Leto? Where are you, Leto?*

She sensed a diminishing in the dark. It began with shadows. Dimensions separated, became new thorns of awareness. White. A line under a door.

*I'm on the floor.*

People walking. She sensed it through the floor.

Jessica squeezed back the memory of terror. *I must remain calm, alert, and prepared. I may get only one chance.* Again, she forced the inner calmness.

The ungainly thumping of her heartbeats evened, shaping out time. She counted back. *I was unconscious about an hour.* She closed her eyes, focused her awareness onto the approaching footsteps.

*Four people.*

She counted the differences in their steps.

*I must pretend I'm still unconscious.* She relaxed against the cold floor, testing her body's readiness, heard a door open, sensed increased light through her eyelids.

Feet approached: someone standing over her.

"You are awake," rumbled a basso voice. "Do not pretend."

She opened her eyes.

The Baron Vladimir Harkonnen stood over her. Around them, she recognized the cellar room where Paul had slept, saw his cot at one side— empty. Suspensor lamps were brought in by guards, distributed near the open door. There was a glare of light in the hallway beyond that hurt her eyes.

She looked up at the Baron. He wore a yellow cape that bulged over his portable suspensors. The fat cheeks were two cherubic mounds beneath spider-black eyes.

"The drug was timed," he rumbled. "We knew to the minute when you'd be coming out of it."

*How could that be?* she wondered. *They'd have to know my exact weight, my metabolism, my . . . . Yueh!*

"Such a pity you must remain gagged," the Baron said. "We could have such an interesting conversation."

*Yueh's the only one it could be,* she thought. *How?*

The Baron glanced behind him at the door. "Come in, Piter."

She had never before seen the man who entered to stand beside the Baron, but the face was known—and the man: *Piter de Vried, the Mentat-Assassin.* She studied him—hawk features, blue-ink eyes that suggested he was a native of Arrakis, but subtleties of movement and stance told her he was not. And his flesh was too well firmed with water. He was tall, though slender, and something about him suggested effeminacy.

"Such a pity we cannot have our conversation, my dear Lady Jessica," the Baron said. "However, I'm aware of your abilities." He glanced at the Mentat. "Isn't that true, Piter?"

"As you say, Baron," the man said.

The voice was tenor. It touched her spine with a wash of coldness. She had never heard such a chill voice. To one with the Bene Gesserit training the voice screamed: *Killer!*

"I have a surprise for Piter," the Baron said. "He thinks he has come here to collect his reward—you, Lady Jessica. But I wish to demonstrate a thing: that he does not really want you."

"You play with me, Baron?" Piter asked, and he smiled.

Seeing that smile, Jessica wondered that the Baron did not leap to defend himself from this Piter. Then she corrected herself. The Baron could not read that smile. He did not have the Training.

"In many ways, Piter is quite naive," the Baron said. "He doesn't admit to himself what a deadly creature you are, Lady Jessica. I'd show him, but it'd be a foolish risk." The Baron smiled at Piter, whose face had become a waiting mask. "I know what Piter really wants. Piter wants power."

"You promised I could have *her*," Piter said. The tenor voice had lost some of its cold reserve.

Jessica heard the clue-tones in the man's voice, allowed herself an inward shudder. *How could the Baron have made such an animal out of a Mentat?*

"I give you a choice, Piter," the Baron said.

"What choice?"

The Baron snapped fat fingers. "This woman and exile from the Imperium, or the Duchy of Atreides on Arrakis to rule as you see fit in my name."

Jessica watched the Baron's spider eyes study Piter.

"You could be Duke here in all but name," the Baron said.

*Is my Leto dead, then?* Jessica asked herself. She felt a silent wail begin somewhere in her mind.

The Baron kept his attention on the Mentat. "Understand yourself, Piter. You want her because she was a Duke's woman, a symbol of his power—beautiful, useful, exquisitely trained for her role. But an entire duchy, Piter! That's more than a symbol; that's the reality. With it you could have many women . . . and more."

"You do not joke with Piter?"

The Baron turned with that dancing lightness the suspensors gave him. "Joke? I? Remember—*I* am giving up the boy. You heard what the traitor said about the lad's training. They are alike, this mother and son—deadly." The Baron smiled. "I must go now. I will send in the guard I've reserved for this moment. He's stone deaf. His orders will be to convey you on the first leg of your journey into exile. He will subdue this woman if he sees her gain control of you. He'll not permit you to untie her gag until you're off Arrakis. If you choose not to leave . . . he has other orders."

"You don't have to leave," Piter said. "I've chosen."

"Ah, hah!" the Baron chortled. "Such quick decision can mean only one thing."

"I will take the duchy," Piter said.

And Jessica thought: *Doesn't Piter know the Baron's lying to him? But—how could he know? He's a twisted Mentat.*

The Baron glanced down at Jessica. "Is it not wonderful that I know Piter so well? I wagered with my Master at Arms that this would be Piter's choice. Hah! Well, I leave now. This is much better. Ah-h, much better. You understand, Lady Jessica? I hold no rancor toward you. It's a necessity. Much better this way. Yes. And I've not *actually* ordered you destroyed. When it's asked of me what happened to you, I can shrug it off in all truth."

"You leave it to me then?" Piter asked.

"The guard I send you will take your orders," the Baron said. "Whatever's done I leave to you." He stared at Piter. "Yes. There will be no blood on my hands here. It's your decision. Yes. I know nothing of it. You will wait until I've gone before doing whatever you must do. Yes. Well . . . ah, yes. Yes. Good."

*He fears the questioning of a Truthsayer,* Jessica thought. *Who? Ah-h-h, the Reverend Mother Gaius Helen, of course! If he knows he must face her questions, then the Emperor is in on this for sure. Ah-h-h-h, my poor Leto.*

With one last glance at Jessica, the Baron turned, went out the door. She followed him with her eyes, thinking: *It's as the Reverend Mother warned—too potent an adversary.*

Two Harkonnen troopers entered. Another, his face a scarred mask, followed and stood in the doorway with drawn lasgun.

*The deaf one,* Jessica thought, studying the scarred face. *The Baron knows I could use the Voice on any other man.*

Scarface looked at Piter. "We've the boy on a litter outside. What are your orders?"

Piter spoke to Jessica. "I'd thought of binding you by a threat held over your son, but I begin to see that would not have worked. I let emotion cloud reason. Bad policy for a Mentat." He looked at the first pair of troopers, turning so the deaf one could read his lips: "Take them into the desert as the traitor suggested for the boy. His plan is a good one. The worms will destroy all evidence. Their bodies must never be found."

"You don't wish to dispatch them yourself?" Scarface asked.

*He reads lips,* Jessica thought.

"I follow my Baron's example," Piter said. "Take them where the traitor said."

Jessica heard the harsh Mentat control in Piter's voice, thought: *He, too, fears the Truthsayer.*

Piter shrugged, turned, and went through the doorway. He hesitated there, and Jessica thought he might turn back for a last look at her, but he went out without turning.

"Me, I wouldn't like the thought of facing that Truthsayer after this night's work," Scarface said.

"You ain't likely ever to run into that old witch," one of the other troopers said. He went around to Jessica's head, bent over her. "It ain't getting our work done standing around here chattering. Take her feet and—"

"Why'n't we kill 'em here?" Scarface asked.

"Too messy," the first one said. "Unless you wants to strangle 'em. Me, I likes a nice straightforward job. Drop 'em on the desert like that traitor said, cut 'em once or twice, leave the evidence for the worms. Nothing to clean up afterward."

"Yeah . . . well, I guess you're right," Scarface said.

Jessica listened to them, watching, registering. But the gag blocked her Voice, and there was the deaf one to consider.

Scarface holstered his lasgun, took her feet. They lifted her like a sack of grain, maneuvered her through the door and dumped her onto a suspensor-buoyed litter with another bound figure. As they turned her, fitting her to the litter, she saw her companion's face—Paul! He was bound, but not gagged. His face was no more than ten centimeters from hers, eyes closed, his breathing even.

*Is he drugged?* she wondered.

The troopers lifted the litter, and Paul's eyes opened the smallest fraction— dark slits staring at her.

*He mustn't try the Voice!* she prayed. *The deaf guard!*

Paul's eyes closed.

He had been practicing the awareness-breathing, calming his mind, listening to their captors. The deaf one posed a problem, but Paul contained his despair. The mind-calming Bene Gesserit regimen his mother had taught him kept him poised, ready to expand any opportunity.

Paul allowed himself another slit-eyed inspection of his mother's face. She appeared unharmed. Gagged, though.

He wondered who could've captured her. His own captivity was plain enough—to bed with a capsule prescribed by Yueh, awaking to find himself bound to this litter. Perhaps a similar thing had befallen her. Logic said the traitor was Yueh, but he held final decision in abeyance. There was no understanding it—a Suk doctor a traitor.

The litter tipped slightly as the Harkonnen troopers maneuvered it through a doorway into starlit night. A suspensor-buoy rasped against the doorway. Then they were on sand, feet grating in it. A 'thopter wing loomed overhead, blotting the stars. The litter settled to the ground.

Paul's eyes adjusted to the faint light. He recognized the deaf trooper as the man who opened the 'thopter door, peered inside at the green gloom illuminated by the instrument panel.

"This the 'thopter we're supposed to use?" he asked, and turned to watch his companion's lips.

"It's the one the traitor said was fixed for desert work," the other said.

Scarface nodded. "But it's one of them little liaison jobs. Ain't room in there for more'n them an' two of us."

"Two's enough," said the litter-bearer, moving up close and presenting his lips for reading. "We can take care of it from here on, Kinet."

"The Baron he told me to make sure what happened to them two," Scarface said.

"What you so worried about?" asked another trooper from behind the litter-bearer.

"She is a Bene Gesserit witch," the deaf one said. "They have powers."

"Ah-h-h . . . ." The litter-bearer made the sign of the fist at his ear. "One of them, eh? Know whatcha mean."

The trooper behind him grunted. "She'll be worm meat soon enough. Don't suppose even a Bene Gesserit witch has powers over one of them big worms. Eh, Czigo?" He nudged the litter-bearer.

"Yee-up," the litter-bearer said. He returned to the litter, took Jessica's shoulders. "C'mon, Kinet. You can go along if you wants to make sure what happens."

"It is nice of you to invite me, Czigo," Scarface said.

Jessica felt herself lifted, the wing shadow spinning—stars. She was pushed into the rear of the 'thopter, her *krimskell* fiber bindings examined, and she was strapped down. Paul was jammed in beside her, strapped securely, and she noted his bonds were simple rope.

Scarface, the deaf one they called Kinet, took his place in front. The litter-bearer, the one they called Czigo, came around and took the other front seat.

Kinet closed his door, bent to the controls. The 'thopter took off in a wing-tucked surge, headed south over the Shield Wall. Czigo tapped his companion's shoulder, said: "Whyn't you turn around and keep an eye on them two?"

"Sure you know the way to go?" Kinet watched Czigo's lips.

"I listened to the traitor same's you."

Kinet swiveled his seat. Jessica saw the glint of starlight on a lasgun in his hand. The 'thopter's light-walled interior seemed to collect illumination as her eyes adjusted, but the guard's scarred face remained dim. Jessica tested her seat belt, found it loose. She felt roughness in the strap against her left arm, realized the strap had been almost severed, would snap at a sudden jerk.

*Has someone been at this 'thopter, preparing it for us?* she wondered. *Who?* Slowly, she twisted her bound feet clear of Paul's.

"Sure do seem a shame to waste a good-looking woman like this," Scarface said. "You ever have any highborn types?" He turned to look at the pilot.

"Bene Gesserit ain't all highborn," the pilot said.

"But they all look heighty."

*He can see me plain enough,* Jessica thought. She brought her bound legs up onto the seat, curled into a sinuous ball, staring at Scarface.

"Real pretty, she is," Kinet said. He wet his lips with his tongue. "Sure do seem a shame." He looked at Czigo.

"You thinking what I think you're thinking?" the pilot asked.

"Who'd be to know?" the guard asked. "Afterward . . . ." He shrugged. "I just never had me no highborns. Might never get a chancet like this one again."

"You lay a hand on my mother . . . ." Paul grated. He glared at Scarface.

"Hey!" the pilot laughed. "Cub's got a bark. Ain't got no bite, though."

And Jessica thought: *Paul's pitching his voice too high. It may work, though.*

They flew on in silence.

*These poor fools,* Jessica thought, studying her guards and reviewing the Baron's words. *They'll be killed as soon as they report success on their mission. The Baron wants no witnesses.*

The 'thopter banked over the southern rim of the Shield Wall, and Jessica saw a moonshadowed expanse of sand beneath them.

"This oughta be far enough," the pilot said. "The traitor said to put 'em on the sand anywhere near the Shield Wall." He dipped the craft toward the dunes in a long, falling stoop, brought it up stiffly over the desert surface.

Jessica saw Paul begin taking the rhythmic breaths of the calming exercise. He closed his eyes, opened them. Jessica stared, helpless to aid him. *He hasn't mastered the Voice yet,* she thought, *if he fails . . . .*

The 'thopter touched sand with a soft lurch, and Jessica, looking north back across the Shield Wall, saw a shadow of wings settle out of sight up there.

*Someone's following us!* she thought. *Who!* Then: *The ones the Baron set to watch this pair. And there'll be watchers for the watchers, too.*

Czigo shut off his wing rotors. Silence flooded in upon them.

Jessica turned her head. She could see out the window beyond Scarface a dim glow of light from a rising moon, a frosted rim of rock rising from the desert. Sandblast ridges streaked its sides.

Paul cleared his throat.

The pilot said: "Now, Kinet?"

"I dunno, Czigo."

Czigo turned, said: "Ah-h-h, look." He reached out for Jessica's skirt.

"Remove her gag," Paul commanded.

Jessica felt the words rolling in the air. The tone, the timbre excellent— imperative, very sharp. A slightly lower pitch would have been better, but it could still fall within this man's spectrum.

Czigo shifted his hand up to the band around Jessica's mouth, slipped the knot on the gag.

"Stop that!" Kinet ordered.

"Ah, shut your trap," Czigo said. "Her hands're tied." He freed the knot and the binding dropped. His eyes glittered as he studied Jessica.

Kinet put a hand on the pilot's arm. "Look, Czigo, no need to . . . ."

Jessica twisted her neck, spat out the gag. She pitched her voice in low, intimate tones. "Gentlemen! No need to *fight* over me." At the same time, she writhed sinuously for Kinet's benefit.

She saw them grow tense, knowing that in this instant they were convinced of the need to fight over her. Their disagreement required no other reason. In their minds, they *were* fighting over her.

She held her face high in the instrument glow to be sure Kinet would read her lips, said: "You mustn't disagree." They drew farther apart, glanced warily at each other. "Is any woman worth fighting over?" she asked.

By uttering the words, by being there, she made herself infinitely worth their fighting.

Paul clamped his lips tightly closed, forced himself to be silent. There had been the one chance for him to succeed with the Voice. Now—everything depended on his mother whose experience went so far beyond his own.

"Yeah," Scarface said. "No need to fight over . . . ."

His hand flashed toward the pilot's neck. The blow was met by a splash of metal that caught the arm and in the same motion slammed into Kinet's chest.

Scarface groaned, sagged backward against the door.

"Thought I was some dummy didn't know that trick," Czigo said. He brought back his hand, revealing the knife. It glittered in reflected moonlight.

"Now for the cub," he said and leaned toward Paul.

"No need for that," Jessica murmured.

Czigo hesitated.

"Wouldn't you rather have me cooperative?" Jessica asked. "Give the boy a chance." Her lip curled in a sneer. "Little enough chance he'd have out there in that sand. Give him that and . . . ." She smiled. "You could find yourself well rewarded."

Czigo glanced left, right, returned his attention to Jessica. "I've heard me what can happen to a man in this desert," he said. "Boy might find the knife a kindness."

"Is it so much I ask?" Jessica pleaded.

"You're trying to trick me," Czigo muttered.

"I don't want to see my son die," Jessica said. "Is that a trick?"

Czigo moved back, elbowed the door latch. He grabbed Paul, dragged him across the seat, pushed him half out the door and held the knife poised. "What'll y' do, cub, if I cut y'r bonds?"

"He'll leave here immediately and head for those rocks," Jessica said.

"Is that what y'll do, cub?" Czigo asked.

Paul's voice was properly surly. "Yes."

The knife moved down, slashed the bindings of his legs. Paul felt the hand on his back to hurl him down onto the sand, feigned a lurch against the door-frame for purchase, turned as though to catch himself, lashed out with his right foot.

The toe was aimed with a precision that did credit to his long years of training, as though all of that training focused on this instant. Almost every muscle of his body cooperated in the placement of it. The tip struck the soft part of Czigo's abdomen just below the sternum, slammed upward with terrible force over the liver and through the diaphragm to crush the right ventricle of the man's heart.

With one gurgling scream, the guard jerked backward across the seats. Paul, unable to use his hands, continued his tumble onto the sand, landing with a roll that took up the force and brought him back to his feet in one motion. He drove back into the cabin, found the knife and held it in his teeth while his mother sawed her bonds. She took the blade and freed his hands.

"I could've handled him," she said. "He'd have had to cut my bindings. That was a foolish risk."

"I saw the opening and used it," he said.

She heard the harsh control in his voice, said: "Yueh's house sign is scrawled on the ceiling of this cabin."

He looked up, saw the curling symbol.

"Get out and let us study the craft," she said. "There's a bundle under the pilot's seat. I felt it when we got in."

"Bomb?"

"Doubt it. There's something peculiar here."

Paul leaped out to the sand and Jessica followed. She turned, reached under the seat for the strange bundle, seeing Czigo's feet close to her face, feeling dampness on the bundle as she removed it, realizing the dampness was the pilot's blood.

*Waste of moisture,* she thought, knowing that this was Arrakeen thinking.

Paul stared around them, saw the rock scarp lifting out of the desert like a beach rising from the sea, wind-carved palisades beyond. He turned back as his mother lifted the bundle from the 'thopter, saw her stare across the dunes toward the Shield Wall. He looked to see what drew her attention, saw another 'thopter swooping toward them, realized they'd not have time to clear the bodies out of this 'thopter and escape.

"Run, Paul!" Jessica shouted. "It's Harkonnens!"

*Arrakis teaches the attitude of the knife—chopping off what's incomplete and saying: "Now, it's complete because it's ended here."*

**—from "Collected Sayings of Muad'Dib"
by the Princess Irulan**

A man in Harkonnen uniform skidded to a stop at the end of the hall, stared in at Yueh, taking in at a single glance Mapes' body, the sprawled form of the Duke, Yueh standing there. The man held a lasgun in his right hand. There was a casual air of brutality about him, a sense of toughness and poise that sent a shiver through Yueh.

*Sardaukar,* Yueh thought. *A Bashar by the look of him. Probably one of the Emperor's own sent here to keep an eye on things. No matter what the uniform, there's no disguising them.*

"You're Yueh," the man said. He looked speculatively at the Suk School ring on the Doctor's hair, stared once at the diamond tattoo and then met Yueh's eyes.

"I am Yueh," the Doctor said.

"You can relax, Yueh," the man said. "When you dropped the house shields we came right in. Everything's under control here. Is this the Duke?"

"This is the Duke."

"Dead?"

"Merely unconscious. I suggest you tie him."

"Did you do for these others?" He glanced back down the hall where Mapes' body lay.

"More's the pity," Yueh muttered.

"Pity!" the Sardaukar sneered. He advanced, looked down at Leto. "So that's the great Red Duke."

*If I had doubts about what this man is, that would end them,* Yueh thought. *Only the Emperor calls the Atreides the Red Dukes.*

The Sardaukar reached down, cut the red hawk insignia from Leto's uniform. "Little souvenir," he said. "Where's the ducal signet ring?"

"He doesn't have it on him," Yueh said.

"I can see that!" the Sardaukar snapped.

Yueh stiffened, swallowed. *If they press me, bring in a Truthsayer, they'll find out about the ring, about the 'thopter I prepared—all will fail.*

"Sometimes the Duke sent the ring with a messenger as surety that an order came directly from him," Yueh said.

"Must be damned trusted messengers," the Sardaukar muttered.

"Aren't you going to tie him?" Yueh ventured.

"How long'll he be unconscious?"

"Two hours or so. I wasn't as precise with his dosage as I was for the woman and boy."

The Sardaukar spurned the Duke with his toe. "This was nothing to fear even when awake. When will the woman and boy awaken?"

"About ten minutes."

"So soon?"

"I was told the Baron would arrive immediately behind his men."

"So he will. You'll wait outside, Yueh." He shot a hard glance at Yueh. "Now!"

Yueh glanced at Leto. "What about . . . ."

"He'll be delivered all properly trussed like a roast for the oven." Again, the Sardaukar looked at the diamond tattoo on Yueh's forehead. "You're known; you'll be safe enough in the halls. We've no more time for chit-chat, traitor. I hear the others coming."

*Traitor,* Yueh thought. He lowered his gaze, pressed past the Sardaukar, knowing this as a foretaste of how history would remember him: *Yueh the traitor.*

He passed more bodies on his way to the front entrance and glanced at them, fearful that one might be Paul or Jessica. All were house troopers or wore Harkonnen uniform.

Harkonnen guards came alert, staring at him as he emerged from the front entrance into flame-lighted night. The palms along the road had been fired to illuminate the house. Black smoke from the flammables used to ignite the trees poured upward through orange flames.

"It's the traitor," someone said.

"The Baron will want to see you soon," another said.

*I must get to the 'thopter,* Yueh thought. *I must put the ducal signet where Paul will find it.* And fear struck him: *If Idaho suspects me or grows impatient—if he doesn't wait and go exactly where I told him—Jessica and Paul will not be saved from the carnage. I'll be denied even the smallest relief from my act.*

The Harkonnen guard released his arm, said: "Wait over there out of the way."

Abruptly, Yueh saw himself as cast away in this place of destruction, spared nothing, given not the smallest pity. *Idaho must not fail!*

Another guard bumped into him, barked: "Stay out of the way, you!"

*Even when they've profited by me they despise me,* Yueh thought. He straightened himself as he was pushed aside, regained some of his dignity.

"Wait for the Baron!" a guard officer snarled.

Yueh nodded, walked with controlled casualness along the front of the house, turned the corner into shadows out of sight of the burning palms. Quickly, every step betraying his anxiety, Yueh made for the rear yard beneath the conservatory where the 'thopter waited—the craft they had placed there to carry away Paul and his mother.

A guard stood at the open rear door of the house, his attention focused on the lighted hall and men banging through there, searching from room to room.

How confident they were!

Yueh hugged the shadows, worked his way around the 'thopter, eased open the door on the side away from the guard. He felt under the front seats for the Fremkit he had hidden there, lifted a flap and slipped in the ducal signet. He felt the crinkling of the spice paper there, the note he had written, pressed the ring into the paper. He removed his hand, resealed the pack.

Softly, Yueh closed the 'thopter door, worked his way back to the corner of the house and around toward the flaming trees.

*Now, it is done,* he thought.

Once more, he emerged into the light of the blazing palms. He pulled his cloak around him, stared at the flames. *Soon I will know. Soon I will see the Baron and I will know. And the Baron—he will encounter a small tooth.*

> There is a legend that the instant the Duke Leto Atreides died a meteor
> streaked across the skies above his ancestral palace on Caladan.
>
> **—the Princess Irulan: "Introduction to**
> **A Child's History of Muad'Dib"**

The Baron Vladimir Harkonnen stood at a viewport of the grounded lighter he was using as a command post. Out the port he saw the flame-lighted night of Arrakeen. His attention focused on the distant Shield Wall where his secret weapon was doing its work.

Explosive artillery.

The guns nibbled at the caves where the Duke's fighting men had retreated for a last-ditch stand. Slowly measured bites of orange glare, showers of rock and dust in the brief illumination—and the Duke's men were being sealed off to die by starvation, caught like animals in their burrows.

The Baron could feel the distant chomping—a drumbeat carried to him through the ship's metal: *broomp . . . broomp.* Then: *BROOMP-broomp!*

*Who would think of reviving artillery in this day of shields?* The thought was a chuckle in his mind. *But it was predictable the Duke's men would run for those caves. And the Emperor will appreciate my cleverness in preserving the lives of our mutual force.*

He adjusted one of the little suspensors that guarded his fat body against the pull of gravity. A smile creased his mouth, pulled at the lines of his jowls.

*A pity to waste such fighting men as the Duke's,* he thought. He smiled more broadly, laughing at himself. *Pity should be cruel!* He nodded. Failure was, by definition, expendable. The whole universe sat there, open to the man who could make the right decisions. The uncertain rabbits had to be exposed, made to run for their burrows. Else how could you control them and breed them? He pictured his fighting men as bees routing the rabbits. And he thought: *The day hums sweetly when you have enough bees working for you.*

A door opened behind him. The Baron studied the reflection in the night-blackened viewport before turning.

Piter de Vries advanced into the chamber followed by Umman Kudu, the captain of the Baron's personal guard. There was a motion of men just outside the door, the mutton faces of his guard, their expressions carefully sheeplike in his presence.

The Baron turned.

Piter touched finger to forelock in his mocking salute. "Good news, m'Lord. The Sardaukar have brought in the Duke."

"Of course they have," the Baron rumbled.

He studied the somber mask of villainy on Piter's effeminate face. And the eyes: those shaded slits of bluest blue-in-blue.

*Soon I must remove him,* the Baron thought. *He has almost outlasted his usefulness, almost reached the point of positive danger to my person. First, though, he must make the people of Arrakis hate him. Then—they will welcome my darling Feyd-Rautha as a savior.*

The Baron shifted his attention to the guard captain—Umman Kudu: scissors-line of jaw muscles, chin like a boot toe—a man to be trusted because the captain's vices were known.

"First, where is the traitor who gave me the Duke?" the Baron asked. "I must give the traitor his reward."

Piter turned on one toe, motioned to the guard outside.

A bit of black movement there and Yueh walked through. His motions were stiff and stringy. The mustache drooped beside his purple lips. Only the old eyes seemed alive. Yueh came to a stop three paces into the room, obeying a motion from Piter, and stood there staring across the open space at the Baron.

"Ah-h-h, Dr. Yueh."

"M'Lord Harkonnen."

"You've given us the Duke, I hear."

"My half of the bargain, m'Lord."

The Baron looked at Piter.

Piter nodded.

The Baron looked back at Yueh. "The letter of the bargain, eh? And I . . . . ." He spat the words out: "What was I to do in return?"

"You remember quite well, m'Lord Harkonnen."

And Yueh allowed himself to think now, hearing the loud silence of clocks in his mind. He had seen the subtle betrayals in the Baron's manner. Wanna was indeed dead—gone far beyond their reach. Otherwise, there'd still be a hold on the weak doctor. The Baron's manner showed there was no hold; it was ended.

"Do I?" the Baron asked.

"You promised to deliver my Wanna from her agony."

The Baron nodded. "Oh, yes. Now, I remember. So I did. That was my promise. That was how we bent the Imperial Conditioning. You couldn't endure seeing your Bene Gesserit witch grovel in Piter's pain amplifiers. Well, the Baron Vladimir Harkonnen always keeps his promises. I told you I'd free her from the agony and permit you to join her. So be it." He waved a hand at Piter.

Piter's blue eyes took on a glazed look. His movement was catlike in its sudden fluidity. The knife in his hand glistened like a claw as it flashed into Yueh's back.

The old man stiffened, never taking his attention from the Baron.

"So join her!" the Baron spat.

Yueh stood, swaying. His lips moved with careful precision, and his voice came in oddly measured cadence: "You . . . think . . . you . . . de . . . feated . . . me. You . . . think . . . I . . . did . . . not . . . know . . . what . . . I . . . bought . . . for . . . my . . . Wanna."

He toppled. No bending or softening. It was like a tree falling.

"So join her," the Baron repeated. But his words were like a weak echo.

Yueh had filled him with a sense of foreboding. He whipped his attention to Piter, watched the man wipe the blade on a scrap of cloth, watched the creamy look of satisfaction in the blue eyes.

*So that's how he kills by his own hand,* the Baron thought. *It's well to know.*

"He *did* give us the Duke?" the Baron asked.

"Of a certainty, my Lord," Piter said.

"Then get him in here!"

Piter glanced at the guard captain, who whirled to obey.

The Baron looked down at Yueh. From the way the man had fallen, you could suspect oak in him instead of bones.

"I never could bring myself to trust a traitor," the Baron said. "Not even a traitor I created."

He glanced at the night-shrouded viewport. That black bag of stillness out there was his, the Baron knew. There was no more crump of artillery against the Shield Wall caves; the burrow traps were sealed off. Quite suddenly, the Baron's mind could conceive of nothing more beautiful than that utter emptiness of black. Unless it were white on the black. Plated white on the black. Porcelain white.

But there was still the feeling of doubt.

What had the old fool of a doctor meant? Of course, he'd probably known what would happen to him in the end. But that bit about thinking he'd been defeated: *"You think you defeated me."*

What had he meant?

The Duke Leto Atreides came through the door. His arms were bound in chains, the eagle face streaked with dirt. His uniform was torn where someone had ripped off his insignia. There were tatters at his waist where the shield belt had been removed without first freeing the uniform ties. The Duke's eyes held a glazed insane look.

"Wel-l-l-l," the Baron said. He hesitated, drawing in a deep breath. He knew he had spoken too loudly. This moment, long-envisioned, had lost some of its savor.

*Damn that cursed doctor through all eternity!*

"I believe the good Duke is drugged," Piter said. "That's how Yueh caught him for us." Piter turned to the Duke. "Aren't you drugged, my dear Duke?"

The voice was far away. Leto could feel the chains, the ache of muscles, his cracked lips, his burning cheeks, the dry taste of thirst whispering its grit in his mouth. But sounds were dull, hidden by a cottony blanket. And he saw only dim shapes through the blanket.

"What of the woman and the boy, Piter?" the Baron asked. "Any word yet?"

Piter's tongue darted over his lips.

"You've heard something!" the Baron snapped. "What?"

Piter glanced at the guard captain, back to the Baron. "The men who were sent to do the job, m'Lord—they've . . . ah . . . been . . . ah . . . found."

"Well, they report everything satisfactory?"

"They're dead, m'Lord."

"Of course they are! What I want to know is—"

"They were dead when found, m'Lord."

The Baron's face went livid. "And the woman and boy?"

"No sign, m'Lord, but there was a worm. It came while the scene was being investigated. Perhaps it's as we wished—an accident. Possibly—"

"We do not deal in possibilities, Piter. What of the missing 'thopter? Does that suggest anything to my Mentat?"

"One of the Duke's men obviously escaped in it, m'Lord. Killed our pilot and escaped."

"Which of the Duke's men?"

"It was a clean, silent killing, m'Lord. Hawat, perhaps, or that Halleck one. Possibly Idaho. Or any top lieutenant."

"Possibilities," the Baron muttered. He glanced at the swaying, drugged figure of the Duke.

"The situation is in hand, m'Lord," Piter said.

"No, it isn't! Where is that stupid planetologist? Where is this man Kynes?"

"We've word where to find him and he's been sent for, m'Lord."

"I don't like the way the Emperor's servant is helping us," the Baron muttered.

They were words through a cottony blanket, but some of them burned in Leto's mind. *Woman and boy—no sign.* Paul and Jessica had escaped. And the fate of Hawat, Halleck, and Idaho remained an unknown. There was still hope.

"Where is the ducal signet ring?" the Baron demanded. "His finger is bare."

"The Sardaukar say it was not on him when he was taken, my Lord," the guard captain said.

"You killed the doctor too soon," the Baron said. "That was a mistake. You should've warned me, Piter. You moved too precipitately for the good of our enterprise." He scowled. "Possibilities!"

The thought hung like a sine wave in Leto's mind: *Paul and Jessica have escaped!* And there was something else in his memory: a bargain. He could almost remember it.

*The tooth!*

He remembered part of it now: *a pill of poison gas shaped into a false tooth.*

Someone had told him to remember the tooth. The tooth was in his mouth. He could feel its shape with his tongue. All he had to do was bite sharply on it.

*Not yet!*

The someone had told him to wait until he was near the Baron. Who had told him? He couldn't remember.

"How long will he remain drugged like this?" the Baron asked.

"Perhaps another hour, m'Lord."

"Perhaps," the Baron muttered. Again, he turned to the night-blackened window. "I am hungry."

*That's the Baron, that fuzzy gray shape there,* Leto thought. The shape danced back and forth, swaying with the movement of the room. And the room expanded and contracted. It grew brighter and darker. It folded into blackness and faded.

Time became a sequence of layers for the Duke. He drifted up through them. *I must wait.*

There was a table. Leto saw the table quite clearly. And a gross, fat man on the other side of the table, the remains of a meal in front of him. Leto felt himself sitting in a chair across from the fat man, felt the chains, the straps that held his tingling body in the chair. He was aware there had been a passage of time, but its length escaped him.

"I believe he's coming around, Baron."

*A silky voice, that one. That was Piter.*

"So I see, Piter."

*A rumbling basso: the Baron.*

Leto sensed increasing definition in his surroundings. The chair beneath him took on firmness, the bindings were sharper.

And he saw the Baron clearly now. Leto watched the movements of the man's hands: compulsive touchings—the edge of a plate, the handle of a spoon, a finger tracing the fold of a jowl.

Leto watched the moving hand, fascinated by it.

"You can hear me, Duke Leto," the Baron said. "I know you can hear me. We want to know from you where to find your concubine and the child you sired on her."

No sign escaped Leto, but the words were a wash of calmness through him. *It's true, then: they don't have Paul and Jessica.*

"This is not a child's game we play," the Baron rumbled. "You must know that." He leaned toward Leto, studying the face. It pained the Baron that this could not be handled privately, just between the two of them. To have others see royalty in such straits—it set a bad precedent.

Leto could feel strength returning. And now, the memory of the false tooth stood out in his mind like a steeple in a flat landscape. The nerve-shaped capsule within that tooth—the poison gas—he remembered who had put the deadly weapon in his mouth.

*Yueh.*

Drug-fogged memory of seeing a limp corpse dragged past him in this room hung like a vapor in Leto's mind. He knew it had been Yueh.

"Do you hear that noise, Duke Leto?" the Baron asked.

Leto grew conscious of a frog sound, the burred mewling of someone's agony.

"We caught one of your men disguised as a Fremen," the Baron said. "We penetrated the disguise quite easily: the eyes, you know. He insists he was sent among the Fremen to spy on them. I've lived for a time on this planet, cher cousin. One does not spy on those ragged scum of the desert. Tell me, did you buy their help? Did you send your woman and son to them?"

Leto felt fear tighten his chest. *If Yueh sent them to the desert folk . . . the search won't stop until they're found.*

"Come, come," the Baron said. "We don't have much time and pain is quick. Please don't bring it to this, my dear Duke." The Baron looked up at Piter who stood at Leto's shoulder. "Piter doesn't have all his tools here, but I'm sure he could improvise."

"Improvisation is sometimes the best, Baron."

*That silky, insinuating voice!* Leto heard it at his ear.

"You had an emergency plan," the Baron said. "Where have your woman and the boy been sent?" He looked at Leto's hand. "Your ring is missing. Does the boy have it?"

The Baron looked up, stared into Leto's eyes.

"You don't answer," he said. "Will you force me to do a thing I do not want to do? Piter will use simple, direct methods. I agree they're sometimes the best, but it's not good that *you* should be subjected to such things."

"Hot tallow on the back, perhaps, or on the eyelids," Piter said. "Perhaps on other portions of the body. It's especially effective when the subject doesn't know where the tallow will fall next. It's a good method and there's a sort of beauty in the pattern of pus-white blisters on naked skin, eh, Baron?"

"Exquisite," the Baron said, and his voice sounded sour.

*Those touching fingers!* Leto watched the fat hands, the glittering jewels on baby-fat hands—their compulsive wandering.

The sounds of agony coming through the door behind him gnawed at the Duke's nerves. *Who is it they caught?* he wondered. *Could it have been Idaho?*

"Believe me, cher cousin," the Baron said. "I do not want it to come to this."

"You think of nerve couriers racing to summon help that cannot come," Piter said. "There's artistry in this, you know."

"You're a superb artist," the Baron growled. "Now, have the decency to be silent."

Leto suddenly recalled a thing Gurney Halleck had said once, seeing a picture of the Baron: "'*And I stood upon the sand of the sea and saw a beast rise up out of the sea . . . and upon his heads the name of blasphemy.*'"

"We waste time, Baron," Piter said.

"Perhaps."

The Baron nodded. "You know, my dear Leto, you'll tell us in the end where they are. There's a level of pain that'll buy you."

*He's most likely correct*, Leto thought. *Were it not for the tooth . . . and the fact that I truly don't know where they are.*

The Baron picked up a sliver of meat, pressed the morsel into his mouth, chewed slowly, swallowed. *We must try a new tack*, he thought.

"Observe this prize person who denies he's for hire," the Baron said. "Observe him, Piter."

And the Baron thought: *Yes! See him there, this man who believes he cannot be bought. See him detained there by a million shares of himself sold in dribbles every second of his life! If you took him up now and shook him, he'd rattle inside. Emptied! Sold out! What difference how he dies now?*

The frog sounds in the background stopped.

The Baron saw Umman Kudu, the guard captain, appear in the doorway across the room, shake his head. The captive hadn't produced the needed information. Another failure. Time to quit stalling with this fool Duke, this stupid soft fool who didn't realize how much hell there was so near him—only a nerve's thickness away.

This thought calmed the Baron, overcoming his reluctance to have a royal person subjected to pain. He saw himself suddenly as a surgeon exercising endless supple scissor dissections—cutting away the masks from fools, exposing the hell beneath.

*Rabbits, all of them!*

And how they cowered when they saw the carnivore!

Leto stared across the table, wondering why he waited. The tooth would end it all quickly. Still—it had been good, much of this life. He found himself remembering an antenna kite updangling in the shell-blue sky of Caladan, and Paul laughing with joy at the sight of it. And he remembered sunrise here on Arrakis—colored strata of the Shield Wall mellowed by dust haze.

"Too bad," the Baron muttered. He pushed himself back from the table, stood up lightly in his suspensors and hesitated, seeing a change come over the Duke. He saw the man draw in a deep breath, the jawline stiffen, the ripple of a muscle there as the Duke clamped his mouth shut.

*How he fears me!* the Baron thought.

Shocked by fear that the Baron might escape him, Leto bit hard on the capsule tooth, felt it break. He opened his mouth, expelled the biting vapor he could taste as it formed on his tongue. The Baron grew smaller, a figure seen in a tightening tunnel. Leto heard a gasp beside his ear—the silky-voiced one: Piter.

*It got him, too!*

"Piter! What's wrong?"

The rumbling voice was far away.

Leto sensed memories rolling in his mind—the old toothless mutterings of hags. The room, the table, the Baron, a pair of terrified eyes—blue within blue, the eyes—all compressed around him in ruined symmetry.

There was a man with a boot-toe chin, a toy man falling. The toy man had a broken nose slanted to the left: an offbeat metronome caught forever at the start of an upward stroke. Leto heard the crash of crockery—so distant—a roaring in his ears. His mind was a bin without end, catching everything. Everything that had ever been: every shout, every whisper, every . . . silence.

One thought remained to him. Leto saw it in formless light on rays of black: *The day the flesh shapes and the flesh the day shapes.* The thought struck him with a sense of fullness he knew he could never explain.

Silence.

The Baron stood with his back against his private door, his own bolt hole behind the table. He had slammed it on a room full of dead men. His senses took in guards swarming around him. *Did I breathe it?* he asked himself. *Whatever it was in there, did it get me, too?*

Sounds returned to him . . . and reason. He heard someone shouting orders—gas masks . . . keep a door closed . . . get blowers going.

*The others fell quickly,* he thought. I'm still standing. I'm still breathing. *Merciless hell! That was close!*

He could analyze it now. His shield had been activated, set low but still enough to slow molecular interchange across the field barrier. And he had been pushing himself away from the table . . . that and Piter's shocked gasp which had brought the guard captain darting forward into his own doom.

Chance and the warning in a dying man's gasp—these had saved him.

The Baron felt no gratitude to Piter. The fool had got himself killed. And that stupid guard captain! He'd said he scoped everyone before bringing them into the Baron's presence! How had it been possible for the Duke. . . ? No warning. Not even from the poison snooper over the table—until it was too late. How?

*Well, no matter now,* the Baron thought, his mind firming. *The next guard captain will begin by finding answers to these questions.*

He grew aware of more activity down the hall—around the corner at the other door to that room of death. The Baron pushed himself away from his own door, studied the lackeys around him. They stood there staring, silent, waiting for the Baron's reaction.

*Would the Baron be angry?*

And the Baron realized only a few seconds had passed since his flight from that terrible room.

Some of the guards had weapons leveled at the door. Some were directing their ferocity toward the empty hall that stretched away toward the noises around the corner to their right.

A man came striding around that corner, gas mask dangling by its straps at his neck, his eyes intent on the overhead poison snoopers that lined this corridor. He was yellow-haired, flat of face with green eyes. Crisp lines radiated from his thick-lipped mouth. He looked like some water creature misplaced among those who walked the land.

The Baron stared at the approaching man, recalling the name: Nefud. Iakin Nefud. Guard corporal. Nefud was addicted to semuta, the drug-music combination that played itself in the deepest consciousness. A useful item of information, that.

The man stopped in front of the Baron, saluted. "Corridor's clear, m'Lord. I was outside watching and saw that it must be poison gas. Ventilators in your room were pulling air in from these corridors." He glanced up at the snooper over the Baron's head. "None of the stuff escaped. We have the room cleaned out now. What are your orders?"

The Baron recognized the man's voice—the one who'd been shouting orders. *Efficient, this corporal,* he thought.

"They're all dead in there?" the Baron asked.

"Yes, m'Lord."

*Well, we must adjust,* the Baron thought.

"First," he said, "let me congratulate you, Nefud. You're the new captain of my guard. And I hope you'll take to heart the lesson to be learned from the fate of your predecessor."

The Baron watched the awareness grow in his newly promoted guardsman. Nefud knew he'd never again be without his semuta.

Nefud nodded. "My Lord knows I'll devote myself entirely to his safety."

"Yes. Well, to business. I suspect the Duke had something in his mouth. You will find out what that something was, how it was used, who helped him put it there. You'll take every precaution—"

He broke off, his chain of thought shattered by a disturbance in the corridor behind him—guards at the door to the lift from the lower levels of the frigate trying to hold back a tall colonel bashar who had just emerged from the lift.

The Baron couldn't place the colonel bashar's face: thin with mouth like a slash in leather, twin ink spots for eyes.

"Get your hands off me, you pack of carrion-eaters!" the man roared, and he dashed the guards aside.

*Ah-h-h, one of the Sardaukar,* the Baron thought.

The colonel bashar came striding toward the Baron, whose eyes went to slits of apprehension. The Sardaukar officers filled him with unease. They all seemed to look like relatives of the Duke . . . the late Duke. And their manners with the Baron!

The colonel bashar planted himself half a pace in front of the Baron, hands on hips. The guard hovered behind him in twitching uncertainty.

The Baron noted the absence of salute, the disdain in the Sardaukar's manner, and his unease grew. There was only the one legion of them locally—ten brigades—reinforcing the Harkonnen legions, but the Baron did not fool himself. That one legion was perfectly capable of turning on the Harkonnens and overcoming them.

"Tell your men they are not to prevent me from seeing you, Baron," the Sardaukar growled. "My men brought you the Atreides Duke before I could discuss his fate with you. We will discuss it now."

*I must not lose face before my men,* the Baron thought.

"So?" It was a coldly controlled word, and the Baron felt proud of it.

"My Emperor has charged me to make certain his royal cousin dies cleanly without agony," the colonel bashar said.

"Such were the Imperial orders to me," the Baron lied. "Did you think I'd disobey?"

"I'm to report to my Emperor what I see with my own eyes," the Sardaukar said.

"The Duke's already dead," the Baron snapped, and he waved a hand to dismiss the fellow.

The colonel bashar remained planted facing the Baron. Not by flicker of eye or muscle did he acknowledge he had been dismissed. "How?" he growled.

*Really!* the Baron thought. *This is too much.*

"By his own hand, if you must know," the Baron said. "He took poison."

"I will see the body now," the colonel bashar said.

The Baron raised his gaze to the ceiling in feigned exasperation while his thoughts raced. *Damnation! This sharp-eyed Sardaukar will see the room before a thing's been changed!*

"Now," the Sardaukar growled. "I'll see it with my own eyes."

There was no preventing it, the Baron realized. The Sardaukar would see all. He'd know the Duke had killed Harkonnen men . . . that the Baron most likely had escaped by a narrow margin. There was the evidence of the dinner remnants on the table, and the dead Duke across from it with destruction around him.

No preventing it at all.

"I'll not be put off," the colonel bashar snarled.

"You're not being put off," the Baron said, and he stared into the Sardaukar's obsidian eyes. "I hide nothing from my Emperor." He nodded to Nefud. "The colonel bashar is to see everything, at once. Take him in by the door where you stood, Nefud."

"This way, sir," Nefud said.

Slowly, insolently, the Sardaukar moved around the Baron, shouldered a way through the guardsmen.

*Insufferable,* the Baron thought. *Now, the Emperor will know how I slipped up. He'll recognize it as a sign of weakness.*

And it was agonizing to realize that the Emperor and his Sardaukar were alike in their disdain for weakness. The Baron chewed at his lower lip, consoling himself that the Emperor, at least, had not learned of the Atreides raid on Giedi Prime, the destruction of the Harkonnen spice stores there.

*Damn that slippery Duke!*

The Baron watched the retreating backs—the arrogant Sardaukar and the stocky, efficient Nefud.

*We must adjust,* the Baron thought. *I'll have to put Rabban over this damnable planet once more. Without restraint. I must spend my own Harkonnen blood to put Arrakis into a proper condition for accepting Feyd-Rautha. Damn that Piter! He would get himself killed before I was through with him.*

The Baron sighed.

*And I must send at once to Tleielax for a new Mentat. They undoubtedly have the new one ready for me by now.*

One of the guardsmen beside him coughed.

The Baron turned toward the man. "I am hungry."

"Yes, m' Lord."

"And I wish to be diverted while you're clearing out that room and studying its secrets for me," the Baron rumbled.

The guardsman lowered his eyes. "What diversion does m'Lord wish?"

"I'll be in my sleeping chambers," the Baron said. "Bring me that young fellow we bought on Gamont, the one with the lovely eyes. Drug him well. I don't feel like wrestling."

"Yes, m'Lord."

The Baron turned away, began moving with his bouncing, suspensor-buoyed pace toward his chambers. *Yes,* he thought. *The one with the lovely eyes, the one who looks so much like the young Paul Atreides.*

*O Seas of Caladan,*
*O people of Duke Leto—*
*Citadel of Leto fallen,*
*Fallen forever . . .*

**—from "Songs of Muad'Dib" by the Princess Irulan**

Paul felt that all his past, every experience before this night, had become sand curling in an hourglass. He sat near his mother hugging his knees within a small fabric and plastic hutment—a stilltent—that had come, like the Fremen clothing they now wore, from the pack left in the 'thopter.

There was no doubt in Paul's mind who had put the Fremkit there, who had directed the course of the 'thopter carrying them captive.

*Yueh.*

The traitor doctor had sent them directly into the hands of Duncan Idaho.

Paul stared out the transparent end of the stilltent at the moonshadowed rocks that ringed this place where Idaho had hidden them.

*Hiding like a child when I'm now the Duke,* Paul thought. He felt the thought gall him, but could not deny the wisdom in what they did.

Something had happened to his awareness this night—he saw with sharpened clarity every circumstance and occurrence around him. He felt unable to stop the inflow of data or the cold precision with which each new item was added to his knowledge and the computation was centered in his awareness. It was Mentat power and more.

Paul thought back to the moment of impotent rage as the strange 'thopter dived out of the night onto them, stooping like a giant hawk above the desert with wind screaming through its wings. The thing in Paul's mind had happened then. The 'thopter had skidded and slewed across a sand ridge toward the running figures—his mother and himself. Paul remembered how the smell of burned sulfur from abrasion of 'thopter skids against sand had drifted across them.

His mother, he knew, had turned, expected to meet a lasgun in the hands of Harkonnen mercenaries, and had recognized Duncan Idaho leaning out the 'thopter's open door shouting: "Hurry! There's wormsign south of you!"

But Paul had known as he turned who piloted the 'thopter. An accumulation of minutiae in the way it was flown, the dash of the landing—clues so small even his mother hadn't detected them—had told Paul *precisely* who sat at those controls.

Across the stilltent from Paul, Jessica stirred, said: "There can be only one explanation. The Harkonnens held Yueh's wife. He hated the Harkonnens! I cannot be wrong about that. You read his note. But why has he saved us from the carnage?"

*She is only now seeing it and that poorly,* Paul thought. The thought was a shock. He had known this fact as a by-the-way thing while reading the note that had accompanied the ducal signet in the pack.

"Do not try to forgive me," Yueh had written. "I do not want your forgiveness. I already have enough burdens. What I have done was done without malice or hope of another's understanding. It is my own tahaddi al-burhan, my ultimate test. I give you the Atreides ducal signet as token that I write truly. By the time you read this, Duke Leto will be dead. Take consolation from my assurance that he did not die alone, that one we hate above all others died with him."

It had not been addressed or signed, but there'd been no mistaking the familiar scrawl—Yueh's.

Remembering the letter, Paul re-experienced the distress of that moment—a thing sharp and strange that seemed to happen outside his new mental alertness. He had read that his father was dead, known the truth of the words, but had felt them as no more than another datum to be entered in his mind and used.

*I loved my father,* Paul thought, and knew this for truth. *I should mourn him. I should feel something.*

But he felt nothing except: *Here's an important fact.*

It was one with all the other facts.

All the while his mind was adding sense impressions, extrapolating, computing.

Halleck's words came back to Paul: *"Mood's a thing for cattle or for making love. You fight when the necessity arises, no matter your mood."*

*Perhaps that's it,* Paul thought. *I'll mourn my father later . . . when there's time.*

But he felt no letup in the cold precision of his being. He sensed that his new awareness was only a beginning, that it was growing. The sense of terrible purpose he'd first experienced in his ordeal with the Reverend Mother Gaius Helen Mohiam pervaded him. His right hand—the hand of remembered pain—tingled and throbbed.

*Is this what it is to be their Kwisatz Haderach?* he wondered.

"For a while, I thought Hawat had failed us again," Jessica said. "I thought perhaps Yueh wasn't a Suk doctor."

"He was everything we thought him . . . and more," Paul said. And he thought: *Why is she so slow seeing these things?* He said, "If Idaho doesn't get through to Kynes, we'll be—"

"He's not our only hope," she said.

"Such was not my suggestion," he said.

She heard the steel in his voice, the sense of command, and stared across the grey darkness of the stilltent at him. Paul was a silhouette against moonfrosted rocks seen through the tent's transparent end.

"Others among your father's men will have escaped," she said. "We must regather them, find—"

"We will depend upon ourselves," he said. "Our immediate concern is our family atomics. We must get them before the Harkonnens can search them out."

"Not likely they'll be found," she said, "the way they were hidden."

"It must not be left to chance."

And she thought: *Blackmail with the family atomics as a threat to the planet and its spice—that's what he has in mind. But all he can hope for then is escape into renegade anonymity.*

His mother's words had provoked another train of thought in Paul—a duke's concern for all the people they'd lost this night. *People are the true strength of a Great House,* Paul thought. And he remembered Hawat's words: *"Parting with people is a sadness; a place is only a place."*

"They're using Sardaukar," Jessica said. "We must wait until the Sardaukar have been withdrawn."

"They think us caught between the desert and the Sardaukar," Paul said. "They intend that there be no Atreides survivors—total extermination. Do not count on any of our people escaping."

"They cannot go on indefinitely risking exposure of the Emperor's part in this."

"Can't they?"

"Some of our people are bound to escape."

"Are they?"

Jessica turned away, frightened of the bitter strength in her son's voice, hearing the precise assessment of chances. She sensed that his mind had leaped ahead of her, that it now saw more in some respects than she did. She had helped train the intelligence which did this, but now she found herself fearful of it. Her thoughts turned, seeking toward the lost sanctuary of her Duke, and tears burned her eyes.

*This is the way it had to be, Leto,* she thought. *"A time of love and a time of grief."* She rested her hand on her abdomen, awareness focused on the embryo there. *I have the Atreides daughter I was ordered to produce, but the Reverend Mother was wrong: a daughter wouldn't have saved my Leto. This child is only life reaching for the future in the midst of death. I conceived out of instinct and not out of obedience.*

"Try the communinet receiver again," Paul said.

*The mind goes on working no matter how we try to hold it back,* she thought.

Jessica found the tiny receiver Idaho had left for them, flipped its switch. A green light glowed on the instrument's face. Tinny screeching came from its speaker. She reduced the volume, hunted across the bands. A voice speaking Atreides battle language came into the tent.

". . . back and regroup at the ridge. Fedor reports no survivors in Carthag and the Guild Bank has been sacked."

*Carthag!* Jessica thought. *That was a Harkonnen hotbed.*

"They're Sardaukar," the voice said. "Watch out for Sardaukar in Atreides uniforms. They're . . . ."

A roaring filled the speaker, then silence.

"Try the other bands," Paul said.

"Do you realize what that means?" Jessica asked.

"I expected it. They want the Guild to blame us for destruction of their bank. With the Guild against us, we're trapped on Arrakis. Try the other bands."

She weighed his words: *"I expected it."* What had happened to him? Slowly, Jessica returned to the instrument. As she moved the bandslide, they caught glimpses of violence in the few voices calling out in Atreides battle language: ". . . fall back . . . ." ". . . try to regroup at . . . ." ". . . trapped in a cave at . . . ."

And there was no mistaking the victorious exultation in the Harkonnen gibberish that poured from the other bands. Sharp commands, battle reports. There wasn't enough of it for Jessica to register and break the language, but the tone was obvious.

Harkonnen victory.

Paul shook the pack beside him, hearing the two literjons of water gurgle there. He took a deep breath, looked up through the transparent end of the tent at the rock escarpment outlined against the stars. His left hand felt the sphincter-seal of the tent's entrance. "It'll be dawn soon," he said. "We can wait through the day for Idaho, but not through another night. In the desert, you must travel by night and rest in shade through the day."

Remembered lore insinuated itself into Jessica's mind: *Without a stillsuit, a man sitting in shade on the desert needs five liters of water a day to maintain body weight.* She felt the slick-soft skin of the stillsuit against her body, thinking how their lives depended on these garments.

"If we leave here, Idaho can't find us," she said.

"There are ways to make any man talk," he said. "If Idaho hasn't returned by dawn, we must consider the possibility he has been captured. How long do you think he could hold out?"

The question required no answer, and she sat in silence.

Paul lifted the seal on the pack, pulled out a tiny micromanual with glowtab and magnifier. Green and orange letters leaped up at him from the pages: "literjons, stilltent, energy caps, recaths, sandsnork, binoculars, stillsuit repkit, baradye pistol, sinkchart, filt-plugs, paracompass, maker hooks, thumpers, Fremkit, fire pillar . . . ."

So many things for survival on the desert.

Presently, he put the manual aside on the tent floor.

"Where can we possibly go?" Jessica asked.

"My father spoke of *desert power*," Paul said. "The Harkonnens cannot rule this planet without it. They've never ruled this planet, nor shall they. Not even with ten thousand legions of Sardaukar."

"Paul, you can't think that—"

"We've all the evidence in our hands," he said. "Right here in this tent—the tent itself, this pack and its contents, these stillsuits. We know the Guild wants a prohibitive price for weather satellites. We know that—"

"What've weather satellites to do with it?" she asked. "They couldn't possibly . . . ." She broke off.

Paul sensed the hyperalertness of his mind reading her reactions, computing on minutiae. "You see it now," he said. "Satellites watch the terrain below. There are things in the deep desert that will not bear frequent inspection."

"You're suggesting the Guild itself controls this planet?"

She was so slow.

"No!" he said. "The Fremen! They're paying the Guild for privacy, paying in a coin that's freely available to anyone with desert power—spice. This is more than a second-approximation answer; it's the straight-line computation. Depend on it."

"Paul," Jessica said, "you're not a Mentat yet; you can't know for sure how—"

"I'll never be a Mentat," he said. "I'm something else . . . a freak."

"Paul! How can you say such—"

"Leave me alone!"

He turned away from her, looking out into the night. *Why can't I mourn?* he wondered. He felt that every fiber of his being craved this release, but it would be denied him forever.

Jessica had never heard such distress in her son's voice. She wanted to reach out to him, hold him, comfort him, help him—but she sensed there was nothing she could do. He had to solve this problem by himself.

The glowing tab of the Fremkit manual between them on the tent floor caught her eye. She lifted it, glanced at the flyleaf, reading: "Manual of 'The Friendly Desert,' the place full of life. Here are the ayat and burhan of Life. Believe, and al-Lat shall never burn you."

*It reads like the Azhar Book,* she thought, recalling her studies of the Great Secrets. *Has a Manipulator of Religions been on Arrakis?*

Paul lifted the paracompass from the pack, returned it, said: "Think of all these special-application Fremen machines. They show unrivaled sophistication. Admit it. the culture that made these things betrays depths no one suspected."

Hesitating, still worried by the harshness in his voice, Jessica returned to the book, studied an illustrated constellation from the Arrakeen sky: "Muad'Dib: The Mouse," and noted that the tail pointed north.

Paul stared into the tent's darkness at the dimly discerned movements of his mother revealed by the manual's glowtab. *Now is the time to carry out my father's wish,* he thought. *I must give her his message now while she has time for grief. Grief would inconvenience us later.* And he found himself shocked by precise logic.

"Mother," he said.

"Yes?"

She heard the change in his voice, felt coldness in her entrails at the sound. Never had she heard such harsh control.

"My father is dead," he said.

She searching within herself for the coupling of fact and fact and fact—the Bene Gesserit way of assessing data—and it came to her: the sensation of terrifying loss.

Jessica nodded, unable to speak.

"My father charged me once," Paul said, "to give you a message if anything happened to him. He feared you might believe he distrusted you."

*That useless suspicion,* she thought.

"He wanted you to know he never suspected you," Paul said, and explained the deception, adding: "He wanted you to know he always trusted you completely, always loved you and cherished you. He said he would sooner have mistrusted himself and he had but one regret—that he never made you his Duchess."

She brushed the tears coursing down her cheeks, thought: *What a stupid waste of the body's water!* But she knew this thought for what it was—the attempt to retreat from grief into anger. *Leto, my Leto,* she thought. *What terrible things we do to those we love!* With a violent motion, she extinguished the little manual's glowtab.

Sobs shook her.

Paul heard his mother's grief and felt the emptiness within himself. *I have no grief,* he thought. *Why? Why?* He felt the inability to grieve as a terrible flaw.

*"A time to get and a time to lose, "* Jessica thought, quoting to herself from the O.C. Bible. *"A time to keep and a time to cast away; a time for love and a time to hate; a time of war and a time of peace."*

Paul's mind had gone on in its chilling precision. He saw the avenues ahead of them on this hostile planet. Without even the safety valve of dreaming, he focused his prescient awareness, seeing it as a computation of most probable futures, but with something more, an edge of mystery—as though his mind dipped into some timeless stratum and sampled the winds of the future.

Abruptly, as though he had found a necessary key, Paul's mind climbed another notch in awareness. He felt himself clinging to this new level, clutching at a precarious hold and peering about. It was as though he existed within a globe with avenues radiating away in all directions . . . yet this only approximated the sensation.

He remembered once seeing a gauze kerchief blowing in the wind and now he sensed the future as though it twisted across some surface as undulant and impermanent as that of the windblown kerchief.

He saw people.

He felt the heat and cold of uncounted probabilities.

He knew names and places, experienced emotions without number, reviewed data of innumerable unexplored crannies. There was time to probe and test and taste, but no time to shape.

The thing was a spectrum of possibilities from the most remote past to the most remote future—from the most probable to the most improbable. He saw his own death in countless ways. He saw new planets, new cultures.

People.

People.

He saw them in such swarms they could not be listed, yet his mind catalogued them.

Even the Guildsmen.

And he thought: *The Guild—there'd be a way for us, my strangeness accepted as a familiar thing of high value, always with an assured supply of the now-necessary spice.*

But the idea of living out his life in the mind-groping-ahead-through-possible-futures that guided hurtling spaceships appalled him. It *was* a way, though. And in meeting the *possible future* that contained Guildsmen he recognized his own strangeness.

*I have another kind of sight. I see another kind of terrain: the available paths.*

The awareness conveyed both reassurance and alarm—so many places on that other kind of terrain dipped or turned out of his sight.

As swiftly as it had come, the sensation slipped away from him, and he realized the entire experience had taken the space of a heartbeat.

Yet, his own personal awareness had been turned over, illuminated in a terrifying way. He stared around him.

Night still covered the stilltent within its rock-enclosed hideaway. His mother's grief could still be heard.

His own lack of grief could still be felt . . . that hollow place somewhere separated from his mind, which went on in its steady pace—dealing with data, evaluating, computing, submitting answers in something like the Mentat way.

And now he saw that he had a wealth of data few such minds ever before had encompassed. But this made the empty place within him no easier to bear. He felt that something must shatter. It was as though a clockwork control for a bomb had been set to ticking within him. It went on about its business no matter what he wanted. It recorded minuscule shadings of difference around him—a slight change in moisture, a fractional fall in temperature, the progress of an insect across their stilltent roof, the solemn approach of dawn in the starlight patch of sky he could see out the tent's transparent end.

The emptiness was unbearable. Knowing how the clockwork had been set in motion made no difference. He could look to his own past and see the start of it—the training, the sharpening of talents, the refined pressures of sophisticated disciplines, even exposure to the O.C. Bible at a critical moment . . . and, lastly, the heavy intake of spice. And he could look ahead—the most terrifying direction—to see where it all pointed.

*I'm a monster!* he thought. *A freak!*

"No," he said. Then: "No. No! NO!"

He found that he was pounding the tent floor with his fists. (The implacable part of him recorded this as an interesting emotional datum and fed it into computation.)

"Paul!"

His mother was beside him, holding his hands, her face a gray blob peering at him. "Paul, what's wrong?"

"You!" he said.

"I'm here, Paul," she said. "It's all right."

"What have you done to me?" he demanded.

In a burst of clarity, she sensed some of the roots in the question, said: "I gave birth to you."

It was, from instinct as much as her own subtle knowledge, the precisely correct answer to calm him. He felt her hands holding him, focused on the dim outline of her face. (Certain gene traces in her facial structure were noted in the new way by his onflowing mind, the clues added to other data, and a final-summation answer put forward.)

"Let go of me," he said.

She heard the iron in his voice, obeyed. "Do you want to tell me what's wrong, Paul?"

"Did you know what you were doing when you trained me?" he asked.

*There's no more childhood in his voice,* she thought. And she said: "I hoped the thing any parent hopes—that you'd be . . . superior, different."

"Different?"

She heard the bitterness in his tone, said: "Paul, I—"

"You didn't want a son!" he said. "You wanted a Kwisatz Haderach! You wanted a male Bene Gesserit!"

She recoiled from his bitterness. "But Paul . . . ."

"Did you ever consult my father in this?"

She spoke gently out of the freshness of her grief: "Whatever you are, Paul, the heredity is as much your father as me."

"But not the training," he said. "Not the things that . . . awakened . . . the sleeper."

"Sleeper?"

"It's here." He put a hand on his head and then to his breast. "In me. It goes on and on and on and on and—"

"Paul!"

She had heard the hysteria edging his voice.

"Listen to me," he said. "You wanted the Reverend Mother to hear about my dreams? You listen in her place now. I've just had a *waking* dream. Do you know why?"

"You must calm yourself," she said. "If there's—"

"The spice," he said. "It's in everything here—the air, the soil, the food. The *geriatric* spice. It's like the Truthsayer drug. It's a poison!"

She stiffened.

His voice lowered and he repeated: "A poison—so subtle, so insidious . . . so irreversible. It won't even kill you unless you stop taking it. We can't leave Arrakis unless we take part of Arrakis with us."

The terrifying *presence* of his voice brooked no dispute.

"You and the spice," Paul said. "The spice changes anyone who gets this much of it, but thanks to *you*, I could bring the change to consciousness. I don't get to leave it in the unconscious where its disturbance can be blanked out. I can *see* it."

"Paul, you—"

"I *see* it!" he repeated.

She heard madness in his voice, didn't know what to do.

But he spoke again, and she heard the iron control return to him: "We're trapped here."

*We're trapped here,* she agreed.

And she accepted the truth of his words. No pressure of the Bene Gesserit, no trickery or artifice could pry them completely free from Arrakis: the spice was addictive. Her body had known the fact long before her mind awakened to it.

*So here we live out our lives,* she thought, *on this hell-planet. The place is prepared for us, if we can evade the Harkonnens. And there's no doubt of my course: a broodmare preserving an important bloodline for the Bene Gesserit Plan.*

"I must tell you about my waking dream," Paul said. (Now there was fury in his voice.) "To be sure you accept what I say, I'll tell you first I know you'll bear a daughter, my sister, here on Arrakis."

Jessica placed her hands against the tent floor, pressed back against the curving fabric wall to still a pang of fear. She knew her pregnancy could not show yet. Only her own Bene Gesserit training had allowed her to read the first faint signals of her body, to know of the embryo only a few weeks old.

"Only to serve," Jessica whispered, clinging to the Bene Gesserit motto. "We exist only to serve."

"We'll find a home among the Fremen," Paul said, "where your Missionaria Protectiva has bought us a bolt hole."

*They've prepared a way for us in the desert,* Jessica told herself. *But how can he know of the Missionaria Protectiva?* She found it increasingly difficult to subdue her terror at the overpowering strangeness in Paul.

He studied the dark shadow of her, seeing her fear and every reaction with his new awareness as though she were outlined in blinding light. A beginning of compassion for her crept over him.

"The things that can happen here, I cannot begin to tell you," he said. "I cannot even begin to tell myself, although I've seen them. This *sense* of the future—I seem to have no control over it. The thing just happens. The immediate future—say, a year—I can see some of that . . . a *road* as broad as our Central Avenue on Caladan. Some places I don't see . . . shadowed places . . . as though it went behind a hill" (and again he thought of the surface of a blowing kerchief) ". . . and there are branchings . . . ."

He fell silent as memory of that *seeing* filled him. No prescient dream, no experience of his life had quite prepared him for the totality with which the veil had been ripped away to reveal naked time.

Recalling the experience, he recognized his own terrible purpose—the pressure of his life spreading outward like an expanding bubble . . . time retreating before it . . . .

Jessica found the tent's glowtab control, activated it.

Dim green light drove back the shadows, easing her fear. She looked at Paul's face, his eyes—the inward stare. And she knew where she had seen such a look before: pictured in records of disasters—on the faces of children who experienced starvation or terrible injury. The eyes were like pits, mouth a straight line, cheeks indrawn.

*It's the look of terrible awareness,* she thought, *of someone forced to the knowledge of his own mortality.*

He was, indeed, no longer a child.

The underlying import of his words began to take over in her mind, pushing all else aside. Paul could see ahead, a way of escape for them.

"There's a way to evade the Harkonnens," she said.

"The Harkonnens!" he sneered. "Put those twisted humans out of your mind." He stared at his mother, studying the lines of her face in the light of the glowtab. The lines betrayed her.

She said: "You shouldn't refer to people as humans without—"

"Don't be so sure you know where to draw the line," he said. "We carry our past with us. And, mother mine, there's a thing you don't know and should—*we* are Harkonnens."

Her mind did a terrifying thing: it blanked out as though it needed to shut off all sensation. But Paul's voice went on at that implacable pace, dragging her with it.

"When next you find a mirror, study your face—study mine now. The traces are there if you don't blind yourself. Look at my hands, the set of my bones. And if none of this convinces you, then take my word for it. I've walked the future, I've looked at a record, I've seen a place, I have all the data. We're Harkonnens."

"A . . . renegade branch of the family," she said. "That's it, isn't it? Some Harkonnen cousin who—"

"You're the Baron's own daughter," he said, and watched the way she pressed her hands to her mouth. "The Baron sampled many pleasures in his youth, and once permitted himself to be seduced. But it was for the genetic purposes of the Bene Gesserit, by one of *you.*"

The way he said *you* struck her like a slap. But it set her mind to working and she could not deny his words. So many blank ends of meaning in her past reached out now and linked. The daughter the Bene Gesserit wanted—it wasn't to end the old Atreides-Harkonnen feud, but to fix some genetic factor in their lines. *What?* She groped for an answer.

As though he saw inside her mind, Paul said: "They thought they were reaching for me. But I'm not what they expected, and I've arrived before my time. And *they* don't know it."

Jessica pressed her hands to her mouth.

*Great Mother! He's the Kwisatz Haderach!*

She felt exposed and naked before him, realizing then that he saw her with eyes from which little could be hidden. And *that*, she knew, was the basis of her fear.

"You're thinking I'm the Kwisatz Haderach," he said. "Put that out of your mind. I'm something unexpected."

*I must get word out to one of the schools,* she thought. *The mating index may show what has happened.*

"They won't learn about me until it's too late," he said.

She sought to divert him, lowered her hands and said: "We'll find a place among the Fremen?"

"The Fremen have a saying they credit to Shai-hulud, Old Father Eternity," he said. "They say: 'Be prepared to appreciate what you meet.'"

And he thought: *Yes, mother mine—among the Fremen. You'll acquire the blue eyes and a callus beside your lovely nose from the filter tube to your stillsuit . . . and you'll bear my sister: St. Alia of the Knife.*

"If you're not the Kwisatz Haderach," Jessica said, "what—"

"You couldn't possibly know," he said. "You won't believe it until you see it."

And he thought: *I'm a seed.*

He suddenly saw how fertile was the ground into which he had fallen, and with this realization, the terrible purpose filled him, creeping through the empty place within, threatening to choke him with grief.

He had seen two main branchings along the way ahead—in one he confronted an evil old Baron and said: "Hello, Grandfather." The thought of that path and what lay along it sickened him.

The other path held long patches of gray obscurity except for peaks of violence. He had seen a warrior religion there, a fire spreading across the universe with the Atreides green and black banner waving at the head of fanatic legions drunk on spice liquor. Gurney Halleck and a few others of his father's men—a pitiful few—were among them, all marked by the hawk symbol from the shrine of his father's skull.

"I can't go that way," he muttered. "That's what the old witches of your schools really want."

"I don't understand you, Paul," his mother said.

He remained silent, thinking like the seed he was, thinking with the race consciousness he had first experienced as terrible purpose. He found that he no longer could hate the Bene Gesserit or the Emperor or even the Harkonnens. They were all caught up in the need of their race to renew its scattered inheritance, to cross and mingle and infuse their bloodlines in a great new pooling of genes. And the race knew only one sure way for this—the ancient way, the tried and certain way that rolled over everything in its path: jihad.

*Surely I cannot choose that way,* he thought.

But he saw again in his mind's eye the shrine of his father's skull and the violence with the green and black banner waving in its midst.

Jessica cleared her throat, worried by his silence. "Then . . . the Fremen will give us sanctuary?"

He looked up, staring across the green-lighted tent at the inbred, patrician lines of her face. "Yes," he said. "That's one of the ways." He nodded. "Yes. They'll call me . . . Muad'Dib, 'The One Who Points the Way.' Yes . . . that's what they'll call me."

And he closed his eyes, thinking: *Now, my father, I can mourn you.* And he felt the tears coursing down his cheeks.

# MUAD'DIB

---

*When my father, the Padishah Emperor, heard of Duke Leto's death and the manner of it, he went into such a rage as we had never before seen. He blamed my mother and the compact forced on him to place a Bene Gesserit on the throne. He blamed the Guild and the evil old Baron. He blamed everyone in sight, not excepting even me, for he said I was a witch like all the others. And when I sought to comfort him, saying it was done according to an older law of self-preservation to which even the most ancient rulers gave allegiance, he sneered at me and asked if I thought him a weakling. I saw then that he had been aroused to this passion not by concern over the dead Duke but by what that death implied for all royalty. As I look back on it, I think there may have been some prescience in my father, too, for it is certain that his line and Muad'Dib's shared common ancestry.*

—**"In My Father's House," by the Princess Irulan**

"Now Harkonnen shall kill Harkonnen," Paul whispered.

He had awakened shortly before nightfall, sitting up in the sealed and darkened stilltent. As he spoke, he heard the vague stirrings of his mother where she slept against the tent's opposite wall.

Paul glanced at the proximity detector on the floor, studying the dials illuminated in the blackness by phosphor tubes.

"It should be night soon," his mother said. "Why don't you lift the tent shades?"

Paul realized then that her breathing had been different for some time, that she had lain silent in the darkness until certain he was awake.

"Lifting the shades wouldn't help," he said. "There's been a storm. The tent's covered by sand. I'll dig us out soon."

"No sign of Duncan yet?"

"None."

Paul rubbed absently at the ducal signet on his thumb, and a sudden rage against the very substance of this planet which had helped kill his father set him trembling.

"I heard the storm begin," Jessica said.

The undemanding emptiness of her words helped restore some of his calm. His mind focused on the storm as he had seen it begin through the transparent end of their stilltent—cold dribbles of sand crossing the basin, then runnels and tails furrowing the sky. He had looked up to a rock spire, seen it change shape under the blast, becoming a low, cheddar-colored wedge. Sand funneled into their basin had shadowed the sky with dull curry, then blotted out all light as the tent was covered.

Tent bows had creaked once as they accepted the pressure, then—silence broken only by the dim bellows wheezing of their sand snorkel pumping air from the surface.

"Try the receiver again," Jessica said.

"No use," he said.

He found his stillsuit's watertube in its clip at his neck, drew a warm swallow into his mouth, and he thought that here he truly began an Arrakeen existence—living on reclaimed moisture from his own breath and body. It was flat and tasteless water, but it soothed his throat.

Jessica heard Paul drinking, felt the slickness of her own stillsuit clinging to her body, but she refused to accept her thirst. To accept it would require awakening fully into the terrible necessities of Arrakis where they must guard even fractional traces of moisture, hoarding the few drops in the tent's catchpockets, begrudging a breath wasted on the open air.

So much easier to drift back down into sleep.

But there had been a dream in this day's sleep, and she shivered at memory of it. She had held dreaming hands beneath sandflow where a name had been written: *Duke Leto Atreides.* The name had blurred with the sand and she had moved to restore it, but the first letter filled before the last was begun.

The sand would not stop.

Her dream became wailing: louder and louder. That ridiculous wailing— part of her mind had realized the sound was her own voice as a tiny child, little more than a baby. A woman not quite visible to memory was going away.

*My unknown mother,* Jessica thought. *The Bene Gesserit who bore me and gave me to the Sisters because that's what she was commanded to do. Was she glad to rid herself of a Harkonnen child?*

"The place to hit them is in the spice," Paul said.

*How can he think of attack at a time like this?* she asked herself.

"An entire planet full of spice," she said. "How can you hit them there?"

She heard him stirring, the sound of their pack being dragged across the tent floor.

"It was sea power and air power on Caladan," he said. "Here, it's *desert power*. The Fremen are the key."

His voice came from the vicinity of the tent's sphincter. Her Bene Gesserit training sensed in his tone an unresolved bitterness toward her.

*All his life he has been trained to hate Harkonnens,* she thought. *Now, he finds he is Harkonnen . . . because of me. How little he knows me! I was my Duke's only woman. I accepted his life and his values even to defying my Bene Gesserit orders.*

The tent's glowtab came alight under Paul's hand, filled the domed area with green radiance. Paul crouched at the sphincter, his stillsuit hood adjusted for the open desert—forehead capped, mouth filter in place, nose plugs adjusted. Only his dark eyes were visible: a narrow band of face that turned once toward her and away.

"Secure yourself for the open," he said, and his voice was blurred behind the filter.

Jessica pulled the filter across her mouth, began adjusting her hood as she watched Paul break the tent seal.

Sand rasped as he opened the sphincter and a burred fizzle of grains ran into the tent before he could immobilize it with a static compaction tool. A hole grew in the sandwall as the tool realigned the grains. He slipped out and her ears followed his progress to the surface.

*What will we find out there?* she wondered. *Harkonnen troops and the Sardaukar, those are dangers we can expect. But what of the dangers we don't know?*

She thought of the compaction tool and the other strange instruments in the pack. Each of these tools suddenly stood in her mind as a sign of mysterious dangers.

She felt then a hot breeze from surface sand touch her cheeks where they were exposed above the filter.

"Pass up the pack." It was Paul's voice, low and guarded.

She moved to obey, heard the water literjons gurgle as she shoved the pack across the floor. She peered upward, saw Paul framed against stars.

"Here," he said and reached down, pulled the pack to the surface.

Now she saw only the circle of stars. They were like the luminous tips of weapons aimed down at her. A shower of meteors crossed her patch of night. The meteors seemed to her like a warning, like tiger stripes, like luminous grave slats clabbering her blood. And she felt the chill of the price on their heads.

"Hurry up," Paul said. "I want to collapse the tent."

A shower of sand from the surface brushed her left hand. *How much sand will the hand hold?* she asked herself.

"Shall I help you?" Paul asked.

"No."

She swallowed in a dry throat, slipped into the hole, felt static-packed sand rasp under her hands. Paul reached down, took her arm. She stood beside him on a smooth patch of starlit desert, stared around. Sand almost brimmed their basin, leaving only a dim lip of surrounding rock. She probed the farther darkness with her trained senses.

Noise of small animals.

Birds.

A fall of dislodged sand and faint creature sounds within it.

Paul collapsed their tent, recovering it up the hole.

Starlight displaced just enough of the night to charge each shadow with menace. She looked at patches of blackness.

*Black is a blind remembering,* she thought. *You listen for pack sounds, for the cries of those who hunted your ancestors in a past so ancient only your most primitive cells remember. The ears see. The nostrils see.*

Presently, Paul stood beside her, said: "Duncan told me that if he was captured, he could hold out . . . this long. We must leave here now." He shouldered the pack, crossed to the shallow lip of the basin, climbed to a ledge that looked down on open desert.

Jessica followed automatically, noting how she now lived in her son's orbit.

*For now is my grief heavier than the sands of the seas,* she thought. *This world has emptied me of all but the oldest purpose: tomorrow's life. I live now for my young Duke and the daughter yet to be.*

She felt the sand drag her feet as she climbed to Paul's side.

He looked north across a line of rocks, studying a distant escarpment.

The faraway rock profile was like an ancient battleship of the seas outlined by stars. The long swish of it lifted on an invisible wave with syllables of boomerang antennae, funnels arcing back, a pi-shaped upthrusting at the stern.

An orange glare burst above the silhouette and a line of brilliant purple cut downward toward the glare.

Another line of purple!

And another upthrusting orange glare!

It was like an ancient naval battle, remembered shellfire, and the sight held them staring.

"Pillars of fire," Paul whispered.

A ring of red eyes lifted over the distant rock. Lines of purple laced the sky.

"Jetflares and lasguns," Jessica said.

The dust-reddened first moon of Arrakis lifted above the horizon to their left and they saw a storm trail there—a ribbon of movement over the desert.

"It must be Harkonnen 'thopters hunting us," Paul said. "The way they're cutting up the desert . . . it's as though they were making certain they stamped out whatever's there . . . the way you'd stamp out a nest of insects."

"Or a nest of Atreides," Jessica said.

"We must seek cover," Paul said. "We'll head south and keep to the rocks. If they caught us in the open . . . ." He turned, adjusting the pack to his shoulders. "They're killing anything that moves."

He took one step along the ledge and, in that instant, heard the low hiss of gliding aircraft, saw the dark shapes of ornithopters above them.

---

*My father once told me that respect for the truth comes close to being the basis for all morality. "Something cannot emerge from nothing," he said. This is profound thinking if you understand how unstable "the truth" can be.*

**—from "Conversations with Muad'Dib"
by the Princess Irulan**

"I've always prided myself on seeing things the way they truly are," Thufir Hawat said. "That's the curse of being a Mentat. You can't stop analyzing your data."

The leathered old face appeared composed in the predawn dimness as he spoke. His sapho-stained lips were drawn into a straight line with radial creases spreading upward.

A robed man squatted silently on sand across from Hawat, apparently unmoved by the words.

The two crouched beneath a rock overhang that looked down on a wide, shallow sink. Dawn was spreading over the shattered outline of cliffs across the basin, touching everything with pink. It was cold under the overhang, a dry and penetrating chill left over from the night. There had been a warm wind just before dawn, but now it was cold. Hawat could hear teeth chattering behind him among the few troopers remaining in his force.

The man squatting across from Hawat was a Fremen who had come across the sink in the first light of false dawn, skittering over the sand, blending into the dunes, his movements barely discernible.

The Fremen extended a finger to the sand between them, drew a figure there. It looked like a bowl with an arrow spilling out of it. "There are many Harkonnen patrols," he said. He lifted his finger, pointed upward across the cliffs that Hawat and his men had descended.

Hawat nodded.

*Many patrols. Yes.*

But still he did not know what this Fremen wanted and this rankled. Mentat training was supposed to give a man the power to see motives.

This had been the worst night of Hawat's life. He had been at Tsimpo, a garrison village, buffer outpost for the former capital city, Carthag, when the reports of attack began arriving. At first, he'd thought: *It's a raid. The Harkonnens are testing.*

But report followed report—faster and faster.

Two legions landed at Carthag.

Five legions—fifty brigades!—attacking the Duke's main base at Arrakeen.

A legion at Arsunt.

Two battle groups at Splintered Rock.

Then the reports became more detailed—there were Imperial Sardaukar among the attackers—possibly two legions of them. And it became clear that the invaders knew precisely which weight of arms to send where. Precisely! Superb intelligence.

Hawat's shocked fury had mounted until it threatened the smooth functioning of his Mentat capabilities. The size of the attack struck his mind like a physical blow.

Now, hiding beneath a bit of desert rock, he nodded to himself, pulled his torn and slashed tunic around him as though warding off the cold shadows.

*The size of the attack.*

He had always expected their enemy to hire an occasional lighter from the Guild for probing raids. That was an ordinary enough gambit in this kind of House-to-House warfare. Lighters landed and took off on Arrakis regularly to transport the spice for House Atreides. Hawat had taken precautions against random raids by false spice lighters. For a full attack they'd expected no more than ten brigades.

But there were more than two thousand ships down on Arrakis at the last count—not just lighters, but frigates, scouts, monitors, crushers, troop-carriers, dump-boxes . . . .

More than a hundred brigades—ten legions!

The entire spice income of Arrakis for fifty years might just cover the cost of such a venture.

It *might.*

*I underestimated what the Baron was willing to spend in attacking us,* Hawat thought. *I failed my Duke.*

Then there was the matter of the traitor.

*I will live long enough to see her strangled!* he thought. *I should've killed that Bene Gesserit witch when I had the chance.* There was no doubt in his mind who had betrayed them—the Lady Jessica. She fitted all the facts available.

"Your man Gurney Halleck and part of his force are safe with our smuggler friends," the Fremen said.

"Good."

*So Gurney will get off this hell planet. We're not all gone.*

Hawat glanced back at the huddle of his men. He had started the night just past with three hundred of his finest. Of those, an even twenty remained and half of them were wounded. Some of them slept now, standing up, leaning against the rock, sprawled on the sand beneath the rock. Their last 'thopter, the one they'd been using as a ground-effect machine to carry their wounded, had given out just before dawn. They had cut it up with lasguns and hidden the pieces, then worked their way down into this hiding place at the edge of the basin.

Hawat had only a rough idea of their location—some two hundred kilometers southeast of Arrakeen. The main traveled ways between the Shield Wall sietch communities were somewhere south of them.

The Fremen across from Hawat threw back his hood and stillsuit cap to reveal sandy hair and beard. The hair was combed straight back from a high, thin forehead. He had the unreadable total blue eyes of the spice diet. Beard and mustache were stained at one side of the mouth, his hair matted there by pressure of the looping catchtube from his nose plugs.

The man removed his plugs, readjusted them. He rubbed at a scar beside his nose.

"If you cross the sink here this night," the Fremen said, "you must not use shields. There is a break in the wall . . . ." He turned on his heels, pointed south. ". . . there, and it is open sand down to the erg. Shields will attract a . . . ." He hesitated. ". . . worm. They don't often come in here, but a shield will bring one every time."

*He said worm,* Hawat thought. *He was going to say something else. What? And what does he want of us?*

Hawat sighed.

He could not recall ever before being this tired. It was a muscle weariness that energy pills were unable to ease.

Those damnable Sardaukar!

With a self-accusing bitterness, he faced the thought of the soldier-fanatics and the Imperial treachery they represented. His own Mentat assessment of the data told him how little chance he had ever to present evidence of this treachery before the High Council of the Landsraad where justice might be done.

"Do you wish to go to the smugglers?" the Fremen asked.

"Is it possible?"

"The way is long."

*"Fremen don't like to say no,"* Idaho had told him once.

Hawat said: "You haven't told me whether your people can help my wounded."

"They are wounded."

*The same damned answer every time!*

"We know they're wounded!" Hawat snapped. "That's not the—"

"Peace, friend," the Fremen cautioned. "What do your wounded say? Are there those among them who can see the water need of your tribe?"

"We haven't talked about water," Hawat said. "We—"

"I can understand your reluctance," the Fremen said. "They are your friends, your tribesmen. Do you have water?"

"Not enough."

The Fremen gestured to Hawat's tunic, the skin exposed beneath it. "You were caught in-sietch, without your suits. You must make a water decision, friend."

"Can we hire your help?"

The Fremen shrugged. "You have no water." He glanced at the group behind Hawat. "How many of your wounded would you spend?"

Hawat fell silent, staring at the man. He could see as a Mentat that their communication was out of phase. Word-sounds were not being linked up here in the normal manner.

"I am Thufir Hawat," he said. "I can speak for my Duke. I will make promissory commitment now for your help. I wish a limited form of help, preserving my force long enough only to kill a traitor who thinks herself beyond vengeance."

"You wish our siding in a vendetta?"

"The vendetta I'll handle myself. I wish to be freed of responsibility for my wounded that I may get about it."

The Fremen scowled. "How can you be responsible for your wounded? They are their own responsibility. The water's at issue, Thufir Hawat. Would you have me take that decision away from you?"

The man put a hand to a weapon concealed beneath his robe.

Hawat tensed, wondering: *Is this betrayal here?*

"What do you fear?" the Fremen demanded.

*These people and their disconcerting directness!* Hawat spoke cautiously. "There's a price on my head."

"Ah-h-h-h." The Fremen removed his hand from his weapon. "You think we have the Byzantine corruption. You don't know us. The Harkonnens have not water enough to buy the smallest child among us."

*But they had the price of Guild passage for more than two thousand fighting ships,* Hawat thought. And the size of that price still staggered him.

"We both fight Harkonnens," Hawat said. "Should we not share the problems and ways of meeting the battle issue?"

"We are sharing," the Fremen said. "I have seen you fight Harkonnens. You are good. There've been times I'd have appreciated your arm beside me."

"Say where my arm may help you," Hawat said.

"Who knows?" the Fremen asked. "There are Harkonnen forces everywhere. But you still have not made the water decision or put it to your wounded."

*I must be cautious,* Hawat told himself. *There's a thing here that's not understood.*

He said: "Will you show me your way, the Arrakeen way?"

"Stranger-thinking," the Fremen said, and there was a sneer in his tone. He pointed to the northwest across the clifftop. "We watched you come across the sand last night." He lowered his arm. "You keep your force on the slipface of the dunes. Bad. You have no stillsuits, no water. You will not last long."

"The ways of Arrakis don't come easily," Hawat said.

"Truth. But we've killed Harkonnens."

"What do you do with your own wounded?" Hawat demanded.

"Does a man not know when he is worth saving?" the Fremen asked. "Your wounded know you have no water." He tilted his head, looking sideways up at Hawat. "This is clearly a time for water decision. Both wounded and unwounded must look to the tribe's future."

*The tribe's future,* Hawat thought. *The tribe of Atreides. There's sense in that.* He forced himself to the question he had been avoiding.

"Have you word of my Duke or his son?"

Unreadable blue eyes stared upward into Hawat's. "Word?"

"Their fate!" Hawat snapped.

"Fate is the same for everyone," the Fremen said. "Your Duke, it is said, has met his fate. As to the Lisan al-Gaib, his son, that is in Liet's hands. Liet has not said."

*I knew the answer without asking,* Hawat thought.

He glanced back at his men. They were all awake now. They had heard. They were staring out across the sand, the realization in their expressions: there was no returning to Caladan for them, and now Arrakis was lost.

Hawat turned back to the Fremen. "Have you heard of Duncan Idaho?"

"He was in the great house when the shield went down," the Fremen said. "This I've heard . . . no more."

*She dropped the shield and let in the Harkonnens,* he thought. *I was the one who sat with my back to a door. How could she do this when it meant turning against her own son? But . . . who knows how a Bene Gesserit witch thinks . . . if you can call it thinking?*

Hawat tried to swallow in a dry throat. "When will you hear about the boy?"

"We know little of what happens in Arrakeen," the Fremen said. He shrugged. "Who knows?"

"You have ways of finding out?"

"Perhaps." The Fremen rubbed at the scar beside his nose. "Tell me, Thufir

Hawat, do you have knowledge of the big weapons the Harkonnens used?"

*The artillery,* Hawat thought bitterly. *Who could have guessed they'd use artillery in this day of shields?*

"You refer to the artillery they used to trap our people in the caves," he said. "I've . . . theoretical knowledge of such explosive weapons."

"Any man who retreats into a cave which has only one opening deserves to die," the Fremen said. "Why do you ask about these weapons?"

"Liet wishes it."

*Is that what he wants from us?* Hawat wondered. He said: "Did you come here seeking information about the big guns?"

"Liet wished to see one of the weapons for himself."

"Then you should just go take one," Hawat sneered.

"Yes," the Fremen said. "We took one. We have it hidden where Stilgar can study it for Liet and where Liet can see it for himself if he wishes. But I doubt he'll want to: the weapon is not a very good one. Poor design for Arrakis."

"You . . . took one?" Hawat asked.

"It was a good fight," the Fremen said. "We lost only two men and spilled the water from more than a hundred of theirs."

*There were Sardaukar at every gun,* Hawat thought. *This desert madman speaks casually of losing only two men against Sardaukar!*

"We would not have lost the two except for those others fighting beside the Harkonnens," the Fremen said. "Some of those were good fighters."

One of Hawat's men limped forward, looked down at the squatting Fremen. "Are you talking about Sardaukar?"

"He's talking about Sardaukar," Hawat said.

"Sardaukar!" the Fremen said, and there appeared to be glee in his voice. "Ah-h-h, so that's what they are! This was a good night indeed. Sardaukar. Which legion? Do you know?"

"We . . . don't know," Hawat said.

"Sardaukar," the Fremen mused. "Yet they wear Harkonnen clothing. Is this not strange?"

"The Emperor does not wish it known he fights against a Great House," Hawat said.

"But *you* know they are Sardaukar."

"Who am I?" Hawat asked bitterly.

"You are Thufir Hawat," the man said matter-of-factly. "Well, we would have learned it in time. We've sent three of them captive to be questioned by Liet's men."

Hawat's aide spoke slowly, disbelief in every word: "You . . . *captured* Sardaukar?"

"Only three of them," the Fremen said. "They fought well."

*If only we'd had the time to link up with these Fremen,* Hawat thought. It was a sour lament in his mind. *If only we could've trained them and armed them. Great Mother, what a fighting force we'd have had!*

"Perhaps you delay because of worry over the Lisan al-Gaib," the Fremen said. "If he is truly the Lisan al-Gaib, harm cannot touch him. Do not spend thoughts on a matter which has not been proved."

"I serve the . . . Lisan al-Gaib," Hawat said. "His welfare is my concern. I've pledged myself to this."

"You are pledged to his water?"

Hawat glanced at his aide, who was still staring at the Fremen, returned his attention to the squatting figure. "To his water, yes."

"You wish to return to Arrakeen, to the place of his water?"

"To . . . yes, to the place of his water."

"Why did you not say at first it was a water matter?" The Fremen stood up, seated his nose plugs firmly.

Hawat motioned with his head for his aide to return to the others. With a tired shrug, the man obeyed. Hawat heard a low-voiced conversation arise among the men.

The Fremen said: "There is always a way to water."

Behind Hawat, a man cursed. Hawat's aide called: "Thufir! Arkie just died."

The Fremen put a fist to his ear. "The bond of water! It's a sign!" He stared at Hawat. "We have a place nearby for accepting the water. Shall I call my men?"

The aide returned to Hawat's side, said: "Thufir, a couple of the men left wives in Arrakeen. They're . . . well, you know how it is at a time like this."

The Fremen still held his fist to his ear. "Is it the bond of water, Thufir Hawat?" he demanded.

Hawat's mind was racing. He sensed now the direction of the Fremen's words, but feared the reaction of the tired men under the rock overhang when they understood it.

"The bond of water," Hawat said.

"Let our tribes be joined," the Fremen said, and he lowered his fist.

As though that were the signal, four men slid and dropped down from the rocks above them. They darted back under the overhang, rolled the dead man in a loose robe, lifted him and began running with him along the cliff wall to the right. Spurts of dust lifted around their running feet.

It was over before Hawat's tired men could gather their wits. The group with the body hanging like a sack in its enfolding robe was gone around a turn in the cliff.

One of Hawat's men shouted: "Where they going with Arkie? He was—"

"They're taking him to . . . bury him," Hawat said.

"Fremen don't bury their dead!" the man barked. "Don't you try any tricks on us, Thufir. We know what they do. Arkie was one of—"

"Paradise were sure for a man who died in the service of Lisan al-Gaib," the Fremen said. "If it is the Lisan al-Gaib you serve, as you have said it, why raise mourning cries? The memory of one who died in this fashion will live as long as the memory of man endures."

But Hawat's men advanced, angry looks on their faces. One had captured a lasgun. He started to draw it.

"Stop right where you are!" Hawat barked. He fought down the sick fatigue that gripped his muscles. "These people respect our dead. Customs differ, but the meaning's the same."

"They're going to render Arkie down for his water," the man with the lasgun snarled.

"Is it that your men wish to attend the ceremony?" the Fremen asked.

*He doesn't even see the problem*, Hawat thought. The naïveté of the Fremen was frightening.

"They're concerned for a respected comrade," Hawat said.

"We will treat your comrade with the same reverence we treat our own," the Fremen said. "This is the bond of water. We know the rites. A man's flesh is his own; the water belongs to the tribe."

Hawat spoke quickly as the man with the lasgun advanced another step. "Will you now help our wounded?"

"One does not question the bond," the Fremen said. "We will do for you what a tribe does for its own. First, we must get all of you suited and see to the necessities."

The man with the lasgun hesitated.

Hawat's aide said: "Are we buying help with Arkie's . . . water?"

"Not buying," Hawat said. "We've joined these people."

"Customs differ," one of his men muttered.

Hawat began to relax.

"And they'll help us get to Arrakeen?"

"We will kill Harkonnens," the Fremen said. He grinned. "And Sardaukar." He stepped backward, cupped his hands beside his ears and tipped his head back, listening. Presently, he lowered his hands, said: "An aircraft comes. Conceal yourselves beneath the rock and remain motionless."

At a gesture from Hawat, his men obeyed.

The Fremen took Hawat's arm, pressed him back with the others. "We will fight in the time of fighting," the man said. He reached beneath his robes, brought out a small cage, lifted a creature from it.

Hawat recognized a tiny bat. The bat turned its head and Hawat saw its blue-within-blue eyes.

The Fremen stroked the bat, soothing it, crooning to it. He bent over the animal's head, allowed a drop of saliva to fall from his tongue into the bat's upturned mouth. The bat stretched its wings, but remained on the Fremen's open hand. The man took a tiny tube, held it beside the bat's head and chattered into the tube; then, lifting the creature high, he threw it upward.

The bat swooped away beside the cliff and was lost to sight.

The Fremen folded the cage, thrust it beneath his robe. Again, he bent his head, listening. "They quarter the high country," he said. "One wonders who they seek up there."

"It's known that we retreated this direction," Hawat said.

"One should never presume one is the sole object of a hunt," the Fremen said. "Watch the other side of the basin. You will see a thing."

Time passed.

Some of Hawat's men stirred, whispering.

"Remain silent as frightened animals," the Fremen hissed.

Hawat discerned movement near the opposite cliff—flitting blurs of tan on tan.

"My little friend carried his message," the Fremen said. "He is a good messenger—day or night. I'll be unhappy to lose that one."

The movement across the sink faded away. On the entire four to five kilometer expanse of sand nothing remained but the growing pressure of the day's heat—blurred columns of rising air.

"Be most silent now," the Fremen whispered.

A file of plodding figures emerged from a break in the opposite cliff, headed directly across the sink. To Hawat, they appeared to be Fremen, but a curiously inept band. He counted six men making heavy going of it over the dunes.

A "thwok-thwok" of ornithopter wings sounded high to the right behind Hawat's group. The craft came over the cliff wall above them—an Atreides 'thopter with Harkonnen battle colors splashed on it. The 'thopter swooped toward the men crossing the sink.

The group there stopped on a dune crest, waved.

The 'thopter circled once over them in a tight curve, came back for a dust-shrouded landing in front of the Fremen. Five men swarmed from the 'thopter and Hawat saw the dust-repellent shimmering of shields and, in their motions, the hard competence of Sardaukar.

"Aiihh! They use their stupid shields," the Fremen beside Hawat hissed. He glanced toward the open south wall of the sink.

"They are Sardaukar," Hawat whispered.

"Good."

The Sardaukar approached the waiting group of Fremen in an enclosing half-circle. Sun glinted on blades held ready. The Fremen stood in a compact group, apparently indifferent.

Abruptly, the sand around the two groups sprouted Fremen. They were at the ornithopter, then in it. Where the two groups had met at the dune crest, a dust cloud partly obscured violent motion.

Presently, dust settled. Only Fremen remained standing.

"They left only three men in their 'thopter," the Fremen beside Hawat said. "That was fortunate. I don't believe we had to damage the craft in taking it."

Behind Hawat, one of his men whispered: "Those were Sardaukar!"

"Did you notice how well they fought?" the Fremen asked.

Hawat took a deep breath. He smelled the burned dust around him, felt the heat, the dryness. In a voice to match that dryness, he said: "Yes, they fought well, indeed."

The captured 'thopter took off with a lurching flap of wings, angled upward to the south in a steep, wing-tucked climb.

*So these Fremen can handle 'thopters, too,* Hawat thought.

On the distant dune, a Fremen waved a square of green cloth: once . . . twice.

"More come!" the Fremen beside Hawat barked. "Be ready. I'd hoped to have us away without more inconvenience."

*Inconvenience!* Hawat thought.

He saw two more 'thopters swooping from high in the west onto an area of sand suddenly devoid of visible Fremen. Only eight splotches of blue—the bodies of the Sardaukar in Harkonnen uniforms—remained at the scene of violence.

Another 'thopter glided in over the cliff wall above Hawat. He drew in a sharp breath as he saw it—a big troop carrier. It flew with the slow, spreading-wing heaviness of a full load—like a giant bird coming to its nest.

In the distance, the purple finger of a lasgun beam flicked from one of the diving 'thopters. It laced across the sand, raising a sharp trail of dust.

"The cowards!" the Fremen beside Hawat rasped.

The troop carrier settled toward the patch of blue-clad bodies. Its wings crept out to full reach, began the cupping action of a quick stop.

Hawat's attention was caught by a flash of sun on metal to the south, a 'thopter plummeting there in a power dive, wings folded flat against its sides, its jets a golden flare against the dark silvered gray of the sky. It plunged like an arrow toward the troop carrier which was unshielded because of the lasgun activity around it. Straight into the carrier the diving 'thopter plunged.

A flaming roar shook the basin. Rocks tumbled from the cliff walls all around. A geyser of red-orange shot skyward from the sand where the carrier and its companion 'thopters had been—everything there caught in the flame.

*It was the Fremen who took off in that captured 'thopter,* Hawat thought. *He deliberately sacrificed himself to get that carrier. Great Mother! What are these Fremen?*

"A reasonable exchange," said the Fremen beside Hawat. "There must've been three hundred men in that carrier. Now, we must see to their water and make plans to get another aircraft." He started to step out of their rock-shadowed concealment.

A rain of blue uniforms came over the cliff wall in front of him, falling in low-suspensor slowness. In the flashing instant, Hawat had time to see that they were Sardaukar, hard faces set in battle frenzy, that they were unshielded and each carried a knife in one hand, a stunner in the other.

A thrown knife caught Hawat's Fremen companion in the throat, hurling him backward, twisting face down. Hawat had only time to draw his own knife before blackness of a stunner projectile felled him.

> *Muad'Dib could, indeed, see the Future, but you must understand the limits of this power. Think of sight. You have eyes, yet cannot see without light. If you are on the floor of a valley, you cannot see beyond your valley. Just so, Muad'Dib could not always choose to look across the mysterious terrain. He tells us, that a single obscure decision of prophecy, perhaps the choice of one word over another, could change the entire aspect of the future. He tells us "The vision of time is broad, but when you pass through it, time becomes a narrow door." And always he fought the temptation to choose a clear, safe course, warning "That path leads ever down into stagnation."*
>
> **—from "Arrakis Awakening" by the Princess Irulan**

As the ornithopters glided out of the night above them, Paul grabbed his mother's arm, snapped: "Don't move!"

Then he saw the lead craft in the moonlight, the way its wings cupped to brake for landing, the reckless dash of the hands at the controls.

"It's Idaho," he breathed.

The craft and its companions settled into the basin like a covey of birds coming to nest. Idaho was out of his 'thopter and running toward them before the dust settled. Two figures in Fremen robes followed him. Paul recognized one: the tall, sandy-bearded Kynes.

"This way!" Kynes called and he veered left.

Behind Kynes, other Fremen were throwing fabric covers over their ornithopters. The craft became a row of shallow dunes.

Idaho skidded to a stop in front of Paul, saluted. "M'Lord, the Fremen have a temporary hiding place nearby where we—"

"What about that back there?"

Paul pointed to the violence above the distant cliff—the jetflares, the purple beams of lasguns lacing the desert.

A rare smile touched Idaho's round, placid face. "M'Lord . . . Sire, I've left them a little sur—"

Glaring white light filled the desert—bright as a sun, etching their shadows onto the rock floor of the ledge. In one sweeping motion, Idaho had Paul's arm in one hand, Jessica's shoulder in the other, hurling them down off the ledge into the basin. They sprawled together in the sand as the roar of an explosion thundered over them. Its shock wave tumbled chips off the rock ledge they had vacated.

Idaho sat up, brushed sand from himself.

"Not the family atomics!" Jessica said. "I thought—"

"You planted a shield back there," Paul said.

"A big one turned to full force," Idaho said. "A lasgun beam touched it and . . . ." He shrugged.

"Subatomic fusion," Jessica said. "That's a dangerous weapon."

"Not weapon, m'Lady, defense. That scum will think twice before using lasguns another time."

The Fremen from the ornithopters stopped above them. One called in a low voice: "We should get under cover, friends."

Paul got to his feet as Idaho helped Jessica up.

"That blast *will* attract considerable attention, Sire," Idaho said.

*Sire,* Paul thought.

The word had such a strange sound when directed at him. Sire had always been his father.

He felt himself touched briefly by his powers of prescience, seeing himself infected by the wild race consciousness that was moving the human universe toward chaos. The vision left him shaken, and he allowed Idaho to guide him along the edge of the basin to a rock projection. Fremen there were opening a way down into the sand with their compaction tools.

"May I take your pack, Sire?" Idaho asked.

"It's not heavy, Duncan," Paul said.

"You have no body shield," Idaho said. "Do you wish mine?" He glanced at the distant cliff. "Not likely there'll be any more lasgun activity about."

"Keep your shield, Duncan. Your right arm is shield enough for me."

Jessica saw the way the praise took effect, how Idaho moved closer to Paul, and she thought: *Such a sure hand my son has with his people.*

The Fremen removed a rock plug that opened a passage down into the native basement complex of the desert. A camouflage cover was rigged for the opening.

"This way," one of the Fremen said, and he led them down rock steps into darkness.

Behind them, the cover blotted out the moonlight. A dim green glow came alive ahead, revealing the steps and rock walls, a turn to the left. Robed Fremen were all around them now, pressing downward. They rounded the corner, found another down-slanting passage. It opened into a rough cave chamber.

Kynes stood before them, jubba hood thrown back. The neck of his stillsuit glistening in the green light. His long hair and beard were mussed. The blue eyes without whites were a darkness under heavy brows.

In the moment of encounter, Kynes wondered at himself: *Why am I helping these people? It's the most dangerous thing I've ever done. It could doom me with them.*

Then he looked squarely at Paul, seeing the boy who had taken on the mantle of manhood, masking grief, suppressing all except the position that now must be assumed—the dukedom. And Kynes realized in that moment the dukedom still existed and solely because of this youth—and this was not a thing to be taken lightly.

Jessica glanced once around the chamber, registering it on her senses in the Bene Gesserit way—a laboratory, a civil place full of angles and squares in the ancient manner.

"This is one of the Imperial Ecological Testing Stations my father wanted as advance bases," Paul said.

*His father wanted!* Kynes thought.

And again Kynes wondered at himself. *Am I foolish to aid these fugitives? Why am I doing it? It'd be so easy to take them now, to buy the Harkonnen trust with them.*

Paul followed his mother's example, gestalting the room, seeing the workbench down one side, the walls of featureless rock. Instruments lined the bench—dials glowing, wire gridex planes with fluting glass emerging from them. An ozone smell permeated the place.

Some of the Fremen moved on around a concealing angle in the chamber and new sounds started there—machine coughs, the whinnies of spinning belts and multidrives.

Paul looked to the end of the room, saw cages with small animals in them stacked against the wall.

"You've recognized this place correctly," Kynes said. "For what would you use such a place, Paul Atreides?"

"To make this planet a fit place for humans," Paul said.

*Perhaps that's why I help them,* Kynes thought.

The machine sounds abruptly hummed away to silence. Into this void there came a thin animal squeak from the cages. It was cut off abruptly as though in embarrassment.

Paul returned his attention to the cages, saw that the animals were brown-winged bats. An automatic feeder extended from the side wall across the cages.

A Fremen emerged from the hidden area of the chamber, spoke to Kynes: "Liet, the field-generator equipment is not working. I am unable to mask us from proximity detectors."

"Can you repair it?" Kynes asked.

"Not quickly. The parts . . . ." The man shrugged.

"Yes," Kynes said. "Then we'll do without machinery. Get a hand pump for air out to the surface."

"Immediately." The man hurried away.

Kynes turned back to Paul. "You gave a good answer."

Jessica marked the easy rumble of the man's voice. It was a *royal* voice, accustomed to command. And she had not missed the reference to him as Liet. Liet was the Fremen alter ego, the other face of the tame planetologist.

"We're most grateful for your help, Doctor Kynes," she said.

"Mm-m-m, we'll see," Kynes said. He nodded to one of his men. "Spice coffee in my quarters, Shamir."

"At once, Liet," the man said.

Kynes indicated an arched opening in a side wall of the chamber. "If you please?"

Jessica allowed herself a regal nod before accepting. She saw Paul give a hand signal to Idaho, telling him to mount guard here.

The passage, two paces deep, opened through a heavy door into a square office lighted by golden glowglobes. Jessica passed her hand across the door as she entered, was startled to identify plasteel.

Paul stepped three paces into the room, dropped his pack to the floor. He heard the door close behind him, studied the place—about eight meters to a side, walls of natural rock, curry-colored, broken by metal filing cabinets on their right. A low desk with milk glass top shot full of yellow bubbles occupied the room's center. Four suspensor chairs ringed the desk.

Kynes moved around Paul, held a chair for Jessica. She sat down, noting the way her son examined the room.

Paul remained standing for another eyeblink. A faint anomaly in the room's air currents told him there was a secret exit to their right behind the filing cabinets.

"Will you sit down, Paul Atreides?" Kynes asked.

*How carefully he avoids my title,* Paul thought. But he accepted the chair, remained silent while Kynes sat down.

"You sense that Arrakis could be a paradise," Kynes said. "Yet, as you see, the Imperium sends here only its trained hatchetmen, its seekers after the spice!"

Paul held up his thumb with its ducal signet. "Do you see this ring?"

"Yes."

"Do you know its significance?"

Jessica turned sharply to stare at her son.

"Your father lies dead in the ruins of Arrakeen," Kynes said. "You are technically the Duke."

"I'm a soldier of the Imperium," Paul said, "*technically* a hatchetman."

Kynes' face darkened. "Even with the Emperor's Sardaukar standing over your father's body?"

"The Sardaukar are one thing, the legal source of my authority is another," Paul said.

"Arrakis has its own way of determining who wears the mantle of authority," Kynes said.

And Jessica, turning back to look at him, thought: *There's steel in this man that no one has taken the temper out of . . . and we've need of steel. Paul's doing a dangerous thing.*

Paul said: "The Sardaukar on Arrakis are a measure of how much our beloved Emperor feared my father. Now, *I* will give the Padishah Emperor reasons to fear the—"

"Lad," Kynes said, "there are things you don't—"

"You will address me as Sire or my Lord," Paul said.

*Gently,* Jessica thought.

Kynes stared at Paul, and Jessica noted the glint of admiration in the planetologist's face, the touch of humor there.

"Sire," Kynes said.

"I am an embarrassment to the Emperor," Paul said. "I am an embarrassment to all who would divide Arrakis as their spoil. As I live, I shall continue to be such an embarrassment that I stick in their throats and choke them to death!"

"Words," Kynes said.

Paul stared at him. Presently, Paul said: "You have a legend of the Lisan al-Gaib here, the Voice from the Outer World, the one who will lead the Fremen to paradise. Your men have—"

"Superstition!" Kynes said.

"Perhaps," Paul agreed. "Yet perhaps not. Superstitions sometimes have strange roots and stranger branchings."

"You have a plan," Kynes said. "This much is obvious . . . *Sire.*"

"Could your Fremen provide me with proof positive that the Sardaukar are here in Harkonnen uniform?"

"Quite likely."

"The Emperor will put a Harkonnen back in power here," Paul said. "Perhaps even Beast Rabban. Let him. Once he has involved himself beyond escaping his guilt, let the Emperor face the possibility of a Bill of Particulars laid before the Landsraad. Let him answer there where—"

"Paul!" said Jessica.

"Granted that the Landsraad High Council accepts your case," Kynes said, "there could be only one outcome: general warfare between the Imperium and the Great Houses."

"Chaos," Jessica said.

"But I'd present my case to the Emperor," Paul said, "and give him an alternative to chaos."

Jessica spoke in a dry tone: "Blackmail?"

"One of the tools of statecraft, as you've said yourself," Paul said, and Jessica heard the bitterness in his voice. "The Emperor has no sons, only daughters."

"You'd aim for the throne?" Jessica asked.

"The Emperor will not risk having the Imperium shattered by total war," Paul said. "Planets blasted, disorder everywhere—he'll not risk that."

"This is a desperate gamble you propose," Kynes said.

"What do the Great Houses of the Landsraad fear most?" Paul asked. "They fear most what is happening here right now on Arrakis—the Sardaukar picking them off one by one. That's why there *is* a Landsraad. This is the glue of the Great Convention. Only in union do they match the Imperial forces."

"But they're—"

"This is what they fear," Paul said. "Arrakis would become a rallying cry. Each of them would see himself in my father—cut out of the herd and killed."

Kynes spoke to Jessica: "Would his plan work?"

"I'm no Mentat," Jessica said.

"But you are Bene Gesserit."

She shot a probing stare at him, said: "His plan has good points and bad points . . . as any plan would at this stage. A plan depends as much upon execution as it does upon concept."

"'Law is the ultimate science,'" Paul quoted. "Thus it reads above the Emperor's door. I propose to show him law."

"And I'm not sure I could trust the person who conceived this plan," Kynes said. "Arrakis has its own plan that we—"

"From the throne," Paul said, "I could make a paradise of Arrakis with the wave of a hand. This is the coin I offer for your support."

Kynes stiffened. "My loyalty's not for sale, *Sire*."

Paul stared across the desk at him, meeting the cold glare of those blue-within-blue eyes, studying the bearded face, the commanding appearance. A harsh smile touched Paul's lips and he said: "Well spoken. I apologize."

Kynes met Paul's stare and, presently, said: "No Harkonnen ever admitted error. Perhaps you're not like them, Atreides."

"It could be a fault in their education," Paul said. "You say you're not for sale, but I believe I've the coin you'll accept. For your loyalty I offer *my* loyalty to you . . . totally."

*My son has the Atreides sincerity,* Jessica thought. *He has that tremendous, almost naïve honor—and what a powerful force that truly is.*

She saw that Paul's words had shaken Kynes.

"This is nonsense," Kynes said. "You're just a boy and—"

"I'm the Duke," Paul said. "I'm an Atreides. No Atreides has ever broken such a bond."

Kynes swallowed.

"When I say totally," Paul said, "I mean without reservation. I would give my life for you."

"Sire!" Kynes said, and the word was torn from him, but Jessica saw that he was not now speaking to a boy of fifteen, but to a man, to a superior. Now Kynes meant the word.

*In this moment he'd give his life for Paul,* she thought. *How do the Atreides accomplish this so quickly, so easily?*

"I know you mean this," Kynes said. "Yet the Harkon—"

The door behind Paul slammed open. He whirled to see reeling violence—shouting, the clash of steel, wax-image faces grimacing in the passage.

With his mother beside him, Paul leaped for the door, seeing Idaho blocking the passage, his blood-pitted eyes there visible through a shield blur, claw hands beyond him, arcs of steel chopping futilely at the shield. There was the orange fire-mouth of a stunner repelled by the shield. Idaho's blades were through it all, flick-flicking, red dripping from them.

Then Kynes was beside Paul and they threw their weight against the door.

Paul had one last glimpse of Idaho standing against a swarm of Harkonnen uniforms—his jerking, controlled staggers, the black goat hair with a red blossom of death in it. Then the door was closed and there came a snick as Kynes threw the bolts.

"I appear to've decided," Kynes said.

"Someone detected your machinery before it was shut down," Paul said. He pulled his mother away from the door, met the despair in her eyes.

"I should've suspected trouble when the coffee failed to arrive," Kynes said.

"You've a bolt hole out of here," Paul said. "Shall we use it?"

Kynes took a deep breath, said: "This door should hold for at least twenty minutes against all but a lasgun."

"They'll not use a lasgun for fear we've shields on this side," Paul said.

"Those were Sardaukar in Harkonnen uniform," Jessica whispered.

They could hear pounding on the door now, rhythmic blows.

Kynes indicated the cabinets against the right-hand wall, said: "This way." He crossed to the first cabinet, opened a drawer, manipulated a handle within it. The entire wall of cabinets swung open to expose the black mouth of a tunnel. "This door also is plasteel," Kynes said.

"You were well prepared," Jessica said.

"We lived under the Harkonnens for eighty years," Kynes said. He herded them into the darkness, closed the door.

In the sudden blackness, Jessica saw a luminous arrow on the floor ahead of her.

Kynes' voice came from behind them: "We'll separate here. This wall is tougher. It'll stand for at least an hour. Follow the arrows like that one on the floor. They'll be extinguished by your passage. They lead through a maze to another exit where I've secreted a 'thopter. There's a storm across the desert tonight. Your only hope is to run for that storm, dive into the top of it, ride with it. My people have done this in stealing 'thopters. If you stay high in the storm you'll survive."

"What of you?" Paul asked.

"I'll try to escape another way. If I'm captured . . . well, I'm still Imperial Planetologist. I can say I was your captive."

*Running like cowards,* Paul thought. *But how else can I live to avenge my father?* He turned to face the door.

Jessica heard him move, said: "Duncan's dead, Paul. You saw the wound. You can do nothing for him."

"I'll take full payment for them all one day," Paul said.

"Not unless you hurry now," Kynes said.

Paul felt the man's hand on his shoulder.

"Where will we meet, Kynes?" Paul asked.

"I'll send the Fremen searching for you. The storm's path is known. Hurry now, and the Great Mother give you speed and luck."

They heard him go, a scrambling in the blackness.

Jessica found Paul's hand, pulled him gently. "We must not get separated," she said.

"Yes."

He followed her across the first arrow, seeing it go black as they touched it. Another arrow beckoned ahead.

They crossed it, saw it extinguish itself, saw another arrow ahead.

They were running now.

*Plans within plans within plans within plans,* Jessica thought. *Have we become part of someone else's plan now?*

The arrows led them around turnings, past side openings only dimly sensed in the faint luminescence. Their way slanted downward for a time, then up, ever up. They came finally to steps, rounded a corner and were brought short by a glowing wall with a dark handle visible in its center.

Paul pressed the handle.

The wall swung away from them. Light flared to reveal a rock-hewn cavern with an ornithopter squatting in its center. A flat gray wall with a doorsign on it loomed beyond the aircraft.

"Where did Kynes go?" Jessica asked.

"He did what any good guerrilla leader would," Paul said. "He separated us into two parties and arranged that he couldn't reveal where we are if he's captured. He won't really know."

Paul drew her into the room, noting how their feet kicked up dust on the floor.

"No one's been here for a long time," he said.

"He seemed confident the Fremen could find us," she said.

"I share that confidence."

Paul released her hand, crossed to the ornithopter's left door, opened it, and secured his pack in the rear. "This ship's proximity masked," he said. "Instrument panel has remote door control, light control. Eighty years under the Harkonnens taught them to be thorough."

Jessica leaned against the craft's other side, catching her breath.

"The Harkonnens will have a covering force over this area," she said. "They're not stupid." She considered her direction sense, pointed right. "The storm we saw is that way."

Paul nodded, fighting an abrupt reluctance to move. He knew its cause, but found no help in the knowledge. Somewhere this night he had passed a decision-nexus into the deep unknown. He knew the time-area surrounding them, but the here-and-now existed as a place of mystery. It was as though he had seen himself from a distance go out of sight down into a valley. Of the countless paths up out of that valley, some might carry a Paul Atreides back into sight, but many would not.

"The longer we wait the better prepared they'll be," Jessica said.

"Get in and strap yourself down," he said.

He joined her in the ornithopter, still wrestling with the thought that this was *blind* ground, unseen in any prescient vision. And he realized with an abrupt sense of shock that he had been giving more and more reliance to prescient memory and it had weakened him for this particular emergency.

"If you rely only on your eyes, your other senses weaken." It was a Bene Gesserit axiom. He took it to himself now, promising never again to fall into that trap . . . if he lived through this.

Paul fastened his safety harness, saw that his mother was secure, checked the aircraft. The wings were at full spread-rest, their delicate metal interleavings extended. He touched the retractor bar, watched the wings shorten for jet-boost take-off the way Gurney Halleck had taught him. The starter switch moved easily. Dials on the instrument panel came alive as the jetpods were armed. Turbines began their low hissing.

"Ready?" he asked.

"Yes."

He touched the remote control for lights.

Darkness blanketed them.

His hand was a shadow against the luminous dials as he tripped the remote door control. Grating sounded ahead of them. A cascade of sand swished away to silence. A dusty breeze touched Paul's cheeks. He closed his door, feeling the sudden pressure.

A wide patch of dust-blurred stars framed in angular darkness appeared where the door-wall had been. Starlight defined a shelf beyond, a suggestion of sand ripples.

Paul depressed the glowing action-sequence switch on his panel. The wings snapped back and down, hurling the 'thopter out of its nest. Power surged from the jetpods as the wings locked into lift attitude.

Jessica let her hands ride lightly on the dual controls, feeling the sureness of her son's movements. She was frightened, yet exhilarated. *Now, Paul's training is our only hope,* she thought. *His youth and swiftness.*

Paul fed more power to the jetpods. The 'thopter banked, sinking them into their seats as a dark wall lifted against the stars ahead. He gave the craft more wing, more power. Another burst of lifting wingbeats and they came out over rocks, silver-frosted angles and outcroppings in the starlight. The dust-reddened second moon showed itself above the horizon to their right, defining the ribbon trail of the storm.

Paul's hands danced over the controls. Wings snicked in to beetle stubs. G-force pulled at their flesh as the craft came around in a tight bank.

"Jetflares behind us!" Jessica said.

"I saw them."

He slammed the power arm forward.

Their 'thopter leaped like a frightened animal, surged southwest toward the storm and the great curve of desert. In the near distance, Paul saw scattered shadows telling where the line of rocks ended, the basement complex sinking beneath the dunes. Beyond stretched moonlit fingernail shadows—dunes diminishing one into another.

And above the horizon climbed the flat immensity of the storm like a wall against the stars.

Something jarred the 'thopter.

"Shellburst!" Jessica gasped. "They're using some kind of projectile weapon."

She saw a sudden animal grin on Paul's face. "They seem to be avoiding their lasguns," he said.

"But we've no shields!"

"Do they know that?"

Again the 'thopter shuddered.

Paul twisted to peer back. "Only one of them appears to be fast enough to keep up with us."

He returned his attention to their course, watching the storm wall grow high in front of them. It loomed like a tangible solid.

"Projectile launchers, rockets, all the ancient weaponry—that's one thing we'll give the Fremen," Paul whispered.

"The storm," Jessica said. "Hadn't you better turn?"

"What about the ship behind us?"

"He's pulling up."

"Now!"

Paul stubbed the wings, banked hard left into the deceptively slow boiling of the storm wall, felt his cheeks pull in the G-force.

They appeared to glide into a slow clouding of dust that grew heavier and heavier until it blotted out the desert and the moon. The aircraft became a long, horizontal whisper of darkness lighted only by the green luminosity of the instrument panel.

Through Jessica's mind flashed all the warnings about such storms—that they cut metal like butter, etched flesh to bone and ate away the bones. She felt the buffeting of dust-blanketed wind. It twisted them as Paul fought the controls. She saw him chop the power, felt the ship buck. The metal around them hissed and trembled.

"Sand!" Jessica shouted.

She saw the negative shake of his head in the light from the panel. "Not much sand this high."

But she could feel them sinking deeper into the maelstrom.

Paul sent the wings to their full soaring length, heard them creak with the strain. He kept his eyes fixed on the instruments, gliding by instinct, fighting for altitude.

The sound of their passage diminished.

The 'thopter began rolling off to the left. Paul focused on the glowing globe within the attitude curve, fought his craft back to level flight.

Jessica had the eerie feeling that they were standing still, that all motion was external. A vague tan flowing against the windows, a rumbling hiss reminded her of the powers around them.

*Winds to seven or eight hundred kilometers an hour,* she thought. Adrenalin edginess gnawed at her. *I must not fear,* she told herself, mouthing the words of the Bene Gesserit litany. *Fear is the mind-killer.*

Slowly her long years of training prevailed.

Calmness returned.

"We have the tiger by the tail," Paul whispered. "We can't go down, can't land . . . and I don't think I can lift us out of this. We'll have to ride it out."

Calmness drained out of her. Jessica felt her teeth chattering, clamped them together. Then she heard Paul's voice, low and controlled, reciting the litany:

"Fear is the mind-killer. Fear is the little death that brings total obliteration. I will face my fear. I will permit it to pass over me and through me. And when it has gone past me I will turn to see fear's path. Where the fear has gone there will be nothing. Only I will remain."

*What do you despise? By this are you truly known.*

**—from "Manual of Muad'Dib" by the Princess Irulan**

"They are dead, Baron," said Iakin Nefud, the guard captain. "Both the woman and the boy are certainly dead."

The Baron Vladimir Harkonnen sat up in the sleep suspensors of his private quarters. Beyond these quarters and enclosing him like a multishelled egg stretched the space frigate he had grounded on Arrakis. Here in his quarters, though, the ship's harsh metal was disguised with draperies, with fabric paddings and rare art objects.

"It is a certainty," the guard captain said. "They are dead."

The Baron shifted his gross body in the suspensors, focused his attention on an ebaline statue of a leaping boy in a niche across the room. Sleep faded from him. He straightened the padded suspensor beneath the fat folds of his neck, stared across the single glowglobe of his bedchamber to the doorway where Captain Nefud stood blocked by the pentashield.

"They're certainly dead, Baron," the man repeated.

The Baron noted the trace of semuta dullness in Nefud's eyes. It was obvious the man had been deep within the drug's rapture when he received this report, and had stopped only to take the antidote before rushing here.

"I have a full report," Nefud said.

*Let him sweat a little,* the Baron thought. *One must always keep the tools of statecraft sharp and ready. Power and fear—sharp and ready.*

"Have you seen their bodies?" the Baron rumbled.

Nefud hesitated.

"Well?"

"M'Lord . . . they were seen to dive into a sandstorm . . . winds over eight hundred kilometers. Nothing survives such a storm, m'Lord. Nothing! One of our own craft was destroyed in the pursuit."

The Baron stared at Nefud, noting the nervous twitch in the scissors line of the man's jaw muscles, the way the chin moved as Nefud swallowed.

"You have seen the bodies?" the Baron asked.

"M'Lord—"

"For what purpose do you come here rattling your armor?" the Baron roared. "To tell me a thing is certain when it is not? Do you think I'll praise you for such stupidity, give you another promotion?"

Nefud's face went bone pale.

*Look at that chicken,* the Baron thought. *I am surrounded by such useless clods. If I scattered sand before this creature and told him it was grain, he'd peck at it.*

"The man Idaho led us to them, then?" the Baron asked.

"Yes, m'Lord!"

*Look how he blurts out his answer,* the Baron thought. He said: "They were attempting to flee to the Fremen, eh?"

"Yes, m'Lord."

"Is there more to this . . . report?"

"The Imperial Planetologist, Kynes, is involved, m'Lord. Idaho joined this Kynes under mysterious circumstances . . . I might even say *suspicious* circumstances."

"So?"

"They . . . ah, fled together to a place in the desert where it's apparent the boy and his mother were hiding. In the excitement of the chase, several of our groups were caught in a lasgun-shield explosion."

"How many did we lose?"

"I'm . . . ah, not sure yet, m'Lord."

*He's lying,* the Baron thought. *It must've been pretty bad.*

"The Imperial lackey, this Kynes," the Baron said. "He was playing a double game, eh?"

"I'd stake my reputation on it, m'Lord."

*His reputation!*

"Have the man killed," the Baron said.

"M'Lord! Kynes is the *Imperial* Planetologist, His Majesty's own serv—"

"Make it look like an accident, then!"

"M'Lord, there were Sardaukar with our forces in the subjugation of this Fremen nest. They have Kynes in custody now."

"Get him away from them. Say I wish to question him."

"If they demur?"

"They will not if you handle it correctly."

Nefud swallowed. "Yes, m'Lord."

"The man must die," the Baron rumbled. "He tried to help my enemies."

Nefud shifted from one foot to the other.

"Well?"

"M'Lord, the Sardaukar have . . . two persons in custody who might be of interest to you. They've caught the Duke's Master of Assassins."

"Hawat? Thufir Hawat?"

"I've seen the captive myself, m'Lord. 'Tis Hawat."

"I'd not've believed it possible!"

"They say he was knocked out by a stunner, m'Lord. In the desert where he couldn't use his shield. He's virtually unharmed. If we can get our hands on him, he'll provide great sport."

"This is a Mentat you speak of," the Baron growled. "One doesn't waste a Mentat. Has he spoken? What does he say of his defeat? Could he know the extent of . . . but no."

"He has spoken only enough, m'Lord, to reveal his belief that the Lady Jessica was his betrayer."

"Ah-h-h-h-h."

The Baron sank back, thinking; then: "You're sure? It's the Lady Jessica who attracts his anger?"

"He said it in my presence, m'Lord."

"Let him think she's alive, then."

"But, m'Lord—"

"Be quiet. I wish Hawat treated kindly. He must be told nothing of the late Doctor Yueh, his true betrayer. Let it be said that Doctor Yueh died defending his Duke. In a way, this may even be true. We will, instead, feed his suspicions against the Lady Jessica."

"M'Lord, I don't—"

"The way to control and direct a Mentat, Nefud, is through his information. False information—false results."

"Yes, m'Lord, but . . . ."

"Is Hawat hungry? Thirsty?"

"M'Lord, Hawat's still in the hands of the Sardaukar!"

"Yes. Indeed, yes. But the Sardaukar will be as anxious to get information from Hawat as I am. I've noticed a thing about our allies, Nefud. They're not very devious . . . politically. I do believe this is a deliberate thing; the Emperor wants it that way. Yes. I do believe it. You will remind the Sardaukar commander of my renown at obtaining information from reluctant subjects."

Nefud looked unhappy. "Yes, m'Lord."

"You will tell the Sardaukar commander that I wish to question both Hawat and this Kynes at the same time, playing one off against the other. He can understand that much, I think."

"Yes, m'Lord."

"And once we have them in our hands . . . ." The Baron nodded.

"M'Lord, the Sardaukar will want an observer with you during any . . . questioning."

"I'm sure we can produce an emergency to draw off any unwanted observers, Nefud."

"I understand, m'Lord. That's when Kynes can have his accident."

"Both Kynes and Hawat will have accidents then, Nefud. But only Kynes will have a real accident. It's Hawat I want. Ah, yes."

Nefud blinked, swallowed. He appeared about to ask a question, but remained silent.

"Hawat will be given both food and drink," the Baron said. "Treated with kindness, with sympathy. In his water you will administer the residual poison developed by the late Piter de Vried. *And* you will see that the antidote becomes a regular part of Hawat's diet from this point on . . . unless I say otherwise."

"The antidote, yes." Nefud shook his head. "But—"

"Don't be dense, Nefud. The Duke almost killed me with that poison-capsule tooth. The gas he exhaled into my presence deprived me of my most valuable Mentat, Piter. I need a replacement."

"Hawat?"

"Hawat."

"But—"

"You're going to say Hawat's completely loyal to the Atreides. True, but the Atreides are dead. We will woo him. He must be convinced he's not to blame for the Duke's demise. It was all the doing of that Bene Gesserit witch. He had an inferior master, one whose reason was clouded by emotion. Mentats admire the ability to calculate without emotion, Nefud. We will woo the formidable Thufir Hawat."

"Woo him. Yes, m'Lord."

"Hawat, unfortunately, had a master whose resources were poor, one who could not elevate a Mentat to the sublime peaks of reasoning that are a Mentat's right. Hawat will see a certain element of truth in this. The Duke couldn't afford the most efficient spies to provide his Mentat with the required information." The Baron stared at Nefud. "Let us never deceive ourselves, Nefud. The truth is a powerful weapon. We know how we overwhelmed the Atreides. Hawat knows, too. We did it with wealth."

"With wealth. Yes, m'Lord."

"We will woo Hawat," the Baron said. "We will hide him from the Sardaukar. And we will hold in reserve . . . the withdrawal of the antidote for the poison. There's no way of removing the residual poison. And, Nefud, Hawat need never suspect. The antidote will not betray itself to a poison snooper. Hawat can scan his food as he pleases and detect no trace of poison."

Nefud's eyes opened wide with understanding.

"The absence of a thing," the Baron said, "this can be as deadly as the *presence.* The absence of air, eh? The absence of water? The absence of anything else we're addicted to." The Baron nodded. "You understand me, Nefud?"

Nefud swallowed. "Yes, m'Lord."

"Then get busy. Find the Sardaukar commander and set things in motion."

"At once, m'Lord." Nefud bowed, turned, and hurried away.

*Hawat by my side!* the Baron thought. *The Sardaukar will give him to me. If they suspect anything at all it's that I wish to destroy the Mentat. And this suspicion I'll confirm! The fools! One of the most formidable Mentats in all history, a Mentat trained to kill, and they'll toss him to me like some silly toy to be broken. I will show them what use can be made of such a toy.*

The Baron reached beneath a drapery beside his suspensor bed, pressed a button to summon his older nephew, Rabban. He sat back, smiling.

*And all the Atreides dead!*

The stupid guard captain had been right, of course. Certainly, nothing survived in the path of a sandblast storm on Arrakis. Not an ornithopter . . . or its occupants. The woman and the boy were dead. The bribes in the right places, the *unthinkable* expenditure to bring overwhelming military force down onto one planet . . . all the sly reports tailored for the Emperor's ears alone, all the careful scheming were here at last coming to full fruition.

*Power and fear—fear and power!*

The Baron could see the path ahead of him. One day, a Harkonnen would be Emperor. Not himself, and no spawn of his loins. But a Harkonnen. Not this Rabban he'd summoned, of course. But Rabban's younger brother, young Feyd-Rautha. There was a sharpness to the boy that the Baron enjoyed . . . a ferocity.

*A lovely boy,* the Baron thought. *A year or two more—say, by the time he's seventeen, I'll know for certain whether he's the tool that House Harkonnen requires to gain the throne.*

"M'Lord Baron."

The man who stood outside the doorfield of the Baron's bedchamber was low built, gross of face and body, with the Harkonnen paternal line's narrow-set eyes and bulge of shoulders. There was yet some rigidity in his fat, but it was obvious to the eye that he'd come one day to the portable suspensors for carrying his excess weight.

*A muscle-minded tank-brain,* the Baron thought. *No Mentat, my nephew . . . not a Piter de Vries, but perhaps something more precisely devised for the task at hand. If I give him freedom to do it, he'll grind over everything in his path. Oh, how he'll be hated here on Arrakis!*

"My dear Rabban," the Baron said. He released the doorfield, but pointedly kept his body shield at full strength, knowing that the shimmer of it would be visible above the bedside glowglobe.

"You summoned me," Rabban said. He stepped into the room, flicked a glance past the air disturbance of the body shield, searched for a suspensor chair, found none.

"Stand closer where I can see you easily," the Baron said.

Rabban advanced another step, thinking that the damnable old man had deliberately removed all chairs, forcing a visitor to stand.

"The Atreides are dead," the Baron said. "The last of them. That's why I summoned you here to Arrakis. This planet is again yours."

Rabban blinked. "But I thought you were going to advance Piter de Vried to the—"

"Piter, too, is dead."

"Piter?"

"Piter."

The Baron reactivated the doorfield, blanked it against all energy penetration.

"You finally tired of him, eh?" Rabban asked.

His voice fell flat and lifeless in the energy-blanketed room.

"I will say a thing to you just this once," the Baron rumbled. "You insinuate that I obliterated Piter as one obliterates a trifle." He snapped fat fingers. "Just like that, eh? I am not so stupid, Nephew. I will take it unkindly if ever again you suggest by word or action that I am so stupid."

Fear showed in the squinting of Rabban's eyes. He knew within certain limits how far the old Baron would go against family. Seldom to the point of death unless there were outrageous profit or provocation in it. But family punishments could be painful.

"Forgive me, m'Lord Baron," Rabban said. He lowered his eyes as much to hide his own anger as to show subservience.

"You do not fool me, Rabban," the Baron said.

Rabban kept his eyes lowered, swallowed.

"I make a point," the Baron said. "Never obliterate a man unthinkingly, the way an entire fief might do it through some *due process of law*. Always do it for an overriding purpose—and *know your purpose!*"

Anger spoke in Rabban: "But you obliterated the traitor, Yueh! I saw his body being carried out as I arrived last night."

Rabban stared at his uncle, suddenly frightened by the sound of those words.

But the Baron smiled. "I'm very careful about dangerous weapons," he said. "Doctor Yueh was a traitor. He gave me the Duke." Strength poured into the Baron's voice. "*I* suborned a doctor of the Suk School! The *Inner* School! You hear, boy? But that's a wild sort of weapon to leave lying about. I didn't obliterate him casually."

"Does the Emperor know you suborned a Suk doctor?"

*That was a penetrating question,* the Baron thought. *Have I misjudged this nephew?*

"The Emperor doesn't know it yet," the Baron said. "But his Sardaukar are sure to report it to him. Before that happens, though, I'll have my own report in his hands through CHOAM Company channels. I will explain that I *luckily* discovered a doctor who pretended to the conditioning. A false doctor, you understand? Since everyone *knows* you cannot counter the conditioning of a Suk School, this will be accepted."

"Ah-h-h, I see," Rabban murmured.

And the Baron thought: *Indeed, I hope you do see. I hope you do see how vital it is that this remain secret.* The Baron suddenly wondered at himself. *Why did I do that? Why did I boast to this fool nephew of mine—the nephew I must use and discard?* The Baron felt anger at himself. He felt betrayed.

"It must be kept secret," Rabban said. "I understand."

The Baron sighed. "I give you different instructions about Arrakis this time, Nephew. When last you ruled this place, I held you in strong rein. This time, I have only one requirement."

"M'Lord?"

"Income."

"Income?"

"Have you any idea, Rabban, how much we spent to bring such military force to bear on the Atreides? Do you have even the first inkling of how much the Guild charges for military transport?"

"Expensive, eh?"

"Expensive!"

The Baron shot a fat arm toward Rabban. "If you squeeze Arrakis for every cent it can give us for sixty years, you'll just barely repay us!"

Rabban opened his mouth, closed it without speaking.

"Expensive," the Baron sneered. "The damnable Guild monopoly on space would've ruined us if I hadn't planned for this expense long ago. You should know, Rabban, that *we* bore the entire brunt of it. We even paid for transport of the Sardaukar."

And not for the first time, the Baron wondered if there ever would come a day when the Guild might be circumvented. They were insidious—bleeding off just enough to keep the host from objecting until they had you in their fist where they could force you to pay and pay and pay.

Always, the exorbitant demands rode upon military ventures. "Hazard rates," the oily Guild agents explained. And for every agent you managed to insert as a watchdog in the Guild Bank structure, they put two agents into your system.

*Insufferable!*

"Income, then," Rabban said.

The Baron lowered his arm, made a fist. "You must squeeze."

"And I may do anything I wish as long as I squeeze?"

"Anything."

"The cannons you brought," Rabban said. "Could I—"

"I'm removing them," the Baron said.

"But you—"

"You won't need such toys. They were a special innovation and are now useless. We need the metal. They cannot go against a shield, Rabban. They were merely the unexpected. It was predictable that the Duke's men would retreat into cliff caves on this abominable planet. Our cannon merely sealed them in."

"The Fremen don't use shields."

"You may keep some lasguns if you wish."

"Yes, m'Lord. And I have a free hand."

"As long as you squeeze."

Rabban's smile was gloating. "I understand perfectly, m'Lord."

"You understand nothing perfectly," the Baron growled. "Let us have that clear at the outset. What you *do* understand is how to carry out my orders. Has it occurred to you, nephew, that there are at least five million persons on this planet?"

"Does m'Lord forget that I was his regent-siridar here before? And if m'Lord will forgive me, his estimate may be low. It's difficult to count a population scattered among sinks and pans the way they are here. And when you consider the Fremen of—"

"The Fremen aren't worth considering!"

"Forgive me, m'Lord, but the Sardaukar believe otherwise."

The Baron hesitated, staring at his nephew. "You know something?"

"M'Lord had retired when I arrived last night. I . . . ah, took the liberty of contacting some of my lieutenants from . . . ah, before. They've been acting as guides to the Sardaukar. They report that a Fremen band ambushed a Sardaukar force somewhere southeast of here and wiped it out."

"Wiped out a Sardaukar force?"

"Yes, m'Lord."

"Impossible!"

Rabban shrugged.

"Fremen defeating Sardaukar," the Baron sneered.

"I repeat only what was reported to me," Rabban said. "It is said this Fremen force already had captured the Duke's redoubtable Thufir Hawat."

"Ah-h-h-h-h-h."

The Baron nodded, smiling.

"I believe the report," Rabban said. "You've no idea what a problem the Fremen were."

"Perhaps, but these weren't Fremen your lieutenants saw. They must've been Atreides men trained by Hawat and disguised as Fremen. It's the only possible answer."

Again, Rabban shrugged. "Well, the Sardaukar think they were Fremen. The Sardaukar already have launched a pogrom to wipe out all Fremen."

"Good!"

"But—"

"It'll keep the Sardaukar occupied. And we'll soon have Hawat. I know it! I can feel it! Ah, this has been a day! The Sardaukar off hunting a few useless desert bands while we get the real prize!"

"M'Lord . . . ." Rabban hesitated, frowning. "I've always felt that we underestimated the Fremen, both in numbers and in—"

"Ignore them, boy! They're rabble. It's the populous towns, cities, and villages that concern us. A great many people there, eh?"

"A great many, m'Lord."

"They worry me, Rabban."

"Worry you?"

"Oh . . . ninety per cent of them are of no concern. But there are always a few . . . Houses Minor and so on, people of ambition who might try a dangerous thing. If one of them should get off Arrakis with an unpleasant story about what happened here, I'd be most displeased. Have you any idea how displeased I'd be?"

Rabban swallowed.

"You must take immediate measures to hold a hostage from each House Minor," the Baron said. "As far as anyone off Arrakis must learn, this was straightforward House-to-House battle. The Sardaukar had no part in it, you understand? The Duke was offered the usual quarter and exile, but he died in an unfortunate accident before he could accept. He was about to accept, though. That is the story. And any rumor that there were Sardaukar here, it must be laughed at."

"As the Emperor wishes it," Rabban said.

"As the Emperor wishes it."

"What about the smugglers?"

"No one believes smugglers, Rabban. They are tolerated, but not believed. At any rate, you'll be spreading some bribes in that quarter . . . and taking other measures which I'm sure you can think of."

"Yes, m'Lord."

"Two things from Arrakis, then, Rabban: income and a merciless fist. You must show no mercy here. Think of these clods as what they are—slaves envious of their masters and waiting only the opportunity to rebel. Not the slightest vestige of pity or mercy must you show them."

"Can one exterminate an entire planet?" Rabban asked.

"Exterminate?" Surprise showed in the swift turning of the Baron's head. "Who said anything about exterminating?"

"Well, I presumed you were going to bring in new stock and—"

"I said *squeeze*, Nephew, not exterminate. Don't waste the population, merely drive them into utter submission. You must be the carnivore, my boy." He smiled, a baby's expression in the dimple-fat face. "A carnivore never stops. Show no mercy. Never stop. Mercy is a chimera. It can be defeated by the stomach rumbling its hunger, by the throat crying its thirst. You must be always hungry and thirsty." The Baron caressed his bulges beneath the suspensors. "Like me."

"I see, m'Lord."

Rabban swung his gaze left and right.

"It's all clear then, Nephew?"

"Except for one thing, Uncle: the planetologist, Kynes."

"Ah, yes, Kynes."

"He's the Emperor's man, m'Lord. He can come and go as he pleases. And he's very close to the Fremen . . . married one."

"Kynes will be dead by tomorrow's nightfall."

"That's dangerous work, Uncle, killing an Imperial servant."

"How do you think I've come this far this quickly?" the Baron demanded. His voice was low, charged with unspeakable adjectives. "Besides, you need never have feared Kynes would leave Arrakis. You're forgetting that he's addicted to the spice."

"Of course!"

"Those who know will do nothing to endanger their supply," the Baron said. "Kynes certainly must know."

"I forgot," Rabban said.

They stared at each other in silence.

Presently, the Baron said: "Incidentally, you will make my own supply one of your first concerns. I've quite a stockpile of private stuff, but that suicide raid by the Duke's men got most of what we'd stored for sale."

Rabban nodded. "Yes, m'Lord."

The Baron brightened. "Now, tomorrow morning, you will assemble what remains of organization here and you'll say to them: 'Our Sublime Padishah Emperor has charged me to take possession of this planet and end all dispute.'"

"I understand, m'Lord."

"This time, I'm sure you do. We will discuss it in more detail tomorrow. Now, leave me to finish my sleep."

The Baron deactivated his doorfield, watched his nephew out of sight.

*A tank-brain,* the Baron thought. *Muscle-minded tank-brain. They will be bloody pulp here when he's through with them. Then, when I send in Feyd-Rautha to take the load off them, they'll cheer their rescuer. Beloved Feyd-Rautha. Benign Feyd-Rautha, the compassionate one who saves them from a beast. Feyd-Rautha, a man to follow and die for. The boy will know by that time how to oppress with impunity. I'm sure he's the one we need. He'll learn. And such a lovely body. Really a lovely boy.*

> *At the age of fifteen, he had already learned silence.*
>
> **—from "A Child's History of Muad'Dib"**
> **by the Princess Irulan**

As Paul fought the 'thopter's controls he grew aware that he was sorting out the interwoven storm forces, his more than Mentat awareness computing on the basis of fractional minutiae. He felt dust fronts, billowings, mixings of turbulence, an occasional vortex.

The cabin interior was an angry box lighted by the green radiance of instrument dials. The tan flow of dust outside appeared featureless, but his inner sense began to *see* through the curtain.

*I must find the right vortex,* he thought.

For a long time now he had sensed the storm's power diminishing, but still it shook them. He waited out another turbulence.

The vortex began as an abrupt billowing that rattled the entire ship. Paul defied all fear to bank the 'thopter left.

Jessica saw the maneuver on the attitude globe.

"Paul!" she screamed.

The vortex turned them, twisting, tipping. It lifted the 'thopter like a chip on a geyser, spewed them up and out—a winged speck within a core of winding dust lighted by the second moon.

Paul looked down, saw the dust-defined pillar of hot wind that had disgorged them, saw the dying storm trailing away like a dry river into the desert—moon-gray motion growing smaller and smaller below as they rode the updraft.

"We're out of it," Jessica whispered.

Paul turned their craft away from the dust in swooping rhythm while he scanned the night sky.

"We've given them the slip," he said.

Jessica felt her heart pounding. She forced herself to calmness, looked at the diminishing storm. Her time sense said they had ridden within that compounding of elemental forces almost four hours, but part of her mind computed the passage as a lifetime. She felt reborn.

*It was like the litany,* she thought. *We faced it and did not resist. The storm passed through us and around us. It's gone, but we remain.*

"I don't like the sound of our wing motion," Paul said. "We suffered some damage in there."

He felt the grating, injured flight through his hands on the controls. They were out of the storm, but still not out into the full view of his prescient vision. Yet, they had escaped, and Paul sensed himself trembling on the verge of a revelation.

He shivered.

The sensation was magnetic and terrifying, and he found himself caught on the question of what caused this trembling awareness. Part of it, he felt, was the spice-saturated diet of Arrakis. But he thought part of it could be the litany, as though the words had a power of their own.

*"I shall not fear . . . ."*

Cause and effect: he was alive despite malignant forces, and he felt himself poised on a brink of self-awareness that could not have been without the litany's magic.

Words from the Orange Catholic Bible rang through his memory: *"What senses do we lack that we cannot see or hear another world all around us?"*

"There's rock all around," Jessica said.

Paul focused on the 'thopter's launching, shook his head to clear it. He looked where his mother pointed, saw uplifting rock shapes black on the sand ahead and to the right. He felt wind around his ankles, a stirring of dust in the cabin. There was a hole somewhere, more of the storm's doing.

"Better set us down on sand," Jessica said. "The wings might not take full brake."

He nodded toward a place ahead where sandblasted ridges lifted into moonlight above the dunes. "I'll set us down near those rocks. Check your safety harness."

She obeyed, thinking: *We've water and stillsuits. If we can find food, we can survive a long time on this desert. Fremen live here. What they can do we can do.*

"Run for those rocks the instant we're stopped," Paul said. "I'll take the pack."

"Run for . . . ." She fell silent, nodded. "Worms."

"Our friends, the worms," he corrected her. "They'll get this 'thopter. There'll be no evidence of where we landed."

*How direct his thinking,* she thought.

They glided lower . . . lower . . .

There came a rushing sense of motion to their passage—blurred shadows of dunes, rocks lifting like islands. The 'thopter touched a dune top with a soft lurch, skipped a sand valley, touched another dune.

*He's killing our speed against the sand,* Jessica thought, and permitted herself to admire his competence.

"Brace yourself!" Paul warned.

He pulled back on the wing brakes, gently at first, then harder and harder. He felt them cup the air, their aspect ratio dropping faster and faster. Wind screamed through the lapped coverts and primaries of the wings' leaves.

Abruptly, with only the faintest lurch of warning, the left wing, weakened by the storm, twisted upward and in, slamming across the side of the 'thopter. The craft skidded across a dune top, twisting to the left. It tumbled down the opposite face to bury its nose in the next dune amid a cascade of sand. They lay stopped on the broken wing side, the right wing pointing toward the stars.

Paul jerked off his safety harness, hurled himself upward across his mother, wrenching the door open. Sand poured around them into the cabin, bringing a dry smell of burned flint. He grabbed the pack from the rear, saw that his mother was free of her harness. She stepped up onto the side of the right-hand seat and out onto the 'thopter's metal skin. Paul followed, dragging the pack by its straps.

"Run!" he ordered.

He pointed up the dune face and beyond it where they could see a rock tower undercut by sandblast winds.

Jessica leaped off the 'thopter and ran, scrambling and sliding up the dune. She heard Paul's panting progress behind. They came out onto a sand ridge that curved away toward the rocks.

"Follow the ridge," Paul ordered. "It'll be faster."

They slogged toward the rocks, sand gripping their feet.

A new sound began to impress itself on them: a muted whisper, a hissing, an abrasive slithering.

"Worm," Paul said.

It grew louder.

"Faster!" Paul gasped.

The first rock shingle, like a beach slanting from the sand, lay no more than ten meters ahead when they heard metal crunch and shatter behind them.

Paul shifted his pack to his right arm, holding it by the straps. It slapped his side as he ran. He took his mother's arm with his other hand. They scrambled onto the lifting rock, up a pebble-littered surface through a twisted, wind-carved channel. Breath came dry and gasping in their throats.

"I can't run any farther," Jessica panted.

Paul stopped, pressed her into a gut of rock, turned and looked down onto the desert. A mound-in-motion ran parallel to their rock island—moonlit ripples, sand waves, a cresting burrow almost level with Paul's eyes at a distance of about a kilometer. The flattened dunes of its track curved once—a short loop crossing the patch of desert where they had abandoned their wrecked ornithopter.

Where the worm had been there was no sign of the aircraft.

The burrow mound moved outward into the desert, coursed back across its own path, questing.

"It's bigger than a Guild spaceship," Paul whispered. "I was told worms grew large in the deep desert, but I didn't realize . . . how big."

"Nor I," Jessica breathed.

Again, the thing turned out away from the rocks, sped now with a curving track toward the horizon. They listened until the sound of its passage was lost in gentle sand stirrings around them.

Paul took a deep breath, looked up at the moon-frosted escarpment, and quoted from the Kitab al-Ibar: "Travel by night and rest in black shade through the day." He looked at his mother. "We still have a few hours of night. Can you go on?"

"In a moment."

Paul stepped out onto the rock shingle, shouldered the pack and adjusted its straps. He stood a moment with a paracompass in his hands.

"Whenever you're ready," he said.

She pushed herself away from the rock, feeling her strength return. "Which direction?"

"Where this ridge leads." He pointed.

"Deep into the desert," she said.

"The Fremen desert," Paul whispered.

And he paused, shaken by the remembered high relief imagery of a prescient vision he had experienced on Caladan. He had seen this desert. But the *set* of the vision had been subtly different, like an optical image that had disappeared into his consciousness, been absorbed by memory, and now failed of perfect registry when projected onto the real scene. The vision appeared to have shifted and aproached him from a different angle while he remained motionless.

*Idaho was with us in the vision,* he remembered. *But now Idaho is dead.*

"Do you see a way to go?" Jessica asked, mistaking his hesitation.

"No," he said, "but we'll go anyway."

He settled his shoulders more firmly in the pack, struck out up a sand-carved channel in the rock. The channel opened onto a moonlit floor of rock with benched ledges climbing away to the south.

Paul headed for the first ledge, clambered onto it. Jessica followed.

She noted presently how their passage became a matter of the immediate and particular—the sand pockets between rocks where their steps were slowed, the wind-carved ridge that cut their hands, the obstruction that forced a choice: Go over or go around? The terrain enforced its own rhythms. They spoke only when necessary and then with the hoarse voices of their exertion.

"Careful here—this ledge is slippery with sand."

"Watch you don't hit your head against this overhang."

"Stay below this ridge; the moon's at our backs and it'd show our movement to anyone out there."

Paul stopped in a bight of rock, leaned the pack against a narrow ledge.

Jessica leaned beside him, thankful for the moment of rest. She heard Paul pulling at his stillsuit tube, sipped her own reclaimed water. It tasted brackish, and she remembered the waters of Caladan—a tall fountain enclosing a curve of sky, such a richness of moisture that it hadn't been noticed for itself . . . only for its shape, or its reflection, or its sound as she stopped beside it.

*To stop*, she thought. *To rest . . . truly rest.*

It occurred to her that mercy was the ability to stop, if only for a moment. There was no mercy where there could be no stopping.

Paul pushed away from the rock ledge, turned, and climbed over a sloping surface. Jessica followed with a sigh.

They slid down onto a wide shelf that led around a sheer rock face. Again, they fell into the disjointed rhythm of movement across this broken land.

Jessica felt that the night was dominated by degrees of smallness in substances beneath their feet and hands—boulders or pea gravel or flaked rock or pea sand or sand itself or grit or dust or gossamer powder.

The powder clogged nose filters and had to be blown out. Pea sand and pea gravel rolled on a hard surface and could spill the unwary. Rock flakes cut.

And the omnipresent sand patches dragged against their feet.

Paul stopped abruptly on a rock shelf, steadied his mother as she stumbled into him.

He was pointing left and she looked along his arm to see that they stood atop a cliff with the desert stretched out like a static ocean some two hundred meters below. It lay there full of moon-silvered waves—shadows of angles that lapsed into curves and, in the distance, lifted to the misted gray blur of another escarpment.

"Open desert," she said.

"A wide place to cross," Paul said, and his voice was muffled by the filter trap across his face.

Jessica glanced left and right—nothing but sand below.

Paul stared straight ahead across the open dunes, watching the movement of shadows in the moon's passage. "About three or four kilometers across," he said.

"Worms," she said.

"Sure to be."

She focused on her weariness, the muscle ache that dulled her senses. "Shall we rest and eat?"

Paul slipped out of the pack, sat down and leaned against it. Jessica supported herself by a hand on his shoulder as she sank to the rock beside him. She felt Paul turn as she settled herself, heard him scrabbling in the pack.

"Here," he said.

His hand felt dry against hers as he pressed two energy capsules into her palm.

She swallowed them with a grudging spit of water from her stillsuit tube.

"Drink all your water," Paul said. "Axiom: the best place to conserve your water is in your body. It keeps your energy up. You're stronger. Trust your stillsuit."

She obeyed, drained her catchpockets, feeling energy return. She thought then how peaceful it was here in this moment of their tiredness, and she recalled once hearing the minstrel-warrior Gurney Halleck say, "Better a dry morsel and quietness therewith than a house full of sacrifice and strife."

Jessica repeated the words to Paul.

"That was Gurney," he said.

She caught the tone of his voice, the way he spoke as of someone dead, thought: *And well poor Gurney might be dead.* The Atreides forces were either dead or captive or lost like themelves in this waterless void.

"Gurney always had the right quotation," Paul said. "I can hear him now: 'And I will make the rivers dry, and sell the land into the hand of the wicked: and I will make the land waste, and all that is therein, by the hand of strangers.'"

Jessica closed her eyes, found herself moved close to tears by the pathos in her son's voice.

Presently, Paul said: "How do you . . . feel?"

She recognized that his question was directed at her pregnancy, said: "Your sister won't be born for many months yet. I still feel . . . physically adequate."

And she thought: *How stiffly formal I speak to my own son!* Then, because it was the Bene Gesserit way to seek within for the answer to such an oddity, she searched and found the source of her formality: *I'm afraid of my son; I fear his strangeness; I fear what he may see ahead of us, what he may tell me.*

Paul pulled his hood down over his eyes, listened to the bug-hustling sounds of the night. His lungs were charged with his own silence. His nose itched. He rubbed it, removed the filter and grew conscious of the rich smell of cinnamon.

"There's melange spice nearby," he said.

An eider wind feathered Paul's cheeks, ruffled the folds of his burnoose. But this wind carried no threat of storm; already he could sense the difference.

"Dawn soon," he said.

Jessica nodded.

"There's a way to get safely across that open sand," Paul said. "The Fremen do it."

"The worms?"

"If we were to plant a thumper from our Fremkit back in the rocks here," Paul said. "It'd keep a worm occupied for a time."

She glanced at the stretch of moonlighted desert between them and the other escarpment. "Four kilometers' worth of time?"

"Perhaps. And if we crossed there making only *natural* sounds, the kind that don't attract the worms . . . ."

Paul studied the open desert, questing in his prescient memory, probing the mysterious allusions to thumpers and maker hooks in the Fremkit manual that had come with their escape pack. He found it odd that all he sensed was pervasive terror at thought of the worms. He knew as though it lay just at the edge of his awareness that the worms were to be respected and not feared . . . if . . . if . . . .

He shook his head.

"It'd have to be sounds without rhythm," Jessica said.

"What? Oh. Yes. If we broke our steps . . . the sand itself must shift down at times. Worms can't investigate every little sound. We should be fully rested before we try it, though."

He looked across at that other rock wall, seeing the passage of time in the vertical moonshadows there. "It'll be dawn within the hour."

"Where'll we spend the day?" she asked.

Paul turned left, pointed. "The cliff curves back north over there. You can see by the way it's wind-cut that's the windward face. There'll be crevasses there, deep ones."

"Had we better get started?" she asked.

He stood, helped her to her feet. "Are you rested enough for a climb down? I want to get as close as possible to the desert floor before we camp."

"Enough." She nodded for him to lead the way.

He hesitated, then lifted the pack, settled it onto his shoulders and turned along the cliff.

*If only we had suspensors,* Jessica thought. *It'd be such a simple matter to jump down there. But perhaps suspensors are another thing to avoid in the open desert. Maybe they attract the worms the way a shield does.*

They came to a series of shelves dropping down and, beyond them, saw a fissure with its ledge outlined by moonshadow leading along the vestibule.

Paul led the way down, moving cautiously but hurrying because it was obvious the moonlight could not last much longer. They wound down into a world of deeper and deeper shadows. Hints of rock shape climbed to the stars around them. The fissure narrowed to some ten meters' width at the brink of a dim gray sandslope that slanted downward into darkness.

"Can we go down?" Jessica whispered.

"I think so."

He tested the surface with one foot.

"We can slide down," he said. "I'll go first. Wait until you hear me stop."

"Careful," she said.

He stepped onto the slope and slid and slipped down its soft surface onto an almost level floor of packed sand. The place was deep within the rock walls.

There came the sound of sand sliding behind him. He tried to see up the slope in the darkness, was almost knocked over by the cascade. It trailed away to silence.

"Mother?" he said.

There was no answer.

"Mother?"

He dropped the pack, hurled himself up the slope, scrambling; digging, throwing sand like a wild man. "Mother!" he gasped. "Mother, where are you?"

Another cascade of sand swept down on him, burying him to the hips. He wrenched himself out of it.

*She's been caught in the sandslide,* he thought. *Buried in it. I must be calm and work this out carefully. She won't smother immediately. She'll compose herself in bindu suspension to reduce her oxygen needs. She knows I'll dig for her.*

In the Bene Gesserit way she had taught him, Paul stilled the savage beating of his heart, set his mind as a blank slate upon which the past few moments could write themselves. Every partial shift and twist of the slide replayed itself in his memory, moving with an interior stateliness that contrasted with the fractional second of real time required for the total recall.

Presently, Paul moved slantwise up the slope, probing cautiously until he found the wall of the fissure, an outcurve of rock there. He began to dig, moving the sand with care not to dislodge another slide. A piece of fabric came under his hands. He followed it, found an arm. Gently, he traced the arm, exposed her face.

"Do you hear me?" he whispered.

No answer.

He dug faster, freed her shoulders. She was limp beneath his hands, but he detected a slow heartbeat.

*Bindu suspension,* he told himself.

He cleared the sand away to her waist, draped her arms over his shoulders and pulled downslope, slowly at first, then dragging her as fast as he could, feeling the sand give way above. Faster and faster he pulled her, gasping with the effort, fighting to keep his balance. He was out on the hard-packed floor of the fissure then, swinging her to his shoulder and breaking into a staggering run as the entire sandslope came down with a loud hiss that echoed and was magnified within the rock walls.

He stopped at the end of the fissure where it looked out on the desert's marching dunes some thirty meters below. Gently, he lowered her to the sand, uttered the word to bring her out of the catalepsis.

She awakened slowly, taking deeper and deeper breaths.

"I knew you'd find me," she whispered.

He looked back up the fissure. "It might have been kinder if I hadn't."

"Paul!"

"I lost the pack," he said. "It's buried under a hundred tons of sand . . . at least."

"Everything?"

"The spare water, the stilltent—everything that counts." He touched a pocket. "I still have the paracompass." He fumbled at the waist sash. "Knife and binoculars. We can get a good look around the place where we'll die."

In that instant, the sun lifted above the horizon somewhere to the left beyond the end of the fissure. Colors blinked in the sand out on the open desert. A chorus of birds held forth their songs from hidden places among the rocks.

But Jessica had eyes only for the despair in Paul's face. She edged her voice with scorn, said: "Is this the way you were taught?"

"Don't you understand?" he asked. "Everything we need to survive in this place is under that sand."

"You found me," she said, and now her voice was soft, reasonable.

Paul squatted back on his heels.

Presently, he looked up the fissure at the new slope, studying it, marking the looseness of the sand.

"If we could immobilize a small area of that slope and the upper face of a hole dug into the sand, we might be able to put down a shaft to the pack. Water might do it, but we don't have enough water for . . . ." He broke off, then: "Foam."

Jessica held herself to stillness lest she disturb the hyperfunctioning of his mind.

Paul looked out at the open dunes, searching with his nostrils as well as his eyes, finding the direction and then centering his attention on a darkened patch of sand below them.

"Spice," he said. "Its essence—highly alkaline. And I have the paracompass. Its power pack is acid-base."

Jessica sat up straight against the rock.

Paul ignored her, leaped to his feet, and was off down the wind-compacted surface that spilled from the end of the fissure to the desert's floor.

She watched the way he walked, breaking his stride—step . . . pause, step-step . . . slide . . . pause . . .

There was no rhythm to it that might tell a marauding worm something not of the desert moved here.

Paul reached the spice patch, shoveled a mound of it into a fold of his robe, returned to the fissure. He spilled the spice onto the sand in front of Jessica, squatted and began dismantling the paracompass, using the point of his knife. The compass face came off. He removed his sash, spread the compass parts on it, lifted out the power pack. The dial mechanism came out next, leaving an empty dished compartment in the instrument.

"You'll need water," Jessica said.

Paul took the catchtube from his neck, sucked up a mouthful, expelled it into the dished compartment.

*If this fails, that's water wasted,* Jessica thought. *But it won't matter then, anyway.*

With his knife, Paul cut open the power pack, spilled its crystals into the water. They foamed slightly, subsided.

Jessica's eyes caught motion above them. She looked up to see a line of hawks along the rim of the fissure. They perched there staring down at the open water.

*Great Mother!* she thought. *They can sense water even at that distance!*

Paul had the cover back on the paracompass, leaving off the reset button which gave a small hole into the liquid. Taking the reworked instrument in one hand, a handful of spice in the other, Paul went back up the fissure, studying the lay of the slope. His robe billowed gently without the sash to hold it. He waded part way up the slope, kicking off sand rivulets, spurts of dust.

Presently, he stopped, pressed a pinch of the spice into the paracompass, shook the instrument case.

Green foam boiled out of the hole where the reset button had been. Paul aimed it at the slope, spread a low dike there, began kicking away the sand beneath it, immobilizing the opened face with more foam.

Jessica moved to a position below him, called out: "May I help?"

"Come up and dig," he said. "We've about three meters to go. It's going to be a near thing." As he spoke, the foam stopped billowing from the instrument.

"Quickly," Paul said. "No telling how long this foam will hold the sand."

Jessica scrambled up beside Paul as he sifted another pinch of spice into the hole, shook the paracompass case. Again, foam boiled from it.

As Paul directed the foam barrier, Jessica dug with her hands, hurling the sand down the slope. "How deep?" she panted.

"About three meters," he said. "And I can only approximate the position. We may have to widen this hole." He moved a step aside, slipping in loose sand. "Slant your digging backward. Don't go straight down."

Jessica obeyed.

Slowly, the hole went down, reaching a level even with the floor of the basin and still no sign of the pack.

*Could I have miscalculated?* Paul asked himself. *I'm the one that panicked originally and caused this mistake. Has that warped my ability?*

He looked at the paracompass. Less than two ounces of the acid infusion remained.

Jessica straightened in the hole, rubbed a foam-stained hand across her cheek. Her eyes met Paul's.

"The upper face," Paul said. "Gently, now." He added another pinch of spice to the container, sent the foam boiling around Jessica's hands as she began cutting a vertical face in the upper slant of the hole. On the second pass, her hands encountered something hard. Slowly, she worked out a length of strap with a plastic buckle.

"Don't move any more of it," Paul said and his voice was almost a whisper. "We're out of foam."

Jessica held the strap in one hand, looked up at him.

Paul threw the empty paracompass down onto the floor of the basin, said: "Give me your other hand. Now listen carefully. I'm going to pull you to the side and downhill. Don't let go of that strap. We won't get much more spill from the top. This slope has stabilized itself. All I'm going to aim for is to keep your head free of the sand. Once that hole's filled, we can dig you out and pull up the pack."

"I understand," she said.

"Ready?"

"Ready." She tensed her fingers on the strap.

With one surge, Paul had her half out of the hole, holding her head up as the foam barrier gave way and sand spilled down. When it had subsided, Jessica remained buried to the waist, her left arm and shoulder still under the sand, her chin protected on a fold of Paul's robe. Her shoulder ached from the strain put on it.

"I still have the strap," she said.

Slowly, Paul worked his hand into the sand beside her, found the strap. "Together," he said. "Steady pressure. We mustn't break it."

More sand spilled down as they worked the pack up. When the strap cleared the surface, Paul stopped, freed his mother from the sand. Together then they pulled the pack downslope and out of its trap.

In a few minutes they stood on the floor of the fissure holding the pack between them.

Paul looked at his mother. Foam stained her face, her robe. Sand was caked to her where the foam had dried. She looked as though she had been a target for balls of wet, green sand.

"You look a mess," he said.

"You're not so pretty yourself," she said.

They started to laugh, then sobered.

"That shouldn't have happened," Paul said. "I was careless."

She shrugged, feeling caked sand fall away from her robe.

"I'll put up the tent," he said. "Better slip off that robe and shake it out." He turned away, taking the pack.

Jessica nodded, suddenly too tired to answer.

"There're anchor holes in the rock," Paul said. "Someone's tented here before."

*Why not?* she thought as she brushed at her robe. This was a likely place—deep in rock walls and facing another cliff some four kilometers away—far enough above the desert to avoid worms but close enough for easy access before a crossing.

She turned, seeing that Paul had the tent up, its rib-domed hemisphere blending with the rock walls of the fissure. Paul stepped past her, lifting his binoculars. He adjusted their internal pressure with a quick twist, focused the oil lenses on the other cliff lifting golden tan in morning light across open sand.

Jessica watched as he studied that apocalyptic landscape, his eyes probing into sand rivers and canyons.

"There are growing things over there," he said.

Jessica found the spare binoculars in the pack beside the tent, moved up beside Paul.

"There," he said, holding the binoculars with one hand and pointing with the other.

She looked where he pointed.

"Saguaro," she said. "Scrawny stuff."

"There may be people nearby," Paul said.

"That could be the remains of a botanical testing station," she warned.

"This is pretty far south into the desert," he said. He lowered his binoculars, rubbed beneath his filter baffle, feeling how dry and chapped his lips were, sensing the dusty taste of thirst in his mouth. "This has the feeling of a Fremen place," he said.

"Are we certain the Fremen will be friendly?" she asked.

"Kynes promised their help."

*But there's desperation in the people of this desert,* she thought. *I felt some of it myself today. Desperate people might kill us for our water.*

She closed her eyes and, against this wasteland, conjured in her mind a scene from Caladan. There had been a vacation trip once on Caladan—she and the Duke Leto, before Paul's birth. They'd flown over the southern jungles, above the weed-wild shouting leaves and rice paddies of the deltas. And they had seen the ant lines in the greenery—man-gangs carrying their loads on suspensor-buoyed shoulder poles. And in the sea reaches there'd been the white petals of trimaran dhows.

All of it gone.

Jessica opened her eyes to the desert stillness, to the mounting warmth of the day. Restless heat devils were beginning to set the air aquiver out on the open sand. The other rock face across from them was like a thing seen through cheap glass.

A spill of sand spread its brief curtain across the open end of the fissure. The sand hissed down, loosed by puffs of morning breeze, by the hawks that were beginning to lift away from the clifftop. When the sandfall was gone, she still heard it hissing. It grew louder, a sound that once heard, was never forgotten.

"Worm," Paul whispered.

It came from their right with an uncaring majesty that could not be ignored. A twisting burrow-mound of sand cut through the dunes within their field of vision. The mound lifted in front, dusting away like a bow wave in water. Then it was gone, coursing off to the left.

The sound diminished, died.

"I've seen space frigates that were smaller," Paul whispered.

She nodded, continuing to stare across the desert. Where the worm had passed there remained that tantalizing gap. It flowed bitterly endless before them, beckoning beneath its horizontal collapse of skyline.

"When we've rested," Jessica said, "we should continue with your lessons."

He suppressed a sudden anger, said: "Mother, don't you think we could do without . . . ."

"Today you panicked," she said. "You know your mind and bindu-nervature perhaps better than I do, but you've much yet to learn about your body's prana-musculature. The body does things of itself sometimes, Paul, and I can teach you about this. You must learn to control every muscle, every fiber of your body. You need review of the hands. We'll start with finger muscles, palm tendons, and tip sensitivity." She turned away. "Come, into the tent, now."

He flexed the fingers of his left hand, watching her crawl through the sphincter valve, knowing that he could not deflect her from this determination . . . that he must agree.

*Whatever has been done to me, I've been a party to it,* he thought.

Review of the hand!

He looked at his hand. How inadequate it appeared when measured against such creatures as that worm.

*We came from Caladan—a paradise world for our form of life. There existed no need on Caladan to build a physical paradise or a paradise of the mind—we could see the actuality all around us. And the price we paid was the price men have always paid for achieving a paradise in this life—we went soft, we lost our edge.*

**—from "Muad'Dib: Conversations" by the Princess Irulan**

"So you're the great Gurney Halleck," the man said.

Halleck stood staring across the round cavern office at the smuggler seated behind a metal desk. The man wore Fremen robes and had the half-tint blue eyes that told of off-planet foods in his diet. The office duplicated a space frigate's master control center—communications and viewscreens along a thirty-degree arc of wall, remote arming and firing banks adjoining, and the desk formed as a wall projection—part of the remaining curve.

"I am Staban Tuek, son of Esmar Tuek," the smuggler said.

"Then you're the one I owe thanks for the help we've received," Halleck said.

"Ah-h-h, gratitude," the smuggler said. "Sit down."

A ship-type bucket seat emerged from the wall beside the screens and Halleck sank onto it with a sigh, feeling his weariness. He could see his own reflection now in a dark surface beside the smuggler and scowled at the lines of fatigue in his lumpy face. The inkvine scar along his jaw writhed with the scowl.

Halleck turned from his reflection, stared at Tuek. He saw the family resemblance in the smuggler now—the father's heavy, overhanging eyebrows and rock planes of cheeks and nose.

"Your men tell me your father is dead, killed by the Harkonnens," Halleck said.

"By the Harkonnens or by a traitor among your people," Tuek said.

Anger overcame part of Halleck's fatigue. He straightened, said: "Can you name the traitor?"

"We are not sure."

"Thufir Hawat suspected the Lady Jessica."

"Ah-h-h, the Bene Gesserit witch . . . perhaps. But Hawat is now a Harkonnen captive."

"I heard." Halleck took a deep breath. "It appears we've a deal more killing ahead of us."

"We will do nothing to attract attention to us," Tuek said.

Halleck stiffened. "But—"

"You and those of your men we've saved are welcome to sanctuary among us," Tuek said. "You speak of gratitude. Very well; work off your debt to us. We can always use good men. We'll destroy you out of hand, though, if you make the slightest open move against the Harkonnens.'

"But they killed your father, man!"

"Perhaps. And if so, I'll give you my father's answer to those who act without thinking: 'A stone is heavy and the sand is weighty; but a fool's wrath is heavier than them both.'"

"You mean to do nothing about it, then?" Halleck sneered.

"You did not hear me say that. I merely say I will protect our contract with the Guild. The Guild requires that we play a circumspect game. There are other ways of destroying a foe."

"Ah-h-h-h-h."

"Ah, indeed. If you've a mind to seek out the witch, have at it. But I warn you that you're probably too late . . . and we doubt she's the one you want anyway."

"Hawat made few mistakes."

"He allowed himself to fall into Harkonnen hands."

"You think *he's* the traitor?"

Tuek shrugged. "This is academic. We think the witch is dead. At least the Harkonnens believe it."

"You seem to know a great deal about the Harkonnens."

"Hints and suggestions . . . rumors and hunches."

"We are seventy-four men," Halleck said. "If you seriously wish us to enlist with you, you must believe our Duke is dead."

"His body has been seen."

"And the boy, too—young Master Paul?" Halleck tried to swallow, found a lump in his throat.

"According to the last word we had, he was lost with his mother in a desert storm. Likely not even their bones will ever be found."

"So the witch is dead then . . . all dead."

Tuek nodded. "And Beast Rabban, so they say, will sit once more in the seat of power here on Dune."

"The Count Rabban of Lankiveil?"

"Yes."

It took Halleck a moment to put down the upsurge of rage that threatened to overcome him. He spoke with panting breath: "I've a score of my own against Rabban. I owe him for the lives of my family . . . ." He rubbed at the scar along his jaw. ". . . and for this . . . ."

"One does not risk everything to settle a score prematurely," Tuek said. He frowned, watching the play of muscles along Halleck's jaw, the sudden withdrawal in the man's shed-lidded eyes.

"I know . . . I know." Halleck took a deep breath.

"You and your men can work out your passage off Arrakis by serving with us. There are many places to—"

"I release my men from any bond to me; they can choose for themselves. With Rabban here—I stay."

"In your mood, I'm not sure we want you to stay."

Halleck stared at the smuggler. "You doubt my word?"

"No-o-o . . . ."

"You've saved me from the Harkonnens. I gave loyalty to the Duke Leto for no greater reason. I'll stay on Arrakis—with you . . . or with the Fremen."

"Whether a thought is spoken or not it is a real thing and it has power," Tuek said. "You might find the line between life and death among the Fremen to be too sharp and quick."

Halleck closed his eyes briefly, feeling the weariness surge up in him. "Where is the Lord who led us through the land of deserts and of pits?" he murmured.

"Move slowly and the day of your revenge will come," Tuek said. "Speed is a device of Shaitan. Cool your sorrow—we've the diversions for it; three things there are that ease the heart—water, green grass, and the beauty of woman."

Halleck opened his eyes. "I would prefer the blood of Rabban Harkonnen flowing about my feet." He stared at Tuek. "You think that day will come?"

"I have little to do with how you'll meet tomorrow, Gurney Halleck. I can only help you meet today."

"Then I'll accept that help and stay until the day you tell me to revenge your father and all the others who—"

"Listen to me, *fighting man,*" Tuek said. He leaned forward over his desk, his shoulders level with his ears, eyes intent. The smuggler's face was suddenly like weathered stone. "My father's water—I'll buy that back myself, with my own blade."

Halleck stared back at Tuek. In that moment the smuggler reminded him of Duke Leto: a leader of men, courageous, secure in his own position and his own course. He was like the Duke . . . before Arrakis.

"Do you wish my blade beside you?" Halleck asked.

Tuek sat back, relaxed, studying Halleck silently.

"Do you think of me as *fighting man?*" Halleck pressed.

"You're the only one of the Duke's lieutenants to escape," Tuek said. "Your enemy was overwhelming, yet you rolled with him . . . . You defeated him the way we defeat Arrakis."

"Eh?"

"We live on sufferance down here, Gurney Halleck," Tuek said. "Arrakis is our enemy."

"One enemy at a time, is that it?"

"That's it."

"Is that the way the Fremen make out?"

"Perhaps."

"You said I might find life with the Fremen too tough. They live in the desert, in the open, is that why?"

"Who knows where the Fremen live? For us, the Central Plateau is a no-man's land. But I wish to talk more about—"

"I'm told that the Guild seldom routes spice lighters in over the desert," Halleck said. "But there are rumors that you can see bits of greenery here and there if you know where to look."

"Rumors!" Tuek sneered. "Do you wish to choose now between me and the Fremen? We have a measure of security, our own sietch carved out of the rock, our own hidden basins. We live the lives of civilized men. The Fremen are a few ragged bands that *we* use as spice-hunters."

"But they can kill Harkonnens."

"And do you wish to know the result? Even now they are being hunted down like animals—with lasguns, because they have no shields. They are being exterminated. Why? Because they killed Harkonnens."

"Was it Harkonnens they killed?" Halleck asked.

"What do you mean?"

"Haven't you heard that there may've been Sardaukar with the Harkonnens?"

"More rumors."

"But a pogrom—that isn't like the Harkonnens. A pogrom is wasteful."

"I believe what I see with my own eyes," Tuek said. "Make your choice, fighting man. Me or the Fremen. I will promise you sanctuary and a chance to draw the blood we both want. Be sure of that. The Fremen will offer you only the life of the hunted."

Halleck hesitated, sensing wisdom and sympathy in Tuek's words, yet troubled for no reason he could explain.

"Trust your own abilities," Tuek said. "Whose decisions brought your force through the battle? Yours. Decide."

"It must be," Halleck said. "The Duke and his son are dead?"

"The Harkonnens believe it. Where such things are concerned, I incline to trust the Harkonnens." A grim smile touched Tuek's mouth. "But it's about the only trust I give them."

"Then it must be," Halleck repeated. He held out his right hand, palm up and thumb folded flat against it in the traditional gesture. "I give you my sword."

"Accepted."

"Do you wish me to persuade my men?"

"You'd let them make their own decision?"

"They've followed me this far, but most are Caladan-born. Arrakis isn't what they thought it'd be. Here, they've lost everything except their lives. I'd prefer they decided for themselves now."

"Now is no time for you to falter," Tuek said. "They've followed you this far."

"You need them, is that it?"

"We can always use experienced fighting men . . . in these times more than ever."

"You've accepted my sword. Do you wish me to persuade them?"

"I think they'll follow you, Gurney Halleck."

" 'Tis to be hoped."

"Indeed."

"I may make my own decision in this, then?"

"Your own decision."

Halleck pushed himself up from the bucket seat, feeling how much of his reserve strength even that small effort required. "For now, I'll see to their quarters and well-being," he said.

"Consult my quartermaster," Tuek said. "Drisq is his name. Tell him it's my wish that you receive every courtesy. I'll join you myself presently. I've some off-shipments of spice to see to first."

"Fortune passes everywhere," Halleck said.

"Everywhere," Tuek said. "A time of upset is a rare opportunity for our business."

Halleck nodded, heard the faint sussuration and felt the air shift as a lockport swung open beside him. He turned, ducked through it and out of the office.

He found himself in the assembly hall through which he and his men had been led by Tuek's aides. It was a long, fairly narrow area chewed out of the native rock, its smooth surface betraying the use of cutteray burners for the job. The ceiling stretched away high enough to continue the natural supporting curve of the rock and to permit internal air-convection currents. Weapons racks and lockers lined the walls.

Halleck noted with a touch of pride that those of his men still able to stand were standing—no relaxation in weariness and defeat for them. Smuggler medics were moving among them tending the wounded. Litter cases were assembled in one area down to the left, each wounded man with an Atreides companion.

The Atreides training—*"We care for our own!"*—it held like a core of native rock in them, Halleck noted.

One of his lieutenants stepped forward carrying Halleck's nine-string baliset out of its case. The man snapped a salute, said: "Sir, the medics here say there's no hope for Mattai. They have no bone and organ banks here—only outpost medicine. Mattai can't last, they say, and he has a request of you."

"What is it?"

The lieutenant thrust the baliset forward. "Mattai wants a song to ease his going, sir. He says you'll know the one . . . he's asked it of you often enough." The lieutenant swallowed. "It's the one called 'My Woman,' sir. If you—"

"I know." Halleck took the baliset, flicked the multipick out of its catch on the fingerboard. He drew a soft chord from the instrument, found that someone had already tuned it. There was a burning in his eyes, but he drove that out of his thoughts as he strolled forward, strumming the tune, forcing himself to smile casually.

Several of his men and a smuggler medic were bent over one of the litters. One of the men began singing softly as Halleck approached, catching the counter-beat with the ease of long familiarity:

"My woman stands at her window,
Curved lines 'gainst square glass.
Uprais'd arms . . . bent . . . downfolded
'Gainst sunset red and golded—
Come to me . . .

Come to me, warm arms of my lass.
For me . . .
For me, the warm arms of my lass."

The singer stopped, reached out a bandaged arm and closed the eyelids of the man on the litter.

Halleck drew a final soft chord from the baliset, thinking: *Now we are seventy-three.*

*Family life of the Royal Creche is difficult for many people to understand, but I shall try to give you a capsule view of it. My father had only one real friend, I think. That was Count Hasimir Fenring, the genetic-eunuch and one of the deadliest fighters in the Imperium. The Count, a dapper and ugly little man, brought a new slave-concubine to my father one day and I was dispatched by my mother to spy on the proceedings. All of us spied on my father as a matter of self-protection. One of the slave-concubines permitted my father under the Bene Gesserit–Guild agreement could not, of course, bear a Royal Successor, but the intrigues were constant and oppressive in their similarity. We became adept, my mother and sisters and I, at avoiding subtle instruments of death. It may seem a dreadful thing to say, but I'm not at all sure my father was innocent in all these attempts. A Royal Family is not like other families. Here was a new slave-concubine, then, red-haired like my father, willowy and graceful. She had a dancer's muscles, and her training obviously had included neuro-enticement. My father looked at her for a long time as she postured unclothed before him. Finally he said: "She is too beautiful. We will save her as a gift." You have no idea how much consternation this restraint created in the Royal Creche. Subtlety and self-control were, after all, the most deadly threats to us all.*

—**"In My Father's House" by the Princess Irulan**

Paul stood outside the stilltent in the late afternoon. The crevasse where he had pitched their camp lay in deep shadow. He stared out across the open sand at the distant cliff, wondering if he should waken his mother, who lay asleep in the tent.

Folds upon folds of dunes spread beyond their shelter. Away from the setting sun, the dunes exposed greased shadows so black they were like bits of night.

And the flatness.

His mind searched for something tall in that landscape. But there was no persuading tallness out of heat-addled air and that horizon—no bloom or gently shaken thing to mark the passage of a breeze . . . only dunes and that distant cliff beneath a sky of burnished silver-blue.

*What if there isn't one of the abandoned testing stations across there?* he wondered. *What if there are no Fremen, either, and the plants we see are only an accident?*

Within the tent, Jessica awakened, turned onto her back and peered sidelong out the transparent end at Paul. He stood with his back to her and something about his stance reminded her of his father. She sensed the well of grief rising within her and turned away.

Presently she adjusted her stillsuit, refreshed herself with water from the tent's catchpocket, and slipped out to stand and stretch the sleep from her muscles.

Paul spoke without turning: "I find myself enjoying the quiet here."

*How the mind gears itself for its environment,* she thought. And she recalled a Bene Gesserit axiom: *"The mind can go either direction under stress—toward positive or toward negative: on or off. Think of it as a spectrum whose extremes are unconsciousness at the negative end and hyperconsciousness at the positive end. The way the mind will lean under stress is strongly influenced by training."*

"It could be a good life here," Paul said.

She tried to see the desert through his eyes, seeking to encompass all the rigors this planet accepted as commonplace, wondering at the possible futures Paul had glimpsed. *One could be alone out here,* she thought, *without fear of someone behind you, without fear of the hunter.*

She stepped past Paul, lifted her binoculars, adjusted the oil lenses and studied the escarpment across from them. Yes, saguaro in the arroyos and other spiny growth . . . and a matting of low grasses, yellow-green in the shadows.

"I'll strike camp," Paul said.

Jessica nodded, walked to the fissure's mouth where she could get a sweep of the desert, and swung her binoculars to the left. A salt pan glared white there with a blending of dirty tan at its edges—a field of white out here where white was death. But the pan said another thing: *water.* At some time water had flowed across that glaring white. She lowered her binoculars, adjusted her burnoose, listened for a moment to the sound of Paul's movements.

The sun dipped lower. Shadows stretched across the salt pan. Lines of wild color spread over the sunset horizon. Color streamed into a toe of darkness testing the sand. Coal-colored shadows spread, and the thick collapse of night blotted the desert.

Stars!

She stared up at them, sensing Paul's movements as he came up beside her. The desert night focused upward with a feeling of lift toward the stars. The weight of the day receded. There came a brief flurry of breeze across her face.

"The first moon will be up soon," Paul said. "The pack's ready. I've planted the thumper."

*We could be lost forever in this hellplace,* she thought. And no one to know.

The night wind spread sand runnels that grated across her face, bringing the smell of cinnamon: a shower of odors in the dark.

"Smell that," Paul said.

"I can smell it even through the filter," she said. "Riches. But will it buy water?" She pointed across the basin. "There are no artificial lights across there."

"Fremen would be hidden in a sietch behind those rocks," he said.

A sill of silver pushed above the horizon to their right: the first moon. It lifted into view, the hand pattern plain on its face. Jessica studied the white-silver of sand exposed in the light.

"I planted the thumper in the deepest part of the crevasse," Paul said. "Whenever I light its candle it'll give us about thirty minutes."

"Thirty minutes?"

"Before it starts calling . . . a . . . worm."

"Oh. I'm ready to go."

He slipped away from her side and she heard his progress back up their fissure.

*The night is a tunnel,* she thought, *a hole into tomorrow . . . if we're to have a tomorrow.* She shook her head. *Why must I be so morbid? I was trained better than that!*

Paul returned, took up the pack, led the way down to the first spreading dune where he stopped and listened as his mother came up behind him. He heard her soft progress and the cold single-grain dribbles of sand—the desert's own code spelling out its measure of safety.

"We must walk without rhythm," Paul said and he called up memory of men walking the sand . . . both prescient memory and real memory.

"Watch how I do it," he said. "This is how Fremen walk the sand."

He stepped out onto the windward face of the dune, following the curve of it, moved with a dragging pace.

Jessica studied his progress for ten steps, followed, imitating him. She saw the sense of it: they must sound like the natural shifting of sand . . . like the wind. But muscles protested this unnatural, broken pattern: Step . . . drag . . . drag . . . step . . . step . . . wait . . . drag . . . step . . .

Time stretched out around them. The rock face ahead seemed to grow no nearer. The one behind still towered high.

"Lump! Lump! Lump! Lump!"

It was a drumming from the cliff behind.

"The thumper," Paul hissed.

Its pounding continued and they found difficulty avoiding the rhythm of it in their stride.

"Lump . . . lump . . . lump . . . lump . . . ."

They moved in a moonlit bowl punctured by that hollow thumping. Down and up through spilling dunes: step . . . drag . . . wait . . . step. . . . Across pea sand that rolled under their feet: drag . . . wait . . . step . . . .

And all the while their ears searched for a special hissing.

The sound, when it came, started so low that their own dragging passage masked it. But it grew . . . louder and louder . . . out of the west.

"Lump . . . lump . . . lump . . . lump . . . ." drummed the thumper.

The hissing approach spread across the night behind them. They turned their heads as they walked, saw the mound of the coursing worm.

"Keep moving," Paul whispered. "Don't look back."

A grating sound of fury exploded from the rock shadows they had left. It was a flailing avalanche of noise.

"Keep moving," Paul repeated.

He saw that they had reached an unmarked point where the two rock faces—the one ahead and the one behind—appeared equally remote.

And still behind them, that whipping, frenzied tearing of rocks dominated the night.

They moved on and on and on . . . . Muscles reached a stage of mechanical aching that seemed to stretch out indefinitely, but Paul saw that the beckoning escarpment ahead of them had climbed higher.

Jessica moved in a void of concentration, aware that the pressure of her will alone kept her walking. Dryness ached in her mouth, but the sounds behind drove away all hope of stopping for a sip from her stillsuit's catchpockets.

"Lump . . . lump . . . ."

Renewed frenzy erupted from the distant cliff, drowning out the thumper. Silence!

"Faster," Paul whispered.

She nodded, knowing he did not see the gesture, but needing the action to tell herself that it was necessary to demand even more from muscles that already were being taxed to their limits—the unnatural movement . . . .

The rock face of safety ahead of them climbed into the stars, and Paul saw a plane of flat sand stretching out at the base. He stepped onto it, stumbled in his fatigue, righted himself with an involuntary outthrusting of a foot.

Resonant booming shook the sand around them.

Paul lurched sideways two steps.

"Boom! Boom!"

"Drum sand!" Jessica hissed.

Paul recovered his balance. A sweeping glance took in the sand around them, the rock escarpment perhaps two hundred meters away.

Behind them, he heard a hissing—like the wind, like a riptide where there was no water.

"Run!" Jessica screamed. "Paul, run!"

They ran.

Drumsound boomed beneath their feet. Then they were out of it and into pea gravel. For a time, the running was a relief to muscles that ached from unfamiliar, rhythmless use. Here was action that could be understood. Here was rhythm. But sand and gravel dragged at their feet. And the hissing approach of the worm was storm sound that grew around them.

Jessica stumbled to her knees. All she could think of was the fatigue and the sound and the terror.

Paul dragged her up.

They ran on, hand in hand.

A thin pole jutted from the sand ahead of them. They passed it, saw another. Jessica's mind failed to register on the poles until they were past.

There was another—wind-etched surface thrust up from a crack in rock. Another.

*Rock!*

She felt it through her feet, the shock of unresisting surface, gained new strength from the firmer footing.

A deep crack stretched its vertical shadow upward into the cliff ahead of them. They sprinted for it, crowded into the narrow hole.

Behind them, the sound of the worm's passage stopped.

Jessica and Paul turned, peered out onto the desert.

Where the dunes began, perhaps fifty meters away at the foot of a rock beach, a silver-gray curve broached from the desert, sending rivers of sand and dust cascading all around. It lifted higher, resolved into a giant, questing mouth. It was a round, black hole with edges glistening in the moonlight.

The mouth snaked toward the narrow crack where Paul and Jessica huddled. Cinnamon yelled in their nostrils. Moonlight flashed from crystal teeth.

Back and forth the great mouth wove.

Paul stilled his breathing.

Jessica crouched staring.

It took intense concentration of her Bene Gesserit training to put down the primal terrors, subduing a race-memory fear that threatened to fill her mind.

Paul felt a kind of elation. In some recent instant, he had crossed a time barrier into more unknown territory. He could sense the darkness ahead, nothing revealed to his inner eye. It was as though some step he had taken had plunged him into a well . . . or into the trough of a wave where the future was invisible. The landscape had undergone a profound shifting.

Instead of frightening him, the sensation of time-darkness forced a hyper-acceleration of his other senses. He found himself registering every available aspect of the thing that lifted from the sand there seeking him. Its mouth was some eighty meters in diameter . . . crystal teeth with the curved shape of crysknives glinting around the rim . . . the bellows breath of cinnamon, subtle aldehydes . . . acids . . . .

The worm blotted out the moonlight as it brushed the rocks above them. A shower of small stones and sand cascaded into the narrow hiding place.

Paul crowded his mother farther back.

Cinnamon!

The smell of it flooded across him.

*What has the worm to do with the spice, melange?* he asked himself. And he remembered Liet-Kynes betraying a veiled reference to some association between worm and spice.

"Barrrroooom!"

It was like a peal of dry thunder coming from far off to their right.

Again: "Barrrroooom!"

The worm drew back onto the sand, lay there momentarily, its crystal teeth weaving moonflashes.

"Lump! Lump! Lump! Lump!"

*Another thumper!* Paul thought.

Again it sounded off to their right.

A shudder passed through the worm. It drew farther away into the sand. Only a mounded upper curve remained like half a bell mouth, the curve of a tunnel rearing above the dunes.

Sand rasped.

The creature sank farther, retreating, turning. It became a mound of cresting sand that curved away through a saddle in the dunes.

Paul stepped out of the crack, watched the sand wave recede across the waste toward the new thumper summons.

Jessica followed, listening: "Lump . . . lump . . . lump . . . lump . . . lump . . . ."

Presently the sound stopped.

Paul found the tube into his stillsuit, sipped at the reclaimed water.

Jessica focused on his action, but her mind felt blank with fatigue and the aftermath of terror. "Has it gone for sure?" she whispered.

"Somebody called it," Paul said. "Fremen."

She felt herself recovering. "It was so big!"

"Not as big as the one that got our 'thopter."

"Are you sure it was Fremen?"

"They used a thumper."

"Why would they help us?"

"Maybe they weren't helping us. Maybe they were just calling a worm."

"Why?"

An answer lay poised at the edge of his awareness, but refused to come. He had a vision in his mind of something to do with the telescoping barbed sticks in their packs—the "maker hooks."

"Why would they call a worm?" Jessica asked.

A breath of fear touched his mind, and he forced himself to turn away from his mother, to look up the cliff. "We'd better find a way up there before daylight." He pointed. "Those poles we passed—there are more of them."

She looked, following the line of his hand, saw the poles—wind-scratched markers—made out the shadow of a narrow ledge that twisted into a crevasse high above them.

"They mark a way up the cliff," Paul said. He settled his shoulders into the pack, crossed to the foot of the ledge and began the climb upward.

Jessica waited a moment, resting, restoring her strength; then she followed.

Up they climbed, following the guide poles until the ledge dwindled to a narrow lip at the mouth of a dark crevasse.

Paul tipped his head to peer into the shadowed place. He could feel the precarious hold his feet had on the slender ledge, but forced himself to slow caution. He saw only darkness within the crevasse. It stretched away upward, open to the stars at the top. His ears searched, found only sounds he could expect—a tiny spill of sand, an insect *brrr*, the patter of a small running creature. He tested the darkness in the crevasse with one foot, found rock beneath a gritting surface. Slowly, he inched around the corner, signaled for his mother to follow. He grasped a loose edge of her robe, helped her around.

They looked upward at starlight framed by two rock lips. Paul saw his mother beside him as a cloudy gray movement. "If we could only risk a light," he whispered.

"We have other senses than eyes," she said.

Paul slid a foot forward, shifted his weight, and probed with the other foot, met an obstruction. He lifted his foot, found a step, pulled himself up onto it. He reached back, felt his mother's arm, tugged at her robe for her to follow.

Another step.

"It goes on up to the top, I think," he whispered.

*Shallow and even steps,* Jessica thought. *Man-carved beyond a doubt.*

She followed the shadowy movement of Paul's progress, feeling out the steps. Rock walls narrowed until her shoulders almost brushed them. The steps ended in a slitted defile about twenty meters long, its floor level, and this opened onto a shallow, moonlit basin.

Paul stepped out into the rim of the basin, whispered: "What a beautiful place."

Jessica could only stare in silent agreement from her position a step behind him.

In spite of weariness, the irritation of recaths and nose plugs and the confinement of the stillsuit, in spite of fear and the aching desire for rest, this basin's beauty filled her senses, forcing her to stop and admire it.

"Like a fairyland," Paul whispered.

Jessica nodded.

Spreading away in front of her stretched desert growth—bushes, cacti, tiny clumps of leaves—all trembling in the moonlight. The ringwalls were dark to her left, moonfrosted on her right.

"This must be a Fremen place," Paul said.

"There would have to be people for this many plants to survive," she agreed. She uncapped the tube to her stillsuit's catchpockets, sipped at it. Warm, faintly acrid wetness slipped down her throat. She marked how it refreshed her. The tube's cap grated against flakes of sand as she replaced it.

Movement caught Paul's attention—to his right and down on the basin floor curving out beneath them. He stared down through smoke bushes and weeds into a wedged slab sand-surface of moonlight inhabited by an *up-hop, jump, pop-hop* of tiny motion.

"Mice!" he hissed.

*Pop-hop-hop!* they went, into shadows and out.

Something fell soundlessly past their eyes into the mice. There came a thin screech, a flapping of wings, and a ghostly gray bird lifted away across the basin with a small, dark shadow in its talons.

*We needed that reminder,* Jessica thought.

Paul continued to stare across the basin. He inhaled, sensed the softly cutting contralto smell of sage climbing the night. The predatory bird—he thought of it as the way of this desert. It had brought a stillness to the basin so unuttered that the blue-milk moonlight could almost be heard flowing across sentinel saguaro and spiked paintbush. There was a low humming of light here more basic in its harmony than any other music in his universe.

"We'd better find a place to pitch the tent," he said. "Tomorrow we can try to find the Fremen who—"

"Most intruders here regret finding the Fremen!"

It was a heavy masculine voice chopping across his words, shattering the moment. The voice came from above them and to their right.

"Please do not run, intruders," the voice said as Paul made to withdraw into the defile. "If you run you'll only waste your body's water."

*They want us for the water of our flesh!* Jessica thought. Her muscles overrode all fatigue, flowed into maximum readiness without external betrayal. She pinpointed the location of the voice, thinking: *Such stealth! I didn't hear him.* And she realized that the owner of that voice had permitted himself only the small sounds, the natural sounds of the desert.

Another voice called from the basin's rim to their left. "Make it quick, Stil. Get their water and let's be on our way. We've little enough time before dawn."

Paul, less conditioned to emergency response than his mother, felt chagrin that he had stiffened and tried to withdraw, that he had clouded his abilities by a momentary panic. He forced himself now to obey her teachings: relax, then fall into the semblance of relaxation, then into the arrested whipsnap of muscles that can slash in any direction.

Still, he felt the edge of fear within him and knew its source. This was blind time, no future he had seen . . . and they were caught between wild Fremen whose only interest was the water carried in the flesh of two unshielded bodies.

*This Fremen religious adaptation, then, is the source of what we now recognize as "The Pillars of the Universe," whose Qizara Tafwid are among us all with signs and proofs and prophecy. They bring us the Arrakeen mystical fusion whose profound beauty is typified by the stirring music built on the old forms, but stamped with the new awakening. Who has not heard and been deeply moved by "The Old Man's Hymn"?*

> *I drove my feet through a desert*
> *Whose mirage fluttered like a host.*
> *Voracious for glory, greedy for danger,*
> *I roamed the horizons of al-Kulab,*
> *Watching time level mountains*
> *In its search and its hunger for me.*
> *And I saw the sparrows swiftly approach,*
> *Bolder than the onrushing wolf.*
> *They spread in the tree of my youth.*
> *I heard the flock in my branches*
> *And was caught on their beaks and claws!*

**—from "Arrakis Awakening" by the Princess Irulan**

The man crawled across a dunetop. He was a mote caught in the glare of the noon sun. He was dressed only in torn remnants of a jubba cloak, his skin bare to the heat through the tatters. The hood had been ripped from the cloak, but the man had fashioned a turban from a torn strip of cloth. Wisps of sandy hair protruded from it, matched by a sparse beard and thick brows. Beneath the blue-within-blue eyes, remains of a dark stain spread down to his cheeks. A matted depression across mustache and beard showed where a stillsuit tube had marked out its path from nose to catchpockets.

The man stopped half across the dunecrest, arms stretched down the slipface. Blood had clotted on his back and on his arms and legs. Patches of yellow-gray sand clung to the wounds. Slowly, he brought his hands under him, pushed himself to his feet, stood there swaying. And even in this almost-random action there remained a trace of once-precise movement.

"I am Liet-Kynes," he said, addressing himself to the empty horizon, and his voice was a hoarse caricature of the strength it had known. "I am His Imperial Majesty's Planetologist," he whispered, "planetry ecologist for Arrakis. I am steward of this land."

He stumbled, fell sideways along the crusty surface of the windward face. His hands dug feebly into the sand.

*I am steward of this sand,* he thought.

He realized that he was semi-delirious, that he should dig himself into the sand, find the relatively cool underlayer and cover himself with it. But he could still smell the rank, semisweet esthers of a pre-spice pocket somewhere underneath this sand. He knew the peril within this fact more certainly than any other Fremen. If he could smell the pre-spice mass, that meant the gasses deep under the sand were nearing explosive pressure. He had to get away from here.

His hands made weak scrabbling motions along the dune face.

A thought spread across his mind—clear, distinct: *The real wealth of a planet is in its landscape, how we take part in that basic source of civilization— agriculture.*

And he thought how strange it was that his mind, long fixed on a single track, could not get off that track. The Harkonnen troopers had left him here without water or stillsuit, thinking a worm would get him if the desert didn't. They had thought it amusing to leave him alive to die by inches at the impersonal hands of his planet.

*The Harkonnens always did find it difficult to kill Fremen,* he thought. *We don't die easily. I should be dead now . . . I will be dead soon . . . but I can't stop being an ecologist.*

"The highest function of ecology is understanding consequences."

The voice shocked him because he recognized it and knew the owner of it was dead. It was the voice of his father who had been planetologist here before him—his father long dead, killed in the cave-in at Plaster Basin.

"Got yourself into quite a fix here, Son," his father said. "You should've known the consequences of trying to help the child of that Duke."

*I'm delirious,* Kynes thought.

The voice seemed to come from his right. Kynes scraped his face through sand, turning to look in that direction—nothing except a curving stretch of dune dancing with heat devils in the full glare of the sun.

"The more life there is within a system, the more niches there are for life," his father said. And the voice came now from his left, from behind him.

*Why does he keep moving around?* Kynes asked himself. *Doesn't he want me to see him?*

"Life improves the capacity of the environment to sustain life," his father said. "Life makes needed nutrients more readily available. It binds more energy into the system through the tremendous chemical interplay from organism to organism."

*Why does he keep harping on the same subject?* Kynes asked himself. *I knew that before I was ten.*

Desert hawks, carrion-eaters in this land as were most wild creatures, began to circle over him. Kynes saw a shadow pass near his hand, forced his head farther around to look upward. The birds were a blurred patch on silver-blue sky—distant flecks of soot floating above him.

"We are generalists," his father said. "You can't draw neat lines around planet-wide problems. Planetology is a cut-and-fit science."

*What's he trying to tell me?* Kynes wondered. *Is there some consequence I failed to see?*

His cheek slumped back against the hot sand, and he smelled the burned rock odor beneath the pre-spice gasses. From some corner of logic in his mind, a thought formed: *Those are carrion-eater birds over me. Perhaps some of my Fremen will see them and come to investigate.*

"To the working planetologist, his most important tool is human beings," his father said. "You must cultivate ecological literacy among the people. That's why I've created this entirely new form of ecological notation."

*He's repeating things he said to me when I was a child,* Kynes thought.

He began to feel cool, but that corner of logic in his mind told him: *The sun is overhead. You have no stillsuit and you're hot; the sun is burning the moisture out of your body.*

His fingers clawed feebly at the sand.

*They couldn't even leave me a stillsuit!*

"The presence of moisture in the air helps prevent too-rapid evaporation from living bodies," his father said.

*Why does he keep repeating the obvious?* Kynes wondered.

He tried to think of moisture in the air—grass covering this dune . . . open water somewhere beneath him, a long qanat flowing with water across the desert, and trees lining it . . . He had never seen water open to the sky except in text illustratons. Open water . . . irrigation water . . . it took five thousand cubic meters of water to irrigate one hectare of land per growing season, he remembered.

"Our first goal on Arrakis," his father said, "is grassland provinces. We will start with these mutated poverty grasses. When we have moisture locked in grasslands, we'll move on to start upland forests, then a few open bodies of water—small at first—and situated along lines of prevailing winds with windtrap moisture precipitators spaced in the lines to recapture what the wind steals. We must create a true sirocco—a moist wind—but we will never get away from the necessity for windtraps."

*Always lecturing me,* Kynes thought. *Why doesn't he shut up? Can't he see I'm dying?*

"You will die, too," his father said, "if you don't get off the bubble that's forming right now deep underneath you. It's there and you know it. You can smell the pre-spice gasses. You know the little makers are beginning to lose some of their water into the mass."

The thought of that water beneath him was maddening. He imagined it now—sealed off in strata of porous rock by the leathery half-plant, half-animal little makers—and the thin rupture that was pouring a cool stream of clearest, pure, liquid, soothing water into . . . .

*A pre-spice mass!*

He inhaled, smelling the rank sweetness. The odor was much richer around him than it had been.

Kynes pushed himself to his knees, heard a bird screech, the hurried flapping of wings.

*This is spice desert,* he thought. *There must be Fremen about even in the day sun. Surely they can see the birds and will investigate.*

"Movement across the landscape is a necessity for animal life," his father said. "Nomad peoples follow the same necessity. Lines of movement adjust to physical needs for water, food, minerals. We must control this movement now, align it for our purposes."

"Shut up, old man," Kynes muttered.

"We must do a thing on Arrakis never before attempted for an entire planet," his father said. "We must use man as a constructive ecological force—inserting adapted terraform life: a planet here, an animal there, a man in that place—to transform the water cycle, to build a new kind of landscape."

"Shut up!" Kynes croaked.

"It was lines of movement that gave us the first clue to the relationship between worms and spice," his father said.

*A worm,* Kynes thought with a surge of hope. *A maker's sure to come when this bubble bursts. But I have no hooks. How can I mount a big maker without hooks?*

He could feel frustration sapping what little strength remained to him. Water so near—only a hundred meters or so beneath him; a worm sure to come, but no way to trap it on the surface and use it.

Kynes pitched forward onto the sand, returning to the shallow depression his movements had defined. He felt sand hot against his left cheek, but the sensation was remote.

"The Arrakeen environment built itself into the evolutionary pattern of native life forms," his father said. "How strange that so few people ever looked up from the spice long enough to wonder at the near-ideal nitrogen-oxygen-$CO_2$ balance being maintained here in the absence of large areas of plant cover. The energy sphere of the planet is there to see and understand—a relentless process, but a process nonetheless. There is a gap in it? Then something occupies that gap. Science is made up of so many things that appear obvious after they are explained. I knew the little maker was there, deep in the sand, long before I ever saw it."

"Please stop lecturing me, Father," Kynes whispered.

A hawk landed on the sand near his outstretched hand. Kynes saw it fold its wings, tip its head to stare at him. He summoned the energy to croak at it. The bird hopped away two steps, but continued to stare at him.

"Men and their works have been a disease on the surface of their planets before now," his father said. "Nature tends to compensate for diseases, to remove or encapsulate them, to incorporate them into the system in her own way."

The hawk lowered its head, stretched its wings, refolded them. It transferred its attention to his outstretched hand.

Kynes found that he no longer had the strength to croak at it.

"The historical system of mutual pillage and extortion stops here on Arrakis," his father said. "You cannot go on forever stealing what you need without regard to those who come after. The physical qualities of a planet are written into its economic and political record. We have the record in front of us and our course is obvious."

*He never could stop lecturing,* Kynes thought. *Lecturing, lecturing, lecturing—always lecturing.*

The hawk hopped one step closer to Kynes' outstretched hand, turned its head first one way and then the other to study the exposed flesh.

"Arrakis is a one-crop planet," his father said. "One crop. It supports a ruling class that lives as ruling classes have lived in all times while, beneath them, a semihuman mass of semislaves exists on the leavings. It's the masses and the leavings that occupy our attention. These are far more valuable than has ever been suspected."

"I'm ignoring you, Father," Kynes whispered. "Go away."

And he thought: *Surely there must be some of my Fremen near. They cannot help but see the birds over me. They will investigate if only to see if there's moisture available.*

"The masses of Arrakis will know that we work to make the land flow with water," his father said. "Most of them, of course, will have only a semimystical understanding of how we intend to do this. Many, not understanding the prohibitive mass-ratio problem, may even think we'll bring water from some other planet rich in it. Let them think anything they wish as long as they believe in us."

*In a minute I'll get up and tell him what I think of him,* Kynes thought. *Standing there lecturing me when he should be helping me.*

The bird took another hop closer to Kynes' outstretched hand. Two more hawks drifted down to the sand behind it.

"Religion and law among our masses must be one and the same," his father said. "An act of disobedience must be a sin and require religious penalties. This will have the dual benefit of bringing both greater obedience and greater bravery. We must depend not so much on the bravery of individuals, you see, as upon the bravery of a whole population."

*Where is my population now when I need it most?* Kynes thought. He summoned all his strength, moved his hand a finger's width toward the nearest hawk. It hopped backward among its companions and all stood poised for flight.

"Our timetable will achieve the stature of a natural phenomenon," his father said. "A planet's life is a vast, tightly interwoven fabric. Vegetation and animal changes will be determined at first by the raw physical forces we manipulate. As they establish themselves, though, our changes will become controlling influences in their own right—and we will have to deal with them, too. Keep in mind, though, that we need control only three per cent of the energy surface—only three per cent—to tip the entire structure over into our self-sustaining system."

*Why aren't you helping me?* Kynes wondered. *Always the same: when I need you most, you fail me.* He wanted to turn his head, to stare in the direction of his father's voice, stare the old man down. Muscles refused to answer his demand.

Kynes saw the hawk move. It approached his hand, a cautious step at a time while its companions waited in mock indifference. The hawk stopped only a hop away from his hand.

A profound clarity filled Kynes' mind. He saw quite suddenly a potential for Arrakis that his father had never seen. The possibilities along that different path flooded through him.

"No more terrible disaster could befall your people than for them to fall into the hands of a Hero," his father said.

*Reading my mind!* Kynes thought. *Well . . . let him.*

*The messages already have been sent to my sietch villages,* he thought. *Nothing can stop them. If the Duke's son is alive they'll find him and protect him as I have commanded. They may discard the woman, his mother, but they'll save the boy.*

The hawk took one hop that brought it within slashing distance of his hand. It tipped its head to examine the supine flesh. Abruptly, it straightened, stretched its head upward and with a single screech, leaped into the air and banked away overhead with its companions behind it.

*They've come!* Kynes thought. *My Fremen have found me!*

Then he heard the sand rumbling.

Every Fremen knew the sound, could distinguish it immediately from the noises of worms or other desert life. Somewhere beneath him, the pre-spice mass had accumulated enough water and organic matter from the little makers, had reached the critical stage of wild growth. A gigantic bubble of carbon dioxide was forming deep in the sand, heaving upward in an enormous "blow" with a dust whirlpool at its center. It would exchange what had been formed deep in the sand for whatever lay on the surface.

The hawks circled overhead screeching their frustration. They knew what was happening. Any desert creature would know.

*And I am a desert creature,* Kynes thought. *You see me, Father? I am a desert creature.*

He felt the bubble lift him, felt it break and the dust whirlpool engulf him, dragging him down into cool darkness. For a moment, the sensation of coolness and the moisture were blessed relief. Then, as his planet killed him, it occurred to Kynes that his father and all the other scientists were wrong, that the most persistent principles of the universe were accident and error.

Even the hawks could appreciate these facts.

*Prophecy and prescience—How can they be put to the test in the face of the unanswered questions? Consider: How much is actual prediction of the "wave form" (as Muad'Dib referred to his vision-image) and how much is the prophet shaping the future to fit the prophecy? What of the harmonics inherent in the act of prophecy? Does the prophet see the future or does he see a line of weakness, a fault or cleavage that he may shatter with words or decisions as a diamond-cutter shatters his gem with a blow of a knife?*

**—"Private Reflections on Muad'Dib"**
**by the Princess Irulan**

*"Get their water,"* the man calling out of the night had said. And Paul fought down his fear, glanced at his mother. His trained eyes saw her readiness for battle, the waiting whipsnap of her muscles.

"It would be regrettable should we have to destroy you out of hand," the voice above them said.

*That's the one who spoke to us first,* Jessica thought. *There are at least two of them—one to our right and one on our left.*

"Cignoro hrobosa sukares hin mange la pchagavas doi me kamavas na beslas lele pal hrobas!"

It was the man to their right calling out across the basin.

To Paul, the words were gibberish, but out of her Bene Gesserit training, Jessica recognized the speech. It was Chakobsa, one of the ancient hunting languages, and the man above them was saying that perhaps these were the strangers they sought.

In the sudden silence that followed the calling voice, the hoop-wheel face of the second moon—faintly ivory blue—rolled over the rocks across the basin, bright and peering.

Scrambling sounds came from the rocks—above and to both sides . . . dark motions in the moonlight. Many figures flowed through the shadows.

*A whole troop!* Paul thought with a sudden pang.

A tall man in a mottled burnoose stepped in front of Jessica. His mouth baffle was thrown aside for clear speech, revealing a heavy beard in the sidelight of the moon, but face and eyes were hidden in the overhang of his hood.

"What have we here—jinn or human?" he asked.

And Jessica heard the true-banter in his voice, she allowed herself a faint hope. This was the voice of command, the voice that had first shocked them with its intrusion from the night.

"Human, I warrant," the man said.

Jessica sensed rather than saw the knife hidden in the fold of the man's robe. She permitted herself one bitter regret that she and Paul had no shields.

"Do you also speak?" the man asked.

Jessica put all the royal arrogance at her command into her manner and voice. Reply was urgent, but she had not heard enough of this man to be certain she had a register on his culture and weaknesses.

"Who comes on us like criminals out of the night?" she demanded.

The burnoose-hooded head showed tension in a sudden twist, then slow relaxation that revealed much. The man had good control.

Paul shifted away from his mother to separate them as targets and give each of them a clearer arena of action.

The hooded head turned at Paul's movement, opening a wedge of face to moonlight. Jessica saw a sharp nose, one glinting eye—*dark, so dark the eye, without any white in it*—a heavy brow and upturned mustache.

"A likely cub," the man said. "If you're fugitives from the Harkonnens, it may be you're welcome among us. What is it, boy?"

The possibilities flashed through Paul's mind: *A trick? A fact?* Immediate decision was needed.

"Why should you welcome fugitives?" he demanded.

"A child who thinks and speaks like a man," the tall man said. "Well, now to answer your question, my young wali, I am one who does not pay the fai, the water tribute, to the Harkonnens. That is why I might welcome a fugitive."

*He knows who we are,* Paul thought. *There's concealment in his voice.*

"I am Stilgar, the Fremen," the tall man said. "Does that speed your tongue, boy?"

*It is the same voice,* Paul thought. And he remembered the Council with this man seeking the body of a friend slain by the Harkonnens.

"I know you, Stilgar," Paul said. "I was with my father in Council when you came for the water of your friend. You took away with you my father's man, Duncan Idaho—an exchange of friends."

"And Idaho abandoned us to return to his Duke," Stilgar said.

Jessica heard the shading of disgust in his voice, held herself prepared for attack.

The voice from the rocks above them called: "We waste time here, Stil."

"This is the Duke's son," Stilgar barked. "He's certainly the one Liet told us to seek."

"But . . . a child, Stil."

"The Duke was a man and this lad used a thumper," Stilgar said. "That was a brave crossing he made in the path of *shai-hulud.*"

And Jessica heard him excluding her from his thoughts. Had he already passed sentence?

"We haven't time for the test," the voice above them protested.

"Yet he could be the Lisan al-Gaib," Stilgar said.

*He's looking for an omen!* Jessica thought.

"But the woman," the voice above them said.

Jessica readied herself anew. There had been death in that voice.

"Yes, the woman," Stilgar said. "And her water."

"You know the law," said the voice from the rocks. "One who cannot live with the desert—"

"Be quiet," Stilgar said. "Times change."

"Did Liet *command* this?" asked the voice from the rocks.

"You heard the voice of the cielago, Jamis," Stilgar said. "Why do you press me?"

And Jessica thought: *Cielago!* The clue of the tongue opened wide avenues of understanding: this was the language of Ilm and Fiqh, and cielago meant *bat*, a small flying mammal. *Voice of the cielago:* they had received a distrans message to seek Paul and herself.

"I but remind you of your duties, friend Stilgar," said the voice above them.

"My duty is the strength of the tribe," Stilgar said. "That is my only duty. I need no one to remind me of it. This child-man interests me. He is full-fleshed. He has lived on much water. He has lived away from the father sun. He has not the eyes of the ibad. Yet he does not speak or act like a weakling of the pans. Nor did his father. How can this be?"

"We cannot stay out here all night arguing," said the voice from the rocks. "If a patrol—"

"I will not tell you again, Jamis, to be quiet," Stilgar said.

The man above them remained silent, but Jessica heard him moving, crossing by a leap over a defile and working his way down to the basin floor on their left.

"The voice of the cielago suggested there'd be value to us in saving you two," Stilgar said. "I can see possibility in this strong boy-man: he is young and can learn. But what of yourself, woman?" He stared at Jessica.

*I have his voice and pattern registered now,* Jessica thought. *I could control him with a word, but he's a strong man . . . worth much more to us unblunted and with full freedom of action. We shall see.*

"I am the mother of this boy," Jessica said. "In part, his strength which you admire is the product of my training."

"The strength of a woman can be boundless," Stilgar said. "Certain it is in a Reverend Mother. Are you a Reverend Mother?"

For the moment, Jessica put aside the implications of the question, answered truthfully, "No."

"Are you trained in the ways of the desert?"

"No, but many consider my training valuable."

"We make our own judgments on value," Stilgar said.

"Every man has the right to his own judgments," she said.

"It is well that you see the reason," Stilgar said. "We cannot dally here to test you, woman. Do you understand? We'd not want your shade to plague us. I will take the boy-man, your son, and he shall have my countenance, sanctuary in my tribe. But for you, woman—you understand there is nothing personal in this? It is the rule, Istislah, in the general interest. Is that not enough?"

Paul took a half-step forward. "What are you talking about?"

Stilgar flicked a glance across Paul, but kept his attention on Jessica. "Unless you've been deep-trained from childhood to live here, you could bring destruction onto an entire tribe. It is the law, and we cannot carry useless . . . ."

Jessica's motion started as a slumping, deceptive faint to the ground. It was the obvious thing for a weak outworlder to do, and the obvious slows an opponent's reactions. It takes an instant to interpret a known thing when that thing is exposed as something unknown. She shifted as she saw his right shoulder drop to bring a weapon within the folds of his robe to bear on her new position.

A turn, a slash of her arm, a whirling of mingled robes, and she was against the rocks with the man helpless in front of her.

At his mother's first movement, Paul backed two steps. As she attacked, he dove for shadows. A bearded man rose up in his path, half-crouched, lunging forward with a weapon in one hand. Paul took the man beneath the sternum with a straight-hand jab, sidestepped and chopped the base of his neck, relieving him of the weapon as he fell.

Then Paul was into the shadows, scrambling upward among the rocks, the weapon tucked into his waist sash. He had recognized it in spite of its unfamiliar shape—a projectile weapon, and that said many things about this place, another clue that shields were not used here.

*They will concentrate on my mother and that Stilgar fellow. She can handle him. I must get to a safe vantage point where I can threaten them and give her time to escape.*

There came a chorus of sharp spring-clicks from the basin. Projectiles whined off the rocks around him. One of them flicked his robe. He squeezed around a corner in the rocks, found himself in a narrow vertical crack, began inching upward—his back against one side, his feet against the other—slowly, as silently as he could.

The roar of Stilgar's voice echoed up to him: "Get back, you worm-headed lice! She'll break my neck if you come near!"

A voice out of the basin said: "The boy got away, Stil. What are we—"

"Of course he got away, you sand-brained . . . Ugh-h-h! Easy, woman!"

"Tell them to stop hunting my son," Jessica said.

"They've stopped, woman. He got away as you intended him to. Great gods below! Why didn't you say you were a weirding woman and a fighter?"

"Tell your men to fall back," Jessica said. "Tell them to go out into the basin where I can see them . . . and you'd better believe that I know how many of them there are."

And she thought: *This is the delicate moment, but if this man is as sharp-minded as I think him, we have a chance.*

Paul inched his way upward, found a narrow ledge on which he could rest and look down into the basin. Stilgar's voice came up to him.

"And if I refuse? How can you . . . ugh-h-h! Leave be, woman! We mean no harm to you, now. Great gods! If you can do this to the strongest of us, you're worth ten times your weight of water."

*Now, the test of reason,* Jessica thought. She said: "You ask after the Lisan al-Gaib."

"You could be the folk of the legend," he said, "but I'll believe that when it's been tested. All I know now is that you came here with that stupid Duke who. . . . Aiee-e-e! Woman! I care not if you kill me! He was honorable and brave, but it was stupid to put himself in the way of the Harkonnen fist!"

Silence.

Presently, Jessica said: "He had no choice, but we'll not argue it. Now, tell that man of yours behind the bush over there to stop trying to bring his weapon to bear on me, or I'll rid the universe of you and take him next."

"You there!" Stilgar roared. "Do as she says!"

"But, Stil—"

"Do as she says, you wormfaced, crawling, sand-brained piece of lizard turd! Do it or I'll help her dismember you! Can't you see the worth of this woman?"

The man at the bush straightened from his partial concealment, lowered his weapon.

"He has obeyed," Stilgar said.

"Now," Jessica said, "explain clearly to your people what it is you wish of me. I want no young hothead to make a foolish mistake."

"When we slip into the villages and towns we must mask our origin, blend with the pan and graben folk," Stilgar said. "We carry no weapons, for the crysknife is sacred. But you, woman, you have the weirding ability of battle. We'd only heard of it and many doubted, but one cannot doubt what he sees with his own eyes. You mastered an armed Fremen. *This* is a weapon no search could expose."

There was a stirring in the basin as Stilgar's words sank home.

"And if I agree to teach you the . . . weirding way?"

"My countenance for you as well as your son."

"How can we be sure of the truth in your promise?"

Stilgar's voice lost some of its subtle undertone of reasoning, took on an edge of bitterness. "Out here, woman, we carry no paper for contracts. We make no evening promises to be broken at dawn. When a man says a thing, that's the contract. As leader of my people, I've put them in bond to my word. Teach us this weirding way and you have sanctuary with us as long as you wish. Your water shall mingle with our water."

"Can you speak for all Fremen?" Jessica asked.

"In time, that may be. But only my brother, Liet, speaks for all Fremen. Here, I promise only secrecy. My people will not speak of you to any other sietch. The Harkonnens have returned to Dune in force and your Duke is dead. It is said that you two died in a Mother storm. The hunter does not seek dead game."

*There's safety in that,* Jessica thought. *But these people have good communications and a message could be sent.*

"I presume there was a reward offered for us," she said.

Stilgar remained silent, and she could almost see the thoughts turning over in his head, sensing the shifts of his muscles beneath her hands.

Presently, he said: "I will say it once more: I've given the tribe's word-bond. My people know your worth to us now. What could the Harkonnens give us? Our freedom? Hah! No, you are the taqwa, that which buys us more than all the spice in the Harkonnen coffers."

"Then I shall teach you my way of battle," Jessica said, and she sensed the unconscious ritual-intensity of her own words.

"Now, you will release me?"

"So be it," Jessica said. She released her hold on him, stepped aside in full view of the band in the basin. *This is the test-mashed,* she thought. *But Paul must know about them even if I die for his knowledge.*

In the waiting silence, Paul inched forward to get a better view of where his mother stood. As he moved, he heard heavy breathing, suddenly stilled, above him in the vertical crack of the rock, and sensed a faint shadow there outlined against the stars.

Stilgar's voice came up from the basin: "You, up there! Stop hunting the boy. He'll come down presently."

The voice of a young boy or girl sounded from the darkness above Paul: "But, Stil, he can't be far from—"

"I said leave him be, Chani! You spawn of a lizard!"

There came a whispered imprecation from above Paul and a low voice: "Call *me* spawn of a lizard!" But the shadow pulled back out of view.

Paul returned his attention to the basin, picking out the gray-shadowed movement of Stilgar beside his mother.

"Come in, all of you," Stilgar called. He turned to Jessica. "And now I'll ask you how *we* may be certain you'll fulfill your half of our bargain? You're the one's lived with papers and empty contracts and such as—"

"We of the Bene Gesserit don't break our vows any more than you do," Jessica said.

There was a protracted silence, then a multiple hissing of voices: "A Bene Gesserit witch!"

Paul brought his captured weapon from his sash, trained it on the dark figure of Stilgar, but the man and his companions remained immobile, staring at Jessica.

"It *is* the legend," someone said.

"It was said that the Shadout Mapes gave this report on you," Stilgar said. "But a thing so important must be tested. If you are the Bene Gesserit of the legend whose son will lead us to paradise . . . ." He shrugged.

Jessica sighed, thinking: *So our Missionaria Protectiva even planted religious safety valves all through this hell hole. Ah, well . . . it'll help, and that's what it was meant to do.*

She said: "The seeress who brought you the legend, she gave it under the binding of karama and ijaz, the miracle and the inimitability of the prophecy— this I know. Do you wish to see a sign?"

His nostrils flared in the moonlight. "We cannot tarry for the rites," he whispered.

Jessica recalled a chart Kynes had shown her while arranging emergency escape routes. How long ago it seemed. There had been a place called "Sietch Tabr" on the chart and beside it the notation: "Stilgar."

"Perhaps when we get to Sietch Tabr," she said.

The revelation shook him, and Jessica thought: *If only he knew the tricks we use! She must've been good, that Bene Gesserit of the Missionaria Protectiva. These Fremen are beautifully prepared to believe in us.*

Stilgar shifted uneasily. "We must go now."

She nodded, letting him know that they left with her permission.

He looked up at the cliff almost directly at the rock ledge where Paul crouched. "You there, lad: you may come down now." He returned his attention to Jessica, spoke with an apologetic tone: "Your son made an incredible amount of noise climbing. He has much to learn lest he endanger us all, but he's young."

"No doubt we have much to teach each other," Jessica said. "Meanwhile, you'd best see to your companion out there. My noisy son was a bit rough in disarming him."

Stilgar whirled, his hood flapping. "Where?"

"Beyond those bushes." She pointed.

Stilgar touched two of his men. "See to it." He glanced at his companions, identifying them. "Jamis is missing." He turned to Jessica. "Even your cub knows the weirding way."

"And you'll notice that my son hasn't stirred from up there as you ordered," Jessica said.

The two men Stilgar had sent returned supporting a third who stumbled and gasped between them. Stilgar gave them a flicking glance, returned his attention to Jessica. "The son will take only your orders, eh? Good. He knows discipline."

"Paul, you may come down now," Jessica said.

Paul stood up, emerging into moonlight above his concealing cleft, slipped the Fremen weapon back into his sash. As he turned, another figure arose from the rocks to face him.

In the moonlight and reflection off gray stone, Paul saw a small figure in Fremen robes, a shadowed face peering out at him from the hood, and the muzzle of one of the projectile weapons aimed at him from a fold of robe.

"I am Chani, daughter of Liet."

The voice was lilting, half filled with laughter.

"I would not have permitted you to harm my companions," she said.

Paul swallowed. The figure in front of him turned into the moon's path and he saw an elfin face, black pits of eyes. The familiarity of that face, the features out of numberless visions in his earliest prescience, shocked Paul to stillness. He remembered the angry bravado with which he had once described this face-from-a-dream, telling the Reverend Mother Gaius Helen Mohiam: "I will meet her."

And here was the face, but in no meeting he had ever dreamed.

"You were as noisy as shai-hulud in a rage," she said. "And you took the most difficult way up here. Follow me; I'll show you an easier way down."

He scrambled out of the cleft, followed the swirling of her robe across a tumbled landscape. She moved like a gazelle, dancing over the rocks. Paul felt hot blood in his face, was thankful for the darkness.

*That girl!* She was like a touch of destiny. He felt caught up on a wave, in tune with a motion that lifted all his spirits.

They stood presently amid the Fremen on the basin floor.

Jessica turned a wry smile on Paul, but spoke to Stilgar: "This will be a good exchange of teachings. I hope you and your people feel no anger at our violence. It seemed . . . necessary. You were about to . . . make a mistake."

"To save one from a mistake is a gift of paradise," Stilgar said. He touched his lips with his left hand, lifted the weapon from Paul's waist with the other, tossed it to a companion. "You will have your own maula pistol, lad, when you've earned it."

Paul started to speak, hesitated, remembering his mother's teaching: *"Beginnings are such delicate times."*

"My son has what weapons he needs," Jessica said. She stared at Stilgar, forcing him to think of how Paul had acquired the pistol.

Stilgar glanced at the man Paul had subdued—Jamis. The man stood at one side, head lowered, breathing heavily. "You are a difficult woman," Stilgar said. He held out his left hand to a companion, snapped his fingers. "Kushti bakka te."

*More Chakobsa*, Jessica thought.

The companion pressed two squares of gauze into Stilgar's hand. Stilgar ran them through his fingers, fixed one around Jessica's neck beneath her hood, fitted the other around Paul's neck in the same way.

"Now you wear the kerchief of the bakka," he said. "If we become separated, you will be recognized as belonging to Stilgar's sietch. We will talk of weapons another time."

He moved out through his band now, inspecting them, giving Paul's Fremkit pack to one of his men to carry.

*Bakka*, Jessica thought, recognizing the religious term: *bakka—the weeper*. She sensed how the symbolism of the kerchiefs united this band. *Why should weeping unite them?* she asked herself.

Stilgar came to the young girl who had embarrassed Paul, said: "Chani, take the child-man under your wing. Keep him out of trouble."

Chani touched Paul's arm. "Come along, child-man."

Paul hid the anger in his voice, said: "My name is Paul. It were well you—"

"We'll give you a name, manling," Stilgar said, "in the time of the mihna, at the test of aql."

*The test of reason*, Jessica translated. The sudden need of Paul's ascendancy overrode all other consideration, and she barked, "My son's been tested with the gom jabbar!"

In the stillness that followed, she knew she had struck to the heart of them.

"There's much we don't know of each other," Stilgar said. "But we tarry overlong. Day-sun mustn't find us in the open." He crossed to the man Paul had struck down, said, "Jamis, can you travel?"

A grunt answered him. "Surprised me, he did. 'Twas an accident. I can travel."

"No accident," Stilgar said. "I'll hold you responsible with Chani for the lad's safety, Jamis. These people have my countenance."

Jessica stared at the man, Jamis. His was the voice that had argued with Stilgar from the rocks. His was the voice with death in it. And Stilgar had seen fit to reinforce his order with this Jamis.

Stilgar flicked a testing glance across the group, motioned two men out. "Larus and Farrukh, you are to hide our tracks. See that we leave no trace. Extra care—we have two with us who've not been trained." He turned, hand upheld and aimed across the basin. "In squad line with flankers—move out. We must be at Cave of the Ridges before dawn."

Jessica fell into step beside Stilgar, counting heads. There were forty Fremen—she and Paul made it forty-two. And she thought: *They travel as a military company—even the girl, Chani.*

Paul took a place in the line behind Chani. He had put down the black feeling at being caught by a girl. In his mind now was the memory called up by his mother's barked reminder: "My son's been tested with the gom jabbar!" He found that his hand tingled with remembered pain.

"Watch where you go," Chani hissed. "Do not brush against a bush lest you leave a thread to show our passage."

Paul swallowed, nodded.

Jessica listened to the sounds of the troop, hearing her own footsteps and Paul's, marveling at the way the Fremen moved. They were forty people crossing the basin with only the sounds natural to the place—ghostly feluccas, their robes flitting through the shadows. Their destination was Sietch Tabr—Stilgar's sietch.

She turned the word over in her mind: sietch. It was a Chakobsa word, unchanged from the old hunting language of countless centuries. Sietch: a meeting place in time of danger. The profound implications of the word and the language were just beginning to register with her after the tension of their encounter.

"We move well," Stilgar said. "With Shai-hulud's favor, we'll reach Cave of the Ridges before dawn."

Jessica nodded, conserving her strength, sensing the terrible fatigue she held at bay by force of will . . . and, she admitted it: by the force of elation. Her mind focused on the value of this troop, seeing what was revealed here about the Fremen culture.

*All of them,* she thought, *an entire culture trained to military order. What a priceless thing is here for an outcast Duke!*

> The Fremen were supreme in that quality the ancients called "span-nungsbogen"—which is the self-imposed delay between desire for a thing and the act of reaching out to grasp that thing.

> **—from "The Wisdom of Muad'Dib"**
> **by the Princess Irulan**

They approached Cave of the Ridges at dawnbreak, moving through a split in the basin wall so narrow they had to turn sideways to negotiate it. Jessica saw Stilgar detach guards in the thin dawnlight, saw them for a moment as they began their scrambling climb up the cliff.

Paul turned his head upward as he walked, seeing the tapestry of this planet cut in cross section where the narrow cleft gaped toward gray-blue sky.

Chani pulled at his robe to hurry him, said: "Quickly. It is already light."

"The men who climbed above us, where are they going?" Paul whispered.

"The first daywatch," she said. "Hurry now!"

*A guard left outside,* Paul thought. *Wise. But it would've been wiser still for us to approach this place in separate bands. Less chance of losing the whole troop.* He paused in the thought, realizing that this was guerrilla thinking, and he remembered his father's fear that the Atreides might become a guerrilla house.

"Faster," Chani whispered.

Paul sped his steps, hearing the swish of robes behind. And he thought of the words of the sirat from Yueh's tiny O.C. Bible.

*"Paradise on my right, Hell on my left and the Angel of Death behind."* He rolled the quotation in his mind.

They rounded a corner where the passage widened. Stilgar stood at one side motioning them into a low hole that opened at right angles.

"Quickly!" he hissed. "We're like rabbits in a cage if a patrol catches us here."

Paul bent for the opening, followed Chani into a cave illuminated by thin gray light from somewhere ahead.

"You can stand up," she said.

He straightened, studied the place: a deep and wide area with domed ceiling that curved away just out of a man's handreach. The troop spread out through shadows. Paul saw his mother come up on one side, saw her examine their companions. And he noted how she failed to blend with the Fremen even though her garb was identical. The way she moved—such a sense of power and grace.

"Find a place to rest and stay out of the way, child-man," Chani said. "Here's food." She pressed two leaf-wrapped morsels into his hand. They reeked of spice.

Stilgar came up behind Jessica, called an order to a group on the left. "Get the doorseal in place and see to moisture security." He turned to another Fremen: "Lemil, get glowglobes." He took Jessica's arm. "I wish to show you something, weirding woman." He led her around a curve of rock toward the light source.

Jessica found herself looking out across the wide lip of another opening to the cave, an opening high in a cliff wall—looking out across another basin about ten or twelve kilometers wide. The basin was shielded by high rock walls. Sparse clumps of plant growth were scattered around it.

As she looked at the dawn-gray basin, the sun lifted over the far escarpment illuminating a biscuit-colored landscape of rocks and sand. And she noted how the sun of Arrakis appeared to leap over the horizon.

*It's because we want to hold it back,* she thought. *Night is safer than day.* There came over her then a longing for a rainbow in this place that would never see rain. *I must suppress such longings,* she thought. *They're a weakness. I no longer can afford weaknesses.*

Stilgar gripped her arm, pointed across the basin. "There! There you see proper Druses."

She looked where he pointed, saw movement: people on the basin floor scattering at the daylight into the shadows of the opposite cliffwall. In spite of the distance, their movements were plain in the clear air. She lifted her binoculars from beneath her robe, focused the oil lenses on the distant people. Kerchiefs fluttered like a flight of multicolored butterflies.

"That is home," Stilgar said. "We will be there this night." He stared across the basin, tugging at his mustache. "My people stayed out overlate working. That means there are no patrols about. I'll signal them later and they'll prepare for us."

"Your people show good discipline," Jessica said. She lowered the binoculars, saw that Stilgar was looking at them.

"They obey the preservation of the tribe," he said. "It is the way we choose among us for a leader. The leader is the one who is the strongest, the one who brings water and security." He lifted his attention to her face.

She returned his stare, noted the whiteless eyes, the stained eyepits, the dust-rimmed beard and mustache, the line of the catchtube curving down from his nostrils into his stillsuit.

"Have I compromised your leadership by besting you, Stilgar?" she asked.

"You did not call me out," he said.

"It's important that a leader keep the respect of his troop," she said.

"Isn't a one of those sandlice I cannot handle," Stilgar said. "When you bested me, you bested us all. Now, they hope to learn from you . . . the weirding way . . . and some are curious to see if you intend to call me out."

She weighed the implications. "By besting you in formal battle?"

He nodded. "I'd advise you against this because they'd not follow you. You're not of the sand. They saw this in our night's passage."

"Practical people," she said.

"True enough." He glanced at the basin. "We know our needs. But not many are thinking deep thoughts now this close to home. We've been out overlong arranging to deliver our spice quota to the free traders for the cursed Guild . . . may their faces be forever black."

Jessica stopped in the act of turning away from him, looked back up into his face. "The Guild? What has the Guild to do with your spice?"

"It's Liet's command," Stilgar said. "We know the reason, but the taste of it sours us. We bribe the Guild with a monstrous payment in spice to keep our skies clear of satellites and such that none may spy what we do to the face of Arrakis."

She weighed out her words, remembering that Paul had said this must be the reason Arrakeen skies were clear of satellites. "And what is it you do to the face of Arrakis that must not be seen?"

"We change it . . . slowly but with certainty . . . to make it fit for human life. Our generation will not see it, nor our children nor our children's children nor the grandchildren of their children . . . but it will come." He stared with veiled eyes out over the basin. "Open water and tall green plants and people walking freely without stillsuits."

*So that's the dream of this Liet-Kynes,* she thought. And she said: "Bribes are dangerous; they have a way of growing larger and larger."

"They grow," he said, "but the slow way is the safe way."

Jessica turned, looked out over the basin, trying to see it the way Stilgar was seeing it in his imagination. She saw only the grayed mustard stain of distant rocks and a sudden hazy motion in the sky above the cliffs.

"Ah-h-h-h," Stilgar said.

She thought at first it must be a patrol vehicle, then realized it was a mirage—another landscape hovering over the desert-sand and a distant wavering of greenery and in the middle distance a long worm traveling the surface with what looked like Fremen robes fluttering on its back.

The mirage faded.

"It would be better to ride," Stilgar said, "but we cannot permit a maker into this basin. Thus, we must walk again tonight."

*Maker—their word for worm,* she thought.

She measured the import of his words, the statement that they could not *permit* a worm into this basin. She knew what she had seen in the mirage—Fremen riding on the back of a giant worm. It took heavy control not to betray her shock at the implications.

"We must be getting back to the others," Stilgar said. "Else my people may suspect I dally with you. Some already are jealous that my hands tasted your loveliness when we struggled last night in Tuono Basin."

"That will be enough of that!" Jessica snapped.

"No offense," Stilgar said, and his voice was mild. "Women among us are not taken against their will . . . and with you . . . ." He shrugged. ". . . even that convention isn't required."

"You will keep in mind that I was a duke's lady," she said, but her voice was calmer.

"As you wish," he said. "It's time to seal off this opening, to permit relaxation of stillsuit discipline. My people need to rest in comfort this day. Their families will give them little rest on the morrow."

Silence fell between them.

Jessica stared out into the sunlight. She had heard what she had heard in Stilgar's voice—the unspoken offer of more than his *countenance.* Did he need a wife? She realized she could step into that place with him. It would be one way to end conflict over tribal leadership—female properly aligned with male.

But what of Paul then? Who could tell yet what rules of parenthood prevailed here? And what of the unborn daughter she had carried these few weeks? What of a dead Duke's daughter? And she permitted herself to face fully the significance of this other child growing within her, to see her own motives in permitting the conception. She knew what it was—she had succumbed to that profound drive shared by all creatures who are faced with death—the drive to seek immortality through progeny. The fertility drive of the species had overpowered them.

Jessica glanced at Stilgar, saw that he was studying her, waiting. *A daughter born here to a woman wed to such a one as this man—what would be the fate of such a daughter?* she asked herself. *Would he try to limit the necessities that a Bene Gesserit must follow?*

Stilgar cleared his throat and revealed then that he understood some of the questions in her mind. "What is important for a leader is that which makes him a leader. It is the needs of his people. If you teach me your powers, there may come a day when one of us must challenge the other. I would prefer some alternative."

"There are several alternatives?" she asked.

"The Sayyadina," he said. "Our Reverend Mother is old."

*Their Reverend Mother!*

Before she could probe this, he said: "I do not necessarily offer myself as mate. This is nothing personal, for you are beautiful and desirable. But should you become one of my women, that might lead some of my young men to believe that I'm too much concerned with pleasures of the flesh and not enough concerned with the tribe's needs. Even now they listen to us and watch us."

*A man who weighs his decisions, who thinks of consequences,* she thought.

"There are those among my young men who have reached the age of wild spirits," he said. "They must be eased through this period. I must leave no great reasons around for them to challenge me. Because I would have to maim and kill among them. This is not the proper course for a leader if it can be avoided with honor. A leader, you see, is one of the things that distinguishes a mob from a people. He maintains the level of individuals. Too few individuals, and a people reverts to a mob."

His words, the depth of their awareness, the fact that he spoke as much to her as to those who secretly listened, forced her to re-evaluate him.

*He has stature,* she thought. *Where did he learn such inner balance?*

"The law that demands our form of choosing a leader is a just law," Stilgar said. "But it does not follow that justice is always the thing a people needs. What we truly need now is time to grow and prosper, to spread our force over more land."

*What is his ancestry?* she wondered. *Whence comes such breeding?* She said: "Stilgar, I underestimated you."

"Such was my suspicion," he said.

"Each of us apparently underestimated the other," she said.

"I should like an end to this," he said. "I should like friendship with you . . . and trust. I should like that respect for each other which grows in the breast without demand for the huddlings of sex."

"I understand," she said.

"Do you trust me?" 

"I hear your sincerity."

"Among us," he said, "the Sayyadina, when they are not the formal leaders, hold a special place of honor. They teach. They maintain the strength of God here." He touched his breast.

*Now I must probe this Reverend Mother mystery,* she thought. And she said: "You spoke of your Reverend Mother . . . and I've heard words of legend and prophecy."

"It is said that a Bene Gesserit and her offspring hold the key to our future," he said.

"Do you believe I am that one?"

She watched his face, thinking: *The young reed dies so easily. Beginnings are times of such great peril.*

"We do not know," he said.

She nodded, thinking: *He's an honorable man. He wants a sign from me, but he'll not tip fate by telling me the sign.*

Jessica turned her head, stared down into the basin at the golden shadows, the purple shadows, the vibrations of dust-mote air across the lip of their cave. Her mind was filled suddenly with feline prudence. She knew the cant of the Missionaria Protectiva, knew how to adapt the techniques of legend and fear and hope to her emergency needs, but she sensed wild changes here . . . as though someone had been in among these Fremen and capitalized on the Missionaria Protectiva's imprint.

Stilgar cleared his throat.

She sensed his impatience, knew that the day moved ahead and men waited to seal off this opening. This was a time for boldness on her part, and she realized what she needed: some dar al-hikman, some school of translation that would give her . . . .

"Adab," she whispered.

Her mind felt as though it had rolled over within her. She recognized the sensation with a quickening of pulse. Nothing in all the Bene Gesserit training carried such a signal of recognition. It could be only the adab, the demanding memory that comes upon you of itself. She gave herself up to it, allowing the words to flow from her.

"Ibn qirtaiba," she said, "as far as the spot where the dust ends." She stretched out an arm from her robe, seeing Stilgar's eyes go wide. She heard a rustling of many robes in the background. "I see a . . . Fremen with the book of examples," she intoned. "He reads to al-Lat, the sun whom he defied and subjugated. He reads to the Sadus of the Trial and this is what he reads:

"Mine enemies are like green blades eaten down
That did stand in the path of the tempest.
Hast thou not seen what our Lord did?
He sent the pestilence among them
That did lay schemes against us.
They are like birds scattered by the huntsman.
Their schemes are like pellets of poison
That every mouth rejects."

A trembling passed through her. She dropped her arm.

Back to her from the inner cave's shadows came a whispered response of many voices: "Their works have been overturned."

"The fire of God mount over thy heart," she said. And she thought: *Now, it goes in the proper channel.*

"The fire of God set alight," came the response.

She nodded. "Thine enemies shall fall," she said.

"Bi-la kaifa," they answered.

In the sudden hush, Stilgar bowed to her. "Sayyadina," he said. "If the Shai-hulud grant, then you may yet pass within to become a Reverend Mother."

*Pass within,* she thought. *An odd way of putting it. But the rest of it fitted into the cant well enough.* And she felt a cynical bitterness at what she had done. *Our Missionaria Protectiva seldom fails. A place was prepared for us in this wilderness. The prayer of the salat has carved out our hiding place. Now . . . I must play the part of Auliya, the Friend of God . . . Sayyadina to rogue peoples who've been so heavily imprinted with our Bene Gesserit soothsay they even call their chief priestesses Reverend Mothers.*

Paul stood beside Chani in the shadows of the inner cave. He could still taste the morsel she had fed him—bird flesh and grain bound with spice honey and encased in a leaf. In tasting it he had realized he never before had eaten such a concentration of spice essence and there had been a moment of fear. He knew what this essence could do to him—the *spice change* that pushed his mind into prescient awareness.

"Bi-la kaifa," Chani whispered.

He looked at her, seeing the awe with which the Fremen appeared to accept his mother's words. Only the man called Jamis seemed to stand aloof from the ceremony, holding himself apart with arms folded across his breast.

"Duy yakha hin mange," Chani whispered. "Duy punra hin mange. I have two eyes. I have two feet."

And she stared at Paul with a look of wonder.

Paul took a deep breath, trying to still the tempest within him. His mother's words had locked onto the working of the spice essence, and he had felt her voice rise and fall within him like the shadows of an open fire. Through it all, he had sensed the edge of cynicism in her—he knew her so well!—but nothing could stop this thing that had begun with a morsel of food.

*Terrible purpose!*

He sensed it, the race consciousness that he could not escape. There was the sharpened clarity, the inflow of data, the cold precision of his awareness. He sank to the floor, sitting with his back against rock, giving himself up to it. Awareness flowed into that timeless stratum where he could view time, sensing the available paths, the winds of the future . . . the winds of the past: the one-eyed vision of the future—all combined in a trinocular vision that permitted him to see time-become-space.

There was danger, he felt, of overrunning himself, and he had to hold onto his awareness of the present, sensing the blurred deflection of experience, the flowing moment, the continual solidification of that-which-is into the perpetual-was.

In grasping the present, he felt for the first time the massive steadiness of time's movement everywhere complicated by shifting currents, waves, surges, and countersurges, like surf against rocky cliffs. It gave him a new understanding of his prescience, and he saw the source of blind time, the source of error in it, with an immediate sensation of fear.

The prescience, he realized, was an illumination that incorporated the limits of what it revealed—at once a source of accuracy and meaningful error. A kind of Heisenberg indeterminacy intervened: the expenditure of energy that revealed what he saw, changed what he saw.

And what he saw was a time nexus within this cave, a boiling of possibilities focused here, wherein the most minute action—the wink of an eye, a careless word, a misplaced grain of sand—moved a gigantic lever across the known universe. He saw violence with the outcome subject to so many variables that his slightest movement created vast shiftings in the pattern.

The vision made him want to freeze into immobility, but this, too, was action with its consequences.

The countless consequences—lines fanned out from this cave, and along most of these consequence-lines he saw his own dead body with blood flowing from a gaping knife wound.

*My father, the Padishah Emperor, was 72 yet looked no more than 35 the year he encompassed the death of Duke Leto and gave Arrakis back to the Harkonnens. He seldom appeared in public wearing other than a Sardaukar uniform and a Burseg's black helmet with the Imperial lion in gold upon its crest. The uniform was an open reminder of where his power lay. He was not always that blatant, though. When he wanted, he could radiate charm and sincerity, but I often wonder in these later days if anything about him was as it seemed. I think now he was a man fighting constantly to escape the bars of an invisible cage. You must remember that he was an emperor, father-head of a dynasty that reached back into the dimmest history. But we denied him a legal son. Was this not the most terrible defeat a ruler ever suffered? My mother obeyed her Sister Superiors where the Lady Jessica disobeyed. Which of them was the stronger? History already has answered.*

**—"In My Father's House" by the Princess Irulan**

Jessica awakened in cave darkness, sensing the stir of Fremen around her, smelling the acrid stillsuit odor. Her inner timesense told her it would soon be night outside, but the cave remained in blackness, shielded from the desert by the plastic hoods that trapped their body moisture within this space.

She realized that she had permitted herself the utterly relaxing sleep of great fatigue, and this suggested something of her own unconscious assessment on personal security within Stilgar's troop. She turned in the hammock that had been fashioned of her robe, slipped her feet to the rock floor and into her desert boots.

*I must remember to fasten the boots slip-fashion to help my stillsuit's pumping action,* she thought. *There are so many things to remember.*

She could still taste their morning meal—the morsel of bird flesh and grain bound within a leaf with spice honey—and it came to her that the use of time was turned around here: night was the day of activity and day was the time of rest.

*Night conceals; night is safest.*

She unhooked her robe from its hammock pegs in a rock alcove, fumbled with the fabric in the dark until she found the top, slipped into it.

How to get a message out to the Bene Gesserit? she wondered. They would have to be told of the two strays in Arrakeen sanctuary.

Glowglobes came alight farther into the cave. She saw people moving there, Paul among them already dressed and with his hood thrown back to reveal the aquiline Atreides profile.

He had acted so strangely before they retired, she thought. *Withdrawn.* He was like one come back from the dead, not yet fully aware of his return, his eyes half shut and glassy with the inward stare. It made her think of his warning about the spice-impregnated diet: *addictive.*

*Are there side effects?* she wondered. *He said it had something to do with his prescient faculty, but he has been strangely silent about what he sees.*

Stilgar came from shadows to her right, crossed to the group beneath the glowglobes. She marked how he fingered his beard and the watchful, cat-stalking look of him.

Abrupt fear shot through Jessica as her senses awakened to the tensions visible in the people gathered around Paul—the stiff movements, the ritual positions.

"They have my countenance!" Stilgar rumbled.

Jessica recognized the man Stilgar confronted—Jamis! She saw then the rage in Jamis—the tight set of his shoulders.

*Jamis, the man Paul bested!* she thought.

"You know the rule, Stilgar," Jamis said.

"Who knows it better?" Stilgar asked, and she heard the tone of placation in his voice, the attempt to smooth something over.

"I choose the combat," Jamis growled.

Jessica sped across the cave, grasped Stilgar's arm. "What is this?" she asked.

"It is the amtal rule," Stilgar said. "Jamis is demanding the right to test your part in the legend."

"She must be championed," Jamis said. "If her champion wins, that's the truth in it. But it's said . . . ." He glanced across the press of people. ". . . that she'd need no champion from the Fremen—which can mean only that she brings her own champion."

*He's talking of single combat with Paul!* Jessica thought.

She released Stilgar's arm, took a half-step forward. "I'm always my own champion," she said. "The meaning's simple enough for . . . ."

"You'll not tell us our ways!" Jamis snapped. "Not without more proof than I've seen. Stilgar could've told you what to say last morning. He could've filled your mind full of the coddle and you could've bird-talked it to us, hoping to make a false way among us."

*I can take him,* Jessica thought, *but that might conflict with the way they interpret the legend.* And again she wondered at the way the Missionaria Protectiva's work had been twisted on this planet.

Stilgar looked at Jessica, spoke in a low voice but one designed to carry to the crowd's fringe. "Jamis is one to hold a grudge, Sayyadina. Your son bested him and—"

"It was an accident!" Jamis roared. "There was witch-force at Tuono Basin and I'll prove it now!"

". . . and I've bested him myself," Stilgar continued. "He seeks by this tahaddi challenge to get back at me as well. There's too much of violence in Jamis for him ever to make a good leader—too much ghafla, the distraction. He gives his mouth to the rules and his heart to the sarfa, the turning away. No, he could never make a good leader. I've preserved him this long because he's useful in a fight as such, but when he gets this carving anger on him he's dangerous to his own society."

"Stilgar-r-r-r!" Jamis rumbled.

And Jessica saw what Stilgar was doing, trying to enrage Jamis, to take the challenge away from Paul.

Stilgar faced Jamis, and again Jessica heard the soothing in the rumbling voice. "Jamis, he's but a boy. He's—"

"You named him a man," Jamis said. "His mother *says* he's been through the gom jabbar. He's full-fleshed and with a surfeit of water. The ones who carried their pack say there's literjons of water in it. Literjons! And us sipping our catch-pockets the instant they show dewsparkle."

Stilgar glanced at Jessica. "Is this true? Is there water in your pack?"

"Yes."

"Literjons of it?"

"Two literjons."

"What was intended with this wealth?"

*Wealth?* she thought. She shook her head, feeling the coldness in his voice.

"Where I was born, water fell from the sky and ran over the land in wide rivers," she said. "There were oceans of it so broad you could not see the other shore. I've not been trained to your water discipline. I never before had to think of it this way."

A sighing gasp arose from the people around them: "Water fell from the sky . . . it ran *over* the land."

"Did you know there're those among us who've lost from their catch-pockets by accident and will be in sore trouble before we reach Tabr this night?"

"How could I know?" Jessica shook her head. "If they're in need, give them water from our pack."

"Is that what you intended with this wealth?"

"I intended it to save life," she said.

"Then we accept your blessing, Sayyadina."

"You'll not buy us off with water," Jamis growled. "Nor will you anger me against yourself, Stilgar. I see you trying to make me call you out before I've proved my words."

Stilgar faced Jamis. "Are you determined to press this fight against a child, Jamis?" His voice was low, venomous.

"She must be championed."

"Even though she has my countenance?"

"I invoke the amtal rule," Jamis said. "It's my right."

Stilgar nodded. "Then, if the boy does not carve you down, you'll answer to my knife afterward. And this time I'll not hold back the blade as I've done before."

"You cannot do this thing," Jessica said. "Paul's just—"

"You must not interfere, Sayyadina," Stilgar said. "Oh, I know you can take me and, therefore, can take anyone among us, but you cannot best us all united. This must be; it is the amtal rule."

Jessica fell silent, staring at him in the green light of the glowglobes, seeing the demoniacal stiffness that had taken over his expression. She shifted her attention to Jamis, saw the brooding look to his brows and thought: *I should've seen that before. He broods. He's the silent kind, one who works himself up inside. I should've been prepared.*

"If you harm my son," she said, "You'll have me to meet. I call you out now. I'll carve you into a joint of—"

"Mother." Paul stepped forward, touched her sleeve. "Perhaps if I explain to Jamis how—"

"Explain!" Jamis sneered.

Paul fell silent, staring at the man. He felt no fear of him. Jamis appeared clumsy in his movements and he had fallen so easily in their night encounter on the sand. But Paul still felt the nexus-boiling of this cave, still remembered the prescient visions of himself dead under a knife. There had been so few avenues of escape for him in that vision . . . .

Stilgar said: "Sayyadina, you must step back now where—"

"Stop calling her Sayyadina!" Jamis said. "That's yet to be proved. So she knows the prayer! What's that? Every child among us knows it."

*He has talked enough,* Jessica thought. *I've the key to him. I could immobilize him with a word.* She hesitated. *But I cannot stop them all.*

"You will answer to me then," Jessica said, and she pitched her voice in a twisting tone with a little whine in it and a catch at the end.

Jamis stared at her, fright visible on his face.

"I'll teach you agony," she said in the same tone. "Remember *that* as you fight. You'll have agony such as will make the gom jabbar a happy memory by comparison. You will writhe with your entire—"

"She tries a spell on me!" Jamis gasped. He put his clenched right fist beside his ear. "I invoke the silence on her!"

"So be it then," Stilgar said. He cast a warning glance at Jessica. "If you speak again, Sayyadina, we'll know it's your witchcraft and you'll be forfeit." He nodded for her to step back.

Jessica felt hands pulling her, helping her back, and she sensed they were not unkindly. She saw Paul being separated from the throng, the elfin-faced Chani whispering in his ear as she nodded toward Jamis.

A ring formed within the troop. More glowglobes were brought and all of them tuned to the yellow band.

Jamis stepped into the ring, slipped out of his robe and tossed it to someone in the crowd. He stood there in a cloudy gray slickness of stillsuit that was patched and marked by tucks and gathers. For a moment, he bent with his mouth to his shoulder, drinking from a catchpocket tube. Presently he straightened, peeled off and detached the suit, handed it carefully into the crowd. He stood waiting, clad in loincloth and some tight fabric over his feet, a crysknife in his right hand.

Jessica saw the girl-child Chani helping Paul, saw her press a crysknife handle into his palm, saw him heft it, testing the weight and balance. And it came to Jessica that Paul had been trained in prana and bindu, the nerve and the fiber—that he had been taught fighting in a deadly school, his teachers men like Duncan Idaho and Gurney Halleck, men who were legends in their own lifetimes. The boy knew the devious ways of the Bene Gesserit and he looked supple and confident.

*But he's only fifteen,* she thought. *And he has no shield. I must stop this. Somehow, there must be a way to . . . .* She looked up, saw Stilgar watching her.

"You cannot stop it," he said. "You must not speak."

She put a hand over her mouth, thinking: *I've planted fear in Jamis' mind. It'll slow him some . . . perhaps. If I could only pray—truly pray.*

Paul stood alone now just into the ring, clad in the fighting trunks he'd worn under his stillsuit. He held a crysknife in his right hand; his feet were bare against the sand-gritted rock. Idaho had warned him time and again: *"When in doubt of your surface, bare feet are best."* And there were Chani's words of instruction still in the front of his consciousness: *"Jamis turns to the right with his knife after a parry. It's a habit we've all seen. And he'll aim for the eyes to catch a blink in which to slash you. And he can fight either hand; look out for a knife shift."*

But the strongest in Paul so that he felt it with his entire body was the training and the instinctual reaction mechanism that had been hammered into him day after day, hour after hour on the practice floor.

Gurney Halleck's words were there to remember: *"The good knife fighter thinks on point and blade and shearing-guard simultaneously. The point can also cut; the blade can also stab; the shearing-guard can also trap your opponent's blade."*

Paul glanced at the crysknife. There was no shearing-guard; only the slim round ring of the handle with its raised lips to protect the hand. And even so, he realized that he did not know the breaking tension of this blade, did not even know if it *could* be broken.

Jamis began sidling to the right along the edge of the ring opposite Paul.

Paul crouched, realizing then that he had no shield, but was trained to fighting with its subtle field around him, trained to react on defense with utmost speed while his attack would be timed to the controlled slowness necessary for penetrating the enemy's shield. In spite of constant warning from his trainers not to depend on the shield's mindless blunting of attack speed, he knew that shield-awareness was part of him.

Jamis called out in ritual challenge: "May thy knife chip and shatter!"

*This knife will break then,* Paul thought.

He cautioned himself that Jamis also was without shield, but the man wasn't trained to its use, had no shield-fighter inhibitions.

Paul stared across the ring at Jamis. The man's body looked like knotted whipcord on a dried skeleton. His crysknife shone milky yellow in the light of the glowglobes.

Fear coursed through Paul. He felt suddenly alone and naked standing in dull yellow light within this ring of people. Prescience had fed his knowledge with countless experiences, hinted at the strongest currents of the future and the strings of decision that guided them, but this was the *real-now*. This was death hanging on an infinite number of miniscule mischances.

Anything could tip the future here, he realized. Someone coughing in the troop of watchers, a distraction. A variation in a glowglobe's brilliance, a deceptive shadow.

*I'm afraid,* Paul told himself.

And he circled warily opposite Jamis, repeating to himself the Bene Gesserit litany against fear. *"Fear is the mind-killer . . . ."* It was a cool bath washing over him. He felt muscles unite themselves, become poised and ready.

"I'll sheath my knife in your blood," Jamis snarled. And in the middle of the last word, he pounced.

Jessica saw the motion, stifled an outcry.

Where the man struck there was only empty air and Paul stood now behind Jamis with a clear shot at the exposed back.

*Now, Paul! Now!* Jessica screamed it in her mind.

Paul's motion was slowly timed, beautifully fluid, but so slow it gave Jamis the margin to twist away, backing and turning to the right.

Paul withdrew, crouching low. "First, you must find my blood," he said.

Jessica recognized the shield-fighter timing in her son, and it came over her what a two-edged thing that was. The boy's reactions were those of youth and trained to a peak these people had never seen. But the attack was trained, too, and conditioned by the necessities of penetrating a shield barrier. A shield would repel too fast a blow, admit only the slowly deceptive counter. It needed control and trickery to get through a shield.

*Does Paul see it?* she asked herself. *He must!*

Again Jamis attacked, ink-dark eyes glaring, his body a yellow blur under the glowglobes.

And again Paul slipped away to return too slowly on the attack.

And again.

And again.

Each time, Paul's counterblow came an instant late.

And Jessica saw a thing she hoped Jamis did not see. Paul's defensive reactions were blindingly fast, but they moved each time at the precisely correct angle they would take if a shield were helping deflect part of Jamis' blow.

"Is your son playing with that poor fool?" Stilgar asked. He waved her to silence before she could respond. "Sorry; you must remain silent."

Now the two figures on the rock floor circled each other: Jamis with knife hand held far forward and tipped up slightly; Paul crouched with knife held low.

Again, Jamis pounced, and this time he twisted to the right where Paul had been dodging.

Instead of faking back and out, Paul met the man's knife hand on the point of his own blade. Then the boy was gone, twisting away to the left and thankful for Chani's warning.

Jamis backed into the center of the circle, rubbing his knife hand. Blood dripped from the injury for a moment, stopped. His eyes were wide and staring—two blue-black holes—studying Paul with a new wariness in the dull light of the glowglobes.

"Ah, that one hurt," Stilgar murmured.

Paul crouched at the ready and, as he had been trained to do after first blood, called out: "Do you yield?"

"Hah!" Jamis cried.

An angry murmur arose from the troop.

"Hold!" Stilgar called out. "The lad doesn't know our rule." Then, to Paul: "There can be no yielding in the tahaddi-challenge. Death is the test of it."

Jessica saw Paul swallow hard. And she thought: *He's never killed a man like this . . . in the hot blood of a knife fight. Can he do it?*

Paul circled slowly right, forced by Jamis' movement. The prescient knowledge of the time-boiling variables in this cave came back to plague him now. His new understanding told him there were too many swiftly compressed decisions in this fight for any clear channel ahead to show itself.

Variable piled on variable—that was why this cave lay as a blurred nexus in his path. It was like a gigantic rock in the flood, creating maelstroms in the current around it.

"Have an end to it, lad," Stilgar muttered. "Don't play with him."

Paul crept farther into the ring, relying on his own edge in speed.

Jamis backed now that the realization swept over him—that this was no soft offworlder in the tahaddi ring, easy prey for a Fremen crysknife.

Jessica saw the shadow of desperation in the man's face. *Now is when he's most dangerous*, she thought. *Now he's desperate and can do anything. He sees that this is not like a child of his own people, but a fighting machine born and trained to it from infancy. Now the fear I planted in him has come to bloom.*

And she found in herself a sense of pity for Jamis—an emotion tempered by awareness of the immediate peril to her son.

*Jamis could do anything . . . any unpredictable thing,* she told herself. She wondered then if Paul had glimpsed this future, if he were reliving this experience. But she saw the way her son moved, the beads of perspiration on his face and shoulders, the careful wariness visible in the flow of muscles. And for the first time she sensed, without understanding it, the uncertainty factor in Paul's gift.

Paul pressed the fight now, circling but not attacking. He had seen the fear in his opponent. Memory of Duncan Idaho's voice flowed through Paul's awareness: *"When your opponent fears you, then's the moment when you give the fear its own rein, give it the time to work on him. Let it become terror. The terrified man fights himself. Eventually, he attacks in desperation. That is the most dangerous moment, but the terrified man can be trusted usually to make a fatal mistake. You are being trained here to detect these mistakes and use them."*

The crowd in the cavern began to mutter.

*They think Paul's toying with Jamis,* Jessica thought. *They think Paul's being needlessly cruel.*

But she sensed also the undercurrent of crowd excitement, their enjoyment of the spectacle. And she could see the pressure building up in Jamis. The moment when it became too much for him to contain was as apparent to her as it was to Jamis . . . or to Paul.

Jamis leaped high, feinting and striking down with his right hand, but the hand was empty. The crysknife had been shifted to his left hand.

Jessica gasped.

But Paul had been warned by Chani: *"Jamis fights with either hand."* And the depth of his training had taken in that trick *en passant.* *"Keep the mind on the knife and not on the hand that holds it,"* Gurney Halleck had told him time and again. *"The knife is more dangerous than the hand and the knife can be in either hand."*

And Paul had seen Jamis' mistake: bad footwork so that it took the man a heartbeat longer to recover from his leap, which had been intended to confuse Paul and hide the knife shift.

Except for the low yellow light of the glowglobes and the inky eyes of the staring troop, it was similar to a session on the practice floor. Shields didn't count where the body's own movement could be used against it. Paul shifted his own knife in a blurred motion, slipped sideways and thrust upward where Jamis' chest was descending—then away to watch the man crumple.

Jamis fell like a limp rag, face down, gasped once and turned his face toward Paul, then lay still on the rock floor. His dead eyes stared out like beads of dark glass.

*"Killing with the point lacks artistry,"* Idaho had once told Paul, *"but don't let that hold your hand when the opening presents itself."*

The troop rushed forward, filling the ring, pushing Paul aside. They hid Jamis in a frenzy of huddling activity. Presently a group of them hurried back into the depths of the cavern carrying a burden wrapped in a robe.

And there was no body on the rock floor.

Jessica pressed through toward her son. She felt that she swam in a sea of robed and stinking backs, a throng strangely silent.

*Now is the terrible moment,* she thought. *He has killed a man in clear superiority of mind and muscle. He must not grow to enjoy such a victory.*

She forced herself through the last of the troop and into a small open space where two bearded Fremen were helping Paul into his stillsuit.

Jessica stared at her son. Paul's eyes were bright. He breathed heavily, permitting the ministrations to his body rather than helping them.

"Him against Jamis and not a mark on him," one of the men muttered.

Chani stood at one side, her eyes focused on Paul. Jessica saw the girl's excitement, the admiration in the elfin face.

*It must be done now and swiftly,* Jessica thought.

She compressed ultimate scorn into her voice and manner, said: "We-l-l, now—how does it feel to be a killer?"

Paul stiffened as though he had been struck. He met his mother's cold glare and his face darkened with a rush of blood. Involuntarily he glanced toward the place on the cavern floor where Jamis had lain.

Stilgar pressed through to Jessica's side, returning from the cave depths where the body of Jamis had been taken. He spoke to Paul in a bitter, controlled tone: "When the time comes for you to call me out and try for my burda, do not think you will play with me the way you played with Jamis."

Jessica sensed the way her own words and Stilgar's sank into Paul, doing their harsh work on the boy. The mistake these people made—it served a purpose now. She searched the faces around them as Paul was doing, seeing what he saw. Admiration, yes, and fear . . . and in some—loathing. She looked at Stilgar, saw his fatalism, knew how the fight had seemed to him.

Paul looked at his mother. "You know what it was," he said.

She heard the return to sanity, the remorse in his voice. Jessica swept her glance across the troop, said: "Paul has never killed a man with a naked blade."

Stilgar faced her, disbelief in his face.

"I wasn't playing with him," Paul said. He pressed in front of his mother, straightening his robe, glanced at the dark place of Jamis' blood on the cavern floor. "I did not want to kill him."

Jessica saw belief come slowly to Stilgar, saw the relief in him as he tugged at his beard with a deeply veined hand. She heard muttering awareness spread through the troop.

"That's why y' asked him to yield," Stilgar said. "I see. Our ways are different, but you'll see the sense in them. I thought we'd admitted a scorpion into our midst." He hesitated, then: "And I shall not call you lad the more."

A voice from the troop called out: "Needs a naming, Stil."

Stilgar nodded, tugging at his beard. "I see strength in you . . . like the strength beneath a pillar." Again he paused, then: "You shall be known among us as Usul, the base of the pillar. This is your secret name, your troop name. We of Sietch Tabr may use it, but none other may so presume . . .Usul."

Murmuring went through the troop: "Good choice, that . . . strong . . . bring us luck." And Jessica sensed the acceptance, knowing she was included in it with her champion. She was indeed Sayyadina.

"Now, what name of manhood do *you* choose for us to call you openly?" Stilgar asked.

Paul glanced at his mother, back to Stilgar. Bits and pieces of this moment registered on his prescient *memory*, but he felt the differences as though they were physical, a pressure forcing him through the narrow door of the present.

"How do you call among you the little mouse, the mouse that jumps?" Paul asked, remembering the *pop-hop* of motion at Tuono Basin. He illustrated with one hand.

A chuckle sounded through the troop.

"We call that one muad'dib," Stilgar said.

Jessica gasped. It was the name Paul had told her, saying that the Fremen would accept them and call him thus. She felt a sudden fear *of* her son and *for* him.

Paul swallowed. He felt that he played a part already played over countless times in his mind . . . yet . . . there were differences. He could see himself perched on a dizzying summit, having experienced much and possessed of a profound store of knowledge, but all around him was abyss.

And again he remembered the vision of fanatic legions following the green and black banner of the Atreides, pillaging and burning across the universe in the name of their prophet Muad'Dib.

*That must not happen,* he told himself.

"Is that the name you wish, Muad'Dib?" Stilgar asked.

"I am an Atreides," Paul whispered, and then louder: "It's not right that I give up entirely the name my father gave me. Could I be known among you as Paul-Muad'Dib?"

"You are Paul-Muad'Dib," Stilgar said.

And Paul thought: *That was in no vision of mine. I did a different thing.*

But he felt that the abyss remained all around him.

Again a murmuring response went through the troop as man turned to man: "Wisdom with strength . . . Couldn't ask more . . . It's the legend for sure . . . Lisan al-Gaib . . . Lisan al-Gaib . . . ."

"I will tell you a thing about your new name," Stilgar said. "The choice pleases us. Muad'Dib is wise in the ways of the desert. Muad'Dib creates his own water. Muad'Dib hides from the sun and travels in the cool night. Muad'Dib is fruitful and multiplies over the land. Muad'Dib we call 'instructor-of-boys.' That is a powerful base on which to build your life, Paul-Muad'Dib, who is Usul among us. We welcome you."

Stilgar touched Paul's forehead with one palm, withdrew his hand, embraced Paul and murmured, "Usul."

As Stilgar released him, another member of the troop embraced Paul, repeating his new troop name. And Paul was passed from embrace to embrace through the troop, hearing the voices, the shadings of tone: "Usul . . . Usul . . . Usul." Already, he could place some of them by name. And there was Chani who pressed her cheek against his as she held him and said his name.

Presently Paul stood again before Stilgar, who said: "Now you are of the Ichwan Bedwine, our brother." His face hardened, and he spoke with command in his voice. "And now, Paul-Muad'Dib, tighten up that stillsuit." He glanced at Chani. "Chani! Paul-Muad'Dib's nose plugs are as poor a fit as I've ever seen! I thought I ordered you to see after him!"

"I hadn't the makings, Stil," she said. "There's Jamis', of course, but—"

"Enough of that!"

"Then I'll share one of mine," she said. "I can make do with one until—"

"You will not," Stilgar said. "I know there are spares among us. Where are the spares? Are we a troop together or a band of savages?"

Hands reached out from the troop offering hard, fibrous objects. Stilgar selected four, handed them to Chani. "Fit these to Usul and the Sayyadina."

A voice lifted from the back of the troop: "What of the water, Stil? What of the literjons in their pack?"

"I know your need, Farok," Stilgar said. He glanced at Jessica. She nodded.

"Broach one for those that need it," Stilgar said. "Watermaster . . . where is a watermaster? Ah, Shimoom, care for the measuring of what is needed. The necessity and no more. This water is the dower property of the Sayyadina and will be repaid in the sietch at field rates less pack fees."

"What is this repayment at field rates?" Jessica asked.

"Ten for one," Stilgar said.

"But—"

"It's a wise rule as you'll come to see," Stilgar said.

A rustling of robes marked movement at the back of the troop as men turned to get the water.

Stilgar held up a hand, and there was silence. "As to Jamis," he said, "I order the full ceremony. Jamis was our companion and brother of the Ichwan Bedwine. There shall be no turning away without the respect due one who proved our fortune by his tahaddi-challenge. I invoke the rite . . . at sunset, when the dark shall cover him."

Paul, hearing these words, realized that he had plunged once more into the abyss . . . blind time. There was no past occupying the future in his mind . . . except . . . except . . . he could still sense the green and black Atreides banner waving . . . somewhere ahead . . . still see the jihad's bloody swords and fanatic legions.

*It will not be,* he told himself. *I cannot let it be.*

*God created Arrakis to train the faithful.*

**—from "The Wisdom of Muad'Dib"
by the Princess Irulan**

In the stillness of the cavern, Jessica heard the scrape of sand on rock as people moved, the distant bird calls that Stilgar had said were the signals of his watchmen.

The great plastic hood-seals had been removed from the cave's openings. She could see the march of evening shadows across the lip of rock in front of her and the open basin beyond. She sensed the daylight leaving them, sensed it in the dry heat as well as the shadows. She knew her trained awareness soon would give her what these Fremen obviously had—the ability to sense even the slightest change in the air's moisture.

How they had scurried to tighten their stillsuits when the cave was opened!

Deep within the cave, someone began chanting:

"Ima trava okolo!
I korenja okolo!"

Jessica translated silently: *"These are ashes! And these are roots!"*

The funeral ceremony for Jamis was beginning.

She looked out at the Arrakeen sunset, at the banked decks of color in the sky. Night was beginning to utter its shadows along the distant rocks and the dunes.

Yet the heat persisted.

Heat forced her thoughts onto water and the observed fact that this whole people could be trained to be thirsty only at given times.

Thirst.

She could remember moonlit waves on Caladan throwing white robes over rocks . . . and the wind heavy with dampness. Now the breeze that fingered her robes seared the patches of exposed skin at cheeks and forehead. The new nose plugs irritated her, and she found herself overly conscious of the tube that trailed down across her face into the suit, recovering her breath's moisture.

The suit itself was a sweatbox.

*"Your suit will be more comfortable when you've adjusted to lower water content in your body,"* Stilgar had said.

She knew he was right, but the knowledge made this moment no more comfortable. The unconscious preoccupation with water here weighed on her mind. *No,* she corrected herself: *it was preoccupation with* moisture.

And that was a more subtle and profound matter.

She heard approaching footsteps, turned to see Paul come out of the cave's depths trailed by the elfin-faced Chani.

*There's another thing,* Jessica thought. *Paul must be cautioned about their women. One of these desert women would not do as wife to a Duke. As concubine, yes, but not as wife.*

Then she wondered at herself, thinking: *Have I been infected with his schemes?* And she saw how well she had been conditioned. *I can think of the marital needs of royalty without once weighing my own concubinage. Yet . . . I was more than concubine.*

"Mother."

Paul stopped in front of her. Chani stood at his elbow.

"Mother, do you know what they're doing back there?"

Jessica looked at the dark patch of his eyes staring out from the hood. "I think so."

"Chani showed me . . . because I'm supposed to see it and give my . . . permission for the weighing of the water."

Jessica looked at Chani.

"They're recovering Jamis' water," Chani said, and her thin voice came out nasal past the nose plugs. "It's the rule. The flesh belongs to the person, but his water belongs to the tribe . . . except in the combat."

"They say the water's mine," Paul said.

Jessica wondered why this should make her suddenly alert and cautious.

"Combat water belongs to the winner," Chani said. "It's because you have to fight in the open without stillsuits. The winner has to get his water back that he loses while fighting."

"I don't want his water," Paul muttered. He felt that he was a part of many images moving simultaneously in a fragmenting way that was disconcerting to the inner eye. He could not be certain what he would do, but of one thing he was positive: he did not want the water distilled out of Jamis' flesh.

"It's . . . water," Chani said.

Jessica marveled at the way she said it. *"Water."* So much meaning in a simple sound. A Bene Gesserit axiom came to Jessica's mind: *"Survival is the ability to swim in strange water."* And Jessica thought: *Paul and I, we must find the currents and patterns in these strange waters . . . if we're to survive.*

"You will accept the water," Jessica said.

She recognized the tone in her voice. She had used that same tone once with Leto, telling her lost Duke that he would accept a large sum offered for his support in a questionable venture—because money maintained power for the Atreides.

On Arrakis, water was money. She saw that clearly.

Paul remained silent, knowing then that he would do as she ordered—not because she ordered it, but because her tone of voice had forced him to re-evaluate. To refuse the water would be to break with accepted Fremen practice.

Presently Paul recalled the words of 467 Kalima in Yueh's O.C. Bible. He said: "From water does all life begin."

Jessica stared at him. *Where did he learn that quotation?* she asked herself. *He hasn't studied the mysteries.*

"Thus it is spoken," Chani said. "Giudichar mantene: It is written in the Shah-Nama that water was the first of all things created."

For no reason she could explain (and *this* bothered her more than the sensation), Jessica suddenly shuddered. She turned away to hide her confusion and was just in time to see the sunset. A violent calamity of color spilled over the sky as the sun dipped beneath the horizon.

"It is time!"

The voice was Stilgar's ringing in the cavern. "Jamis' weapon has been killed. Jamis has been called by Him, by Shai-hulud, who has ordained the phases for the moons that daily wane and—in the end—appear as bent and withered twigs." Stilgar's voice lowered. "Thus it is with Jamis."

Silence fell like a blanket on the cavern.

Jessica saw the gray-shadow movement of Stilgar like a ghost figure within the inner reaches. She glanced at the basin, sensing the coolness.

"The friends of Jamis will approach," Stilgar said.

Men moved behind Jessica, dropping a curtain across the opening. A single glowglobe was lighted overhead far back in the cave. Its yellow glow picked out an inflowing of human figures. Jessica heard the rustling of the robes.

Chani took a step away as though pulled by the light.

Jessica bent close to Paul's ear, speaking in the family code: "Follow their lead; do as they do. It will be a simple ceremony to placate the shade of Jamis."

*It will be more than that,* Paul thought. And he felt a wrenching sensation within his awareness as though he were trying to grasp some thing in motion and render it motionless.

Chani glided back to Jessica's side, took her hand. "Come, Sayyadina. We must sit apart."

Paul watched them move off into the shadows, leaving him alone. He felt abandoned.

The men who had fixed the curtain came up beside him.

"Come, Usul."

He allowed himself to be guided forward, to be pushed into a circle of people being formed around Stilgar, who stood beneath the glowglobe and beside a bundled, curving, and angular shape gathered beneath a robe on the rock floor.

The troop crouched down at a gesture from Stilgar, their robes hissing with the movement. Paul settled with them, watching Stilgar, noting the way the overhead globe made pits of his eyes and brightened the touch of green fabric at his neck. Paul shifted his attention to the robe-covered mound at Stilgar's feet, recognized the handle of a baliset protruding from the fabric.

"The spirit leaves the body's water when the first moon rises," Stilgar intoned. "Thus it is spoken. When we see the first moon rise this night, whom will it summon?"

"Jamis," the troop responded.

Stilgar turned full circle on one heel, passing his gaze across the ring of faces. "I was a friend of Jamis," he said. "When the hawk plane stooped upon us at Hole-in-the-Rock, it was Jamis pulled me to safety."

He bent over the pile beside him, lifted away the robe. "I take this robe as a friend of Jamis—leader's right." He draped the robe over a shoulder, straightening.

Now, Paul saw the contents of the mound exposed: the pale glistening gray of a stillsuit, a battered literjon, a kerchief with a small book in its center, the bladeless handle of a crysknife, an empty sheath, a folded pack, a paracompass, a distrans, a thumper, a pile of fist-sized metallic hooks, an assortment of what looked like small rocks within a fold of cloth, a clump of bundled feathers . . . and the baliset exposed beside the folded pack.

*So Jamis played the baliset,* Paul thought. The instrument reminded him of Gurney Halleck and all that was lost. Paul knew with his memory of the future in the past that some chance-lines could produce a meeting with Halleck, but the reunions were few and shadowed. They puzzled him. The uncertainty factor touched him with wonder. *Does it mean that something I will do . . . that I may do, could destroy Gurney . . . or bring him back to life . . . or . . . .*

Paul swallowed, shook his head.

Again, Stilgar bent over the mound.

"For Jamis' woman and for the guards," he said. The small rocks and the book were taken into the folds of his robe.

"Leader's right," the troop intoned.

"The marker for Jamis' coffee service," Stilgar said, and he lifted a flat disc of green metal. "That it shall be given to Usul in suitable ceremony when we return to the sietch."

"Leader's right," the troop intoned.

Lastly, he took the crysknife handle and stood with it. "For the funeral plain," he said.

"For the funeral plain," the troop responded.

At her place in the circle across from Paul, Jessica nodded, recognizing the ancient source of the rite, and she thought: *The meeting between ignorance and knowledge, between brutality and culture—it begins in the dignity with which we treat our dead.* She looked across at Paul, wondering: *Will he see it? Will he know what to do?*

"We are friends of Jamis," Stilgar said. "We are not wailing for our dead like a pack of garvarg."

A gray-bearded man to Paul's left stood up. "I was a friend of Jamis," he said. He crossed to the mound, lifted the distrans. "When our water went below minim at the siege of Two Birds, Jamis shared." The man returned to his place in the circle.

*Am I supposed to say I was a friend of Jamis?* Paul wondered. *Do they expect me to take something from that pile?* He saw faces turn toward him, turn away. *They expect it!*

Another man across from Paul arose, went to the pack and removed the paracompass. "I was a friend of Jamis," he said. "When the patrol caught us at Bight-of-the-Cliff and I was wounded, Jamis drew them off so the wounded could be saved." He returned to his place in the circle.

Again, the faces turned toward Paul, and he saw the expectancy in them, lowered his eyes. An elbow nudged him and a voice hissed: "Would you bring the destruction on us?"

*How can I say I was his friend?* Paul wondered.

Another figure arose from the circle opposite Paul and, as the hooded face came into the light, he recognized his mother. She removed a kerchief from the mound. "I was a friend of Jamis," she said. "When the spirit of spirits within him saw the needs of truth, that spirit withdrew and spared my son." She returned to her place.

And Paul recalled the scorn in his mother's voice as she had confronted him after the fight. *"How does it feel to be a killer?"*

Again, he saw the faces turned toward him, felt the anger and fear in the troop. A passage his mother had once filmbooked for him on "The Cult of the Dead" flickered through Paul's mind. He knew what he had to do.

Slowly, Paul got to his feet.

A sigh passed around the circle.

Paul felt the diminishment of his *self* as he advanced into the center of the circle. It was as though he lost a fragment of himself and sought it here. He bent over the mound of belongings, lifted out the baliset. A string twanged softly as it struck against something in the pile.

"I was a friend of Jamis," Paul whispered.

He felt tears burning his eyes, forced more volume into his voice. "Jamis taught me . . . that . . . when you kill . . . you pay for it. I wish I'd known Jamis better."

Blindly, he groped his way back to his place in the circle, sank to the rock floor.

A voice hissed: "He sheds tears!"

It was taken up around the ring: "Usul gives moisture to the dead!"

He felt fingers touch his damp cheek, heard the awed whispers.

Jessica, hearing the voices, felt the depth of the experience, realized what terrible inhibitions there must be against shedding tears. She focused on the words: *"He gives moisture to the dead."* It was a gift to the shadow world—tears. They would be sacred beyond a doubt.

Nothing on this planet had so forcefully hammered into her the ultimate value of water. Not the water-sellers, not the dried skins of the natives, not stillsuits or the rules of water discipline. Here there was a substance more precious than all others—it was life itself and entwined all around with symbolism and ritual.

Water.

"I touched his cheek," someone whispered. "I felt the gift."

At first, the fingers touching his face frightened Paul. He clutched the cold handle of the baliset, feeling the strings bite his palm. Then he saw the faces beyond the groping hands—the eyes wide and wondering.

Presently, the hands withdrew. The funeral ceremony resumed. But now there was a subtle space around Paul, a drawing back as the troop honored him by a respectful isolation.

The ceremony ended with a low chant:

"Full moon calls thee—
Shai-hulud shalt thou see;
Red the night, dusky sky,
Bloody death didst thou die.
We pray to a moon: she is round—
Luck with us will then abound,
What we seek for shall be found
In the land of solid ground."

A bulging sack remained at Stilgar's feet. He crouched, placed his palms against it. Someone came up beside him, crouched at his elbow, and Paul recognized Chani's face in the hood shadow.

"Jamis carried thirty-three liters and seven and three-thirty-seconds drachms of the tribe's water," Chani said. "I bless it now in the presence of a Sayyadina. Ekkeri-akairi, this is the water, fillissin-follasy of Paul-Muad'Dib! Kivi a-kavi, never the more, nakalas! Nakelas! to be measured and counted, ukair-an! by the heartbeats jan-jan-jan of our friend . . . Jamis."

In an abrupt and profound silence, Chani turned, stared at Paul. Presently she said: "Where I am flame be thou the coals. Where I am dew be thou the water."

"Bi-lal kaifa," intoned the troop.

"To Paul-Muad'Dib goes this portion," Chani said. "May he guard it for the tribe, preserving it against careless loss. May he be generous with it in time of need. May he pass it on in his time for the good of the tribe."

"Bi-lal kaifa," intoned the troop.

*I must accept that water,* Paul thought. Slowly, he arose, made his way to Chani's side. Stilgar stepped back to make room for him, took the baliset gently from his hand.

"Kneel," Chani said.

Paul knelt.

She guided his hands to the waterbag, held them against the resilient surface. "With this water the tribe entrusts thee," she said. "Jamis is gone from it. Take it in peace." She stood, pulling Paul up with her.

Stilgar returned the baliset, extended a small pile of metal rings in one palm. Paul looked at them, seeing the different sizes, the way the light of the glowglobe reflected off them.

Chani took the largest ring, held it on a finger. "Thirty liters," she said. One by one, she took the others, showing each to Paul, counting them. "Two liters; one liter; seven watercounters of one drachm each; one watercounter of three-thirty-seconds drachms. In all—thirty-three liters and seven and three-thirty-seconds drachms."

She held them up on her finger for Paul to see.

"Do you accept them?" Stilgar asked.

Paul swallowed, nodded. "Yes."

"Later," Chani said. "I will show you how to tie them in a kerchief so they won't rattle and give you away when you need silence." She extended her hand.

"Will you . . . hold them for me?" Paul asked.

Chani turned a startled glance on Stilgar.

He smiled, said, "Paul-Muad'Dib who is Usul does not yet know our ways, Chani. Hold his watercounters without commitment until it's time to show him the manner of carrying them."

She nodded, whipped a ribbon of cloth from beneath her robe, linked the rings onto it with an intricate over and under weaving, hesitated, then stuffed them into the sash beneath her robe.

*I missed something there,* Paul thought. He sensed the feeling of humor around him, something bantering in it, and his mind linked up a prescient memory: *watercounters offered to a woman—courtship ritual.*

"Watermasters," Stilgar said.

The troop arose in a hissing of robes. Two men stepped out, lifted the waterbag. Stilgar took down the glowglobe, led the way with it into the depths of the cave.

Paul was pressed in behind Chani, noted the buttery glow of light over rock walls, the way the shadows danced, and he felt the troop's lift of spirits contained in a hushed air of expectancy.

Jessica, pulled into the end of the troop by eager hands, hemmed around by jostling bodies, suppressed a moment of panic. She had recognized fragments of the ritual, identified the shards of Chakobsa and Bhotani-jib in the words, and she knew the wild violence that could explode out of these seemingly simple moments.

*Jan-jan-jan,* she thought. *Go-go-go.*

It was like a child's game that had lost all inhibition in adult hands.

Stilgar stopped at a yellow rock wall. He pressed an outcropping and the wall swung silently away from him, opening along an irregular crack. He led the way through past a dark honeycomb lattice that directed a cool wash of air across Paul when he passed it.

Paul turned a questioning stare on Chani, tugged her arm. "That air felt damp," he said.

"Sh-h-h-h," she whispered.

But a man behind them said: "Plenty of moisture in the trap tonight. Jamis' way of telling us he's satisfied."

Jessica passed through the secret door, heard it close behind. She saw how the Fremen slowed while passing the honeycomb lattice, felt the dampness of the air as she came opposite it.

*Windtrap!* she thought. *They've a concealed windtrap somewhere on the surface to funnel air down here into cooler regions and precipitate the moisture from it.*

They passed through another rock door with latticework above it, and the door closed behind them. The draft of air at their backs carried a sensation of moisture clearly perceptible to both Jessica and Paul.

At the head of the troop, the glowglobe in Stilgar's hands dropped below the level of the heads in front of Paul. Presently he felt steps beneath his feet, curving down to the left. Light reflected back up across hooded heads and a winding movement of people spiraling down the steps.

Jessica sensed mounting tension in the people around her, a pressure of silence that rasped her nerves with its urgency.

The steps ended and the troop passed through another low door. The light of the glowblobe was swallowed in a great open space with a high curved ceiling.

Paul felt Chani's hand on his arm, heard a faint dripping sound in the chill air, felt an utter stillness come over the Fremen in the cathedral presence of water.

*I have seen this place in a dream,* he thought.

The thought was both reassuring and frustrating. Somewhere ahead of him on this path, the fantastic hordes cut their glory path across the universe in his name. The green and black Atreides banner would become a symbol of terror. Wild legions would charge into battle screaming their war cry: "Muad'Dib!"

*It must not be,* he thought. *I cannot let it happen.*

But he could feel the demanding race consciousness within him, his own terrible purpose, and he knew that no small thing could deflect the juggernaut. It was gathering weight and momentum. If he died this instant, the thing would go on through his mother and his unborn sister. Nothing less than the deaths of all the troop gathered here and now—himself and his mother included—could stop the thing.

Paul stared around him, saw the troop spread out in a line. They pressed him forward against a low barrier carved from native rock. Beyond the barrier in the glow of Stilgar's globe, Paul saw an unruffled dark surface of water. It stretched away into shadows—deep and black—the far wall only faintly visible, perhaps a hundred meters away.

Jessica felt the dry pulling of skin on her cheeks and forehead relaxing in the presence of moisture. The water pool was deep; she could sense its deepness, and resisted a desire to dip her hands into it.

A splashing sounded on her left. She looked down the shadowy line of Fremen, saw Stilgar with Paul standing beside him and the watermasters emptying their load into the pool through a flowmeter. The meter was a round gray eye above the pool's rim. She saw its glowing pointer move as the water flowed through it, saw the pointer stop at thirty-three liters, seven and three-thirty-seconds drachms.

*Superb accuracy in water measurement,* Jessica thought. And she noted that the walls of the meter trough held no trace of moisture after the water's passage. The water flowed off those walls without binding tension. She saw a profound clue to Fremen technology in the simple fact: they were perfectionists.

Jessica worked her way down the barrier to Stilgar's side. Way was made for her with casual courtesy. She noted the withdrawn look in Paul's eyes, but the mystery of this great pool of water dominated her thoughts.

Stilgar looked at her. "There were those among us in need of water," he said, "yet they would come here and not touch this water. Do you know that?"

"I believe it," she said.

He looked at the pool. "We have more than thirty-eight million decaliters here," he said. "Walled off from the little makers, hidden and preserved."

"A treasure trove," she said.

Stilgar lifted the globe to look into her eyes. "It is greater than treasure. We have thousands of such caches. Only a few of us know them all." He cocked his head to one side. The globe cast a yellow-shadowed glow across face and beard. "Hear that?"

They listened.

The dripping of water precipitated from the windtrap filled the room with its presence. Jessica saw that the entire troop was caught up in a rapture of listening. Only Paul seemed to stand remote from it.

To Paul, the sound was like moments ticking away. He could feel time flowing through him, the instants never to be recaptured. He sensed a need for decision, but felt powerless to move.

"It has been calculated with precision," Stilgar whispered. "We know to within a million decaliters how much we need. When we have it, we shall change the face of Arrakis."

A hushed whisper of response lifted from the troop: "Bi-lal kaifa."

"We will trap the dunes beneath grass plantings," Stilgar said, his voice growing stonger. "We will tie the water into the soil with trees and undergrowth."

"Bi-lal kaifa," intoned the troop.

"Each year the polar ice retreats," Stilgar said.

"Bi-lal kaifa," they chanted.

"We will make a homeworld of Arrakis—with melting lenses at the poles, with lakes in the temperate zones, and only the deep desert for the maker and his spice."

"Bi-lal kaifa."

"And no man ever again shall want for water. It shall be his for dipping from well or pond or lake or canal. It shall run down through the qanats to feed our plants. It shall be there for any man to take. It shall be his for holding out his hand."

"Bi-lal kaifa."

Jessica felt the religious ritual in the words, noted her own instinctively awed response. *They're in league with the future,* she thought. *They have their mountain to climb. This is the scientist's dream . . . and these simple people, these peasants, are filled with it.*

Her thoughts turned to Liet-Kynes, the Emperor's planetary ecologist, the man who had gone native—and she wondered at him. This was a dream to capture men's souls, and she could sense the hand of the ecologist in it. This was a dream for which men would die willingly. It was another of the essential ingredients that she felt her son needed: people with a goal. Such people would be easy to imbue with fervor and fanaticism. They could be wielded like a sword to win back Paul's place for him.

"We leave now," Stilgar said, "and wait for the first moon's rising. When Jamis is safely on his way, we will go home."

Whispering their reluctance, the troop fell in behind him, turned back along the water barrier and up the stairs.

And Paul, walking behind Chani, felt that a vital moment had passed him, that he had missed an essential decision and was now caught up in his own myth. He knew he had seen this place before, experienced it in a fragment of prescient dream on faraway Caladan, but details of the place were being filled in now that he had not seen. He felt a new sense of wonder at the limits of his gift. It was as though he rode within the wave of time, sometimes in its trough, sometimes on a crest—and all around him the other waves lifted and fell, revealing and then hiding what they bore on their surface.

Through it all, the wild jihad still loomed ahead of him, the violence and the slaughter. It was like a promontory above the surf.

The troop filed through the last door into the main cavern. The door was sealed. Lights were extinguished, hoods removed from the cavern openings, revealing the night and the stars that had come over the desert.

Jessica moved to the dry lip of the cavern's edge, looked up at the stars. They were sharp and near. She felt the stirring of the troop around her, heard the sound of a baliset being tuned somewhere behind her, and Paul's voice humming the pitch. There was a melancholy in his tone that she did not like.

Chani's voice intruded from the deep cave darkness: "Tell me about the waters of your birthworld, Paul-Muad'Dib."

And Paul: "Another time, Chani. I promise."
*Such sadness.*
"It's a good baliset," Chani said.
"Very good," Paul said. "Do you think Jamis'll mind my using it?"
*He speaks of the dead in the present tense,* Jessica thought. The implications disturbed her.
A man's voice intruded: "He liked music betimes, Jamis did."
"Then sing me one of your songs," Chani pleaded.
*Such feminine allure in that girl-child's voice,* Jessica thought. *I must caution Paul about their women . . . and soon.*
"This was a song of a friend of mine," Paul said. "I expect he's dead now, Gurney is. He called it his evensong."
The troop grew still, listening as Paul's voice lifted in a sweet boy tenor with the baliset tinkling and strumming beneath it:

"This clear time of seeing embers—
A gold-bright sun's lost in first dusk.
What frenzied senses, desp'rate musk
Are consort of rememb'ring."

Jessica felt the verbal music in her breast—pagan and charged with sounds that made her suddenly and intensely aware of herself, feeling her own body and its needs. She listened with a tense stillness.

"Night's pearl-censered requi-em . . .
'Tis for us!
What joys run, then—
Bright in your eyes—
What flower-spangled amores
Pull at our hearts . . .
What flower-spangled amores
Fill our desires."

And Jessica heard the after-stillness that hummed in the air with the last note. *Why does my son sing a love song to that girl-child?* she asked herself. She felt an abrupt fear. She could sense life flowing around her and she had no grasp on its reins. *Why did he choose that song?* she wondered. *The instincts are true sometimes. Why did he do this?*
Paul sat silently in the darkness, a single stark thought dominating his awareness: *My mother is my enemy. She does not know it, but she is. She is bringing the jihad. She bore me; she trained me. She is my enemy.*

> *The concept of progress acts as a protective mechanism to shield us from the terrors of the future.*
>
> **—from "Collected Sayings of Muad'Dib"**
> **by the Princess Irulan**

On his seventeenth birthday, Feyd-Rautha Harkonnen killed his one hundredth slave-gladiator in the family games. Visiting observers from the Imperial
Court—a Count and Lady Fenring—were on the Harkonnen homeworld of
Giedi Prime for the event, invited to sit that afternoon with the immediate
family in the golden box above the triangular arena.

In honor of the na-Baron's nativity and to remind all Harkonnens and
subjects that Feyd-Rautha was heir-designate, it was holiday on Giedi Prime.
The old Baron had decreed a meridian-to-meridian rest from labors, and effort
had been spent in the family city of Harko to create the illusion of gaiety:
banners flew from buildings, new paint had been splashed on the walls along
Court Way.

But off the main way, Count Fenring and his lady noted the rubbish heaps,
the scabrous brown walls reflected in the dark puddles of the streets, and the
furtive scurrying of the people.

In the Baron's blue-walled keep, there was fearful perfection, but the Count
and his lady saw the price being paid—guards everywhere and weapons with
that special sheen that told a trained eye they were in regular use. There were
checkpoints for routine passage from area to area even within the keep. The
servants revealed their military training in the way they walked, in the set of
their shoulders . . . in the way their eyes watched and watched and watched.

"The pressure's on," the Count hummed to his lady in their secret language.
"The Baron is just beginning to see the price he really paid to rid himself of the
Duke Leto."

"Sometime I must recount for you the legend of the phoenix," she said.

They were in the reception hall of the keep waiting to go to the family games.
It was not a large hall—perhaps forty meters long and half that in width—but
false pillars along the sides had been shaped with an abrupt taper, and the
ceiling had a subtle arch, all giving the illusion of much greater space.

"Ah-h-h, here comes the Baron," the Count said.

The Baron moved down the length of the hall with that peculiar waddling-
glide imparted by the necessities of guiding suspensor-hung weight. His jowls
bobbed up and down; the suspensors jiggled and shifted beneath his orange
robe. Rings glittered on his hands and opafires shone where they had been
woven into the robe.

At the Baron's elbow walked Feyd-Rautha. His dark hair was dressed in close
ringlets that seemed incongruously gay above sullen eyes. He wore a tight-
fitting black tunic and snug trousers with a suggestion of bell at the bottom.
Soft-soled slippers covered his small feet.

Lady Fenring, noting the young man's poise and the sure flow of muscles
beneath the tunic, thought: *Here's one who won't let himself go to fat.*

The Baron stopped in front of them, took Feyd-Rautha's arm in a possessive
grip, said, "My nephew, the na-Baron, Feyd-Rautha Harkonnen." And,
turning his baby-fat face toward Feyd-Rautha, he said, "The Count and Lady
Fenring of whom I've spoken."

Feyd-Rautha dipped his head with the required courtesy. He stared at the
Lady Fenring. She was golden-haired and willowy, her perfection of figure

clothed in a flowing gown of ecru—simple fitness of form without ornament. Gray-green eyes stared back at him. She had that Bene Gesserit serene repose about her that the young man found subtly disturbing.

"Um-m-m-m-ah-hm-m-m-m," said the Count. He studied Feyd-Rautha. "The, hm-m-m-m, *precise* young man, ah, my . . . hm-m-m-m . . . dear?" The Count glanced at the Baron. "My dear Baron, you say you've spoken of us to this *precise* young man? What did you say?"

"I told my nephew of the great esteem our Emperor holds for you, Count Fenring," the Baron said. And he thought: *Mark him well, Feyd! A killer with the manners of a rabbit—this is the most dangerous kind.*

"Of course!" said the Count, and he smiled at his lady.

Feyd-Rautha found the man's actions and words almost insulting. They stopped just short of something overt that would require notice. The young man focused his attention on the Count: a small man, weak-looking. The face was weaselish with overlarge dark eyes. There was gray at the temples. And his movements—he moved a hand or turned his head one way, then he spoke another way. It was difficult to follow.

"Um-m-m-m-ah-h-h-hm-m-m, you come upon such, mm-m-m, precise-ness so rarely," the Count said, addressing the Baron's shoulder. "I . . . ah, congratulate you on the hm-m-m perfection of your ah-h-h heir. In the light of the hm-m-m elder, one might say."

"You are too kind," the Baron said. He bowed, but Feyd-Rautha noted that his uncle's eyes did not agree with the courtesy.

"When you're mm-m-m ironic, that ah-h-h suggests you're hm-m-m-m thinking deep thoughts," the Count said.

*There he goes again,* Feyd-Rautha thought. *It sounds like he's being insulting, but there's nothing you can call out for satisfaction.*

Listening to the man gave Feyd-Rautha the feeling his head was being pushed through mush . . . *um-m-m-ah-h-h-hm-m-m-m!* Feyd-Rautha turned his attention back to the Lady Fenring.

"We're ah-h-h taking up too much of this young man's time," she said. "I understand he's to appear in the arena today."

*By the houris of the Imperial hareem, she's a lovely one!* Feyd-Rautha thought. He said: "I shall make a kill for you this day, my Lady. I shall make the dedication in the arena, with your permission."

She returned his stare serenely, but her voice carried whiplash as she said: "You do *not* have my permission."

"Feyd!" the Baron said. And he thought: *That imp! Does he want this deadly Count to call him out?*

But the Count only smiled and said: "Hm-m-m-m-um-m-m."

"You really *must* be getting ready for the arena, Feyd," the Baron said. "You must be rested and not take any foolish risks."

Feyd-Rautha bowed, his face dark with resentment. "I'm sure everything will be as you wish, Uncle." He nodded to Count Fenring. "Sir." To the lady: "My Lady." And he turned, strode out of the hall, barely glancing at the knot of Families Minor near the double doors.

"He's so young," the Baron sighed.

"Um-m-m-m-ah indeed hmmm," the Count said.

And the Lady Fenring thought: *Can that be the young man the Reverend Mother meant! Is that a bloodline we must preserve?*

"We've more than an hour before going to the arena," the Baron said. "Perhaps we could have our little talk now, Count Fenring." He tipped his gross head to the right. "There's a considerable amount of progress to be discussed."

And the Baron thought: *Let us see now how the Emperor's errand boy gets across whatever message he carries without ever being so crass as to speak it right out.*

The Count spoke to his lady: "Um-m-m-m-ah-h-h-hm-m-m, you mm-m will ah-h-h excuse us, my dear?"

"Each day, some time each hour, brings change," she said. "Mm-m-m-m." And she smiled sweetly at the Baron before turning away. Her long skirts swished and she walked with a straight-backed regal stride toward the double doors at the end of the hall.

The Baron noted how all conversation among the Houses Minor there stopped at her approach, how the eyes followed her. *Bene Gesserit!* the Baron thought. *The universe would be better rid of them all!*

"There's a cone of silence between two of the pillars over here on our left," the Baron said. "We can talk there without fear of being overheard." He led the way with his waddling gait into the sound-deadening field, feeling the noises of the keep become dull and distant.

The Count moved up beside the Baron, and they turned, facing the wall so their lips could not be read.

"We're not satisfied with the way you ordered the Sardaukar off Arrakis," the Count said.

*Straight talk!* the Baron thought.

"The Sardaukar could not stay longer without risking that *others* would find out how the Emperor helped me," the Baron said.

"But your nephew Rabban does not appear to be pressing strongly enough toward a solution of the Fremen problem."

"What does the Emperor wish?" the Baron asked. "There cannot be more than a handful of Fremen left on Arrakis. The southern desert is uninhabitable. The northern desert is swept regularly by our patrols."

"Who says the southern desert is uninhabitable?"

"Your own planetologist said it, my dear Count."

"But Doctor Kynes is dead."

"Ah, yes . . . unfortunate, that."

"We've word from an overflight across the southern reaches," the Count said. "There's evidence of plant life."

"Has the Guild then agreed to a watch from space?"

"You know better than that, Baron. The Emperor cannot legally post a watch on Arrakis."

"And *I* cannot afford it," the Baron said. "Who made this overflight?"

"A . . . smuggler."

"Someone has lied to you, Count," the Baron said. "Smugglers cannot navigate the southern reaches any better than can Rabban's men. Storms, sand-static, and all that, you know. Navigation markers are knocked out faster than they can be installed."

"We'll discuss various types of static another time," the Count said.

*Ah-h-h-h,* the Baron thought. "Have you found some mistake in my accounting then?" he demanded.

"When you imagine mistakes there can be no self-defense," the Count said.

*He's deliberately trying to arouse my anger,* the Baron thought. He took two deep breaths to calm himself. He could smell his own sweat, and the harness of the suspensors beneath his robe felt suddenly itchy and galling.

"The Emperor cannot be unhappy about the death of the concubine and the boy," the Baron said. "They fled into the desert. There was a storm."

"Yes, there were so many convenient accidents," the Count agreed.

"I do not like your tone, Count," the Baron said.

"Anger is one thing, violence another," the Count said. "Let me caution you: Should an unfortunate accident occur to me here the Great Houses all would learn what you did on Arrakis. They've long suspected how you do business."

"The only recent business I can recall," the Baron said, "was transportation of several legions of Sardaukar to Arrakis."

"You think you could hold that over the Emperor's head?"

"I wouldn't think of it!"

The Count smiled. "Sardaukar commanders could be found who'd confess they acted without orders because they wanted a battle with your Fremen scum."

"Many might doubt such a confession," the Baron said, but the threat staggered him. *Are Sardaukar truly that disciplined?* he wondered.

"The Emperor does wish to audit your books," the Count said.

"Any time."

"You . . . . ah . . . have no objections?"

"None. My CHOAM Company directorship will bear the closest scrunity." And he thought: *Let him bring a false accusation against me and have it exposed. I shall stand there, promethean, saying: "Behold me, I am wronged." Then let him bring any other accusation against me, even a true one. The Great Houses will not believe a seond attack from an accuser once proved wrong.*

"No doubt your books will bear the closest scrutiny," the Count muttered.

"Why is the Emperor so interested in exterminating the Fremen?" the Baron asked.

"You wish the subject to be changed, eh?" The Count shrugged. "It is the Sardaukar who wish it, not the Emperor. They needed practice in killing . . . and they hate to see a task left undone."

*Does he think to frighten me by reminding me that he is supported by bloodthirsty killers?* the Baron wondered.

"A certain amount of killing has always been an arm of business," the Baron said, "but a line has to be drawn somewhere. Someone must be left to work the spice."

The Count emitted a short, barking laugh. "You think you can harness the Fremen?"

"There never were enough of them for that," the Baron said. "But the killing has made the rest of my population uneasy. It's reaching the point where I'm considering another solution to the Arrakeen problem, my dear Fenring. And I must confess the Emperor deserves credit for the inspiration."

"Ah-h-h?"

"You see, Count, I have the Emperor's prison planet, Salusa Secundus, to inspire me."

The Count stared at him with glittering intensity. "What possible connection is there between Arrakis and Salusa Secundus?"

The Baron felt the alertness in Fenring's eyes, said: "No connection yet."

"Yet?"

"You must admit it'd be a way to develop a substantial work force on Arrakis—use the place as a prison planet."

"You anticipate an increase in prisoners?"

"There has been unrest," the Baron admitted. "I've had to squeeze rather severely, Fenring. After all, you know the price I paid that damnable Guild to transport our mutual force to Arrakis. That money has to come from *somewhere*."

"I suggest you not use Arrakis as a prison planet without the Emperor's permission, Baron."

"Of course not," the Baron said, and he wondered at the sudden chill in Fenring's voice.

"Another matter," the Count said. "We learn that Duke Leto's Mentat, Thufir Hawat, is not dead but in your employ."

"I could not bring myself to waste him," the Baron said.

"You lied to our Sardaukar commander when you said Hawat was dead."

"Only a white lie, my dear Count. I hadn't the stomach for a long argument with the man."

"Was Hawat the real traitor?"

"Oh, goodness, no! It was the false doctor." The Baron wiped at perspiration on his neck. "You must understand, Fenring, I was without a Mentat. You know that. I've never been without a Mentat. It was most unsettling."

"How could you get Hawat to shift allegiance?"

"His Duke was dead." The Baron forced a smile. "There's nothing to fear from Hawat, my dear Count. The Mentat's flesh has been impregnated with a latent poison. We administer an antidote in his meals. Without the antidote, the poison is triggered—he'd die in a few days."

"Withdraw the antidote," the Count said.

"But he's useful!"

"And he knows too many things no living man should know."

"You said the Emperor doesn't fear exposure."

"Don't play games with me, Baron!"

"When I see such an order above the Imperial seal I'll obey it," the Baron said. "But I'll not submit to your whim."

"You think it whim?"

"What else can it be? The Emperor has obligations to me, too, Fenring. I rid him of the troublesome Duke."

"With the help of a few Sardaukar."

"Where else would the Emperor have found a House to provide the disguising uniforms to hide his hand in this matter?"

"He has asked himself the same question, Baron, but with a slightly different emphasis."

The Baron studied Fenring, noting the stiffness of jaw muscles, the careful control. "Ah-h-h, now," the Baron said. "I hope the Emperor doesn't believe he can move against *me* in total secrecy."

"He hopes it won't become necessary."

"The Emperor cannot believe I threaten him!" The Baron permitted anger and grief to edge his voice, thinking: *Let him wrong me in that! I could place myself on the throne while still beating my breast over how I'd been wronged.*

The Count's voice went dry and remote as he said: "The Emperor believes what his senses tell him."

"Dare the Emperor charge me with treason before a full Landsraad Council?" And the Baron held his breath with the hope of it.

"The Emperor need *dare* nothing."

The Baron whirled away in his suspensors to hide his expression. *It could happen in my lifetime!* he thought. *Emperor! Let him wrong me! Then—the bribes and coercion, the rallying of the Great Houses: they'd flock to my banner like peasants running for shelter. The thing they fear above all else is the Emperor's Sardaukar loosed upon them one House at a time.*

"It's the Emperor's sincere hope he'll never have to charge you with treason," the Count said.

The Baron found it difficult to keep irony out of his voice and permit only the expresson of hurt, but he managed. "I've been a most loyal subject. These words hurt me beyond my capacity to express."

"Um-m-m-m-ah-hm-m-m," said the Count.

The Baron kept his back to the Count, nodding. Presently he said, "It's time to go to the arena."

"Indeed," said the Count.

They moved out of the cone of silence and, side by side, walked toward the clumps of Houses Minor at the end of the hall. A bell began a slow tolling somewhere in the keep—twenty-minute warning for the arena gathering.

"The Houses Minor wait for you to lead them," the Count said, nodding toward the people they approached.

*Double meaning . . . double meaning,* the Baron thought.

He looked up at the new talismans flanking the exit to his hall—the mounted bull's head and the oil painting of the Old Duke Atreides, the late Duke Leto's father. They filled the Baron with an odd sense of foreboding, and he wondered what thoughts these talismans had inspired in the Duke Leto as they hung in the halls of Caladan and then on Arrakis—the bravura father and the head of the bull that had killed him.

"Mankind has ah only one mm-m-m science," the Count said as they picked up their parade of followers and emerged from the hall into the waiting room—a narrow space with high windows and floor of patterned white and purple tile.

"And what science is that?" the Baron asked.

"It's the um-m-m-ah-h science of ah-h-h discontent," the Count said.

The Houses Minor behind them, sheep-faced and responsive, laughed with just the right tone of appreciation, but the sound carried a note of discord as it collided with the sudden blast of motors that came to them when pages threw open the outer doors, revealing the line of ground cars, their guidon pennants whipping in a breeze.

The Baron raised his voice to surmount the sudden noise, said, "I hope you'll not be discontented with the performance of my nephew today, Count Fenring."

"I ah-h-h am filled um-m-m only with a hm-m-m sense of anticipation, yes," the Count said. "Always in the ah-h-h proces verval, one um-m-m-ah-h-h must consider the ah-h-h office of origin."

The Baron hid his sudden stiffening of surprise by stumbling on the first step down from the exit. *Proces verbal! That was a report of a crime against the Imperium!*

But the Count chuckled to make it seem a joke, and patted the Baron's arm.

All the way to the arena, though, the Baron sat back among the armored cushions of his car, casting covert glances at the Count beside him, wondering why the Emperor's *errand boy* had thought it necessary to make that particular kind of joke in front of the Houses Minor. It was obvious that Fenring seldom did anything he felt to be unnecessary, or used two words where one would do, or held himself to a single meaning in a single phrase.

They were seated in the golden box above the triangular arena—horns blaring, the tiers above and around them jammed with a hubbub of people and waving pennants—when the answer came to the Baron.

"My dear Baron," the Count said, leaning close to his ear, "you know, don't you, that the Emperor has not given official sanction to your choice of heir?"

The Baron felt himself to be within a sudden personal cone of silence produced by his own shock. He stared at Fenring, barely seeing the Count's lady come through the guards beyond to join the party in the golden box.

"That's really why I'm here today," the Count said. "The Emperor wishes me to report on whether you've chosen a worthy successor. There's nothing like the arena to expose the true person from beneath the mask, eh?"

"The Emperor promised me free choice of heir!" the Baron grated.

"We shall see," Fenring said, and turned away to greet his lady. She sat down, smiling at the Baron, then giving her attention to the sand floor beneath them where Feyd-Rautha was emerging in giles and tights—the black glove and the long knife in his right hand, the white glove and the short knife in his left hand.

"White for poison, black for purity," the Lady Fenring said. "A curious custom, isn't it, my love?"

"Um-m-m-m," the Count said.

The greeting cheer lifted from the family galleries, and Feyd-Rautha paused to accept it, looking up and scanning the faces—seeing his cousines and cousins, the demibrothers, the concubines and out-freyn relations. They were so many pink trumpet mouths yammering amidst a flutter of colorful clothing and banners.

It came to Feyd-Rautha then that the packed ranks of faces would look just as avidly at his blood as at that of the slave-gladiator. There was not a doubt of the outcome in this fight, of course. Here was only the form of danger without its substance—yet . . . .

Feyd-Rautha held up his knives to the sun, saluted the three corners of the arena in the ancient manner. The short knife in white-gloved hand (white, the sign of poison) went first into its sheath. Then the long blade in the black-gloved hand—the pure blade that now was unpure, his secret weapon to turn this day into a purely personal victory: poison on the black blade.

The adjustment of his body shield took only a moment, and he paused to sense the skin-tightening at his forehead assuring him he was properly guarded.

This moment carried its own suspense, and Feyd-Rautha dragged it out with the sure hand of a showman, nodding to his handlers and distractors, checking their equipment with a measuring stare—gyves in place with their prickles sharp and glistening, the barbs and hooks waving with their blue streamers.

Feyd-Rautha signaled the musicians.

The slow march began, sonorous with its ancient pomp, and Feyd-Rautha led his troupe across the arena for obeisance at the foot of his uncle's box. He caught the ceremonial key as it was thrown.

The music stopped.

Into the abrupt silence, he stepped back two paces, raised the key and shouted: "I dedicate this truth to . . . ." And he paused, knowing his uncle would think: *The young fool's going to dedicate to Lady Fenring after all and cause a ruckus!*

". . . to my uncle and patron, the Baron Vladimir Harkonnen!" Feyd-Rautha shouted.

And he was delighted to see his uncle sigh.

The music resumed at the quick-march, and Feyd-Rautha led his men scampering back across the arena to the prudence door that admitted only those wearing the proper identification band. Feyd-Rautha prided himself that he never used the pru-door and seldom needed distractors. But it was good to know they were available this day—special plans sometimes involved special dangers.

Again, silence settled over the arena.

Feyd-Rautha turned, faced the big red door across from him through which the gladiator would emerge.

The special gladiator.

The plan Thufir Hawat had devised was admirably simple and direct, Feyd-Rautha thought. The slave would not be drugged—that was the danger.

Instead, a key word had been drummed into the man's unconscious to immobilize his muscles at a critical instant. Feyd-Rautha rolled the vital word in his mind, mouthing it without sound: "Scum!" To the audience, it would appear that an undrugged slave had been slipped into the arena to kill the na-Baron. And all the carefully arranged evidence would point to the slavemaster.

A low humming arose from the red door's servo-motors as they were armed for opening.

Feud-Rautha focused all his awareness on the door. This first moment was the critical one. The appearance of the gladiator as he emerged told the trained eye much it needed to know. All gladiators were supposed to be hyped on elacca drug to come out kill-ready in fighting stance—but you had to watch how they hefted the knife, which way they turned in defense, whether they were actually aware of the audience in the stands. The way a slave cocked his head could give the most vital clue to counter and feint.

The red door slammed open.

Out charged a tall, muscular man with shaved head and darkly pitted eyes. His skin was carrot-colored as it should be from the elacca drug, but Feyd-Rautha knew the color was paint. The slave wore green leotards and the red belt of a semishield—the belt's arrow pointing left to indicate the slave's left side was shielded. He held his knife sword-fashion, cocked slightly outward in the stance of a trained fighter. Slowly, he advanced into the arena, turning his shielded side toward Feyd-Rautha and the group at the pru-door.

"I like not the look of this one," said one of Feyd-Rautha's barb-men. "Are you sure he's drugged, m'Lord?"

"He has the color," Feyd-Rautha said.

"Yet he stands like a fighter," said another helper.

Feyd-Rautha advanced two steps onto the sand, studied this slave.

"What has he done to his arm?" asked one of the distractors.

Feyd-Rautha's attention went to a bloody scratch on the man's left forearm, followed the arm down to the hand as it pointed to a design drawn in blood on the left hip of the green leotards—a wet shape there; the formalized outline of a hawk.

Hawk!

Feyd-Rautha looked up into the darkly pitted eyes, saw them glaring at him with uncommon alertness.

*It's one of Duke Leto's fighting men we took on Arrakis!* Feyd-Rautha thought. *No simple gladiator this!* A chill ran through him, and he wondered if Hawat had another plan for this arena—a feint within a feint within a feint. And only the slavemaster prepared to take the blame!

Feyd-Rautha's chief handler spoke at his ear: "I like not the look on that one, m'Lord. Let me set a barb or two in his left arm to try him."

"I'll set my own barbs," Feyd-Rautha said. He took a pair of long, hooked shafts from the handler, hefted them, testing the balance. These barbs, too, were supposed to be drugged—but not this time, and the chief handler might die because of that. But it was all part of the plan.

*"You'll come out of this a hero,"* Hawat had said. *"Killed your gladiator man*

*to man and in spite of treachery. The slavemaster will be executed and your man will step into his spot."*

Feyd-Rautha advanced another five paces into the arena, playing out the moment, studying the slave. Already, he knew, the experts in the stands above him were aware that something was wrong. The gladiator had the correct skin color for a drugged man, but he stood his ground and did not tremble. The afficionados would be whispering among themselves now: "See how he stands. He should be agitated—attacking or retreating. See how he conserves his strength, how he waits. He should not wait."

Feyd-Rautha felt his own excitement kindle. *Let there be treachery in Hawat's mind,* he thought. *I can handle this slave. And it's my long knife that carries the poison this time, not the short one. Even Hawat doesn't know that.*

"Hai, Harkonnen!" the slave called. "Are you prepared to die?"

Deathly stillness gripped the arena. *Slaves did not issue the challenge!*

Now, Feyd-Rautha had a clear view of the gladiator's eyes, saw the cold ferocity of despair in them. He marked the way the man stood, loose and ready, muscles prepared for victory. The slave grapevine had carried Hawat's message to this one: *"You'll get a true chance to kill the na-Baron."* That much of the scheme was as they'd planned it, then.

A tight smile crossed Feyd-Rautha's mouth. He lifted the barbs, seeing success for his plans in the way the gladiator stood.

"Hai! Hai!" the slave challenged, and crept forward two steps.

*No one in the galleries can mistake it now,* Feyd-Rautha thought.

This slave should have been partly crippled by drug-induced terror. Every movement should have betrayed his inner knowledge that there was no hope for him—he could not win. He should have been filled with the stories of the poisons the na-Baron chose for the blade in his white-gloved hand. The na-Baron never gave quick death; he delighted in demonstrating rare poisons, could stand in the arena pointing out interesting side effects on a writhing victim. There was fear in the slave, yes—but not terror.

Feyd-Rautha lifted the barbs high, nodded in an almost-greeting.

The gladiator pounced.

His feint and defensive counter were as good as any Feyd-Rautha had ever seen. A timed side blow missed by the barest fraction from severing the tendons of the na-Baron's left leg.

Feyd-Rautha danced away, leaving a barbed shaft in the slave's right forearm, the hooks completely buried in flesh where the man could not withdraw them without ripping tendons.

A concerted gasp lifted from the galleries.

The sound filled Feyd-Rautha with elation.

He knew now what his uncle was experiencing, sitting up there with the Fenrings, the observers from the Imperial Court, beside him. There could be no interference with this fight. The forms must be observed in front of witnesses. And the Baron would interpret the events in the arena only one way—threat to himself.

The slave backed, holding knife in teeth and lashing the barbed shaft to his arm with the pennant. "I do not feel your needle!" he shouted. Again he crept forward, knife ready, left side presented, the body bent backward to give it the greatest surface of protection from the half-shield.

That action, too, didn't escape the galleries. Sharp cries came from the family boxes, Feyd-Rautha's handlers were calling out to ask if he needed them.

He waved them back to the pru-door.

*I'll give them a show such as they've never had before,* Feyd-Rautha thought. *No tame killing where they can sit back and admire the style. This'll be something to take them by the guts and twist them. When I'm Baron they'll remember this day and won't be a one of them can escape fear of me because of this day.*

Feyd-Rautha gave ground slowly before the gladiator's crablike advance. Arena sand grated underfoot. He heard the slave's panting, smelled his own sweat and a faint odor of blood on the air.

Steadily, the na-Baron moved backward, turning to the right, his second barb ready. The slave danced sideways. Feyd-Rautha appeared to stumble, heard the scream from the galleries.

Again, the slave pounced.

*Gods, what a fighting man!* Feyd-Rautha thought as he leaped aside. Only youth's quickness saved him, but he left the second barb buried in the deltoid muscle of the slave's right arm.

Shrill cheers rained from the galleries.

*They cheer me now,* Feyd-Rautha thought. He heard the wildness in the voices just as Hawat had said he would. They'd never cheered a family fighter that way before. And he thought with an edge of grimness on a thing Hawat had told him: *"It's easier to be terrified by an enemy you admire."*

Swiftly, Feyd-Rautha retreated to the center of the arena where all could see clearly. He drew his long blade, crouched and waited for the advancing slave.

The man took only the time to lash the second barb tight to his arm, then sped in pursuit.

*Let the family see me do this thing,* Feyd-Rautha thought. *I am their enemy: let them think of me as they see me now.*

He drew his short blade.

"I do not fear you, Harkonnen swine," the gladiator said. "Your tortures cannot hurt a dead man. I can be dead on my own blade before a handler lays finger to my flesh. And I'll have you dead beside me!"

Feyd-Rautha grinned, offered now the long blade, the one with the poison. "Try this one," he said, and feinted with the short blade in his other hand.

The slave shifted knife hands, turned inside both parry and feint to grapple the na-Baron's short blade—the one in the white gloved hand that tradition said should carry the poison.

"You will die, Harkonnen," the gladiator gasped.

They struggled sideways across the sand. Where Feyd-Rautha's shield met the slave's halfshield, a blue glow marked the contact. The air around them filled with ozone from the fields.

"Die on your own poison!" the slave grated.

He began forcing the white-gloved hand inward, turning the blade he thought carried the poison.

*Let them see this!* Feyd-Rautha thought. He brought down the long blade, felt it clang uselessly against the barbed shaft lashed to the slave's arm.

Feyd-Rautha felt a moment of desperation. He had not thought the barbed shafts would be an advantage for the slave. But they gave the man another shield. And the strength of this gladiator! The short blade was being forced inward inexorably, and Feyd-Rautha focused on the fact that a man could also die on an unpoisoned blade.

"Scum!" Feyd-Rautha gasped.

At the key word, the gladiator's muscles obeyed with a momentary slackness. It was enough for Feyd-Rautha. He opened a space between them sufficient for the long blade. Its poisoned tip flicked out, drew a red line down the slave's chest. There was instant agony in the poison. The man disengaged himself, staggered backward.

*Now, let my dear family watch,* Feyd-Rautha thought. *Let them think on this slave who tried to turn the knife he thought poisoned and use it against me. Let them wonder how a gladiator could come into this arena ready for such an attempt. And let them always be aware they cannot know for sure which of my hands carries the poison.*

Feyd-Rautha stood in silence, watching the slowed motions of the slave. The man moved within a hesitation-awareness. There was an orthographic thing on his face now for every watcher to recognize. The death was written there. The slave knew it had been done to him and he knew how it had been done. The wrong blade had carried the poison.

"You!" the man moaned.

Feyd-Rautha drew back to give death its space. The paralyzing drug in the poison had yet to take full effect, but the man's slowness told of its advance.

The slave staggered forward as though drawn by a string—one dragging step at a time. Each step was the only step in his universe. He still clutched his knife, but its point wavered.

"One day . . . one . . . of us . . . will . . . get . . . you," he gasped.

A sad little moue contorted his mouth. He sat, sagged, then stiffened and rolled away from Feyd-Rautha, face down.

Feyd-Rautha advanced in the silent arena, put a toe under the gladiator and rolled him onto his back to give the galleries a clear view of the face when the poison began its twisting, wrenching work on the muscles. But the gladiator came over with his own knife protruding from his breast.

In spite of the frustration, there was for Feyd-Rautha a measure of admiration for the effort this slave had managed in overcoming the paralysis to do this thing to himself. With the admiration came the realization that here was *truly* a thing to fear.

*That which makes a man superhuman is terrifying.*

As he focused on this thought, Feyd-Rautha became conscious of the eruption of noise from the stands and galleries around him. They were cheering with utter abandon.

Feyd-Rautha turned, looking up at them.

All were cheering except the Baron, who sat with hand to chin in deep contemplation—and the Count and his lady, both of whom were staring down at him, their faces masked by smiles.

Count Fenring turned to his lady, said: "Ah-h-h-um-m-m, a resourceful um-m-m-m young man. Eh, mm-m-m-ah, my dear?"

"His ah-h-h synaptic responses are very swift," she said.

The Baron looked at her, at the Count, returned his attention to the arena: *If someone could get that close to one of mine!* Rage began to replace his fear. *I'll have the slavemaster dead over a slow fire this night . . . and if this Count and his lady had a hand in it . . . .*

The conversation in the Baron's box was remote movement to Feyd-Rautha, the voices drowned in the foot-stamping chant that came now from all around:

"Head! Head! Head! Head!"

The Baron scowled, seeing the way Feyd-Rautha turned to him. Languidly, controlling his rage with difficulty, the Baron waved his hand toward the young man standing in the arena beside the sprawled body of the slave. *Give the boy a head. He earned it by exposing the slavemaster.*

Feyd-Rautha saw the signal of agreement, thought: *They think they honor me. Let them see what I think!*

He saw his handlers approaching with a saw-knife to do the honors, waved them back, repeated the gesture as they hesitated. *They think they honor me with just a head!* he thought. He bent and crossed the gladiator's hands around the protruding knife handle, then removed the knife and placed it in the limp hands.

It was done in an instant, and he straightened, beckoned his handlers. "Bury this slave intact with his knife in his hands," he said. "The man earned it."

In the golden box, Count Fenring leaned close to the Baron, said: "A grand gesture, that—true bravura. Your nephew has style as well as courage."

"He insults the crowd by refusing the head," the Baron muttered.

"Not at all," Lady Fenring said. She turned, looking up at the tiers around them.

And the Baron noted the line of her neck—a truly lovely flowing of muscles—like a young boy's.

"They like what your nephew did," she said.

As the import of Feyd-Rautha's gesture penetrated to the most distant seats, as the people saw the handlers carrying off the dead gladiator intact, the Baron watched them and realized she had interpreted the reaction correctly. The people were going wild, beating on each other, screaming and stamping.

The Baron spoke wearily. "I shall have to order a fete. You cannot send people home like this, their energies unspent. They must see that I share their elation." He gave a hand signal to the guard, and a servant above them dipped the Harkonnen orange pennant over the box—once, twice, three times—signal for a fete.

Feyd-Rautha crossed the arena to stand beneath the golden box, his weapons sheathed, arms hanging at his sides. Above the undiminished frenzy of the crowd, he called: "A fete, Uncle?"

The noise began to subside as people saw the conversation and waited.

"In your honor, Feyd!" the Baron called down. And again, he caused the pennant to be dipped in signal.

Across the arena, the pru-barriers had been dropped and young men were leaping down into the arena, racing toward Feyd-Rautha.

"You ordered the pru-shields dropped, Baron?" the Count asked.

"No one will harm the lad," the Baron said. "He's a hero."

The first of the charging mass reached Feyd-Rautha, lifted him on their shoulders, began parading around the arena.

"He could walk unarmed and unshielded through the poorest quarters of Harko tonight," the Baron said. "They'd give him the last of their food and drink just for his company."

The Baron pushed himself from his chair, settled his weight into his suspensors. "You will forgive me, please. There are matters that require my immediate attention. The guard will see you to the keep."

The Count arose, bowed. "Certainly, Baron. We're looking forward to the fete. I've ah-h-h-mm-m-m never seen a Harkonnen fete."

"Yes," the Baron said. "The fete." He turned, was enveloped by guards as he stepped into the private exit from the box.

A guard captain bowed to Count Fenring. "Your orders, my Lord?"

"We will ah-h-h wait for the worst mm-m-m crush to um-m-m pass," the Count said.

"Yes, m'Lord." The man bowed himself back three paces.

Count Fenring faced his lady, spoke again in their personal humming-code tongue: "You saw it, of course?"

In the same humming tongue, she said: "The lad knew the gladiator wouldn't be drugged. There was a moment of fear, yes, but no surprise."

"It was planned," he said. "The entire performance."

"Without a doubt."

"It stinks of Hawat."

"Indeed," she said.

"I demanded earlier that the Baron eliminate Hawat."

"That was an error, my dear."

"I see that now."

"The Harkonnens may have a new Baron ere long."

"If that's Hawat's plan."

"That will bear examination, true," she said.

"The young one will be more amenable to control."

"For us . . . after tonight," she said.

"You don't anticipate difficulty seducing him, my little brood-mother?"

"No, my love. You saw how he looked at me."

"Yes, and I can see now why we must have that bloodline."

"Indeed, and it's obvious we must have a hold on him. I'll plant deep in his deepest self the necessary prana-bindu phrases to bend him."

"We'll leave as soon as possible—as soon as you're sure," he said.

She shuddered. "By all means. I should not want to bear a child in this terrible place."

"The things we do in the name of humanity," he said.

"Yours is the easy part," she said.

"There *are* some ancient prejudices I overcome," he said. "They're quite primordial, you know."

"My poor dear," she said, and patted his cheek. "You know this is the only way to be sure of saving that bloodline."

He spoke in a dry voice: "I quite understand what we do."

"We won't fail," she said.

"Guilt starts as a feeling of failure," he reminded.

"There'll be no guilt," she said. "Hypno-ligation of that Feyd-Rautha's psyche and his child in my womb—then we go."

"That uncle," he said. "Have you ever seen such distortion?"

"He's pretty fierce," she said, "but the nephew could well grow to be worse."

"Thanks to that uncle. You know, when you think what this lad could've been with some other upbringing—with the Atreides code to guide him, for example."

"It's sad," she said.

"Would that we could've saved both the Atreides youth and this one. From what I heard of that young Paul—a most admirable lad, good union of breeding and training." He shook his head. "But we shouldn't waste sorrow over the aristocracy of misfortune."

"There's a Bene Gesserit saying," she said.

"You have sayings for everything!" he protested.

"You'll like this one," she said. "It goes: 'Do not count a human dead until you've seen his body. And even then you can make a mistake.'"

*Muad'Dib tells us in "A Time of Reflection" that his first collisions with Arrakeen necessities were the true beginnings of his education. He learned then how to pole the sand for its weather, learned the language of the wind's needles stinging his skin, learned how the nose can buzz with sand-itch and how to gather his body's precious moisture around him to guard it and preserve it. As his eyes assumed the blue of the Ibad, he learned the Chakobsa way.*

**—Stilgar's preface to "Muad'Dib, the Man"
by the Princess Irulan**

Stilgar's troop returning to the sietch with its two strays from the desert climbed out of the basin in the waning light of the first moon. The robed figures hurried with the smell of home in their nostrils. Dawn's gray line behind them was brightest at the notch in their horizon-calendar that marked the middle of autumn, the month of Caprock.

Wind-raked dead leaves strewed the cliffbase where the sietch children had been gathering them, but the sounds of the troop's passage (except for occasional blunderings by Paul and his mother) could not be distinguished from the natural sounds of the night.

Paul wiped sweat-caked dust from his forehead, felt a tug at his arm, heard Chani's voice hissing: "Do as I told you: bring the fold of your hood down over your forehead! Leave only the eyes exposed. You waste moisture."

A whispered command behind them demanded silence: "The desert hears you!"

A bird chirruped from the rocks high above them.

The troop stopped, and Paul sensed abrupt tension.

There came a faint thumping from the rocks, a sound no louder than mice jumping in the sand.

Again, the bird chirruped.

A stir passed through the troop's ranks. And again, the mouse-thumping pecked its way across the sand.

Once more, the bird chirruped.

The troop resumed its climb up into a crack in the rocks, but there was a stillness of breath about the Fremen now that filled Paul with caution, and he noted covert glances toward Chani, the way she seemed to withdraw, pulling in upon herself.

There was rock underfoot now, a faint gray swishing of robes around them, and Paul sensed a relaxing of discipline, but still that quiet-of-the-person about Chani and the others. He followed a shadow shape—up steps, a turn, more steps, into a tunnel, past two moisture-sealed doors and into a globe-lighted narrow passage with yellow rock walls and ceiling.

All around him, Paul saw the Fremen throwing back their hoods, removing nose plugs, breathing deeply. Someone sighed. Paul looked for Chani, found that she had left his side. He was hemmed in by a press of robed bodies. Someone jostled him, said, "Excuse me, Usul. What a crush! It's always this way."

On his left, the narrow bearded face of the one called Farok turned toward Paul. The stained eyepits and blue darkness of eyes appeared even darker under the yellow globes. "Throw off your hood, Usul," Farok said. "You're home." And he helped Paul, releasing the hood catch, elbowing a space around them.

Paul slipped out his nose plugs, swung the mouth baffle aside. The odor of the place assailed him: unwashed bodies, distillate esthers of reclaimed wastes, everywhere the sour effluvia of humanity with, over it all, a turbulence of spice and spicelike harmonics.

"Why are we waiting, Farok?" Paul asked.

"For the Reverend Mother, I think. You heard the message—poor Chani."

*Poor Chani?* Paul asked himself. He looked around, wondering where she was, where his mother had got to in all this crush.

Farok took a deep breath. "The smells of home," he said.

Paul saw that the man was enjoying the stink of this air, that there was no irony in his tone. He heard his mother cough then, and her voice came back to him through the press of the troop: "How rich the odors of your sietch, Stilgar.

I see you do much working with the spice . . . you make paper . . . plastics . . . and isn't that chemical explosives?"

"You know this from what you smell?" It was another man's voice.

And Paul realized she was speaking for his benefit, that she wanted him to make a quick acceptance of this assault on his nostrils.

There came a buzz of activity at the head of the troop and a prolonged indrawn breath that seemed to pass through the Fremen, and Paul heard hushed voices back down the line: "It's true then—Liet is dead."

*Liet,* Paul thought. Then: *Chani, daughter of Liet.* The pieces fell together in his mind. Liet was the Fremen name of the planetologist.

Paul looked at Farok, asked: "Is it the Liet known as Kynes?"

"There is only one Liet," Farok said.

Paul turned, stared at the robed back of a Fremen in front of him. *Then Liet-Kynes is dead,* he thought.

"It was Harkonnen treachery," someone hissed. "They made it seem an accident . . . lost in the desert . . . a 'thopter crash . . . ."

Paul felt a burst of anger. The man who had befriended them, helped save them from the Harkonnen hunters, the man who had sent his Fremen cohorts searching for two strays in the desert . . . another victim of the Harkonnens.

"Does Usul hunger yet for revenge?" Farok said.

Before Paul could answer, there came a low call and the troop swept forward into a wider chamber, carrying Paul with them. He found himself in an open space confronted by Stilgar and a strange woman wearing a flowing wrap-around garment of brilliant orange and green. Her arms were bare to the shoulders, and he could see she wore no stillsuit. Her skin was a pale olive. Dark hair swept back from her high forehead, throwing emphasis on sharp cheekbones and aquiline nose between the dense darkness of her eyes.

She turned toward him, and Paul saw golden rings threaded with water tallies dangling from her ears.

"*This* bested my Jamis?" she demanded.

"Be silent, Harah," Stilgar said. "It was Jamis' doing—*he* invoked the tahaddi al-burhan."

"He's not but a boy!" she said. She gave her head a sharp shake from side to side, setting the water tallies to jingling. "My children made fatherless by another child? Surely, 'twas an accident!"

"Usul, how many years have you?" Stilgar asked.

"Fifteen standard," Paul said.

Stilgar swept his eyes over the troop. "Is there one among you cares to challenge me?"

Silence.

Stilgar looked at the woman. "Until I've learned his weirding ways, I'd not challenge him."

She returned his stare. "But—"

"You saw the stranger woman who went with Chani to the Reverend Mother?" Stilgar asked. "She's an out-freyn Sayyadina, mother to this lad. The mother and son are masters of the weirding ways of battle."

"Lisan al-Gaib," the woman whispered. Her eyes held awe as she turned them back toward Paul.

*The legend again,* Paul thought.

"Perhaps," Stilgar said. "It hasn't been tested, though." He returned his attention to Paul: "Usul, it's our way that you've now the responsibility for Jamis' woman here and for his two sons. His yali . . . his quarters, are yours. His coffee service is yours . . . and this, his woman."

Paul studied the woman, wondering: *Why isn't she mourning her man? Why does she show no hate for me?* Abruptly, he saw that the Fremen were staring at him, waiting.

Someone whispered: "There's work to do. Say how you accept her."

Stilgar said: "Do you accept Harah as woman or servant?"

Harah lifted her arms, turning slowly on one heel. "I am still young, Usul. It's said I still look as young as when I was with Geoff . . . before Jamis bested him."

*Jamis killed another to win her,* Paul thought.

Paul said: "If I accept her as servant, may I yet change my mind at a later time?"

"You'd have a year to change your decision," Stilgar said. "After that, she's a free woman to choose as she wishes . . . or you could free her to choose for herself at any time. But she's your responsibility, no matter what, for one year . . . and you'll always share some responsibility for the sons of Jamis."

"I accept her as servant," Paul said.

Harah stamped a foot, shook her shoulders with anger. "But I'm young!"

Stilgar looked at Paul, said: "Caution's a worthy trait in a man who'd lead."

"But I'm young!" Harah repeated.

"Be silent," Stilgar commanded. "If a thing has merit, it'll be. Show Usul to his quarters and see he has fresh clothing and a place to rest."

"Oh-h-h-h!" she said.

Paul had registered enough of her to have a first approximation. He felt the impatience of the troop, knew many things were being delayed here. He wondered if he dared ask the whereabouts of his mother and Chani, saw from Stilgar's nervous stance that it would be a mistake.

He faced Harah, pitched his voice with tone and tremolo to accent her fear and awe, said: "Show me my quarters, Harah! We will discuss your youth another time."

She backed away two steps, cast a frightened glance at Stilgar. "He has the weirding voice," she husked.

"Stilgar," Paul said. "Chani's father put heavy obligation on me. If there's anything . . . ."

"It'll be decided in council," Stilgar said. "You can speak then." He nodded in dismissal, turned away with the rest of the troop following him.

Paul took Harah's arm, noting how cool her flesh seemed, feeling her tremble. "I'll not harm you, Harah," he said. "Show me our quarters." And he smoothed his voice with relaxants.

"You'll not cast me out when the year's gone?" she said. "I know for true I'm not as young as once I was."

"As long as I live you'll have a place with me," he said. He released her arm. "Come now, where are our quarters?"

She turned, led the way down the passage, turning right into a wide cross tunnel lighted by evenly spaced yellow overhead globes. The stone floor was smooth, swept clean of sand.

Paul moved up beside her, studied the aquiline profile as they walked. "You do not hate me, Harah?"

"Why should I hate you?"

She nodded to a cluster of children who stared at them from the raised ledge of a side passage. Paul glimpsed adult shapes behind the children partly hidden by filmy hangings.

"I . . . bested Jamis."

"Stilgar said the ceremony was held and you're a friend of Jamis." She glanced sidelong at him. "Stilgar said you gave moisture to the dead. Is that truth?"

"Yes."

"It's more than I'll do . . . can do."

"Don't you mourn him?"

"In the time of mourning, I'll mourn him."

They passed an arched opening. Paul looked through it at men and women working with stand-mounted machinery in a large, bright chamber. There seemed an extra tempo of urgency to them.

"What're they doing in there?" Paul asked.

She glanced back as they passed beyond the arch, said: "They hurry to finish the quota in the plastics shop before we flee. We need many dew collectors for the planting."

"Flee?"

"Until the butchers stop hunting us or are driven from our land."

Paul caught himself in a stumble, sensing an arrested instant of time, remembering a fragment, a visual projection of prescience—but it was displaced, like a montage in motion. The bits of his prescient memory were not quite as he remembered them.

"The Sardaukar hunt us," he said.

"They'll not find much excepting an empty sietch or two," she said. "And they'll find their share of death in the sand."

"They'll find this place?" he asked.

"Likely."

"Yet we take the time to . . . ." He motioned with his head toward the arch now far behind them. ". . . make . . . dew collectors?"

"The planting goes on."

"What're dew collectors?" he asked.

The glance she turned on him was full of surprise. "Don't they teach you anything in the . . . wherever it is you come from?"

"Not about dew collectors."

"Hai!" she said, and there was a whole conversation in the one word.

"Well, what are they?"

"Each bush, each weed you see out there in the erg," she said, "how do you suppose it lives when we leave it? Each is planted most tenderly in its own little pit. The pits are filled with smooth ovals of chromoplastic. Light turns them white. You can see them glistening in the dawn if you look down from a high place. White reflects. But when Old Father Sun departs, the chromoplastic reverts to transparency in the dark. It cools with extreme rapidity. The surface condenses moisture out of the air. That moisture trickles down to keep our plants alive."

"Dew collectors," he muttered, enchanted by the simple beauty of such a scheme.

"I'll mourn Jamis in the proper time for it," she said, as though her mind had not left the question. "He was a good man, Jamis, but quick to anger. A good provider, Jamis, and a wonder with the children. He made no separation between Geoff's boy, my firstborn, and his own true son. They were equal in his eyes." She turned a questing stare on Paul. "Would it be that way with you, Usul?"

"We don't have that problem."

"But if—"

"Harah!"

She recoiled at the harsh edge in his voice.

They passed another brightly lighted room visible through an arch on their left. "What's made there?" he asked.

"They repair the weaving machinery," she said. "But it must be dismantled by tonight." She gestured at a tunnel branching to their left. "Through there and beyond, that's food processing and stillsuit maintenance." She looked at Paul. "Your suit looks new. But if it needs work, I'm good with suits. I work in the factory in season."

They began coming on knots of people now and thicker clusterings of openings in the tunnel's sides. A file of men and women passed them carrying packs that gurgled heavily, the smell of spice strong about them.

"They'll not get our water," Harah said. "Or our spice. You can be sure of that."

Paul glanced at the openings in the tunnel walls, seeing the heavy carpets on the raised ledges, glimpses of rooms with bright fabrics on the walls, piled cushions. People in the openings fell silent at their approach, followed Paul with untamed stares.

"The people find it strange you bested Jamis," Harah said. "Likely you'll have some proving to do when we're settled in a new sietch."

"I don't like killing," he said.

"Thus Stilgar tells it," she said, but her voice betrayed her disbelief.

A shrill chanting grew louder ahead of them. They came to another side opening wider than any of the others Paul had seen. He slowed his pace, staring in at a room crowded with children sitting cross-legged on a maroon-carpeted floor.

At a chalkboard against the far wall stood a woman in a yellow wrap-around, a projecto-stylus in one hand. The board was filled with designs—circles, wedges and curves, snake tracks and squares, flowing arcs split by parallel lines. The woman pointed to the designs one after the other as fast as she could move the stylus, and the children chanted in rhythm with her moving hand.

Paul listened, hearing the voices grow dimmer behind as he moved deeper into the sietch with Harah.

"Tree," the children chanted. "Tree, grass, dune, wind, mountain, hill, fire, lightning, rock, rocks, dust, sand, heat, shelter, heat, full, winter, cold, empty, erosion, summer, cavern, day, tension, moon, night, caprock, sandtide, slope, planting, binder . . . ."

"You conduct classes at a time like this?" Paul asked.

Her face went somber and grief edged her voice: "What Liet taught us, we cannot pause an instant in that. Liet who is dead must not be forgotten. It's the Chakobsa way."

She crossed the tunnel to the left, stepped up onto a ledge, parted gauzy orange hangings and stood aside: "Your yali is ready for you, Usul."

Paul hesitated before joining her on the ledge. He felt a sudden reluctance to be alone with this woman. It came to him that he was surrounded by a way of life that could only be understood by postulating an ecology of ideas and values. He felt that this Fremen world was fishing for him, trying to snare him in its ways. And he knew what lay in that snare—the wild jihad, the religious war he felt he should avoid at any cost.

"This is your yali," Harah said. "Why do you hesitate?"

Paul nodded, joined her on the ledge. He lifted the hangings across from her, feeling metal fibers in the fabric, followed her into a short entrance way and then into a larger room, square, about six meters to a side—thick blue carpets on the floor, blue and green fabrics hiding the rock walls, glowglobes tuned to yellow overhead bobbing against draped yellow ceiling fabrics.

The effect was that of an ancient tent.

Harah stood in front of him, left hand on hip, her eyes studying his face. "The children are with a friend," she said. "They will present themselves later."

Paul masked his unease beneath a quick scanning of the room. Thin hangings to the right, he saw, partly concealed a larger room with cushions piled around the walls. He felt a soft breeze from an air duct, saw the outlet cunningly hidden in a pattern of hangings directly ahead of him.

"Do you wish me to help you remove your stillsuit?" Harah asked.

"No . . . thank you."

"Shall I bring food?"

"Yes."

"There is a reclamation chamber off the other room." She gestured. "For your comfort and convenience when you're out of your stillsuit."

"You said we have to leave this sietch," Paul said. "Shouldn't we be packing or something?"

"It will be done in its time," she said. "The butchers have yet to penetrate to our region."

Still she hesitated, staring at him.

"What is it?" he demanded.

"You've not the eyes of the Ibad," she said. "It's strange but not entirely unattractive."

"Get the food," he said. "I'm hungry."

She smiled at him—a knowing, woman's smile that he found disquieting. "I am your servant," she said, and whirled away in one lithe motion, ducking behind a heavy wall hanging that revealed another narrow passage before falling back into place.

Feeling angry with himself, Paul brushed through the thin hanging on the right and into the larger room. He stood there a moment caught by uncertainty. And he wondered where Chani was . . . Chani who had just lost her father.

*We're alike in that,* he thought.

A wailing cry sounded from the outer corridors, its volume muffled by the intervening hangings. It was repeated, a bit more distant. And again. Paul realized someone was calling the time. He focused on the fact that he had seen no clocks.

The faint smell of burning creosote bush came to his nostrils, riding on the omnipresent stink of the sietch. Paul saw that he had already suppressed the odorous assault on his senses.

And he wondered again about his mother, how the moving montage of the future would incorporate her . . . and the daughter she bore. Mutable time-awareness danced around him. He shook his head sharply, focusing his attention on the evidences that spoke of profound depth and breadth in this Fremen culture that had swallowed them.

With its subtle oddities.

He had seen a thing about the caverns and this room, a thing that suggested far greater differences than anything he had yet encountered.

There was no sign of a poison snooper here, no indication of their use anywhere in the cave warren. Yet he could smell poisons in the sietch stench—strong ones, common ones.

He heard a rustle of hangings, thought it was Harah returning with food, and turned to watch her. Instead, from beneath a displaced pattern of hangings, he saw two young boys—perhaps aged nine and ten—staring out at him with greedy eyes. Each wore a small kindjal-type crysknife, rested a hand on the hilt.

And Paul recalled the stories of the Fremen—that their children fought as ferociously as the adults.

> *The hands move, the lips move—*
> *Ideas gush from his words,*
> *And his eyes devour!*
> *He is an island of Selfdom.*

**—description from "A Manual of Muad'Dib"**
**by the Princess Irulan**

Phosphortubes in the faraway upper reaches of the cavern cast a dim light onto the thronged interior, hinting at the great size of this rock-enclosed space . . . larger, Jessica saw, than even the Gathering Hall of her Bene Gesserit school. She estimated there were more than five thousand people gathered out there beneath the ledge where she stood with Stilgar.

And more were coming.

The air was murmurous with people.

"Your son has been summoned from his rest, Sayyadina," Stilgar said. "Do you wish him to share in your decision?"

"Could he change my decision?"

"Certainly, the air with which you speak comes from your own lungs, but—"

"The decision stands," she said.

But she felt misgivings, wondering if she should use Paul as an excuse for backing out of a dangerous course. There was an unborn daughter to think of as well. What endangered the flesh of the mother endangered the flesh of the daughter.

Men came with rolled carpets, grunting under the weight of them, stirring up dust as the loads were dropped onto the ledge.

Stilgar took her arm, led her back into the acoustical horn that formed the rear limits of the ledge. He indicated a rock bench within the horn. "The Reverend Mother will sit here, but you may rest yourself until she comes."

"I prefer to stand," Jessica said.

She watched the men unroll the carpets, covering the ledge, looked out at the crowd. There were at least ten thousand people on the rock floor now.

And still they came.

Out on the desert, she knew, it already was red nightfall, but here in the cavern hall was perpetual twilight, a gray vastness thronged with people come to see her risk her life.

A way was opened through the crowd to her right, and she saw Paul approaching flanked by two small boys. There was a swaggering air of self-importance about the children. They kept hands on knives, scowled at the wall of people on either side.

"The sons of Jamis who are now the sons of Usul," Stilgar said. "They take their escort duties seriously." He ventured a smile at Jessica.

Jessica recognized the effort to lighten her mood and was grateful for it, but could not take her mind from the danger that confronted her.

*I had no choice but to do this,* she thought. *We must move swiftly if we're to secure our place among these Fremen.*

Paul climbed to the ledge, leaving the children below. He stopped in front of his mother, glanced at Stilgar, back to Jessica. "What is happening? I thought I was being summoned to council."

Stilgar raised a hand for silence, gestured to his left where another way had been opened in the throng. Chani came down the lane opened there, her elfin face set in lines of grief. She had removed her stillsuit and wore a graceful blue wraparound that exposed her thin arms. Near the shoulder on her left arm, a green kerchief had been tied.

*Green for mourning,* Paul thought.

It was one of the customs the two sons of Jamis had explained to him by indirection, telling him they wore no green because they accepted him as guardian-father.

"Are you the Lisan al-Gaib?" they had asked. And Paul had sensed the jihad in their words, shrugged off the question with one of his own—learning then that Kaleff, the elder of the two, was ten, and the natural son of Geoff. Orlop, the younger, was eight, the natural son of Jamis.

It had been a strange day with these two standing guard over him because he asked it, keeping away the curious, allowing him the time to nurse his thoughts and prescient memories, to plan a way to prevent the jihad.

Now, standing beside his mother on the cavern ledge and looking out at the throng, he wondered if any plan could prevent the wild outpouring of fanatic legions.

Chani, nearing the ledge, was followed at a distance by four women carrying another woman in a litter.

Jessica ignored Chani's approach, focusing all her attention on the woman in the litter—a crone, a wrinkled and shriveled ancient thing in a black gown with hood thrown back to reveal the tight knot of gray hair and the stringy neck.

The litter-carriers deposited their burden gently on the ledge from below, and Chani helped the old woman to her feet.

*So this is their Reverend Mother,* Jessica thought.

The old woman leaned heavily on Chani as she hobbled toward Jessica, looking like a collection of sticks draped in the black robe. She stopped in front of Jessica, peered upward for a long moment before speaking in a husky whisper.

"So you're the one." The old head nodded precariously on the thin neck. "The Shadout Mapes was right to pity you."

Jessica spoke quickly, scornfully: "I need no one's pity."

"That remains to be seen," husked the old woman. She turned with surprising quickness and faced the throng. "Tell them, Stilgar."

"Must I?" he asked.

"We are the people of Misr," the old woman rasped. "Since our Sunni ancestors fled from Nilotic al-Ourouba, we have known flight and death. The young go on that our people shall not die."

Stilgar took a deep breath, stepped forward two paces.

Jessica felt the hush come over the crowded cavern—some twenty thousand people now, standing silently, almost without movement. It made her feel suddenly small and filled with caution.

"Tonight we must leave this sietch that has sheltered us for so long and go south into the desert," Stilgar said. His voice boomed out across the uplifted faces, reverberating with the force given it by the acoustical horn behind the ledge.

Still the throng remained silent.

"The Reverend Mother tells me she cannot survive another hajra," Stilgar said. "We have lived before without a Reverend Mother, but it is not good for people to seek a new home in such straits."

Now, the throng stirred, rippling with whispers and currents of disquiet.

"That this may not come to pass," Stilgar said, "our new Sayyadina, Jessica of the Weirding, has consented to enter the rite at this time. She will attempt to pass within that we not lose the strength of our Reverend Mother."

*Jessica of the Weirding,* Jessica thought. She saw Paul staring at her, his eyes filled with questions, but his mouth held silent by all the strangeness around them.

*If I die in the attempt, what will become of him?* Jessica asked herself. Again she felt the misgivings fill her mind.

Chani led the old Reverend Mother to a rock bench deep in the acoustical horn, returned to stand beside Stilgar.

"That we may not lose all if Jessica of the Weirding should fail," Stilgar said, "Chani, daughter of Liet, will be consecrated in the Sayyadina at this time." He stepped one pace to the side.

From deep in the acoustical horn, the old woman's voice came out to them, an amplified whisper, harsh and penetrating: "Chani has returned from her hajra—Chani has seen the waters."

A sussurant response arose from the crowd: "She has seen the waters."

"I consecrate the daughter of Liet in the Sayyadina," husked the old woman.

"She is accepted," the crowd responded.

Paul barely heard the ceremony, his attention still centered on what had been said of his mother.

*If she should fail?*

He turned and looked back at the one they called Reverend Mother, studying the dried crone features, the fathomless blue fixation of her eyes. She looked as though a breeze would blow her away, yet there was that about her which suggested she might stand untouched in the path of a coriolis storm. She carried the same aura of power that he remembered from the Reverend Mother Gaius Helen Mohiam who had tested him with agony in the way of the gom jabbar.

"I, the Reverend Mother Ramallo, whose voice speaks as a multitude, say this to you," the old woman said. "It is fitting Chani enter the Sayyadina."

"It is fitting," the crowd responded.

The old woman nodded, whispered: "I give her the silver skies, the golden desert and its shining rocks, the green fields that will be. I give these to Sayyadina Chani. And lest she forget that she's servant of us all, to her fall the menial tasks in this Ceremony of the Seed. Let it be as Shai-hulud will have it." She lifted a brown-stick arm, dropped it.

Jessica, feeling the ceremony close around her with a current that swept her beyond all turning back, glanced once at Paul's question-filled face, then prepared herself for the ordeal.

"Let the watermasters come forward," Chani said with only the slightest quaver of uncertainty in her girl-child voice.

Now, Jessica felt herself at the focus of danger, knowing its presence in the watchfulness of the throng, in the silence.

A band of men made its way through a serpentine path opened in the crowd, moving up from the back in pairs. Each pair carried a small skin sack, perhaps twice the size of a human head. The sacks sloshed heavily.

The two leaders deposited their load at Chani's feet on the ledge and stepped back.

Jessica looked at the sack, then at the men. They had their hoods thrown back, exposing long hair tied in a roll at the base of the neck. The black pits of their eyes stared back at her without wavering.

A furry redolence of cinnamon arose from the sack, wafted across Jessica. *The spice?* she wondered.

"Is there water?" Chani asked.

The watermaster on the left, a man with a purple scar line across the bridge of his nose, nodded once. "There is water, Sayyadina," he said, "but we cannot drink of it."

"Is there seed?" Chani asked.

"There is seed," the man said.

Chani knelt and put her hands to the sloshing sack. "Blessed is the water and its seed."

There was familiarity to the rite, and Jessica looked back at the Reverend Mother Ramallo. The old woman's eyes were closed and she sat hunched over as though asleep.

"Sayyadina Jessica," Chani said.

Jessica turned to see the girl staring up at her.

"Have you tasted the blessed water?" Chani asked.

Before Jessica could answer, Chani said: "It is not possible that you have tasted the blessed water. You are outworlder and unprivileged."

A sigh passed through the crowd, a sussuration of robes that made the nape hairs creep on Jessica's neck.

"The crop was large and the maker has been destroyed," Chani said. She began unfastening a coiled spout fixed to the top of the sloshing sack.

Now, Jessica felt the sense of danger boiling around her. She glanced at Paul, saw that he was caught up in the mystery of the ritual and had eyes only for Chani.

*Has he seen this moment in time?* Jessica wondered. She rested a hand on her abdomen, thinking of the unborn daughter there, asking herself: *Do I have the right to risk us both?*

Chani lifted the spout toward Jessica, said: "Here is the Water of Life, the water that is greater than water—Kan, the water that frees the soul. If you be a Reverend Mother, it opens the universe to you. Let Shai-hulud judge now."

Jessica felt herself torn between duty to her unborn child and duty to Paul. For Paul, she knew, she should take that spout and drink of the sack's contents, but as she bent to the proffered spout, her senses told her its peril.

The stuff in the sack had a bitter smell subtly akin to many poisons that she knew, but unlike them, too.

"You must drink it now," Chani said.

*There's no turning back*, Jessica reminded herself. But nothing in all her Bene Gesserit training came into her mind to help her through this instant.

*What is it?* Jessica asked herself. *Liquor? A drug?*

She bent over the spout, smelled the esthers of cinnamon, remembering then the drunkenness of Duncan Idaho. *Spice liquor?* she asked herself. She took the siphon tube in her mouth, pulled up only the most minuscule sip. It tasted of the spice, a faint bite acrid on the tongue.

Chani pressed down on the skin bag. A great gulp of the stuff surged into Jessica's mouth and before she could help herself, she swallowed it, fighting to retain her calmness and dignity.

"To accept a little death is worse than death itself," Chani said. She stared at Jessica, waiting.

And Jessica stared back, still holding the spout in her mouth. She tasted the sack's contents in her nostrils, in the roof of her mouth, in her cheeks, in her eyes—a biting sweetness, now.

*Cool.*

Again, Chani sent the liquid gushing into Jessica's mouth.

*Delicate.*

Jessica studied Chani's face—elfin features—seeing the traces of Liet-Kynes there as yet unfixed by time.

*This is a drug they feed me*, Jessica told herself.

But it was unlike any other drug of her experience, and Bene Gesserit training included the taste of many drugs.

Chani's features were so clear, as though outlined in light.

*A drug.*

Whirling silence settled around Jessica. Every fiber of her body accepted the fact that something profound had happened to it. She felt that she was a conscious mote, smaller than any subatomic particle, yet capable of motion and of sensing her surroundings. Like an abrupt revelation—the curtains whipped away—she realized she had become aware of a psychokinesthetic extension of herself. She was the mote, yet not the mote.

The cavern remained around her—the people. She sensed them: Paul, Chani, Stilgar, the Reverend Mother Ramallo.

*Reverend Mother!*

At the school there had been rumors that some did not survive the Reverend Mother ordeal, that the drug took them.

Jessica focused her attention on the Reverend Mother Ramallo, aware now that all this was happening in a frozen instant of time—suspended time for her alone.

*Why is time suspended?* she asked herself. She stared at the frozen expressions around her, seeing a dust mote above Chani's head, stopped there.

Waiting.

The answer to this instant came like an explosion in her consciousness: her personal time was suspended to save her life.

She focused on the psychokinesthetic extension of herself, looking within, and was confronted immediately with a cellular core, a pit of blackness from which she recoiled.

*That is the place where we cannot look,* she thought. *There is the place the Reverend Mothers are so reluctant to mention—the place where only a Kwisatz Haderach may look.*

This realization returned a small measure of confidence, and again she ventured to focus on the psychokinesthetic extension, becoming a mote-self that searched within her for danger.

She found it within the drug she had swallowed.

The stuff was dancing particles within her, its motions so rapid that even frozen time could not stop them. Dancing particles. She began recognizing familiar structures, atomic linkages: a carbon atom here, helical wavering . . . a glucose molecule. An entire chain of molecules confronted her, and she recognized a protein . . . a methyl-protein configuration.

*Ah-h-h!*

It was a soundless mental sigh within her as she saw the nature of the poison.

With her psychokinesthetic probing, she moved into it, shifted an oxygen mote, allowed another carbon mote to link, reattached a linkage of oxygen . . . hydrogen.

The change spread . . . faster and faster as the catalyzed reaction opened its surface of contact.

The suspension of time relaxed its hold upon her, and she sensed motion. The tube spout from the sack was touched to her mouth—gently, collecting a drop of moisture.

*Chani's taking the catalyst from my body to change the poison in that sack,* Jessica thought. *Why?*

Someone eased her to a sitting position. She saw the old Reverend Mother Ramallo being brought to sit beside her on the carpeted ledge. A dry hand touched her neck.

And there was another psychokinesthetic mote within her awareness! Jessica tried to reject it, but the mote swept closer . . . closer.

They touched!

It was like an ultimate *simpatico*, being two people at once: not telepathy, but mutual awareness.

*With the old Reverend Mother!*

But Jessica saw that the Reverend Mother didn't think of herself as old. An image unfolded before the mutual mind's eye: a young girl with a dancing spirit and tender humor.

Within the mutual awareness, the young girl said, "Yes, that is how I am."

Jessica could only accept the words, not respond to them.

"You'll have it all soon, Jessica," the inward image said.

*This is hallucination,* Jessica told herself.

"You know better than that," the inward image said. "Swiftly now, do not fight me. There isn't much time. We . . . ." There came a long pause, then: "You should've told us you were pregnant!"

Jessica found the voice that talked within the mutual awareness: "Why?"

"This changes both of you! Holy Mother, what have we done?"

Jessica sensed a forced shift in the mutual awareness, saw another mote-presence with the inward eye. The other mote darted wildly here, there, circling. It radiated pure terror.

"You'll have to be strong," the old Reverend Mother's image-presence said. "Be thankful it's a daughter you carry. This would've killed a male fetus. Now . . . carefully, gently . . . touch your daughter-presence. Be your daughter-presence. Absorb the fear . . . soothe . . . use your courage and your strength . . . gently now . . . gently . . . ."

The other whirling mote swept near, and Jessica compelled herself to touch it.

Terror threatened to overwhelm her.

She fought it the only way she knew: *"I shall not fear. Fear is the mind killer . . . ."*

The litany brought a semblance of calm. The other mote lay quiescent against her.

*Words won't work,* Jessica told herself.

She reduced herself to basic emotional reactions, radiated love, comfort, a warm snuggling of protection.

The terror receded.

Again, the presence of the old Reverend Mother asserted itself, but now there was a tripling of mutual awareness—two active and one that lay quietly absorbing.

"Time compels me," the Reverend Mother said within the awareness. "I have much to give you. And I do not know if your daughter can accept all this while remaining sane. But it must be: the needs of the tribe are paramount."

"What—"

"Remain silent and accept!"

Experiences began to unroll before Jessica. It was like a lecture strip in a subliminal training projector at the Bene Gesserit school . . . but faster . . . blindingly faster.

Yet . . . distinct.

She knew each experience as it happened: there was a lover—virile, bearded, with the dark Fremen eyes, and Jessica saw his strength and tenderness, all of him in one blink-moment, through the Reverend Mother's memory.

There was no time now to think of what this might be doing to the daughter fetus, only time to accept and record. The experiences poured in on Jessica—birth, life, death—important matters and unimportant, an outpouring of single-view time.

*Why should a fall of sand from a clifftop stick in the memory?* she asked herself.

Too late, Jessica saw what was happening: the old woman was dying and, in dying, pouring her experiences into Jessica's awareness as water is poured into a cup. The other mote faded back into pre-birth awareness as Jessica watched it.

And, dying-in-conception, the old Reverend Mother left her life in Jessica's memory with one last sighing blur of words.

"I've been a long time waiting for you," she said. "Here is my life."

There it was, encapsuled, all of it.

Even the moment of death.

*I am now a Reverend Mother,* Jessica realized.

And she knew with a generalized awareness that she had become, in truth, precisely what was meant by a Bene Gesserit Reverend Mother. The poison drug had transformed her.

This wasn't exactly how they did it at the Bene Gesserit school, she knew. No one had ever introduced her to the mysteries of it, but she knew.

The end result was the same.

Jessica sensed the daughter-mote still touching her inner awareness, probed it without response.

A terrible sense of loneliness crept through Jessica in the realization of what had happened to her. She saw her own life as a pattern that had slowed and all life around her speeded up so that the dancing interplay became clearer.

The sensation of mote-awareness faded slightly, its intensity easing as her body relaxed from the threat of the poison, but still she felt that *other* mote, touching it with a sense of guilt at what she had allowed to happen to it.

*I did it, my poor, unformed, dear little daughter. I brought you into this universe and exposed your awareness to all its varieties without any defenses.*

A tiny outflowing of love-comfort, like a reflection of what she had poured into it, came from the other mote.

Before Jessica could respond, she felt the adab presence of demanding memory. There was something that needed doing. She groped for it, realizing she was being impeded by a muzziness of the changed drug permeating her senses.

*I could change that,* she thought. *I could take away the drug action and make it harmless.* But she sensed this would be an error. *I'm within a rite of joining.*

Then she knew what she had to do.

Jessica opened her eyes, gestured to the watersack now being held above her by Chani.

"It has been blessed," Jessica said. "Mingle the waters, let the change come to all, that the people may partake and share in the blessing."

*Let the catalyst do its work,* she thought. *Let the people drink of it and have their awareness of each other heightened for awhile. The drug is safe now . . . now that a Reverend Mother has changed it.*

Still, the demanding memory worked on her, thrusting. There was another thing she had to do, she realized, but the drug made it difficult to focus.

*Ah-h-h-h-h . . . the old Reverend Mother.*

"I have met the Reverend Mother Ramallo," Jessica said. "She is gone, but she remains. Let her memory be honored in the rite."

*Now, where did I get those words?* Jessica wondered.

And she realized they came from another memory, the *life* that had been given to her and now was part of herself. Something about that gift felt incomplete, though.

*"Let them have their orgy,"* the other-memory said within her. "They've little enough pleasure out of living. Yes, and you and I need this little time to become acquainted before I recede and pour out through your memories. Already, I feel myself being tied to bits of you. Ah-h-h, you've a mind filled with interesting things. So many things I'd never imagined."

And the memory-mind encapsulated within her opened itself to Jessica, permitting a view down a wide corridor to other Reverend Mothers within other Reverend Mothers within other Reverend Mothers until there seemed no end to them.

Jessica recoiled, fearing she would become lost in an ocean of oneness. Still, the corridor remained, revealing to Jessica that the Fremen culture was far older than she had suspected.

There had been Fremen on Poritrin, she saw, a people grown soft with an easy planet, fair game for Imperial raiders to harvest and plant human colonies on Bela Tegeuse and Salusa Secundus.

Oh, the wailing Jessica sensed in *that* parting.

Far down the corridor, an image-voice screamed: "They denied us the Hajj!"

Jessica saw the slave cribs on Bela Tegeuse down that inner corridor, saw the weeding out and the selecting that spread men to Rossak and Harmonthep. Scenes of brutal ferocity opened to her like the petals of a terrible flower. And she saw the thread of the past carried by Sayyadina after Sayyadina—first by word of mouth, hidden in the sand chanteys, then refined through their own Reverend Mothers with the discovery of the poison drug on Rossak . . . and now developed to subtle strength on Arrakis in the discovery of the Water of Life.

Far down the inner corridor, another voice screamed: "Never to forgive! Never to forget!"

But Jessica's attention was focused on the revelation of the Water of Life, seeing its source: the liquid exhalation of a dying sandworm, a maker. And as she saw the killing of it in her new memory, she suppressed a gasp.

The creature was drowned!

"Mother, are you all right?"

Paul's voice intruded on her, and Jessica struggled out of the inner awareness to stare up at him, conscious of duty to him, but resenting his presence.

*I'm like a person whose hands were kept numb, without sensation from the first moment of awareness—until one day the ability to feel is forced into them.*

The thought hung in her mind, an enclosing awareness.

*And I say: "Look! I have hands!" But the people all around me say: "What are hands?"*

"Are you all right?" Paul repeated.

"Yes."

"Is this all right for me to drink?" He gestured to the sack in Chani's hands. "They want me to drink it."

She heard the hidden meaning in his words, realized he had detected the poison in the original, unchanged substance, that he was concerned for her. It occurred to Jessica then to wonder about the limits of Paul's prescience. His question revealed much to her.

"You may drink it," she said. "It has been changed." And she looked beyond him to see Stilgar staring down at her, the dark-dark eyes studying.

"Now, we know you cannot be false," he said.

She sensed hidden meaning here, too, but the muzziness of the drug was overpowering her senses. How warm it was and soothing. How beneficent these Fremen to bring her into the fold of such companionship.

Paul saw the drug take hold of his mother.

He searched his memory—the fixed past, the flux-lines of the possible futures. It was like scanning through arrested instants of time, disconcerting to the lens of the inner eye. The fragments were difficult to understand when snatched out of the flux.

This drug—he could assemble knowledge about it, understand what it was doing to his mother, but the knowledge lacked a natural rhythm, lacked a system of mutual reflection.

He realized suddenly that it was one thing to see the past occupying the present, but the true test of prescience was to see the past in the future.

Things persisted in not being what they seemed.

"Drink it," Chani said. She waved the hornspout of a watersack under his nose.

Paul straightened, staring at Chani. He felt carnival excitement in the air. He knew what would happen if he drank this spice drug with its quintessence of the substance that brought the change onto him. He would return to the vision of pure time, of time-become-space. It would perch him on the dizzying summit and defy him to understand.

From behind Chani, Stilgar said: "Drink it, lad. You delay the rite."

Paul listened to the crowd then, hearing the wildness in their voices—"Lisan al-Gaib," they said. "Muad'Dib!" He looked down at his mother. She appeared peacefully asleep in a sitting position—her breathing even and deep. A phrase out of the future that was his lonely past came into his mind: *"She sleeps in the Waters of Life."*

Chani tugged at his sleeve.

Paul took the hornspout into his mouth, hearing the people shout. He felt the liquid gush into his throat as Chani pressed the sack, sensed giddiness in the fumes. Chani removed the spout, handed the sack into hands that reached for it from the floor of the cavern. His eyes focused on her arm, the green band of mourning there.

As she straightened, Chani saw the direction of his gaze, said: "I can mourn him even in the happiness of the waters. This was something he gave us." She put her hand into his, pulling him along the ledge. "We are alike in a thing, Usul: We have each lost a father to the Harkonnens."

Paul followed her. He felt that his head had been separated from his body and restored with odd connections. His legs were remote and rubbery.

They entered a narrow side passage, its walls dimly lighted by spaced out glowglobes. Paul felt the drug beginning to have its unique effect on him, opening time like a flower. He found need to steady himself against Chani as they turned through another shadowed tunnel. The mixture of whipcord and softness he felt beneath her robe stirred his blood. The sensation mingled with the work of the drug, folding future and past into the present, leaving him the thinnest margin of trinocular focus.

"I know you, Chani," he whispered. "We've sat upon a ledge above the sand while I soothed your fears. We've caressed in the dark of the sietch. We've . . . ." He found himself losing focus, tried to shake his head, stumbled.

Chani steadied him, led him through thick hangings into the yellow warmth of a private apartment—low tables, cushions, a sleeping pad beneath an orange spread.

Paul grew aware that they had stopped, that Chani stood facing him, and that her eyes betrayed a look of quiet terror.

"You must tell me," she whispered.

"You are Sihaya," he said, "the desert spring."

"When the tribe shares the Water," she said, "we're together—all of us. We . . . share. I can . . . sense the others with me, but I'm afraid to share with you."

"Why?"

He tried to focus on her, but past and future were merging into the present, blurring her image. He saw her in countless ways and positions and settings.

"There's something frightening in you," she said. "When I took you away from the others . . . I did it because I could feel what the others wanted. You . . . press on people. You . . . make us *see* things!"

He forced himself to speak distinctly: "What do you see?"

She looked down at her hands. "I see a child . . . in my arms. It's our child, yours and mine." She put a hand to her mouth. "How can I know every feature of you?"

*They've a little of the talent,* his mind told him. *But they suppress it because it terrifies.*

In a moment of clarity, he saw how Chani was trembling.

"What is it you want to say?" he asked.

"Usul," she whispered, and still she trembled.

"You cannot back into the future," he said.

A profound compassion for her swept through him. He pulled her against him, stroked her head. "Chani, Chani, don't fear."

"Usul, help me," she cried.

As she spoke, he felt the drug complete its work within him, ripping away the curtains to let him see the distant gray turmoil of his future.

"You're so quiet," Chani said.

He held himself poised in the awareness, seeing time stretch out in its weird dimension, delicately balanced yet whirling, narrow yet spread like a net gathering countless worlds and forces, a tightwire that he must walk, yet a teeter-totter on which he balanced.

On one side he could see the Imperium, a Harkonnen called Feyd-Rautha who flashed toward him like a deadly blade, the Sardaukar raging off their planet to spread pogrom on Arrakis, the Guild conniving and plotting, the Bene Gesserit with their scheme of selective breeding. They lay massed like a thunderhead on his horizon, held back by no more than the Fremen and their Muad'Dib, the sleeping giant Fremen poised for their wild crusade across the universe.

Paul felt himself at the center, at the pivot where the whole structure turned, walking a thin wire of peace with a measure of happiness, Chani at his side. He could see it stretching ahead of him, a time of relative quiet in a hidden sietch, a moment of peace between periods of violence.

"There's no other place for peace," he said.

"Usul, you're crying," Chani murmured. "Usul, my strength, do you give moisture to the dead? To whose dead?"

"To ones not yet dead," he said.

"Then let them have their time of life," she said.

He sensed through the drug fog how right she was, pulled her against him with savage pressure. "Sihaya!" he said.

She put a palm against his cheek. "I'm no longer afraid, Usul. Look at me. I see what you see when you hold me thus."

"What do you see?" he demanded.

"I see us giving love to each other in a time of quiet between storms. It's what we were meant to do."

The drug had him again and he thought: *So many times you've given me comfort and forgetfulness.* He felt anew the hyperillumination with its high-relief imagery of time, sensed his future becoming memories—the tender indignities of physical love, the sharing and communion of selves, the softness and the violence.

"You're the strong one, Chani," he muttered. "Stay with me."

"Always," she said, and kissed his cheek.

# THE PROPHET

---

*No woman, no man, no child ever was deeply intimate with my father. The closest anyone ever came to casual camaraderie with the Padishah Emperor was the relationship offered by Count Hasimir Fenring, a companion from childhood. The measure of Count Fenring's friendship may be seen first in a positive thing: he allayed the Landsraad's suspicions after the Arrakis affair. It cost more than a billion solaris in spice bribes, so my mother said, and there were other gifts as well: slave women, royal honors, and tokens of rank. The second major evidence of the Count's friendship was negative. He refused to kill a man even though it was within his capabilities and my father commanded it. I will relate this presently.*

**—"Count Fenring: A Profile" by the Princess Irulan**

The Baron Vladimir Harkonnen raged down the corridor from his private apartments, flitting through patches of late afternoon sunlight that poured down from high windows. He bobbed and twisted in his supensors with violent movements.

Past the private kitchen he stormed—past the library, past the small reception room and into the servants' antechamber where the evening relaxation had already set in.

The guard captain, Iakin Nefud, squatted on a divan across the chamber, the stupor of semuta dullness in his flat face, the eerie wailing of semuta music around him. His own court sat near to do his bidding.

"Nefud!" the Baron roared.

Men scrambled.

Nefud stood, his face composed by the narcotic but with an overlay of paleness that told of his fear. The semuta music had stopped.

"My Lord Baron," Nefud said. Only the drug kept the trembling out of his voice.

The Baron scanned the faces around him, seeing the looks of frantic quiet in them. He returned his attention to Nefud, and spoke in a silken tone:

"How long have you been my guard captain, Nefud?"

Nefud swallowed. "Since Arrakis, my Lord. Almost two years."

"And have you always anticipated dangers to my person?"

"Such has been my only desire, my Lord."

"Then where is Feyd-Rautha?" the Baron roared.

Nefud recoiled. "M'Lord?"

"You do not consider Feyd-Rautha a danger to my person?" Again, the voice was silken.

Nefud wet his lips with his tongue. Some of the semuta dullness left his eyes. "Feyd-Rautha's in the slave quarters, my Lord."

"With the women again, eh?" The Baron trembled with the effort of supressing anger.

"Sire, it could be he's—"

"Silence!"

The Baron advanced another step into the antechamber, noting how the men moved back, clearing a subtle space around Nefud, dissociating themselves from the object of wrath.

"Did I not command you to know precisely where the na-Baron was at all times?" the Baron asked. He moved a step closer. "Did I not say to you that you were to know *precisely* what the na-Baron was saying at all times—and to whom?" Another step. "Did I not say to you that you were to tell me whenever he went into the quarters of the slave women?"

Nefud swallowed. Perspiration stood out on his forehead.

The Baron held his voice flat, almost devoid of emphasis: "Did I not say these things to you?"

Nefud nodded.

"And did I not say to you that you were to check all slave boys sent to me and that you were to do this yourself . . . *personally?*"

Again, Nefud nodded.

"Did you, perchance, not see the blemish on the thigh of the one sent me this evening?" the Baron asked. "Is it possible you—"

"Uncle."

The Baron whirled, stared at Feyd-Rautha standing in the doorway. The presence of his nephew here, now—the look of hurry that the young man could not quite conceal—all revealed much. Feyd-Rautha had his own spy system focused on the Baron.

"There is a body in my chambers that I wish removed," the Baron said, and he kept his hand at the projectile weapon beneath his robes, thankful that his shield was the best.

Feyd-Rautha glanced at two guardsmen against the right wall, nodded. The two detached themselves, scurried out the door and down the hall toward the Baron's apartments.

*Those two, eh?* the Baron thought. *Ah, this young monster has much to learn yet about conspiracy!*

"I presume you left matters peaceful in the slave quarters, Feyd," the Baron said.

"I've been playing cheops with the slavemaster," Feyd-Rautha said, and he thought: *What has gone wrong? The boy we sent to my uncle has obviously been killed. But he was perfect for the job. Even Hawat couldn't have made a better choice. The boy was perfect!*

"Playing pyramid chess," the Baron said. "How nice. Did you win?"

"I . . . ah, yes, Uncle." And Feyd-Rautha strove to contain his disquiet.

The Baron snapped his fingers. "Nefud, you wish to be restored to my good graces?"

"Sire, what have I done?" Nefud quavered.

"That's unimportant now," the Baron said. "Feyd has beaten the slave-master at cheops. Did you hear that?"

"Yes . . . Sire."

"I wish you to take three men and go to the slavemaster," the Baron said. "Garrotte the slavemaster. Bring his body to me when you've finished that I may see it was done properly. We cannot have such inept chess players in our employ."

Feyd-Rautha went pale, took a step forward. "But, Uncle I—"

"Later, Feyd," the Baron said, and waved a hand. "Later."

The two guards who had gone to the Baron's quarters for the slaveboy's body staggered past the antechamber door with their load sagging between them, arms trailing. The Baron watched until they were out of sight.

Nefud stepped up beside the Baron. "You wish me to kill the slavemaster, now, my Lord?"

"Now," the Baron said. "And when you've finished, add those two who just passed to your list. I don't like the way they carried that body. One should do such things neatly. I'll wish to see their carcasses, too."

Nefud said, "My Lord, is it anything that I've—"

"Do as your master has ordered," Feyd-Rautha said. And he thought: *All I can hope for now is to save my own skin.*

*Good!* the Baron thought. *He yet knows how to cut his losses.* And the Baron smiled inwardly at himself, thinking: *The lad knows, too, what will please me and be most apt to stay my wrath from falling on him. He knows I must preserve him. Who else do I have who could take the reins I must leave someday? I have no other as capable. But he must learn! And I must preserve myself while he's learning.*

Nefud signaled men to assist him, led them out the door.

"Would you accompany me to my chambers, Feyd?" the Baron asked.

"I am yours to command," Feyd-Rautha said. He bowed, thinking: *I'm caught.*

"After you," the Baron said, and he gestured to the door.

Feyd-Rautha indicated his fear by only the barest hesitation. *Have I failed utterly?* he asked himself. *Will he slip a poisoned blade into my back . . . slowly, through the shield? Does he have an alternative successor?*

*Let him experience this moment of terror,* the Baron thought as he walked along behind his nephew. *He will succeed me, but at a time of my choosing. I'll not have him throwing away what I've built!*

Feyd-Rautha tried not to walk too swiftly. He felt the skin crawling on his back as though his body itself wondered when the blow would come. His muscles alternately tensed and relaxed.

"Have you heard the latest word from Arrakis?" the Baron asked.

"No, Uncle."

Feyd-Rautha forced himself not to look back. He turned down the hall out of the servants' wing.

"They've a new prophet or religious leader of some kind among the Fremen," the Baron said. "They call him Muad'Dib. Very funny, really. It means 'the Mouse.' I've told Rabban to let them have their religion. It'll keep them occupied."

"That's very interesting, Uncle," Feyd-Rautha said. He turned into the private corridor to his uncle's quarters, wondering: *Why does he talk about religion? Is it some subtle hint to me?*

"Yes, isn't it?" the Baron said.

They came into the Baron's apartments through the reception salon to the bedchamber. Subtle signs of a struggle greeted them there—a suspensor lamp displaced, a bedcushion on the floor, a soother-reel spilled open across a bedstand.

"It was a clever plan," the Baron said. He kept his body shield tuned to maximum, stopped, facing his nephew. "But not clever enough. Tell me, Feyd, why didn't you strike me down yourself? You've had opportunity enough."

Feyd-Rautha found a suspensor chair, accomplished a mental shrug as he sat down in it without being asked.

*I must be bold now,* he thought.

"You taught me that my own hands must remain clean," he said.

"Ah, yes," the Baron said. "When you face the Emperor, you must be able to say truthfully that you did not do the deed. The witch at the Emperor's elbow will hear your words and know their truth or falsehood. Yes. I warned you about that."

"Why haven't you ever bought a Bene Gesserit, Uncle?" Feyd-Rautha asked. "With a Truthsayer at your side—"

"You know my tastes!" the Baron snapped.

Feyd-Rautha studied his uncle, said: "Still, one would be valuable for—"

"I trust them not!" the Baron snarled. "And stop trying to change the subject!"

Feyd-Rautha spoke mildly: "As you wish, Uncle."

"I remember a time in the arena several years ago," the Baron said. "It seemed there that day a slave had been set to kill you. Is that truly how it was?"

"It's been so long ago, Uncle. After all, I—"

"No evasions, please," the Baron said, and the tightness of his voice exposed the rein on his anger.

Feyd-Rautha looked at his uncle, thinking: *He knows, else he wouldn't ask.*

"It was a sham, Uncle. I arranged it to discredit your slavemaster."

"Very clever," the Baron said. "Brave, too. That slave-gladiator almost took you, didn't he?"

"Yes."

"If you had finesse and subtlety to match such courage, you'd be truly formidable." The Baron shook his head from side to side. And as he had done many times since that terrible day on Arrakis, he found himself regretting the loss of Piter, the Mentat. There'd been a man of delicate, devilish subtlety. It hadn't saved him, though. Again, the Baron shook his head. Fate was sometimes inscrutable.

Feyd-Rautha glanced around the bedchamber, studying the signs of the struggle, wondering how his uncle had overcome the slave they'd prepared so carefully.

"How did I best him?" the Baron asked. "Ah-h-h, now, Feyd—let me keep some weapons to preserve in my old age. It's better we used this time to strike a bargain."

Feyd-Rautha stared at him. *A bargain! He means to keep me as his heir for certain, then. Else why bargain. One bargains with equals or near equals!*

"What bargain, Uncle?" And Feyd-Rautha felt proud that his voice remained calm and reasonable, betraying none of the elation that filled him.

The Baron, too, noted the control. He nodded. "You're good material, Feyd. I don't waste good material. You persist, however, in refusing to learn my true value to you. You are obstinate. You do not see why I should be preserved as someone of the utmost value to you. This . . . ." He gestured at the evidence of the struggle in the bedchamber. "This was foolishness. I do not reward foolishness."

*Get to the point, you old fool!* Feyd-Rautha thought.

"You think of me as an old fool," the Baron said. "I must dissuade you of that."

"You speak of a bargain."

"Ah, the impatience of youth," the Baron said. "Well, this is the substance of it, then: You will cease these foolish attempts on my life. And I, when you are ready for it, will step aside in your favor. I will retire to an advisory position, leaving you in the seat of power."

"Retire, Uncle?"

"You still think me the fool," the Baron said, "and this but confirms it, eh? You think I'm begging you! Step cautiously, Feyd. This old fool saw through the shielded needle you'd planted in that slave boy's thigh. Right where I'd put my hand on it, eh? The smallest pressure and—snick! A poison needle in the old fool's palm! Ah-h-h, Feyd . . . ."

The Baron shook his head, thinking: *It would've worked, too, if Hawat hadn't warned me. Well, let the lad believe I saw the plot on my own. In a way, I did. I was the one who saved Hawat from the wreckage of Arrakis. And this lad needs greater respect for my prowess.*

Feyd-Rautha remained silent, struggling with himself. *Is he being truthful? Does he really mean to retire? Why not? I'm sure to succeed him one day if I move carefully. He can't live forever. Perhaps it was foolish to try hurrying the process.*

"You speak of a bargain," Feyd-Rautha said. "What pledge do we give to bind it?"

"How can we trust each other, eh?" the Baron asked. "Well, Feyd, as for you: I'm setting Thufir Hawat to watch over you. I trust Hawat's Mentat capabilities in this. Do you understand me? And as for me, you'll have to take me on faith. But I can't live forever, can I, Feyd? And perhaps you should begin to suspect now that there're things I know which you *should* know."

"I give you my pledge and what do you give me?" Feyd-Rautha asked.

"I let you go on living," the Baron said.

Again, Feyd-Rautha studied his uncle. *He sets Hawat over me! What would he say if I told him Hawat planned the trick with the gladiator that cost him his slavemaster? He'd likely say I was lying in the attempt to discredit Hawat. No, the good Thufir is a Mentat and has anticipated this moment.*

"Well, what do you say?" the Baron asked.

"What can I say? I accept, of course."

And Feyd-Rautha thought: *Hawat! He plays both ends against the middle . . . is that it? Has he moved to my uncle's camp because I didn't counsel with him over the slave boy attempt?*

"You haven't said anything about my setting Hawat to watch you," the Baron said.

Feyd-Rautha betrayed anger by a flaring of nostrils. The name of Hawat had been a danger signal in the Harkonnen family for so many years . . . and now it had a new meaning: still dangerous.

"Hawat's a dangerous toy," Feyd-Rautha said.

"Toy! Don't be stupid. I know what I have in Hawat and how to control it. Hawat has deep emotions, Feyd. The man without emotions is the one to fear. But deep emotions . . . ah, now, those can be bent to your needs."

"Uncle, I don't understand you."

"Yes, that's plain enough."

Only a flicker of eyelids betrayed the passage of resentment through Feyd-Rautha.

"And you do not understand Hawat," the Baron said.

*Nor do you!* Feyd-Rautha thought.

"Who does Hawat blame for his present circumstances?" the Baron asked. "Me? Certainly. But he was an Atreides tool and bested me for years until the Imperium took a hand. That's how he sees it. His hate for me is a casual thing now. He believes he can best me any time. Believing this, he is bested. For I direct his attention where I want it—against the Imperium."

Tensions of a new understanding drew tight lines across Feyd-Rautha's forehead, thinned his mouth. "Against the Emperor?"

*Let my dear nephew try the taste of that,* the Baron thought. *Let him say to himself: "The Emperor Feyd-Rautha Harkonnen!" Let him ask himself how much that's worth. Surely it must be worth the life of one old uncle who could make that dream come to pass!*

Slowly, Feyd-Rautha wet his lips with his tongue. Could it be true what the old fool was saying? There was more here than there seemed to be.

"And what has Hawat to do with this?" Feyd-Rautha asked.

"He thinks he uses us to wreak his revenge upon the Emperor."

"And when that's accomplished?"

"He does not think beyond revenge. Hawat's a man who must serve others, and doesn't even know this about himself."

"I've learned much from Hawat," Feyd-Rautha agreed, and felt the truth of the words as he spoke them. "But the more I learn, the more I feel we should dispose of him . . . and soon."

"You don't like the idea of his watching you?"

"Hawat watches everybody."

"And he may put you on a throne. Hawat is subtle. He is dangerous, devious. But I'll not yet withhold the antidote from him. A sword is dangerous, too, Feyd. We have the scabbard for this one, though. The poison's in him. When we withdraw the antidote, death will sheathe him."

"In a way, it's like the arena," Feyd-Rautha said. "Feints within feints within feints. You watch to see which way the gladiator leans, which way he looks, how he holds his knife."

He nodded to himself, seeing that these words pleased his uncle, but thinking: *Yes! Like the arena! And the cutting edge is the mind!*

"Now you see how you need me," the Baron said. "I'm yet of use, Feyd."

*A sword to be wielded until he's too blunt for use,* Feyd-Rautha thought.

"Yes, Uncle," he said.

"And now," the Baron said, "we will go down to the slave quarters, we two. And I will watch while you, with your own hands, kill all the women in the pleasure wing."

"Uncle!"

"There will be other women, Feyd. But I have said that you do not make a mistake casually with me."

Feyd-Rautha's face darkened. "Uncle, you—"

"You will accept your punishment and learn something from it," the Baron said.

Feyd-Rautha met the gloating stare in his uncle's eyes. *And I must remember this night,* he thought. *And remembering it, I must remember other nights.*

"You will not refuse," the Baron said.

*What could you do if I refused, old man?* Feyd-Rautha asked himself. But he knew there might be some other punishment, perhaps a more subtle one, a more brutal lever to bend him.

"I know you, Feyd," the Baron said. "You will not refuse."

*All right,* Feyd-Rautha thought. *I need you now. I see that. The bargain's made. But I'll not always need you. And . . . someday . . .*

> *Deep in the human unconscious is a pervasive need for a logical universe that makes sense. But the real universe is always one step beyond logic.*
>
> **—from "The Sayings of Muad'Dib"**
> **by the Princess Irulan**

*I've sat across from many rulers of Great Houses, but never seen a more gross and dangerous pig than this one,* Thufir Hawat told himself.

"You may speak plainly with me, Hawat," the Baron rumbled. He leaned back in his suspensor chair, the eyes in their folds of fat boring into Hawat.

The old Mentat looked down at the table between him and the Baron Vladimir Harkonnen, noting the opulence of its grain. Even this was a factor to consider in assessing the Baron, as were the red walls of this private conference room and the faint sweet herb scent that hung on the air, masking a deeper musk.

"You didn't have me send that warning to Rabban as an idle whim," the Baron said.

Hawat's leathery old face remained impassive, betraying none of the loathing he felt. "I suspect many things, my Lord," he said.

"Yes. Well, I wish to know how Arrakis figures in your suspicions about Salusa Secundus. It is not enough that you say to me the Emperor is in a ferment about some association between Arrakis and his mysterious prison planet. Now, I rushed the warning out to Rabban only because the courier had to leave on that Heighliner. You said there could be no delay. Well and good. But now I will have an explanation."

*He babbles too much,* Hawat thought. *He's not like Leto who could tell me a thing with the lift of an eyebrow or the wave of a hand. Nor like the old Duke who could express an entire sentence in the way he accented a single word. This is a clod! Destroying him will be a service to mankind.*

"You will not leave here until I've had a full and complete explanation," the Baron said.

"You speak too casually of Salusa Secundus," Hawat said.

"It's a penal colony," the Baron said. "The worst riff-raff in the galaxy are sent to Salusa Secundus. What else do we need to know?"

"That conditions on the prison planet are more oppressive than anywhere else," Hawat said. "You hear that the mortality rate among new prisoners is higher than sixty per cent. You hear all this and do not ask questions?"

"The Emperor doesn't permit the Great Houses to inspect his prison," the Baron growled. "But he hasn't seen into my dungeons, either."

"And curiosity about Salusa Secundus is . . . ah . . . ." Hawat put a bony finger to his lips. ". . . . discouraged."

"So he's not proud of some of the things he must do there!"

Hawat allowed the faintest of smiles to touch his dark lips. His eyes glinted in the glowtube light as he stared at the Baron. "And you've never wondered where the Emperor gets his Sardaukar?"

The Baron pursed his fat lips. This gave his features the look of a pouting baby, and his voice carried a tone of petulance as he said: "Why . . . he recruits . . . that is to say, there are the levies and he enlists from—"

"Faaa!" Hawat snapped. "The stories you hear about the exploits of the Sardaukar, they're not rumors, are they? Those are first-hand accounts from the limited number of survivors who've fought against the Sardaukar, eh?"

"The Sardaukar are excellent fighting men, no doubt of it," the Baron said. "But I think my own legions—"

"A pack of holiday excursionists by comparison!" Hawat snarled. "You think I don't know why the Emperor turned against House Atreides?"

"This is not a realm open to your speculation," the Baron warned.

*Is it possible that even he doesn't know what motivated the Emperor in this?* Hawat asked himself.

"Any area is open to my speculation if it does what you've hired me to do," Hawat said. "I am a Mentat. You do not withhold information or computation lines from a Mentat."

For a long minute, the Baron stared at him, then: "Say what you must say, Mentat."

"The Padishah Emperor turned against House Atreides because the Duke's Warmasters Gurney Halleck and Duncan Idaho had trained a fighting force—a *small* fighting force—to within a hair as good as the Sardaukar. Some of them were even better. And the Duke was in a position to enlarge his force, to make it every bit as strong as the Emperor's."

The Baron weighed this disclosure, then: "What has Arrakis to do with this?"

"It provides a pool of recruits already conditioned to the bitterest survival training."

The Baron shook his head. "You cannot mean the Fremen?"

"I mean the Fremen."

"Hah! Then why warn Rabban? There cannot be more than a handful of Fremen left after the Sardaukar pogrom and Rabban's oppression."

Hawat continued to stare at him silently.

"Not more than a handful!" the Baron repeated. "Rabban killed six thousand of them last year alone!"

Still, Hawat stared at him.

"And the year before it was nine thousand," the Baron said. "And before they left, the Sardaukar must've accounted for at least twenty thousand."

"What are Rabban's troop losses for the past two years?" Hawat asked.

The Baron rubbed his jowls. "Well, he has been recruiting rather heavily, to be sure. His agents make rather extravagant promises and—"

"Shall we say thirty thousand in round numbers?" Hawat asked.

"That would seem a little high," the Baron said.

"Quite the contrary," Hawat said. "I can read between the lines of Rabban's reports as well as you can. And you certainly must've understood my reports from our agents."

"Arrakis is a fierce planet," the Baron said. "Storm losses can—"

"We both know the figure for storm accretion," Hawat said.

"What if he has lost thirty thousand?" the Baron demanded, and blood darkened his face.

"By your own count," Hawat said, "he killed fifteen thousand over two years while losing twice that number. You say the Sardaukar accounted for another twenty thousand, possibly a few more. And I've seen the transportation manifests for their return from Arrakis. If they killed twenty thousand, they lost almost five for one. Why won't you face these figures, Baron, and understand what they mean?"

The Baron spoke in a coldly measured cadence: "This is your job, Mentat. What do they mean?"

"I gave you Duncan Idaho's head count on the sietch he visited," Hawat said. "It all fits. If they had just two hundred and fifty such sietch communities, their population would be about five million. My best estimate is that they had at least twice that many communities. You scatter your population on such a planet."

"Ten million?"

The Baron's jowls quivered with amazement.

"At least."

The Baron pursed his fat lips. The beady eyes stared without wavering at Hawat. *Is this true Mentat computation?* he wondered. *How could this be and no one suspect?*

"We haven't even cut heavily into their birth-rate–growth figure," Hawat said. "We've just weeded out some of their less successful specimens, leaving the strong to grow stronger—just like on Salusa Secundus."

"Salusa Secundus!" the Baron barked. "What has this to do with the Emperor's prison planet?"

"A man who survives Salusa Secundus starts out being tougher than most others," Hawat said. "When you add the very best military training—"

"Nonsense! By your argument, *I* could recruit from among the Fremen after the way they've been oppressed by my nephew."

Hawat spoke in a mild voice: "Don't you oppress any of your troops?"

"Well . . . I . . . but—"

"Oppression is a relative thing," Hawat said. "Your fighting men are much better off than those around them, heh? They see unpleasant alternative to being soldiers of the Baron, heh?"

The Baron fell silent, eyes unfocused. The possibilities—had Rabban unwittingly given House Harkonnen its ultimate weapon?

Presently he said: "How could you be sure of the loyalty of such recruits?"

"I would take them in small groups, not larger than platoon strength," Hawat said. "I'd remove them from their oppressive situation and isolate them with a training cadre of people who understood their background, preferably people who had preceded them from the same oppressive situation. Then I'd fill them with the mystique that their planet had really been a secret training ground to produce just such superior beings as themselves. And all the while, I'd show them what such superior beings could earn: rich living, beautiful women, fine mansions . . . whatever they desired."

The Baron began to nod. "The way the Sardaukar live at home."

"The recruits come to believe in time that such a place as Salusa Secundus is justified because it produced them—the elite. The commonest Sardaukar trooper lives a life, in many respects, as exalted as that of any member of a Great House."

"Such an idea!" the Baron whispered.

"You begin to share my suspicions," Hawat said.

"Where did such a thing start?" the Baron asked.

"Ah, yes: Where did House Corrino originate? Were there people on Salusa Secundus before the Emperor sent his first contingents of prisoners there? Even the Duke Leto, a cousin on the distaff side, never knew for sure. Such questions were not encouraged."

The Baron's eyes glazed with thought. "Yes, a very carefully kept secret. They'd use every device of—"

"Besides, what's there to conceal?" Hawat asked. "That the Padishah Emperor has a prison planet? Everyone knows this. That he has—"

"Count Fenring!" the Baron blurted.

Hawat broke off, studied the Baron with a puzzled frown. "What of Count Fenring?"

"At my nephew's birthday several years ago," the Baron said. "This Imperial popinjay, Count Fenring, came as official observer and to . . . ah, conclude a business arrangement between the Emperor and myself."

"So?"

"I . . . ah, during one of our conversations, I believe I said something about making a prison planet of Arrakis. Fenring—"

"What did you say exactly?" Hawat asked.

"Exactly? That was quite a while ago and—"

"My Lord Baron, if you wish to make the best use of my services, you must give me adequate information. Wasn't this conversation recorded?"

The Baron's face darkened with anger. "You're as bad as Piter! I don't like these—"

"Piter is no longer with you, my Lord," Hawat said. "As to that, whatever *did* happen to Piter?"

"He became too familiar, too demanding of me," the Baron said.

"You assure me you don't waste a useful man," Hawat said. "Will you waste me by threats and quibbling? We were discussing what you said to Count Fenring."

Slowly, the Baron composed his features. *When the time comes,* he thought, *I'll remember his manner with me. Yes. I will remember.*

"One moment," the Baron said, and he thought back to the meeting in his great hall. It helped to visualize the cone of silence in which they had stood. "I said something like this," the Baron said. " 'The Emperor knows a certain amount of killing has always been an arm of business.' I was referring to our work force losses. Then I said something about considering another solution to the Arrakeen problem and I said the Emperor's prison planet inspired me to emulate him."

"Witch blood!" Hawat snapped. "What did Fenring say?"

"That's when he began questioning me about you."

Hawat sat back, closed his eyes in thought. "So that's why they started looking into Arrakis," he said. "Well, the thing's done." He opened his eyes. "They must have spies all over Arrakis by now. Two years!"

"But certainly my innocent suggestion that—"

"Nothing is innocent in an Emperor's eyes! What were your instructions to Rabban?"

"Merely that he should teach Arrakis to fear us."

Hawat shook his head. "You now have two alternatives, Baron. You can kill off the natives, wipe them out entirely, or—"

"Waste an entire work force?"

"Would you prefer to have the Emperor and those Great Houses he can still swing behind him come in here and perform a currettement, scrape out Giedi Prime like a hollow gourd?"

The Baron studied his Mentat, then: "He wouldn't dare!"

"Wouldn't he?"

The Baron's lips quivered. "What is your alternative?"

"Abandon your dear nephew, Rabban."

"Aband . . . ." The Baron broke off, stared at Hawat.

"Send him no more troops, no aid of any kind. Don't answer his messages other than to say you've heard of the terrible way he's handled things on Arrakis and you intend to take corrective measures as soon as you're able. I'll arrange to have some of your messages intercepted by Imperial spies."

"But what of the spice, the revenues, the—"

"Demand your baronial profits, but be careful how you make your demands. Require fixed sums of Rabban. We can—"

The Baron turned his hands palms up. "But how can I be certain that my weasel nephew isn't—"

"We still have our spies on Arrakis. Tell Rabban he either meets the spice quotas you set him or he'll be replaced."

"I know my nephew," the Baron said. "This would only make him oppress the population even more."

"Of course he will!" Hawat snapped. "You don't want that stopped now! You merely want your own hands clean. Let Rabban make your Salusa Secundus for you. There's no need even to send him any prisoners. He has all the population required. If Rabban is driving his people to meet your spice quotas, then the Emperor need suspect no other motive. That's reason enough for putting the planet on the rack. And you, Baron, will not show by word or action that there's any other reason for this."

The Baron could not keep the sly tone of admiration out of his voice. "Ah, Hawat, you are a devious one. Now, how do we move into Arrakis and make use of what Rabban prepares?"

"That's the simplest thing of all, Baron. If you set each year's quota a bit higher than the one before, matters will soon reach a head there. Production will drop off. You can remove Rabban and take over yourself . . . to correct the mess."

"It fits," the Baron said. "But I can feel myself tiring of all this. I'm preparing another to take over Arrakis for me."

Hawat studied the fat face across from him. Slowly the old soldier-spy began to nod his head. "Feyd-Rautha," he said. "So that's the reason for the oppression now. You're very devious yourself, Baron. Perhaps we can incorporate these two schemes. Yes. Your Feyd-Rautha can go to Arrakis as their savior. He can win the populace. Yes."

The Baron smiled. And behind his smile, he asked himself: *Now, how does this fit in with Hawat's personal scheming?*

And, Hawat, seeing that he was dismissed, arose and left the red-walled room. As he walked, he could not put down the disturbing unknowns that cropped into every computation about Arrakis. This new religious leader that Gurney Halleck hinted at from his hiding place among the smugglers, this Muad'Dib.

*Perhaps I should not have told the Baron to let this religion flourish where it will, even among the folk of pan and graben,* he told himself. *But it's well known that repression makes a religion flourish.*

And he thought about Halleck's reports on Fremen battle tactics. The tactics smacked of Halleck himself . . . and Idaho . . . and even of Hawat.

*Did Idaho survive?* he asked himself.

But this was a futile question. He did not yet ask himself if it was possible that Paul had survived. He knew the Baron was convinced that all Atreides were dead. The Bene Gesserit witch had been his weapon, the Baron admitted. And that could only mean an end to all—even to the woman's own son.

*What a poisonous hate she must've had for the Atreides,* he thought. *Something like the hate I hold for this Baron. Will my blow be as final and complete as hers?*

> There is in all things a pattern that is part of our universe. It has symmetry, elegance, and grace—those qualities you find always in that which the true artist captures. You can find it in the turning of the seasons, in the way sand trails along a ridge, in the branch clusters of the creosote bush or the pattern of its leaves. We try to copy these patterns in our lives and our society, seeking the rhythms, the dances, the forms that comfort. Yet, it is possible to see peril in the finding of ultimate perfection. It is clear that the ultimate pattern contains its own fixity. In such perfection, all things move toward death.

> **—from "The Collected Sayings of Muad'Dib"**
> **by the Princess Irulan**

Paul-Muad'Dib remembered that there had been a meal heavy with spice essence. He clung to this memory because it was an anchor point and he could tell himself from this vantage that his immediate experience must be a dream.

*I am a theater of processes,* he told himself. *I am a prey to the imperfect vision, to the race consciousness and its terrible purpose.*

Yet, he could not escape the fear that he had somehow overrun himself, lost his position in time, so that past and future and present mingled without distinction. It was a kind of visual fatigue and it came, he knew, from the constant necessity of holding the prescient future as a kind of memory that was in itself a thing intrinsically of the past.

*Chani prepared the meal for me,* he told himself.

Yet Chani was deep in the south—in the cold country where the sun was hot—secreted in one of the new sietch strongholds, safe with their son, Leto II.

Or, was that a thing yet to happen?

No, he reassured himself, for Alia-the-Strange-One, his sister, had gone there with his mother and with Chani—a twenty-thumper trip into the south, riding a Reverend Mother's palanquin fixed to the back of a wild maker.

He shied away from thought of riding the giant worms, asking himself: *Or is Alia yet to be born?*

*I was on razzia,* Paul recalled. *We went raiding to recover the water of our dead in Arrakeen. And I found the remains of my father in the funeral pyre. I enshrined the skull of my father in a Fremen rock overlooking Harg Pass.*

Or was that a thing yet to be?

*My wounds are real,* Paul told himself. *My scars are real. The shrine of my father's skull is real.*

Still in the dreamlike state, Paul remembered that Harah, Jamis' wife, had intruded on him once to say there'd been a fight in the sietch corridor. That had been the interim sietch before the women and children had been sent into the deep south. Harah had stood there in the entrance to the inner chamber, the black wings of her hair tied back by water rings on a chain. She had held aside the chamber's hangings and told him that Chani had just killed someone.

*This happened,* Paul told himself. *This was real, not born out of its time and subject to change.*

Paul remembered he had rushed out to find Chani standing beneath the yellow globes of the corridor, clad in a brilliant blue wraparound robe with hood thrown back, a flush of exertion on her elfin features. She had been sheathing her crysknife. A huddled group had been hurrying away down the corridor with a burden.

And Paul remembered telling himself: You always know when they're carrying a body.

Chani's water rings, worn openly in sietch on a cord around her neck, tinkled as she turned toward him.

"Chani, what is this?" he asked.

"I dispatched one who came to challenge you in single combat, Usul."

"*You* killed him?"

"Yes. But perhaps I should've left him for Harah."

(And Paul recalled how the faces of the people around them had showed appreciation for these words. Even Harah had laughed.)

"But he came to challenge *me!*"

"You trained me yourself in the weirding way, Usul."

"Certainly! But you shouldn't—"

"I was born in the desert, Usul. I know how to use a crysknife."

He suppressed his anger, tried to talk reasonably. "This may all be true, Chani, but—"

"I am no longer a child hunting scorpions in the sietch by the light of a handglobe, Usul. I do not play games."

Paul glared at her, caught by the odd ferocity beneath her casual attitude.

"He was not worthy, Usul," Chani said. "I'd not disturb your meditations with the likes of him." She moved closer, looking at him out of the corners of her eyes, dropping her voice so that only he might hear. "And, beloved, when it's learned that a challenger may face *me* and be brought to shameful death by Muad'Dib's woman, there'll be fewer challengers."

*Yes,* Paul told himself, *that had certainly happened. It was true-past. And the number of challengers testing the new blade of Muad'Dib did drop dramatically.*

Somewhere, in a world not-of-the-dream, there was a hint of motion, the cry of a nightbird.

*I dream,* Paul reassured himself. *It's the spice meal.*

Still, there was about him a feeling of abandonment. He wondered if it might be possible that his ruh-spirit had slipped over somehow into the world where the Fremen believed he had his true existence—into the alam al-mithal, the world of similitudes, that metaphysical realm where all physical limitations were removed. And he knew fear at the thought of such a place, because removal of all limitations meant removal of all points of reference. In the landscape of a myth he could not orient himself and say: "I am I because I am here."

His mother had said once: "The people are divided, some of them, in how they think of you."

*I must be waking from the dream,* Paul told himself. For this had happened— these words from his mother, the Lady Jessica who was now a Reverend Mother of the Fremen, these words had passed through reality.

Jessica was fearful of the religious relationship between himself and the Fremen, Paul knew. She didn't like the fact that people of both sietch and graben referred to Muad'Dib as *Him.* And she went questioning among the tribes, sending out her sayyadina spies, collecting their answers and brooding on them.

She had quoted a Bene Gesserit proverb to him: "When religion and politics travel in the same cart, the riders believe nothing can stand in their way. Their movement becomes headlong—faster and faster and faster. They put aside all thoughts of obstacles and forget that a precipice does not show itself to the man in a blind rush until it's too late."

Paul recalled that he had sat there in his mother's quarters, in the inner chamber shrouded by dark hangings with their surfaces covered by woven patterns out of Fremen mythology. He had sat there, hearing her out, noting the way she was always observing—even when her eyes were lowered. Her oval face had new lines in it at the corners of the mouth, but the hair was still like polished bronze. The wide-set green eyes, though, hid beneath their over-casting of spice-imbued blue.

"The Fremen have a simple, practical religion," he said.

"Nothing about religion is simple," she warned.

But Paul, seeing the clouded future that still hung over them, found himself swayed by anger. He could only say: "Religion unifies our forces. It's our mystique."

"You deliberately cultivate this air, this bravura," she charged. "You never cease indoctrinating."

"Thus you yourself taught me," he said.

But she had been full of contentions and arguments that day. It had been the day of the circumcision ceremony for little Leto. Paul had understood some of the reasons for her upset. She had never accepted his liaison—the "marriage of youth"—with Chani. But Chani had produced an Atreides son, and Jessica had found herself unable to reject the child and the mother.

Jessica had stirred finally under his stare, said: "You think me an unnatural mother."

"Of course not."

"I see the way you watch me when I'm with your sister. You don't understand about your sister."

"I know why Alia is different," he said. "She was unborn, part of you, when you changed the Water of Life. She—"

"You know nothing of it!"

And Paul, suddenly unable to express the knowledge gained out of its time, said only: "I don't think you unnatural."

She saw his distress, said: "There is a thing, Son."

"Yes?"

"I do love your Chani. I accept her."

This was real, Paul told himself. This wasn't the imperfect vision to be changed by the twistings out of time's own birth.

The reassurance gave him a new hold on his world. Bits of solid reality began to dip through the dream state into his awareness. He knew suddenly that he was in a hiereg, a desert camp. Chani had planted their stilltent on flour-sand for its softness. That could only mean Chani was near by—Chani, his soul, Chani his sihaya, sweet as the desert spring, Chani up from the palmaries of the deep south.

Now, he remembered her singing a sand chanty to him in the time for sleep.

> "O my soul,
> Have no taste for Paradise this night,
> And I swear by Shai-hulud
> You will go there,
> Obedient to my love."

And she had sung the walking song lovers shared on the sand, its rhythm like the drag of the dunes against the feet:

> "Tell me of thine eyes
> And I will tell thee of thy heart.
> Tell me of thy feet
> And I will tell thee of thy hands.
> Tell me of thy sleeping
> And I will tell thee of thy waking.

Tell me of thy desires
And I will tell thee of thy need."

He had heard someone strumming a baliset in another tent. And he'd thought then of Gurney Halleck. Reminded by the familiar instrument, he had thought of Gurney whose face he had seen in a smuggler band, but who had not seen him, could not see him or know of him lest that inadvertently lead the Harkonnens to the son of the Duke they had killed.

But the style of the player in the night, the distinctiveness of the fingers on the baliset's strings, brought the real musician back to Paul's memory. It had been Chatt the Leaper, captain of the Fedaykin, leader of the death commandos who guarded Muad'Dib.

*We are in the desert*, Paul remembered. *We are in the central erg beyond the Harkonnen patrols. I am here to walk the sand, to lure a maker and mount him by my own cunning that I may be a Fremen entire.*

He felt now the maula pistol at his belt, the crysknife. He felt the silence surrounding him.

It was that special pre-morning silence when the nightbirds had gone and the day creatures had not yet signaled their alertness to their enemy, the sun.

"You must ride the sand in the light of day that Shai-hulud shall see and know you have no fear," Stilgar had said. "Thus we turn our time around and set ourselves to sleep this night."

Quietly, Paul sat up, feeling the looseness of a slacked stillsuit around his body, the shadowed stilltent beyond. So softly he moved, yet Chani heard him.

She spoke from the tent's gloom, another shadow there: "It's not yet full light, beloved."

"Sihaya," he said, speaking with half a laugh in his voice.

"You call me your desert spring," she said, "but this day I'm thy goad. I am the sayyadina who watches that the rites be obeyed."

He began tightening his stillsuit. "You told me once the words of the Kitab al-Ibar," he said. "You told me: 'Woman is thy field; go then to thy field and till it.'"

"I am the mother of thy firstborn," she agreed.

He saw her in the grayness matching him movement for movement, securing her stillsuit for the open desert. "You should get all the rest you can," she said.

He recognized her love for him speaking then and chided her gently: "The Sayyadina of the Watch does not caution or warn the candidate."

She slid across to his side, touched his cheek with her palm. "Today, I am both the watcher and the woman."

"You should've left this duty to another," he said.

"Waiting is bad enough at best," she said. "I'd sooner be at thy side."

He kissed her palm before securing the faceflap of his suit, then turned and cracked the seal of the tent. The air that came in to them held the chill not-quite-dryness that would precipitate trace dew in the dawn. With it came the smell of a pre-spice mass, the mass they had detected off to the northeast, and that told them there would be a maker nearby.

Paul crawled through the sphincter opening, stood on the sand and stretched the sleep from his muscles. A faint green-pearl luminescence etched the eastern horizon. The tents of his troop were small false dunes around him in the gloom. He saw movement off to the left—the guard, and knew they had seen him.

They knew the peril he faced this day. Each Fremen had faced it. They gave him this last few moments of isolation now that he might prepare himself.

*It must be done today,* he told himself.

He thought of the power he wielded in the face of the pogrom—the old men who sent their sons to him to be trained in the weirding way of battle, the old men who listened to him now in council and followed his plans, the men who returned to pay him that highest Fremen compliment: "Your plan worked, Muad'Dib."

Yet the meanest and smallest of the Fremen warriors could do a thing that he had never done. And Paul knew his leadership suffered from the omnipresent knowledge of this difference between them.

He had not ridden the maker.

Oh, he'd gone up with the others for training trips and raids, but he had not made his own voyage. Until he did, his world was bounded by the abilities of others. No true Fremen could permit this. Until he did this thing himself, even the great southlands—the area some twenty thumpers beyond the erg—were denied him unless he ordered a palanquin and rode like a Reverend Mother or one of the sick and wounded.

Memory returned to him of his wrestling with his inner awareness during the night. He saw a strange parallel here—if he mastered the maker, his rule was strengthened; if he mastered the inward eye, this carried its own measure of command. But beyond them both lay the clouded area, the Great Unrest where all the universe seemed embroiled.

The differences in the ways he comprehended the universe haunted him—accuracy matched with inaccuracy. He saw it *in situ.* Yet, when it was born, when it came into the pressures of reality, the *now* had its own life and grew with its own subtle differences. Terrible purpose remained. Race consciousness remained. And over all loomed the jihad, bloody and wild.

Chani joined him outside the tent, hugging her elbows, looking up at him from the corners of her eyes the way she did when she studied his mood.

"Tell me again about the waters of thy birthworld, Usul," she said.

He saw that she was trying to distract him, ease his mind of tensions before the deadly test. It was growing lighter, and he noted that some of his Fedaykin were already striking their tents.

"I'd rather you told me about the sietch and about our son," he said. "Does Leto yet hold my mother in his palm?"

"It's Alia he holds as well," she said. "And he grows rapidly. He'll be a big man."

"What's it like in the south?" he asked.

"When you ride the maker you'll see for yourself," she said.

"But I wish to see it first through your eyes."

"It's powerfully lonely," she said.

He touched the nezhoni scarf at her forehead where it protruded from her stillsuit cap. "Why will you not talk about the sietch?"

"I have talked about it. The sietch is a lonely place without our men. It's a place of work. We labor in the factories and the potting rooms. There are weapons to be made, poles to plant that we may forecast the weather, spice to collect for the bribes. There are dunes to be planted to make them grow and to anchor them. There are fabrics and rugs to make, fuel cells to charge. There are children to train that the tribe's strength may never be lost."

"Is nothing then pleasant in the sietch?" he asked.

"The children are pleasant. We observe the rites. We have sufficient food. Sometimes one of us may come north to be with her man. Life must go on."

"My sister, Alia—is she accepted by the people?"

Chani turned toward him in the growing dawnlight. Her eyes bored into him. "It's a thing to be discussed another time, beloved."

"Let us discuss it now."

"You should conserve your energies for the test," she said.

He saw that he had touched something sensitive, hearing the withdrawal in her voice. "The unknown brings its own worries," he said.

Presently she nodded, said, "There is yet . . . misunderstanding because of Alia's strangeness. The women are fearful because a child little more than an infant talks . . . of things that only an adult should know. They do not understand the . . . change in the womb that made Alia . . . different."

"There is trouble?" he asked. And he thought: *I've seen visions of trouble over Alia.*

Chani looked toward the growing line of the sunrise. "Some of the women banded to appeal to the Reverend Mother. They demanded she exorcise the demon in her daughter. They quoted the scripture: 'Suffer not a witch to live among us.'"

"And what did my mother say to them?"

"She recited the law and sent the women away abashed. She said: 'If Alia incites trouble, it is the fault of authority for not foreseeing and preventing the trouble.' And she tried to explain how the change had worked on Alia in the womb. But the women were angry because they had been embarrassed. They went away muttering."

*There will be trouble because of Alia,* he thought.

A crystal blowing of sand touched the exposed portions of his face, bringing the scent of the pre-spice mass. "El Sayal, the rain of sand that brings the morning," he said.

He looked out across the gray light of the desert landscape, the landscape beyond pity, the sand that was form absorbed in itself. Dry lightning streaked a dark corner to the south—sign that a storm had built up its static charge there. The roll of thunder boomed long after.

"The voice that beautifies the land," Chani said.

More of his men were stirring out of their tents. Guards were coming in from the rims. Everything around him moved smoothly in the ancient routine that required no orders.

"Give as few orders as possible," his father had told him . . . once . . . long ago. "Once you've given orders on a subject, you must always give orders on that subject."

The Fremen knew this rule instinctively.

The troop's watermaster began the morning chanty, adding to it now the call for the rite to initiate a sandrider.

"The world is a carcass," the man chanted, his voice wailing across the dunes. "Who can turn away the Angel of Death? What Shai-hulud has decreed must be."

Paul listened, recognizing that these were the words that also began the death chant of his Fedaykin, the words the death commandos recited as they hurled themselves into battle.

*Will there be a rock shrine here this day to mark the passing of another soul?* Paul asked himself. *Will Fremen stop here in the future, each to add another stone and think on Muad'Dib who died in this place?*

He knew this was among the alternatives today, a *fact* along lines of the future radiating from this position in time-space. The imperfect vision plagued him. The more he resisted his terrible purpose and fought against the coming of the jihad, the greater the turmoil that wove through his prescience. His entire future was becoming like a river hurtling toward a chasm—the violent nexus beyond which all was fog and clouds.

"Stilgar approaches," Chani said. "I must stand apart now, beloved. Now, I must be Sayyadina and observe the rite that it may be reported truly in the Chronicles." She looked up at him and, for a moment, her reserve slipped, then she had herself under control. "When this is past, I shall prepare thy breakfast with my own hands," she said. She turned away.

Stilgar moved toward him across the flour sand, stirring up little dust puddles. The dark niches of his eyes remained steady on Paul with their untamed stare. The glimpse of black beard above the stillsuit mask, the lines of craggy cheeks, could have been wind-etched from the native rock for all their movement.

The man carried Paul's banner on its staff—the green and black banner with a water tube in the staff—that already was a legend in the land. Half pridefully, Paul thought: *I cannot do the simplest thing without its becoming a legend. They will mark how I parted from Chani, how I greet Stilgar—every move I make this day. Live or die, it is a legend. I must not die. Then it will be only legend and nothing to stop the jihad.*

Stilgar planted the staff in the sand beside Paul, dropped his hands to his sides. The blue-within-blue eyes remained level and intent. And Paul thought how his own eyes already were assuming this mask of color from the spice.

"They denied us the Hajj," Stilgar said with ritual solemnity.

As Chani had taught him, Paul responded: "Who can deny a Fremen the right to walk or ride where he wills?"

"I am a Naib," Stilgar said, "never to be taken alive. I am a leg of the death tripod that will destroy our foes."

Silence settled over them.

Paul glanced at the other Fremen scattered over the sand beyond Stilgar, the way they stood without moving for this moment of personal prayer. And he thought of how the Fremen were a people whose living consisted of killing, an entire people who had lived with rage and grief all of their days, never once considering what might take the place of either—except for a dream with which Liet-Kynes had infused them before his death.

"Where is the Lord who led us through the land of desert and of pits?" Stilgar asked.

"He is ever with us," the Fremen chanted.

Stilgar squared his shoulders, stepped closer to Paul and lowered his voice. "Now, remember what I told you. Do it simply and directly—nothing fancy. Among our people, we ride the maker at the age of twelve. You are more than six years beyond that age and not born to this life. You don't have to impress anyone with your courage. We know you are brave. All you must do is call the maker and ride him."

"I will remember," Paul said.

"See that you do. I'll not have you shame my teaching."

Stilgar pulled a plastic rod about a meter long from beneath his robe. The thing was pointed at one end, had a spring-wound clapper at the other end. "I prepared this thumper myself. It's a good one. Take it."

Paul felt the warm smoothness of the plastic as he accepted the thumper.

"Shishakli has your hooks," Stilgar said. "He'll hand them to you as you step out onto that dune over there." He pointed to his right. "Call a big maker, Usul. Show us the way."

Paul marked the tone of Stilgar's voice—half ritual and half that of a worried friend.

In that instant, the sun seemed to bound above the horizon. The sky took on the silvered gray-blue that warned this would be a day of extreme heat and dryness even for Arrakis.

"It is the time of the scalding day," Stilgar said, and now his voice was entirely ritual. "Go, Usul, and ride the maker, travel the sand as a leader of men."

Paul saluted his banner, noting how the green and black flag hung limply now that the dawn wind had died. He turned toward the dune Stilgar had indicated—a dirty tan slope with an S-track crest. Already, most of the troop was moving out in the opposite direction, climbing the other dune that had sheltered their camp.

One robed figure remained in Paul's path: Shishakli, a squad leader of the Fedaykin, only his slope-lidded eyes visible between stillsuit cap and mask.

Shishakli presented two thin, whiplike shafts as Paul approached. The shafts were about a meter and a half long with glistening plasteel hooks at one end, roughened at the other end for a firm grip.

Paul accepted them both in his left hand as required by the ritual.

"They are my own hooks," Shishakli said in a husky voice. "They never have failed."

Paul nodded, maintaining the necessary silence, moved past the man and up the dune slope. At the crest, he glanced back, saw the troop scattering like a flight of insects, their robes fluttering. He stood alone now on the sandy ridge with only the horizon in front of him, the flat and unmoving horizon. This was a good dune Stilgar had chosen, higher than its companions for the viewpoint vantage.

Stooping, Paul planted the thumper deep into the windward face where the sand was compacted and would give maximum transmission to the drumming. Then he hesitated, reviewing the lessons, reviewing the life-and-death necessities that faced him.

When he threw the latch, the thumper would begin its summons. Across the sand, a giant worm—a maker—would hear and come to the drumming. With the whiplike hook-staffs, Paul knew, he could mount the maker's high curving back. For as long as a forward edge of a worm's ring segment was held open by a hook, open to admit abrasive sand into the more sensitive interior, the creature would not retreat beneath the desert. It would, in fact, roll its gigantic body to bring the opened segment as far away from the desert surface as possible.

*I am a sandrider,* Paul told himself.

He glanced down at the hooks in his left hand, thinking that he had only to shift those hooks down the curve of a maker's immense side to make the creature roll and turn, guiding it where he willed. He had seen it done. He had been helped up the side of a worm for a short ride in training. The captive worm could be ridden until it lay exhausted and quiescent upon the desert surface and a new maker must be summoned.

Once he was past this test, Paul knew, he was qualified to make the twenty-thumper journey into the southland—to rest and restore himself—into the south where the women and the families had been hidden from the pogrom among the new palmaries and sietch warrens.

He lifted his head and looked to the south, reminding himself that the maker summoned wild from the erg was an unknown quantity, and the one who summoned it was equally unknown to the test.

"You must gauge the approaching maker carefully," Stilgar had explained. "You must stand close enough that you can mount it as it passes, yet not so close that it engulfs you."

With abrupt decision, Paul released the thumper's latch. The clapper began revolving and the summons drummed through the sand, a measured "lump . . . lump . . . lump . . . ."

He straightened, scanning the horizon, remembering Stilgar's words: "Judge the line of approach carefully. Remember, a worm seldom makes an unseen approach to a thumper. Listen all the same. You may often hear it before you see it."

And Chani's words of caution, whispered at night when her fear for him overcame her, filled his mind: "When you take your stand along the maker's path, you must remain utterly still. You must think like a patch of sand. Hide beneath your cloak and become a little dune in your very essence."

Slowly, he scanned the horizon, listening, watching for the signs he had been taught.

It came from the southeast, a distant hissing, a sand-whisper. Presently he saw the faraway outline of the creature's track against the dawnlight and realized he had never before seen a maker this large, never heard of one this size. It appeared to be more than half a league long, and the rise of the sandwave at its cresting head was like the approach of a mountain.

*This is nothing I have seen by vision or in life,* Paul cautioned himself. He hurried across the path of the thing to take his stand, caught up entirely by the rushing needs of this moment.

> *"Control the coinage and the courts—let the rabble have the rest."* Thus the *Padishah Emperor advises you. And he tells you: "If you want profits, you must rule." There is truth in these words, but I ask myself: "Who are the rabble and who are the ruled?"*

**—Muad'Dib's Secret Message to the Landsraad**
**from "Arrakis Awakening" by the Princess Irulan**

A thought came unbidden to Jessica's mind: *Paul will be undergoing his sand-rider test at any moment now. They try to conceal this fact from me, but it's obvious.*

*And Chani has gone on some mysterious errand.*

Jessica sat in her resting chamber, catching a moment of quiet between the night's classes. It was a pleasant chamber, but not as large as the one she had enjoyed in Sietch Tabr before their flight from the pogrom. Still, this place had thick rugs on the floor, soft cushions, a low coffee table near at hand, multicolored hangings on the walls, and soft yellow glowglobes overhead. The room was permeated with the distinctive acrid furry odor of a Fremen sietch that she had come to associate with a sense of security.

Yet she knew she would never overcome a feeling of being in an alien place. It was the harshness that the rugs and hangings attempted to conceal.

A faint tinkling-drumming-slapping penetrated to the resting chamber. Jessica knew it for a birth celebration, probably Subiay's. Her time was near. And Jessica knew she'd see the baby soon enough—a blue-eyed cherub brought to the Reverend Mother for blessing. She knew also that her daughter, Alia, would be at the celebration and would report on it.

It was not yet time for the nightly prayer of parting. They wouldn't have started a birth celebration near the time of ceremony that mourned the slave raids of Poritrin, Bela Tegeuse, Rossak, and Harmonthep.

Jessica sighed. She knew she was trying to keep her thoughts off her son and the dangers he faced—the pit traps with their poisoned barbs, the Harkonnen raids (although these were growing fewer as the Fremen took their toll of aircraft and raiders with the new weapons Paul had given them), and the natural dangers of the desert—makers and thirst and dust chasms.

She thought of calling for coffee and with the thought came that ever present awareness of paradox in the Fremen way of life: how well they lived in these sietch caverns compared to the graben pyons; yet, how much more they endured in the open hajr of the desert than anything the Harkonnen bondsmen endured.

A dark hand inserted itself through the hangings beside her, deposited a cup upon the table and withdrew. From the cup arose the aroma of spiced coffee.

*An offering from the birth celebration,* Jessica thought.

She took the coffee and sipped it, smiling at herself. *In what other society of our universe, she asked herself, could a person of my station accept an anonymous drink and quaff that drink without fear? I could alter any poison now before it did me harm, of course, but the donor doesn't realize this.*

She drained the cup, feeling the energy and lift of its contents—hot and delicious.

And she wondered what other society would have such a natural regard for her privacy and comfort that the giver would intrude only enought to deposit the gift and not inflict her with the donor? Respect and love had sent the gift—with only a slight tinge of fear.

Another element of the incident forced itself into her awareness: she had thought of coffee and it had appeared. There was nothing of telepathy here, she knew. It was the tau, the oneness of the sietch community, a compensation from the subtle poison of the spice diet they shared. The great mass of the people could never hope to attain the enlightenment the spice seed brought to her; they had not been trained and prepared for it. Their minds rejected what they could not understand or encompass. Still they felt and reacted sometimes like a single organism.

And the thought of coincidence never entered their minds.

*Has Paul passed his test on the sand?* Jessica asked herself. *He's capable, but accident can strike down even the most capable.*

The waiting.

*It's the dreariness,* she thought. *You can wait just so long. Then the dreariness of the waiting overcomes you.*

There was all manner of waiting in their lives.

*More than two years we've been here,* she thought, *and twice that number at least to go before we can even hope to think of trying to wrest Arrakis from the Harkonnen governor, the Mudir Nahya, the Beast Rabban.*

"Reverend Mother?"

The voice from outside the hangings at her door was that of Harah, the other woman in Paul's menage.

"Yes, Harah."

The hangings parted and Harah seemed to glide through them. She wore sietch sandals, a red-yellow wraparound that exposed her arms almost to the shoulders. Her black hair was parted in the middle and swept back like the wings of an insect, flat and oily against her head. The jutting, predatory features were drawn into an intense frown.

Behind Harah came Alia, a girl-child of about two years.

Seeing her daughter, Jessica was caught as she frequently was by Alia's resemblance to Paul at that age—the same wide-eyed solemnity to her questing look, the dark hair and firmness of mouth. But there were subtle differences, too, and it was in these that most adults found Alia disquieting. The child—little more than a toddler—carried herself with a calmness and awareness beyond her years. Adults were shocked to find her laughing at a subtle play of words between the sexes. Or they'd catch themselves listening to her half-lisping voice, still blurred as it was by an unformed soft palate, and discover in her words sly remarks that could only be based on experiences no two-year-old had ever encountered.

Harah sank to a cushion with an exasperated sigh, frowned at the child.

"Alia." Jessica motioned to her daughter.

The child crossed to a cushion beside her mother, sank to it and clasped her mother's hand. The contact of flesh restored that mutual awareness they had shared since before Alia's birth. It wasn't a matter of shared thoughts—although there were bursts of that if they touched while Jessica was changing the spice poison for a ceremony. It was something larger, an immediate awareness of another living spark, a sharp and poignant thing, a nerve-*sympatico* that made them emotionally one.

In the formal manner that befitted a member of her son's household, Jessica said: "Subakh ul kuhar, Harah. This night finds you well?"

With the same traditional formality, she said: "Subakh un nar. I am well." The words were almost toneless. Again, she sighed.

Jessica sensed amusement from Alia.

"My brother's ghanima is annoyed with me," Alia said in her half-lisp.

Jessica marked the term Alia used to refer to Harah—ghanima. In the subtleties of the Fremen tongue, the word meant "something acquired in battle" and with the added overtone that the something no longer was used for its original purpose. An ornament, a spearhead used as a curtain weight.

Harah scowled at the child. "Don't try to insult me, child. I know my place."

"What have you done this time, Alia?" Jessica asked.

Harah answered: "Not only has she refused to play with the other children today, but she intruded where . . . ."

"I hid behind the hangings and watched Subiay's child being born," Alia said. "It's a boy. He cried and cried. What a set of lungs! When he'd cried long enough—"

"She came out and touched him," Harah said, "and he stopped crying. Everyone knows a Fremen baby must get his crying done at birth if he's in sietch because he can never cry again lest he betray us on hajr."

"He'd cried enough," Alia said. "I just wanted to feel his spark, his life. That's all. And when he felt me he didn't want to cry anymore."

"It's just made more talk among the people," Harah said.

"Subiay's boy is healthy?" Jessica asked. She saw that something was troubling Harah deeply and wondered at it.

"Healthy as any mother could ask," Harah said. "They know Alia didn't hurt him. They didn't so much mind her touching him. He settled down right away and was happy. It was . . . ." Harah shrugged.

"It's the strangeness of my daughter, is that it?" Jessica asked. "It's the way she speaks of things beyond her years and of things no child her age could know—things of the past."

"How could she know what a child looked like on Bela Tegeuse?" Harah demanded.

"But he does!" Alia said. "Subiay's boy looks just like the son of Mitha born before the parting."

"Alia!" Jessica said. "I warned you."

"But, Mother, I saw it and it was true and . . . ."

Jessica shook her head, seeing the signs of disturbance in Harah's face. *What have I borne?* Jessica asked herself. *A daughter who knew at birth everything that I knew . . . and more: everything revealed to her out of the corridors of the past by the Reverend Mothers within me.*

"It's not just the things she says," Harah said. "It's the exercises, too: the way she sits and stares at a rock, moving only one muscle beside her nose, or a muscle on the back of a finger, or—"

"Those are the Bene Gesserit training," Jessica said. "You know that, Harah. Would you deny my daughter her inheritance?"

"Reverend Mother, you know these things don't matter to me," Harah said. "It's the people and the way they mutter. I feel danger in it. They say your daughter's a demon, that other children refuse to play with her, that she's—"

"She has so little in common with the other children," Jessica said. "She's no demon. It's just the—"

"Of course she's not!"

Jessica found herself surprised at the vehemence in Harah's tone, glanced down at Alia. The child appeared lost in thought, radiating a sense of . . . waiting. Jessica returned her attention to Harah.

"I respect the fact that you're a member of my son's household," Jessica said. (Alia stirred against her hand.) "You may speak openly with me of whatever's troubling you."

"I will not be a member of your son's household much longer," Harah said. "I've waited this long for the sake of my sons, the special training *they* receive as the children of Usul. It's little enough I could give them since it's known I don't share your son's bed."

Again Alia stirred beside her, half-sleeping, warm.

"You'd have made a good companion for my son, though," Jessica said. And she added to herself because such thoughts were ever with her: *Companion . . . not a wife.* Jessica's thoughts went then straight to the center, to the pang that came from the common talk in the sietch that her son's companionship with Chani had become the permanent thing, the marriage.

*I love Chani,* Jessica thought, but she reminded herself that love might have to step aside for royal necessity. Royal marriages had other reasons than love.

"You think I don't know what you plan for your son?" Harah asked.

"What do you mean?" Jessica demanded.

"You plan to unite the tribes under *Him,*" Harah said.

"Is that bad?"

"I see danger for him . . . and Alia is part of that danger."

Alia nestled closer to her mother, eyes opened now and studying Harah.

"I've watched you two together," Harah said, "the way you touch. And Alia is like my own flesh because she's sister to one who is like my brother. I've watched over her and guarded her from the time she was a mere baby, from the time of the razzia when we fled here. I've seen many things about her."

Jessica nodded, feeling disquiet begin to grow in Alia beside her.

"You know what I mean," Harah said. "The way she knew from the first what we were saying to her. When has there been another baby who knew the water discipline so young? What other baby's first words to her nurse were: 'I love you, Harah'?"

Harah stared at Alia. "Why do you think I accept her insults? I know there's no malice in them."

Alia looked up at her mother.

"Yes, I have reasoning powers, Reverend Mother," Harah said. "I could have been of the sayyadina. I have seen what I have seen."

"Harah . . . ." Jessica shrugged. "I don't know what to say." And she felt surprised at herself, because this literally was true.

Alia straightened, squared her shoulders. Jessica felt the sense of waiting ended, an emotion compounded of decision and sadness.

"We made a mistake," Alia said. "Now we need Harah."

"It was the ceremony of the seed," Harah said, "when you changed the Water of Life, Reverend Mother, when Alia was yet unborn within you."

*Need Harah?* Jessica asked herself.

"Who else can talk among the people and make them begin to understand me?" Alia asked.

"What would you have her do?" Jessica asked.

"She already knows what to do," Alia said.

"I will tell them the truth," Harah said. Her face seemed suddenly old and sad with its olive skin drawn into frown wrinkles, a witchery in the sharp features. "I will tell them that Alia only pretends to be a little girl, that she has never been a little girl."

Alia shook her head. Tears ran down her cheeks, and Jessica felt the wave of sadness from her daughter as though the emotion were her own.

"I know I'm a freak," Alia whispered. The adult summation coming from the child mouth was like a bitter confirmation.

"You're not a freak!" Harah snapped. "Who dared say you're a freak?"

Again, Jessica marveled at the fierce note of protectiveness in Harah's voice. Jessica saw then that Alia had judged correctly—they did need Harah. The tribe would understand Harah—both her words and her emotions—for it was obvious she loved Alia as though this were her own child.

"Who said it?" Harah repeated.

"Nobody."

Alia used a corner of Jessica's aba to wipe the tears from her face. She smoothed the robe where she had dampened and crumpled it.

"Then don't you say it," Harah ordered.

"Yes, Harah."

"Now," Harah said, "you may tell me what it was like so that I may tell the others. Tell me what it is that happened to you."

Alia swallowed, looked up at her mother.

Jessica nodded.

"One day I woke up," Alia said. "It was like waking from sleep except that I could not remember going to sleep. I was in a warm, dark place. And I was frightened."

Listening to the half-lisping voice of her daughter, Jessica remembered that day in the big cavern.

"When I was frightened," Alia said, "I tried to escape, but there was no way to escape. Then I saw a spark,. . . but it wasn't exactly like seeing it. The spark was just there with me and I felt the spark's emotions . . . soothing me, comforting me, telling me that way that everything would be all right. That was my mother."

Harah rubbed at her eyes, smiled reassuringly at Alia. Yet there was a look of wildness in the eyes of the Fremen woman, an intensity as though they, too, were trying to hear Alia's words.

And Jessica thought: *What do we really know of how such a one thinks. . . . out of her unique experiences and training and ancestry?*

"Just when I felt safe and reassured," Alia said, "there was another spark with us . . . and everything was happening at once. The other spark was the old Reverend Mother. She was . . . trading lives with my mother . . . everything . . . and I was there with them, seeing it all . . . everything. And it was over, and I was them and all the others and myself . . . only it took me a long time to find myself again. There were so many others."

"It was a cruel thing," Jessica said. "No being should wake into consciousness thus. The wonder of it is you could accept all that happened to you."

"I couldn't do anything else!" Alia said. "I didn't know how to reject or hide my consciousness . . . or shut it off . . . everything just happened . . . everything . . . ."

"We didn't know," Harah murmured. "When we gave your mother the Water to change, we didn't know you existed within her."

"Don't be sad about it, Harah," Alia said. "I shouldn't feel sorry for myself. After all, there's cause for happiness here: I'm a Reverend Mother. The tribe has two Rev . . . ."

She broke off, tipping her head to listen.

Harah rocked back on her heels against the sitting cushion, stared at Alia, bringing her attention then up to Jessica's face.

"Didn't you suspect?" Jessica asked.

"Sh-h-h-h," Alia said.

A distant rhythmic chanting came to them then through the hangings that separated them from the sietch corridors. It grew louder, carrying distinct sounds now: "Ya! Ya! Yawm! Ya! Ya! Yawm! Mu zein, Wallah! Ya! Ya! Yawm! Mu zein, Wallah!"

The chanters passed the outer entrance, and their voices boomed through to the inner apartments. Slowly the sound receded.

When the sound had dimmed sufficiently, Jessica began the ritual, the sadness in her voice: "It was Ramadhan and April on Bela Tegeuse."

"My family sat in their pool courtyard," Harah said, "in air breathed by the moisture that arose from the spray of a fountain. There was a tree of portyguls, round and deep in color, near at hand. There was a basket with mish mish and baklawa and mugs of liban—all manner of good things to eat. In our gardens and in our flocks, there was peace . . . peace in all the land."

"Life was full with happiness until the raiders came," Alia said.

"Blood ran cold at the screams of friends," Jessica said. And she felt the memories rushing through her out of all those other pasts she shared.

"La, la, la, the women cried," said Harah.

"The raiders came through the mushtamal, rushing at us with their knives dripping red from the lives of our men," Jessica said.

Silence came over the three of them as it was in all the apartments of the sietch, the silence while they remembered and kept their grief thus fresh.

Presently, Harah uttered the ritual ending to the ceremony, giving the words a harshness that Jessica had never before heard in them.

"We will never forgive and we will never forget," Harah said.

In the thoughtful quiet that followed her words, they heard a muttering of people, the swish of many robes. Jessica sensed someone standing beyond the hangings that shielded her chamber.

"Reverend Mother?"

A woman's voice, and Jessica recognized it: the voice of Tharthar, one of Stilgar's wives.

"What is it, Tharthar?"

"There is trouble, Reverend Mother."

Jessica felt a constriction at her heart, an abrupt fear for Paul. "Paul. . ." she gasped.

Tharthar spread the hangings, stepped into the chamber. Jessica glimpsed a press of people in the outer room before the hangings fell. She looked up at Tharthar—a small, dark woman in a red-figured robe of black, the total blue of her eyes trained fixedly on Jessica, the nostrils of her tiny nose dilated to reveal the plug scars.

"What is it?" Jessica demanded.

"There is word from the sand," Tharthar said. "Usul meets the maker for his test . . . it is today. The young men say he cannot fail, he will be a sand-rider by nightfall. The young men are banding for a razzia. They will raid in the north and meet Usul there. They say they will raise the cry then. They say they will force him to call out Stilgar and assume command of the tribes."

*Gathering water, planting the dunes, changing their world slowly but surely—these are no longer enough,* Jessica thought. *The little raids, the certain raids—these are no longer enough now that Paul and I have trained them. They feel their power. They want to fight.*

Tharthar shifted from one foot to the other, cleared her throat.

*We know the need for cautious waiting,* Jessica thought, *but there's the core of our frustration. We know also the harm that waiting extended too long can do to us. We lose our sense of purpose if the waiting's prolonged.*

"The young men say if Usul does not call out Stilgar, then he must be afraid," Tharthar said.

She lowered her gaze.

"So that's the way of it," Jessica muttered. And she thought: *Well, I saw it coming. As did Stilgar.*

Again, Tharthar cleared her throat. "Even my brother, Shoab, says it," she said. "They will leave Usul no choice."

*Then it has come,* Jessica thought. *And Paul will have to handle it himself. The Reverend Mother dare not become involved in the succession.*

Alia freed her hand from her mother's, said: "I will go with Tharthar and listen to the young men. Perhaps there is a way."

Jessica met Tharthar's gaze, but spoke to Alia: "Go, then. And report to me as soon as you can."

"We do not want this thing to happen, Reverend Mother," Tharthar said.

"We do not want it," Jessica agreed. "The tribe needs *all* its strength." She glanced at Harah. "Will you go with them?"

Harah answered the unspoken part of the question: "Tharthar will allow no harm to befall Alia. She knows we will soon be wives together, she and I, to share the same man. We have talked, Tharthar and I." Harah looked up at Tharthar, back to Jessica. "We have an understanding."

Tharthar held out a hand for Alia, said: "We must hurry. The young men are leaving."

They pressed through the hangings, the child's hand in the small woman's hand, but the child seemed to be leading.

"If Paul-Muad'Dib slays Stilgar, this will not serve the tribe," Harah said. "Always before, it has been the way of succession, but times have changed."

"Times have changed for you, as well," Jessica said.

"You cannot think I doubt the outcome of such a battle," Harah said. "Usul could not but win."

"That was my meaning," Jessica said.

"And you think my personal feelings enter into my judgment," Harah said. She shook her head, her water rings tinkling at her neck. "How wrong you are. Perhaps you think, as well, that I regret not being the chosen of Usul, that I am jealous of Chani?"

"You make your own choice as you are able," Jessica said.

"I pity Chani," Harah said.

Jessica stiffened. "What do you mean?"

"I know what you think of Chani," Harah said. "You think she is not the wife for your son."

Jessica settled back, relaxed on her cushions. She shrugged. "Perhaps."

"You could be right," Harah said. "If you are, you may find a surprising ally—Chani herself. She wants whatever is best for *Him.*"

Jessica swallowed past a sudden tightening in her throat. "Chani's very dear to me," she said. "She could be no—"

"Your rugs are very dirty in here," Harah said. She swept her gaze around the floor, avoiding Jessica's eyes. "So many people tramping through here all the time. You really should have them cleaned more often."

> *You cannot avoid the interplay of politics within an orthodox religion. This power struggle permeates the training, educating and disciplining of the orthodox community. Because of this pressure, the leaders of such a community inevitably must face that ultimate internal question: to succumb to complete opportunism as the price of maintaining their rule, or risk sacrificing themselves for the sake of the orthodox ethic.*

**—from "Muad'Dib: The Religious Issues"
by the Princess Irulan**

Paul waited on the sand outside the gigantic maker's line of approach. *I must not wait like a smuggler—impatient and jittering,* he reminded himself. *I must be part of the desert.*

The thing was only minutes away now, filling the morning with the friction-hissing of its passage. Its great teeth within the cavern-circle of its mouth spread like some enormous flower. The spice odor from it dominated the air.

Paul's stillsuit rode easily on his body and he was only distantly aware of his nose plugs, the breathing mask. Stilgar's teaching, the painstaking hours on the sand, overshadowed all else.

"How far outside the maker's radius must you stand in pea sand?" Stilgar had asked him.

And he had answered correctly: "Half a meter for every meter of the maker's diameter."

"Why?"

"To avoid the vortex of its passage and still have time to run in and mount it."

"You've ridden the little ones bred for the seed and the Water of Life," Stilgar had said. "But what you'll summon for your test is a wild maker, an old man of the desert. You must have proper respect for such a one."

Now the thumper's deep drumming blended with the hiss of the approaching worm. Paul breathed deeply, smelling mineral bitterness even through his filters. The wild maker, the old man of the desert, loomed almost on him. Its cresting front segments threw a sandwave that would sweep across his knees.

*Come up, you lovely monster,* he thought. *Up. You hear me calling. Come up. Come up.*

The wave lifted his feet. Surface dust swept across him. He steadied himself, his world dominated by the passage of that sand-clouded curving wall, that segmented cliff, the ring lines sharply defined in it.

Paul lifted his hooks, sighted along them, leaned in. He felt them bite and pull. He leaped upward, planting his feet against that wall, leaning out against the clinging barbs. This was the true instant of the testing: if he had planted the hooks correctly at the leading edge of a ring segment, opening the segment, the worm would not roll down and crush him.

The worm slowed. It glided across the thumper, silencing it. Slowly, it began to roll—up, up—bringing those irritant barbs as high as possible, away from the sand that threatened the soft inner lapping of its ring segment.

Paul found himself riding upright atop the worm. He felt exultant, like an emperor surveying his world. He suppressed a sudden urge to cavort there, to turn the worm, to show off his mastery of this creature.

Suddenly he understood why Stilgar had warned him once about brash young men who danced and played with these monsters, doing handstands on their backs, removing both hooks and replanting them before the worm could spill them.

Leaving one hook in place, Paul released the other and planted it lower down the side. When the second hook was firm and tested, he brought down the first one, thus worked his way down the side. The maker rolled, and as it rolled, it turned, coming around the sweep of flour sand where the others waited.

Paul saw them come up, using their hooks to climb, but avoiding the sensitive ring edges until they were on top. They rode at last in a triple line behind him, steadied against their hooks.

Stilgar moved up through the ranks, checked the positioning of Paul's hooks, glanced up at Paul's smiling face.

"You did it, eh?" Stilgar asked, raising his voice above the hiss of their passage. "That's what you think? You did it?" He straightened. "Now I tell you that was a very sloppy job. We have twelve-year-olds who do better. There was drumsand to your left where you waited. You could not retreat there if the worm turned that way."

The smile slipped from Paul's face. "I saw the drumsand."

"Then why did you not signal for one of us to take up position secondary to you? It was a thing you could do even in the test."

Paul swallowed, faced into the wind of their passage.

"You think it bad of me to say this now," Stilgar said. "It is my duty. I think of your worth to the troop. If you had stumbled into that drumsand, the maker would've turned toward you."

In spite of a surge of anger, Paul knew that Stilgar spoke the truth. It took a long minute and the full effort of the training he had received from his mother for Paul to recapture a feeling of calm. "I apologize," he said. "It will not happen again."

"In a tight position, always leave yourself a secondary, someone to take the maker if you cannot," Stilgar said. "Remember that we work together. That way, we're certain. We work together, eh?"

He slapped Paul's shoulder.

"We work together," Paul agreed.

"Now," Stilgar said, and his voice was harsh, "show me you know how to handle a maker. Which side are we on?"

Paul glanced down at the scaled ring surface on which they stood, noted the character and size of the scales, the way they grew larger off to his right, smaller to his left. Every worm, he knew, moved characteristically with one side up more frequently. As it grew older, the characteristic up-side became an almost constant thing. Bottom scales grew larger, heavier, smoother. Top scales could be told by size alone on a big worm.

Shifting his hooks, Paul moved to the left. He motioned flankers down to open segments along the side and keep the worm on a straight course as it rolled. When he had it turned, he motioned two steersmen out of the line and into positions ahead.

"Ach, haiiiii-yoh!" he shouted in the traditional call. The left-side steersman opened a ring segment there.

In a majestic circle, the maker turned to protect its opened segment. Full around it came and when it was headed back to the south, Paul shouted: "Geyrat!"

The steersman released his hook. The maker lined out in a straight course.

Stilgar said: "Very good, Paul-Muad'Dib. With plenty of practice, you may yet become a sandrider."

Paul frowned, thinking: *Was I not first up?*

From behind him there came sudden laughter. The troops began chanting, flinging his name against the sky.

"Muad'Dib! Muad'Dib! Muad'Dib! Muad'Dib!"

And far to the rear along the worm's surface, Paul heard the beat of the goaders pounding the tail segments. The worm began picking up speed. Their robes flapped in the wind. The abrasive sound of their passage increased.

Paul looked back through the troop, found Chani's face among them. He looked at her as he spoke to Stilgar. "Then I am a sandrider, Stil?"

"Hal yawm! You are a sandrider this day."

"Then I may choose our destination?"

"That's the way of it."

"And I am a Fremen born this day here in the Habbanya erg. I have had no life before this day. I was as a child until this day."

"Not quite a child," Stilgar said. He fastened a corner of his hood where the wind was whipping it.

"But there was a cork sealing off my world, and that cork has been pulled."

"There is no cork."

"I would go south, Stilgar—twenty thumpers. I would see this land we make, this land that I've only seen through the eyes of others."

*And I would see my son and my family,* he thought. *I need time now to consider the future that is a past within my mind. The turmoil comes and if I'm not where I can unravel it, the thing will run wild.*

Stilgar looked at him with a steady, measuring gaze. Paul kept his attention on Chani, seeing the interest quicken in her face, noting also the excitement his words had kindled in the troop.

"The men are eager to raid with you in the Harkonnen sinks," Stilgar said. "The sinks are only a thumper away."

"The Fedaykin have raided with me," Paul said. "They'll raid with me again until no Harkonnen breathes Arrakeen air."

Stilgar studied him as they rode, and Paul realized the man was seeing this moment through the memory of how he had risen to command of the Tabr sietch and to leadership of the Council of Leaders now that Liet-Kynes was dead.

*He has heard the reports of unrest among the young Fremen,* Paul thought.

"Do you wish a gathering of the leaders?" Stilgar asked.

Eyes blazed among the young men of the troop. They swayed as they rode, and they watched. And Paul saw the look of unrest in Chani's glance, the way she looked from Stilgar, who was her uncle, to Paul-Muad'Dib, who was her mate.

"You cannot guess what I want," Paul said.

And he thought: *I cannot back down. I must hold control over these people.*

"You are mudir of the sandride this day," Stilgar said. Cold formality rang in his voice. "How do you use this power?"

*We need time to relax, time for cool reflection,* Paul thought.

"We shall go south," Paul said.

"Even if I say we shall return back to the north when this day is over?"

"We shall go south," Paul repeated.

A sense of inevitable dignity enfolded Stilgar as he pulled his robe tightly around him. "There will be a Gathering," he said. "I will send the messages."

*He thinks I will call him out,* Paul thought. *And he knows he cannot stand against me.*

Paul faced south, feeling the wind against his exposed cheeks, thinking of the necessities that went into his decisions.

*They do not know how it is,* he thought.

But he knew he could not let any consideration deflect him. He had to remain on the central line of the time storm he could see in the future. There would come an instant when it could be unraveled, but only if he were where he could cut the central knot of it.

*I will not call him out if it can be helped,* he thought. *If there's another way to prevent the jihad . . . .*

"We'll camp for the evening meal and prayer at Cave of Birds beneath Habbanya Ridge," Stilgar said. He steadied himself with one hook against the swaying of the maker, gestured ahead at a low rock barrier rising out of the desert.

Paul studied the cliff, the great streaks of rock crossing it like waves. No green, no blossom softened that rigid horizon. Beyond it stretched the way to the southern desert—a course of at least ten days and nights, as fast as they could goad the makers.

Twenty thumpers.

The way led far beyond the Harkonnen patrols. He knew how it would be. The dreams had shown him. One day, as they went, there'd be a faint change of color on the far horizon—such a slight change that he might feel he was imagining it out of his hopes—and there would be the new sietch.

"Does my decision suit Muad'Dib?" Stilgar asked. Only the faintest touch of sarcasm tinged his voice, but Fremen ears around them, alert to every tone in a bird's cry or a cielago's piping message, heard the sarcasm and watched Paul to see what he would do.

"Stilgar heard me swear my loyalty to him when we consecrated the Fedaykin," Paul said. "My death commandos know I spoke with honor. Does Stilgar doubt it?"

Real pain exposed itself in Paul's voice. Stilgar heard it and lowered his gaze.

"Usul, the companion of my sietch, him I would never doubt," Stilgar said. "But you are Paul-Muad'Dib, the Atreides Duke, and you are the Lisan al-Gaib, the Voice from the Outer World. These men I don't even know."

Paul turned away to watch the Habbanya Ridge climb out of the desert. The maker beneath them still felt strong and willing. It could carry them almost twice the distance of any other in Fremen experience. He knew it. There was nothing outside the stories told to children that could match this old man of the desert. It was the stuff of a new legend, Paul realized.

A hand gripped his shoulder.

Paul looked at it, followed the arm to the face beyond it—the dark eyes of Stilgar exposed between filter mask and stillsuit hood.

"The one who led Tabr sietch before me," Stilgar said, "he was my friend. We shared dangers. He owed me his life many a time . . . and I owed him mine."

"I am your friend, Stilgar," Paul said.

"No man doubts it," Stilgar said. He removed his hand, shrugged. "It's the way."

Paul saw that Stilgar was too immersed in the Fremen way to consider the possibility of any other. Here a leader took the reins from the dead hands of his predecessor, or slew among the strongest of his tribe if a leader died in the desert. Stilgar had risen to be a naib in that way.

"We should leave this maker in deep sand," Paul said.

"Yes," Stilgar agreed. "We could walk to the cave from here."

"We've ridden him far enough that he'll bury himself and sulk for a day or so," Paul said.

"You're the mudir of the sandride," Stilgar said. "Say when we . . ." He broke off, stared at the eastern sky.

Paul whirled. The spice-blue overcast on his eyes made the sky appear dark, a richly filtered azure against which a distant rhythmic flashing stood out in sharp contrast.

Ornithopter!

"One small 'thopter," Stilgar said.

"Could be a scout," Paul said. "Do you think they've seen us."

"At this distance we're just a worm on the surface," Stilgar said. He motioned with his left hand. "Off. Scatter on the sand."

The troop began working down the worm's sides, dropping off, blending with the sand beneath their cloaks. Paul marked where Chani dropped. Presently, only he and Stilgar remained.

"First up, last off," Paul said.

Stilgar nodded, dropped down the side on his hooks, leaped onto the sand. Paul waited until the maker was safely clear of the scatter area, then released his hooks. This was the tricky moment with a worm not completely exhausted.

Freed of its goads and hooks, the big worm began burrowing into the sand. Paul ran lightly back along its broad surface, judged his moment carefully and leaped off. He landed running, lunged against the slipface of a dune the way he had been taught, and hid himself beneath the cascade of sand over his robe.

Now, the waiting . . . .

Paul turned gently, exposed a crack of sky beneath a crease in his robe. He imagined the others back along their path doing the same.

He heard the beat of the 'thopter's wings before he saw it. There was a whisper of jetpods and it came over his patch of desert, turned in a broad arc toward the ridge.

An unmarked 'thopter, Paul noted.

It flew out of sight beyond Habbanya Ridge.

A bird cry sounded over the desert. Another.

Paul shook himelf free of sand, climbed to the dune top. Other figures stood out in a line trailing away from the ridge. He recognized Chani and Stilgar among them.

Stilgar signaled toward the ridge.

They gathered and began the sandwalk, gliding over the surface in a broken rhythm that would disturb no maker. Stilgar paced himself beside Paul along the windpacked crest of a dune.

"It was a smuggler craft," Stilgar said.

"So it seemed," Paul said. "But this is deep into the desert for smugglers."

"They've their difficulties with patrols, too," Stilgar said.

"If they come this deep, they may go deeper," Paul said.

"True."

"It wouldn't be well for them to see what they could see if they ventured too deep into the south. Smugglers sell information, too."

"They were hunting spice, don't you think?" Stilgar asked.

"There will be a wing and a crawler waiting somewhere for that one," Paul said. "We've spice. Let's bait a patch of sand and catch us some smugglers. They should be taught that this is our land and our men need practice with the new weapons."

"Now, Usul speaks," Stilgar said. "Usul thinks Fremen."

*But Usul must give way to decisions that match a terrible purpose,* Paul thought. And the storm was gathering.

> *When law and duty are one, united by religion, you never become fully conscious, fully aware of yourself. You are always a little less than an individual.*

> **—from "Muad'Dib: The Ninety-nine Wonders of The
> Universe" by the Princess Irulan**

The smuggler's spice factory with its parent carrier and ring of drone ornithopters came over a lifting of dunes like a swarm of insects following its queen. Ahead of the swarm lay one of the low rock ridges that lifted from the desert floor like small imitations of the Shield Wall. The dry beaches of the ridge were swept clean by a recent storm.

In the con-bubble of the factory, Gurney Halleck leaned forward, adjusted the oil lenses of his binoculars and examined the landscape. Beyond the ridge, he could see a dark patch that might be a spiceblow, and he gave the signal to a hovering ornithopter that sent it to investigate.

The 'thopter waggled its wings to indicate it had the signal. It broke away from the swarm, sped down toward the darkened sand, circled the area with its detectors dangling close to the surface.

Almost immediately, it went through the wing-tucked dip and circle that told the waiting factory that spice had been found.

Gurney sheathed his binoculars, knowing the others had seen the signal. He liked this spot. The ridge offered some shielding and protection. This was deep in the desert, an unlikely place for an ambush . . . still . . . . Gurney signaled for a crew to hover over the ridge, to scan it, sent reserves to take up station in pattern around the area—not too high because then they could be seen from afar by Harkonnen detectors.

He doubted, though, that Harkonnen patrols would be this far south. This was still Fremen country.

Gurney checked his weapons, damning the fate that made shields useless out here. Anything that summoned a worm had to be avoided at all costs. He rubbed the inkvine scar along his jaw, studying the scene, decided it would be safest to lead a ground party through the ridge. Inspection on foot was still the most certain. You couldn't be too careful when Fremen and Harkonnen were at each other's throats.

It was Fremen that worried him here. They didn't mind trading for all the spice you could afford, but they were devils on the warpath if you stepped foot where they forbade you to go. And they were so devilishly cunning of late.

It annoyed Gurney, the cunning and adroitness in battle of these natives. They displayed a sophistication in warfare as good as anything he had ever encountered, and he had been trained by the best fighters in the universe then seasoned in battles where only the superior few survived.

Again Gurney scanned the landscape, wondering why he felt uneasy. Perhaps it was the worm they had seen . . . but that was on the other side of the ridge.

A head popped up into the con-bubble beside Gurney—the factory commander, a one-eyed old pirate with full beard, the blue eyes and milky teeth of a space diet.

"Looks like a rich patch, sir," the factory commander said. "Shall I take 'er in?"

"Come down at the edge of that ridge," Gurney ordered. "Let me disembark with my men. You can tractor out to the spice from there. We'll have a look at that rock."

"Aye."

"In case of trouble," Gurney said, "save the factory. We'll lift in the 'thopters."

The factory commander saluted. "Aye, sir." He popped back down through the hatch.

Again Gurney scanned the horizon. He had to respect the possibility that there were Fremen here and he was trespassing. Fremen worried him, their toughness and unpredictability. Many things about this business worried him, but the rewards were great. The fact that he couldn't send spotters high overhead worried him, too. The necessity of radio silence added to his uneasiness.

The factory crawler turned, began to descend. Gently it glided down to the dry beach at the foot of the ridge. Treads touched sand.

Gurney opened the bubble dome, released his safety straps. The instant the factory stopped, he was out, slamming the bubble closed behind him, scrambling out over the tread guards to swing down to the sand beyond the emergency netting. The five men of his personal guard were out with him, emerging from the nose hatch. Others released the factory's carrier wing. It detached, lifted away to fly in a parking circle low overhead.

Immediately the big factory crawler lurched off, swinging away from the ridge toward the dark patch of spice out on the sand.

A 'thopter swooped down near by, skidded to a stop. Another followed and another. They disgorged Gurney's platoon and lifted to hoverflight.

Gurney tested his muscles in his stillsuit, stretching. He left the filter mask off his face, losing moisture for the sake of a greater need—the carrying power of his voice if he had to shout commands. He began climbing up into the rocks, checking the terrain—pebbles and pea sand underfoot, the smell of spice.

*Good site for an emergency base,* he thought. *Might be sensible to bury a few supplies here.*

He glanced back, watching his men spread out as they followed him. Good men, even the new ones he hadn't had time to test. Good men. Didn't have to be told every time what to do. Not a shield glimmer showed on any of them. No cowards in this bunch, carrying shields into the desert where a worm could sense the field and come to rob them of the spice they found.

From this slight elevation in the rocks, Gurney could see the spice patch about half a kilometer away and the crawler just reaching the near edge. He glanced up at the coverflight, noting the altitude—not too high. He nodded to himself, turned to resume his climb up the ridge.

In that instant, the ridge erupted.

Twelve roaring paths of flame streaked upward to the hovering 'thopters and carrier wing. There came a blasting of metal from the factory crawler, and the rocks around Gurney were full of hooded fighting men.

Gurney had time to think: *By the horns of the Great Mother! Rockets! They dare to use rockets!*

Then he was face to face with a hooded figure who crouched low, crysknife at the ready. Two more men stood waiting on the rocks above to left and right.

Only the eyes of the fighting man ahead of him were visible to Gurney between hood and veil of sand-colored burnoose, but the crouch and readiness warned him that here was a trained fighting man. The eyes were the blue-in-blue of the deep-desert Fremen.

Gurney moved one hand toward his own knife, kept his eyes fixed on the other's knife. If they dared use rockets, they'd have other projectile weapons. This moment argued extreme caution. He could tell by sound alone that at least part of his skycover had been knocked out. There were gruntings, too, the noise of several struggles behind him.

The eyes of the fighting man ahead of Gurney followed the motion of hand toward knife, came back to glare into Gurney's eyes.

"Leave the knife in its sheath, Gurney Halleck," the man said.

Gurney hesitated. That voice sounded oddly familiar even through a stillsuit filter.

"You know my name?" he said.

"You've no need of a knife with me, Gurney," the man said. He straightened, slipped his crysknife into its sheath back beneath his robe. "Tell your men to stop their useless resistance."

The man threw his hood back, swung the filter aside.

The shock of what he saw froze Gurney's muscles. He thought at first he was looking at a ghost image of Duke Leto Atreides. Full recognition came slowly.

"Paul," he whispered. Then louder: "Is it truly Paul?"

"Don't you trust your own eyes?" Paul asked.

"They said you were dead," Gurney rasped. He took a half-step forward.

"Tell your men to submit," Paul commanded. He waved toward the lower reaches of the ridge.

Gurney turned, reluctant to take his eyes off Paul. He saw only a few knots of struggle. Hooded desert men seemed to be everywhere around. The factory crawler lay silent with Fremen standing atop it. There were no aircraft overhead.

"Stop the fighting," Gurney bellowed. He took a deep breath, cupped his hands for a megaphone. "This is Gurney Halleck! Stop the fight!"

Slowly, warily, the struggling figures separated. Eyes turned toward him, questioning.

"These are friends," Gurney called.

"Fine friends!" someone shouted back. "Half our people murdered."

"It's a mistake," Gurney said. "Don't add to it."

He turned back to Paul, stared into the youth's blue-blue Fremen eyes.

A smile touched Paul's mouth, but there was a hardness in the expression that reminded Gurney of the Old Duke, Paul's grandfather. Gurney saw then the sinewy harshness in Paul that had never before been seen in an Atreides—a leathery look to the skin, a squint to the eyes and calculation in the glance that seemed to weigh everything in sight.

"They said you were dead," Gurney repeated.

"And it seemed the best protection to let them think so," Paul said.

Gurney realized that was all the apology he'd ever get for having been abandoned to his own resources, left to believe his young Duke . . . his friend, was dead. He wondered then if there were anything left here of the boy he had known and trained in the ways of fighting men.

Paul took a step closer to Gurney, found that his eyes were smarting. "Gurney . . . ."

It seemed to happen of itself, and they were embracing, pounding each other on the back, feeling the reassurance of solid flesh.

"You young pup! You young pup!" Gurney kept saying.

And Paul: "Gurney, man! Gurney, man!"

Presently, they stepped apart, looked at each other. Gurney took a deep breath. "So you're why the Fremen have grown so wise in battle tactics. I might've known. They keep doing things I could've planned myself. If I'd only known . . . ." He shook his head. "If you'd only got word to me, lad. Nothing would've stopped me. I'd have come arunning and . . . ."

A look in Paul's eyes stopped him . . . the hard, weighing stare.

Gurney sighed. "Sure, and there'd have been those who wondered why Gurney Halleck went arunning, and some would've done more than question. They'd have gone hunting for answers."

Paul nodded, glanced to the waiting Fremen around them—the looks of curious appraisal on the faces of the Fedaykin. He turned from the death commandos back to Gurney. Finding his former swordmaster filled him with elation. He saw it as a good omen, a sign that he was on the course of the future where all was well.

*With Gurney at my side . . . .*

Paul glanced down the ridge past the Fedaykin, studied the smuggler crew who had come with Halleck.

"How do your men stand, Gurney?" he asked.

"They're smugglers all," Gurney said. "They stand where the profit is."

"Little enough profit in our venture," Paul said, and he noted the subtle finger signal flashed to him by Gurney's right hand—the old hand code out of their past. There were men to fear and distrust in the smuggler crew.

Paul pulled at his lip to indicate he understood, looked up at the men standing guard above them on the rocks. He saw Stilgar there. Memory of the unsolved problem with Stilgar cooled some of Paul's elation.

"Stilgar," he said, "this is Gurney Halleck of whom you've heard me speak. My father's master-of-arms, one of the swordmasters who instructed me, an old friend. He can be trusted in any venture."

"I hear," Stilgar said. "You are his Duke."

Paul stared at the dark visage above him, wondering at the reasons which had impelled Stilgar to say just that. *His Duke.* There had been a strange, subtle intonation in Stilgar's voice, as though he would rather have said something else. And that wasn't like Stilgar, who was a leader of Fremen, a man who spoke his mind.

*My Duke!* Gurney thought. He looked anew at Paul. *Yes, with Leto dead, the title fell on Paul's shoulders.*

The pattern of the Fremen war on Arrakis began to take on new shape in Gurney's mind. *My Duke!* A place that had been dead within him began coming alive. Only part of his awareness focused on Paul's ordering the smuggler crew disarmed until they could be questioned.

Gurney's mind returned to the command when he heard some of his men protesting. He shook his head, whirled. "Are you men deaf?" he barked. "This is the rightful Duke of Arrakis. Do as he commands."

Grumbling, the smugglers submitted.

Paul moved up beside Gurney, spoke in a low voice. "I'd not have expected you to walk into this trap, Gurney."

"I'm properly chastened," Gurney said. "I'll wager yon patch of spice is little more than a sand grain's thickness, a bait to lure us."

"That's a wager you'd win," Paul said. He looked down at the men being disarmed. "Are there any more of my father's men among your crew?"

"None. We're spread thin. There're a few among the free traders. Most have spent their profits to leave this place.

"But you stayed."

"I stayed."

"Because Rabban is here," Paul said.

"I thought I had nothing left but revenge," Gurney said.

An oddly chopped cry sounded from the ridgetop. Gurney looked up to see a Fremen waving his kerchief.

"A maker comes," Paul said. He moved out to a point of rock with Gurney following, looked off to the southwest. The burrow mound of a worm could be seen in the middle distance, a dust-crowned track that cut directly through the dunes on a course toward the ridge.

"He's big enough," Paul said.

A clattering sound lifted from the factory crawler below them. It turned on its treads like a giant insect, lumbered toward the rocks.

"Too bad we couldn't have saved the carryall," Paul said.

Gurney glanced at him, looked back to the patches of smoke and debris out on the desert where carryall and ornithopters had been brought down by Fremen rockets. He felt a sudden pang for the men lost there—his men, and he said: "Your father would've been more concerned for the men he couldn't save."

Paul shot a hard stare at him, lowered his gaze. Presently, he said: "They were your friends, Gurney. I understand. To us, though, they were trespassers who might see things they shouldn't see. You must understand that."

"I understand it well enough," Gurney said. "Now, I'm curious to see what I shouldn't."

Paul looked up to see the old and well-remembered wolfish grin on Halleck's face, the ripple of the inkvine scar along the man's jaw.

Gurney nodded toward the desert below them. Fremen were going about their business all over the landscape. It struck him that none of them appeared worried by the approach of the worm.

A thumping sounded from the open dunes beyond the baited patch of spice—a deep drumming that seemed to be heard through their feet. Gurney saw Fremen spread out across the sand there in the path of the worm.

The worm came on like some great sandfish, cresting the surface, its rings rippling and twisting. In a moment, from his vantage point above the desert, Gurney saw the taking of a worm—the daring leap of the first hookman, the turning of the creature, the way an entire band of men went up the scaly, glistening curve of the worm's side.

"There's one of the things you shouldn't have seen," Paul said.

"There've been stories and rumors," Gurney said. "But it's not a thing easy to believe without seeing it." He shook his head. "The creature all men on Arrakis fear, you treat it like a riding animal."

"You heard my father speak of desert power," Paul said. "There it is. The surface of this planet is ours. No storm nor creature nor condition can stop us."

*Us,* Gurney thought. *He means the Fremen. He speaks of himself as one of them.* Again, Gurney looked at the spice blue in Paul's eyes. His own eyes, he knew, had a touch of the color, but smugglers could get offworld foods and there was a subtle caste implication in the tone of the eyes among them. They spoke of "the touch of the spicebrush" to mean a man had gone too native. And there was always a hint of distrust in the idea.

"There was a time when we did not ride the maker in the light of day in these latitudes," Paul said. "But Rabban has little enough air cover left that he can waste it looking for a few specks in the sand." He looked at Gurney. "Your aircraft were a shock to us here."

*To us . . . to us . . . .*

Gurney shook his head to drive out such thoughts. "We weren't the shock to you that you were to us," he said.

"What's the talk of Rabban in the sinks and villages?" Paul asked.

"They say they've fortified the graben villages to the point where you cannot harm them. They say they need only sit inside their defenses while you wear yourselves out in futile attack."

"In a word," Paul said, "they're immobilized."

"While you can go where you will," Gurney said.

"It's a tactic I learned from you," Paul said. "They've lost the initiative, which means they've lost the war."

Gurney smiled, a slow, knowing expression.

"Our enemy is exactly where I want him to be," Paul said. He glanced at Gurney. "Well, Gurney, do you enlist with me for the finish of this campaign?"

"Enlist?" Gurney stared at him. "My Lord, I've never left your service. You're the one left me . . . to think you dead. And I, being cast adrift, made what shrift I could, waiting for the moment I might sell my life for what it's worth—the death of Rabban."

An embarrassed silence settled over Paul.

A woman came climbing up the rocks toward them, her eyes between stillsuit hood and face mask flicking between Paul and his companion. She stopped in front of Paul. Gurney noted the possessive air about her, the way she stood close to Paul.

"Chani," Paul said, "this is Gurney Halleck. You've heard me speak of him."

She looked at Halleck, back to Paul. "I have heard."

"Where did the men go on the maker?" Paul asked.

"They but diverted it to give us time to save the equipment."

"Well then . . . ." Paul broke off, sniffed the air.

"There's wind coming," Chani said.

A voice called out from the ridgetop above them: "Ho, there—the wind!"

Gurney saw a quickening of motion among the Fremen now—a rushing about and sense of hurry. A thing the worm had not ignited was brought about by fear of the wind. The factory crawler lumbered up onto the dry beach below them and a way was opened for it among the rocks . . . and the rocks closed behind it so neatly that the passage escaped his eyes.

"Have you many such hiding places?" Gurney asked.

"Many times many," Paul said. He looked at Chani. "Find Korba. Tell him that Gurney has warned me there are men among this smuggler crew who're not to be trusted."

She looked once at Gurney, back to Paul, nodded, and was off down the rocks, leaping with a gazelle-like agility.

"She is your woman," Gurney said.

"The mother of my firstborn," Paul said. "There's another Leto among the Atreides."

Gurney accepted this with only a widening of the eyes.

Paul watched the action around them with a critical eye. A curry color dominated the southern sky now and there came fitful bursts and gusts of wind that whipped dust around their heads.

"Seal your suit," Paul said. And he fastened the mask and hood about his face.

Gurney obeyed, thankful for the filters.

Paul spoke, his voice muffled by the filter: "Which of your crew don't you trust, Gurney?"

"There're some new recruits," Gurney said. "Offworlders . . . ." He hesitated, wondering at himself suddenly. *Offworlders*. The word had come so easily to his tongue.

"Yes?" Paul said.

"They're not like the usual fortune-hunting lot we get," Gurney said. "They're tougher."

"Harkonnen spies?" Paul asked.

"I think, m'Lord, that they report to no Harkonnen. I suspect they're men of the Imperial service. They have a hint of Salusa Secundus about them."

Paul shot a sharp glance at him. "Sardaukar?"

Gurney shrugged. "They could be, but it's well masked."

Paul nodded, thinking how easily Gurney had fallen back into the pattern of Atreides retainer . . . but with subtle reservations . . . differences. Arrakis had changed him, too.

Two hooded Fremen emerged from the broken rock below them, began climbing upward. One of them carried a large black bundle over one shoulder.

"Where are my crew now?" Gurney asked.

"Secure in the rocks below us," Paul said. "We've a cave here—Cave of Birds. We'll decide what to do with them after the storm."

A voice called from above them: "Muad'Dib!"

Paul turned at the call, saw a Fremen guard motioning them down to the cave. Paul signaled he had heard.

Gurney was studying him with a new expression. "You're Muad'Dib?" he asked. "You're the will-o'-the-sand?"

"It's my Fremen name," Paul said.

Gurney turned away, feeling an oppressive sense of foreboding. Half his own crew dead on the sand, the others captive. He did not care about the new recruits, the suspicious ones, but among the others were good men, friends, people for whom he felt responsible. *"We'll decide what to do with them after the storm."* That's what Paul had said, Muad'Dib had said. And Gurney recalled the stories told of Muad'Dib, the Lisan al-Gaib—how he had taken the skin of a Harkonnen officer to make his drumheads, how he was surrounded by death commandos, Fedaykin who leaped into battle with their death chants on their lips.

*Him.*

The two Fremen climbing up the rocks leaped lightly to a shelf in front of Paul. The dark-faced one said: "All secure, Muad'Dib. We best get below now."

"Right."

Gurney noted the tone of the man's voice—half command and half request. This was the man called Stilgar, another figure of the new Fremen legends.

Paul looked at the bundle the other man carried, said: "Korba, what's in the bundle?"

Stilgar answered: " 'Twas in the crawler. It had the initial of your friend here and it contains a baliset. Many times have I heard you speak of the prowess of Gurney Halleck on the baliset."

Gurney studied the speaker, seeing the edge of black beard above the stillsuit mask, the hawk stare, the chiseled nose.

"You've a companion who thinks, m'Lord," Gurney said. "Thank you, Stilgar."

Stilgar signaled for his companion to pass the bundle to Gurney, said: "Thank your Lord Duke. His countenance earns your admittance here."

Gurney accepted the bundle, puzzled by the hard undertones in this conversation. There was an air of challenge about the man, and Gurney wondered if it could be a feeling of jealousy in the Fremen. Here was someone called Gurney Halleck who'd known Paul even in the times before Arrakis, a man who shared a camaraderie that Stilgar could never invade.

"You are two I'd have be friends," Paul said.

"Stilgar, the Fremen, is a name of renown," Gurney said. "Any killer of Harkonnens I'd feel honored to count among my friends."

"Will you touch hands with my friend Gurney Halleck, Stilgar?" Paul asked.

Slowly, Stilgar extended his hand, gripped the heavy calluses of Gurney's swordhand. "There're few who haven't heard the name of Gurney Halleck," he said, and released his grip. He turned to Paul. "The storm comes rushing."

"At once," Paul said.

Stilgar turned away, led them down through the rocks, a twisting and turning path into a shadowed cleft that admitted them to the low entrance of a cave. Men hurried to fasten a doorseal behind them. Glowglobes showed a broad, dome-ceilinged space with a raised ledge on one side and a passage leading off from it.

Paul leaped to the ledge with Gurney right behind him, led the way into the passage. The others headed for another passage opposite the entrance. Paul led the way through an anteroom and into a chamber with dark, wine-colored hangings on its walls.

"We can have some privacy here for a while," Paul said. "The others will respect my—"

An alarm cymbal clanged from the outer chamber, was followed by shouting and clashing of weapons. Paul whirled, ran back through the anteroom and out onto the atrium lip above the outer chamber. Gurney was right behind him, weapon drawn.

Beneath them on the floor of the cave swirled a melee of struggling figures. Paul stood an instant assessing the scene, separating the Fremen robes and bourkas from the costumes of those they opposed. Senses that his mother had trained to detect the most subtle clues picked out a significant fact—the Fremen fought against men wearing smuggler robes, but the smugglers were crouched in trios, backed into triangles where pressed.

That habit of close fighting was a trademark of the Imperial Sardaukar.

A Fedaykin in the crowd saw Paul, and his battlecry was lifted to echo in the chamber: "Muad'Dib! Muad'Dib! Muad'Dib!"

Another eye had also picked Paul out. A black knife came hurtling toward him. Paul dodged, heard the knife clatter against stone behind him, glanced to see Gurney retrieve it.

The triangular knots were being pressed back now.

Gurney held the knife up in front of Paul's eyes, pointed to the hairline yellow coil of Imperial color, the golden lion crest, multifaceted eyes at the pommel.

Sardaukar for certain.

Paul stepped out to the lip of the ledge. Only three of the Sardaukar remained. Bloody rag mounds of Sardaukar and Fremen lay in a twisted pattern across the chamber.

"Hold!" Paul shouted. "The Duke Paul Atreides commands you to hold!"

The fighting wavered, hesitated.

"You Sardaukar!" Paul called to the remaining group. "By whose orders do you threaten a ruling Duke?" And, quickly, as his men started to press in around the Sardaukar: "Hold, I say!"

One of the cornered trio straightened. "Who says we're Sardaukar?" he demanded.

Paul took the knife from Gurney, held it aloft. "This says you're Sardaukar."

"Then who says you're a ruling Duke?" the man demanded.

Paul gestured to the Fedaykin. "These men say I'm a ruling Duke. Your own emperor bestowed Arrakis on House Atreides. I am House Atreides."

The Sardaukar stood silent, fidgeting.

Paul studied the man—tall, flat-featured, with a pale scar across half his left cheek. Anger and confusion were betrayed in his manner, but still there was that pride about him without which a Sardaukar appeared undressed—and with which he could appear fully clothed though naked.

Paul glanced to one of his Fedaykin lieutenants, said: "Korba, how came they to have weapons?"

"They held back knives concealed in cunning pockets within their stillsuits," the lieutenant said.

Paul surveyed the dead and wounded across the chamber, brought his attention back to the lieutenant. There was no need for words. The lieutenant lowered his eyes.

"Where is Chani?" Paul asked and waited, breath held, for the answer.

"Stilgar spirited her aside." He nodded toward the other passage, glanced at the dead and wounded. "I hold myself responsible for this mistake, Muad'Dib."

"How many of these Sardaukar were there, Gurney?" Paul asked.

"Ten."

Paul leaped lightly to the floor of the chamber, strode across to stand within striking distance of the Sardaukar spokesman.

A tense air came over the Fedaykin. They did not like him thus exposed to danger. This was the thing they were pledged to prevent because the Fremen wished to preserve the wisdom of Muad'Dib.

Without turning, Paul spoke to his lieutenant: "How many are our casualties?"

"Four wounded, two dead, Muad'Dib."

Paul saw motion beyond the Sardaukar, Chani and Stilgar were standing in the other passage. He returned his attention to the Sardaukar, staring into the offworld whites of the spokesman's eyes. "You, what is your name?" Paul demanded.

The man stiffened, glanced left and right.

"Don't try it," Paul said. "It's obvious to me that you were ordered to seek out and destroy Muad'Dib. I'll warrant you were the ones suggested seeking spice in the deep desert."

A gasp from Gurney behind him brought a thin smile to Paul's lips.

Blood suffused the Sardaukar's face.

"What you see before you is more than Muad'Dib," Paul said. "Seven of you are dead for two of us. Three for one. Pretty good against Sardaukar, eh?"

The man came up on his toes, sank back as the Fedaykin pressed forward.

"I asked your name," Paul said, and he called up the subtleties of Voice: "Tell me your name!"

"Captain Aramsham, Imperial Sardaukar!" the man snapped. His jaw dropped. He stared at Paul in confusion. The manner about him that had dismissed this cavern as a barbarian warren melted away.

"Well, Captain Aramsham," Paul said, "The Harkonnens would pay dearly to learn what you now know. And the Emperor—what he wouldn't give to learn an Atreides still lives despite his treachery."

The captain glanced left and right at the two men remaining to him. Paul could almost see the thoughts turning over in the man's head. Sardaukar did not submit, but the Emperor *had* to learn of this threat.

Still using the Voice, Paul said: "Submit, Captain."

The man at the captain's left leaped without warning toward Paul, met the flashing impact of his own captain's knife in his chest. The attacker hit the floor in a sodden heap with the knife still in him.

The captain faced his sole remaining companion. "I decide what best serves His Majesty," he said. "Understood?"

The other Sardaukar's shoulders slumped.

"Drop your weapon," the captain said.

The Sardaukar obeyed.

The captain returned his attention to Paul. "I have killed a friend for you," he said. "Let us always remember that."

"You're my prisoners," Paul said. "You submitted to me. Whether you live or die is of no importance." He motioned to his guard to take the two Sardaukar, signaled the lieutenant who had searched the prisoners.

The guard moved in, hustled the Sardaukar away.

Paul bent toward his lieutenant.

"Muad'Dib," the man said, "I failed you in . . . ."

"The failure was mine, Korba," Paul said. "I should've warned you what to seek. In the future, when searching Sardaukar, remember this. Remember, too, that each has a false toenail or two that can be combined with other items secreted about their bodies to make an effective transmitter. They'll have more than one false tooth. They carry coils of shigawire in their hair—so fine you can barely detect it, yet strong enough to garrotte a man and cut off his head in the process. With Sardaukar, you must scan them, scope them—both reflex and hard ray—cut off every scrap of body hair. And when you're through, be certain you haven't discovered everything."

He looked up at Gurney, who had moved close to listen.

"Then we best kill them," the lieutenant said.

Paul shook his head, still looking at Gurney. "No. I want them to escape."

Gurney stared at him. "Sire . . . ." he breathed.

"Yes?"

"Your man here is right. Kill those prisoners at once. Destroy all evidence of them. You've shamed Imperial Sardaukar! When the Emperor learns that he'll not rest until he has you over a slow fire."

"The Emperor's not likely to have that power over me," Paul said. He spoke slowly, coldly. Something had happened inside him while he faced the Sardaukar. A sum of decisions had accumulated in his awareness. "Gurney," he said, "are there many Guildsmen around Rabban?"

Gurney straightened, eyes narrowed. "Your question makes no . . . ."

"Are there?" Paul barked.

"Arrakis is crawling with Guild agents. They're buying spice as though it were the most precious thing in the universe. Why else do you think we ventured this far into . . . ."

"It is the most precious thing in the universe," Paul said. "To them." He looked toward Stilgar and Chani who now were crossing the chamber toward him. "And we control it, Gurney."

"The Harkonnens control it!" Gurney protested.

"The people who can destroy a thing, they control it," Paul said. He waved a hand to silence further remarks from Gurney, nodded to Stilgar who stopped in front of Paul, Chani beside him.

Paul took the Sardaukar knife in his left hand, presented it to Stilgar. "You live for the good of the tribe," Paul said. "Could you draw my life's blood with that knife?"

"For the good of the tribe," Stilgar growled.

"Then use that knife," Paul said.

"Are you calling me out?" Stilgar demanded.

"If I do," Paul said, "I shall stand there without weapon and let you slay me." Stilgar drew in a quick, sharp breath.

Chani said, "Usul!" then glanced at Gurney, back to Paul.

While Stilgar was still weighing his words, Paul said: "You are Stilgar, a fighting man. When the Sardaukar began fighting here, you were not in the front of battle. Your first thought was to protect Chani."

"She's my niece," Stilgar said. "If there'd been any doubt of your Fedaykin handling those scum . . . ."

"Why was your first thought of Chani?" Paul demanded.

"It wasn't!"

"Oh?"

"It was of you," Stilgar admitted.

"Do you think you could lift your hand against me?" Paul asked.

Stilgar began to tremble. "It's the way," he muttered.

"It's the way to kill offworld strangers found in the desert and take their water as a gift from Shai-hulud," Paul said. "Yet you permitted two such to live one night, my mother and myself."

As Stilgar remained silent, trembling, staring at him, Paul said: "Ways change, Stil. You have changed them yourself."

Stilgar looked down at the yellow emblem on the knife he held.

"When I am Duke on Arrakeen with Chani by my side, do you think I'll have time to concern myself with every detail of governing Tabr sietch?" Paul asked. "Do you concern yourself with the internal problems of every family?"

Stilgar continued staring at the knife.

"Do you think I wish to cut off my right arm?" Paul demanded.

Slowly, Stilgar looked up at him.

"You!" Paul said. "Do you think I wish to deprive myself or the tribe of your wisdom and strength?"

In a low voice, Stilgar said: "The young man of my tribe whose name is known to me, this young man I could kill on the challenge floor, Shai-hulud willing. The Lisan al-Gaib, him I could not harm. You knew this when you handed me this knife."

"I knew it," Paul agreed.

Stilgar opened his hand. The knife clattered against the stone of the floor. "Ways change," he said.

"Chani," Paul said, "go to my mother, send her here that her counsel will be available in—"

"But you said we would go to the south!" she protested.

"I was wrong," he said. "The Harkonnens are not there. The war is not there."

She took a deep breath, accepting this as a desert woman accepted all necessities in the midst of a life involved with death.

"You will give my mother a message for her ears alone," Paul said. "Tell her that Stilgar acknowledges me Duke of Arrakis, but a way must be found to make the young men accept this without combat."

Chani glanced at Stilgar.

"Do as he says," Stilgar growled. "We both know he could overcome me . . . and I could not raise my hand against him . . . for the good of the tribe."

"I shall return with your mother," Chani said.

"Send her," Paul said. "Stilgar's instinct was right. I am stronger when you are safe. You will remain in the sietch."

She started to protest, swallowed it.

"Sihaya," Paul said, using his intimate name for her. He whirled away to the right, met Gurney's glaring eyes.

The interchange between Paul and the older Fremen had passed as though in a cloud around Gurney since Paul's reference to his mother.

"Your mother," Gurney said.

"Idaho saved us the night of the raid," Paul said, distracted by the parting with Chani. "Right now we've—"

"What of Duncan Idaho, m'Lord?" Gurney asked.

"He's dead—buying us a bit of time to escape."

*The she-witch alive!* Gurney thought. *The one I swore vengeance against, alive! And it's obvious Duke Paul doesn't know what manner of creature gave him birth. The evil one! Betrayed his own father to the Harkonnens!*

Paul pressed past him, jumped up to the ledge. He glanced back, noted that the wounded and dead had been removed, and he thought bitterly that here was another chapter in the legend of Paul-Muad'Dib. *I didn't even draw my knife, but it'll be said of this day I slew twenty Sardaukar by my own hand.*

Gurney followed with Stilgar, stepping on ground that he did not even feel. The cavern with its yellow light of glowglobes was forced out of his thoughts by rage. *The she-witch alive while those she betrayed are bones in lonesome graves. I must contrive it that Paul learns the truth about her before I slay her.*

*How often it is that the angry man rages denial of what his inner self is telling him.*

—"The Collected Sayings of Muad'Dib"
by the Princess Irulan

The crowd in the cavern assembly chamber radiated that pack feeling Jessica had sensed the day Paul killed Jamis. There was murmuring nervousness in the voices. Little cliques gathered like knots among the robes.

Jessica tucked a message cylinder beneath her robe as she emerged to the ledge from Paul's private quarters. She felt rested after the long journey up from the south, but still rankled that Paul would not yet permit them to use the captured ornithopters.

"We do not have full control of the air," he had said. "And we must not become dependent upon offworld fuel. Both fuel and aircraft must be gathered and saved for the day of maximum effort."

Paul stood with a group of the younger men near the ledge. The pale light of glowglobes gave the scene a tinge of unreality. It was like a tableau, but with the added dimension of warren smells, the whispers, the sounds of shuffling feet.

She studied her son, wondering why he had not yet trotted out his surprise—Gurney Halleck. Thought of Gurney disturbed her with its memories of an easier past—days of love and beauty with Paul's father.

Stilgar waited with a small group of his own at the other end of the ledge. There was a feeling of inevitable dignity about him, the way he stood without talking.

*We must not lose that man,* Jessica thought. *Paul's plan must work. Anything else would be highest tragedy.*

She strode down the ledge, passing Stilgar without a glance, stepped down into the crowd. A way was made for her as she headed toward Paul. And silence followed her.

She knew the meaning of the silence—the unspoken questions of the people, awe of the Reverend Mother.

The young men drew back from Paul as she came up to him, and she found herself momentarily dismayed by the new deference they paid him. *"All men beneath your position covet your station,"* went the Bene Gesserit axiom. But she found no covetousness in these faces. They were held at a distance by the religious ferment around Paul's leadership. And she recalled another Bene Gesserit saying: *"Prophets have a way of dying by violence."*

Paul looked at her.

"It's time," she said, and passed the message cylinder to him.

One of Paul's companions, bolder than the others, glanced across at Stilgar, said: "Are you going to call him out, Muad'Dib? Now's the time for sure. They'll think you a coward if you—"

"Who dares call me coward?" Paul demanded. His hand flashed to his crysknife hilt.

Bated silence came over the group, spreading out into the crowd.

"There's work to do," Paul said as the man drew back from him. Paul turned away, shouldered through the crowd to the ledge, leaped lightly up to it and faced the people.

"Do it!" someone shrieked.

Murmurs and whispers arose behind the shriek.

Paul waited for silence. It came slowly amidst scattered shufflings and coughs. When it was quiet in the cavern, Paul lifted his chin, spoke in a voice that carried to the farthest corners.

"You are tired of waiting," Paul said.

Again, he waited while the cries of response died out.

*Indeed, they are tired of waiting,* Paul thought. He hefted the message cylinder, thinking of what it contained. His mother had showed it to him, explaining how it had been taken from a Harkonnen courier.

The message was explicit: Rabban was being abandoned to his own resources here on Arrakis! He could not call for help or reinforcements!

Again, Paul raised his voice: "You think it's time I called out Stilgar and changed the leadership of the troops!" Before they could respond, Paul hurled his voice at them in anger: "Do you think the Lisan al-Gaib that stupid?"

There was stunned silence.

*He's accepting the religious mantle,* Jessica thought. *He must not do it!*

"It's the way!" someone shouted.

Paul spoke dryly, probing the emotional undercurrents. "Ways change."

An angry voice lifted from a corner of the cavern: "We'll say what's to change!"

There were scattered shouts of agreement through the throng.

"As you wish," Paul said.

And Jessica heard the subtle intonations as he used the powers of Voice she had taught him.

"You will say," he agreed. "But first you will hear my say."

Stilgar moved along the ledge, his bearded face impassive. "That is the way, too," he said. "The voice of any Fremen may be heard in Council. Paul-Muad'Dib is a Fremen."

"The good of the tribe, that is the most important thing, eh?" Paul asked.

Still with that flat-voiced dignity, Stilgar said: "Thus our steps are guided."

"All right," Paul said. "Then, who rules this troop of our tribe—and who rules all the tribes and troops through the fighting instructors we've trained in the weirding way?"

Paul waited, looking over the heads of the throng. No answer came.

Presently, he said: "Does Stilgar rule all this? He says himself that he does not. Do I rule? Even Stilgar does my bidding on occasion, and the sages, the wisest of the wise, listen to me and honor me in Council."

There was shuffling silence among the crowd.

"So," Paul said. "Does my mother rule?" He pointed down to Jessica in her black robes of office among them. "Stilgar and all the other troop leaders ask her advice in almost every major decision. You know this. But does a Reverend Mother walk the sand or lead a razzia against the Harkonnens?"

Frowns creased the foreheads of those Paul could see, but still there were angry murmurs.

*This is a dangerous way to do it,* Jessica thought, but she remembered the message cylinder and what it implied. And she saw Paul's intent: Go right to the depth of their uncertainty, dispose of that, and all the rest must follow.

"No man recognizes leadership without the challenge and the combat, eh?" Paul asked.

"That's the way!" someone shouted.

"What's our goal?" Paul asked. "To unseat Rabban, the Harkonnen beast, and remake our world into a place where we may raise our families in happiness amidst an abundance of water—is this our goal?"

"Hard tasks need hard ways," someone shouted.

"Do you smash your knife before a battle?" Paul demanded. "I say this as fact, not meaning it as boast or challenge: there isn't a man here, Stilgar included, who could stand against me in single combat. This is Stilgar's own admission. He knows it, so do you all."

Again, the angry mutters lifted from the crowd.

"Many of you have been with me on the practice floor," Paul said. "You know this isn't idle boast. I say it because it's fact known to us all, and I'd be foolish not to see it for myself. I began training in these ways earlier than you did and my teachers were tougher than any you've ever seen. How else do you think I bested Jamis at an age when your boys are still fighting only mock battles?"

*He's using the Voice well,* Jessica thought, *but that's not enough with these people. They've good insulation against vocal control. He must catch them also with logic.*

"So," Paul said, "we come to this." He lifted the message cylinder, removed its scrap of tape. "This was taken from a Harkonnen courier. Its authenticity is beyond question. It is addressed to Rabban. It tells him that his request for new troops is denied, that his spice harvest is far below quota, that he must wring more spice from Arrakis with the people he has."

Stilgar moved up beside Paul.

"How many of you see what this means?" Paul asked. "Stilgar saw it immediately."

"They're cut off!" someone shouted.

Paul pushed message and cylinder into his sash. From his neck he took a braided shigawire cord and removed a ring from the cord, holding the ring aloft.

"This was my father's ducal signet," he said. "I swore never to wear it again until I was ready to lead my troops over all of Arrakis and claim it as my rightful fief." He put the ring on his finger, clenched his fist.

Utter stillness gripped the cavern.

"Who rules here?" Paul asked. He raised his fist. "I rule here! I rule on every square inch of Arrakis! This is my ducal fief whether the Emperor says yea or nay! He gave it to my father and it comes to me through my father!"

Paul lifted himself onto his toes, settled back to his heels. He studied the crowd, feeling their temper.

*Almost,* he thought.

"There are men here who will hold positions of importance on Arrakis when I claim those Imperial rights which are mine," Paul said. "Stilgar is one of those men. Not because I wish to bribe him! Not out of gratitude, though I'm one of many here who owe him life for life. No! But because he's wise and strong. Because he governs this troop by his own intelligence and not just by rules. Do you think me stupid? Do you think I'll cut off my right arm and leave it bloody on the floor of this cavern just to provide you with a circus?"

Paul swept a hard gaze across the throng. "Who is there here to say I'm not the rightful ruler on Arrakis? Must I prove it by leaving every Fremen tribe in the erg without a leader?"

Beside Paul, Stilgar stirred, looked at him questioningly.

"Will I subtract from our strength when we need it most?" Paul asked. "I am your ruler, and I say to you that it is time we stopped killing off our best men and started killing our real enemies—the Harkonnens!"

In one blurred motion, Stilgar had his crysknife out and pointed over the heads of the throng. "Long live Duke Paul-Muad'Dib!" he shouted.

A deafening roar filled the cavern, echoed and re-echoed. They were cheering and chanting: "Ya hya chouhada! Muad'Dib! Muad'Dib! Muad'Dib! Ya hya chouhada!"

Jessica translated it to herself: *"Long live the fighters of Muad'Dib!"* The scene she and Paul and Stilgar had cooked up between them had worked as they'd planned.

The tumult died slowly.

When silence was restored, Paul faced Stilgar, said: "Kneel, Stilgar."

Stilgar dropped to his knees on the ledge.

"Hand me your crysknife," Paul said.

Stilgar obeyed.

*This was not as we planned it,* Jessica thought.

"Repeat after me, Stilgar," Paul said, and he called up the words of investiture as he had heard his own father use them. "I, Stilgar, take this knife from the hands of my Duke."

"I, Stilgar, take this knife from the hands of my Duke," Stilgar said, and accepted the milky blade from Paul.

"Where my Duke commands, there shall I place this blade," Paul said.

Stilgar repeated the words, speaking slowly and solemnly.

Remembering the source of the rite, Jessica blinked back tears, shook her head. *I know the reasons for this,* she thought. *I shouldn't let it stir me.*

"I dedicate this blade to the cause of my Duke and the death of his enemies for as long as our blood shall flow," Paul said.

Stilgar repeated it after him.

"Kiss the blade," Paul ordered.

Stilgar obeyed, then, in the Fremen manner, kissed Paul's knife arm. At a nod from Paul, he sheathed the blade, got to his feet.

A sighing whisper of awe passed through the crowd, and Jessica heard the words: "The prophecy—A Bene Gesserit shall show the way and a Reverend

Mother shall see it." And, from farther away: "She shows us through her son!"

"Stilgar leads this tribe," Paul said. "Let no man mistake that. He commands with my voice. What he tells you, it is as though I told you."

*Wise,* Jessica thought. *The tribal commander must lose no face among those who should obey him.*

Paul lowered his voice, said: "Stilgar, I want sandwalkers out this night and cielagos sent to summon a Council Gathering. When you've sent them, bring Chatt, Korba and Otheym and two other lieutenants of your own choosing. Bring them to my quarters for battle planning. We must have a victory to show the Council of Leaders when they arrive."

Paul nodded for his mother to accompany him, led the way down off the ledge and through the throng toward the central passage and the living chambers that had been prepared there. As Paul pressed through the crowd, hands reached out to touch him. Voices called out to him.

"My knife goes where Stilgar commands it, Paul-Muad'Dib! Let us fight soon, Paul-Muad'Dib! Let us wet our world with the blood of Harkonnens!"

Feeling the emotions of the throng, Jessica sensed the fighting edge of these people. They could not be more ready. *We are taking them at the crest,* she thought.

In the inner chamber, Paul motioned his mother to be seated, said: "Wait here." And he ducked through the hangings to the side passage.

It was quiet in the chamber after Paul had gone, so quiet behind the hangings that not even the faint soughing of the wind pumps that circulated air in the sietch penetrated to where she sat.

*He is going to bring Gurney Halleck here,* she thought. And she wondered at the strange mingling of emotions that filled her. Gurney and his music had been a part of so many pleasant times on Caladan before the move to Arrakis. She felt that Caladan had happened to some other person. In the nearly three years since then, she had *become* another person. Having to confront Gurney forced a reassessment of the changes.

Paul's coffee service, the fluted alloy of silver and jasmium that he had inherited from Jamis, rested on a low table to her right. She stared at it, thinking of how many hands had touched that metal. Chani had served Paul from it within the month.

*What can his desert woman do for a Duke except serve him coffee?* she asked herself. *She brings him no power, no family. Paul has only one major chance—to ally himself with a powerful Great House, perhaps even with the Imperial family. There are marriagable princesses, after all, and every one of them Bene Gesserit-trained.*

Jessica imagined herself leaving the rigors of Arrakis for the life of power and security she could know as mother of a royal consort. She glanced at the thick hangings that obscured the rock of this cavern cell, thinking of how she had come here—riding amidst a host of worms, the palanquins and pack platforms piled high with necessities for the coming campaign.

*As long as Chani lives, Paul will not see his duty,* Jessica thought. *She has given him a son and that is enough.*

A sudden longing to see her grandson, the child whose likeness carried so much of the grandfather's features—so like Leto, swept through her. Jessica placed her palms against her cheeks, began the ritual breathing that stilled emotion and clarified the mind, then bent forward from the waist in the devotional exercise that prepared the body for the mind's demands.

Paul's choice of this Cave of Birds as his command post could not be questioned, she knew. It was ideal. And to the north lay Wind Pass opening onto a protected village in a cliff-walled sink. It was a key village, home of artisans and technicians, maintenance center for an entire Harkonnen defensive sector.

A cough sounded outside the chamber hangings. Jessica straightened, took a deep breath, exhaled slowly.

"Enter," she said.

Draperies were flung aside and Gurney Halleck bounded into the room. She had only time for a glimpse of his face with its odd grimace, then he was behind her, lifting her to her feet with one brawny arm beneath her chin.

"Gurney, you fool, what are you doing?" she demanded.

Then she felt the touch of the knife tip against her back. Chill awareness spread out from that knife tip. She knew in that instant that Gurney meant to kill her. *Why?* She could think of no reason, for he wasn't the kind to turn traitor. But she felt certain of his intention. Knowing it, her mind churned. Here was no man to be overcome easily. Here was a killer wary of the Voice, wary of every combat stratagem, wary of every trick of death and violence. Here was an instrument she herself had helped train with subtle hints and suggestions.

"You thought you had escaped, eh, witch?" Gurney snarled.

Before she could turn the question over in her mind or try to answer, the curtains parted and Paul entered.

"Here he is, Moth—" Paul broke off, taking in the tensions of the scene.

"You will stand where you are, m'Lord," Gurney said.

"What . . . ." Paul shook his head.

Jessica started to speak, felt the arm tighten against her throat.

"You will speak only when I permit it, witch," Gurney said. "I want only one thing from you for your son to hear it, and I am prepared to send this knife into your heart by reflex at the first sign of a counter against me. Your voice will remain in a monotone. Certain muscles you will not tense or move. You will act with the most extreme caution to gain yourself a few more seconds of life. And I assure you, these are all you have."

Paul took a step forward. "Gurney, man, what is—"

"Stop right where you are!" Gurney snapped. "One more step and she's dead."

Paul's hand slipped to his knife hilt. He spoke in deadly quiet: "You had best explain yourself, Gurney."

"I swore an oath to slay the betrayer of your father," Gurney said. "Do you think I can forget the man who rescued me from a Harkonnen slave pit, gave me freedom, life, and honor . . . and gave friendship, a thing I prized above all else. I have his betrayer under my knife. No one can stop me from—"

"You couldn't be more wrong, Gurney," Paul said.

And Jessica thought: *So that's it! What irony!*

"Wrong, am I?" Gurney demanded. "Let us hear it from the woman herself. And let her remember that I have bribed and spied and cheated to confirm this charge. I've even pushed semuta on a Harkonnen guard captain to get part of the story."

Jessica felt the arm at her throat ease slightly, but before she could speak, Paul said: "The betrayer was Yueh. I tell you this once, Gurney. The evidence is complete, cannot be controverted. It was Yueh. I do not care how you came by your suspicion—for it can be nothing else—but if you harm my mother . . . ." Paul lifted his crysknife from its scabbard, held the blade in front of him. ". . . I'll have your blood."

"Yueh was a conditioned medic, fit for a royal house," Gurney snarled. "He could not turn traitor!"

"I know a way to remove that conditioning," Paul said.

"Evidence," Gurney insisted.

"The evidence is not here," Paul said. "It's in Tabr sietch, far to the south, but if—"

"This is a trick," Gurney snarled, and his arm tightened on Jessica's throat.

"No trick, Gurney," Paul said, and his voice carried such a note of terrible sadness that the sound tore at Jessica's heart.

"I saw the message captured from the Harkonnen agent," Gurney said. "The note pointed directly at—"

"I saw it, too," Paul said. "My father showed it to me the night he explained why it had to be a Harkonnen trick aimed at making him suspect the woman he loved."

"Ayah!" Gurney said. "You've not—"

"Be quiet," Paul said, and the monotone stillness of his words carried more command than Jessica had ever heard in another voice.

*He has the Great Control,* she thought.

Gurney's arm trembled against her neck. The point of the knife at her back moved with uncertainty.

"What you have not done," Paul said, "is heard my mother sobbing in the night over her lost Duke. You have not seen her eyes stab flame when she speaks of killing Harkonnens."

*So he has listened,* she thought. Tears blinded her eyes.

"What you have not done," Paul went on, "is remembered the lessons you learned in a Harkonnen slave pit. You speak of pride in my father's friendship! Didn't you learn the difference between Harkonnen and Atreides so that you could smell a Harkonnen trick by the stink they left on it? Didn't you learn that Atreides loyalty is bought with love while the Harkonnen coin is hate? Couldn't you see through to the very nature of this betrayal?"

"But Yueh?" Gurney muttered.

"The evidence we have is Yueh's own message to us admitting his treachery," Paul said. "I swear this to you by the love I hold for you, a love I will still hold even after I leave you dead on this floor."

Hearing her son, Jessica marveled at the awareness in him, the penetrating insight of his intelligence.

"My father had an instinct for his friends," Paul said. "He gave his love sparingly, but with never an error. His weakness lay in misunderstanding hatred. He thought anyone who hated Harkonnens could not betray him." He glanced at his mother. "She knows this. I've given her my father's message that he never distrusted her."

Jessica felt herself losing control, bit at her lower lip. Seeing the stiff formality in Paul, she realized what these words were costing him. She wanted to run to him, cradle his head against her breast as she never had done. But the arm against her throat had ceased its trembling; the knife point at her back pressed still and sharp.

"One of the most terrible moments in a boy's life," Paul said, "is when he discovers his father and mother are human beings who share a love that he can never quite taste. It's a loss, an awakening to the fact that the world is *there* and *here* and we are in it alone. The moment carries its own truth; you can't evade it. I *heard* my father when he spoke of my mother. She's not the betrayer, Gurney."

Jessica found her voice, said: "Gurney, release me." There was no special command in the words, no trick to play on his weaknesses, but Gurney's hand fell away. She crossed to Paul, stood in front of him, not touching him.

"Paul," she said, "there are other awakenings in this universe. I suddenly see how I've used you and twisted you and manipulated you to set you on a course of my choosing . . . a course I had to choose—if that's any excuse—because of my own training." She swallowed past a lump in her throat, looked up into her son's eyes. "Paul . . . I want you to do something for me: choose the course of happiness. Your desert woman, marry her if that's your wish. Defy everyone and everything to do this. But choose your own course. I . . . ."

She broke off, stopped by the low sound of muttering behind her.

*Gurney!*

She saw Paul's eyes directed beyond her, turned.

Gurney stood in the same spot, but had sheathed his knife, pulled the robe away from his breast to expose the slick grayness of an issue stillsuit, the type the smugglers traded for among the sietch warrens.

"Put your knife right here in my breast," Gurney muttered. "I say kill me and have done with it. I've besmirched my name. I've betrayed my own Duke! The finest—"

"Be still!" Paul said.

Gurney stared at him.

"Close that robe and stop acting like a fool," Paul said. "I've had enough foolishness for one day."

"Kill me, I say!" Gurney raged.

"You know me better than that," Paul said. "How many kinds of an idiot do you think I am? Must I go through this with every man I need?"

Gurney looked at Jessica, spoke in a forlorn, pleading note so unlike him: "Then you, my Lady, please . . . you kill me."

Jessica crossed to him, put her hands on his shoulders. "Gurney, why do you insist the Atreides must kill those they love?" Gently, she pulled the spread robe out of his fingers, closed and fastened the fabric over his chest.

Gurney spoke brokenly: "But . . . I . . . ."

"You thought you were doing a thing for Leto," she said, "and for this I honor you."

"My Lady," Gurney said. He dropped his chin to his chest, squeezed his eyelids closed against the tears.

"Let us think of this as a misunderstanding among old friends," she said, and Paul heard the soothers, the adjusting tones in her voice. "It's over and we can be thankful we'll never again have that sort of misunderstanding between us."

Gurney opened eyes bright with moisture, looked down at her.

"The Gurney Halleck I knew was a man adept with both blade and baliset," Jessica said. "It was the man of the baliset I most admired. Doesn't that Gurney Halleck remember how I used to enjoy listening by the hour while he played for me? Do you still have a baliset, Gurney?"

"I've a new one," Gurney said. "Brought from Chusuk, a sweet instrument. Plays like a genuine Varota, though there's no signature on it. I think myself it was made by a student of Varota's who . . . ." He broke off. "What can I say to you, my Lady? Here we prattle about—"

"Not prattle, Gurney," Paul said. He crossed to stand beside his mother, eye to eye with Gurney. "Not prattle, but a thing that brings happiness between friends. I'd take it a kindness if you'd play for her now. Battle planning can wait a little while. We'll not be going into the fight till tomorrow at any rate."

"I . . . I'll get my baliset," Gurney said. "It's in the passage." He stepped around them and through the hangings.

Paul put a hand on his mother's arm, found that she was trembling.

"It's over, Mother," he said.

Without turning her head, she looked up at him from the corners of her eyes. "Over?"

"Of course. Gurney's . . . ."

"Gurney? Oh . . . yes." She lowered her gaze.

The hangings rustled as Gurney returned with his baliset. He began tuning it, avoiding their eyes. The hangings on the walls dulled the echoes, making the instrument sound small and intimate.

Paul led his mother to a cushion, seated her there with her back to the thick draperies of the wall. He was suddenly struck by how old she seemed to him with the beginnings of desert-dried lines in her face, the stretching at the corners of her blue-veiled eyes.

*She's tired,* he thought. *We must find some way to ease her burdens.*

Gurney strummed a chord.

Paul glanced at him, said: "I've . . . things that need my attention. Wait here for me."

Gurney nodded. His mind seemed far away, as though he dwelled for this moment beneath the open skies of Caladan with cloud fleece on the horizon promising rain.

Paul forced himself to turn away, let himself out through the heavy hangings over the side passage. He heard Gurney take up a tune behind him, and paused a moment outside the room to listen to the muted music.

"Orchards and vineyards,
And full-breasted houris,
And a cup overflowing before me.
Why do I babble of battles,
And mountains reduced to dust?
Why do I feel these tears?

Heavens stand open
And scatter their riches;
My hands need but gather their wealth.
Why do I think of an ambush,
And poison in molten cup?
Why do I feel my years?

Love's arms beckon
With their naked delights,
And Eden's promise of ecstasies.
Why do I remember the scars,
Dream of old transgressions . . .
And why do I sleep with fears?"

A robed Fedaykin courier appeared from a corner of the passage ahead of Paul. The man had hood thrown back and fastenings of his stillsuit hanging loose about his neck, proof that he had come just now from the open desert.

Paul motioned for him to stop, left the hangings of the door and moved down the passage to the courier.

The man bowed, hands clasped in front of him the way he might greet a Reverend Mother or sayyadina of the rites. He said: "Muad'Dib, leaders are beginning to arrive for the Council."

"So soon?"

"These are the ones Stilgar sent for earlier when it was thought . . . ." He shrugged.

"I see." Paul glanced back toward the faint sound of the baliset, thinking of the old song that his mother favored—an odd stretching of happy tune and sad words. "Stilgar will come here soon with others. Show them where my mother waits."

"I will wait here, Muad'Dib," the courier said.

"Yes . . . yes, do that."

Paul pressed past the man toward the depths of the cavern, headed for the place that each such cavern had—a place near its water-holding basin. There would be a small shai-hulud in this place, a creature no more than nine meters long, kept stunted and trapped by surrounding water ditches. The maker, after emerging from its little maker vector, avoided water for the poison it was. And the drowning of a maker was the greatest Fremen secret because it produced the substance of their union—the Water of Life, the poison that could only be changed by a Reverend Mother.

The decision had come to Paul while he faced the tension of danger to his mother. No line of the future he had ever seen carried that moment of peril from Gurney Halleck. The future—the gray-cloud-future—with its feeling that the entire universe rolled toward a boiling nexus hung around him like a phantom world.

*I must see it,* he thought.

His body had slowly acquired a certain spice tolerance that made prescient visions fewer and fewer . . . dimmer and dimmer. The solution appeared obvious to him.

*I will drown the maker. We will see now whether I'm the Kwisatz Haderach who can survive the test that the Reverend Mothers have survived.*

> *And it came to pass in the third year of the Desert War that Paul-Muad'Dib lay alone in the Cave of Birds beneath the kiswa hangings of an inner cell. And he lay as one dead, caught up in the revelation of the Water of Life, his being translated beyond the boundaries of time by the poison that gives life. Thus was the prophecy made true that the Lisan al-Gaib might be both dead and alive.*

**—"Collected Legends of Arrakis" by the Princess Irulan**

Chani came up out of the Habbanya basin in the predawn darkness, hearing the 'thopter that had brought her from the south go whir-whirring off to a hiding place in the vastness. Around her, the escort kept its distance, fanning out into the rocks of the ridge to probe for dangers—and giving the mate of Muad'Dib, the mother of his firstborn, the thing she had requested: a moment to walk alone.

*Why did he summon me?* she asked herself. *He told me before that I must remain in the south with little Leto and Alia.*

She gathered her robe and leaped lightly up across a barrier rock and onto the climbing path that only the desert-trained could recognize in the darkness. Pebbles slithered underfoot and she danced across them without considering the nimbleness required.

The climb was exhilarating, easing the fears that had fermented in her because of her escort's silent withdrawal and the fact that a precious 'thopter had been sent for her. She felt the inner leaping at the nearness of reunion with Paul-Muad'Dib, her Usul. His name might be a battle cry over all the land: *"Muad'Dib! Muad'Dib! Muad'Dib!"* But she knew a different man by a different name—the father of her son, the tender lover.

A great figure loomed out of the rocks above her, beckoning for speed. She quickened her pace. Dawn birds already were calling and lifting into the sky. A dim spread of light grew across the eastern horizon.

The figure above was not one of her own escort. *Otheym?* she wondered, marking a familiarity of movement and manner. She came up to him, recognized in the growing light the broad, flat features of the Fedaykin lieutenant, his hood open and mouth filter loosely fastened the way one did sometimes when venturing out onto the desert for only a moment.

"Hurry," he hissed, and led her down the secret crevasse into the hidden cave. "It will be light soon," he whispered as he held a doorseal open for her. "The Harkonnens have been making desperation patrols over some of this region. We dare not chance discovery now."

They emerged into the narrow side-passage entrance to the Cave of Birds. Glowglobes came alight. Otheym pressed past her, said: "Follow me. Quickly, now."

They sped down the passage, through another valve door, another passage and through hangings into what had been the Sayyadina's alcove in the days when this was an overday rest cave. Rugs and cushions now covered the floor. Woven hangings with the red figure of a hawk hid the rock walls. A low field desk at one side was strewn with papers from which lifted the aroma of their spice origin.

The Reverend Mother sat alone directly opposite the entrance. She looked up with the inward stare that made the uninitiated tremble.

Otheym pressed palms together, said: "I have brought Chani." He bowed, retreated through the hangings.

And Jessica thought: *How do I tell Chani?*

"How is my grandson?" Jessica asked.

*So it's to be the ritual greeting,* Chani thought, and her fears returned. *Where is Muad'Dib? Why isn't he here to greet me?*

"He is healthy and happy, my mother," Chani said. "I left him with Alia in the care of Harah."

*My mother,* Jessica thought. *Yes, she has the right to call me that in the formal greeting. She has given me a grandson.*

"I hear a gift of cloth has been sent from Coanua sietch," Jessica said.

"It is lovely cloth," Chani said.

"Does Alia send a message?"

"No message. But the sietch moves more smoothly now that the people are beginning to accept the miracle of her status."

*Why does she drag this out so?* Chani wondered. *Something was so urgent that they sent a 'thopter for me. Now, we drag through the formalities!*

"We must have some of the new cloth cut into garments for little Leto," Jessica said.

"Whatever you wish, my mother," Chani said. She lowered her gaze. "Is there news of battles?" She held her face expressionless that Jessica might not see the betrayal—that this was a question about Paul-Muad'Dib.

"New victories," Jessica said. "Rabban has sent cautious overtures about a truce. His messengers have been returned without their water. Rabban has even lightened the burdens of the people in some of the sink villages. But he is too late. The people know he does it out of fear of us."

"Thus it goes as Muad'Dib said," Chani said. She stared at Jessica, trying to keep her fears to herself. *I have spoken his name, but she has not responded. One cannot see emotion in that glazed stone she calls a face . . . but she is too frozen. Why is she so still? What has happened to my Usul?*

"I wish we were in the south," Jessica said. "The oases were so beautiful when we left. Do you not long for the day when the whole land may blossom thus?"

"The land is beautiful, true," Chani said. "But there is much grief in it."

"Grief is the price of victory," Jessica said.

*Is she preparing me for grief?* Chani asked herself. She said: "There are so many women without men. There was jealousy when it was learned that I'd been summoned north."

"I summoned you," Jessica said.

Chani felt her heart hammering. She wanted to clap her hands to her ears, fearful of what they might hear. Still, she kept her voice even: "The message was signed Muad'Dib."

"I signed it thus in the presence of his lieutenants," Jessica said. "It was a subterfuge of necessity." And Jessica thought: *This is a brave woman, my Paul's. She holds to the niceties even when fear is almost overwhelming her. Yes. She may be the one we need now.*

Only the slightest tone of resignation crept into Chani's voice as she said: "Now you may say the thing that must be said."

"You were needed here to help me revive Paul," Jessica said. And she thought: *There! I said it in the precisely correct way. Revive. Thus she knows Paul is alive and knows there is peril, all in the same word.*

Chani took only a moment to calm herself, then: "What is it I may do?" She wanted to leap at Jessica, shake her and scream: *"Take me to him!"* But she waited silently for the answer.

"I suspect," Jessica said, "that the Harkonnens have managed to send an agent among us to poison Paul. It's the only explanation that seems to fit. A most unusual poison. I've examined his blood in the most subtle ways without detecting it."

Chani thrust herself forward onto her knees. "Poison? Is he in pain? Could I . . . ."

"He is unconscious," Jessica said. "The processes of his life are so low that they can be detected only with the most refined techniques. I shudder to think what could have happened had I not been the one to discover him. He appears dead to the untrained eye."

"You have reasons other than courtesy for summoning me," Chani said. "I know you, Reverend Mother. What is it you think I may do that you cannot do?"

*She is brave, lovely and, ah-h-h, so perceptive,* Jessica thought. *She'd have made a fine Bene Gesserit.*

"Chani," Jessica said, "you may find this difficult to believe, but I do not know precisely why I sent for you. It was an instinct . . . a basic intuition. The thought came unbidden: 'Send for Chani.'"

For the first time, Chani saw the sadness in Jessica's expression, the unveiled pain modifying the inward stare.

"I've done all I know to do," Jessica said. "That *all* . . . it is so far beyond what is usually supposed as *all* that you would find difficulty imagining it. Yet . . . I failed."

"The old companion, Halleck," Chani asked, "is it possible he's a traitor?"

"Not Gurney," Jessica said.

The two words carried an entire conversation, and Chani saw the searching, the tests . . . the memories of old failures that went into this flat denial.

Chani rocked back onto her feet, stood up, smoothed her desert-stained robe. "Take me to him," she said.

Jessica arose, turned through hangings on the left wall.

Chani followed, found herself in what had been a storeroom, its rock walls concealed now beneath heavy draperies. Paul lay on a field pad against the far wall. A single glowglobe above him illuminated his face. A black robe covered him to the chest, leaving his arms outside it stretched along his sides. He appeared to be unclothed under the robe. The skin exposed looked waxen, rigid. There was no visible movement to him.

Chani suppressed the desire to dash forward, throw herself across him. She found her thoughts, instead, going to her son—Leto. And she realized in this instant that Jessica once had faced such a moment—her man threatened by death, forced in her own mind to consider what might be done to save a young son. The realization formed a sudden bond with the older woman so that Chani reached out and clasped Jessica's hand. The answering grip was painful in its intensity.

"He lives," Jessica said. "I assure you he lives. But the thread of his life is so thin it could easily escape detection. There are some among the leaders already muttering that the mother speaks and not the Reverend Mother, that my son is truly dead and I do not want to give up his water to the tribe."

"How long has he been this way?" Chani asked. She disengaged her hand from Jessica's, moved farther into the room.

"Three weeks," Jessica said. "I spent almost a week trying to revive him. There were meetings, arguments . . . investigations. Then I sent for you. The Fedaykin obey my orders, else I might not have been able to delay the . . . ." She wet her lips with her tongue, watching Chani cross to Paul.

Chani stood over him now, looking down on the soft beard of youth that framed his face, tracing with her eyes the high browline, the strong nose, the shuttered eyes—the features so peaceful in this rigid repose.

"How does he take nourishment?" Chani asked.

"The demands of his flesh are so slight he does not yet need food," Jessica said.

"How many know of what has happened?" Chani asked.

"Only his closest advisers, a few of the leaders, the Fedaykin and, of course, whoever administered the poison."

"There is no clue to the poisoner?"

"And it's not for want of investigating," Jessica said.

"What do the Fedaykin say?" Chani asked.

"They believe Paul is in a sacred trance, gathering his holy powers before the final battles. This is a thought I've cultivated."

Chani lowered herself to her knees beside the pad, bent close to Paul's face. She sensed an immediate difference in the air about his face . . . but it was only the spice, the ubiquitous spice whose odor permeated everything in Fremen life. Still . . . .

"You were not born to the spice as we were," Chani said. "Have you investigated the possibility that his body has rebelled against too much spice in his diet?"

"Allergy reactions are all negative," Jessica said.

She closed her eyes, as much to blot out this scene as because of sudden realization of fatigue. *How long have I been without sleep?* she asked herself. *Too long.*

"When you change the Water of Life," Chani said, "you do it within yourself by the inward awareness. Have you used this awareness to test his blood?"

"Normal Fremen blood," Jessica said. "Completely adapted to the diet and the life here."

Chani sat back on her heels, submerging her fears in thought as she studied Paul's face. This was a trick she had learned from watching the Reverend Mothers. Time could be made to serve the mind. One concentrated the entire attention.

Presently, Chani said: "Is there a maker here?"

"There are several," Jessica said with a touch of weariness. "We are never without them these days. Each victory requires its blessing. Each ceremony before a raid—"

"But Paul-Muad'Dib has held himself aloof from these ceremonies," Chani said.

Jessica nodded to herself, remembering her son's ambivalent feelings toward the spice drug and the prescient awareness it precipitated.

"How did you know this?" Jessica asked.

"It is spoken."

"Too much is spoken," Jessica said bitterly.

"Get me the raw Water of the maker," Chani said.

Jessica stiffened at the tone of command in Chani's voice, then observed the intense concentration in the younger woman and said: "At once." She went out through the hanging to send a waterman.

Chani sat staring at Paul. *If he has tried to do this,* she thought. *And it's the sort of thing he might try . . . .*

Jessica knelt beside Chani, holding out a plain camp ewer. The charged odor of the poison was sharp in Chani's nostrils. She dipped a finger in the fluid, held the finger close to Paul's nose.

The skin along the bridge of his nose wrinkled slightly. Slowly, the nostrils flared.

Jessica gasped.

Chani touched the dampened finger to Paul's upper lip.

He drew in a long, sobbing breath.

"What is this?" Jessica demanded.

"Be still," Chani said. "You must convert a small amount of the sacred water. Quickly!"

Without questioning, because she recognized the tone of awareness in Chani's voice, Jessica lifted the ewer to her mouth, drew in a small sip.

Paul's eyes flew open. He stared upward at Chani.

"It is not necessary for her to change the Water," he said. His voice was weak, but steady.

Jessica, a sip of the fluid on her tongue, found her body rallying, converting the poison almost automatically. In the light elevation the ceremony always imparted, she sensed the life-glow from Paul—a radiation there registering on her senses.

In that instant, she knew.

"You drank the sacred water!" she blurted.

"One drop of it," Paul said. "So small . . . one drop."

"How could you do such a foolish thing?" she demanded.

"He is your son," Chani said.

Jessica glared at her.

A rare smile, warm and full of understanding, touched Paul's lips. "Hear my beloved," he said. "Listen to her, Mother. She knows."

"A thing that others can do, he must do," Chani said.

"When I had the drop in my mouth, when I felt it and smelled it, when I knew what it was doing to me, then I knew I could do the thing that you have done," he said. "Your Bene Gesserit proctors speak of the Kwisatz Haderach, but they cannot begin to guess the many places I have been. In the few minutes I . . . ." He broke off, looking at Chani with a puzzled frown. "Chani? How did you get here? You're supposed to be . . . . Why are you here?"

He tried to push himself onto his elbows. Chani pressed him back gently.

"Please, my Usul," she said.

"I feel so weak," he said. His gaze darted around the room. "How long have I been here?"

"You've been three weeks in a coma so deep that the spark of life seemed to have fled," Jessica said.

"But it was . . . . I took it just a moment ago and . . . ."

"A moment for you, three weeks of fear for me," Jessica said.

"It was only one drop, but I converted it," Paul said. "I changed the Water of Life." And before Chani or Jessica could stop him, he dipped his hand into the ewer they had placed on the floor beside him, and he brought the dripping hand to his mouth, swallowed the palm-cupped liquid.

"Paul!" Jessica screamed.

He grabbed her hand, faced her with a death's head grin, and he sent his awareness surging over her.

The rapport was not as tender, not as sharing, not as encompassing as it had been with Alia and with the Old Reverend Mother in the cavern . . . but it was a rapport: a sense-sharing of the entire being. It shook her, weakened her, and she cowered in her mind, fearful of him.

Aloud, he said: "You speak of a place where you cannot enter? This place which the Reverend Mother cannot face, show it to me."

She shook her head, terrified by the very thought.

"Show it to me!" he commanded.

"No!"

But she could not escape him. Bludgeoned by the terrible force of him, she closed her eyes and focused inward—the-direction-that-is-dark.

Paul's consciousness flowed through and around her and into the darkness. She glimpsed the place dimly before her mind blanked itself away from the terror. Without knowing why, her whole being trembled at what she had seen—a region where a wind blew and sparks glared, where rings of light expanded and contracted, where rows of tumuescent white shapes flowed over and under and around the lights, driven by darkness and a wind out of nowhere.

Presently, she opened her eyes, saw Paul staring up at her. He still held her hand, but the terrible rapport was gone. She quieted her trembling. Paul released her hand. It was as though some crutch had been removed. She staggered up and back, would have fallen had not Chani jumped to support her.

"Reverend Mother!" Chani said. "What is wrong?"

"Tired," Jessica whispered. "So . . . tired."

"Here," Chani said. "Sit here." She helped Jessica to a cushion against the wall.

The strong young arms felt so good to Jessica. She clung to Chani.

"He has, in truth, seen the Water of Life?" Chani asked. She disengaged herself from Jessica's grip.

"He has seen," Jessica whispered. Her mind still rolled and surged from the contact. It was like stepping to solid land after weeks on a heaving sea. She sensed the old Reverend Mother within her . . . and all the others awakened and questioning: *"What was that? What happened? Where was that place?"*

Through it all threaded the realization that her son was the Kwisatz Haderach, the one who could be many places at once. He was the fact out of the Bene Gesserit dream. And the fact gave her no peace.

"What happened?" Chani demanded.

Jessica shook her head.

Paul said: "There is in each of us an ancient force that takes and an ancient force that gives. A man finds little difficulty facing that place within himself where the taking force dwells, but it's almost impossible for him to see into the giving force without changing into something other than man. For a woman, the situation is reversed."

Jessica looked up, found Chani was staring at her while listening to Paul.

"Do you understand me, Mother?" Paul asked.

She could only nod.

"These things are so ancient within us," Paul said, "that they're ground into each separate cell of our bodies. We're shaped by such forces. You can say to yourself, 'Yes, I see how such a thing may be.' But when you look inward and confront the raw force of your own life unshielded, you see your peril. You see that this could overwhelm you. The greatest peril to the Giver is the force that takes. The greatest peril to the Taker is the force that gives. It's as easy to be overwhelmed by giving as by taking."

"And you, my son," Jessica asked, "are you one who gives or one who takes?"

"I'm the fulcrum," he said. "I cannot give without taking and I cannot take without . . . ." He broke off, looking to the wall at his right.

Chani felt a draft against her cheek, turned to see the hangings close.

"It was Otheym," Paul said. "He was listening."

Accepting the words, Chani was touched by some of the prescience that haunted Paul, and she knew a thing-yet-to-be as though it already had occurred. Otheym would speak of what he had seen and heard. Others would spread the story until it was a fire over the land. Paul-Muad'Dib is not as other men, they would say. There can be no more doubt. He is a man, yet he sees through to the Water of Life in the way of a Reverend Mother. He is indeed the Lisan al-Gaib.

"You have seen the future, Paul," Jessica said. "Will you say what you've seen?"

"Not the future," he said. "I've seen the Now." He forced himself to a sitting position, waved Chani aside as she moved to help him. "The space above Arrakis is filled with the ships of the Guild."

Jessica trembled at the certainty in his voice.

"The Padishah Emperor himself is there," Paul said. He looked at the rock ceiling of his cell. "With his favorite Truthsayer and five legions of Sardaukar. The old Baron Vladimir Harkonnen is there with Thufir Hawat beside him and seven ships jammed with every conscript he could muster. Every Great House has its raiders above us . . . waiting."

Chani shook her head, unable to look away from Paul. His strangeness, the flat tone of voice, the way he looked through her, filled her with awe.

Jessica tried to swallow in a dry throat, said: "For what are they waiting?"

Paul looked at her. "For the Guild's permission to land. The Guild will strand on Arrakis any force that lands without permission."

"The Guild's protecting us?" Jessica asked.

"Protecting us! The Guild itself caused this by spreading tales about what we do here and by reducing troop transport fares to a point where even the poorest Houses are up there now waiting to loot us."

Jessica noted the lack of bitterness in his tone, wondered at it. She couldn't doubt his words—they had that same intensity she'd seen in him the night he'd revealed the path of the future that'd taken them among the Fremen.

Paul took a deep breath, said: "Mother, you must change a quantity of the

Water for us. We need the catalyst. Chani, have a scout force sent out . . . to find a pre-spice mass. If we plant a quantity of the Water of Life above a pre-spice mass, do you know what will happen?"

Jessica weighed his words, suddenly saw through to his meaning. "Paul!" she gasped.

"The Water of Death," he said. "It'd be a chain reaction." He pointed to the floor. "Spreading death among the little makers, killing a vector of the life cycle that includes the spice and the makers. Arrakis will become a true desolation—without spice or maker."

Chani put a hand to her mouth, shocked to numb silence by the blasphemy pouring from Paul's lips.

"He who can destroy a thing has the real control of it," Paul said. "We can destroy the spice."

"What stays the Guild's hand?" Jessica whispered.

"They're searching for me," Paul said. "Think of that! The finest Guild navigators, men who can quest ahead through time to find the safest course for the fastest Heighliners, all of them seeking me . . . and unable to find me. How they tremble! They know I have their secret here!" Paul held out his cupped hand. "Without the spice they're blind!"

Chani found her voice. "You said you see the *now!*"

Paul lay back, searching the spread-out *present*, its limits extended into the future and into the past, holding onto the awareness with difficulty as the spice illumination began to fade.

"Go do as I commanded," he said. "The future's becoming as muddled for the Guild as it is for me. The lines of vision are narrowing. Everything focuses here where the spice is . . . where they've dared not interfere before . . . because to interfere was to lose what they must have. But now they're desperate. All paths lead into darkness."

*And that day dawned when Arrakis lay at the hub of the universe with the wheel poised to spin.*

**—from "Arrakis Awakening" by the Princess Irulan**

"Will you look at that thing!" Stilgar whispered.

Paul lay beside him in a slit of rock high on the Shield Wall rim, eye fixed to the collector of a Fremen telescope. The oil lens was focused on a starship lighter exposed by dawn in the basin below them. The tall eastern face of the ship glistened in the flat light of the sun, but the shadow side still showed yellow portholes from glowglobes of the night. Beyond the ship, the city of Arrakeen lay cold and gleaming in the light of the northern sun.

It wasn't the lighter that excited Stilgar's awe, Paul knew, but the construction for which the lighter was only the centerpost. A single metal hutment, many stories tall, reached out in a thousand-meter circle from the base of the lighter—a tent composed of interlocking metal leaves—the temporary lodging place for five legions of Sardaukar and His Imperial Majesty, the Padishah Emperor Shaddam IV.

From his position squatting at Paul's left, Gurney Halleck said: "I count nine levels to it. Must be quite a few Sardaukar in there."

"Five legions," Paul said.

"It grows light," Stilgar hissed. "We like it not, your exposing yourself, Muad'Dib. Let us go back into the rocks now."

"I'm perfectly safe here," Paul said.

"That ship mounts projectile weapons," Gurney said.

"They believe us protected by shields," Paul said. "They wouldn't waste a shot on an unidentified trio even if they saw us."

Paul swung the telescope to scan the far wall of the basin, seeing the pock-marked cliffs, the slides that marked the tombs of so many of his father's troopers. And he had a momentary sense of the fitness of things that the shades of those men should look down on this moment. The Harkonnen forts and towns across the shielded lands lay in Fremen hands or cut away from their source like stalks severed from a plant and left to wither. Only this basin and its city remained to the enemy.

"They might try a sortie by 'thopter," Stilgar said. "If they see us."

"Let them," Paul said. "We've 'thopters to burn today . . . and we know a storm is coming."

He swung the telescope to the far side of the Arrakeen landing field now, to the Harkonnen frigates lined up there with a CHOAM Company banner waving gently from its staff on the ground beneath them. And he thought of the desperation that had forced the Guild to permit these two groups to land while the others were held in reserve. The Guild was like a man testing the sand with his toe to gauge its temperature before erecting a tent.

"Is there anything new to see from here?" Gurney asked. "We should be getting under cover. The storm *is* coming."

Paul returned his attention on the giant hutment. "They've even brought their women," he said. "And lackeys and servants. Ah-h-h, my dear Emperor, how confident you are."

"Men are coming up the secret way," Stilgar said. "It may be Otheym and Korba returning."

"All right, Stil," Paul said. "We'll go back."

But he took one final look around through the telescope—studying the plain with its tall ships, the gleaming metal hutment, the silent city, the frigates of the Harkonnen mercenaries. Then he slid backward around a scarp of rock. His place at the telescope was taken by a Fedaykin guardsman.

Paul emerged into a shallow depression in the Shield Wall's surface. It was a place about thirty meters in diameter and some three meters deep, a natural feature of the rock that the Fremen had hidden beneath a translucent camouflage cover. Communications equipment was clustered around a hole in the wall to the right. Fedaykin guards deployed through the depression waited for Muad'Dib's command to attack.

Two men emerged from the hole by the communications equipment, spoke to the guards there.

Paul glanced at Stilgar, nodded in the direction of the two men. "Get their report, Stil."

Stilgar moved to obey.

Paul crouched with his back to the rock, stretching his muscles, straightened. He saw Stilgar sending the two men back into that dark hole in the rock, thought about the long climb down that narrow man-made tunnel to the floor of the basin.

Stilgar crossed to Paul.

"What was so important that they couldn't send a cielago with the message?" Paul asked.

"They're saving their birds for the battle," Stilgar said. He glanced at the communications equipment, back to Paul. "Even with a tight beam, it is wrong to use those things, Muad'Dib. They can find you by taking a bearing on its emission."

"They'll soon be too busy to find me," Paul said. "What did the men report?"

"Our pet Sardaukar have been released near Old Gap low on the rim and are on their way to their master. The rocket launchers and other projectile weapons are in place. The people are deployed as you ordered. It was all routine."

Paul glanced across the shallow bowl, studying his men in the filtered light admitted by the camouflage cover. He felt time creeping like an insect working its way across an exposed rock.

"It'll take our Sardaukar a little time afoot before they can signal a troop carrier," Paul said. "They are being watched?"

"They are being watched," Stilgar said.

Beside Paul, Gurney Halleck cleared his throat. "Hadn't we best be getting to a place of safety?"

"There is no such place," Paul said. "Is the weather report still favorable?"

"A great grandmother of a storm coming," Stilgar said. "Can you not feel it, Muad'Dib?"

"The air does feel chancy," Paul agreed. "But I like the certainty of poling the weather."

"The storm'll be here in the hour," Stilgar said. He nodded toward the gap that looked out on the Emperor's hutment and the Harkonnen frigates. "They know it there, too. Not a 'thopter in the sky. Everything pulled in and tied down. They've had a report on the weather from their friends in space."

"Any more probing sorties?" Paul asked.

"Nothing since the landing last night," Stilgar said. "They know we're here. I think now they wait to choose their own time."

"We choose the time," Paul said.

Gurney glanced upward, growled: "If *they* let us."

"That fleet'll stay in space," Paul said.

Gurney shook his head.

"They have no choice," Paul said. "We can destroy the spice. The Guild dares not risk that."

"Desperate people are the most dangerous," Gurney said.

"Are we not desperate?" Stilgar asked.

Gurney scowled at him.

"You haven't lived with the Fremen dream," Paul cautioned. "Stil is thinking of all the water we've spent on bribes, the years of waiting we've added before Arrakis can bloom. He's not—"

"Arrrgh," Gurney growled.

"Why's he so gloomy?" Stilgar asked.

"He's always gloomy before a battle," Paul said. "It's the only form of good humor Gurney allows himself."

A slow, wolfish grin spread across Gurney's face, the teeth showing white above the chin cup of his stillsuit. "It glooms me much to think on all the poor Harkonnen souls we'll dispatch unshriven," he said.

Stilgar chuckled. "He talks like a Fedaykin."

"Gurney was born a death commando," Paul said. And he thought: *Yes, let them occupy their minds with small talk before we test ourselves against that force on the plain.* He looked to the gap in the rock wall and back to Gurney, found that the troubadour-warrior had resumed a brooding scowl.

"Worry saps the strength," Paul murmured. "You told me that once, Gurney."

"My Duke," Gurney said, "my chief worry is the atomics. If you use them to blast a hole in the Shield Wall . . . ."

"Those people up there won't use atomics against us," Paul said. "They don't dare . . . and for the same reason that they cannot risk our destroying the source of the spice."

"But the injunction against—"

"The injunction!" Paul barked. "It's fear, not the injunction that keeps the Houses from hurling atomics against each other. The language of the Great Convention is clear enough: 'Use of atomics against humans shall be cause for planetary obliteration.' We're going to blast the Shield Wall, not humans."

"It's too fine a point," Gurney said.

"The hair-splitters up there will welcome any point," Paul said. "Let's talk no more about it."

He turned away, wishing he actually felt that confident. Presently, he said: "What about the city people? Are they in position yet?"

"Yes," Stilgar muttered.

Paul looked at him. "What's eating you?"

"I never knew the city man could be trusted completely," Stilgar said.

"I was a city man myself once," Paul said.

Stilgar stiffened. His face grew dark with blood. "Muad'Dib knows I did not mean—"

"I know what you meant, Stil. But the test of a man isn't what you think he'll do. It's what he actually does. These city people have Fremen blood. It's just that they haven't yet learned how to escape their bondage. We'll teach them."

Stilgar nodded, spoke in a rueful tone: "The habits of a lifetime, Muad'Dib. On the Funeral Plain we learned to despise the men of the communities."

Paul glanced at Gurney, saw him studying Stilgar. "Tell us, Gurney, why were the cityfolk down there driven from their homes by the Sardaukar?"

"An old trick, my Duke. They thought to burden us with refugees."

"It's been so long since guerrillas were effective that the mighty have forgotten how to fight them," Paul said. "The Sardaukar have played into our hands. They grabbed some city women for their sport, decorated their battle standards with the heads of the men who objected. And they've built up a fever of hate among people who otherwise would've looked on the coming battle as no more than a great inconvenience . . . and the possibility of exchanging one set of masters for another. The Sardaukar recruit for us, Stilgar."

"The city people do seem eager," Stilgar said.

"Their hate is fresh and clear," Paul said. "That's why we use them as shock troops."

"The slaughter among them will be fearful," Gurney said.

Stilgar nodded agreement.

"They were told the odds," Paul said. "They know every Sardaukar they kill will be one less for us. You see, gentlemen, they have something to die for. They've discovered they're a people. They're awakening."

A muttered exclamation came from the watcher at the telescope. Paul moved to the rock slit, asked: "What is it out there?"

"A great commotion, Muad'Dib," the watcher hissed. "At that monstrous metal tent. A surface car came from Rimwall West and it was like a hawk into a nest of rock partridge."

"Our captive Sardaukar have arrived," Paul said.

"They've a shield around the entire landing field now," the watcher said. "I can see the air dancing even to the edge of the storage yard where they kept the spice."

"Now they know who it is they fight," Gurney said. "Let the Harkonnen beasts tremble and fret themselves that an Atreides yet lives!"

Paul spoke to the Fedaykin at the telescope. "Watch the flagpole atop the Emperor's ship. If my flag is raised there—"

"It will not be," Gurney said.

Paul saw the puzzled frown on Stilgar's face, said: "If the Emperor recognizes my claim, he'll signal by restoring the Atreides flag to Arrakis. We'll use the second plan then, move only against the Harkonnens. The Sardaukar will stand aside and let us settle the issue between ourselves."

"I've no experience with these offworld things," Stilgar said. "I've heard of them, but it seems unlikely the—"

"You don't need experience to know what they'll do," Gurney said.

"They're sending a new flag up on the tall ship," the watcher said. "The flag is yellow . . . with a black and red circle in the center."

"There's a subtle piece of business," Paul said. "The CHOAM Company flag."

"It's the same as the flag at the other ships," the Fedaykin guard said.

"I don't understand," Stilgar said.

"A subtle piece of business indeed," Gurney said. "Had he sent up the Atreides banner, he'd have had to live by what that meant. Too many observers about. He could've signaled with the Harkonnen flag on his staff—a flat declaration that'd have been. But, no—he sends up the CHOAM rag. He's telling the people up there . . . ." Gurney pointed toward space. ". . . where the profit is. He's saying he doesn't care if it's an Atreides here or not."

"How long till the storm strikes the Shield Wall?" Paul asked.

Stilgar turned away, consulted one of the Fedaykin in the bowl. Presently, he returned, said: "Very soon, Muad'Dib. Sooner than we expected. It's a great-great-grandmother of a storm . . . perhaps even more than you wished."

"It's my storm," Paul said, and saw the silent awe on the faces of the Fedaykin who heard him. "Though it shook the entire world it could not be more than I wished. Will it strike the Shield Wall full on?"

"Close enough to make no difference," Stilgar said.

A courier crossed from the hole that led down into the basin, said: "The Sardaukar and Harkonnen patrols are pulling back, Muad'Dib."

"They expect the storm to spill too much sand into the basin for good visibility," Stilgar said. "They think we'll be in the same fix."

"Tell our gunners to set their sights well before visibility drops," Paul said. "They must knock the nose off every one of those ships as soon as the storm has destroyed the shields." He stepped to the wall of the bowl, pulled back a fold of the camouflage cover and looked up at the sky. The horsetail twistings of blown sand could be seen against the dark of the sky. Paul restored the cover, said: "Start sending our men down, Stil."

"Will you not go with us?" Stilgar asked.

"I'll wait here a bit with the Fedaykin," Paul said.

Stilgar gave a knowing shrug toward Gurney, moved to the hole in the rock wall, was lost in its shadows.

"The trigger that blasts the Shield Wall aside, that I leave in your hands," Paul said. "You will do it?"

"I'll do it."

Paul gestured to a Fedaykin lieutenant, said: "Otheym, start moving the check patrols out of the blast area. They must be out of there before the storm strikes."

The man bowed, followed Stilgar.

Gurney leaned in to the rock slit, spoke to the man at the telescope: "Keep your attention on the south wall. It'll be completely undefended until we blow it."

"Dispatch a cielago with a time signal," Paul ordered.

"Some ground cars are moving toward the south wall," the man at the telescope said. "Some are using projectile weapons, testing. Our people are using body shields as you commanded. The ground cars have stopped."

In the abrupt silence, Paul heard the wind devils playing overhead—the front of the storm. Sand began to drift down into their bowl through gaps in the cover. A burst of wind caught the cover, whipped it away.

Paul motioned his Fedaykin to take shelter, crossed to the men at the communications equipment near the tunnel mouth. Gurney stayed beside him. Paul crouched over the signalmen.

One said: "A great-great-*great* grandmother of a storm, Muad'Dib."

Paul glanced up at the darkening sky, said: "Gurney, have the south wall observers pulled out." He had to repeat his order, shouting above the growing noise of the storm.

Gurney turned to obey.

Paul fastened his face filter, tightened the stillsuit hood.

Gurney returned.

Paul touched his shoulder, pointed to the blast trigger set into the tunnel mouth beyond the signalmen. Gurney went into the tunnel, stopped there, one hand at the trigger, his gaze on Paul.

"We are getting no messages," the signalman beside Paul said. "Much static."

Paul nodded, kept his eye on the time-standard dial in front of the signalman. Presently, Paul looked at Gurney, raised a hand, returned his attention to the dial. The time counter crawled around its final circuit.

"Now!" Paul shouted, and dropped his hand.

Gurney depressed the blast trigger.

It seemed that a full second passed before they felt the ground beneath them ripple and shake. A rumbling sound was added to the storm's roar.

The Fedaykin watcher from the telescope appeared beside Paul, the telescope clutched under one arm. "The Shield Wall is breached, Muad'Dib!" he shouted. "The storm is on them and our gunners already are firing."

Paul thought of the storm sweeping across the basin, the static charge within the wall of sand that destroyed every shield barrier in the enemy camp.

"The storm!" someone shouted. "We must get under cover, Muad'Dib!"

Paul came to his senses, feeling the sand needles sting his exposed cheeks. *We are committed,* he thought. He put an arm around the signalman's shoulder, said: "Leave the equipment! There's more in the tunnel." He felt himself being pulled away, Fedaykin pressed around him to protect him. They squeezed into the tunnel mouth, feeling its comparative silence, turned a corner into a small chamber with glowglobes overhead and another tunnel opening beyond.

Another signalman sat there at his equipment.

"Much static," the man said.

A swirl of sand filled the air around them.

"Seal off this tunnel!" Paul shouted. A sudden pressure of stillness showed that his command had been obeyed. "Is the way down to the basin still open?" Paul asked.

A Fedaykin went to look, returned, said: "The explosion caused a little rock to fall, but the engineers say it is still open. They're cleaning up with lasbeams."

"Tell them to use their hands!" Paul barked. "There are shields active down there!"

"They are being careful, Muad'Dib," the man said, but he turned to obey.

The signalmen from outside pressed past them carrying their equipment.

"I told those men to leave their equipment!" Paul said.

"Fremen do not like to abandon equipment, Muad'Dib," one of his Fedaykin chided.

"Men are more important than equipment now," Paul said. "We'll have more equipment than we can use soon or have no need for any equipment."

Gurney Halleck came up beside him, said: "I heard them say the way down is open. We're very close to the surface here, m'Lord, should the Harkonnens try to retaliate in kind."

"They're in no position to retaliate," Paul said. "They're just now finding out that they have no shields and are unable to get off Arrakis."

"The new command post is all prepared, though, m'Lord," Gurney said.

"They've no need of me in the command post yet," Paul said. "The plan would go ahead without me. We must wait for the—"

"I'm getting a message, Muad'Dib," said the signalman at the communications equipment. The man shook his head, pressed a receiver phone against his ear. "Much static!" He began scribbling on a pad in front of him, shaking his head waiting, writing . . . waiting.

Paul crossed to the signalman's side. The Fedaykin stepped back, giving him room. He looked down at what the man had written, read:

"Raid . . . on Sietch Tabr . . . captives . . . Alia (blank) families of (blank) dead are . . . they (blank) son of Muad'Dib . . . ."

Again, the signalman shook his head.

Paul looked up to see Gurney staring at him.

"The message is garbled," Gurney said. "The static. You don't know that . . . ."

"My son is dead," Paul said, and knew as he spoke that it was true. "My son is dead . . . and Alia is a captive . . . hostage." He felt emptied, a shell without emotions. Everything he touched brought death and grief. And it was like a disease that could spread across the universe.

He could feel the old-man wisdom, the accumulation out of the experiences from countless possible lives. Something seemed to chuckle and rub its hands within him.

And Paul thought: *How little the universe knows about the nature of real cruelty!*

> *And Muad'Dib stood before them, and he said: "Though we deem the captive dead, yet does she live. For her seed is my seed and her voice is my voice. And she sees unto the farthest reaches of possibility. Yea, unto the vale of the unknowable does she see because of me."*

> **—from "Arrakis Awakening" by the Princess Irulan**

The Baron Vladimir Harkonnen stood with eyes downcast in the Imperial audience chamber, the oval selamlik within the Padishah Emperor's hutment.

With covert glances, the Baron had studied the metal-walled room and its occupants—the noukkers, the pages, the guards, the troop of House Sardaukar drawn up around the walls, standing at ease there beneath the bloody and tattered captured battle flags that were the room's only decoration.

Voices sounded from the right of the chamber, echoing out of a high passage: "Make way! Make way for the Royal Person!"

The Padishah Emperor Shaddam IV came out of the passage into the audience chamber followed by his suite. He stood waiting while his throne was brought, ignoring the Baron, seemingly ignoring every person in the room.

The Baron found that he could not ignore the Royal Person, and studied the Emperor for a sign, any clue to the purpose of this audience. The Emperor stood poised, waiting—a slim, elegant figure in a grey Sardaukar uniform with silver and gold trim. His thin face and cold eyes reminded the Baron of the Duke Leto long dead. There was that same look of the predatory bird. But the Emperor's hair was red, not black, and most of that hair was concealed by a Burseg's ebon helmet with the Imperial crest in gold upon its crown.

Pages brought the throne. It was a massive chair carved from a single piece of Hagal quartz—blue-green translucency shot through with streaks of yellow fire. They placed it on the dais and the Emperor mounted, seated himself.

An old woman in a black aba robe with hood drawn down over her forehead detached herself from the Emperor's suite, took up station behind the throne, one scrawny hand resting on the quartz back. Her face peered out of the hood like a witch caricature—sunken cheeks and eyes, an overlong nose, skin mottled and with protruding veins.

The Baron stilled his trembling at sight of her. The presence of the Reverend Mother Gaius Helen Mohiam, the Emperor's Truthsayer, betrayed the importance of this audience. The Baron looked away from her, studied the suite for a clue. There were two of the Guild agents, one tall and fat, one short and fat, both with bland gray eyes. And among the lackeys stood one of the Emperor's daughters, the Princess Irulan, a woman they said was being trained in the deepest of the Bene Gesserit ways, destined to be a Reverend Mother. She was tall, blonde, face of chiseled beauty, green eyes that looked past and through him.

"My dear Baron."

The Emperor had deigned to notice him. The voice was baritone and with exquisite control. It managed to dismiss him while greeting him.

The Baron bowed low, advanced to the required ten paces from the dais. "I came at your summons, Majesty."

"Summons!" the old witch cackled.

"Now, Reverend Mother," the Emperor chided, but he smiled at the Baron's discomfiture, said: "First, you will tell me where you've sent your minion, Thufir Hawat."

The Baron darted his gaze left and right, reviled himself for coming here without his own guards, not that they'd be much use against Sardaukar. Still . . . .

"Well?" the Emperor said.

"He has been gone these five days, Majesty." The Baron shot a glance at the Guild agents, back to the Emperor. "He was to land at a smuggler base and attempt infiltrating the camp of the Fremen fanatic, this Muad'Dib."

"Incredible!" the Emperor said.

One of the witch's clawlike hands tapped the Emperor's shoulder. She leaned forward, whispered in his ear.

The Emperor nodded, said: "Five days, Baron. Tell me, why aren't you worried about his absence?"

"But I *am* worried, Majesty!"

The Emperor continued to stare at him, waiting. The Reverend Mother emitted a cackling laugh.

"What I mean, Majesty," the Baron said, "is that Hawat will be dead within another few hours anyway." And he explained about the latent poison and need for an antidote.

"How clever of you, Baron," the Emperor said. "And where are your nephews, Rabban and the young Feyd-Rautha?"

"The storm comes, Majesty. I sent them to inspect our perimeter lest the Fremen attack under cover of the sand."

"Perimeter," the Emperor said. The word came out as though it puckered his mouth. "The storm won't be much here in the basin, and that Fremen rabble won't attack while I'm here with five legions of Sardaukar."

"Surely not, Majesty," the Baron said, "but error on the side of caution cannot be censured."

"Ah-h-h-h," the Emperor said. "Censure. Then I'm not to speak of how much time this Arrakis nonsense has taken from me? Nor the CHOAM Company profits pouring down this rat hole? Not the court functions and affairs of state I've had to delay—even cancel—because of this stupid affair?"

The Baron lowered his gaze, frightened by the Imperial anger. The delicacy of his position here, alone and dependent upon the Convention and the dictum familia of the Great Houses, fretted him. *Does he mean to kill me?* the Baron asked himself. *He couldn't! Not with the other Great Houses waiting up there, aching for any excuse to gain from this upset on Arrakis.*

"Have you taken hostages?" the Emperor asked.

"It's useless, Majesty," the Baron said. "These mad Fremen hold a burial ceremony for every captive and act as though such a one were already dead."

"So?" the Emperor said.

And the Baron waited, glancing left and right at the metal walls of the selamlik, thinking of the monstrous fanmetal tent around him. Such unlimited wealth it represented that even the Baron was awed. *He brings pages,* the Baron thought, *and useless court lackeys, his women and their companions—hairdressers, designers, everything . . . all the fringe parasites of the Court. All here—fawning, slyly plotting, "roughing it" with the Emperor . . . here to watch him put an end to this affair, to make epigrams over the battles and idolize the wounded.*

"Perhaps you've never sought the right kind of hostages," the Emperor said.

*He knows something,* the Baron thought. Fear sat like a stone in his stomach until he could hardly bear the thought of eating. Yet, the feeling was like hunger, and he poised himself several times in his suspensors on the point of ordering food brought to him. But there was no one here to obey his summons.

"Do you have any idea who this Muad'Dib could be?" the Emperor asked.

"One of the Umma, surely," the Baron said. "A Fremen fanatic, a religious adventurer. They crop up regularly on the fringes of civilization. Your Majesty knows this."

The Emperor glanced at his Truthsayer, turned back to scowl at the Baron. "And you have no other knowledge of this Muad'Dib?"

"A madman," the Baron said. "But all Fremen are a little mad."

"Mad?"

"His people scream his name as they leap into battle. The women throw their babies at us and hurl themselves onto our knives to open a wedge for their men to attack us. They have no . . . no . . . decency!"

"As bad as that," the Emperor murmured, and his tone of derision did not escape the Baron. "Tell me, my dear Baron, have you investigated the southern polar regions of Arrakis?"

The Baron stared up at the Emperor, shocked by the change of subject. "But . . . well, you know, Your Majesty, the entire region is uninhabitable, open to wind and worm. There's not even any spice in those latitudes."

"You've had no reports from spice lighters that patches of greenery appear there?"

"There've always been such reports. Some were investigated—long ago. A few plants were seen. Many 'thopters were lost. Much too costly, Your Majesty. It's a place where men cannot survive for long."

"So," the Emperor said. He snapped his fingers and a door opened at his left behind the throne. Through the door came two Sardaukar herding a girl-child who appeared to be about four years old. She wore a black aba, the hood thrown back to reveal the attachments of a stillsuit hanging free at her throat. Her eyes were Fremen blue, staring out of a soft, round face. She appeared completely unafraid and there was a look to her stare that made the Baron feel uneasy for no reason he could explain.

Even the old Bene Gesserit Truthsayer drew back as the child passed and made a warding sign in her direction. The old witch obviously was shaken by the child's presence.

The Emperor cleared his throat to speak, but the child spoke first—a thin voice with traces of a soft-palate lisp, but clear nonetheless. "So here he is," she said. She advanced to the edge of the dais. "He doesn't appear much, does he—one frightened old fat man too weak to support his own flesh without the help of suspensors."

It was such a totally unexpected statement from the mouth of a child that the Baron stared at her, speechless in spite of his anger. *Is it a midget?* he asked himself.

"My dear Baron," the Emperor said, "become acquainted with the sister of Muad'Dib."

"The sist . . . ." The Baron shifted his attention to the Emperor. "I do not understand."

"I, too, sometimes err on the side of caution," the Emperor said. "It has been reported to me that your *uninhabited* south polar regions exhibit evidence of human activity."

"But that's impossible!" the Baron protested. "The worms . . . there's sand clear to the . . . ."

"These people seem able to avoid the worms," the Emperor said.

The child sat down on the dais beside the throne, dangled her feet over the edge, kicking them. There was such an air of sureness in the way she appraised her surroundings.

The Baron stared at the kicking feet, the way they moved the black robe, the wink of sandals beneath the fabric.

"Unfortunately," the Emperor said, "I only sent five troop carriers with a light attack force to pick up prisoners for questioning. We barely got away with three prisoners and one carrier. Mind you, Baron, my Sardaukar were almost overwhelmed by a force composed mostly of women, children, and old men. This child here was in command of one of the attacking groups."

"You see, Your Majesty!" the Baron said. "You see how they are!"

"I allowed myself to be captured," the child said. "I did not want to face my brother and have to tell him that his son had been killed."

"Only a handful of our men got away," the Emperor said. "Got away! You hear that?"

"We'd have had them, too," the child said, "except for the flames."

"My Sardaukar used the attitudinal jets on their carrier as flame-throwers," the Emperor said. "A move of desperation and the only thing that got them away with their three prisoners. Mark that, my dear Baron: Sardaukar forced to retreat in confusion from women and children and old men!"

"We must attack in force," the Baron rasped. "We must destroy every last vestige of—"

"Silence!" the Emperor roared. He pushed himself forward on his throne. "Do not abuse my intelligence any longer. You stand there in your foolish innocence and—"

"Majesty," the old Truthsayer said.

He waved her to silence. "You say you don't know about the activity we found, not the fighting qualities of these superb people!" The Emperor lifted himself half off his throne. "What do you take me for, Baron?"

The Baron took two backward steps, thinking: *It was Rabban. He has done this to me. Rabban has . . . .*

"And this fake dispute with Duke Leto," the Emperor purred, sinking back into his throne. "How beautifully you maneuvered it."

"Majesty," the Baron pleaded. "What are you—"

"Silence!"

The old Bene Gesserit put a hand on the Emperor's shoulder, leaned close to whisper in his ear.

The child seated on the dais stopped kicking her feet, said: "Make him afraid some more, Shaddam. I shouldn't enjoy this, but I find the pleasure impossible to suppress."

"Quiet, child," the Emperor said. He leaned forward, put a hand on her head, stared at the Baron. "Is it possible, Baron? Could you be as simple-minded as my Truthsayer suggests? Do you not recognize this child, daughter of your ally, Duke Leto?"

"My father was never his ally," the child said. "My father is dead and this old Harkonnen beast has never seen me before."

The Baron was reduced to stupefied glaring. When he found his voice it was only to rasp: "Who?"

"I am Alia, daughter of Duke Leto and the Lady Jessica, sister of Duke Paul-Muad'Dib," the child said. She pushed herself off the dais, dropped to the floor of the audience chamber. "My brother has promised to have your head atop his battle standard and I think he shall."

"Be hush, child," the Emperor said, and he sank back into his throne, hand to chin, studying the Baron.

"I do not take the Emperor's orders," Alia said. She turned, looked up at the old Reverend Mother. "She knows."

The Emperor glanced up at the Truthsayer. "What does she mean?"

"That child is an abomination!" the old woman said. "Her mother deserves a punishment greater than anything in history. Death! It cannot come too quickly for that *child* or for the one who spawned her!" The old woman pointed a finger at Alia. "Get out of my mind!"

"T-P?" the Emperor whispered. He snapped his attention back to Alia. "By the Great Mother!"

"You don't understand, Majesty," the old woman said. "Not telepathy. She's in my mind. She's like the ones before me, the ones who gave me their memories. She stands in my mind! She cannot be there, but she is!"

"What others?" the Emperor demanded. "What's this nonsense?"

The old woman straightened, lowered her pointing hand. "I've said too much, but the fact remains that this *child* who is not a child must be destroyed. Long were we warned against such a one and how to prevent such a birth, but one of our own has betrayed us."

"You babble, old woman," Alia said. "You don't know how it was, yet you rattle on like a purblind fool." Alia closed her eyes, took a deep breath, and held it.

The old Reverend Mother groaned and staggered.

Alia opened her eyes. "That is how it was," she said. "A cosmic accident . . . and you played your part in it."

The Reverend Mother held out both hands, palms pushing the air toward Alia.

"What is happening here?" the Emperor demanded. "Child, can you truly project your thoughts into the mind of another?"

"That's not how it is at all," Alia said. "Unless I'm born as you, I cannot think as you."

"Kill her," the old woman muttered, and clutched the back of the throne for support. "Kill her!" The sunken old eyes glared at Alia.

"Silence," the Emperor said, and he studied Alia. "Child, can you communicate with your brother?"

"My brother knows I'm here," Alia said.

"Can you tell him to surrender as the price of your life?"

Alia smiled up at him with clear innocence. "I shall not do that," she said.

The Baron stumbled forward to stand beside Alia. "Majesty," he pleaded, "I knew nothing of—"

"Interrupt me once more, Baron," the Emperor said, "and you will lose the powers of interruption . . . forever." He kept his attention focused on Alia, studying her through slitted lids. "You will not, eh? Can you read in my mind what I'll do if you disobey me?"

"I've already said I cannot read minds," she said, "but one doesn't need telepathy to read your intentions."

The Emperor scowled. "Child, your cause is hopeless. I have but to rally my forces and reduce this planet to—"

"It's not that simple," Alia said. She looked at the two Guildsmen. "Ask them."

"It is not wise to go against my desires," the Emperor said. "You should not deny me the least thing."

"My brother comes now," Alia said. "Even an Emperor may tremble before Muad'Dib, for he has the strength of righteousness and heaven smiles upon him."

The Emperor surged to his feet. "This play has gone far enough. I will take your brother and this planet and grind them to—"

The room rumbled and shook around them. There came a sudden cascade of sand behind the throne where the hutment was coupled to the Emperor's ship. The abrupt flicker-tightening of skin pressure told of a wide-area shield being activated.

"I told you," Alia said. "My brother comes."

The Emperor stood in front of his throne, right hand pressed to right ear, the servo-receiver there chattering its report on the situation. The Baron moved two steps behind Alia. Sardaukar were leaping into positions at the doors.

"We will fall back into space and reform," the Emperor said. "Baron, my apologies. These madmen are attacking under cover of the storm. We will show them an Emperor's wrath, then." He pointed at Alia. "Give her body to the storm."

As he spoke, Alia fled backward, feigning terror. "Let the storm have what it can take!" she screamed. And she backed into the Baron's arms.

"I have her, Majesty!" the Baron shouted. "Shall I dispatch her now—eeeeeeeeeeeh!" He hurled her to the floor, clutched his left arm.

"I'm sorry, Grandfather," Alia said. "You've met the Atreides gom jabbar." She got to her feet, dropped a dark needle from her hand.

The Baron fell back. His eyes bulged as he stared at a red slash on his left palm. "You . . . you . . . ." He rolled sideways in his suspensors, a sagging mass of flesh supported inches off the floor with head lolling and the mouth hanging open.

"These people are insane," the Emperor snarled. "Quick! Into the ship. We'll purge this planet of every . . . ."

Something sparkled to his left. A roll of ball lightning bounced away from the wall there, crackled as it touched the metal floor. The smell of burned insulation swept through the selamlik.

"The shield!" one of the Sardaukar officers shouted. "The outer shield is down! They . . . ."

His words were drowned in a metallic roaring as the shipwall behind the Emperor trembled and rocked.

"They've shot the nose off our ship!" someone called.

Dust boiled through the room. Under its cover, Alia leaped up, ran toward the outer door.

The Emperor whirled, motioned his people into an emergency door that swung open in the ship's side behind the throne. He flashed a hand signal to a Sardaukar officer leaping through the dust haze. "We will make our stand here!" the Emperor ordered.

Another crash shook the hutment. The double doors banged open at the far side of the chamber admitting wind-blown sand and the sound of shouting. A small, black-robed figure could be seen momentarily against the light—Alia darting out to find a knife and, as befitted her Fremen training, to kill Harkonnen and Sardaukar wounded. House Sardaukar charged through a greened yellow haze toward the opening, weapons ready, forming an arc there to protect the Emperor's retreat.

"Save yourself, Sire!" a Sardaukar officer shouted. "Into the ship!"

But the Emperor stood alone now on his dais pointing toward the doors A forty-meter section of the hutment had been blasted away there and the selamlik's doors opened now onto drifting sand. A dust cloud hung low over the outside world blowing from pastel distances. Static lightning crackled from the cloud and the spark flashes of shields being shorted out by the storm's charge could be seen through the haze. The plain surged with figures in combat—Sardaukar and leaping gyrating robed men who seemed to come down out of the storm.

All this was as a frame for the target of the Emperor's pointing hand.

Out of the sand haze came an orderly mass of flashing shapes—great rising curves with crystal spokes that resolved into the gaping mouths of sandworms, a massed wall of them, each with troops of Fremen riding to the attack. They came in a hissing wedge, robes whipping in the wind as they cut through the melee on the plain.

Onward toward the Emperor's hutment they came while the House Sardaukar stood awed for the first time in their history by an onslaught their minds found difficult to accept.

But the figures leaping from the worm backs were men, and the blades flashing in that ominous yellow light were a thing the Sardaukar had been trained to face. They threw themselves into combat. And it was man to man on the plain of Arrakeen while a picked Sardaukar bodyguard pressed the

Emperor back into the ship, sealed the door on him, and prepared to die at that door as part of his shield.

In the shock of comparative silence within the ship, the Emperor stared at the wide-eyed faces of his suite, seeing his oldest daughter with the flush of exertion on her cheeks, the old Truthsayer standing like a black shadow with her hood pulled about her face, finding at last the faces he sought—the two Guildsmen. They wore the Guild gray, unadorned, and it seemed to fit the calm they maintained despite the high emotions around them.

The taller of the two, though, held a hand to his left eye. As the Emperor watched, someone jostled the Guildsman's arm, the hand moved, and the eye was revealed. The man had lost one of his masking contact lenses, and the eye stared out a total blue so dark as to be almost black.

The smaller of the pair elbowed his way a step nearer the Emperor, said: "We cannot know how it will go." And the taller companion, hand restored to eye, added in a cold voice: "But this Muad'Dib cannot know, either."

The words shocked the Emperor out of his daze. He checked the scorn on his tongue by a visible effort because it did not take a Guild navigator's single-minded focus on the main chance to see the immediate future out on that plain. Were these two so dependent upon their *faculty* that they had lost the use of their eyes and their reason? he wondered.

"Reverend Mother," he said, "we must devise a plan."

She pulled the hood from her face, met his gaze with an unblinking stare. The look that passed between them carried complete understanding. They had one weapon left and both knew it: treachery.

"Summon Count Fenring from his quarters," the Reverend Mother said.

The Padishah Emperor nodded, waved for one of his aides to obey that command.

> *He was warrior and mystic, ogre and saint, the fox and the innocent, chivalrous, ruthless, less than a god, more than a man. There is no measuring Muad'Dib's motives by ordinary standards. In the moment of his triumph, he saw the death prepared for him, yet he accepted the treachery. Can you say he did this out of a sense of justice? Whose justice, then? Remember, we speak now of the Muad'Dib who ordered battle drums made from his enemies' skins, the Maud'Dib who denied the conventions of his ducal past with a wave of the hand, saying merely: "I am the Kwisatz Haderach. That is reason enough."*

**—from "Arrakis Awakening" by the Princess Irulan**

It was to the Arrakeen governor's mansion, the old Residency the Atreides had first occupied on Dune, that they escorted Paul-Muad'Dib on the evening of his victory. The building stood as Rabban had restored it, virtually untouched by the fighting although there had been looting by townspeople. Some of the furnishings in the main hall had been overturned or smashed.

Paul strode through the main entrance with Gurney Halleck and Stilgar a pace behind. Their escort fanned out into the Great Hall, straightening the place and clearing an area for Muad'Dib. One squad began investigating that no sly trap had been planted here.

"I remember the day we first came here with your father," Gurney said. He glanced around at the beams and the high, slitted windows. "I didn't like this place then and I like it less now. One of our caves would be safer."

"Spoken like a true Fremen," Stilgar said, and he marked the cold smile that his words brought to Muad'Dib's lips. "Will you reconsider, Muad'dib?"

"This place is a symbol," Paul said. "Rabban lived here. By occupying this place I seal my victory for all to understand. Send men through the building. Touch nothing. Just be certain no Harkonnen people or toys remain."

"As you command," Stilgar said, and reluctance was heavy in his tone as he turned to obey.

Communications men hurried into the room with their equipment, began setting up near the massive fireplace. The Fremen guard that augmented the surviving Fedaykin took up stations around the room. There was muttering among them, much darting of suspicious glances. This had been too long a place of the enemy for them to accept their presence in it casually.

"Gurney, have an escort bring my mother and Chani," Paul said. "Does Chani know yet about our son?"

"The message was sent, m'Lord."

"Are the makers being taken out of the basin yet?"

"Yes, m'Lord. The storm's almost spent."

"What's the extent of the storm damage?" Paul asked.

"In the direct path—on the landing field and across the spice storage yards of the plain—extensive damage," Gurney said. "As much from battle as from the storm."

"Nothing money won't repair, I presume," Paul said.

"Except for the lives, m'Lord," Gurney said, and there was a tone of reproach in his voice as though to say: *"When did an Atreides worry first about things when people were at stake?"*

But Paul could only focus his attention on the inner eye and the gaps visible to him in the time-wall that still lay across his path. Through each gap the jihad raged away down the corridors of the future.

He sighed, crossed the hall, seeing a chair against the wall. The chair had once stood in the dining hall and might even have held his own father. At the moment, though, it was only an object to rest his weariness and conceal it from the men. He sat down, pulling his robes around his legs, loosening his stillsuit at the neck.

"The Emperor is still holed up in the remains of his ship," Gurney said.

"For now, contain him there," Paul said. "Have they found the Harkonnens yet?"

"They're still examining the dead."

"What reply from the ships up there?" He jerked his chin toward the ceiling.

"No reply yet, m'Lord."

Paul sighed, resting against the back of his chair. Presently, he said: "Bring me a captive Sardaukar. We must send a message to our Emperor. It's time to discuss terms."

"Yes, m'Lord."

Gurney turned away, dropped a hand signal to one of the Fedaykin who took up close-guard position beside Paul.

"Gurney," Paul whispered. "Since we've been rejoined I've yet to hear you produce the proper quotation for the event." He turned, saw Gurney swallow, saw the sudden grim hardening of the man's jaw.

"As you wish, m'Lord," Gurney said. He cleared his throat, rasped: "'And the victory that day was turned into mourning unto all the people: for the people heard say that day how the king was grieved for his son.'"

Paul close his eyes, forcing grief out of his mind, letting it wait as he had once waited to mourn his father. Now, he gave his thoughts over to this day's accumulated discoveries—the mixed futures and the hidden *presence* of Alia within his awareness.

Of all the uses of time-vision, this was the strangest. "I have breasted the future to place my words where only you can hear them," Alia had said. "Even you cannot do that, my brother. I find it an interesting play. And . . . oh, yes—I've killed our grandfather, the demented old Baron. He had very little pain."

Silence. His time sense had seen her withdrawal.

"Muad'Dib."

Paul opened his eyes to see Stilgar's black-bearded visage above him, the dark eyes glaring with battle light.

"You've found the body of the old Baron," Paul said.

A hush of the person settled over Stilgar. "How could you know?" he whispered. "We just found the body in that great pile of metal the Emperor built."

Paul ignored the question, seeing Gurney return accompanied by two Fremen who supported a captive Sardaukar.

"Here's one of them, m'Lord," Gurney said. He signed to the guard to hold the captive five paces in front of Paul.

The Sardaukar's eyes, Paul noted, carried a glazed expression of shock. A blue bruise stretched from the bridge of his nose to the corner of his mouth. He was of the blond, chisel-featured caste, the look that seemed synonymous with rank among the Sardaukar, yet there were no insignia on his torn uiform except the gold buttons with the Imperial crest and the tattered braid of his trousers.

"I think this one's an officer, m'Lord," Gurney said.

Paul nodded, said: "I am the Duke Paul Atreides. Do you understand that, man?"

The Sardaukar stared at him unmoving.

"Speak up," Paul said, "or your Emperor may die."

The man blinked, swallowed.

"Who am I?" Paul demanded.

"You are the Duke Paul Atreides," the man husked.

He seemed too submissive to Paul, but then the Sardaukar had never been prepared for such happenings as this day. They'd never known anything but victory which, Paul realized, could be a weakness in itself. He put that thought aside for later consideration in his own training program.

"I have a message for you to carry to the Emperor," Paul said. And he couched his words in the ancient formula: "I, a Duke of a Great House, an Imperial Kinsman, give my word of bond under the Convention. If the Emperor and his people lay down their arms and come to me here I will guard their lives with my own." Paul held up his left hand with the ducal signet for the Sardaukar to see. "I swear it by this."

The man wet his lips with his tongue, glanced at Gurney.

"Yes," Paul said. "Who but an Atreides could command the allegiance of Gurney Halleck."

"I will carry the message," the Sardaukar said.

"Take him to our forward command post and send him in," Paul said.

"Yes, m'Lord." Gurney motioned for the guard to obey, led them out.

Paul turned back to Stilgar.

"Chani and your mother have arrived," Stilgar said. "Chani has asked time to be alone with her grief. The Reverend Mother sought a moment in the weirding room; I know not why."

"My mother's sick with longing for a planet she may never see," Paul said. "Where water falls from the sky and plants grow so thickly you cannot walk between them."

"Water from the sky," Stilgar whispered.

In that instant, Paul saw how Stilgar had been transformed from the Fremen naib to a *creature* of the Lisan al-Gaib, a receptacle for awe and obedience. It was a lessening of the man, and Paul felt the ghost-wind of the jihad in it.

*I have seen a friend become a worshiper*, he thought.

In a rush of loneliness, Paul glanced around the room, noting how proper and on-review his guards had become in his presence. He sensed the subtle, prideful competition among them—each hoping for notice from Muad'Dib.

*Muad'Dib from whom all blessings flow*, he thought, and it was the bitterest thought of his life. *They sense that I must take the throne*, he thought. *But they cannot know I do it to prevent the jihad.*

Stilgar cleared his throat, said: "Rabban, too, is dead."

Paul nodded.

Guards to the right suddenly snapped aside, standing at attention to open an aisle for Jessica. She wore her black aba and walked with a hint of striding across sand, but Paul noted how this house had restored to her something of what she had once been here—concubine to a ruling duke. Her presence carried some of its old assertiveness.

Jessica stopped in front of Paul, looked down at him. She saw his fatigue and how he hid it, but found no compassion for him. It was as though she had been rendered incapable of *any* emotion for her son.

Jessica had entered the Great Hall wondering why the place refused to fit itself snugly into her memories. It remained a foreign room, as though she had never walked here, never walked here with her beloved Leto, never confronted a drunken Duncan Idaho here—never, never, never . . . .

*There should be a word-tension directly opposite to adab, the demanding memory,* she thought. *There should be a word for memories that deny themselves.*

"Where is Alia?" she asked.

"Out doing what any good Fremen child should be doing in such times," Paul said. "She's killing enemy wounded and marking their bodies for the water-recovery teams."

"Paul!"

"You must understand that she does this out of kindness," he said. "Isn't it odd how we misunderstand the hidden unity of kindness and cruelty?"

Jessica glared at her son, shocked by the profound change in him. *Was it his child's death did this?* she wondered. And she said: "The men tell strange stories of you, Paul. They say you've all the powers of the legend—nothing can be hidden from you, that you see where others cannot see."

"A Bene Gesserit should ask about legends?" he asked.

"I've had a hand in whatever you are," she admitted, "but you mustn't expect me to—"

"How would you like to live billions upon billions of lives?" Paul asked. "There's a fabric of legends for you! Think of all those experiences, the wisdom they'd bring. But wisdom tempers love, doesn't it? And it puts a new shape on hate. How can you tell what's ruthless unless you've plumbed the depths of both cruelty and kindness? You should fear me, Mother. I am the Kwisatz Haderach."

Jessica tried to swallow in a dry throat. Presently, she said: "Once you denied to me that you were the Kwisatz Haderach."

Paul shook his head. "I can deny nothing any more." He looked up into her eyes. "The Emperor and his people come now. They will be announced any moment. Stand beside me. I wish a clear view of them. My future bride will be among them."

"Paul!" Jessica snapped. "Don't make the mistake your father made!"

"She's a princess," Paul said. "She's my key to the throne, and that's all she'll ever be. Mistake? You think because I'm what you made me that I cannot feel the need for revenge?"

"Even on the innocent?" she asked, and she thought: *He must not make the mistakes I made.*

"There are no innocent any more," Paul said.

"Tell that to Chani," Jessica said, and gestured toward the passage from the rear of the Residency.

Chani entered the Great Hall there, walking between the Fremen guards as though unaware of them. Her hood and stillsuit cap were thrown back, face mask fastened aside. She walked with a fragile uncertainty as she crossed the room to stand beside Jessica.

Paul saw the marks of tears on her cheeks—*She gives water to the dead.* He felt a pang of grief strike through him, but it was as though he could only feel this thing through Chani's presence.

"He is dead, beloved," Chani said. "Our son is dead."

Holding himself under stiff control, Paul got to his feet. He reached out, touched Chani's cheek, feeling the dampness of her tears. "He cannot be replaced," Paul said, "but there will be other sons. It is Usul who promises this." Gently, he moved her aside, gestured to Stilgar.

"Muad'Dib," Stilgar said.

"They come from the ship, the Emperor and his people," Paul said. "I will stand here. Assemble the captives in an open space in the center of the room. They will be kept at a distance of ten meters from me unless I command otherwise."

"As you command, Muad'Dib."

As Stilgar turned to obey, Paul heard the awed muttering of Fremen guards: "You see? He knew! No one told him, but he knew!"

The Emperor's entourage could be heard approaching now, his Sardaukar humming one of their marching tunes to keep up their spirits. There came a murmur of voices at the entrance and Gurney Halleck passed through the guard, crossed to confer with Stilgar, then moved to Paul's side, a strange look in his eyes.

*Will I lose Gurney, too?* Paul wondered. *The way I lost Stilgar—losing a friend to gain a creature?*

"They have no throwing weapons," Gurney said. "I've made sure of that myself." He glanced around the room, seeing Paul's preparations. "Feyd-Rautha Harkonnen is with them. Shall I cut him out?"

"Leave him."

"There're some Guild people, too, demanding special privileges, threatening an embargo against Arrakis. I told them I'd give you their message."

"Let them threaten."

"Paul!" Jessica hissed behind him. "He's talking about the Guild!"

"I'll pull their fangs presently," Paul said.

And he thought then about the Guild—the force that had specialized for so long that it had become a parasite, unable to exist independently of the life upon which it fed. They had never dared grasp the sword . . . and now they could not grasp it. They might have taken Arrakis when they realized the error of specializing on the melange awareness-spectrum narcotic for their navigators. They *could* have done this, lived their glorious day and died. Instead, they'd existed from moment to moment, hoping the seas in which they swam might produce a new host when the old one died.

The Guild navigators, gifted with limited prescience, had made the fatal decision: they'd chosen always the clear, safe course that leads ever downward into stagnation.

*Let them look closely at their new host,* Paul thought.

"There's also a Bene Gesserit Reverend Mother who says she's a friend of your mother," Gurney said.

"My mother has no Bene Gesserit friends."

Again, Gurney glanced around the Great Hall, then bent close to Paul's ear. "Thufir Hawat's with 'em, m'Lord. I had no chance to see him alone, but he used our old hand signs to say he's been working with the Harkonnens, thought you were dead. Says he's to be left among 'em."

"You left Thufir among those—"

"He wanted it . . . and I thought it best. If . . . there's something wrong, he's where we can control him. If not—we've an ear on the other side."

Paul thought then of prescient glimpses into the possibilities of this moment—and one time-line where Thufir carried a poisoned needle which the Emperor commanded he use against "this upstart Duke."

The entrance guards stepped aside, formed a short corridor of lances. There came a murmurous swish of garments, feet rasping the sand that had drifted into the Residency.

The Padishah Emperor Shaddam IV led his people into the hall. His burseg helmet had been lost and the red hair stood out in disarray. His uniform's left sleeve had been ripped along the inner seam. He was beltless and without weapons, but his presence moved with him like a force-shield bubble that kept his immediate area open.

A Fremen lance dropped across his path, stopped him where Paul had ordered. The others bunched up behind, a montage of color, of shuffling and of staring faces.

Paul swept his gaze across the group, saw women who hid signs of weeping, saw the lackeys who had come to enjoy the grandstand seats at a Sardaukar victory and now stood choked to silence by defeat. Paul saw the bird-bright eyes of the Reverend Mother Gaius Helen Mohiam glaring beneath her black hood, and beside her the narrow furtiveness of Feyd-Rautha Harkonnen.

*There's a face time betrayed to me,* Paul thought.

He looked beyond Feyd-Rautha then, attracted by a movement, seeing there a narrow, weaselish face he'd never before encountered—not in time or out of it. It was a face he felt he should know and the feeling carried with it a marker of fear.

*Why should I fear that man?* he wondered.

He leaned toward his mother, whispered: "That man to the left of the Reverend Mother, the evil-looking one—who is that?"

Jessica looked, recognizing the face from her Duke's dossiers. "Count Fenring," she said. "The one who was here immediately before us. A genetic-eunuch . . . and a killer."

*The Emperor's errand boy,* Paul thought. And the thought was a shock crashing across his consciousness because he had seen the Emperor in uncounted associations spread through the possible futures—but never once had Count Fenring appeared within those prescient visions.

It occurred to Paul then that he had seen his own dead body along countless reaches of the time web, but never once had he seen his moment of death.

*Have I been denied a glimpse of this man because he is the one who kills me?* Paul wondered.

The thought sent a pang of foreboding through him. He forced his attention away from Fenring, looked now at the remnants of Sardaukar men and officers, the bitterness on their faces and the desperation. Here and there among them, faces caught Paul's attention briefly: Sardaukar officers measuring the preparations within this room, planning and scheming yet for a way to turn defeat into victory.

Paul's attention came at last to a tall blonde woman, green-eyed, a face of patrician beauty, classic in its hauteur, untouched by tears, completely undefeated. Without being told it, Paul knew her—Princess Royal, Bene Gesserit-trained, a face that time vision had shown him in many aspects: Irulan.

*There's my key,* he thought.

Then he saw movement in the clustered people, a face and figure emerged—Thufir Hawat, the seamed old features with darkly stained lips, the hunched shoulders, the look of fragile age about him.

"There's Thufir Hawat," Paul said. "Let him stand free, Gurney."

"M'Lord," Gurney said.

"Let him stand free," Paul repeated.

Gurney nodded.

Hawat shambled forward as a Fremen lance was lifted and replaced behind him. The rheumy eyes peered at Paul, measuring, seeking.

Paul stepped forward one pace, sensed the tense, waiting movement of the Emperor and his people.

Hawat's gaze stabbed past Paul, and the old man said: "Lady Jessica, I but learned this day how I've wronged you in my thoughts. You needn't forgive."

Paul waited, but his mother remained silent.

"Thufir, old friend," Paul said, "as you can see, my back is toward no door."

"The universe is full of doors," Hawat said.

"Am I my father's son?" Paul asked.

"More like your grandfather's," Hawat rasped. "You've his manner and the look of him in your eyes."

"Yet I'm my father's son," Paul said. "For I say to you, Thufir, that in payment for your years of service to my family you may now ask anything you wish of me. Anything at all. Do you need my life now, Thufir? It is yours." Paul stepped forward a pace, hands at his side, seeing the look of awareness grow in Hawat's eyes.

*He realizes that I know of the treachery,* Paul thought.

Pitching his voice to carry in a half-whisper for Hawat's ears alone, Paul said: "I mean this, Thufir. If you're to strike me, do it now."

"I but wanted to stand before you once more, my Duke," Hawat said. And Paul became aware for the first time of the effort the old man exerted to keep from falling. Paul reached out, supported Hawat by the shoulders, feeling the muscle tremors beneath his hands.

"Is there pain, old friend?" Paul asked.

"There is pain, my Duke," Hawat agreed, "but the pleasure is greater." He half turned in Paul's arms, extended his left hand, palm up, toward the Emperor, exposing the tiny needle cupped against the fingers. "See, Majesty?" he called. "See your traitor's needle? Do you think that I who've given my life to service of the Atreides would give them less now?"

Paul staggered as the old man sagged in his arms, felt the death there, the utter flaccidity. Gently, Paul lowered Hawat to the floor, straightened and signed for guardsmen to carry the body away.

Silence held the hall while his command was obeyed.

A look of deadly waiting held the Emperor's face now. Eyes that had never admitted fear admitted it at last.

"Majesty," Paul said, and noted the jerk of surprised attention in the tall Princess Royal. The words had been uttered with the Bene Gesserit controlled atonals, carrying in it every shade of contempt and scorn that Paul could put there.

*Bene Gesserit-trained indeed*, Paul thought.

The Emperor cleared his throat, said: "Perhaps my respected kinsman believes he has things all his own way now. Nothing could be more remote from fact. You have violated the Convention, used atomics against—"

"I used atomics against a natural feature of the desert," Paul said. "It was in my way and I was in a hurry to get to you, Majesty, to ask your explanation for some of your strange activities."

"There's a massed armada of the Great Houses in space over Arrakis right now," the Emperor said. "I've but to say the word and they'll—"

"Oh, yes," Paul said, "I almost forgot about them." He searched through the Emperor's suite until he saw the faces of the two Guildsmen, spoke aside to Gurney. "Are those the Guild agents, Gurney, the two fat ones dressed in gray over there?"

"Yes, m'Lord."

"You two," Paul said, pointing. "Get out of there immediately and dispatch messages that will get that fleet on its way home. After this, you'll ask my permission before—"

"The Guild doesn't take your orders!" the taller of the two barked. He and his companion pushed through to the barrier lances, which were raised at a nod from Paul. The two men stepped out and the taller leveled an arm at Paul, said: "You may very well be under embargo for your—"

"If I hear any more nonsense from either of you," Paul said, "I'll give the order that'll destroy all spice production on Arrakis . . . forever."

"Are you mad?" the tall Guildsman demanded. He fell back half a step.

"You grant that I have the power to do this thing, then?" Paul asked.

The Guildsman seemed to stare into space for a moment, then: "Yes, you could do it, but you must not."

"Ah-h-h," Paul said and nodded to himself. "Guild navigators, both of you, eh?"

"Yes!"

The shorter of the pair said: "You would blind yourself, too, and condemn us all to slow death. Have you any idea what it means to be deprived of the spice liquor once you're addicted?"

"The eye that looks ahead to the safe course is closed forever," Paul said. "The Guild is crippled. Humans become little isolated clusters on their isolated planets. You know, I might do this thing out of pure spite . . . or out of ennui."

"Let us talk this over privately," the taller Guildsman said. "I'm sure we can come to some compromise that is—"

"Send the message to your people over Arrakis," Paul said. "I grow tired of this argument. If that fleet over us doesn't leave soon there'll be no need for us to talk." He nodded toward his communications men at the side of the hall. "You may use our equipment."

"First we must discuss this," the tall Guildsman said. "We cannot just—"

"Do it!" Paul barked. "The power to destroy a thing is the absolute control over it. You've agreed I have that power. We are not here to discuss or to negotiate or to compromise. You will obey my orders or suffer the *immediate* consequences!"

"He means it," the shorter Guildsman said. And Paul saw the fear grip them.

Slowly the two crossed to the Fremen communications equipment.

"Will they obey?" Gurney asked.

"They have a narrow vision of time," Paul said. "They can see ahead to a blank wall marking the consequences of disobedience. Every Guild navigator on every ship over us can look ahead to that same wall. They'll obey."

Paul turned back to look at the Emperor, said: "When they permitted you to mount your father's throne, it was only on the assurance that you'd keep the spice flowing. You've failed them, Majesty. Do you know the consequences?"

"Nobody *permitted* me to—"

"Stop playing the fool," Paul barked. "The Guild is like a village beside a river. They need the water, but can only dip out what they require. They cannot dam the river and control it, because that focuses attention on what they take, it brings down eventual destruction. The spice flow, that's their river, and I have built a dam. But my dam is such that you cannot destroy it without destroying the river."

The Emperor brushed a hand through his red hair, glanced at the backs of the two Guildsmen.

"Even your Bene Gesserit Truthsayer is trembling," Paul said. "There are other poisons the Reverend Mothers can use for their tricks, but once they've used the spice liquor, the others no longer work."

The old woman pulled her shapeless black robes around her, pressed forward out of the crowd to stand at the barrier lances.

"Reverend Mother Gaius Helen Mohiam," Paul said. "It has been a long time since Caladan, hasn't it?"

She looked past him at his mother, said: "Well, Jessica, I see that your son is indeed the one. For that you can be forgiven even the abomination of your daughter."

Paul stilled a cold, piercing anger, said: "You've never had the right or cause to forgive my mother anything!"

The old woman locked eyes with him.

"Try your tricks on me, old witch," Paul said. "Where's your gom jabbar? Try looking into that place where you dare not look! You'll find me there staring out at you!"

The old woman dropped her gaze.

"Have you nothing to say?" Paul demanded.

"I welcomed you to the ranks of humans," she muttered. "Don't besmirch that."

Paul raised his voice: "Observe her, comrades! This is a Bene Gesserit Reverend Mother, patient in a patient cause. She could wait with her sisters—ninety generations for the proper combination of genes and environment to produce the one person their schemes required. Observe her! She knows now that the ninety generations have produced that person. Here I stand . . . but . . . I . . . will . . . never . . . do . . . her . . . bidding!"

"Jessica!" the old woman screamed. "Silence him!"

"Silence him yourself," Jessica said.

Paul glared at the old woman. "For your part in all this I could gladly have you strangled," he said. "You couldn't prevent it!" he snapped as she stiffened in rage. "But I think it better punishment that you live out your years never able to touch me or bend me to a single thing your scheming desires."

"Jessica, what have you done?" the old woman demanded.

"I'll give you only one thing," Paul said. "You saw part of what the race needs, but how poorly you saw it. You think to control human breeding and intermix a select few according to your master plan! How little you understand of what—"

"You mustn't speak of these things!" the old woman hissed.

"Silence!" Paul roared. The word seemed to take substance as it twisted through the air between them under Paul's control.

The old woman reeled back into the arms of those behind her, face blank with shock at the power with which he had seized her psyche. "Jessica," she whispered. "Jessica."

"I remember your gom jabbar," Paul said. "You remember mine. I can kill you with a word."

The Fremen around the hall glanced knowingly at each other. Did the legend not say: "*And his word shall carry death eternal to those who stand against righteousness.*"?

Paul turned his attention to the tall Princess Royal standing beside her Emperor father. Keeping his eyes focused on her, he said: "Majesty, we both know the way out of our difficulty."

The Emperor glanced at his daughter, back to Paul. "You dare? You! An adventurer without family, a nobody from—"

"You've already admitted who I am," Paul said. "Royal kinsman, you said. Let's stop this nonsense."

"I am your ruler," the Emperor said.

Paul glanced at the Guildsmen standing now at the communications equipment and facing him. One of them nodded.

"I could force it," Paul said.

"You will not dare!" the Emperor grated.

Paul merely stared at him.

The Princess Royal put a hand on her father's arm. "Father," she said, and her voice was silky soft, soothing.

"Don't try your tricks on me," the Emperor said. He looked at her. "You don't need to do this, Daughter. We've other resources that—"

"But here's a man fit to be your son," she said.

The old Reverend Mother, her composure regained, forced her way to the Emperor's side, leaned close to his ear and whispered.

"She pleads your case," Jessica said.

Paul continued to look at the golden-haired Princess. Aside to his mother, he said: "That's Irulan, the oldest, isn't it?"

"Yes."

Chani moved up on Paul's other side, said: "Do you wish me to leave, Muad'Dib?"

He glanced at her. "Leave? You'll never again leave my side."

"There's nothing binding between us," Chani said.

Paul looked down at her for a silent moment, then: "Speak only truth with me, my Sihaya." As she started to reply, he silenced her with a finger to her lips. "That which binds us cannot be loosed," he said. "Now, watch these matters closely for I wish to see this room later through your wisdom."

The Emperor and his Truthsayer were carrying on a heated, low-voiced argument.

Paul spoke to his mother: "She reminds him that it's part of their agreement to place a Bene Gesserit on the throne, and Irulan is the one they've groomed for it."

"Was that their plan?" Jessica said.

"Isn't it obvious?" Paul asked.

"I see the signs!" Jessica snapped. "My question was meant to remind you that you should not try to teach me those matters in which I instructed you."

Paul glanced at her, caught a cold smile on her lips.

Gurney Halleck leaned between them, said: "I remind you, m'Lord, that there's a Harkonnen in that bunch." He nodded toward the dark-haired Feyd-Rautha pressed against a barrier lance on the left. "The one with the squinting eyes there on the left. As evil a face as ever I saw. You promised me once that—"

"Thank you, Gurney," Paul said.

"It's the na-Baron . . . Baron, now that the old man's dead," Gurney said. "He'll do for what I've in—"

"Can you take him, Gurney?"

"M'Lord jests!"

"That argument between the Emperor and his witch has gone on long enough, don't you think, Mother?"

She nodded. "Indeed."

Paul raised his voice, called out to the Emperor: "Majesty, is there a Harkonnen among you?"

Royal disdain revealed itself in the way the Emperor turned to look at Paul. "I believe my entourage has been placed under the protection of your ducal word," he said.

"My question was for information only," Paul said. "I wish to know if a Harkonnen is officially a part of your entourage or if a Harkonnen is merely hiding behind a technicality out of cowardice."

The Emperor's smile was calculating. "Anyone accepted into the Imperial company is a member of my entourage."

"You have the word of a Duke," Paul said, "but Muad'Dib is another matter. *He* may not recognize your definition of what constitutes an entourage. My friend Gurney Halleck wishes to kill a Harkonnen. If he—"

"Kanly!" Feyd-Rautha shouted. He pressed against the barrier lance. "Your father named this vendetta, Atreides. You call me coward while you hide among your women and offer to send a lackey against me!"

The old Truthsayer whispered something fiercely into the Emperor's ear, but he pushed her aside, said: "Kanly, is it? There are strict rules for kanly."

"Paul, put a stop to this," Jessica said.

"M'Lord," Gurney said, "you promised me my day against the Harkonnens."

"You've had your day against them," Paul said and he felt a harlequin abandon take over his emotions. He slipped his robe and hood from his shoulders, handed them to his mother with his belt and crysknife, began unstrapping his stillsuit. He sensed now that the universe focused on this moment.

"There's no need for this," Jessica said. "There are easier ways, Paul."

Paul stepped out of his stillsuit, slipped the crysknife from its sheath in his mother's hands. "I know," he said. "Poison, an assassin, all the old familiar ways."

"You promised me a Harkonnen!" Gurney hissed, and Paul marked the rage in the man's face, the way the inkvine scar stood out dark and ridged. "You owe it to me, m'Lord!"

"Have you suffered more from them than I?" Paul asked.

"My sister," Gurney rasped. "My years in the slave pits—"

"My father," Paul said. "My good friends and companions, Thufir Hawat and Duncan Idaho, my years as a fugitive without rank or succor . . . and one more thing: it is now kanly and you know as well as I the rules that must prevail."

Halleck's shoulders sagged. "M'Lord, if that swine . . . he's no more than a beast you'd spurn with your foot and discard the shoe because it'd been contaminated. Call in an executioner, if you must, or let me do it, but don't offer yourself to—"

"Muad'Dib need not do this thing," Chani said.

He glanced at her, saw the fear for him in her eyes. "But the Duke Paul must," he said.

"This is a Harkonnen animal!" Gurney rasped.

Paul hesitated on the point of revealing his own Harkonnen ancestry, stopped at a sharp look from his mother, said merely: "But this being has human shape, Gurney, and deserves human doubt."

Gurney said: "If he so much as—"

"Please stand aside," Paul said. He hefted the crysknife, pushed Gurney gently aside.

"Gurney!" Jessica said. She touched Gurney's arm. "He's like his grandfather in this mood. Don't distract him. It's the only thing you can do for him now." and she thought: *Great Mother! What irony.*

The Emperor was studying Feyd-Rautha, seeing the heavy shoulders, the thick muscles. He turned to look at Paul—a stringy whipcord of a youth, not as desiccated as the Arrakeen natives, but with ribs there to count, and sunken in the flanks so that the ripple and gather of muscles could be followed under the skin.

Jessica leaned close to Paul, pitched her voice for his ears alone: "One thing, Son. Sometimes a dangerous person is prepared by the Bene Gesserit, a word implanted into the deepest recesses by the old pleasure-pain methods. The word-sound most frequently used is Uroshnor. If this one's been prepared, as I strongly suspect, that word uttered in his ear will render his muscles flaccid and—"

"I want no special advantage for this one," Paul said. "Step back out of my way."

Gurney spoke to her: "Why is he doing this? Does he think to get himself killed and achieve martyrdom? This Fremen religious prattle, is that what clouds his reason?"

Jessica hid her face in her hands, realizing that she did not know fully why Paul took this course. She could feel death in the room and knew that the changed Paul was capable of such a thing as Gurney suggested. Every talent within her focused on the need to protect her son, but there was nothing she could do.

"Is it this religious prattle?" Gurney insisted.

"Be silent," Jessica whispered. "And pray."

The Emperor's face was touched by an abrupt smile. "If Feyd-Rautha Harkonnen . . . of my entourage . . . so wishes," he said, "I relieve him of all restraint and give him freedom to choose his own course in this." The Emperor waved a hand toward Paul's Fedaykin guards. "One of your rabble has my belt and short blade. If Feyd-Rautha wishes it, he may meet you with my blade in his hand."

"I wish it," Feyd-Rautha said, and Paul saw the elation on the man's face.

*He's overconfident,* Paul thought. *There's a natural advantage I can accept.*

"Get the Emperor's blade," Paul said, and watched as his command was obeyed. "Put it on the floor there." He indicated a place with his foot. "Clear the Imperial rabble back against the wall and let the Harkonnen stand clear."

A flurry of robes, scraping of feet, low-voiced commands and protests accompanied obedience to Paul's command. The Guildsmen remained standing near the communications equipment. They frowned at Paul in obvious indecision.

*They're accustomed to seeing the future,* Paul thought. *In this place and time they're blind . . . even as I am.* And he sampled the time-winds, sensing the turmoil, the storm nexus that now focused on this moment place. Even the faint gaps were closed now. Here was the unborn jihad, he knew. Here was the race consciousness that he had known once as his own terrible purpose. Here was reason enough for a Kwisatz Haderach or a Lisan al-Gaib or even the halting schemes of the Bene Gesserit. The race of humans had felt its own dormancy, sensed itself grown stale and knew now only the need to experience turmoil in which the genes would mingle and the strong new mixtures survive. All humans were alive as an unconscious single organism in this moment, experiencing a kind of sexual heat that could override any barrier.

And Paul saw how futile were any efforts of his to change any smallest bit of this. He had thought to oppose the jihad within himself, but the jihad would be. His legions would rage out from Arrakis even without him. They needed only the legend he already had become. He had shown them the way, given them mastery even over the Guild which must have the spice to exist.

A sense of failure pervaded him, and he saw through it that Feyd-Rautha Harkonnen had slipped out of the torn uniform, stripped down to a fighting girdle with a mail core.

*This is the climax,* Paul thought. *From here, the future will open, the clouds part onto a kind of glory. And if I die here, they'll say I sacrificed myself that my spirit might lead them. And if I live, they'll say nothing can oppose Muad'Dib.*

"Is the Atreides ready?" Feyd-Rautha called, using the words of the ancient kanly ritual.

Paul chose to answer him in the Fremen way: "May thy knife chip and shatter!" He pointed to the Emperor's blade on the floor, indicating that Feyd-Rautha should advance and take it.

Keeping his attention on Paul, Feyd-Rautha picked up the knife, balancing it a moment in his hand to get the feel of it. Excitement kindled in him. This was a fight he had dreamed about—man against man, skill against skill with no shields intervening. He could see a way to power opening before him because the Emperor surely would reward whoever killed this troublesome duke. The reward might even be that haughty daughter and a share of the throne. And this yokel duke, this back-world adventurer could not possibly be a match for a Harkonnen trained in every device and every treachery by a thousand arena combats. And the yokel had no way of knowing he faced more weapons than a knife here.

*Let us see if you're proof against poison!* Feyd-Rautha thought. He saluted Paul with the Emperor's blade, said: "Meet your death, fool."

"Shall we fight, cousin?" Paul asked. And he cat-footed forward, eyes on the waiting blade, his body crouched low with his own milk-white crysknife pointing out as though an extension of his arm.

They circled each other, bare feet grating on the floor, watching with eyes intent for the slightest opening.

"How beautifully you dance," Feyd-Rautha said.

*He's a talker,* Paul thought. *There's another weakness. He grows uneasy in the face of silence.*

"Have you been shriven?" Feyd-Rautha asked.

Still, Paul circled in silence.

And the old Reverend Mother, watching the fight from the press of the Emperor's suite, felt herself trembling. The Atreides youth had called the Harkonnen cousin. It could only mean he knew the ancestry they shared, easy to understand because he was the Kwisatz Haderach. But the words forced her to focus on the only thing that mattered to her here.

This could be a major catastrophe for the Bene Gesserit breeding scheme.

She had seen something of what Paul had seen here, that Feyd-Rautha might kill but not be victorious. Another thought, though, almost overwhelmed her. Two end products of this long and costly program faced each other in a fight to the death that might easily claim both of them. If both died here that would leave only Feyd-Rautha's bastard daughter, still a baby, an unknown, an unmeasured factor, and Alia, the abomination.

"Perhaps you have only pagan rites here," Feyd-Rautha said. "Would you like the Emperor's Truthsayer to prepare your spirit for its journey?"

Paul smiled, circling to the right, alert, his black thoughts suppressed by the needs of the moment.

Feyd-Rautha leaped, feinting with right hand, but with the knife shifted in a blur to his left hand.

Paul dodged easily, noting the shield-conditioned hesitation in Feyd-Rautha's thrust. Still, it was not as great a shield conditioning as some Paul had seen, and he sensed that Feyd-Rautha had fought before against unshielded foes.

"Does an Atreides run or stand and fight?" Feyd-Rautha asked.

Paul resumed his silent circling. Idaho's words came back to him, the words of training from the long-ago practice floor on Caladan: *"Use the first moments in study. You may miss many an opportunity for quick victory this way, but the moments of study are insurance of success. Take your time and be sure."*

"Perhaps you think this dance prolongs your life a few moments," Feyd-Rautha said. "Well and good." He stopped the circling, straightened.

Paul had seen enough for a first approximation. Feyd-Rautha led to the left side, presenting the right hip as though the mailed fighting girdle could protect his entire side. It was the action of a man trained to the shield and with a knife in both hands.

*Or* . . . And Paul hesitated . . . the girdle was more than it *seemed*.

The Harkonnen appeared too confident against a man who'd this day led the forces of victory against Sardaukar legions.

Feyd-Rautha noted the hesitation, said: "Why prolong the inevitable? You but keep me from exercising my rights over this ball of dirt."

*If it's a flip-dart,* Paul thought, *it's a cunning one. The girdle shows no signs of tampering.*

"Why don't you speak?" Feyd-Rautha demanded.

Paul resumed his probing circle, allowing himself a cold smile at the tone of unease in Feyd-Rautha's voice, evidence that the pressure of silence was building.

"You smile, eh?" Feyd-Rautha asked. And he leaped in mid-sentence.

Expecting the slight hesitation, Paul almost failed to evade the downflash of blade, felt its tip scratch his left arm. He silenced the sudden pain there, his mind flooded with realization that the earlier hesitation had been a trick—an overfeint. Here was more of an opponent than he had expected. There would be tricks within tricks within tricks.

"Your own Thufir Hawat taught me some of my skills," Feyd-Rautha said. "He gave me first blood. Too bad the old fool didn't live to see it."

And Paul recalled that Idaho had once said, *"Expect only what happens in the fight. That way you'll never be surprised."*

Again the two circled each other, crouched, cautious.

Paul saw the return of elation to his opponent, wondered at it. Did a scratch signify that much to the man? Unless there were poison on the blade! But how could there be? His own men had handled the weapon, snooped it before passing it. They were too well trained to miss an obvious thing like that.

"That woman you were talking to over there," Feyd-Rautha said. "The little one. Is she something special to you? A pet perhaps? Will she deserve my special attentions?"

Paul remained silent, probing with his inner senses, examining the blood from the wound, finding a trace of soporific from the Emperor's blade. He realigned his own metabolism to match this threat and change the molecules of the soporific, but he felt a thrill of doubt. They'd been prepared with soporific on a blade. A soporific. Nothing to alert a poison snooper, but strong enough to slow the muscles it touched. His enemies had their own plans within plans, their own stacked treacheries.

Again Feyd-Rautha leaped, stabbing.

Paul, the smile frozen on his face, feinted with slowness as though inhibited by the drug and at the last instant dodged to meet the downflashing arm on the crysknife point.

Feyd-Rautha ducked sideways and was out and away, his blade shifted to his left hand, and the measure of him that only a slight paleness of jaw betrayed the acid pain where Paul had cut him.

*Let him know his own moment of doubt,* Paul thought. *Let him suspect poison.*

"Treachery!" Feyd-Rautha shouted. "He's poisoned me! I do feel poison in my arm!"

Paul dropped his cloak of silence, said: "Only a little acid to counter the soporific on the Emperor's blade."

Feyd-Rautha matched Paul's cold smile, lifted blade in left hand for a mock salute. His eyes glared rage behind the knife.

Paul shifted his crysknife to his left hand, matching his opponent. Again, they circled, probing.

Feyd-Rautha began closing the space between them, edging in, knife held high, anger showing itself in squint of eye and set of jaw. He feinted right and under, and they were pressed against each other, knife hands gripped, straining.

Paul, cautious of Feyd-Rautha's right hip where he suspected a poison flip-dart, forced the turn to the right. He almost failed to see the needle point flick out beneath the belt line. A shift and a giving in Feyd-Rautha's motion warned him. The tiny point missed Paul's flesh by the barest fraction.

*On the left hip!*

*Treachery within treachery within treachery,* Paul reminded himself. Using Bene Gesserit-trained muscles, he sagged to catch a reflex in Feyd-Rautha, but the necessity of avoiding the tiny point jutting from his opponent's hip threw Paul off just enough that he missed his footing and found himself thrown hard to the floor, Feyd-Rautha on top.

"You see it there on my hip?" Feyd-Rautha whispered. "Your death, fool." And he began twisting himself around, forcing the poisoned needle closer and closer. "It'll stop your muscles and my knife will finish you. There'll be never a trace left to detect!"

Paul strained, hearing the silent screams in his mind, his cell-stamped ancestors demanding that he use the secret word to slow Feyd-Rautha, to save himself.

"I will not say it!" Paul gasped.

Feyd-Rautha gaped at him, caught in the merest fraction of hesitation. It was enough for Paul to find the weakness of balance in one of his opponent's leg muscles, and their positions were reversed. Feyd-Rautha lay partly underneath with right hip high, unable to turn because of the tiny needle point caught against the floor beneath him.

Paul twisted his left hand free, aided by the lubrication of blood from his arm, thrust once hard up underneath Feyd-Rautha's jaw. The point slid home into the brain. Feyd-Rautha jerked and sagged back, still held partly on his side by the needle imbedded in the floor.

Breathing deeply to restore his calm, Paul pushed himself away and got to his feet. He stood over the body, knife in hand, raised his eyes with deliberate slowness to look across the room at the Emperor.

"Majesty," Paul said, "your force is reduced by one more. Shall we now shed sham and pretense? Shall we now discuss what must be? Your daughter wed to me and the way opened for an Atreides to sit on the throne."

The Emperor turned, looked at Count Fenring. The Count met his stare—gray eyes against green. The thought lay there clearly between them, their association so long that understanding could be achieved with a glance.

*Kill this upstart for me, the Emperor was saying. The Atreides is young and resourceful, yes—but he is also tired from long effort and he'd be no match for you anyway. Call him out now . . . you know the way of it. Kill him.*

Slowly, Fenring moved his head, a prolonged turning until he faced Paul.

"Do it!" the Emperor hissed.

The Count focused on Paul, seeing with eyes his Lady Margot had trained in the Bene Gesserit way, aware of the mystery and hidden grandeur about this Atreides youth.

*I could kill him,* Fenring thought—and he knew this for a truth.

Something in his own secretive depths stayed the Count then, and he glimpsed briefly, inadequately, the advantage he held over Paul—a way of hiding from the youth, a furtiveness of person and motives that no eye could penetrate.

Paul, aware of some of this from the way the time nexus boiled, understood at last why he had never seen Fenring along the webs of prescience. Fenring was one of the might-have-beens, an almost–Kwisatz Haderach, crippled by a flaw in the genetic pattern—a eunuch, his talent concentrated into furtiveness and inner seclusion. A deep compassion for the Count flowed through Paul, the first sense of brotherhood he'd ever experienced.

Fenring, reading Paul's emotion, said, "Majesty, I must refuse."

Rage overcame Shaddam IV. He took two short steps through the entourage, cuffed Fenring viciously across the jaw.

A dark flush spread up and over the Count's face. He looked directly at the Emperor, spoke with deliberate lack of emphasis: "We have been friends, Majesty. What I do now is out of friendship. I shall forget that you struck me."

Paul cleared his throat, said: "We were speaking of the throne, Majesty."

The Emperor whirled, glared at Paul. "I sit on the throne!" he barked.

"You shall have a throne on Salusa Secundus," Paul said.

"I put down my arms and came here on your word of bond!" the Emperor shouted. "You dare threaten—"

"Your person is safe in my presence," Paul said. "An Atreides promised it. Muad'Dib, however, sentences you to your prison planet. But have no fear, Majesty. I will ease the harshness of the place with all the powers at my disposal. It shall become a garden world, full of gentle things."

As the hidden import of Paul's words grew in the Emperor's mind, he glared across the room at Paul. "Now we see true motives," he sneered.

"Indeed," Paul said.

"And what of Arrakis?" the Emperor asked. "Another garden world full of gentle things?"

"The Fremen have the word of Muad'Dib," Paul said. "There will be flowing water here open to the sky and green oases rich with good things. But we have the spice to think of, too. Thus there will always be desert on Arrakis . . . and fierce winds, and trials to toughen a man. We Fremen have a saying: 'God created Arrakis to train the faithful.' One cannot go against the word of God."

The old Truthsayer, the Reverend Mother Gaius Helen Mohiam, had her own view of the hidden meaning in Paul's words now. She glimpsed the jihad and said: "You cannot loose these people upon the universe!"

"You will think back to the gentle ways of the Sardaukar!" Paul snapped.

"You cannot," she whispered.

"You're a Truthsayer," Paul said. "Review your words." He glanced at the Princess Royal, back to the Emperor. "Best were done quickly, Majesty."

The Emperor turned a stricken look upon his daughter. She touched his arm, spoke soothingly: "For this I was trained, Father."

He took a deep breath.

"You cannot stay this thing," the old Truthsayer muttered.

The Emperor straightened, standing stiffly with a look of remembered dignity. "Who will negotiate for you, kinsman?" he asked.

Paul turned, saw his mother, her eyes heavy-lidded, standing with Chani in a squad of Fedaykin guards. He crossed to them, stood looking down at Chani.

"I know the reasons," Chani whispered. "If it must be . . . Usul."

Paul, hearing the secret tears in her voice, touched her cheek. "My Sihaya need fear nothing, ever," he whispered. He dropped his arm, faced his mother. "You will negotiate for me, Mother, with Chani by your side. She has wisdom and sharp eyes. And it is wisely said that no one bargains tougher than a Fremen. She will be looking through the eyes of her love for me and with the thought of her sons to be, what they will need. Listen to her."

Jessica sensed the harsh calculation in her son, put down a shudder. "What are your instructions?" she asked.

"The Emperor's entire CHOAM Company holdings as dowry," he said.

"Entire?" She was shocked almost speechless.

"He is to be stripped. I'll want an earldom and CHOAM directorship for Gurney Halleck, and him in the fief of Caladan. There will be titles and attendant power for every surviving Atreides man, not excepting the lowliest trooper."

"What of the Fremen?" Jessica asked.

"The Fremen are mine," Paul said. "What they receive shall be dispensed by Muad'Dib. It'll begin with Stilgar as Governor on Arrakis, but that can wait."

"And for me?" Jessica asked.

"Is there something you wish?"

"Perhaps Caladan," she said, looking at Gurney. "I'm not certain. I've become too much the Fremen . . . and the Reverend Mother. I need a time of peace and stillness in which to think."

"*That* you shall have," Paul said, "and anything else that Gurney or I can give you."

Jessica nodded, feeling suddenly old and tired. She looked at Chani. "And for the royal concubine?"

"No title for me," Chani whispered. "Nothing. I beg of you."

Paul stared down into her eyes, remembering her suddenly as she had stood once with little Leto in her arms, their child now dead in this violence. "I swear to you now," he whispered, "that you'll need no title. That woman over there will be my wife and you but a concubine because this is a political thing and we must weld peace out of this moment, enlist the Great Houses of the Landsraad. We must obey the forms. Yet that princess shall have no more of me than my name. No child of mine nor touch nor softness of glance, nor instant of desire."

"So you say now," Chani said. She glanced across the room at the tall princess.

"Do you know so little of my son?" Jessica whispered. "See that princess standing there, so haughty and confident. They say she has pretensions of a literary nature. Let us hope she finds solace in such things; she'll have little else." A bitter laugh escaped Jessica. "Think on it, Chani: that princess will have the name, yet she'll live as less than a concubine—never to know a moment of tenderness from the man to whom she's bound. While we, Chani, we who carry the name of concubine—history will call us wives."

# DUNE MESSIAH

*Such a rich store of myths enfolds Paul Muad'Dib, the Mentat Emperor,
and his sister, Alia, it is difficult to see the real persons behind these veils. But
there were, after all, a man born Paul Atreides and a woman born Alia. Their
flesh was subject to space and time. And even though their oracular powers
placed them beyond the usual limits of time and space, they came from human
stock. They experienced real events which left real traces upon a real
universe. To understand them, it must be seen that their catastrophe was the
catastrophe of all mankind. This work is dedicated, then, not to Muad'Dib or
his sister, but to their heirs—to all of us.*

**—Dedication in the Muad'Dib Concordance as
copied from the Tabla Memorium of the
Mahdi Spirit Cult**

Muad'Dib's Imperial reign generated more historians than any other era in
human history. Most of them argued a particular viewpoint, jealous and
sectarian, but it says something about the peculiar impact of this man that he
aroused such passions on so many diverse worlds.

Of course, he contained the ingredients of history, ideal and idealized. This
man, born Paul Atreides in an ancient Great Family, received the deep *prana-
bindu* training from the Lady Jessica, his Bene Gesserit mother, and had
through this a superb control over muscles and nerves. But more than that, he
was a *mentat*, an intellect whose capacities surpassed those of the religiously
proscribed mechanical computers used by the ancients.

Above all else, Muad'Dib was the *Kwisatz Haderach* which the Sisterhood's
breeding program had sought across thousands of generations.

The Kwisatz Haderach, then, the one who could be "many places at once,"
this prophet, this man through whom the Bene Gesserit hoped to control
human destiny—this man became Emperor Muad'Dib and executed a
marriage of convenience with a daughter of the Padishah Emperor he had
defeated.

Think on the paradox, the failure implicit in this moment, for you surely have
read other histories and know the surface facts. Muad'Dib's wild Fremen did,
indeed, overwhelm the Padishah Shaddam IV. They toppled the Sardaukar
legions, the allied forces of the Great Houses, the Harkonnen armies and the
mercenaries bought with money voted in the Landsraad. He brought the
Spacing Guild to its knees and placed his own sister, Alia, on the religious
throne the Bene Gesserit had thought their own.

He did all these things and more.

Muad'Dib's Qizarate missionaries carried their religious war across space in a Jihad whose major impetus endured only twelve standard years, but in that time, religious colonialism brought all but a fraction of the human universe under one rule.

He did this because capture of Arrakis, that planet known more often as Dune, gave him a monopoly over the ultimate coin of the realm—the geriatric spice, melange, the poison that gave life.

Here was another ingredient of ideal history: a material whose psychic chemistry unraveled Time. Without melange, the Sisterhood's Reverend Mothers could not perform their feats of observation and human control. Without melange, the Guild's Steersmen could not navigate across space. Without melange, billions upon billions of Imperial citizens would die of addictive withdrawal.

Without melange, Paul Muad'Dib could not prophesy.

We know this moment of supreme power contained failure. There can be only one answer, that completely accurate and total prediction is lethal.

Other histories say Muad'Dib was defeated by obvious plotters—the Guild, the Sisterhood and the scientific amoralists of the Bene Tleilax with their Face-Dancer disguises. Other histories point out the spies in Muad'Dib's household. They make much of the Dune Tarot which clouded Muad'Dib's powers of prophecy. Some show how Muad'Dib was made to accept the services of a *ghola*, the flesh brought back from the dead and trained to destroy him. But certainly they must know this ghola was Duncan Idaho, the Atreides lieutenant who perished saving the life of the young Paul.

Yet, they delineate the Qizarate cabal guided by Korba the Panegyrist. They take us step by step through Korba's plan to make a martyr of Muad'Dib and place the blame on Chani, the Fremen concubine.

How can any of this explain the facts as history has revealed them? They cannot. Only through the lethal nature of prophecy can we understand the failure of such enormous and far-seeing power.

Hopefully, other historians will learn something from this revelation.

> —Analysis of History: Muad'Dib
> by Bronso of Ix

> *There exists no separation between gods and men; one blends softly casual into the other.*
>
> **—Proverbs of Muad'Dib**

Despite the murderous nature of the plot he hoped to devise, the thoughts of Scytale, the Tleilaxu Face Dancer, returned again and again to rueful compassion.

*I shall regret causing death and misery to Muad'Dib*, he told himself.

He kept this benignity carefully hidden from his fellow conspirators. Such feelings told him, though, that he found it easier to identify with the victim than with the attackers—a thing characteristic of the Tleilaxu.

Scytale stood in bemused silence somewhat apart from the others. The argument about psychic poison had been going on for some time now. It was energetic and vehement, but polite in that blindly compulsive way adepts of the Great Schools always adopted for matters close to their dogma.

"When you think you have him skewered, right then you'll find him unwounded!"

That was the old Reverend Mother of the Bene Gesserit, Gaius Helen Mohiam, their hostess here on Wallach IX. She was a black-robed stick figure, a witch crone seated in a floater chair at Scytale's left. Her aba hood had been thrown back to expose a leathery face beneath silver hair. Deeply pocketed eyes stared out of skull-mask features.

They were using a *mirabhasa* language, honed phalange consonants and jointed vowels. It was an instrument for conveying fine emotional subtleties. Edric, the Guild Steersman, replied to the Reverend Mother now with a vocal curtsy contained in a sneer—a lovely touch of disdainful politeness.

Scytale looked at the Guild envoy. Edric swam in a container of orange gas only a few paces away. His container sat in the center of the transparent dome which the Bene Gesserit had built for this meeting. The Guildsman was an elongated figure, vaguely humanoid with finned feet and hugely fanned membranous hands—a fish in a strange sea. His tank's vents emitted a pale orange cloud rich with the smell of the geriatric spice, melange.

"If we go on this way, we'll die of stupidity!"

That was the fourth person present—the *potential* member of the conspiracy —Princess Irulan, wife (*but not mate*, Scytale reminded himself) of their mutual foe. She stood at a corner of Edric's tank, a tall blond beauty, splendid in a robe of blue whale fur and matching hat. Gold buttons glittered at her ears. She carried herself with an aristocrat's hauteur, but something in the absorbed smoothness of her features betrayed the controls of her Bene Gesserit background.

Scytale's mind turned from nuances of language and faces to nuances of location. All around the dome lay hills mangy with melting snow which reflected mottled wet blueness from the small blue-white sun hanging at the meridian.

*Why this particular place?* Scytale wondered. The Bene Gesserit seldom did anything casually. Take the dome's open plan: a more conventional and confining space might've inflicted the Guildsman with claustrophobic nervousness. Inhibitions in his psyche were those of birth and life off-planet in open space.

To have built this place especially for Edric, though—what a sharp finger that pointed at his weakness.

What here, Scytale wondered, was aimed at me?

"Have you nothing to say for yourself, Scytale?" the Reverend Mother demanded.

"You wish to draw me into this fools' fight?" Scytale asked. "Very well.

We're dealing with a potential messiah. You don't launch a frontal attack upon such a one. Martyrdom would defeat us."

They all stared at him.

"You think that's the only danger?" the Reverend Mother demanded, voice wheezing.

Scytale shrugged. He had chosen a bland, round-faced appearance for this meeting, jolly features and vapid full lips, the body of a bloated dumpling. It occurred to him now, as he studied his fellow conspirators, that he had made an ideal choice—out of instinct perhaps. He alone in this group could manipulate fleshly appearance across a wide spectrum of bodily shapes and features. He was the human chameleon, a Face Dancer, and the shape he wore now invited others to judge him too lightly.

"Well?" the Reverend Mother pressed.

"I was enjoying the silence," Scytale said. "Our hostilities are better left unvoiced."

The Reverend Mother drew back, and Scytale saw her reassessing him. They were all products of profound prana-bindu training, capable of muscle and nerve control that few humans ever achieved. But Scytale, a Face Dancer, had muscles and nerve linkages the others didn't even possess plus a special quality of *sympatico*, a mimic's insight with which he could put on the psyche of another as well as the other's appearance.

Scytale gave her enough time to complete the reassessment, said: "Poison!" He uttered the word with the atonals which said he alone understood its secret meaning.

The Guildsman stirred and his voice rolled from the glittering speaker globe which orbited a corner of his tank above Irulan. "We're discussing *psychic* poison, not a physical one."

Scytale laughed. Mirabhasa laughter could flay an opponent and he held nothing back now.

Irulan smiled in appreciation, but the corners of the Reverend Mother's eyes revealed a faint hint of anger.

"Stop that!" Mohiam rasped.

Scytale stopped, but he had their attention now, Edric in a silent rage, the Reverend Mother alert in her anger, Irulan amused but puzzled.

"Our friend Edric suggests," Scytale said, "that a pair of Bene Gesserit witches trained in all their subtle ways have not learned the true uses of deception."

Mohiam turned to stare out at the cold hills of her Bene Gesserit homeworld. She was beginning to see the vital thing here, Scytale realized. That was good. Irulan, though, was another matter.

"Are you one of us or not, Scytale?" Edric asked. He stared out of tiny rodent eyes.

"My allegiance is not the issue," Scytale said. He kept his attention on Irulan. "You are wondering, Princess, if this was why you came all those parsecs, risked so much?"

She nodded agreement.

"Was it to bandy platitudes with a humanoid fish or dispute with a fat Tleilaxu Face Dancer?" Scytale asked.

She stepped away from Edric's tank, shaking her head in annoyance at the thick odor of melange.

Edric took this moment to pop a melange pill into his mouth. He ate the spice and breathed it and, no doubt, drank it, Scytale noted. Understandable, because the spice heightened a Steersman's prescience, gave him the power to guide a Guild heighliner across space at translight speeds. With spice awareness he found that line of the ship's future which avoided peril. Edric smelled another kind of peril now, but his crutch of prescience might not find it.

"I think it was a mistake for me to come here," Irulan said.

The Reverend Mother turned, opened her eyes, closed them, a curiously reptilian gesture.

Scytale shifted his gaze from Irulan to the tank, inviting the Princess to share his viewpoint. She would, Scytale knew, see Edric as a repellent figure: the bold stare, those monstrous feet and hands moving softly in the gas, the smoky swirling of orange eddies around him. She would wonder about his sex habits, thinking how odd it would be to mate with such a one. Even the field-force generator which recreated for Edric the weightlessness of space would set him apart from her now.

"Princess," Scytale said, "because of Edric here, your husband's oracular sight cannot stumble upon certain incidents, including this one . . . presumably."

"Presumably," Irulan said.

Eyes closed, the Reverend Mother nodded. "The phenomenon of prescience is poorly understood even by its initiates," she said.

"I am a full Guild Navigator and have the Power," Edric said.

Again, the Reverend Mother opened her eyes. This time, she stared at the Face Dancer, eyes probing with that peculiar Bene Gesserit intensity. She was weighing minutiae.

"No, Reverend Mother," Scytale murmured, "I am not as simple as I appeared."

"We don't understand this Power of second sight," Irulan said. "There's a point. Edric says my husband cannot see, know or predict what happens within the sphere of a Navigator's influence. But how far does that influence extend?"

"There are people and things in our universe which I know only by their effects," Edric said, his fish mouth held in a thin line. "I know they have been here . . . there . . . somewhere. As water creatures stir up the currents in their passage, so the prescient stir up Time. I have seen where your husband has been; never have I seen him nor the people who truly share his aims and loyalties. This is the concealment which an adept gives to those who are his."

"Irulan is not yours," Scytale said. And he looked sideways at the Princess.

"We all know why the conspiracy must be conducted only in my presence," Edric said.

Using the voice mode for describing a machine, Irulan said: "You have your uses, apparently."

*She sees him now for what he is*, Scytale thought. *Good!*

"The future is a thing to be shaped," Scytale said. "Hold that thought, Princess."

Irulan glanced at the Face Dancer.

"People who share Paul's aims and loyalties," she said. "Certain of his Fremen legionaries, then, wear his cloak. I have seen him prophesy for them, heard their cries of adulation for their Mahdi, their Muad'Dib."

*It has occurred to her*, Scytale thought, *that she is on trial here, that a judgment remains to be made which could preserve her or destroy her. She sees the trap we set for her.*

Momentarily, Scytale's gaze locked with that of the Reverend Mother and he experienced the odd realization that they had shared this thought about Irulan. The Bene Gesserit, of course, had briefed their Princess, primed her with the *lie adroit*. But the moment always came when a Bene Gesserit must trust her own training and instincts.

"Princess, I know what it is you most desire from the Emperor," Edric said.

"Who does not know it?" Irulan asked.

"You wish to be the founding mother of the royal dynasty," Edric said, as though he had not heard her. "Unless you join us, that will never happen. Take my oracular word on it. The Emperor married you for political reasons, but you'll never share his bed."

"So the oracle is also a voyeur," Irulan sneered.

"The Emperor is more firmly wedded to his Fremen concubine than he is to you!" Edric snapped.

"And she gives him no heir," Irulan said.

"Reason is the first victim of strong emotion," Scytale murmured. He sensed the outpouring of Irulan's anger, saw his admonition take effect.

"She gives him no heir," Irulan said, her voice measuring out controlled calmness, "because I am secretly administering a contraceptive. Is that the sort of admission you wanted from me?"

"It'd not be a thing for the Emperor to discover," Edric said, smiling.

"I have lies ready for him," Irulan said. "He may have truthsense, but some lies are easier to believe than the truth."

"You must make the choice, Princess," Scytale said, "but understand what it is protects you."

"Paul is fair with me," she said. "I sit in his Council."

"In the twelve years you've been his Princess Consort," Edric asked, "has he shown you the slightest warmth?"

Irulan shook her head.

"He deposed your father with his infamous Fremen horde, married you to fix his claim to the throne, yet he has never crowned you Empress," Edric said.

"Edric tries to sway you with emotion, Princess," Scytale said. "Is that not interesting?"

She glanced at the Face Dancer, saw the bold smile on his features, answered it with raised eyebrows. She was fully aware now, Scytale saw, that if she left this conference under Edric's sway, part of their plot, these moments might be concealed from Paul's oracular vision. If she withheld commitment, though . . .

"Does it seem to you, Princess," Scytale asked, "that Edric holds undue sway in our conspiracy?"

"I've already agreed," Edric said, "that I'll defer to the best judgment offered in our councils."

"And who chooses the best judgment?" Scytale asked.

"Do you wish the Princess to leave here without joining us?" Edric asked.

"He wishes her commitment to be a real one," the Reverend Mother growled. "There should be no trickery between us."

Irulan, Scytale saw, had relaxed into a thinking posture, hands concealed in the sleeves of her robe. She would be thinking now of the bait Edric had offered: *to found a royal dynasty!* She would be wondering what scheme the conspirators had provided to protect themselves from her. She would be weighing many things.

"Scytale," Irulan said presently, "it is said that you Tleilaxu have an odd system of honor: your victims must always have a means of escape."

"If they can but find it," Scytale agreed.

"Am I a victim?" Irulan asked.

A burst of laughter escaped Scytale.

The Reverend Mother snorted.

"Princess," Edric said, his voice softly persuasive, "you already are one of us, have no fear of that. Do you not spy upon the Imperial Household for your Bene Gesserit superiors?"

"Paul knows I report to my teachers," she said.

"But don't you give them the material for strong propaganda against your Emperor?" Edric asked.

*Not "our" Emperor*, Scytale noted. *"Your" Emperor. Irulan is too much the Bene Gesserit to miss that slip.*

"The question is one of powers and how they may be used," Scytale said, moving closer to the Guildsman's tank. "We of the Tleilaxu believe that in all the universe there is only the insatiable appetite of matter, that energy is the only true *solid*. And energy learns. Hear me well, Princess: energy learns. This, we call power."

"You haven't convinced me we can defeat the Emperor," Irulan said.

"We haven't even convinced ourselves," Scytale said.

"Everywhere we turn," Irulan said, "his power confronts us. He's the Kwisatz Haderach, the one who can be many places at once. He's the Mahdi whose merest whim is absolute command to his Qizarate missionaries. He's the mentat whose computational mind surpasses the greatest ancient computers. He is Muad'Dib whose orders to the Fremen legions depopulate planets. He possesses oracular vision which sees into the future. He has that gene pattern which we Bene Gesserits covet for—"

"We know his attributes," the Reverend Mother interrupted. "And we know the abomination, his sister Alia, possesses this gene pattern. But they're also humans, both of them. Thus, they have weaknesses."

"And where are those human weaknesses?" the Face Dancer asked. "Shall we search for them in the religious arm of his Jihad? Can the Emperor's Qizara be turned against him? What about the civil authority of the Great Houses? Can the Landsraad Congress do more than raise a verbal clamor?"

"I suggest the Combine Honnete Ober Advancer Mercantiles," Edric said, turning in his tank. "CHOAM is business and business follows profits."

"Or perhaps the Emperor's mother," Scytale said. "The Lady Jessica, I understand, remains on Caladan, but is in frequent communication with her son."

"That traitorous bitch," Mohiam said, voice level. "Would I might disown my own hands which trained her."

"Our conspiracy requires a lever," Scytale said.

"We are more than conspirators," the Reverend Mother countered.

"Ah, yes," Scytale agreed. "We are energetic and we learn quickly. This makes us the one true hope, the certain salvation of humankind." He spoke in the speech mode for absolute conviction, which was perhaps the ultimate sneer coming as it did, from a Tleilaxu.

Only the Reverend Mother appeared to understand the subtlety. "Why?" she asked, directing the question at Scytale.

Before the Face Dancer could answer, Edric cleared his throat, said: "Let us not bandy philosophical nonsense. Every question can be boiled down to the one: 'Why is there anything?' Every religious, business and governmental question has the single derivative: 'Who will exercise the power?' Alliances, combines, complexes, they all chase mirages unless they go for the power. All else is nonsense, as most thinking beings come to realize."

Scytale shrugged, a gesture designed solely for the Reverend Mother. Edric had answered her question for him. The pontificating fool was their major weakness. To make sure the Reverend Mother understood, Scytale said: "Listening carefully to the teacher, one acquires an education."

The Reverend Mother nodded slowly.

"Princess," Edric said, "make your choice. You have been chosen as an instrument of destiny, the very finest . . . ."

"Save your praise for those who can be swayed by it," Irulan said. "Earlier, you mentioned a ghost, a revenant with which we may contaminate the Emperor. Explain this."

"The Atreides will defeat himself!" Edric crowed.

"Stop talking riddles!" Irulan snapped. "What is this ghost?"

"A very unusual ghost," Edric said. "It has a body and a name. The body—that's the flesh of a renowned swordmaster known as Duncan Idaho. The name . . . ."

"Idaho's dead," Irulan said. "Paul has mourned the loss often in my presence. He saw Idaho killed by my father's Sardaukar."

"Even in defeat," Edric said, "your father's Sardaukar did not abandon wisdom. Let us suppose a wise Sardaukar commander recognized the swordmaster in a corpse his men had slain. What then? There exist uses for such flesh and training . . . if one acts swiftly."

"A Tleilaxu ghola," Irulan whispered, looking sideways at Scytale.

Scytale, observing her attention, exercised his Face-Dancer powers—shape flowing into shape, flesh moving and readjusting. Presently, a slender man stood before her. The face remained somewhat round, but darker and with slightly flattened features. High cheekbones formed shelves for eyes with definite epicanthic folds. The hair was black and unruly.

"A ghola of this appearance," Edric said, pointing to Scytale.

"Or merely another Face Dancer?" Irulan asked.

"No Face Dancer," Edric said. "A Face Dancer risks exposure under prolonged surveillance. No; let us assume that our wise Sardaukar commander had Idaho's corpse preserved for the axolotl tanks. Why not? This corpse held the flesh and nerves of one of the finest swordsmen in history, an adviser to the Atreides, a military genius. What a waste to lose all that training and ability when it might be revived as an instructor for the Sardaukar."

"I heard not a whisper of this and I was one of my father's confidantes," Irulan said.

"Ahh, but your father was a defeated man and within a few hours you had been sold to the new Emperor," Edric said.

"Was it done?" she demanded.

With a maddening air of complacency, Edric said: "Let us presume that our wise Sardaukar commander, knowing the need for speed, immediately sent the preserved flesh of Idaho to the Bene Tleilax. Let us suppose further that the commander and his men died before conveying this information to your father—who couldn't have made much use of it anyway. There would remain then a physical fact, a bit of flesh which had been sent off to the Tleilaxu. There was only one way for it to be sent, of course, on a heighliner. We of the Guild naturally know every cargo we transport. Learning of this one, would we not think it additional wisdom to purchase the ghola as a gift befitting an Emperor?"

"You've done it then," Irulan said.

Scytale, who had resumed his roly-poly first appearance, said: "As our long-winded friend indicates, we've done it."

"How has Idaho been conditioned?" Irulan asked.

"Idaho?" Edric asked, looking at the Tleilaxu. "Do you know of an Idaho, Scytale?"

"We sold you a creature called Hayt," Scytale said.

"Ah, yes—Hayt," Edric said. "Why did you sell him to us?"

"Because we once bred a Kwisatz Haderach of our own," Scytale said.

With a quick movement of her old head, the Reverend Mother looked up at him. "You didn't tell us that!" she accused.

"You didn't ask," Scytale said.

"How did you overcome your Kwisatz Haderach?" Irulan asked.

"A creature who has spent his life creating one particular representation of his selfdom will die rather than become the antithesis of that representation," Scytale said.

"I do not understand," Edric ventured.

"He killed himself," the Reverend Mother growled.

"Follow me well, Reverend Mother," Scytale warned, using a voice mode which said: You are not a sex object, have never been a sex object, cannot be a sex object.

The Tleilaxu waited for the blatant emphasis to sink in. She must not mistake his intent. Realization must pass through anger into awareness that the Tleilaxu certainly could not make such an accusation, knowing as he must the breeding requirements of the Sisterhood. His words, though, contained a gutter insult, completely out of character for a Tleilaxu.

Swiftly, using the mirabhasa placative mode, Edric tried to smooth over the moment. "Scytale, you told us you sold Hayt because you shared our desire on how to use him."

"Edric, you will remain silent until I give you permission to speak," Scytale said. And as the Guildsman started to protest, the Reverend Mother snapped: "Shut up, Edric!"

The Guildsman drew back into his tank in flailing agitation.

"Our own transient emotions aren't pertinent to a solution of the mutual problem," Scytale said. "They cloud reasoning because the only relevant emotion is the basic fear which brought us to this meeting."

"We understand," Irulan said, glancing at the Reverend Mother.

"You must see the dangerous limitations of our shield," Scytale said. "The oracle cannot chance upon what it cannot understand."

"You are devious, Scytale," Irulan said.

*How devious she must not guess*, Scytale thought. *When this is done, we will possess a Kwisatz Haderach we can control. These others will possess nothing.*

"What was the origin of your Kwisatz Haderach?" the Reverend Mother asked.

"We've dabbled in various pure essences," Scytale said. "Pure good and pure evil. A pure villain who delights only in creating pain and terror can be quite educational."

"The old Baron Harkonnen, our Emperor's grandfather, was he a Tleilaxu creation?" Irulan asked.

"Not one of ours," Scytale said. "But then nature often produces creations as deadly as ours. We merely produce them under conditions where we can study them."

"I will not be passed by and treated this way!" Edric protested. "Who is it hides this meeting from—"

"You see?" Scytale asked. "Whose best judgment conceals us? What judgment?"

"I wish to discuss our mode of giving Hayt to the Emperor," Edric insisted. "It's my understanding that Hayt reflects the old morality that the Atreides learned on his birthworld. Hayt is supposed to make it easy for the Emperor to enlarge his moral nature, to delineate the positive-negative elements of life and religion."

Scytale smiled, passing a benign gaze over his companions. They were as he'd been led to expect. The old Reverend Mother wielded her emotions like a scythe. Irulan had been well trained for a task at which she had failed, a flawed Bene Gesserit creation. Edric was no more (and no less) than the magician's hand: he might conceal and distract. For now, Edric relapsed into sullen silence as the others ignored him.

"Do I understand that this Hayt is intended to poison Paul's psyche?" Irulan asked.

"More or less," Scytale said.

"And what of the Qizarate?" Irulan asked.

"It requires only the slightest shift in emphasis, a glissade of the emotions, to transform envy into enmity," Scytale said.

"And CHOAM?" Irulan asked.

"They will rally round profit," Scytale said.

"What of the other power groups?"

"One invokes the name of government," Scytale said. "We will annex the less powerful in the name of morality and progress. Our opposition will die of its own entanglements."

"Alia, too?"

"Hayt is a multi-purpose ghola," Scytale said. "The Emperor's sister is of an age when she can be distracted by a charming male designed for that purpose. She will be attracted by his maleness and by his abilities as a mentat."

Mohiam allowed her old eyes to go wide in surprise. "The ghola's a mentat? That's a dangerous move."

"To be accurate," Irulan said, "a mentat must have accurate data. What if Paul asks him to define the purpose behind our gift?"

"Hayt will tell the truth," Scytale said. "It makes no difference."

"So you leave an escape door open for Paul," Irulan said.

"A mentat!" Mohiam muttered.

Scytale glanced at the old Reverend Mother, seeing the ancient hates which colored her responses. From the days of the Butlerian Jihad when "thinking machines" had been wiped from most of the universe, computers had inspired distrust. Old emotions colored the human computer as well.

"I do not like the way you smile," Mohiam said abruptly, speaking in the truth mode as she glared up at Scytale.

In the same mode, Scytale said: "And I think less of what pleases you. But we must work together. We all see that." He glanced at the Guildsman. "Don't we, Edric?"

"You teach painful lessons," Edric said. "I presume you wished to make it plain that I must not assert myself against the combined judgments of my fellow conspirators."

"You see, he can be taught," Scytale said.

"I see other things as well," Edric growled. "The Atreides holds a monopoly on the spice. Without it I cannot probe the future. The Bene Gesserit lose their truthsense. We have stockpiles, but these are finite. Melange is a powerful coin."

"Our civilization has more than one coin," Scytale said. "Thus, the law of supply and demand fails."

"You think to steal the secret of it," Mohiam wheezed. "And him with a planet guarded by his mad Fremen!"

"The Fremen are civil, educated and ignorant," Scytale said. "They're not mad. They're trained to believe, not to know. Belief can be manipulated. Only knowledge is dangerous."

"But will I be left with something to father a royal dynasty?" Irulan asked. They all heard the commitment in her voice, but only Edric smiled at it.

"Something," Scytale said. "Something."

"It means the end of this Atreides as a ruling force," Edric said.

"I should imagine that others less gifted as oracles have made that prediction," Scytale said. "For them, *mektub al mellah*, as the Fremen say."

"The thing was written with salt," Irulan translated.

As she spoke, Scytale recognized what the Bene Gesserit had arrayed here for him—a beautiful and intelligent female who could never be his. *Ah, well,* he thought, *perhaps I'll copy her for another.*

---

*Every civilization must contend with an unconscious force which can block, betray or countermand almost any conscious intention of the collectivity.*

**—Tleilaxu Theorem (unproven)**

Paul sat on the edge of his bed and began stripping off his desert boots. They smelled rancid from the lubricant which eased the action of the heel-powered pumps that drove his stillsuit. It was late. He had prolonged his nighttime walk and caused worry for those who loved him. Admittedly, the walks were dangerous, but it was a kind of danger he could recognize and meet immediately. Something compelling and attractive surrounded walking anonymously at night in the streets of Arrakeen.

He tossed the boots into the corner beneath the room's lone glowglobe, attacked the seal strips of his stillsuit. Gods below, how tired he was! The tiredness stopped at his muscles, though, and left his mind seething. Watching the mundane activities of everyday life filled him with profound envy. Most of that nameless flowing life outside the walls of his Keep couldn't be shared by an Emperor—but . . . to walk down a public street without attracting attention: what a privilege! To pass by the clamoring of mendicant pilgrims, to hear a Fremen curse a shopkeeper: "You have damp hands!". . . .

Paul smiled at the memory, slipped out of his stillsuit.

He stood naked and oddly attuned to his world. Dune was a world of paradox now—a world under siege, yet the center of power. To come under siege, he decided, was the inevitable fate of power. He stare down at the green carpeting, feeling its rough texture against his soles.

The streets had been ankle deep in sand blown over the Shield Wall on the stratus wind. Foot traffic had churned it into choking dust which clogged stillsuit filters. He could smell the dust even now despite a blower cleaning at the portals of his Keep. It was an odor full of desert memories.

*Other days . . . other dangers.*

Compared to those other days, the peril in his lonely walks remained minor. But, putting on a stillsuit, he put on the desert. The suit with all its apparatus for reclaiming his body's moisture guided his thoughts in subtle ways, fixed his movements in a desert pattern. He became wild Fremen. More than a disguise, the suit made of him a stranger to his city self. In the stillsuit, he abandoned security and put on the old skills of violence. Pilgrims and townfolk passed him then with eyes downcast. They left the wild ones strictly alone out of prudence. If the desert had a face for city folk, it was a Fremen face concealed by a stillsuit's mouth-nose filters.

In truth, there existed now only the small danger that someone from the old *sietch* days might mark him by his walk, by his odor or by his eyes. Even then, the chances of meeting an enemy remained small.

A swish of door hangings and a wash of light broke his reverie. Chani entered bearing his coffee service on a platinum tray. Two slaved glowglobes followed her, darting to their positions: one at the head of their bed, one hovering beside her to light her work.

Chani moved with an ageless air of fragile power—so self-contained, so vulnerable. Something about the way she bent over the coffee service reminded him then of their first days. Her features remained darkly elfin, seemingly unmarked by their years—unless one examined the outer corners of her whiteless eyes, noting the lines there: "sandtracks," the Fremen of the desert called them.

Steam wafted from the pot as she lifted the lid by its Hagar emerald knob. He could tell the coffee wasn't yet ready by the way she replaced the lid. The pot—fluting silver female shape, pregnant—had come to him as a *ghanima*, a spoil of battle won when he'd slain the former owner in single combat. Jamis, that'd been the man's name . . . Jamis. What an odd immortality death had earned for Jamis. Knowing death to be inevitable, had Jamis carried that particular one in his mind?

Chani put out cups: blue pottery squatting like attendants beneath the immense pot. There were three cups: one for each drinker and one for all the former owners.

"It'll only be a moment," she said.

She looked at him then, and Paul wondered how he appeared in her eyes. Was he yet the exotic offworlder, slim and wiry but water-fat when compared to Fremen? Had he remained the Usul of his tribal name who'd taken her in "Fremen *tau*" while they'd been fugitives in the desert?

Paul stared down at his own body: hard muscles, slender . . . a few more scars, but essentially the same despite twelve years as Emperor. Looking up, he glimpsed his face in a shelf mirror—blue-blue Fremen eyes, mark of spice addiction; a sharp Atreides nose. He looked the proper grandson for an Atreides who'd died in the bull ring creating a spectacle for his people.

Something the old man had said slipped then into Paul's mind: *"One who rules assumes irrevocable responsibility for the ruled. You are a husbandman. This demands, at times, a selfless act of love which may only be amusing to those you rule."*

People still remembered that old man with affection.

*And what have I done for the Atreides name?* Paul asked himself. *I've loosed the wolf among the sheep.*

For a moment, he contemplated all the death and violence going on in his name.

"Into bed now!" Chani said in a sharp tone of command that Paul knew would've shocked his Imperial subjects.

He obeyed, lay back with his hands behind his head, letting himself be lulled by the pleasant familiarity of Chani's movements.

The room around them struck him suddenly with amusement. It was not at all what the populace must imagine as the Emperor's bedchamber. The yellow light of restless glowglobes moved the shadows in an array of colored glass jars on a shelf behind Chani. Paul named their contents silently—the dry ingredients of the desert pharmacopoeia, unguents, incense, mementos . . . a pinch of sand from Sietch Tabr, a lock of hair from their firstborn . . . long dead . . . twelve years dead . . . an innocent bystander killed in the battle that had made Paul Emperor.

The rich odor of spice-coffee filled the room. Paul inhaled, his glance falling on a yellow bowl beside the tray where Chani was preparing the coffee. The bowl held ground nuts. The inevitable poison-snooper mounted beneath the table waved its insect arms over the food. The snooper angered him. They'd never needed snoopers in the desert days!

"Coffee's ready," Chani said. "Are you hungry?"

His angry denial was drowned in the whistling scream of a spice lighter hurling itself spaceward from the field outside Arrakeen.

Chani saw his anger, though, poured their coffee, put a cup near his hand. She sat down on the foot of the bed, exposed his legs, began rubbing them where the muscles were knotted from walking in the stillsuit. Softly, with a casual air which did not deceive him, she said: "Let us discuss Irulan's desire for a child."

Paul's eyes snapped wide open. He studied Chani carefully. "Irulan's been back from Wallach less than two days," he said. "Has she been at you already?"

"We've not discussed her frustrations," Chani said.

Paul forced his mind to mental alertness, examined Chani in the harsh light of observational minutiae, the Bene Gesserit Way his mother had taught him in violation of her vows. It was a thing he didn't like doing with Chani. Part of her hold on him lay in the fact he so seldom needed his tension-building powers with her. Chani mostly avoided indiscreet questions. She maintained a Fremen sense of good manners. Hers were more often practical questions. What interested Chani were facts which bore on the position of her man—his strength in Council, the loyalty of his legions, the abilities and talents of his allies. Her memory held catalogs of names and cross-indexed details. She could rattle off the major weakness of every known enemy, the potential dispositions of opposing forces, battle plans of their military leaders, the tooling and production capacities of basic industries.

Why now, Paul wondered, did she ask about Irulan?

"I've troubled your mind," Chani said. "That wasn't my intention."

"What was your intention?"

She smiled shyly, meeting his gaze. "If you're angered, love, please don't hide it."

Paul sank back against the headboard. "Shall I put her away?" he asked. "Her use is limited now and I don't like the things I sense about her trip home to the Sisterhood."

"You'll not put her away," Chani said. She went on massaging his legs, spoke matter-of-factly: "You've said many times she's your contact with our enemies, that you can read their plans through her actions."

"Then why ask about her desire for a child?"

"I think it'd disconcert our enemies and put Irulan in a vulnerable position should you make her pregnant."

He read by the movements of her hands on his legs what that statement had cost her. A lump rose in his throat. Softly, he said: "Chani, beloved, I swore an oath never to take her into my bed. A child would give her too much power. Would you have her displace you?"

"I have no place."

"Not so, Sihaya, my desert springtime. What is this sudden concern for Irulan?"

"It's concern for you, not for her! If she carried an Atreides child, her friends would question her loyalties. The less trust our enemies place in her, the less use she is to them."

"A child for her could mean your death," Paul said. "You know the plotting in this place." A movement of his arm encompassed the Keep.

"You must have an heir!" she husked.

"Ahhh," he said.

So that was it: Chani had not produced a child for him. Someone else, then, must do it. Why not Irulan? That was the way Chani's mind worked. And it must be done in an act of love because all the Empire avowed strong taboos against artificial ways. Chani had come to a Fremen decision.

Paul studied her face in this new light. It was a face he knew better in some ways than his own. He had seen this face soft with passion, in the sweetness of sleep, awash in fears and angers and griefs.

He closed his eyes, and Chani came into his memories as a girl once more—veiled in springtime, singing, waking from sleep beside him—so perfect that the very vision of her consumed him. In his memory, she smiled . . . shyly at first, then strained against the vision as though she longed to escape.

Paul's mouth went dry. For a moment, his nostrils tasted the smoke of a devastated future and the voice of another kind of vision commanding him to disengage . . . disengage . . . disengage. His prophetic visions had been eavesdropping on eternity for such a long while, catching snatches of foreign tongues, listening to stones and to flesh not his own. Since the day of his first encounter with terrible purpose, he had peered at the future, hoping to find peace.

There existed a way, of course. He knew it by heart without knowing the heart of it—a rote future, strict in its instructions to him: disengage, disengage, disengage . . . .

Paul opened his eyes, looked at the decision in Chani's face. She had stopped massaging his legs, sat still now—purest Fremen. Her features remained familiar beneath the blue *nezhoni* scarf she often wore about her hair in the privacy of their chambers. But the mask of decision sat on her, an ancient and alien-to-him way of thinking. Fremen women had shared their men for thousands of years—not always in peace but with a way of making the fact nondestructive. Something mysteriously Fremen in this fashion had happened in Chani.

"You'll give me the only heir I want," he said.

"You've *seen* this?" she asked, making it obvious by her emphasis that she referred to prescience.

As he had done many times, Paul wondered how he could explain the delicacy of the oracle, the Timelines without number which vision waved before him on an undulating fabric. He sighed, remembered water lifted from a river in the hollow of his hands—trembling, draining. Memory drenched his face in it. How could he drench himself in futures growing increasingly obscure from the pressure of too many oracles?

"You've not *seen* it, then," Chani said.

That vision-future scarce any longer accessible to him except at the expenditure of life-draining effort, what could it show them except grief? Paul asked himself. He felt that he occupied an inhospitable middle zone, a wasted place where his emotions drifted, swayed, swept outward in unchecked restlessness.

Chani covered his legs, said: "An heir to House Atreides, this is not something you leave to chance or one woman."

That was a thing his mother might've said, Paul thought. He wondered if the Lady Jessica had been in secret communication with Chani. His mother would think in terms of House Atreides. It was a pattern bred and conditioned into her by the Bene Gesserit, and would hold true even now when her powers were turned against the Sisterhood.

"You listened when Irulan came to me today," he accused.

"I listened." She spoke without looking at him.

Paul focused his memory on the encounter with Irulan. He'd let himself into the family salon, noted an unfinished robe on Chani's loom. There'd been an acrid wormsmell to the place, an evil odor which almost hid the underlying cinnamon bite of melange. Someone had spilled unchanged spice essence and left it to combine there with a spice-based rug. It had not been a felicitous combination. Spice essence had dissolved the rug. Oily marks lay congealed on the plastone floor where the rug had been. He'd thought to send for someone to clean away the mess, but Harah, Stilgar's wife and Chani's closest feminine friend, had slipped in to announce Irulan.

He'd been forced to conduct the interview in the presence of that evil smell, unable to escape a Fremen superstition that evil smells foretold disaster.

Harah withdrew as Irulan entered.

"Welcome," Paul said.

Irulan wore a robe of gray whale fur. She pulled it close, touched a hand to her hair. He could see her wondering at his mild tone. The angry words she'd obviously prepared for this meeting could be sensed leaving her mind in a welter of second thoughts.

"You came to report that the Sisterhood has lost its last vestige of morality," he said.

"Isn't it dangerous to be that ridiculous?" she asked.

"To be ridiculous and dangerous, a questionable alliance," he said. His renegade Bene Gesserit training detected her putting down an impulse to withdraw. The effort exposed a brief glimpse of underlying fear, and he saw she'd been assigned a task not to her liking.

"They expect a bit too much from a princess of the blood royal," he said.

Irulan grew very still and Paul became aware that she had locked herself into a viselike control. A heavy burden, indeed, he thought. And he wondered why prescient visions had given him no glimpse of this possible future.

Slowly, Irulan relaxed. There was no point in surrendering to fear, no point in retreat, she had decided.

"You've allowed the weather to fall into a very primitive pattern," she said, rubbing her arms through the robe. "It was dry and there was a sandstorm today. Are you never going to let it rain here?"

"You didn't come here to talk about the weather," Paul said. He felt that he had been submerged in double meanings. Was Irulan trying to tell him something which her training would not permit her to say openly? It seemed that way. He felt that he had been cast adrift suddenly and now must thrash his way back to some steady place.

"I must have a child," she said.

He shook his head from side to side.

"I must have my way!" she snapped. "If need be, I'll find another father for my child. I'll cuckold you and dare you to expose me."

"Cuckold me all you wish," he said, "but no child."

"How can you stop me?"

With a smile of utmost kindness, he said: "I'd have you garrotted, if it came to that."

Shocked silence held her for a moment and Paul sensed Chani listening behind the heavy draperies into their private apartments.

"I am your wife," Irulan whispered.

"Let us not play these silly games," he said. "You play a part, no more. We both know who my wife is."

"And I am a convenience, nothing more," she said, voice heavy with bitterness.

"I have no wish to be cruel to you," he said.

"You chose me for this position."

"Not I," he said. "Fate chose you. Your father chose you. The Bene Gesserit chose you. The Guild chose you. And they have chosen you once more. For what have they chosen you, Irulan?"

"Why can't I have your child?"

"Because that's a role for which you weren't chosen."

"It's my right to bear the royal heir! My father was—"

"Your father was and is a beast. We both know he'd lost almost all touch with the humanity he was supposed to rule and protect."

"Was he hated less than you're hated?" she flared.

"A good question," he agreed, a sardonic smile touching the edges of his mouth.

"You say you've no wish to be cruel to me, yet . . . ."

"And that's why I agree that you can take any lover you choose. But understand me well: take a lover, but bring no sour-fathered child into my household. I would deny such a child. I don't begrudge you any male alliance as long as you are discreet . . . and childless. I'd be silly to feel otherwise under the circumstances. But don't presume upon this license which I freely bestow. Where the throne is concerned, I control what blood is heir to it. The Bene Gesserit doesn't control this, nor does the Guild. This is one of the privileges I won when I smashed your father's Sardaukar legions out there on the Plain of Arrakeen."

"It's on your head, then," Irulan said. She whirled and swept out of the chamber.

Remembering the encounter now, Paul brought his awareness out of it and focused on Chani seated beside him on their bed. He could understand his ambivalent feelings about Irulan, understand Chani's Fremen decision. Under other circumstances Chani and Irulan might have been friends.

"What have you decided?" Chani asked.

"No child," he said.

Chani made the Fremen crysknife sign with the index finger and thumb of her right hand.

"It could come to that," he agreed.

"You don't think a child would solve anything with Irulan?" she asked.

"Only a fool would think that."

"I am not a fool, my love."

Anger possessed him. "I've never said you were! But this isn't some damned romantic novel we're discussing. That's a real princess down the hall. She was raised in all the nasty intrigues of an Imperial Court. Plotting is as natural to her as writing her stupid histories!"

"They are not stupid, love."

"Probably not." He brought his anger under control, took her hand in his. "Sorry. But that woman has many plots—plots within plots. Give in to one of her ambitions and you could advance another of them."

Her voice mild, Chani said: "Haven't I always said as much?"

"Yes, of course you have." He stared at her. "Then what are you really trying to say to me?"

She lay down beside him, placed her head against his neck. "They have come to a decision on how to fight you," she said. "Irulan reeks of secret decisions."

Paul stroked her hair.

Chani had peeled away the dross.

Terrible purpose brushed him. It was a *coriolis* wind in his soul. It whistled through the framework of his being. His body knew things then never learned in consciousness.

"Chani, beloved," he whispered, "do you know what I'd spend to end the Jihad—to separate myself from the damnable godhead the Qizarate forces onto me?"

She trembled. "You have but to command it," she said.

"Oh, no. Even if I died now, my name would still lead them. When I think of the Atreides name tied to this religious butchery . . . ."

"But you're the Emperor! You've—"

"I'm a figurehead. When godhead's given, that's the one thing the so-called god no longer controls." A bitter laugh shook him. He sensed the future looking back at him out of dynasties not even dreamed. He felt his being cast out, crying, unchained from the rings of fate—only his name continued. "I was chosen," he said. "Perhaps at birth . . . certainly before I had much say in it. I was chosen."

"Then un-choose," she said.

His arm tightened around her shoulder. "In time, beloved. Give me yet a little time."

Unshed tears burned his eyes.

"We should return to Sietch Tabr," Chani said. "There's too much to contend with in this tent of stone."

He nodded, his chin moving against the smooth fabric of the scarf which covered her hair. The soothing spice smell of her filled his nostrils.

Sietch. The ancient Chakobsa word absorbed him: a place of retreat and safety in a time of peril. Chani's suggestion made him long for vistas of open sand, for clean distances where one could see an enemy coming from a long way off.

"The tribes expect Muad'Dib to return to them," she said. She lifted her head to look at him. "You belong to us."

"I belong to a vision," he whispered.

He thought then of the Jihad, of the gene mingling across parsecs and the vision which told him how he might end it. Should he pay the price? All the hatefulness would evaporate, dying as fires die—ember by ember. But . . . oh! The terrifying price!

*I never wanted to be a god,* he thought. *I wanted only to disappear like a jewel of trace dew caught by the morning. I wanted to escape the angels and the damned—alone . . . as though by an oversight.*

"Will we go back to the Sietch?" Chani pressed.

"Yes," he whispered. And he thought: *I must pay the price.*

Chani heaved a deep sigh, settled back against him.

*I've loitered,* he thought. And he saw how he'd been hemmed in by boundaries of love and the Jihad. And what was one life, no matter how beloved, against all the lives the Jihad was certain to take? Could single misery be weighed against the agony of multitudes?

428 THE GREAT DUNE TRILOGY

"Love?" Chani said, questioning.

He put a hand against her lips.

*I'll yield up myself,* he thought. *I'll rush out while I yet have the strength, fly through a space a bird might not find.* It was a useless thought, and he knew it. The Jihad would follow his ghost.

What could he answer? he wondered. How explain when people taxed him with brutal foolishness? Who might understand?

*I wanted only to look back and say: "There! There's an existence which couldn't hold me. See! I vanish! No restraint or net of human devising can trap me ever again. I renounce my religion! This glorious instant is mine! I'm free!"*

*What empty words!*

"A big worm was seen below the Shield Wall yesterday," Chani said. "More than a hundred meters long, they say. Such big ones come rarely into this region any more. The water repels them, I suppose. They say this one came to summon Muad'Dib home to his desert." She pinched his chest. "Don't laugh at me!"

"I'm not laughing."

Paul, caught by wonder at the persistent Fremen mythos, felt a heart constriction, a thing inflicted upon his lifeline: *adab,* the demanding memory. He recalled his childhood room on Caladan then . . . dark night in the stone chamber . . . a vision! It'd been one of his earliest prescient moments. He felt his mind dive into the vision, saw through a veiled cloud-memory (vision-within-vision) a line of Fremen, their robes trimmed with dust. They paraded past a gap in tall rocks. They carried a long, cloth-wrapped burden.

And Paul heard himself say in the vision: "It was mostly sweet . . . but you were the sweetest of all . . . ."

Adab released him.

"You're so quiet," Chani whispered. "What is it?"

Paul shuddered, sat up, face averted.

"You're angry because I've been to the desert's edge," Chani said.

He shook his head without speaking.

"I only went because I want a child," Chani said.

Paul was unable to speak. He felt himself consumed by the raw power of that early vision. Terrible purpose! In that moment, his whole life was a limb shaken by the departure of a bird . . . and the bird was *chance.* Free will.

*I succumbed to the lure of the oracle,* he thought.

And he sensed that succumbing to this lure might be to fix himself upon a single-track life. Could it be, he wondered, that the oracle didn't *tell* the future? Could it be that the oracle *made* the future? Had he exposed his life to some web of underlying threads, trapped himself there in that long-ago awakening, victim of a spider-future which even now advanced upon him with terrifying jaws.

A Bene Gesserit axiom slipped into his mind: *To use raw power is to make yourself infinitely vulnerable to greater powers.*

"I know it angers you," Chani said, touching his arm. "It's true that the tribes have revived the old rites and the blood sacrifices, but I took no part in those."

Paul inhaled a deep, trembling breath. The torrent of his vision dissipated, became a deep, still place whose currents moved with absorbing power beyond his reach.

"Please," Chani begged. "I want a child, our child. Is that a terrible thing?"

Paul caressed her arm where she touched him, pulled away. He climbed from the bed, extinguished the glowglobes, crossed to the balcony window, opened the draperies. The deep desert could not intrude here except by its odors. A windowless wall climbed to the night sky across from him. Moonlight slanted down into an enclosed garden, sentinel trees and broad leaves, wet foliage. He could see a fish pond reflecting stars among the leaves, pockets of white floral brilliance in the shadows. Momentarily, he saw the garden through Fremen eyes: alien, menacing, dangerous in its waste of water.

He thought of the Water Sellers, their way destroyed by the lavish dispensing from his hands. They hated him. He'd slain the past. And there were others, even those who'd fought for the sols to buy precious water, who hated him for changing the old ways. As the ecological pattern dictated by Muad'Dib remade the planet's landscape, human resistance increased. Was it not presumptuous, he wondered, to think he could make over an entire planet—everything growing where and how he told it to grow? Even if he succeeded, what of the universe waiting out there? Did it fear similar treatment?

Abruptly, he closed the draperies, sealed the ventilators. He turned toward Chani in the darkness, felt her waiting there. Her water rings tinkled like the almsbells of pilgrims. He groped his way to the sound, encountered her outstretched arms.

"Beloved," she whispered. "Have I troubled you?"

Her arms enclosed his future as they enclosed him.

"Not you," he said. "Oh . . . not you."

*The advent of the Field Process shield and the lasgun with their explosive interaction, deadly to attacker and attacked, placed the current determinatives on weapons technology. We need not go into the special role of atomics. The fact that any Family in my Empire could so deploy its atomics as to destroy the planetary bases of fifty or more other Families causes some nervousness, true. But all of us possess precautionary plans for devastating retaliation. Guild and Landsraad contain the keys which hold this force in check. No, my concern goes to the development of humans as special weapons. Here is a virtually unlimited field which a few powers are developing.*

**—Muad'Dib: Lecture to the War College
from The Stilgar Chronicle**

The old man stood in his doorway peering out with blue-in-blue eyes. The eyes were veiled by that native suspicion all desert folk held for strangers. Bitter lines tortured the edges of his mouth where it could be seen through a fringe of white beard. He wore no stillsuit and it said much that he ignored this fact in the full knowledge of the moisture pouring from his house through the open door.

Scytale bowed, gave the greeting signal of the conspiracy.

From somewhere behind the old man came the sound of a rebec wailing through the atonal dissonance of *semuta* music. The old man's manner carried no drug dullness, an indication that semuta was the weakness of another. It seemed strange to Scytale, though, to find that sophisticated vice in this place.

"Greetings from afar," Scytale said, smiling through the flat-featured face he had chosen for this encounter. It occurred to him, then, that this old man might recognize the chosen face. Some of the older Fremen here on Dune had known Duncan Idaho.

The choice of features, which he had thought amusing, might have been a mistake, Scytale decided. But he dared not change the face out here. He cast nervous glances up and down the street. Would the old man never invite him inside?

"Did you know my son?" the old man asked.

That, at least, was one of the countersigns. Scytale made the proper response, all the time keeping his eyes alert for any suspicious circumstance in his surroundings. He did not like his position here. The street was a cul-de-sac ending in this house. The houses all around had been built for veterans of the Jihad. They formed a suburb of Arrakeen which stretched into the Imperial Basin past Tiemag. The walls which hemmed in this street presented blank faces of dun plasmeld broken by dark shadows of sealed doorways and, here and there, scrawled obscenities. Beside this very door someone had chalked a pronouncement that one Beris had brought back to Arrakis a loathsome disease which deprived him of his manhood.

"Do you come in partnership," the old man asked.

"Alone," Scytale said.

The old man cleared his throat, still hesitating in that maddening way.

Scytale cautioned himself to patience. Contact in this fashion carried its own dangers. Perhaps the old man knew some reason for carrying on this way. It was the proper hour, though. The pale sun stood almost directly overhead. People of this quarter remained sealed in their houses to sleep through the hot part of the day.

Was it the new neighbor who bothered the old man? Scytale wondered. The adjoining house, he knew, had been assigned to Otheym, once a member of Muad'Dib's dreaded Fedaykin death commandos. And Bijaz, the catalyst-dwarf, waited with Otheym.

Scytale returned his gaze to the old man, noted the empty sleeve dangling from the left shoulder and the lack of a stillsuit. An air of command hung about this old man. He'd been no foot slogger in the Jihad.

"May I know the visitor's name?" the old man asked.

Scytale suppressed a sigh of relief. He was to be accepted, after all. "I am Zaal," he said, giving the name assigned him for this mission.

"I am Farok," the old man said, "once Bashar of the Ninth Legion in the Jihad. Does this mean anything to you?"

Scytale read menace in the words, said: "You were born in Sietch Tabr with allegiance to Stilgar."

Farok relaxed, stepped aside. "You are welcome in my house."

Scytale slipped past him into a shadowy atrium—blue tile floor, glittering designs worked in crystal on the walls. Beyond the atrium was a covered courtyard. Light admitted by translucent filters spread an opalescence as silvery as the white-night of First Moon. The street door grated into its moisture seals behind him.

"We were a noble people," Farok said, leading the way toward the courtyard. "We were not of the cast-out. We lived in no *graben* village . . . such as this! We had a proper sietch in the Shield Wall above Habbanya Ridge. One worm could carry us into Kedem, the inner desert."

"Not like this," Scytale agreed, realizing now what had brought Farok into the conspiracy. The Fremen longed for the old days and the old ways.

They entered the courtyard.

Farok struggled with an intense dislike for his visitor, Scytale realized. Fremen distrusted eyes that were not the total blue of the Ibad. Offworlders, Fremen said, had unfocused eyes which saw things they were not supposed to see.

The semuta music had stopped at their entrance. It was replaced now by the strum of a baliset, first a nine-scale chord, then the clear notes of a song which was popular on the Naraj worlds.

As his eyes adjusted to the light, Scytale saw a youth sitting cross-legged on a low divan beneath arches to his right. The youth's eyes were empty sockets. With that uncanny facility of the blind, he began singing the moment Scytale focused on him. The voice was high and sweet:

"A wind has blown the land away
And blown the sky away
And all the men!
Who is this wind?
The trees stand unbent,
Drinking where men drank.
I've known too many worlds,
Too many men,
Too many trees,
Too many winds."

Those were not the original words of the song, Scytale noted. Farok led him away from the youth and under the arches on the opposite side, indicated cushions scattered over the tile floor. The tile was worked into designs of sea creatures.

"There is a cushion once occupied in sietch by Muad'Dib," Farok said, indicating a round, black mound. "It is yours now."

"I am in your debt," Scytale said, sinking to the black mound. He smiled. Farok displayed wisdom. A sage spoke of loyalty even while listening to songs of hidden meaning and words with secret messages. Who could deny the terrifying powers of the tyrant Emperor?

Inserting his words across the song without breaking the meter, Farok said: "Does my son's music disturb you?"

Scytale gestured to a cushion facing him, put his back against a cool pillar. "I enjoy music."

"My son lost his eyes in the conquest of Naraj," Farok said. "He was nursed there and should have stayed. No woman of the People will have him thus. I find it curious, though, to know I have grandchildren on Naraj that I may never see. Do you know the Naraj worlds, Zaal?"

"In my youth, I toured there with a troupe of my fellow Face Dancers," Scytale said.

"You are a Face Dancer, then," Farok said. "I had wondered at your features. They reminded me of a man I knew here once."

"Duncan Idaho?"

"That one, yes. A swordmaster in the Emperor's pay."

"He was killed, so it is said."

"So it is said," Farok agreed. "Are you truly a man, then? I've heard stories about Face Dancers that . . . ." He shrugged.

"We are Jadacha hermaphrodites," Scytale said, "either sex at will. For the present, I am a man."

Farok pursed his lips in thought, then: "May I call for refreshments? Do you desire water? Iced fruit?"

"Talk will suffice," Scytale said.

"The guest's wish is a command," Farok said, settling to the cushion which faced Scytale.

"Blessed is Abu d' Dhur, Father of the Indefinite Roads of Time," Scytale said. And he thought: *There! I've told him straight out that I come from a Guild Steersman and wear the Steersman's concealment.*

"Thrice blessed," Farok said, folding his hands into his lap in the ritual clasp. They were old, heavily veined hands.

"An object seen from a distance betrays only its principle," Scytale said, revealing that he wished to discuss the Emperor's fortress Keep.

"That which is dark and evil may be seen for evil at any distance," Farok said, advising delay.

*Why?* Scytale wondered. But he said: "How did your son lose his eyes?"

"The Naraj defenders used a stone burner," Farok said. "My son was too close. Cursed atomics! Even the stone burner should be outlawed."

"It skirts the intent of the law," Scytale agreed. And he thought: *A stone burner on Naraj! We weren't told of that. Why does this old man speak of stone burners here?*

"I offered to buy Tleilaxu eyes for him from your master," Farok said. "But there's a story in the legions that Tleilaxu eyes enslave their users. My son told me that such eyes are metal and he is flesh, that such a union must be sinful."

"The principle of an object must fit its original intent," Scytale said, trying to turn the conversation back to the information he sought.

Farok's lips went thin, but he nodded. "Speak openly of what you wish," he said. "We must put our trust in your Steersman."

"Have you ever entered the Imperial Keep?" Scytale asked.

"I was there for the feast celebrating the Molitor victory. It was cold in all that stone despite the best Ixian space heaters. We slept on the terrace of Alia's Fane the night before. He has trees in there, you know—trees from many worlds. We Bashars were dressed in our finest green robes and had our table set apart. We ate and drank too much. I was disgusted with some of the things I saw. The walking wounded came, dragging themselves along on their crutches. I do not think our Muad'Dib knows how many men he has maimed."

"You objected to the feast?" Scytale asked, speaking from a knowledge of the Fremen orgies which were ignited by spice-beer.

"It was not like the mingling of our souls in the sietch," Farok said. "There was no tau. For entertainment, the troops had slave girls, and the men shared the stories of their battles and their wounds."

"So you were inside that great pile of stone," Scytale said.

"Muad'Dib came out to us on the terrace," Farok said. " 'Good fortune to us all,' he said. The greeting drill of the desert in that place!"

"Do you know the location of his private apartments?" Scytale asked.

"Deep inside," Farok said. "Somewhere deep inside. I am told he and Chani live a nomadic life and that all within the walls of their Keep. Out to the Great Hall he comes for the public audiences. He has reception halls and formal meeting places, a whole wing for his personal guard, places for the ceremonies and an inner section for communications. There is a room far beneath his fortress, I am told, where he keeps a stunted worm surrounded by a water moat with which to poison it. Here is where he reads the future."

*Myth all tangled up with facts*, Scytale thought.

"The apparatus of government accompanies him everywhere," Farok grumbled. "Clerks and attendants and attendants for the attendants. He trusts only the ones such as Stilgar who were very close to him in the old days."

"Not you," Scytale said.

"I think he has forgotten my existence," Farok said.

"How does he come and go when he leaves that building?" Scytale asked.

"He has a tiny 'thopter landing which juts from an inner wall," Farok said. "I am told Muad'Dib will not permit another to handle the controls for a landing there. It requires an approach, so it is said, where the slightest miscalculation would plunge him down a sheer cliff of wall into one of his accursed gardens."

Scytale nodded. This, most likely, was true. Such an aerial entry to the Emperor's quarters would carry a certain measure of security. The Atreides were superb pilots all.

"He uses men to carry his *distrans* messages," Farok said. "It demeans men to implant wave translators in them. A man's voice should be his own to command. It should not carry another man's message hidden within its sounds."

Scytale shrugged. All great powers used the distrans in this age. One could never tell what obstacle might be placed between sender and addressee. The distrans defied political cryptology because it relied on subtle distortions of natural sound patterns which could be scrambled with enormous intricacy.

"Even his tax officials use this method," Farok complained. "In my day, the distrans was implanted only in the lower animals."

*But revenue information must be kept secret,* Scytale thought. *More than one government has fallen because people discovered the real extent of official wealth.*

"How do the Fremen cohorts feel now about Muad'Dib's Jihad?" Scytale asked. "Do they object to making a god out of their Emperor?"

"Most of them don't even consider this," Farok said. "They think of the Jihad the way I thought of it—most of them. It is a source of strange experiences, adventure, wealth. This graben hovel in which I live"—Farok gestured at the courtyard—"it cost sixty lidas of spice. Ninety kontars! There was a time when I could not even imagine such riches." He shook his head.

Across the courtyard, the blind youth took up the notes of a love ballad on his baliset.

*Ninety kontars,* Scytale thought. *How strange. Great riches, certainly. Farok's hovel would be a palace on many another world, but all things were relative—even the kontar. Did Farok, for example, know whence came his measure for this weight of spice? Did he ever think to himself that one and a half kontar once limited a camel load? Not likely. Farok might never even have heard of a camel or of the Golden Age of Earth.*

His words oddly in rhythm to the melody of his son's baliset, Farok said: "I owned a crysknife, water rings to ten liters, my own lance which had been my father's, a coffee service, a bottle made of red glass older than any memory in my sietch. I had my own share of our spice, but no money. I was rich and did not know it. Two wives I had: one plain and dear to me, the other stupid and obstinate, but with form and face of an angel. I was a Fremen Naib, a rider of worms, master of the leviathan and of the sand."

The youth across the courtyard picked up the beat of his melody.

"I knew many things without the need to think about them," Farok said. "I knew there was water far beneath our sand, held there in bondage by the Little Makers. I knew that my ancestors sacrificed virgins to Shai-hulud . . . before Liet-Kynes made us stop. It was wrong of us to stop. I had seen the jewels in the mouth of a worm. My soul had four gates and I knew them all."

He fell silent, musing.

"Then the Atreides came with his witch mother," Scytale said.

"The Atreides came," Farok agreed. "The one we named Usul in our sietch, his private name among us. Our Muad'Dib, our Mahdi! And when he called for the Jihad, I was one of those who asked: 'Why should I go to fight there? I have no relatives there.' But other men went—young men, friends, companions of my childhood. When they returned, they spoke of wizardry, of the power in this Atreides *savior.* He fought our enemy, the Harkonnen. Liet-Kynes, who had promised us a paradise upon our planet, blessed him. It was said this Atreides came to change our world and our universe, that he was the man to make the golden flower blossom in the night."

Farok held up his hands, examined the palms. "Men pointed to First Moon and said: 'His soul is there.' Thus, he was called Muad'Dib. I did not understand all this."

He lowered his hands, stared across the courtyard at his son. "I had no thoughts in my head. There were thoughts only in my heart and my belly and my loins."

Again, the tempo of the background music increased.

"Do you know why I enlisted in the Jihad?" The old eyes stared hard at Scytale. "I heard there was a thing called a sea. It is very hard to believe in a sea when you have lived only here among our dunes. We have no seas. Men of Dune had never known a sea. We had our wind-traps. We collected water for the great change Liet-Kynes promised us . . . this great change Muad'Dib is bringing with a wave of his hand. I could imagine a *qanat*, water flowing across the land in a canal. From this, my mind could picture a river. But a sea?"

Farok gazed at the translucent cover of his courtyard as though trying to probe into the universe beyond. "A sea," he said, voice low. "It was too much for my mind to picture. Yet, men I knew said they had seen this marvel. I thought they lied, but I had to know for myself. It was for this reason that I enlisted."

The youth struck a loud final chord on the baliset, took up a new song with an oddly undulating rhythm.

"Did you find your sea?" Scytale asked.

Farok remained silent and Scytale thought the old man had not heard. The baliset music rose around them and fell like a tidal movement. Farok breathed to its rhythm.

"There was a sunset," Farok said presently. "One of the elder artists might have painted such a sunset. It had red in it the color of the glass in my bottle. There was gold . . . blue. It was on the world they call Enfeil, the one where I led my legion to victory. We came out of a mountain pass where the air was sick with water. I could scarcely breathe it. And there below me was the thing my friends had told me about: water as far as I could see and farther. We marched down to it. I waded out into it and drank. It was bitter and made me ill. But the wonder of it has never left me."

Scytale found himself sharing the old Fremen's awe.

"I immersed myself in that sea," Farok said, looking down at the water creatures worked into the tiles of his floor. "One man sank beneath that water . . . another man arose from it. I felt that I could remember a past which had never been. I stared around me with eyes which could accept anything . . . anything at all. I saw a body in the water—one of the defenders we had slain. There was a log nearby supported on that water, a piece of a great tree. I can close my eyes now and see that log. It was black on one end from a fire. And there was a piece of cloth in that water—no more than a yellow rag . . . torn, dirty. I looked at all these things and I understood why they had come to this place. It was for me to see them."

Farok turned slowly, stared into Scytale's eyes. "The universe is unfinished, you know," he said.

*This one is garrulous, but deep*, Scytale thought. And he said: "I can see it made a profound impression on you."

"You are a Tleilaxu," Farok said. "You have seen many seas. I have seen only this one, yet I know a thing about seas which you do not."

Scytale found himself in the grip of an odd feeling of disquiet.

"The Mother of Chaos was born in a sea," Farok said. "A Qizara Tafwid stood nearby when I came dripping from that water. He had not entered the sea. He stood on the sand . . . it was wet sand . . . with some of my men who shared his fear. He watched me with eyes that knew I had learned something which was denied to him. I had become a sea creature and I frightened him. The sea healed me of the Jihad and I think he saw this."

Scytale realized that somewhere in this recital the music had stopped. He found it disturbing that he could not place the instant when the baliset had fallen silent.

As though it were relevant to what he'd been recounting, Farok said: "Every gate is guarded. There's no way into the Emperor's fortress."

"That's its weakness," Scytale said.

Farok stretched his neck upward, peering.

"There's a way in," Scytale explained. "The fact that most men—including, we may hope, the Emperor—believe otherwise . . . that's to our advantage." He rubbed his lips, feeling the strangeness of the visage he'd chosen. The musician's silence bothered him. Did it mean Farok's son was through transmitting? That had been the way of it, naturally: the message condensed and transmitted within the music. It had been impressed upon Scytale's own neural system, there to be triggered at the proper moment by the distrans embedded in his adrenal cortex. If it was ended, he had become a container of unknown words. He was a vessel sloshing with data: every cell of the conspiracy here on Arrakis, every name, every contact phrase—all the vital information.

With this information, they could brave Arrakis, capture a sandworm, begin the culture of melange somewhere beyond Muad'Dib's writ. They could break the monopoly as they broke Muad'Dib. They could do many things with this information.

"We have the woman here," Farok said. "Do you wish to see her now?"

"I've seen her," Scytale said. "I've studied her with care. Where is she?"

Farok snapped his fingers.

The youth took up his rebec, drew the bow across it. Semuta music wailed from the strings. As though drawn by the sound, a young woman in a blue robe emerged from a doorway behind the musician. Narcotic dullness filled her eyes which were the total blue of the Ibad. She was a Fremen, addicted to the spice, and now caught by an offworld vice. Her awareness lay deep within the semuta, lost somewhere and riding the ecstasy of the music.

"Otheym's daughter," Farok said. "My son gave her the narcotic in the hope of winning a woman of the People for himself despite his blindness. As you can see, his victory is empty. Semuta has taken what he hoped to gain."

"Her father doesn't know?" Scytale asked.

"She doesn't even know," Farok said. "My son supplies false memories with which she accounts to herself for her visits. She thinks herself in love with him. This is what her family believes. They are outraged because he is not a complete man, but they won't interfere, of course."

The music trailed away to silence.

At a gesture from the musician, the young woman seated herself beside him, bent close to listen as he murmured to her.

"What will you do with her?" Farok asked.

Once more, Scytale studied the courtyard. "Who else is in this house?" he asked.

"We are all here now," Farok said. "You've not told me what you'll do with the woman. It is my son who wishes to know."

As though about to answer, Scytale extended his right arm. From the sleeve of his robe, a glistening needle darted, embedded itself in Farok's neck. There was no outcry, no change of posture. Farok would be dead in a minute, but he sat unmoving, frozen by the dart's poison.

Slowly, Scytale climbed to his feet, crossed to the blind musician. The youth was still murmuring to the young woman when the dart whipped into him.

Scytale took the young woman's arm, urged her gently to her feet, shifted his own appearance before she looked at him. She came erect, focused on him.

"What is it, Farok?" she asked.

"My son is tired and must rest," Scytale said. "Come. We'll go out the back way."

"We had such a nice talk," she said. "I think I've convinced him to get Tleilaxu eyes. It'd make a man of him again."

"Haven't I said it many times?" Scytale asked, urging her into a rear chamber.

His voice, he noted with pride, matched his features precisely. It unmistakably was the voice of the old Fremen, who certainly was dead by this time.

Scytale sighed. It had been done with sympathy, he told himself, and the victims certainly had known their peril. Now, the young woman would have to be given her chance.

> *Empires do not suffer emptiness of purpose at the time of their creation. It is when they have become established that aims are lost and replaced by vague ritual.*

**—Words of Muad'Dib
by Princess Irulan**

It was going to be a bad session, this meeting of the Imperial Council, Alia realized. She sensed contention gathering force, storing up energy—the way

Irulan refused to look at Chani, Stilgar's nervous shuffling of papers, the scowls Paul directed at Korba the Qizara.

She seated herself at the end of the golden council table so she could look out the balcony windows at the dusty light of the afternoon.

Korba, interrupted by her entrance, went on with something he'd been saying to Paul. "What I mean, m'Lord, is that there aren't as many gods as once there were."

Alia laughed, throwing her head back. The movement dropped the black hood of her aba robe. Her features lay exposed—blue-in-blue "spice eyes," her mother's oval face beneath a cap of bronze hair, small nose, mouth wide and generous.

Korba's cheeks went almost the color of his orange robe. He glared at Alia, an angry gnome, bald and fuming.

"Do you know what's being said about your brother?" he demanded.

"I know what's being said about your Qizarate," Alia countered. "You're not divines, you're god's spies."

Korba glanced at Paul for support, said: "We are sent by the writ of Muad'Dib, that He shall know the truth of His people and they shall know the truth of Him."

"Spies," Alia said.

Korba pursed his lips in injured silence.

Paul looked at his sister, wondering why she provoked Korba. Abruptly, he saw that Alia had passed into womanhood, beautiful with the first blazing innocence of youth. He found himself surprised that he hadn't noticed it until this moment. She was fifteen—almost sixteen, a Reverend Mother without motherhood, virgin priestess, object of fearful veneration for the superstitious masses—Alia of the Knife.

"This is not the time or place for your sister's levity," Irulan said.

Paul ignored her, nodded to Korba. "The square's full of pilgrims. Go out and lead their prayer."

"But they expect *you*, m'Lord," Korba said.

"Put on your turban," Paul said. "They'll never know at this distance."

Irulan smothered irritation at being ignored, watched Korba arise to obey. She'd had the the sudden disquieting thought that Edric might not hide her actions from Alia. *What do we really know of the sister?* she wondered.

Chani, hands tightly clasped in her lap, glanced across the table at Stilgar, her uncle, Paul's Minister of State. Did the old Fremen Naib ever long for the simpler life of his desert sietch? she wondered. Stilgar's black hair, she noted, had begun to gray at the edges, but his eyes beneath heavy brows remained far-seeing. It was the eagle stare of the wild, and his beard still carried the catchtube indentation of life in a stillsuit.

Made nervous by Chani's attention, Stilgar looked around the Council Chamber. His gaze fell on the balcony window and Korba standing outside. Korba raised outstretched arms for the benediction and a trick of the afternoon sun cast a red halo onto the window behind him. For a moment, Stilgar saw the Court Qizara as a figure crucified on a fiery wheel. Korba lowered his arms, destroyed the illusion, but Stilgar remained shaken by it. His thoughts went in angry frustration to the fawning supplicants waiting in the Audience Hall, and to the hateful pomp which surrounded Muad'Dib's throne.

Convening with the Emperor, one hoped for a fault in him, to find mistakes, Stilgar thought. He felt this might be sacrilege, but wanted it anyway.

Distant crowd murmuring entered the chamber as Korba returned. The balcony door thumped into its seals behind him, shutting off the sound.

Paul's gaze followed the Qizara. Korba took his seat at Paul's left, dark features composed, eyes glazed by fanaticism. He'd enjoyed that moment of religious power.

"The spirit presence has been invoked," he said.

"Thank the lord for that," Alia said.

Korba's lips went white.

Again, Paul studied his sister, wondered at her motives. Her innocence masked deception, he told himself. She'd come out of the same Bene Gesserit breeding program as he had. What had the Kwisatz Haderach genetics produced in her? There was always that mysterious difference: she'd been an embryo in the womb when her mother had survived the raw melange poison. Mother and unborn daughter had become Reverend Mothers simultaneously. But simultaneity didn't carry identity.

Of the experience, Alia said that in one terrifying instant she had awakened to consciousness, her memory absorbing the uncounted other-lives which her mother was assimilating.

"I became my mother and all the others," she said. "I was unformed, unborn, but I became an old woman then and there."

Sensing his thoughts on her, Alia smiled at Paul. His expression softened. *How could anyone react to Korba with other than cynical humor?* he asked himself. *What is more ridiculous than a Death Commando transformed into a priest?*

Stilgar tapped his papers. "If my liege permits," he said. "These are matters urgent and dire."

"The Tupile Treaty?" Paul asked.

"The Guild maintains that we must sign this treaty without knowing the precise location of the Tupile Entente," Stilgar said. "They've some support from Landsraad delegates."

"What pressures have you brought to bear?" Irulan asked.

"Those pressures which my Emperor has designated for this enterprise," Stilgar said. The stiff formality of his reply contained all his disapproval of the Princess Consort.

"My Lord and husband," Irulan said, turning to Paul, forcing him to acknowledge her.

*Emphasizing the titular difference in front of Chani,* Paul thought, *is a weakness.* In such moments, he shared Stilgar's dislike for Irulan, but sympathy tempered his emotions. What was Irulan but a Bene Gesserit pawn?

"Yes?" Paul said.

Irulan stared at him. "If you withheld their melange . . . ."

Chani shook her head in dissent.

"We tread with caution," Paul said. "Tupile remains the place of sanctuary for defeated Great Houses. It symbolizes a last resort, a final place of safety for all our subjects. Exposing the sanctuary makes it vulnerable."

"If they can hide people they can hide other things," Stilgar rumbled. "An army, perhaps, or the beginnings of melange culture which—"

"You don't back people into a corner," Alia said. "Not if you want them to remain peaceful." Ruefully, she saw that she'd been drawn into the contention which she'd foreseen.

"So we've spent ten years negotiating for nothing," Irulan said.

"None of my brother's actions is for nothing," Alia said.

Irulan picked up a scribe, gripped it with white-knuckled intensity. Paul saw her marshal emotional control in the Bene Gesserit way: the penetrating inward stare, deep breathing. He could almost hear her repeating the litany. Presently, she said: "What have we gained?"

"We've kept the Guild off balance," Chani said.

"We want to avoid a showdown confrontation with our enemies," Alia said. "We have no special desire to kill them. There's enough butchery going on under the Atreides banner."

*She feels it, too,* Paul thought. Strange, what a sense of compelling responsibility they both felt for that brawling, idolatrous universe with its ecstasies of tranquility and wild motion. *Must we protect them from themselves?* he wondered. *They play with nothingness every moment—empty lives, empty words. They ask too much of me.* His throat felt tight and full. How many moments would he lose? What sons? What dreams? Was it worth the price his vision had revealed? Who would ask the living of some far distant future, who would say to them: "But for Muad'Dib, you would not be here."

"Denying them their melange would solve nothing," Chani said. "So the Guild's navigators would lose their ability to see into timespace. Your Sisters of the Bene Gesserit would lose their truthsense. Some people might die before their time. Communication would break down. Who could be blamed?"

"They wouldn't let it come to that," Irulan said.

"Wouldn't they?" Chani asked. "Why not? Who could blame the Guild? They'd be helpless, demonstrably so."

"We'll sign the treaty as it stands," Paul said.

"M'Lord," Stilgar said, concentrating on his hands, "there is a question in our minds."

"Yes?" Paul gave the old Fremen his full attention.

"You have certain . . . powers," Stilgar said. "Can you not locate the Entente despite the Guild?"

*Powers!* Paul thought. Stilgar couldn't just say: *"You're prescient. Can't you trace a path in the future that leads to Tupile?"*

Paul looked at the golden surface of the table. Always the same problem: How could he express the limits of the inexpressible? Should he speak of fragmentation, the natural destiny of all power? How could someone who'd never experienced the spice change of prescience conceive an awareness containing no localized spacetime, no personal image-vector nor associated sensory captives?

He looked at Alia, found her attention on Irulan. Alia sensed his movement, glanced at him, nodded toward Irulan. Ahhh, yes: any answer they gave would find its way into one of Irulan's special reports to the Bene Gesserit. They never gave up seeking an answer to their Kwisatz Haderach.

Stilgar, though, deserved an answer of some kind. For that matter, so did Irulan.

"The uninitiated try to conceive of prescience as obeying a *Natural Law*," Paul said. He steepled his hands in front of him. "But it'd be just as correct to say it's heaven speaking to us, that being able to read the future is a harmonious act of man's being. In other words, prediction is a natural consequence in the wave of the present. It wears the guise of nature, you see. But such powers cannot be used from an attitude that prestates aims and purposes. Does a chip caught in a wave say where it's going? There's no cause and effect in the oracle. Causes become occasions or convections and confluences, places where the currents meet. Accepting prescience, you fill your being with concepts repugnant to the intellect. Your intellectual consciousness, therefore, rejects them. In rejecting, intellect becomes a part of the processes, and is subjugated."

"You cannot do it?" Stilgar asked.

"Were I to seek Tupile with prescience," Paul said, speaking directly to Irulan, "this might hide Tupile."

"Chaos!" Irulan protested. "It has no . . . no . . . consistency."

"I did say it obeys no Natural Law," Paul said.

"Then there are limits to what you can see or do with your powers?" Irulan asked.

Before Paul could answer, Alia said: "Dear Irulan, prescience has no limits. Not consistent? Consistency isn't a necessary aspect of the universe."

"But he said . . ."

"How can my brother give you explicit information about the limits of something which has no limits? The boundaries escape the intellect."

*That was a nasty thing for Alia to do*, Paul thought. It would alarm Irulan, who had such a careful consciousness, so dependent upon values derived from precise limits. His gaze went to Korba, who sat in a pose of religious reverie—*listening with the soul*. How could the Qizarate use this exchange? More religious mystery? Something to evoke awe? No doubt.

"Then you'll sign the treaty in its present form?" Stilgar asked.

Paul smiled. The issue of the oracle, by Stilgar's judgment, had been closed. Stilgar aimed only at victory, not at discovering truth. Peace, justice and a sound coinage—these anchored Stilgar's universe. He wanted something visible and real—a signature on a treaty.

"I'll sign it," Paul said.

Stilgar took up a fresh folder. "The latest communication from our field commanders in Sector Ixian speaks of agitation for a constitution." The old Fremen glanced at Chani, who shrugged.

Irulan, who had closed her eyes and put both hands to her forehead in mnemonic impressment, opened her eyes, studied Paul intently.

"The Ixian Confederacy offers submission," Stilgar said, "but their negotiators question the amount of the Imperial Tax which they—"

"They want a legal limit to my Imperial will," Paul said. "Who would govern me, the Landsraad or CHOAM?"

Stilgar removed from the folder a note on *instroy* paper. "One of our agents sent this memorandum from a caucus of the CHOAM minority." He read the cipher in a flat voice: "The Throne must be stopped in its attempt at a power monopoly. We must tell the truth about the Atreides, how he maneuvers behind the triple sham of Landsraad legislation, religious sanction and bureaucratic efficiency." He pushed the note back into the folder.

"A constitution," Chani murmured.

Paul glanced at her, back to Stilgar. *Thus the Jihad falters*, Paul thought, *but not soon enough to save me.* The thought produced emotional tensions. He remembered his earliest visions of the Jihad-to-be, the terror and revulsion he'd experienced. Now, of course, he knew visions of greater terrors. He had lived with the real violence. He had seen his Fremen, charged with mystical strength, sweep all before them in the religious war. The Jihad gained a new perspective. It was finite, of course, a brief spasm when measured against eternity, but beyond lay horrors to overshadow anything in the past.

*All in my name*, Paul thought.

"Perhaps they could be given the *form* of a constitution," Chani suggested. "It needn't be actual."

"Deceit *is* a tool of statecraft," Irulan agreed.

"There are limits to power, as those who put their hopes in a constitution always discover," Paul said.

Korba straightened from his reverent pose. "M'Lord?"

"Yes?" And Paul thought, *Here now! Here's one who may harbor secret sympathies for an imagined rule of Law.*

"We could begin with a religious constitution," Korba said, "something for the faithful who—"

"No!" Paul snapped. "We will make this an Order in Council. Are you recording this, Irulan?"

"Yes, m'Lord," Irulan said, voice frigid with dislike for the menial role he forced upon her.

"Constitutions become the ultimate tyranny," Paul said. "They're organized power on such a scale as to be overwhelming. The constitution is social power mobilized and it has no conscience. It can crush the highest and the lowest, removing all dignity and individuality. It has an unstable balance point and no limitations. I, however, have limitations. In my desire to provide an ultimate protection for my people, I forbid a constitution. Order in Council, this date, etcetera, etcetera."

"What of the Ixian concern about the tax, m'Lord?" Stilgar asked.

Paul forced his attention away from the brooding, angry look on Korba's face, said: "You've a proposal, Stil?"

"We must have control of taxes, Sire."

"Our price to the Guild for my signature on the Tupile Treaty," Paul said, "is the submission of the Ixian Confederacy to our tax. The Confederacy cannot trade without Guild transport. They'll pay."

"Very good, m'Lord." Stilgar produced another folder, cleared his throat. "The Qizarate's report on Salusa Secundus. Irulan's father has been putting his legions through landing maneuvers."

Irulan found something of interest in the palm of her left hand. A pulse throbbed at her neck.

"Irulan," Paul asked, "do you persist in arguing that your father's one legion is nothing more than a toy?"

"What could he do with only one legion?" she asked. She stared at him out of slitted eyes.

"He could get himself killed," Chani said.

Paul nodded. "And I'd be blamed."

"I know a few commanders in the Jihad," Alia said, "who'd pounce if they learned of this."

"But it's only his police force!" Irulan protested.

"Then they have no need for landing manuevers," Paul said. "I suggest that your next little note to your father contain a frank and direct discussion of my views about his delicate position."

She lowered her gaze. "Yes, m'Lord. I hope that will be the end of it. My father would make a good martyr."

"Mmmmmm," Paul said. "My sister wouldn't send a message to those commanders she mentioned unless I ordered it."

"An attack on my father carries dangers other than the obvious military ones," Irulan said. "People are beginning to look back on his reign with a certain nostalgia."

"You'll go too far one day," Chani said in her deadly serious Fremen voice.

"Enough!" Paul ordered.

He weighed Irulan's revelation about public nostalgia—ah, now! that'd carried a note of truth. Once more, Irulan had proved her worth.

"The Bene Gesserit send a formal supplication," Stilgar said, presenting another folder. "They wish to consult you about the preservation of your bloodline."

Chani glanced sideways at the folder as though it contained a deadly device.

"Send the Sisterhood the usual excuses," Paul said.

"Must we?" Irulan demanded.

"Perhaps . . . this is the time to discuss it," Chani said.

Paul shook his head sharply. They couldn't know that this was part of the price he had not yet decided to pay.

But Chani wasn't to be stopped. "I have been to the prayer wall of Sietch Tabr where I was born," she said. "I have submitted to doctors. I have knelt in the desert and sent my thoughts into the depths where dwells Shai-hulud. Yet"—she shrugged—"nothing avails."

*Science and superstition, all have failed her,* Paul thought. *Do I fail her, too, by not telling her what bearing an heir to House Atreides will precipitate?* He looked up to find an expression of pity in Alia's eyes. The idea of pity from his sister repelled him. Had she, too, seen that terrifying future?

"My Lord must know the dangers to his realm when he has no heir," Irulan said, using her Bene Gesserit powers of voice with an oily persuasiveness. "These things are naturally difficult to discuss, but they must be brought into the open. An Emperor is more than a man. His figure leads the realm. Should he die without an heir, civil strife must follow. As you love your people, you cannot leave them thus?"

Paul pushed himself away from the table, strode to the balcony windows. A wind was flattening the smoke of the city's fires out there. The sky presented a darkening silver-blue softened by the evening fall of dust from the Shield Wall. He stared southward at the escarpment which protected his northern lands from the coriolis wind, and he wondered why his own peace of mind could find no such shield.

The Council sat silently waiting behind him, aware of how close to rage he was.

Paul sensed time rushing upon him. He tried to force himself into a tranquility of many balances where he might shape a new future.

*Disengage . . . disengage . . . disengage,* he thought. What would happen if he took Chani, just picked up and left with her, sought sanctuary on Tupile? His name would remain behind. The Jihad would find new and more terrible centers upon which to turn. He'd be blamed for that, too. He felt suddenly fearful that in reaching for any new thing he might let fall what was most precious, that even the slightest noise from him might send the universe crashing back, receding until he never could recapture any piece of it.

Below him, the square had become the setting for a band of pilgrims in the green and white of the hajj. They wended their way like a disjointed snake behind a striding Arrakeen guide. They reminded Paul that his reception hall would be packed with supplicants by now. Pilgrims! Their exercise in homelessness had become a disgusting source of wealth for his Imperium. The hajj filled the spaceways with religious tramps. They came and they came and they came.

*How did I set this in motion?* he asked himself.

It had, of course, set itself in motion. It was in the genes which might labor for centuries to achieve this brief spasm.

Driven by that deepest religious instinct, the people came, seeking their resurrection. The pilgrimage ended here—"Arrakis, the place of rebirth, the place to die." .

Snide old Fremen said he wanted the pilgrims for their water.

What was it the pilgrims really sought? Paul wondered. They said they came to a holy place. But they must know the universe contained no Eden-source, no Tupile for the soul. They called Arrakis the place of the unknown where all mysteries were explained. This was a link between their universe and the next. And the frightening thing was that they appeared to go away satisfied.

*What do they find here?* Paul asked himself.

Often in their religious ecstasy, they filled the streets with screeching like some odd aviary. In fact, the Fremen called them "passage birds." And the few who died here were "winged souls."

With a sigh, Paul thought how each new planet his legions subjugated opened new sources of pilgrims. They came out of gratitude for "the peace of Muad'Dib."

*Everywhere there is peace,* Paul thought. *Everywhere . . . except in the heart of Muad'Dib.*

He felt that some element of himself lay immersed in frosty hoar-darkness without end. His prescient power had tampered with the image of the universe held by all mankind. He had shaken the safe cosmos and replaced security with his Jihad. He had out-fought and out-thought and out-predicted the universe of men, but a certainty filled him that this universe still eluded him.

This planet beneath him which he had commanded be remade from desert into a water-rich paradise, it was alive. It had a pulse as dynamic as that of any human. It fought him, resisted, slipped away from his commands . . .

A hand crept into Paul's. He looked down to see Chani peering up at him, concern in her eyes. Those eyes drank him, and she whispered: "Please, love, do not battle with your ruh-self." An outpouring of emotion swept upward from her hand, buoyed him.

"Sihaya," he whispered.

"We must go to the desert soon," she said in a low voice.

He squeezed her hand, released it, returned to the table where he remained standing.

Chani took her seat.

Irulan stared at the papers in front of Stilgar, her mouth a tight line.

"Irulan proposes herself as mother of the Imperial heir," Paul said. He glanced at Chani, back to Irulan, who refused to meet his gaze. "We all know she holds no love for me."

Irulan went very still.

"I know the political arguments," Paul said. "It's the human arguments which concern me. I think if the Princess Consort were not bound by the commands of the Bene Gesserit, if she did not seek this out of desires for personal power, my reaction would be very different. As matters stand, though, I reject this proposal."

Irulan took a deep, shaky breath.

Paul, resuming his seat, thought he had never seen her under such poor control. Leaning toward her, he said: "Irulan, I am truly sorry."

She lifted her chin, a look of pure fury in her eyes. "I don't want your pity!" she hissed. And turning to Stilgar: "Is there more that's urgent and dire?"

Holding his gaze firmly on Paul, Stilgar said: "One more matter, m'Lord. The Guild again proposes a formal embassy here on Arrakis."

"One of the deep-space kind?" Korba asked, his voice full of fanatic loathing.

"Presumably," Stilgar said.

"A matter to be considered with the utmost care, m'Lord," Korba warned.

"The Council of Naibs would not like it, an actual Guildsman here on Arrakis. They contaminate the very ground they touch."

"They live in tanks and don't touch the ground," Paul said, letting his voice reveal irritation.

"The Naibs might take matters into their own hands, m'Lord," Korba said.

Paul glared at him.

"They are Fremen, after all, m'Lord," Korba insisted. "We well remember how the Guild brought those who oppressed us. We have not forgotten the way they blackmailed a spice ransom from us to keep our secrets from our enemies. They drained us of every—"

"Enough!" Paul snapped. "Do you think *I* have forgotten?"

As though he had just awakened to the import of his own words, Korba stuttered unintelligibly, then: "M'Lord, forgive me. I did not mean to imply you are not a Fremen. I did not . . ."

"They'll send a Steersman," Paul said. "It isn't likely a Steersman would come here if he could see danger in it."

Her mouth dry with sudden fear, Irulan said: "You've . . . *seen* a Steersman come here?"

"Of course I haven't *seen* a Steersman," Paul said, mimicking her tone. "But I can see where one's been and where one's going. Let them send us a Steersman. Perhaps I have a use for such a one."

"So ordered," Stilgar said.

And Irulan, hiding a smile behind her hand, thought: *It's true then. Our Emperor cannot see a Steersman. They are mutually blind. The conspiracy is hidden.*

*"Once more the drama begins."*

**—The Emperor Paul Muad'Dib
on his ascension to the Lion Throne**

Alia peered down from her spy window into the great reception hall to watch the advance of the Guild entourage.

The sharply silver light of noon poured through clerestory windows onto a floor worked in green, blue and egg-shell tiles to simulate a bayou with water plants and, here and there, a splash of exotic color to indicate bird or animal.

Guildsmen moved across the tile pattern like hunters stalking their prey in a strange jungle. They formed a moving design of gray robes, black robes, orange robes—all arrayed in a deceptively random way around the transparent tank where the Steersman-Ambassador swam in his orange gas. The tank slid on its supporting field, towed by two gray-robed attendants, like a rectangular ship being warped into its dock.

Directly beneath her, Paul sat on the Lion Throne on its raised dais. He wore the new formal crown with its fish and fist emblems. The jeweled golden robes of state covered his body. The shimmering of a personal shield surrounded him. Two wings of bodyguards fanned out on both sides along the dais and down the steps. Stilgar stood two steps below Paul's right hand in a white robe with a yellow rope for a belt.

Sibling empathy told her that Paul seethed with the same agitation she was experiencing, although she doubted another could detect it. His attention remained on an orange-robed attendant whose blindly staring metal eyes looked neither to right nor to left. This attendant walked at the right front corner of the Ambassador's troupe like a military outrider. A rather flat face beneath curly black hair, such of his figure as could be seen beneath the orange robe, every gesture shouted a familiar identity.

It was Duncan Idaho.

It could not be Duncan Idaho, yet it was.

Captive memories absorbed in the womb during the moment of her mother's spice change identified this man for Alia by a rihani decipherment which cut through all camouflage. Paul was seeing him, she knew, out of countless personal experiences, out of gratitudes and youthful sharing.

It was Duncan.

Alia shuddered. There could be only one answer: this was a Tleilaxu ghola, a being reconstructed from the dead flesh of the original. That original had perished saving Paul. This could only be a product of the axolotl tanks.

The ghola walked with the cock-footed alertness of a master swordsman. He came to a halt as the Ambassador's tank glided to a stop ten paces from the steps of the dais.

In the Bene Gesserit way she could not escape, Alia read Paul's disquiet. He no longer looked at the figure out of his past. Not looking, his whole being stared. Muscles strained against restrictions as he nodded to the Guild Ambassador, said: "I am told your name is Edric. We welcome you to our Court in the hope this will bring new understanding between us."

The Steersman assumed a sybaritic reclining pose in his orange gas, popped a melange capsule into his mouth before meeting Paul's gaze. The tiny transducer orbiting a corner of the Guildsman's tank reproduced a coughing sound, then the rasping, uninvolved voice: "I abase myself before my Emperor and beg leave to present my credentials and offer a small gift."

An aide passed a scroll up to Stilgar, who studied it, scowling, then nodded to Paul. Both Stilgar and Paul turned then toward the ghola standing patiently below the dais.

"Indeed my Emperor has discerned the gift," Edric said.

"We are pleased to accept your credentials," Paul said. "Explain the gift."

Edric rolled in the tank, bringing his attention to bear on the ghola. "This is a man called Hayt," he said, spelling the name. "According to our investigators, he has a most curious history. He was killed here on Arrakis . . . a grievous head-wound which required many months of regrowth. The body was sold to the Bene Tleilax as that of a master swordsman, an adept of the Ginaz School. It came to our attention that this must be Duncan Idaho, the trusted retainer of your household. We bought him as a gift befitting an Emperor." Edric peered up at Paul. "Is it not Idaho, Sire?"

Restraint and caution gripped Paul's voice. "He has the aspect of Idaho."

*Does Paul see something I don't?* Alia wondered. *No! It's Duncan!*

The man called Hayt stood impassively, metal eyes fixed straight ahead, body relaxed. No sign escaped him to indicate he knew himself to be the object of discussion.

"According to our best knowledge, it's Idaho," Edric said.

"He's called Hayt now," Paul said. "A curious name."

"Sire, there's no divining how or why the Tleilaxu bestow names," Edric said. "But names can be changed. The Tleilaxu name is of little importance."

*This is a Tleilaxu thing,* Paul thought. *There's the problem.* The Bene Tleilax held little attachment to phenomenal nature. Good and evil carried strange meanings in their philosophy. What might they have incorporated in Idaho's flesh—out of design or whim?

Paul glanced at Stilgar, noted the Fremen's superstitious awe. It was an emotion echoed all through his Fremen guard. Stilgar's mind would be speculating about the loathsome habits of Guildsmen, of Tleilaxu and of gholas.

Turning toward the ghola, Paul said; "Hayt, is that your only name?"

A serene smile spread over the ghola's dark features. The metal eyes lifted, centered on Paul, but maintained their mechanical stare. "That is how I am called, my Lord: Hayt."

In her dark spy hole, Alia trembled. It was Idaho's voice, a quality of sound so precise she sensed its imprint upon her cells.

"May it please my Lord," the ghola added, "if I say his voice gives me pleasure. This is a sign, say the Bene Tleilax, that I have heard the voice . . . before."

"But you don't know this for sure," Paul said.

"I know nothing of my past for sure, my Lord. It was explained that I can have no memory of my former life. All that remains from before is the pattern set by the genes. There are, however, niches into which once-familiar things may fit. There are voices, places, foods, faces, sounds, actions—a sword in my hand, the controls of a 'thopter . . ."

Noting how intently the Guildsmen watched this exchange, Paul asked: "Do you understand that you're a gift?"

"It was explained to me, my Lord."

Paul sat back, hands resting on the arms of the throne.

*What debt do I owe Duncan's flesh?* he wondered. *The man died saving my life. But this is not Idaho, this is a ghola.* Yet, here were body and mind which had taught Paul to fly a 'thopter as though the wings grew from his own shoulders. Paul knew he could not pick up a sword without leaning on the harsh education Idaho had given him. A ghola. This was flesh full of false impressions, easily misread. Old associations would persist. *Duncan Idaho.* It wasn't so much a mask the ghola wore as it was a loose, concealing garment of personality which moved in a way different from whatever the Tleilaxu had hidden here.

"How might you serve us?" Paul asked.

"In any way my Lord's wishes and my capabilities agree."

Alia, watching from her vantage point, was touched by the ghola's air of diffidence. She detected nothing feigned. Something ultimately innocent shone from the new Duncan Idaho. The original had been worldly, devil-may-care. But this flesh had been cleansed of all that. It was a pure surface upon which the Tleilaxu had written . . . what?

She sensed the hidden perils in this gift then. This was a Tleilaxu thing. The Tleilaxu displayed a disturbing lack of inhibitions in what they created. Unbridled curiosity might guide their actions. They boasted they could make *anything* from the proper human raw material—devils or saints. They sold killer-mentats. They'd produced a killer medic, overcoming the Suk inhibitions against the taking of human life to do it. Their wares included willing menials, pliant sex toys for any whim, soldiers, generals, philosophers, even an occasional moralist.

Paul stirred, looked at Edric. "How has this *gift* been trained?" he asked.

"If it please my Lord," Edric said, "it amused the Tleilaxu to train this ghola as a mentat and philosopher of the Zensunni. Thus, they sought to increase his abilities with the sword."

"Did they succeed?"

"I do not know, my Lord."

Paul weighed the answer. Truthsense told him Edric sincerely believed the ghola to be Idaho. But there was more. The waters of Time through which this oracular Steersman moved suggested dangers without revealing them. *Hayt.* The Tleilaxu name spoke of peril. Paul felt himself tempted to reject the gift. Even as he felt the temptation, he knew he couldn't choose that way. This flesh made demands on House Atreides—a fact the enemy knew well.

"Zensunni philosopher," Paul mused, once more looking at the ghola. "You've examined your own role and motives?"

"I approach my service in an attitude of humility, Sire. I am a cleansed mind washed free of the imperatives from my human past."

"Would you prefer we called you Hayt or Duncan Idaho?"

"My Lord may call me what he wishes, for I am not a name."

"But do you *enjoy* the name Duncan Idaho?"

"I think that was my name, Sire. It fits within me. Yet . . . it stirs up curious responses. One's name, I think, must carry much that's unpleasant along with the pleasant."

"What gives you the most pleasure?" Paul asked.

Unexpectedly, the ghola laughed, said: "Looking for signs in others which reveal my former self."

"Do you see such signs here?"

"Oh, yes, my Lord. Your man Stilgar there is caught between suspicion and admiration. He was friend to my former self, but this ghola flesh repels him. You, my Lord, admired the man I was . . . and you trusted him."

"Cleansed mind," Paul said. "How can a cleansed mind put itself in bondage to us?"

"Bondage, my Lord? The cleansed mind makes decisions in the presence of unknowns and without cause and effect. Is this bondage?"

Paul scowled. It was a Zensunni saying, cryptic, apt—immersed in a creed which denied objective function in all mental activity. *Without cause and effect!* Such thoughts shocked the mind. *Unknowns?* Unknowns lay in every decision, even in the oracular vision.

"You'd prefer we called you Duncan Idaho?" Paul asked.

"We live by differences, my Lord. Choose a name for me."

"Let your Tleilaxu name stand," Paul said. "Hayt—there's a name inspires caution."

Hayt bowed, moved back one step.

And Alia wondered: *How did he know the interview was over? I knew it because I know my brother. But there was no sign a stranger could read. Did the Duncan Idaho in him know?*

Paul turned toward the Ambassador, said: "Quarters have been set aside for your embassy. It is our desire to have a private consultation with you at the earliest opportunity. We will send for you. Let us inform you further, before you hear it from an inaccurate source, that a Reverend Mother of the Sisterhood, Gaius Helen Mohiam, has been removed from the heighliner which brought you. It was done at our command. Her presence on your ship will be an item in our talks."

A wave of Paul's left hand dismissed the envoy. "Hayt," Paul said, "stay here."

The Ambassador's attendants backed away, towing the tank. Edric became orange motion in orange gas—eyes, a mouth, gently waving limbs.

Paul watched until the last Guildsman was gone, the great doors swinging closed behind them.

*I've done it now*, Paul thought. *I've accepted the ghola.* The Tleilaxu creation was bait, no doubt of it. Very likely the old hag of a Reverend Mother played the same role. But it was the time of the tarot which he'd forecast in an early vision. The damnable tarot! It muddied the waters of Time until the prescient strained to detect moments but an hour off. Many a fish took the bait and escaped, he reminded himself. And the tarot worked for him as well as against him. What he could not see, others might not detect as well.

The ghola stood, head cocked to one side, waiting.

Stilgar moved across the steps, hid the ghola from Paul's view. In Chakobsa, the hunting language of their sietch days, Stilgar said: "That creature in the tank gives me the shudders, Sire, but this *gift!* Send it away!"

In the same tongue, Paul said: "I cannot."

"Idaho's dead," Stilgar argued. "This isn't Idaho. Let me take its water for the tribe."

"The ghola is my problem, Stil. Your problem is our prisoner. I want the Reverend Mother guarded most carefully by the men I trained to resist the wiles of Voice."

"I like this not, Sire."

"I'll be cautious, Stil. See that you are, too."

"Very well, Sire." Stilgar stepped down to the floor of the hall, passed close to Hayt, sniffed him and strode out.

*Evil can be detected by its smell,* Paul thought. Stilgar had planted the green and white Atreides banner on a dozen worlds, but remained superstitious Fremen, proof against any sophistication.

Paul studied the gift.

"Duncan, Duncan," he whispered. "What have they done to you?"

"They gave me life, m'Lord," Hayt said.

"But why were you trained and given to us?" Paul asked.

Hayt pursed his lips, then: "They intend me to destroy you."

The statement's candor shook Paul. But then, how else could a Zensunni-mentat respond? Even in a ghola, a mentat could speak no less than the truth, especially out of Zensunni inner calm. This was a human computer, mind and nervous system fitted to the tasks relegated long ago to hated mechanical devices. To condition him also as a Zensunni meant a double ration of honesty . . . unless the Tleilaxu had built something even more odd into this flesh.

Why, for example, the mechanical eyes? Tleilaxu boasted their metal eyes improved on the original. Strange, then, that more Tleilaxu didn't wear them out of choice.

Paul glanced up at Alia's spy hole, longed for her presence and advice, for counsel not clouded by feelings of responsibility and debt.

Once more, he looked at the ghola. This was no frivolous gift. It gave honest answers to dangerous questions.

*It makes no difference that I know this is a weapon to be used against me,* Paul thought.

"What should I do to protect myself from you?" Paul asked. It was direct speech, no royal "we," but a question as he might have put it to the old Duncan Idaho.

"Send me away, m'Lord."

Paul shook his head from side to side. "How are you to destroy me?"

Hayt looked at the guards, who'd moved closer to Paul after Stilgar's departure. He turned, cast his gaze around the hall, brought his metal eyes back to bear on Paul, nodded.

"This is a place where a man draws away from people," Hayt said. "It speaks of such power that one can contemplate it comfortably only in the remembrance that all things are finite. Did my Lord's oracular powers plot his course into this place?"

Paul drummed his fingers against the throne's arms. The mentat sought data, but the question disturbed him. "I came to this position by strong decisions . . . not always out of my other . . . abilities."

"Strong decisions," Hayt said. "These temper a man's life. One can take the temper from fine metal by heating it and allowing it to cool without quenching."

"Do you divert me with Zensunni prattle?" Paul asked.

"Zensunni has other avenues to explore, Sire, than diversion and display."

Paul wet his lips with his tongue, drew in a deep breath, set his own thoughts into the counterbalance poise of the mentat. Negative answers arose around him. It wasn't expected that he'd go haring after the ghola to the exclusion of other duties. No, that wasn't it. Why a *Zensunni*-mentat? Philosophy... words ... contemplation ... inward searching ... He felt the weakness of his data.

"We need more data," he muttered.

"The facts needed by a mentat do not brush off onto one as you might gather pollen on your robe while passing through a field of flowers," Hayt said. "One chooses his pollen carefully, examines it under powerful amplification."

"You must teach me this Zensunni way with rhetoric," Paul said.

The metallic eyes glittered at him for a moment, then: "M'Lord, perhaps that's what was intended."

*To blunt my will with words and ideas?* Paul wondered.

"Ideas are most to be feared when they become actions," Paul said.

"Send me away, Sire," Hayt said, and it was Duncan Idaho's voice full of concern for "the young master."

Paul felt trapped by that voice. He couldn't send that voice away, even when it came from a ghola. "You will stay," he said, "and we'll both exercise caution."

Hayt bowed in submission.

Paul glanced up at the spy hole, eyes pleading for Alia to take this *gift* off his hands and ferret out its secrets. Gholas were ghosts to frighten children. He'd never thought to know one. To know this one, he had to set himself above all compassion ... and he wasn't certain he could do it. *Duncan ... Duncan ...* Where was Idaho in this shaped-to-measure flesh? It wasn't flesh ... it was a shroud in fleshly shape! Idaho lay dead forever on the floor of an Arrakeen cavern. His ghost stared out of metal eyes. Two beings stood side by side in this revenant flesh. One was a threat with its force and nature hidden behind unique veils.

Closing his eyes, Paul allowed old visions to sift through his awareness. He sensed the spirits of love and hate spouting there in a rolling sea from which no rock lifted above the chaos. No place at all from which to survey turmoil.

*Why has no vision shown me this new Duncan Idaho?* he asked himself. *What concealed Time from an oracle? Other oracles, obviously.*

Paul opened his eyes, asked: "Hayt, do you have the power of prescience?"

"No, m'Lord."

Sincerity spoke in that voice. It was possible the ghola didn't know he possessed this ability, of course. But that'd hamper his working as a mentat. What was the hidden design?

Old visions surged around Paul. Would he have to choose the terrible way? Distorted Time hinted at this ghola in that hideous future. Would that way close in upon him no matter what he did?

*Disengage ... disengage ... disengage ...*

The thought tolled in his mind.

In her position above Paul, Alia sat with chin cupped in left hand, stared down at the ghola. A magnetic attraction about this Hayt reached up to her. Tleilaxu restoration had given him youth, an innocent intensity which called out to her. She'd understood Paul's unspoken plea. When oracles failed, one turned to real spies and physical powers. She wondered, though, at her own eagerness to accept this challenge. She felt a positive desire to be near this *new* man, perhaps to touch him.

*He's a danger to both of us,* she thought.

*Truth suffers from too much analysis.*

**—Ancient Fremen Saying**

"Reverend Mother, I shudder to see you in such circumstances," Irulan said.

She stood just inside the cell door, measuring the various capacities of the room in her Bene Gesserit way. It was a three-meter cube carved with cutterays from the veined brown rock beneath Paul's Keep. For furnishings, it contained one flimsy basket chair occupied now by the Reverend Mother Gaius Helen Mohiam, a pallet with a brown cover upon which had been spread a deck of the new Dune Tarot cards, a metered water tap above a reclamation basin, a Fremen privy with moisture seals. It was all sparse, primitive. Yellow light came from anchored and caged glowglobes at the four corners of the ceiling.

"You've sent word to the Lady Jessica?" the Reverend Mother asked.

"Yes, but I don't expect her to lift one finger against her firstborn," Irulan said. She glanced at the cards. They spoke of the powerful turning their backs on supplicants. The card of the Great Worm lay beneath Desolate Sand. Patience was counseled. *Did one require the tarot to see this?* she asked herself.

A guard stood outside watching them through a meta-glass window in the door. Irulan knew there'd be other monitors on this encounter. She had put in much thought and planning before daring to come here. To have stayed away carried its own perils, though.

The Reverend Mother had been engaged in *prajna* meditation interspersed with examinations of the tarot. Despite a feeling that she would never leave Arrakis alive, she had achieved a measure of calm through this. One's oracular powers might be small, but muddy water was muddy water. And there was always the Litany Against Fear.

She had yet to assimilate the import of the actions which had precipitated her into this cell. Dark suspicions brooded in her mind (and the tarot hinted at confirmations). Was it possible the Guild had planned this?

A yellow-robed Qizara, head shaved for a turban, beady eyes of total blue in a bland round face, skin leathered by the wind and sun of Arrakis, had awaited her on the heighliner's reception bridge. He had looked up from a bulb of spice-coffee being served by an obsequious steward, studied her a moment, put down the coffee bulb.

"You are the Reverend Mother Gaius Helen Mohiam?"

To replay those words in her mind was to bring that moment alive in the memory. Her throat had constricted with an unmanageable spasm of fear. How had one of the Emperor's minions learned of her presence on the heighliner?

"It came to our attention that you were aboard," the Qizara said. "Have you forgotten that you are denied permission to set foot on the holy planet?"

"I am not on Arrakis," she said. "I'm a passenger on a Guild heighliner in free space."

"There is no such thing as free space, Madame."

She read hate mingled with profound suspicion in his tone.

"Muad'Dib rules everywhere," he said.

"Arrakis is not my destination," she insisted.

"Arrakis is the destination of everyone," he said. And she feared for a moment that he would launch into a recital of the mystical itinerary which pilgrims followed. (This very ship had carried thousands of them.)

But the Qizara had pulled a golden amulet from beneath his robe, kissed it, touched it to his forehead and placed it to his right ear, listened. Presently, he restored the amulet to its hidden place.

"You are ordered to gather your luggage and accompany me to Arrakis."

"But I have business elsewhere!"

In that moment, she suspected Guild perfidy . . . or exposure through some transcendent power of the Emperor or his sister. Perhaps the Steersman did not conceal the conspiracy, after all. The abomination, Alia, certainly possessed the abilities of a Bene Gesserit Reverend Mother. What happened when those powers were coupled with the forces which worked in her brother?

"At once!" the Qizara snapped.

Everything in her cried out against setting foot once more on that accursed desert planet. Here was where the Lady Jessica had turned against the Sisterhood. Here was where they'd lost Paul Atreides, the Kwisatz Haderach they'd sought through long generations of careful breeding.

"At once," she agreed.

"There's little time," the Qizara said. "When the Emperor commands, all his subjects obey."

*So the order had come from Paul!*

She thought of protesting to the heighliner's Navigator-Commander, but the futility of such a gesture stopped her. What could the Guild do?

"The Emperor has said I must die if I set foot on Dune," she said, making a last desperate effort. "You spoke of this yourself. You are condemning me if you take me down there."

"Say no more," the Qizara ordered. "The thing is ordained."

That was how they always spoke of Imperial commands, she knew. *Ordained!* The holy ruler whose eyes could pierce the future had spoken. What must be must be. He had seen it, had He not?

With the sick feeling that she was caught in a web of her own spinning, she had turned to obey.

And the web had become a cell which Irulan could visit. She saw that Irulan had aged somewhat since their meeting on Wallach IX. New lines of worry spread from the corners of her eyes. Well . . . time to see if this Sister of the Bene Gesserit could obey her vows.

"I've had worse quarters," the Reverend Mother said. "Do you come from the Emperor?" And she allowed her fingers to move as though in agitation.

Irulan read the moving fingers and her own fingers flashed an answer as she spoke, saying: "No—I came as soon as I heard you were here."

"Won't the Emperor be angry?" the Reverend Mother asked. Again, her fingers moved: imperative, pressing, demanding.

"Let him be angry. You were my teacher in the Sisterhood, just as you were the teacher of his own mother. Does he think I will turn my back on you as she has done?" And Irulan's finger-talk made excuses, begged.

The Reverend Mother sighed. On the surface, it was the sigh of a prisoner bemoaning her fate, but inwardly she felt the response as a comment on Irulan. It was futile to hope the Atreides Emperor's precious gene pattern could be preserved through this instrument. No matter her beauty, this Princess was flawed. Under that veneer of sexual attraction lived a whining shrew more interested in words than in actions. Irulan was still a Bene Gesserit, though, and the Sisterhood reserved certain techniques to use on some of its weaker vessels as insurance that vital instructions would be carried out.

Beneath small talk about a softer pallet, better food, the Reverend Mother brought up her arsenal of persuasion and gave her orders: the brother-sister crossbreeding must be explored. (Irulan almost broke at receiving this command.)

"I must have my chance!" Irulan's fingers pleaded.

"You've had your chance," the Reverend Mother countered. And she was explicit in her instructions: Was the Emperor ever angry with his concubine? His unique powers must make him lonely. To whom could he speak in any hope of being understood? To the sister, obviously. She shared this loneliness. The depth of their communion must be exploited. Opportunities must be created to throw them together in privacy. Intimate encounters must be arranged. The possibility of eliminating the concubine must be explored. Grief dissolved traditional barriers.

Irulan protested. If Chani were killed, suspicion would fasten immediately upon the Princess-Consort. Besides, there were other problems. Chani had fastened upon an ancient Fremen diet supposed to promote fertility and the diet eliminated all opportunity for administering the contraceptive drugs. Lifting the suppressives would make Chani even more fertile.

The Reverend Mother was outraged and concealed it with difficulty while her fingers flashed their demands. Why had this information not been conveyed at the beginning of their conversation? How could Irulan be that stupid? If Chani conceived and bore a son, the Emperor would declare the child his heir!

Irulan protested that she understood the dangers, but the genes might not be totally lost.

*Damn such stupidity!* the Reverend Mother raged. Who knew what suppressions and genetic entanglements Chani might introduce from her wild Fremen strain? The Sisterhood must have only the pure line! And an heir would renew Paul's ambitions, spur him to new efforts in consolidating his Empire. The conspiracy could not afford such a setback.

Defensively, Irulan wanted to know how she could have prevented Chani from trying this diet?

But the Reverend Mother was in no mood for excuses. Irulan received explicit instructions now to meet this new threat. If Chani conceived, an abortifact must be introduced into her food or drink. Either that, or she must be killed. An heir to the throne from that source must be prevented at all costs.

An abortifact would be as dangerous as an open attack on the concubine, Irulan objected. She trembled at the thought of trying to kill Chani.

Was Irulan deterred by danger? the Reverend Mother wanted to know, her finger-talk conveying deep scorn.

Angered, Irulan signaled that she knew her value as an agent in the royal household. Did the conspiracy wish to waste such a valuable agent? Was she to be thrown away? In what other way could they keep this close watch on the Emperor? Or had they introduced another agent into the household? Was that it? Was she to be used now, desperately, and for the last time?

In a war, all values acquired new relationships, the Reverend Mother countered. Their greatest peril was that House Atreides should secure itself with an Imperial line. The Sisterhood could not take such a risk. This went far beyond the danger to the Atreides genetic pattern. Let Paul anchor his family to the throne and the Sisterhood could look forward to centuries of disruption for its programs.

Irulan understood the argument, but she couldn't escape the thought that a decision had been made to spend the Princess-Consort for something of great value. Was there something she should know about the ghola? Irulan ventured.

The Reverend Mother wanted to know if Irulan thought the Sisterhood composed of fools. When had they ever failed to tell Irulan all she *should* know?

It was no answer, but an admission of concealment, Irulan saw. It said she would be told no more than she needed to know.

How could they be certain the ghola was capable of destroying the Emperor? Irulan asked.

She could just as well have asked if melange were capable of destruction, the Reverend Mother countered.

It was a rebuke with a subtle message, Irulan realized. The Bene Gesserit "whip that instructs" informed her that she should have understood long ago this similarity between the spice and the ghola. Melange was valuable, but it exacted a price—addiction. It added years to a life—decades for some—but it was still just another way to die.

The ghola was something of deadly value.

The obvious way to prevent an unwanted birth was to kill the prospective mother before conception, the Reverend Mother signaled, returning to the attack.

*Of course*, Irulan thought. *If you decide to spend a certain sum, get as much for it as you can.*

The Reverend Mother's eyes, dark with the blue brilliance of her melange addiction, stared up at Irulan, measuring, waiting, observing minutiae.

*She reads me clearly,* Irulan thought with dismay. *She trained me and observed me in that training. She knows I realize what decision has been taken here. She only observes now to see how I will take this knowledge. Well, I will take it as a Bene Gesserit and a princess.*

Irulan managed a smile, pulled herself erect, thought of the evocative opening passage of the Litany Against Fear:

*"I must not fear. Fear is the mind-killer. Fear is the little-death that brings total obliteration. I will face my fear . . ."*

When calmness had returned, she thought: *Let them spend me. I will show them what a princess is worth. Perhaps I'll buy them more than they expected.*

After a few more empty vocalizations to bind off the interview, Irulan departed.

When she had gone, the Reverend Mother returned to her tarot cards, laying them out in the fire-eddy pattern. Immediately, she got the Kwisatz Haderach of the Major Arcana and the card lay coupled with the Eight of Ships: the sibyl hoodwinked and betrayed. These were not cards of good omen: they spoke of concealed resources for her enemies.

She turned away from the cards, sat in agitation, wondering if Irulan might yet destroy them.

---

*The Fremen see her as the Earth Figure, a demigoddess whose special charge is to protect the tribes through her powers of violence. She is Reverend Mother to their Reverend Mothers. To pilgrims who seek her out with demands that she restore virility or make the barren fruitful, she is a form of anti-mentat. She feeds on that strong human desire for the mysterious. She is living proof that the "analytic" has limits. She represents ultimate tension. She is the virgin-harlot—witty, vulgar, cruel, as destructive in her whims as a coriolis storm.*

**—St. Alia of the Knife**
**as taken from The Irulan Report**

---

Alia stood like a black-robed sentinel figure on the south platform of her temple, the Fane of the Oracle which Paul's Fremen cohorts had built for her against a wall of his stronghold.

She hated this part of her life, but knew no way to evade the temple without bringing down destruction upon them all. The pilgrims (damn them!) grew more numerous every day. The temple's lower porch was crowded with them. Vendors moved among the pilgrims, and there were minor sorcerers, haruspices, diviners, all working their trade in pitiful imitation of Paul Muad'Dib and his sister.

Red and green packages containing the new Dune Tarot were prominent among the vendors' wares, Alia saw. She wondered about the tarot. Who was feeding this device into the Arrakeen market? Why had the tarot sprung to prominence at this particular time and place? Was it to muddy Time? Spice addiction always conveyed some sensitivity to prediction. Fremen were notoriously fey. Was it an accident that so many of them dabbled in portents and omens here and now? She decided to seek an answer at the first opportunity.

There was a wind from the southeast, a small leftover wind blunted by the scarp of the Shield Wall which loomed high in these northern reaches. The rim glowed orange through a thin dust haze underlighted by the late afternoon sun. It was a hot wind against her cheeks and it made her homesick for the sand, for the security of open spaces.

The last of the day's mob began descending the broad greenstone steps of the lower porch, singly and in groups, a few pausing to stare at the keepsakes and holy amulets on the street vendors' racks, some consulting one last minor sorcerer. Pilgrims, supplicants, townfolk, Fremen, vendors closing up for the day—they formed a straggling line that trailed off into the palm-lined avenue which led to the heart of the city.

Alia's eyes picked out the Fremen, marking the frozen looks of superstitious awe on their faces, the half-wild way they kept their distance from the others. They were her strength and her peril. They still captured giant worms for transport, for sport and for sacrifice. They resented the offworld pilgrims, barely tolerated the townfolk of graben and *pan,* hated the cynicism they saw in the street vendors. One did not jostle a wild Fremen, even in a mob such as the ones which swarmed to Alia's Fane. There were no knifings in the Sacred Precincts, but bodies had been found . . . later.

The departing swarm had stirred up dust. The flinty odor came to Alia's nostrils, ignited another pang of longing for the open *bled.* Her sense of the past, she realized, had been sharpened by the coming of the ghola. There'd been much pleasure in those untrammeled days before her brother had mounted the throne—time for joking, time for small things, time to enjoy a cool morning or a sunset, time . . . time . . . time . . . Even danger had been good in those days—clean danger from known sources. No need then to strain the limits of prescience, to peer through murky veils for frustrating glimpses of the future.

Wild Fremen said it well: "Four things cannot be hidden—love, smoke, a pillar of fire and a man striding across the open bled."

With an abrupt feeling of revulsion, Alia retreated from the platform into the shadows of the Fane, strode along the balcony which looked down into the glistening opalescence of her Hall of Oracles. Sand on the tiles rasped beneath her feet. *Supplicants always tracked sand into the Sacred Chambers!* She ignored attendants, guards, postulants, the Qizarate's omnipresent priest-sycophants, plunged into the spiral passage which twisted upward to her private quarters. There, amidst divans, deep rugs, tent hangings and mementos of the desert, she dismissed the Fremen amazons Stilgar had assigned as her personal guardians. *Watchdogs, more likely!* When they had gone, muttering and objecting, but more fearful of her than they were of Stilgar, she stripped off her robe, leaving only the sheathed crysknife on its thong around her neck, strewed garments behind as she made for the bath.

He was near, she knew—that shadow-figure of a man she could sense in her future, but could not see. It angered her that no power of prescience could put flesh on that figure. He could be sensed only at unexpected moments while she scanned the lives of others. Or she came upon a smoky outline in solitary darkness when innocence lay coupled with desire. He stood just beyond an unfixed horizon, and she felt that if she strained her talents to an unexpected intensity she might see him. He was *there*—a constant assault on her awareness: fierce, dangerous, immoral.

Moist warm air surrounded her in the bath. Here was a habit she had learned from the memory-entities of the uncounted Reverend Mothers who were strung out in her awareness like pearls on a glowing necklace. Water, warm water in a sunken tub, accepted her skin as she slid into it. Green tiles with figures of red fish worked into a sea pattern surrounded the water. Such an abundance of water occupied this space that a Fremen of old would have been outraged to see it used merely for washing human flesh.

*He* was near.

It was lust in tension with chastity, she thought. Her flesh desired a mate. Sex held no casual mystery for a Reverend Mother who had presided at the sietch orgies. The *tau* awareness of her *other-selves* could supply any detail her curiosity required. This feeling of nearness could be nothing other than flesh reaching for flesh.

Need for action fought lethargy in the warm water.

Abruptly, Alia climbed dripping from the bath, strode wet and naked into the training chamber which adjoined her bedroom. The chamber, oblong and skylighted, contained the gross and subtle instruments which toned a Bene Gesserit adept into ultimate physical and mental awareness/preparedness. There were mnemonic amplifiers, digit mills from Ix to strengthen and sensitize fingers and toes, odor synthesizers, tactility sensitizers, temperature gradient fields, pattern betrayers to prevent her falling into detectable habits, alpha-wave-response trainers, blink-synchronizers to tone abilities in light/dark/spectrum analysis . . .

In ten-centimeter letters along one wall, written by her own hand in mnemonic paint, stood the key reminder from the Bene Gesserit Creed:

"Before us, all methods of learning were tainted by instinct. We learned how to learn. Before us, instinct-ridden researchers possessed a limited attention span—often no longer than a single lifetime. Projects stretching across fifty or more lifetimes never occurred to them. The concept of total muscle/nerve training had not entered awareness."

As she moved into the training room, Alia caught her own reflection multiplied thousands of times in the crystal prisms of a fencing mirror swinging in the heart of a target dummy. She saw the long sword waiting on its brackets against the target, and she thought: *Yes! I'll work myself to exhaustion—drain the flesh and clear the mind.*

The sword felt right in her hand. She slipped the crysknife from its sheath at her neck, held it sinister, tapped the activating stud with the sword tip. Resistance came alive as the aura of the target shield built up, pushing her weapon slowly and firmly away.

Prisms glittered. The target slipped to her left.

Alia followed with the tip of the long blade, thinking as she often did that the thing could almost be alive. But it was only servomotors and complex reflector circuits designed to lure the eyes away from danger, to confuse and teach. It was an instrument geared to react as she reacted, an anti-self which moved as she moved, balancing light on its prisms, shifting its target, offering its counter-blade.

Many blades appeared to lunge at her from the prisms, but only one was real. She countered the real one, slipped the sword past shield resistance to tap the target. A marker light came alive: red and glistening among the prisms . . . more distraction.

Again the thing attacked, moving at one-marker speed now, just a bit faster than it had at the beginning.

She parried and, against all caution, moved into the danger zone, scored with the crysknife.

Two lights glowed from the prisms.

Again, the thing increased speed, moving out on its rollers, drawn like a magnet to the motions of her body and the tip of her sword.

Attack—parry—counter.

Attack—parry—counter . . .

She had four lights alive in there now, and the thing was becoming more dangerous, moving faster with each light, offering more areas of confusion.

Five lights.

Sweat glistened on her naked skin. She existed now in a universe whose dimensions were outlined by the threatening blade, the target, bare feet against the practice floor, senses/nerves/muscles—motion against motion.

Attack—parry—counter.

Six lights . . . seven . . .

Eight!

She had never before risked eight.

In a recess of her mind there grew a sense of urgency, a crying out against such wildness as this. The instrument of prisms and target could not think, feel caution or remorse. And it carried a real blade. To go against less defeated the purpose of such training. That attacking blade could maim and it could kill. But the finest swordsmen in the Imperium never went against more than seven lights.

Nine!

Alia experienced a sense of supreme exaltation. Attacking blade and target became blurs among blurs. She felt that the sword in her hand had come alive. She was an anti-target. She did not move the blade; it moved her.

Ten!

Eleven!

Something flashed past her shoulder, slowed at the shield aura around the target, slid through and tripped the deactivating stud. The lights darkened. Prisms and target twisted their way to stillness.

Alia whirled, angered by the intrusion, but her reaction was thrown into tension by awareness of the supreme ability which had hurled that knife. It had been a throw timed to exquisite nicety—just fast enough to get through the shield zone and not too fast to be deflected.

And it had touched a one-millimeter spot within an eleven-light target.

Alia found her own emotions and tensions running down in a manner not unlike that of the target dummy. She was not at all surprised to see who had thrown the knife.

Paul stood just inside the training room doorway, Stilgar three steps behind him. Her brother's eyes were squinted in anger.

Alia, growing conscious of her nudity, thought to cover herself, found the idea amusing. What the eyes had seen could not be erased. Slowly, she replaced the crysknife in its sheath at her neck.

"I might've known," she said.

"I presume you know how dangerous that was," Paul said. He took his time reading the reactions on her face and body: the flush of her exertions coloring her skin, the wet fullness of her lips. There was a disquieting femaleness about her that he had never considered in his sister. He found it odd that he could look at a person who was this close to him and no longer recognize her in the identity framework which had seemed so fixed and familiar.

"That was madness," Stilgar rasped, coming up to stand beside Paul.

The words were angry, but Alia heard awe in his voice, saw it in his eyes.

"Eleven lights," Paul said, shaking his head.

"I'd have made it twelve if you hadn't interfered," she said. She began to pale under his close regard, added: "And why do the damned things have that many lights if we're not supposed to try for them?"

"A Bene Gesserit should ask the reasoning behind an open-ended system?" Paul asked.

"I suppose you never tried for more than seven!" she said, anger returning. His attentive posture began to annoy her.

"Just once," Paul said. "Gurney Halleck caught me on ten. My punishment was sufficiently embarrassing that I won't tell you what he did. And speaking of embarrassment . . ."

"Next time, perhaps you'll have yourselves announced," she said. She brushed past Paul into the bedroom, found a loose gray robe, slipped into it, began brushing her hair before a wall mirror. She felt sweaty, sad, a post-coitum kind of sadness that left her with a desire to bathe once more . . . and to sleep. "Why're you here?" she asked.

"My Lord," Stilgar said. There was an odd inflection in his voice that brought Alia around to stare at him.

"We're here at Irulan's suggestion," Paul said, "as strange as that may seem. She believes, and information in Stil's possession appears to confirm it, that our enemies are about to make a major try for—"

"My Lord!" Stilgar said, his voice sharper.

As her brother turned, questioning, Alia continued to look at the old Fremen Naib. Something about him now made her intensely aware that he was one of the primitives. Stilgar believed in a supernatural world very near him. It spoke to him in a simple pagan tongue dispelling all doubts. The natural universe in which he stood was fierce, unstoppable, and it lacked the common morality of the Imperium.

"Yes, Stil," Paul said. "Do you want to tell her why we came?"

"This isn't the time to talk of why we came," Stilgar said.

"What's wrong, Stil?"

Stilgar continued to stare at Alia. "Sire, are you blind?"

Paul turned back to his sister, a feeling of unease beginning to fill him. Of all his aides, only Stilgar dared speak to him in that tone, but even Stilgar measured the occasion by its need.

"This one must have a mate!" Stilgar blurted. "There'll be trouble if she's not wed, and that soon."

Alia whirled away, her face suddenly hot. *How did he touch me?* she wondered. Bene Gesserit self-control had been powerless to prevent her reaction. How had Stilgar done that? He hadn't the power of the Voice. She felt dismayed and angry.

"Listen to the great Stilgar!" Alia said, keeping her back to them, aware of a shrewish quality in her voice and unable to hide it. "Advice to maidens from Stilgar, the Fremen!"

"As I love you both, I must speak," Stilgar said, a profound dignity in his tone. "I did not become a chieftain among the Fremen by being blind to what moves men and women together. One needs no mysterious powers for this."

Paul weighed Stilgar's meaning, reviewed what they had seen here and his own undeniable male reaction to his own sister. Yes—there'd been a ruttish air about Alia, something wildly wanton. What had made her enter the practice floor in the nude? And risking her life in that foolhardy way! Eleven lights in the fencing prisms! That brainless automaton loomed in his mind with all the aspects of an ancient horror creature. Its possession was the shibboleth of this age, but it carried also the taint of old immorality. Once, they'd been guided by an artificial intelligence, computer brains. The Butlerian Jihad had ended that, but it hadn't ended the aura of aristocratic vice which enclosed such things.

Stilgar was right, of course. They must find a mate for Alia.

"I will see to it," Paul said. "Alia and I will discuss this later—privately."

Alia turned around, focused on Paul. Knowing how his mind worked, she realized she'd been the subject of a mentat decision, uncounted bits falling together in that human-computer analysis. There was an inexorable quality to this realization—a movement like the movement of planets. It carried something of the order of the universe in it, inevitable and terrifying.

"Sire," Stilgar said, "perhaps we'd—"

"Not now!" Paul snapped. "We've other problems at the moment."

Aware that she dared not try to match logic with her brother, Alia put the past few moments aside, Bene Gesserit fashion, said: "Irulan sent you?" She found herself experiencing menace in that thought.

"Indirectly," Paul said. "The information she gives us confirms our suspicion that the Guild is about to try for a sandworm."

"They'll try to capture a small one and attempt to start the spice cycle on some other world," Stilgar said. "It means they've found a world they consider suitable."

"It means they have Fremen accomplices!" Alia argued. "No offworlder could capture a worm!"

"That goes without saying," Stilgar said.

"No, it doesn't," Alia said. She was outraged by such obtuseness. "Paul, certainly you . . ."

"The rot is setting in," Paul said. "We've known that for quite some time. I've never *seen* this other world, though, and that bothers me. If they—"

"*That* bothers you?" Alia demanded. "It means only that they've clouded its location with Steersmen the way they hide their sanctuaries."

Stilgar opened his mouth, closed it without speaking. He had the overwhelming sensation that his idols had admitted blasphemous weakness.

Paul, sensing Stilgar's disquiet, said: "We've an immediate problem! I want your opinion, Alia. Stilgar suggests we expand our patrols in the open bled and reinforce the sietch watch. It's just possible we could spot a landing party and prevent the—"

"With a Steersman guiding them?" Alia asked.

"They *are* desperate, aren't they?" Paul agreed. "*That* is why I'm here."

"What've they *seen* that we haven't?" Alia asked.

"Precisely."

Alia nodded, remembering her thoughts about the new Dune Tarot. Quickly, she recounted her fears.

"Throwing a blanket over us," Paul said.

"With adequate patrols," Stilgar ventured, "we might prevent the—"

"We prevent nothing . . . forever," Alia said. She didn't like the *feel* of the way Stilgar's mind was working now. He had narrowed his scope, eliminated obvious essentials. This was not the Stilgar she remembered.

"We must count on their getting a worm," Paul said. "Whether they can start the melange cycle on another planet is a different question. They'll need more than a worm."

Stilgar looked from brother to sister. Out of ecological thinking that had been ground into him by sietch life, he grasped their meaning. A captive worm couldn't live except with a bit of Arrakis—sand plankton, Little Makers and all. The Guild's problem was large, but not impossible. His own growing uncertainty lay in a different area.

"Then your visions do not detect the Guild at its work?" he asked.

"Damnation!" Paul exploded.

Alia studied Stilgar, sensing the savage sideshow of ideas taking place in his mind. He was hung on a rack of enchantment. Magic! Magic! To glimpse the future was to steal terrifying fire from a sacred flame. It held the attraction of ultimate peril, souls ventured and lost. One brought back from the formless, dangerous distances something with form and power. But Stilgar was beginning to sense other forces, perhaps greater powers beyond that unknown horizon. His Queen Witch and Sorcerer Friend betrayed dangerous weaknesses.

'Stilgar," Alia said, fighting to hold him, "you stand in a valley between dunes. I stand on the crest. I see where you do not see. And, among other things, I see mountains which conceal the distances."

"There are things hidden from you," Stilgar said. "This you've always said."

"All power is limited," Alia said.

"And danger may come from behind the mountains," Stilgar said.

"It's *something* on that order," Alia said.

Stilgar nodded, his gaze fastened on Paul's face. "But whatever comes from behind the mountains must cross the dunes."

> The most dangerous game in the universe is to govern from an oracular base. We do not consider ourselves wise enough or brave enough to play that game. The measures detailed here for regulation in lesser matters are as near as we dare venture to the brink of government. For our purposes, we borrow a definition from the Bene Gesserit and we consider the various worlds as gene pools, sources of teachings and teachers, sources of the possible. Our goal is not to rule, but to tap these gene pools, to learn, and to free ourselves from all restraints imposed by dependency and government.

> —"The Orgy as a Tool of Statecraft,"
> Chapter Three of the The Steersman's Guide

"Is that where your father died?" Edric asked, sending a beam pointer from his tank to a jeweled marker on one of the relief maps adorning a wall of Paul's reception salon.

"That's the shrine of his skull," Paul said. "My father died a prisoner on a Harkonnen frigate in the sink below us."

"Oh, yes: I recall the story now," Edric said. "Something about killing the old Baron Harkonnen, his mortal enemy." Hoping he didn't betray too much of the terror which small enclosures such as this room imposed upon him, Edric rolled over in the orange gas, directed his gaze at Paul, who sat alone on a long divan of striped gray and black.

"My sister killed the Baron," Paul said, voice and manner dry, "just before the battle of Arrakeen."

And why, he wondered, did the Guild man-fish reopen old wounds in this place and at this time?

The Steersman appeared to be fighting a losing battle to contain his nervous energies. Gone were the languid fish motions of their earlier encounter. Edric's tiny eyes jerked here . . . there, questing and measuring. The one attendant who had accompanied him in here stood apart near the line of houseguards ranging the end wall at Paul's left. The attendant worried Paul—hulking, thick-necked, blunt and vacant face. The man had entered the salon, nudging Edric's tank along on its supporting field, walking with a strangler's gait, arms akimbo.

*Scytale,* Edric had called him. *Scytale, an aide.*

The aide's surface shouted stupidity, but the eyes betrayed him. They laughed at everything they saw.

"Your concubine appeared to enjoy the performance of the Face Dancers," Edric said. "It pleases me that I could provide that small entertainment. I particularly enjoyed her reaction to seeing her own features simultaneously repeated by the whole troupe."

"Isn't there a warning against Guildsmen bearing gifts?" Paul asked.

And he thought of the performance out there in the Great Hall. The dancers had entered in the costumes and guise of the Dune Tarot, flinging themselves about in seemingly random patterns that devolved into fire eddies and ancient prognostic designs. Then had come the rulers—a parade of kings and emperors like faces on coins, formal and stiff in outline, but curiously fluid. And the jokes: a copy of Paul's own face and body, Chani repeated across the floor of the Hall, even Stilgar, who had grunted and shudddered while others laughed.

"But our gifts have the kindest intent," Edric protested.

"How kindly can you be?" Paul asked. "The ghola you gave us believes he was designed to destroy us."

"Destroy you, Sire?" Edric asked, all bland attention. "Can one destroy a god?"

Stilgar, entering on the last words, stopped, glared at the guards. They were much farther from Paul than he liked. Angrily he motioned them closer.

"It's all right, Stil," Paul said, lifting a hand. "Just a friendly discussion. Why don't you move the Ambassador's tank over by the end of my divan?"

Stilgar, weighing the order, saw that it would put the Steersman's tank between Paul and the hulking aide, much too close to Paul, but . . .

"It's all right, Stil," Paul repeated, and he gave the private hand-signal which made the order an imperative.

Moving with obvious reluctance, Stilgar pushed the tank closer to Paul. He didn't like the feel of the container or the heavily perfumed smell of melange around it. He took up a position at the corner of the tank beneath the orbiting device through which the Steersman spoke.

"To kill a god," Paul said. "That's very interesting. But who says I'm a god?"

"Those who worship you," Edric said, glancing pointedly at Stilgar.

"Is this what you believe?" Paul asked.

"What I believe is of no moment, Sire," Edric said. "It seems to most observers, however, that you conspire to make a god of yourself. And one might ask if that is something any mortal can do . . . safely?"

Paul studied the Guildsman. Repellent creature, but perceptive. It was a question Paul had asked himself time and again. But he had seen enough alternate Timelines to know of worse possibilities than accepting godhead for himself. Much worse. These were not, however, the normal avenues for a Steersman to probe. Curious. Why had that question been asked? What could Edric hope to gain by such effrontery? Paul's thoughts went *flick* (the association of Tleilaxu would be behind this move)—*flick* (the Jihad's recent Sembou victory would bear on Edric's action)—*flick* (various Bene Gesserit credos showed themselves here) *flick* . . .

A process involving thousands of information bits poured flickering through his computational awareness. It required perhaps three seconds.

"Does a Steersman question the guidelines of prescience?" Paul asked, putting Edric on the weakest ground.

This disturbed the Steersman, but he covered well, coming up with what sounded like a long aphorism: "No man of intelligence questions the fact of prescience, Sire. Oracular vision has been known to men since most ancient times. It has a way of entangling us when we least suspect. Luckily, there are other forces in our universe."

"Greater than prescience?" Paul asked, pressing him.

"If prescience alone existed and did everything, Sire, it would annihilate itself. Nothing but prescience? Where could it be applied except to its own degenerating movements?"

"There's always the human situation," Paul agreed.

"A precarious thing at best," Edric said, "without confusing it by hallucinations."

"Are my visions no more than hallucinations?" Paul asked, mock sadness in his voice. "Or do you imply that my worshipers hallucinate?"

Stilgar, sensing the mounting tensions, moved a step nearer Paul, fixed his attention on the Guildsman reclining in the tank.

"You twist my words, Sire," Edric protested. An odd sense of violence lay suspended in the words.

*Violence here?* Paul wondered. *They wouldn't dare! Unless* (and he glanced at his guards) *the forces which protected him were to be used in replacing him.*

"But you accuse me of conspiring to make a god of myself," Paul said, pitching his voice that only Edric and Stilgar might hear. "Conspire?"

"A poor choice of word, perhaps, my Lord," Edric said.

"But significant," Paul said. "It says you expect the worst of me."

Edric arched his neck, stared sideways at Stilgar with a look of apprehension. "People always expect the worst of the rich and powerful, Sire. It is said one can always tell an aristocrat: he reveals only those of his vices which will make him popular."

A tremor passed across Stilgar's face.

Paul looked up at the movement, sensing the thoughts and angers whispering in Stilgar's mind. How dared this Guildsman talk thus to Muad'Dib?

"You're not joking, of course," Paul said.

"Joking, Sire?"

Paul grew aware of dryness in his mouth. He felt that there were too many people in this room, that the air he breathed had passed through too many lungs. The taint of melange from Edric's tank felt threatening.

"Who might my accomplices be in such a conspiracy?" Paul asked presently. "Do you nominate the Qizarate?"

Edric's shrug stirred the orange gas around his head. He no longer appeared concerned by Stilgar, although the Fremen continued to glare at him.

"Are you suggesting that my missionaries of the Holy Orders, *all of them,* are preaching falsehood?" Paul insisted.

"It could be a question of self-interest and sincerity," Edric said.

Stilgar put a hand to the crysknife beneath his robe.

Paul shook his head, said: "Then you accuse me of insincerity."

"I'm not sure that *accuse* is the proper word, Sire."

*The boldness of this creature!* Paul thought. And he said: "Accused or not, you're saying my bishops and I are no better than power-hungry brigands."

"Power-hungry, Sire?" Again, Edric looked at Stilgar. "Power tends to isolate those who hold too much of it. Eventually, they lose touch with reality . . . and fall."

"M'Lord," Stilgar growled, "you've had men executed for less!"

"Men, yes," Paul agreed. "But this is a Guild Ambassador."

"He accuses you of an unholy fraud!" Stilgar said.

"His thinking interests me, Stil," Paul said. "Contain your anger and remain alert."

"As Muad'Dib commands."

"Tell me, Steersman," Paul said, "how could we maintain this hypothetical fraud over such enormous distances of space and time without the means to watch every missionary, to examine every nuance in every Qizarate priory and temple?"

"What is time to you?" Edric asked.

Stilgar frowned in obvious puzzlement. And he thought: *Muad'Dib has often said he sees past the veils of time. What is the Guildsman really saying?*

"Wouldn't the structure of such a fraud begin to show holes?' Paul asked. "Significant disagreements, schisms . . . doubts, confessions of guilt—surely fraud could not suppress all these."

"What religion and self-interest cannot hide, governments can," Edric said.

"Are you testing the limits of my tolerance?" Paul asked.

"Do my arguments lack all merit?" Edric countered.

*Does he want us to kill him?* Paul wondered. *Is Edric offering himself as a sacrifice?*

"I prefer the cynical view," Paul said, testing. "You obviously are trained in all the lying tricks of statecraft, the double meanings and the power words. Language is nothing more than a weapon to you and, thus, you test my armor."

"The cynical view," Edric said, a smile stretching his mouth. "And rulers are notoriously cynical where religions are concerned. Religion, too, is a weapon. What manner of weapon is religion when it becomes the government?"

Paul felt himself go inwardly still, a profound caution gripping him. To whom was Edric speaking? Damnable clever words, heavy with manipulation leverages—that undertone of comfortable humor, the unspoken air of shared secrets: his manner said he and Paul were two sophisticates, men of a wider universe who understood things not granted common folk. With a feeling of shock, Paul realized that he had not been the main target for all this rhetoric.

This affliction visited upon the court had been speaking for the benefit of others—speaking to Stilgar, to the household guards . . . perhaps even to the hulking aide.

"Religious *mana* was thrust upon me," Paul said. "I did not seek it." And he thought: *There! Let this man-fish think himself victorious in our battle of words!*

"Then why have you not disavowed it, Sire?" Edric asked.

"Because of my sister, Alia," Paul said, watching Edric carefully. "She is a goddess. Let me urge caution where Alia is concerned lest she strike you dead with her glance."

A gloating smile began forming on Edric's mouth, was replaced by a look of shock.

"I am deadly serious," Paul said, watching the shock spread, seeing Stilgar nod.

In a bleak voice, Edric said: "You have mauled my confidence in you, Sire. And no doubt that was your intent."

"Do not be certain you know my intent," Paul said, and he signaled Stilgar that the audience was at an end.

To Stilgar's questioning gesture asking if Edric were to be assassinated, Paul gave a negative hand-sign, amplified it with an imperative lest Stilgar take matters into his own hands.

Scytale, Edric's aide, moved to the rear corner of the tank, nudged it toward the door. When he came opposite Paul, he stopped, turned that laughing gaze on Paul, said: "If my Lord permits?"

"Yes, what is it?" Paul asked, noting how Stilgar moved close in answer to the implied menace from this man.

"Some say," Scytale said, "that people cling to Imperial leadership because space is infinite. They feel lonely without a unifying symbol. For a lonely people, the Emperor is a definite place. They can turn toward him and say: 'See, there He is. He makes us one.' Perhaps religion serves the same purpose, m'Lord."

Scytale nodded pleasantly, gave Edric's tank another nudge. They moved out of the salon, Edric supine in his tank, eyes closed. The Steersman appeared spent, all his nervous energies exhausted.

Paul stared after the shambling figure of Scytale, wondering at the man's words. A peculiar fellow, that Scytale, he thought. While he was speaking, he had radiated a feeling of many people—as though his entire genetic inheritance lay exposed on his skin.

"That was odd," Stilgar said, speaking to no one in particular.

Paul arose from the divan as a guard closed the door behind Edric and the escort.

"Odd," Stilgar repeated. A vein throbbed at his temple.

Paul dimmed the salon's lights, moved to a window which opened onto an angled cliff of his Keep. Lights glittered far below—pigmy movement. A work gang moved down there bringing giant plasmeld blocks to repair a facade of Alia's temple which had been damaged by a freak twisting of a sandblast wind.

"That was a foolish thing, Usul, inviting that creature in these chambers," Stilgar said.

*Usul,* Paul thought. *My sietch name. Stilgar reminds me that he ruled over me once, that he saved me from the desert.*

"Why did you do it?" Stilgar asked, speaking from close behind Paul.

"Data," Paul said. "I need more data."

"Is it not dangerous to try meeting this threat *only* as a mentat?"

*That was perceptive,* Paul thought.

Mentat computation remained finite. You couldn't say something boundless within the boundaries of any language. Mentat abilities had their uses, though. He said as much now, daring Stilgar to refute his argument.

"There's always something outside," Stilgar said. "Some things best *kept* outside."

"Or inside," Paul said. And he accepted for a moment his own oracular/mentat summation. Outside, yes. And inside: here lay the true horror. How could he protect himself from himself? They certainly were setting him up to destroy himself, but this was a position hemmed in by even more terrifying possibilities.

His reverie was broken by the sound of rapid footsteps. The figure of Korba the Qizara surged through the doorway backlighted by the brilliant illumination in the hallways. He entered as though hurled by an unseen force and came to an almost immediate halt when he encountered the salon's gloom. His hands appeared to be full of shigawire reels. They glittered in the light from the hall, strange little round jewels that were extinguished as a guardsman's hand came into view, closed the door.

"Is that you, m'Lord?" Korba asked, peering into the shadows.

"What is it?" Stilgar asked.

"Stilgar?"

"We're both here. What is it?"

"I'm disturbed by this reception for the Guildsman."

"Disturbed?" Paul asked.

"The people say, m'Lord, that you honor our enemies."

"Is that all?" Paul said. "Are those the reels I asked you to bring earlier?" He indicated the shigawire orbs in Korba's hands.

"Reels . . . oh! Yes, m'Lord. These are the histories. Will you view them here?"

"I've viewed them. I want them for Stilgar here."

"For me?" Stilgar asked. He felt resentment grow at what he interpreted as caprice on Paul's part. Histories! Stilgar had sought out Paul earlier to discuss the logistics computations for the Zabulon conquest. The Guild Ambassador's presence had intervened. And now—Korba with histories!

"How much history do you know?" Paul mused aloud, studying the shadowy figure beside him.

"M'Lord, I can name every world our people touched in their migrations. I know the reaches of Imperial . . ."

"The Golden Age of Earth, have you ever studied that?"

"Earth? Golden Age?" Stilgar was irritated and puzzled. Why would Paul wish to discuss myths from the dawn of time? Stilgar's mind still felt crammed with Zabulon data—computations from the staff mentats: two hundred and five attack frigates with thirty legions, support battalions, pacification cadres, Qizarate missionaries . . . the food requirements (he had the figures right here in his mind) and melange . . . weaponry, uniforms, medals . . . urns for the ashes of the dead . . . the number of specialists—men to produce raw materials of propaganda, clerks, accountants . . . spies . . . and spies upon the spies . . .

"I brought the pulse-synchronizer attachment, also, m'Lord," Korba ventured. He obviously sensed the tensions building between Paul and Stilgar and was disturbed by them.

Stilgar shook his head from side to side. *Pulse-synchronizer?* Why would Paul wish him to use a mnemonic flutter-system on a shigawire projector? Why scan for specific data in histories? This was mentat work! As usual, Stilgar found he couldn't escape a deep suspicion at the thought of using a projector and attachments. The thing always immersed him in disturbing sensations, an overwhelming shower of data which his mind sorted out later, surprising him with information he had not known he possessed.

"Sire, I came with the Zabulon computations," Stilgar said.

"Dehydrate the Zabulon computations!" Paul snapped, using the obscene Fremen term which meant that here was moisture no man could demean himself by touching.

"M'Lord!"

"Stilgar," Paul said, "you urgently need a sense of balance which can come only from an understanding of long-term effects. What little information we have about the old times, the pittance of data which the Butlerians left us, Korba has brought it for you. Start with the Genghis Khan."

"Genghis . . . Khan? Was he of the Sardaukar, m'Lord?"

"Oh, long before that. He killed . . . perhaps four million."

"He must've had formidable weaponry to kill that many, Sire. Lasbeams, perhaps, or . . ."

"He didn't kill them himself, Stil. He killed the way I kill, by sending out his legions. There's another emperor I want you to note in passing—a Hitler. He killed more than six million. Pretty good for those days."

"Killed . . . by his legions?" Stilgar asked.

"Yes."

"Not very impressive statistics, m'Lord."

"Very good, Stil." Paul glanced at the reels in Korba's hands. Korba stood with them as though he wished he could drop them and flee. "Statistics: at a conservative estimate, I've killed sixty-one billion, sterilized ninety planets, completely demoralized five hundred others. I've wiped out the followers of forty religions which had existed since—"

"Unbelievers!" Korba protested. "Unbelievers all!"

"No," Paul said. "Believers."

"My Liege makes a joke," Korba said, voice trembling. "The Jihad has brought ten thousand worlds into the shining light of—"

"Into the darkness," Paul said. "We'll be a hundred generations recovering from Muad'Dib's Jihad. I find it hard to imagine that anyone will ever surpass this." A barking laugh erupted from his throat.

"What amuses Muad'Dib?" Stilgar asked.

"I am not amused. I merely had a sudden vision of the Emperor Hitler saying something similar. No doubt he did."

"No other ruler ever had your powers," Korba argued. "Who would dare challenge you? Your legions control the known universe and all the—"

"The legions control," Paul said. "I wonder if they know this?"

"You control your legions, Sire," Stilgar interrupted, and it was obvious from the tone of his voice that he suddenly felt his own position in that chain of command, his own hand guiding all that power.

Having set Stilgar's thoughts in motion along the track he wanted, Paul turned his full attention to Korba, said: "Put the reels down here on the divan." As Korba obeyed, Paul said: "How goes the reception, Korba? Does my sister have everything well in hand?"

"Yes, m'Lord." Korba's tone was wary. "And Chani watches from the spy hole. She suspects there may be Sardaukar in the Guild entourage."

"No doubt she's correct," Paul said. "The jackals gather."

"Bannerjee," Stilgar said, naming the chief of Paul's Security detail, "was worried earlier that some of them might try to penetrate the private areas of the Keep."

"Have they?"

"Not yet."

"But there was some confusion in the formal gardens," Korba said.

"What sort of confusion?" Stilgar demanded.

Paul nodded.

"Strangers coming and going," Korba said, "trampling the plants, whispered conversations—I heard reports of some disturbing remarks."

"Such as?" Paul asked.

"*Is this the way our taxes are spent?* I'm told the Ambassador himself asked that question."

"I don't find that surprising," Paul said. "Were there many strangers in the gardens?"

"Dozens, m'Lord."

"Bannerjee stationed picked troopers at the vulnerable doors, m'Lord," Stilgar said. He turned as he spoke, allowing the salon's single remaining light to illuminate half his face. The peculiar lighting, the face, all touched a node of memory in Paul's mind—something from the desert. Paul didn't bother bringing it to full recall, his attention being focused on how Stilgar had pulled back mentally. The Fremen had a tight-skinned forehead which mirrored almost every thought flickering across his mind. He was suspicious now, profoundly suspicious of his Emperor's odd behavior.

"I don't like the intrusion into the gardens," Paul said. "Courtesy to guests is one thing, and the formal necessities of greeting an envoy, but this . . ."

"I'll see to removing them," Korba said. "Immediately."

"Wait!" Paul ordered as Korba started to turn.

In the abrupt stillness of the moment, Stilgar edged himself into a position where he could study Paul's face. It was deftly done. Paul admired the way of it, an achievement devoid of any forwardness. It was a Fremen thing: slyness touched by respect for another's privacy, a movement of necessity.

"What time is it?" Paul asked.

"Almost midnight, Sire," Korba said.

"Korba, I think you may be my finest creation," Paul said.

"Sire!" There was injury in Korba's voice.

"Do you feel awe of me?" Paul asked.

"You are Paul Muad'Dib who was Usul in our sietch," Korba said. "You know my devotion to—"

"Have you ever felt like an apostle?" Paul asked.

Korba obviously misunderstood the words, but correctly interpreted the tone. "My emperor knows I have a clean conscience!"

"Shai-hulud save us," Paul murmured.

The questioning silence of the moment was broken by the sound of someone whistling as he walked down the outer hall. The whistling was stilled by a guardsman's barked command as it came opposite the door.

"Korba, I think you may survive all this," Paul said. And he read the growing light of understanding on Stilgar's face.

"The strangers in the gardens, Sire?" Stilgar asked.

"Ahh, yes," Paul said. "Have Bannerjee put them out, Stil. Korba will assist."

"Me, Sire?" Korba betrayed deep disquiet.

"Some of my friends have forgotten they once were Fremen," Paul said, speaking to Korba, but designing his words for Stilgar. "You will mark down the ones Chani identifies as Sardaukar and you will have them killed. Do it yourself. I want it done quietly and without undue disturbance. We must keep in mind that there's more to religion and government than approving treaties and sermons."

"I obey the orders of Muad'Dib," Korba whispered.

"The Zabulon computations?" Stilgar asked.

"Tomorrow," Paul said. "And when the strangers are removed from the gardens, announce that the reception is ended. The party's over, Stil."

"I understand, m'Lord."

"I'm sure you do," Paul said.

> *Here lies a toppled god–*
> *His fall was not a small one.*
> *We did but build his pedestal,*
> *A narrow and a tall one.*

**—Tleilaxu Epigram**

Alia crouched, resting elbows on knees, chin on fists, stared at the body on the dune—a few bones and some tattered flesh that once had been a young woman. The hands, the head, most of the upper torso were gone—eaten by the coriolis wind. The sand all around bore the tracks of her brother's medics and questors. They were gone now, all excepting the mortuary attendants who stood to one side with Hayt, the ghola, waiting for her to finish her mysterious perusal of what had been written here.

A wheat-colored sky enfolded the scene in the glaucous light common to midafternoon for these latitudes.

The body had been discovered several hours earlier by a low-flying courier whose instruments had detected a faint water trace where none should be. His call had brought the experts. And they had learned—what? That this had been a woman of about twenty years, Fremen, addicted to semuta . . . and she had died here in the crucible of the desert from the effects of a subtle poison of Tleilaxu origin.

To die in the desert was a common enough occurrence. But a Fremen addicted to semuta, this was such a rarity that Paul had sent her to examine the scene in the ways their mother had taught them.

Alia felt that she had accomplished nothing here except to cast her own aura of mystery about a scene that was already mysterious enough. She heard the ghola's feet stir the sand, looked at him. His attention rested momentarily upon the escort 'thopters circling overhead like a flock of ravens.

*Beware of the Guild bearing gifts,* Alia thought.

The mortuary 'thopter and her own craft stood on the sand near a rock outcropping behind the ghola. Focusing on the grounded 'thopters filled Alia with a craving to be airborne and away from here.

But Paul had thought she might see something here which others would miss. She squirmed in her stillsuit. It felt raspingly unfamiliar after all the suitless months of city life. She studied the ghola, wondering if he might know something important about this peculiar death. A lock of his black-goat hair, she saw, had escaped his stillsuit hood. She sensed her hand longing to tuck that hair back into place.

As though lured by this thought, his gleaming gray metal eyes turned toward her. The eyes set her trembling and she tore her gaze away from him.

A Fremen woman had died here from a poison called "the throat of hell."

A Fremen addicted to semuta.

She shared Paul's disquiet at this conjunction.

The mortuary attendants waited patiently. This corpse contained not enough water for them to salvage. They felt no need to hurry. And they'd believe that Alia, through some glyptic art, was reading a strange truth in these remains.

No strange truth came to her.

There was only a distant feeling of anger deep within her at the obvious thoughts in the attendants' minds. It was a product of the damned religious mystery. She and her brother could not be *people*. They had to be something more. The Bene Gesserit had seen to that by manipulating Atreides ancestry. Their mother had contributed to it by thrusting them onto the path of witchery.

And Paul perpetuated the difference.

The Reverend Mothers encapsulated in Alia's memories stirred restlessly, provoking adab flashes of thought: *"Peace, Little One! You are what you are. There are compensations."*

Compensations!

She summoned the ghola with a gesture.

He stopped beside her, attentive, patient.

"What do you see in this?" she asked.

"We may never learn who it was died here," he said. "The head, the teeth are gone. The hands . . . Unlikely such a one had a genetic record somewhere to which her cells could be matched."

"Tleilaxu poison," she said. "What do you make of that?"

"Many people buy such poisons."

"True enough. And this flesh is too far gone to be regrown as was done with your body."

"Even if you could trust the Tleilaxu to do it," he said.

She nodded, stood. "You will fly me back to the city now."

When they were airborne and pointed north, she said: "You fly exactly as Duncan Idaho did."

He cast a speculative glance at her. "Others have told me this."

"What are you thinking now?" she asked.

"Many things."

"Stop dodging my question, damn you!"

"Which question?"

She glared at him.

He saw the glare, shrugged.

How like Duncan Idaho, that gesture, she thought. Accusingly, her voice thick and with a catch in it, she said: "I merely wanted your reactions voiced to play my own thoughts against them. That young woman's death bothers me."

"I was not thinking about that."

"What were you thinking about?"

"About the strange emotions I feel when people speak of the one I may have been."

"May have been?"

"The Tleilaxu are very clever."

"Not that clever. You were Duncan Idaho."

"Very likely. It's the prime computation."

"So you get emotional?"

"To a degree. I feel eagerness. I'm uneasy. There's a tendency to tremble and I must devote effort to controlling it. I get . . . flashes of imagery."

"What imagery?"

"It's too rapid to recognize. Flashes. Spasms . . . almost memories."

"Aren't you curious about such memories?"

"Of course. Curiosity urges me forward, but I move against a heavy reluctance. I think: 'What if I'm not the one they believe me to be?' I don't like that thought."

"And this is all you were thinking?"

"You know better than that, Alia."

*How dare he use my given name?* She felt anger rise and go down beneath the memory of the way he'd spoken: softly throbbing undertones, casual male confidence. A muscle twitched along her jaw. She clenched her teeth.

"Isn't that El Kuds down there?" he asked, dipping a wing briefly, causing a sudden flurry in their escort.

She looked down at their shadows rippling across the promontory above Harg Pass, at the cliff and the rock pyramid containing the skull of her father. *El Kuds—the Holy Place.*

"That's the Holy Place," she said.

"I must visit that place one day," he said. "Nearness to your father's remains may bring memories I can capture."

She saw suddenly how strong must be this need to know who he'd been. It was a central compulsion with him. She looked back at the rocks, the cliff with its base sloping into a dry beach and a sea of sand—cinnamon rock lifting from the dunes like a ship breasting waves.

"Circle back," she said.

"The escort . . ."

"They'll follow. Swing under them."

He obeyed.

"Do you truly serve my brother?" she asked, when he was on the new course, the escort following.

"I serve the Atreides," he said, his tone formal.

And she saw his right hand lift, fall—almost the old salute of Caladan. A pensive look came over his face. She watched him peer down at the rock pyramid.

"What bothers you?" she asked.

His lips moved. A voice emerged, brittle, tight: "He was . . . he was . . ." A tear slid down his cheek.

Alia found herself stilled by Fremen awe. He gave water to the dead! Compulsively, she touched a finger to his cheek, felt the tear.

"Duncan," she whispered.

He appeared locked to the 'thopter controls, gaze fastened to the tomb below.

She raised her voice: "Duncan!"

He swallowed, shook his head, looked at her, the metal eyes glistening. "I . . . felt . . . an arm . . . on my shoulders," he whispered. "I felt it! An arm." His throat worked. "It was . . . a friend. It was . . . my friend."

"Who?"

"I don't know. I think it was . . . I don't know."

The call light began flashing in front of Alia, their escort captain wanting to know why they returned to the desert. She took the microphone, explained that they had paid a brief homage to her father's tomb. The captain reminded her that it was late.

"We will go to Arrakeen now," she said, replacing the microphone.

Hayt took a deep breath, banked their 'thopter around to the north.

"It was my father's arm you felt, wasn't it?" she asked.

"Perhaps."

His voice was that of the mentat computing probabilities, and she saw he had regained his composure.

"Are you aware of how I know my father?" she asked.

"I have some idea."

"Let me make it clear," she said. Briefly, she explained how she had awakened to Reverend Mother awareness before birth, a terrified fetus with the knowledge of countless lives embedded in her nerve cells—and all this after the death of her father.

"I know my father as my mother knew him," she said. "In every last detail of every experience she shared with him. In a way, I am my mother. I have all her memories up to the moment when she drank the Water of Life and entered the trance of transmigration."

"Your brother explained something of this."

"He did? Why?"

"I asked."

"Why?"

"A mentat requires data."

"Oh." She looked down at the flat expanse of the Shield Wall—tortured rock, pits and crevices.

He saw the direction of her gaze, said: "A very exposed place, that down there."

"But an easy place to hide," she said. She looked at him. "It reminds me of a human mind . . . with all its concealments."

"Ahhh," he said.

"Ahhh? What does that mean—ahhh?" She was suddenly angry with him and the reason for it escaped her.

"You'd like to know what my mind conceals," he said. It was a statement, not a question.

"How do you know I haven't exposed you for what you are by my powers of prescience?" she demanded.

"Have you?" He seemed genuinely curious.

"No!"

"Sibyls have limits," he said.

He appeared to be amused and this reduced Alia's anger. "Amused? Have you no respect for my powers?" she asked. The question sounded weakly argumentative even to her own ears.

"I respect your omens and portents perhaps more than you think," he said. "I was in the audience for your Morning Ritual."

"And what does that signify?"

"You've great ability with symbols," he said, keeping his attention on the 'thopter's controls. "That's a Bene Gesserit thing, I'd say. But, as with many witches, you've become careless of your powers."

She felt a spasm of fear, blared: "How dare you?"

"I dare much more than my makers anticipated," he said. "Because of that rare fact, I remain with your brother."

Alia studied the steel balls which were his eyes: no human expression there. The stillsuit hood concealed the line of his jaw. His mouth remained firm, though. Great strength in it . . . and determination. His words had carried a reassuring intensity. ". . . dare much more . . ." That was a thing Duncan Idaho might have said. Had the Tleilaxu fashioned their ghola better than they knew—or was this mere sham, part of his conditioning?

"Explain yourself, ghola," she commanded.

"Know thyself, is that thy commandment?" he asked.

Again, she felt that he was amused. "Don't bandy words with me, you . . . you *thing!*" she said. She put a hand to the crysknife in its throat sheath. "Why were you given to my brother?"

"Your brother tells me that you watched the presentation," he said. "You've heard me answer that question for him."

"Answer it again . . . for me!"

"I am intended to destroy him."

"Is that the mentat speaking?"

"You knew the answer to that without asking," he chided. "And you know, as well, that such a gift wasn't necessary. Your brother already was destroying himself quite adequately."

She weighed these words, her hand remaining on the haft of her knife. A tricky answer, but there was sincerity in the voice.

"Then why such a gift?" she probed.

"It may have amused the Tleilaxu. And, it is true, that the Guild asked for me as a gift."

"Why?"

"Same answer."

"How am I careless of my powers?"

"How are you employing them?" he countered.

His question slashed through to her own misgivings. She took her hand away from the knife, asked: "Why do you say my brother was destroying himself?"

"Oh, come now, child! Where are these vaunted powers? Have you no ability to reason?"

Controlling anger, she said: "Reason *for* me, mentat."

"Very well." He glanced around at their escort, returned his attention to their course. The plain of Arrakeen was beginning to show beyond the northern rim of the Shield Wall. The pattern of the pan and graben villages remained indistinct beneath a dust pall, but the distant gleam of Arrakeen could be discerned.

"Symptoms," he said. "Your brother keeps an official Panegyrist who—"

"Who was a gift of the Fremen Naibs!"

"An odd gift from friends," he said. "Why would they surround him with flattery and servility? Have you really listened to this Panegyrist? *'The people are illuminated by Muad'Dib. The Umma Regent, our Emperor, came out of*

*darkness to shine resplendently upon all men. He is our Sire. He is precious water*
*from an endless fountain. He spills joy for all the universe to drink.'* Pah!"

Speaking softly, Alia said: "If I but repeated your words for our Fremen
escort, they'd hack you into bird feed."

"Then tell them."

"My brother rules by the natural law of heaven!"

"You don't believe that, so why say it?"

"How do you know what I believe?" She experienced trembling that no Bene
Gesserit powers could control. This ghola was having an effect she hadn't
anticipated.

"You commanded me to reason as a mentat," he reminded her.

"No mentat knows what I believe!" She took two deep, shuddering breaths.
"How dare you judge us?"

"Judge you? I don't judge."

"You've no idea how we were taught!"

"Both of you were taught to govern," he said. "You were conditioned to an
overweening thirst for power. You were imbued with a shrewd grasp of politics
and a deep understanding for the uses of war and ritual. Natural law? What
natural law? That myth haunts human history. Haunts! It's a ghost. It's
insubstantial, unreal. Is your Jihad a natural law?"

"Mentat jabber," she sneered.

"I'm a servant of the Atreides and I speak with candor," he said.

"Servant? We've no servants; only disciples."

"And I am a disciple of awareness," he said. "Understand that, child, and
you—"

"Don't call me child!" she snapped. She slipped her crysknife half out of its
sheath.

"I stand corrected." He glanced at her, smiled, returned his attention to
piloting the 'thopter. The cliff-sided structure of the Atreides Keep could be
made out now, dominating the northern suburbs of Arrakeen. "You are
something ancient in flesh that is little more than a child," he said. "And the
flesh is disturbed by its new womanhood."

"I don't know why I listen to you," she growled, but she let the crysknife fall
back into its sheath, wiped her palm on her robe. The palm, wet with
perspiration, disturbed her sense of Fremen frugality. Such a waste of the
body's moisture!

"You listen because you know I'm devoted to your brother," he said. "My
actions are clear and easily understood."

"Nothing about you is clear and easily understood. You're the most
complex creature I've ever seen. How do I know what the Tleilaxu built
into you?"

"By mistake or intent," he said, "they gave me freedom to mold myself."

"You retreat into Zensunni parables," she accused. "The wise man molds
himself—the fool lives only to die." Her voice was heavy with mimicry.
"Disciple of awareness!"

"Men cannot separate means and enlightenment," he said.

"You speak riddles!"

"I speak to the opening mind."

"I'm going to repeat all this to Paul."

"He's heard most of it already."

She found herself overwhelmed by curiosity. "How is it you're still alive . . . and free? What did he say?"

"He laughed. And he said, 'People don't want a bookkeeper for an Emperor; they want a master, someone who'll protect them from change.' But he agreed that destruction of his Empire arises from himself."

"Why would he say such things?"

"Because I convinced him I understand his problem and will help him."

"What could you possibly have said to do that?"

He remained silent, banking the 'thopter into the downwind leg for a landing at the guard complex on the roof of the Keep.

"I demand you tell me what you said!"

"I'm not sure you could take it."

"I'll be the judge of that! I command you to speak at once!"

"Permit me to land us first," he said. And not waiting for her permission, he turned onto the base leg, brought the wings into optimum lift, settled gently onto the bright orange pad atop the roof.

"Now," Alia said. "Speak."

"I told him that to endure onself may be the hardest task in the universe."

She shook her head. "That's . . . that's . . ."

"A bitter pill," he said, watching the guards run toward them across the roof, taking up their escort positions.

"Bitter nonsense!"

"The greatest palatinate earl and the lowliest stipendiary serf share the same problem. You cannot hire a mentat or any other intellect to solve it for you. There's no writ of inquest or calling of witnesses to provide answers. No servant—or disciple—can dress the wound. You dress it yourself or continue bleeding for all to see."

She whirled away from him, realizing in the instant of action what this betrayed about her own feelings. Without wile of voice or witch-wrought trickery, he had reached into her psyche once more. How did he do this?

"What have you told him to do?" she whispered.

"I told him to judge, to impose order."

Alia stared out at the guard, marking how patiently they waited—how orderly. "To dispense justice," she murmured.

"Not that!" he snapped. "I suggested that he judge, no more, guided by one principle, perhaps . . ."

"And that?"

"To keep his friends and destroy his enemies."

"To judge unjustly, then."

"What is justice? Two forces collide. Each may have the right in his own sphere. And here's where an Emperor commands orderly solutions. Those collisions he cannot prevent—he solves."

"How?"

"In the simplest way: he decides."

"Keeping his friends and destroying his enemies."

"Isn't that stability? People want order, this kind or some other. They sit in the prison of their hungers and see that war has become the sport of the rich. That's a dangerous form of sophistication. It's disorderly."

"I will suggest to my brother that you are much too dangerous and must be destroyed," she said, turning to face him.

"A solution I've already suggested," he said.

"And that's why you are dangerous," she said, measuring out her words. "You've mastered your passions."

"That is *not* why I'm dangerous." Before she could move, he leaned across, gripped her chin in one hand, planted his lips on hers.

It was a gentle kiss, brief. He pulled away and she stared at him with a shock leavened by glimpses of spasmodic grins on the faces of her guardsmen still standing at orderly attention outside.

Alia put a finger to her lips. There'd been such a sense of familiarity about that kiss. His lips had been flesh of a future she'd seen in some prescient byway. Breast heaving, she said: "I should have you flayed."

"Because I'm dangerous?"

"Because you presume too much!"

"I presume nothing. I take nothing which is not first offered to me. Be glad I did not take all that was offered." He opened his door, slid out. "Come along. We've dallied too long on a fool's errand." He strode toward the entrance dome beyond the pad.

Alia leaped out, ran to match his stride. "I'll tell him everything you've said and everything you did," she said.

"Good." He held the door for her.

"He will order you executed," she said, slipping into the dome.

"Why? Because I took the kiss I wanted?" He followed her, his movement forcing her back. The door slid closed behind him.

"The kiss *you* wanted!" Outrage filled her.

"All right, Alia. The kiss you wanted, then." He started to move around her toward the drop field.

As though his movement had propelled her into heightened awareness, she realized his candor—the utter truthfulness of him. *The kiss I wanted,* she told herself. *True.*

"Your truthfulness, that's what's dangerous," she said, following him.

"You return to the ways of wisdom," he said, not breaking his stride. "A mentat could not 've stated the matter more directly. Now: what is it you saw in the desert?"

She grabbed his arm, forcing him to a halt. He'd done it again: shocked her mind into sharpened awareness.

"I can't explain it," she said, "but I keep thinking of the Face Dancers. Why is that?"

"That is why your brother sent you to the desert," he said, nodding. "Tell him of this persistent thought."

"But why?" She shook her head. "Why Face Dancers?"

"There's a young woman dead out there," he said. "Perhaps no young woman is reported missing among the Fremen."

> *I think what a joy it is to be alive, and I wonder if I'll ever leap inward to the root of this flesh and know myself as once I was. The root is there. Whether any act of mine can find it, that remains tangled in the future. But all things a man can do are mine. Any act of mine may do it.*

> **—The Ghola Speaks**
> **Alia's Commentary**

As he lay immersed in the screaming odor of the spice, staring inward through the oracular trance, Paul saw the moon become an elongated sphere. It rolled and twisted, hissing—the terrible hissing of a star being quenched in an infinite sea—down . . . down . . . down . . . like a ball thrown by a child.

It was gone.

This moon had not set. Realization engulfed him. It was gone: no moon. The earth quaked like an animal shaking its skin. Terror swept over him.

Paul jerked upright on his pallet, eyes wide open, staring. Part of him looked outward, part inward. Outwardly, he saw the plasmeld grillwork which vented his private room, and he knew he lay beside a stonelike abyss of his Keep. Inwardly, he continued to see the moon fall.

*Out! Out!*

His grillwork of plasmeld looked onto the blazing light of noon across Arrakeen. Inward—there lay blackest night. A shower of sweet odors from a garden roof nibbled at his senses, but no floral perfume could roll back that fallen moon.

Paul swung his feet to the cold surface of the floor, peered through the grillwork. He could see directly across to the gentle arc of a footbridge constructed of crystal-stabilized gold and platinum. Fire jewels from far Cedon decorated the bridge. It led to the galleries of the inner city across a pool and fountain filled with waterflowers. If he stood, Paul knew, he could look down into petals as clean and red as fresh blood whirling, turning there—disks of ambient color tossed on an emerald freshet.

His eyes absorbed the scene without pulling him from spice thralldom.

*That terrible vision of a lost moon.*

The vision suggested a monstrous loss of individual security. Perhaps he'd seen his civilization fall, toppled by its own pretensions.

*A moon . . . a moon . . . a falling moon.*

It had taken a massive dose of the spice essence to penetrate the mud thrown up by the tarot. All it had shown him was a falling moon and the hateful way he'd known from the beginning. To buy an end for the Jihad, to silence the volcano of butchery, he must discredit himself.

*Disengage . . . disengage . . . disengage . . .*

Floral perfume from the garden roof reminded him of Chani. He longed for her arms now, for the clinging arms of love and forgetfulness. But even Chani could not exorcise this vision. What would Chani say if he went to her with the statement that he had a particular death in mind? Knowing it to be inevitable, why not choose an aristocrat's death, ending life on a secret flourish, squandering any years that might have been? To die before coming to the end of willpower, was that not an aristocrat's choice?

He stood, crossed to the lapped opening in the grillwork, went out onto a balcony which looked upward to flowers and vines trailing from the garden. His mouth held the dryness of a desert march.

*Moon . . . moon—where is that moon?*

He thought of Alia's description, the young woman's body found in the dunes. A Fremen addicted to semuta! Everything fitted the hateful pattern.

*You do not take from this universe,* he thought. *It grants what it will.*

The remains of a conch shell from the seas of Mother Earth lay on a low table beside the balcony rail. He took its lustrous smoothness into his hands, tried to feel backward in Time. The pearl surface reflected glittering moons of light. He tore his gaze from it, peered upward past the garden to a sky become a conflagration—trails of rainbow dust shining in the silver sun.

*My Fremen call themselves "Children of the moon,"* he thought.

He put down the conch, strode along the balcony. Did that terrifying moon hold out hope of escape? He probed for meaning in the region of mystic communion. He felt weak, shaken, still gripped by the spice.

At the north end of his plasmeld chasm, he came in sight of the lower buildings of the government warren. Foot traffic thronged the roof walks. He felt that the people moved there like a frieze against a background of doors, walls, tile designs. The people were tiles! When he blinked, he could hold them frozen in his mind. A frieze.

*A moon falls and is gone.*

A feeling came over him that the city out there had been translated into an odd symbol for his universe. The buildings he could see had been erected on the plain where his Fremen had obliterated the Sardaukar legions. Ground once trampled by battles rang now to the rushing clamor of business.

Keeping to the balcony's outer edge, Paul strode around the corner. Now, his vista was a suburb where city structures lost themselves in rocks and the blowing sand of the desert. Alia's temple dominated the foreground; green and black hangings along its two-thousand-meter sides displayed the moon symbol of Muad'Dib.

*A falling moon.*

Paul passed a hand across his forehead and eyes. The symbol-metropolis oppressed him. He despised his own thoughts. Such vacillation in another would have aroused his anger.

He loathed his city!

Rage rooted in boredom flickered and simmered deep within him, nurtured by decisions that couldn't be avoided. He knew which path his feet must follow. He'd seen it enough times, hadn't he? *Seen* it! Once . . . long ago, he'd thought of himself as an inventor of government. But the invention had fallen into old patterns. It was like some hideous contrivance with plastic memory. Shape it any way you wanted, but relax for a moment, and it snapped into the ancient forms. Forces at work beyond his reach in human breasts eluded and defied him.

Paul stared out across the rooftops. What treasures of untrammeled life lay beneath those roofs? He glimpsed leaf-green places, open plantings amidst the chalk-red and gold of the roofs. Green, the gift of Muad'Dib and his water. Orchards and groves lay within his view—open plantings to rival those of fabled Lebanon.

"Muad'Dib spends water like a madman," Fremen said.

Paul put his hands over his eyes.

*The moon fell.*

He dropped his hands, stared at his metropolis with clarified vision. Buildings took on an aura of monstrous imperial barbarity. They stood enormous and bright beneath the northern sun. Colossi! Every extravagance of architecture a demented history could produce lay within his view: terraces of mesa proportion, squares as large as some cities, parks, premises, bits of cultured wilderness.

Superb artistry abutted inexplicable prodigies of dismal tastelessness. Details impressed themselves upon him: a postern out of most ancient Baghdad . . . a dome dreamed in mythical Damascus . . . an arch from the low gravity of Atar . . . harmonious elevations and queer depths. All created an effect of unrivaled magnificence.

*A moon! A moon! A moon!*

Frustration tangled him. He felt the pressure of mass-unconscious, that burgeoning sweep of humankind across his universe. They rushed upon him with a force like a gigantic tidal bore. He sensed the vast migrations at work in human affairs: eddies, currents, gene flows. No dams of abstinence, no seizures of impotence nor maledictions could stop it.

Muad'Dib's Jihad was less than an eye-blink in this larger movement. The Bene Gesserit swimming in this tide, that corporate entity trading in genes, was trapped in the torrent as he was. Visions of a falling moon must be measured against other legends, other visions in a universe where even the seemingly eternal stars waned, flickered, died . . .

What mattered a single moon in such a universe?

Far within his fortress citadel, so deep within that the sound sometimes lost itself in the flow of city noises, a ten-string rebaba tinkled with a song of the Jihad, a lament for a woman left behind on Arrakis:

> *Her hips are dunes curved by the wind,*
> *Her eyes shine like summer heat,*
> *Two braids of hair hang down her back–*

*Rich with water rings, her hair!*
*My hands remember her skin,*
*Fragrant as amber, flower-scented.*
*Eyelids tremble with memories . . .*
*I am stricken by love's white flame!*

The song sickened him. A tune for stupid creatures lost in sentimentality! As well sing to the dune-impregnated corpse Alia had seen.

A figure moved in shadows of the balcony's grillwork. Paul whirled.

The ghola emerged into the sun's full glare. His metal eyes glittered.

"Is it Duncan Idaho or the man called Hayt?" Paul asked.

The ghola came to a stop two paces from him. "Which would my Lord prefer?"

The voice carried a soft ring of caution.

"Play the Zensunni," Paul said bitterly. *Meanings within meanings!* What could a Zensunni philosopher say or do to change one jot of the reality unrolling before them at this instant?

"My Lord is troubled."

Paul turned away, stared at the Shield Wall's distant scarp, saw wind-carved arches and buttresses, terrible mimicry of his city. Nature playing a joke on him! *See what I can build!* He recognized a slash in the distant massif, a place where sand spilled from a crevasse, and thought: *There! Right there, we fought Sardaukar!*

"What troubles my Lord?" the ghola asked.

"A vision," Paul whispered.

"Ahhhhh, when the Tleilaxu first awakened me, I had visions. I was restless, lonely . . . not really knowing I was lonely. Not then. My visions revealed nothing! The Tleilaxu told me it was an intrusion of the flesh which men and gholas all suffer, a sickness, no more."

Paul turned, studied the ghola's eyes, those pitted, steely balls without expression. What visions did those eyes see?

"Duncan . . . Duncan . . ." Paul whispered.

"I am called Hayt."

"I saw a moon fall," Paul said. "It was gone, destroyed. I heard a great hissing. The earth shook."

"You are drunk on too much time," the ghola said.

"I ask for the Zensunni and get the mentat!" Paul said. "Very well! Play my vision through your logic, mentat. Analyze it and reduce it to mere words laid out for burial."

"Burial, indeed," the ghola said. "You run from death. You strain at the next instant, refuse to live here and now. Augury! What a crutch for an Emperor!"

Paul found himself fascinated by a well-remembered mole on the ghola's chin.

"Trying to live in this future," the ghola said, "do you give substance to such a future? Do you make it real?"

"If I go the way of my vision-future, I'll be alive *then*," Paul muttered. "What makes you think I want to live there?"

The ghola shrugged. "You asked me for a substantial answer."

"Where is there substance in a universe composed of events?" Paul asked. "Is there a final answer? Doesn't each solution produce new questions?"

"You've digested so much time you have delusions of immortality," the ghola said. "Even *your* Empire, my Lord, must live its time and die."

"Don't parade smoke-blackened altars before me," Paul growled. "I've heard enough sad histories of gods and messiahs. Why should I need special powers to forecast ruins of my own like all those others? The lowliest servant of my kitchens could do this." He shook his head. "The moon fell!"

"You've not brought your mind to rest at its beginning," the ghola said.

"Is that how you destroy me?" Paul demanded. "Prevent me from collecting my thoughts?"

"Can you collect chaos?" the ghola asked. "We Zensunni say: 'Not collecting, that is the ultimate gathering.' What can you gather without gathering yourself?"

"I'm deviled by a vision and you spew nonsense!" Paul raged. "What do you know of prescience?"

"I've seen the oracle at work," the ghola said. "I've seen those who seek signs and omens for their individual destiny. They fear what they seek."

"My falling moon is real," Paul whispered. He took a trembling breath. "It moves. It moves."

"Men always fear things which move by themselves," the ghola said. "You fear your own powers. Things fall into your head from nowhere. When they fall out, where do they go?"

"You comfort me with thorns," Paul growled.

An inner illumination came over the ghola's face. For a moment, he became pure Duncan Idaho. "I give you what comfort I can," he said.

Paul wondered at that momentary spasm. Had the ghola felt grief which his mind rejected? Had Hayt put down a vision of his own?

"My moon has a name," Paul whispered.

He let the vision flow over him then. Though his whole being shrieked, no sound escaped him. He was afraid to speak, fearful that his voice might betray him. The air of this terrifying future was thick with Chani's absence. Flesh that had cried in ecstasy, eyes that had burned him with their desire, the voice that had charmed him because it played no tricks of subtle control—all gone, back into the water and the sand.

Slowly, Paul turned away, looked out at the present and the plaza before Alia's temple. Three shaven-headed pilgrims entered from the processional avenue. They wore grimy yellow robes and hurried with their heads bent against the afternoon's wind. One walked with a limp, dragging his left foot. They beat their way against the wind, rounded a corner and were gone from his sight.

Just as his moon would go, they were gone. Still, his vision lay before him. Its terrible purpose gave him no choice.

*The flesh surrenders itself,* he thought. *Eternity takes back its own. Our bodies stirred these waters briefly, danced with a certain intoxication before the love of life and self, dealt with a few strange ideas, then submitted to the instruments of Time. What can we say of this? I occurred. I am not . . . yet, I occurred.*

*"You do not beg the sun for mercy."*

**—Muad'Dib's Travail
from The Stilgar Commentary**

One moment of incompetence can be fatal, the Reverend Mother Gaius Helen Mohiam reminded herself.

She hobbled along, apparently unconcerned, within a ring of Fremen guards. One of those behind her, she knew, was a deaf-mute immune to any wiles of Voice. No doubt he'd been charged to kill her at the slightest provocation.

Why had Paul summoned her? she wondered. Was he about to pass sentence? She remembered the day long ago when she'd tested him . . . the child Kwisatz Haderach. He was a deep one.

Damn his mother for all eternity! It was her fault the Bene Gesserit had lost their hold on this gene line.

Silence surged along the vaulted passages ahead of her entourage. She sensed the word being passed. Paul would hear the silence. He'd know of her coming before it was announced. She didn't delude herself with ideas that her powers exceeded his.

Damn him!

She begrudged the burdens age had imposed on her: the aching joints, responses not as quick as once they'd been, muscles not as elastic as the whipcords of her youth. A long day lay behind her and a long life. She'd spent this day with the Dune Tarot in a fruitless search for some clue to her own fate. But the cards were sluggish.

The guards herded her around a corner into another of the seemingly endless vaulted passages. Triangular metaglass windows on her left gave a view upward to trellised vines and indigo flowers in deep shadows cast by the afternoon sun. Tiles lay underfoot—figures of water creatures from exotic planets. Water reminders everywhere. Wealth . . . riches.

Robed figures passed across another hall in front of her, cast covert glances at the Reverend Mother. Recognition was obvious in their manner—and tension.

She kept her attention on the sharp hairline of the guard immediately in front: young flesh, pink creases at the uniform collar.

The immensity of this ighir citadel began to impress her. Passages . . . passages . . . They passed an open doorway from which emerged the sound of timbur and flute playing soft, elder music. A glance showed her blue-in-blue Fremen eyes staring from the room. She sensed in them the ferment of legendary revolts stirring in wild genes.

There lay the measure of her personal burden, she knew. A Bene Gesserit could not escape awareness of the genes and their possibilities. She was touched by a feeling of loss: that stubborn fool of an Atreides! How could he deny the jewels of posterity within his loins? a Kwisatz Haderach! Born out of his time, true, but real—as real as his abomination of a sister . . . and there lay a dangerous unknown. A wild Reverend Mother spawned without Bene Gesserit inhibitions, holding no loyalty to orderly development of the genes. She shared her brother's powers, no doubt—and more.

The size of the citadel began to oppress her. Would the passages never end? The place reeked of terrifying physical power. No planet, no civilization in all human history had ever before seen such man-made immensity. A dozen ancient cities could be hidden in its walls!

They passed oval doors with winking lights. She recognized them for Ixian handiwork: pneumatic transport orifices. Why was she being marched all this distance, then? The answer began to shape itself in her mind: to oppress her in preparation for this audience with the Emperor.

A small clue, but it joined other subtle indications—the relative suppression and selection of words by her escort, the traces of primitive shyness in their eyes when they called her *Reverend Mother,* the cold and bland, essentially odorless nature of these halls—all combined to reveal much that a Bene Gesserit could interpret.

Paul wanted something from her!

She concealed a feeling of elation. A bargaining lever existed. It remained only to find the nature of that lever and test its strength. Some levers had moved things greater than this citadel. A finger's touch had been known to topple civilizations.

The Reverend Mother reminded herself then of Scytale's assessment: *When a creature has developed into one thing, he will choose death rather than change into his opposite.*

The passages through which she was being escorted grew larger by subtle stages—tricks of arching, graduated amplification of pillared supports, displacement of the triangular windows by larger, oblong shapes. Ahead of her, finally, loomed double doors centered in the far wall of a tall antechamber. She sensed that the doors were *very* large, and was forced to suppress a gasp as her trained awareness measured out the true proportions. The doorway stood at least eighty meters high, half that in width.

As she approached with her escort, the doors swung inward—an immense and silent movement of hidden machinery. She recognized more Ixian handiwork. Through that towering doorway she marched with her guards into the Grand Reception Hall of the Emperor Paul Atreides—"Muad'Dib, before whom all people are dwarfed." Now, she saw the effect of that popular saying at work.

As she advanced toward Paul on the distant throne, the Reverend Mother found herself more impressed by the architectural subtleties of her surroundings than she was by the immensities. The space was large: it could've housed the entire citadel of any ruler in human history. The open sweep of the room said much about hidden structural forces balanced with nicety. Trusses and supporting beams behind these walls and the faraway domed ceiling must surpass anything ever before attempted. Everything spoke of engineering genius.

Without seeming to do so, the hall grew smaller at its far end, refusing to dwarf Paul on his throne centered on a dais. An untrained awareness, shocked by surrounding proportions, would see him at first as many times larger than his actual size. Colors played upon the unprotected psyche: Paul's green throne had been cut from a single Hagar emerald. It suggested growing things and, out of the Fremen mythos, reflected the mourning color. It whispered that here sat he who could make you mourn—life and death in one symbol, a clever stress of opposites. Behind the throne, draperies cascaded in burnt orange, curried gold of Dune earth, and cinnamon flecks of melange. To a trained eye, the symbolism was obvious, but it contained hammer blows to beat down the uninitiated.

Time played its role here.

The Reverend Mother measured the minutes required to approach the Imperial Presence at her hobbling pace. You had time to be cowed. Any tendency toward resentment would be squeezed out of you by the unbridled power which focused down upon your person. You might start the long march toward that throne as a human of dignity, but you ended the march as a gnat.

Aides and attendants stood around the Emperor in a curiously ordered sequence—attentive household guardsmen along the draped back wall, that abomination, Alia, two steps below Paul and on his left hand; Stilgar, the Imperial lackey, on the step directly below Alia; and on the right, one step up from the floor of the hall, a solitary figure: the fleshly revenant of Duncan Idaho, the ghola. She marked older Fremen among the guardsmen, bearded Naibs with stillsuit scars on their noses, sheathed crysknives at their waists, a few maula pistols, even some lasguns. Those must be trusted men, she thought, to carry lasguns in Paul's presence when he obviously wore a shield generator. She could see the shimmering of its field around him. One burst of a lasgun into that field and the entire citadel would be a hole in the ground.

Her guard stopped ten paces from the foot of the dais, parted to open an unobstructed view of the Emperor. She noted now the absence of Chani and Irulan, wondered at it. He held no important audience without them, so it was said.

Paul nodded to her, silent, measuring.

Immediately, she decided to take the offensive, said: "So the great Paul Atreides deigns to see the one he banished."

Paul smiled wryly, thinking: *She knows I want something from her.* That knowledge had been inevitable, she being who she was. He recognized her powers. The Bene Gesserit didn't become Reverend Mothers by chance.

"Shall we dispense with fencing?" he asked.

Would it be this easy? she wondered. And she said: "Name the thing you want."

Stilgar stirred, cast a sharp glance at Paul. The Imperial lackey didn't like her tone.

"Stilgar wants me to send you away," Paul said.

"Not kill me?" she asked. "I would've expected something more direct from a Fremen Naib."

Stilgar scowled, said: "Often, I must speak otherwise than I think. That is called diplomacy."

"Then let us dispense with diplomacy as well," she said. "Was it necessary to have me walk all that distance? I am an old woman."

"You had to be shown how callous I can be," Paul said. "That way, you'll appreciate magnanimity."

"You dare such gaucheries with a Bene Gesserit?" she asked.

"Gross actions carry their own messages," Paul said.

She hesitated, weighed his words. So—he might yet dispense with her . . . grossly, obviously, if she . . . if she what?

"Say what it is you want from me," she muttered.

Alia glanced at her brother, nodded toward the draperies behind the throne. She knew Paul's reasoning in this, but disliked it all the same. Call it *wild prophecy:* She felt pregnant with reluctance to take part in this bargaining.

"You must be careful how you speak to me, old woman," Paul said.

*He called me old woman when he was a stripling,* the Reverend Mother thought. *Does he remind me now of my hand in his past? The decision I made then, must I remake it here?* She felt the weight of decision, a physical thing that set her knees to trembling. Muscles cried their fatigue.

"It was a long walk," Paul said, "and I can see that you're tired. We will retire to my private chamber behind the throne. You may sit there." He gave a hand-signal to Stilgar, arose.

Stilgar and the ghola converged on her, helped her up the steps, followed Paul through a passage concealed by the draperies. She realized then why he had greeted her in the hall: a dumb-show for the guards and Naibs. He feared them, then. And now—now, he displayed kindly benevolence, daring such wiles on a Bene Gesserit. Or was it daring? She sensed another presence behind, glanced back to see Alia following. The younger woman's eyes held a brooding, baleful cast. The Reverend Mother shuddered.

The private chamber at the end of the passage was a twenty-meter cube of plasmeld, yellow glowglobes for light, the deep orange hangings of a desert stilltent around the walls. It contained divans, soft cushions, a faint odor of melange, crystal water flagons on a low table. It felt cramped, tiny after the outer hall.

Paul seated her on a divan, stood over her, studying the ancient face—steely teeth, eyes that hid more than they revealed, deeply wrinkled skin. He indicated a water flagon. She shook her head, dislodging a wisp of gray hair.

In a low voice, Paul said: "I wish to bargain with you for the life of my beloved."

Stilgar cleared his throat.

Alia fingered the handle of the crysknife sheathed at her neck.

The ghola remained at the door, face impassive, metal eyes pointed at the air above the Reverend Mother's head.

"Have you had a vision of my hand in her death?" the Reverend Mother asked. She kept her attention on the ghola, oddly disturbed by him. Why should she feel threatened by the ghola? He was a tool of the conspiracy.

"I know what it is you want from me," Paul said, avoiding her question.

*Then he only suspects,* she thought. The Reverend Mother looked down at the tips of her shoes exposed by a fold of her robe. Black . . . black . . . shoes and robe showed marks of her confinement: stains, wrinkles. She lifted her chin, met an angry glare in Paul's eyes. Elation surged through her, but she hid the emotion behind pursed lips, slitted eyelids.

"What coin do you offer?" she asked.

"You may have my seed, but not my person," Paul said. "Irulan banished and inseminated by artificial—"

"You dare!" the Reverend Mother flared, stiffening.

Stilgar took a half step forward.

Disconcertingly, the ghola smiled. And now Alia was studying him.

"We'll not discuss the things your Sisterhood forbids," Paul said. "I will listen to no talk of sins, abominations or the beliefs left over from past Jihads. You may have my seed for your plans, but no child of Irulan's will sit on my throne."

"Your throne," she sneered.

"*My* throne."

"Then who will bear the Imperial heir?"

"Chani."

"She is barren."

"She is with child."

An involuntary indrawn breath exposed her shock. "You lie!" she snapped.

Paul held up a restraining hand as Stilgar surged forward.

"We've known for two days that she carries my child."

"But Irulan . . ."

"By artificial means only. That's my offer."

The Reverend Mother closed her eyes to hide his face. Damnation! To cast the genetic dice in such a way! Loathing boiled in her breast. The teaching of the Bene Gesserit, the lessons of the Butlerian Jihad—all proscribed such an act. One did not demean the highest aspirations of humankind. No machine could function in the way of a human mind. No word or deed could imply that men might be bred on the level of animals.

"Your decision," Paul said.

She shook her head. The genes, the precious Atreides genes—only these were important. Need went deeper than proscription. For the Sisterhood, mating mingled more than sperm and ovum. One aimed to capture the psyche.

The Reverend Mother understood now the subtle depths of Paul's offer. He would make the Bene Gesserit party to an act which would bring down popular wrath . . . were it ever discovered. They could not admit such paternity if the

Emperor denied it. This coin might save the Atreides genes for the Sisterhood, but it would never buy a throne.

She swept her gaze around the room, studying each face: Stilgar, passive and waiting now; the ghola frozen at some inward place; Alia watching the ghola . . . and Paul—wrath beneath a shallow veneer.

"This is your only offer?" she asked.

"My only offer."

She glanced at the ghola, caught by a brief movement of muscles across his cheeks. Emotion? "You, ghola," she said. "Should such an offer be made? Having been made, should it be accepted? Function as the mentat for us."

The metallic eyes turned to Paul.

"Answer as you will," Paul said.

The ghola returned his gleaming attention to the Reverend Mother, shocked her once more by smiling. "An offer is only as good as the real thing it buys," he said. "The exchange offered here is life-for-life, a high order of business."

Alia brushed a strand of coppery hair from her forehead, said: "And what else is hidden in this bargain?"

The Reverend Mother refused to look at Alia, but the words burned in her mind. Yes, far deeper implications lay here. The sister was an abomination, true, but there could be no denying her status as a Reverend Mother with all the title implied. Gaius Helen Mohiam felt herself in this instant to be not one single person, but all the others who sat like tiny congeries in her memory. They were alert, every Reverend Mother she had absorbed in becoming a Priestess of the Sisterhood. Alia would be standing in the same situation here.

"What else?" the ghola asked. "One wonders why the witches of the Bene Gesserit have not used Tleilaxu methods."

Gaius Helen Mohiam and all the Reverend Mothers within her shuddered. Yes, the Tleilaxu did loathsome things. If one let down the barriers to artificial insemination, was the next step a Tleilaxu one—controlled mutation?

Paul, observing the play of emotion around him, felt abruptly that he no longer knew these people. He could see only strangers. Even Alia was a stranger.

Alia said: "If we set the Atreides genes adrift in a Bene Gesserit river, who knows what may result?"

Gaius Helen Mohiam's head snapped around, and she met Alia's gaze. For a flashing instant, they were two Reverend Mothers together, communing on a single thought: *What lay behind any Tleilaxu action? The ghola was a Tleilaxu thing. Had he put this plan into Paul's mind? Would Paul attempt to bargain directly with the Bene Tleilax?*

She broke her gaze from Alia's, feeling her own ambivalence and inadequacies. The pitfall of Bene Gesserit training, she reminded herself, lay in the powers granted: such powers predisposed one to vanity and pride. But power deluded those who used it. One tended to believe power could overcome any barrier . . . including one's own ignorance.

Only one thing stood paramount here for the Bene Gesserit, she told herself. That was the pyramid of generations which had reached an apex in Paul

Atreides . . . and in his abomination of a sister. A wrong choice here and the pyramid would have to be rebuilt . . . starting generations back in the parallel lines and with breeding specimens lacking the choicest characteristics.

*Controlled mutation,* she thought. *Did the Tleilaxu really practice it? How tempting!* She shook her head, the better to rid it of such thoughts.

"You reject my proposal?" Paul asked.

"I'm thinking," she said.

And again, she looked at the sister. The optimum cross for this female Atreides had been lost . . . killed by Paul. Another possibility remained, however—one which would *cement* the desired characteristic into an offspring. Paul dared offer animal breeding to the Bene Gesserit! How much was he really prepared to pay for his Chani's life? Would he accept a cross with his own sister?

Sparring for time, the Reverend Mother said: "Tell me, oh flawless exemplar of all that's holy, has Irulan anything to say of your proposal?"

"Irulan will do what you tell her to do," Paul growled.

*True enough,* Mohiam thought. She firmed her jaw, offered a new gambit: "There are two Atreides."

Paul, sensing something of what lay in the old witch's mind, felt blood darken his face. "Careful what you suggest," he said.

"You'd just *use* Irulan to gain your own ends, eh?" she asked.

"Wasn't she trained to be used?" Paul asked.

*And we trained her, that's what he's saying,* Mohiam thought. *Well . . . Irulan's a divided coin. Was there another way to spend such a coin?*

"Will you put Chani's child on the throne?" the Reverend Mother asked.

"On *my* throne," Paul said. He glanced at Alia, wondering suddenly if she knew the divergent possibilities in this exchange. Alia stood with eyes closed, an odd stillness-of-person about her. With what inner force did she commune? Seeing his sister thus, Paul felt he'd been cast adrift. Alia stood on a shore that was receding from him.

The Reverend Mother made her decision, said: "This is too much for one person to decide. I must consult with my Council on Wallach. Will you permit a message?"

*As though she needed my permission!* Paul thought.

He said: "Agreed, then. But don't delay too long. I will not sit idly by while you debate."

"Will you bargain with the Bene Tleilax?" the ghola asked, his voice a sharp intrusion.

Alia's eyes popped open and she stared at the ghola as though she'd been awakened by a dangerous intruder.

"I've made no such decision," Paul said. "What I will do is go into the desert as soon as it can be arranged. Our child will be born in sietch."

"A wise decision," Stilgar intoned.

Alia refused to look at Stilgar. It was a wrong decision. She could feel this in every cell. Paul *must* know it. Why had he fixed himself upon such a path?

"Have the Bene Tleilax offered their services?" Alia asked. She saw Mohiam hanging on the answer.

Paul shook his head. "No." He glanced at Stilgar. "Stil, arrange for the message to be sent to Wallach."

"At once, m'Lord."

Paul turned away, waited while Stilgar summoned guards, left with the old witch. He sensed Alia debating whether to confront him with more questions. She turned, instead, to the ghola.

"Mentat," she said, "will the Tleilaxu bid for favor with my brother?"

The ghola shrugged.

Paul felt his attention wander. *The Tleilaxu? No . . . not in the way Alia meant.* Her question revealed, though, that she had not seen the alternatives here. Well . . . vision varied from sibyl to sibyl. Why not a variance from brother to sister? Wandering . . . wandering . . . He came back from each thought with a start to pick up shards of the nearby conversation.

". . . must know what the Tleilaxu . . ."

". . . the fullness of data is always . . ."

". . . healthy doubts where . . ."

Paul turned, looked at his sister, caught her attention. He knew she would see tears on his face and wonder at them. Let her wonder. Wondering was a kindness now. He glanced at the ghola, seeing only Duncan Idaho despite the metallic eyes. Sorrow and compassion warred in Paul. What might those metal eyes record?

*There are many degrees of sight and many degrees of blindness,* Paul thought. His mind turned to a paraphrase of the passage from the Orange Catholic Bible: *What senses do we lack that we cannot see another world all around us?*

Were those metal eyes another sense than sight?

Alia crossed to her brother, sensing his utter sadness. She touched a tear on his cheek with a Fremen gesture of awe, said: "We must not grieve for those dear to us before their passing."

"Before their passing," Paul whispered. "Tell me, little sister, what is *before?*"

> "I've had a bellyful of the god and priest business! You think I don't see my own mythos? Consult your data once more, Hayt. I've insinuated my rites into the most elementary human acts. The people eat in the name of Muad'Dib! They make love in my name, are born in my name—cross the street in my name. A roof beam cannot be raised in the lowliest hovel of far Gangishree without invoking the blessing of Muad'Dib!"
>
> **—Book of Diatribes**
> **from the Hayt Chronicle**

"You risk much leaving your post and coming to me here at this time," Edric said, glaring through the walls of his tank at the Face Dancer.

"How weak and narrow is your thinking," Scytale said. "Who is it who comes to visit you?"

Edric hesitated, observing the hulk shape, heavy eyelids, blunt face. It was early in the day and Edric's metabolism had not yet cycled from night repose into full melange consumption.

"This is not the shape which walked the streets?" Edric asked.

"One would not look twice at some of the figures I have been today," Scytale said.

*The chameleon thinks a change of shape will hide him from anything,* Edric thought with rare insight. And he wondered if his presence in the conspiracy truly hid them from all oracular powers. The Emperor's sister, now . . .

Edric shook his head, stirring the orange gas of his tank, said: "Why are you here?"

"The gift must be prodded to swifter action," Scytale said.

"That cannot be done."

"A way must be found," Scytale insisted.

"Why?"

"Things are not to my liking. The Emperor is trying to split us. Already he has made his bid to the Bene Gesserit."

"Oh, *that.*"

"That! You must prod the ghola to . . ."

"You fashioned him, Tleilaxu," Edric said. "You know better than to ask this." He paused, moved closer to the transparent wall of his tank. "Or did you lie to us about this gift?"

"Lie?"

"You said the weapon was to be aimed and released, nothing more. Once the ghola was given we could not tamper."

"Any ghola can be disturbed," Scytale said. "You need do nothing more than question him about his original being."

"What will this do?"

"It will stir him to actions which will serve our purposes."

"He is a mentat with powers of logic and reason," Edric objected. "He may guess what I'm doing . . . or the sister. If her attention is focused upon—"

"Do you hide us from the sibyl or don't you?" Scytale asked.

"I'm not afraid of oracles," Edric said. "I'm concerned with logic, with real spies, with the physical powers of the Imperium, with the control of the spice, with—"

"One can contemplate the Emperor and his powers comfortably if one remembers that all things are finite," Scytale said.

Oddly, the Steersman recoiled in agitation, threshing his limbs like some weird newt. Scytale fought a sense of loathing at the sight. The Guild Navigator wore his usual dark leotard bulging at the belt with various containers. Yet . . . he gave the impression of nakedness when he moved. It was the swimming, reaching movements, Scytale decided, and he was struck once more by the delicate linkages of their conspiracy. They were not a compatible group. That was weakness.

Edric's agitation subsided. He stared out at Scytale, vision colored by the orange gas which sustained him. What plot did the Face Dancer hold in reserve to save himself? Edric wondered. The Tleilaxu was not acting in a predictable fashion. Evil omen.

Something in the Navigator's voice and actions told Scytale that the Guildsman feared the sister more than the Emperor. This was an abrupt thought flashed on the screen of awareness. Disturbing. Had they overlooked something important about Alia? Would the ghola be sufficient weapon to destroy both?

"You know what is said of Alia?" Scytale asked, probing.

"What do you mean?" Again, the fish-man was agitated.

"Never have philosophy and culture had such a patroness," Scytale said. "Pleaure and beauty unite in—"

"What is enduring about beauty and pleasure?" Edric demanded. "We will destroy both Atreides. Culture! They dispense culture the better to rule. Beauty! They promote the beauty which enslaves. They create a literate ignorance—easiest thing of all. They leave nothing to chance. Chains! Everything they do forges chains, enslaves. But slaves always revolt."

"The sister may wed and produce offspring," Scytale said.

"Why do you speak of the sister?" Edric asked.

"The Emperor may choose a mate for her," Scytale said.

"Let him choose. Already, it is too late."

"Even you cannot invent the next moment," Scytale warned. "You are not a creator . . . any more than are the Atreides." He nodded. "We must not presume too much."

"We aren't the ones to flap our tongues about creation," Edric protested. "We aren't the rabble trying to make a messiah out of Muad'Dib. What is this nonsense? Why are you raising such questions?"

"It's this planet," Scytale said. "*It* raises questions."

"Planets don't speak!"

"This one does."

"Oh?"

"It speaks of creation. Sand blowing in the night, that is creation."

"Sand blowing . . ."

"When you awaken, the first light shows you the new world—all fresh and ready for your tracks."

*Untracked sand?* Edric thought. *Creation?* He felt knotted with sudden anxiety. The confinement of his tank, the surrounding room, everything closed in upon him, constricted him.

*Tracks in sand.*

"You talk like a Fremen," Edric said.

"This is a Fremen thought and it's instructive," Scytale agreed. "They speak of Muad'Dib's Jihad as leaving tracks in the universe in the same way that a Fremen tracks new sand. They've marked out a trail in men's lives."

"So?"

"Another night comes," Scytale said. "Winds blow."

"Yes," Edric said, "the Jihad is finite. Muad'Dib has used his Jihad and—"

"He didn't use the Jihad," Scytale said. "The Jihad used him. I think he would've stopped it if he could."

"If he could? All he had to do was—"

"Oh, be still!" Scytale barked. "You can't stop a mental epidemic. It leaps from person to person across parsecs. It's overwhelmingly contagious. It strikes at the unprotected side, in the place where we lodge the fragments of other such plagues. Who can stop such a thing? Muad'Dib hasn't the antidote. The thing has roots in chaos. Can orders reach there?"

"Have you been infected, then?" Edric asked. He turned slowly in the orange gas, wondering why Scytale's words carried such a tone of fear. Had the Face Dancer broken from the conspiracy? There was no way to peer into the future and examine this now. The future had become a muddy stream, clogged with prophets.

"We're all contaminated," Scytale said, and he reminded himself that Edric's intelligence had severe limits. How could this point be made so that the Guildsman would understand it?

"But when we destroy him," Edric said, "the contag—"

"I should leave you in this ignorance," Scytale said. "But my duties will not permit it. Besides, it's dangerous to all of us."

Edric recoiled, steadied himself with a kick of one webbed foot which sent the orange gas whipping around his legs. "You speak strangely," he said.

"This whole thing is explosive," Scytale said in a calmer voice. "It's ready to shatter. When it goes, it will send bits of itself out through the centuries. Don't you see this?"

"We've dealt with religions before," Edric protested. "If this new—"

"It is *not* just a religion!" Scytale said, wondering what the Reverend Mother would say to this harsh education of their fellow conspirator. "Religious government is something else. Muad'Dib has crowded his Qizarate in everywhere, displaced the old functions of government. But he has no permanent civil service, no interlocking embassies. He has bishoprics, islands of authority. At the center of each island is a man. Men learn how to gain and hold personal power. Men are jealous."

"When they're divided, we'll absorb them one by one," Edric said with a complacent smile. "Cut off the head and the body will fall to—"

"This body has two heads," Scytale said.

"The sister . . . who may wed."

"Who will certainly wed."

"I don't like your tone, Scytale."

"And I don't like your ignorance."

"What if she does wed? Will that shake our plans?"

"It will shake the universe."

"But they're not unique. I, myself, possess powers which—"

"You're an infant. You toddle where they stride."

"They are *not* unique!"

"You forget, Guildsman, that we once made a kwisatz haderach. This is a being filled by the spectacle of Time. It is a form of existence which cannot be threatened without enclosing yourself in the identical threat. Muad'Dib knows we would attack his Chani. We must move faster than we have. You must get to the ghola, prod him as I have instructed."

"And if I do not?"

"We will feel the thunderbolt."

> *Oh, worm of many teeth,*
> *Canst thou deny what has no cure?*
> *The flesh and breath which lure thee*
> *To the ground of all beginnings*
> *Feed on monsters twisting in a door of fire!*
> *Thou hast no robe in all thy attire*
> *To cover intoxications of divinity*
> *Or hide the burnings of desire!*

**—Wormsong**
**from The Dunebook**

Paul had worked up a sweat on the practice floor using crysknife and short sword against the ghola. He stood now at a window looking down into the temple plaza, tried to imagine the scene with Chani at the clinic. She'd been taken ill at midmorning, the sixth week of her pregnancy. The medics were the best. They'd call when they had news.

Murky afternoon sandclouds darkened the sky over the plaza. Fremen called such weather "dirty air."

Would the medics never call? Each second struggled past, reluctant to enter his universe.

Waiting . . . waiting . . . The Bene Gesserit sent no word from Wallach. Deliberately delaying, of course.

Prescient vision had recorded these moments, but he shielded his awareness from the oracle, preferring the role here of a Timefish swimming not where he willed, but where the currents carried him. Destiny permitted no struggles now.

The ghola could be heard racking weapons, examining the equipment. Paul sighed, put a hand to his own belt, deactivated his shield. The tingling passage of its field ran down against his skin.

He'd face events when Chani came, Paul told himself. Time enough then to accept the fact that what he'd concealed from her had prolonged her life. Was it evil, he wondered, to prefer Chani to an heir? By what right did he make her choice for her? Foolish thoughts! Who could hesitate, given the alternatives— slave pits, torture, agonizing sorrow . . . and worse.

He heard the door open, Chani's footsteps.

Paul turned.

Murder sat on Chani's face. The wide Fremen belt which gathered the waist of her golden robe, the water rings worn as a necklace, one hand at her hip (never far from the knife), the trenchant stare which was her first inspection of any room—everything about her stood now only as a background for violence.

He opened his arms as she came to him, gathered her close.

"Someone," she rasped, speaking against his breast, "has been feeding me a contraceptive for a long time . . . before I began the new diet. There'll be problems with this birth because of it."

"But there are remedies?" he asked.

"Dangerous remedies. I know the source of that poison! I'll have her blood."

"My Sihaya," he whispered, holding her close to calm a sudden trembling. "You'll bear the heir we want. Isn't that enough?"

"My life burns faster," she said, pressing against him. "The birth now controls my life. The medics told me it goes at a terrible pace. I must eat and eat . . . and take more spice, as well . . . eat it, drink it. I'll kill her for this—"

Paul kissed her cheek. "No, my Sihaya. You'll kill no one." And he thought: *Irulan prolonged your life, beloved. For you, the time of birth is the time of death.*

He felt hidden grief drain his marrow then, empty his life into a black flask.

Chani pushed away from him. "She cannot be forgiven!"

"Who said anything about forgiving?"

"Then why shouldn't I kill her?"

It was such a flat, Fremen question that Paul felt himself almost overcome by a hysterical desire to laugh. He covered it by saying: "It wouldn't help."

"You've *seen* that?"

Paul felt his belly tighten with vision-memory.

"What I've seen . . . what I've seen . . ." he muttered. Every aspect of surrounding events fitted a present which paralyzed him. He felt chained to a future which, exposed too often, had locked onto him like a greedy succubus. Tight dryness clogged his throat. Had he followed the witchcall of his own oracle, he wondered, until it'd spilled him into a merciless present?

"Tell me what you've *seen,*" Chani said.

"I can't."

"Why mustn't I kill her?"

"Because I ask it."

He watched her accept this. She did it the way sand accepted water: absorbing and concealing. Was there obedience beneath that hot, angry surface? he wondered. And he realized then that life in the royal Keep had left Chani unchanged. She'd merely stopped here for a time, inhabited a way station on a journey with her man. Nothing of the desert had been taken from her.

Chani stepped away from him then, glanced at the ghola who stood waiting near the diamond circle of the practice floor.

"You've been crossing blades with him?" she asked.

"And I'm better for it."

Her gaze went to the circle on the floor, back to the ghola's metallic eyes.

"I don't like it," she said.

"He's not intended to do me violence," Paul said.

"You've seen *that?*"

"I've not *seen* it!"

"Then how do you know?"

"Because he's more than ghola; he's Duncan Idaho."

"The Bene Tleilax made him."

"They made more than they intended."

She shook her head. A corner of her nezhoni scarf rubbed the collar of her robe. "How can you change the fact that he is ghola?"

"Hayt," Paul said, "are you the tool of my undoing?"

"If the substance of here and now is changed, the future is changed," the ghola said.

"That is no answer!" Chani objected.

Paul raised his voice: "How will I die, Hayt?"

Light glinted from the artificial eyes. "It is said, m'Lord, that you will die of money and power."

Chani stiffened. "How dare he speak thus to you?"

"The mentat is truthful," Paul said.

"Was Duncan Idaho a real friend?" she asked.

"He gave his life for me."

"It is sad," Chani whispered, "that a ghola cannot be restored to his original being."

"Would you convert me?" the ghola asked, directing his gaze to Chani.

"What does he mean?" Chani asked.

"To be converted is to be turned around," Paul said. "But there's no going back."

"Every man carries his own past with him," Hayt said.

"And every ghola?" Paul asked.

"In a way, m'Lord."

"Then what of that past in your secret flesh?" Paul asked.

Chani saw how the question disturbed the ghola. His movements quickened, hands clenched into fists. She glanced at Paul, wondering why he probed thus. Was there a way to restore this creature to the man he'd been?

"Has a ghola ever remembered his real past?" Chani asked.

"Many attempts have been made," Hayt said, his gaze fixed on the floor near his feet. "No ghola has ever been restored to his former being."

"But you long for this to happen," Paul said.

The blank surfaces of the ghola's eyes came up to center on Paul with a pressing intensity. "Yes!"

Voice soft, Paul said: "If there's a way . . ."

"This flesh," Hayt said, touching left hand to forehead in a curious saluting movement, "is not the flesh of my original birth. It is . . . reborn. Only the shape is familiar. A Face Dancer might do as well."

"Not as well," Paul said. "And you're not a Face Dancer."

"That is true, m'Lord."

"Whence comes your shape?"

"The genetic imprint of the original cells."

"Somewhere," Paul said, "there's a plastic something which remembers the shape of Duncan Idaho. It's said the ancients probed this region before the Butlerian Jihad. What's the extent of this memory, Hayt? What did it learn from the original?"

The ghola shrugged.

"What if he wasn't Idaho?" Chani asked.

"He was."

"Can you be certain?" she asked.

"He is Duncan in every aspect. I cannot imagine a force strong enough to hold that shape thus without any relaxation or any deviation."

"M'Lord!" Hayt objected. "Because we cannot imagine a thing, that doesn't exclude it from reality. There are things I must do as a ghola that I would not do as a man."

Keeping his attention on Chani, Paul said: "You see?"

She nodded.

Paul turned away, fighting deep sadness. He crossed to the balcony windows, drew the draperies. Lights came on in the sudden gloom. He pulled the sash of his robe tight, listened for sounds behind him.

Nothing.

He turned. Chani stood as though entranced, her gaze centered on the ghola.

Hayt, Paul saw, had retreated to some inner chamber of his being—had gone back to the ghola place.

Chani turned at the sound of Paul's return. She still felt the thralldom of the instant Paul had precipitated. For a brief moment, the ghola had been an intense, vital human being. For that moment, he had been someone she did not fear—indeed, someone she liked and admired. Now, she understood Paul's purpose in this probing. He had wanted her to see the *man* in the ghola flesh.

She stared at Paul. "That man, was that Duncan Idaho?"

"That was Duncan Idaho. He is still there."

"Would *he* have allowed Irulan to go on living?" Chani asked.

*The water didn't sink too deep,* Paul thought. And he said: "If I commanded it."

"I don't understand," she said. "Shouldn't you be angry?"

"I am angry."

"You don't sound . . . angry. You sound sorrowful."

He closed his eyes. "Yes. That, too."

"You're my man," she said. "I know this, but suddenly I don't understand you."

Abruptly, Paul felt that he walked down a long cavern. His flesh moved—one foot and then another—but his thoughts went elsewhere. "I don't understand myself," he whispered. When he opened his eyes, he found that he had moved away from Chani.

She spoke from somewhere behind him. "Beloved, I'll not ask again what you've *seen*. I only know I'm to give you the heir we want."

He nodded, then: "I've known that from the beginning." He turned, studied her. Chani seemed very far away.

She drew herself up, placed a hand on her abdomen. "I'm hungry. The medics tell me I must eat three or four times what I ate before. I'm frightened, beloved. It goes too fast."

*Too fast,* he agreed. *This fetus knows the necessity for speed.*

> *The audacious nature of Muad'Dib's actions may be seen in the fact that He knew from the beginning whither He was bound, yet not once did He step aside from that path. He put it clearly when He said: "I tell you that I come now to my time of testing when it will be shown that I am the Ultimate Servant." Thus He weaves all into One, that both friend and foe may worship Him. It is for this reason and this reason only that His Apostles prayed: "Lord, save us from the other paths which Muad'Dib covered with the Waters of His Life." Those "other paths" may be imagined only with the deepest revulsion.*

> **—from The Yiam-el-Din**
> **(Book of Judgment)**

The messenger was a young woman—her face, name and family known to Chani—which was how she'd penetrated Imperial Security.

Chani had done no more than identify her for a Security Officer named Bannerjee, who then arranged the meeting with Muad'Dib. Bannerjee acted out of instinct and the assurance that the young woman's father had been a member of the Emperor's Death Commandos, the dreaded Fedaykin, in the days before the Jihad. Otherwise, he might have ignored her plea that her message was intended only for the ears of Muad'Dib.

She was, of course, screened and searched before the meeting in Paul's private office. Even so, Bannerjee accompanied her, hand on knife, other hand on her arm.

It was almost midday when they brought her into the room—an odd space, mixture of desert-Fremen and Family-Aristocrat. *Hiereg* hangings lined three walls: delicate tapestries adorned with figures out of Fremen mythology. A view screen covered the fourth wall, a silver-gray surface behind an oval desk whose top held only one object, a Fremen sandclock built into an *orrery*. The orrery, a suspensor mechanism from Ix, carried both moons of Arrakis in the classic Worm Trine aligned with the sun.

Paul, standing beside the desk, glanced at Bannerjee. The Security Officer was one of those who'd come up through the Fremen Constabulary, winning his place on brains and proven loyalty despite the smuggler ancestry attested by his name. He was a solid figure, almost fat. Wisps of black hair fell down over the dark, wet-appearing skin of his forehead like the crest of an exotic bird. His eyes were blue-blue and steady in a gaze which could look upon happiness or atrocity without change of expression. Both Chani and Stilgar trusted him. Paul knew that if he told Bannerjee to throttle the girl immediately, Bannerjee would do it.

"Sire, here is the messenger girl," Bannerjee said. "M'Lady Chani said she sent word to you."

"Yes." Paul nodded curtly.

Oddly, the girl didn't look at him. Her attention remained on the orrery. She was dark-skinned, of medium height, her figure concealed beneath a robe whose rich wine fabric and simple cut spoke of wealth. Her blue-black hair was held in a narrow band of material which matched the robe. The robe concealed her hands. Paul suspected that the hands were tightly clasped. It would be in character. Everything about her would be in character—including the robe: a last piece of finery saved for such a moment.

Paul motioned Bannerjee aside. He hesitated before obeying. Now, the girl moved—one step forward. When she moved there was grace. Still, her eyes avoided him.

Paul cleared his throat.

Now the girl lifted her gaze, the whiteless eyes widening with just the right shade of awe. She had an odd little face with delicate chin, a sense of reserve in the way she held her small mouth. The eyes appeared abnormally large above slanted cheeks. There was a cheerless air about her, something which said she seldom smiled. The corners of her eyes even held a faint yellow misting which could have been from dust irritation or the tracery of semuta.

Everything was in character.

"You asked to see me," Paul said.

The moment of supreme test for this girl-shape had come. Scytale had put on the shape, the mannerisms, the sex, the voice—everything his abilities could grasp and assume. But this was a female known to Muad'Dib in the sietch days. She'd been a child, then, but she and Muad'Dib shared common experiences. Certain areas of memory must be avoided delicately. It was the most exacting part Scytale had ever attempted.

"I am Otheym's Lichna of Berk al Dib."

The girl's voice came out small, but firm, giving name, father and pedigree.

Paul nodded. He saw how Chani had been fooled. The timbre of voice, everything reproduced with exactitude. Had it not been for his own Bene Gesserit training in voice and for the web of *dao* in which oracular vision enfolded him, this Face-Dancer disguise might have gulled even him.

Training exposed certain discrepancies: the girl was older than her known years: too much control tuned the vocal cords; set of neck and shoulders missed by a fraction the subtle hauteur of Fremen poise. But there were niceties, too: the rich robe had been patched to betray actual status . . . and the features were beautifully exact. They spoke a certain sympathy of this Face Dancer for the role being played.

"Rest in my home, daughter of Otheym," Paul said in formal Fremen greeting. "You are welcome as water after a dry crossing."

The faintest of relaxations exposed the confidence this apparent acceptance had conveyed.

"I bring a message," she said.

"A man's messenger is as himself," Paul said.

Scytale breathed softly. It went well, but now came the crucial task: the Atreides must be guided onto that special path. He must lose his Fremen concubine in circumstances where no other shared the blame. The failure must belong only to the *omnipotent* Muad'Dib. He had to be led into an ultimate realization of his failure and thence to acceptance of the Tleilaxu alternative.

"I am the smoke which banishes sleep in the night," Scytale said, employing a Fedaykin code phrase: *I bear bad tidings.*

Paul fought to maintain calmness. He felt naked, his soul abandoned in a groping-time concealed from every vision. Powerful oracles hid this Face Dancer. Only the edges of these moments were known to Paul. He knew only what he could *not* do. He could not slay this Face Dancer. That would precipitate the future which must be avoided at all cost. Somehow, a way must be found to reach into the darkness and change the terrifying pattern.

"Give me your message," Paul said.

Bannerjee moved to place himself where he could watch the girl's face. She seemed to notice him for the first time and her gaze went to the knife handle beneath the Security Officer's hand.

"The innocent do not believe in evil," she said, looking squarely at Bannerjee.

*Ahhh, well done,* Paul thought. It was what the real Lichna would've said. He felt a momentary pang for the real daughter of Otheym—dead now, a corpse in the sand. There was no time for such emotions, though. He scowled.

Bannerjee kept his attention on the girl.

"I was told to deliver my message in secret," she said.

"Why?" Bannerjee demanded, voice harsh, probing.

"Because it is my father's wish."

"This is my friend," Paul said. "Am I not a Fremen? Then my friend may hear anything I hear."

Scytale composed the girl-shape. Was this a true Fremen custom . . . or was it a test?

"The Emperor may make his own rules," Scytale said. "This is the message: My father wishes you to come to him, bringing Chani."

"Why must I bring Chani?"

"She is your woman and a Sayyadina. This is a Water matter, by the rules of our tribes. She must attest it that my father speaks according to the Fremen Way."

*There truly are Fremen in the conspiracy,* Paul thought. This moment fitted the shape of things to come for sure. And he had no alternative but to commit himself to this course.

"Of what will your father speak?" Paul asked.

"He will speak of a plot against you—a plot among the Fremen."

"Why doesn't he bring that message in person?" Bannerjee demanded.

She kept her gaze on Paul. "My father cannot come here. The plotters suspect him. He'd not survive the journey."

"Could he not divulge the plot to you?" Bannerjee asked. "How came he to risk his daughter on such a mission?"

"The details are locked in a distrans carrier that only Muad'Dib may open," she said. "This much I know."

"Why not send the distrans, then?" Paul asked.

"It is a human distrans," she said.

"I'll go, then," Paul said. "But I'll go alone."

"Chani must come with you!"

"Chani is with child."

"When has a Fremen woman refused to . . ."

"My enemies fed her a subtle poison," Paul said. "It will be a difficult birth. Her health will not permit her to accompany me now."

Before Scytale could still them, strange emotions passed over the girl-features: frustration, anger. Scytale was reminded that every victim must have a way of escape—even such a one as Muad'Dib. The conspiracy had not failed, though. This Atreides remained in the net. He was a creature who had developed firmly into one pattern. He'd destroy himself before changing into the opposite of that pattern. That had been the way with the Tleilaxu Kwisatz Haderach. It'd be the way with this one. And then . . . the ghola.

"Let me ask Chani to decide this," she said.

"I have decided it," Paul said. "You will accompany me in Chani's stead."

"It requires a Sayyadina of the Rite!"

"Are you not Chani's friend?"

*Boxed!* Scytale thought. *Does he suspect? No. He's being Fremen-cautious. And the contraceptive is a fact. Well—there are other ways.*

"My father told me I was not to return," Scytale said, "that I was to seek asylum with you. He said you'd not risk me."

Paul nodded. It was beautifully in character. He couldn't deny this asylum. She'd plead Fremen obedience to a father's command.

"I'll take Stilgar's wife, Harah," Paul said. "You'll tell us the way to your father."

"How do you know you can trust Stilgar's wife?"

"I know it."

"But I don't."

Paul pursed his lips, then: "Does your mother live?"

"My true mother has gone to Shai-hulud. My second mother still lives and cares for my father. Why?"

"She's of Sietch Tabr?"

"Yes."

"I remember her," Paul said. "She will serve in Chani's place." He motioned to Bannerjee. "Have attendants take Otheym's Lichna to suitable quarters."

Bannerjee nodded. *Attendants.* The key word meant that this messenger must be put under special guard. He took her arm. She resisted.

"How will you go to my father?" she pleaded.

"You'll describe the way to Bannerjee," Paul said. "He is my friend."

"No! My father has commanded it! I cannot!"

"Bannerjee?" Paul said.

Bannerjee paused. Paul saw the man searching that encyclopedic memory which had helped bring him to his position of trust. "I know a guide who can take you to Otheym," Bannerjee said.

"Then I'll go alone," Paul said.

"Sire, if you . . ."

"Otheym wants it this way," Paul said, barely concealing the irony which consumed him.

"Sire, it's too dangerous," Bannerjee protested.

"Even an Emperor must accept some risks," Paul said. "The decision is made. Do as I've commanded."

Reluctantly, Bannerjee led the Face Dancer from the room.

Paul turned toward the blank screen behind his desk. He felt that he waited for the arrival of a rock on its blind journey from some height.

Should he tell Bannerjee about the messenger's true nature? he wondered. No! Such an incident hadn't been written on the screen of his vision. Any deviation here carried precipitate violence. A moment of fulcrum had to be found, a place where he could will himself out of the vision.

*If such a moment existed . . .*

> *No matter how exotic human civilization becomes, no matter the develop-*
> *ments of life and society nor the complexity of the machine/human interface,*
> *there always come interludes of lonely power when the course of humankind,*
> *the very future of humankind, depends upon the relatively simple actions of*
> *single individuals.*

> **—from The Tleilaxu Godbuk**

As he crossed over on the high footbridge from his Keep to the Qizarate Office Building, Paul added a limp to his walk. It was almost sunset and he walked through long shadows that helped conceal him, but sharp eyes still might detect something in his carriage that identified him. He wore a shield, but it was not activated, his aides having decided that the shimmer of it might arouse suspicions.

Paul glanced left. Strings of sandclouds lay across the sunset like slatted shutters. The air was hiereg dry through his stillsuit filters.

He wasn't really alone out here, but the web of Security hadn't been this loose around him since he'd ceased walking the streets alone in the night. Ornithopters with night scanners drifted far overhead in seemingly random pattern, all of them tied to his movements through a transmitter concealed in his clothing. Picked men walked the streets below. Others had fanned out through the city after seeing the Emperor in his disguise—Fremen costume down to the stillsuit and *temag* desert boots, the darkened features. His cheeks had been distorted with plastene inserts. A catchtube ran down along his left jaw.

As he reached the opposite end of the bridge, Paul glanced back, noted a movement beside the stone lattice that concealed a balcony of his private quarters. Chani, no doubt. "Hunting for sand in the desert," she'd called this venture.

How little she understood the bitter choice. Selecting among agonies, he thought, made even lesser agonies near unbearable.

For a blurred, emotionally painful moment, he relived their parting. At the last instant, Chani had experienced a tau-glimpse of his feelings, but she had misinterpreted. She had thought his emotions were those experienced in the parting of loved ones when one entered the dangerous unknown.

*Would that I did not know,* he thought.

He had crossed the bridge now and entered the upper passageway through the office building. There were fixed glowglobes here and people hurrying on business. The Qizarate never slept. Paul found his attention caught by the signs above doorways, as though he were seeing them for the first time: *Speed Merchants. Wind Stills and Retorts. Prophetic Prospects. Tests of Faith. Religious Supply. Weaponry . . . Propagation of the Faith . . .*

A more honest label would've been *Propagation of the Bureaucracy,* he thought.

A type of religious civil servant had sprung up all through his universe. This new man of the Qizarate was more often a convert. He seldom displaced a Fremen in the key posts, but he was filling all the interstices. He used melange as much to show he could afford it as for the geriatric benefits. He stood apart from his rulers—Emperor, Guild, Bene Gesserit, Landsraad, Family or Qizarate. His gods were Routine and Records. He was served by mentats and prodigious filing systems. Expediency was the first word in his catechism, although he gave proper lip-service to the precepts of the Butlerians. Machines could not be fashioned in the image of a man's mind, he said, but he betrayed by every action that he preferred machines to men, statistics to individuals, the faraway general view to the intimate personal touch requiring imagination and initiative.

As Paul emerged onto the ramp at the far side of the building, he heard the bells calling the Evening Rite at Alia's Fane.

There was an odd feeling of permanence about the bells.

The temple across the thronged square was new, its rituals of recent devising, but there was something about this setting in a desert sink at the edge of Arrakeen—something in the way wind-driven sand had begun to weather stones and plastene, something in the haphazard way buildings had gone up around the Fane. Everything conspired to produce the impression that this was a very old place full of traditions and mystery.

He was down into the press of people now—committed. The only guide his Security force could find had insisted it be done this way. Security hadn't liked Paul's ready agreement. Stilgar had liked it even less. And Chani had objected most of all.

The crowd around him, even while its members brushed against him, glanced his way unseeing and passed on, gave him a curious freedom of movement. It was the way they'd been conditioned to treat a Fremen, he knew. He carried himself like a man of the inner desert. Such men were quick to anger.

As he moved into the quickening flow to the temple steps, the crush of people became even greater. Those all around could not help but press against him now, but he found himself the target for ritual apologies: "Your pardon, noble sir. I cannot prevent this discourtesy." "Pardon, sir; this crush of people is the worst I've ever seen." "I abase myself, holy citizen. A lout shoved me."

Paul ignored the words after the first few. There was no feeling in them except a kind of ritual fear. He found himself, instead, thinking that he had come a long way from his boyhood days in Caladan Castle. Where had he put his foot on the path that led to this journey across a crowded square on a planet so far from Caladan? Had he really put his foot on a path? He could not say he had acted at any point in his life for one specific reason. The motives and impinging forces had been complex—more complex possibly than any other set of goads in human history. He had the heady feeling here that he might still avoid the fate he could see so clearly along this path. But the crowd pushed him forward and he experienced the dizzy sense that he had lost his way, lost personal direction over his life.

The crowd flowed with him up the steps now into the temple portico. Voices grew hushed. The smell of fear grew stronger—acrid, sweaty.

Acolytes had already begun the service within the temple. Their plain chant dominated the other sounds—whispers, rustle of garments, shuffling feet, coughs—telling the story of the Far Places visited by the Priestess in her holy trance.

"She rides the sandworm of space!
She guides through all storms
Into the land of gentle winds.
Though we sleep by the snake's den,
She guards our dreaming souls.
Shunning the desert heat,
She hides us in a cool hollow.
The gleaming of her white teeth
Guides us in the night.
By the braids of her hair
We are lifted up to heaven!
Sweet fragrance, flower-scented,
Surrounds us in her presence."

*Balak!* Paul thought, thinking in Fremen. *Look out! She can be filled with angry passion, too.*

The temple portico was lined with tall, slender glowtubes simulating candle flame. They flickered. The flickering stirred ancestral memories in Paul even while he knew that was the intent. This setting was an atavism, subtly contrived, effective. He hated his own hand in it.

The crowd flowed with him through tall metal doors into the gigantic nave, a gloomy place with the flickering lights far away overhead, a brilliantly illuminated altar at the far end. Behind the altar, a deceptively simple affair of black wood encrusted with sand patterns from the Fremen mythology, hidden lights played on the field of a pru-door to create a rainbow borealis. The seven rows of chanting acolytes ranked below that spectral curtain took on an eerie quality: black robes, white faces, mouths moving in unison.

Paul studied the pilgrims around him, suddenly envious of their intentness, their air of listening to truths he could not hear. It seemed to him that they gained something here which was denied to him, something mysteriously healing.

He tried to inch his way closer to the altar, was stopped by a hand on his arm. Paul whipped his gaze around, met the probing stare of an ancient Fremen— blue-blue eyes beneath overhanging brows, recognition in them. A name flashed into Paul's mind: Rasir, a companion from the sietch days.

In the press of the crowd, Paul knew he was completely vulnerable if Rasir planned violence.

The old man pressed close, one hand beneath a sand-grimed robe—grasping the hilt of a crysknife, no doubt. Paul set himself as best he could to resist attack. The old man moved his head toward Paul's ear, whispered: "We will go with the others."

It was the signal to identify his guide. Paul nodded.

Rasir drew back, faced the altar.

"She comes from the east," the acolytes chanted. "The sun stands at her back. All things are exposed. In the full glare of light—her eyes miss no thing, neither light nor dark."

A wailing rebaba jarred across the voices, stilled them, receded into silence. With an electric abruptness, the crowd surged forward several meters. They were packed into a tight mass of flesh now, the air heavy with their breathing and the scent of spice.

"Shai-hulud writes on clean sand!" the acolytes shouted.

Paul felt his own breath catch in unison with those around him. A feminine chorus began singing faintly from the shadows behind the shimmering pru-door: "Alia . . . Alia . . . Alia . . ." It grew louder and louder, fell to a sudden silence.

Again—voices beginning vesper-soft:

"She stills all storms—
Her eyes kill our enemies,
And torment the unbelievers.
From the spires of Tuono
Where dawnlight strikes
And clear water runs,
You see her shadow.
In the shining summer heat
She serves us bread and milk—
Cool, fragrant with spices,
Her eyes melt our enemies,
Torment our oppressors

And pierce all mysteries.
She is Alia . . . Alia . . . Alia . . . Alia . . . ."

Slowly, the voices trailed off.

Paul felt sickened. *What are we doing?* he asked himself. Alia was a child witch, but she was growing older. And he thought: *Growing older is to grow more wicked.*

The collective mental atmosphere of the temple ate at his psyche. He could sense that element of himself which was one with those all around him, but the differences formed a deadly contradiction. He stood immersed, isolated in a personal sin which he could never expiate. The immensity of the universe outside the temple flooded his awareness. How could one man, one ritual, hope to knit such immensity into a garment fitted to all men?

Paul shuddered.

The universe opposed him at every step. It eluded his grasp, conceived countless disguises to delude him. That universe would never agree with any shape he gave it.

A profound hush spread through the temple.

Alia emerged from the darkness behind the shimmering rainbows. She wore a yellow robe trimmed in Atreides green—yellow for sunlight, green for the death which produced life. Paul experienced the sudden surprising thought that Alia had emerged here just for him, for him alone. He stared across the mob in the temple at his sister. She *was* his sister. He knew her ritual and its roots, but he had never before stood out here with the pilgrims, watched her through their eyes. Here, performing the mystery of this place, he saw that she partook of the universe which opposed him.

Acolytes brought her a golden chalice.

Alia raised the chalice.

With part of his awareness, Paul knew that the chalice contained the unaltered melange, the subtle poison, her sacrament of the oracle.

Her gaze on the chalice, Alia spoke. Her voice caressed the ears, flower sound, flowing and musical:

"In the beginning, we were empty," she said.

"Ignorant of all things," the chorus sang.

"We did not know the Power that abides in every place," Alia said.

"And in every Time," the chorus sang.

"Here is the Power," Alia said, raising the chalice slightly.

"It brings us joy," sang the chorus.

*And it brings us distress,* Paul thought.

"It awakens the soul," Alia said.

"It dispels all doubts," the chorus sang.

"In worlds, we perish," Alia said.

"In the Power, we survive," sang the chorus.

Alia put the chalice to her lips, drank.

To his astonishment, Paul found he was holding his breath like the meanest pilgrim of this mob. Despite every shred of personal knowledge about the experience Alia was undergoing, he had been caught in the tao-web. He felt himself remembering how that fiery poison coursed into the body. Memory unfolded the time-stopping when awareness became a mote which changed the poison. He reexperienced the awakening into timelessness where all things were possible. He *knew* Alia's present experience, yet he saw now that he did not know it. Mystery blinded the eyes.

Alia trembled, sank to her knees.

Paul exhaled with the enraptured pilgrims. He nodded. Part of the veil began to lift from him. Absorbed in the bliss of a vision, he had forgotten that each vision belonged to all those who were still on-the-way, still to become. In the vision, one passed through a darkness, unable to distinguish reality from insubstantial accident. One hungered for absolutes which could never be.

Hungering, one lost the present.

Alia swayed with the rapture of spice change.

Paul felt that some transcendental presence spoke to him, saying: "Look! See there! See what you've ignored?" In that instant, he thought he looked through other eyes, that he saw an imagery and rhythm in this place which no artist or poet could reproduce. It was vital and beautiful, a glaring light that exposed all power-gluttony . . . even his own.

Alia spoke. Her amplified voice boomed across the nave.

"Luminous night," she cried.

A moan swept like a wave through the crush of pilgrims.

"Nothing hides in such a night!" Alia said. "What rare light is this darkness? You cannot fix your gaze upon it! Senses cannot record it. No words describe it." Her voice lowered. "The abyss remains. It is pregnant with all the things yet to be. Ahhhhh, what gentle violence!"

Paul felt that he waited for some private signal from his sister. It could be any action or word, something of wizardry and mystical processes, an outward streaming that would fit him like an arrow into a cosmic bow. This instant lay like quivering mercury in his awareness.

"There will be sadness," Alia intoned. "I remind you that all things are but a beginning, forever beginning. Worlds wait to be conquered. Some within the sound of my voice will attain exalted destinies. You will sneer at the past, forgetting what I tell you now: within all differences there is unity."

Paul suppressed a cry of disappointment as Alia lowered her head. She had not said the thing he waited to hear. His body felt like a dry shell, a husk abandoned by some desert insect.

Others must feel something similar, he thought. He sensed the restlessness about him. Abruptly, a woman in the mob, someone far down in the nave to Paul's left, cried out, a wordless noise of anguish.

Alia lifted her head and Paul had the giddy sensation that the distance between them collapsed, that he stared directly into her glazed eyes only inches away from her.

"Who summons me?" Alia asked.

"I do," the woman cried. "I do, Alia. Oh, Alia, help me. They say my son was killed on Muritan. Is he gone? Will I never see my son again . . . never?"

"You try to walk backward in the sand," Alia intoned. "Nothing is lost. Everything returns later, but you may not recognize the changed form that returns."

"Alia, I don't understand!" the woman wailed.

"You live in the air but you do not see it," Alia said, sharpness in her voice. "Are you a lizard? Your voice has the Fremen accent. Does a Fremen try to bring back the dead? What do we need from our dead except their water?"

Down in the center of the nave, a man in a rich red cloak lifted both hands, the sleeves falling to expose white-clad arms. "Alia," he shouted, "I have had a business proposal. Should I accept?"

"You come here like a beggar," Alia said. "You look for the golden bowl but you will find only a dagger."

"I have been asked to kill a man!" a voice shouted from off to the right—a deep voice with sietch tones. "Should I accept? Accepting, would I succeed?"

"Beginning and end are a single thing," Alia snapped. "Have I not told you this before? You didn't come here to ask that question. What is it you cannot believe that you must come here and cry out against it?"

"She's in a fierce mood tonight," a woman near Paul muttered. "Have you ever seen her this angry?"

*She knows I'm out here,* Paul thought. *Did she see something in the vision that angered her? Is she raging at me?*

"Alia," a man directly in front of Paul called. "Tell these businessmen and faint-hearts how long your brother will rule!"

"I permit you to look around that corner by yourself," Alia snarled. "You carry your prejudice in your mouth! It is because my brother rides the worm of chaos that you have roof and water!"

With a fierce gesture, clutching her robe, Alia whirled away, strode through the shimmering ribbons of light, was lost in the darkness behind.

Immediately, the acolytes took up the closing chant, but their rhythm was off. Obviously, they'd been caught by the unexpected ending of the rite. An incoherent mumbling arose on all sides of the crowd. Paul felt the stirring around him—restless, dissatisfied.

"It was that fool with his stupid question about business," a woman near Paul muttered. "The hypocrite!"

What had Alia seen? What track through the future?

Something had happened here tonight, souring the rite of the oracle. Usually, the crowd clamored for Alia to answer their pitiful questions. They came as beggars to the oracle, yes. He had heard them thus many times as he'd watched, hidden in the darkness behind the altar. What had been different about this night?

The old Fremen tugged Paul's sleeve, nodded toward the exit. The crowd already was beginning to push in that direction. Paul allowed himself to be pressed along with them, the guide's hand upon his sleeve. There was the feeling in him then that his body had become the manifestation of some power he could no longer control. He had become a non-being, a stillness which moved itself. At the core of the non-being, there he existed, allowing himself to be led through the streets of his city, following a track so familiar to his visions that it froze his heart with grief.

*I should know what Alia saw,* he thought. *I have seen it enough times myself. And she didn't cry out against it . . . she saw the alternatives, too.*

> *Production growth and income growth must not get out of step in my Empire. That is the substance of my command. There are to be no balance-of-payment difficulties between the different spheres of influence. And the reason for this is simply because I command it. I want to emphasize my authority in this area. I am the supreme energy-eater of this domain, and will remain so, alive or dead. My Government is the economy.*

> **—Order in Council**
> **The Emperor Paul Muad'Dib**

"I will leave you here," the old man said, taking his hand from Paul's sleeve. "It is on the right, second door from the far end. Go with Shai-hulud, Muad'Dib . . . and remember when you were Usul."

Paul's guide slipped away into the darkness.

There would be Security men somewhere out there waiting to grab the guide and take the man to a place of questioning, Paul knew. But Paul found himself hoping the old Fremen would escape.

There were stars overhead and the distant light of First Moon somewhere beyond the Shield Wall. But this place was not the open desert where a man could sight on a star to guide his course. The old man had brought him into one of the new suburbs; this much Paul recognized.

This street now was thick with sand blown in from encroaching dunes. A dim light glowed from a single public suspensor globe far down the street. It gave enough illumination to show that this was a dead-end street.

The air around him was thick with the smell of a reclamation still. The thing must be poorly capped for its fetid odors to escape, loosing a dangerously wasteful amount of moisture into the night air. How careless his people had grown, Paul thought. They were millionaires of water—forgetful of the days when a man on Arrakis could have been killed for just an eighth share of the water in his body.

*Why am I hesitating?* Paul wondered. *It is the second door from the far end. I knew that without being told. But this thing must be played out with precision. So . . . I hesitate.*

The noise of an argument arose suddenly from the corner house on Paul's left. A woman there berated someone: the new wing of their house leaked dust, she complained. Did he think water fell from heaven? If dust came in, moisture got out.

*Some remember,* Paul thought.

He moved down the street and the quarrel faded away behind.

*Water from heaven!* he thought.

Some Fremen had seen that wonder on other worlds. He had seen it himself, had ordered it for Arrakis, but the memory of it felt like something that had occurred to another person. Rain, it was called. Abruptly, he recalled a rainstorm on his birthworld—clouds thick and gray in the sky of Caladan, an electric storm presence, moist air, the big wet drops drumming on skylights. It ran in rivulets off the eaves. Storm drains took the water away to a river which ran muddy and turgid past the Family orchards . . . trees there with their barren branches glistening wetly.

Paul's foot caught in a low drift of sand across the street. For an instant, he felt mud clinging to the shoes of his childhood. Then he was back in the sand, in the dust-clotted, wind-muffled darkness with the Future hanging over him, taunting. He could feel the aridity of life around him like an accusation. *You did this!* They'd become a civilization of dry-eyed watchers and tale-tellers, people who solved all problems with power . . . and more power . . . and still more power—hating every erg of it.

Rough stones came underfoot. His vision remembered them. The dark rectangle of a doorway appeared on his right—black in black: Otheym's house, Fate's house, a place different from the ones around it only in the role Time had chosen for it. It was a strange place to be marked down in history.

The door opened to his knock. The gap revealed the dull green light of an atrium. A dwarf peered out, ancient face on a child's body, an apparition prescience had never seen.

"You've come then," the apparition said. The dwarf stepped aside, no awe in his manner, merely the gloating of a slow smile. "Come in! Come in!"

Paul hesitated. There'd been no dwarf in the vision, but all else remained identical. Visions could contain such disparities and still hold true to their original plunge into infinity. But the difference dared him to hope. He glanced back up the street at the creamy pearl glistening of his moon swimming out of jagged shadows. The moon haunted him. How did it fall?

"Come in," the dwarf insisted.

Paul entered, heard the door thud into its moisture seals behind. The dwarf passed him, led the way, enormous feet slapping the floor, opened the delicate lattice gate into the roofed central courtyard, gestured. "They await, Sire."

*Sire,* Paul thought. *He knows me, then.*

Before Paul could explore this discovery, the dwarf slipped away down a side passage. Hope was a dervish wind whirling, dancing in Paul. He headed across the courtyard. It was a dark and gloomy place, the smell of sickness and defeat in it. He felt daunted by the atmosphere. Was it defeat to choose a lesser evil? he wondered. How far down this track had he come?

Light poured from a narrow doorway in the far wall. He put down the feeling of watchers and evil smells, entered the doorway into a small room. It was a barren place by Fremen standards with heireg hangings on only two walls. Opposite the door, a man sat on carmine cushions beneath the best hanging. A feminine figure hovered in shadows behind another doorway in a barren wall to the left.

Paul felt vision-trapped. This was the way it'd gone. Where was the dwarf? Where was the difference?

His senses absorbed the room in a single gestalten sweep. The place had received painstaking care despite its poor furnishings. Hooks and rods across the barren walls showed where hangings had been removed. Pilgrims paid enormous prices for authentic Fremen artifacts, Paul reminded himself. Rich pilgrims counted desert tapestries as treasures, true marks of a hajj.

Paul felt that the barren walls accused him with their fresh gypsum wash. The threadbare condition of the two remaining hangings amplified the sense of guilt.

A narrow shelf occupied the wall on his right. It held a row of portraits— mostly bearded Fremen, some in stillsuits with their catchtubes dangling, some in Imperial uniforms posed against exotic offworld backgrounds. The most common scene was a seascape.

The Fremen on the cushions cleared his throat, forcing Paul to look at him. It was Otheym precisely as the vision had revealed him: neck grown scrawny, a bird thing which appeared too weak to support the large head. The face was a lopsided ruin—networks of crisscrossed scars on the left cheek below a drooping, wet eye, but clear skin on the other side and a straight, blue-in-blue Fremen gaze. A long kedge of a nose bisected the face.

Otheym's cushion sat in the center of a threadbare rug, brown with maroon and gold threads. The cushion fabric betrayed splotches of wear and patching, but every bit of metal around the seated figure shone from polishing—the portrait frames, shelf lip and brackets, the pedestal of a low table on the right.

Paul nodded to the clear half of Otheym's face, said: "Good luck to you and your dwelling place." It was the greeting of an old friend and sietch mate.

"So I see you once more, Usul."

The voice speaking his tribal name whined with an old man's quavering. The dull drooping eye on the ruined side of the face moved above the parchment skin and scars. Gray bristles stubbled that side and the jawline there hung with scabrous peelings. Otheym's mouth twisted as he spoke, the gap exposing silvery metal teeth.

"Muad'Dib always answers the call of a Fedaykin," Paul said.

The woman in the doorway shadows moved, said: "So Stilgar boasts."

She came forward into the light, an older version of the Lichna which the Face Dancer had copied. Paul recalled then that Otheym had married sisters. Her hair was gray, nose grown witch-sharp. Weavers' calluses ran along her forefingers and thumbs. A Fremen woman would've displayed such marks proudly in the sietch days, but she saw his attention on her hands, hid them under a fold of her pale blue robe.

Paul remembered her name then—Dhuri. The shock was he remembered her as a child, not as she'd been in his vision of these moments. It was the whine that edged her voice, Paul told himself. She'd whined even as a child.

"You see me here," Paul said. "Would I be here if Stilgar hadn't approved?" He turned toward Otheym. "I carry your water burden, Otheym. Command me."

This was the straight Fremen talk of sietch brothers.

Otheym produced a shaky nod, almost too much for that thin neck. He lifted a liver-marked left hand, pointed to the ruin of his face. "I caught the splitting disease on Tarahell, Usul," he wheezed. "Right after the victory when we'd all . . ." A fit of coughing stopped his voice.

"The tribe will collect his water soon," Dhuri said. She crossed to Otheym, propped pillows behind him, held his shoulder to steady him until the coughing passed. She wasn't really very old, Paul saw, but a look of lost hopes ringed her mouth, bitterness lay in her eyes.

"I'll summon doctors," Paul said.

Dhuri turned, hand on hip. "We've had medical men, as good as any you could summon." She sent an involuntary glance to the barren wall on her left.

*And the medical men were costly,* Paul thought.

He felt edgy, constrained by the vision but aware that minor differences had crept in. How could he exploit the differences? Time came out of its skein with subtle changes, but the background fabric held oppressive sameness. He knew with terrifying certainty that if he tried to break out of the enclosing pattern here, it'd become a thing of terrible violence. The power in this deceptively gentle flow of Time oppressed him.

"Say what you want of me," he growled.

"Couldn't it be that Otheym needed a friend to stand by him in this time?" Dhuri asked. "Does a Fedaykin have to consign his flesh to strangers?"

*We shared Sietch Tabr,* Paul reminded himself. *She has the right to berate me for apparent callousness.*

"What I can do I will do," Paul said.

Another fit of coughing shook Otheym. When it had passed, he gasped: "There's treachery, Usul. Fremen plot against you." His mouth worked then without sound. Spittle escaped his lips. Dhuri wiped his mouth with a corner of her robe, and Paul saw how her face betrayed anger at such waste of moisture.

Frustrated rage threatened to overwhelm Paul then. *That Otheym should be spent thus! A Fedaykin deserved better.* But no choice remained—not for a Death Commando or his Emperor. They walked occam's razor in this room. The slightest misstep multiplied horrors—not just for themselves, but for all humankind, even for those who would destroy them.

Paul squeezed calmness into his mind, looked at Dhuri. The expression of terrible longing with which she gazed at Otheym strengthened Paul. *Chani must never look at me that way,* he told himself.

"Lichna spoke of a message," Paul said.

"My dwarf," Otheym wheezed. "I bought him on . . . on . . . on a world . . . I forget. He's a human distrans, a toy discarded by the Tleilaxu. He's recorded all the names . . . the traitors . . ."

Otheym fell silent, trembling.

"You speak of Lichna," Dhuri said. "When you arrived, we knew she'd reached you safely. If you're thinking of this new burden Otheym places upon you, Lichna is the sum of that burden. An even exchange, Usul: take the dwarf and go."

Paul suppressed a shudder, closed his eyes. *Lichna!* The real daughter had perished in the desert, a semuta-wracked body abandoned to the sand and the wind.

Opening his eyes, Paul said: "You could've come to me at any time for . . ."

"Otheym stayed away that he might be numbered among those who hate you, Usul," Dhuri said. "The house to the south of us at the end of the street, that is a gathering place for your foes. It's why we took this hovel."

"Then summon the dwarf and we'll leave," Paul said.

"You've not listened well," Dhuri said.

"You must take the dwarf to a safe place," Otheym said, an odd strength in his voice. "He carries the only record of the traitors. No one suspects his talent. They think I keep him for amusement."

"We cannot leave," Dhuri said. "Only you and the dwarf. It's known . . . how poor we are. We've said we're selling the dwarf. They'll take you for the buyer. It's your only chance."

Paul consulted his memory of the vision: in it, he'd left here with the names of the traitors, but never seeing how those names were carried. The dwarf obviously moved under the protection of another oracle. It occurred to Paul then that all creatures must carry some kind of destiny stamped out by purposes of varying strengths, by the fixation of training and disposition. From the moment the Jihad had chosen him, he'd felt himself hemmed in by the forces of a multitude. Their fixed purposes demanded and controlled his course. Any delusions of Free Will he harbored now must be merely the prisoner rattling his cage. His curse lay in the fact that he *saw* the cage. He *saw* it!

He listened now to the emptiness of this house: only the four of them in it—Dhuri, Otheym, the dwarf and himself. He inhaled the fear and tension of his companions, sensed the watchers—his own force hovering in 'thopters far overhead . . . and those others . . . next door.

*I was wrong to hope,* Paul thought. But thinking of hope brought him a twisted *sense* of hope, and he felt that he might yet seize his moment.

"Summon the dwarf," he said.

"Bijaz!" Dhuri called.

"You call me?" The dwarf stepped into the room from the courtyard, an alert expression of worry on his face.

"You have a new master, Bijaz," Dhuri said. She stared at Paul. "You may call him . . . Usul."

"Usul, that's the base of the pillar," Bijaz said, translating. "How can Usul be base when I'm the basest thing living?"

"He always speaks thus," Otheym apologized.

"I don't speak," Bijaz said. "I operate a machine called language. It creaks and groans, but is mine own."

*A Tleilaxu toy, learned and alert,* Paul thought. *The Bene Tleilax never threw away something this valuable.* He turned, studied the dwarf. Round melange eyes returned his stare.

"What other talents have you, Bijaz?" Paul asked.

"I know when we should leave," Bijaz said. "It's a talent few men have. There's a time for endings—and that's a good beginning. Let us begin to go, Usul."

Paul examined his vision memory: no dwarf, but the little man's words fitted the occasion.

"At the door, you called me Sire," Paul said. "You know me, then?"

"You've sired, Sire," Bijaz said, grinning. "You are much more than the base Usul. You're the Atreides emperor, Paul Muad'Dib. And you are my finger." He held up the index finger of his right hand.

"Bijaz!" Dhuri snapped. "You tempt fate."

"I tempt my finger, " Bijaz protested, voice squeaking. He pointed at Usul. "I point at Usul. Is my finger not Usul himself? Or is it a reflection of something more base?" He brought the finger close to his eyes, examined it with a mocking grin, first one side then the other. "Ahhh, it's merely a finger, after all."

"He often rattles on thus," Dhuri said, worry in her voice. "I think it's why he was discarded by the Tleilaxu."

"I'll not be patronized," Bijaz said, "yet I have a new patron. How strange the workings of the finger." He peered at Dhuri and Otheym, eyes oddly bright. "A weak glue bound us, Otheym. A few tears and we part." The dwarf's big feet rasped on the floor as he whirled completely around, stopped facing Paul. "Ahhh, patron! I came the long way around to find you."

Paul nodded.

"You'll be kind, Usul?" Bijaz asked. "I'm a person, you know. Persons come in many shapes and sizes. This be but one of them. I'm weak of muscle, but strong of mouth; cheap to feed, but costly to fill. Empty me as you will, there's still more in me than men put there."

"We've no time for your stupid riddles," Dhuri growled. "You should be gone."

"I'm riddled with conundrums," Bijaz said, "but not all of them stupid. To be gone, Usul, is to be a bygone. Yes? Let us let bygones be bygones. Dhuri speaks truth, and I've the talent for hearing that, too."

"You've truthsense?" Paul asked, determined now to wait out the clockwork of his vision. Anything was better than shattering these moments and producing the new consequences. There remained things for Otheym to say lest Time be diverted into even more horrifying channels.

"I've now-sense," Bijaz said.

Paul noted that the dwarf had grown more nervous. Was the little man aware of things about to happen? Could Bijaz be his own oracle?

"Did you inquire of Lichna?" Otheym asked suddenly, peering up at Dhuri with his one good eye.

"Lichna is safe," Dhuri said.

Paul lowered his head, lest his expression betray the lie. Safe! Lichna was ashes in a secret grave.

"That's good then," Otheym said, taking Paul's lowered head for a nod of agreement. "One good thing among the evils, Usul. I don't like the world we're making, you know that? It was better when we were alone in the desert with only the Harkonnens for enemy."

"There's but a thin line between many an enemy and many a friend," Bijaz said. "Where that line stops, there's no beginning and no end. Let's end it, my friends." He moved to Paul's side, jittered from one foot to the other.

"What's *now*-sense?" Paul asked, dragging out these moments, goading the dwarf.

"Now!" Bijaz said, trembling. "Now! Now!" He tugged at Paul's robe. "Let us go now!"

"His mouth rattles, but there's no harm in him," Otheym said, affection in his voice, the one good eye staring at Bijaz.

"Even a rattle can signal departure," Bijaz said. "And so can tears. Let's be gone while there's time to begin."

"Bijaz, what do you fear?" Paul asked.

"I fear the spirit seeking me now," Bijaz muttered. Perspiration stood out on his forehead. His cheeks twitched. "I fear the one who thinks not and will have no body except mine—and that one gone back into itself! I fear the things I see and the things I do not see."

*This dwarf does possess the power of prescience,* Paul thought. Bijaz shared the terrifying oracle. Did he share the oracle's fate, as well? How potent was the dwarf's power? Did he have the little prescience of those who dabbled in the Dune Tarot? Or was it something greater? How much had he seen?

"Best you go," Dhuri said. "Bijaz is right."

"Every minute we linger," Bijaz said, "prolongs . . . prolongs the present!"

*Every minute I linger defers my guilt,* Paul thought. A worm's poisonous breath, its teeth dripping dust, had washed over him. It had happened long ago, but he inhaled the memory of it now—spice and bitterness. He could sense his own worm waiting—"the urn of the desert."

"These are troubled times," he said, addressing himself to Otheym's judgment of their world.

"Fremen know what to do in time of trouble," Dhuri said.

Otheym contributed a shaky nod.

Paul glanced at Dhuri. He'd not expected gratitude, would have been burdened by it more than he could bear, but Otheym's bitterness and the passionate resentment he saw in Dhuri's eyes shook his resolve. Was *anything* worth this price?

"Delay serves no purpose," Dhuri said.

"Do what you must, Usul," Otheym wheezed.

Paul sighed. The words of the vision had been spoken. "There'll be an accounting," he said to complete it. Turning, he strode from the room, heard Bijaz foot-slapping behind.

"Bygones, bygones," Bijaz muttered as they went. "Let bygones fall where they may. This has been a dirty day."

*The convoluted wording of legalisms grew up around the necessity to hide from
ourselves the violence we intend toward each other. Between depriving a man
of one hour from his life and depriving him of his life there exists only a
difference of degree. You have done violence to him, consumed his energy.
Elaborate euphemisms may conceal your intent to kill, but behind any use of
power over another the ultimate assumption remains: "I feed on your
energy."*

**—Addenda to Orders in Council
The Emperor Paul Muad'Dib**

First Moon stood high over the city as Paul, his shield activated and
shimmering around him, emerged from the cul-de-sac. A wind off the massif
whirled sand and dust down the narrow street, causing Bijaz to blink and shield
his eyes.

"We must hurry," the dwarf muttered. "Hurry! Hurry!"

"You sense danger?" Paul asked, probing.

"I *know* danger!"

An abrupt sense of peril very near was followed almost immediately by a
figure joining them out of a doorway.

Bijaz crouched and whimpered.

It was only Stilgar moving like a war machine, head thrust forward, feet
striking the street solidly.

Swiftly, Paul explained the value of the dwarf, handed Bijaz over to Stilgar.
The pace of the vision moved here with great rapidity. Stilgar sped away with
Bijaz. Security Guards enveloped Paul. Orders were given to send men down
the street toward the house beyond Otheym's. The men hurried to obey,
shadows among shadows.

*More sacrifices,* Paul thought.

"We want live prisoners," one of the guard officers hissed.

The sound was a vision-echo in Paul's ears. It went with solid precision
here—vision/reality, tick for tick. Ornithopters drifted down across the
moon.

The night was full of Imperial troopers attacking.

A soft hiss grew out of the other sounds, climbed to a roar while they still
heard the sibilance. It picked up a terra-cotta glow that hid the stars, engulfed
the moon.

Paul, knowing that sound and glow from the earliest nightmare glimpses of
his vision, felt an odd sense of fulfillment. It went the way it must.

"Stone burner!" someone screamed.

"Stone burner!" The cry was all around him. "Stone burner . . . stone
burner . . ."

Because it was required of him, Paul threw a protective arm across his face,
dove for the low lip of a curb. It already was too late, of course.

Where Otheym's house had been there stood now a pillar of fire, a blinding jet roaring at the heavens. It gave off a dirty brilliance which threw into sharp relief every ballet movement of the fighting and fleeing men, the tipping retreat of ornithopters.

For every member of this frantic throng it was too late.

The ground grew hot beneath Paul. He heard the sound of running stop. Men threw themselves down all around him, every one of them aware that there was no point in running. The first damage had been done: and now they must wait out the extent of the stone burner's potency. The things's radiation, which no man could outrun, already had penetrated their flesh. The peculiar result of stone-burner radiation already was at work in them. What else this weapon might do now lay in the planning of the men who had used it, the men who had defied the Great Convention to use it.

"Gods . . . a stone burner," someone whimpered. "I . . . don't . . . want . . . to . . . be . . . blind."

"Who does?" The harsh voice of a trooper far down the street.

"The Tleilaxu will sell many eyes here," someone near Paul growled. "Now shut up and wait!"

They waited.

Paul remained silent, thinking what this weapon implied. Too much fuel in it and it'd cut its way into the planet's core. Dune's molten level lay deep, but the more dangerous for that. Such pressures released and out of control might split a planet, scattering lifeless bits and pieces through space.

"I think it's dying down a bit," someone said.

"It's just digging deeper," Paul cautioned. "Stay put, all of you. Stilgar will be sending help."

"Stilgar got away?"

"Stilgar got away."

"The ground's hot," someone complained.

"They dared use atomics!" a trooper near Paul protested.

"The sound's diminishing," someone down the street said.

Paul ignored the words, concentrated on his fingertips against the street. He could feel the rolling-rumbling of the thing—deep . . . deep . . .

"My eyes!" someone cried. "I can't see!"

*Someone closer to it than I was,* Paul thought. He still could see to the end of the cul-de-sac when he lifted his head, although there was a mistiness across the scene. A red-yellow glow filled the area where Otheym's house and its neighbor had been. Pieces of adjoining buildings made dark patterns as they crumbled into the glowing pit.

Paul climbed to his feet. He felt the stone burner die, silence beneath him. His body was wet with perspiration against the stillsuit's slickness—too much for the suit to accommodate. The air he drew into his lungs carried the heat and sulfur stench of the burner.

As he looked at the troopers beginning to stand up around him, the mist on Paul's eyes faded into darkness. He summoned up his oracular vision of these moments, then turned and strode along the track that Time had carved for him, fitting himself into the vision so tightly that it could not escape. He felt himself grow aware of this place as a multitudinous possession, reality welded to prediction.

Moans and groans of his troopers arose all around him as the men realized their blindness.

"Hold fast!" Paul shouted. "Help is coming!" And, as the complaints persisted, he said: "This is Muad'Dib! I command you to hold fast! Help comes!"

Silence.

Then, true to his vision, a nearby guardsman said: "Is it truly the Emperor? Which of you can see? Tell me."

"None of us has eyes," Paul said. "They have taken my eyes, as well, but not my vision. I can *see* you standing there, a dirty wall within touching distance on your left. Now wait bravely. Stilgar comes with our friends."

The thwock-thwock of many 'thopters grew louder all around. There was the sound of hurrying feet. Paul *watched* his friends come, matching their sounds to his oracular vision.

"Stilgar!" Paul shouted, waving an arm. "Over here!"

"Thanks to Shai-hulud," Stilgar cried, running up to Paul. "You're not . . ." In the sudden silence, Paul's vision showed him Stilgar staring with an expression of agony at the ruined eyes of his friend and Emperor. "Oh, m'Lord," Stilgar groaned. "Usul . . . Usul . . . Usul . . ."

"What of the stone burner?" one of the newcomers shouted.

"It's ended," Paul said, raising his voice. He gestured. "Get up there now and rescue the ones who were closest to it. Put up barriers. Lively now!" He turned back to Stilgar.

"Do you *see*, m'Lord?" Stilgar asked, wonder in his tone. "How can you see?"

For answer, Paul put a finger out to touch Stilgar's cheek above the stillsuit mouthcap, felt tears. "You need give no moisture to me, old friend," Paul said. "I am not dead."

"But your eyes!"

"They've blinded my body, but not my vision," Paul said. "Ah, Stil, I live in an apocalyptic dream. My steps fit into it so precisely that I fear most of all I will grow bored reliving the thing so exactly."

"Usul, I don't, I don't . . ."

"Don't try to understand it. Accept it. I am in the world beyond this world here. For me, they are the same. I need no hand to guide me. I see every movement all around me. I see every expression of your face. I have no eyes, yet I see."

Stilgar shook his head sharply. "Sire, we must conceal your affliction from—"

"We hide it from no man," Paul said.

"But the law . . ."

"We live by the Atreides Law now, Stil. The Fremen Law that the blind should be abandoned in the desert applies only to the blind. I am not blind. I live in the cycle of being where the war of good and evil has its arena. We are at a turning point in the succession of ages and we have our parts to play."

In a sudden stillness, Paul heard one of the wounded being led past him. "It was terrible," the man groaned, "a great fury of fire."

"None of these men shall be taken into the desert," Paul said. "You hear me, Stil?"

"I hear you, m'Lord."

"They are to be fitted with new eyes at my expense."

"It will be done, m'Lord."

Paul, hearing the awe grow in Stilgar's voice, said: "I will be at the Command 'thopter. Take charge here."

"Yes, m'Lord."

Paul stepped around Stilgar, strode down the street. His vision told him every movement, every irregularity beneath his feet, every face he encountered. He gave orders as he moved, pointing to men of his personal entourage, calling out names, summoning to himself the ones who represented the intimate apparatus of government. He could feel the terror grow behind him, the fearful whispers.

"His eyes!"

"But he looked right at you, called you by name!"

At the Command 'thopter, he deactivated his personal shield, reached into the machine and took the microphone from the hand of a startled communications officer, issued a swift string of orders, thrust the microphone back into the officer's hand. Turning, Paul summoned a weapons specialist, one of the eager and brilliant new breed who remembered sietch life only dimly.

"They used a stone burner," Paul said.

After the briefest pause, the man said: "So I was told, Sire."

"You know what that means, of course."

"The fuel could only have been atomic."

Paul nodded, thinking of how this man's mind must be racing. Atomics. The Great Convention prohibited such weapons. Discovery of the perpetrator would bring down the combined retributive assault of the Great Houses. Old feuds would be forgotten, discarded in the face of this threat and the ancient fears it aroused.

"It cannot have been manufactured without leaving some traces," Paul said. "You will assemble the proper equipment and search out the place where the stone burner was made."

"At once, Sire." With one last fearful glance, the man sped away.

"M'Lord," the communications officer ventured from behind him. "Your eyes . . ."

Paul turned, reached into the 'thopter, returned the command set to his personal band. "Call Chani," he ordered. "Tell her . . . tell her I am alive and will be with her soon."

*Now the forces gather,* Paul thought. And he noted how strong was the smell of fear in the perspiration all around.

*He has gone from Alia,*
*The womb of heaven!*
*Holy, holy, holy!*
*Fire-sand leagues*
*Confront our lord.*
*He can see*
*Without eyes!*
*A demon upon him!*
*Holy, holy, holy*
*Equation:*
*He solved for*
*Martyrdom!*

**—The Moon Falls Down**
**Songs of Muad'Dib**

After seven days of radiating fevered activity, the Keep took on an unnatural quiet. On this morning, there were people about, but they spoke in whispers, heads close together, and they walked softly. Some scurried with an oddly furtive gait. The sight of a guard detail coming in from the forecourt drew questioning looks and frowns at the noise which the newcomers brought with their trampling about and stacking of weapons. The newcomers caught the mood of the interior, though, and began moving in that furtive way.

Talk of the stone burner still floated around: "He said the fire had blue-green in it and a smell out of hell."

"Elpa is a fool! He says he'll commit suicide rather than take Tleilaxu eyes."

"I don't like talk of eyes."

"Muad'Dib passed me and called me by name!"

"How does *He* see without eyes?"

"People are leaving, had you heard? There's great fear. The Naibs say they'll go to Sietch Makab for a Grand Council."

"What've they done with the Panegyrist?"

"I saw them take him into the chamber where the Naibs are meeting. Imagine Korba a prisoner!"

Chani had arisen early, awakened by a stillness in the Keep. Awakening, she'd found Paul sitting up beside her, his eyeless sockets aimed at some formless place beyond the far wall of their bedchamber. What the stone burner had done with its peculiar affinity for eye tissue, all that ruined flesh had been removed. Injections and unguents had saved the stronger flesh around the sockets, but she felt that the radiation had gone deeper.

Ravenous hunger seized her as she sat up. She fed on the food kept by the bedside—spicebread, a heavy cheese.

Paul gestured at the food. "Beloved, there was no way to spare you this. Believe me."

Chani stilled a fit of trembling when he aimed those empty sockets at her. She'd given up asking him to explain. He spoke so oddly: *"I was baptized in sand and it cost me the knack of believing. Who trades in faiths anymore? Who'll buy? Who'll sell?"*

What could he mean by such words?

He refused even to consider Tleilaxu eyes, although he bought them with a lavish hand for the men who'd shared his affliction.

Hunger satisfied, Chani slipped from bed, glanced back at Paul, noted his tiredness. Grim lines framed his mouth. The dark hair stood up, mussed from a sleep that hadn't healed. He appeared so saturnine and remote. The back and forth of waking and sleeping did nothing to change this. She forced herself to turn away, whispered: "My love . . . my love . . ."

He leaned over, pulled her back into the bed, kissed her cheeks. "Soon we'll go back to our desert," he whispered. "Only a few things remain to be done here."

She trembled at the finality in his voice.

He tightened his arms around her, murmured: "Don't fear me, my Sihaya. Forget mystery and accept love. There's no mystery about love. It comes from life. Can't you feel that?"

"Yes."

She put a palm against his chest, counting his heartbeats. His love cried out to the Fremen spirit in her—torrential, outpouring, savage. A magnetic power enveloped her.

"I promise you a thing, beloved," he said. "A child of ours will rule such an empire that mine will fade in comparison. Such achievements of living and art and sublime—"

"We're here now!" she protested, fighting a dry sob. "And . . . I feel we have so little . . . time."

"We have eternity, beloved."

"*You* may have eternity. I have only now."

"But this *is* eternity." He stroked her forehead.

She pressed against him, lips on his neck. The pressure agitated the life in her womb. She felt it stir.

Paul felt it, too. He put a hand on her abdomen, said: "Ahh, little ruler of the universe, wait your time. This moment is mine."

She wondered then why he always spoke of the life within her as singular. Hadn't the medics told him? She searched back in her own memory, curious that the subject had never arisen between them. Surely, he must know she carried twins. She hesitated on the point of raising this question. He *must* know. He knew everything. He knew all the things that were herself. His hands, his mouth—all of him knew her.

Presently, she said: "Yes, love. This is forever . . . this is real." And she closed her eyes tightly lest sight of his dark sockets stretch her soul from paradise to hell. No matter the *rihani* magic in which he'd enciphered their lives, his flesh remained real, his caresses could not be denied.

When they arose to dress for the day, she said: "If the people only knew your love . . ."

But his mood had changed. "You can't build politics on love," he said.

"People aren't concerned with love; it's too disordered. They prefer despotism. Too much freedom breeds chaos. We can't have that, can we? And how do you make despotism lovable?"

"You're not a despot!" she protested, tying her scarf. "Your laws are just."

"Ahh, laws," he said. He crossed to the window, pulled back the draperies as though he could look out. "What's law? Control? Law filters chaos and what drips through? Serenity? Law—our highest ideal and our basest nature. Don't look too closely at the law. Do, and you'll find the rationalized interpretations, the legal casuistry, the precedents of convenience. You'll find the serenity, which is just another word for death."

Chani's mouth drew into a tight line. She couldn't deny his wisdom and sagacity, but these moods frightened her. He turned upon himself and she sensed internal wars. It was as though he took the Fremen maxim, *"Never to forgive—never to forget,"* and whipped his own flesh with it.

She crossed to his side, stared past him at an angle. The growing heat of the day had begun pulling the north wind out of these protected latitudes. The wind painted a false sky full of ochre plumes and sheets of crystal, strange designs in rushing gold and red. High and cold, the wind broke against the Shield Wall with fountains of dust.

Paul felt Chani's warmth beside him. Momentarily, he lowered a curtain of forgetfulness across his vision. He might just be standing here with his eyes closed. Time refused to stand still for him, though. He inhaled darkness— starless, tearless. His affliction dissolved substance until all that remained was astonishment at the way sounds condensed his universe. Everything around him leaned on his lonely sense of hearing, falling back only when he touched objects: the drapery, Chani's hand . . . He caught himself listening for Chani's breaths.

Where was the insecurity of things that were only probable? he asked himself. His mind carried such a burden of mutilated memories. For every instant of reality there existed countless projections, things fated never to be. An invisible self within him remembered the false pasts, their burden threatening at times to overwhelm the present.

Chani leaned against his arm.

He felt his body through her touch: dead flesh carried by time eddies. He reeked of memories that had glimpsed eternity. To see eternity was to be exposed to eternity's whims, oppressed by endless dimensions. The oracle's false immortality demanded retribution: Past and Future became simultaneous.

Once more, the vision arose from its black pit, locked onto him. It was his eyes. It moved his muscles. It guided him into the next moment, the next hour, the next day . . . until he felt himself to be always *there!*

"It's time we were going," Chani said. "The Council . . ."

"Alia will be there to stand in my place."

"Does she know what to do?"

"She knows."

Alia's day began with a guard squadron swarming into the parade yard below her quarters. She stared down at a scene of frantic confusion, clamorous and intimidating babble. The scene became intelligible only when she recognized the prisoner they'd brought: Korba, the Panegyrist.

She made her morning toilet, moving occasionally to the window, keeping watch on the progress of impatience down there. Her gaze kept straying to Korba. She tried to remember him as the rough and bearded commander of the third wave in the battle of Arrakeen. It was impossible. Korba had become an immaculate fop dressed now in a Parato silk robe of exquisite cut. It lay open to the waist, revealing a beautifully laundered ruff and embroidered undercoat set with green gems. A purple belt gathered the waist. The sleeves poking through the robe's armhole slits had been tailored into rivulet ridges of dark green and black velvet.

A few Naibs had come out to observe the treatment accorded a fellow Fremen. They'd brought on the clamor, exciting Korba to protest his innocence. Alia moved her gaze across the Fremen faces, trying to recapture memories of the original men. The present blotted out the past. They'd all become hedonists, samplers of pleasures most men couldn't even imagine.

Their uneasy glances, she saw, strayed often to the doorway into the chamber where they would meet. They were thinking of Muad'Dib's blind-sight, a new manifestation of mysterious powers. By their law, a blind man should be abandoned in the desert, his water given up to Shai-hulud. But eyeless Muad'Dib saw them. They disliked buildings, too, and felt vulnerable in space built above the ground. Give them a proper cave cut from rock, then they could relax—but not here, not with this new Muad'Dib waiting *inside*.

As she turned to go down to the meeting, she saw the letter where she'd left it on a table by the door: the latest message from their mother. Despite the special reverence held for Caladan as the place of Paul's birth, the Lady Jessica had emphasized her refusal to make her planet a stop on the hajj.

"No doubt my son is an epochal figure of history," she'd written, "but I cannot see this as an excuse for submitting to a rabble invasion."

Alia touched the letter, experienced an odd sensation of mutual contact. This paper had been in her mother's hands. Such an archaic device, the letter—but personal in a way no recording could achieve. Written in the Atreides Battle Tongue, it represented an almost invulnerable privacy of communication.

Thinking of her mother afflicted Alia with the usual inward blurring. The spice change that had mixed the psyches of mother and daughter forced her at times to think of Paul as a son to whom she had given birth. The capsule-complex of oneness could present her own father as a lover. Ghost shadows cavorted in her mind, people of possibility.

Alia reviewed the letter as she walked down the ramp to the antechamber where her guard amazons waited.

"You produce a deadly paradox," Jessica had written. "Government cannot be religious and self-assertive at the same time. Religious experience needs a spontaneity which laws inevitably suppress. And you cannot govern without laws. Your laws eventually must replace morality, replace conscience, replace even the religion by which you think to govern. Sacred ritual must spring from praise and holy yearnings which hammer out a significant morality. Government, on the other hand, is a cultural organism particularly attractive to doubts, questions and contentions. I see the day coming when ceremony must take the place of faith and symbolism replaces morality."

The smell of spice-coffee greeted Alia in the antechamber. Four guard amazons in green watchrobes came to attention as she entered. They fell into step behind her, striding firmly in the bravado of their youth, eyes alert for trouble. They had zealot faces untouched by awe. They radiated that special Fremen quality of violence: they could kill casually with no sense of guilt.

*In this, I am different,* Alia thought. *The Atreides name has enough dirt on it without that.*

Word preceded her. A waiting page darted off as she entered the lower hall, running to summon the full guard detail. The hall stretched out windowless and gloomy, illuminated only by a few subdued glowglobes. Abruptly, the doors to the parade yard opened wide at the far end to admit a glaring shaft of daylight. The guard with Korba in their midst wavered into view from the outside with the light behind them.

"Where is Stilgar?" Alia demanded.

"Already inside," one of her amazons said.

Alia led the way into the chamber. It was one of the Keep's more pretentious meeting places. A high balcony with rows of soft seats occupied one side. Across from the balcony, orange draperies had been pulled back from tall windows. Bright sunlight poured through from an open space with a garden and a fountain. At the near end of the chamber on her right stood a dais with a single massive chair.

Moving to the chair, Alia glanced back and up, saw the gallery filled with Naibs.

Household guardsmen packed the open space beneath the gallery, Stilgar moving among them with a quiet word here, a command there. He gave no sign that he'd seen Alia enter.

Korba was brought in, seated at a low table with cushions beside it on the chamber floor below the dais. Despite his finery, the Panegyrist gave the appearance now of a surly, sleepy old man huddled up in his robes as against the outer cold. Two guardsmen took up positions behind him.

Stilgar approached the dais as Alia seated herself.

"Where is Muad'Dib?" he asked.

"My brother has delegated me to preside as Reverend Mother," Alia said.

Hearing this, the Naibs in the gallery began raising their voices in protest.

"Silence!" Alia commanded. In the abrupt quiet, she said: "Is it not Fremen law that a Reverend Mother presides when life and death are at issue?"

As the gravity of her statement penetrated, stillness came over the Naibs, but Alia marked angry stares across the rows of faces. She named them in her mind for discussion in Council—Hobars, Rajifiri, Tasmin, Saajid, Umbu, Legg . . . The names carried pieces of Dune in them: Umbu Sietch, Tasmin Sink, Hobars Gap . . .

She turned her attention to Korba.

Observing her attention, Korba lifted his chin, said: "I protest my innocence."

"Stilgar, read the charges," Alia said.

Stilgar produced a brown spicepaper scroll, stepped forward. He began reading, a solemn flourish in his voice as though to hidden rhythms. He gave the words an incisive quality, clear and full of probity:

". . .that you did conspire with traitors to accomplish the destruction of our Lord and Emperor; that you did meet in vile secrecy with diverse enemies of the realm; that you . . ."

Korba kept shaking his head with a look of pained anger.

Alia listened broodingly, chin planted on her left fist, head cocked to that side, the other arm extended along the chair arm. Bits of the formal procedure began dropping out of her awareness, screened by her own feelings of disquiet.

". . . venerable tradition . . . support of the legions and all Fremen everywhere . . . violence met with violence according to the Law . . . majesty of the Imperial Person . . . forfeit all rights to . . ."

It was nonsense, she thought. Nonsense! All of it—nonsense . . . nonsense . . . nonsense . . .

Stilgar finished: "Thus the issue is brought to judgment."

In the immediate silence, Korba rocked forward, hands gripping his knees, veined neck stretched as though he were preparing to leap. His tongue flicked between his teeth as he spoke.

"Not by word or deed have I been traitor to my Fremen vows! I demand to confront my accuser!"

*A simple enough protest,* Alia thought.

And she saw that it had produced a considerable effect on the Naibs. They knew Korba. He was one of them. To become a Naib, he'd proved his Fremen courage and caution. Not brilliant, Korba, but reliable. Not one to lead a Jihad, perhaps, but a good choice as supply officer. Not a crusader, but one who cherished the old Fremen virtues: *The Tribe is paramount.*

Otheym's bitter words as Paul had recited them swept through Alia's mind. She scanned the gallery. Any of those men might see himself in Korba's place—some for good reason. But an innocent Naib was as dangerous as a guilty one here.

Korba felt it, too. "Who accuses me?" he demanded. "I have a Fremen right to confront my accuser."

"Perhaps you accuse yourself," Alia said.

Before he could mask it, mystical terror lay briefly on Korba's face. It was there for anyone to read: *With her powers, Alia had but to accuse him herself, saying she brought the evidence from the shadow region,* the alam al-mythal.

"Our enemies have Fremen allies," Alia pressed. "Water traps have been destroyed, qanats blasted, plantings poisoned and storage basins plundered . . ."

"And now—they've stolen a worm from the desert, taken it to another world!"

The voice of this intrusion was known to all of them—Muad'Dib. Paul came through the doorway from the hall, pressed through the guard ranks and crossed to Alia's side. Chani, accompanying him, remained on the sidelines.

"M'Lord," Stilgar said, refusing to look at Paul's face.

Paul aimed his empty sockets at the gallery, then down to Korba. "What, Korba—no words of praise?"

Muttering could be heard in the gallery. It grew louder, isolated words and phrases audible: ". . . law for the blind . . . Fremen way . . . in the desert . . . who breaks . . ."

"Who says I'm blind?" Paul demanded. He faced the gallery. "You, Rajifiri? I see you're wearing gold today, and that blue shirt beneath it which still has dust on it from the streets. You always were untidy."

Rajifiri made a warding gesture, three fingers against evil.

"Point those fingers at yourself!" Paul shouted. "We know where the evil is!" He turned back to Korba. "There's guilt on your face, Korba."

"Not my guilt! I may've associated with the guilty, but no . . ." He broke off, shot a frightened look at the gallery.

Taking her cue from Paul, Alia arose, stepped down to the floor of the chamber, advanced to the edge of Korba's table. From a range of less than a meter, she stared down at him, silent and intimidating.

Korba cowered under the burden of eyes. He fidgeted, shot anxious glances at the gallery.

"Whose eyes do you seek up there?" Paul asked.

"You cannot see!" Korba blurted.

Paul put down a momentary feeling of pity for Korba. The man lay trapped in the vision's snare as securely as any of those present. He played a part, no more.

"I don't need eyes to see you," Paul said. And he began describing Korba, every movement, every twitch, every alarmed and pleading look at the gallery.

Desperation grew in Korba.

Watching him, Alia saw he might break any second. Someone in the gallery must realize how near he was to breaking, she thought. Who? She studied the faces of the Naibs, noting small betrayals in the masked faces . . . angers, fears, uncertainties . . . guilts.

Paul fell silent.

Korba mustered a pitiful air of pomposity to plead: "Who accuses me?"

"Otheym accuses you," Alia said.

"But Otheym's dead!" Korba protested.

"How did you know that?" Paul asked. "Through your spy system? Oh, yes! We know about your spies and couriers. We know who brought the stone burner here from Tarahell."

"It was for the defense of the Qizarate!" Korba blurted.

"Is that how it got into traitorous hands?" Paul asked.

"It was stolen and we . . ." Korba fell silent, swallowed. His gaze darted left and right. "Everyone knows I've been the voice of love for Muad'Dib." He stared at the gallery. "How can a dead man accuse a Fremen?"

"Otheym's voice isn't dead," Alia said. She stopped as Paul touched her arm.

"Otheym sent us his voice," Paul said. "It gives the names, the acts of treachery, the meeting places and the times. Do you miss certain faces in the Council of Naibs, Korba? Where are Merkur and Fash? Keke the Lame isn't with us today. And Takim, where is he?"

Korba shook his head from side to side.

"They've fled Arrakis with the stolen worm," Paul said. "Even if I freed you now, Korba, Shai-hulud would have your water for your part in this. Why don't I free you, Korba? Think of all those men whose eyes were taken, the men who cannot see as I see. They have families and friends, Korba. Where could you hide from them?"

"It was an accident," Korba pleaded. "Anyway, they're getting Tleilaxu . . ." Again, he subsided.

"Who knows what bondage goes with metal eyes?" Paul asked.

The Naibs in their gallery began exchanging whispered comments, speaking behind raised hands. They gazed coldly at Korba now.

"Defense of the Qizarate," Paul murmured, returning to Korba's plea. "A device which either destroys a planet or produces J-rays to blind those too near it. Which effect, Korba, did you conceive as a defense? Does the Qizarate rely on stopping the eyes of all observers?"

"It was a curiosity, m'Lord," Korba pleaded. "We knew the Old Law said that only Families could possess atomics, but the Qizarate obeyed . . . obeyed . . ."

"Obeyed you," Paul said. "A curiosity, indeed."

"Even if it's only the voice of my accuser, you must face me with it!" Korba said. "A Fremen has rights."

"He speaks truth, Sire," Stilgar said.

Alia glanced sharply at Stilgar.

"The law is the law," Stilgar said, sensing Alia's protest. He began quoting Fremen Law, interspersing his own comments on how the Law pertained.

Alia experienced the odd sensation she was hearing Stilgar's words before he spoke them. How could he be this credulous? Stilgar had never appeared more official and conservative, more intent on adhering to the Dune Code. His chin was outthrust, aggressive. His mouth chopped. Was there really nothing in him but this outrageous pomposity?

"Korba is a Fremen and must be judged by Fremen Law," Stilgar concluded.

Alia turned away, looked out at the day shadows dropping down the wall across from the garden. She felt drained by frustration. They'd dragged this thing along well into midmorning. Now, what? Korba had relaxed. The Panegyrist's manner said he'd suffered an unjust attack, that everything he'd done had been for love of Muad'Dib. She glanced at Korba, surprised a look of sly self-importance sliding across his face.

He might almost have received a message, she thought. He acted the part of a man who'd heard friends shout: *"Hold fast! Help is on its way!"*

For an instant, they'd held this thing in their hands—the information out of the dwarf, the clues that others were in the plot, the names of informants. But the critical moment had flown. *Stilgar? Surely not Stilgar.* She turned, stared at the old Fremen.

Stilgar met her gaze without flinching.

"Thank you, Stil," Paul said, "for reminding us of the Law."

Stilgar inclined his head. He moved close, shaped silent words in a way he knew both Paul and Alia could read. *I'll wring him dry and then take care of the matter.*

Paul nodded, signaled the guardsmen behind Korba.

"Remove Korba to a maximum security cell," Paul said. "No visitors except counsel. As counsel, I appoint Stilgar."

"Let me choose my own counsel!" Korba shouted.

Paul whirled. "You deny the fairness and judgment of Stilgar?"

"Oh, no, m'Lord, but . . ."

"Take him away!" Paul barked.

The guardsmen lifted Korba off the cushions, herded him out.

With new mutterings, the Naibs began quitting their gallery. Attendants came from beneath the gallery, crossed to the windows and drew the orange draperies. Orange gloom took over the chamber.

"Paul," Alia said.

"When we precipitate violence," Paul said, "it'll be when we have full control of it. Thank you, Stil; you played your part well. Alia, I'm certain, has identified the Naibs who were with him. They couldn't help giving themselves away."

"You cooked this up between you?" Alia demanded.

"Had I ordered Korba slain out of hand, the Naibs would have understood," Paul said. "But this formal procedure without strict adherence to Fremen Law—they felt their own rights threatened. Which Naibs were with him, Alia?"

"Rajifiri for certain," she said, voice low. "And Saajid, but . . ."

"Give Stilgar the complete list," Paul said.

Alia swallowed in a dry throat, sharing the general fear of Paul in this moment. She knew how he moved among them without eyes, but the delicacy of it daunted her. To see their forms in the air of his vision! She sensed her person shimmering for him in a sidereal time whose accord with reality depended entirely on his words and actions. He held them all in the palm of his vision!

"It's past time for your morning audience, Sire," Stilgar said. "Many people—curious . . . afraid . . ."

"Are you afraid, Stil?"

It was barely a whisper: "Yes."

"You're my friend and have nothing to fear from me," Paul said.

Stilgar swallowed. "Yes, m'Lord."

"Alia, take the morning audience," Paul said. "Stilgar, give the signal."

Stilgar obeyed.

A flurry of movement erupted at the great doors. A crowd was pressed back from the shadowy room to permit entrance of officials. Many things began happening all at once: the household guard elbowing and shoving back the press of Supplicants, garishly robed Pleaders trying to break through, shouts, curses. Pleaders waved the papers of their calling. The Clerk of the Assemblage strode ahead of them through the opening cleared by the guard. He carried the List of Preferences, those who'd be permitted to approach the Throne. The Clerk, a wiry Fremen named Tecrube, carried himself with weary cynicism, flaunting his shaven head, clumped whiskers.

Alia moved to intercept him, giving Paul time to slip away with Chani through the private passage behind the dais. She experienced a momentary distrust of Tecrube at the prying curiosity in the stare he sent after Paul.

"I speak for my brother today," she said. "Have the Supplicants approach one at a time."

"Yes, m'Lady." He turned to arrange his throng.

"I can remember a time when you wouldn't have mistaken your brother's purpose here," Stilgar said.

"I was distracted," she said. "There's been a dramatic change in you, Stil. What is it?"

Stilgar drew himself up, shocked. One changed, of course. But dramatically? This was a particular view of himself that he'd never encountered. Drama was a questionable thing. Imported entertainers of dubious loyalty and more dubious virtue were dramatic. Enemies of the Empire employed drama in their attempts to sway the fickle populace. Korba had slipped away from Fremen virtues to employ drama for the Qizarate. And he'd die for that.

"You're being perverse," Stilgar said. "Do you distrust me?"

The distress in his voice softened her expression, but not her tone. "You *know* I don't distrust you. I've always agreed with my brother that once matters were in Stilgar's hands we could safely forget them."

"Then why do you say I've . . . changed?"

"You're preparing to disobey my brother," she said. "I can read it in you. I only hope it doesn't destroy you both."

The first of the Pleaders and Supplicants were approaching now. She turned away before Stilgar could respond. His face, though, was filled with the things she'd sensed in her mother's letter—the replacement of morality and conscience with law.

*"You produce a deadly paradox."*

> Tibana was an apologist for Socratic Christianity, probably a native of IV Anbus who lived between the eighth and ninth centuries before Corrino, likely in the second reign of Dalamak. Of his writings, only a portion survives from which this fragment is taken: "The hearts of all men dwell in the same wilderness."

**—from The Dunebuk of Irulan**

"You are Bijaz," the ghola said, entering the small chamber where the dwarf was held under guard. "I am called Hayt."

A strong contingent of the household guard had come in with the ghola to take over the evening watch. Sand carried by the sunset wind had stung their cheeks while they crossed the outer yard, made them blink and hurry. They could be heard in the passage outside now exchanging the banter and ritual of their tasks.

"You are not Hayt," the dwarf said. "You are Duncan Idaho. I was there when they put your dead flesh into the tank and I was there when they removed it, alive and ready for training."

The ghola swallowed in a throat suddenly dry. The bright glowglobes of the chamber lost their yellowness in the room's green hangings. The light showed beads of perspiration on the dwarf's forehead. Bijaz seemed a creature of odd integrity, as though the purpose fashioned into him by the Tleilaxu were projected out through his skin. There was power beneath the dwarf's mask of cowardice and frivolity.

"Muad'Dib has charged me to question you to determine what it is the Tleilaxu intend you to do here," Hayt said.

"Tleilaxu, Tleilaxu," the dwarf sang. "I am the Tleilaxu, you dolt! For that matter, so are you."

Hayt stared at the dwarf. Bijaz radiated a charismatic alertness that made the observer think of ancient idols.

"You hear that guard outside?" Hayt asked. "If I gave them the order, they'd strangle you."

"Hai! Hai!" Bijaz cried. "What a callous lout you've become. And you said you came seeking truth."

Hayt found he didn't like the look of secret repose beneath the dwarf's expression. "Perhaps I only seek the future," he said.

"Well spoken," Bijaz said. "Now we know each other. When two thieves meet they need no introduction."

"So we're thieves," Hayt said. "What do we steal?"

"Not thieves, but dice," Bijaz said. "And you came here to read my spots. I, in turn, read yours. And lo! You have two faces!"

"Did you really see me go into the Tleilaxu tanks?" Hayt asked, fighting an odd reluctance to ask that question.

"Did I not say it?" Bijaz demanded. The dwarf bounced to his feet. "We had a terrific struggle with you. The flesh did not want to come back."

Hayt felt suddenly that he existed in a dream controlled by some other mind, and that he might momentarily forget this to become lost in the convolutions of that mind.

Bijaz tipped his head slyly to one side, walked all around the ghola, staring up at him. "Excitement kindles old patterns in you," Bijaz said. "You are the pursuer who doesn't want to find what he pursues."

"You're a weapon aimed at Muad'Dib," Hayt said, swiveling to follow the dwarf. "What is it you're to do?"

"Nothing!" Bijaz said, stopping. "I give you a common answer to a common question."

"Then you were aimed at Alia," Hayt said. "Is she your target?"

"They call her Hawt, the Fish Monster, on the outworlds," Bijaz said. "How is it I hear your blood boiling when you speak of her?"

"So they call her Hawt," the ghola said, studying Bijaz for any clue to his purpose. The dwarf made such odd responses.

"She is the virgin-harlot," Bijaz said. "She is vulgar, witty, knowledgeable to a depth that terrifies, cruel when she is most kind, unthinking while she thinks, and when she seeks to build she is as destructive as a coriolis storm."

"So you came here to speak out against Alia," Hayt said.

"Against her?" Bijaz sank to a cushion against the wall. "I came here to be captured by the magnetism of her physical beauty." He grinned, a saurian expression in the big-featured face.

"To attack Alia is to attack her brother," Hayt said.

"That is so clear it is difficult to see," Bijaz said. "In truth, Emperor and sister are one person back to back, one being, half male and half female."

"That is a thing we've heard said by the Fremen of the deep desert," Hayt said. "And those are the ones who've revived the blood sacrifice to Shai-hulud. How is it you repeat their nonsense?"

"You dare say nonsense?" Bijaz demanded. "You, who are both man and mask? Ahh, but the dice cannot read their own spots. I forget this. And you are doubly confused because you serve the Atreides double-being. Your senses are not as close to the answer as your mind is."

"Do you preach that false ritual about Muad'Dib to your guards?" Hayt asked, his voice low. He felt his mind being tangled by the dwarf's words.

"They preach to me!" Bijaz said. "And they pray. Why should they not? All of us should pray. Do we not live in the shadow of the most dangerous creation the universe has ever seen?"

"Dangerous creation . . ."

"Their own mother refuses to live on the same planet with them!"

"Why don't you answer me straight out?" Hayt demanded. "You know we have other ways of questioning you. We'll get our answers . . . one way or another."

"But I have answered you! Have I not said the myth is real? Am I the wind that carries death in its belly? No! I am words! Such words as the lightning which strikes from the sand in a dark sky. I have said: 'Blow out the lamp! Day is here!' And you keep saying: 'Give me a lamp so I can find the day.'"

"You play a dangerous game with me," Hayt said. "Did you think I could not understand these Zensunni ideas? You leave tracks as clear as those of a bird in mud."

Bijaz began to giggle.

"Why do you laugh?" Hayt demanded.

"Because I have teeth and wish I had not," Bijaz managed between giggles. "Having no teeth, I could not gnash them."

"And now I know your target," Hayt said. "You were aimed at me."

"And I've hit it right on!" Bijaz said. "You made such a big target, how could I miss?" He nodded as though to himself. "Now I will sing to you." He began to hum, a keening, whining monotonous theme, repeated over and over.

Hayt stiffened, experiencing odd pains that played up and down his spine. He stared at the face of the dwarf, seeing youthful eyes in an old face. The eyes were the center of a network of knobby white lines which ran to the hollows below his temples. Such a large head! Every feature focused on the pursed-up mouth from which that monotonous noise issued. The sound made Hayt think of ancient rituals, folk memories, old words and customs, half-forgotten meanings in lost mutterings. Something vital was happening here—a bloody play of ideas across Time. Elder ideas lay tangled in the dwarf's singing. It was like a blazing light in the distance, coming nearer and nearer, illuminating life across a span of centuries.

"What are you doing to me?" Hayt gasped.

"You are the instrument I was taught to play," Bijaz said. "I am playing you. Let me tell you the names of the other traitors among the Naibs. They are Bikouros and Cahueit. There is Djedida, who was secretary to Korba. There is Abumojandis, the aide to Bannerjee. Even now, one of them could be sinking a blade into your Muad'Dib."

Hayt shook his head from side to side. He found it too difficult to talk.

"We are like brothers," Bijaz said, interrupting his monotonous hum once more. "We grew in the same tank: I first and then you."

Hayt's metal eyes inflicted him with a sudden burning pain. Flickering red haze surrounded everything he saw. He felt he had been cut away from every immediate sense except the pain, and he experienced his surroundings through a thin separation like windblown gauze. All had become accident, the chance involvement of inanimate matter. His own will was no more than a subtle, shifting thing. It lived without breath and was intelligible only as an inward illumination.

With a clarity born of desperation, he broke through the gauze curtain with the lonely sense of sight. His attention focused like a blazing light under Bijaz. Hayt felt that his eyes cut through layers of the dwarf, seeing the little man as a hired intellect, and beneath that, a creature imprisoned by hungers and cravings which lay huddled in the eyes—layer after layer, until finally, there was only an entity-aspect being manipulated by symbols.

"We are upon a battleground," Bijaz said. "You may speak of it."

His voice freed by the command, Hayt said: "You cannot force me to slay Muad'Dib."

"I have heard the Bene Gesserit say," Bijaz said, "that there is nothing firm, nothing balanced, nothing durable in all the universe—that nothing remains in its state, that each day, sometimes each hour, brings change."

Hayt shook his head dumbly from side to side.

"You believed the silly Emperor was the prize we sought," Bijaz said. "How little you understand our masters, the Tleilaxu. The Guild and Bene Gesserit believe we produce artifacts. In reality, we produce tools and services. Anything can be a tool—poverty, war. War is useful because it is effective in so many areas. It stimulates the metabolism. It enforces government. It diffuses genetic strains. It possesses a vitality such as nothing else in the universe. Only those who recognize the value of war and exercise it have any degree of self-determination."

In an oddly placid voice, Hayt said: "Strange thoughts coming from you, almost enough to make me believe in a vengeful Providence. What restitution was exacted to create you? It would make a fascinating story, doubtless with an even more extraordinary epilogue."

"Magnificent!" Bijaz chortled. "You attack—therefore you have willpower and exercise self-determination."

"You're trying to awaken violence in me," Hayt said in a panting voice.

Bijaz denied this with a shake of the head. "Awaken, yes; violence, no. You are a disciple of awareness by training, so you have said. I have an awareness to awaken in you, Duncan Idaho."

"Hayt!"

"Duncan Idaho. Killer extraordinary. Lover of many women. Swordsman soldier. Atreides field-hand on the field of battle. Duncan Idaho."

"The past cannot be awakened."

"Cannot?"

"It has never been done!"

"True, but our masters defy the idea that something cannot be done. Always, they seek the proper tool, the right application of effort, the services of the proper—"

"You hide your real purpose! You throw up a screen of words and they mean nothing!"

"There is a Duncan Idaho in you," Bijaz said. "It will submit to emotion or to dispassionate examination, but submit it will. This awareness will rise through a screen of suppression and selection out of the dark past which dogs your footsteps. It goads you even now while it holds you back. There exists that being within you upon which awareness must focus and which you will obey."

"The Tleilaxu think I'm still their slave, but I—"

"Quiet, slave!" Bijaz said in that whining voice.

Hayt found himself frozen in silence.

"Now we are down to bedrock," Bijaz said. "I know you feel it. And these are the power-words to manipulate you . . . I think they will have sufficient leverage."

Hayt felt the perspiration pouring down his cheeks, the trembling of his chest and arms, but he was powerless to move.

"One day," Bijaz said, "the Emperor will come to you. He will say: 'She is gone.' The grief mask will occupy his face. He will give water to the dead, as they call their tears hereabouts. And you will say, using my voice: 'Master! Oh, Master!'"

Hayt's jaw and throat ached with the locking of his muscles. He could only twist his head in a brief arc from side to side.

"You will say, 'I carry a message from Bijaz.'" The dwarf grimaced. "Poor Bijaz, who has no mind . . . poor Bijaz, a drum stuffed with messages, an essence for others to use . . . pound on Bijaz and he produces a noise . . ."

Again, he grimaced. "You think me a hypocrite, Duncan Idaho! I am not! I can grieve, too. But the time has come to substitute swords for words."

A hiccup shook Hayt.

Bijaz giggled, then: "Ah, thank you, Duncan, thank you. The demands of the body save us. As the Emperor carries the blood of the Harkonnens in his veins, he will do as we demand. He will turn into a spitting machine, a biter of words that ring with a lovely noise to our masters."

Hayt blinked, thinking how the dwarf appeared like an alert little animal, a thing of spite and rare intelligence. *Harkonnen blood in the Atreides?*

"You think of Beast Rabban, the vile Harkonnen, and you glare," Bijaz said. "You are like the Fremen in this. When words fail, the sword is always at hand, eh? You think of the torture inflicted upon your family by the Harkonnens. And, through his mother, your precious Paul is a Harkonnen! You would not find it difficult to slay a Harkonnen, now would you?"

Bitter frustration coursed through the ghola. Was it anger? Why should this cause anger?

"Ohhh," Bijaz said, and: "Ahhhh, hah! Click-click. There is more to the message. It is a trade the Tleilaxu offer your precious Paul Atreides. Our masters will restore his beloved. A sister to yourself—another ghola."

Hayt felt suddenly that he existed in a universe occupied only by his own heartbeats.

"A ghola," Bijaz said. "It will be the flesh of his beloved. She will bear his children. She will love only him. We can even improve on the original if he so desires. Did ever a man have greater opportunity to regain what he'd lost? It is a bargain he will leap to strike."

Bijaz nodded, eyes drooping as though tiring. Then: "He will be tempted . . . and in his distraction, you will move close. In the instant, you will strike! Two gholas, not one! That is what our masters demand!" The dwarf cleared his throat, nodded once more, said: "Speak."

"I will not do it," Hayt said.

"But Duncan Idaho would," Bijaz said. "It will be the moment of supreme vulnerability for this descendant of the Harkonnens. Do not forget this. You will suggest improvements to his beloved—perhaps a deathless heart, gentler emotions. You will offer asylum as you move close to him—a planet of his choice somewhere beyond the Imperium. Think of it! His beloved restored. No more need for tears and a place of idyls to live out his years."

"A costly package," Hayt said, probing. "He'll ask the price."

"Tell him he must renounce his godhead and discredit the Qizarate. He must discredit himself, his sister."

"Nothing more?" Hayt asked, sneering.

"He must relinquish his CHOAM holdings, naturally."

"Naturally."

"And if you're not yet close enough to strike, speak of how much the Tleilaxu admire what he has taught them about the possibilities of religion. Tell him the Tleilaxu have a department of religious engineering, shaping religions to particular needs."

"How very clever," Hayt said.

"You think yourself free to sneer and disobey me," Bijaz said. He cocked his head slyly to one side: "Don't deny it . . ."

"They made you well, little animal," Hayt said.

"And you as well," the dwarf said. "You will tell him to hurry. Flesh decays and her flesh must be preserved in a cryological tank."

Hayt felt himself floundering, caught in a matrix of objects he could not recognize. The dwarf appeared so sure of himself! There had to be a flaw in the Tleilaxu logic. In making their ghola, they'd keyed him to the voice of Bijaz, but . . . But what? Logic/matrix/object . . . How easy it was to mistake clear reasoning for correct reasoning! Was Tleilaxu logic distorted?

Bijaz smiled, listened, as though to a hidden voice. "Now you will forget," he said. "When the moment comes, you will remember. He will say: 'She is gone.' Duncan Idaho will awaken then."

The dwarf clapped his hands together.

Hayt grunted, feeling that he had been interrupted in the middle of a thought . . . or perhaps in the middle of a sentence. What was it? Something about . . . targets?

"You think to confuse me and manipulate me," he said.

"How is that?" Bijaz asked.

"I am your target and you can't deny it," Hayt said.

"I would not think of denying it."

"What is it you'd try to do with me?"

"A kindness," Bijaz said. "A simple kindness."

*The sequential nature of actual events is not illuminated with lengthy precision by the powers of prescience except under the most extraordinary circumstances. The oracle grasps incidents cut out of their historic chain. Eternity moves. It inflicts itself upon the oracle and the supplicant alike. Let Muad'Dib's subjects doubt his majesty and his oracular visions. Let them deny his powers. Let them never doubt Eternity.*

**—The Dune Gospels**

Hayt watched Alia emerge from her temple and cross the plaza. Her guard was bunched close, fierce expressions on their faces to mask the lines molded by good living and complacency.

A heliograph of 'thopter wings flashed in the bright afternoon sun above the temple, part of the Royal Guard with Muad'Dib's fist-symbol on its fuselage.

Hayt returned his gaze to Alia. She looked out of place here in the city, he thought. Her proper setting was the desert—open, untrammeled space. An odd thing about her came back to him as he watched her approach: Alia appeared thoughtful only when she smiled. It was a trick of the eyes, he decided, recalling a cameo memory of her as she'd appeared at the reception for the Guild

Ambassador: haughty against a background of music and brittle conversation among extravagant gowns and uniforms. And Alia had been wearing white, dazzling, a bright garment of chastity. He had looked down upon her from a window as she crossed an inner garden with its formal pond, its fluting fountains, fronds of pampas grass and a white belvedere.

Entirely wrong . . . all wrong. She belonged in the desert.

Hayt drew in a ragged breath. Alia moved out of his view then as she did now. He waited, clenching and unclenching his fists. The interview with Bijaz had left him uneasy.

He heard Alia's entourage pass outside the room where he waited. She went into the Family quarters.

Now he tried to focus on the thing about her which troubled him. The way she'd walked across the plaza? Yes. She'd moved like a hunted creature fleeing some predator. He stepped out onto the connecting balcony, walked along it behind the plasmeld sunscreen, stopped while still in concealing shadows. Alia stood at the balustrade overlooking her temple.

He looked where she was looking—out over the city. He saw rectangles, blocks of color, creeping movements of life and sound. Structures gleamed, shimmered. Heat patterns spiraled off the rooftops. There was a boy across the way bouncing a ball in a cul-de-sac formed by a buttressed massif at a corner of the temple. Back and forth the ball went.

Alia, too, watched the ball. She felt a compelling identity with that ball—back and forth . . . back and forth. She sensed herself bouncing through corridors of Time.

The potion of melange she'd drained just before leaving the temple was the largest she'd ever attempted—a massive overdose. Even before beginning to take effect, it had terrified her.

*Why did I do it?* she asked herself.

One made a choice between dangers. Was that it? This was the way to penetrate the fog spread over the future by that damnable Dune Tarot. A barrier existed. It must be breached. She had acted out of a necessity to see where it was her brother walked with his eyeless stride.

The familiar melange fugue state began creeping into her awareness. She took a deep breath, experienced a brittle form of calm, poised and selfless.

*Possession of second sight has a tendency to make one a dangerous fatalist,* she thought. Unfortunately, there existed no abstract leverage, no calculus of prescience. Visions of the future could not be manipulated as formulas. One had to enter them, risking life and sanity.

A figure moved from the harsh shadows of the adjoining balcony. The ghola! In her heightened awareness, Alia saw him with intense clarity—the dark, lively features dominated by those glistening metal eyes. He was a union of terrifying opposites, something put together in a shocking, linear way. He was shadow and blazing light, a product of the process which had revived his dead flesh . . . and of something intensely pure . . . innocent.

He was innocence under siege!

"Have you been there all along, Duncan?" she asked.

"So I'm to be Duncan," he said. "Why?"

"Don't question me," she said.

And she thought, looking at him, that the Tleilaxu had left no corner of their ghola unfinished.

"Only gods can safely risk perfection," she said. "It's a dangerous thing for a man."

"Duncan died," he said, wishing she would not call him that. "I am Hayt."

She studied his artificial eyes, wondering what they saw. Observed closely, they betrayed tiny black pockmarks, little wells of darkness in the glittering metal. Facets! The universe shimmered around her and lurched. She steadied herself with a hand on the sun-warmed surface of the balustrade. Ahhhh, the melange moved swiftly.

"Are you ill?" Hayt asked. He moved closer, the steely eyes opened wide, staring.

*Who spoke?* she wondered. Was it Duncan Idaho? Was it the mentat-ghola or the Zensunni philosopher? Or was it a Tleilaxu pawn more dangerous than any Guild Steersman? Her brother knew.

Again, she looked at the ghola. There was something inactive about him now, a latent something. He was saturated with waiting and with powers beyond their common life.

"Out of my mother, I am like the Bene Gesserit," she said. "Do you know that?"

"I know it."

"I use their powers, think as they think. Part of me knows the sacred urgency of the breeding program . . . and its products."

She blinked, feeling part of her awareness begin to move freely in Time.

"It's said that the Bene Gesserit never let go," he said. And he watched her closely, noting how white her knuckles were where she gripped the edge of the balcony.

"Have I stumbled?" she asked.

He marked how deeply she breathed, with tension in every movement, the glazed appearance of her eyes.

"When you stumble," he said, "you may regain your balance by jumping beyond the thing that tripped you."

"The Bene Gesserit stumbled," she said. "Now they wish to regain their balance by leaping beyond my brother. They want Chani's baby . . . or mine."

"Are you with child?"

She struggled to fix herself in a timespace relationship to this question. With child? When? Where?

"I see . . . my child," she whispered.

She moved away from the balcony's edge, turned her head to look at the ghola. He had a face of salt, bitter eyes—two circles of glistening lead . . . and, as he turned away from the light to follow her movement, blue shadows.

"What . . . do you see with such eyes?" she whispered.

"What other eyes see," he said.

His words rang in her ears, stretching her awareness. She felt that she reached across the universe—such a stretching . . . out . . . out. She lay intertwined with all Time.

"You've taken the spice, a large dose," he said.

"Why can't I see him?" she muttered. The womb of all creation held her captive. "Tell me, Duncan, why I cannot see him."

"Who can't you see?"

"I cannot see the father of my children. I'm lost in a Tarot fog. Help me."

Mentat logic offered its prime computation, and he said: "The Bene Gesserit want a mating between you and your brother. It would lock the genetic . . ."

A wail escaped her. "The egg in the flesh," she gasped. A sensation of chill swept over her, followed by intense heat. The unseen mate of her darkest dreams! Flesh of her flesh that the oracle could not reveal—would it come to that?

"Have you risked a dangerous dose of the spice?" he asked. Something within him fought to express the utmost terror at the thought that an Atreides woman might die, that Paul might face him with the knowledge that a female of the royal family had . . . gone.

"You don't know what it's like to hunt the future," she said. "Sometimes I glimpse myself . . . but I get in my own way. I cannot see through myself." She lowered her head, shook it from side to side.

"How much of the spice did you take?" he asked.

"Nature abhors prescience," she said, raising her head. "Did you know that, Duncan?"

He spoke softly, reasonably, as to a small child: "Tell me how much of the spice you took." He took hold of her shoulder with his left hand.

"Words are such gross machinery, so primitive and ambiguous," she said. She pulled away from his hand.

"You must tell me," he said.

"Look at the Shield Wall," she commanded, pointing. She sent her gaze along her own outstretched hand, trembled as the landscape crumbled in an overwhelming vision—a sandcastle destroyed by invisible waves. She averted her eyes, was transfixed by the appearance of the ghola's face. His features crawled, became aged, then young . . . aged . . . young. He was life itself, assertive, endless . . . She turned to flee, but he grabbed her left wrist.

"I am going to summon a doctor," he said.

"No! You must let me have the vision! I have to know!"

"You are going inside now," he said.

She stared down at his hand. Where their flesh touched, she felt an electric presence that both lured and frightened her. She jerked free, gasped: "You can't hold the whirlwind!"

"You must have medical help!" he snapped.

"Don't you understand?" she demanded. "My vision's incomplete, just fragments. It flickers and jumps. I have to remember the future. Can't you see that?"

"What is the future if you die?" he asked, forcing her gently into the Family chambers.

"Words . . . words," she muttered. "I can't explain it. One thing is the occasion of another thing, but there's no cause . . . no effect. We can't leave the universe as it was. Try as we may, there's a gap."

"Stretch out here," he commanded.

*He is so dense!* she thought.

Cool shadows enveloped her. She felt her own muscles crawling like worms—a firm bed that she knew to be insubstantial. Only space was permanent. Nothing else had substance. The bed flowed with many bodies, all of them her own. Time became a multiple sensation, overloaded. It presented no single reaction for her to abstract. It was Time. It moved. The whole universe slipped backward, forward, sideways.

"It has no thing-aspect," she explained. "You can't get under it or around it. There's no place to get leverage."

There came a fluttering of people all around her. Many someones held her left hand. She looked at her own moving flesh, followed a twining arm out to a fluid mask of face: Duncan Idaho! His eyes were . . . wrong, but it was Duncan—child-man-adolescent-child-man-adolescent . . . Every line of his features betrayed concern for her.

"Duncan, don't be afraid," she whispered.

He squeezed her hand, nodded. "Be still," he said.

And he thought: *She must not die! She must not! No Atreides woman can die!* He shook his head sharply. Such thoughts defied mentat logic. Death was a necessity that life might continue.

*The ghola loves me,* Alia thought.

The thought became bedrock to which she might cling. He was a familiar face with a solid room behind him. She recognized one of the bedrooms in Paul's suite.

A fixed, immutable person did something with a tube in her throat. She fought against retching.

"We got her in time," a voice said, and she recognized the tones of a Family medic. "You should've called me sooner." There was suspicion in the medic's voice. She felt the tube slide out of her throat—a snake, a shimmering cord.

"The slapshot will make her sleep," the medic said. "I'll send one of her attendants to—"

"I will stay with her," the ghola said.

"That is not seemly!" the medic snapped.

"Stay . . . Duncan," Alia whispered.

He stroked her hand to tell her he'd heard. "M'Lady," the medic said, "it'd be better if . . ."

"You do not tell me what is best," she rasped. Her throat ached with each syllable.

"M'Lady," the medic said, voice accusing, "*you* know the dangers of consuming too much melange. I can only assume someone gave it to you without—"

"You are a fool," she rasped. "Would you deny me my visions? I knew what I took and why." She put a hand to her throat. "Leave us. At once!"

The medic pulled out of her field of vision, said: "I will send word to your brother."

She felt him leave, turned her attention to the ghola. The vision lay clearly in her awareness now, a culture medium in which the present grew outward. She sensed the ghola move in that play of Time, no longer cryptic, fixed now against a recognizable background.

*He is the crucible,* she thought. *He is danger and salvation.*

And she shuddered, knowing she saw the vision her brother had seen. Unwanted tears burned her eyes. She shook her head sharply. No tears! They wasted moisture and, worse, distracted the harsh flow of vision. Paul must be stopped! Once, just once, she had bridged Time to place her voice where he would pass. But stress and mutability would not permit that here. The web of Time passed through her brother now like rays of light through a lens. He stood at the focus and he knew it. He had gathered all the lines to himself and would not permit them to escape or change.

"Why?" she muttered. "Is it hate? Does he strike out at Time itself because it hurt him? Is that it . . . hate?"

Thinking he heard her speak his name, the ghola said: "M'Lady?"

"If I could only burn this thing out of me!" she cried. "I didn't want to be different."

"Please, Alia," he murmured. "Let yourself sleep."

"I wanted to be able to laugh," she whispered. Tears slid down her cheeks. "But I'm sister to an Emperor who's worshiped as a god. People fear me. I never wanted to be feared."

He wiped the tears from her face.

"I don't want to be part of history," she whispered. "I just want to be loved . . . and to love."

"You are loved," he said.

"Ahhh, loyal, loyal Duncan," she said.

"Please, don't call me that," he pleaded.

"But you are," she said. "And loyalty is a valued commodity. It can be sold . . . not bought, but sold."

"I don't like your cynicism," he said.

"Damn your logic! It's true!"

"Sleep," he said.

"Do you love me, Duncan?" she asked.

"Yes."

"Is that one of those lies," she asked, "one of the lies that are easier to believe than the truth? Why am I afraid to believe you?"

"You fear my differences as you fear your own."

"Be a man, not a mentat!" she snarled.

"I am a mentat and a man."

"Will you make me your woman, then?"

"I will do what love demands."

"And loyalty?"

"And loyalty."

"That's where you're dangerous," she said.

Her words disturbed him. No sign of the disturbance arose to his face, no muscle trembled—but she knew it. Vision-memory exposed the disturbance. She felt she had missed part of the vision, though, that she should remember something else from the future. There existed another perception which did not go precisely by the senses, a thing which fell into her head from nowhere the way prescience did. It lay in the Time shadows—infinitely painful.

Emotion! That was it—emotion! It had appeared in the vision, not directly, but as a product from which she could infer what lay behind. She had been possessed by emotion—a single constriction made up of fear, grief and love. They lay there in the vision, all collected into a single epidemic body, overpowering and primordial.

"Duncan, don't let me go," she whispered.

"Sleep," he said. "Don't fight it."

"I must . . . I must. He's the bait in his own trap. He's the servant of power and terror. Violence . . . deification is a prison enclosing him. He'll lose . . . everything. It'll tear him apart."

"You speak of Paul?"

"They drive him to destroy himself," she gasped, arching her back. "Too much weight, too much grief. They seduce him away from love." She sank back to the bed. "They're creating a universe where he won't permit himself to live."

"Who is doing this?"

"He is! Ohhh, you're so dense. He's part of the pattern. And it's too late . . . too late . . . too late . . ."

As she spoke, she felt her awareness descend, layer by layer. It came to rest directly behind her navel. Body and mind separated and merged in a storehouse of relic visions—moving, moving . . . She heard a fetal heartbeat, a child of the future. The melange still possessed her, then, setting her adrift in Time. She knew she had tasted the life of a child not yet conceived. One thing certain about this child—it would suffer the same awakening she had suffered. It would be an aware, thinking entity before birth.

*There exists a limit to the force even the most powerful may apply without destroying themselves. Judging this limit is the true artistry of government. Misuse of power is the fatal sin. The law cannot be a tool of vengeance, never a hostage, nor a fortification against the martyrs it has created. You cannot threaten any individual and escape the consequences.*

**—Muad'Dib on Law
The Stilgar Commentary**

Chani stared out at the morning desert framed in the fault cleft below Sietch Tabr. She wore no stillsuit, and this made her feel unprotected here in the desert. The sietch grotto's entrance lay hidden in the buttressed cliff above and behind her.

The desert . . . the desert . . . She felt that the desert had followed her wherever she had gone. Coming back to the desert was not so much a homecoming as a turning around to see what had always been there.

A painful constriction surged through her abdomen. The birth would be soon. She fought down the pain, wanting this moment alone with her desert.

Dawn stillness gripped the land. Shadows fled among the dunes and terraces of the Shield Wall all around. Daylight lunged over the high scarp and plunged her up to her eyes in a bleak landscape stretching beneath a washed blue sky. The scene matched the feeling of dreadful cynicism which had tormented her since the moment she'd learned of Paul's blindness.

*Why are we here?* she wondered.

It was not a hajra, a journey of seeking. Paul sought nothing here except, perhaps, a place for her to give birth. He had summoned odd companions for this journey, she thought—Bijaz, the Tleilaxu dwarf; the ghola, Hayt, who might be Duncan Idaho's revenant; Edric, the Guild Steersman-Ambassador; Gauis Helen Mohiam, the Bene Gesserit Reverend Mother he so obviously hated; Lichna, Otheym's strange daughter, who seemed unable to move beyond the watchful eyes of guards; Stilgar, her uncle of the Naibs, and his favorite wife, Harah . . . and Irulan . . . Alia . . .

The sound of wind through the rocks accompanied her thoughts. The desert day had become yellow on yellow, tan on tan, gray on gray.

Why such a strange mixture of companions?

"We have forgotten," Paul had said in response to her question, "that the word 'company' originally meant traveling companions. We are a company."

"But what value are they?"

"There!" he'd said, turning his frightful sockets toward her. "We've lost that clear, single-note of living. If it cannot be bottled, beaten, pointed or hoarded, we give it no value."

Hurt, she'd said: "That's not what I meant."

"Ahhh, dearest one," he'd said, soothing, "we are so money-rich and so life-poor. I am evil, obstinate, stupid . . ."

"You are not!"

"That, too, is true. But my hands are blue with time. I think . . . I think I tried to invent life, not realizing it'd already been invented."

And he'd touched her abdomen to feel the new life there.

Remembering, she placed both hands over her abdomen and trembled, sorry that she'd asked Paul to bring her here.

The desert wind had stirred up evil odors from the fringe plantings which anchored the dunes at the cliff base. Fremen superstition gripped her: *evil odors, evil times.* She faced into the wind, saw a worm appear outside the plantings. It arose like the prow of a demon ship out of the dunes, threshed sand, smelled the water deadly to its kind, and fled beneath a long, burrowing mound.

She hated the water then, inspired by the worm's fear. Water, once the spirit-soul of Arrakis, had become a poison. Water brought pestilence. Only the desert was clean.

Below her, a Fremen work gang appeared. They climbed to the sietch's middle entrance, and she saw that they had muddy feet.

*Fremen with muddy feet!*

The children of the sietch began singing to the morning above her, their voices piping from the upper entrance. The voices made her feel time fleeing from her like hawks before the wind. She shuddered.

What storms did Paul *see* with his eyeless vision?

She sensed a vicious madman in him, someone weary of songs and polemics.

The sky, she noted, had become crystal gray filled with alabaster rays, bizarre designs etched across the heavens by windborne sand. A line of gleaming white in the south caught her attention. Eyes suddenly alerted, she interpreted the sign: White sky in the south: Shai-hulud's mouth. A storm came, big wind. She felt the warning breeze, a crystal blowing of sand against her cheeks. The incense of death came on the wind: odors of water flowing in qanats, sweating sand, flint. The water—that was why Shai-hulud sent his coriolis wind.

Hawks appeared in the cleft where she stood, seeking safety from the wind. They were brown as the rocks and with scarlet in their wings. She felt her spirit go out to them: they had a place to hide; she had none.

"M'Lady, the wind comes!"

She turned, saw the ghola calling to her outside the upper entrance to the sietch. Fremen fears gripped her. Clean death and the body's water claimed for the tribe, these she understood. But . . . something brought back from death . . .

Windblown sand whipped at her, reddened her cheeks. She glanced over her shoulder at the frightful band of dust across the sky. The desert beneath the storm had taken on a tawny, restless appearance as though dune waves beat on a tempest shore the way Paul had once described a sea. She hesitated, caught by a feeling of the desert's transience. Measured against eternity, this was no more than a caldron. Dune surf thundered against cliffs.

The storm out there had become a universal thing for her—all the animals hiding from it . . . nothing left of the desert but its own private sounds: blown sand scraping along rock, a wind-surge whistling, the gallop of a boulder tumbled suddenly from its hill—then! somewhere out of sight, a capsized worm thumping its idiot way aright and slithering off to its dry depths.

It was only a moment as her life measured time, but in that moment she felt this planet being swept away—cosmic dust, part of other waves.

"We must hurry," the ghola said from right beside her.

She sensed fear in him then, concern for her safety.

"It'll shred the flesh from your bones," he said, as though he needed to explain such a storm to *her*.

Her fear of him dispelled by his obvious concern, Chani allowed the ghola to help her up the rock stairway to the sietch. They entered the twisting baffle which protected the entrance. Attendants opened the moisture seals, closed them behind.

Sietch odors assaulted her nostrils. The place was a ferment of nasal memories—the warren closeness of bodies, rank esters of the reclamation stills, familiar food aromas, the flinty burning of machines at work . . . and through it all, the omnipresent spice; melange everywhere.

She took a deep breath. "Home."

The ghola took his hand from her arm, stood aside, a patient figure now, almost as though turned off when not in use. Yet . . . he watched.

Chani hesitated in the entrance chamber, puzzled by something she could not name. This was truly her home. As a child, she'd hunted scorpions here by glowglobe light. Something was changed, though . . .

"Shouldn't you be going to your quarters, m'Lady?" the ghola asked.

As though ignited by his words, a rippling birth constriction seized her abdomen. She fought against revealing it.

"M'Lady?" the ghola said.

"Why is Paul afraid for me to bear our children?" she asked.

"It is a natural thing to fear for your safety," the ghola said.

She put a hand to her cheek where the sand had reddened it. "And he doesn't fear for the children?"

"M'Lady, he cannot think of a child without remembering that your firstborn was slain by the Sardaukar."

She studied the ghola—flat face, unreadable mechanical eyes. Was he truly Duncan Idaho, this creature? Was he friend to anyone? Had he spoken truthfully now?

"You should be with the medics," the ghola said.

Again, she heard the fear for her safety in his voice. She felt abruptly that her mind lay undefended, ready to be invaded by shocking perceptions.

"Hayt, I'm afraid," she whispered. "Where is my Usul?"

"Affairs of state detain him," the ghola said.

She nodded, thinking of the government apparatus which had accompanied them in a great flight of ornithopters. Abruptly, she realized what puzzled her about the sietch: outworld odors. The clerks and aides had brought their own perfumes into this environment, aromas of diet and clothing, of exotic toiletries. They were an undercurrent of odors here.

Chani shook herself, concealing an urge to bitter laughter. Even the smells changed in Muad'Dib's presence!

"There were pressing matters which he could not defer," the ghola said, misreading her hesitation.

"Yes . . . yes, I understand. I came with that swarm, too."

Recalling the flight from Arrakeen, she admitted to herself now that she had not expected to survive it. Paul had insisted on piloting his own 'thopter. Eyeless, he had guided the machine here. After that experience, she knew nothing he did could surprise her.

Another pain fanned out through her abdomen.

The ghola saw her indrawn breath, the tightening of her cheeks, said: "Is it your time?"

"I . . . yes, it is."

"You must not delay," he said. He grasped her arm, hurried her down the hall.

She sensed panic in him, said: "There's time."

He seemed not to hear. "The Zensunni approach to birth," he said, urging her even faster, "is to wait without purpose in the state of highest tension. Do not compete with what is happening. To compete is to prepare for failure. Do not be trapped by the need to achieve anything. This way, you achieve everything."

While he spoke, they reached the entrance to her quarters. He thrust her through the hangings, cried out: "Harah! Harah! It is Chani's time. Summon the medics!"

His call brought attendants running. There was a great bustling of people in which Chani felt herself an isolated island of calm . . . until the next pain came.

Hayt, dismissed to the outer passage, took time to wonder at his own actions. He felt fixated at some point of time where all truths were only temporary. Panic lay beneath his actions, he realized. Panic centered not on the possibility that Chani might die, but that Paul should come to him afterward . . . filled with grief . . . his loved one . . . gone . . . gone . . .

*Something cannot emerge from nothing,* the ghola told himself. *From what does this panic emerge?*

He felt that his mentat faculties had been dulled, let out a long, shuddering breath. A psychic shadow passed over him. In the emotional darkness of it, he felt himself waiting for some absolute sound—the snap of a branch in a jungle.

A sigh shook him. Danger had passed without striking.

Slowly, marshaling his powers, shedding bits of inhibition, he sank into mentat awareness. He forced it—not the best way—but somehow necessary. Ghost shadows moved within him in place of people. He was a trans-shipping station for every datum he had ever encountered. His being was inhabited by creatures of possibility. They passed in revue to be compared, judged.

Perspiration broke out on his forehead.

Thoughts with fuzzy edges feathered away into darkness—unknown. Infinite systems! A mentat could not function without realizing he worked in infinite systems. Fixed knowledge could not surround the infinite. *Everywhere* could not be brought into finite perspective. Instead, he must *become* the infinite—momentarily.

In one gestalten spasm, he had it, seeing Bijaz seated before him blazing from some inner fire.

*Bijaz!*

The dwarf had done something to him!

Hayt felt himself teetering on the lip of a deadly pit. He projected the mentat computation line forward, seeing what could develop out of his own actions.

"A compulsion!" he gasped. "I've been rigged with a compulsion!"

A blue-robed courier, passing as Hayt spoke, hesitated. "Did you say something, sirra?"

Not looking at him, the ghola nodded. "I said everything."

> *There was a man so wise,*
> *He jumped into*
> *A sandy place*
> *And burnt out both his eyes!*
> *And when he knew his eyes were gone,*
> *He offered no complaint.*
> *He summoned up a vision*
> *And made himself a saint.*

> **—Children's Verse**
> **from History of Muad'Dib**

Paul stood in darkness outside the sietch. Oracular vision told him it was night, that moonlight silhouetted the shrine atop Chin Rock high on his left. This was a memory-saturated place, his first sietch, where he and Chani . . .

*I must not think of Chani,* he told himself.

The thinning cup of his vision told him of changes all around—a cluster of palms far down to the right, the black-silver line of a qanat carrying water through dunes piled up by that morning's storm.

*Water flowing in the desert!* He recalled another kind of water flowing in a river of his birthworld, Caladan. He hadn't realized then the treasure of such a flow, even the murky slithering in a qanat across a desert basin. Treasure.

With a delicate cough, an aide came up behind.

Paul held out his hands for a magnaboard with a single sheet of metallic paper on it. He moved as sluggishly as the qanat's water. The vision flowed, but he found himself increasingly reluctant to move with it.

"Pardon, Sire," the aide said. "The Semboule Treaty—your signature?"

"I can read it!" Paul snapped. He scrawled "Atreides Imper." in the proper place, returned the board, thrusting it directly into the aide's outstretched hand, aware of the fear this inspired.

The man fled.

Paul turned away. *Ugly, barren land!* He imagined it sun-soaked and monstrous with heat, a place of sandslides and the drowned darkness of dust pools, blowdevils unreeling tiny dunes across the rocks, their narrow bellies full of ochre crystals. But it was a rich land, too: big, exploding out of narrow places with vistas of storm-trodden emptiness, rampart cliffs and tumbledown ridges.

All it required was water . . . and love.

Life changed those irascible wastes into shapes of grace and movement, he thought. That was the message of the desert. Contrast stunned him with realization. He wanted to turn to the aides massed in the sietch entrance, shout at them: If you need something to worship, then worship life—all life, every last crawling bit of it! We're all in this beauty together!

They wouldn't understand. In the desert, they were endlessly desert. Growing things performed no green ballet for them.

He clenched his fists at his sides, trying to halt the vision. He wanted to flee from his own mind. It was a beast come to devour him! Awareness lay in him, sodden, heavy with all the living it had sponged up, saturated with too many experiences.

Desperately, Paul squeezed his thoughts outward.

*Stars!*

Awareness turned over at the thought of all those stars above him—an infinite volume. A man must be half mad to imagine he could rule even a teardrop of that volume. He couldn't begin to imagine the number of subjects his Imperium claimed.

Subjects? Worshipers and enemies, more likely. Did any among them see beyond rigid beliefs? Where was one man who'd escaped the narrow destiny of his prejudices? Not even an Emperor escaped. He'd lived a take-everything life, tried to create a universe in his own image. But the exultant universe was breaking across him at last with its silent waves.

*I spit on Dune!* he thought. *I give it my moisture!*

This myth he'd made out of intricate movements and imagination, out of moonlight and love, out of prayers older than Adam, and gray cliffs and crimson shadows, laments and rivers of martyrs—what had it come to at last? When the waves receded, the shores of Time would spread out there clean, empty, shining with infinite grains of memory and little else. Was this the golden genesis of man?

Sand scuffed against rocks told him that the ghola had joined him.

"You've been avoiding me today, Duncan," Paul said.

"It's dangerous for you to call me that," the ghola said.

"I know."

"I . . . came to warn you, m'Lord."

"I know."

The story of the compulsion Bijaz had put on him poured from the ghola then.

"Do you know the nature of the compulsion?" Paul asked.

"Violence."

Paul felt himself arriving at a place which had claimed him from the beginning. He stood suspended. The Jihad had seized him, fixed him onto a glidepath from which the terrible gravity of the Future would never release him.

"There'll be no violence from Duncan," Paul whispered.

"But, Sire . . ."

"Tell me what you see around us," Paul said.

"M'Lord?"

"The desert—how is it tonight?"

"Don't you *see* it?"

"I have no eyes, Duncan."

"But . . ."

"I've only my vision," Paul said, "and wish I didn't have it. I'm dying of prescience, did you know that, Duncan?"

"Perhaps . . . what you fear won't happen," the ghola said.

"What? Deny my own oracle? How can I when I've seen it fulfilled thousands of times? People call it a power, a gift. It's an affliction! It won't let me leave my life where I found it!"

"M'Lord," the ghola muttered, "I . . . it isn't . . . young master, you don't . . . I . . ." He fell silent.

Paul sensed the ghola's confusion, said: "What'd you call me, Duncan?"

"What? What? I . . . for a moment, I . . ."

"You called me 'young master.'"

"I did, yes."

"That's what Duncan always called me." Paul reached out, touched the ghola's face. "Was that part of your Tleilaxu training?"

"No."

Paul lowered his hand. "What, then?"

"It came from . . . me."

"Do you serve two masters?"

"Perhaps."

"Free yourself from the ghola, Duncan."

"How?"

"You're human. Do a human thing."

"I'm a ghola!"

"But your flesh is human. Duncan's in there."

"*Something's* in there."

"I care not how you do it," Paul said, "but you'll do it."

"You've foreknowledge?"

"Foreknowledge be damned!" Paul turned away. His vision hurtled forward now, gaps in it, but it wasn't a thing to be stopped.

"M'Lord, if you've—"

"Quiet!" Paul held up a hand. "Did you hear that?"

"Hear what, m'Lord?"

Paul shook his head. Duncan hadn't heard it. Had he only imagined the sound? It'd been his tribal name called from the desert—far away and low: "Usul . . . Uuuussssuuuulllll . . ."

"What is it, m'Lord?"

Paul shook his head. He felt watched. Something out there in the night shadows knew he was here. Something? No—some*one*.

"It was mostly sweet," he whispered, "and you were the sweetest of all."

"What'd you say, m'Lord?"

"It's the future," Paul said.

That amorphous human universe out there had undergone a spurt of motion, dancing to the tune of his vision. It had struck a powerful note then. The ghost-echoes might endure.

"I don't understand, m'Lord," the ghola said.

"A Fremen dies when he's too long from the desert," Paul said. "They call it the 'water sickness.' Isn't that odd?"

"That's very odd."

Paul strained at memories, tried to recall the sound of Chani breathing beside him in the night. *Where is there comfort?* he wondered. All he could remember was Chani at breakfast the day they'd left for the desert. She'd been restless, irritable.

"Why do you wear that old jacket?" she'd demanded, eyeing the black uniform coat with its red hawk crest beneath his Fremen robes. "You're an Emperor!"

"Even an Emperor has his favorite clothing," he'd said.

For no reason he could explain, this had brought real tears to Chani's eyes—the second time in her life when Fremen inhibitions had been shattered.

Now, in the darkness, Paul rubbed his own cheeks, felt moisture there. *Who gives moisture to the dead?* he wondered. It was his own face, yet not his. The wind chilled the wet skin. A frail dream formed, broke. What was this swelling in his breast? Was it something he'd eaten? How bitter and plaintive was this other self, giving moisture to the dead. The wind bristled with sand. The skin, dry now, was his own. But whose was the quivering which remained?

They heard the wailing then, far away in the sietch depths. It grew louder . . . louder . . .

The ghola whirled at a sudden glare of light, someone flinging wide the entrance seals. In the light, he saw a man with a raffish grin—no! Not a grin, but a grimace of grief! It was a Fedaykin lieutenant named Tandis. Behind him came a press of many people, all fallen silent now that they saw Muad'Dib.

"Chani . . ." Tandis said.

"Is dead," Paul whispered. "I heard her call."

He turned toward the sietch. He knew this place. It was a place where he could not hide. His onrushing vision illuminated the entire Fremen mob. He *saw* Tandis, felt the Fedaykin's grief, the fear and anger.

"She is gone," Paul said.

The ghola heard the words out of a blazing corona. They burned his chest, his backbone, the sockets of his metal eyes. He felt his right hand move toward the knife at his belt. His own thinking became strange, disjointed. He was a puppet held fast by strings reaching down from that awful corona. He moved to another's commands, to another's desires. The strings jerked his arms, his legs, his jaw. Sounds came squeezing out of his mouth, a terrifying repetitive noise—

"Hraak! Hraak! Hraak!"

The knife came up to strike. In that instant, he grabbed his own voice, shaped rasping words: "Run! Young master, run!"

"We will not run," Paul said. "We'll move with dignity. We'll do what must be done."

The ghola's muscles locked. He shuddered, swayed.

". . . *what must be done!*" The words rolled in his mind like a great fish surfacing. ". . . *what must be done!*" Ahhh, that had sounded like the old Duke, Paul's grandfather. The young master had some of the old man in him. ". . . *what must be done!*"

The words began to unfold in the ghola's consciousness. A sensation of living two lives simultaneously spread out through his awareness: Hayt/Idaho/Hayt/ Idaho . . . He became a motionless chain of relative existence, singular, alone. Old memories flooded his mind. He marked them, adjusted them to new understandings, made a beginning at the integration of a new awareness. A new *persona* achieved a temporary form of internal tyranny. The masculating 'synthesis remained charged with potential disorder, but events pressed him to the temporary adjustment. The young master needed him.

It was done then. He knew himself as Duncan Idaho, remembering everything of Hayt as though it had been stored secretly in him and ignited by a flaming catalyst. The corona dissolved. He shed the Tleilaxu compusions.

"Stay close to me, Duncan," Paul said. "I'll need to depend on you for many things." And, as Idaho continued to stand entranced: "Duncan!"

"Yes, I am Duncan."

"Of course you are! This was the moment when you came back. We'll go inside now."

Idaho fell into step beside Paul. It was like the old times, yet not like them. Now that he stood free of the Tleilaxu, he could appreciate what they had given him. Zensunni training permitted him to overcome the shock of events. The mentat accomplishment formed a counterbalance. He put off all fear, standing above the source. His entire consciousness looked outward from a position of infinite wonder: he had been dead; he was alive.

"Sire," the Fedaykin Tandis said as they approached him, "the woman, Lichna, says she must see you. I told her to wait."

"Thank you," Paul said. "The birth . . ."

"I spoke to the medics," Tandis said, falling into step. "They said you have two children, both of them alive and sound."

"Two?" Paul stumbled, caught himself on Idaho's arm.

"A boy and a girl," Tandis said. "I saw them. They're good Fremen babies."

"How . . . how did she die?" Paul whispered.

"M'Lord?" Tandis bent close.

"Chani?" Paul said.

"It was the birth, m'Lord," Tandis husked. "They said her body was drained by the speed of it. I don't understand, but that is what they said."

"Take me to her," Paul whispered.

"M'Lord?"

"Take me to her!"

"That's where we're going, m'Lord." Again, Tandis bent close to Paul. "Why does your ghola carry a bared knife?"

"Duncan, put away your knife," Paul said. "The time for violence is past."

As he spoke, Paul felt closer to the sound of his voice than to the mechanism which had created the sound. Two babies! The vision had contained but one.

Yet, these moments went as the vision went. There was a person here who felt grief and anger. Someone. His own awareness lay in the grip of an awful treadmill, replaying his life from memory.

*Two babies?*

Again he stumbled. *Chani, Chani,* he thought. *There was no other way. Chani, beloved, believe me that this death was quicker for you . . . and kinder. They'd have held our children hostage, displayed you in a cage and slave pits, reviled you with the blame for my death. This way . . . this way we destroy them and save our children.*

*Children?*

Once more, he stumbled.

*I permitted this,* he thought. *I should feel guilty.*

The sound of noisy confusion filled the cavern ahead of them. It grew louder precisely as he remembered it growing louder. Yes, this was the pattern, the inexorable pattern, even with two children.

*Chani is dead,* he told himself.

At some faraway instant in a past which he had shared with others, this future had reached down to him. It had chivvied him and herded him into a chasm whose walls grew narrower and narrower. He could feel them closing in on him. This was the way the vision went.

*Chani is dead. I should abandon myself to grief.*

But that was *not* the way the vision went.

"Has Alia been summoned?" he asked.

"She is with Chani's friends," Tandis said.

Paul sensed the mob pressing back to give him passage. Their silence moved ahead of him like a wave. The noisy confusion began dying down. A sense of congested emotion filled the sietch. He wanted to remove the people from his vision, found it impossible. Every face turning to follow him carried its special imprint. They were pitiless with curiosity, those faces. They felt grief, yes, but he understood the cruelty which drenched them. They were watching the articulate become dumb, the wise become a fool. Didn't the clown always appeal to cruelty?

This was more than a deathwatch, less than a wake.

Paul felt his soul begging for respite, but still the vision moved him. *Just a little farther now,* he told himself. Black, visionless dark awaited him just ahead. There lay the place ripped out of the vision by grief and guilt, the place where the moon fell.

He stumbled into it, would've fallen had Idaho not taken his arm in a fierce grip, a solid presence knowing how to share his grief in silence.

"Here is the place," Tandis said.

"Watch your step, Sire," Idaho said, helping him over an entrance lip. Hangings brushed Paul's face. Idaho pulled him to a halt. Paul felt the room then, a reflection against his cheeks and ears. It was a rock-walled space with the rock hidden behind tapestries.

"Where is Chani?" Paul whispered.

Harah's voice answered him: "She is right here, Usul."

Paul heaved a trembling sigh. He had feared her body already had been removed to the stills where Fremen reclaimed the water of the tribe. Was that the way the vision went? He felt abandoned in his blindness.

"The children?" Paul asked.

"They are here, too, m'Lord," Idaho said.

"You have beautiful twins, Usul," Harah said, "a boy and a girl. See? We have them here in a creche."

*Two children,* Paul thought wonderingly. The vision had contained only a daughter. He cast himself adrift from Idaho's arm, moved toward the place where Harah had spoken, stumbled into a hard surface. His hands explored it: the metaglass outlines of a creche.

Someone took his left arm. "Usul?" It was Harah. She guided his hand into the creche. He felt soft-soft flesh. It was so warm! He felt ribs, breathing.

"That is your son," Harah whispered. She moved his hand. "And this is your daughter." Her hand tightened on his. "Usul, are you truly blind now?"

He knew what she was thinking. *The blind must be abandoned in the desert.* Fremen tribes carried no dead weight.

"Take me to Chani," Paul said, ignoring her question.

Harah turned him, guided him to the left.

Paul felt himself accepting now the fact that Chani was dead. He had taken his place in a universe he did not want, wearing flesh that did not fit. Every breath he drew bruised his emotions. *Two children!* He wondered if he had committed himself to a passage where his vision would never return. It seemed unimportant.

"Where is my brother?"

It was Alia's voice behind him. He heard the rush of her, the overwhelming presence as she took his arm from Harah.

"I must speak to you!" Alia hissed.

"In a moment," Paul said.

"Now! It's about Lichna."

"I know," Paul said. "In a moment."

"You don't have a moment!"

"I have many moments."

"But Chani doesn't!"

"Be still!" he ordered. "Chani is dead." He put a hand across her mouth as she started to protest. "I order you to be still!" He felt her subside and removed his hand. "Describe what you see," he said.

"Paul!" Frustration and tears battled in her voice.

"Never mind," he said. And he forced himself to inner stillness, opened the eyes of his vision to this moment. Yes—it was still here. Chani's body lay on a pallet within a ring of light. Someone had straightened her white robe, smoothed it trying to hide the blood from the birth. No matter; he could not turn his awareness from the vision of her face: such a mirror of eternity in the still features!

He turned away, but the vision moved with him. She was gone . . . never to return. The air, the universe, all vacant—everywhere vacant. Was this the essence of his penance? he wondered. He wanted tears, but they would not come. Had he lived too long a Fremen? This death demanded its moisture!

Nearby, a baby cried and was hushed. The sound pulled a curtain on his vision. Paul welcomed the darkness. *This is another world,* he thought. *Two children.*

The thought came out of some lost oracular trance. He tried to recapture the timeless mind-dilation of the melange, but awareness fell short. No burst of the future came into this new consciousness. He felt himself rejecting the future—any future.

"Goodbye, my Sihara," he whispered.

Alia's voice, harsh and demanding, came from somewhere behind him. "I've brought Lichna!"

Paul turned. "That's not Lichna," he said. "That's a Face Dancer. Lichna's dead."

"But hear what she says," Alia said.

Slowly, Paul moved toward his sister's voice.

"I'm not surprised to find you alive, Atreides." The voice was like Lichna's, but with subtle differences, as though the speaker used Lichna's vocal cords, but no longer bothered to control them sufficiently. Paul found himself struck by an odd note of honesty in the voice.

"Not surprised?" Paul asked.

"I am Scytale, a Tleilaxu of the Face Dancers, and I would know a thing before we bargain. Is that a ghola I see behind you, or Duncan Idaho?"

"It's Duncan Idaho," Paul said. "And I will not bargain with you."

"I think you'll bargain," Scytale said.

"Duncan," Paul said, speaking over his shoulder, "will you kill this Tleilaxu if I ask it?"

"Yes, m'Lord." There was the suppressed rage of a berserker in Idaho's voice.

"Wait!" Alia said. "You don't know what you're rejecting."

"But I do know," Paul said.

"So it's truly Duncan Idaho of the Atreides," Scytale said. "We found the lever! A ghola *can* regain his past."

Paul heard footsteps. Someone brushed past him on the left. Scytale's voice came from behind him now. "What do you remember of your past, Duncan?"

"Everything. From my childhood on. I even remember you at the tank when they removed me from it," Idaho said.

"Wonderful," Scytale breathed. "Wonderful."

Paul heard the voice moving. *I need a vision,* he thought. Darkness frustrated him. Bene Gesserit training warned him of terrifying menace in Scytale, yet the creature remained a voice, a shadow of movement—entirely beyond him.

"Are these the Atreides babies?" Scytale asked.

"Harah!" Paul cried. "Get her away from there!"

"Stay where you are!" Scytale shouted. "All of you! I warn you, a Face Dancer can move faster than you suspect. My knife can have both these lives before you touch me."

Paul felt someone touch his right arm, then move off to the right.

"That's far enough, Alia," Scytale said.

"Alia," Paul said. "Don't."

"It's my fault," Alia groaned. "My fault!"

"Atreides," Scytale said, "shall we bargain now?"

Behind him, Paul heard a single hoarse curse. His throat constricted at the suppressed violence in Idaho's voice. Idaho must not break! Scytale would kill the babies!

"To strike a bargain, one requires a thing to sell," Scytale said. "Not so, Atreides? Will you have your Chani back? We can restore her to you. A ghola, Atreides. A ghola *with full memory!* But we must hurry. Call your friends to bring a cryologic tank to preserve the flesh."

*To hear Chani's voice once more,* Paul thought. *To feel her presence beside me. Ahhh, that's why they gave me Idaho as a ghola, to let me discover how much the re-creation is like the original. But now—full restoration . . . at their price. I'd be a Tleilaxu tool forevermore. And Chani . . . chained to the same fate by a threat to our children, exposed once more to the Qizarate's plotting . . .*

"What pressures would you use to restore Chani's memory to her?" Paul asked, fighting to keep his voice calm. "Would you condition her to . . . to kill one of her own children?"

"We use whatever pressures we need," Scytale said. "What say you, Atreides?"

"Alia," Paul said, "bargain with this *thing.* I cannot bargain with what I cannot see."

"A wise choice," Scytale gloated. "Well, Alia, what do you offer me as your brother's agent?"

Paul lowered his head, bringing himself to stillness within stillness. He'd glimpsed something just then—like a vision, but not a vision. It had been a knife close to him. There!

"Give me a moment to think," Alia said.

"My knife is patient," Scytale said, "but Chani's flesh is not. Take a *reasonable* amount of time."

Paul felt himself blinking. It could not be . . . but it was! He felt eyes! Their vantage point was odd and they moved in an erratic way. *There!* The knife swam into his view. With a breath-stilling shock, Paul recognized the viewpoint. It was that of one of his children! he was seeing Scytale's knife hand from within the creche! It glittered only inches from him. Yes—and he could see himself across the room, as well—head down, standing quietly, a figure of no menace, ignored by the others in this room.

"To begin, you might assign us all your CHOAM holdings," Scytale suggested.

"All of them?" Alia protested.

"All."

Watching himself through the eyes in the creche, Paul slipped his crysknife from its belt sheath. The movement produced a strange sensation of duality. He measured the distance, the angle. There'd be no second chance. He prepared his body then in the Bene Gesserit way, armed himself like a cocked spring for a single concentrated movement, a *prajna* thing requiring all his muscles balanced in one exquisite unity.

The crysknife leaped from his hand. The milky blur of it flashed into Scytale's right eye, jerked the Face Dancer's head back. Scytale threw both hands up and staggered backward against the wall. His knife clattered off the ceiling, to hit the floor. Scytale rebounded from the wall; he fell face forward, dead before he touched the floor.

Still through the eyes in the creche, Paul watched the faces in the room turn toward his eyeless figure, read the combined shock. Then Alia rushed to the creche, bent over it and hid the view from him.

"Oh, they're safe," Alia said. "They're safe."

"M'Lord," Idaho whispered, "was *that* part of your vision?"

"No." He waved a hand in Idaho's direction. "Let it be."

"Forgive me, Paul," Alia said. "But when that creature said they could . . . revive . . ."

"There are some prices an Atreides cannot pay," Paul said. "You know that."

"I know," she sighed. "But I was tempted . . ."

"Who was not tempted?" Paul asked.

He turned away from them, groped his way to a wall, leaned against it and tried to understand what he had done. *How? How? The eyes in the creche!* He felt poised on the brink of terrifying revelation.

*"My eyes, father."*

The word-shapings shimmered before his sightless vision.

"My son!" Paul whispered, too low for any to hear. "You're . . . aware."

*"Yes, father. Look!"*

Paul sagged against the wall in a spasm of dizziness. He felt that he'd been upended and drained. His own life whipped past him. He saw his father. He *was* his father. And the grandfather, and the grandfathers before that. His awareness tumbled through a mind-shattering corridor of his whole male line.

"How?" he asked silently.

Faint word-shapings appeared, faded and were gone, as though the strain was too great. Paul wiped saliva from the corner of his mouth. He remembered the awakening of Alia in the Lady Jessica's womb. But there had been no Water of Life, no overdose of melange this time . . . or had there? Had Chani's hunger been for that? Or was this somehow the genetic product of his line, foreseen by the Reverend Mother Gaius Helen Mohiam?

Paul felt himself in the creche then, with Alia cooing over him. Her hands soothed him. Her face loomed, a giant thing directly over him. She turned him then and he saw his creche companion—a girl with that bony-ribbed look of strength which came from a desert heritage. She had a full head of tawny red hair. As he stared, she opened her eyes. Those eyes! Chani peered out of her eyes . . . and the Lady Jessica. A multitude peered out of those eyes.

"Look at that," Alia said. "They're staring at each other."

"Babies can't focus at this age," Harah said.

"I could," Alia said.

Slowly, Paul felt himself being disengaged from that endless awareness. He was back at his own wailing wall then, leaning against it. Idaho shook his shoulder gently.

"M'Lord?"

"Let my son be called Leto for my father," Paul said, straightening.

"At the time of naming," Harah said, "I will stand beside you as a friend of the mother and give that name."

"And my daughter," Paul said. "Let her be called Ghanima."

"Usul!" Harah objected. "Ghanima's an ill-omened name."

"It saved your life," Paul said. "What matter that Alia made fun of you with that name? My daughter is Ghanima, a spoil of war."

Paul heard wheels squeak behind him then—the pallet with Chani's body being removed. The chant of the Water Rite began.

"Hal yawm!" Harah said. "I must leave now if I am to be the observer of the holy truth and stand beside my friend for the last time. Her water belongs to the tribe."

"Her water belongs to the tribe," Paul murmured. He heard Harah leave. He groped outward and found Idaho's sleeve. "Take me to my quarters, Duncan."

Inside his quarters, he shook himself free gently. It was a time to be alone. But before Idaho could leave there was a disturbance at the door.

"Master!" It was Bijaz calling from the doorway.

"Duncan," Paul said, "let him come two paces forward. Kill him if he comes farther."

"Ayyah," Idaho said.

"Duncan is it?" Bijaz asked. "Is it *truly* Duncan Idaho?"

"It is," Idaho said. "I remember."

"Then Scytale's plan succeeded!"

"Scytale is dead," Paul said.

"But I am not and the plan is not," Bijaz said. "By the tank in which I grew! It can be done! I shall have my pasts—all of them. It needs only the right trigger."

"Trigger?" Paul asked.

"The compulsion to kill you," Idaho said, rage thick in his voice. "Mentat computation: They found that I thought of you as the son I never had. Rather than slay you, the true Duncan Idaho would take over the ghola body. But . . . it might have failed. Tell me, dwarf, if your plan had failed, if I'd killed him, what then?"

"Oh . . . then we'd have bargained with the sister to save her brother. But this way the bargaining is better."

Paul took a shuddering breath. He could hear the mourners moving down the last passage now toward the deep rooms and the water stills.

"It's not too late, m'Lord," Bijaz said. "Will you have your love back? We can restore her to you. A ghola, yes. But now—we hold out the full restoration. Shall we summon servants with a cryological tank, preserve the flesh of your beloved . . ."

It was harder now, Paul found. He had exhausted his powers in the first Tleilaxu temptation. And now all that was for nothing! To feel Chani's presence once more . . .

"Silence him," Paul told Idaho, speaking in Atreides battle tongue. He heard Idaho move toward the door.

"Master!" Bijaz squeaked.

"As you love me," Paul said, still in battle tongue, "do me this favor: Kill him before I succumb!"

"Noooooo . . ." Bijaz screamed.

The sound stopped abruptly with a frightened grunt.

"I did him the kindness," Idaho said.

Paul bent his head, listening. He no longer could hear the mourners. He thought of the ancient Fremen rite being performed now deep in the sietch, far down in the room of the death-still where the tribe recovered its water.

"There was no choice," Paul said. "You understand that, Duncan?"

"I understand."

"There are some things no one can bear. I meddled in all the possible futures I could create until, finally, they created me."

"M'Lord, you shouldn't . . ."

"There are problems in this universe for which there are no answers," Paul said. "Nothing. Nothing can be done."

As he spoke, Paul felt his link with the vision shatter. His mind cowered, overwhelmed by infinite possibilities. His lost vision became like the wind, blowing where it willed.

*We say of Muad'Dib that he has gone on a journey into that land where we walk without footprints.*

**—Preamble to the Qizarate Creed**

There was a dike of water against the sand, an outer limit for the plantings of the sietch holding. A rock bridge came next and then the open desert beneath Idaho's feet. The promontory of Sietch Tabr dominated the night sky behind him. The light of both moons frosted its high rim. An orchard had been brought right down to the water.

Idaho paused on the desert side and stared back at flowered branches over silent water—reflections and reality—four moons. The stillsuit felt greasy against his skin. Wet flint odors invaded his nostrils past the filters. There was a malignant simpering to the wind through the orchard. He listened for night sounds. Kangaroo mice inhabited the grass at the water verge; a hawk owl bounced its droning call into the cliff shadows; the wind-broken hiss of a sandfall came from the open bled.

Idaho turned toward the sound.

He could see no movement out there on the moonlit dunes.

It was Tandis who had brought Paul this far. Then the man had returned to tell his account. And Paul had walked out into the desert—like a Fremen.

"He was blind—truly blind," Tandis had said, as though that explained it. "Before that, he had the vision which he told to us . . . but . . ."

A shrug. Blind Fremen were abandoned in the desert. Muad'Dib might be Emperor, but he was also Fremen. Had he not made provision that Fremen guard and raise his children? He was Fremen.

It was a skeleton desert here, Idaho saw. Moon-silvered ribs of rock showed through the sand; then the dunes began.

*I should not have left him alone, not even for a minute,* Idaho thought. *I knew what was in his mind.*

"He told me the future no longer needed his physical presence," Tandis had reported. "When he left me, he called back. 'Now I am free' were his words."

*Damn them!* Idaho thought.

The Fremen had refused to send 'thopters or searchers of any kind. Rescue was against their ancient customs.

"There will be a worm for Muad'Dib," they said. And they began the chant for those committed to the desert, the ones whose water went to Shaihulud: "Mother of sand, father of Time, beginning of Life, grant him passage."

Idaho seated himself on a flat rock and stared at the desert. The night out there was filled with camouflage patterns. There was no way to tell where Paul had gone.

"Now I am free."

Idaho spoke the words aloud, surprised by the sound of his own voice. For a time, he let his mind run, remembering a day when he'd taken the child Paul to the sea market on Caladan, the dazzling glare of a sun on water, the sea's riches brought up dead, there to be sold. Idaho remembered Gurney Halleck playing music of the baliset for them—pleasure, laughter. Rhythms pranced in his awareness, leading his mind like a thrall down channels of remembered delight.

Gurney Halleck. Gurney would blame him for this tragedy.

Memory music faded.

He recalled Paul's words: *"There are problems in this universe for which there are no answers."*

Idaho began to wonder how Paul would die out there in the desert. Quickly, killed by a worm? Slowly, in the sun? Some of the Fremen back there in the sietch had said Muad'Dib would never die, that he had entered the ruh-world where all possible futures existed, that he would be present henceforth in the *alam al-mythal,* wandering there endlessly even after his flesh had ceased to be.

*He'll die and I'm powerless to prevent it,* Idaho thought.

He began to realize that there might be a certain fastidious courtesy in dying without a trace—no remains, nothing, and an entire planet for a tomb.

*Mentat, solve thyself,* he thought.

Words intruded on his memory—the ritual words of the Fedaykin lieu-tenant, posting a guard over Muad'Dib's children: "It shall be the solemn duty of the officer in charge . . ."

The plodding, self-important language of government enraged him. It had seduced the Fremen. It had seduced everyone. A man, a great man, was dying out there, but language plodded on . . . and on . . . and on . . .

What had happened, he wondered, to all the clean meanings that screened out nonsense? Somewhere, in some lost *where* which the Imperium had created, they'd been walled off, sealed against chance rediscovery. His mind quested for solutions, mentat fashion. Patterns of knowledge glistened there. Lorelei hair might shimmer thus, beckoning . . . beckoning the enchanted seaman into emerald caverns. . .

With an abrupt start, Idaho drew back from catatonic forgetfulness.

*So!* he thought. *Rather than face my failure, I would disappear within myself!*

The instant of that almost-plunge remained in his memory. Examining it, he felt his life stretch out as long as the existence of the universe. Real flesh lay condensed, finite in its emerald cavern of awareness, but infinite life had shared his being.

Idaho stood up, feeling cleansed by the desert. Sand was beginning to chatter in the wind, pecking at the surfaces of leaves in the orchard behind him. There was the dry and abrasive smell of dust in the night air. His robe whipped to the pulse of a sudden gust.

Somewhere far out in the bled, Idaho realized, a mother storm raged, lifting vortices of winding dust in hissing violence—a giant worm of sand powerful enough to cut flesh from bones.

*He will become one with the desert,* Idaho thought. *The desert will fulfill him.*

It was a Zensunni thought washing through his mind like clear water. Paul would go on marching out there, he knew. An Atreides would not give himself up completely to destiny, not even in the full awareness of the inevitable.

A touch of prescience came over Idaho then, and he saw that people of the future would speak of Paul in terms of seas. Despite a life soaked in dust, water would follow him. "His flesh foundered," they would say, "but he swam on."

Behind Idaho, a man cleared his throat.

Idaho turned to discern the figure of Stilgar standing on the bridge over the qanat.

"He will not be found," Stilgar said. "Yet all men will find him."

"The desert takes him—and deifies him," Idaho said. "Yet he was an interloper here. He brought an alien chemistry to this planet—water."

"The desert imposes its own rhythms," Stilgar said. "We welcomed him, called him our Mahdi, our Muad'Dib, and gave him his secret name, Base of the Pillar: Usul."

"Still, he was not born a Fremen."

"And that does not change the fact that we claimed him . . . and have claimed him finally." Stilgar put a hand on Idaho's shoulder. "All men are interlopers, old friend."

"You're a deep one, aren't you, Stil?"

"Deep enough. I can see how we clutter the universe with our migrations. Muad'Dib gave us something uncluttered. Men will remember his Jihad for that, at least."

"He won't give up to the desert," Idaho said. "He's blind, but he won't give up. He's a man of honor and principle. He was Atreides-trained."

"And his water will be poured on the sand," Stilgar said. "Come." He pulled gently at Idaho's arm. "Alia is back and is asking for you."

"She was with you at Sietch Makab?"

"Yes—she helped whip those soft Naibs into line. They take her orders now . . . as I do."

"What orders?"

"She commanded the execution of the traitors."

"Oh." Idaho suppressed a feeling of vertigo as he looked up at the promontory. "Which traitors?"

"The Guildsman, the Reverend Mother Mohiam, Korba . . . a few others."

"You slew a Reverend Mother?"

"I did. Muad'Dib left word that it should not be done." He shrugged. "But I disobeyed him, as Alia knew I would."

Idaho stared again into the desert, feeling himself become whole, one person capable of seeing the pattern of what Paul had created. *Judgment strategy*, the Atreides called it in their training manuals. *People are subordinate to government, but the ruled influence the rulers.* Did the ruled have any concept, he wondered, of what they had helped create here?

"Alia . . ." Stilgar said, clearing his throat. He sounded embarrassed. "She needs the comfort of your presence."

"And she is the government," Idaho murmured.

"A regency, no more."

"Fortune passes everywhere, as her father often said," Idaho muttered.

"We make our bargain with the future," Stilgar said. "Will you come now? We need you back there." Again, he sounded embarrassed. "She is . . . distraught. She cries out against her brother one moment, mourns him the next."

"Presently," Idaho promised. He heard Stilgar leave. He stood facing into the rising wind, letting the grains of sand rattle against the stillsuit.

Mentat awareness projected the outflowing patterns into the future. The possibilities dazzled him. Paul had set in motion a whirling vortex and nothing could stand in its path.

The Bene Tleilax and the Guild had overplayed their hands and had lost, were discredited. The Qizarate was shaken by the treason of Korba and others high within it. And Paul's final voluntary act, his ultimate acceptance of their customs, had ensured the loyalty of the Fremen to him and to his house. He was one of them forever now.

"Paul is gone!" Alia's voice choked. She had come up almost silently to where Idaho stood and was now beside hm. "He was a fool, Duncan!"

"Don't say that!" he snapped.

"The whole universe will say it before I'm through," she said.

"Why, for the love of heaven?"

"For the love of my brother, not of heaven."

Zensunni insight dilated his awareness. He could sense that there was no vision in her—had been none since Chani's death. "You practice an odd love," he said.

"Love? Duncan, he had but to step off the track! What matter that the rest of the universe would have come shattering down behind him? He'd have been safe . . . and Chani with him!"

"Then . . . why didn't he?"

"For the love of heaven," she whispered. Then, more loudly, she said: "Paul's entire life was a struggle to escape his Jihad and its deification. At least, he's free of it. He chose this!"

"Ah, yes—the oracle." Idaho shook his head in wonder. "Even Chani's death. His moon fell."

"He *was* a fool, wasn't he, Duncan?"

Idaho's throat tightened with suppressed grief.

"Such a fool!" Alia gasped, her control breaking. "He'll live forever while we must die!"

"Alia, don't . . ."

"It's just grief," she said, voice low. "Just grief. Do you know what I must do for him? I must save the life of the Princess Irulan. That one! You should hear *her* grief. Wailing, giving moisture to the dead; she swears she loved him and knew it not. She reviles her Sisterhood, says she'll spend her life teaching Paul's children."

"You trust her?"

"She reeks of trustworthiness!"

"Ahhh," Idaho murmured. The final pattern unreeled before his awareness like a design on fabric. The defection of the Princess Irulan was the last step. It left the Bene Gesserit with no remaining lever against the Atreides heirs.

Alia began to sob, leaned against him, face pressed into his chest. "Ohhh, Duncan, Duncan! He's gone!"

Idaho put his lips against her hair. "Please," he whispered. He felt her grief mingling with his like two streams entering the same pool.

"I need you, Duncan," she sobbed. "Love me!"

"I do," he whispered.

She lifted her head, peered at the moon-frosted outline of his face. "I know, Duncan. Love knows love."

Her words sent a shudder through him, a feeling of estrangement from his old self. He had come out here looking for one thing and had found another. It was as though he'd lurched into a room full of familiar people only to realize too late that he knew none of them.

She pushed away from him, took his hand. "Will you come with me, Duncan?"

"Wherever you lead," he said.

She led him back across the qanat into the darkness at the base of the massif and its Place of Safety.

# EPILOGUE

---

*No bitter stench of funeral-still for Muad'Dib.*
*No knell nor solemn rite to free the mind*
*From avaricious shadows.*
*He is the fool saint,*
*The golden stranger living forever*
*On the edge of reason.*
*Let your guard fall and he is there!*
*His crimson peace and sovereign pallor*
*Strike into our universe on prophetic webs*
*To the verge of a quiet glance—there!*
*Out of bristling star-jungles:*
*Mysterious, lethal, an oracle without eyes,*
*Catspaw of prophecy, whose voice never dies!*
*Shai-hulud, he awaits thee upon a strand*
*Where couples walk and fix, eye to eye,*
*The delicious ennui of love.*
*He strides through the long cavern of time,*
*Scattering the fool-self of his dream.*

**—The Ghola's Hymn**

# CHILDREN OF DUNE

FOR BEV:
Out of the wonderful commitment of our love
and to share her beauty and her wisdom
for she truly inspired this book.

*Muad'Dib's teachings have become the playground of scholastics, of the superstitious and the corrupt. He taught a balanced way of life, a philosophy with which a human can meet problems arising from an ever-changing universe. He said humankind is still evolving, in a process which will never end. He said this evolution moves on changing principles which are known only to eternity. How can corrupted reasoning play with such an essence?*

**—Words of the Mentat
Duncan Idaho**

A spot of light appeared on the deep red rug which covered the raw rock of the cave floor. The light glowed without apparent source, having its existence only on the red fabric surface woven of spice fiber. A questing circle about two centimeters in diameter, it moved erratically—now elongated, now an oval. Encountering the deep green side of a bed, it leaped upward, folded itself across the bed's surface.

Beneath the green covering lay a child with rusty hair, face still round with baby fat, a generous mouth—a figure lacking the lean sparseness of Fremen tradition, but not as water-fat as an off-worlder. As the light passed across closed eyelids, the small figure stirred. The light winked out.

Now there was only the sound of even breathing and, faint behind it, a reassuring drip-drip-drip of water collecting in a catchbasin from the windstill far above the cave.

Again the light appeared in the chamber—slightly larger, a few lumens brighter. This time there was a suggestion of source and movement to it: a hooded figure filled the arched doorway at the chamber's edge and the light originated there. Once more the light flowed around the chamber, testing, questing. There was a sense of menace in it, a restless dissatisfaction. It avoided the sleeping child, paused on the gridded air inlet at an upper corner, probed a bulge in the green and gold wall hangings which softened the enclosing rock.

Presently the light winked out. The hooded figure moved with a betraying swish of fabric, took up a station at one side of the arched doorway. Anyone aware of the routine here in Sietch Tabr would have suspected at once that this must be Stilgar, Naib of the Sietch, guardian of the orphaned twins who would one day take up the mantle of their father, Paul Muad'Dib. Stilgar often made night inspections of the twins' quarters, always going first to the chamber where Ghanima slept and ending here in the adjoining room, where he could reassure himself that Leto was not threatened.

*I'm an old fool,* Stilgar thought.

He fingered the cold surface of the light projector before restoring it to the loop in his belt sash. The projector irritated him even while he depended upon it. The thing was a subtle instrument of the Imperium, a device to detect the presence of large living bodies. It had shown only the sleeping children in the royal bedchambers.

Stilgar knew his thoughts and emotions were like the light. He could not still a restless inner projection. Some greater power controlled *that* movement. It projected him into this moment where he sensed the accumulated peril. Here lay the magnet for dreams of grandeur throughout the known universe. Here lay temporal riches, secular authority and that most powerful of all mystic talismans: the divine authenticity of Muad'Dib's religious bequest. In these twins—Leto and his sister Ghanima—an awesome power focused. While they lived, Muad'Dib, though dead, lived in them.

These were not merely nine-year-old children; they were a natural force, objects of veneration and fear. They were the children of Paul Atreides, who had become Muad'Dib, the Mahdi of all the Fremen. Muad'Dib had ignited an explosion of humanity; Fremen had spread from this planet in a jihad, carrying their fervor across the human universe in a wave of religious government whose scope and ubiquitous authority had left its mark on every planet.

*Yet these children of Muad'Dib are flesh and blood,* Stilgar thought. *Two simple thrusts of my knife would still their hearts. Their water would return to the tribe.*

His wayward mind fell into turmoil at such a thought.

*To kill Muad'Dib's children!*

But the years had made him wise in introspection. Stilgar knew the origin of such a terrible thought. It came from the left hand of the damned, not from the right hand of the blessed. The *ayat* and *burhan* of Life held few mysteries for him. Once he'd been proud to think of himself as Fremen, to think of the desert as a friend, to name his planet Dune in his thoughts and not Arrakis, as it was marked on all the Imperial star charts.

*How simple things were when our Messiah was only a dream,* he thought. *By finding our Mahdi we loosed upon the universe countless messianic dreams. Every people subjugated by the jihad now dreams of a leader to come.*

Stilgar glanced into the darkened bedchamber.

*If my knife liberated all of those people, would they make a messiah of me?*

Leto could be heard stirring restlessly in his bed.

Stilgar sighed. He had never known the Atreides grandfather whose name this child had taken. But many said the moral strength of Muad'Dib had come from that source. Would that terrifying quality of *rightness* skip a generation now? Stilgar found himself unable to answer this question.

He thought: *Sietch Tabr is mine. I rule here. I am a Naib of the Fremen. Without me there would have been no Muad'Dib. These twins, now . . . through Chani, their mother and my kinswoman, my blood flows in their veins. I am there with Muad'Dib and Chani and all the others. What have we done to our universe?*

Stilgar could not explain why such thoughts came to him in the night and why they made him feel so guilty. He crouched within his hooded robe. Reality was not at all like the dream. The Friendly Desert, which once had spread from pole to pole, was reduced to half its former size. The mystic paradise of spreading greenery filled him with dismay. It was not like the dream. And as his planet changed, he knew he had changed. He had become a far more subtle person than the one-time sietch chieftain. He was aware now of many things—of statecraft and profound consequences in the smallest decisions. Yet he felt this knowledge and subtlety as a thin veneer covering an iron core of simpler, more deterministic awareness. And that older core called out to him, pleaded with him for a return to cleaner values.

The morning sounds of the sietch began intruding upon his thoughts. People were beginning to move about in the cavern. He felt a breeze against his cheeks: people were going out through the doorseals into the predawn darkness. The breeze spoke of carelessness as it spoke of the time. Warren dwellers no longer maintained the tight water discipline of the old days. Why should they, when rain had been recorded on this planet, when clouds were seen, when eight Fremen had been inundated and killed by a flash flood in a wadi? Until that event, the word *drowned* had not existed in the language of Dune. But this was no longer Dune; this was Arrakis . . . and it was the morning of an eventful day.

He thought: *Jessica, mother of Muad'Dib and grandmother of these royal twins, returns to our planet today. Why does she end her self-imposed exile at this time? Why does she leave the softness and security of Caladan for the danger of Arrakis?*

And there were other worries: Would she sense Stilgar's doubts? She was a Bene Gesserit witch, graduate of the Sisterhood's deepest training, and a Reverend Mother in her own right. Such females were acute and they were dangerous. Would she order him to fall upon his own knife as the Umma-Protector of Liet-Kynes had been ordered?

*Would I obey her?* he wondered.

He could not answer that question, but now he thought about Liet-Kynes, the planetologist who had first dreamed of transforming the planetwide desert of Dune into the human-supportive green planet which it was becoming. Liet-Kynes had been Chani's father. Without him there would have been no dream, no Chani, no royal twins. The workings of this fragile chain dismayed Stilgar.

*How have we met in this place?* he asked himself. *How have we combined? For what purpose? Is it my duty to end it all, to shatter that great combination?*

Stilgar admitted the terrible urging within him now. He could make that choice, denying love and family to do what a Naib must do on occasion: make a deadly decision for the good of the tribe. By one view, such a murder represented ultimate betrayal and atrocity. *To kill mere children!* Yet they were not mere children. They had eaten melange, and shared in the sietch orgy, had probed the desert for sandtrout and played the other games of Fremen children. . . . And they sat in the Royal Council. Children of such tender years, yet wise enough to sit in the Council. They might be children in flesh, but they were ancient in experience, born with a totality of genetic memory, a terrifying awareness which set their Aunt Alia and themselves apart from all other living humans.

Many times in many nights had Stilgar found his mind circling this *difference* shared by the twins and their aunt; many times had he been awakened from sleep by these torments, coming here to the twins' bedchamber with his dreams unfinished. Now his doubts came to focus. Failure to make a decision was in itself a decision—he knew this. These twins and their aunt had awakened in the womb, knowing there all of the memories passed on to them by their ancestors. Spice addiction had done this, spice addiction of the mothers—the Lady Jessica and Chani. The Lady Jessica had borne a son, Muad'Dib, before her addiction. Alia had come after the addiction. That was clear in retrospect. The countless generations of selective breeding directed by the Bene Gesserits had achieved Muad'Dib, but nowhere in the Sisterhood's plans had they allowed for melange. Oh, they knew about this possibility, but they feared it and called it *Abomination*. That was the most dismaying fact. Abomination. They must possess reasons for such a judgment. And if they said Alia was an Abomination, then that must apply equally to the twins, because Chani, too, had been addicted, her body saturated with spice, and her genes had somehow complemented those of Muad'Dib.

Stilgar's thoughts moved in ferment. There could be no doubt these twins went beyond their father. But in which direction? The boy spoke of an ability to *be* his father—and had proved it. Even as an infant, Leto had revealed memories which only Muad'Dib should have known. Were there other ancestors waiting in that vast spectrum of memories—ancestors whose beliefs and habits created unspeakable dangers for living humans?

Abominations, the holy witches of the Bene Gesserit said. Yet the Sisterhood coveted the genophase of these children. The witches wanted sperm and ovum without the disturbing flesh which carried them. Was that why the Lady Jessica returned at this time? She had broken with the Sisterhood to support her Ducal mate, but rumor said she had returned to the Bene Gesserit ways.

*I could end all of these dreams,* Stilgar thought. *How simple it would be.*

And yet again he wondered at himself that he could contemplate such a choice. Were Muad'Dib's twins responsible for the reality which obliterated the dreams of others? No. They were merely the lens through which light poured to reveal new shapes in the universe.

In torment, his mind reverted to primary Fremen beliefs, and he thought: *God's command comes; so seek not to hasten it. God's it is to show the way; and some do swerve from it.*

It was the religion of Muad'Dib which upset Stilgar most. Why did they make a god of Muad'Dib? Why deify a man known to be flesh? Muad'Dib's *Golden Elixir of Life* had created a bureaucratic monster which sat astride human affairs. Government and religion united, and breaking a law became sin. A smell of blasphemy arose like smoke around any questioning of governmental edicts. The guilt of rebellion invoked hellfire and self-righteous judgments.

Yet it was men who created these governmental edicts.

Stilgar shook his head sadly, not seeing the attendants who had moved into the Royal Antechamber for their morning duties.

He fingered the crysknife at his waist, thinking of the past it symbolized, thinking that more than once he had sympathized with rebels whose abortive uprisings had been crushed by his own orders. Confusion washed through his mind and he wished he knew how to obliterate it, returning to the simplicities represented by the knife. But the universe would not turn backward. It was a great engine projected upon the gray void of nonexistence. His knife, if it brought the deaths of the twins, would only reverberate against that void, weaving new complexities to echo through human history, creating new surges of chaos, inviting humankind to attempt other forms of order and disorder.

Stilgar sighed, growing aware of the movements around him. Yes, these attendants represented a kind of order which was bound around Muad'Dib's twins. They moved from one moment to the next, meeting whatever necessities occurred there. *Best to emulate them,* Stilgar told himself. *Best meet what comes when it comes.*

*I am an attendant yet,* he told himself. *And my master is God the Merciful, the Compassionate.* And he quoted to himself: *"Surely, We have put on their necks fetters up to the chin, so their heads are raised; and We have put before them a barrier and behind them a barrier; and We have covered them, so they do not see."*

Thus was it written in the old Fremen religion.

Stilgar nodded to himself.

To *see,* to anticipate the next moment as Muad'Dib had done with his awesome visions of the future, added a counter-force to human affairs. It created new places for decisions. To be unfettered, yes, that might well indicate a whim of God. Another complexity beyond ordinary human reach.

Stilgar removed his hand from the knife. His fingers tingled with remembrance of it. But the blade which once had glistened in a sandworm's gaping mouth remained in its sheath. Stilgar knew he would not draw this blade now to kill the twins. He had reached a decision. Better to retain that one old virtue which he still cherished: loyalty. Better the complexities one thought he knew than the complexities which defied understanding. Better the now than the future of a dream. The bitter taste in his mouth told Stilgar how empty and revolting some dreams could be.

*No! No more dreams!*

CHALLENGE: *"Have you seen The Preacher?"*
RESPONSE: *"I have seen a sandworm."*
CHALLENGE: *"What about that sandworm?"*
RESPONSE: *"It gives us the air we breathe."*
CHALLENGE: *"Then why do we destroy its land?"*
RESPONSE: *"Because Shai-Hulud* [sandworm deified] *orders it."*

**—Riddles of Arrakis
by Harq al-Ada**

As was the Fremen custom, the Atreides twins arose an hour before dawn. They yawned and stretched in secret unison in their adjoining chambers, feeling the activity of the cave-warren around them. They could hear attendants in the antechamber preparing breakfast, a simple gruel with dates and nuts blended in liquid skimmed from partially fermented spice. There were glowglobes in the antechamber and a soft yellow light entered through the open archways of the bedchambers. The twins dressed swiftly in the soft light, each hearing the other nearby. As they had agreed, they donned stillsuits against the desert's parching winds.

Presently the royal pair met in the antechamber, noting the sudden stillness of the attendants. Leto, it was observed, wore a black-edged tan cape over his stillsuit's grey slickness. His sister wore a green cape. The neck of each cape was held by a clasp in the form of an Atreides hawk—gold with red jewels for eyes.

Seeing this finery, Harah, who was one of Stilgar's wives, said: "I see you have dressed to honor your grandmother." Leto picked up his breakfast bowl before looking at Harah's dark and wind-creased face. He shook his head. Then: "How do you know it's not ourselves we honor?"

Harah met his taunting stare without flinching, said: "My eyes are just as blue as yours!"

Ghanima laughed aloud. Harah was always an adept at the Fremen challenge-game. In one sentence, she had said: "Don't taunt me, boy. You may be royalty, but we both bear the stigma of melange-addiction—eyes without whites. What Fremen needs more finery or more honor than that?"

Leto smiled, shook his head ruefully. "Harah, my love, if you were but younger and not already Stilgar's, I'd make you my own."

Harah accepted the small victory easily, signaling the other attendants to continue preparing the chambers for this day's important activities. "Eat your breakfasts," she said. "You'll need the energy today."

"Then you agree that we're not too fine for our grandmother?" Ghanima asked, speaking around a mouthful of gruel.

"Don't fear her, Ghani," Harah said.

Leto gulped a mouthful of gruel, sent a probing stare at Harah. The woman was infernally folk-wise, seeing through the game of finery so quickly. "Will she believe we fear her?" Leto asked.

"Like as not," Harah said. "She was our Reverend Mother, remember. I know her ways."

"How was Alia dressed?" Ghanima asked.

"I've not seen her." Harah spoke shortly, turning away.

Leto and Ghanima exchanged a look of shared secrets, bent quickly to their breakfast. Presently they went out into the great central passage.

Ghanima spoke in one of the ancient languages they shared in genetic memory: "So today we have a grandmother."

"It bothers Alia greatly," Leto said.

"Who likes to give up such authority?" Ghanima asked.

Leto laughed softly, an oddly adult sound from flesh so young. "It's more than that."

"Will her mother's eyes observe what we have observed?"

"And why not?" Leto asked.

"Yes . . . . That could be what Alia fears."

"Who knows Abomination better than Abomination?" Leto asked.

"We could be wrong, you know," Ghanima said.

"But we're not." And he quoted from the Bene Gesserit Azhar Book: "It is with reason and terrible experience that we call the pre-born *Abomination*. For who knows what lost and damned persona out of our evil past may take over the living flesh?"

"I know the history of it," Ghanima said. "But if that's true, why don't we suffer from this inner assault?"

"Perhaps our parents stand guard within us," Leto said.

"Then why not guardians for Alia as well?"

"I don't know. It could be because one of her parents remains among the living. It could be simply that we are still young and strong. Perhaps when we're older and more cynical . . ."

"We must take great care with this grandmother," Ghanima said.

"And not discuss this Preacher who wanders our planet speaking heresy?"

"You don't really think he's our father!"

"I make no judgment on it, but Alia fears him."

Ghanima shook her head sharply. "I don't believe this Abomination nonsense!"

"You've just as many memories as I have," Leto said. "You can believe what you want to believe."

"You think it's because we haven't dared the spice trance and Alia has," Ghanima said.

"That's exactly what I think."

They fell silent, moving out into the flow of people in the central passage. It was cool in Sietch Tabr, but the stillsuits were warm and the twins kept their condenser hoods thrown back from their red hair. Their faces betrayed the stamp of shared genes: generous mouths, widely set eyes of spice addict blue-on-blue.

Leto was the first to note the approach of their Aunt Alia.

"Here she comes now," he said, shifting to Atreides battle language as a warning.

Ghanima nodded to her aunt as Alia stopped in front of them, said: "A *spoil of war* greets her illustrious relative." Using the same Chakobsa language, Ghanima emphasized the meaning of her own name—*Spoil of War*.

"You see, Beloved Aunt," Leto said, "we prepare ourselves for today's encounter with your mother."

Alia, the one person in the teeming royal household who harbored not the faintest surprise at adult behavior from these children, glared from one to the other. Then: "Hold your tongues, both of you!"

Alia's bronze hair was pulled back into two golden water rings. Her oval face held a frown, the wide mouth with its downturned hint of self-indulgence was held in a tight line. Worry wrinkles fanned the corners of her blue-on-blue eyes.

"I've warned both of you how to behave today," Alia said. "You know the reasons as well as I."

"We know your reasons, but you may not know ours," Ghanima said.

"Ghani!" Alia growled.

Leto glared at his aunt, said: "Today of all days, we will not pretend to be simpering infants!"

"No one wants you to simper," Alia said. "But we think it unwise for you to provoke dangerous thoughts in my mother. Irulan agrees with me. Who knows what role the Lady Jessica will choose? She is, after all, Bene Gesserit."

Leto shook his head, wondering: *Why does Alia not see what we suspect? Is she too far gone?* And he made special note of the subtle gene-markers on Alia's face which betrayed the presence of her maternal grandfather. The Baron Vladimir Harkonnen had not been a pleasant person. At this observation, Leto felt the vague stirrings of his own disquiet, thinking: *My own ancestor, too.*

He said: "The Lady Jessica was trained to rule."

Ghanima nodded. "Why does she choose this time to come back?"

Alia scowled. Then: "Is it possible she merely wants to see her grandchildren?"

Ghanima thought: *That's what you hope, my dear aunt. But it's damned well not likely.*

"She cannot rule here," Alia said. "She has Caladan. That should be enough."

Ghanima spoke placatingly: "When our father went into the desert to die, he left you as Regent. He . . ."

"Have you any complaint?" Alia demanded.

"It was a reasonable choice," Leto said, following his sister's lead. "You were the one person who knew what it was like to be born as we were born."

"It's rumored that my mother has returned to the Sisterhood," Alia said, "and you both know what the Bene Gesserit think about . . . ."

"Abomination," Leto said.

"Yes!" Alia bit the word off.

"Once a witch, always a witch—so it's said," Ghanima said.

*Sister, you play a dangerous game,* Leto thought, but he followed her lead, saying: "Our grandmother was a woman of greater simplicity than others of her kind. You share her memories, Alia; surely you must know what to expect."

"Simplicity!" Alia said, shaking her head, looking around her at the thronged passage, then back to the twins. "If my mother were less complex, neither of you would be here—nor I. I would have been her firstborn and none of this . . . ." A shrug, half shudder, moved her shoulders. "I warn you two, be very careful what you do today." Alia looked up. "Here comes my guard."

"And you still don't think it safe for us to accompany you to the spaceport?" Leto asked.

"Wait here," Alia said. "I'll bring her back."

Leto exchanged a look with his sister, said: "You've told us many times that the memories we hold from those who've passed before us lack a certain usefulness until we've experienced enough with our own flesh to make them reality. My sister and I believe this. We anticipate dangerous changes with the arrival of our grandmother."

"Don't stop believing that," Alia said. She turned away to be enclosed by her guards and they moved swiftly down the passage toward the State Entrance where ornithopters awaited them.

Ghanima wiped a tear from her right eye.

"Water for the dead?" Leto whispered, taking his sister's arm.

Ghanima drew in a deep, sighing breath, thinking of how she had observed her aunt, using the way she knew best from her own accumulation of ancestral experiences. "Spice trance did it?" she asked, knowing what Leto would say.

"Do you have a better suggestion?"

"For the sake of argument, why didn't our father . . . or even our grandmother succumb?"

He studied her a moment. Then: "You know the answer as well as I do. They had secure personalities by the time they came to Arrakis. The spice trance—well . . ." He shrugged. "They weren't born into this world already possessed of their ancestors. Alia, though . . ."

"Why didn't she believe the Bene Gesserit warnings?" Ghanima chewed her lower lip. "Alia had the same information to draw upon that we do."

"They already were calling her Abomination," Leto said. "Don't you find it tempting to find out if you're stronger than all of those . . ."

"No, I don't!" Ghanima looked away from her brother's probing stare, shuddered. She had only to consult her genetic memories and the Sisterhood's warnings took on vivid shape. The pre-born observably tended to become adults of nasty habits. And the likely cause . . . Again she shuddered.

"Pity we don't have a few pre-born in our ancestry," Leto said.

"Perhaps we do."

"But we'd . . . Ahh, yes, the old unanswered question: Do we really have open access to every ancestor's total file of experiences?"

From his own inner turmoil, Leto knew how his conversation must be disturbing his sister. They'd considered this question many times, always without conclusion. He said: "We must delay and delay and delay every time she urges the trance upon us. Extreme caution with a spice overdose; that's our best course."

"An overdose would have to be pretty large," Ghanima said.

"Our tolerance is probably high," he agreed. "Look how much Alia requires."

"I pity her," Ghanima said. "The lure of it must've been subtle and insidious, creeping up on her until . . ."

"She's a victim, yes," Leto said. "Abomination."

"We could be wrong."

"True."

"I always wonder," Ghanima mused, "if the next ancestral memory I seek will be the one which . . ."

"The past is no farther away than your pillow," Leto said.

"We must make the opportunity to discuss this with our grandmother."

"So her memory within me urges," Leto said.

Ghanima met his gaze. Then: "Too much knowledge never makes for simple decisions."

*The sietch at the desert's rim*
*Was Liet's, was Kynes's,*
*Was Stilgar's, was Muad'Dib's*
*And, once more, was Stilgar's.*
*The Naibs one by one sleep in the sand,*
*But the sietch endures.*

**—from a Fremen song**

Alia felt her heart pounding as she walked away from the twins. For a few pulsing seconds, she had felt herself near compulsion to stay with them and beg their help. What a foolish weakness! Memory of it sent a warning stillness through Alia. Would these twins dare practice prescience? The path which had engulfed their father must lure them—spice trance with its visions of the future wavering like gauze blown on a fickle wind.

*Why cannot I see the future?* Alia wondered. *Much as I try, why does it elude me?*

The twins must be made to try, she told herself. They could be lured into it. They had the curiosity of children and it was linked to memories which traversed millennia.

*Just as I have,* Alia thought.

Her guards opened the moisture seals at the State Entrance of the sietch, stood aside as she emerged onto the landing lip where the ornithopters waited. There was a wind from the desert blowing dust across the sky, but the day was bright. Emerging from the glowglobes of the sietch into the daylight sent her thoughts outward.

Why was the Lady Jessica returning at this moment? Had stories been carried to Caladan, stories of how the Regency was . . .

"We must hurry, My Lady," one of her guards said, raising his voice above the wind sounds.

Alia allowed herself to be helped into her ornithopter and secured the safety harness, but her thoughts went leaping ahead.

*Why now?*

As the ornithopter's wings dipped and the craft went skidding into the air, she felt the pomp and power of her position as physical things—but they were fragile, oh, how fragile!

Why now, when her plans were not completed?

The dust mists drifted, lifting, and she could see the bright sunlight upon the changing landscape of the planet: broad reaches of green vegetation where parched earth had once dominated.

*Without a vision of the future, I could fail. Oh, what magic I could perform if only I could see as Paul saw! Not for me the bitterness which prescient visions brought.*

A tormenting hunger shuddered through her and she wished she could put aside the power. Oh, to be as others were—blind in that safest of all blindnesses, living only the hypnoidal half-life into which birth-shock precipitated most humans. But no! She had been born an Atreides, victim of that eons-deep awareness inflicted by her mother's spice addiction.

*Why does my mother return today?*

Gurney Halleck would be with her—ever the devoted servant, the hired killer of ugly mien, loyal and straightforward, a musician who played murder with a sliptip, or entertained with equal ease upon his nine-string baliset. Some said he'd become her mother's lover. That would be a thing to ferret out; it might prove a most valuable leverage.

The wish to be as others were left her.

*Leto must be lured into the spice trance.*

She recalled asking the boy how he would deal with Gurney Halleck. And Leto, sensing undercurrents in her question, had said Halleck was loyal "to a fault," adding: "He adored . . . my father."

She'd noted the small hesitation. Leto had almost said "me" instead of "my father." Yes, it was hard at times to separate the genetic memory from the chord of living flesh. Gurney Halleck would not make that separation easier for Leto.

A harsh smile touched Alia's lips.

Gurney had chosen to return to Caladan with the Lady Jessica after Paul's death. His return would tangle many things. Coming back to Arrakis, he would add his own complexities to the existing lines. He had served Paul's father—and thus the succession went: Leto I to Paul to Leto II. And out of the Bene Gesserit breeding program: Jessica to Alia to Ghanima—a branching line. Gurney, adding to the confusion of identities, might prove valuable.

*What would he do if he discovered we carry the blood of Harkonnens, the Harkonnens he hates so bitterly?*

The smile on Alia's lips became introspective. The twins were, after all, children. They were like children with countless parents, whose memories belonged both to others and to self. They would stand at the lip of Sietch Tabr and watch the track of their grandmother's ship landing in the Arrakeen Basin. That burning mark of a ship's passage visible on the sky—would it make Jessica's arrival more real for her grandchildren?"

*My mother will ask me about their training,* Alia thought. *Do I mix* prana bindu *disciplines with a judicious hand? And I will tell her that they train themselves—just as I did. I will quote her grandson to her: "Among the responsibilities of command is the necessity to punish . . . but only when the victim demands it."*

It came to Alia then that if she could only focus the Lady Jessica's attention sharply enough onto the twins, others might escape a closer inspection.

Such a thing could be done. Leto was very like Paul. And why not? He could be Paul whenever he chose. Even Ghanima possessed this shattering ability.

*Just as I can be my mother or any of the others who've shared their lives with us.*

She veered away from this thought, staring out at the passing landscape of the Shield Wall. Then: *How was it to leave the warm safety of water-rich Caladan and return to Arrakis, to this desert planet where her Duke was murdered and her son died a martyr?*

Why did the Lady Jessica come back at this time?

Alia found no answer—nothing certain. She could share another's ego-awareness, but when experiences went their separate ways, then motives diverged as well. The stuff of decisions lay in the private actions taken by individuals. For the pre-born, the *many-born* Atreides, this remained the paramount reality, in itself another kind of birth: it was the absolute separation of living, breathing flesh when that flesh left the womb which had afflicted it with multiple awareness.

Alia saw nothing strange in loving and hating her mother simultaneously. It was a necessity, a required balance without room for guilt or blame. Where could loving or hating stop? Was one to blame the Bene Gesserit because they set the Lady Jessica upon a certain course? Guilt and blame grew diffuse when memory covered millennia. The Sisterhood had only been seeking to breed a Kwisatz Haderach: the male counterpart of a fully developed Reverend Mother . . . and more—a human of superior sensitivity and awareness, the Kwisatz Haderach who could be many places simultaneously. And the Lady Jessica, merely a pawn in that breeding program, had the bad taste to fall in love with the breeding partner to whom she had been assigned. Responsive to her beloved Duke's wishes, she produced a son instead of the daughter which the Sisterhood had commanded as the firstborn.

*Leaving me to be born after she became addicted to the spice! And now they don't want me. Now they fear me! With good reason . . .*

They'd achieved Paul, their Kwisatz Haderach, one lifetime too early—a minor miscalculation in a plan that extended. And now they had another problem: the Abomination, who carried the precious genes they'd sought for so many generations.

Alia felt a shadow pass across her, glanced upward. Her escort was assuming the high guard position preparatory to landing. She shook her head in wonderment at her wandering thoughts. What good was served by calling up old lifetimes and rubbing their mistakes together? This was a new lifetime.

Duncan Idaho had put his memtat awareness to the question of why Jessica returned at this time, evaluating the problem in the human-computer fashion which was his gift. He said she returned to take over the twins for the Sisterhood. The twins, too, carried those precious genes. Duncan could well be right. That might be enough to take the Lady Jessica out of her self-imposed seclusion on Caladan. If the Sisterhood commanded . . . Well, why else would she come back to the scenes of so much that must be shatteringly painful to her?

"We shall see," Alia muttered.

She felt the ornithopter touch down on the roof of her Keep, a positive and jarring punctuation which filled her with grim anticipation.

> melange (me'-lange *also* ma,lanj) *n-s, origin uncertain (thought to derive from ancient Terran Franzh): a. mixture of spices; b. spice of Arrakis (Dune) with geriatric properties first noted by Yanshuph Ashkoko, royal chemist in reign of Shakkad the Wise; Arrakeen melange, found only in deepest desert*

*sands of Arrakis, linked to prophetic visions of Paul Muad'Dib (Atreides), first Fremen Mahdi; also employed by Spacing Guild Navigators and the Bene Gesserit.*

—Dictionary Royal
fifth edition

The two big cats came over the rocky ridge in the dawn light, loping easily. They were not really into the passionate hunt as yet, merely looking over their territory. They were called Laza tigers, a special breed brought here to the planet Salusa Secundus almost eight thousand years past. Genetic manipulation of the ancient Terran stock had erased some of the original tiger features and refined other elements. The fangs remained long. Their faces were wide, eyes alert and intelligent. The paws were enlarged to give them support on uneven terrain and their sheathed claws could extend some ten centimeters, sharpened at the ends into razor tips by abrasive compression of the sheath. Their coats were a flat and even tan which made them almost invisible against sand.

They differed in another way from their ancestors: servo-stimulators had been implanted in their brains while they were cubs. The stimulators made them pawns of whoever possessed the transmitter.

It was cold and as the cats paused to scan the terrain, their breath made fog on the air. Around them lay a region of Salusa Secundus left sere and barren, a place which harbored a scant few sandtrout smuggled from Arrakis and kept precariously alive in the dream that the melange monopoly might be broken. Where the cats stood, the landscape was marked by tan rocks and a scattering of sparse bushes, silvery green in the long shadows of the morning sun.

With only the slightest movement the cats grew suddenly alert. Their eyes turned slowly left, then their heads turned. Far down in the scarred land two children struggled up a dry wash, hand in hand. The children appeared to be of an age, perhaps nine or ten standard years. They were red-haired and wore stillsuits partly covered by rich white bourkas which bore all around the hem and at the forehead the hawk crest of the House Atreides worked in flame-jewel threads. As they walked, the children chattered happily and their voices carried clearly to the hunting cats. The Laza tigers knew this game; they had played it before, but they remained quiescent, awaiting the triggering of the chase signal in their servo-stimulators.

Now a man appeared on the ridgetop behind the cats. He stopped and surveyed the scene: cats, children. The man wore a Sardaukar working uniform in gray and black with insignia of a Levenbrech, aide to a Bashar. A harness passed behind his neck and under his arms to carry the servo-transmitter in a thin package against his chest where the keys could be reached easily by either hand.

The cats did not turn at his approach. They knew this man by sound and smell. He scrambled down to stop two paces from the cats, mopped his forehead. The air was cold, but this was hot work. Again his pale eyes surveyed the scene: cats, children. He pushed a damp strand of blond hair back under his black working helmet, touched the implanted microphone in his throat.

"The cats have them in sight."

The answering voice came to him through receivers implanted behind each ear. "We see them."

"This time?" the Levenbrech asked.

"Will they do it without a chase command?" the voice countered.

"They're ready," the Levenbrech said.

"Very well. Let us see if four conditioning sessions will be enough."

"Tell me when you're ready."

"Any time."

"Now, then," the Levenbrech said.

He touched a red key on the right-hand side of his servo-transmitter, first releasing a bar which shielded the key. Now the cats stood without any transmitted restraints. He held his hand over a black key below the red one, ready to stop the animals should they turn on him. But they took no notice of him, crouched, and began working their way down the ridge toward the children. Their great paws slid out in smooth gliding motions.

The Levenbrech squatted to observe, knowing that somewhere around him a hidden transeye carried the entire scene to a secret monitor within the Keep where his Prince lived.

Presently the cats began to lope, then to run.

The children, intent on climbing through the rocky terrain, still had not seen their peril. One of them laughed, a high and piping sound in the clear air. The other child stumbled and, recovering balance, turned and saw the cats. The child pointed. "Look!"

Both children stopped and stared at the interesting intrusion into their lives. They were still standing when the Laza tigers hit them, one cat to each child. The children died with a casual abruptness, necks broken swiftly. The cats began to feed.

"Shall I recall them?' the Levenbrech asked.

"Let them finish. They did well. I knew they would; this pair is superb."

"Best I've ever seen," the Levenbrech agreed.

"Very good, then. Transport is being sent for you. We will sign off now."

The Levenbrech stood and stretched. He refrained from looking directly off to the high ground on his left where a telltale glitter had revealed the location of the transeye, which had relayed his fine performance to his Bashar far away in the green lands of the Capitol. The Levenbrech smiled. There would be a promotion for this day's work. Already he could feel a Bator's insignia at his neck—and someday, Burseg . . . Even, one day, Bashar. People who served well in the corps of Farad'n, grandson of the late Shaddam IV, earned rich promotions. One day, when the Prince was seated on his rightful throne, there would be even greater promotions. A Bashar's rank might not be the end of it. There were Baronies and Earldoms to be had on the many worlds of this realm . . . once the twin Atreides were removed.

*The Fremen must return to his original faith, to his genius in forming human
communities; he must return to the past, where that lesson of survival was
learned in the struggle with Arrakis. The only business of the Fremen should
be that of opening his soul to the inner teachings. The worlds of the Imperium,
the Landsraad and the CHOAM Confederacy have no message to give him.
They will only rob him of his soul.*

**—The Preacher at Arrakeen**

All around the Lady Jessica, reaching far out into the dun flatness of the landing
plain upon which her transport rested, crackling and sighing after its dive from
space, stood an ocean of humanity. She estimated half a million people were
there and perhaps only a third of them pilgrims. They stook in awesome silence,
attention fixed on the transport's exit platform, whose shadowy hatchway
concealed her and her party.

It lacked two hours until noon, but already the air above that throng reflected
a dusty shimmering in promise of the day's heat.

Jessica touched her silver-flecked copper hair where it framed her oval face
beneath the aba hood of a Reverend Mother. She knew she did not look her best
after the long trip, and the black of the aba was not her best color. But she had
worn this garment here before. The significance of the aba robe would not be
lost upon the Fremen. She sighed. Space travel did not agree with her, and
there'd been that added burden of memories—the other trip from Caladan to
Arrakis when her Duke had been forced into this fief against his better
judgment.

Slowly, probing with her Bene Gesserit-trained ability to detect significant
minutiae, she scanned the sea of people. There were stillsuit hoods of dull gray,
garments of Fremen from the deep desert; there were white-robed pilgrims
with penitence marks on their shoulders; there were scattered pockets of rich
merchants, hoodless in light clothing to flaunt their disdain for water loss in
Arrakeen's parching air . . . and there was the delegation from the Society of
the Faithful, green robed and heavily hooded, standing aloof within the
sanctity of their own group.

Only when she lifted her gaze from the crowd did the scene take on any
similarity to that which had greeted her upon her arrival with her beloved
Duke. How long ago had that been? *More than twenty years.* She did not like to
think of those intervening heartbeats. Time lay within her like a dead weight,
and it was as though her years away from this planet had never been.

*Once more into the dragon's mouth,* she thought.

Here, upon this plain, her son had wrested the Imperium from the late
Shaddam IV. A convulsion of history had imprinted this place into men's
minds and beliefs.

She heard the restless stirring of the entourage behind her and again she
sighed. They must wait for Alia, who had been delayed. Alia's party could be
seen now approaching from the far edge of the throng, creating a human wave
as a wedge of Royal Guards opened a passage.

Jessica scanned the landscape once more. Many differences submitted to her searching stare. A prayer balcony had been added to the landing field's control tower. And visible far off to the left across the plain stood the awesome pile of plasteel which Paul had built as his fortress—his "sietch above the sand." It was the largest integrated single construction ever to rise from the hand of man. Entire cities could have been housed within its walls and room to spare. Now it housed the most powerful governing force in the Imperium, Alia's "Society of the Faithful," which she had built upon her brother's body.

*That place must go,* Jessica thought.

Alia's delegation had reached the foot of the exit ramp and stood there expectantly. Jessica recognized Stilgar's craggy features. And God forfend! There stood the Princess Irulan hiding her savagery in that seductive body with its cap of golden hair exposed by a vagrant breeze. Irulan seemed not to have aged a day; it was an affront. And there, at the point of the wedge, was Alia, her features impudently youthful, her eyes staring upward into the hatchway's shadows. Jessica's mouth drew into a straight line and she scanned her daughter's face. A leaden sensation pulsed through Jessica's body and she heard the surf of her own life within her ears. The rumors were true! Horrible! Horrible! Alia had fallen into the forbidden way. The evidence was there for the initiate to read. *Abomination!*

In the few moments it took her to recover, Jessica realized how much she had hoped to find the rumors false.

*What of the twins?* she asked herself. *Are they lost, too?*

Slowly, as befitted the mother of a god, Jessica moved out of the shadows and onto the lip of the ramp. Her entourage remained behind as instructed. These next few moments were the crucial ones. Jessica stood alone in full view of the throng. She heard Gurney Halleck cough nervously behind her. Gurney had objected: *"Not even a shield on you? Gods below, woman! You're insane!"*

But among Gurney's most valuable features was a core of obedience. He would say his piece and then he would obey. Now he obeyed.

The human sea emitted a sound like the hiss of a giant sandworm as Jessica emerged. She raised her arms in the benedictory to which the priesthood had conditioned the Imperium. With significant pockets of tardiness but still like one giant organism, the people sank to their knees. Even the official party complied.

Jessica had marked out the places of delay, and she knew that other eyes behind her and among her agents in the throng had memorized a temporary map with which to seek out the tardy.

As Jessica remained with her arms upraised, Gurney and his men emerged. They moved swiftly past her down the ramp, ignoring the official party's startled looks, joining the agents who identified themselves by handsign. Quickly they fanned out through the human sea, leaping knots of kneeling figures, dashing through narrow lanes. A few of their targets saw the danger and tried to flee. They were the easiest: a thrown knife, a garrotte loop and the runners went down. Others were herded out of the press, hands bound, feet hobbled.

Through it all, Jessica stood with arms outstretched, blessing by her presence, keeping the throng subservient. She read the signs of spreading rumors though, and knew the dominant one because it had been planted: *"The Reverend Mother returns to weed out the slackers. Bless the mother of our Lord!"*

When it was over—a few dead bodies sprawled on the sand, captives removed to holding pens beneath the landing tower—Jessica lowered her arms. Perhaps three minutes had elapsed. She knew there was little likelihood Gurney and his men had taken any of the ringleaders, the ones who posed the most potent threat. They would be the alert and sensitive ones. But the captives would contain some interesting fish as well as the usual culls and dullards.

Jessica lowered her arms and, cheering, the people surged to their feet.

As though nothing untoward had happened, Jessica walked alone down the ramp, avoiding her daughter, singling out Stilgar for concentrated attention. The black beard which fanned out across the neck of his stillsuit hood like a wild delta contained flecks of gray, but his eyes carried that same whiteless intensity they'd presented to her on their first encounter in the desert. Stilgar knew what had just occurred, and approved. Here stood a true Fremen Naib, a leader of men and capable of bloody decisions. His first words were completely in character.

"Welcome home, My Lady. It's always a pleasure to see direct and effective action."

Jessica allowed herself a tiny smile. "Close the port, Stil. No one leaves until we've questioned those we took."

"It's already done, My Lady," Stilgar said. "Gurney's man and I planned this together."

"Those were your men, then, the ones who helped."

"Some of them, My Lady."

She read the hidden reservations, nodded. "You studied me pretty well in those old days, Stil."

"As you once were at pains to tell me, My Lady, one observes the survivors and learns from them."

Alia stepped forward then and Stilgar stood aside while Jessica confronted her daughter.

Knowing there was no way to hide what she had learned, Jessica did not even try concealment. Alia could read the minutiae when she needed, could read as well as any adept of the Sisterhood. She would already know by Jessica's behavior what had been seen and interpreted. They were enemies for whom the word *mortal* touched only the surface.

Alia chose anger as the easiest and most proper reaction.

"How dare you plan an action such as this without consulting me?" she demanded, pushing her face close to Jessica's.

Jessica spoke mildly: "As you've just heard, Gurney didn't even let me in on the whole plan. It was thought . . ."

"And you, Stilgar!" Alia said, rounding on him. "To whom are *you* loyal?"

"My oath is to Muad'Dib's children," Stilgar said, speaking stiffly. "We have removed a threat to them."

"And why doesn't that fill you with joy . . . daughter?" Jessica asked.

Alia blinked, glanced once at her mother, suppressed the inner tempest, and even managed a straight-toothed smile. "I *am* filled with joy . . . mother," she said. And to her own surprise, Alia found that she *was* happy, experiencing a terrible delight that it was all out in the open at last between herself and her mother. The moment she had dreaded was past and the power balance had not really been changed. "We will discuss this in more detail at a more convenient time," Alia said, speaking both to her mother and Stilgar.

"But of course," Jessica said, turning with a movement of dismissal to face the Princess Irulan.

For a few brief heartbeats, Jessica and the Princess stood silently studying each other—two Bene Gesserits who had broken with the Sisterhood for the same reason: love . . . both of them for love of men who now were dead. This Princess had loved Paul in vain, becoming his wife but not his mate. And now she lived only for the children given to Paul by his Fremen concubine, Chani.

Jessica spoke first: "Where are my grandchildren?"

"At Sietch Tabr."

"Too dangerous for them here; I understand."

Irulan permitted herself a faint nod. She had observed the interchange between Jessica and Alia, but put upon it an interpretation for which Alia had prepared her. *"Jessica has returned to the Sisterhood and we both know they have plans for Paul's children."* Irulan had never been the most accomplished adept in the Bene Gesserit—valuable more for the fact that she was a daughter of Shaddam IV than for any other reason; often too proud to exert herself in extending her capabilities. Now she chose sides with an abruptness which did no credit to her training.

"Really, Jessica," Irulan said, "the Royal Council should have been consulted. It was wrong of you to work only through—"

"Am I to believe none of you trust Stilgar?" Jessica asked.

Irulan possessed the wit to realize there could be no answer to such a question. She was glad that the priestly delegates, unable to contain their impatience any longer, pressed forward. She exchanged a glance with Alia, thinking: *Jessica's as haughty and certain of herself as ever!* A Bene Gesserit axiom arose unbidden in her mind, though: *"The haughty do but build castle walls behind which they try to hide their doubts and fears."* Could that be true of Jessica? Surely not. Then it must be a pose. But for what purpose? The question disturbed Irulan.

The priests were noisy in their possession of Muad'Dib's mother. Some only touched her arms, but most bowed low and spoke greetings. At last the leaders of the delegation took their turn with the Most Holy Reverend Mother, accepting the ordained role—"The first shall be last"—with practiced smiles, telling her that the official Lustration ceremony awaited her at the Keep, Paul's old fortress-stronghold.

Jessica studied the pair, finding them repellent. One was called Javid, a young man of surly features and round cheeks, shadowed eyes which could not hide the suspicions lurking in their depths. The other was Zebataleph, second son of a Naib she'd known in her Fremen days, as he was quick to remind her. He was easily classified: jollity linked with ruthlessness, a thin face with blond beard, an air about him of secret excitements and powerful knowledge. Javid she judged far more dangerous of the two, a man of private counsel, simultaneously magnetic and—she could find no other word—*repellent*. She found his accents strange, full of old Fremen pronunciations, as though he'd come from some isolated pocket of his people.

"Tell me, Javid," she said, "whence come you?"

"I am but a simple Fremen of the desert," he said, every syllable giving the lie to the statement.

Zebataleph intruded with an offensive deference, almost mocking: "We have much to discuss of the old days, My Lady. I was one of the first, you know, to recognize the holy nature of your son's mission."

"But you weren't one of his Fedaykin," she said.

"No, My Lady. I possessed a more philosophic bent; I studied for the priesthood."

*And insured the preservation of your skin,* she thought.

Javid said: "They await us at the Keep, My Lady."

Again she found the strangeness of his accent an open question demanding an answer. "Who awaits us?" she asked.

"The Convocation of the Faith, all those who keep bright the name and the deeds of your holy son," Javid said.

Jessica glanced around her, saw Alia smiling at Javid, asked: "Is this man one of your appointees, daughter?"

Alia nodded. "A man destined for great deeds."

But Jessica saw that Javid had no pleasure in this attention, marked him for Gurney's special study. And there came Gurney with five trusted men, signaling that they had the suspicious laggards under interrogation. He walked with the rolling stride of a powerful man, glance flicking left, right, all around, every muscle flowing through the relaxed alertness she had taught him out of the Bene Gesserit *prana-bindu* manual. He was an ugly lump of trained reflexes, a killer, and altogether terrifying to some, but Jessica loved him and prized him above all other living men. The scar of an inkvine whip rippled along his jaw, giving him a sinister appearance, but a smile softened his face as he saw Stilgar.

"Well done, Stil," he said. And they gripped arms in the Fremen fashion.

"The Lustration," Javid said, touching Jessica's arm.

Jessica drew back, chose her words carefully in the controlled power of Voice, her tone and delivery calculated for a precise emotional effect upon Javid and Zebataleph: "I returned to Dune to see my grandchildren. Must we take time for this priestly nonsense?"

Zebataleph reacted with shock, his mouth dropping open, eyes alarmed, glancing about at those who had heard. The eyes marked each listener: *Priestly nonsense!* What effect would such words have, coming from the mother of their messiah?

Javid, however, confirmed Jessica's assessment. His mouth hardened, then smiled. The eyes did not smile, nor did they waver to mark the listeners. Javid already knew each member of this party. He had an earshot map of those who would be watched with special care from this point onward. Only seconds later, Javid stopped smiling with an abruptness which said he knew how he had betrayed himself. Javid had not failed to do his homework: he knew the observational powers possessed by the Lady Jessica. A short, jerking nod of his head acknowledged those powers.

In a lightning flash of mentation, Jessica weighed the necessities. A subtle hand signal to Gurney would bring Javid's death. It could be done here for effect, or in quiet later, and be made to appear an accident.

She thought: *When we try to conceal our innermost drives, the entire being screams betrayal.* Bene Gesserit training turned upon this revelation—raising the adepts above it and teaching them to read the open flesh of others. She saw Javid's intelligence as valuable, a temporary weight in the balance. If he could be won over, he could be the link she needed, the line into the Arrakeen priesthood. And he was Alia's man.

Jessica said: "My official party must remain small. We have room for one addition, however. Javid, you will join us. Zebataleph, I am sorry. And, Javid . . . I will attend this—this ceremony—if you insist."

Javid allowed himself a deep breath and a low-voiced "As Muad'Dib's mother commands." He glanced to Alia, to Zebataleph, back to Jessica. "It pains me to delay the reunion with your grandchildren, but there are, ahhh, reasons of state . . ."

Jessica thought: *Good. He's a businessman above all else. Once we've determined the proper coinage, we'll buy him.* And she found herself enjoying the fact that he insisted on his precious ceremony. This little victory would give him power with his fellows, and they both knew it. Accepting his Lustration could be a down payment on later services.

"I presume you've arranged transportation," she said.

> *I give you the desert chameleon, whose ability to blend itself into the background tells you all you need to know about the roots of ecology and the foundations of a personal identity.*

> **—Book of Diatribes**
> **from the Hayt Chronicle**

Leto sat playing a small baliset which had been sent to him on his fifth birthday by that consummate artist of the instrument, Gurney Halleck. In four years of practice, Leto had achieved a certain fluency, although the two bass side strings still gave him trouble. He had found the baliset soothing, however, for particular feelings of upset—a fact which had not escaped Ghanima. He sat now in twilight on a rock shelf at the southernmost extremity of the craggy outcropping which sheltered Sietch Tabr. Softly he strummed the baliset.

Ghanima stood behind him, her small figure radiating protest. She had not wanted to come here into the open after learning from Stilgar that their grandmother was delayed in Arrakeen. She particularly objected to coming here with nightfall near. Attempting to hurry her brother, she asked: "Well, what is it?"

For answer, he began another tune.

For the first time since accepting the gift, Leto felt intensely aware that this baliset had originated with a master craftsman on Caladan. He possessed inherited memories which could inflict him with profound nostalgia for that beautiful planet where House Atreides had ruled. Leto had but to relax his inner barriers in the presence of this music and he would hear memories from those times when Gurney had employed the baliset to beguile his friend and charge, Paul Atreides. With the baliset sounding in his own hands, Leto felt himself more and more dominated by his father's psychical presence. Still he played, relating more strongly to the instrument with every second that passed. He sensed the absolute idealized summation within himself which *knew* how to play this baliset, though nine-year-old muscles had not yet been conditioned to that inner awareness.

Ghanima tapped her foot impatiently, unaware that she matched the rhythm of her brother's playing.

Setting his mouth in a grimace of concentration, Leto broke from the familiar music and tried a song more ancient than any even Gurney had played. It had been old when Fremen migrated to their fifth planet. The words echoed a Zensunni theme, and he heard them in his memory while his fingers elicited a faltering version of the tune.

> *"Nature's beauteous form*
> *Contains a lovely essence*
> *Called by some—decay.*
> *By this lovely presence*
> *New life finds its way.*
> *Tears shed silently*
> *Are but water of the soul:*
> *They bring new life*
> *To the pain of being—*
> *A separation from that seeing*
> *Which death makes whole."*

Ghanima spoke behind him as he strummed the final note. "There's a mucky old song. Why that one?"

"Because it fits."

"Will you play it for Gurney?"

"Perhaps."

"He'll call it moody nonsense."

"I know."

Leto peered back over his shoulder at Ghanima. There was no surprise in him that she knew the song and its lyrics, but he felt a sudden onset of awe at the singleness of their twinned lives. One of them could die and yet remain alive in the other's consciousness, every shared memory intact; they were that close. He found himself frightened by the timeless web of that closeness, broke his gaze away from her. The web contained gaps, he knew. His fear arose from the newest of those gaps. He felt their lives beginning to separate and wondered: *How can I tell her of this thing which has happened only to me?*

He peered out over the desert, seeing the deep shadows behind the barachans—those high, crescent-shaped migratory dunes which moved like waves around Arrakis. This was *Kedem,* the inner desert, and its dunes were rarely marked these days by the irregularities of a giant worm's progress. Sunset drew bloody streaks over the dunes, imparting a fiery light to the shadow edges. A hawk falling from the crimson sky captured his awareness as it captured a rock partridge in flight.

Directly beneath him on the desert floor plants grew in a profusion of greens, watered by a qanat which flowed partly in the open, partly in covered tunnels. The water came from giant windtrap collectors behind him on the highest point of rock. The green flag of the Atreides flew openly there.

*Water and green.*

The new symbols of Arrakis: water and green.

A diamond-shaped oasis of planted dunes spread beneath his high perch, focusing his attention into sharp Fremen awareness. The bell call of a nightbird came from the cliff below him, and it amplified the sensation that he lived this moment out of a wild past.

*Nous avons changé tout cela,* he thought, falling easily into one of the ancient tongues which he and Ghanima employed in private. *"We have altered all of that."* He sighed. *Oublier je ne puis. "I cannot forget."*

Beyond the oasis, he could see in this failing light the land Fremen called "The Emptiness"—the land where nothing grows, the land never fertile. Water and the great ecological plan were changing that. There were places now on Arrakis where one could see the plush green velvet of forested hills. Forests on Arrakis! Some in the new generation found it difficult to imagine dunes beneath those undulant green hills. To such young eyes there was no shock value in seeing the flat foliage of rain trees. But Leto found himself thinking now in the Old Fremen manner, wary of change, fearful in the presence of the new.

He said: "The children tell me they seldom find sandtrout here near the surface anymore."

"What's that supposed to indicate?" Ghanima asked. There was petulance in her tone.

"Things are beginning to change very swiftly," he said.

Again the bird chimed in the cliff, and night fell upon the desert as the hawk had fallen upon the partridge. Night often subjected him to an assault of memories—all of those inner lives clamoring for their moment. Ghanima didn't object to this phenomenon in quite the way he did. She knew his disquiet, though, and he felt her hand touch his shoulder in sympathy.

He struck an angry chord from the baliset.

How could he tell her what was happening to him?

Within his head were wars, uncounted lives parceling out their ancient memories: violent accidents, love's languor, the colors of many places and many faces . . . the buried sorrows and leaping joys of multitudes. He heard elegies to springs on planets which no longer existed, green dances and firelight, wails and halloos, a harvest of conversations without number.

Their assault was hardest to bear at nightfall in the open.

"Shouldn't we be going in?" she asked.

He shook his head, and she felt the movement, realizing at last that his troubles went deeper than she had suspected.

*Why do I so often greet the night out here?* he asked himself. He did not feel Ghanima withdraw her hand.

"You know why you torment yourself this way," she said.

He heard the gentle chiding in her voice. Yes, he knew. The answer lay there in his awareness, obvious: *Because that great known-unknown within moves me like a wave.* He felt the cresting of his past as though he rode a surfboard. He had his father's time-spread memories of prescience superimposed upon everything else, yet he wanted all of those pasts. He wanted them. And they were so very dangerous. He knew that completely now with this new thing which he would have to tell Ghanima.

The desert was beginning to glow under the rising light of First Moon. He stared out at the false immobility of sand furls reaching into infinity. To his left, in the near distance, lay The Attendant, a rock outcropping which sandblast winds had reduced to a low, sinuous shape like a dark worm striking through the dunes. Someday the rock beneath him would be cut down to such a shape and Sietch Tabr would be no more, except in the memories of someone like himself. He did not doubt that there would be someone like himself.

"Why're you staring at The Attendant?" Ghanima asked.

He shrugged. In defiance of their guardians' orders, he and Ghanima often went to The Attendant. They had discovered a secret hiding place there, and Leto knew now why that place lured them.

Beneath him, its distance foreshortened by darkness, an open stretch of qanat gleamed in moonlight; its surface rippled with movements of predator fish which Fremen always planted in their stored water to keep out the sandtrout.

"I stand between fish and worm," he murmured.

"What?"

He repeated it louder.

She put a hand to her mouth, beginning to suspect the thing which moved him. Her father had acted thus; she had but to peer inward and compare.

Leto shuddered. Memories which fastened him to places his flesh had never known presented him with answers to questions he had not asked. He saw relationships and unfolding events against a gigantic inner screen. The sandworm of Dune would not cross water; water poisoned it. Yet water had been known here in prehistoric times. White gypsum pans attested to bygone lakes and seas. Wells, deep-drilled, found water which sandtrout sealed off. As clearly as if he'd witnessed the events, he saw what had happened on this planet and it filled him with foreboding for the cataclysmic changes which human intervention was bringing.

His voice barely above a whisper, he said: "I know what happened, Ghanima."

She bent close to him. "Yes?"

"The sandtrout . . ."

He fell silent and she wondered why he kept referring to the haploid phase of the planet's giant sandworm, but she dared not prod him.

"The sandtrout," he repeated, "was introduced here from some other place. This was a wet planet then. They proliferated beyond the capability of existing ecosystems to deal with them. Sandtrout encysted the available free water, made this a desert planet . . . and they did it to survive. In a planet sufficiently dry, they could move to their sandworm phase."

"The sandtrout?" She shook her head, not doubting him, but unwilling to search those depths where he gathered such information. And she thought: *Sandtrout?* Many times in this flesh and other had she played the childhood game, poling for sandtrout, teasing them into a thin glove membrane before taking them to the deathstill for their water. It was difficult to think of this mindless little creature as a shaper of enormous events.

Leto nodded to himself. Fremen had always known to plant predator fish in their water cisterns. The haploid sandtrout actively resisted great accumulations of water near the planet's surface; predators swam in that qanat below him. Their sandworm vector could handle small amounts of water—the amounts held in cellular bondage by human flesh, for example. But confronted by large bodies of water, their chemical factories went wild, exploded in the death-transformation which produced the dangerous melange concentrate, the ultimate awareness drug employed in a diluted fraction for the sietch orgy. That pure concentrate had taken Paul Muad'Dib through the walls of Time, deep into the well of dissolution which no other male had ever dared.

Ghanima sensed her brother trembling where he sat in front of her. "What have you done?" she demanded.

But he would not leave his own train of revelation. "Fewer sandtrout—the ecological transformation of the planet . . ."

"They resist it, of course," she said, and now she began to understand the fear in his voice, drawn into this thing against her will.

"When the sandtrout go, so do all the worms," he said. "The tribes must be warned."

"No more spice," she said.

Words merely touched high points of the system danger which they both saw hanging over human intrusion into Dune's ancient relationships.

"It's the thing Alia knows," he said. "It's why she gloats."

"How can you be sure of that?"

"I'm sure."

Now she knew for certain what disturbed him, and she felt the knowledge chill her.

"The tribes won't believe us if she denies it," he said.

His statement went to the primary problem of their existence: What Fremen expected wisdom from a nine-year-old? Alia, growing farther and farther from her own inner sharing each day, played upon this.

"We must convince Stilgar," Ghanima said.

As one, their heads turned and they stared out over the moonlit desert. It was a different place now, changed by just a few moments of awareness. Human interplay with that environment had never been more apparent to them. They felt themselves as integral parts of a dynamic system held in delicately balanced order. The new outlook involved a real change of consciousness which flooded them with observations. As Liet-Kynes had said, the universe was a place of constant conversation between animal populations. The haploid sandtrout had spoken to them as human animals.

"The tribes would understand a threat to water," Leto said.

"But it's a threat to more than water. It's a—" She fell silent, understanding the deeper meaning of his words. Water was the ultimate power symbol on Arrakis. At their roots Fremen remained special-application animals, desert survivors, governance experts under conditions of stress. And as water became plentiful, a strange symbol transfer came over them even while they understood the old necessities.

"You mean a threat to power," she corrected him.

"Of course."

"But will they believe us?"

"If they see it happening, if they see the imbalance."

"Balance," she said, and repeated her father's words from long ago: "It's what distinguishes a people from a mob."

Her words called up their father in him and he said: "Economics versus beauty—a story older than Sheba." He sighed, looked over his shoulder at her. "I'm beginning to have prescient dreams, Ghani."

A sharp gasp escaped her.

He said: "When Stilgar told us our grandmother was delayed—I already knew that moment. Now my other dreams are suspect."

"Leto . . ." She shook her head, eyes damp. "It came later for our father. Don't you think it might be—"

"I've dreamed myself enclosed in armor and racing across the dunes," he said. "And I've been to Jacurutu."

"Jacu . . ." She cleared her throat. "That old myth!"

"A real place. Ghani! I must find this man they call The Preacher. I must find him and question him."

"You think he's . . . our father?"

"Ask yourself that question."

"It'd be just like him," she agreed, "but . . ."

"I don't like the things I know I'll do," he said. "For the first time in my life I understand my father."

She felt excluded from his thoughts, said: "The Preacher's probably just an old mystic."

"I pray for that," he whispered. "Oh, how I pray for that!" He rocked forward, got to his feet. The baliset hummed in his hand as he moved. "Would that he were only Gabriel without a horn." He stared silently at the moonlit desert.

She turned to look where he looked, saw the foxfire glow of rotting vegetation at the edge of the sietch plantings, then the clean blending into lines of dunes. That was a living place out there. Even when the desert slept, something remained awake in it. She sensed that wakefulness, hearing animals below her drinking at the qanat. Leto's revelation had transformed the night: this was a living moment, a time to discover regularities within perpetual change, an instant in which to feel that long movement from their Terranic past, all of it encapsulated in her memories.

"Why Jacurutu?" she asked, and the flatness of her tone shattered the mood.

"Why . . . I don't know. When Stilgar first told us how they killed the people there and made the place tabu, I thought . . . what you thought. But danger comes from there now . . . and The Preacher."

She didn't respond, didn't demand that he share more of his prescient dreams with her, and she knew how much this told him of her terror. That way led to Abomination and they both knew it. The word hung unspoken between them as he turned and led the way back over the rocks to the sietch entrance. *Abomination.*

> *The Universe is God's. It is one thing, a wholeness against which all separations may be identified. Transient life, even that self-aware and reasoning life which we call sentient, holds only fragile trusteeship on any portion of the wholeness.*
>
> **—Commentaries from the C.E.T.**
> **(Commission of Ecumenical Translators)**

Halleck used hand signals to convey the actual message while speaking aloud of other matters. He didn't like the small anteroom the priests had assigned for this report, knowing it would be crawling with spy devices. Let them try to break the tiny hand signals, though. The Atreides had used this means of communication for centuries without anyone the wiser.

Night had fallen outside, but the room had no windows, depending upon glowglobes at the upper corners.

"Many of those we took were Alia's people." Halleck signaled, watching Jessica's face as he spoke aloud, telling her the interrogation still continued.

"It was as you anticipated then," Jessica replied, her fingers winking. She nodded and spoke an open reply: "I'll expect a full report when you're satisfied, Gurney."

"Of course, My Lady," he said, and his fingers continued: "There is another thing, quite disturbing. Under the deep drugs, some of our captives talked of Jacurutu and, as they spoke the name, they died."

"A conditioned heart-stopper?" Jessica's fingers asked. And she said: "Have you released any of the captives?"

"A few, My Lady—the more obvious culls." And his fingers darted: "We suspect a heart-compulsion but are not yet certain. The autopsies aren't completed. I thought you should know about this thing of Jacurutu, however, and came immediately."

"My Duke and I always thought Jacurutu an interesting legend probably based on fact," Jessica's fingers said, and she ignored the usual tug of sorrow as she spoke of her long-dead love.

"Do you have orders?" Halleck asked, speaking aloud.

Jessica answered in kind, telling him to return to the landing field and report when he had positive information, but her fingers conveyed another message: "Resume contact with your friends among the smugglers. If Jacurutu exists, they'll support themselves by selling spice. There'd be no other market for them except for the smugglers."

Halleck bowed his head briefly while his fingers said: "I've already set this course in motion, My Lady." And because he could not ignore the training of a lifetime, added: "Be very careful in this place. Alia is your enemy and most of the priesthood belongs to her."

"Not Javid," Jessica's fingers responded. "He hates the Atreides. I doubt anyone but an adept could detect it, but I'm positive of it. He conspires and Alia doesn't know of it."

"I'm assigning additional guards to your person," Halleck said, speaking aloud, avoiding the light spark of displeasure which Jessica's eyes betrayed. "There are dangers, I'm certain. Will you spend the night here?"

"We'll go later to Sietch Tabr," she said and hesitated, on the point of telling him not to send more guards, but she held her silence. Gurney's instincts were to be trusted. More than one Atreides had learned this, both to his pleasure and his sorrow. "I have one more meeting—with the Master of Novitiates this time," she said. "That's the last one and I'll be happily shut of this place."

---

*And I beheld another beast coming up out of the sand; and he had two horns like a lamb, but his mouth was fanged and fiery as the dragon and his body shimmered and burned with great heat while it did hiss like the serpent.*

**—Revised Orange Catholic Bible**

---

He called himself *The Preacher*, and there had come to be an awesome fear among many on Arrakis that he might be Muad'Dib returned from the desert, not dead at all. Muad'Dib could be alive; for who had seen his body? For that matter, who saw any body that the desert took? But still—Muad'Dib? Points of comparison could be made, although no one from the old days came forward and said: "Yes, I see that this is Muad'Dib. I know him."

Still . . . Like Muad'Dib, The Preacher was blind, his eye sockets black and scarred in a way that could have been done by a stone burner. And his voice conveyed that crackling penetration, that same compelling force which demanded a response from deep within you. Many remarked this. He was lean, this Preacher, his leathery face seamed, his hair grizzled. But the deep desert did that to many people. You had only to look about you and see this proven. And there was another fact for contention: The Preacher was led by a young Fremen, a lad without known sietch who said, when questioned, that he worked for hire. It was argued that Muad'Dib, knowing the future, had not needed such a guide except at the very end, when his grief overcame him. But he'd needed a guide then; everyone knew it.

The Preacher had appeared one winter morning in the streets of Arrakeen, a brown and ridge-veined hand on the shoulder of his guide. The lad, who gave his name as Assan Tariq, moved through the flint-smelling dust of the early swarming, leading his charge with the practiced agility of the warren-born, never once losing contact.

It was observed that the blind man wore a traditional bourka over a stillsuit which bore the mark about it of those once made only in the sietch caves of the deepest desert. It wasn't like the shabby suits being turned out these days. The nose tube which captured moisture from his breath for the recycling layers beneath the bourka was wrapped in braid, and it was the black vine braid so seldom seen anymore. The suit's mask across the lower half of his face carried green patches etched by the blown sand. All in all, this Preacher was a figure from Dune's past.

Many among the early crowds of that winter day had noted his passage. After all, a blind Fremen remained a rarity. Fremen law still consigned the blind to Shai-Hulud. The wording of the Law, although it was less honored in these modern, water-soft times, remained unchanged from the earliest days. The blind were a gift to Shai-Hulud. They were to be exposed in the open *bled* for the great worms to devour. When it was done—and there were stories which got back to the cities—it was always done out where the largest worms still ruled, those called Old Men of the Desert. A blind Fremen, then, was a curiosity, and people paused to watch the passing of this odd pair.

The lad appeared about fourteen standard, one of the new breed who wore modified stillsuits; it left the face open to the moisture-robbing air. He had slender features, the all-blue spice-tinted eyes, a nubbin nose, and that innocuous look of innocence which so often masks cynical knowledge in the young. In contrast, the blind man was a reminder of times almost forgotten—long in stride and with a wiriness that spoke of many years on the sand with only his feet or a captive worm to carry him. He held his head in that stiff-necked rigidity which some of the blind cannot put off. The hooded head moved only when he cocked an ear at an interesting sound.

Through the day's gathering crowds the strange pair came, arriving at last on the steps which led up like terraced hectares to the escarpment which was Alia's Temple, a fitting companion to Paul's Keep. Up the steps The Preacher went until he and his young guide came to the third landing, where pilgrims of the Hajj awaited the morning opening of those gigantic doors above them. They were doors large enough to have admitted an entire cathedral from one of the ancient religions. Passing through them was said to reduce a pilgrim's soul to *motedom,* sufficiently small that it could pass through the eye of a needle and enter heaven.

At the edge of the third landing The Preacher turned, and it was as though he looked about him, seeing with his empty eye sockets the foppish city dwellers, some of them Fremen, with garments which simulated stillsuits but were only decorative fabrics, *seeing* the eager pilgrims fresh off the Guild space transports and awaiting that first step on the devotion which would ensure them a place in paradise.

The landing was a noisy place: there were Mahdi Spirit Cultists in green robes and carrying live hawks trained to screech a "call to heaven." Food was being sold by shouting vendors. Many things were being offered for sale, the voices shouting in competitive stridence: there was the Dune Tarot with its booklets of commentaries imprinted on shigawire. One vendor had exotic bits of cloth "guaranteed to have been touched by Muad'Dib himself!" Another had vials of water "certified to have come from Sietch Tabr, where Muad'Dib lived." Through it all there were conversations in a hundred or more dialects of Galach interspersed with harsh gutturals and squeaks of *outrine* languages which were gathered under the Holy Imperium. Face dancers and little people from the suspected artisan planets of the Tleilaxu bounced and gyrated through the throng in bright clothing. There were lean faces and fat, water-rich faces. The susurration of nervous feet came from the gritty plasteel which formed the wide steps. And occasionally a keening voice would rise out of the cacophony in prayer—"Mua-a-a-ad'Dib! Mua-a-a-d'Dib! Greet my soul's entreaty! You, who are God's anointed, greet my soul! Mua-a-a-ad'Dib!"

Nearby among the pilgrims, two mummers played for a few coins, reciting the lines of the currently popular "Disputation of Armistead and Leandgrah."

The Preacher cocked his head to listen.

The mummers were middle-aged city men with bored voices. At a word of command, the young guide described them to The Preacher. They were garbed in loose robes, not even deigning to simulate stillsuits on their water-rich bodies. Assan Tariq thought this amusing, but The Preacher reprimanded him.

The mummer who played the part of Leandgrah was just concluding his oration: "Bah! The universe can be grasped only by the sentient hand. That hand is what drives your precious brain, and it drives everything else that derives from the brain. You see what you have created, you *become* sentient, only after the hand has done its work!"

A scattering of applause greeted his performance.

The Preacher sniffed and his nostrils recorded the rich odors of this place: uncapped esters of poorly adjusted stillsuits, masking musks of diverse origin, the common flinty dust, exhalations of uncounted exotic diets and the aromas of rare incense which already had been ignited within Alia's Temple and now drifted down over the steps in cleverly directed currents. The Preacher's thoughts were mirrored on his face as he absorbed his surroundings: *We have come to this, we Fremen!*

A sudden diversion rippled through the crowd on the landing. Sand Dancers had come into the plaza at the foot of the steps, half a hundred of them tethered to each other by elacca ropes. They obviously had been dancing thus for days, seeking a state of ecstasy. Foam dribbled from their mouths as they jerked and stamped to their secret music. A full third of them dangled unconscious from the ropes, tugged back and forth by the others like dolls on strings. One of these dolls had come awake, though, and the crowd apparently knew what to expect.

"I have *see-ee-een!*" the newly awakened dancer shrieked. "I have *see-ee-een!*" He resisted the pull of the other dancers, darted his wild gaze right and left. "Where this city is, there will be only sand! I have *see-ee-een!*"

A great swelling laugh went up from the onlookers. Even the new pilgrims joined it.

This was too much for The Preacher. He raised both arms and roared in a voice which surely had commanded worm riders: *"Silence!"* The entire throng in the plaza went still at that battle cry.

The Preacher pointed a thin hand toward the dancers, and the illusion that he actually saw them was uncanny. "Did you not hear that man? Blasphemers and idolaters! All of you! The religion of Muad'Dib is not Muad'Dib. He spurns it as he spurns you! Sand will cover this place. Sand will cover you."

Saying this, he dropped his arms, put a hand on his young guide's shoulder, and commanded: "Take me from this place."

Perhaps it was The Preacher's choice of words: *He spurns it as he spurns you!* Perhaps it was his tone, certainly something more than human, a vocality trained surely in the arts of the Bene Gesserit Voice which commanded by mere nuances of subtle inflection. Perhaps it was only the inherent mysticism of this place where Muad'Dib had lived and walked and ruled. Someone called out from the landing, shouting at The Preacher's receding back in a voice that trembled with religious awe: "Is that Muad'Dib come back to us?"

The Preacher stopped, reached into the purse beneath his bourka, and removed an object which only those nearby recognized. It was a desert-mummified human hand, one of the planet's jokes on mortality which occasionally turned up in the sand and were universally regarded as communications from Shai-Hulud. The hand had been desiccated into a tight fist which ended in white bone scarred by sandblast winds.

"I bring the Hand of God, and that is all I bring!" The Preacher shouted. "I speak for the Hand of God. I am The Preacher."

Some took him to mean that the hand was Muad'Dib's, but others fastened on that commanding presence and the terrible voice—and that was how Arrakis came to know his name. But it was not the last time his voice was heard.

---

*It is commonly reported, my dear Georad, that there exists great natural virtue in the melange experience. Perhaps this is true. There remains within me, however, profound doubts that every use of melange always brings virtue. Meseems that certain persons have corrupted the use of melange in defiance of God. In the words of the Ecumenon, they have disfigured the soul. They skim the surface of melange and believe thereby to attain grace. They deride their fellows, do great harm to godliness, and they distort the meaning of this abundant gift maliciously, surely a mutilation beyond the power of man to restore. To be truly at one with the virtue of the spice, uncorrupted in all ways, full of goodly honor, a man must permit his deeds and his words to agree. When your actions describe a system of evil consequences, you should be judged by those consequences and not by your explanations. It is thus that we should judge Muad'Dib.*

**—The Pedant Heresy**

It was a small room tinged with the odor of ozone and reduced to a shadowy greyness by dimmed glowglobes and the metallic blue light of a single transeye monitoring screen. The screen was about a meter wide and only two-thirds of a meter in height. It revealed in remote detail a barren, rocky valley with two Laza tigers feeding on the bloody remnants of a recent kill. On the hillside above the tigers could be seen a slender man in Sardaukar working uniform, Levenbrech insignia at his collar. He wore a servo-control keyboard against his chest.

One veriform suspensor chair faced the screen, occupied by a fair-haired woman of indeterminate age. She had a heart-shaped face and slender hands which gripped the chair arms as she watched. The fullness of a white robe trimmed in gold concealed her figure. A pace to her right stood a blocky man dressed in the bronze and gold uniform of a Bashar Aide in the old Imperial Sardaukar. His greying hair had been closely cropped over square, emotionless features.

The woman coughed, said: "It went as you predicted, Tyekanik."

"Assuredly, Princess," the Bashar Aide said, his voice hoarse.

She smiled at the tension in his voice, asked: "Tell me, Tyekanik, how will my son like the sound of Emperor Farad'n I?"

"The title suits him, Princess."

"That was not my question."

"He might not approve some of the things done to gain him that, ahh, title."

"Then again . . ." She turned, peered up through the gloom at him. "You served my father well. It was not your fault that he lost the throne to the Atreides. But surely the sting of that loss must be felt as keenly by you as by any—"

"Does the Princess Wensicia have some special task for me?" Tyekanik asked. His voice remained hoarse, but there was a sharp edge to it now.

"You have a bad habit of interrupting me," she said.

Now he smiled, displaying thick teeth which glistened in the light of the screen. "At times you remind me of your father," he said. "Always these circumlocutions before a request for a delicate . . . ahh, assignment."

She jerked her gaze away from him to conceal anger, asked: "Do you really think those Lazas will put my son on the throne?"

"It's distinctly possible, Princess. You must admit that the bastard get of

Paul Atreides would be no more than juicy morsels for those two. And with those twins gone . . ." He shrugged.

"The grandson of Shaddam IV becomes the logical successor," she said. "That is if we can remove the objections of the Fremen, the Landsraad and CHOAM, not to mention any surviving Atreides who might—"

"Javid assures me that his people can take care of Alia quite easily. I do not count the Lady Jessica as an Atreides. Who else remains?"

"Landsraad and CHOAM will go where the profit goes," she said, "but what of the Fremen?"

"We'll drown them in their Muad'Dib's religion!"

"Easier said than done, my dear Tyekanik."

"I see," he said. "We're back to that old argument."

"House Corrino has done worse things to gain power," she said.

"But to embrace this . . . this Mahdi's religion!"

"My son respects you," she said.

"Princess, I long for the day when House Corrino returns to its rightful seat of power. So does every remaining Sardaukar here on Salusa. But if you—"

"Tyekanik! This is the planet Salusa *Secundus*. Do not fall into the lazy ways which spread through our Imperium. Full name, complete title—attention to every detail. Those attributes will send the Atreides lifeblood into the sands of Arrakis. Every detail, Tyekanik!"

He knew what she was doing with this attack. It was part of the shifty trickiness she'd learned from her sister, Irulan. But he felt himself losing ground.

"Do you hear me, Tyekanik?"

"I hear, Princess."

"I want you to embrace this Muad'Dib religion," she said.

"Princess, I would walk into fire for you, but this . . ."

"That is an order, Tyekanik!"

He swallowed, stared into the screen. The Laza tigers had finished feeding and now lay on the sand completing their toilet, long tongues moving across their forepaws.

"An *order*, Tyekanik—do you understand me?"

"I hear and obey, Princess." His voice did not change tone.

She sighed. "Ohh, if my father were only alive . . ."

"Yes, Princess."

"Don't mock me, Tyekanik. I know how distasteful this is to you. But if you set the example . . ."

"He may not follow, Princess."

"He'll follow." She pointed at the screen. "It occurs to me that the Levenbrech out there could be a problem."

"A problem? How is that?"

"How many people know this thing of the tigers?"

"That Levenbrech who is their trainer . . . one transport pilot, you and of course . . ." He tapped his own chest.

"What about the buyers?"

"They know nothing. What is it you fear, Princess?"

"My son is, well, sensitive."

"Sardaukar do not reveal secrets," he said.

"Neither do dead men." She reached forward and depressed a red key beneath the lighted screen.

Immediately the Laza tigers raised their heads. They got to their feet and looked up the hill at the Levenbrech. Moving as one, they turned and began a scrambling run up the hillside.

Appearing calm at first, the Levenbrech depressed a key on his console. His movements were assured but, as the cats continued their dash toward him, he became more frenzied, pressing the key harder and harder. A look of startled awareness came over his features and his hand jerked toward the working knife at his waist. The movement came too late. A raking claw hit his chest and sent him sprawling. As he fell, the other tiger took his neck in one great-fanged bite and shook him. His spine snapped.

"Attention to detail," the Princess said. She turned, stiffened as Tyekanik drew his knife. But he presented the blade to her, handle foremost.

"Perhaps you'd like to use my knife to attend to another detail," he said.

"Put that back in its sheath and don't act the fool!" she raged. "Sometimes, Tyekanik, you try me to the—"

"That was a good man out there, Princess. One of my best."

"One of *my* best," she corrected him.

He drew a deep, trembling breath, sheathed his knife. "And what of my transport pilot?"

"This will be ascribed to an accident," she said. "You will advise him to employ the utmost caution when he brings those tigers back to us. And of course, when he has delivered our pets to Javid's people on the transport . . ." She looked at his knife.

"Is that an order, Princess?"

"It is."

"Shall I, then, fall on my knife, or will you take care of that, ahhh, detail?"

She spoke with a false calm, her voice heavy: "Tyekanik, were I not absolutely convinced that you *would* fall on your knife at my command, you would not be standing here beside me—armed."

He swallowed, stared at the screen. The tigers once more were feeding.

She refused to look at the scene, continued to stare at Tyekanik as she said: "You will, as well, tell our buyers not to bring us any more matched pairs of children who fit the necessary description."

"As you command, Princess."

"Don't use that tone with me, Tyekanik."

"Yes, Princess."

Her lips drew into a straight line. Then: "How many more of those paired costumes do we have?"

"Six sets of the robes, complete with stillsuits and the sand shoes, all with the Atreides insignia worked into them."

"Fabrics as rich as the ones on that pair?" she nodded toward the screen.

"Fit for royalty, Princess."

"Attention to detail," she said. "The garments will be dispatched to Arrakis as gifts for our royal cousins. They will be gifts from my son, do you understand me, Tyekanik?"

"Completely, Princess."

"Have him inscribe a suitable note. It should say that he sends these few paltry garments as tokens of his devotion to House Atreides. Something on that order."

"And the occasion?"

"There must be a birthday or holy day or something, Tyekanik. I leave that to you. I trust you, my friend."

He stared at her silently.

Her face hardened. "Surely you must know that? Who else can I trust since the death of my husband?"

He shrugged, thinking how closely she emulated the spider. It would not do to get on intimate terms with her, as he now suspected his Levenbrech had done.

"And Tyekanik," she said, "one more detail."

"Yes, Princess."

"My son is being trained to rule. There will come a time when he must grasp the sword in his own hands. You will know when that moment arrives. I'll wish to be informed immediately."

"As you command, Princess."

She leaned back, peered knowingly at Tyekanik. "You do not approve of me, I know that. It is unimportant to me as long as you remember the lesson of the Levenbrech."

"He was very good with animals, but disposable; yes, Princess."

"That is not what I mean!"

"It isn't? Then . . . I don't understand."

"An army," she said, "is composed of disposable, completely replaceable parts. That is the lesson of the Levenbrech."

"Replaceable parts," he said. "Including the supreme command?"

"Without the supreme command there is seldom a reason for an army, Tyekanik. That is why you will immediately embrace this Mahdi religion and, at the same time, begin the campaign to convert my son."

"At once, Princess. I presume you don't want me to stint his education in the other martial arts at the expense of this, ahh, religion?"

She pushed herself out of the chair, strode around him, paused at the door, and spoke without looking back. "Someday you will try my patience once too often, Tyekanik." With that, she let herself out.

*Either we abandon the long-honored Theory of Relativity, or we cease to believe that we can engage in continued accurate prediction of the future. Indeed, knowing the future raises a host of questions which cannot be answered under conventional assumptions unless one first projects an Observer outside of*

*Time and, second, nullifies all movement. If you accept the Theory of Relativity, it can be shown that Time and the Observer must stand still in relationship to each other or inaccuracies will intervene. This would seem to say that it is impossible to engage in accurate prediction of the future. How, then, do we explain the continued seeking after this visionary goal by respected scientists? How, then, do we explain Muad'Dib?*

**—Lectures on Prescience
By Harq al-Ada**

"I must tell you something," Jessica said, "even though I know my telling will remind you of many experiences from our mutual past, and that this will place you in jeopardy."

She paused to see how Ghanima was taking this.

They sat alone, just the two of them, occupying low cushions in a chamber of Sietch Tabr. It had required considerable skill to maneuver this meeting, and Jessica was not at all certain that she had been alone in the maneuvering. Ghanima had seemed to anticipate and augment every step.

It was almost two hours after daylight, and the excitement of greeting and all of the recognitions were past. Jessica forced her pulse back to a steady pace and focused her attention into this rock-walled room with its dark hangings and yellow cushions. To meet the accumulated tensions, she found herself for the first time in years recalling the Litany Against Fear from the Bene Gesserit rite.

*"I must not fear. Fear is the mind-killer. Fear is the little-death that brings total obliteration. I will face my fear. I will permit it to pass over me and through me. And when it has gone past I will turn the inner eye to see its path. Where the fear has gone there will be nothing. Only I will remain."*

She did this silently and took a deep, calming breath.

"It helps at times," Ghanima said. "The Litany, I mean."

Jessica closed her eyes to hide the shock of this insight. It had been a long time since anyone had been able to read her that intimately. The realization was disconcerting, especially when it was ignited by an intellect which hid behind a mask of childhood.

Having faced her fear, though, Jessica opened her eyes and knew the source of turmoil: *I fear for my grandchildren.* Neither of these children betrayed the stigmata of Abomination which Alia flaunted, although Leto showed every sign of some terrifying concealment. It was for that reason he'd been deftly excluded from this meeting.

On impulse, Jessica put aside her ingrained emotional masks, knowing them to be of little use here, barriers to communication. Not since those loving moments with her Duke had she lowered these barriers, and she found the action both relief and pain. There remained facts which no curse or prayer or litany could wash from existence. Flight would not leave such facts behind. They could not be ignored. Elements of Paul's vision had been rearranged and the times had caught up with his children. They were a magnet in the void; evil and all the sad misuses of power collected around them.

Ghanima, watching the play of emotions across her grandmother's face, marveled that Jessica had let down her controls.

With catching movements of their heads remarkably synchronized, both turned, eyes met, and they stared deeply, probingly at each other. Thoughts without spoken words passed between them.

Jessica: *I wish you to see my fear.*

Ghanima: *Now I know you love me.*

It was a swift moment of utter trust.

Jessica said: "When your father was but a boy, I brought a Reverend Mother to Caladan to test him."

Ghanima nodded. The memory of it was extremely vivid.

"We Bene Gesserits were always cautious to make sure that the children we raised were human and not animal. One cannot always tell by exterior appearances."

"It's the way you were trained," Ghanima said, and the memory flooded into her mind: that old Bene Gesserit, Gaius Helen Mohiam. She'd come to Castle Caladan with her poisoned gom jabbar and her box of burning pain. Paul's hand (Ghanima's own hand in the shared memory) screamed with the agony of that box while the old woman talked calmly of immediate death if the hand were withdrawn from the pain. And there had been no doubt of the death in that needle held ready against the child's neck while the aged voice droned its rationale:

"*You've heard of animals chewing off a leg to escape a trap. There's an animal kind of trick. A human would remain in the trap, endure the pain, feigning death that he might kill the trapper and remove a threat to his kind.*"

Ghanima shook her head against the remembered pain. The burning! The burning! Paul had imagined his skin curling black on that agonized hand within the box, flesh crisping and dropping away until only charred bones remained. And it had been a trick—the hand unharmed. But sweat stood out on Ghanima's forehead at the memory.

"Of course you remember this in a way that I cannot," Jessica said.

For a moment, memory-driven, Ghanima saw her grandmother in a different light: what this woman might do out of the driving necessities of that early conditioning in the Bene Gesserit schools! It raised new questions about Jessica's return to Arrakis.

"It would be stupid to repeat such a test on you or your brother," Jessica said. "You already know the way it went. I must assume you are human, that you will not misuse your inherited powers."

"But you don't make that assumption at all," Ghanima said.

Jessica blinked, realized that the barriers had been creeping back in place, dropped them once more. She asked: "Will you believe my love for you?"

"Yes." Ghanima raised a hand as Jessica started to speak. "But that love wouldn't stop you from destroying us. Oh, I know the reasoning: 'Better the animal-human die than it re-create itself.' And that's especially true if the animal-human bears the name Atreides."

"You at least are human," Jessica blurted. "I trust my instinct on this."

Ghanima saw the truth in this, said: "But you're not sure of Leto."

"I'm not."

"Abomination?"

Jessica could only nod.

Ghanima said: "Not yet, at least. We both know the danger of it, though. We can see the way of it in Alia."

Jessica cupped her hands over her eyes, thought: *Even love can't protect us from unwanted facts.* And she knew that she still loved her daughter, crying out silently against fate: *Alia! Oh, Alia! I am sorry for my part in your destruction.*

Ghanima cleared her throat loudly.

Jessica lowered her hands, thought: *I may mourn my poor daughter, but there are other necessities now.* She said: "So you've recognized what happened to Alia."

"Leto and I watched it happen. We were powerless to prevent it, although we discussed many possibilities."

"You're sure that your brother is free of this curse?"

"I'm sure."

The quiet assurance in that statement could not be denied. Jessica found herself accepting it. Then: "How is it you've escaped?"

Ghanima explained the theory upon which she and Leto had settled, that their avoiding of the spice trance while Alia entered it often made the difference. She went on to reveal his dreams and the plans they'd discussed—even Jacurutu.

Jessica nodded. "Alia is an Atreides, though, and that poses enormous problems."

Ghanima fell silent before the sudden realization that Jessica still mourned her Duke as though his death had been but yesterday, that she would guard his name and memory against all threats. Personal memories from the Duke's own lifetime fled through Ghanima's awareness to reinforce this assessment, to soften it with understanding.

"Now," Jessica said, voice brisk, "what about this Preacher? I heard some disquieting reports yesterday after that damnable Lustration."

Ghanima shrugged. "He could be—"

"Paul?"

"Yes, but we haven't seen him to examine."

"Javid laughs at the rumors," Jessica said.

Ghanima hesitated. Then: "Do you trust this Javid?"

A grim smile touched Jessica's lips. "No more than you do."

"Leto says Javid laughs at the wrong things," Ghanima said.

"So much for Javid's laughter," Jessica said. "But do you actually entertain the notion that my son is still alive, that he has returned in this guise?"

"We say it's possible. And Leto . . ." Ghanima found her mouth suddenly dry, remembered fears clutching her breast. She forced herself to overcome them, recounted Leto's other revelations of prescient dreams.

Jessica moved her head from side to side as though wounded.

Ghanima said: "Leto says he must find this Preacher and make sure."

"Yes . . . Of course. I should never have left here. It was cowardly of me."

"Why do you blame yourself? You had reached a limit. I know that. Leto knows it. Even Alia may know it."

Jessica put a hand to her own throat, rubbed it briefly. Then: "Yes, the problem of Alia."

"She works a strange attraction on Leto," Ghanima said. "That's why I helped you meet alone with me. He agrees that she is beyond hope, but still he finds ways to be with her and . . . study her. And . . . it's very disturbing. When I try to talk against this, he falls asleep. He—"

"Is she drugging him?"

"No-o-o." Ghanima shook her head. "But he has this odd empathy for her. And . . . in his sleep, he often mutters *Jacurutu*."

"That again!" And Jessica found herself recounting Gurney's report about the conspirators exposed at the landing field.

"I sometimes fear Alia wants Leto to seek out Jacurutu," Ghanima said. "And I always thought it only a legend. You know it, of course."

Jessica shuddered. "Terrible story. Terrible."

"What must we do?" Ghanima asked. "I fear to search all of my memories, all of my lives . . ."

"Ghani! I warn you against that. You mustn't risk—"

"It may happen even if I don't risk it. How do we know what really happened to Alia?"

"No! You could be spared that . . . that *possession*." She ground the word out. "Well . . . Jacurutu, is it? I've sent Gurney to find the place—if it exists."

"But how can he . . . Oh! Of course: the smugglers."

Jessica found herself silenced by this further example of how Ghanima's mind worked in concert with what must be an inner awareness of others. *Of me!* How truly strange it was, Jessica thought, that this young flesh could carry all of Paul's memories, at least until the moment of Paul's spermal separation from his own past. It was an invasion of privacy against which something primal in Jessica rebelled. Momentarily she felt herself sinking into the absolute and unswerving Bene Gesserit judgment: *Abomination!* But there was a sweetness about this child, a willingness to sacrifice for her brother, which could not be denied.

*We are one life reaching out into a dark future,* Jessica thought. *We are one blood.* And she girded herself to accept the events which she and Gurney Halleck had set in motion. Leto must be separated from his sister, must be trained as the Sisterhood insisted.

> *I hear the wind blowing across the desert and I see the moons of a winter night rising like great ships in the void. To them I make my vow: I will be resolute and make an art of government; I will balance my inherited past and become a perfect storehouse of my relic memories. And I will be known for kindliness more than for knowledge. My face will shine down the corridors of time for as long as humans exist.*

**—Leto's Vow**
**After Harq al-Ada**

When she had been quite young, Alia Atreides had practiced for hours in the *prana-bindu* trance, trying to strengthen her own private personality against the onslaught of *all those others*. She knew the problem—melange could not be escaped in a sietch warren. It infested everything: food, water, air, even the fabrics against which she cried at night. Very early she recognized the uses of the sietch orgy where the tribe drank the death-water of a worm. In the orgy, Fremen released the accumulated pressures of their own genetic memories, and they denied those memories. She saw her companions being temporarily possessed in the orgy.

For her, there was no such release, no denial. She had possessed full consciousness long before birth. With that consciousness came a cataclysmic awareness of her circumstances: womb-locked into intense, inescapable contact with the personas of all her ancestors and of those identities death-transmitted in spice-*tau* to the Lady Jessica. Before birth, Alia had contained every bit of the knowledge required in a Bene Gesserit Reverend Mother—plus much, much more from *all those others*.

In that knowledge lay recognition of a terrible reality—Abomination. The totality of that knowledge weakened her. The pre-born did not escape. Still she'd fought against the more terrifying of her ancestors, winning for a time a Pyrrhic victory which had lasted through childhood. She'd known a private personality, but it had no immunity against casual intrusions from those who lived their reflected lives through her.

*Thus will I be one day,* she thought. This thought chilled her. To walk and dissemble through the life of a child from her own loins, intruding, grasping at consciousness to add a quantum of experience.

Fear stalked her childhood. It persisted into puberty. She had fought it, never asking for help. Who would understand the help she required? Not her mother, who could never quite drive away that specter of Bene Gesserit judgment: the pre-born were Abomination.

There had come that night when her brother walked alone into the desert seeking death, giving himself to Shai-Hulud as blind Fremen were supposed to do. Within the month, Alia had been married to Paul's swordmaster, Duncan Idaho, a mentat brought back from the dead by the arts of the Tleilaxu. Her mother fled back to Caladan. Paul's twins were Alia's legal charge.

And she controlled the Regency.

Pressures of responsibility had driven the old fears away and she had been wide open to the inner lives, demanding their advice, plunging into spice trance in search of guiding visions.

The crisis came on a day like many others in the spring month of Laab, a clear morning at Muad'Dib's Keep with a cold wind blowing down from the pole. Alia still wore the yellow for mourning, the color of the sterile sun. More and more these past few weeks she'd been denying the inner voice of her mother, who tended to sneer at preparation for the coming Holy Days to be centered on the Temple.

The inner-awareness of Jessica faded, faded . . . sinking away at last with a faceless demand that Alia would be better occupied working on the Atreides

Law. New lives began to clamor for their moment of consciousness. Alia felt
that she had opened a bottomless pit, and faces arose out of it like a swarm of
locusts, until she came at last to focus on one who was like a beast: the old Baron
Harkonnen. In terrified outrage she had screamed out against all of that inner
clamor, winning a temporary silence.

On this morning, Alia took her pre-breakfast walk through the Keep's roof
garden. In a new attempt to win the inner battle, she tried to hold her entire
awareness within Choda's admonition to the Zensunni:

*"Leaving the ladder, one may fall upward!"*

But the morning's glow along the cliffs of the Shield Wall kept distracting
her. Plantings of resilient fuzz-grass filled the garden's pathways. When she
looked away from the Shield Wall she saw dew on the grass, the catch of all the
moisture which had passed here in the night. It reflected her own passage as of a
multitude.

That multitude made her giddy. Each reflection carried the imprint of a face
from the inner multitude.

She tried to focus her mind on what the grass implied. The presence of
plentiful dew told her how far the ecological transformation had progressed on
Arrakis. The climate of these nothern latitudes was growing warmer;
atmospheric carbon dioxide was on the increase. She reminded herself how
many new hectares would be put under green plants in the coming year—and it
required thirty-seven thousand cubic feet of water to irrigate just one
hectare.

Despite every attempt at mundane thoughts, she could not drive away the
sharklike circling of all those others within her.

She put her hands to her forehead and pressed.

Her temple guards had brought her a prisoner to judge at sunset the previous
day: one Essas Paymon, a dark little man ostensibly in the pay of a house minor,
the Nebiros, who traded in holy artifacts and small manufactured items for
decoration. Actually Paymon was known to be a CHOAM spy whose task was
to assess the yearly spice crop. Alia had been on the point of sending him into
the dungeons when he'd protested loudly "the injustice of the Atreides." That
could have brought him an immediate sentence of death on the hanging tripod,
but Alia had been caught by his boldness. She'd spoken sternly from her
Throne of Judgment, trying to frighten him into revealing more than he'd
already told her inquisitors.

"Why are our spice crops of such interest to the Combine Honnete?" she'd
demanded. "Tell us and we may spare you."

"I only collect something for which there is a market," Paymon said. "I know
nothing of what is done with my harvest."

"And for this petty profit you interfere with our royal plans?" Alia
demanded.

"Royalty never considers that we might have plans, too," he countered.

Alia, captivated by his desperate audacity, said: "Essas Paymon, will you
work for me?"

At this a grin whitened his dark face, and he said: "You were about to obliterate me without a qualm. What is my new value that you should suddenly make a market for it?"

"You've a simple and practical value," she said. "You're bold and you're for hire to the highest bidder. I can bid higher than any other in the Empire."

At which, he named a remarkable sum which he required for his services, but Alia laughed and countered with a figure she considered more reasonable and undoubtedly far more than he'd ever before received. She added: "And, of course, I throw in the gift of your life upon which, I presume, you place an even more inordinate value."

"A bargain!" Paymon cried and, at a signal from Alia, was led away by her priestly Master of Appointments, Ziarenko Javid.

Less than an hour later, as Alia prepared to leave the Judgment Hall, Javid came hurrying to report that Paymon had been overheard to mutter the fateful lines from the Orange Catholic Bible: *"Maleficos non patieris vivere."*

"Thou shalt not suffer a witch to live," Alia translated. So that was his gratitude! He was one of those who plotted against her very life! In a flush of rage such as she'd never before experienced, she ordered Paymon's immediate execution, sending his body to the Temple deathstill where his water, at least, would be of some value in the priestly coffers.

And all night long Paymon's dark face haunted her.

She tried all of her tricks against this persistent, accusing image, reciting the *Bu Ji* from the Fremen Book of Kreos: "Nothing occurs! Nothing occurs!" But Paymon took her through a wearing night into this giddy new day, where she could see that his face had joined those in the jeweled reflections from the dew.

A female guard called her to breakfast from the roof door behind a low hedge of mimosa. Alia sighed. She felt small choice between hells: the outcry within her mind or the outcry from her attendants—all were pointless voices, but persistent in their demands, hourglass noises that she would like to silence with the edge of a knife.

Ignoring the guard, Alia stared across the roof garden toward the Shield Wall. A *bahada* had left its broad outwash like a detrital fan upon the sheltered floor of her domain. The delta of sand spread out before her gaze, outlined by the morning sun. It came to her that an uninitiated eye might see that broad fan as evidence of a river's flow, but it was no more than the place where her brother had shattered the Shield Wall with the Atreides Family atomics, opening a path from the desert for the sandworms which had carried his Fremen troops to shocking victory over his Imperial predecessor, Shaddam IV. Now a broad qanat flowed with water on the Shield Wall's far side to block off sandworm intrusions. Sandworms would not cross open water; it poisoned them.

*Would that I had such a barrier within my mind,* she thought.

The thought increased her giddy sensation of being separated from reality. *Sandworms! Sandworms!*

Her memory presented a collection of sandworm images: mighty Shai-Hulud, the demiurge of the Fremen, deadly beast of the desert's depths whose outpourings included the priceless spice. How odd it was, this sandworm, to grow from a flat and leathery sandtrout, she thought. They were like the flocking multitude within her awareness. The sandtrout, when linked edge to edge against the planet's bedrock, formed living cisterns; they held back the water that their sandworm vector might live. Alia could feel the analogy: some of *those others* within her mind held back dangerous forces which could destroy her.

Again the guard called her to breakfast, a note of impatience apparent.

Angrily Alia turned, waved a dismissal signal.

The guard obeyed, but the roof door slammed.

At the sound of the slamming door, Alia felt herself caught by everything she had attempted to deny. The other lives welled up within her like a hideous tide. Each demanding life pressed its face against her vision centers—a cloud of faces. Some presented mange-spotted skin, other were callous and full of sooty shadows; there were mouths like moist lozenges. The pressure of the swarm washed over her in a current which demanded that she float free and plunge into them.

"No," she whispered. "No . . . no . . . no . . ."

She would have collapsed onto the path but for a bench beside her which accepted her sagging body. She tried to sit, could not, stretched out on the cold plasteel, still whispering denial.

The tide continued to rise within her.

She felt attuned to the slightest show of attention, aware of the risk, but alert for every exclamation from those guarded mouths which clamored within her. They were a cacophony of demand for her attention: *"Me! Me!"* *"No, me!"* And she knew that if she once gave her attention, gave it completely, she would be lost. To behold one face out of the multitude and follow the voice of that face would be to be held by that egocentrism which shared her existence.

"Prescience does this to you," a voice whispered.

She covered her ears with her hands, thinking: *I'm not prescient! The trance doesn't work for me!*

But the voice persisted: *"It might work, if you had help."*

"No . . . no," she whispered.

Other voices wove around her mind: "I, Agamemnon, your ancestor, demand audience!"

"No . . . no." She pressed her hands against her ears until the flesh answered her with pain.

An insane cackle within her head asked: "What has become of Ovid? Simple. He's John Bartlett's ibid!"

The names were meaningless in her extremity. She wanted to scream against them and against all the other voices but could not find her own voice.

Her guard, sent back to the roof by senior attendants, peered once more from the doorway behind the mimosa, saw Alia on the bench, spoke to a companion: "Ahhh, she is resting. You noted that she didn't sleep well last night. It is good for her to take the *zaha*, the morning siesta."

Alia did not hear her guard. Her awareness was caught by shrieks of singing: "Merry old birds are we, hurrah!" the voices echoed against the inside of her skull and she thought: *I'm going insane. I'm losing my mind.*

Her feet made feeble fleeing motions against the bench. She felt that if she could only command her body to run, she might escape. She had to escape lest any part of that inner tide sweep her into silence, forever contaminating her soul. But her body would not obey. The mightiest forces in the Imperial universe would obey her slightest whim, but her body would not.

An inner voice chuckled. Then: "From one viewpoint, child, each incident of creation represents a catastrophe." It was a basso voice which rumbled against her eyes, and again that chuckle as though deriding its own pontification. "My dear child, I will help you, but you must help me in return."

Against the swelling background clamor behind that basso voice, Alia spoke through chattering teeth: "Who . . . who . . ."

A face formed itself upon her awareness. It was a smiling face of such fatness that it could have been a baby's except for the glittering eagerness of the eyes. She tried to pull back, but achieved only a longer view which included the body attached to that face. The body was grossly, immensely fat, clothed in a robe which revealed by subtle bulges beneath it that this fat had required the support of portable suspensors.

"You see," the basso voice rumbled, "it is only your maternal grandfather. You know me. I was the Baron Vladimir Harkonnen."

"You're . . . you're dead!" she gasped.

"But, of course, my dear! *Most* of us within you are dead. But none of the others are really willing to help you. They don't understand you."

"Go away," she pleaded. "Oh, please go away."

"But you need help, granddaughter," the Baron's voice argued.

*How remarkable he looks,* she thought, watching the projection of the Baron against her closed eyelids.

"I'm willing to help you," the Baron wheedled. "The others in here would only fight to take over your entire consciousness. Any one of them would try to drive you out. But me . . . I want only a little corner of my own."

Again the other lives within her lifted their clamor. The tide once more threatened to engulf her and she heard her mother's voice screeching. And Alia thought: *She's not dead.*

"Shut up!" the Baron commanded.

Alia felt her own desires reinforcing that command, making it felt throughout her awareness.

Inner silence washed through her like a cool bath and she felt her hammering heart begin slowing to its normal pace. Soothingly the Baron's voice intruded: "You see? Together, we're invincible. You help me and I help you."

"What . . . what do you want?" she whispered.

A pensive look came over the fat face against her closed eyelids. "Ahhh, my darling granddaughter," he said, "I wish only a few simple pleasures. Give me but an occasional moment of contact with your senses. No one else need ever know. Let me feel but a small corner of your life when, for example, you are enfolded in the arms of your lover. Is that not a small price to ask?"

"Y-yes."

"Good, good," the Baron chortled. "In return, my darling granddaughter, I can serve you in many ways. I can advise you, help you with my counsel. You will be invincible within and without. You will sweep away all opposition. History will forget your brother and cherish you. The future will be yours."

"You . . . won't let . . . the . . . the others take over?"

"They cannot stand against us! Singly we can be overcome, but together we command. I will demonstrate. Listen."

And the Baron fell silent, withdrawing his image, his inner presence. Not one memory, face, or voice of the other lives intruded.

Alia allowed herself a trembling sigh.

Accompanying that sigh came a thought. It forced itself into her awareness as though it were her own, but she sensed silent voices behind it.

*The old Baron was evil. He murdered your father. He would've killed you and Paul. He tried to and failed.*

The Baron's voice came to her without a face: "Of course I would've killed you. Didn't you stand in my way? But that argument is ended. You've won it, child! You're the new truth."

She felt herself nodding and her cheek moved scratchingly against the harsh surface of the bench.

His words were reasonable, she thought. A Bene Gesserit precept reinforced the reasonable character of his words: *"The purpose of argument is to change the nature of truth."*

*Yes . . . that was the way the Bene Gesserit would have it.*

"Precisely!" the Baron said. "And I am dead while you are alive. I have only a fragile existence. I'm a mere memory-self within you. I am yours to command. And how little I ask in return for the profound advice which is mine to deliver."

"What do you advise me to do now?" she asked, testing.

"You're worried about the judgment you gave last night," he said. "You wonder if Paymon's words were reported truthfully. Perhaps Javid saw in this Paymon a threat to his position of trust. Is this not the doubt which assails you?"

"Y-yes."

"And your doubt is based on acute observation, is it not? Javid behaves with increasing intimacy toward your person. Even Duncan has noted it, hasn't he?"

"You know he has."

"Very well, then. Take Javid for your lover and—"

"No!"

"You worry about Duncan? But your husband is a mentat mystic. He cannot be touched or harmed by activities of the flesh. Have you not felt sometimes how distant he is from you?"

"B-but he . . ."

"Duncan's mentat part would understand should he ever have need to know the device you employed in destroying Javid."

"Destroy . . ."

"Certainly! Dangerous tools may be used, but they should be cast aside when they grow too dangerous."

"Then . . . why should . . . I mean . . ."

"Ahhh, you precious dunce! Because of the value contained in the lesson."

"I don't understand."

"Values, my dear grandchild, depend for their acceptance upon their success. Javid's obedience must be unconditional, his acceptance of your authority absolute, and his—"

"The morality of this *lesson* escapes—"

"Don't be dense, grandchild! Morality must always be based on practicality. Render unto Caesar and all that nonsense. A victory is useless unless it reflects your deepest wishes. Is it not true that you have admired Javid's manliness?"

Alia swallowed, hating the admission, but forced to it by her complete nakedness before the inner-watcher. "Ye-es."

"Good!" How jovial the word sounded within her head. "Now we begin to understand each other. When you have him helpless, then, in your bed, convinced that you are *his* thrall, you will ask him about Paymon. Do it jokingly: a rich laugh between you. And when he admits the deception, you will slip a crysknife between his ribs. Ahhh, the flow of blood can add so much to your satis—"

"No," she whispered, her mouth dry with horror. "No . . . no . . . no . . . ."

"Then I will do it for you," the Baron argued. "It must be done; you admit that. If you but set up the conditions, I will assume temporary sway over . . ."

"No!"

"Your fear is so transparent, granddaughter. My sway of your senses cannot be else but temporary. There are others, now, who could mimic you to a perfection that . . . But you know this. With me, ahhh, people would spy out my presence immediately. You know the Fremen Law for those possessed. You'd be slain out of hand. Yes—even you. And you know I do not want *that* to happen. I'll take care of Javid for you and, once it's done, I'll step aside. You need only . . ."

"How is this good advice?"

"It rids you of a dangerous tool. And, child, it sets up the working relationship between us, a relationship which can only teach you well about future judgments which—"

"Teach me?"

"Naturally!"

Alia put her hands over her eyes, trying to think, knowing that any thought might be known to this presence within her, that a thought might originate with that presence and be taken as her own.

"You worry yourself needlessly," the Baron wheedled. "This Paymon fellow, now, was—"

"What I did was wrong! I was tired and acted hastily. I should've sought confirmation of—"

"You did right! Your judgments cannot be based on any such foolish abstract as that Atreides notion of equality. That's what kept you sleepless, not Paymon's death. You make a good decision! He was another dangerous tool. You acted to maintain order in your society. Now there's a good reason for judgments, not this *justice* nonsense! There's no such thing as equal justice anywhere. It's unsettling to a society when you try to achieve such a false balance."

Alia felt pleasure at this defense of her judgment against Paymon, but shocked at the amoral concept behind the argument. "Equal justice was an Atreides . . . was . . ." She took her hands from her eyes, but kept her eyes closed.

"All of your priestly judges should be admonished about this error," the Baron argued. "Decisions must be weighed only as to their merit in maintaining an orderly society. Past civilizations without number have foundered on the rocks of equal justice. Such foolishness destroys the natural hierarchies which are far more important. Any individual takes on significance only in his relationship to your total society. Unless that society be ordered in logical steps, no one can find a place in it— not the lowliest or the highest. Come, come, grandchild! You must be the stern mother of your people. It's your duty to maintain order."

"Everything Paul did was to . . ."

"Your brother's dead, a failure!"

"So are you!"

"True . . . but with me it was an accident beyond my designing. Come now, let us take care of this Javid as I have outlined for you."

She felt her body grow warm at the thought, spoke quickly: "I must think about it." And she thought: *If it's done, it'll be only to put Javid in his place. No need to kill him for that. And the fool might just give himself away . . . in my bed.*

"To whom do you talk, My Lady?" a voice asked.

For a confused moment, Alia thought this another intrusion by those clamorous multitudes within, but recognition of the voice opened her eyes. Ziarenka Valefor, chief of Alia's guardian amazons, stood beside the bench, a worried frown on her weathered Fremen features.

"I speak to my inner voices," Alia said, sitting up on the bench. She felt refreshed, buoyed up by the silencing of that distracting inner clamor.

"Your inner voices, My Lady. Yes." Ziarenka's eyes glistened at this information. Everyone knew the Holy Alia drew upon inner resources available to no other person.

"Bring Javid to my quarters," Alia said. "There's a serious matter I must discuss with him."

"To your quarters, My Lady?"

"Yes! To my private chamber."

"As My Lady commands." The guard turned to obey.

"One moment," Alia said. "Has Master Idaho already gone to Sietch Tabr?"

"Yes, My Lady. He left before dawn as you instructed. Do you wish me to send for . . ."

"No. I will manage this myself. And Zia, no one must know that Javid is being brought to me. Do it yourself. This is a very serious matter."

The guard touched the crysknife at her waist. "My Lady, is there a threat to—"

"Yes, there's a threat, and Javid may be at the heart of it."

"Ohhh, My Lady, perhaps I should not bring—"

"Zia! Do you think me incapable of handling such a one?"

A lupine smile touched the guard's mouth. "Forgive me, My Lady. I will bring him to your private chamber at once, but . . . with My Lady's permission, I will mount guard outside your door."

"You only," Alia said.

"Yes, My Lady. I go at once."

Alia nodded to herself, watching Ziarenka's retreating back. Javid was not loved among her guards, then. Another mark against him. But he was still valuable—very valuable. He was her key to Jacurutu and with that place, well . . .

"Perhaps you were right, Baron," she whispered.

"You see!" the voice within her chortled. "Ahhh, this will be a pleasant service to you, child, and it's only the beginning . . ."

> *These are illusions of popular history which a successful religion must promote: Evil men never prosper; only the brave deserve the fair; honesty is the best policy; actions speak louder than words; virtue always triumphs; a good deed is its own reward; any bad human can be reformed; religious talismans protect one from demon possession; only females understand the ancient mysteries; the rich are doomed to unhappiness . . .*

**—From the Instruction Manual:
Missionaria Protectiva**

"I am called Muriz," the leathery Fremen said.

He sat on cavern rock in the glow of a spice lamp whose fluttering light revealed damp walls and dark holes which were passages from this place. Sounds of dripping water could be heard down one of those passages and, although water sounds were essential to the Fremen paradise, the six bound men facing Muriz took no pleasure from the rhythmic dripping. There was the musty smell of a deathstill in the chamber.

A youth of perhaps fourteen standard years came out of the passage and stood at Muriz's left hand. An unsheathed crysknife reflected pale yellow from the spice lamp as the youth lifted the blade and pointed it briefly at each of the bound men.

With a gesture toward the youth, Muriz said: "This is my son, Assan Tariq, who is about to undergo his test of manhood."

Muriz cleared his throat, stared once at each of the six captives. They sat in a loose semicircle across from him, tightly restrained with spice-fiber ropes which held their legs crossed, their hands behind them. The bindings terminated in a tight noose at each man's throat. Their stillsuits had been cut away at the neck.

The bound men stared back at Muriz without flinching. Two of them wore loose off-world garments which marked them as wealthy residents of an Arrakeen city. These two had skin which was smoother, lighter than that of their companions, whose sere features and bony frames marked them as desert-born.

Muriz resembled the desert dwellers, but his eyes were more deeply sunken, whiteless pits which not even the glow of the spice lamp touched. His son appeared an unformed copy of the man, with a flatness of face which did not quite hide the turmoil boiling within him.

"Among the Cast Out we have a special test for manhood," Muriz said. "One day my son will be a judge in Shuloch. We must know that he can act as he must. Our judges cannot forget Jacurutu and our day of despair. Kralizec, the Typhoon Struggle, lives in, our hearts." It was all spoken with the flat intonation of ritual.

One of the soft-featured city dwellers across from Muriz stirred, said: "You do wrong to threaten us and bind us captive. We came peacefully on *umma*."

Muriz nodded. "You came in search of a personal religious awakening? Good. You shall have that awakening."

The soft-featured man said: "If we—"

Beside him a darker desert Fremen snapped: "Be silent, fool! These are the water stealers. These are the ones we thought we'd wiped out."

"That old story," the soft-featured captive said.

"Jacurutu is more than a story," Muriz said. Once more he gestured to his son. "I have presented Assan Tariq. I am *arifa* in this place, your only judge. My son, too, will be trained to detect demons. The old ways are best."

"That's why we came into the deep desert," the soft-featured man protested. "We chose the old way, wandering in—"

"With paid guides," Muriz said, gesturing to the darker captives. "You would buy your way into heaven?" Muriz glanced up at his son. "Assan, are you prepared?"

"I have reflected long upon that night when men came and murdered our people," Assan said. His voice projected an uneasy straining. "They owe us water."

"Your father gives you six of them," Muriz said. "Their water is ours. Their shades are yours, your guardians forevermore. Their shades will warn you of demons. They will be your slaves when you cross over into the *alam al-mythal*. What do you say, my son?"

"I thank my father," Assan said. He took a short step forward. "I accept manhood among the Cast Out. This water is our water."

As he finished speaking, the youth crossed to the captives. Starting on the left, he gripped the man's hair and drove the crysknife up under the chin into the brain. It was skillfully done to spill the minimum blood. Only the one soft-featured city Fremen protested, squalling as the youth grabbed his hair. The others spat at Assan Tariq in the old way, saying by this: *"See how little I value my water when it is taken by animals!"*

When it was done, Muriz clapped his hands once. Attendants came and began removing the bodies, taking them to the deathstill where they could be rendered for their water.

Muriz arose, looked at his son who stood breathing deeply, watching the attendants remove the bodies. "Now you are a man," Muriz said. "The water of our enemies will feed slaves. And, my son . . ."

Assan Tariq turned an alert and pouncing look upon his father. The youth's lips were drawn back in a tight smile.

"The Preacher must not know of this," Muriz said.

"I understand, father."

"You did it well," Muriz said. "Those who stumble upon Shuloch must not survive."

"As you say, father."

"You are trusted with important duties," Muriz said. "I am proud of you."

> *A sophisticated human can become primitive. What this really means is that the human's way of life changes. Old values change, become linked to the landscape with its plants and animals. This new existence requires a working knowledge of those multiplex and cross-linked events usually referred to as nature. It requires a measure of respect for the inertial power within such natural systems. When a human gains this working knowledge and respect, that is called "being primitive." The converse, of course, is equally true: the primitive can become sophisticated, but not without accepting dreadful psychological damage.*

> **—The Leto Commentary**
> **After Harq al-Ada**

"How can we be sure?" Ghanima asked. "This is very dangerous."

"We've tested it before," Leto argued.

"It may not be the same this time. What if—"

"It's the only way open to us," Leto said. "You agree we can't go the way of the spice."

Ghanima sighed. She did not like this thrust and parry of words, but knew the necessity which pressed her brother. She also knew the fearful source of her own reluctance. They had but to look at Alia and know the perils of that inner world.

"Well?" Leto asked.

Again she sighed.

They sat cross-legged in one of their private places, a narrow opening from the cave to the cliff where often their mother and father had watched the sun set over the *bled*. It was two hours past the evening meal, a time when the twins were expected to exercise their bodies and their minds. They had chosen to flex their minds.

"I will try it alone if you refuse to help," Leto said.

Ghanima looked away from him toward the black hangings of the moisture seals which guarded this opening in the rock. Leto continued to stare out over the desert.

They had been speaking for some time in a language so ancient that even its name remained unknown in these times. The language gave their thoughts a privacy which no other human could penetrate. Even Alia, who avoided the intricacies of her inner world, lacked the mental linkages which would allow her to grasp any more than an occasional word.

Leto inhaled deeply, taking in the distinctive furry odor of a Fremen cavern-sietch which persisted in this windless alcove. The murmurous hubbub of the sietch and its damp heat were absent here, and both felt this as a relief.

"I agree we need guidance," Ghanima said. "But if we—"

"Ghani! We need more than guidance. We need protection."

"Perhaps there is no protection." She looked directly at her brother, met that gaze in his eyes like the waiting watchfulness of a predator. His eyes belied the placidity of his features.

"We must escape possession," Leto said. He used the special infinitive of the ancient language, a form strictly neutral in voice and tense but profoundly active in its implications.

Ghanima correctly interpreted his argument.

"Mohw'pwium d'mi hish pash moh'm ka," she intoned. *The capture of my soul is the capture of a thousand souls.*

"Much more than that," he countered.

"Knowing the dangers, you persist." She made it a statement, not a question.

"Wabun 'k wabunat!" he said. *Rising, thou risest!*

He felt his choice as an obvious necessity. Doing this thing, it were best done actively. They must wind the past into the present and allow it to unreel into their future.

"Muriyat," she conceded, her voice low. *It must be done lovingly.*

"Of course." He waved a hand to encompass total acceptance. "Then we will consult as our parents did."

Ghanima remained silent, tried to swallow past a lump in her throat. Instinctively she glanced south toward the great open *erg* which was showing a dim grey pattern of dunes in the last of the day's light. In that direction her father had gone on his last walk into the desert.

Leto stared downward over the cliff edge at the green of the sietch oasis. All was dusk down there, but he knew its shapes and colors: blossoms of copper, gold, red, yellow, rust, and russet spread right out to the rock markers which outlined the extent of the qanat-watered plantings. Beyond the rock markers stretched a stinking band of dead Arrakeen life, killed by foreign plants and too much water, now forming a barrier against the desert.

Presently Ghanima said: "I am ready. Let us begin."

"Yes, damn all!" He reached out, touched her arm to soften the exclamation, said: "Please, Ghani . . . Sing that song. It makes this easier for me."

Ghanima hitched herself closer to him, circled his waist with her left arm. She drew in two deep breaths, cleared her throat, and began singing in a clear piping voice the words her mother had so often sung for their father:

"Here I redeem the pledge thou gavest;
I pour sweet water upon thee.
Life shall prevail in this windless place:
My love, thou shalt live in a palace,
Thy enemies shall fall to emptiness.
We travel this path together
Which love has traced for thee.
Surely well do I show the way
For my love is thy palace . . ."

Her voice fell into the desert silence which even a whisper might despoil, and Leto felt himself sinking, sinking—becoming the father whose memories spread like an overlayer in the genes of his immediate past.

*For this brief space, I must be Paul,* he told himself. *This is not Ghani beside me; it is my beloved Chani, whose wise counsel has saved us both many a time.*

For her part, Ghanima had slipped into the persona-memory of her mother with frightening ease, as she had known she would. How much easier this was for the female—and how much more dangerous.

In a voice turned suddenly husky, Ghanima said: "Look there, beloved!"

First Moon had risen and, against its cold light, they saw an arc of orange fire falling upward into space. The transport which had brought the Lady Jessica, laden now with spice, was returning to its mother-cluster in orbit.

The keenest of remembrances ran through Leto then, bringing memories like bright bell-sounds. For a flickering instant he was another Leto—Jessica's Duke. Necessity pushed those memories aside, but not before he felt the piercing of the love and the pain.

*I must be Paul,* he reminded himself.

The transformation came over him with a frightening duality, as though Leto were a dark screen against which his father was projected. He felt both his own flesh and his father's, and the flickering differences threatened to overcome him.

"Help me, father," he whispered.

The flickering disturbance passed and now there was another imprint upon his awareness, while his own identity as Leto stood at one side as an observer.

"My last vision has not yet come to pass," he said, and the voice was Paul's. He turned to Ghanima. "You know what I saw."

She touched his cheek with her right hand. "Did you walk into the desert to die, beloved? Is that what you did?"

"It may be that I did, but that vision . . . Would that not be reason enough to stay alive?"

"But blind?" she asked.

"Even so."

"Where could you go?"

He took a deep, shuddering breath. "Jacurutu."

"Beloved!" Tears began flowing down her cheeks.

"Muad'Dib, the hero, must be destroyed utterly," he said. "Otherwise this child cannot bring us back from chaos."

"The Golden Path," she said. "It is not a good vision."

"It's the only possible vision."

"Alia has failed, then . . ."

"Utterly. You see the record of it."

"Your mother has returned too late." She nodded, and it was Chani's wise expression on the childish face of Ghanima. "Could there not be another vision? Perhaps if—"

"No, beloved. Not yet. This child cannot peer into the future yet and return safely."

Again a shuddering breath disturbed his body, and Leto-observer felt the deep longing of his father to live once more in vital flesh, to make living decisions and . . . How desperate the need to unmake past mistakes!

"Father!" Leto called, and it was as though he shouted echoingly within his own skull.

It was a profound act of will which Leto felt then: the slow, clinging withdrawal of his father's internal presence, the release of senses and muscles.

"Beloved," Chani's voice whispered beside him, and the withdrawal slowed. "What is happening?"

"Don't go yet," Leto said, and it was his own voice, rasping and uncertain, still his own. Then: "Chani, you must tell us: How do we avoid . . . what has happened to Alia?"

It was Paul-within who answered him, though, with words which fell upon his inner ear, halting and with long pauses: "There is no certainty. You . . . saw . . . what . . . almost . . . happened . . . with . . . me."

"But Alia . . ."

"The damned Baron has her!"

Leto felt his throat burning with dryness. " Is he . . . have I . . ."

"He's in you . . . but . . . I . . . we cannot . . . sometimes we sense . . . each other, but you . . ."

"Can you not read my thoughts?" Leto asked. "Would you know then if . . . he . . ."

"Sometimes I can feel your thoughts . . . but I . . . we live only through . . . the . . . reflection of . . . your awareness. Your memory creates us. The danger . . . it is a precise memory. And . . . those of us . . . those of us who loved power . . . and gathered it at . . . any price . . . those can be . . . more precise."

"Stronger?" Leto whispered.

"Stronger."

"I know your vision," Leto said. "Rather than let him have me, I'll become you."

"Not that!"

Leto nodded to himself, sensing the enormous will-force his father had required to withdraw, recognizing the consequences of failure. *Any* possession reduced the possessed to Abomination. The recognition gave him a renewed sense of strength, and he felt his own body with abnormal acuteness and a deeply drawn awareness of past mistakes: his own and those of his ancestors. It was the uncertainties which weakened—he saw this now. For an instant, temptation warred with fear within him. This flesh possessed the ability to transform melange into a vision of the future. With the spice, he could breathe the future, shatter Time's veils. He found the temptation difficult to shed, clasped his hands and sank into the *prana-bindu* awareness. His flesh negated the temptation. His flesh wore the deep knowledge learned in blood by Paul. Those who sought the future hoped to gain the winning gamble on tomorrow's race. Instead they found themselves trapped into a lifetime whose every heartbeat and anguished wail was known. Paul's final vision had shown the precarious way out of that trap, and Leto knew now that he had no other choice but to follow that way.

"The joy of living, its beauty is all bound up in the fact that life can surprise you," he said.

A soft voice whispered in his ear: "I've always known that beauty."

Leto turned his head, stared into Ghanima's eyes which glistened in the bright moonlight. He saw Chani looking back at him. "Mother," he said, "you must withdraw."

"Ahhh, the temptation!" she said, and kissed him.

He pushed her away. "Would you take your daughter's life?" he demanded.

"It's so easy . . . so foolishly easy," she said.

Leto, feeling panic begin to grip him, remembered what an effort of will his father's persona-within had required to abandon the flesh. Was Ghanima lost in that observer-world where he had watched and listened, learning what he had required from his father?

"I will despise you, mother," he said.

"Others won't despise me," she said. "Be my beloved."

"If I do . . . you know what you both will become," he said. "My father will despise you."

"Never!"

"I will!"

The sound was jerked out of his throat without his volition and it carried all the old overtones of Voice which Paul had learned from his witch mother.

"Don't say it," she moaned.

"I will despise you!"

"Please . . . please don't say it."

Leto rubbed his throat, feeling the muscles become once more his own. "He will despise you. He will turn his back on you. He will go into the desert again."

"No . . . no . . ."

She shook her head from side to side.

"You must leave, mother," he said.

"No . . . no . . ." But the voice lacked its original force.

Leto watched his sister's face. How the muscles twitched! Emotions fled across the flesh at the turmoil within her.

"Leave," he whispered. "Leave."

"No-o-o-o . . ."

He gripped her arm, felt the tremors which pulsed through her muscles, the nerves twitching. She writhed, tried to pull away, but he held tightly to her arm, whispering: "Leave . . . leave . . ."

And all the time, Leto berated himself for talking Ghani into this *parent game* which once they'd played often, but she had lately resisted. It was true that the female had more weakness in that inner assault, he realized. There lay the origin of the Bene Gesserit fear.

Hours passed and still Ghanima's body trembled and twitched with the inner battle, but now his sister's voice joined the argument. He heard her talking to that imago within, the pleading.

"Mother . . . please—" And once: "You've seen Alia! Will you become another Alia?"

At last Ghanima leaned against him, whispered: "She has accepted it. She's gone."

He stroked her head. "Ghani, I'm sorry. I'm sorry. I'll never ask you to do that again. I was selfish. Forgive me."

"There's nothing to forgive," she said, and her voice came panting as though after great physical exertion. "We've learned much that we needed to know."

"She spoke to you of many things," he said. "We'll share it later when—"

"No! We'll do it now. You were right."

"My Golden Path?"

"Your damned Golden Path!"

"Logic's useless unless it's armed with essential data," he said. "But I—"

"Grandmother came back to guide our education and to see if we'd been . . . contaminated."

"That's what Duncan says. There's nothing new in—"

"Prime computation," she agreed, her voice strengthened. She pulled away from him, looked out at the desert which lay in a predawn hush. This battle . . . this knowledge, had cost them a night. The Royal Guard beyond the moisture seal must have had much to explain. Leto had charged that nothing disturb them.

"People often learn subtlety as they age," Leto said. "What is it we're learning with all of this agedness to draw upon?"

"The universe as we see it is never quite the exact physical universe," she said. "We mustn't perceive this grandmother just as a grandmother."

"That'd be dangerous," he agreed. "But my ques—"

"There's something beyond subtlety," she said. "We must have a place in our awareness to perceive what we can't preconceive. That's why . . . my mother spoke to me often of Jessica. At the last, when we were both reconciled to the inner exchange, she said many things." Ghanima sighed.

"We *know* she's our grandmother," he said. "You were with her for hours yesterday. Is that why—"

"If we allow it, our *knowing* will determine how we react to her," Ghanima said. "That's what my mother kept warning me. She quoted our grandmother once and—" Ghanima touched his arm. "—I heard the echo of it within me in our grandmother's voice."

"Warning you," Leto said. He found this thought disturbing. Was nothing in this world dependable?

"Most deadly errors arise from obsolete assumptions," Ghanima said. "That's what my mother kept quoting."

"That's pure Bene Gesserit."

"If . . . if Jessica has gone back to the Sisterhood completely . . ."

"That'd be very dangerous to us," he said, completing the thought. "We carry the blood of their Kwisatz Haderach—their male Bene Gesserit."

"They won't abandon that search," she said, "but they may abandon us. Our grandmother could be the instrument."

"There's another way," he said.

"Yes—the two of us . . . mated. But they know what recessives might complicate that pairing."

"It's a gamble they must've discussed."

"And with our grandmother, at that. I don't like that way."

"Nor I."

"Still, it's not the first time a royal line has tried to . . ."

"It repels me," he said, shuddering.

She felt the movement, fell silent.

"Power," he said.

And in that strange alchemy of their similarities she knew where his thoughts had been. "The power of the Kwisatz Haderach must fail," she agreed.

"Used in their way," he said.

In that instant, day came to the desert beyond their vantage point. They sensed the heat beginning. Colors leaped forth from the plantings beneath the cliff. Grey-green leaves sent spiked shadows along the ground. The low morning light of Dune's silvery sun revealed the verdant oasis full of golden and purple shadows in the well of the sheltering cliffs.

Leto stood, stretched.

"The Golden Path, then," Ghanima said, and she spoke as much to herself as to him, knowing how their father's last vision met and melted into Leto's dreams.

Something brushed against the moisture seals behind them and voices could be heard murmuring there.

Leto reverted to the ancient language they used for privacy: "L'ii ani howr samis sm'kwi owr samit sut."

That was where the decision lodged itself in their awareness. Literally: *We will accompany each other into deathliness, though only one may return to report it.*

Ghanima stood then and, together, they returned through the moisture seals to the sietch, where the guards roused themselves and fell in behind as the twins headed toward their own quarters. The throngs parted before them with a difference on this morning, exchanging glances with the guards. Spending the night alone above the desert was an old Fremen custom for the holy sages. All the Uma had practiced this form of vigil. Paul Muad'Dib had done it . . . and Alia. Now the royal twins had begun.

Leto noted the difference, mentioned it to Ghanima.

"They don't know what we've decided for them," she said. "They don't really know."

Still in the private language, he said: "It requires the most fortuitous beginning."

Ghanima hesitated a moment to form her thoughts. Then: "In that time, mourning for the sibling, it must be exactly real—even to the making of the tomb. The heart must follow the sleep lest there be no awakening."

In the ancient tongue it was an extremely convoluted statement, employing a pronominal object separated from the infinitive. It was a syntax which allowed each set of internal phrases to turn upon itself, becoming several different meanings, all definite and quite distinct but subtly interrelated. In part, what she had said was that they risked death with Leto's plan and, real or simulated, it made no difference. The resultant change would be like death, literally: "funeral murder." And there was an added meaning to the whole which pointed accusatively at whoever *survived* to report, that is: *act out the living part.* Any misstep there would negate the entire plan, and Leto's Golden Path would become a dead end.

"Extremely delicate," Leto agreed. He parted the hangings for them as they entered their own anteroom.

Activity among their attendants paused only for a heartbeat as the twins crossed to the arched passage which led into the quarters assigned to the Lady Jessica.

"You are not Osiris," Ghanima reminded him.

"Nor will I try to be."

Ghanima took his arm to stop him. "Alia darsatay haunus m'smow," she warned.

Leto stared into his sister's eyes. Indeed, Alia's actions did give off a foul smell which their grandmother must have noted. He smiled appreciatively at Ghanima. She had mixed the ancient tongue with Fremen superstition to call up a most basic tribal omen. *M'smow,* the foul odor of a summer night, was the harbinger of death at the hands of demons. And Isis had been the demon-goddess of death to the people whose tongue they now spoke.

"We Atreides have a reputation for audacity to maintain," he said.

"So we'll *take* what we need," she said.

"It's that or become petitioners before our own Regency," he said. "Alia would enjoy that."

"But our plan . . ." She let it trail off.

*Our plan,* he thought. She shared it completely now. He said: "I think of our plan as the toil of the shaduf."

Ghanima glanced back at the anteroom through which they'd passed, smelling the furry odors of morning with their sense of eternal beginning. She liked the way Leto had employed their private language. *Toil of the shaduf.* It was a pledge. He'd called their plan agricultural work of a very menial kind: fertilizing, irrigating, weeding, transplanting, pruning—yet with the Fremen implication that this labor occurred simultaneously in Another World where it symbolized cultivating the richness of the soul.

Ghanima studied her brother as they hesitated here in the rock passage. It had grown increasingly obvious to her that he was pleading on two levels: one, for the Golden Path of his vision and their father's, and two, that she allow him free reign to carry out the extremely dangerous myth-creation which the plan generated. This frightened her. Was there more to his private vision that he had not shared? Could he see himself as the potentially deified figure to lead humankind into a rebirth—like father, like son? The cult of Muad'Dib had turned sour, fermenting in Alia's mismanagement and the unbridled license of a military priesthood which rode the Fremen power. Leto wanted regeneration.

*He's hiding something from me,* she realized.

She reviewed what he had told her of his dream. It held such iridescent reality that he might walk around for hours afterward in a daze. The dream never varied, he said.

*"I am on sand in bright yellow daylight, yet there is no sun. Then I realize that I am the sun. My light shines out as a Golden Path. When I realize this, I move out of myself. I turn, expecting to see myself as the sun. But I am not the sun; I am a stick figure, a child's drawing with zigzag lightning lines for eyes, stick legs and stick arms. There is a scepter in my left hand, and it's a real scepter—much more detailed in its reality than the stick figure which holds it. The scepter moves, and this terrifies me. As it moves, I feel myself awaken, yet I know I'm still dreaming. I realize then that my skin is encased in something—an armor which moves as my skin moves. I cannot see this armor, but I feel it. My terror leaves me then, for this armor gives me the strength of ten thousand men."*

As Ghanima stared at him, Leto tried to pull away, to continue their course toward Jessica's quarters. Ghanima resisted.

"This Golden Path could be no better than any other path," she said.

Leto looked at the rock floor between them, feeling the strong return of Ghanima's doubts. "I must do it," he said.

"Alia is possessed," she said. "That could happen to us. It could already have happened and we might not know it."

"No." He shook his head, met her gaze. "Alia resisted. That gave the powers within her their strength. By her own strength she was overcome. We've dared to search within, to seek out the old languages and the old knowledge. We're already amalgams of those lives within us. We don't resist; we ride with them. This was what I learned from our father last night. It's what I had to learn."

"He said nothing of that within me."

"You listened to our mother. It's what we—"

"And I almost lost."

"Is she still strong within you?" Fear tightened his face.

"Yes . . . but now I think she guards me with her love. You were very good when you argued with her." And Ghanima thought about the reflected mother-within, said: "Our mother exists now for me in the *alam al-mythal* with the others, but she has tasted the fruit of hell. Now I can listen to her without fear. As to the others . . ."

"Yes," he said. "And I listened to my father, but I think I'm really following the counsel of the grandfather for whom I was named. Perhaps the name makes it easy."

"Are you counseled to speak to our grandmother of the Golden Path?"

Leto waited while an attendant pressed past them with a basket-tray carrying the Lady Jessica's breakfast. A strong smell of spice filled the air as the attendant passed.

"She lives in us and in her own flesh," Leto said. "Her counsel can be consulted twice."

"Not by me," Ghanima protested. "I'm not risking that again."

"Then by me."

"I thought we agreed that she's gone back to the Sisterhood."

"Indeed. Bene Gesserit at her beginning, her own creature in the middle, and Bene Gesserit at the end. But remember that she, too, carries Harkonnen blood and is closer to it than we are, that she has experienced a form of this inner sharing which we have."

"A very shallow form," Ghanima said. "And you haven't answered my question."

"I don't think I'll mention the Golden Path."

"I may."

"Ghani!"

"We don't need any more Atreides gods! We need a space for some humanity!"

"Have I ever denied it?"

"No." She took a deep breath and looked away from him. Attendants peered in at them from the anteroom, hearing the argument by its tone but unable to understand the ancient words.

"We have to do it," he said. "If we fail to act, we might just as well fall upon our knives." He used the Fremen form which carried the meaning of "spill our water into the tribal cistern."

Once more Ghanima looked at him. She was forced to agree. But she felt trapped within a construction of many walls. They both knew a day of reckoning lay across their path no matter what they did. Ghanima knew this with a certainty reinforced by the data garnered from those other memory-lives, but now she feared the strength which she gave those other psyches by using the data of their experiences. They lurked like harpies within her, shadow demons waiting in ambush.

Except for her mother, who had held the fleshly power and had renounced it. Ghanima still felt shaken by that inner struggle, knowing she would have lost but for Leto's persuasiveness.

Leto said his Golden Path led out of this trap. Except for the nagging realization that he withheld something from his vision, she could only accept his sincerity. He needed her fertile creativity to enrich the plan.

"We'll be tested," he said, knowing where her doubts led.

"Not in the spice."

"Perhaps even there. Surely, in the desert and in the Trial of Possession."

"You never mentioned the Trial of Possession!" she accused. "Is that part of your dream?"

He tried to swallow in a dry throat, cursed this betrayal. "Yes."

"Then we will be . . . possessed?"

"No."

She thought about the Trial—that ancient Fremen examination whose ending most often brought hideous death. Then this plan had other complexities. It would take them onto an edge where a plunge to either side might not be countenanced by the human mind and that mind remain sane.

Knowing where her thoughts meandered, Leto said: "Power attracts the psychotics. Always. That's what we have to avoid within ourselves."

"You're sure we won't be . . . possessed?"

"Not if we create the Golden Path."

Still doubtful, she said: "I'll not bear your children, Leto."

He shook his head, suppressing the inner betrayals, lapsed into the royal-formal form of the ancient tongue: "Sister mine, I love you more dearly than myself, but that is not the tender of my desires."

"Very well, then let us return to another argument before we join our grandmother. A knife slipped into Alia might settle most of our problems."

"If you believe that, you believe we can walk in mud and leave no tracks," he said. "Besides, when has Alia ever given anyone an opportunity?"

"There is talk about this Javid."

"Does Duncan show any signs of growing horns?"

Ghanima shrugged. "One poison, two poison." It was the common label applied to the royal habit of cataloguing companions by their threat to your person, a mark of rulers everywhere.

"We must do it my way," he said.

"The other way might be cleaner."

By her reply, he knew she had finally suppressed her doubts and come around to agreement with his plan. The realization brought him no happiness. He found himself looking at his own hands, wondering if the dirt would cling.

*This was Muad'Dib's achievement: He saw the subliminal reservoir of each individual as an unconscious bank of memories going back to the primal cell of our common genesis. Each of us, he said, can measure out his distance from that common origin. Seeing this and telling of it, he made the audacious leap of decision. Muad'Dib set himself the task of integrating genetic memory into ongoing evaluation. Thus did he break through Time's veils, making a single thing of the future and the past. That was Muad'Dib's creation embodied in his son and his daughter.*

—**Testament of Arrakis**
**by Harq al-Ada**

Farad'n strode through the garden compound of his grandfather's royal palace, watching his shadow grow shorter as the sun of Salusa Secundus climbed toward noon. He had to stretch himself a bit to keep step with the tall Bashar who accompanied him.

"I have doubts, Tyekanik," he said. "Oh, there's no denying the attractions of a throne, but—" He drew in a deep breath. "—I have so many interests."

Tyekanik, fresh from a savage argument with Farad'n's mother, glanced sidelong at the Prince, noting how the lad's flesh was firming as he approached his eighteenth birthday. There was less and less of Wensicia in him with each passing day and more and more of old Shaddam, who had preferred his private pursuits to the responsibilities of royalty. That was what had cost him the throne in the end, of course. He'd grown soft in the ways of command.

"You have to make a choice," Tyekanik said. "Oh, doubtless there'll be time for some of your interests, but . . ."

Farad'n chewed his lower lip. Duty held him here, but he felt frustrated. He would far rather have gone to the rock enclave where the sandtrout experiments were being conducted. Now *there* was a project with enormous potential: wrest the spice monopoly from the Atreides and anything might happen.

"You're sure these twins will be . . . eliminated?"

"Nothing absolutely certain, My Prince, but the prospects are good."

Farad'n shrugged. Assassination remained a fact of royal life. The language was filled with the subtle permutations of ways to eliminate important personages. By a single word, one could distinguish between poison in drink or poison in food. He presumed the elimination of the Atreides twins would be accomplished by a poison. It was not a pleasant thought. By all accounts the twins were a most interesting pair.

"Would we have to move to Arrakis?" Farad'n asked.

"It's the best choice, put us at the point of greatest pressure." Farad'n appeared to be avoiding some question and Tyekanik wondered what it might be.

"I'm troubled, Tyekanik," Farad'n said, speaking as they rounded a hedge corner and approached a fountain surrounded by giant black roses. Gardeners could be heard snipping beyond the hedges.

"Yes?" Tyekanik prompted.

"This, ah, religion which you've professed . . ."

"Nothing strange about that, My Prince," Tyekanik said and hoped his voice remained firm. "This religion speaks to the warrior in me. It's a fitting religion for a Sardaukar." That, at least, was true.

"Yesss . . . But my mother seems so pleased by it." *Damn Wensicia!* he thought. *She's made her son suspicious.*

"I care not what your mother thinks," Tyekanik said. "A man's religion is his own affair. Perhaps she sees something in this that may help to put you on the throne."

"That was my thought," Farad'n said.

*Ahhh, this is a sharp lad!* Tyekanik thought. He said: "Look into the religion for yourself; you'll see at once why I chose it."

"Still . . . Muad'Dib's preachings? He was an Atreides, after all."

"I can only say that the ways of God are mysterious," Tyekanik said.

"I see. Tell me, Tyek, why'd you ask me to walk with you just now? It's almost noon and usually you're off to someplace or other at my mother's command this time of day."

Tyekanik stopped at a stone bench which looked upon the fountain and the giant roses beyond. The splashing water soothed him and he kept his attention upon it as he spoke. "My Prince, I've done something which your mother may not like." And he thought: *If he believes that, her damnable scheme will work.* Tyekanik almost hoped Wensicia's scheme would fail. *Bringing that damnable Preacher here. She was insane. And the cost!*

As Tyekanik remained silent, waiting, Farad'n asked: "All right, Tyek, what've you done?"

"I've brought a practitioner of oneiromancy," Tyekanik said.

Farad'n shot a sharp glance at his companion. Some of the older Sardaukar played the dream-interpretation game, had done so increasingly since their defeat by that "Supreme Dreamer," Muad'Dib. Somewhere within their dreams, they reasoned, might lay a way back to power and glory. But Tyekanik had always eschewed this play.

"This doesn't sound like you, Tyek," Farad'n said.

"Then I can only speak from my new religion," he said, addressing the fountain. To speak of religion was, of course, why they'd risked bringing The Preacher here.

"Then speak from this religion," Farad'n said.

"As My Prince commands." He turned, looked at this youthful holder of all the dreams which now were distilled into the path which House Corrino would follow. "Church and state, My Prince, even scientific reason and faith, and even more: progress and tradition—all of these are reconciled in the teachings of Muad'Dib. He taught that there are no intransigent opposites except in the beliefs of men and, sometimes, in their dreams. One discovers the future in the past, and both are part of a whole."

In spite of doubts which he could not dispel, Farad'n found himself impressed by these words. He heard a note of reluctant sincerity in Tyekanik's voice, as though the man spoke against inner compulsions.

"And that's why you bring me this . . . this interpreter of dreams?"

"Yes, My Prince. Perhaps your dream penetrates Time. You win back your consciousness of your inner being when you recognize the universe as a coherent whole. Your dreams . . . well . . ."

"But I spoke idly of my dreams," Farad'n protested. "They are a curiosity, no more. I never once suspected that you . . ."

"My Prince, nothing you do can be unimportant."

"That's very flattering, Tyek. Do you really believe this fellow can see into the heart of great mysteries?"

"I do, My Prince."

"Then let my mother be displeased."

"You will see him?"

"Of course—since you've brought him to displease my mother."

*Does he mock me?* Tyekanik wondered. And he said: "I must warn you that the old man wears a mask. It is an Ixian device which enables the sightless to see with their skin."

"He is blind?"

"Yes, My Prince."

"Does he know who I am?"

"I told him, My Prince."

"Very well. Let us go to him."

"If My Prince will wait a moment here, I will bring the man to him."

Farad'n looked around the fountain garden, smiled. As good a place as any for this foolishness. "Have you told him what I dreamed?"

"Only in general terms, My Prince. He will ask you for a personal accounting."

"Oh, very well. I'll wait here. Bring the fellow."

Farad'n turned his back, heard Tyekanik retire in haste. A gardener could be seen working just beyond the hedge, the top of a brown-capped head, the flashing of shears poking above the greenery. The movement was hypnotic.

*This dream business is nonsense,* Farad'n thought. *It was wrong of Tyek to do this without consulting me. Strange that Tyek should get religion at his age. And now it's dreams.*

Presently he heard footsteps behind him, Tyekanik's familiar positive stride and a more dragging gait. Farad'n turned, stared at the approaching dream interpreter. The Ixian mask was a black, gauzy affair which concealed the face from the forehead to below the chin. There were no eye slits in the mask. If one were to believe the Ixian boasts, the entire mask was a single eye.

Tyekanik stopped two paces from Farad'n, but the masked old man approached to less than a pace.

"The interpreter of dreams," Tykanik said.

Farad'n nodded.

The masked old man coughed in a remote grunting fashion, as though trying to bring something up from his stomach.

Farad'n was acutely conscious of a sour spice smell from the old man. It emanated from the long grey robe which covered his body.

"Is that mask truly a part of your flesh?" Farad'n asked, realizing he was trying to delay the subject of dreams.

"While I wear it," the old man said, and his voice carried a bitter twang and just a suggestion of Fremen accent. "Your dream," he said. "Tell me."

Farad'n shrugged. *Why not?* That was why Tyek had brought the old man. Or was it? Doubts gripped Farad'n and he asked: "Are you truly a practitioner of oneiromancy?"

"I have come to interpret your dream, Puissant Lord."

Again Farad'n shrugged. This masked figure made him nervous and he glanced at Tyekanik, who remained where he had stopped, arms folded, staring at the fountain.

"Your dream, then," the old man pressed.

Farad'n inhaled deeply, began to relate the dream. It became easier to talk as he got fully into it. He told about the water flowing upward in the well, about the worlds which were atoms dancing in his head, about the snake which transformed itself into a sandworm and exploded in a cloud of dust. Telling about the snake, he was surprised to discover, required more effort. A terrible reluctance inhibited him and this made him angry as he spoke.

The old man remained impassive as Farad'n at last fell silent. The black gauze mask moved slightly to his breathing. Farad'n waited. The silence continued.

Presently Farad'n asked: "Aren't you going to interpret my dream?"

"I have interpreted it," he said, his voice seeming to come from a long distance.

"Well?" Farad'n heard his own voice squeaking, telling him the tension his dream had produced.

Still the old man remained impassively silent.

"Tell me, then!" The anger was obvious in his tone.

"I said I'd interpret," the old man said. "I did not agree to tell you my interpretation."

Even Tyekanik was moved by this, dropping his arms into balled fists at his sides. "What?" he grated.

"I did not say I'd reveal my interpretation," the old man said.

"You wish more pay?" Farad'n asked.

"I did not ask pay when I was brought here." A certain cold pride in the response softened Farad'n's anger. This was a brave old man, at any rate. He must know death could follow disobedience.

"Allow me, My Prince," Tyekanik said as Farad'n started to speak. Then: "Will you tell us why you won't reveal your interpretation?"

"Yes, My Lords. The dream tells me there would be no purpose in explaining these things."

Farad'n could not contain himself. "Are you saying I already know the meaning of my dream?"

"Perhaps you do, My Lord, but that is not my gist."

Tyekanik moved up to stand beside Farad'n. Both glared at the old man. "Explain yourself," Tyekanik said.

"Indeed," Farad'n said.

"If I were to speak of this dream, to explore these matters of water and dust, snakes and worms, to analyze the atoms which dance in your head as they do in mine—ahh, Puissant Lord, my words would only confuse you and you would insist upon misunderstanding."

"Do you fear that your words might anger me?" Farad'n demanded.

"My Lord! You're already angry."

"Is it that you don't trust us?" Tyekanik asked.

"That is very close to the mark, My Lord. I do not trust either of you and for the simple reason that you do not trust yourselves."

"You walk dangerously close to the edge," Tyekanik said. "Men have been killed for behavior less abusive than yours."

Farad'n nodded, said: "Don't tempt us to anger."

"The fatal consequences of Corrino anger are well known, My Lord of Salusa Secundus," the old man said.

Tyekanik put a restraining hand on Farad'n's arm, asked: "Are you trying to goad us into killing you?"

Farad'n had not thought of that, felt a chill now as he considered what such behavior might mean. Was this old man who called himself Preacher . . . was he more than he appeared? What might be the consequences of his death? Martyrs could be dangerous creations.

"I doubt that you'll kill me no matter what I say," The Preacher said. "I think you know my value, Bashar, and your Prince now suspects it."

"You absolutely refuse to interpret his dream?" Tyekanik asked.

"I *have* interpreted it."

"And you will not reveal what you see in it?"

"Do you blame me, My Lord?"

"How can you be valuable to me?" Farad'n asked.

The Preacher held out his right hand. "If I but beckon with this hand, Duncan Idaho will come to me and he will obey me."

"What idle boast is this?" Farad'n asked.

But Tyekanik shook his head, recalling his argument with Wensicia. He said: "My Prince, it could be true. This Preacher has many followers on Dune."

"Why didn't you tell me he was from that place?" Farad'n asked.

Before Tyekanik could answer, The Preacher addressed Farad'n: "My Lord, you must not feel guilty about Arrakis. You are but a product of your times. This is a special pleading which any man may make when his guilts assail him."

"Guilts!" Farad'n was outraged.

The Preacher only shrugged.

Oddly, this shifted Farad'n from outrage to amusement. He laughed, throwing his head back, drawing a startled glance from Tyekanik. Then: "I like you, Preacher."

"This gratifies me, Prince," the old man said.

Suppressing a chuckle, Farad'n said: "We'll find you an apartment here in the palace. You will be my official interpreter of dreams—even though you never give me a word of interpretation. And you can advise me about Dune. I have great curiosity about that place."

"This I cannot do, Prince."

An edge of his anger returned. Farad'n glared at the black mask. "And why not, pray tell?"

"My Prince," Tyekanik said, again touching Farad'n's arm.

"What is it, Tyek?"

"We brought him here under bonded agreement with the Guild. He is to be returned to Dune."

"I am summoned back to Arrakis," The Preacher said.

"Who summons you?" Farad'n demanded.

"A power greater than thine, Prince."

Farad'n shot a questioning glance at Tyekanik. "Is he an Atreides spy?"

"Not likely, My Prince. Alia has put a price on his head."

"If it's not the Atreides, then who summons you?" Farad'n asked, returning his attention to The Preacher.

"A power greater than the Atreides."

A chuckle escaped Farad'n. This was only mystic nonsense. How could Tyek be fooled by such stuff? This Preacher had been *summoned*—most likely by a dream. Of what importance were dreams?

"This has been a waste of time, Tyek," Farad'n said. "Why did you subject me to this . . . this farce?"

"There is a double price here, My Prince," Tyekanik said. "This interpreter of dreams promised me to deliver Duncan Idaho as an agent of House Corrino. All he asked was to meet you and interpret your dream." And Tyekanik added to himself: *Or so he told Wensicia!* New doubts assailed the Bashar.

"Why is my dream so important to you, old man?" Farad'n asked.

"Your dream tells me that great events move toward a logical conclusion," The Preacher said. "I must hasten my return."

Mocking, Farad'n said: "And you will remain inscrutable, giving me no advice."

"Advice, Prince, is a dangerous commodity. But I will venture a few words which you may take as advice or in any other way which pleases you."

"By all means," Farad'n said.

The Preacher held his masked face rigidly confronting Farad'n. "Governments may rise and fall for reasons which appear insignificant, Prince. What small events! An argument between two women . . . which way the wind blows on a certain day . . . a sneeze, a cough, the length of a garment or the chance collision of a fleck of sand and a courtier's eye. It is not always the majestic concerns of Imperial ministers which dictate the course of history, nor is it necessarily the pontifications of priests which move the hands of God."

Farad'n found himself profoundly stirred by these words and could not explain his emotion.

Tyekanik, however, had focused on one phrase. Why did this Preacher speak of a garment? Tyekanik's mind focused on the Imperial costumes dispatched to the Atreides twins, the tigers trained to attack. Was this old man voicing a subtle warning? How much did he know?

"How is this advice?" Farad'n asked.

"If you would succeed," The Preacher said, "you must reduce your strategy to its point of application. Where does one apply strategy? At a particular place and with a particular people in mind. But even with the greatest concern for minutiae, some small detail with no significance attached to it will escape you. Can your strategy, Prince, be reduced to the ambitions of a regional governor's wife?"

His voice cold, Tyekanik interrupted: "Why do you harp upon strategy, Preacher? What is it you think My Prince will have?"

"He is being led to desire a throne," The Preacher said. "I wish him good luck, but he will need much more than luck."

"These are dangerous words," Farad'n said. "How is it you dare such words?"

"Ambitions tend to remain undisturbed by realities," The Preacher said. "I dare such words because you stand at a crossroad. You could become admirable. But now you are surrounded by those who do not seek moral justifications, by advisers who are strategy-oriented. You are young and strong and tough, but you lack a certain advanced training by which your character might evolve. This is sad because you have weaknesses whose dimensions I have described."

"What do you mean?" Tyekanik demanded.

"Have a care when you speak," Farad'n said. "What is this weakness?"

"You've given no thought to the kind of society you might prefer," The Preacher said. "You do not consider the hopes of your subjects. Even the form of the Imperium which you seek has little shape in your imaginings." He turned his masked face toward Tyekanik. "Your eye is upon the power, not upon its subtle uses and its perils. Your future is filled, thus, with manifest unknowns: with arguing women, with coughs and windy days. How can you create an epoch when you cannot see every detail? Your tough mind will not serve you. This is where you are weak."

Farad'n studied the old man for a long space, wondering at the deeper issues implied by such thoughts, at the persistence of such discredited concepts. Morality! Social goals! These were myths to put beside belief in an upward movement of evolution.

Tyekanik said: "We've had enough words. What of the price agreed upon, Preacher?"

"Duncan Idaho is yours," The Preacher said. "Have a care how you use him. He is a jewel beyond price."

"Oh, we've a suitable mission for him," Tyekanik said. He glanced at Farad'n. "By your leave, My Prince?"

"Send him packing before I change my mind," Farad'n said. Then, glaring at Tyekanik: "I don't like the way you've used me, Tyek!"

"Forgive him, Prince," The Preacher said. "Your faithful Bashar does God's will without even knowing it." Bowing, The Preacher departed, and Tyekanik hurried to see him away.

Farad'n watched the retreating backs, thought: *I must look into this religion which Tyek espouses.* And he smiled ruefully. *What a dream interpreter! But what matter? My dream was not an important thing.*

> *And he saw a vision of armor. The armor was not his own skin; it was stronger than plasteel. Nothing penetrated his armor—not knife or poison or sand, not the dust of the desert or its desiccating heat. In his right hand he carried the power to make the Coriolis storm, to shake the earth and erode it into nothing. His eyes were fixed upon the Golden Path and in his left hand he carried the scepter of absolute mastery. And beyond the Golden Path, his eyes looked into eternity which he knew to be the food of his soul and of his everlasting flesh.*

**—Heighia, My Brother's Dream
from The Book of Ghanima**

"It'd be better for me never to become Emperor," Leto said. "Oh, I don't imply that I've made my father's mistake and peered into the future with a glass of spice. I say this thing out of selfishness. My sister and I desperately need a time of freedom when we can learn how to live with what we are."

He fell silent, stared questioningly at the Lady Jessica. He'd spoken his piece as he and Ghanima had agreed. Now what would be their grandmother's response?

Jessica studied her grandson in the low light of glowglobes which illuminated her quarters in Sietch Tabr. It was still early morning of her second day here and she'd already had disturbing reports that the twins had spent a night of vigil outside the sietch. What were they doing? She had not slept well and she felt fatigue acids demanding that she come down from the hyper-level which had sustained her through all the demanding necessities since that crucial performance at the spaceport. This was the sietch of her nightmares—but outside, that was not the desert she remembered. *Where have all the flowers come from?* And the air around her felt too damp. Stillsuit discipline was lax among the young.

"What are you, child, that you need time to learn about yourself?" she asked.

He shook his head gently, knowing it to be a bizarre gesture of adulthood on a child's body, reminding himself that he must keep this woman off balance. "First, I am not a child. Oh . . ." He touched his chest. "This is a child's body; no doubt of that. But *I* am not a child."

Jessica chewed her upper lip, disregarding what this betrayed. Her Duke, so many years dead on this accursed planet, had laughed at her when she did this. *"Your one unbridled response,"* he'd called that chewing of the lip. *"It tells me that you're disturbed, and I must kiss those lips to still their fluttering."*

Now this grandson who bore the name of her Duke shocked her into heart-pounding stillness merely by smiling and saying: "You are disturbed; I see it by the fluttering of those lips."

It required the most profound discipline of her Bene Gesserit training to restore a semblance of calm. She managed: "Do you taunt me?"

"Taunt you? Never. But I must make it clear to you how much we differ. Let me remind you of that sietch orgy so long ago when the Old Reverend Mother gave you her lives and her memories. She tuned herself to you and gave you that . . . that long chain of sausages, each one a person. You have them yet. So you know something of what Ghanima and I experience."

"And Alia?" Jessica asked, testing him.

"Didn't you discuss that with Ghani?"

"I wish to discuss it with you."

"Very well. Alia denied what she was and became that which she feared. The *past-within* cannot be relegated to the unconscious. That is a dangerous course for any human, but for us who are pre-born, it is worse than death. And that is all I will say about Alia."

"So you're not a child," Jessica said.

"I'm millions of years old. That requires adjustments which humans have never before been called upon to make."

Jessica nodded, calmer now, much more cautious than she'd been with Ghanima. And where was Ghanima? Why had Leto come here alone?

"Well, grandmother," he said, "are we Abominations or are we the hope of the Atreides?"

Jessica ignored the question. "Where is your sister?"

"She distracts Alia to keep us from being disturbed. It is necessary. But Ghani would say nothing more to you than I've said. Didn't you observe that yesterday?"

"What I observed yesterday is my affair. Why do you prattle about Abomination?"

"Prattle? Don't give me your Bene Gesserit cant, grandmother. I'll feed it back to you, word for word, right out of your own memories. I want more than the fluttering of your lips."

Jessica shook her head, feeling the coldness of this . . . *person* who carried her blood. The resources at his disposal daunted her. She tried to match his tone, asked: "What do you know of my intentions?"

He sniffed. "You needn't inquire whether I've made the mistake my father made. I've not looked outside our garden of time—at least not by seeking it out. Leave absolute knowledge of the future to those moments of *déjà vu* which any human may experience. I *know* the trap of prescience. My father's life tells me what I need to know about it. No, grandmother: to know the future absolutely is to be trapped into that future absolutely. It collapses time. Present becomes future. I require more freedom than that."

Jessica felt her tongue twitch with unspoken words. How could she respond to him with something he didn't already know? This was monstrous! *He's me! He's my beloved Leto!* This thought shocked her. Momentarily she wondered if the childish mask might not lapse into those dear features and resurrect . . . *No!*

Leto lowered his head, looked upward to study her. Yes, she could be maneuvered after all. He said: "When you think of prescience, which I hope is rarely, you're probably no different from any other. Most people imagine how nice it would be to know tomorrow's quotation on the price of whale fur. Or whether a Harkonnen will once more govern their homeworld of Giedi Prime? But of course *we* know the Harkonnens without prescience, don't we, grandmother?"

She refused to rise to his baiting. Of course he would know about the cursed Harkonnen blood in his ancestry.

"Who is a Harkonnen?" he asked, goading. "Who is Beast Rabban? Any one of us, eh? But I digress. I speak the popular myth of prescience: to *know* the future absolutely! All of it! What fortunes could be made—and lost—on such absolute knowledge, eh? The rabble believes this. They believe that if a little bit is good, more must be better. How excellent! And if you handed one of them the complete scenario of his life, the unvarying dialogue up to his moment of death —what a hellish gift that'd be. What utter boredom! Every living instant he'd be replaying what he knew absolutely. No deviation. He could anticipate every response, every utterance—over and over and over and over and over and . . ."

Leto shook his head. "Ignorance has its advantages. A universe of surprises is what I pray for!"

It was a long speech and, as she listened, Jessica marveled at how his mannerisms, his intonations, echoed his father—her lost son. Even the ideas: these were things Paul might have said.

"You remind me of your father," she said.

"Is that hurtful to you?"

"In a way, but it's reassuring to know he lives on in you."

"How little you understand of how he lives on in me."

Jessica found his tone flat but dripping bitterness. She lifted her chin to look directly at him.

"Or how your Duke lives in me," Leto said. "Grandmother, Ghanima is *you*! She's you to such an extent that your life holds not a single secret from her up to the instant you bore our father. And me! What a catalogue of fleshly recordings am I. There are moments when it is too much to bear. You come here to judge us? You come here to judge Alia? Better that we judge you!"

Jessica demanded answer of herself and found none. What was he doing? Why this emphasis on his difference? Did he court rejection? Had he reached Alia's condition—Abomination?

"This disturbs you," he said.

"It disturbs me." She permitted herself a futile shrug. "Yes, it disturbs me—and for reasons you know full well. I'm sure you've reviewed my Bene Gesserit training. Ghanima admits it. I know Alia . . . did. You know the consequences of your *difference*."

He peered upward at her with disturbing intensity. "Almost, we did not take this tack with you," he said, and there was a sense of her own fatigue in his voice. "We know the fluttering of your lips as your lover knew them. Any bedchamber endearment your Duke whispered is ours to recall at will. You've accepted this intellectually, no doubt. But I warn you that intellectual acceptance is not enough. If any of us becomes Abomination—it could be you within us who creates it! Or my father . . . or mother! Your Duke! Any one of us could possess us—and the condition would be the same."

Jessica felt a burning in her chest, dampness in her eyes. "Leto . . ." she managed, allowing herself to use his name at last. She found the pain less than she'd imagined it would be, forced herself to continue. "What is it you want of me?"

"I would teach my grandmother."

"Teach me what?"

"Last night, Ghani and I played the mother-father roles almost to our destruction, but we learned much. There are things one can know, given an awareness of conditions. Actions can be predicted. Alia, now—it's well nigh certainty that she's plotting to abduct you."

Jessica blinked, shocked by the swift accusation. She knew this trick well, had employed it many times: set a person up along one line of reasoning, then introduce the shocker from another line. She recovered with a sharp intake of breath.

"I know what Alia has been doing . . . what she *is*, but . . ."

"Grandmother, pity her. Use your heart as well as your intelligence. You've done that before. You pose a threat, and Alia wants the Imperium for her own—at least, the thing she has become wants this."

"How do I know this isn't another Abomination speaking?"

He shrugged. "That's where your heart comes in. Ghani and I know how she fell. It isn't easy to adjust to the clamor of that inner multitude. Suppress their egos and they will come crowding back every time you invoke a memory. One day—" He swallowed in a dry throat. "—a strong one from that inner pack decides it's time to share the flesh."

"And there's nothing you can do?" She asked the question although she feared the answer.

"We believe there is something . . . yes. We cannot succumb to the spice; that's paramount. And we must not suppress the past entirely. We must use it, make an amalgam of it. Finally we will mix them all into ourselves. We will no longer be our original selves—*but we will not be possessed.*"

"You speak of a plot to adbuct me."

"It's obvious. Wensicia is ambitious for her son. Alia is ambitious for herself, and . . ."

"Alia and Farad'n?"

"That's not indicated," he said. "But Alia and Wensicia run parallel courses right now. Wensicia has a sister in Alia's house. What simpler thing than a message to—"

"You know of such a message?"

"As though I'd seen it and read its every word."

"But you've not seen such a message?"

"No need. I have only to know that the Atreides are all here together on Arrakis. All of the water in one cistern." He gestured to encompass the planet.

"House Corrino wouldn't dare attack us here!"

"Alia would profit if they did." A sneer in his voice provoked her.

"I won't be patronized by my own grandson!" she said.

"Then dammit, woman, stop thinking of me as your grandson! Think of me as your *Duke* Leto!" Tone and facial expression, even the abrupt hand gesture, were so exact that she fell silent in confusion.

In a dry, remote voice, Leto said: "I tried to prepare you. Give me that, at least."

"Why would Alia abduct me?"

"To blame it on House Corrino, of course."

"I don't believe it. Even for her, this would be . . . monstrous! Too dangerous! How could she do it without . . . I cannot believe this!"

"When it happens, you'll believe. Ahh, grandmother, Ghani and I have but to eavesdrop within ourselves and we *know*. It's simple self-preservation. How else can we even guess at the mistakes being made around us?"

"I do not for a minute accept that abduction is part of Alia's—"

"Gods below! How can you, a Bene Gesserit, be this dense? The whole

Imperium suspects why you're here. Wensicia's propagandists are all prepared to discredit you. Alia can't wait for that to happen. If you go down, House Atreides could suffer a mortal blow."

"What does the whole Imperium suspect?"

She measured out the words as coldly as possible, knowing she could not sway this *unchild* with any wile of Voice.

"The Lady Jessica plans to breed those twins together!" he rasped. "That's what the Sisterhood wants. Incest!"

She blinked. "Idle rumor." She swallowed. "The Bene Gesserits will not let such a rumor run wild in the Imperium. We still have some influence. Remember that."

"Rumor? What rumor? You've certainly held your options open on interbreeding us." He shook his head as she started to speak. "Don't deny it. Let us pass puberty still living in the same household and *you* in that household and your *influence* will be no more than a rag waved in the face of a sandworm."

"Do you believe us to be such utter fools?" Jessica asked.

"Indeed I do. Your Sisterhood is nothing but a bunch of damn' fool old women who haven't thought beyond their precious breeding program! Ghani and I know the leverage they have. Do *you* think *us* fools?"

"Leverage?"

"They know you're a Harkonnen! It'll be in their breeding records: Jessica out of Tanidia Nerus by the Baron Vladimir Harkonnen. That record *accidentally* made public would pull your teeth to—"

"You think the Sisterhood would stoop to blackmail?"

"I *know* they would. Oh, they coated it sweetly. They told you to investigate the rumors about your daughter. They fed your curiosity and your fears. They invoked your sense of responsibility, made you feel guilty because you'd fled back to Caladan. And they offered you the prospect of *saving* your grandchildren."

Jessica could only stare at him in silence. It was as though he'd eavesdropped on the emotional meetings with her Proctors from the Sisterhood. She felt completely subdued by his words, and now began to accept the possibility that he spoke the truth when he said Alia planned abduction.

"You see, grandmother, I have a difficult decision to make," he said. "Do I follow the Atreides mystique? Do I live for my subjects . . . and die for them? Or do I choose another course—one which would permit me to live thousands of years?"

Jessica recoiled involuntarily. These words spoken so easily touched on a subject the Bene Gesserits made almost unthinkable. Many Reverend Mothers could choose that course . . . or try it. The manipulation of internal chemistry was available to initiates of the Sisterhood. But if one did it, sooner or later all would try it. There could be no concealing such an accumulation of ageless women. They knew for a certainty that this course would lead them to destruction. Short-lived humanity would turn upon them. No—it was unthinkable.

"I don't like the trend of your thoughts," she said.

"You don't understand my thoughts," he said. "Ghani and I . . ." He shook his head. "Alia had it in her grasp and threw it away."

"Are you sure of that? I've already sent word to the Sisterhood that Alia practices the unthinkable. Look at her! She's not aged a day since last I . . ."

"Oh, that!" He dismissed Bene Gesserit body balance with a wave of his hand. "I'm speaking of something else—a perfection of being far beyond anything humans have ever before achieved."

Jessica remained silent, aghast at how easily he'd lifted her disclosure from her. He'd known surely that such a message represented a death sentence on Alia. And no matter how he changed the words, he could only be talking about committing the same offense. Didn't he know the peril of his words?

"You must explain," she said finally.

"How?" he asked. "Unless you understand that Time isn't what it appears, I can't even begin to explain. My father suspected it. He stood at the edge of realization, but fell back. Now it's up to Ghani and me."

"I insist that you explain," Jessica said and she fingered the poisoned needle she held beneath a fold of her robe. It was the gom jabbar, so deadly that the slightest prick of it killed within seonds. And she thought: *They warned me I might have to use it.* The thought sent the muscles of her arm trembling in waves and she was thankful for the concealing robe.

"Very well," he sighed. "First, as to Time: there is no difference between ten thousand years and one year; no difference between one hundred thousand years and a heartbeat. No difference. That is the first fact about Time. And the second fact: the entire universe with all of its Time is within me."

"What nonsense is this?" she demanded.

"You see? You don't understand. I will try to explain in another way, then." He raised his right hand to illustrate, moving it as he spoke. "We go forward, we come back."

"Those words explain nothing!"

"That is correct," he said. "There are things which words cannot explain. You must experience them without words. But you are not prepared for such a venture, just as when you look at me you do not see me."

"But . . . I'm looking directly at you. Of course I see you!" She glared at him. His words reflected knowledge of the Zensunni Codex as she'd been taught it in the Bene Gesserit schools: play of words to confuse one's understanding of philosophy.

"Some things occur beyond your control," he said.

"How does that explain this . . . this *perfection* which is so far beyond other human experiences?"

He nodded. "If one delays old age or death by the use of melange or by that learned adjustment of fleshly balance which you Bene Gesserits so rightly fear, such a delay invokes only an illusion of control. Whether one walks rapidly through the sietch or slowly, one traverses the sietch. And that passage of time is experienced internally."

"Why do you bandy words this way? I cut my wisdom teeth on such nonsense long before even your father was born."

"But only the teeth grew," he said.

"Words! Words!"

"Ahhh, you're very close!"

"Hah!"

"Grandmother?"

"Yes?"

He held his silence for a long space. Then: "You see? You can still respond as yourself." He smiled at her. "But you cannot see past the shadows. I am here." Again he smiled. "My father came very near to this. When he lived, he lived, but when he died, he failed to die."

"What're you saying?"

"Show me his body!"

"Do you think this Preacher . . ."

"Possible, but even so, that is not his body."

"You've explained nothing," she accused.

"Just as I warned you."

"Then why . . ."

"You asked. You had to be shown. Now let us return to Alia and her plan of abduction for—"

"Are you planning the unthinkable?" she demanded, holding the poisonous gom jabbar at the ready beneath her robe.

"Will you be her executioner?" he asked, his voice deceptively mild. He pointed a finger at the hand beneath her robe. "Do you think she'll permit you to use that? Or do you think I'd let you use it?"

Jessica found she could not swallow.

"In answer to your question," he said, "I do not plan the unthinkable. I am not that stupid. But I am shocked at you. You dare judge Alia. Of course she's broken the precious Bene Gesserit commandment! What'd you expect? You ran out on her, left her as queen here in all but name. All of that power! So you ran back to Caladan to nurse your wounds in Gurney's arms. Good enough. But who are you to judge Alia?"

"I tell you, I will not dis—"

"Oh, shut up!" He looked away from her in disgust. But his words had been uttered in that special Bene Gesserit way—the controlling *Voice*. It silenced her as though a hand had been clapped over her mouth. She thought: *Who'd know how to hit me with Voice better than this one?* It was a mitigating argument which eased her wounded feelings. As many times as she'd used Voice on others, she'd never expected to be suceptible to it . . . not ever again . . . not since the school days when . . .

He turned back to her. "I'm sorry. I just happen to know how blindly you can be expected to react when—"

"Blindly? Me?" She was more outraged by this than she'd been by his exquisite use of Voice against her.

"You," he said. "Blindly. If you've any honesty left in you at all, you'll recognize your own reactions. I call your name and you say, 'Yes?' I silence your tongue. I invoke all your Bene Gesserit myths. Look inward the way you were taught. That, at least, is something you can do for your—"

"How dare you! What do you know of . . ." Her voice trailed off. Of course he knew!

"Look inward, I say!" His voice was imperious.

Again, his voice enthralled her. She found her senses stilled, felt a quickening of breath. Just beyond awareness lurked a pounding heart, the panting of . . . Abruptly she realized that the quickened breath, the pounding heart, were not latent, not held at bay by her Bene Gesserit control. Eyes widening in shocked awareness, she felt her own flesh obeying other commands. Slowly she recovered her poise, but the realization remained. This *unchild* had been playing her like a fine instrument throughout their interview.

"Now you know how profoundly you were conditioned by your precious Bene Gesserits," he said.

She could only nod. Her belief in words lay shattered. Leto had forced her to look her physical universe squarely in the face, and she'd come away shaken, her mind running with a new awareness. *"Show me his body!"* He'd shown her her own body as though it were newborn. Not since her earliest schooling days on Wallach, not since those terrifying days before the Duke's buyers came for her, not since then had she felt such trembling uncertainty about her next moments.

"You will allow yourself to be abducted," Leto said.

"But—"

"I'm not asking for discussion on this point," he said. "You will allow it. Think of this as a command from your Duke. You'll see the purpose when it's done. You're going to confront a very interesting student."

Leto stood, nodded. He said: "Some actions have an end but no beginning; some begin but do not end. It all depends upon where the observer is standing." Turning, he left her chambers.

In the second anteroom, Leto met Ghanima hurrying into their private quarters. She stopped as she saw him, said: "Alia's busy with the Convocation of the Faith." She looked a question at the passage which led to Jessica's quarters.

"It worked," Leto said.

> Atrocity is recognized as such by victim and perpetrator alike, by all who
> learn about it at whatever remove. Atrocity has no excuses, no mitigating
> argument. Atrocity never balances or rectifies the past. Atrocity merely arms
> the future for more atrocity. It is self-perpetuating upon itself—a barbarous
> form of incest. Whoever commits atrocity also commits those future atrocities
> thus bred.
>
> **—The Apocrypha of Muad'Dib**

Shortly after noon, when most of the pilgrims had wandered off to refresh themselves in whatever cooling shade and source of libation they could find, The Preacher entered the great square below Alia's Temple. He came on the arm of his surrogate eyes, young Assan Tariq. In a pocket beneath his flowing robes, The Preacher carried the black gauze mask he'd worn on Salusa Secundus. It amused him to think that the mask and the boy served the same purpose—disguise. While he needed surrogate eyes, doubts remained alive.

*Let the myth grow, but keep doubts alive,* he thought.

No one must discover that the mask was merely cloth, not an Ixian artifact at all. His hand must not slip from Assan Tariq's bony shoulder. Let The Preacher once walk as the sighted despite his eyeless sockets, and all doubts would dissolve. The small hope he nursed would be dead. Each day he prayed for a change, something different over which he might stumble, but even Salusa Secundus had been a pebble, every aspect known. Nothing changed; nothing could be changed . . . yet.

Many people marked his passage past the shops and arcades, noting the way he turned his head from side to side, holding it centered on a doorway or a person. The movements of his head were not always blind-natural, and this added to the growing myth.

Alia watched from a concealed slit in the towering battlement of her temple. She searched that scarred visage far below for some sign—a sure sign of identity. Every rumor was reported to her. Each new one came with its thrill of fear.

She'd thought her order to take The Preacher captive would remain secret, but that, too, came back to her now as a rumor. Even among her guards, someone could not remain silent. She hoped now that the guards would follow her new orders and not take this robed mystery captive in a public place where it could be seen and reported.

It was dusty hot in the square. The Preacher's young guide had pulled the veil of his robe up around his nose, leaving only the dark eyes and a thin patch of forehead exposed. The veil bulged with the outline of a stillsuit's catchtube. This told Alia that they'd come in from the desert. Where did they hide out there?

The Preacher wore no veil protection from the searing air. He had even dropped the catchtube flap of his stillsuit. His face lay open to the sunlight and the heat shiverings which lifted off the square's paving blocks in visible waves.

At the Temple steps there stood a group of nine pilgrims making their departure obeisance. The shadowed edge of the square held perhaps fifty more persons, mostly pilgrims devoting themselves to various penances imposed by the priesthood. Among the onlookers could be seen messengers and a few merchants who'd not yet made enough sales to close up for the worst of the day's heat.

Watching from the open slit, Alia felt the drenching heat and knew herself to be caught between thinking and sensation, the way she'd often seen her brother caught. The temptation to consult within herself rang like an ominous humming in her head. The Baron was there: dutiful, but always ready to play upon her terrors when rational judgment failed and the things around her lost their sense of past, present, and future.

*What if that's Paul down there?* she asked herself.

"Nonsense!" the voice within her said.

But the reports of The Preacher's words could not be doubted. *Heresy!* It terrified her to think that Paul himself might bring down the structure built on his name.

*Why not?*

She thought of what she'd said in Council just that morning, turning viciously upon Irulan, who'd urged acceptance of the gift of clothing from House Corrino.

"All gifts to the twins will be examined thoroughly, just as always," Irulan had argued.

"And when we find the gift harmless?" Alia had cried.

Somehow that had been the most frightening thing of all: to find that the gift carried no threat.

In the end they'd accepted the fine clothing and had gone on to the other issue: Was the Lady Jessica to be given a position on the Council? Alia had managed to delay a vote.

She thought of this as she stared down at The Preacher.

Things which happened to her Regency now were like the underside of that transformation they inflicted upon this planet. Dune had once symbolized the power of ultimate desert. That power dwindled physically, but the myth of its power grew apace. Only the ocean-desert remained, the great Mother Desert of the inner planet, with its rim of thorn bushes, which Fremen still called Queen of Night. Behind the thorn bushes arose soft green hills bending down to the sand. All the hills were man-made. Every last one of them had been planted by men who had labored like crawling insects. The green of those hills was almost overpowering to someone raised, as Alia had been, in the tradition of dun-shaded sand. In her mind, as in the minds of all Fremen, the ocean-desert still held Dune in a grip which would never relax. She had only to close her eyes and she would see that desert.

Open eyes at the desert edge saw now the verdant hills, marsh slime reaching out green pseudopods toward the sand—but the other desert remained as powerful as ever.

Alia shook her head, stared down at The Preacher.

He had mounted the first of the terraced steps below the Temple and turned to face the almost deserted square. Alia touched the button beside her window which would amplify voices from below. She felt a wave of self-pity, seeing herself held here in loneliness. Whom could she trust? She'd thought Stilgar remained reliable, but Stilgar had been infected by this blind man.

"You know how he counts?" Stilgar had asked her. "I heard him counting coins as he paid his guide. It's very strange to my Fremen ears, and that's a terrible thing. He counts 'shuc, ishcai, qimsa, chuascu, picha, sucta, and so on. I've not heard counting like that since the old days in the desert."

From this, Alia knew that Stilgar could not be sent to do the job which must be done. And she would have to be circumspect with her guards where the slightest emphasis from the Regency tended to be taken as absolute command.

What was he doing down there, this Preacher?

The surrounding marketplace beneath its protective balconies and arched arcade still presented a gaudy face: merchandise left on display with a few boys to watch over it. Some few merchants remained awake there sniffing for the spice-biscuit money of the back country or the jingle in a pilgrim's purse.

Alia studied The Preacher's back. He appeared poised for speech, but something withheld his voice.

*Why do I stand here watching that ruin in ancient flesh?* she asked herself. *That mortal wreckage down there cannot be the "vessel of magnificence" which once was my brother.*

Frustration bordering on anger filled her. How could she find out about The Preacher, find out for certain *without finding out?* She was trapped. She dared not reveal more than a passing curiosity about this heretic.

Irulan felt it. She'd lost her famous Bene Gesserit poise and screamed in Council: "We've lost the power to think well of ourselves!"

Even Stilgar had been shocked.

Javid had brought them back to their senses: "We don't have time for such nonsense!"

Javid was right. What did it matter how they thought of themselves? All that concerned them was holding onto the Imperial power.

But Irulan, recovering her poise, had been even more devastating: "We've lost something vital, I tell you. When we lost it, we lost the ability to make good decisions. We fall upon decisions these days the way we fall upon an enemy—or wait and wait, which is a form of giving up, and we allow the decisions of others to move us. Have we forgotten that we were the ones who set this current flowing?"

And all over the question of whether to accept a gift from House Corrino.

*Irulan will have to be disposed of,* Alia decided.

What was that old man down there waiting for? He called himself a preacher. Why didn't he preach?

*Irulan was wrong about our decision-making,* Alia told herself. *I can still make proper decisions!* The person with life-and-death decisions to make must make decisions or remain caught in the pendulum. Paul had always said that stasis was the most dangerous of those things which were not natural. The only permanence was fluid. Change was all that mattered.

*I'll show them change!* Alia thought.

The Preacher raised his arms in benediction.

A few of those remaining in the square moved closer to him, and Alia noted the slowness of that movement. Yes, the rumors were out that The Preacher had aroused Alia's displeasure. She bent closer to the Ixian speaker beside her spy hole. The speaker brought her the murmurings of the people in the square, the sound of wind, the scratching of feet on sand.

"I bring you four messages!" The Preacher said.

His voice blared from Alia's speaker, and she turned down the volume.

"Each message is for a certain person," The Preacher said. "The first message is for Alia, the suzerain of this place." He pointed behind him toward her spy hole. "I bring her a warning: You, who held the secret of duration in your loins, have sold your future for an empty purse!"

*How dare he?* Alia thought. But his words froze her.

"My second message," The Preacher said, "is for Stilgar, the Fremen Naib, who believes he can translate the power of the tribes into the power of the Imperium. My warning to you, Stilgar: The most dangerous of all creations is a rigid code of ethics. It will turn upon you and drive you into exile!"

*He has gone too far!* Alia thought. *I must send the guards for him no matter the consequences.* But her hands remained at her sides.

The Preacher turned to face the Temple, climbed to the second step and once more whirled to face the square, all the time keeping his left hand upon the shoulder of his guide. He called out now: "My third message is for the Princess Irulan. Princess! Humiliation is a thing which no person can forget. I warn you to flee!"

*What's he saying?* Alia asked herself. *We humiliated Irulan, but . . . Why does he warn her to flee? My decision was just made!* A thrill of fear shot through Alia. How did The Preacher know?

"My fourth message is for Duncan Idaho," he shouted. "Duncan! You were taught to believe that loyalty buys loyalty. Ohh, Duncan, do not believe in history, because history is impelled by whatever passes for money. Duncan! Take your horns and do what you know best how to do."

Alia chewed the back of her right hand. *Horns!* She wanted to reach out and press the button which would summon guards, but her hand refused to move.

"Now I will preach to you," The Preacher said. "This is a sermon of the desert. I direct it to the ears of Muad'Dib's priesthood, those who practice the ecumenism of the sword. Ohhh, you believers in manifest destiny! Know you not that manifest destiny has its demoniac side? You cry out that you find yourselves exalted merely to have lived in the blessed generations of Muad'Dib. I say to you that you have abandoned Muad'Dib. Holiness has replaced love in your religion! You court the vengeance of the desert!"

The Preacher lowered his head as though in prayer.

Alia felt herself shivering with awareness. Gods below! That voice! It had been cracked by years in the burning sands, but it could be the remnant of Paul's voice.

Once more The Preacher raised his head. His voice boomed out over the square where more people had begun to gather, attracted by this oddity out of the past.

"Thus it is written!" The Preacher shouted. "They who pray for dew at the desert's edge shall bring forth the deluge! They shall not escape their fate through powers of reason! Reason arises from pride that a man may not know in this way when he has done evil." He lowered his voice. "It was said of Muad'Dib that he died of prescience, that knowledge of the future killed him and he passed from the universe of reality into the *alam al-mythal*. I say to you that this is the illusion of Maya. Such thoughts have no independent reality. They cannot go out from you and do real things: Muad'Dib said of himself that he possessed no Rihani magic with which to encipher the universe. Do not doubt him."

Again The Preacher raised his arms, lifted his voice in a stentorian bellow: "I warn the priesthood of Muad'Dib! The fire on the cliff shall burn you! They who learn the lesson of self-deception too well shall perish by that deception. The blood of a brother cannot be cleansed away!"

He had lowered his arms, found his young guide, and was leaving the square before Alia could break herself from the trembling immobility which had overcome her. Such fearless heresy! It must be Paul. She had to warn her guards. They dared not move against this *Preacher* openly. The evidence in the square below her confirmed this.

Despite the heresy, no one moved to stop the departing Preacher. No Temple guard leaped to pursue him. No pilgrim tried to stop him. That charismatic blind man! Everyone who saw or heard him felt his power, the reflection of divine talent.

In spite of the day's heat, Alia felt suddenly cold. She felt the thin edge of her grip on the Imperium as a physical thing. She gripped the edge of her spy hole window as though to hold her power, thinking of its fragility. The balance of Landsraad, CHOAM, and Fremen arms held the core of power, while Spacing Guild and Bene Gesserit dealt silently in the shadows. The forbidden seepage of technological development which came from the edges of humankind's farthest migrations nibbled at the central power. Products permitted the Ixian and Tleilaxu factories could not relieve the pressure. And always in the wings there stood Farad'n of House Corrino, inheritor of Shaddam IV's titles and claims.

Without the Fremen, without House Atreides' monopoly on the geriatric spice, her grip would loosen. All the power would dissolve. She could feel it slipping from her right now. People heeded this Preacher. It would be dangerous to silence him; just as dangerous as it was to let him continue preaching such words as he'd shouted across her square today. She could see the first omens of her own defeat and the pattern of the problem stood out clearly in her mind. The Bene Gesserits had codified the problem:

"A large populace held in check by a small but powerful force is quite a common situation in our universe. And we know the major conditions wherein this large populace may turn upon its keepers—

"One: When they find a leader. This is the most volatile threat to the powerful; they must retain control of leaders.

"Two: When the populace recognizes its chains. Keep the populace blind and unquestioning.

"Three: When the populace perceives a hope of escape from bondage. They must never even believe that escape is possible!"

Alia shook her head, feeling her cheeks tremble with the force of movement. The signs were here in her populace. Every report she received from her spies throughout the Imperium reinforced her certain knowledge. Unceasing warfare of the Fremen Jihad left its mark everywhere. Wherever "the ecumenism of the sword" had touched, people retained the attitude of a subject population: defensive, concealing, evasive. All manifestations of authority—and this meant essentially *religious* authority—became subject to resentment. Oh, pilgrims still came in their thronging millions, and some among them were probably devout. But for the most part, pilgrimage had other motivations than devotion. Most often it was a canny surety for the future. It emphasized obedience and gained a real form of power which was easily translated into wealth. The Hajji who returned from Arrakis came home to new authority, new social status. The Hajji could make profitable economic decisions which the planet-bound of his homeworld dared not challenge.

Alia knew the popular riddle: "What do you see inside the empty purse brought home from Dune?" And the answer: "The eyes of Muad'Dib (fire diamonds)."

The traditional ways to counter growing unrest paraded themselves before Alia's awareness: people had to be taught that opposition was always punished and assistance to the ruler was always rewarded. Imperial forces must be shifted in random fashion. Major adjuncts to Imperial power had to be concealed. Every movement by which the Regency countered potential attack required delicate timing to keep the opposition off balance.

*Have I lost my sense of timing?* she wondered.

"What idle speculation is this?" a voice within her asked. She felt herself growing calmer. Yes, the Baron's plan was a good one. We eliminate the threat of the Lady Jessica and, at the same time, we discredit House Corrino. Yes.

The Preacher could be dealt with later. She understood his posture. The symbolism was clear. He was the ancient spirit of unbridled speculation, the spirit of heresy alive and functioning in her desert of orthodoxy. That was his strength. It didn't matter whether he was Paul . . . as long as that could be kept in doubt. But her Bene Gesserit knowledge told Alia that his strength would contain the key to his weakness.

*The Preacher has a flaw which we will find. I will have him spied upon, watched every moment. And if the opportunity arises, he will be discredited.*

---

> I will not argue with the Fremen claims that they are divinely inspired to transmit a religious revelation. It is their concurrent claim to ideological revelation which inspires me to shower them with derision. Of course, they make the dual claim in the hope that it will strengthen their mandarinate and help them to endure in a universe which finds them increasingly oppressive. It is in the name of all those oppressed people that I warn the Fremen: short-term expediency always fails in the long term.
>
> **—The Preacher at Arrakeen**

Leto had come up in the night with Stilgar to the narrow ledge at the crest of the low rock outcropping which Sietch Tabr called The Attendant. Under the waning light of Second Moon, the ledge gave them a panoramic view—the Shield Wall with Mount Idaho to the north, the Great Flat to the south and rolling dunes eastward toward Habbanya Ridge. Winding dust, the aftermath of a storm, hid the southern horizon. Moonlight frosted the rim of the Shield Wall.

Stilgar had come against his will, joining the secretive venture finally because Leto aroused his curiosity. Why was it necessary to risk a sand crossing in the night? The lad had threatened to sneak away and make the journey alone if Stilgar refused. The way of it bothered him profoundly, though. Two such important targets alone in the night!

Leto squatted on the ledge facing south toward the flat. Occasionally he pounded his knee as though in frustration.

Stilgar waited. He was good at silent waiting, and stood two paces to one side of his charge, arms folded, his robes moving softly in the night breeze.

For Leto, the sand crossing represented a response to inner desperation, a need to seek a new alignment for his life in a silent conflict which Ghanima could no longer risk. He had maneuvered Stilgar into sharing the journey because there were things Stilgar had to know in preparation for the days ahead.

Again Leto pounded his knee. It was difficult to know a beginning! He felt, at times, like an extension of those countless other lives, all as real and immediate as his own. In the flow of those lives there was no ending, no accomplishment—only eternal beginning. They could be a mob, too, clamoring at him as though he were a single window through which each desired to peer. And there lay the peril which had destroyed Alia.

Leto stared outward at the moonlight silvering the storm remnants. Folds and overfolds of dunes spread across the flat: silica grit measured out by the winds, mounded into waves—pea sand, grit sand, pebbles. He felt himself caught in one of those poised moments just before dawn. Time pressed at him. It was already the month of Akkad and behind him lay the last of an interminable waiting time: long hot days and hot dry winds, nights like this one tormented by gusts and endless blowings from the furnace lands of the Hawkbled. He glanced over his shoulder toward the Shield Wall, a broken line in starlight. Beyond that wall in the Northern Sink lay the focus of his problems.

Once more he looked to the desert. As he stared into the hot darkness, day dawned, the sun rising out of dust scarves and placing a touch of lime into the storm's red streamers. He closed his eyes, willing himself to see how this day would appear from Arrakeen, and the city lay there in his consciousness, caught up like a scattering of boxes between the light and the new shadows. Desert . . . boxes . . . desert . . . boxes . . .

When he opened his eyes, the desert remained: a spreading curry expanse of wind-kicked sand. Oily shadows along the base of each dune reached out like rays of the night just past. They linked one time with the other. He thought of the night, squatting here with Stilgar restless beside him, the older man worried at the silence and the unexplained reasons for coming to this place. Stilgar must have many memories of passing this way with his beloved Muad'Dib. Even now Stilgar was moving, scanning all around, alert for dangers. Stilgar did not like the open in daylight. He was pure old Fremen in that.

Leto's mind was reluctant to leave the night and the clean exertions of a sand crossing. Once here in the rocks, the night had taken on its black stillness. He sympathized with Stilgar's daylight fears. Black was a single thing even when it contained boiling terrors. Light could be many things. Night held its fear smells and its things which came with slithering sounds. Dimensions separated in the night, everything amplified—thorns sharper, blades more cutting. But terrors of the day could be worse.

Stilgar cleared his throat.

Leto spoke without turning: "I have a very serious problem, Stil."

"So I surmised." The voice beside Leto came low and wary. The child had sounded disturbingly of the father. It was a thing of forbidden magic which touched a cord of revulsion in Stilgar. Fremen knew the terrors of *possession*. Those found possessed were rightfully killed and their water cast upon the sand lest it contaminate the tribal cistern. The dead should remain dead. It was correct to find one's immortality in children, but children had no right to assume too exact a shape from their past.

"My problem is that my father left so many things undone," Leto said. "Especially the focus of our lives. The Empire cannot go on this way, Stil, without a proper focus for human life. I am speaking of life, you understand? Life, not death."

"Once, when he was troubled by a vision, your father spoke in this vein to me," Stilgar said.

Leto found himself tempted to pass off that questioning fear beside him with a light response, perhaps a suggestion that they break their fast. He realized that he was very hungry. They had eaten the previous noon and Leto had insisted on fasting through the night. But another hunger drew him now.

*The trouble with my life is the trouble with this place,* Leto thought. *No preliminary creation. I just go back and back and back until distances fade away. I cannot see the horizon; I cannot see Habbanya Ridge. I can't find the original place of testing.*

"There's really no substitute for prescience," Leto said. "Perhaps I should risk the spice . . ."

"And be destroyed as your father was?"

"A dilemma," Leto said.

"Once your father confided in me that knowing the future too well was to be locked into that future to the exclusion of any freedom to change."

"The paradox which is our problem," Leto said. "It's a subtle and powerful thing, prescience. The future becomes now. To be sighted in the land of the blind carries its own perils. If you try to interpret what you see for the blind, you tend to forget that the blind possess an inherent movement conditioned by their blindness. They are like a monstrous machine moving along its own path. They have their own momentum, their own fixations. I fear the blind, Stil. I fear them. They can so easily crush anything in their path."

Stilgar stared at the desert. Lime dawn had become steel day. He said: "Why have we come to this place?"

"Because I wanted you to see the place where I may die."

Stilgar tensed. Then: "So you *have* had a vision!"

"Perhaps it was only a dream."

"Why do we come to such a dangerous place?" Stilgar glared down at his charge. "We will return at once."

"I won't die today, Stil."

"No? What was this vision?"

"I saw three paths," Leto said. His voice came out with the sleepy sound of remembrance. "One of those futures requires me to kill our grandmother."

Stilgar shot a sharp glance back toward Sietch Tabr, as though he feared the Lady Jessica could hear them across the sandy distance. "Why?"

"To keep from losing the spice monopoly."

"I don't understand."

"Nor do I. But that is the thought of my dream when I use the knife."

"Oh." Stilgar understood the use of a knife. He drew a deep breath. "What is the second path?"

"Ghani and I marry to seal the Atreides bloodline."

"*Ghaaa!*" Stilgar expelled his breath in a violent expression of distate.

"It was usual in ancient times for kings and queens to do this," Leto said. "Ghani and I have decided we will not breed."

"I warn you to hold fast in that decision!" There was death in Stilgar's voice.

By Fremen Law, incest was punishable by death on the hanging tripod. He cleared his throat, asked: "And the third path?"

"I am called to reduce my father to human stature."

"He was my friend, Muad'Dib," Stilgar muttered.

"He was your god! I must undeify him."

Stilgar turned his back on the desert, stared toward the oasis of his beloved Sietch Tabr. Such talk always disturbed him.

Leto sensed the sweaty smell of Stilgar's movement. It was such a temptation to avoid the purposeful things which had to be said here. They could talk half the day away, moving from the specific to the abstract as though drawn away from real decisions, from those immediate necessities which confronted them. And there was no doubt that House Corrino posed a real threat to real lives—his own and Ghani's. But everything he did now had to be weighed and tested against the secret necessities. Stilgar once had voted to have Farad'n assassinated, holding out for the subtle application of chaumurky: poison administered in a drink. Farad'n was known to be partial to certain sweet liquors. That could not be permitted.

"If I die here, Stil," Leto said, "you must beware of Alia. She is no longer your friend."

"What is this talk of death and your aunt?" Now Stilgar was truly outraged. *Kill the Lady Jessica! Beware of Alia! Die in this place!*

"Small men change their faces at her command," Leto said. "A ruler need not be a prophet, Stil. Nor even godlike. A ruler need only be sensitive. I brought you here with me to clarify what our Imperium requires. It requires good government. That does not depend upon laws or precedent, but upon the personal qualities of whoever governs."

"The Regency handles its Imperial duties quite well," Stilgar said. "When you come of age—"

"I *am* of age! I'm the oldest person here! You're a puling infant beside me. I can remember times more than fifty centuries past. Hah! I can even remember when we Fremen were on Thurgrod."

"Why do you play with such fancies?" Stilgar demanded, his tone peremptory.

Leto nodded to himself. Why indeed? Why recount his memories of those other centuries? Today's Fremen were his immediate problem, most of them still only half-tamed savages, prone to laugh at unlucky innocence.

"The crysknife dissolves at the death of its owner," Leto said. "Muad'Dib has dissolved. Why are the Fremen still alive?"

It was one of those abrupt thought changes which so confounded Stilgar. He found himself temporarily dumb. Such words contained meaning, but their intent eluded him.

"I am expected to be Emperor, but I must be the servant," Leto said. He glanced across his shoulder at Stilgar. "My grandfather for whom I was named added new words to his coat of arms when he came here to Dune: 'Here I am; here I remain.' "

"He had no choice," Stilgar said.

"Very good, Stil. Nor have I any choice. I should be the Emperor by birth, by the fitness of my understanding, by all that has gone into me. I even know what the Imperium requires: good government."

"Naib has an ancient meaning," Stilgar said. "It is 'servant of the Sietch.' "

"I remember your training, Stil," Leto said. "For proper government, the tribe must have ways to choose men whose lives reflect the way a government should behave."

From the depths of his Fremen soul, Stilgar said: "You'll assume the Imperial Mantle if it's meet. First you must prove that you can behave in the fashion of a ruler!"

Unexpectedly, Leto laughed. Then: "Do you doubt my sincerity, Stil?"

"Of course not."

"My birthright?"

"You are who you are."

"And if I do what is expected of me, that is the measure of my sincerity, eh?"

"It is the Fremen practice."

"Then I cannot have inner feelings to guide my behavior?"

"I don't understand what—"

"If I always behave with propriety, no matter what it costs me to suppress my own desires, then that is the measure of me."

"Such is the essence of self-control, youngster."

"Youngster!" Leto shook his head. "Ahhh, Stil, you provide me with the key to a rational ethic of government. I must be constant, every action rooted in the traditions of the past."

"That is proper."

"But my past goes deeper than yours!"

"What difference—"

"I have no first person singular, Stil. I am a multiple person with memories of traditions more ancient than you could imagine. That's my burden, Stil. I'm past-directed. I'm abrim with innate knowledge which resists newness and change. Yet Muad'Dib changed all this." He gestured at the desert, his arm sweeping to encompass the Shield Wall behind him.

Stilgar turned to peer at the Shield Wall. A village had been built beneath the wall since Muad'Dib's time, houses to shelter a planetology crew helping spread plant life into the desert. Stilgar stared at the man-made intrusion into the landscape. Change? Yes. There was an alignment to the village, a trueness which offended him. He stood silently, ignoring the itching of grit particles under his stillsuit. That village was an offense against the thing this planet had been. Suddenly Stilgar wanted a circular howling of wind to leap over the dunes and obliterate that place. The sensation left him trembling.

Leto said: "Have you noticed, Stil, that the new stillsuits are of sloppy manufacture? Our water loss is too high."

Stilgar stopped himself on the point of asking: *Have I not said it?* Instead he said: "Our people grow increasingly dependent upon the pills."

Leto nodded. The pills shifted body temperature, reduced water loss. They were cheaper and easier than stillsuits. But they inflicted the user with other burdens, among them a tendency to slowed reaction time, occasional blurred vision.

"Is that why we came out here?" Stilgar asked. "To discuss stillsuit manufacture?"

"Why not?" Leto asked. "Since you will not face what I must talk about."

"Why must I beware of your aunt?" Anger edged his voice.

"Because she plays upon the old Fremen desire to resist change, yet would bring more terrible change than you can imagine."

"You make much out of little! She's a proper Fremen."

"Ahhh, then the proper Fremen holds to the ways of the past and I have an ancient past. Stil, were I to give free reign to this inclination, I would demand a closed society, completely dependent upon the sacred ways of the past. I would control migration, explaining that this fosters new ideas, and new ideas are a threat to the entire structure of life. Each little planetary polis would go its own way, becoming what it would. Finally the Empire would shatter under the weight of its differences."

Stilgar tried to swallow in a dry throat. These were words which Muad'Dib might have produced. They had his ring to them. They were paradox, frightening. But if one allowed any change . . . He shook his head.

"The past may show the right way to behave if you live in the past, Stil, but circumstances change."

Stilgar could only agree that circumstances did change. How must one behave then? He looked beyond Leto, seeing the desert and not seeing it. Muad'Dib had walked there. The flat was a place of golden shadows as the sun climbed, purple shadows, gritty rivulets crested in dust vapors. The dust fog which usually hung over Habbanya Ridge was visible in the far distance now, and the desert between presented his eyes with dunes diminishing, one curve into another. Through the smoky shimmer of heat he saw the plants which crept out from the desert edge. Muad'Dib had caused life to sprout in that desolate place. Copper, gold, red flowers, yellow flowers, rust and russet, grey-green leaves, spikes and harsh shadows beneath bushes. The motion of the day's heat set shadows quivering, vibrating in the air.

Presently Stilgar said: "I am only a leader of Fremen; you are the son of a Duke."

"Not knowing what you said, you said it," Leto said.

Stilgar scowled. Once, long ago, Muad'Dib had chided him thus.

"You remember it, don't you, Stil?" Leto asked. "We were under Habbanya Ridge and the Sardaukar captain—remember him: Aramsham? He killed his friend to save himself. And you warned several times that day about preserving the lives of Sardaukar who'd seen our secret ways. Finally you said they would surely reveal what they'd seen; they must be killed. And my father said: 'Not knowing what you said, you said it.' And you were hurt. You told him you were only a *simple* leader of Fremen. Dukes must know more important things."

Stilgar stared down at Leto. *We were under Habbanya Ridge! We!* This . . . this child, not even conceived on that day, knew what had taken place in exact detail, the kind of detail which could only be known to someone who had been there. It was only another proof that these Atreides children could not be judged by ordinary standards.

"Now you will listen to me," Leto said. "If I die or disappear in the desert, you are to flee from Sietch Tabr. I command it. You are to take Ghani and—"

"You are not yet my Duke! You're a . . . a child!"

"I'm an adult in a child's flesh," Leto said. He pointed down to a narrow crack in the rocks below them. "If I die here, it will be in that place. You will see the blood. You will known then. Take my sister and—"

"I'm doubling your guard," Stilgar said. "You're not coming out here again. We are leaving now and you—"

"Stil! You cannot hold me. Turn your mind once more to the time at Habbanya Ridge. Remember? The factory crawler was out there on the sand and a big Maker was coming. There was no way to save the crawler from the worm. And my father was annoyed that he couldn't save that crawler. But Gurney could think only of the men he'd lost in the sand. Remember what he said: 'Your father would've been more concerned for the men he couldn't save.' Stil, I charge you to save people. They're more important than things. And Ghani is the most precious of all because, without me, she is the only hope for the Atreides."

"I will hear no more," Stilgar said. He turned and began climbing down the rocks toward the oasis across the sand. He heard Leto following. Presently Leto passed him and, glancing back, said:

"Have you noticed, Stil, how beautiful the young women are this year?"

*The life of a single human, as the life of a family or an entire people, persists as memory. My people must come to see this as part of their maturing process. They are people as organism, and in this persistent memory they store more and more experiences in a subliminal reservoir. Humankind hopes to call upon this material if it is needed for a changing universe. But much that is stored can be lost in that chance play of accident which we call "fate." Much may not be integrated into evolutionary relationships, and thus may not be evaluated and keyed into activity by those ongoing environmental changes which inflict themselves upon flesh. The species can forget! This is the special value of the Kwisatz Haderach which the Bene Gesserits never suspected: the Kwisatz Haderach cannot forget.*

—The Book of Leto
After Harq al-Ada

Stilgar could not explain it, but he found Leto's casual observation profoundly disturbing. It ground through his awareness all the way back across the sand to Sietch Tabr, taking precedence over everything else Leto had said out there on The Attendant.

Indeed, the young women of Arrakis were very beautiful that year. And the young men, too. Their faces glowed serenely with water-richness. Their eyes looked outward and far. They exposed their features often without any pretense of stillsuit masks and the snaking lines of catchtubes. Frequently they did not even wear stillsuits in the open, preferring the new garments which, as they moved, offered flickering suggestions of the lithe young bodies beneath.

Such human beauty was set off against the new beauty of the landscape. By contrast with the old Arrakis, the eye could be spellbound by its collision with a tiny clump of green twigs growing among red-brown rocks. And the old sietch warrens of the cave-metropolis culture, complete with elaborate seals and moisture traps at every entrance, were giving way to open villages built often of mud bricks. Mud bricks!

*Why did I want the village destroyed?* Stilgar wondered, and he stumbled as he walked.

He knew himself to be of a dying breed. Old Fremen gasped in wonder at the prodigality of their planet—water wasted into the air for no more than its ability to mold building bricks. The water for a single one-family dwelling would keep an entire sietch alive for a year.

The new buildings even had transparent windows to let in the sun's heat and to desiccate the bodies within. Such windows opened outward.

New Fremen within their mud homes could look out upon their landscape. They no longer were enclosed and huddling in a sietch. Where the new vision moved, there also moved the imagination. Stilgar could feel this. The new vision joined Fremen to the rest of the Imperial universe, conditioned them to unbounded space. Once they'd been tied to water-poor Arrakis by their enslavement to its bitter necessities. They'd not shared that open-mindedness which conditioned inhabitants on most planets of the Imperium.

Stilgar could see the changes contrasting with his own doubts and fears. In the old days it had been a rare Fremen who even considered the possibility that he might leave Arrakis to begin a new life on one of the water-rich worlds. They'd not even been permitted the *dream* of escape.

He watched Leto's moving back as the youth walked ahead. Leto had spoken of prohibitions against movement off-planet. Well, that had always been a reality for most other-worlders, even where the dream was permitted as a safety valve. But planetary serfdom had reached its peak here on Arrakis. Fremen had turned inward, barricaded in their minds as they were barricaded in their cave warrens.

The very meaning of sietch—a place of sanctuary in times of trouble—had been perverted here into a monstrous confinement for an entire population.

Leto spoke the truth: Muad'Dib had changed all that.

Stilgar felt lost. He could feel his old beliefs crumbling. The new outward vision produced life which desired to move away from containment.

*"How beautiful the young women are this year."*

The old ways (*My ways!* he admitted) had forced his people to ignore all history except that which turned inward onto their own travail. The old Fremen had read history out of their own terrible migrations, their flights from persecution into persecution. The old planetary government had followed the stated policy of the old Imperium. They had suppressed creativity and all sense of progress, of evolution. Prosperity had been dangerous to the old Imperium and its holders of power.

With an abrupt shock, Stilgar realized that these things were equally dangerous to the course which Alia was setting.

Again Stilgar stumbled and fell farther behind Leto.

In the old ways and old religions, there'd been no future, only an endless *now*. Before Muad'Dib, Stilgar saw, the Fremen had been conditioned to believe in failure, never in the possibility of accomplishment. Well . . . they'd believed Liet-Kynes, but he'd set a forty-generation timescale. That was no accomplishment; that was a dream which, he saw now, had also turned inward.

*Muad'Dib had changed that!*

During the Jihad, Fremen had learned much about the old Padishah Emperor, Shaddam IV. The eighty-first Padishah of House Corrino to occupy the Golden Lion Throne and reign over this Imperium of uncounted worlds had used Arrakis as a testing place for those policies which he'd hoped to implement in the rest of his empire. His planetary governors on Arrakis had cultivated a persistent pessimism to bolster their power base. They'd made sure that everyone on Arrakis, even the free-roaming Fremen, became familiar with numerous cases of injustice and insoluble problems; they had been taught to think of themselves as a helpless people for whom there was no succor.

*"How beautiful the young women are this year!"*

As he watched Leto's retreating back, Stilgar began to wonder how the youth had set these thoughts flowing—and just by uttering a seemingly simple statement. Because of that statement, Stilgar found himself viewing Alia and his own role on the Council in an entirely different way.

Alia was fond of saying that old ways gave ground slowly. Stilgar admitted to himself that he'd always found this statement vaguely reassuring. Change was dangerous. Invention must be suppressed. Individual willpower must be denied. What other function did the priesthood serve than to deny individual will?

Alia kept saying that opportunities for open competition had to be reduced to manageable limits. But that meant the recurrent threat of technology could only be used to confine populations—just as it had served its ancient masters. Any permitted technology had to be rooted in ritual. Otherwise . . . otherwise . . .

Again Stilgar stumbled. He was at the qanat now and saw Leto waiting beneath the apricot orchard which grew along the flowing water. Stilgar heard his feet moving through uncut grass.

*Uncut grass!*

*What can I believe?* Stilgar asked himself.

It was proper for a Fremen of his generation to believe that individuals needed a profound sense of their own limitations. Traditions were surely the most controlling element in a secure society. People had to know the boundaries of their time, of their society, of their territory. What was wrong with the sietch as a model for all thinking? A sense of enclosure should pervade every individual choice—should fence in the family, the community, and every step taken by a proper government.

Stilgar came to a stop and stared across the orchard at Leto. The youth stood there, regarding him with a smile.

*Does he know the turmoil in my head?* Stilgar wondered.

And the old Fremen Naib tried to fall back on the traditional catechism of his people. Each aspect of life required a single form, its inherent circularity based on secret inner knowledge of what will work and what will not work. The model for life, for the community, for every element of the larger society right up to and beyond the peaks of government—that model had to be the sietch and its counterpart in the sand: Shai-Hulud. The giant sandworm was surely a most formidable creature, but when threatened it hid in the impenetrable deeps.

*Change is dangerous!* Stilgar told himself. Sameness and stability were the proper goals of government.

But the young men and women were beautiful.

And they remembered the words of Muad'Dib as he deposed Shaddam IV: "It's not long life to the Emperor that I seek; it's long life to the Imperium."

*Isn't that what I've been saying to myself?* Stilgar wondered.

He resumed walking, headed toward the sietch entrance slightly to Leto's right. The youth moved to intercept him.

Muad'Dib had said another thing, Stilgar reminded himself: *"Just as individuals are born, mature, breed, and die, so do societies and civilizations and governments."*

Dangerous or not, there would be change. The beautiful young Fremen knew this. They could look outward and see it, prepare for it.

Stilgar was forced to stop. It was either that or walk right over Leto.

The youth peered up at him owlishly, said: "You see, Stil? Tradition isn't the absolute guide you thought it was."

*A Fremen dies when he is too long from the desert; this we call "the water sickness."*

**—Stilgar, the Commentaries**

"It is difficult for me, asking you to do this," Alia said. "But . . . I must insure that there's an empire for Paul's children to inherit. There's no other reason for the Regency."

Alia turned from where she was seated at a mirror completing her morning toilet. She looked at her husband, measuring how he absorbed these words. Duncan Idaho deserved careful study in these moments; there was no doubt that he'd become something far more subtle and dangerous than the one-time swordmaster of House Atreides. The outer appearance remained similar—the black goat hair over sharp dark features—but in the long years since his awakening from the ghola state he had undergone an inner metamorphosis.

She wondered now, as she had wondered many times, what the ghola rebirth-after-death might have hidden in the secret loneliness of him. Before the Tleilaxu had worked their subtle science on him, Duncan's reactions had borne clear labels for the Atreides—loyalty, fanatic adherence to the moral code of his mercenary forebears, swift to anger and swift to recover. He had been implacable in his resolve for revenge against House Harkonnen. And he had died saving Paul. But the Tleilaxu had bought his body from the Sardaukar and, in their regeneration vats, they had grown a zombie-katrundo: the flesh of Duncan Idaho, but none of his conscious memories. He'd been trained as a mentat and sent as a gift, a human computer for Paul, a fine tool equipped with a hypnotic compulsion to slay his owner. The flesh of Duncan Idaho had resisted that compulsion and, in the intolerable stress, his cellular past had come back to him.

Alia had decided long ago that it was dangerous to think of him as Duncan in the privacy of her thoughts. Better to think of him by his ghola name, Hayt. Far better. And it was essential that he get not the slightest glimpse of the old Baron Harkonnen sitting there in her mind.

Duncan saw Alia studying him, turned away. Love could not hide the changes in her, nor conceal from him the transparency of her motives. The many-faceted metal eyes which the Tleilaxu had given him were cruel in their ability to penetrate deception. They limned her now as a gloating, almost masculine figure, and he could not stand to see her thus.

"Why do you turn away?" Alia asked.

"I must think about this thing," he said. "The Lady Jessica is . . . an Atreides."

"And your loyalty is to House Atreides, not to me," Alia pouted.

"Don't put such fickle interpretations into me," he said.

Alia pursed her lips. Had she moved too rapidly?

Duncan crossed to the chambered opening which looked down on a corner of the Temple plaza. He could see pilgrims beginning to gather there, the Arrakeen traders moving in to feed on the edges like a pack of predators upon a herd of beasts. He focused on a particular group of tradesmen, spice-fiber baskets over their arms, Fremen mercenaries a pace behind them. They moved with a stolid force through the gathering throng.

"They sell pieces of etched marble," he said, pointing. "Did you know that? They set the pieces out in the desert to be etched by stormsands. Sometimes they find interesting patterns in the stone. They call it a new art form, very popular: genuine storm-etched marble from Dune. I bought a piece of it last week—a golden tree with five tassels, lovely but very fragile."

"Don't change the subject," Alia said.

"I haven't changed the subject," he said. "It's beautiful, but it's not art. Humans create art by their own violence, by their own volition." He put his right hand on the windowsill. "The twins detest this city and I'm afraid I see their point."

"I fail to see the association," Alia said. "The abduction of my mother is not a real abduction. She will be safe as your captive."

"This city was built by the blind," he said. "Did you know that Leto and Stilgar went out from Sietch Tabr into the desert last week? They were gone the whole night."

"It was reported to me," she said. "These baubles from the sand—would you have me prohibit their sale?"

"That'd be bad for business," he said, turning. "Do you know what Stilgar said when I asked why they went out on the sand that way? He said Leto wished to commune with the spirit of Muad'Dib."

Alia felt the sudden coldness of panic, looked in the mirror a moment to recover. Leto would not venture from the sietch at night for such nonsense. Was it a conspiracy?

Idaho put a hand over his eyes to blot out the sight of her, said: "Stilgar told me he went along with Leto because he still believes in Muad'Dib."

"Of course he does!"

Idaho chuckled, a hollow sound. "He said he still believes because Muad'Dib was always for the little people."

"What did you say to that?" Alia asked, her voice betraying her fear.

Idaho dropped his hand from his eyes. "I said, 'That must make you one of the little people.'"

"Duncan! That's a dangerous game. Bait *that* Fremen Naib and you could awaken a beast to destroy us all."

"He still believes in Muad'Dib," Idaho said. "That's our protection."

"What was his reply?"

"He said he knew his own mind."

"I see."

"No . . . I don't believe you do. Things that bite have longer teeth than Stilgar's."

"I don't understand you today, Duncan. I ask you to do a very important thing, a thing vital to . . . What is all of this rambling?"

How petulant she sounded. He turned back to the chambered window. "When I was trained as a mentat . . . It is very difficult, Alia, to learn how to work your own mind. You learn first that the mind must be allowed to work itself. That's very strange. You can work your own muscles, exercise them, strengthen them, but the mind acts of itself. Sometimes, when you have learned this about the mind, it shows you things you do not want to see."

"And that's why you tried to insult Stilgar?"

"Stilgar doesn't know his own mind; he doesn't let it run free."

"Except in the spice orgy."

"Not even there. That's what makes him a Naib. To be a leader of men, he controls and limits his reactions. He does what is expected of him. Once you know this, you know Stilgar and you can measure the length of his teeth."

"That's the Fremen way," she said. "Well, Duncan, will you do it, or won't you? She must be taken and it must be made to look like the work of House Corrino."

He remained silent, weighing her tone and arguments in his mentat way. This abduction plan spoke of a coldness and a cruelty whose dimensions, thus revealed, shocked him. Risk her own mother's life for the reasons thus far produced? Alia was lying. Perhaps the whisperings about Alia and Javid were true. This thought produced an icy hardness in his stomach.

"You're the only one I can trust for this," Alia said.

"I know that," he said.

She took this as acceptance, smiled at herself in the mirror.

"You know," Idaho said, "the mentat learns to look at every human as a series of relationships."

Alia did not respond. She sat, caught in a personal memory which drew a blank expression on her face. Idaho, glancing over his shoulder at her, saw the expression and shuddered. It was as though she communed with voices heard only by herself.

"Relationships," he whispered.

And he thought: *One must cast off old agonies as a snake casts off its skin— only to grow a new set and accept all of their limitations. It was the same with governments—even the Regency. Old governments can be traced like discarded molts. I must carry out this scheme, but not in the way Alia commands.*

Presently Alia shook her shoulders, said: "Leto should not be going out like that in these times. I will reprimand him."

"Not even with Stilgar?"

"Not even with him."

She arose from her mirror, crossed to where Idaho stood beside the window, put a hand on his arm.

He repressed a shiver, reduced this reaction to a mentat computation. Something in her revolted him.

Something in her.

He could not bring himself to look at her. He smelled the melange of her cosmetics, cleared his throat.

She said: "I will be busy today examining Farad'n's gifts."

"The clothing?"

"Yes. Nothing he does is what it seems. And we must remember that his Bashar, Tyekanik, is an adept of chaumurky, chaumas, and all the other subtleties of royal assassination."

"The price of power," he said, pulling away from her. "But we're still mobile and Farad'n is not."

She studied his chiseled profile. Sometimes the workings of his mind were difficult to fathom. Was he thinking only that freedom of action gave life to a military power? Well, life on Arrakis had been too secure for too long. Senses once whetted by omnipresent dangers could degenerate when not used.

"Yes," she said, "we still have the Fremen."

"Mobility," he repeated. "We cannot degenerate into infantry. That'd be foolish."

His tone annoyed her, and she said: "Farad'n will use any means to destroy us."

"Ahhh, that's it," he said. "That's a form of initiative, a mobility which we didn't have in the old days. We had a code, the code of House Atreides. We always paid our way and let the enemy be the pillagers. That restriction no longer holds, of course. We're equally mobile, House Atreides and House Corrino."

"We abduct my mother to save her from harm as much as for any other reason," Alia said. "We still live by the code!"

He looked down at her. She knew the dangers of inciting a mentat to compute. Didn't she realize what he had computed? Yet . . . he still loved her. He brushed a hand across his eyes. How youthful she looked. The Lady Jessica was correct: Alia gave the appearance of not having aged a day in their years together. She still possessed the soft features of her Bene Gesserit mother, but her eyes were Atreides—measuring, demanding, hawklike. And now something possessed of cruel calculation lurked behind those eyes.

Idaho had served House Atreides for too many years not to understand the family's strengths as well as their weaknesses. But this thing in Alia, this was new. The Atreides might play a devious game against enemies, but never against friends and allies, and not at all against Family. It was ground into the Atreides manner: support your own populace to the best of your ability; show them how much better they lived under the Atreides. Demonstrate your love for your friends by the candor of your behavior with them. What Alia asked now, though, was not Atreides. He felt this with all of his body's flesh and nerve structure. He was a unit, indivisible, feeling this alien attitude in Alia.

Abruptly his mentat sensorium clicked into full awareness and his mind leaped into the frozen trance where Time did not exist; only the computation existed. Alia would recognize what had happened to him, but that could not be helped. He gave himself up to the computation.

Computation: A *reflected* Lady Jessica lived out a pseudo-life in Alia's awareness. He saw this as he saw the reflected pre-ghola Duncan Idaho which remained a constant in his own awareness. Alia had this awareness by being one of the pre-born. He had it out of the Tleilaxu regeneration tanks. Yet Alia denied that reflection, risked her mother's life. Therefore Alia was not in contact with that pseudo-Jessica within. Therefore Alia was *completely* possessed by another pseudo-life to the exclusion of all others.

*Possessed!*

*Alien!*

*Abomination!*

Mentat fashion, he accepted this, turned to other facets of his problem. All of the Atreides were on this one planet. Would House Corrino risk attack from space? His mind flashed through the review of those conventions which had ended primitive forms of warfare:

One—All planets were vulnerable to attack from space; ergo: retaliation/revenge facilities were set up off-planet by every House Major. Farad'n would know that the Atreides had not omitted this elementary precaution.

Two—Force shields were a complete defense against projectiles and explosives of non-atomic type, the basic reason why hand-to-hand conflict had reentered human combat. But infantry had its limits. House Corrino might have brought their Sardaukar back to a pre-Arrakeen edge, but they still could be no match for the abandoned ferocity of the Fremen.

Three—Planetary feudalism remained in constant danger from a large technical class, but the effects of the Butlerian Jihad continued as a damper on technological excesses. Ixians, Tleilaxu, and a few scattered outer planets were the only possible threat in this regard, and they were planet-vulnerable to the combined wrath of the rest of the Imperium. The Butlerian Jihad would not be undone. Mechanized warfare required a large technical class. The Atreides Imperium had channeled this force into other pursuits. No large technical class existed unwatched. And the Empire remained safely feudalist, naturally, since that was the best social form for spreading over widely dispersed wild frontiers—new planets.

Duncan felt his mentat awareness coruscate as it shot through memory data *of itself*, completely impervious to the passage of time. Arriving at the conviction that House Corrino would not risk an *illegal* atomic attack, he did this in flash-computation, the main decisional pathway, but he was perfectly aware of the elements which went into this conviction: The Imperium commanded as many nuclear and allied weapons as all the Great Houses combined. At least half the Great Houses would react without thinking if House Corrino broke the Convention. The Atreides off-planet retaliation system would be joined by overwhelming force and no need to summon any of them. Fear would do the calling. Salusa Secundus and its allies would vanish in hot clouds. House Corrino would not risk such a holocaust. They were undoubtedly sincere in subscribing to the argument that nuclear weapons were a reserve held for one purpose: defense of humankind should a threatening "other intelligence" ever be enountered.

The computational thoughts had clean edges, sharp relief. There were no blurred between-places. Alia chose abduction and terror because she had become alien, non-Atreides. House Corrino was a threat, but not in the ways which Alia argued in Council. Alia wanted the Lady Jessica removed because that searing Bene Gesserit intelligence had seen what only now had become clear to him.

Idaho shook himself out of the mentat trance, saw Alia standing in front of him, a coldly measuring expression on her face.

"Wouldn't you rather the Lady Jessica were killed?" he asked.

The alien-flash of her joy lay exposed before his eyes for a brief instant before being covered by false outrage. "Duncan!"

Yes, this alien-Alia preferred matricide.

"You are afraid *of* your mother, not *for* her," he said.

She spoke without a change in her measuring stare. "Of course I am. She has reported about me to the Sisterhood."

"What do you mean?"

"Don't you know the greatest temptation for a Bene Gesserit?" She moved closer to him, seductive, looked upward at him through her lashes. "I thought only to keep myself strong and alert for the sake of the twins."

"You speak of temptation," he said, his voice mentat-flat.

"It's the thing which the Sisterhood hides most deeply, the thing they most fear. It's why they call me *Abomination*. They know their inhibitions won't hold me back. Temptation—they always speak with heavy emphasis: *Great Temptation*. You see, we who employ the Bene Gesserit teachings can influence such things as the internal adjustment of enzyme balance within our bodies. It can prolong youth—far longer than with melange. Do you see the consequences should many Bene Gesserits do this? It would be noticed. I'm sure you compute the accuracy of what I'm saying. Melange is what makes us the target for so many plots. We control a substance which prolongs life. What if it became known that Bene Gesserits controlled an even more potent secret? You see! Not one Reverend Mother would be safe. Abduction and torture of Bene Gesserits would become a most common activity."

"You've accomplished this enzyme balancing." It was a statement, not a question.

"I've defied the Sisterhood! My mother's reports to the Sisterhood will make the Bene Gesserits unswerving allies of House Corrino."

*How very plausible,* he thought.

He tested: "But surely your own mother would not turn against you!"

"She was Bene Gesserit long before she was my mother. Duncan, she permitted her own son, my brother, to undergo the test of the *gom jabbar!* She arranged it! And she knew he might not survive it! Bene Gesserits have always been short on faith and long on pragmatism. She'll act against me if she believes it's in the best interests of the Sisterhood."

He nodded. How convincing she was. It was a sad thought.

"We must hold the initiative," she said. "That's our sharpest weapon."

"There's the problem of Gurney Halleck," he said. "Do I have to kill my old friend?"

"Gurney's off on some spy errand in the desert," she said, knowing Idaho already was aware of this. "He's safely out of the way."

"Very odd," he said, "the Regent Governor of Caladan running errands here on Arrakis."

"Why not?" Alia demanded. "He's her lover—in his dreams if not in fact."

"Yes, of course." And he wondered that she did not hear the insincerity in his voice.

"When will you abduct her?" Alia asked.

"It's better that you don't know."

"Yes . . . yes, I see. Where'll you take her?"

"Where she cannot be found. Depend upon it; she won't be left here to threaten you."

The glee in Alia's eyes could not be mistaken. "But where will . . ."

"If you do not know, then you can answer before a Truthsayer, if necessary, that you do not know where she is."

"Ahhh, clever, Duncan."

*Now she believes I will kill the Lady Jessica,* he thought And he said: "Goodbye, beloved."

She did not hear the finality in his voice, even kissed him lightly as he left.

And all the way down through the sietchlike maze of Temple corridors, Idaho brushed at his eyes. Tleilaxu eyes were not immune to tears.


> *You have loved Caladan*
> *And lamented its lost host—*
> *But pain discovers*
> *New lovers cannot erase*
> *Those forever ghost.*

**—Refrain from The Habbanya Lament**


Stilgar quadrupled the sietch guard around the twins, but he knew it was useless. The lad was like his Atreides namesake, the grandfather Leto. Everyone who'd known the original Duke remarked on it. Leto had the measuring look about him, and caution, yes, but all of it had to be evaluated against that latent wildness, the susceptibility to dangerous decisions.

Ghanima was more like her mother. There was Chani's red hair, the set of Chani's eyes, and a calculating way about her when she adjusted to difficulties. She often said that she only did what she had to do, but where Leto led she would follow.

And Leto was going to lead them into danger.

Not once did Stilgar think of taking his problem to Alia. That ruled out Irulan, who ran to Alia with anything and everything. In coming to his decision, Stilgar realized he had accepted the possibility that Leto judged Alia correctly.

*She uses people in a casual and callous way,* he thought. *She even uses Duncan that way. It isn't so much that she'd turn on me and kill me. She'd discard me.*

Meanwhile the guard was strengthened and Stilgar stalked his sietch like a robed specter, prying everywhere. All the time, his mind seethed with the doubts Leto had planted there. If one could not depend upon tradition, then where was the rock upon which to anchor his life?

On the afternoon of the Convocation of Welcome for the Lady Jessica, Stilgar spied Ghanima standing with her grandmother at the entrance lip to the sietch's great assembly chamber. It was early and Alia had not yet arrived, but people already were thronging into the chamber, casting surreptitious glances at the child and adult as they passed.

Stilgar paused in a shadowed alcove out of the crowd flow and watched the pair of them, unable to hear their words above the murmuring throb of an assembling multitude. The people of many tribes would be here today to welcome back their old Reverend Mother. But he stared at Ghanima. Her eyes, the way they danced when she spoke! The movement fascinated him. Those deep blue, steady, demanding, measuring eyes. And that way of throwing her red-gold hair off her shoulder with a twist of her head: that was Chani. It was a ghostly resurrection, an uncanny resemblance.

Slowly Stilgar drew closer and took up his station in another alcove.

He could not associate Ghanima's observing manner with any other child of his experience—except her brother. Where was Leto? Stilgar glanced back up the crowded passage. His guards would have spread an alarm if anything were amiss. He shook his head. These twins assaulted his sanity. They were a constant abrasion against his peace of mind. He could almost hate them. Kin were not immune from one's hatred, but blood (and its precious water) carried demands for one's countenance which transcended most other concerns. These twins existed as his greatest responsibility.

Dust-filtered brown light came from the cavernous assembly chamber beyond Ghanima and Jessica. It touched the child's shoulders and the new white robe she wore, backlighting her hair as she turned to peer into the passage at the people thronging past.

*Why did Leto afflict me with these doubts?* he wondered. There was no doubt that it had been done deliberately. *Perhaps Leto wanted me to have a small share of his own mental experience.* Stilgar *knew* why the twins were different, but had always found his reasoning processes unable to accept what he knew. He had never experienced the womb as prison to an awakened consciousness—a living awareness from the second month of gestation, so it was said.

Leto had once said that his memory was like "an internal holograph, expanding in size and in detail from that original shocked awakening, but never changing shape or outline."

For the first time, as he watched Ghanima and the Lady Jessica, Stilgar began to understand what it must be like to live in such a scrambled web of memories, unable to retreat or find a sealed room of the mind. Faced with such a condition, one had to integrate madness, to select and reject from a multitude of offerings in a system where answers changed as fast as the questions.

There could be no fixed tradition. There could be no absolute answers to double-faced questions. What works? That which does not work. What does not work? That which works. He recognized this pattern. It was the old Fremen game of riddles. Question: "It brings death and life." Answer: "The Coriolis wind."

*Why did Leto want me to understand this?* Stilgar asked himself. From his cautious probings, Stilgar knew that the twins shared a common view of their difference: they thought of it as affliction. *The birth canal would be a draining place to such a one,* he thought. Ignorance reduces the shock of some experiences, but they would have no ignorance about birth. What would it be like to live a life where you knew all of the things that *could* go wrong? You would face a constant war with doubts. You would resent your difference from your fellows. It would be pleasant to inflict others with even a taste of that difference. "Why me?" would be your first unanswered question.

*And what have I been asking myself?* Stilgar thought. A wry smile touched his lips. *Why me?*

Seeing the twins in this new way, he understood the dangerous chances they took with their uncompleted bodies. Ghanima had put it to him succinctly once after he'd berated her for climbing the precipitous west face to the rim above Sietch Tabr.

"Why should I fear death? I've been there before—many times."

*How can I presume to teach such children?* Stilgar wondered. *How can anyone presume?*

Oddly, Jessica's thoughts were moving in a similar vein as she talked to her granddaughter. She'd been thinking how difficult it must be to carry mature minds in immature bodies. The body would have to learn what the mind already knew it could do—aligning responses and reflexes. The old Bene Gesserit *prana-bindu* regimen would be available to them, but even there the mind would run where the flesh could not. Gurney had a supremely difficult task carrying out her orders.

"Stilgar is watching us from an alcove back there," Ghanima said.

Jessica did not turn. But she found herself confounded by what she heard in Ghanima's voice. Ghanima loved the old Fremen as one would love a parent. Even while she spoke lightly of him and teased him, she loved him. The realization forced Jessica to see the old Naib in a new light, understanding in a gestalten revelation what the twins and Stilgar shared. This new Arrakis did not fit Stilgar well, Jessica realized. No more than this new universe fitted her grandchildren.

Unwanted and undemanded, a Bene Gesserit saying flowed through Jessica's mind: "*To suspect your own mortality is to know the beginning of terror; to learn irrefutably that you are mortal is to know the end of terror.*"

Yes, death would not be a hard yoke to wear, but life was a slow fire to Stilgar and the twins. Each found an ill-fitting world and longed for other ways where variations might be known without threat. They were children of Abraham, learning more from a hawk stooping over the desert than from any book yet written.

Leto had confounded Jessica only that morning as they'd stood beside the qanat which flowed below the sietch. He'd said: "Water traps us, grandmother. We'd be better off living like dust because then the wind could carry us higher than the highest cliffs of the Shield Wall."

Although she was familiar with such devious maturity from the mouths of these children, Jessica had been caught by this utterance, but had managed: "Your father might've said that."

And Leto, throwing a handful of sand into the air to watch it fall: "Yes, he might've. But my father did not consider then how quickly water makes everything fall back to the ground from which it came."

Now, standing beside Ghanima in the sietch, Jessica felt the shock of those words anew. She turned, glanced back at the still-flowing throng, let her gaze wander across Stilgar's shadowy shape in the alcove. Stilgar was no tame Fremen, trained only to carry twigs to the nest. He was still a hawk. When he thought of the color red, he did not think of flowers but of blood

"You're so quiet, suddenly," Ghanima said. "Is something wrong?"

Jessica shook her head. "It's something Leto said this morning, that's all."

"When you went out to the plantings? What'd he say?"

Jessica thought of the curious look of adult wisdom which had come over Leto's face out there in the morning. It was the same look which came over Ghanima's face right now. "He was recalling the time when Gurney came back from the smugglers to the Atreides banner," Jessica said.

"Then you were talking about Stilgar," Ghanima said.

Jessica did not question how this insight occurred. The twins appeared capable of reproducing each other's thought trains at will.

"Yes, we were," Jessica. "Stilgar didn't like to hear Gurney calling . . . Paul his Duke, but Gurney's presence forced this upon all of the Fremen. Gurney kept saying 'My Duke.' "

"I see," Ghanima said. "And of course, Leto observed that *he* was not yet Stilgar's Duke."

"That's right."

"You know what he was doing to you, of course," Ghanima said.

"I'm not sure I do," Jessica admitted, and she found this admission particularly disturbing because it had not occurred to her that Leto was doing anything at all to her.

"He was trying to ignite your memories of our father," Ghanima said. "Leto's always hungry to know our father from the viewpoints of others who knew him."

"But . . . doesn't Leto have . . ."

"Oh, he can listen to the *inner life*. Certainly. But that's not the same. You spoke about him, of course. Our father, I mean. You spoke of him as your son."

"Yes." Jessica clipped it off. She did not like the feeling that these twins could turn her on and off at will, open her memories for observation, touch any emotion which attracted their interest. Ghanima might be doing that right now!

"Leto said something to disturb you," Ghanima said.

Jessica found herself shocked at the necessity to suppress anger. "Yes . . . he did."

"You don't like the fact that he knows our father as our mother knew him, and knows our mother as our father knew her," Ghanima said. "You don't like what that implies—what we may know about you."

"I'd never really thought about it that way before," Jessica said, finding her voice stiff.

"It's the knowledge of sensual things which usually disturbs," Ghanima said. "It's your conditioning. You find it extremely difficult to think of us as anything but children. But there's nothing our parents did together, in public or in private, that we would not know."

For a brief instant Jessica found herself returning to the reaction which had come over her out there beside the qanat, but now she focused that reaction upon Ghanima.

"He probably spoke of your Duke's 'rutting sensuality,' " Ghanima said. "Sometimes Leto needs a bridle on his mouth!"

*Is there nothing these twins cannot profane?* Jessica wondered, moving from shock to outrage to revulsion. How dared they speak of *her* Leto's sensuality? Of course a man and woman who loved each other would share the pleasure of their bodies! It was a private and beautiful thing, not to be paraded in casual conversation between a child and an adult.

*Child and adult!*

Abruptly Jessica realized that neither Leto nor Ghanima had done this casually.

As Jessica remained silent, Ghanima said: 'We've shocked you. I apologize for both of us. Knowing Leto, I know he didn't consider apologizing. Sometimes when he's following a particular scent, he forgets how different we are . . . from you, for instance."

Jessica thought: *And that is why you both do this, of course. You are teaching me!* And she wondered then: *Who else are you teaching? Stilgar? Duncan?*

"Leto tries to see things as you see them," Ghanima said. "Memories are not enough. When you try the hardest, just then, you most often fail."

Jessica sighed.

Ghanima touched her grandmother's arm. "Your son left many things unsaid which yet must be said, even to you. Forgive us, but he loved you. Don't you know that?"

Jessica turned away to hide the tears glistening in her eyes.

"He knew your fears," Ghanima said. "Just as he knew Stilgar's fears. Dear Stil. Our father was his 'Doctor of Beasts' and Stil was no more than the green snail hidden in its shell." She hummed the tune from which she'd taken these words. The music hurled the lyrics against Jessica's awareness without compromise:

"O Doctor of Beasts,
To a green snail shell
With its timid miracle

Hidden, awaiting death,
You come as a deity!
Even snails know
That gods obliterate,
And cures bring pain,
That heaven is seen
Through a door of flame.
O Doctor of Beasts,
I am the man-snail
Who sees your single eye
Peering into my shell!
Why, Muad'Dib? Why?"

Ghanima said: "Unfortunately, our father left many man-snails in our universe."

*The assumption that humans exist within an essentially impermanent universe, taken as an operational precept, demands that the intellect become a totally aware balancing instrument. But the intellect cannot react thus without involving the entire organism. Such an organism may be recognized by its burning, driving behavior. And thus it is with a society treated as organism. But here we encounter an old inertia. Societies move to the goading of ancient, reactive impulses. They demand permanence. Any attempt to display the universe of impermanence arouses rejection patterns, fear, anger, and despair. Then how do we explain the acceptance of prescience? Simply: the giver of prescient visions, because he speaks of an absolute (permanent) realization, may be greeted with joy by humankind even while predicting the most dire events.*

—**The Book of Leto**
**After Harq al-Ada**

"It's like fighting in the dark," Alia said.

She paced the Council Chamber in angry strides, moving from the tall silvery draperies which softened the morning sun at the eastern windows to the divans grouped beneath decorated wall panels at the room's opposite end. Her sandals crossed spice-fiber rugs, parquet wood, tiles of giant garnet and, once more, rugs. At last she stood over Irulan and Idaho, who sat facing each other on divans of grey whale fur.

Idaho had resisted returning from Tabr, but she had sent peremptory orders. The abduction of Jessica was more important than ever now, but it had to wait. Idaho's mentat perceptions were required.

"These things are cut from the same pattern," Alia said. "They stink of a far-reaching plot."

"Perhaps not," Irulan ventured, but she glanced questioningly at Idaho.

Alia's face lapsed into an undisguised sneer. How could Irulan be that innocent? Unless . . . Alia bent a sharp and questioning stare onto the Princess. Irulan wore a simple black aba robe which matched the shadows in her spice-indigo eyes. Her blonde hair was tied in a tight coil at the nape of her neck, accenting a face thinned and toughened by years on Arrakis. She still retained the haughtiness she'd learned in the court of her father, Shaddam IV, and Alia often felt that this prideful attitude could mask the thoughts of a conspirator.

Idaho lounged in the black-and-green uniform of an Atreides House Guard, no insignia. It was an affectation which was secretly resented by many of Alia's actual guards, especially the amazons, who gloried in the insignia of office. They did not like the plain presence of the ghola-swordmaster-mentat, the more so because he was the husband of their mistress.

"So the tribes want the Lady Jessica reinstated into the Regency Council," Idaho said. "How can that—"

"They make unanimous demand!" Alia said, pointing to an embossed sheet of spice-paper on the divan beside Irulan. "Farad'n is one thing, but this . . . this has the stink of other alignments!"

"What does Stilgar think?" Irulan asked.

"His signature's on that paper!" Alia said.

"But if he . . ."

"How could he deny the mother of his god?" Alia sneered.

Idaho looked up at her, thinking: *That's awfully close to the edge with Irulan!* Again he wondered why Alia had brought him back here when she knew that he was needed at Sietch Tabr if the abduction plot were to be carried off. Was it possible she'd heard about the message sent to him by The Preacher? This thought filled his breast with turmoil. How could that mendicant mystic know the secret signal by which Paul Atreides had always summoned his swordmaster? Idaho longed to leave this pointless meeting and return to the search for an answer to that question.

"There's no doubt that The Preacher has been off-planet," Alia said. "The Guild wouldn't dare deceive us in such a thing. I will have him—"

"Careful!" Irulan said.

"Indeed, have a care," Idaho said. "Half the planet believe him to be—" He shrugged. "—your brother." And Idaho hoped he had carried this off with a properly casual attitude. How had the man known that signal?

"But if he's a courier, or a spy of the—"

"He's made contact with no one from CHOAM or House Corrino," Irulan said. "We can be sure of—"

"We can be sure of nothing!" Alia did not try to hide her scorn. She turned her back on Irulan, faced Idaho. He knew why he was here! Why didn't he perform as expected? He was in Council because Irulan was here. The history which had brought a Princess of House Corrino into the Atreides fold could never be forgotten. Allegiance, once changed, could change again. Duncan's mentat powers should be searching for flaws, for subtle deviations in Irulan's behavior.

Idaho stirred, glanced at Irulan. There were times when he resented the straight-line necessities imposed on mentat performance. He knew what Alia was thinking. Irulan would know it as well. But this Princess-wife to Paul Muad'Dib had overcome the decisions which had made her less than the royal concubine, Chani. There could be no doubt of Irulan's devotion to the royal twins. She had renounced family and Bene Gesserit in dedication to the Atreides.

"My mother is part of this plot!" Alia insisted. "For what other reason would the Sisterhood send her back here at a time such as this?"

"Hysteria isn't going to help us," Idaho said.

Alia whirled away from him, as he'd known she would. It helped him that he did not have to look at that once-beloved face which was now so twisted by alien possession.

"Well," Irulan said, "the Guild can't be completely trusted for—"

"The Guild!" Alia sneered.

"We can't rule out the enmity of the Guild or the Bene Gesserit," Idaho said. "But we must assign them special categories as essentially passive combatants. The Guild will live up to its basic rule: Never Govern. They're a parasitic growth, and they know it. They won't do anything to kill the organism which keeps them alive."

"Their idea of which organism keeps them alive may be different from ours," Irulan drawled. It was the closest she ever came to a sneer, that lazy tone of voice which said: "You missed a point, mentat."

Alia appeared puzzled. She had not expected Irulan to take this tack. It was not the kind of view which a conspirator would want examined.

"No doubt," Idaho said. "But the Guild won't come out overtly against House Atreides. The Sisterhood, on the other hand, might risk a certain kind of political break which—"

"If they do, it'll be through a front: someone or some group they can disavow," Irulan said. "The Bene Gesserit haven't existed all these centuries without knowing the value of self-effacement. They prefer being behind the throne, not on it."

*Self-effacement?* Alia wondered. Was that Irulan's choice?

"Precisely the point I make about the Guild," Idaho said. He found the necessities of argument and explanation helpful. They kept his mind from other problems.

Alia strode back toward the sunlit windows. She knew Idaho's blind spot; every mentat had it. They had to make pronouncements. This brought about a tendency to depend upon absolutes, to see finite limits. They knew this about themselves. It was part of their training. Yet they continued to act beyond self-limiting parameters. *I should've left him at Sietch Tabr,* Alia thought. *It would've been better to just turn Irulan over to Javid for questioning.*

Within her skull, Alia heard a rumbling voice: "Exactly!"

*Shut up! Shut up! Shut up!* she thought. A dangerous mistake beckoned her in these moments and she could not recognize its outlines. All she could sense was the danger. Idaho had to help her out of this predicament. He was a mentat. Mentats were necessary. The human-computer replaced the mechanical devices destroyed by the Butlerian Jihad. *Thou shalt not make a machine in the likeness of a human mind!* But Alia longed now for a compliant machine. They could not have suffered from Idaho's limitations. You could never distrust a machine.

Alia heard Irulan's drawling voice.

"A feint within a feint within a feint within a feint," Irulan said. "We all know the accepted pattern of attack upon power. I don't blame Alia for her suspicions. Of course she suspects everyone—even us. Ignore that for the moment, though. What remains as the prime arena of motives, the most fertile source of danger to the Regency?"

"CHOAM," Idaho said, his voice mentat-flat.

Alia allowed herself a grim smile. The Combine Honnete Ober Advancer Mercantiles! But House Atreides dominated CHOAM with fifty-one per cent of its shares. The Priesthood of Muad'Dib held another five per cent, pragmatic acceptance by the Great Houses that Dune controlled the priceless melange. Not without reason was the spice often called "the secret coinage." Without melange, the Spacing Guild's heighliners could not move. Melange precipitated the "navigation trance" by which a translight pathway could be "seen" before it was traveled. Without melange and its amplification of the human immunogenic system, life expectancy for the very rich degenerated by a factor of at least four. Even the vast middle class of the Imperium ate diluted melange in small sprinklings with at least one meal a day.

But Alia had heard the mentat sincerity in Idaho's voice, a sound which she'd been awaiting with terrible expectancy.

CHOAM. The Combine Honnete was much more than House Atreides, much more than Dune, much more than the Priesthood or melange. It was inkvines, whale fur, shigawire, Ixian artifacts and entertainers, trade in people and places, the Hajj, those products which came from the borderline legality of Tleilaxu technology; it was addictive drugs and medical techniques; it was transportation (the Guild) and all of the supercomplex commerce of an empire which encompassed thousands of known planets plus some which fed secretly at the fringes, permitted there for services rendered. When Idaho said CHOAM, he spoke of a constant ferment, intrigue within intrigue, a play of powers where the shift of one duodecimal point in interest payments could change the ownership of an entire planet.

Alia returned to stand over the two seated on the divans. "Something specific about CHOAM bothers you?" she asked.

"There's always the heavy speculative stockpiling of spice by certain Houses," Irulan said.

Alia slapped her hands against her own thighs, then gestured at the embossed spice-paper beside Irulan. "That *demand* doesn't intrigue you, coming as it does—"

"All right!" Idaho barked. "Out with it. What're you withholding? You know better than to deny the data and still expect me to function as—"

"There has been a recent very significant increase in trade for people with four specific specialties," Alia said. And she wondered if this would be truly new information for this pair.

"Which specialties?" Irulan asked.

"Swordmasters, twisted mentats from Tleilax, conditioned medics from the Suk school, and fincap accountants, most especially the latter. Why would questionable bookkeeping be in demand right now?" She directed the question at Idaho.

*Function as a mentat!* he thought. Well, that was better than dwelling on what Alia had become. He focused on her words, replaying them in his mind mentat fashion. *Swordmasters?* That had been his own calling once. Swordmasters were, of course, more than personal fighters. They could repair force shields, plan military campaigns, design military support facilities, improvise weapons. *Twisted mentats?* The Tleilaxu persisted in this hoax, obviously. As a mentat himself, Idaho knew the fragile insecurity of Tleilaxu *twisting*. Great Houses which bought such mentats hoped to control them absolutely. Impossible! Even Piter de Vries, who'd served the Harkonnens in their assault on House Atreides, had maintained his own essential dignity, accepting death rather than surrender his inner core of selfdom at the end. *Suk doctors?* Their conditioning supposedly guaranteed them against disloyalty to their owner-patients. Suk doctors came very expensive. Increased purchase of Suks would involve substantial exchanges of funds.

Idaho weighed these facts against an increase in fincap accountants.

"Prime computation," he said, indicating a heavily weighted assurance that he spoke of inductive fact. "There's been a recent increase in wealth among the Houses Minor. Some have to be moving quietly toward Great House status. Such wealth could only come from specific shifts in political alignments."

"We come at last to the Landsraad," Alia said, voicing her own belief.

"The next Landsraad session is almost two standard years away," Irulan reminded her.

"But political bargaining never ceases," Alia said. "And I'll warrant some among those tribal signatories—" She gestured at the paper beside Irulan. "—are among the Houses Minor who've shifted their alignment."

"Perhaps," Irulan said.

"The Landsraad," Alia said. "What better front for the Bene Gesserits? And what better agent for the Sisterhood than my own mother?" Alia planted herself directly in front of Idaho. "Well, Duncan?"

*Why not function as a mentat?* Idaho asked himself. He saw the tenor of Alia's suspicions now. After all, Duncan Idaho had been personal house guard to the Lady Jessica for many years.

"Duncan?" Alia pressed.

"You should inquire closely after any advisory legislation which may be under preparation for the next session of the Landsraad," Idaho said. "They might take the legal position that a Regency can't veto certain kinds of legislation—specifically, adjustments of taxation and the policing of cartels. There are others, but . . ."

"Not a very good pragmatic bet on their part if they take that position," Irulan said.

"I agree," Alia said. "The Sardaukar have no teeth and we still have our Fremen legions."

"Careful, Alia," Idaho said. "Our enemies would like nothing better than to make us appear monstrous. No matter how many legions you command, power ultimately rides on popular suffrance in an empire as scattered as this one."

"Popular suffrance?" Irulan asked.

"You mean Great House suffrance," Alia said.

"And how many Great Houses will we face under this new alliance?" Idaho asked. "Money is collecting in strange places!"

"The fringes?" Irulan asked.

Idaho shrugged. It was an unanswerable question. All of them suspected that one day the Tleilaxu or technological tinkerers on the Imperial fringes would nullify the Holtzmann Effect. On that day, shields would be useless. The whole precarious balance which maintained planetary feudatories would collapse.

Alia refused to consider that possibility. "We'll ride with what we have," she said. "And what we have is certain knowledge throughout the CHOAM directorate that *we* can destroy the spice if they force us to it. They won't risk that."

"Back to CHOAM again," Irulan said.

"Unless someone has managed to duplicate the sandtrout-sandworm cycle on another planet," Idaho said. He looked speculatively at Irulan, excited by this question. "Salusa Secundus?"

"My contacts there remain reliable," Irulan said. "Not Salusa."

"Then my answer stands," Alia said, staring at Idaho. "We ride with what we have."

*My move,* Idaho thought. He said: "Why'd you drag me away from *important work?* You could've worked this out yourself."

"Don't take that tone with me!" Alia snapped.

Idaho's eyes went wide. For an instant, he'd seen the alien on Alia's face, and it was a disconcerting sight. He turned his attention to Irulan, but she had not seen—or gave that appearance.

"I don't need an elementary education," Alia said, her voice still edged with alien anger.

Idaho managed a rueful smile, but his breast ached.

"We never get far from wealth and all of its masks when we deal with power," Irulan drawled. "Paul was a social mutation and, as such, we have to remember that he shifted the old balance of wealth."

"Such mutations are not irreversible," Alia said, turning away from them as though she'd not exposed her terrible difference. "Wherever there's wealth in this empire, they know this."

"They also know," Irulan said, "that there are three people who could perpetuate that mutation: the twins and . . ." She pointed at Alia.

*Are they insane, this pair?* Idaho wondered.

"They will try to assassinate me!" Alia rasped.

And Idaho sat in shocked silence, his mentat awareness whirling. Assassinate

Alia? Why? They could discredit her too easily. They could cut her out of the Fremen pack and hunt her down at will. But the twins, now . . . He knew he was not in the proper mentat calm for such an assessment, but he had to try. He had to be as precise as possible. At the same time, he knew that precise thinking contained undigested absolutes. Nature was not precise. The universe was not precise when reduced to his scale; it was vague and fuzzy, full of unexpected movements and changes. Humankind as a whole had to be entered into this computation as a natural phenomenon. And the whole process of precise analysis represented a chopping off, a remove from the ongoing current of the universe. He had to get at that current, see it in motion.

"We were right to focus on CHOAM and the Landsraad," Irulan drawled. "And Duncan's suggestion offers a first line of inquiry for—"

"Money as a translation of energy can't be separated from the energy it expresses," Alia said. "We all know this. But we have to answer three specific questions: When? Using what weapons? Where?"

*The twins . . . the twins,* Idaho thought. *It's the twins who're in danger, not Alia.*

"You're not interested in who or how?" Irulan asked.

"If House Corrino or CHOAM or any other group employs human instruments on this planet," Alia said, "we stand a better than sixty per cent chance of finding them before they act. Knowing when they'll act and where gives us a bigger leverage on those odds. How? That's just asking *what weapons?*"

*Why can't they see it as I see it?* Idaho wondered.

"All right," Irulan said. "When?"

"When attention is focused on someone else," Alia said.

"Attention was focused on your mother at the Convocation," Irulan said. "There was no attempt."

"Wrong place," Alia said.

*What is she doing?* Idaho wondered.

"Where, then?" Irulan asked.

"Right here in the Keep," Alia said. "It's the place where I'd feel most secure and least on my guard."

"What weapons?" Irulan asked.

"Conventional—something a Fremen might have on his person: poisoned crysknife, maula pistol, a—"

"They've not tried a hunter-seeker in a long while," Irulan said.

"Wouldn't work in a crowd," Alia said. "There'll have to be a crowd."

"Biological weapon?" Irulan asked.

"An infectious agent?" Alia asked, not masking her incredulity. How could Irulan think an infectious agent would succeed against the immunological barriers which protected an Atreides?

"I was thinking more in the line of some animal," Irulan said. "A small pet, say, trained to bite a specific victim, inflicting a poison with its bite."

"The House ferrets will prevent that," Alia said.

"One of *them,* then?" Irulan asked.

"Couldn't be done. The House ferrets would reject an outsider, kill it. You know that."

"I was just exploring possibilities in the hope that—"

"I'll alert my guards," Alia said.

As Alia said *guards*, Idaho put a hand over his Tleilaxu eyes, trying to prevent the demanding involvement which swept over him. It was Rhajia, the movement of Infinity as expressed by Life, the latent cup of total immersion in mentat awareness which lay in wait for every mentat. It threw his awareness onto the universe like a net, falling, defining the shapes within it. He saw the twins crouching in darkness while giant claws raked the air about them.

"No," he whispered.

"What?" Alia looked at him as though surprised to find him still there.

He took his hands from his eyes.

"The garments that House Corrino sent?" he asked. "Have they been sent on to the twins?"

"Of course," Irulan said. "They're perfectly safe."

"No one's going to try for the twins at Sietch Tabr," Alia said. "Not with all those Stilgar-trained guards around."

Idaho stared at her. He had no particular datum to reinforce an argument based on mentat computation, but he knew. *He knew.* This thing he'd experienced came very close to the visionary power which Paul had known. Neither Irulan nor Alia would believe it, coming from him.

"I'd like to alert the port authorities against allowing the importation of any outside animals," he said.

"You're not taking Irulan's suggestion seriously," Alia protested.

"Why take any chances?" he asked.

"Tell that to the smugglers," Alia said. "I'll put my dependence on the House ferrets."

Idaho shook his head. What could House ferrets do against claws the size of those he envisioned? But Alia was right. Bribes in the right places, one acquiescent Guild navigator, and any place in the Empty Quarter became a landing port. The Guild would resist a front position in any attack on House Atreides, but if the price were high enough . . . Well, the Guild could only be thought of as something like a geological barrier which made attacks difficult, but not impossible. They could always protest that they were just "a transportation agency." How could they know to what use a particular cargo would be put?

Alia broke the silence with a purely Fremen gesture, a raised fist with thumb horizontal. She accompanied the gesture with a traditional expletive which meant, "I give Typhoon Conflict." She obviously saw herself as the only logical target for assassins, and the gesture protested a universe full of undigested threats. She was saying she would hurl the death wind at anyone who attacked her.

Idaho felt the hopelessness of any protest. He saw that she no longer suspected him. He was going back to Tabr and she expected a perfectly executed abduction of the Lady Jessica. He lifted himself from the divan in an adrenalin surge of anger, thinking: *If only Alia were the target! If only assassins could get to her!* For an instant, he rested his hand on his own knife, but it was not in him to do this. Far better, though, that she die a martyr than live to be discredited and hounded into a sandy grave.

"Yes," Alia said, misinterpreting his expression as concern for her. "You'd best hurry back to Tabr." And she thought: *How foolish of me to suspect Duncan! He's mine, not Jessica's!* It had been the demand from the tribes that'd upset her, Alia thought. She waved an airy goodbye to Idaho as he left.

Idaho left the Council Chamber feeling hopeless. Not only was Alia blind with her alien possession, but she became more insane with each crisis. She'd already passed her danger point and was doomed. But what could be done for the twins? Whom could he convince? Stilgar? And what could Stilgar do that he wasn't already doing?

*The Lady Jessica, then?*

Yes, he'd explore that possibility—but she, too, might be far gone in plotting with her Sisterhood. He carried few illusions about that Atreides concubine. She might do anything at the command of the Bene Gesserits—even turn against her own grandchildren.

> Good government never depends upon laws, but upon the personal qualities of those who govern. The machinery of government is always subordinate to the will of those who administer that machinery. The most important element of government, therefore, is the method of choosing leaders.

> **—Law and Governance**
> **The Spacing Guild Manual**

*Why does Alia wish me to share the morning audience?* Jessica wondered. *They've not voted me back into the Council.*

Jessica stood in the anteroom to the Keep's Great Hall. The anteroom itself would have been a great hall anywhere other than Arrakis. Following the Atreides lead, buildings in Arrakeen had become ever more gigantic as wealth and power concentrated, and this room epitomized her misgivings. She did not like this anteroom with its tiled floor depicting her son's victory over Shaddam IV.

She caught a reflection of her own face in the polished plasteel door which led into the Great Hall. Returning to Dune forced such comparisons upon her, and Jessica noted only the signs of aging in her own features: the oval face had developed tiny lines and the eyes were more brittle in their indigo reflection. She could remember when there had been white around the blue of her eyes. Only the careful ministrations of a professional dresser maintained the polished bronze of her hair. Her nose remained small, mouth generous, and her body was still slender, but even the Bene Gesserit-trained muscles had a tendency toward slowing with the passage of time. Some might not note this and say:

"You haven't changed a bit!" But the Sisterhood's training was a two-edged sword; small changes seldom escaped the notice of people thus trained.

And the lack of small changes in Alia had not escaped Jessica's notice.

Javid, the master of Alia's appointments, stood at the great door, being very official this morning. He was a robed genie with a cynical smile on his round face. Javid struck Jessica as a paradox: a well-fed Fremen. Noting her attention upon him, Javid smiled knowingly, shrugged. His attendance in Jessica's entourage had been short, as he'd known it would be. He hated Atreides, but he was Alia's man in more ways than one, if the rumors were to be believed.

Jessica saw the shrug, thought: *This is the age of the shrug. He knows I've heard all the stories about him and he doesn't care. Our civilization could well die of indifference within it before succumbing to external attack.*

The guards Gurney had assigned her before leaving for the smugglers and the desert hadn't liked her coming here without their attendance. But Jessica felt oddly safe. Let someone make a martyr of her in this place; Alia wouldn't survive it. Alia would know that.

When Jessica failed to respond to his shrug and smile, Javid coughed, a belching disturbance of his larynx which could only have been achieved with practice. It was like a secret language. It said: "We understand the nonsense of all this pomp, My Lady. Isn't it wonderful what humans can be made to believe!"

*Wonderful!* Jessica agreed, but her face gave no indication of the thought.

The anteroom was quite full now, all of the morning's permitted suppliants having received their right of entrance from Javid's people. The outer doors had been closed. Suppliants and attendants kept a polite distance from Jessica, but observed that she wore the formal black aba of a Fremen Reverend Mother. This would raise many questions. No mark of Muad'Dib's priesthood could be seen on her person. Conversations hummed as the people divided their attention between Jessica and the small side door through which Alia would come to lead them into the Great Hall. It was obvious to Jessica that the old pattern which defined where the Regency's powers lay had been shaken.

*I did that just by coming here,* she thought. *But I came because Alia invited me.*

Reading the signs of disturbance, Jessica realized Alia was deliberately prolonging this moment, allowing the subtle currents to run their course here. Alia would be watching from a spy hole, of course. Few subtleties of Alia's behavior escaped Jessica, and she felt with each passing minute how right she'd been to accept the mission which the Sisterhood had pressed upon her.

"Matters cannot be allowed to continue in this way," the leader of the Bene Gesserit delegation had argued. "Surely the signs of decay have not escaped you—you of all people! We know why you left us, but we know also how you were trained. Nothing was stinted in your education. You are an adept of the Panoplia Prophetica and you must know when the souring of a powerful religion threatens us all."

Jessica had pursed her lips in thought while staring out a window at the soft signs of spring at Castle Caladan. She did not like to direct her thinking in such a logical fashion. One of the first lessons of the Sisterhood had been to reserve an attitude of questioning distrust for anything which came in the guise of logic. But the members of the delegation had known that, too.

How moist the air had been that morning, Jessica thought, looking around Alia's anteroom. How fresh and moist. Here there was a sweaty dampness to the air which evoked a sense of uneasiness in Jessica, and she thought: *I've reverted to Fremen ways.* The air was too moist in this sietch-above-ground. What was wrong with the Master of the Stills? Paul would never have permitted such laxness.

She noted that Javid, his shiny face alert and composed, appeared not to have noticed the fault of dampness in the anteroom's air. Bad training for one born on Arrakis.

The members of the Bene Gesserit delegation had wanted to know if she required proofs of their allegations. She'd given them an angry answer out of their own manuals: "All proofs inevitably lead to propositions which have no proof! All things are known because we want to believe in them."

"But we have submitted these questions to mentats," the delegation's leader had protested.

Jessica had stared at the woman, astonished. "I marvel that you have reached your present station and not yet learned the limits of mentats," Jessica had said.

At which the delegation had relaxed. Apparently it had all been a test, and she had passed. They'd feared, of course, that she had lost all touch with those balancing abilities which were at the core of Bene Gesserit training.

Now Jessica became softly alert as Javid left his door station and approached her. He bowed. "My Lady. It occurred to me that you might not've heard the latest exploit of The Preacher."

"I get daily reports on everything which occurs here," Jessica said. *Let him take that back to Alia!*

Javid smiled. "Then you know he rails against your family. Only last night, he preached in the south suburb and no one dared touch him. You know why, of course."

"Because they think he's my son come back to them," Jessica said, her voice bored.

"This question has not yet been put to the mentat Idaho," Javid said. "Perhaps that should be done and the thing settled."

Jessica thought: *Here's one who truly doesn't know a mentat's limits, although he dares put horns on one—in his dreams if not in fact.*

"Mentats share the fallibilities of those who use them," she said. "The human mind, as is the case with the mind of any animal, is a resonator. It responds to resonances in the environment. The mentat has learned to extend his awareness across many parallel loops of causality and to proceed along those loops for long chains of consequences." *Let him chew on that!*

"This Preacher doesn't disturb you, then?" Javid asked, his voice abruptly formal and portentous.

"I find him a healthy sign," she said. "I don't want him bothered."

Javid clearly had not expected that blunt a response. He tried to smile, failed.

Then: "The ruling Council of the church which deifies thy son will, of course, bow to your wishes if you insist. But certainly some explanation—"

"Perhaps you'd rather I explained how *I* fit into your schemes," she said.

Javid stared at her narrowly. "Madame, I see no logical reason why thou refusest to denounce this Preacher. He cannot be thy son. I make a reasonable request: denounce him."

*This is a set piece,* Jessica thought. *Alia put him up to it.*

She said: "No."

"But he defiles the name of thy son! He preaches abominable things, cries out against thy holy daughter. He incites the populace against us. When asked, he said that even thou possessest the nature of evil and that thy—"

"Enough of this nonsense!" Jessica said. "Tell Alia that I refuse. I've heard nothing but tales of this Preacher since returning. He bores me."

"Does it bore thee, Madame, to learn that in his latest defilement he has said that thou wilt not turn against him? And here, clearly, thou—"

"Evil as I am, I still won't denounce him," she said.

"It is no joking matter, Madame!"

Jessica waved him away angrily. "Begone!" She spoke with sufficient carrying power that others heard, forcing him to obey.

His eyes glared with rage, but he managed a stiff bow and returned to his position at the door.

This argument fitted neatly into the observations Jessica already had made. When he spoke of Alia, Javid's voice carried the husky undertones of a lover; no mistaking it. The rumors no doubt were true. Alia had allowed her life to degenerate in a terrible way. Observing this, Jessica began to harbor the suspicion that Alia was a willing participant in Abomination. Was it a perverse will to self-destruction? Because surely Alia was working to destroy herself and the power base which fed on her brother's teachings.

Faint stirrings of unease began to grow apparent in the anteroom. The aficionados of this place would know when Alia delayed too long, and by now they'd all heard about Jessica's peremptory dismissal of Alia's favorite.

Jessica sighed. She felt that her body had walked into this place with her soul creeping behind. Movements among the courtiers were so transparent! The seeking out of important people was a dance like the wind through a field of cereal stalks. The cultivated inhabitants of this place furrowed their brows and gave pragmatic rating numbers to the importance of each of their fellows. Obviously her rebuff of Javid had hurt him; few spoke to him now. But the others! Her trained eye could read the rating numbers in the satellites attending the powerful.

*They do not attend me because I am dangerous,* she thought. *I have the stink of someone Alia fears.*

Jesica glanced around the room, seeing eyes turn away. They were such seriously futile people that she found herself wanting to cry out against their ready-made justifications for pointless lives. Oh, if only The Preacher could see this room as it looked now!

A fragment of nearby conversation caught her attention. A tall, slender Priest was addressing his coterie, no doubt supplicants here under his auspices. "Often I must speak otherwise than I think," he said. "This is called diplomacy."

The resultant laughter was too loud, too quickly silenced. People in the group saw that Jessica had overheard.

*My Duke would have transported such a one to the farthest available hellhole!* Jessica thought. *I've returned none too soon.*

She knew now that she'd lived on faraway Caladan in an insulated capsule which had allowed only the most blatant of Alia's excesses to intrude. *I contributed to my own dream-existence,* she thought. Caladan had been something like that insulation provided by a really first-class frigate riding securely in the hold of a Guild heighliner. Only the most violent maneuvers could be felt, and those as mere softened movements.

*How seductive it is to live in peace,* she thought.

The more she saw of Alia's court, the more sympathy Jessica felt for the words reported as coming from this blind Preacher. Yes, Paul might have said such words on seeing what had become of his realm. And Jessica wondered what Gurney had found out among the smugglers.

Her first reaction to Arrakeen had been the right one, Jessica realized. On that first ride into the city with Javid, her attention had been caught by armored screens around dwellings, the heavily guarded pathways and alleys, the patient watchers at every turn, the tall walls and indications of deep underground places revealed by thick foundations. Arrakeen had become an ungenerous place, a contained place, unreasonable and self-righteous in its harsh outlines.

Abruptly the anteroom's small side door opened. A vanguard of priestess amazons spewed into the room with Alia shielded behind them, haughty and moving with a confined awareness of real and terrible power. Alia's face was composed; no emotion betrayed itself as her gaze caught and held her mother's. But both knew the battle had been joined.

At Javid's command, the giant doors into the great Hall were opened, moving with a silent and inevitable sense of hidden energies.

Alia came to her mother's side as the guards enfolded them.

"Shall we go in now, mother?" Alia asked.

"It's high time," Jessica said. And she thought, seeing the sense of gloating in Alia's eyes: *She thinks she can destroy me and remain unscathed! She's mad!*

And Jessica wondered if that might not have been what Idaho had wanted. He'd sent a message, but she'd been unable to respond. Such an enigmatic message: *"Danger. Must see you."* It had been written in a variant of the old Chakobsa where the particular word chosen to denote danger signified a plot.

*I'll see him immediately when I return to Tabr,* she thought.

> *This is the fallacy of power: ultimately it is effective only in an absolute, a limited universe. But the basic lesson of our relativistic universe is that things change. Any power must always meet a greater power. Paul Muad'Dib taught this lesson to the Sardaukar on the Plains of Arrakeen. His descendants have yet to learn the lesson for themselves.*

**—The Preacher at Arrakeen**

The first supplicant for the morning audience was a Kadeshian troubadour, a pilgrim of the Hajj whose purse had been emptied by Arrakeen mercenaries. He stood on the watergreen stone of the chamber floor with no air of begging about him.

Jessica admired his boldness from where she sat with Alia atop the seven-step platform. Identical thrones had been placed here for mother and daughter, and Jessica made particular note of the fact that Alia sat on the right, the *masculine* position.

As for the Kadeshian troubadour, it was obvious that Javid's people had passed him for just this quality he now displayed, his boldness. The troubadour was expected to provide some entertainment for the courtiers of the Great Hall; it was the payment he'd make in lieu of the money he no longer possessed.

From the report of the Priest-Advocate who now pled the troubadour's case, the Kadeshian had retained only the clothing on his back and the baliset slung over one shoulder on a leather cord.

"He says he was fed a dark drink," the Advocate said, barely hiding the smile which sought to twist his lips. "If it please your Holiness, the drink left him helpless but awake while his purse was cut."

Jessica studied the troubadour while the Advocate droned on and on with a false subservience, his voice full of mucky morals. The Kadeshian was tall, easily two meters. He had a roving eye which showed intelligent alertness and humor. His golden hair was worn to the shoulders in the style of his planet, and there was a sense of virile strength in the broad chest and neatly tapering body which a grey Hajj robe could not conceal. His name was given as Tagir Mohandis and he was descended from merchant engineers, proud of his ancestry and himself.

Alia finally cut off the pleading with a hand wave, spoke without turning: "The Lady Jessica will render first judgment in honor of her return to us."

"Thank you, daughter," Jessica said, stating the order of ascendancy to all who heard. *Daughter!* So this Tagir Mohandis was part of their plan. Or was he an innocent dupe? This judgment was designed to open attack on herself, Jessica realized. It was obvious in Alia's attitude.

"Do you play that instrument well?" Jessica asked, indicating the nine-string baliset on the troubadour's shoulder.

"As well as the great Gurney Halleck himself!" Tagir Mohandis spoke loudly for all in the hall to hear, and his words evoked an interested stir among the courtiers.

"You seek the gift of transport money," Jessica said. "Where would that money take you?"

"To Salusa Secundus and Farad'n's court," Mohandis said. "I've heard he seeks troubadors and minstrels, that he supports the arts and builds a great renaissance of cultivated life around him."

Jessica refrained from glancing at Alia. They'd known, of course, what Mohandis would ask. She found herself enjoying this byplay. Did they think her unable to meet this thrust?"

"Will you play for your passage?" Jessica asked. "My terms are Fremen terms. If I enjoy your music, I may keep you here to smooth away my cares; if your music offends me, I may send you to toil in the desert for your passage money. If I deem your playing just right for Farad'n, who is said to be an enemy of the Atreides, then I will send you to him with my blessing. Will you play on these terms, Tagir Mohandis?"

He threw his head back in a great roaring laugh. His blond hair danced as he unslung the baliset and tuned it deftly to indicate acceptance of her challenge.

The crowd in the chamber started to press closer, but were held back by courtiers and guards.

Presently Mohandis strummed a note, holding the bass hum of the side strings with a fine attention to their compelling vibration. Then, lifting his voice in a mellow tenor, he sang, obviously improvising, but his touch so deft that Jessica was enthralled before she focused on his lyrics:

"You say you long for Caladan seas,
Where once you ruled, Atreides,
Without surcease—
But exiles dwell in stranger-lands!

You say 'twere bitter, men so rude,
To sell your dreams of Shai-Hulud,
For tasteless food—
And exiles, dwell in stranger-lands.

You make Arrakis grow infirm,
Silence the passage of the worm
And end your term—
As exiles, dwell in stranger-lands.

Alia! They name you Coan-Teen,
That spirit who is never seen
Until—"

*"Enough!"* Alia screamed. She pushed herself half out of her throne. "I'll have you—"

"Alia!" Jessica spoke just loud enough, voice pitched just right to avoid confrontation while gaining full attention. It was a masterful use of Voice and all who heard it recognized the trained powers in this demonstration. Alia sank back into her seat and Jessica noted that she showed not the slightest discomfiture.

*This, too, was anticipated,* Jessica thought. *How very interesting.*

"The judgment on this first one is mine," Jessica reminded her.

"Very well," Alia's words were barely audible.

"I find this one a fitting gift for Farad'n," Jessica said. "He has a tongue which cuts like a crysknife. Such bloodletting as that tongue can administer would be healthy for our own court, but I'd rather he ministered to House Corrino."

A light rippling of laughter spread through the hall.

Alia permitted herself a snorting exhalation. "Do you know what he called me?"

"He didn't call you anything, daughter. He but reported that which he or anyone else could hear in the streets. There they call you Coan-Teen . . . ."

"The female death-spirit who walks without feet," Alia snarled.

"If you put away those who report accurately, you'll keep only those who know what you want to hear," Jessica said, her voice sweet. "I can think of nothing more poisonous than to rot in the stink of your own reflections."

Audible gasps came from those immediately below the thrones.

Jessica focused on Mohandis, who remained silent, standing completely uncowed. He awaited whatever judgment was passed upon him as though it did not matter. Mohandis was exactly the kind of man her Duke would have chosen to have by his side in troubled times: one who acted with confidence of his own judgment, but accepted whatever befell, even death, without berating his fate. Then why had he chosen this course?

"Why did you sing those particular words?" Jessica asked him.

He lifted his head to speak clearly: "I'd heard that the Atreides were honorable and open-minded. I'd a thought to test it and perhaps to stay here in your service, thereby having the time to seek out those who robbed me and deal with them in my own fashion."

"He dares test *us*!" Alia muttered.

"Why not?" Jessica asked.

She smiled down at the troubadour to signal goodwill. He had come into this hall only because it offered him opportunity for another adventure, another passage through his universe. Jessica found herself tempted to bind him to her own entourage, but Alia's reaction boded evil for brave Mohandis. There were also those signs which said this was the course expected of the Lady Jessica—take a brave and handsome troubadour into her service as she'd taken brave Gurney Halleck. Best Mohandis were sent on his way, though it rankled to lose such a fine specimen to Farad'n.

"He shall go to Farad'n," Jessica said. "See that he gets his passage money. Let his tongue draw the blood of House Corrino and see how he survives it."

Alia glowered at the floor, then produced a belated smile. "The wisdom of the Lady Jessica prevails," she said, waving Mohandis away.

*That did not go the way she wanted,* Jessica thought, but there were indicators in Alia's manner that a more potent test remained.

Another supplicant was being brought forward.

Jessica, noting her daughter's reaction, felt the gnawing of doubts. The lesson learned from the twins was needed here. Let Alia be *Abomination,* still she was one of the pre-born. She could know her mother as she knew herself. It did not compute that Alia would misjudge her mother's reactions in the matter of the troubadour. *Why did Alia stage that confrontation? To distract me?*

There was no more time to reflect. The second supplicant had taken his place below the twin thrones, his Advocate at his side.

The supplicant was a Fremen this time, an old man with the sand marks of the desert-born on his face. He was not tall, but had a wiry body and the long *dishdasha* usually worn over a stillsuit gave him a stately appearance. The robe was in keeping with his narrow face and beaked nose, the glaring eyes of blue-on-blue. He wore no stillsuit and seemed uncomfortable without it. The gigantic space of the Audience Hall must seem to him like the dangerous open air which robbed his flesh of its priceless moisture. Under the hood, which had been thrown partly back, he wore the knotted *keffiya* headdress of a Naib.

"I am Ghadhean al-Fali," he said, placing one foot on the steps to the thrones to signify his status above that of the mob. "I was one of Muad'Dib's death commandos and I am here concerning a matter of the desert."

Alia stiffened only slightly, a small betrayal. Al-Fali's name had been on that demand to place Jessica on the Council.

*A matter of the desert!* Jessica thought.

Ghadhean al-Fali had spoken before his Advocate could open the pleading. With that formal Fremen phrase he had placed them on notice that he brought them something of concern to all of Dune—and that he spoke with the authority of a Fedaykin who had offered his life beside that of Paul Muad'Dib. Jessica doubted that this was what Ghadhean al-Fali had told Javid or the Advocate General in seeking audience here. Her guess was confirmed as an official of the Priesthood rushed forward from the rear of the chamber waving the black cloth of intercession.

"My Ladies!" the official called out. "Do not listen to this man! He comes under false—"

Jessica, watching the Priest run toward them, caught a movement out of the corners of her eyes, saw Alia's hand signaling in the Atreides battle language: "*Now!*" Jessica could not determine where the signal was directed, but acted instinctively with a lurch to the left, taking throne and all. She rolled away from the crashing throne as she fell, came to her feet as she heard the sharp *spat* of a maula pistol . . . and again. But she was moving with the first sound, felt something tug at her right sleeve. She drove into the throng of supplicants and courtiers gathered below the dais. Alia, she noted, had not moved.

Surrounded by people, Jessica stopped.

Ghadhean al-Fali, she saw, had dodged to the other side of the dais, but the Advocate remained in his original position.

It had happened with the rapidity of an ambush, but everyone in the Hall knew where trained reflexes should have taken anyone caught by surprise. Alia and the Advocate stood frozen in their exposure.

A disturbance toward the middle of the room caught Jessica's attention and she forced a way through the throng, saw four supplicants holding the Priest official. His black cloth of intercession lay near his feet, a maula pistol exposed in its folds.

Al-Fali thrust his way past Jessica, looked from the pistol to the Priest. The Fremen let out a cry of rage, came up from his belt with an *achag* blow, the fingers of his left hand rigid. They caught the Priest in the throat and he collapsed, strangling. Without a backward glance at the man he had killed, the old Naib turned an angry face toward the dais.

"Dalal-il 'an-nubuwwa!" al-Fali called, placing both palms against his forehead, then lowering them. "The Qadis as-Salif will not let me be silenced! If I do not slay those who interfere, others will slay them!"

*He thinks he was the target,* Jessica realized. She looked down at her sleeve, put a finger in the neat hole left by the maula pellet. Poisoned, no doubt.

The supplicants had dropped the Priest. He lay writhing on the floor, dying with his larynx crushed. Jessica motioned to a pair of shocked courtiers standing at her left, said: "I want that man saved for questioning. If he dies, you die!" As they hesitated, peering toward the dais, she used Voice on them: "Move!"

The pair moved.

Jessica thrust herself to al-Fali's side, nudged him: "You are a fool, Naib! They were after me, not you."

Several people around them heard her. In the immediate shocked silence, al-Fali glanced at the dais with its one toppled throne and Alia still seated on the other. The look of realization which came over his face could've been read by a novice.

"Fedaykin," Jessica said, reminding him of his old service to her family, "we who have been scorched know how to stand back to back."

"Trust me, My Lady," he said, taking her meaning immediately.

A gasp behind Jessica brought her whirling, and she felt al-Fali move to stand with his back to her. A woman in the gaudy garb of a city Fremen was straightening from beside the Priest on the floor. The two courtiers were nowhere to be seen. The woman did not even glance at Jessica, but lifted her voice in the ancient keening of her people—the call for those who serviced the deathstills, the call for them to come and gather a body's water into the tribal cistern. It was a curiously incongruous noise coming from one dressed as this woman was. Jessica felt the persistence of the old ways even as she saw the falseness in this city woman. The creature in the gaudy dress obviously had killed the Priest to make sure he was silenced.

*Why did she bother?* Jessica wondered. *She had only to wait for the man to die of asphyxiation.* The act was a desperate one, a sign of deep fear.

Alia sat forward on the edge of her throne, her eyes aglitter with watchfulness. A slender woman wearing the braid knots of Alia's own guards strode past Jessica, bent over the Priest, straightened, and looked back at the dais. "He is dead."

"Have him removed," Alia called. She motioned to guards below the dais. "Straighten the Lady Jessica's chair."

*So you'll try to brazen it out!* Jessica thought. Did Alia think anyone had been fooled? Al-Fali had spoken of the Qadis as-Salaf, calling on the holy fathers of Fremen mythology as his protectors. But no supernatural agency had brought a maula pistol into this room where no weapons were permitted. A conspiracy involving Javid's people was the only answer, and Alia's unconcern about her own person told everyone she was a part of that conspiracy.

The old Naib spoke over his shoulder to Jessica: "Accept my apologies, My Lady. We of the desert come to you as our last desperate hope, and now we see that you still have need of us."

"Matricide does not sit well on my daughter," Jessica said.

"The tribes will hear of this," al-Fali promised.

"If you have such desperate need of me," Jessica asked, "why did you not approach me at the Convocation in Sietch Tabr?"

"Stilgar would not permit it."

*Ahhh,* Jessica thought, *the rule of the Naibs! In Tabr, Stilgar's word was law.*

The toppled throne had been straightened. Alia motioned for her mother to return, said: "All of you please note the death of that traitor-Priest. Those who threaten me die." She glanced at al-Fali. "My thanks to you, Naib."

"Thanks for a mistake," al-Fali muttered. He looked at Jessica. "You were right. My rage removed one who should've been questioned."

Jessica whispered: "Mark those two courtiers and the woman in the colorful dress, Fedaykin. I want them taken and questioned."

"It will be done," he said.

"If we get out of here alive," Jessica said. "Come, let us go back and play our parts."

"As you say, My Lady."

Together, they returned to the dais, Jessica mounting the steps and resuming her position beside Alia, al-Fali remaining in the supplicant's position below.

"Now," Alia said.

"One moment, daughter," Jessica said. She held up her sleeve, exposed the hole with a finger through it. "The attack was aimed at me. The pellet almost found me even as I was dodging. You will all note that the maula pistol is no longer down there." She pointed. "Who has it?"

There was no response.

"Perhaps it could be traced," Jessica said.

"What nonsense!" Alia said. "*I* was the—"

Jessica half turned toward her daughter, motioned with her left hand. "Someone down there has that pistol. Don't you have a fear that—"

"One of my guards has it!" Alia said.

"Then that guard will bring the weapon to me," Jessica said.

"She's already taken it away."

"How convenient," Jessica said.

"What are you saying?" Alia demanded.

Jessica allowed herself a grim smile. "I am saying that two of your people were charged with saving that *traitor-Priest.* I warned them that they would die if he died. They will die."

"I forbid it!"

Jessica merely shrugged.

"We have a brave Fedaykin here," Alia said, motioning toward al-Fali. "This argument can wait."

"It can wait forever," Jessica said, speaking in Chakobsa, her words double-barbed to tell Alia that no argument would stop the death command.

"We shall see!" Alia said. She turned to al-Fali. "Why are you here, Ghadhean al-Fali?"

"To see the mother of Muad'Dib," the Naib said. "What is left of the

Fedaykin, that band of brothers who served her son, pooled their resources to buy my way in here past the avaricous guardians who shield the Atreides from the realities of Arrakis."

Alia said: "Anything the Fedaykin require, they have only—"

"He came to see me," Jessica interrupted. "What is your desperate need, Fedaykin?"

Alia said: "I speak for the Atreides here! What is—"

"Be silent, you murderous Abomination!" Jessica snapped. "You tried to have me killed, *daughter*! I say it for all here to know. You can't have everyone in this hall killed to silence them—as that Priest was silenced. Yes, the Naib's blow would've killed the man, but he could have been saved. He could've been questioned! You have no concern that he was silenced. Spray your protests upon us as you will, your guilt is written in your actions!"

Alia sat in frozen silence, face pale. And Jessica, watching the play of emotions across her daughter's face, saw a terrifyingly familiar movement of Alia's hands, an unconscious response which once had identified a deadly enemy of the Atreides. Alia's fingers moved in a tapping rhythm—little finger twice, index finger three times, ring finger twice, little finger once, ring finger twice . . . and back through the tapping in the same order.

The old Baron!

The focus of Jessica's eyes caught Alia's attention and she glanced down at her hand, held it still, looked back at her mother to see the terrible recognition. A gloating smile locked Alia's mouth.

"So you have your revenge upon us," Jessica whispered.

"Have you gone mad, mother?" Alia asked.

"I wish I had," Jessica said. And she thought: *She knows I will confirm this to the Sisterhood. She knows. She may even suspect I'll tell the Fremen and force her into a Trial of Possession. She cannot let me leave here alive.*

"Our brave Fedaykin waits while we argue," Alia said.

Jessica forced her attention back to the old Naib. She brought her responses under control, said: "You came to see me, Ghadhean."

"Yes, My lady. We of the desert see terrible things happening. The Little Makers come out of the sand as was foretold in the oldest prophecies. Shai-Hulud no longer can be found except in the deeps of the Empty Quarter. We have abandoned our friend, the desert!"

Jessica glanced at Alia, who merely motioned for Jessica to continue. Jessica looked out over the throng in the Chamber, saw the shocked alertness on every face. The import of the fight between mother and daughter had not been lost on this throng, and they must wonder why the audience continued. She returned her attention to al-Fali.

"Ghadean, what is this talk of Little Makers and the scarcity of sandworms?"

"Mother of Moisture," he said, using her old Fremen title, "we were warned of this in the Kitab al-Ibar. We beseech thee. Let it not be forgotten that on the day Muad'Dib died, Arrakis turned by itself! We cannot abandon the desert."

"Hah!" Alia sneered. "The superstitious riffraff of the Inner Desert fear the ecological transformation. They—"

"I hear you, Ghadhean," Jessica said. "If the worms go, the spice goes. If the spice goes, what coin do we have to buy our way?"

Sounds of surprise: gasps and startled whispers could be heard spreading across the Great Hall. The Chamber echoed to the sound.

Alia shrugged. "Superstitious nonsense!"

Al-Fali lifted his right hand to point at Alia. "I speak to the Mother of Moisture, not to the Coan-Teen!"

Alia's hands gripped the arms of her throne, but she remained seated.

Al-Fali looked at Jessica. "Once it was the land where nothing grew. Now there are plants. They spread like lice upon a wound. There have been clouds and rain along the belt of Dune! Rain, My Lady! Oh, precious mother of Muad'Dib, as sleep is death's brother, so is rain on the Belt of Dune. It is the death of us all."

"We do only what Liet-Kynes and Muad'Dib himself designed for us to do," Alia protested. "What is all of this superstitious gabble? We revere the words of Liet-Kynes, who told us: 'I wish to see this entire planet caught up in a net of green plants.' So it will be."

"And what of the worms and the spice?" Jessica asked.

"There'll always be *some* desert," Alia said. "The worms will survive."

*She's lying,* Jessica thought. *Why does she lie?*

"Help us, Mother of Moisture," al-Fali pleaded.

With an abrupt sensation of double vision, Jessica felt her awareness lurch, propelled by the old Naib's words. It was the unmistakable *adab*, the demanding memory which came upon one of itself. It came without qualifications and held her senses immobile while the lesson of the past was impressed upon her awareness. She was caught up in it completely, a fish in the net. Yet she felt the demand of it as a *human-most* moment, each small part a reminder of creation. Every element of the lesson-memory was real but insubstantial in its constant change, and she knew this was the closest she might ever come to experiencing the prescient dietgrasp which had inflicted itself upon her son.

*Alia lied because she was possessed by one who would destroy the Atreides. She was, in herself, the first destruction. Then al-Fali spoke the truth: the sandworms are doomed unless the course of the ecological transformation is modified.*

In the pressure of revelation, Jessica saw the people of the audience reduced to slow motion, their roles identified for her. She could pick the ones charged with seeing that she did not leave here alive! And the path through them lay there in her awareness as though outlined in bright light—confusion among them, one of them feinted to stumble into another, whole groups tangled. She saw, also, that she might leave this Great Hall only to fall into other hands. Alia did not care if she created a martyr. No—the *thing which possessed her* did not care.

Now, in this frozen time, Jessica chose a way to save the old Naib and send him as messenger. The way through the audience remained indelibly clear. How simple it was! They were buffoons with barricaded eyes, their shoulders held in positions of immovable defense. Each position upon the great floor could be seen as an atropic collision from which dead flesh might slough away to reveal skeletons. Their bodies, their clothes, and their faces described individual hells—the insucked breast of concealed terrors, the glittering hook of a jewel become substitute armor; the mouths were judgments full of frightened absolutes, cathedral prisms of eyebrows showing lofty and religious sentiments which their loins denied.

Jessica sensed dissolution in the shaping forces loosed upon Arrakis. Al-Fali's voice had been like a distrans in her soul, awakening a beast from the deepest part of her.

In an eyeblink Jessica moved from the *adab* into the universe of movement, but it was a different universe from the one which had commanded her attention only a second before.

Alia was starting to speak, but Jessica said: "Silence!" Then: "There are those who fear that I have returned without reservation to the Sisterhood. But since that day in the desert when the Fremen gave the gift of life to me and to my son, I have been Fremen!" And she lapsed into the old tongue which only those in this room who could profit by it would understand: "Onsar akhaka zeliman aw maslumen!" *Support your brother in his time of need, whether he be just or unjust!*

Her words had the desired effect, a subtle shifting of positions within the Chamber.

But Jessica raged on: "This Ghadhean al-Fali, an honest Fremen, comes here to tell me what others should have revealed to me. Let no one deny this! The ecological transformation has become a tempest out of control!"

Wordless confirmations could be seen throughout the room.

"And my daughter delights in this!" Jessica said. "Mektub al-mellah! You carve wounds upon my flesh and write there in salt! Why did the Atreides find a home here? Because the *Mohalata* was natural to us. To the Atreides, government was always a protective partnership: *Mohalata*, as the Fremen have always known it. Now look at her!" Jessica pointed at Alia. "She laughs alone at night in contemplation of her own evil! Spice production will fall to nothing, or at best a fraction of its former level! And when word of *that* gets out—"

"We'll have a corner on the most priceless product in the universe!" Alia shouted.

"We'll have a corner on hell!" Jessica raged.

And Alia lapsed into the most ancient Chakobsa, the Atreides private language with its difficult glottal stops and clicks: "Now, you know, *mother!* Did you think a granddaughter of Baron Harkonnen would not appreciate all of the lifetimes you crushed into my awareness before I was even born? When I raged against what you'd done to me, I had only to ask myself what the Baron would've done. And he answered! Understand me, Atreides bitch! He answered *me!*"

Jessica heard the venom and the confirmation of her guess. *Abomination!* Alia had been overwhelmed within, possessed by that *cahueit* of evil, the Baron Vladimir Harkonnen. The Baron himself spoke from her mouth now, uncaring of what was revealed. He wanted her to see his revenge, wanted her to know that he could not be cast out.

*I'm supposed to remain here helpless in my knowledge,* Jessica thought. With the thought, she launched herself onto the path the *adab* had revealed, shouting: "Fedaykin, follow me!"

It turned out there were six Fedaykin in the room, and five of them won through behind her.

> *When I am weaker than you, I ask you for freedom because that is according to your principles; when I am stronger than you, I take away your freedom because that is according to my principles.*

**—Words of an ancient philosopher**
**(Attributed by Harq al-Ada to**
**one Louis Veuillot)**

Leto leaned out the covert exit from the sietch, saw the bight of the cliff towering above his limited view. Late afternoon sunlight cast long shadows in the cliff's vertical striations. A skeleton butterfly flew in and out of the shadows, its webbed wings a transparent lacery against the light. How delicate that butterfly was to exist here, he thought.

Directly ahead of him lay the apricot orchard, with children working there to gather the fallen fruit. Beyond the orchard was the qanat. He and Ghanima had given the slip to their guards by losing themselves in a sudden crush of incoming workers. It had been a relatively simple matter to worm their way down an air passage to its connection with the steps to the covert exit. Now they had only to mingle themselves with the children, work their way to the qanat and drop into the tunnel. There they could move beside the predator fish which kept sandtrout from encysting the tribe's irrigation water. No Fremen would yet think of a human risking accidental immersion in water.

He stepped out of the protective passages. The cliff stretched away on both sides of him, turned horizontal just by the act of his own movement.

Ghanima moved closely behind him. Both carried small fruit baskets woven of spice-fiber, but each basket carried a sealed package: Fremkit, maula pistol, crysknife . . . and the new robes sent by Farad'n.

Ghanima followed her brother into the orchard, mingled with the working children. Stillsuit masks concealed every face. They were just two more workers here, but she felt the action drawing her life away from protective boundaries and known ways. What a simple step it was, that step from one danger into another!

In their baskets those new garments sent by Farad'n conveyed a purpose well understood by both of them. Ghanima had accented this knowledge by sewing their personal motto, *"We Share,"* in Chakobsa above the hawk crest at each breast.

It would be twilight soon and, beyond the qanat which marked off sietch cultivation, there would come a special quality of evening which few places in the universe could match. It would be that softly lighted desert world with its persistent solitude, its saturated sense that each creature in it was alone in a new universe.

"We've been seen," Ghanima whispered, bending to work beside her brother.

"Guards?"

"No—others."

"Good."

"We must move swiftly," she said.

Leto acknowledged this by moving away from the cliff through the orchard. He thought with his father's thoughts: *Everything remains mobile in the desert or perishes.* Far out on the sand he could see The Attendant's outcropping, reminder of the need for mobility. The rocks lay static and rigid in their watchful enigma, fading yearly before the onslaught of wind-driven sand. One day The Attendant would be sand.

As they neared the qanat they heard music from a high entrance of the sietch. It was an old-style Fremen group—two-holed flutes, tambourines, tympani made on spice-plastic drums with skins stretched taut across one end. No one asked what animal on this planet provided that much skin.

*Stilgar will remember what I told him about that cleft in The Attendant,* Leto thought. *He'll come in the dark when it's too late—and then he'll know.*

Presently they were at the qanat. They slipped into an open tube, climbed down the inspection ladder to the service ledge. It was dusky, damp, and cold in the qanat and they could hear the predator fish splashing. Any sandtrout trying to steal this water would find its water-softened inner surface attacked by the fish. Humans must be wary of them, too.

"Careful," Leto said, moving down the slippery ledge. He fastened his memory to times and places his flesh had never known. Ghanima followed.

At the end of the qanat they stripped to their stillsuits and put on the new robes. They left the old Fremen robes behind as they climbed out another inspection tube, wormed their way over and down the far side. There they sat shielded from the sietch, strapped on maula pistols and crysknives, slipped the Fremkit packs onto their shoulders. They no longer could hear the music.

Leto arose, struck out through the valley between the dunes.

Ghanima fell into step behind him, moving with practiced unrhythmical quiet over the open sand.

Below the crest of each dune they bent low and crept across into the hidden lee, there to pause and peer backward seeking pursuit. No hunters had emerged upon the desert by the time they reached the first rocks.

In the shadows of the rocks they worked their way around The Attendant, climbed to a ledge looking out upon the desert. Colors blinked far out on the *bled*. The darkening air held the fragility of fine crystal. The landscape which met their gaze was beyond pity, nowhere did it pause—no hesitation in it at all. The gaze stayed upon no single place in its scanning movements across that immensity.

*It is the horizon of eternity,* Leto thought.

Ghanima crouched beside her brother, thinking: *The attack will come soon.* She listened for the slightest sound, her whole body transformed into a single sense of taut probing.

Leto sat equally alert. He knew now the culmination of all the training which had gone into the lives he shared so intimately. In this wilderness one developed a firm dependence upon the senses, *all* of the senses. Life became a hoard of stored perceptions, each one linked only to momentary survival.

Presently Ghanima climbed up the rocks and peered through a notch at the way they had come. The safety of the sietch seemed a lifetime away, a bulk of dumb cliffs rising out of brown-purple distance, dust-blurred edges at the rim where the last of the sunlight cast its silver streaks. Still no pursuit could be seen in the intervening distance. She returned to Leto's side.

"It'll be a predatory animal," Leto said. "That's my tertiary computation."

"I think you stopped computing too soon," Ghanima said. "It'll be more than one animal. House Corrino has learned not to put all of its hopes into a single bag."

Leto nodded agreement.

His mind felt suddenly heavy with the multitude of lives which his *difference* provided him: all of those lives, his even before birth. He was saturated with living and wanted to flee from his own consciousness. The inner world was a heavy beast which could devour him.

Restlessly he arose, climbed to the notch Ghanima had used, peered at the cliffs of the sietch. Back there, beneath the cliff, he could see how the qanat drew a line between life and death. On the oasis edge he could see camel sage, onion grass, gobi feather grass, wild alfalfa. In the last of the light he could make out the black movements of birds pick-hopping in the alfalfa. The distant grain tassels were ruffled by a wind which drew shadows that moved right up to the orchard. The motion caught at his awareness, and he saw that the shadows hid within their fluid form a larger change, and that larger change gave ransom to the turning rainbows of a silver-dusted sky.

*What will happen out here?* he asked himself.

And he knew it would either be death or the play of death, himself the object. Ghanima would be the one to return, believing the reality of a death she had seen or reporting sincerely from a deep hypnotic compulsion that her brother was, indeed, slain.

The unknowns of this place haunted him. He thought how easy it would be to succumb to the demand for prescience, to risk launching his awareness into an unchanging absolute future. The small vision of his dream was bad enough, though. He knew he dared not risk the larger vision.

Presently, he returned to Ghanima's side.

"No pursuit yet," he said.

"The beasts they send for us will be large," Ghanima said. "We may have time to see them coming."

"Not if they come in the night."

"It'll be dark very soon," she said.

"Yes. It's time we went down into *our* place." He indicated the rocks to their left and below them where wind-sand had eaten a tiny cleft in the basalt. It was large enough to admit them, but small enough to keep out large creatures. Leto felt himself reluctant to go there, but knew it must be done. That was the place he'd pointed out to Stilgar.

"They may really kill us," he said.

"This is the chance we have to take," she said. "We owe it to our father."

"I'm not arguing."

And he thought: *This is the correct path; we do the right thing.* But he knew how dangerous it was to be *right* in this universe. Their survival now demanded vigor and fitness and an understanding of the limitations in every moment. Fremen ways were their best armor, and the Bene Gesserit knowledge was a force held in reserve. They were both thinking now as Atreides-trained battle veterans with no other defenses than a Fremen toughness which was not even hinted at by their childish bodies and their formal attire.

Leto fingered the hilt of the poison-tipped crysknife at his waist. Unconsciously Ghanima duplicated the gesture.

"Shall we go down now?" Ghanima asked. As she spoke she saw the movement far below them, small movement made less threatening by distance. Her stillness alerted Leto before she could utter a warning.

"Tigers," he said.

"Laza tigers," she corrected him.

"They see us," he said.

"We'd better hurry," she said. "A maula would never stop those creatures. They will've been well trained for this."

"They'll have a human director somewhere around," he said, leading the way at a fast lope down the rocks to the left.

Ghanima agreed, but kept it to herself, saving her strength. There'd be a human around somewhere. Those tigers couldn't be allowed to run free until the proper moment.

The tigers moved fast in the last of the light, leaping from rock to rock. They were eye-minded creatures and soon it would be night, the time of the ear-minded. The bell-call of a nightbird came from The Attendant's rocks to emphasize the change. Creatures of the darkness already were hustling in the shadows of the etched crevasses.

Still the tigers remained visible to the running twins. The animals flowed with power, a rippling sense of golden sureness in every movement.

Leto felt that he had stumbled into this place to free himself from his soul. He ran with the sure knowledge that he and Ghanima could reach their narrow notch in time, but his gaze kept returning with fascination to the oncoming beasts.

*One stumble and we're lost,* he thought.

That thought reduced the sureness of his knowledge and he ran faster.

*You Bene Gesserit call your activity of the Panoplia Prophetica a "Science of Religion." Very well. I, a seeker after another kind of scientist, find this an appropriate definition. You do, indeed, build your own myths, but so do all societies. You I must warn, however. You are behaving as so many other misguided scientists have behaved. Your actions reveal that you wish to take something out of [away from] life. It is time you were reminded of that which you so often profess: One cannot have a single thing without its opposite.*

—**The Preacher at Arrakeen:**
**A Message to the Sisterhood**

In the hour before dawn, Jessica sat immobile on a worn rug of spice-cloth. Around her were the bare rocks of an old and poor sietch, one of the original settlements. It lay below the rim of Red Chasm, sheltered from the westerlies of the desert. Al-Fali and his brothers had brought her here; now they awaited word from Stilgar. The Fedaykin had moved cautiously in the matter of communication, however. Stilgar was not to know their location.

The Fedaykin already knew they were under a *procès-verbal*, an official report of crimes against the Imperium. Alia was taking the tack that her mother had been suborned by enemies of the realm, although the Sisterhood had not yet been named. The high-handed, tyrannical nature of Alia's power was out in the open, however, and her belief that because she controlled the Priesthood she controlled the Fremen was about to be tested.

Jessica's message to Stilgar had been direct and simple: *"My daughter is possessed and must be put to the trial."*

Fears destroyed values, though, and it already was known that some Fremen would prefer not to believe this accusation. Their attempts to use the accusation as a passport had brought on two battles during the night, but the ornithopters al-Fali's people had stolen had brought the fugitives to this precarious safety: Red Chasm Sietch. Word was going out to the Fedaykin from here, but fewer than two hundred of them remained on Arrakis. The others held posts throughout the Empire.

Reflecting upon these facts, Jessica wondered if she had come to the place of her death. Some of the Fedaykin believed it, but the death commandos accepted this easily enough. Al-Fali had merely grinned at her when some of his young men voiced their fears.

"When God hath ordained a creature to die in a particular place, He causeth that creature's wants to direct him to that place," the old Naib had said.

The patched curtains at her doorway rustled; al-Fali entered. The old man's narrow, windburned face appeared drawn, his eyes feverish. Obviously he had not rested.

"Someone comes," he said.

"From Stilgar?"

"Perhaps." He lowered his eyes, glanced leftward in the manner of the old Fremen who brought bad news.

"What is it?" Jessica demanded.

"We have word from Tabr that your grandchildren are not there." He spoke without looking at her.

"Alia . . ."

"She has ordered that the twins be given over to her custody, but Sietch Tabr reports that the children are not there. That is all we know."

"Stilgar's sent them into the desert," Jessica said.

"Possibly, but it is known that he was searching for them all through the night. Perhaps it was a trick on his part . . . ."

"That's not Stilgar's way," she said, and thought: *Unless the twins put him up to it.* But that didn't feel right either. She wondered at herself: no sensations of panic to suppress, and her fears for the twins were tempered by what Ghanima had revealed. She peered up at al-Fali, found him studying her with pity in his eyes. She said: "They've gone into the desert by themselves."

"Alone? Those two children!"

She did not bother to explain that "those two children" probably knew more about desert survival than most living Fremen. Her thoughts were fixed, instead, on Leto's odd behavior when he'd insisted that she allow herself to be abducted. She'd put the memory aside, but this moment demanded it. He'd said she would know the moment to obey him.

"The messenger should be in the sietch by now," al-Fali said. "I will bring him to you." He let himself out through the patched curtain.

Jessica stared at the curtain. It was red cloth of spice-fiber, but the patches were blue. The story was that this sietch had refused to profit from Muad'Dib's religion, earning the enmity of Alia's Priesthood. The people here reportedly had put their capital into a scheme to raise dogs as large as ponies, dogs bred for intelligence as guardians of children. The dogs had all died. Some said it was poison and the Priests were blamed.

She shook her head to drive out these reflections, recognizing them for what they were: *gahfla*, the gadfly distraction.

Where had those children gone? To Jacurutu? They had a plan. *They tried to enlighten me to the extent they thought I'd accept,* she remembered. And when they'd reached the limits as they saw them, Leto had commanded her to obey. *He'd* commanded *her!*

Leto had recognized what Alia was doing; that much was obvious. Both twins had spoken of their aunt's "affliction," even when defending her. Alia was gambling on the *rightness* of her position in the Regency. Demanding custody of the twins confirmed that. Jessica found a harsh laugh shaking her own breast. The Reverend Mother Gaius Helen Mohiam had been fond of explaining this particular error to her student, Jessica. *"If you focus your awareness only upon your own rightness, then you invite the forces of opposition to overwhelm you. This is a common error. Even I, your teacher, have made it."*

"And even I, your student, have made it," Jessica whispered to herself.

She heard fabrics whispering in the passage beyond the curtain. Two young Fremen entered, part of the entourage they'd picked up during the night. The two were obviously awed at being in the presence of Muad'Dib's mother. Jessica had read them completely: they were non-thinkers, attaching themselves to any fancied power for the identity which this gave them. Without a reflection from her they were empty. Thus, they were dangerous.

"We were sent ahead by al-Fali to prepare you," one of the young Fremen said.

Jessica felt an abrupt clenching tightness in her breast, but her voice remained calm. "Prepare me for what?"

"Stilgar has sent Duncan Idaho as his messenger."

Jessica pulled her aba hood up over her hair, an unconscious gesture. *Duncan?* But he was Alia's tool.

The Fremen who'd spoken took a half step forward. "Idaho says he has come to take you to safety, but al-Fali does not see how this can be."

"It seems passing strange, indeed," Jessica said. "But there are stranger things in our universe. Bring him."

They glanced at each other but obeyed, leaving together with such a rush that they tore another rent in the worn curtain.

Presently Idaho stepped through the curtain, followed by the two Fremen and al-Fali bringing up the rear, hand on his crysknife. Idaho appeared composed. He wore the dress casuals of the Atreides House Guard, a uniform which had changed little in more than fourteen centuries. Arrakis had replaced the old gold-handled plasteel blade with a crysknife, but that was minor.

"I'm told you wish to help me," Jessica said.

"As odd as that may seem," he said.

"But didn't Alia send you to abduct me?" she asked.

A slight raising of his black eyebrows was the only mark of surprise. The many-faceted Tleilaxu eyes continued to stare at her with glittering intensity. "Those were her orders," he said.

Al-Fali's knuckles went white on his crysknife, but he did not draw.

"I've spent much of this night reviewing the mistakes I made with my daughter," she said.

"There were many," Idaho agreed, "and I shared in most of them."

She saw now that his jaw muscles were trembling.

"It was easy to listen to the arguments which led us astray," Jessica said. "I wanted to leave this place . . .You . . . you wanted a girl you saw as a younger version of me."

He accepted this silently.

"Where are my grandchildren?" she demanded, voice going harsh.

He blinked. Then: "Stilgar believes they have gone into the desert—hiding. Perhaps they saw this crisis coming."

Jessica glanced at al-Fali, who nodded his recognition that she had anticipated this.

"What is Alia doing?" Jessica asked.

"She risks civil war," he said.

"Do you believe it'll come to that?"

Idaho shrugged. "Probably not. These are softer times. There are more people willing to listen to pleasant arguments."

"I agree," she said. "Well and good, what of my grandchildren?"

"Stilgar will find them—if . . ."

"Yes, I see." It was really up to Gurney Halleck then. She turned to look at the rock wall on her left. "Alia grasps the power firmly now." She looked back at Idaho. "You understand? One uses power by grasping it lightly. To grasp too strongly is to be taken over by power, and thus to become its victim."

"As my Duke always told me," Idaho said.

Somehow Jessica knew he meant the older Leto, not Paul. She asked: "Where am I to be taken in this . . . abduction?"

Idaho peered down at her as though trying to see into the shadows created by the hood.

Al-Fali stepped forward: "My Lady, you are not seriously thinking . . ."

"Is it not my right to decide my own fate?" Jessica asked.

"But this . . ." Al-Fali's head nodded toward Idaho.

"This was my loyal guardian before Alia was born," Jessica said. "Before he died saving my son's life and mine. We Atreides always honor certain obligations."

"Then you will go with me?" Idaho asked.

"Where would you take her?" al-Fali asked.

"Best that you don't know," Jessica said.

Al-Fali scowled but remained silent. His face betrayed indecision, an understanding of the wisdom in her words but an unresolved doubt of Idaho's trustworthiness.

"What of the Fedaykin who helped me?" Jessica asked.

"They have Stilgar's countenance if they can get to Tabr," Idaho said. Jessica faced al-Fali: "I command you to go there, my friend. Stilgar can use Fedaykin in the search for my grandchildren."

The old Naib lowered his gaze. "As Muad'Dib's mother commands."

*He's still obeying Paul,* she thought.

"We should be out of here quickly," Idaho said. "The search is certain to include this place, and that early."

Jessica rocked forward and arose with that fluid grace which never quite left the Bene Gesserit, even when they felt the pangs of age. And she felt old now after her night of flight. Even as she moved, her mind remained on that peculiar interview with her grandson. What was he really doing? She shook her head, covered the motion by adjusting her hood. It was too easy to fall into the trap of underestimating Leto. Life with ordinary children conditioned one to a false view of the inheritance which the twins enjoyed.

Her attention was caught by Idaho's pose. He stood in the relaxed preparedness for violence, one foot ahead of the other, a stance which she herself had taught him. She shot a quick look at the two young Fremen, at al-Fali. Doubts still assailed the old Fremen Naib and the two young men felt this.

"I trust this man with my life," she said, addressing herself to al-Fali. "And it is not the first time."

"My Lady," al-Fali protested. "It's just . . ." He glared at Idaho. "He's the husband of the Coan-Teen!"

"And he was trained by my Duke and by me," she said.

"But he's a *ghola*!" The words were torn from al-Fali.

"My son's ghola," she reminded him.

It was too much for a former Fedaykin who'd once pledged himself to support Muad'Dib to the death. He sighed, stepped aside, and motioned the two young men to open the curtains.

Jessica stepped through, Idaho behind her. She turned, spoke to al-Fali in the doorway. "You are to go to Stilgar. He's to be trusted."

"Yes . . . ." But she still heard doubts in the old man's voice.

Idaho touched her arm. "We should go at once. Is there anything you wish to take?"

"Only my common sense," she said.

"Why? Do you fear you're making a mistake?"

She glanced up at him. "You were always the best 'thopter pilot in our service, Duncan."

This did not amuse him. He stepped ahead of her, moving swiftly, retracing the way he'd come. Al-Fali fell into step beside Jessica. "How did you know he came by 'thopter?"

"He wears no stillsuit," Jessica said.

Al-Fali appeared abashed by this obvious perception. He would not be silenced, though. "Our messenger brought him here directly from Stilgar's. They could've been seen."

"Were you seen, Duncan?" Jessica asked Idaho's back.

"You know better than that," he said. "We flew lower than the dune tops."

They turned into a side passage which led downward in spiral steps, debouching finally into an open chamber well-lighted by glowglobes high in the brown rock. A single ornithopter sat facing the far wall, crouched there like an insect waiting to spring. The wall would be false rock, then—a door opening onto the desert. As poor as this sietch was, it still maintained the instruments of secrecy and mobility.

Idaho opened the ornithopter's door for her, helped her into the right-hand seat. As she moved past him, she saw perspiration on his forehead where a lock of the black goat-hair lay tumbled. Unbidden, Jessica found herself recalling that head spouting blood in a noisy cavern. The steely marbles of the Tleilaxu eyes brought her out of that recollection. Nothing was as it seemed anymore. She busied herself fastening her seatbelt.

"It's been a long time since you've flown me, Duncan," she said.

"Long and far time," he said. He was already checking the controls.

Al-Fali and the two younger Fremen waited beside the controls to the false rock, prepared to open it.

"Do you think I harbor doubts about you?" Jessica asked, speaking softly to Idaho.

Idaho kept his attention on an engine instrument, ignited the impellers and watched a needle move. A smile touched his mouth, a quick and harsh gesture in his sharp features, gone as quickly as it had come.

"I am still Atreides," Jessica said. "Alia is not."

"Have no fear," he grated. "I still serve the Atreides."

"Alia is no longer Atreides," Jessica repeated.

"You needn't remind me!" he snarled. "Now shut up and let me fly this thing."

The desperation in his voice was quite unexpected, out of keeping with the Idaho she'd known. Putting down a renewed sense of fear, Jessica asked: "Where are we going, Duncan? You can tell me now."

But he nodded to al-Fali and the false rock opened outward into bright silvery sunlight. The ornithopter leaped outward and up, its wings throbbing with the effort, the jets roaring, and they mounted into an empty sky. Idaho set a southwesterly course toward Sahaya Ridge which could be seen as a dark line upon the sand.

Presently he said: "Do not think harshly of me, My Lady."

"I haven't thought harshly of you since that night you came into our Arrakeen great hall roaring drunk on spice-beer," she said. But his words renewed her doubts, and she fell into the relaxed preparedness of complete *prana-bindu* defense.

"I remember that night well," he said. "I was very young and . . . inexperienced."

"But the best swordmaster in my Duke's retinue."

"Not quite, My Lady. Gurney could best me six times out of ten." He glanced at her. "Where is Gurney?"

"Doing my bidding."

He shook his head.

"Do you know where we're going?" she asked.

"Yes, My Lady."

"Then tell me."

"Very well. I promised that I would create a believable plot against House Atreides. Only one way, really, to do that." He pressed a button on the control wheel and cocoon restraints whipped from Jessica's seat, enfolded her in unbreakable softness, leaving only her head exposed. "I'm taking you to Salusa Secundus," he said. "To Farad'n."

In a rare, uncontrolled spasm, Jessica surged against the restraints, felt them tighten, easing only when she relaxed, but not before she felt the deadly shigawire concealed in the protective sheathing.

"The shigawire release has been disconnected," he said, not looking at her. "Oh yes, and don't try Voice on me. I've come a long way since the days when you could move me that way." He looked at her. "The Tleilaxu armored me against such wiles."

"You're obeying Alia," Jessica said, "and she—"

"Not Alia," he said. "We do The Preacher's bidding. He wants you to teach Farad'n as once you taught . . . Paul."

Jessica remained in frozen silence, remembering Leto's words, that she would find an interesting student. Presently she said: "This Preacher—is he my son?"

Idaho's voice seemed to come from a great distance: "I wish I knew."

*The universe is just there; that's the only way a Fedaykin can view it and remain the master of his senses. The universe neither threatens nor promises. It holds things beyond our sway: the fall of a meteor, the eruption of a spiceblow, growing old and dying. These are the realities of this universe and they must be faced regardless of how you feel about them. You cannot fend off such realities with words. They will come at you in their own wordless way and then, then you will understand what is meant by "life and death." Understanding this, you will be filled with joy.*

**—Muad'Dib to his Fedaykin**

"And those are the things we have set in motion," Wensicia said. "These things were done for *you*."

Farad'n remained motionless, seated across from his mother in her morning room. The sun's golden light came from behind him, casting his shadow on the white-carpeted floor. Light reflected from the wall behind his mother drew a nimbus around her hair. She wore her usual white robe trimmed in gold—reminders of royal days. Her heart-shaped face appeared composed, but he knew she was watching his every reaction. His stomach felt empty, although he'd just come from breakfast.

"You don't approve?" Wensicia asked.

"What is there to disapprove?" he asked.

"Well . . . that we kept this from you until now?"

"Oh, that." He studied his mother, tried to reflect upon his complex position in this matter. He could only think on a thing he had noticed recently, that Tyekanik no longer called her "My Princess." What did he call her? Queen Mother?

*Why do I feel a sense of loss?* he wondered. *What am I losing?* The answer was obvious: he was losing his carefree days, time for those pursuits of the mind which so attracted him. If this plot unfolded by his mother came off, those things would be gone forever. New responsibilities would demand his attention. He found that he resented this deeply. How dared they take such liberties with his time? And without even consulting him!

"Out with it," his mother said. "Something's wrong."

"What if this plan fails?" he asked, saying the first thing that came into his mind.

"How can it fail?"

"I don't know . . . . Any plan can fail. How're you using Idaho in all of this?"

"Idaho? What's this interest in . . . Oh, yes—that mystic fellow Tyek brought here without consulting me. That was wrong of him. The mystic spoke of Idaho, didn't he?"

It was a clumsy lie on her part, and Farad'n found himself staring at his mother in wonderment. She'd known about The Preacher all along!

"It's just that I've never seen a ghola," he said.

She accepted this, said: "We're saving Idaho for something important."

Farad'n chewed silently at his upper lip.

Wensicia found herself reminded of his dead father. Dalak had been like that at times, very inward and complex, difficult to read. Dalak, she reminded herself, had been related to Count Hasimir Fenring, and there'd been something of the dandy and the fanatic in both of them. Would Farad'n follow in that path? She began to regret having Tyek lead the lad into the Arrakeen religion. Who knew where that might take him?

"What does Tyek call you now?" Farad'n asked.

"What's that?" She was startled by this shift.

"I've noticed that he doesn't call you 'My Princess' anymore."

*How observant he is,* she thought, wondering why this filled her with disquiet. *Does he think I've taken Tyek as a lover? Nonsense, it wouldn't matter one way or the other. Then why this question?*

"He calls me 'My Lady'," she said.

"Why?"

"Because that's the custom in all the Great Houses."

*Including the Atreides,* he thought.

"It's less suggestive if overheard," she explained. "Some will think we've given up our legitimate aspirations."

"Who would be that stupid?" he asked.

She pursed her lips, decided to let it pass. A small thing, but great campaigns were made up of many small things.

"The Lady Jessica shouldn't have left Caladan," he said.

She shook her head sharply. What was this? His mind was darting around like a crazy thing! She said: "What do you mean?"

"She shouldn't have gone back to Arrakis," he said. "That's bad strategy. Makes one wonder. Would've been better to have her grandchildren visit her on Caladan."

*He's right,* she thought, dismayed that this had never occurred to her. Tyek would have to explore this immediately. Again she shook her head. *No!* What was Farad'n doing? He must know that the Priesthood would never risk both twins in space.

She said this.

"Is it the Priesthood or the Lady Alia?" he asked, noting that her thoughts had gone where he had wanted. He found exhilaration in this new importance, the mind-games available in political plotting. It had been a long time since his mother's mind had interested him. She was too easily maneuvered.

"You think Alia wants power for herself?" Wensicia asked.

He looked away from her. Of course Alia wanted the power for herself! All of the reports from that accursed planet agreed on this. His thoughts took off on a new course.

"I've been reading about their Planetologist," he said. "There has to be a clue to the sandworms and the haploids in there somewhere, if only . . ."

"Leave that to others now!" she said, beginning to lose patience with him. "Is this all you have to say about the things we've done for you?"

"You didn't do them for me," he said.

"Wha-a-at?"

"You did it for House Corrino," he said, "and you're House Corrino right now. I've not been invested."

"You have responsibilities!" she said. "What about all of the people who depend upon you?"

As if her words put the burden upon him, he felt the weight of all those hopes and dreams which followed House Corrino.

"Yes," he said, "I understand about them, but I find some of the things done in my *name* distasteful."

"Dis . . . How can you say such a thing? We do what any great House would do in promoting its own fortunes!"

"Do you? I think you've been a bit gross. No! Don't interrupt me. If I'm to be an Emperor, then you'd better learn how to listen to me. Do you think I cannot read between the lines? How were those tigers trained?"

She remained speechless at this cutting demonstration of his perceptive abilities.

"I see," he said. "Well, I'll keep Tyek because I know you led him into this. He's a good officer under most circumstances, but he'll fight for his own principles only in a friendly arena."

"His . . . *principles?*"

"The difference between a good officer and a poor one is strength of character and about five heartbeats," he said. "He has to stick by his principles wherever they're challenged."

"The tigers were necessary," she said.

"I'll believe that if they succeed," he said. "But I will not condone what had to be done in training them. Don't protest. It's obvious. They were *conditioned.* You said it yourself."

"What're you going to do?" she asked.

"I'm going to wait and see," he said, "Perhaps I'll become Emperor."

She put a hand to her breast, sighed. For a few moments there he'd terrified her. She'd almost believed he would denounce her. Principles! But he was committed now; she could see that.

Farad'n got up, went to the door and rang for his mother's attendants. He looked back: "We are through, aren't we?"

"Yes." She raised a hand as he started to leave. "Where're you going?"

"To the library. I've become fascinated lately by Corrino history." He left her then, sensing how he carried his new commitment with him.

*Damn her!*

But he knew he was committed. And he recognized that there was a deep emotional difference between history as recorded on shigawire and read at leisure, a deep difference between that kind of history and the history which one lived. This new living history which he felt gathering around him possessed a sense of plunging into an irreversible future. Farad'n could feel himself driven now by the desires of all those whose fortunes rode with him. He found it strange that he could not pin down his own desires in this.

*It is said of Muad'Dib that once when he saw a weed trying to grow between two rocks, he moved one of the rocks. Later, when the weed was seen to be flourishing, he covered it with the remaining rock. "That was its fate," he explained.*

—The Commentaries

"Now!" Ghanima shouted.

Leto, two steps ahead of her in reaching the narrow cut in the rocks, did not hesitate. He dove into the slit, crawled forward until darkness enfolded him. He heard Ghanima drop behind him, a sudden stillness, and her voice, not hurrying or fearful:

"I'm stuck."

He stood up, knowing this would bring his head within reach of questing claws, reversed himself in the narrow passage, crept back until he felt Ghanima's outstretched hand.

"It's my robe," she said. "It's caught."

He heard rocks falling directly below them, pulled on her hand but felt only a small gain.

There was panting below them, a growl.

Leto tensed himself, wedging his hips against the rock, heaved on Ghanima's arm. Cloth ripped and he felt her jerk toward him. She hissed and he knew she felt pain, but he pulled once more, harder. She came farther into the hole, then all the way, dropping beside him. They were too close to the end of the cut, though. He turned, dropped to all fours, scrambled deeper. Ghanima pulled herself along behind him. There was a panting intensity to her movements which told him she'd been hurt. He came to the end of the opening, rolled over and peered upward out the narrow gap of their sanctuary. The opening was about two meters above him, filled with stars. Something large obscured the stars.

A rumbling growl filled the air around the twins. It was deep, menacing, an ancient sound: hunter speaking to its prey.

"How badly are you hurt?" Leto asked, keeping his voice even.

She matched him, tone for tone: "One of them clawed me. Breached my stillsuit along the left leg. I'm bleeding."

"How bad?"

"Vein. I can stop it."

"Use pressure," he said. "Don't move. I'll take care of our friends."

"Careful," she said. "They're bigger than I expected."

Leto unsheathed his crysknife, reached up with it. He knew the tiger would be questing downward, claws raking the narrow passage where its body could not go.

Slowly, slowly, he extended the knife. Abruptly something struck the top of the blade. He felt the blow all along his arm, almost lost his grip on the knife. Blood gushed along his hand, spattered his face, and there came an immediate scream which deafened him. The stars became visible. Something threshed and flung itself down the rocks toward the sand in a violent caterwauling.

Once more, the stars were obscured and he heard the hunter's growl. The second tiger had moved into place, unmindful of its companion's fate.

"They're persistent," Leto said.

"You got one for sure," Ghanima said. "Listen!"

The screams and thrashing convulsions below them were growing fainter. The second tiger remained, though, a curtain against the stars.

Leto sheathed his blade, touched Ghanima's arm. "Give me your knife. I want a fresh tip to make sure of this one."

"Do you think they'll have a third one in reserve?" she asked.

"Not likely. Laza tigers hunt in pairs."

"Just as we do," she said.

"As we do," he agreed. He felt the handle of her crysknife slip into his palm, gripped it tightly. Once more he began that careful upward questing. The blade encountered only empty air, even when he reached into a level dangerous to his body. He withdrew, pondering this.

"Can't you find it?"

"It's not behaving the way the other one did."

"It's still there. Smell it?"

He swallowed in a dry throat. A fetid breath, moist with the musky smell of the cat, assaulted his nostrils. The stars were still blocked from view. Nothing could be heard of the first cat; the crysknife's poison had completed its work.

"I think I'm going to have to stand up," he said.

"No!"

"It has to be teased into reach of the knife."

"Yes, but we agreed that if one of us could avoid being wounded . . ."

"And you're wounded, so you're the one going back," he said.

"But if you're badly injured, I won't be able to leave you," she said.

"Do you have a better idea?"

"Give me back my knife."

"But your leg!"

"I can stand on the good one."

"That thing could take your head off with one sweep. Maybe the maula. . ."

"If there's anyone out there to hear, they'll know we came prepared for—"

"I don't like your taking this risk!" he said.

"Whoever's out there mustn't learn we have maulas—not yet." She touched his arm. "I'll be careful, keep my head down."

As he remained silent, she said: "You know I'm the one who has to do this. Give me back my knife."

Reluctantly he quested with his free hand, found her hand and returned the knife. It was the logical thing to do, but logic warred with every emotion in him.

He felt Ghanima pull away, heard the sandy rasping of her robe against the rock. She gasped, and he knew she must be standing. *Be very careful!* he thought. And he almost pulled her back to insist they use a maula pistol. But that could warn anyone out there that they had such weapons. Worse, it could drive the tiger out of reach, and they'd be trapped in here with a wounded tiger waiting for them in some unknown place out on those rocks.

Ghanima took a deep breath, braced her back against one wall of the cleft. *I must be quick,* she thought. She reached upward with the knife point. Her left leg throbbed where the claws had raked it. She felt the crusting of blood against her skin there and the warmth of a new flow. *Very quick!* She sank her senses into the calm preparation for crisis which the Bene Gesserit Way provided, put pain and all other distractions out of her awareness. The cat must reach down! Slowly she passed the blade along the opening. Where was the damned animal? Once more she raked the air. Nothing. The tiger would have to be lured into attack.

Carefully she probed with her sense of smell. Warm breath came from her left. She poised herself, drew in a deep breath, screamed: "Taqwa!" It was the old Fremen battlecry, its meaning found in the most ancient legends: *"The price of freedom!"* With the cry she tipped the blade and stabbed along the cleft's dark opening. Claws found her elbow before the knife touched flesh, and she had time only to tip her wrist toward the pain before agony raked her arm from elbow to wrist. Through the pain, she felt the poison tip sink into the tiger. The blade was wrenched from her numb fingers. But again the narrow gap of the cleft lay open to the stars and the wailing voice of a dying cat filled the night. They followed it by its death throes, a thrashing passage down the rocks. Presently the death-silence came.

"It got my arm," Ghanima said, trying to bind a loose fold of her robe around the wound.

"Badly?"

"I think so. I can't feel my hand."

"Let me get a light and—"

"Not until we get under cover!"

"I'll hurry."

She heard him twisting to reach his Fremkit, felt the dark slickness of a nightshield as it was slipped over her head, tucked in behind her. He didn't bother to make it moisture tight.

"My knife's on this side," she said. "I can feeel the handle with my knee."

"Leave it for now."

He ignited a single small globe. The brilliance of it made her blink. Leto put the globe on the sandy floor at one side, gasped as he saw her arm. One claw had opened a long, gaping wound which twisted from the elbow along the back of her arm almost to the wrist. The wound described the way she had rotated her arm to present the knife tip to the tiger's paw.

Ghanima glanced once at the wound, closed her eyes and began reciting the litany against fear.

Leto found himself sharing her need, but put aside the clamor of his own emotions while he set about binding up the wound. It had to be done carefully to stop the flow of blood while retaining the appearance of a clumsy job which Ghanima might have done by herself. He made her tie off the knot with her free hand, holding one end of the bandage in her teeth.

"Now let's look at the leg," he said.

She twisted around to present the other wound. It was not as bad: two shallow claw cuts along the calf. They had bled freely into the stillsuit, however. He cleaned it up as best he could, bound the wound beneath the stillsuit. He sealed the suit over the bandage.

"I got sand in it," he said. "Have it treated as soon as you get back."

"Sand in our wounds," she said. "That's an old story for Fremen."

He managed a smile, sat back.

Ghanima took a deep breath. "We've pulled it off."

"Not yet."

She swallowed, fighting to recover from the aftermath of shock. Her face appeared pale in the light of the glowglobe. And she thought: *Yes, we must move fast now. Whoever controlled those tigers could be out there right now.*

Leto, staring at his sister, felt a sudden wrenching sense of loss. It was a deep pain which shot through his breast. He and Ghanima must separate now. For all of those years since birth they had been as one person. But their plan demanded now that they undergo a metamorphosis, going their separate ways into uniqueness where the sharing of daily experiences would never again unite them as they once had been united.

He retreated into the necessarily mundane. "Here's my Fremkit. I took the bandages from it. Someone may look."

"Yes." She exchanged kits with him.

"Someone out there has a transmitter for those cats," he said. "Most likely he'll be waiting near the qanat to make certain of us."

She touched her maula pistol where it sat atop the Fremkit, picked it up and thrust it into the sash beneath her robe. "My robe's torn."

"Yes."

"Searchers may get here soon," he said. "They may have a traitor among them. Best you slip back alone. Get Harah to hide you."

"I'll . . . I'll start the search for the traitor as soon as I get back," she said. She peered into her brother's face, sharing his painful knowledge that from this point on they would accumulate a store of differences. Never again would they be as one, sharing knowledge which no one else could understand.

"I'll go to Jacurutu," he said.

"Fondak," she said.

He nodded his agreement. Jacurutu/Fondak—they had to be the same place. It was the only way the legendary place could have been hidden. Smugglers had done it, of course. How easy for them to convert one label into another, acting under the cover of the unspoken convention by which they were allowed to exist. The ruling family of a planet must always have a back door for escape in extremis. And a small share in smuggling profits kept the channels open. In Fondak/Jacurutu, the smugglers had taken over a completely operative sietch untroubled by a resident population. And they had hidden Jacurutu right out in the open, secure in the taboo which kept Fremen from it.

"No Fremen will think to search for me in such a place," he said. "They'll inquire among the smugglers, of course, but . . ."

"We'll do as we agreed," she said. "it's just . . ."

"I know." Hearing his own voice, Leto realized they were drawing out these last moments of sameness. A wry grin touched his mouth, adding years to his appearance. Ghanima realized she was seeing him through a veil of time, looking at an older Leto. Tears burned her eyes.

"You needn't give water to the dead just yet," he said, brushing a finger against the dampness on her cheeks. "I'll go out far enough that no one will hear, and I'll call a worm." He indicated the collapsed Maker hooks strapped to the outside of his Fremkit. "I'll be at Jacurutu before dawn two days from now."

"Ride swiftly, my old friend," she whispered.

"I'll come back to you, my only friend," he said. "Remember to be careful at the qanat."

"Choose a good worm," she said, giving him the Fremen words of parting. Her left hand extinguished the glowglobe, and the nightseal rustled as she pulled it aside, folded it and tucked it into her kit. She felt him go, hearing only the softest of sounds quickly fading into silence as he crept down the rocks into the desert.

Ghanima steeled herself then for what she had to do. Leto must be dead to her. She had to make herself believe it. There could be no Jacurutu in her mind, no brother out there seeking a place lost in Fremen mythology. From this point onward she could not think of Leto as alive. She must condition herself to react out of a total belief that her brother was dead, killed here by Laza tigers. Not many humans could fool a Truthsayer, but she knew she could do it . . . might have to do it. The multi-lives she and Leto shared had taught them the way: a hypnotic process old in Sheba's time, although she might be the only human alive who could recall Sheba as a reality. The deep compulsions had been designed with care and, for a long time after Leto had gone, Ghanima reworked her self-awareness, building the lonely sister, the surviving twin, until it was a believable totality. As she did this, she found the inner world becoming silent, blanked away from intrusion into her consciousness. It was a side effect she had not expected.

*If only Leto could have lived to learn this,* she thought, and she did not find the thought a paradox. Standing, she peered down at the desert where the tiger had taken Leto. There was a sound growing in the sand out there, a familiar sound to Fremen: the passage of a worm. Rare as they had become in these parts, a worm still came. Perhaps the first cat's death throes . . . . Yes, Leto had killed one cat before the other one got him. It was oddly symbolic that a worm should come. So deep was her compulsion that she saw three dark spots far down on the sand: the two tigers and Leto. Then the worm came and there was only sand with its surface broken into new waves by the passage of Shai-Hulud. It had not been a very large worm . . . but large enough. And her compulsion did not permit her to see a small figure riding on the ringed back.

Fighting her grief, Ghanima sealed her Fremkit, crept cautiously from her hiding place. Hand on her maula pistol, she scanned the area. No sign of a human with a transmitter. She worked her way up the rocks and across to the far side, creeping through moonshadows, waiting and waiting to be sure no assassin lurked in her path.

Across the open space she could see torches at Tabr, the wavering activity of a search. A dark patch moved across the sand toward The Attendant. She chose her path to run far to the north of the approaching party, went down to the sand and moved into the dune shadows. Careful to make her steps fall in a broken rhythm which would not attract a worm, she set out into the lonely distance which separated Tabr from the place where Leto had died. She would have to be careful at the qanat, she knew. Nothing must prevent her from telling how her brother had perished saving her from the tigers.

> *Governments, if they endure, always tend increasingly toward aristocratic*
> *forms. No government in history has been known to evade this pattern. And as*
> *the aristocracy develops, government tends more and more to act exclusively*
> *in the interests of the ruling class—whether that class be hereditary royalty,*
> *oligarchs of financial empires, or entrenched bureaucracy.*

> **—Politics as Repeat Phenomenon:**
> **Bene Gesserit Training Manual**

"Why does he make us this offer?" Farad'n asked. "That's not essential."

He and the Bashar Tyekanik stood in the lounge of Farad'n's private quarters. Wensicia sat at one side on a low blue divan, almost as audience rather than participant. She knew her position and resented it, but Farad'n had undergone a terrifying change since that morning when she'd revealed their plots to him.

It was late afternoon at Corrino Castle and the low light accented the quiet comfort of this lounge—a room lined with actual books reproduced in plastino, with shelves revealing a horde of player spools, data blocks, shigawire reels, mnemonic amplifiers. There were signs all around that this room was much used—worn places on the books, bright metal on the amplifiers, frayed corners on the data blocks. There was only one divan, but many chairs—all of them sensiform floaters designed for unobtrusive comfort.

Farad'n stood with his back to a window. He wore a plain Sardaukar uniform in gray and black with only the golden lion-claw symbols on the wings of his collar as decoration. He had chosen to receive the Bashar and his mother in this room, hoping to create an atmospere of more relaxed communication than could be achieved in a more formal setting. But Tyekanik's constant "My Lord this" and "My Lady that" kept them at a distance.

"My Lord, I don't think he'd make this offer were he unable to deliver," Tyekanik said.

"Of course not!" Wensicia intruded.

Farad'n merely glanced at his mother to silence her, asked: "We've put no pressure on Idaho, made no attempt to seek delivery on The Preacher's promise?"

"None," Tyekanik said.

"Then why does Duncan Idaho, noted all of his life for his fanatic loyalty to the Atreides, offer now to deliver the Lady Jessica into our hands?"

"These rumors of trouble on Arrakis . . ." Wensicia ventured.

"Unconfirmed," Farad'n said. "Is it possible that The Preacher has precipitated this?"

"Possible," Tyekanik said, "but I fail to see a motive."

"He speaks of seeking asylum for her," Farad'n said. "That might follow if those rumors . . ."

"Precisely," his mother said.

"Or it could be a ruse of some sort," Tyekanik said.

"We can make several assumptions and explore them," Farad'n said. "What if Idaho has fallen into disfavor with his Lady Alia?"

"That might explain matters," Wensicia said, "but he—"

"No word yet from the smugglers?" Farad'n interrupted. "Why can't we—"

"Transmission is always slow in this season," Tyekanik said, "and the needs of security . . ."

"Yes, of course, but still . . ." Farad'n shook his head. "I don't like our assumption."

"Don't be too quick to abandon it," Wensicia said. "All of those stories about Alia and that Priest, whatever his name is . . ."

"Javid," Farad'n said. "But the man's obviously—"

"He's been a very valuable source of imformation for us," Wensicia said.

"I was about to say that he's obviously a double agent," Farad'n said. "How could he indict himself in this? He's not to be trusted. There are too many signs . . ."

"I fail to see them," she said.

He was suddenly angry with her denseness. "Take my word for it, mother! The signs are there; I'll explain later."

"I'm afraid I must agree," Tyekanik said.

Wensicia lapsed into hurt silence. How dared they push her out of Council like this? As though she were some light-headed fancy woman with no—

"We mustn't forget that Idaho was once a ghola," Farad'n said. "The Tleilaxu . . ." He glanced sidelong at Tyekanik.

"That avenue will be explored," Tyekanik said. He found himself admiring the way Farad'n's mind worked: alert, questing, sharp. Yes, the Tleilaxu, in restoring life to Idaho, might have planted a powerful barb in him for their own use.

"But I fail to apprehend a Tleilaxu motive," Farad'n said.

"An investment in our fortunes," Tyekanik said. "A small insurance for future favors?"

"Large investment, I'd call it," Farad'n said.

"Dangerous," Wensicia said.

Farad'n had to agree with her. The Lady Jessica's capabilities were notorious in the Empire. After all, she'd been the one who'd trained Muad'Dib.

"If it became known that we hold her," Farad'n said.

"Yes, that'd be a two-edged sword," Tyekanik said. "But it need not be known."

"Let us assume," Farad'n said, "that we accept this offer. What's her value? Can we exchange her for something of greater importance?"

"Not openly," Wensicia said.

"Of course not!" He peered expectantly at Tyekanik.

"That remains to be seen," Tyekanik said.

Farad'n nodded. "Yes. I think if we accept, we should consider the Lady Jessica as money banked for indeterminate use. After all, wealth doesn't necessarily have to be spent on any particular thing. It's just . . . potentially useful."

"She'd be a very dangerous captive," Tyekanik said.

"There is that to consider, indeed," Farad'n said. "I'm told that her Bene Gesserit Ways permit her to manipulate a person just by the subtle employment of her voice."

"Or her body," Wensicia said. "Irulan once divulged to me some of the things she'd learned. She was showing off at the time, and I saw no demonstrations. Still the evidence is pretty conclusive that Bene Gesserits have their ways of achieving their ends."

"Were you suggesting," Farad'n asked, "that she might seduce me?"

Wensicia merely shrugged.

"I'd say she's a little old for that, wouldn't you?" Farad'n asked.

"With a Bene Gesserit, nothing's certain," Tyekanik said.

Farad'n experienced a shiver of excitement tinged with fear. Playing this game to restore House Corrino's high seat of power both attracted and repelled him. How attractive it remained, the urge to retire from this game into his preferred pursuits—historical research and learning the manifest duties for ruling here on Salusa Secundus. The restoration of his Sardaukar forces was a task in itself . . . and for that job, Tyek was still a good tool. One planet was, after all, an enormous responsibility. But the Empire was an even greater responsibility, far more attractive as an instrument of power. And the more he read about Muad'Dib/Paul Atreides, the more fascinated Farad'n became with the uses of power. As titular head of House Corrino, heir of Shaddam IV, what a great achievement it would be to restore his line to the Lion Throne. He wanted that! He wanted it. Farad'n had found that, by repeating this enticing litany to himself several times, he could overcome momentary doubts.

Tyekanik was speaking: ". . . and of course, the Bene Gesserit teach that peace encourages aggression, thus igniting war. The paradox of—"

"How did we get on this subject?" Farad'n asked, bringing his attention back from the arena of speculation.

"Why," Wensicia said sweetly, having noted the wool-gathering expression on her son's face. "I merely asked if Tyek was familiar with the driving philosophy behind the Sisterhood."

"Philosophy should be approached with irreverence," Farad'n said, turning to face Tyekanik. "In regard to Idaho's offer, I think we should inquire further.

When we think we know something, that's precisely the moment when we should look deeper into the thing."

"It will be done," Tyekanik said. He liked this cautious streak in Farad'n, but hoped it did not extend to those military decisions which required speed and precision.

With seeming irrelevancy, Farad'n asked: "Do you know what I find most interesting about the history of Arrakis? It was the custom in primitive times for Fremen to kill on sight anyone not clad in a stillsuit with its easily visible and characteristic hood."

"What is your fascination with the stillsuit?" Tyekanik asked.

"So you've noticed, eh?"

"How could we not notice?" Wensicia asked.

Farad'n sent an irritated glance at his mother. Why did she interrupt like that? He returned his attention to Tyekanik.

"The stillsuit is the key to that planet's character, Tyek. It's the hallmark of Dune. People tend to focus on the physical characteristics: the stillsuit conserves body moisture, recycles it, and makes it possible to exist on such a planet. You now, the Fremen custom was to have one stillsuit for each member of a family, *except* for food gatherers. They had spares. But please note, both of you—" He moved to include his mother in this. "—how garments which appear to be stillsuits, but really aren't, have become high fashion throughout the Empire. It's such a dominant characteristic for humans to copy the conqueror!"

"Do you really find such information valuable?" Tyekanik asked, his tone puzzled.

"Tyek, Tyek—without such information, one cannot govern. I said the stillsuit was the key to their character and it is! It's a conservative thing. The mistakes they make will be conservative mistakes."

Tyekanik glanced at Wensicia, who was staring at her son with a worried frown. This characteristic of Farad'n's both attracted and worried the Bashar. It was so unlike old Shaddam. Now, there had been an essential Sardaukar: a military killer with few inhibitions. But Shaddam had fallen to the Atreides under that damnable Paul. Indeed, what he read of Paul Atreides revealed just such characteristics as Farad'n now displayed. It was possible that Farad'n might hesitate less than the Atreides over brutal necessities, but that was his Sardaukar training.

"Many have governed without using this kind of information," Tyekanik said.

Farad'n merely stared at him for a moment. Then: "Governed and failed."

Tyekanik's mouth drew into a stiff line at this obvious allusion to Shaddam's failure. That had been a Sardaukar failure, too, and no Sardaukar could recall it easily.

Having made his point, Farad'n said: "You see, Tyek, the influence of a planet upon the mass unconscious of its inhabitants has never been fully appreciated. To defeat the Atreides, we must understand not only Caladan but Arrakis: one planet soft and the other a training ground for hard decisions. That was a unique event, that marriage of Atreides and Fremen. We must know how it worked or we won't be able to match it, let alone defeat it."

"What does this have to do with Idaho's offer?" Wensicia demanded.

Farad'n glanced pityingly down at his mother. "We begin their defeat by the kinds of stress we introduce into their society. That's a very powerful tool: stress. And the lack of it is important, too. Did you not mark how the Atreides helped things grow soft and easy here?"

Tyekanik allowed himself a curt nod of agreement. That was a good point. The Sardaukar could not be permitted to grow too soft. This offer from Idaho still bothered him, though. He said: "Perhaps it'd be best to reject the offer."

"Not yet," Wensicia said. "We've a spectrum of choices open to us. Our task is to identify as much of the spectrum as we can. My son is right: we need more information."

Farad'n stared at her, measuring her intent as well as the surface meaning of her words. "But will we know when we've passed the point of no alternate choice?" he asked.

A sour chuckle came from Tyekanik. "If you ask me, we're long past the point of no return."

Farad'n tipped his head back to laugh aloud. "But we still have alternate choices, Tyek! When we come to the end of our rope, that's an important place to recognize!"

> *In this age when the means of human transport include devices which can span the deeps of space in transtime, and other devices which can carry men swiftly over virtually impassable planetary surfaces, it seems odd to think of attempting long journeys afoot. Yet this remains a primary means of travel on Arrakis, a fact attributed partly to preference and partly to the brutal treatment which this planet reserves for anything mechanical. In the strictures of Arrakis, human flesh remains the most durable and reliable resource for the Hajj. Perhaps it is the implicit awareness of this fact which makes Arrakis the ultimate mirror of the soul.*

> **—Handbook of the Hajj**

Slowly, cautiously, Ghanima made her way back to Tabr, holding herself to the deepest shadows of the dunes, crouching in stillness as the search party passed to the south of her. Terrible awareness gripped her: the worm which had taken the tigers and Leto's body, the dangers ahead. He was gone; her twin was gone. She put aside all fears and nurtured her rage. In this, she was pure Fremen. And she knew this, reveling in it.

She understood what was said about Fremen. They were not supposed to have a conscience, having lost it in a burning for revenge against those who had driven them from planet to planet in the long wandering. That was foolishness, of course. Only the rawest primitive had no conscience. Fremen possessed a highly evolved conscience which centered on their own welfare as a people. It was only to outsiders that they seemed brutish—just as outsiders appeared brutish to Fremen. Every Fremen knew very well that he could do a brutal thing and feel no guilt. Fremen did not feel guilt for the same things that aroused such feelings in others. Their rituals provided a freedom from guilts which might otherwise have destroyed them. They knew in their deepest awareness that any transgression could be ascribed, at least in part, to well recognized extenuating circumstances: "the failure of authority," or "a *natural* bad tendency" shared by all humans, or to "bad luck," which any sentient creature should be able to identify as a collision between mortal flesh and the outer chaos of the universe.

In this context Ghanima felt herself to be the pure Fremen, a carefully prepared extension of tribal brutality. She needed only a target—and that, obviously, was House Corrino. She longed to see Farad'n's blood spilled on the ground at her feet.

No enemy awaited her at the qanat. Even the search parties had gone elsewhere. She crossed the water on an earth bridge, crept through tall grass toward the covert exit of the sietch. Abruptly light flared ahead of her and Ghanima threw herself flat on the ground. She peered out through stalks of giant alfalfa. A woman had entered the covert passage from the outside, and someone had remembered to prepare that passage in the way any sietch entrance should be prepared. In troubled times, one greeted anyone entering the sietch with bright light, temporarily blinding the newcomer and giving guards time to decide. But such a greeting was never meant to be broadcast out over the desert. The light visible here meant the outer seals had been left aside.

Ghanima felt a tug of bitterness at this betrayal of sietch security: this flowing light. The ways of the lace-shirt Fremen were to be found everywhere!

The light continued to throw its fan over the ground at the cliff base. A young girl ran out of the orchard's darkness into the light, something fearful about her movements. Ghanima could see the bright circle of a glowglobe within the passage, a halo of insects around it. The light illuminated two dark shadows in the passage: a man and the girl. They were holding hands as they stared into each other's eyes.

Ghanima sensed something wrong about the man and woman there. They were not just two lovers stealing a moment from the search. The light was suspended above and beyond them in the passage. The two talked against a glowing arch, throwing their shadows into the outer night where anyone could be a watcher of their movements. Now and again the man would free a hand. The hand would come gesturing into the light, a sharp and furtive movement which, once completed, returned to the shadows.

Lonely sounds of night creatures filled the darkness around Ghanima, but she screened out such distractions.

What was it about these two?

The man's motions were so static, so careful.

He turned. Reflection from the woman's robe illuminated him, exposing a raw red face with a large blotchy nose. Ghanima drew in a deep, silent breath of recognition. *Palimbasha!* He was a grandson of a Naib whose sons had fallen in Atreides service. The face—and another thing revealed by the open swinging of his robe as he turned—drew for Ghanima a complete picture. He wore a belt beneath the robe, and attached to the belt was a box which glistened with keys and dials. It was an instrument of the Tleilaxu or the Ixians for certain. And it had to be the transmitter which had released the tigers. Palimbasha. This meant that another Naibate family had gone over to House Corrino.

Who was the woman, then? No matter. She was someone being used by Palimbasha.

Unbidden, a Bene Gesserit thought came into Ghanima's mind: *Each planet has its own period, and each life likewise.*

She recalled Palimbasha well, watching him there with that woman, seeing the transmitter, the furtive movements. Palimbasha taught in the sietch school. Mathematics. The man was a mathematical boor. He had attempted to explain Muad'Dib through mathematics until censured by the Priesthood. He was a mind-slaver and his enslaving process could be understood with extreme simplicity: he transferred technical knowledge without a transfer of values.

*I should've suspected him earlier,* she thought. *The signs were all there.*

Then, with an acid tightening of her stomach: *He killed my brother!*

She forced herself to calmness. Palimbasha would kill her, too, if she tried to pass him there in the covert passage. Now she understood the reason for this un-Fremen display of light, this betrayal of the hidden entrance. They were watching by that light to see if either of their victims had escaped. It must be a terrible time of waiting for them, not knowing. And now that Ghanima had seen the transmitter, she could explain certain of the hand motions. Palimbasha was depressing one of the transmitter's keys frequently, an angry gesture.

The presence of this pair said much to Ghanima. Likely every way into the sietch carried a similar watcher in its depths.

She scratched her nose where dust tickled it. Her wounded leg still throbbed and the knife arm ached when it didn't burn. The fingers remained numb. Should it come to a knife, she would have to use the blade in her left hand.

Ghanima thought of using the maula pistol, but its characteristic sound would be sure to attract unwanted attention. Some other way would have to be found.

Palimbasha turned away from the entrance once more. He was a dark object against the light. The woman turned her attention to the outer night while she talked. There was a trained alertness about the woman, a sense that she knew how to look into the shadows, using the edges of her eyes. She was more than just a useful tool, then. She was part of the deeper conspiracy.

Ghanima recalled now that Palimbasha aspired to be a Kaymakam, a political governor under the Regency. He would be part of a larger plan, that was clear. There would be many others with him. Even here in Tabr. Ghanima examined the edges of the problem thus exposed, probed into it. If she could take one of these guardians alive, many others would be forfeit.

The *whiffle* of a small animal drinking at the qanat behind her caught Ghanima's awareness. Natural sounds and natural things. Her memory searched through a strange silent barrier in her mind, found a priestess of Jowf captured in Assyria by Sennacherib. The memories of that priestess told Ghanima what would have to be done here. Palimbasha and his woman there were mere children, wayward and dangerous. They knew nothing of Jowf, knew not even the name of the planet where Sennacherib and the priestess had faded into dust. The thing which was about to happen to the pair of conspirators, if it were explained to them, could only be explained in terms of beginning here.

And ending here.

Rolling onto her side, Ghanima freed her Fremkit, slipped the sandsnorkel from its bindings. She uncapped the sandsnorkel, removed the long filter within it. Now she had an open tube. She selected a needle from the repair pack, unsheathed her cryknife, and inserted the needle into the poison hollow at the knife's tip, that place where once a sandworm's nerve had fitted. Her injured arm made the work difficult. She moved carefully and slowly, handling the poisoned needle with caution while she took a wad of spice-fiber from its chamber in the kit. The needle's shank fitted tightly into the fiber wad, forming a missile which went tightly into the tube of the sandsnorkel.

Holding the weapon flat, Ghanima wormed her way closer to the light, moving slowly to cause minimal disturbance in the alfalfa. As she moved, she studied the insects around the light. Yes, there were piume flies in that fluttering mob. They were notorious biters of human flesh. The poisoned dart might go unnoticed, swatted aside as a biting fly. A decision remained: Which one of those two to take—the man or the woman!

*Muriz.* The name came unbidden into Ghanima's mind. That was the woman's name. It recalled things said about her. She was one of those who fluttered around Palimbasha as the insects fluttered around the light. She was easily swayed, a weak one.

Very well. Palimbasha had chosen the wrong companion for this night.

Ghanima put the tube to her mouth and, with the memory of the priestess of Jowf clearly in her awareness, she sighted carefully, expelled her breath in one strong surge.

Palimbasha batted at his cheek, drew away a hand with a speck of blood on it. The needle was nowhere to be seen, flicked away by the motion of his own hand.

The woman said something soothing and Palimbasha laughed. As he laughed, his legs began to give away beneath him. He sagged against the woman, who tried to support him. She was still staggering with the dead weight when Ghanima came up beside her and pressed the point of an unsheathed cryknife against her waist.

In a conversational tone, Ghanima said: "Make no sudden moves, Muriz. My knife is poisoned. You may let go of Palimbasha now. He is dead."

*In all major socializing forces you will find an underlying movement to gain and maintain power through the use of words. From witch doctor to priest to bureaucrat it is all the same. A governed populace must be conditioned to accept power-words as actual things, to confuse the symbolized system with the tangible universe. In the maintenance of such a power structure, certain symbols are kept out of the reach of common understanding—symbols such as those dealing with economic manipulation or those which define the local interpretation of sanity. Symbol-secrecy of this form leads to the development of fragmented sub-languages, each being a signal that its users are accumulating some form of power. With this insight into a power process, our Imperial Security Force must be ever alert to the formation of sub-languages.*

**—Lectures to the Arrakeen War College
by The Princess Irulan**

"It is perhaps unnecessary to tell you," Farad'n said, "but to avoid any errors I'll announce that a mute has been stationed with orders to kill you both should I show signs of succumbing to witchery."

He did not expect to see any effect from these words. Both the Lady Jessica and Idaho gratified his expectations.

Farad'n had chosen with care the setting for this first examination of the pair, Shaddam's old State Audience Chamber. What it lacked in grandeur it made up for with exotic appointments. Outside it was a winter afternoon, but the windowless chamber's lighting simulated a timeless summer day bathed in golden light from artfully scattered glowglobes of the purest Ixian crystal.

The news from Arrakis filled Farad'n with quiet elation. Leto, the male twin, was dead, killed by an assassin-tiger. Ghanima, the surviving sister, was in the custody of her aunt and reputedly was a hostage. The full report did much to explain the presence of Idaho and the Lady Jessica. Sanctuary was what they wanted. Corrino spies reported an uneasy truce on Arrakis. Alia had agreed to submit herself to a test called "the Trial of Possession," the purpose of which had not been fully explained. However, no date had been set for this trial and two Corrino spies believed it might never take place. This much was certain, though: there had been fighting between desert Fremen and the Imperial Military Fremen, an abortive civil war which had brought government to a temporary standstill. Stilgar's holdings were now neutral ground, designated after an exchange of hostages. Ghanima evidently had been considered one of these hostages, although the working of this remained unclear.

Jessica and Idaho had been brought to the audience securely bound in suspensor chairs. Both were held down by deadly thin strands of shigawire which would cut flesh at the slightest struggle. Two Sardaukar troopers had brought them, checked the bindings, and had gone away silently.

The warning had, indeed, been unnecessary. Jessica had seen the armed mute standing against a wall at her right, an old but efficient projectile weapon in his hand. She allowed her gaze to roam over the room's exotic inlays. The broad leaves of the rare iron bush had been set with eye pearls and interlaced to form the center crescent of the domed ceiling. The floor beneath her was alternate blocks of diamond wood and kabuzu shell arranged within rectangular borders of passaquet bones. These had been set on end, laser-cut and polished. Selected hard materials decorated the walls in stress-woven patterns which outlined the four positions of the Lion symbol claimed by descendants of the late Shaddam IV. The lions were executed in wild gold.

Farad'n had chosen to receive the captives while standing. He wore uniform shorts and a light golden jacket of elf-silk open at the throat. His only decoration was the princely starburst of his royal family worn at the left breast. He was attended by the Bashar Tyekanik wearing Sardaukar dress tans and heavy boots, an ornate lasgun carried in a front holster at the belt buckle. Tyekanik, whose heavy visage was known to Jessica from Bene Gesserit reports, stood three paces to the left and slightly behind Farad'n. A single throne of dark wood sat on the floor near the wall directly behind the two.

"Now," Farad'n said, addressing Jessica, "do you have anything to say?"

"I would inquire why we are bound thus?" Jessica said, indicating the shigawire.

"We have only just now received reports from Arrakis to explain your presence here," Farad'n said. "Perhaps I'll have you released presently." He smiled. "If you—" He broke off as his mother entered by the State doors behind the captives.

Wensicia hurried past Jessica and Idaho without a glance, presented a small message to Farad'n, actuated it. He studied the glowing face, glancing occasionally at Jessica, back to the cube. The glowing face went dark and he returned the cube to his mother, indicated that she should show it to Tyekanik. While she was doing this, he scowled at Jessica.

Presently Wensicia stationed herself at Farad'n's right hand, the darkened cube in her hand, partly concealed in a fold of her white gown.

Jessica glanced to her right at Idaho, but he refused to meet her gaze.

"The Bene Gesserit are displeased with me," Farad'n said. "They believe I was responsible for the death of your grandson."

Jessica held her face emotionless, thinking: *So Ghanima's story is to be trusted, unless . . .* She didn't like the suspected unknowns.

Idaho closed his eyes, opened them to glance at Jessica. She continued to stare at Farad'n. Idaho had told her about his Rhajia vision, but she'd seemed unworried. He didn't know how to catalogue her lack of emotion. She obviously knew something, though, that she wasn't revealing.

"This is the situation," Farad'n said, and he proceeded to explain everything he'd learned about events on Arrakis, leaving out nothing. He concluded: "Your granddaughter survives, but she's reportedly in the custody of the Lady Alia. This should gratify you."

"Did you kill my grandson?" Jessica asked.

Farad'n answered truthfully: "I did not. I recently learned of a plot, but it was not of my making."

Jessica looked at Wensicia, saw the gloating expression on that heart-shaped face, thought: *Her doing! The lioness schemes for her cub.* This was a game the lioness might live to regret.

Returning her attention to Farad'n, Jessica said: "But the Sisterhood believes you killed him."

Farad'n turned to his mother. "Show her the message."

As Wensicia hesitated, he spoke with an edge of anger which Jessica noted for future use. "I said show it to her!"

Face pale, Wensicia presented the message face of the cube to Jessica, activated it. Words flowed across the face, responding to Jessica's eye movements: *"Bene Gesserit Council on Wallach IX files formal protest against House Corrino in assassination of Leto Atreides II. Arguments and showing of evidence are assigned to Landsraad Internal Security Commission. Neutral ground will be chosen and names of judges will be submitted for approval by all parties. Your immediate response required. Sabit Rekush for the Landsraad."*

Wensicia returned to her son's side.

"How do you intend to respond?" Jessica asked.

Wensicia said: "Since my son has not yet been formally invested as head of House Corrino, I will—Where are you going?" This last was addressed to Farad'n who, as she spoke, turned and headed for a side door near the watchful mute.

Farad'n paused, half turned. "I'm going back to my books and the other pursuits which hold much more interest for me."

"How dare you?" Wensicia demanded. A dark flush spread from her neck up across her cheeks.

"I'll dare quite a few things in my own name," Farad'n said. "You have made decisions in my name, decisions which I find extremely distasteful. Either I will make the decisions in my own name from this point on or you can find yourself another heir for House Corrino!"

Jessica passed her gaze swiftly across the participants in this confrontation, seeing the real anger in Farad'n. The Bashar Aide stood stiffly at attention, trying to make it appear that he had heard nothing. Wensicia hesitated on the brink of screaming rage. Farad'n appeared perfectly willing to accept any outcome from his throw of the dice. Jessica rather admired his poise, seeing many things in this confrontation which could be of value to her. It seemed that the decision to send assassin tigers against her grandchildren had been made without Farad'n's knowledge. There could be little doubt of his truthfulness in saying he'd learned of the plot after its inception. There was no mistaking the real anger in his eyes as he stood there, ready to accept any decision.

Wensicia took a deep, trembling breath. Then: "Very well. The formal investiture will take place tomorrow. You may act in advance of it now." She looked at Tyekanik, who refused to meet her gaze.

*There'll be a screaming fight once mother and son get out of here,* Jessica thought. *But I do believe he has won.* She allowed her thoughts to return then to the message from the Landsraad. The Sisterhood had judged their messengers with a finesse which did credit to Bene Gesserit planning. Hidden in the formal notice of protest was a message for Jessica's eyes. The fact of the message said the Sisterhood's spies knew Jessica's situation and they'd gauged Farad'n with a superb nicety to guess he'd show it to his captive.

"I'd like an answer to my question," Jessica said, addressing herself to Farad'n as he returned to face her.

"I shall tell the Landsraad that I had nothing to do with this assassination," Farad'n said. "I will add that I share the Sisterhood's distaste for the manner of it, although I cannot be completely displeased at the outcome. My apologies for any grief this may have caused you. Fortune passes everywhere."

*Fortune passes everywhere!* Jessica thought. That'd been a favorite saying of her Duke, and there'd been something in Farad'n's manner which said he knew this. She forced herself to ignore the possibility that they'd really killed Leto. She had to assume that Ghanima's fears for Leto had motivated a complete revelation of the twins' plan. The smugglers would put Gurney in position to meet Leto then and the Sisterhood's devices would be carried out. Leto had to be tested. He had to be. Without the testing he was doomed as Alia was doomed. And Ghanima. . . Well, that could be faced later. There was no way to send the pre-born before a Reverend Mother Gaius Helen Mohiam.

Jessica allowed herself a deep sigh. "Sooner or later," she said, "it'll occur to someone that you and my granddaughter could unite our two Houses and heal old wounds."

"This has already been mentioned to me as a possibility," Farad'n said, glancing briefly at his mother. "My response was that I'd prefer to await the outcome of recent events on Arrakis. There's no need for a hasty decision."

"There's always the possibility that you've already played into my daughter's hands," Jessica said.

Farad'n stiffened, "Explain!"

"Matters on Arrakis are not as they may seem to you," Jessica said. "Alia plays her own game, Abomination's game. My granddaughter is in danger unless Alia can contrive a way to use her."

"You expect me to believe that you and your daughter oppose each other, that Atreides fights Atreides?"

Jessica looked at Wensicia, back to Farad'n. "Corrino fights Corrino."

A wry smile moved Farad'n's lips. "Well taken. How would I have played into your daughter's hands?"

"By becoming implicated in my grandson's death, by abducting me."

"Abduct . . ."

"Don't trust this witch," Wensicia cautioned.

"I'll choose whom to trust, mother," Farad'n said. "Forgive me, Lady Jessica, but I don't understand this matter of abduction. I'd understood that you and your faithful retainer—"

"Who is Alia's husband," Jessica said.

Farad'n turned a measuring stare on Idaho, looked to the Bashar. "What think you, Tyek?"

The Bashar apparently was having thoughts similar to those Jessica professed. He said: "I like her reasoning. Caution!"

"He's a ghola-mentat," Farad'n said. "We could test him to the death and not find a certain answer."

"But it's a safe working assumption that we may've been tricked," Tyekanik said.

Jessica knew the moment had come to make her move. Now if Idaho's grief only kept him locked in the part he'd chosen. She disliked using him this way, but there were larger considerations.

"To begin with," Jessica said, "I might announce publicly that I came here of my own free choice."

"Interesting," Farad'n said.

"You'd have to trust me and grant me the complete freedom of Salusa Secundus," Jessica said. "There could be no appearance that I spoke out of compulsion."

"No!" Wensicia protested.

Farad'n ignored her. "What reason would you give?"

"That I'm the Sisterhood's plenipotentiary sent here to take over your education."

"But the Sisterhood accuses—"

"That'd require a decisive action from you," Jessica said.

"Don't trust her!" Wensicia said.

With extreme politeness, Farad'n glanced at her, said: "If you interrupt me once more, I'll have Tyek remove you. He heard you consent to the formal investiture. That binds him to *me* now."

"She's a witch, I tell you!" Wensicia looked to the mute against the side wall.

Farad'n hesitated. Then: "Tyek, what think you? Have I been witched?"

"Not in my judgment. She—"

"You've both been witched!"

"Mother." His tone was flat and final.

Wensicia clenched her fists, tried to speak, whirled, and fled the room.

Addressing himself once more to Jessica, Farad'n asked: "Would the Bene Gesserit consent to this?"

"They would."

Farad'n absorbed the implications of this, smiled tightly. "What does the Sisterhood want in all of this?"

"Your marriage to my granddaughter."

Idaho shot a questioning look at Jessica, made as though to speak, but remained silent.

Jessica said: "You were going to say something, Duncan?"

"I was going to say that the Bene Gesserit want what they've always wanted: a universe which won't interfere with them."

"An obvious assumption," Farad'n said, "but I hardly see why you intrude with it."

Idaho's eyebrows managed the shrug which the shigawire would not permit his body. Disconcertingly, he smiled.

Farad'n saw the smile, whirled to confront Idaho. "I amuse you?"

"This whole situation amuses me. Someone in your family has compromised the Spacing Guild by using them to carry instruments of assassination to Arrakis, instruments whose intent could not be concealed. You've offended the Bene Gesserit by killing a male they wanted for their breeding pro—"

"You call me a liar, ghola?"

"No. I believe you didn't know about the plot. But I thought the situation needed bringing into focus."

"Don't forget that he's a mentat," Jessica cautioned.

"My very thought," Farad'n said. Once more he faced Jessica. "Let us say that I free you and you make your announcement. That still leaves the matter of your grandson's death. The mentat is correct."

"Was it your mother?" Jessica asked.

"My Lord!" Tyekanik warned.

"It's all right, Tyek." Farad'n waved a hand easily. "And if I say it was my mother?"

Risking everything in the test of this internal break among the Corrino, Jessica said: "You must denounce her and banish her."

"My Lord," Tyekanik said, "there could be trickery within trickery here."

Idaho said: "And the Lady Jessica and I are the ones who've been tricked."

Farad'n's jaw hardened.

And Jessica thought: *Don't interfere, Duncan! Not now!* But Idaho's own words had sent her own Bene Gesserit abilities at logic into motion. He shocked her. She began to wonder if there were the possibility that she was being used in ways she didn't understand. Ghanima and Leto. . . . The pre-born could draw upon countless inner experiences, a storehouse of advice far more extensive than the living Bene Gesserit depended upon. And there was that other question: Had her own Sisterhood been completely candid with her? They still might not trust her. After all, she'd betrayed them once . . . to her Duke.

Farad'n looked at Idaho with a puzzled frown. "Mentat, I need to know what this Preacher is to you."

"He arranged the passage here. I . . . . We did not exchange ten words. Others acted for him. He could be . . . . He could be Paul Atreides, but I don't have enough data for certainty. All I know for certain is that it was time for me to leave and he had the means."

"You speak of being tricked," Farad'n reminded him.

"Alia expects you to kill us quietly and conceal the evidence of it," Idaho said. "Having rid her of the Lady Jessica, I'm no longer useful. And the Lady Jessica, having served her Sisterhood's purposes, is no longer useful to them. Alia will be calling the Bene Gesserit to account, but they will win."

Jessica closed her eyes in concentration. He was right! She could hear the mentat firmness of his voice, that deep sincerity of pronouncement. The pattern fell into place without a chink. She took two deep breaths and triggered the mnemonic trance, rolled the data through her mind, came out of the trance and opened her eyes. It was done while Farad'n moved from in front of her to a position within half a step of Idaho—a space of no more than three steps.

"Say no more, Duncan," Jessica said, and she thought mournfully of how Leto had warned her against Bene Gesserit conditioning.

Idaho, about to speak, closed his mouth.

"I command here," Farad'n said. "Continue, mentat."

Idaho remained silent.

Farad'n half turned to study Jessica.

She stared at a point on the far wall, reviewing what Idaho and the trance had built. The Bene Gesserit hadn't abandoned the Atreides line, of course. But they wanted control of a Kwisatz Haderach and they'd invested too much in the long breeding program. They wanted the open clash between Atreides and Corrino, a situation where they could step in as arbiters. And Duncan was right. They'd emerge with control of both Ghanima and Farad'n. It was the only compromise possible. The wonder was that Alia hadn't seen it. Jessica swallowed past a tightness in her throat. Alia . . . . Abomination! Ghanima was right to pity her. But who was left to pity Ghanima?

"The Sisterhood has promised to put you on the throne with Ghanima as your mate," Jessica said.

Farad'n took a backward step. Did the witch read minds?

"They worked secretly and not through your mother," Jessica said. "They told you I was not privy to their plan."

Jessica read revelation in Farad'n's face. How open he was. But it was true, the whole structure. Idaho had demonstrated masterful abilities as a mentat in seeing through to the fabric on the limited data available to him.

"So they played a double game and told you," Farad'n said.

"They told me nothing of this," Jessica said. "Duncan was correct: they tricked me." She nodded to herself. It had been a classic delaying action in the Sisterhood's traditional pattern—a reasonable story, easily accepted because it squared with what one might believe of their motives. But they wanted Jessica out of the way—a flawed sister who'd failed them once.

Tyekanik moved to Farad'n's side. "My Lord, these two are too dangerous to—"

"Wait a bit, Tyek," Farad'n said. "There are wheels within wheels here." He faced Jessica. "We've had reasons to believe that Alia might offer herself as my bride."

Idaho gave an involuntary start, controlled himself. Blood began dripping from his left wrist where the shigawire had cut.

Jessica allowed herself a small, eye-widening response. She who'd known the original Leto as lover, father of her children, confidant and friend, saw his trait of cold reasoning filtered now through the twistings of an Abomination.

"Will you accept?" Idaho asked.

"It is being considered."

"Duncan, I told you to be silent," Jessica said. She addressed Farad'n. "Her price was two inconsequential deaths—the two of us."

"We suspected treachery," Farad'n said. "Wasn't it your son who said 'treachery breeds treachery'?"

"The Sisterhood is out to control both Atreides and Corrino," Jessica said. "Isn't that obvious?"

"We're toying now with the idea of accepting your offer, Lady Jessica, but Duncan Idaho should be sent back to his loving wife."

*Pain is a function of nerves,* Idaho reminded himself. *Pain comes as light comes to the eyes. Effort comes from the muscles, not from nerves.* It was an old mentat drill and he completed it in the space of one breath, flexed his right wrist and severed an artery against the shigawire.

Tyekanik leaped to the chair, hit its trip lock to release the bindings, shouted for medical aid. It was revealing that assistants came swarming at once through doors hidden in wall panels.

*There was always a bit of foolishness in Duncan,* Jessica thought.

Farad'n studied Jessica a moment while the medics ministered to Idaho. "I didn't say I was going to accept his Alia."

"That's not why he cut his wrist," Jessica said.

"Oh? I thought he was simply removing himself."

"You're not that stupid," Jessica said. "Stop pretending with me."

He smiled. "I'm well aware that Alia would destroy me. Not even the Bene Gesserit could expect me to accept her."

Jessica bent a weighted stare upon Farad'n. What was this young scion of House Corrino? He didn't play the fool well. Again, she recalled Leto's words that she'd encounter an interesting student. And The Preacher wanted this as well, Idaho said. She wished she'd met this Preacher.

"Will you banish Wensicia?" Jessica asked.

"It seems a reasonable bargain," Farad'n said.

Jessica glanced at Idaho. The medics had finished with him. Less dangerous restraints held him in the floater chair.

"Mentats should beware of absolutes," she said.

"I'm tired," Idaho said. "You've no idea how tired I am."

"When it's overexploited, even loyalty wears out finally," Farad'n said.

Again Jessica shot that measuring stare at him.

Farad'n, seeing this, thought: *In time she'll know me for certain and that could be valuable. A renegade Bene Gesserit of my own! It's the one thing her son had that I don't have. Let her get only a glimpse of me now. She can see the rest later.*

"A fair exchange," Farad'n said. "I accept your offer on your terms." He signaled the mute against the wall with a complex flickering of fingers. The mute nodded. Farad'n bent to the chair's controls, released Jessica.

Tyekanik asked: "My Lord, are you sure?"

"Isn't it what we discussed?" Farad'n asked.

"Yes, but . . ."

Farad'n chuckled, addressed Jessica. "Tyek suspects my sources. But one learns from books and reels only that certain things can be done. Actual learning requires that you do those things."

Jessica mused on this as she lifted herself from the chair. Her mind returned to Farad'n's hand signals. He had an Atreides-style battle language! It spoke of careful analysis. Someone here was consciously copying the Atreides.

"Of course," Jessica said, "you'll want me to teach you as the Bene Gesserit are taught."

Farad'n beamed at her. "The one offer I cannot resist," he said.

> *The password was given to me by a man who died in the dungeons of Arrakeen. You see, that is where I got this ring in the shape of a tortoise. It was in the suk outside the city where I was hidden by the rebels. The password? Oh, that has been changed many times since then. It was "Persistence." And the countersign was "Tortoise." It got me out of there alive. That's why I bought this ring: a reminder.*

**—Tagir Mohandis: Conversations with a Friend**

Leto was far out on the sand when he heard the worm behind him, coming to his thumper there and the dusting of spice he'd spread around the dead tigers. There was a good omen for this beginning of their plan: worms were scarce enough in these parts most times. The worm was not essential, but it helped. There would be no need for Ghanima to explain a missing body.

By this time he knew that Ghanima had worked herself into the belief that he was dead. Only a tiny, isolated capsule of awareness would remain to her, a walled-off memory which could be recalled by words uttered in the ancient language shared only by the two of them in all of this universe. *Secher Nbiw.* If she heard those words: *Golden Path* . . . only then would she remember him. Until then, he was dead.

Now Leto felt truly alone.

He moved with the random walk which made only those sounds natural to the desert. Nothing in his passage would tell that worm back there that human flesh moved here. It was a way of walking so deeply conditioned in him that he didn't need to think about it. The feet moved of themselves, no measurable rhythm to their pacing. Any sound his feet made could be ascribed to the wind, to gravity. No human passed here.

When the worm had done its work behind him, Leto crouched behind a dune's slipface and peered back toward The Attendant. Yes, he was far enough. He planted a thumper and summoned his transportation. The worm came swiftly, giving him barely enough time to position himself before it engulfed the thumper. As it passed, he went up its side on the Maker hooks, opened the sensitive leading edge of a ring, and turned the mindless beast southeastward. It was a small worm, but strong. He could sense the strength in its twisting as it hissed across the dunes. There was a following breeze and he felt the heat of their passage, the friction which the worm converted to the beginnings of spice within itself.

As the worm moved, his mind moved. Stilgar had taken him up for his first worm journey. Leto had only to let his memory flow and he could hear Stilgar's voice: calm and precise, full of politeness from another age. Not for Stilgar the threatening staggers of a Fremen drunk on spice-liquor. Not for Stilgar the loud voice and bluster of these times. No—Stilgar had his duties. He was an instructor of royalty: "In the olden times, the birds were named for their songs. Each wind had its name. A six-klick wind was called a Pastaza, a twenty-klick wind was Cueshma, and a hundred-klick wind was Heinali—Heinali, the man-pusher. Then there was the wind of the demon in the open desert: Hulasikali Wala, the wind that eats flesh."

And Leto, who'd already known these things, had nodded his gratitude at the wisdom of such instruction.

But Stilgar's voice could be filled with many valuable things.

"There were in olden times certain tribes which were known to be water hunters. They were called Iduali, which meant 'water insects,' because those people wouldn't hesitate to steal the water of another Fremen. If they caught you alone in the desert they would not even leave you the water of your flesh. There was this place where they lived: Sietch Jacurutu. That's where the other tribes banded and wiped out the Iduali. That was a long time ago, before Kynes even—in my great-great-grandfather's days. And from that day to this, no Fremen has gone to Jacurutu. It is tabu."

Thus had Leto been reminded of knowledge which lay in his memory. It had been an important lesson about the working of memory. A memory was not enough, even for one whose past was as multiform as his, unless its use was known and its value revealed to judgment. Jacurutu would have water, a wind trap, all of the attributes of a Fremen sietch, plus the value without compare that no Fremen would venture there. Many of the young would not even know such a place as Jacurutu had ever existed. Oh, they would know about Fondak, of course, but that was a smuggler place.

It was a perfect place for the dead to hide—among the smugglers and the dead of another age.

*Thank you, Stilgar.*

The worm tired before dawn. Leto slid off its side and watched it dig itself into the dunes, moving slowly in the familiar pattern of the creatures. It would go deep and sulk.

*I must wait out the day,* he thought.

He stood atop a dune and scanned all around: emptiness, emptiness, emptiness. Only the wavering track of the vanished worm broke the pattern.

The slow cry of a nightbird challenged the first green line of light along the eastern horizon. Leto dug himself into the sand's concealment, inflated a stilltent around his body and sent the tip of a sandsnorkel questing for air.

For a long time before sleep came, he lay in the enforced darkness thinking about the decision he and Ghanima had made. It had not been an easy decision, especially for Ghanima. He had not told her all of his vision, nor all of the reasoning derived from it. It was a vision, not a dream, in his thinking now. But the peculiarity of this thing was that he saw it as a vision of a vision. If any argument existed to convince him that his father still lived, it lay in that vision-vision.

*The life of the prophet locks us into his vision,* Leto thought. *And a prophet could only break out of the vision by creating his death at variance with that vision.* That was how it appeared in Leto's doubled vision, and he pondered this as it related to the choice he had made. *Poor Baptist John,* he thought. *If he'd only had the courage to die some other way. . . . But perhaps his choice had been the bravest one. How do I know what alternatives faced him? I know what alternatives faced my father, though.*

Leto sighed. To turn his back on his father was like betraying a god. But the Atreides Empire needed shaking up. It had fallen into the worst of Paul's vision. How casually it obliterated men. It was done without a second thought. The mainspring of a religious insanity had been wound tight and left ticking.

*And we're locked in my father's vision.*

A way out of that insanity lay along the Golden Path, Leto knew. His father had seen it. But humanity might come out of that Golden Path and look back down it at Muad'Dib's time, seeing that as a better age. Humankind had to experience the alternative to Muad'Dib, though, or never understand its own myths.

*Security . . . peace . . . prosperity . . .*

Given the choice, there was little doubt what most citizens of this Empire would select.

*Though they hate me,* he thought. *Though Ghani hate me.*

His right hand itched, and he thought of the terrible glove in his vision-vision. *It will be,* he thought. *Yes, it will be.*

*Arrakis, give me strength,* he prayed. His planet remained strong and alive beneath him and around him. Its sand pressed close against the stilltent. Dune was a giant counting its massed riches. It was a beguiling entity, both beautiful and grossly ugly. The only coin its merchants really knew was the bloodpulse of their own power, no matter how that power had been amassed. They possessed this planet the way a man might possess a captive mistress, or the way the Bene Gesserits possessed their Sisters.

No wonder Stilgar hated the merchant-priests.

*Thank you, Stilgar.*

Leto recalled then the beauties of the old sietch ways, the life lived before the coming of the Imperium's technocracy, and his mind flowed as he knew Stilgar's dreams flowed. Before the glowglobes and lasers, before the ornithopters and spice-crawlers, there'd been another kind of life: brown-skinned mothers with babies on their hips, lamps which burned spice-oil amidst a heavy fragrance of cinnamon, Naibs who persuaded their people while knowing none could be compelled. It had been a dark swarming of life in rocky burrows . . .

*A terrible glove will restore the balance,* Leto thought.

Presently, he slept.

*I saw his blood and a piece of his robe which had been ripped by sharp claws. His sister reports vividly of the tigers, the sureness of their attack. We have questioned one of the plotters, and others are dead or in custody. Everything points to a Corrino plot. A Truthsayer has attested to this testimony.*

**—Stilgar's Report
to the Landsraad Commission**

Farad'n studied Duncan Idaho through the spy circuit, seeking a clue to that strange man's behavior. It was shortly after noon and Idaho waited outside the quarters assigned to the Lady Jessica, seeking audience with her. Would she see him? She'd know they were spied upon, of course. But would she see him?

Around Farad'n lay the room where Tyekanik had guided the training of the Laza tigers—an illegal room, really, filled as it was with forbidden instruments from the hands of the Tleilaxu and Ixians. By the movement of switches at his right hand, Farad'n could look at Idaho from six different angles, or shift to the interior of the Lady Jessica's suite where the spying facilities were equally sophisticated.

Idaho's eyes bothered Farad'n. Those pitted metal orbs which the Tleilaxu had given their ghola in the regrowth tanks marked their possessor as profoundly different from other humans. Farad'n touched his own eyelids, feeling the hard surfaces of the permanent contact lenses which concealed the total blue of his spice addiction. Idaho's eyes must record a different universe. How could it be otherwise. It almost tempted Farad'n to seek out the Tleilaxu surgeons and answer that question himself.

*Why did Idaho try to kill himself?*

*Was that really what he'd tried? He must've known we wouldn't permit it. Idaho remained a dangerous question mark.*

Tyekanik wanted to keep him on Salusa or kill him. Perhaps that would be best.

Farad'n shifted to a frontal view. Idaho sat on a hard bench outside the door to the Lady Jessica's suite. It was a windowless foyer with light wood walls decorated by lance pennants. Idaho had been on that bench for more than an hour and appeared ready to wait there forever. Farad'n bent close to the screen. The loyal swordmaster of the Atreides, instructor of Paul Muad'Dib, had been treated kindly by his years on Arrakis. He'd arrived with a youthful spring in his step. A steady spice diet must have helped him, of course. And that marvelous metabolic balance which the Tleilaxu tanks always imparted. Did Idaho really remember his past before the tanks? No other whom the Tleilaxu had revived could claim this. What an enigma this Idaho was!

The reports of his death were in the library. The Sardaukar who'd slain him reported his prowess: nineteen of their number dispatched by Idaho before he'd fallen. Nineteen Sardaukar! His flesh had been well worth sending to the regrowth tanks. But the Tleilaxu had made a mentat out of him. What a strange creature lived in that regrown flesh. How did it feel to be a human computer in addition to all of his other talents?

*Why did he try to kill himself?*

Farad'n knew his own talents and held few illusions about them. He was a historian-archaeologist and judge of men. Necessity had forced him to become an expert on those who would serve him—necessity and a careful study of the Atreides. He saw it as the price always demanded of aristocracy. To rule required accurate and incisive judgments about those who wielded your power. More than one ruler had fallen through mistakes and excesses of his underlings.

Careful study of the Atreides revealed a superb talent in choosing servants.

They'd known how to maintain loyalty, how to keep a fine edge on the ardor of their warriors.

Idaho was not acting in character.

*Why?*

Farad'n squinted his eyes, trying to see past the skin of this man. There was a sense of duration about Idaho, a feeling that he could not be worn down. He gave the impression of being self-contained, an organized and firmly integrated whole. The Tleilaxu tanks had set something more than human into motion. Farad'n sensed this. There was a self-renewing movement about the man, as though he acted in accordance with immutable laws, beginning anew at every ending. He moved in a fixed orbit with an endurance about him like that of a planet around a star. He would respond to pressure without breaking—merely shifting his orbit slightly but not really changing anything basic.

*Why did he cut his wrist?*

Whatever his motive, he had done it for the Atreides, for his ruling House. The Atreides were the star of his orbit.

*Somehow he believes that my holding the Lady Jessica here strengthens the Atreides.*

And Farad'n reminded himself: *A mentat thinks this.*

It gave the thought an added depth. Mentats made mistakes, but not often.

Having come to this conclusion, Farad'n almost summoned his aides to have them send the Lady Jessica away with Idaho. He poised himself on the point of acting, withdrew.

Both of those people—the ghola-mentat and the Bene Gesserit witch— remained counters of unknown denomination in this game of power. Idaho must be sent back because that would certainly stir up troubles on Arrakis. Jessica must be kept here, drained of her strange knowledge to benefit House Corrino.

Farad'n knew it was a subtle and deadly game he played. But he had prepared himself for this possibility over the years, ever since he'd realized that he was more intelligent, more sensitive than those around him. It had been a frightening discovery for a child, and he knew the library had been his refuge as well as his teacher.

Doubts ate at him now, though, and he wondered if he was quite up to this game. He'd alienated his mother, lost her counsel, but her decision had always been dangerous to him. Tigers! Their training had been an atrocity and their use had been stupidity. How easy they were to trace! She should be thankful to suffer nothing more than banishment. The Lady Jessica's advice had fitted his needs with a lovely precision there. She must be made to divulge the way of that Atreides thinking.

His doubts began to fade away. He thought of his Sardaukar once more growing tough and resilient through the rigorous training and the denial of luxury which he commanded. His Sardaukar legions remained small, but once more they were a man-to-man match for the Fremen. That served little purpose as long as the limits imposed by the Treaty of Arrakeen governed the relative size of the forces. Fremen could overwhelm him by their numbers—unless they were tied up and weakened by civil war.

It was too soon for a battle of Sardaukar against Fremen. He needed time. He needed new allies from among the discontented Houses Major and the newly powerful from the Houses Minor. He needed access to CHOAM financing. He needed the time for his Sardaukar to grow stronger and the Fremen to grow weaker.

Again Farad'n looked at the screen which revealed the patient ghola. Why did Idaho want to see the Lady Jessica at this time? He would know they were spied upon, that every word, every gesture would be recorded and analyzed. *Why?*

Farad'n glanced away from the screen to the ledge beside his control console. In the pale electronic light he could make out the spools which contained the latest reports from Arrakis. His spies were thorough; he had to give them credit. There was much to give him hope and pleasure in those reports. He closed his eyes, and the high points of those reports passed through his mind in the oddly editorial form to which he'd reduced the spools for his own uses:

*As the planet is made fertile, Fremen are freed of land pressures and their new communities lose the traditional sietch-stronghold character. From infancy, in the old sietch culture, the Fremen was taught by the rota: "Like the knowledge of your own being, the sietch forms a firm base from which you move out into the world and into the universe."*

*The traditional Fremen says: "Look to the Massif," meaning that the master science is the Law. But the new social structure is loosening those old legal restrictions; discipline grows lax. The new Fremen leaders know only their Low Catechism of ancestry plus the history which is camouflaged in the myth structure of their songs. People of the new communities are more volatile, more open; they quarrel more often and are less responsive to authority. The old sietch folk are more disciplined, more inclined to group actions and they tend to work harder; they are more careful of their resources. The old folk still believe that the orderly society is the fulfillment of the individual. The young grow away from this belief. Those remnants of the older culture which remain look at the young and say: "The death wind has etched away their past."*

Farad'n liked the pointedness of his own summary. The new diversity on Arrakis could only bring violence. He had the essential concepts firmly etched into the spools:

*The religion of Muad'Dib is based firmly in the old Fremen sietch cultural tradition while the new culture moves farther and farther from those disciplines.*

Not for the first time, Farad'n asked himself why Tyekanik had embraced that religion. Tyekanik behaved oddly in his new morality. He seemed utterly sincere, but carried along as though against his will. Tyekanik was like one who had stepped into the whirlwind to test it and had been caught up by forces beyond his control. Tyekanik's conversion annoyed Farad'n by its characterless completeness. It was a reversion to very old Sardaukar ways. He warned that the young Fremen might yet revert in a similar way, that the inborn, ingrained traditions would prevail.

Once more Farad'n thought about those report spools. They told of a disquieting thing: the persistence of a cultural remnant from the most ancient

Fremen times—"The Water of Conception." The amniotic fluid of the newborn was saved at birth, distilled into the first water fed to that child. The traditional form required a godmother to serve the water, saying: "Here is the water of thy conception." Even the young Fremen still followed this tradition with their own newborn.

*The water of thy conception.*

Farad'n found himself revolted by the idea of drinking water distilled from the amniotic fluid which had borne him. And he thought about the surviving twin, Ghanima, her mother dead when she'd taken that strange water. Had she reflected later upon that odd link with her past? Probably not. She'd been raised Fremen. What was natural and acceptable to Fremen had been natural and acceptable to her.

Momentarily Farad'n regretted the death of Leto II. It would have been interesting to discuss this point with him. Perhaps an opportunity would come to discuss it with Ghanima.

*Why did Idaho cut his wrists?*

The question persisted every time he glanced at the spy screen. Again doubts assailed Farad'n. He longed for the ability to sink into the mysterious spice trance as Paul Muad'Dib had done, there to seek out the future and *know* the answers to his questions. No matter how much spice he ingested, though, his ordinary awareness persisted in its singular flow of *now*, reflecting a universe of uncertainties.

The spy screen showed a servant opening the Lady Jessica's door. The woman beckoned Idaho, who arose from the bench and went through the door. The servant would file a complete report later, but Farad'n, his curiosity once more fully aroused, touched another switch on his console, watched as Idaho entered the sitting room of the Lady Jessica's quarters.

How calm and contained the mentat appeared. And how fathomless were his ghola eyes.

> *Above all else, the mentat must be a generalist, not a specialist. It is wise to have decisions of great moment monitored by generalists. Experts and specialists lead you quickly into chaos. They are a source of useless nitpicking, the ferocious quibble over a comma. The mentat-generalist, on the other hand, should bring to decision-making a healthy common sense. He must not cut himself off from the broad sweep of what is happening in his universe. He must remain capable of saying: "There's no real mystery about this at the moment. This is what we want now. It may prove wrong later, but we'll correct that when we come to it." The mentat-generalist must understand that anything which we can identify as our universe is merely part of larger phenomena. But the expert looks backward; he looks for living principles, knowing full well that such principles change, that they develop. It is to the characteristics of change itself that the mentat-generalist must look. There can be no permanent catalogue of such change, no handbook or manual. You must look at it with as few preconceptions as possible, asking yourself: "Now what is this thing doing?"*

**—The Mentat Handbook**

It was the day of the Kwisatz Haderach, the first Holy Day of those who followed Muad'Dib. It recognized the deified Paul Atreides as that person who was everywhere simultaneously, the male Bene Gesserit who mingled both male and female ancestry in an inseparable power to become the One-with-All. The faithful called this day *Ayil*, the Sacrifice, to commemorate the death which made his presence "real in all places."

The Preacher chose the early morning of this day to appear once more in the plaza of Alia's temple, defying the order for his arrest which everyone knew had been issued. The delicate truce prevailed between Alia's Priesthood and those desert tribes which had rebelled, but the presence of this truce could be felt as a tangible thing which moved everyone in Arrakeen with uneasiness. The Preacher did not dispel that mood.

It was the twenty-eighth day of official mourning for Muad'Dib's son, six days following the memorial rite at Old Pass which had been delayed by the rebellion. Even the fighting had not stopped the Hajj, though. The Preacher knew the plaza would be heavily thronged on this day. Most pilgrims tried to time their stay on Arrakis to cross *Ayil*, "to feel then the Holy Presence of the Kwisatz Haderach on His day."

The Preacher entered the plaza at first light, finding the place already thronging with the faithful. He kept a hand lightly on the shoulder of his young guide, sensing the cynical pride in the lad's walk. Now, when The Preacher approached, people noticed every nuance of his behavior. Such attention was not entirely distasteful to the young guide. The Preacher merely accepted it as a necessity.

Taking his stance on the third of the Temple's steps, The Preacher waited for the hush to come. When silence had spread like a wave through the throng and the hurrying footsteps of others come to listen could be heard at the plaza's limits, he cleared his throat. It was still morning-cold around him and light had not yet come down into the plaza from the building tops. He felt the grey hush of the great square as he began to speak.

"I have come to give homage and to preach in the memory of Leto Atreides II," he said, calling out in that strong voice so reminiscent of a wormsman from the desert. "I do it in compassion for all who suffer. I say to you what the dead Leto has learned, that tomorrow has not yet happened and may never happen. This moment here is the only observable time and place for us in our universe. I tell you to savor this moment and understand what it teaches. I tell you to learn that a government's growth and its death are apparent in the growth and death of its citizens."

A disturbed murmur passed through the plaza. Did he mock the death of Leto II? They wondered if Priest Guards would rush out now and arrest The Preacher.

Alia knew there would be no such interruption of The Preacher. It was her order that he be left unmolested on this day. She had disguised herself in a good stillsuit with a moisture mask to conceal her nose and mouth, and a common hooded robe to hide her hair. She stood in the second row beneath The Preacher, watching him carefully. Was this Paul? The years might have changed him thus. And he had always been superb with Voice, a fact which made it difficult to identify him by his speech. Paul could not have done it better. She felt that she had to know his identity before she could act against him. How his words dazzled her!

She sensed no irony in The Preacher's statement. He was using the seductive attraction of definite sentences uttered with a driving sincerity. People might stumble only momentarily at his meanings, realizing that he had meant them to stumble, teaching them in this fashion. Indeed, he picked up the crowd's response, saying: "Irony often masks the inability to think beyond one's assumptions. I am not being ironic. Ghanima has said to you that the blood of her brother cannot be washed off. I concur.

"It will be said that Leto has gone where his father went, has done what his father did. Muad'Dib's Church says he chose in behalf of his own humanity a course which might appear absurd and foolhardy, but which history will validate. That history is being rewritten even now.

"I say to you that there is another lesson to be learned from these lives and their endings."

Alia, alert to every nuance, asked herself why The Preacher said *endings* instead of *deaths*. Was he saying that one or both were not truly dead? How could that be? A Truthsayer had confirmed Ghanima's story. What was this Preacher doing, then? Was he making a statement of myth or reality?

"Note this other lesson well!" The Preacher thundered, lifting his arms. "If you would possess your humanity, let go of the universe!"

He lowered his arms, pointed his empty sockets directly at Alia. He seemed to be speaking intimately to her, an action so obvious that several around her turned to peer inquiringly in her direction. Alia shivered at the power in him. This could be Paul. It could!

"But I realize that humans cannot bear very much reality," he said. "Most lives are a flight from selfhood. Most prefer the truths of the stable. You stick your heads into the stanchions and munch contentedly until you die. Others use you for their purposes. Not once do you live outside the stable to lift your head and be your own creature. Muad'Dib came to tell you about that. Without understanding his message, you cannot revere him!"

Someone in the throng, possibly a Priest in disguise, could stand no more. His hoarse male voice was lifted in a shout: "You don't live the life of Muad'Dib! How dare you to tell others how they must revere him!"

"Because he's dead!" The Preacher bellowed.

Alia turned to see who had challenged The Preacher. The man remained hidden from her, but his voice came over the intervening heads in another shout: "If you believe him truly dead, then you are alone from this time forward!"

Surely it was a Priest, Alia thought. But she failed to recognize the voice.

"I come only to ask a simple question," The Preacher said. "Is Muad'Dib's death to be followed by the moral suicide of all men? Is that the inevitable aftermath of a Messiah?"

"Then you admit him Messiah!" the voice from the crowd shouted.

"Why not, since I'm the prophet of his times?" The Preacher asked.

There was such calm assurance in his tone and manner that even his challenger fell silent. The crowd responded with a disturbed murmur, a low animal sound.

"Yes," The Preacher repeated, "I am the prophet of these times."

Alia, concentrating on him, detected the subtle inflections of Voice. He'd certainly controlled the crowd. Was he Bene Gesserit trained? Was this another ploy of the Missionaria Protectiva? Not Paul at all, but just another part of the endless power game?

"I articulate the myth and the dream!" The Preacher shouted. "I am the physician who delivers the child and announces that the child is born. Yet I come to you at a time of death. Does that not disturb you? It should shake your souls!"

Even as she felt anger at his words, Alia understood the pointed way of his speech. With others, she found herself edging closer up the steps, crowding toward this tall man in desert garb. His young guide caught her attention: how bright-eyed and saucy the lad appeared! Would Muad'Dib employ such a cynical youth?

"I mean to disturb you!" The Preacher shouted. "It is my intention! I come here to combat the fraud and illusion of your conventional, institutionalized religion. As with all such religions, your institution moves toward cowardice, it moves toward mediocrity, inertia, and self-satisfaction."

Angry murmurs began to rise in the center of the throng.

Alia felt the tensions and gloatingly wondered if there might not be a riot. Could The Preacher handle these tensions? If not, he could die right here!

"That Priest who challenged me!" The Preacher called, pointing into the crowd.

*He knows!* Alia thought. A thrill ran through her, almost sexual in its undertones. This Preacher played a dangerous game, but he played it consummately.

"You, Priest in your mufti," The Preacher called, "you are a chaplain to the self-satisfied. I come not to challenge Muad'Dib but to challenge you! Is your religion real when it costs you nothing and carries no risk? Is your religion real when you fatten upon it? Is your religion real when you commit atrocities in its name? Whence comes your downward degeneration from the original revelation? Answer me, Priest!"

But the challenger remained silent. And Alia noted that the crowd once more was listening with avid submission to The Preacher's every word. By attacking the Priesthood, he had their sympathy! And if her spies were correct, most of the pilgrims and Fremen on Arrakis believed this man was Muad'Dib.

"The son of Muad'Dib risked!" The Preacher shouted, and Alia heard tears in his voice. "Muad'Dib risked! They paid their price! And what did Muad'Dib achieve? A religion which is doing away with him!"

*How different those words if they come from Paul himself,* Alia thought. *I must find out!* She moved closer up the steps and others moved with her. She pressed through the throng until she could almost reach out and touch this mysterious prophet. She smelled the desert on him, a mixture of spice and flint. Both The Preacher and his young guide were dusty, as though they'd recently come from the *bled*. She could see where The Preacher's hands were deeply veined along the skin protruding from the wrist seals of his stillsuit. She could see that one finger of his left hand had worn a ring; the indentation remained. Paul had worn a ring on that finger: the Atreides Hawk which now reposed in Sietch Tabr. Leto would have worn it had he lived . . . or had she permitted him to ascend the throne.

Again The Preacher aimed his empty sockets at Alia, spoke intimately, but with a voice which carried across the throng.

"Muad'Dib showed you two things: a certain future and an uncertain future. With full awareness, he confronted the ultimate uncertainty of the larger universe. He stepped off *blindly* from his position on this world. He showed us that men must do this always, choosing the uncertain instead of the certain." His voice, Alia noted, took on a pleading tone at the end of this statement.

Alia glanced around, slipped a hand onto the hilt of her crysknife. *If I killed him right now, what would they do?* Again, she felt a thrill rush through her. *If I killed him and revealed myself, denouncing The Preacher as impostor and heretic!*

But what if they proved it was Paul?

Someone pushed Alia even closer to him. She felt herself enthralled by his presence even as she fought to still her anger. Was this Paul? Gods below! What could she do?

"Why has another Leto been taken from us?" The Preacher demanded. There was real pain in his voice. "Answer me if you can! Ahhhh, their message is clear: abandon certainty." He repeated it in a rolling stentorian shout: "Abandon certainty! That's life's deepest command. That's what life's all about. We're a probe into the unknown, into the uncertain. Why can't you hear Muad'Dib? If certainty is knowing absolutely an absolute future, then that's only death disguised! Such a future becomes *now*! He showed you this!"

With a terrifying directness The Preacher reached out, grabbed Alia's arm. It was done without any groping or hesitation. She tried to pull away, but he held her in a painful grip, speaking directly into her face as those around them edged back in confusion.

"What did Paul Atreides tell you, woman?" he demanded.

How does he know I'm a woman? she asked herself. She wanted to sink into her inner lives, ask their protection, but the world within remained frighteningly silent, mesmerized by this figure from their past.

"He told you that completion equals death!" The Preacher shouted. "Absolute prediction is completion . . . is death!"

She tried to pry his fingers away. She wanted to grab her knife and slash him away from her, but dared not. She had never felt this daunted in all of her life.

The Preacher lifted his chin to speak over her to the crowd, shouted: "I give you Muad'Dib's words! He said, 'I'm going to rub your faces in things you try to avoid. I don't find it strange that all you want to believe is only that which comforts you. How else do humans invent the traps which betray us into mediocrity? How else do we define cowardice?' That's what Muad'Dib told you!"

Abruptly he released Alia's arm, thrust her into the crowd. She would have fallen but for the press of people supporting her.

"To exist is to stand out, away from the background," The Preacher said. "You aren't thinking or really existing unless you're willing to risk even your own sanity in the judgment of your existence."

Stepping down, The Preacher once more took Alia's arm—no faltering or hesitation. He was gentler this time, though. Leaning close, he pitched his voice for her ears alone, said: "Stop trying to pull me once more into the background, sister."

Then, hand on his young guide's shoulder, he stepped into the throng. Way was made for the strange pair. Hands reached out to touch The Preacher, but people reached with an awesome tenderness, fearful of what they might find beneath that dusty Fremen robe.

Alia stood alone in her shock as the throng moved out behind The Preacher. Certainty filled her. It was Paul. No doubt remained. It was her brother. She felt what the crowd felt. She had stood in the sacred presence and now her universe tumbled all about her. She wanted to run after him, pleading for him to save her from herself, but she could not move. While others pressed to follow The Preacher and his guide, she stood intoxicated with an absolute despair, a distress so deep that she could only tremble with it, unable to command her own muscles.

*What will I do? What will I do?* she asked

Now she did not even have Duncan to lean upon, nor her mother. The inner lives remained silent. There was Ghanima, held securely under guard within the Keep, but Alia could not bring herself to take this distress to the surviving twin.

*Everyone has turned against me. What can I do?*

> *The one-eyed view of our universe says you must not look far afield for problems. Such problems may never arrive. Instead, tend to the wolf within your fences. The packs ranging outside may not even exist.*

**—The Azhar Book; Shamra I:4**

Jessica awaited Idaho at the window of her sitting room. It was a comfortable room with soft divans and old-fashioned chairs. There wasn't a suspensor in any of her rooms, and the glowglobes were crystal from another age. Her window overlooked a courtyard garden one story down.

She heard the servant open the door, then the sound of Idaho's footsteps on the wood floor, then on the carpet. She listened without turning, kept her gaze upon the dappled light of the courtyard's green floor. The silent, fearful warfare of her emotions must be suppressed now. She took the deep breaths of her *prana-bindu* training, felt the outflow of enforced calmness.

The high sun threw its searchlight along a dustbeam into the courtyard, highlighting the silver wheel of a spiderweb stretched in the branches of a linden tree which reached almost to her window. It was cool within her quarters, but outside the sealed window there was air which trembled with petrified heat. Castle Corrino sat in a stagnant place which belied the greens in her courtyard.

She heard Idaho stop directly behind her.

Without turning, she said: "The gift of words is the gift of deception and illusion, Duncan. Why do you wish words with me?"

"It may be that only one of us will survive," he said.

"And you wish me to make a good report of your efforts?" She turned, saw how calmly he stood there, watching her with those grey metal eyes which held no center of focus. How blank they were!

"Duncan, is it possible that you're jealous of your place in history?"

She spoke accusingly and remembered as she spoke that other time when she'd confronted this man. He'd been drunk then, set to spy upon her, and was torn by conflicting obligations. But that had been a pre-ghola Duncan. This was not the same man at all. This one was not divided in his actions, not torn.

He proved her summation by smiling. "History holds its own court and delivers its own judgments," he said. "I doubt that I'll be concerned when my judgment's handed down."

"Why are you here?" she asked.

"For the same reason you're here, My Lady."

No outward sign betrayed the shocking power of those simple words, but she reflected at a furious pace: *Does he really know why I'm here?* How could he? Only Ghanima knew. Then had he enough data for a mentat computation? That was possible. And what if he said something to give her away? Would he do that if he shared her reason for being here? He must know their every movement, every word was being spied upon by Farad'n or his servants.

"House Atreides has come to a bitter crossroads," she said. "Family turned against itself. You were among my Duke's most loyal men, Duncan. When the Baron Harkonnen—"

"Let us not speak of Harkonnens," he said. "That was another age and your Duke is dead." And he wondered: *Can't she guess that Paul revealed the Harkonnen blood in the Atreides?* What a risk that had been for Paul, but it had bound Duncan Idaho even more firmly to him. The trust in the revelation had been a coin almost too great to imagine. Paul had known what the Baron's people had done to Idaho.

"House Atreides is not dead," Jessica said.

"What is House Atreides?" he asked. "Are you House Atreides? Is it Alia? Ghanima? Is it the people who serve this House? I look at those people and they bear the stamp of a travail beyond words! How can they be Atreides? Your son said it rightly: 'Travail and persecution are the lot of all who follow me.' I would break myself away from that, My Lady."

"Have you really gone over to Farad'n?"

"Isn't that what you've done, My Lady? Didn't you come here to convince Farad'n that a marriage to Ghanima would solve all of our problems?"

*Does he really think that?* she wondered. *Or is he talking for the watchful spies?*

"House Atreides has always been essentially an idea," she said. "You know that, Duncan. We bought loyalty with loyalty."

"Service to the people," Idaho sneered. "Ahhh, many's the time I've heard your Duke say it. He must lie uneasy in his grave, My Lady."

"Do you really think us fallen that low?"

"My Lady, did you not know that there are Fremen rebels—they call themselves 'Maquis of the Inner Desert'—who curse House Atreides and even Muad'Dib?"

"I heard Farad'n's report," she said, wondering where he was leading this conversation and to what point.

"More than that, My Lady. More than Farad'n's report. I've heard their curse myself. Here's the way of it: 'Burning be on you, Atreides! You shall have no souls, nor spirits, nor bodies, nor shades nor magic nor bones, nor hair nor utterances nor words. You shall have no grave, nor house nor hole nor tomb. You shall have no garden, nor tree nor bush. You shall have no water, nor bread nor light nor fire. You shall have no children, nor family nor heirs nor tribe. You shall have no head, nor arms nor legs nor gait nor seed. You shall have no seats on any planet. Your souls shall not be permitted to come up from the depths, and they shall never be among those permitted to live upon the earth. On no day shall you behold Shai-Hulud, but you shall be bound and fettered in the nethermost abomination and your souls shall never enter into the glorious light for ever and ever.' That's the way of the curse, My Lady. Can you imagine such hatred from Fremen? They consign all Atreides to the left hand of the damned, to the Woman-Sun which is full of burning."

Jessica allowed herself a shudder. Idaho undoubtedly had delivered those words with the same voice in which he'd heard the original curse. Why did he expose this to House Corrino? She could picture an outraged Fremen, terrible in his anger, standing before his tribe to vent that ancient curse. Why did Idaho want Farad'n to hear it?

"You make a strong argument for the marriage of Ghanima and Farad'n," she said.

"You always did have a single-minded approach to problems," he said. "Ghanima's Fremen. She can marry only one who pays no *fai*, no tax for protection. House Corrino gave up its entire CHOAM holdings to your son and his heirs. Farad'n exists on Atreides suffrance. And remember when your Duke planted the Hawk flag on Arrakis, remember what he said: 'Here I am; here I remain!' His bones are still there. And Farad'n would have to live on Arrakis, his Sardaukar with him."

Idaho shook his head at the very thought of such an alliance.

"There's an old saying that one peels a problem like an onion," she said, her voice cold. *How dare he patronize me? Unless he's performing for Farad'n's watchful eyes . . .*

"Somehow, I can't see Fremen and Sardaukar sharing a planet," Idaho said. "That's a layer which doesn't come off the onion."

She didn't like the thoughts which Idaho's words might arouse in Farad'n and his advisors, spoke sharply: "House Atreides is still the law in this

Empire!" And she thought: *Does Idaho want Farad'n to believe he can regain the throne without the Atreides?*

"Oh, yes," Idaho said. "I almost forgot. Atreides Law! As translated, of course, by the Priests of the Golden Elixir. I have but to close my eyes and I hear your Duke telling me that real estate is always gained and held by violence or the threat of it. Fortune passes everywhere, as Gurney used to sing it. The end justifies the means? Or do I have my proverbs mixed up? Well, it doesn't matter whether the mailed fist is brandished openly by Fremen legions or Sardaukar, or whether it's hidden in the Atreides Law—the fist is still there. And the onion layer won't come off, My Lady. You know, I wonder which fist Farad'n will demand?"

*What is he doing?* Jessica wondered. House Corrino would soak up this argument and gloat over it!

"So you think the Priests wouldn't let Ghanima marry Farad'n?" Jessica ventured, probing to see where Idaho's words might be leading.

"Let her? Gods below! The Priests will let Alia do whatever she decrees. She could marry Farad'n herself!"

*Is that where he's fishing?* Jessica wondered.

"No, My Lady," Idaho said. "That's not the issue. This Empire's people cannot distinguish between Atreides government and the government of Beast Rabban. Men die every day in Arrakeen's dungeons. I left because I could not give my sword arm another hour to the Atreides! Don't you understand what I'm saying, why I came here to you as the nearest Atreides representative? The Atreides Empire has betrayed your Duke and your son. I loved your daughter, but she went one way and I went another. If it comes down to it, I'll advise Farad'n to accept Ghanima's hand—or Alia's—only on his own terms!"

*Ahhh, he sets the stage for a formal withdrawal with honor from Atreides service,* she thought. But these other matters of which he spoke, could he possibly know how well they did her work for her? She scowled at him. "You know spies are listening to every word, don't you?"

"Spies?" He chuckled. "They listen as I would listen in their place. Don't you know how my loyalties move in a different way? Many's the night I've spent alone in the desert, and the Fremen are right about that place. In the desert, especially at night, you encounter the dangers of hard thinking."

"Is that where you heard Fremen curse us?"

"Yes. Among the al-Ourouba. At The Preacher's bidding I joined them, My Lady. We call ourselves the Zarr Sadus, those who refuse to submit to the Priests. I am here to make formal announcement to an Atreides that I've removed myself to enemy territory."

Jessica studied him, looking for betrayals of minutiae, but Idaho gave no indication that he spoke falsely or with hidden plans. Was it really possible that he'd gone over to Farad'n? She was reminded of her Sisterhood's maxim: *In human affairs, nothing remains enduring; all human affairs revolve in a helix, moving around and out.* If Idaho had really left the Atreides fold, that would explain his present behavior. He was moving around and out. She had to consider this as a possibility.

*But why had he emphasized that he did The Preacher's bidding?*

Jessica's mind raced and, having considered alternatives, she realized she might have to kill Idaho. The plan upon which she had staked her hopes remained so delicate that nothing could be allowed to interfere with it. Nothing. And Idaho's words hinted that he knew her plan. She gauged their relative positions in the room, moving and turning to place herself in position for a lethal blow.

"I've always considered the normalizing effect of the *faufreluches* to be a pillar of our strength," she said. Let him wonder why she shifted their conversation to the system of class distinction. "The Landsraad Council of the Great Houses, the regional Sysselraads, all deserve our—"

"You do not distract me," he said.

And Idaho wondered at how transparent her actions had become. Was it that she had grown lax in concealment, or had he finally breached the walls of her Bene Gesserit training? The latter, he decided, but some of it was in herself—a changing as she aged. It saddened him to see this just the way it saddened him to see the small way the new Fremen differed from the old. The passing of the desert was the passing of something precious to humans and he could not describe this thing, no more than he could describe what had happened to the Lady Jessica.

Jessica stared at Idaho in open astonishment, not trying to conceal her reaction. Could he read her that easily?

"You will not slay me," he said. He used the Fremen words of warning: "Don't throw your blood upon my knife." And he thought: *I've become very much the Fremen.* It gave him a wry sense of continuity to realize how deeply he had accepted the ways of the planet which had harbored his second life.

"I think you'd better leave," she said.

"Not until you accept my withdrawal from Atreides service."

"Accepted!" She bit it off. And only after she'd uttered the word did she realize how much pure reflex had gone into this exchange. She needed time to think and reconsider. How had Idaho known what she would do? She did not believe him capable of leaping Time in the spice way.

Idaho backed away from her until he felt the door behind him. He bowed. "Once more I call you My Lady, and then never again. My advice to Farad'n will be to send you back to Wallach, quietly and quickly, at the earliest practical moment. You are too dangerous a toy to keep around. Although I don't believe he thinks of you as a toy. You are working for the Sisterhood, not for the Atreides. I wonder now if you ever worked for the Atreides. You witches move too deeply and darkly for mere mortals ever to trust."

"A ghola considers himself a mere mortal," she jibed.

"Compared to you," he said.

"Leave!" she ordered.

"Such is my intention." He slipped out the door, passing the curious stare of the servant who'd obviously been listening.

*It's done,* he thought. *And they can read it in only one way.*

*Only in the realm of mathematics can you understand Muad'Dib's precise view of the future. Thus: first, we postulate any number of point-dimensions in space. (This is the classic n-fold extended aggregate, an aggregate of n dimensions.) With this framework, Time as commonly understood becomes an aggregate of one-dimensional properties. Applying this to the Muad'Dib phenomenon, we find that we either are confronted by new properties of Time or (by reduction through the infinity calculus) we are dealing with separate systems which contain n body properties. For Muad'Dib, we assume the latter. As demonstrated by the reduction, the point dimensions of the n-fold can only have separate existence within different frameworks of Time. Separate dimensions of Time are thus demonstrated to coexist. This being the inescapable case, Muad'Dib's predictions required that he perceive the n-fold not as extended aggregate but as an operation within a single framework. In effect, he froze his universe into that one framework which was his view of Time.*

—Palimbasha:
Lectures at Sietch Tabr

Leto lay at the crest of a dune, peering across open sand at a sinuous rock outcropping. The rock lay like an immense worm atop the sand, flat and threatening in the morning sunlight. Nothing stirred there. No bird circled overhead; no animal scampered among the rocks. He could see the slots of a windtrap almost at the center of the "worm's" back. There'd be water here. The rock-worm held the familiar appearance of a sietch shelter, except for the absence of living things. He lay quietly, blending with sand, watching.

One of Gurney Halleck's tunes kept flowing through his mind, monotonously persistent:

*Beneath the hill where the fox runs lightly,*
*A dappled sun shines brightly*
*Where my one love's still.*

*Beneath the hill in the fennel brake*
*I spy my love who cannot wake.*
*He hides in a grave*
*Beneath the hill.*

Where was the entrance to that place? Leto wondered.

He felt the certainty that this must be Jacurutu/Fondak, but there was something wrong here beyond the lack of animal movement. Something flickered at the edges of conscious perception, warning him.

What hid beneath the hill?

Lack of animals was bothersome. It aroused his Fremen sense of caution: *The absence says more than the presence when it comes to desert survival.* But there was a windtrap. There would be water and humans to use it. This was the tabu place which hid behind Fondak's name, its other identity lost even to the memories of most Fremen. And no birds or animals could be seen there.

No humans—yet here the Golden Path began.

His father had once said: "There's unknown all around at every moment. That's where you seek knowledge."

Leto glanced out to his right along the dune crests. There'd been a mother storm recently. Lake Azrak, the gypsum plain, had been exposed from beneath its sandy cover. Fremen superstition said that whoever saw the Biyan, the White Lands, was granted a two-edged wish, a wish which might destroy you. Leto saw only a gypsum plain which told him that open water had existed once here on Arrakis.

As it would exist once more.

He peered upward, swinging his gaze all around in the search for movement. The sky was porous after the storm. Light passing through it generated a sensation of milky presence, of a silver sun lost somewhere above the dust veil which persisted in the high altitudes.

Once more Leto brought his attention back to the sinuous rock. He slipped the binoculars from his Fremkit, focused their motile lenses and peered at the naked greyness, this outcropping where once the men of Jacurutu had lived. Amplification revealed a thorn bush, the one called Queen of Night. The bush nestled in shadows at a cleft which might be an entrance into the old sietch. He scanned the length of the outcropping. The silver sun turned reds into grey, casting a diffuse flatness over the long expanse of rock.

He rolled over, turning his back on Jacurutu, scanned the circle of his surroundings through the binoculars. Nothing in that wilderness preserved the marks of human passage. The wind already had obliterated his tracks, leaving only a vague roundness where he had dropped from his worm in the night.

Again he looked at Jacurutu. Except for the windtrap, there was no sign that men had ever passed this way. And without that sinuous length of rock, there was nothing here to subtract from the bleached sand, a wilderness from horizon to horizon.

Leto felt suddenly that he was in this place because he had refused to be confined in the system which his ancestors bequeathed him. He thought of how people looked at him, that universal mistake in every glance except Ghanima's.

*Except for that ragged mob of other memories, this child was never a child.*

*I must accept the responsibility for the decision we made,* he thought.

Once more he scanned the length of rock. By all the descriptions this had to be Fondak, and no other place could be Jacurutu. He felt a strange resonant relationship with the tabu of this place. In the Bene Gesserit Way, he opened his mind to Jacurutu, seeking to know nothing about it. *Knowing* was a barrier which prevented learning. For a few moments he allowed himself merely to resonate, making no demands, asking no questions.

The problem lay within the lack of animal life, but it was a particular thing which alerted him. He perceived it then: there were no scavenger birds—no eagles, no vultures, no hawks. Even when other life hid, these remained. Every watering place in this desert held its chain of life. At the end of the chain were the omnipresent scavengers. Nothing had come to investigate his presence. How well he knew the "watchdogs of the sietch," that line of crouched birds on the cliff's edge at Tabr, primitive undertakers waiting for flesh. As the Fremen said: "Our competitors." But they said it with no sense of jealousy because questing birds often told when strangers approached.

*What if this Fondak has been abandoned even by the smugglers?*

Leto paused to drink from one of his catchtubes.

*What if there's truly no water here?*

He reviewed his position. He'd run two worms into the sand getting here, riding them with his flail through the night, leaving them half dead. This was the Inner Desert where the smugglers' haven was to be found. If life existed here, if it *could* exist, it would have to be in the presence of water.

*What if there's no water? What if this isn't Fondak/Jacurutu?*

Once more he aimed his binoculars at the windtrap. Its outer edges were sand-etched, in need of maintenance, but enough of it remained. There should be water.

*But what if there isn't?*

An abandoned sietch might lose its water to the air, to any number of catastrophes. Why were there no scavenger birds? Killed for their water? By whom? How could all of them be eliminated? Poison?

*Poisoned water.*

The legend of Jacurutu contained no story of the cistern poisoned, but it might have been. If the original flocks were slain, would they not have been renewed by this time? The Iduali were wiped out generations ago and the stories never mentioned poison. Again he examined the rock with his binoculars. How could an entire sietch have been wiped out? Certainly some must have escaped. All of the inhabitants of a sietch were seldom at home. Parties roamed the desert, trekked to the towns.

With a sigh of resignation Leto put away his binoculars. He slipped down the hidden face of the dune, took extra care to dig in his stilltent and conceal all sign of his intrusion as he prepared to spend the hot hours. The sluggish currents of fatigue stole along his limbs as he sealed himself in the darkness. Within the tent's sweaty confines he spent much of the day drowsing, imagining mistakes he could have made. His dreams were defensive, but there could be no self-defense in this trial he and Ghanima had chosen. Failure would scald their souls. He ate spice-biscuits and slept, awakened to eat once more, to drink and return to sleep. It had been a long journey to this place, a severe test for the muscles of a child.

Toward evening he awoke refreshed, listened for signs of life. He crept out of his sandy shroud. There was dust high in the sky blowing one way, but he could feel sand stinging his cheek from another direction—sure sign there would be a weather change. He sensed a storm coming.

Cautiously he crept to the crest of his dune, peered once more at those enigmatic rocks. The intervening air was yellow. The signs spoke of a Coriolis storm approaching, the wind that carried death in its belly. There'd be a great winding sheet of wind-driven sand that might stretch across four degrees of latitude. The desolate emptiness of the gypsum pan was a yellow surface now, reflecting the dust clouds. The false peace of evening enfolded him. Then the day collapsed and it was night, the quick night of the Inner Desert. The rocks were transformed into angular peaks frosted by the light of First Moon. He felt sandthorns stinging his skin. A peal of dry thunder sounded like an echo from distant drums and, in the space between moonlight and darkness he saw sudden movement: bats. He could hear the stirring of their wings, their tiny squeaks.

*Bats.*

By design or accident, this place conveyed a sense of abandoned desolation. It was where the half-legendary smuggler stronghold should be: Fondak. But what if it were not Fondak? What if the tabu still ruled and this were only the shell of ghostly Jacurutu?

Leto crouched in the lee of his dune and waited for the night to settle into its own rhythms. Patience and caution—caution and patience. For a time he amused himself by reviewing Chaucer's route from London to Canterbury, listing the places from Southwark: two miles to the watering-place of St. Thomas, five miles to Deptford, six miles to Greenwich, thirty miles to Rochester, forty miles to Sittingbourne, fifty-five miles to Boughton under Blean, fifty-eight miles to Harbledown, and sixty miles to Canterbury. It gave him a sense of timeless buoyancy to know that few in his universe would recall Chaucer or know any London except the village on Gansireed. St. Thomas was preserved in the Orange Catholic Bible and the Azhar Book, but Canterbury was gone from the memories of men, as was the planet which had known it. There lay the burden of his memories, of all those lives which threatened to engulf him. He had made that trip to Canterbury once.

His present trip was longer, though, and more dangerous.

Presently he crept over the dune's crest and made his way toward the moonlit rocks. He blended with shadows, slid across the crests, made no sounds that might signal his presence.

The dust had gone as it often did just before a storm, and the night was brilliant. The day had revealed no movement, but he heard small creatures hustling in the darkness as he neared the rocks.

In a valley between two dunes he came upon a family of jerboa which scampered away at his approach. He eased over the next crest, his emotions beset by salty anxieties. That cleft he had seen—did it lead up to an entrance? And there were other concerns: the old-time sietch had always been guarded by traps—poisoned barbs in pits, poisoned spines on plants. He felt himself caught up in the Fremen agrapha: *The earminded night.* And he listened for the slightest sound.

The grey rocks towered above him now, made giant by his nearness. As he listened, he heard birds invisible in that cliff, the soft calling of winged prey. They were the sounds of daybirds, but abroad by night. What had turned their world around? Human predation?

Abruptly Leto froze against the sand. There was fire on the cliff, a ballet of glittering and mysterious gems against the night's black gauze, the sort of signal a sietch might send to wanderers across the *bled*. Who were these occupants of this place? He crept forward into the deepest shadows at the cliff's base, felt along the rock with a hand, sliding his body behind the hand as he sought the fissure he'd seen by daylight. He located it on his eighth step, slipped the sandsnorkel from his kit and probed the darkness. As he moved, something tight and binding dropped over his shoulders and arms, immobilizing him.

*Trapvine!*

He resisted the urge to struggle; that only made the vine pull tighter. He dropped the snorkel, flexed the fingers of his right hand, trying for the knife at his waist. He felt like a bare innocent for not throwing something into that fissure from a distance, testing the darkness for its dangers. His mind had been too occupied by the fire on the cliff.

Each movement tightened the trapvine, but his fingers at last touched the knife hilt. Stealthily, he closed his hand around the hilt, began to slip it free.

Flaring light enveloped him, arresting all movement.

"Ahhh, a fine catch in our net." It was a heavy masculine voice from behind Leto, something vaguely familiar in the tone. Leto tried to turn his head, aware of the vine's dangerous propensity to crush a body which moved too freely.

A hand took his knife before he could see his captor. The hand moved expertly over his body, extracting the small devices he and Ghanima carried as a matter of survival. Nothing escaped the searcher, not even the shigawire garrotte concealed in his hair.

Leto still had not seen the man.

Fingers did something with the trapvine and he found he could breathe easier, but the man said: "Do not struggle, Leto Atreides. I have your water in my cup."

By supreme effort Leto remained calm, said: "You know my name?"

"Of course! When one baits a trap, it's for a purpose. One aims for a specific quarry, not so?"

Leto remained silent, but his thoughts whirled.

"You feel betrayed!" the heavy voice said. Hands turned him around, gently but with an obvious show of strength. An adult male was telling the child what the odds were.

Leto stared up into the glare from twin floater flares, saw the black outline of a stillsuit-masked face, the hood. As his eyes adjusted he made out a dark strip of skin, the utterly shadowed eyes of melange addiction.

"You wonder why we went to all this trouble," the man said. His voice issued from the shielded lower part of his face with a curious muffled quality, as though he tried to conceal an accent.

"I long ago ceased to wonder at the numbers of people who want the Atreides twins dead," Leto said. "Their reasons are obvious."

As he spoke, Leto's mind flung itself against the unknown as against a cage, questing wildly for answers. A baited trap? But who had known except Ghanima? Impossible! Ghanima wouldn't betray her own brother. Then did someone know him well enough to predict his actions? Who? His grandmother? How could she?

"You could not be permitted to go on as you were," the man said. "Very bad. Before ascending the throne, you need to be educated." The whiteless eyes stared down at him. "You wonder how one could presume to educate such a person as yourself? You, with the knowledge of a multitude held there in your memories? That's just it, you see! You think yourself educated, but all you are is a repository of dead lives. You don't yet have a life of your own. You're just a walking surfeit of others, all with one goal—to seek death. Not good in a ruler, being a death seeker. You'd strew your surroundings with corpses. Your father, for example, never understood the—"

"You dare speak of him that way?"

"Many's the time I've dared it. He was only Paul Atreides, after all. Well, boy, welcome to your school."

The man brought a hand from beneath his robe, touched Leto's cheek. Leto felt the jolt of a slapshot and found himself winding downward into a darkness where a green flag waved. It was the green banner of the Atreides with its day and night symbols, its Dune staff which concealed a water tube. He heard the water gurgling as unconsciousness enfolded him. Or was it someone chuckling?

> We can still remember the golden days before Heisenberg, who showed humans the walls enclosing our predestined arguments. The lives within me find this amusing. Knowledge, you see, has no uses without purpose, but purpose is what builds enclosing walls.

> **—Leto Atreides II**
> **His Voice**

Alia found herself speaking harshly to the guards she confronted in the Temple foyer. There were nine of them in the dusty green uniforms of the suburban patrol, and they were still panting and sweating with their exertions. The light of late afternoon came in the door behind them. The area had been cleared of pilgrims.

"So my orders mean nothing to you?" she demanded.

And she wondered at her own anger, not trying to contain it but letting it run. Her body trembled with unleashed tensions. Idaho gone . . . the Lady Jessica . . . no reports . . . only rumors that they were on Salusa. Why hadn't Idaho sent a message? What had he done? Had he learned finally about Javid?

Alia wore the yellow of Arrakeen mourning, the color of the burning sun from Fremen history. In a few minutes she would be leading the second and final funeral procession to Old Gap, there to complete the stone marker for her lost nephew. The work would be completed in the night, fitting homage to one who'd been destined to lead Fremen.

The priestly guards appeared defiant in the face of her anger, not shamed at all. They stood in front of her, outlined by the waning light. The odor of their perspiration was easily detected through the light and inefficient stillsuits of city dwellers. Their leader, a tall blond Kaza with the bourka symbols of the

Cadelam family, flung his stillsuit mask aside to speak more clearly. His voice was full of the prideful intonations to be expected from a scion of the family which once had ruled at Sietch Abbir.

"Certainly we tried to capture him!"

The man was obviously outraged at her attack. "He speaks blasphemy! We know your orders, but we heard him with our own ears!"

"And you failed to catch him," Alia said, her voice low and accusing.

One of the other guards, a short young woman, tried to defend them. "The crowds were thick there! I swear people interfered with us!"

"We'll keep after him," the Cadelam said. "We'll not always fail."

Alia scowled. "Why won't you understand and obey me?"

"My Lady, we—"

"What will you do, scion of the *Cade Lamb*, if you capture him and find him to be, in truth, my brother?"

He obviously did not hear her special emphasis on his name, although he could not be a priestly guard without some education and the wit to go with it. Did he want to sacrifice himself?

The guardsman swallowed, then: "We must kill him ourselves, for he breeds disorder."

The others stood aghast at this, but still defiant. They knew what they had heard.

"He calls upon the tribes to band against you," the Cadelam said.

Alia knew how to handle him now. She spoke in a quiet, matter-of-fact tone: "I see. Then if you must sacrifice yourself this way, taking him openly for all to see who you are and what you do, then I guess you must."

"Sacrifice my . . ." He broke off, glanced at his companions. As Kaza of this group, their appointed leader, he had the right to speak for them, but he showed signs that he wished he'd remained silent. The other guards stirred uncomfortably. In the heat of the chase they'd defied Alia. One could only reflect now upon such defiance of the "Womb of Heaven." With obvious discomfort the guards opened a small space between themselves and their Kaza.

"For the good of the Church, our official reaction would have to be severe," Alia said. "You understand that, don't you?"

"But he—"

"I've heard him myself," she said. "But this is a special case."

"He cannot be Muad'Dib, My Lady!"

*How little you know!* she thought. She said: "We cannot risk taking him in the open, harming him where others could see it. If another opportunity presents itself, of course."

"He's always surrounded by crowds these days!"

"Then I fear you must be patient. Of course, if you insist on defying me . . . ." She left the consequences hanging in the air, unspoken, but well understood. The Cadelam was ambitious, a shining career before him.

"We didn't mean defiance, My Lady." The man had himself under control now. "We acted hastily; I can see that. Forgive us, but he—"

"Nothing has happened; nothing to forgive," she said, using the common

Fremen formula. It was one of the many ways a tribe kept peace in its ranks, and this Cadelam was still Old Fremen enough to remember that. His family carried a long tradition of leadership. Guilt was the Naib's whip, to be used sparingly. Fremen served best when free of guilt or resentment.

He showed his realization of her judgment by bowing his head, saying: "For the good of the tribe; I understand."

"Go refresh yourselves," she said. "The procession begins in a few minutes."

"Yes, My Lady." They bustled away, every movement revealing their relief at this escape.

Within Alia's head a bass voice rumbled: "Ahhhhh, you handled that most adroitly. One or two of them still believe you desire The Preacher dead. They'll find a way."

"Shut up!" she hissed. "Shut up! I should never have listened to you! Look what you've done . . ."

"Set you on the road to immortality," the bass voice said.

She felt it echoing in her skull like a distant ache, thought: *Where can I hide? There's no place to go!*

"Ghanima's knife is sharp," the Baron said. "Remember that."

Alia blinked. Yes, that was something to remember. Ghanima's knife was sharp. That knife might yet cut them out of their present predicament.

> *If you believe certain words, you believe their hidden arguments. When you believe something is right or wrong, true or false, you believe the assumptions in the words which express the arguments. Such assumptions are often full of holes, but remain most precious to the convinced.*

> **—The Open-Ended Proof**
> **from The Panoplia Prophetica**

Leto's mind floated in a stew of fierce odors. He recognized the heavy cinnamon of melange, the confined sweat of working bodies, the acridity of an uncapped deathstill, dust of many sorts with flint dominant. The odors formed a trail through dreamsand, created shapes of fog in a dead land. He knew these odors should tell him something, but part of him could not yet listen.

Thoughts like wraiths floated through his mind: *In this time I have no finished features; I am all of my ancestors. The sun setting into the sand is the sun setting into my soul. Once this multitude within me was great, but that's ended. I'm Fremen and I'll have a Fremen ending. The Golden Path is ended before it began. It's nothing but a windblown trail. We Fremen knew all the tricks to conceal ourselves: we left no feces, no water, no tracks . . . . Now, look at my trail vanish.*

A masculine voice spoke close to his ear: "I could kill you, Atreides. I could kill you, Atreides." It was repeated over and over until it lost meaning, became a wordless thing carried within Leto's dreaming, a litany of sorts: "I could kill you, Atreides."

Leto cleared his throat and felt the reality of this simple act shake his senses. His dry throat managed: "Who . . ."

The voice beside him said: "I'm an educated Fremen and I've killed my man. You took away our gods, Atreides. What do we care about your stinking Muad'Dib? Your god's dead!"

Was that a real Ouraba voice or another part of his dream? Leto opened his eyes, found himself unfettered on a hard couch. He looked upward at rock, dim glowglobes, an unmasked face staring down at him so close he could smell the breath with its familiar odors of a sietch diet. The face was Fremen; no mistaking the dark skin, those sharp features and water-wasted flesh. This was no fat city dweller. Here was a desert Fremen.

"I am Namri, father of Javid," the Fremen said. "Do you know me now, Atreides?"

"I know Javid," Leto husked.

"Yes, your family knows my son well. I am proud of him. You Atreides may know him even better soon."

"What . . ."

"I am one of your schoolmasters, Atreides. I have only one function: I am the one who could kill you. I'd do it gladly. In this school, to graduate is to live; to fail is to be given into my hands."

Leto heard implacable sincerity in that voice. It chilled him. This was a human gom jabbar, a high-handed enemy to test his right of entrance into the human concourse. Leto sensed his grandmother's hand in this and, behind her, the faceless masses of the Bene Gesserit. He writhed at this thought.

"Your education begins with me," Namri said. "That is just. It is fitting. Because it could end with me. Listen to me carefully now. My every word carries your life in it. Everything about me holds your death within it."

Leto shot his glance around the room: rock walls, barren—only this couch, the dim glowglobes, and a dark passage behind Namri.

"You will not get past me," Namri said. And Leto believed him.

"Why're you doing this?" Leto asked.

"That's already been explained. Think what plans are in your head! You are here and you cannot put a future into your present condition. The two don't go together: now and future. But if you really know your past, if you look backward and see where you've been, perhaps there'll be reason once more. If not, there will be your death."

Leto noted that Namri's tone was not unkind, but it was firm and no denying the death in it.

Namri rocked back on his heels, stared at the rock ceiling. "In olden times Fremen faced east at dawn. *Eos*, you know? That's dawn in one of the old tongues."

Bitter pride in his voice, Leto said: "I speak that tongue."

"You have not listened to me, then," Namri said, and there was a knife edge in his voice. "Night was the time of chaos. Day was the time of order. That's how it was in the time of that tongue you say you speak: darkness-disorder, light-order. We Fremen changed that. *Eos* was the light we distrusted. We preferred the light of a moon, or the stars. Light was too much order and that can be fatal. You see what you *Eos*-Atreides have done? Man is a creature of only that light which protects him. The sun was our enemy on Dune." Namri brought his gaze down to Leto's level. "What light do you prefer, Atreides?"

By Namri's poised attitude, Leto sensed that this question carried deep weight. Would the man kill him if he failed to answer correctly? He might. Leto saw Namri's hand resting quietly next to the polished hilt of a crysknife. A ring in the form of a magic tortoise glittered on the Fremen's knife hand.

Leto eased himself up onto his elbows, sent his mind questing into Fremen beliefs. They trusted the Law and loved to hear its lessons expounded in analogy, these old Fremen. The light of the moon?

"I prefer . . . the light of *Lisanu L'haqq,*" Leto said, watching Namri for subtle revelations. The man seemed disappointed, but his hand moved away from his knife. "It is the light of truth, the light of the perfect man in which the influence of al-Mutakallim can clearly be seen," Leto continued. "What other light would a human prefer?"

"You speak as one who recites, not one who believes," Namri said.

And Leto thought: *I did recite.* But he began to sense the drift of Namri's thoughts, how his words were filtered through early training in the ancient riddle game. Thousands of these riddles went into Fremen training, and Leto had but to bend his attention upon this custom to find examples flooding his mind. *"Challenge: Silence? Answer: The friend of the hunted."*

Namri nodded to himself as though he shared this thought, said: "There is a cave which is the cave of life for Fremen. It is an actual cave which the desert has hidden. Shai-Hulud, the great-grandfather of all Fremen, sealed up that cave. My Uncle Ziamad told me about it and he never lied to me. There is such a cave."

Leto heard the challenging silence when Namri finished speaking. *Cave of life?* "My Uncle Stilgar also told me of that cave," Leto said. "It was sealed to keep cowards from hiding there."

The reflection of a glowglobe glittered in Namri's shadowed eyes. He asked: "Would you Atreides open that cave? You seek to control life through a ministry: your Central Ministry for Information, Auqaf and Hajj. The Maulana in charge is called Kausar. He has come a long way from his family's beginnings at the salt mines of Niazi. Tell me, Atreides, what is wrong with your ministry?"

Leto sat up, aware now that he was fully into the riddle game with Namri and that the forfeit was death. The man gave every indication that he'd use that crysknife at the first wrong answer.

Namri, recognizing this awareness in Leto, said: "Believe me, Atreides. I am the clod-crusher. I am the Iron Hammer."

Now Leto understood. Namri saw himself as Mirzabah, the Iron Hammer with which the dead are beaten who cannot reply satisfactorily to the questions they must answer before entry into paradise.

*What was wrong with the central ministry which Alia and her priests had created?*

Leto thought of why he'd come into the desert, and a small hope returned to him that the Golden Path might yet appear in his universe. What this Namri implied by his question was no more than the motive which had driven Muad'Dib's own son into the desert.

"God's it is to show the way," Leto said.

Namri's chin jerked down and he stared sharply at Leto. "Can it be true that you believe this?" he demanded.

"It's why I am here," Leto said.

"To find the way?"

"To find it for myself." Leto put his feet over the edge of the cot. The rock floor was uncarpeted, cold. "The Priests created their ministry to hide the way."

"You speak like a true rebel," Namri said, and he rubbed the tortoise ring on his finger. "We shall see. Listen carefully once more. You know the high Shield Wall at Jalal-ud-Din? That Wall bears my family's marks carved there in the first days. Javid, my son, has seen those marks. Abedi Jalal, my nephew, has seen them. Mujahid Shafqat of the Other Ones, he too has seen our marks. In the season of the storms near Sukkar, I came down with my friend Yakup Abad near that place. The winds were blistering hot like the whirlwinds from which we learned our dances. We did not take time to see the marks because a storm blocked the way. But when the storm passed we saw the vision of Thatta upon the blown sand. The face of Shakir Ali was there for a moment, looking down upon his city of tombs. The vision was gone in the instant, but we all saw it. Tell me, Atreides, where can I find that city of tombs?"

*The whirlwinds from which we learned our dances,* Leto thought. *The vision of Thatta and Shakir Ali.* These were the words of a Zensunni Wanderer, those who considered themselves to be the only true men of the desert.

*And Fremen were forbidden to have tombs.*

"The city of tombs is at the end of the path which all men follow," Leto said. And he dredged up the Zensunni beatifics. "It is in a garden one thousand paces square. There is a fine entry corridor two hundred and thirty-three paces long and one hundred paces wide all paved with marble from ancient Jaipur. Therein dwells ar-Razzaq, he who provides food for all who ask. And on the Day of Reckoning, all who stand up and seek the city of tombs shall not find it. For it is written: That which you know in one world, you shall not find in another."

"Again you recite without belief," Namri sneered. "But I'll accept it for now because I think you know why you're here." A cold smile touched his lips. "I give you a *provisional* future, Atreides."

Leto studied the man warily. Was this another question in disguise?

"Good!" Namri said. "Your awareness has been prepared. I've sunk home the barbs. One more thing, then. Have you heard that they wear imitation stillsuits in the cities of far Kadrish?"

As Namri waited, Leto quested in his mind for a hidden meaning. *Imitation stillsuits? They were worn on many planets.* He said: "The foppish habits of Kadrish are an old story often repeated. The wise animal blends into its surroundings."

Namri nodded slowly. Then: "The one who trapped you and brought you here will see you presently. Do not try to leave this place. It would be your death." Arising as he spoke, Namri went out into the dark passage.

For a long time after he had gone, Leto stared into the passage. He could hear sounds out there, the quiet voices of men on guard duty. Namri's story of the mirage-vision stayed with Leto. It brought up the long desert crossing to this place. It no longer mattered whether this were Jacurutu/Fondak. Namri was not a smuggler. He was something much more potent. And the game Namri played smelled of the Lady Jessica; it stank of the Bene Gesserit. Leto sensed an enclosing peril in this realization. But that dark passage where Namri had gone was the only exit from this room. And outside lay a strange sietch—beyond that, the desert. The harsh severity of that desert, its ordered chaos with mirages and endless dunes, came over Leto as part of the trap in which he was caught. He could recross that sand, but where would flight take him? The thought was like stagnant water. It would not quench his thirst.

> *Because of the one-pointed Time awareness in which the conventional mind remains immersed, humans tend to think of everything in a sequential, word-oriented framework. This mental trap produces very short-term concepts of effectiveness and consequences, a condition of constant, unplanned response to crises.*

**—Liet-Kynes**
**The Arrakis Workbook**

*Words and movements simultaneous,* Jessica reminded herself and she bent her thoughts to those necessary mental preparations for the coming encounter.

The hour was shortly after breakfast, the golden sun of Salusa Secundus just beginning to touch the far wall of the enclosed garden which she could see from her window. She had dressed herself carefully: the black hooded cloak of a Reverend Mother, but it carried the Atreides crest in gold worked into an embroidered ring around the hem and again at the cuff of each sleeve. Jessica arranged the drape of her garment carefully as she turned her back on the window, holding her left arm across her waist to present the Hawk motif of the crest.

Farad'n noted the Atreides symbols, commenting on them as he entered, but he betrayed no anger or surprise. She detected subtle humor in his voice and wondered at it. She saw that he had clad himself in the grey leotard which she had suggested. He sat on the low green divan to which she directed him, relaxing with his right arm along the back.

*Why do I trust her?* he wondered. *This is a Bene Gesserit witch!*

Jessica, reading the thought in the contrast between his relaxed body and the expression on his face, smiled and said: "You trust me because you know our bargain is a good one, and you want what I can teach you."

She saw the pinch of a scowl touch his brow, waved her left hand to calm him. "No, I don't read minds. I read the face, the body, the mannerisms, tone of voice, set of arms. Anyone can do this once they learn the Bene Gesserit Way."

"And you will teach me?"

"I'm sure you've studied the reports about us," she said. "Is there anywhere a report that we fail to deliver on a direct promise?"

"No reports, but . . ."

"We survive in part by the complete confidence which people can have in our truthfulness. That has not changed."

"I find this reasonable," he said. "I'm anxious to begin."

"I'm surprised you've never asked the Bene Gesserit for a teacher," she said. "They would've leaped at the opportunity to put you in their debt."

"My mother would never listen to me when I urged her to do this," he said. "But now . . . ." He shrugged, an eloquent comment on Wensicia's banishment. "Shall we start?"

"It would've been better to begin this when you were much younger," Jessica said. "It'll be harder for you now, and it'll take much longer. You'll have to begin by learning patience, extreme patience. I pray you'll not find it too high a price."

"Not for the reward you offer."

She heard the sincerity, the pressure of expectations, and the touch of awe in his voice. These formed a place to begin. She said: "The art of patience, then—starting with some elementary *prana-bindu* exercises for the legs and arms, for your breathing. We'll leave the hands and fingers for later. Are you ready?"

She seated herself on a stool facing him.

Farad'n nodded, holding an expectant expression on his face to conceal the sudden onset of fear. Tyekanik had warned him that there must be a trick in the Lady Jessica's offer, something brewed by the Sisterhood. "You cannot believe that she has abandoned them again or that they have abandoned her." Farad'n had stopped the argument with an angry outburst for which he'd been immediately sorry. His emotional reaction had made him agree more quickly with Tyekanik's precautions. Farad'n glanced at the corners of the room, the subtle gleam of *jems* in the coving. All that glittered was not *jems*: everything in this room would be recorded and good minds would review every nuance, every word, every movement.

Jessica smiled, noting the direction of his gaze, but not revealing that she knew where his attention had wandered. She said: "To learn patience in the Bene Gesserit Way, you must begin by recognizing the essential, raw instability of our universe. We call nature—meaning this totality in all of its manifestations—the Ultimate Non-Absolute. To free your vision and permit you to recognize this conditional nature's changing ways, you will hold your two hands at arm's length in front of you. Stare at your extended hands, first the palms and then the backs. Examine the fingers, front and back. Do it."

Farad'n complied, but he felt foolish. These were his own hands. He knew them.

"Imagine your hands aging," Jessica said. "They must grow very old in your eyes. Very, very old. Notice how dry the skin . . ."

"My hands don't change," he said. He already could feel the muscles of his upper arms trembling.

"Continue to stare at your hands. Make them old, as old as you can imagine. It may take time. But when you see them age, reverse the process. Make your hands young again—as young as you can make them. Strive to take them from infancy to great age at will, back and forth, back and forth."

"They don't change!" he protested. His shoulders ached.

"If you demand it of your senses, your hands will change," she said. "Concentrate upon visualizing the flow of time which you desire: infancy to age, age to infancy. It may take you hours, days, months. But it can be achieved. Reversing that change-flow will teach you to see every system as something spinning in relative stability . . . only relative."

"I thought I was learning patience." She heard anger in his voice, an edge of frustration.

"And relative stability," she said. "This is the perspective which you create with your own belief, and beliefs can be manipulated by imagination. You've learned only a limited way of looking at the universe. Now you must make the universe your own creation. This will permit you to harness any relative stability to your own uses, to whatever uses you are capable of imagining."

"How long did you say it takes?"

"Patience," she reminded him.

A spontaneous grin touched his lips. His eyes wavered toward her.

"Look at your hands!" she snapped.

The grin vanished. His gaze jerked back to a fixated concentration upon his extended hands.

"What do I do when my arms get tired?" he asked.

"Stop talking and concentrate," she said. "If you become too tired, stop. Return to it after a few minutes of relaxation and exercise. You must persist in this until you succeed. At your present stage, this is more important than you could possibly realize. Learn this lesson or the others will not come."

Farad'n inhaled a deep breath, chewed his lips, stared at his hands. He turned them slowly: front, back, front back . . . . His shoulders trembled with fatigue. Front, back . . . . Nothing changed.

Jessica arose, crossed to the only door.

He spoke without removing his attention from his hands. "Where are you going?"

"You'll work better on this if you're alone. I'll return in about an hour. Patience."

"I know!"

She studied him a moment. How intent he looked. He reminded her with a heart-tugging abruptness of her own lost son. She permitted herself a sigh, said: "When I return I'll give you the exercise lessons to relieve your muscles. Give it time. You'll be astonished at what you can make your body and your senses do."

She let herself out.

The omnipresent guards took up station three paces behind her as she strode down the hall. Their awe and fear were obvious. They were Sardaukar, thrice-warned of her prowess, raised on the stories of their defeat by the Fremen of Arrakis. This witch was a Fremen Reverend Mother, a Bene Gesserit and an Atreides.

Jessica, glancing back, saw their stern faces as a mile-post in her design. She turned away as she came to the stairs, went down them and through a short passage into the garden below her windows.

*Now if only Duncan and Gurney can do their parts,* she thought as she felt the gravel of a pathway beneath her feet, saw the golden light filtered by greenery.

> *You will learn the integrated communication methods as you complete the next step in your mentat education. This is a gestalten function which will overlay data paths in your awareness, resolving complexities and masses of input from the mentat index-catalogue techniques which you already have mastered. Your initial problem will be the breaking tensions arising from the divergent assembly of minutiae/data on specialized subjects. Be warned. Without mentat overlay integration, you can be immersed in the Babel Problem, which is the label we give to the omnipresent dangers of achieving wrong combinations from accurate information.*

> **—The Mentat Handbook**

The sound of fabrics rubbing together sent sparks of awareness through Leto. He was surprised that he had tuned his sensitivity to the point where he automatically identified the fabrics from their sound: the combination came from a Fremen robe rubbing against the coarse hangings of a door curtain. He turned toward the sound. It came from the passage where Namri had gone minutes before. As Leto turned, he saw his captor enter. It was the same man who had taken him prisoner: the same dark strip of skin above the stillsuit mask, the identical searing eyes. The man lifted a hand to his mask, slipped the catchtube from his nostrils, lowered the mask and, in the same motion, flipped his hood back. Even before he focused on the scar of the inkvine whip along the man's jaw, Leto recognized him. The recognition was a totality in his awareness with the search for confirming details coming afterward. No mistake about it, this rolling lump of humanity, this warrior-troubadour, was Gurney Halleck!

Leto clenched his hands into fists, overcome momentarily by the shock of recognition. No Atreides retainer had ever been more loyal. None better at shield fighting. He'd been Paul's trusted confidant and teacher.

He was the Lady Jessica's servant.

These recognitions and more surged through Leto's mind. Gurney was his captor. Gurney and Namri were in this conspiracy together. And Jessica's hand was in it with them.

"I understand you've met our Namri," Halleck said. "Pray believe him, young sir. He has one function and one function only. He's the one capable of killing you should the need arise."

Leto responded automatically with his father's tones: "So you've joined my enemies, Gurney! I never thought the—"

"Try none of your devil tricks on me, lad," Halleck said. "I'm proof against them all. I follow your grandmother's orders. Your education has been planned to the last detail. It was she who approved my selection of Namri. What comes next, painful as it may seem, is at her command."

"And what does she command?"

Halleck lifted a hand from the folds of his robe, exposed a Fremen injector, primitive but efficient. Its transparent tube was charged with blue fluid.

Leto squirmed backward on the cot, was stopped by the rock wall. As he moved, Namri entered, stood beside Halleck with hand on crysknife. Together they blocked the only exit.

"I see you've recognized the spice essence," Halleck said. "You're to take the *worm trip*, lad. You must go through it. Otherwise, what your father dared and you dare not would hang over you for the rest of your days."

Leto shook his head wordlessly. This was the thing he and Ghanima knew could overwhelm them. Gurney was an ignorant fool! How could Jessica . . . Leto felt the father-presence in his memories. It surged into his mind, trying to strip away his defenses. Leto wanted to shriek outrage, could not move his lips. But this was the wordless thing which his pre-born awareness most feared. This was prescient trance, the reading of immutable future with all of its fixity and its terrors. Surely Jessica could not have ordered such an ordeal for her own grandson. But her presence loomed in his mind, filling him with acceptance arguments. Even the litany of fear was pressed upon him with a repetitive droning: *"I must not fear. Fear is the mind-killer. Fear is the little death that brings total obliteration. I will face my fear. I will permit it to pass over me and through me. And when it has gone past . . . ."*

With an oath already ancient when Chaldea was young, Leto tried to move, tried to leap at the two men standing over him, but his muscles refused to obey. As though he already existed in the trance, Leto saw Halleck's hand move, the injector approach. The light of a glowglobe sparkled within the blue fluid. The injector touched Leto's left arm. Pain lanced through him, shot upward to the muscles of his neck, into his head.

Abruptly Leto saw a young woman sitting outside a crude hut in dawnlight. She sat right there in front of him roasting coffee beans to a rose brown, adding cardamom and melange. The voice of a rebeck echoed from somewhere behind him. The music echoed and echoed until it entered his head, still echoing. It suffused his body and he felt himself to be large, very large, not a child at all. And his skin was not his own. He knew that sensation! His skin was not his own. Warmth spread through his body. As abruptly as his first vision, he found himself standing in darkness. It was night. Stars like a rain of embers fell in gusts from a brilliant cosmos.

Part of him knew there was no escaping, but still he tried to fight it until the father-presence intruded. "I will protect you in the trance. The others within will not take you."

Wind tumbled Leto, rolled him, hissing, pouring dust and sand over him, cutting his arms, his face, abrading his clothes, whipping the loose-torn ends of now useless fabric. But he felt no pain and he saw the cuts heal as rapidly as they appeared. Still he rolled with the wind. And his skin was not his own.

*It will happen!* he thought.

But the thought was distant and came as though it were not his own, not really his own; no more than his skin.

The vision absorbed him. It evolved into a stereologic memory which separated past and present, future and present, future and past. Each separation mingled into a trinocular focus which he sensed as the multi-dimensional relief map of his own future existence.

He thought: *Time is a measure of space, just as a range-finder is a measure of space, but measuring locks us into the place we measure.*

He sensed the trance deepening. It came as an amplification of internal consciousness which his self-identity soaked up and through which he felt himself changing. It was living Time and he could not arrest an instant of it. Memory fragments, future and past, deluged him. But they existed as montage-in-motion. Their relationships underwent a constant dance. His memory was a lens, an illuminating searchlight which picked out fragments, isolating them, but forever failing to stop the ceaseless motion and modification which surged into his view.

That which he and Ghanima had planned came through the searchlight, dominating everything, but now it terrified him. Vision reality ached in him. The uncritical inevitability made his ego cringe.

*And his skin was not his own!* Past and present tumbled through him, surging across the barriers of his terror. He could not separate them. One moment he felt himself setting forth on the Butlerian Jihad, eager to destroy any machine which simulated human awareness. That had to be the past—over and done with. Yet his senses hurtled through the experience, absorbing the most minute details. He heard a minister-companion speaking from a pulpit: *"We must negate the machines-that-think. Humans must set their own guidelines. This is not something machines can do. Reasoning depends upon programming, not on hardware, and we are the ultimate program!"*

He heard the voice clearly, knew his surroundings—a vast wooden hall with dark windows. Light came from sputtering flames. And his minister-companion said: *"Our Jihad is a 'dump program.' We dump the things which destroy us as humans!"*

And it was in Leto's mind that the speaker had been a servant of computers, one who knew them and serviced them. But the scene vanished and Ghanima stood in front of him, saying: *"Gurney knows. He told me. They're Duncan's words and Duncan was speaking as a mentat. 'In doing good, avoid notoriety; in doing evil, avoid self-awareness.'"*

That had to be future—far future. But he felt the reality. It was as intense as any past from his multitude of lives. And he whispered: "Isn't that true, father?"

But the father-presence within spoke warningly: *"Don't invite disaster! You're learning stroboscopic awareness now. Without it you could overrun yourself, lose your place-mark in Time."*

And the bas-relief imagery persisted. Intrusions hammered at him. Past-present-now. There was no true separation. He knew he had to flow with this thing, but the flowing terrified him. How could he return to any recognizable place? Yet he felt himself being forced to cease every effort of resistance. He could not grasp his new universe in motionless, labeled bits. No bit would stand still. Things could not be forever ordered and formulated. He had to find the rhythm of change and see between the changes to the changing itself. Without knowing where it began he found himself moving within a gigantic *moment bienheureux*, able to see the past in the future, present in past, the *now* in both past and future. It was the accumulation of centuries experienced between one heartbeat and the next.

Leto's awareness floated free, no objective psyche to compensate for consciousness, no barriers. Namri's "provisional future" remained lightly in his memory, but it shared awareness with many futures. And in this shattering awareness, all of his past, every inner life became his own. With the help of the greatest within him, he dominated. They were *his*.

He thought: *When you study an object from a distance, only its principle may be seen.* He had achieved the distance and he could see his own life now: the multi-past and its memories were his burden, his joy, and his necessity. But the *worm trip* had added another dimension and his father no longer stood guard within him because the need no longer existed. Leto saw through the distances clearly—past and present. And the past presented him with an ultimate ancestor —one who was called Harum and without whom the distant future would not be. These clear distances provided new principles, new dimensions of sharing. Whichever life he now chose, he'd live it out in an autonomous sphere of mass experience, a trail of lives so convoluted that no single lifetime could count the generations of it. Aroused, this mass experience held the power to subdue his selfdom. It could make itself felt upon an individual, a nation, a society or an entire civilization. That, of course, was why Gurney had been taught to fear him; why Namri's knife waited They could not be allowed to see this power within him. No one could ever see it in its fullness—not even Ghanima.

Presently Leto sat up, saw that only Namri remained, watching.

In an old voice Leto said: "There's no single set of limits for all men. Universal prescience is an empty myth. Only the most powerful local currents of Time may be foretold. But in an infinite universe, *local* can be so gigantic that your mind shrinks from it."

Namri shook his head, not understanding.

"Where's Gurney?" Leto asked.

"He left lest he have to watch me slay you."

"Will you slay me, Namri?" It was almost a plea to have the man do it.

Namri took his hand from his knife. "Since you ask me to do it, I will not. If you were indifferent, though . . ."

"The malady of indifference is what destroys many things," Leto said. He nodded to himself. "Yes . . . even civilizations die of it. It's as though that were the price demanded for achieving new levels of complexity or consciousness." He looked up at Namri. "So they told you to look for indifference in me?" And he saw Namri was more than a killer—Namri was devious.

"As a sign of unbridled power," Namri said, but it was a lie.

"Indifferent power, yes." Leto sat up, sighed deeply. "There was no moral grandeur to my father's life, Namri; only a local trap which he built for himself."

> O Paul, thou Muad'Dib,
> Mahdi of all men,
> Thy breath exhaled
> Sent forth the huricen.

**—Songs of Muad'Dib**

"Never!" Ghanima said. "I'd kill him on our wedding night." She spoke with a barbed stubbornness which thus far had resisted all blandishments. Alia and her advisors had been at it half the night, keeping the royal quarters in a state of unrest, sending out for new advisors, for food and drink. The entire Temple and its adjoining Keep seethed with the frustrations of unmade decisions.

Ghanima sat composedly on a green floater chair in her own quarters, a large room with rough tan walls to simulate sietch rock. The ceiling, however, was imbar crystal which flickered with blue light, and the floor was black tile. The furnishings were sparse: a small writing table, five floater chairs and a narrow cot set into an alcove, Fremen fashion. Ghanima wore a robe of yellow mourning.

"You are not a free person who can settle every aspect of her own life," Alia said for perhaps the hundredth time. *The little fool must come to realize this sooner or later! She must approve the betrothal to Farad'n. She must! Let her kill him later, but the betrothal requires open acknowledgment by the Fremen affianced.*

"He killed my brother," Ghanima said, holding to the single note which sustained her. "Everyone knows this. Fremen would spit at the mention of my name were I to consent to this betrothal."

*And that is one of the reasons why you must consent,* Alia thought. She said: "His mother did it. He has banished her for it. What more do you want of him?"

"His blood," Ghanima said. "He's a Corrino."

"He has denounced his own mother," Alia protested. "And why should you worry about the Fremen rabble? They'll accept whatever we tell them to accept. Ghani, the peace of the Empire demands that—"

"I will not consent," Ghanima said. "You cannot announce the betrothal without me."

Irulan, entering the room as Ghanima spoke, glanced inquiringly at Alia and the two female advisors who stood dejectedly beside her. Irulan saw Alia throw up her arms in disgust and drop into a chair facing Ghanima.

"You speak to her, Irulan," Alia said.

Irulan pulled a floater into place, sat down beside Alia.

"You're a Corrino, Irulan," Ghanima said. "Don't press your luck with me." Ghanima got up, crossed to her cot and sat on it cross-legged, glaring back at the women. Irulan, she saw, had dressed in a black aba to match Alia's, the hood thrown back to reveal her golden hair. It was mourning hair under the yellow glow of the floating globes which illuminated the room.

Irulan glanced at Alia, stood up and crossed to stand facing Ghanima. "Ghani, I'd kill him myself if that were the way to solve matters. And Farad'n's my own blood, as you so kindly emphasized. But you have duties far higher than your commitment to Fremen . . ."

"That doesn't sound any better coming from you than it does from my precious aunt," Ghanima said. "The blood of a brother cannot be washed off. That's more than some little Fremen aphorism."

Irulan pressed her lips together. Then: "Farad'n holds your grandmother captive. He holds Duncan and if we don't—"

"I'm not satisfied with your stories of how all this happened," Ghanima said, peering past Irulan at Alia. "Once Duncan died rather than let enemies take my father. Perhaps this new ghola-flesh is no longer the same as—"

"Duncan was charged with protecting your grandmother's life!" Alia said, whirling in her chair. "I'm confident he chose the only way to do that." And she thought: *Duncan! Duncan! You weren't supposed to do it this way.*

Ghanima, reading the overtones of contrivance in Alia's voice, stared across at her aunt. "You're lying, O Womb of Heaven. I've heard about your fight with my grandmother. What is it you fear to tell us about her and your precious Duncan?"

"You've heard it all," Alia said, but she felt a stab of fear at this bald accusation and what it implied. Fatigue had made her careless, she realized. She arose, said: "Everything I know, you know." Turning to Irulan: "You work on her. She must be made to—"

Ghanima interrupted with a coarse Fremen expletive which came shockingly from the immature lips. Into the quick silence she said: "You think me just a mere child, that you have years in which to work on me, that eventually I'll accept. Think again, O Heavenly Regent. You know better than anyone the years I have within me. I'll listen to them, not to you."

Alia barely suppressed an angry retort, stared hard at Ghanima. *Abomination?* Who was this child? A new fear of Ghanima began to rise in Alia. Had she accepted her own compromise with the lives which came to her pre-born? Alia said: "There's time yet for you to see reason."

"There may be time yet for me to see Farad'n's blood spurt around my knife," Ghanima said. "Depend on it. If I'm ever left alone with him, one of us will surely die."

"You think you loved your brother more than I?" Irulan demanded. "You play a fool's game! I was mother to him as I was to you. I was—"

"You never knew him," Ghanima said. "All of you, except at times my *beloved aunt*, persist in thinking us children. You're the fools! Alia knows! Look at her run away from . . ."

"I run from nothing," Alia said, but she turned her back on Irulan and Ghanima, and stared at the two amazons who were pretending not to hear this argument. They'd obviously given up on Ghanima. Perhaps they sympathized with her. Angrily, Alia sent them from the room. Relief was obvious on their faces as they obeyed.

"You run," Ghanima persisted.

"I've chosen a way of life which suits me," Alia said, turning back to stare at Ghanima sitting cross-legged on the cot. Was it possible she'd made that terrible inner compromise? Alia tried to see the signs of it in Ghanima, but was unable to read a single betrayal. Alia wondered then: *Has she seen it in me? But how could she?*

"You feared to be the window for a multitude," Ghanima accused. "But we're the pre-born and we know. You'll be their window, conscious or unconscious. You cannot deny them." And she thought: *Yes, I know you—Abomination. And perhaps I'll go as you have gone, but for now I can only pity you and despise you.*

Silence hung between Ghanima and Alia, an almost palpable thing which alerted the Bene Gesserit training in Irulan. She glanced from one to the other, then: "Why're you so quiet suddenly?"

"I've just had a thought which requires considerable reflection," Alia said.

"Reflect at your leisure, dear aunt," Ghanima sneered.

Alia, putting down fatigue-inflamed anger, said: "Enough for now! Leave her to think. Perhaps she'll come to her senses."

Irulan arose, said: "It's almost dawn anyway. Ghani, before we go, would you care to hear the latest message from Farad'n? He . . ."

"I would not," Ghanima said. "And hereafter, cease calling me by that ridiculous diminutive. Ghani! It merely supports the mistaken assumption that I'm a child you can . . ."

"Why'd you and Alia grow so suddenly quiet?" Irulan asked, reverting to her previous question, but casting it now in a delicate mode of Voice.

Ghanima threw her head back in laughter. "Irulan! You'd try Voice on me?"

"What?" Irulan was taken aback.

"You'd teach your grandmother to suck eggs," Ghanima said.

"I'd what?"

"The fact that I remember the expression and you've never even heard it before should give you pause," Ghanima said. "It was an old expression of scorn when you Bene Gesserit were young. But if that doesn't chasten you, ask yourself what your royal parents could've been thinking of when they named you Irulan? Or is it Ruinal?"

In spite of her training, Irulan flushed. "You're trying to goad me, Ghanima."

"And you tried to use Voice on me. On me! I remember the first human efforts in that direction. I remember *then*, Ruinous Irulan. Now, get out of here, all of you."

But Alia was intrigued now, caught by an inner suggestion which sluffed her fatigue aside. She said: "Perhaps I've a suggestion which could change your mind, Ghani."

"Still Ghani!" A brittle laugh escaped Ghanima, then: "Reflect but a moment: If I desire to kill Farad'n, I need but fall in with your plans. I presume you've thought of that. Beware of *Ghani* in a tractable mood. You see, I'm being utterly candid with you."

"That's what I hoped," Alia said. "If you . . ."

"The blood of a brother cannot be washed away," Ghanima said. "I'll not go before my Fremen loved ones a traitor to that. *Never to forgive, never to forget.* Isn't that our catechism? I warn you here, and I'll say it publicly: you cannot betroth me to Farad'n. Who, knowing me, would believe it? Farad'n himself could not believe it. Fremen, hearing of such a betrothal, would laugh into their sleeves and say; 'See! She lures him into a trap.' If you . . ."

"I understand that," Alia said, moving to Irulan's side. Irulan, she noted, was standing in shocked silence, aware already of where this conversation was headed.

"And so I would be luring him into a trap," Ghanima said. "If that's what you want, I'll agree, but he may not fall. If you wish this false betrothal as the empty coin with which to buy back my grandmother and your precious Duncan, so be it. But it's on your head. Buy them back. Farad'n, though, is mine. Him I'll kill."

Irulan whirled to face Alia before she could speak. "Alia! If we go back on our word . . ." She let it hang there a moment while Alia smilingly reflected on the potential wrath among the Great Houses in Faufreluches Assembled, the destructive consequences to believe in Atreides honor, the loss of religious trust, all of the great and small building blocs which would tumble.

"It'd rule against us," Irulan protested. "All belief in Paul's prophethood would be destroyed. It . . . the Empire . . ."

"Who could dare question our right to decide what is wrong and what is right?" Alia asked, voice mild. "We mediate between good and evil. I need but proclaim . . ."

"You can't do this!" Irulan protested. "Paul's memory . . ."

"Is just another tool of Church and State," Ghanima said. "Don't speak foolishness, Irulan." Ghanima touched the crysknife at her waist, looked up at Alia. "I've misjudged my clever aunt, Regent of all that's Holy in Muad'Dib's Empire. I have, indeed, misjudged you. Lure Farad'n into our parlor if you will."

"This is recklessness," Irulan pleaded.

"You agree to this betrothal, Ghanima?" Alia asked, ignoring Irulan.

"On my terms," Ghanima said, hand still on her crysknife.

"I wash my hands of this," Irulan said, actually wringing her hands. "I was willing to argue for a true betrothal to heal—"

"We'll give you a wound much more difficult to heal, Alia and I," Ghanima said. "Bring him quickly, if he'll come. And perhaps he will. Would he suspect a child of my tender years? Let us plan the formal ceremony of betrothal to require his presence. Let there be an opportunity for me to be alone with him . . . just a minute or two . . ."

Irulan shuddered at this evidence that Ghanima was, after all, Fremen entire, child no different from adult in this terrible bloodiness. After all, Fremen children were accustomed to slay the wounded on the battlefield, releasing women from this chore that they might collect the bodies and haul them away to the deathstills. And Ghanima, speaking with the voice of a Fremen child, piled horror upon horror by the studied maturity of her words, by the ancient sense of vendetta which hung like an aura around her.

"Done," Alia said, and she fought to keep voice and face from betraying her glee. "We'll prepare the formal charter of betrothal. We'll have the signatures witnessed by the proper assemblage from the Great Houses. Farad'n cannot possibly doubt—"

"He'll doubt, but he'll come," Ghanima said. "And he'll have guards. But will they think to guard him from me?"

"For the love of all that Paul tried to do," Irulan protested, "let us at least make Farad'n's death appear an accident, or the result of malice by outside—"

"I'll take joy in displaying my bloody knife to my brethren," Ghanima said.

"Alia, I beg you." Irulan said. "Abandon this rash insanity. Declare *kanly* against Farad'n, anything to—"

"We don't require formal declaration of vendetta against him," Ghanima said. "The whole Empire knows how we must feel." She pointed to the sleeve of her robe. "We wear the yellow of mourning. When I exchange it for the black of a Fremen betrothed, will that fool anyone?"

"Pray that it fools Farad'n," Alia said, "and the delegates of the Great Houses we invite to witness the—"

"Every one of those delegates will turn against you," Irulan said. "You know that!"

"Excellent point," Ghanima said. "Choose those delegates with care, Alia. They must be ones we won't mind eliminating later."

Irulan threw up her arms in despair, turned and fled.

"Have her put under close surveillance lest she try to warn her nephew," Ghanima said.

"Don't try to teach me how to conduct a plot," Alia said. She turned and followed Irulan, but at a slower pace. The guards outside and the waiting aides were sucked up in her wake like sand particles drawn into the vortex of a rising worm.

Ghanima shook her head sadly from side to side as the door closed, thought: *It's as poor Leto and I thought. Gods below! I wish it'd been me the tiger killed instead of him.*

*Many forces sought control of the Atreides twins and, when the death of Leto was announced, this movement of plot and counterplot was amplified. Note the relative motivations: the Sisterhood feared Alia, an adult Abomination, but still wanted those genetic characteristics carried by the Atreides. The Church hierarchy of Auqaf and Hajj saw only the power implicit in control of Muad'Dib's heir. CHOAM wanted a doorway to the wealth of Dune. Farad'n and his Sardaukar sought a return to glory for House Corrino. The Spacing Guild feared the equation Arrakis = melange; without the spice they could not navigate. Jessica wished to repair what her disobedience to the Bene Gesserit had created. Few thought to ask the twins what their plans might be, until it was too late.*

**—The Book of Kreos**

Shortly after the evening meal, Leto saw a man walking past the arched doorway to his chamber, and his mind went with the man. The passage had been left open and Leto had seen some activity out there—spice hampers being wheeled past, three women with the obvious off-world sophistication of dress which marked them as smugglers. This man who took Leto's mind walking might have been no different except that he moved like Stilgar, a much younger Stilgar.

It was a peculiar walk his mind took. Time filled Leto's awareness like a stellar globe. He could see infinite timespaces, but he had to press into his own future before knowing in which moment his flesh lay. His multifaceted memory-lives surged and receded, but they were his now. They were like waves on a beach, but if they rose too high, he could command them and they would retreat, leaving the royal Harum behind.

Now and again he would listen to those memory-lives. One would rise like a prompter, poking its head up out of the stage and calling cues for his behavior. His father came during the mind-walk and said: "You are a child seeking to be a man. When you are a man, you will seek in vain for the child you were."

All the while, he felt his body being plagued by the fleas and lice of an old sietch poorly maintained. None of the attendants who brought his heavily spice-laced food appeared bothered by the creatures. Did these people have immunity from such things, or was it only that they had lived with them so long they could ignore discomfort?

Who were these people assembled around Gurney? How had they come to this place? Was this Jacurutu? His multi-memories produced answers he did not like. They were ugly people and Gurney was the ugliest. Perfection floated here, though, dormant and waiting beneath an ugly surface.

Part of him knew he remained spice-bound, held in bondage by the heavy dosages of melange in every meal. His child's body wanted to rebel while his persona raved with the immediate presence of memories carried over from thousands of eons.

His mind returned from its walk, and he wondered if his body had really stayed behind. Spice confused the senses. He felt the pressures of self-limitations piling up against him like the long barachan dunes of the *bled* slowly building themselves a ramp against a desert cliff. One day a few trickles of sand would flow over the cliff, then more and more and more . . . and only the sand would remain exposed to the sky.

But the cliff would still be there underneath.

*I'm still within the trance,* he thought.

He knew he would come soon to a branching of life and death. His captors kept sending him back into the spice thralldom, unsatisfied with his responses at every return. Always, treacherous Namri waited there with his knife. Leto knew countless pasts and futures, but he had yet to learn what would satisfy Namri . . . or Gurney Halleck. They wanted something outside of the visions. The life and death branching lured Leto. His life, he knew, would have to possess some inner meaning which carried it above the vision circumstances. Thinking of this demand, he felt that his inner awareness was his true being and his outer existence was the trance. This terrified him. He did not want to go back to the sietch with its fleas, its Namri, its Gurney Halleck.

*I'm a coward,* he thought.

But a coward, even a coward, might die bravely with nothing but a gesture. Where was that gesture which could make him whole once more? How could he awaken from trance and vision into the universe which Gurney demanded? Without that turning, without an awakening from aimless visions, he knew he could die in a prison of his own choosing. In this he had at last come to cooperate with his captors. Somewhere he had to find wisdom, an inner balance which would reflect upon the universe and return to him an image of calm strength. Only then might he seek his Golden Path and survive the skin which was not his own.

Someone was playing the baliset out there in the sietch. Leto felt that his body probably heard the music in the present. He sensed the cot beneath his back. He could hear music. It was Gurney at the baliset. No other fingers could quite compare with his mastery of that most difficult instrument. He played an old Fremen song, one called a *hadith* because of its internal narrative and the voice which invoked those patterns required for survival on Arrakis. The song told the story of human occupations within a sietch.

Leto felt the music move him through a marvelous ancient cavern. He saw women trampling spice residue for fuel, curding the spice for fermentation, forming spice-fabrics. Melange was everywhere in the sietch.

Those moments came when Leto could not distinguish between the music and the people of the cavern vision. The whine and slap of a power loom was the whine and slap of the baliset. But his inner eyes beheld fabrics of human hair, the long fur of mutated rats, threads of desert cotton, and strips curled from the skin of birds. He saw a sietch school. The eco-language of Dune raged through his mind on its wings of music. He saw the sun-powered kitchen, the long chamber where stillsuits were made and maintained. He saw weather forecasters reading the sticks they'd brought in from the sand.

Somewhere during this journey, someone brought him food and spooned it into his mouth, holding his head up with a strong arm. He knew this as a real-time sensation, but the marvelous play of motion continued within him.

As though it came in the next instant after the spice-laden food, he saw the hurtling of a sandstorm. Moving images within the sand breath became the golden reflections of a moth's eyes, and his own life was reduced to the viscous trail of a crawling insect.

Words from the Panoplia Prophetica raved through him: "It is said that there is nothing firm, nothing balanced, nothing durable in all the universe—that nothing remains in its state, that each day, some time each hour, brings change."

*The old Missionaria Protectiva knew what they were doing,* he thought. *They knew about Terrible Purposes. They knew how to manipulate people and religions. Even my father didn't escape them, not in the end.*

There lay the clue he'd been seeking. Leto studied it. He felt strength flowing back into his flesh. His entire multifaceted being turned over and looked out upon the universe. He sat up and found himself alone in the gloomy cell with only the light from the outer passage where the man had walked past and taken his mind an eon ago.

"Good fortune to us all!" he called in the traditional Fremen way.

Gurney Halleck appeared in the arched doorway, his head a black silhouette against the light from the outer passage.

"Bring light," Leto said.

"You wish to be tested further?"

Leto laughed. "No. It's my turn to test you."

"We shall see." Halleck turned away, returning in a moment with a bright blue glowglobe in the crook of his left elbow. He released it in the cell, allowing it to drift above their heads.

"Where's Namri?" Leto asked.

"Just outside where I can call him."

"Ahh, Old Father Eternity always waits patiently," Leto said. He felt curiously released, poised on the edge of discovery.

"You call Namri by the name reserved for Shai-Hulud?" Halleck asked.

"His knife's a worm's tooth," Leto said. "Thus, he's Old Father Eternity."

Halleck smiled grimly, but remained silent.

"You still wait to pass judgment on me," Leto said. "And there's no way to exchange information, I'll admit, without making judgments. You can't ask the universe to be exact, though."

A rustling sound behind Halleck alerted Leto to Namri's approach. He stopped half a pace to Halleck's left.

"Ahhh, the left hand of the damned," Leto said.

"It's not wise to joke about the Infinite and the Absolute," Namri growled. He glanced sideways at Halleck.

"Are you God, Namri, that you invoke absolutes?" Leto asked. But he kept his attention on Halleck. Judgment would come from there.

Both men merely stared at him without answering.

"Every judgment teeters on the brink of error," Leto explained. "To claim absolute knowledge is to become monstrous. Knowledge is an unending adventure at the edge of uncertainty."

"What word game is this you play?" Halleck demanded.

"Let him speak," Namri said.

"It's the game Namri initiated with me," Leto said, and saw the old Fremen's head nod agreement. He'd certainly recognized the riddle game. "Our senses always have at least two levels," Leto said.

"Trivia and message," Namri said.

"Excellent!" Leto said. "You gave me trivia; I give you message. I see, I hear, I detect odors, I touch; I feel changes in temperature, taste. I sense the passage of time. I may take emotive samples. Ahhhhh! I am happy. You see, Gurney? Namri? There's no mystery about a human life. It's not a problem to be solved, but a reality to be experienced."

"You try our patience, lad," Namri said. "Is this the place where you wish to die?"

But Halleck put out a restraining hand.

"First, I am not a lad," Leto said. He made the fist sign at his right ear. "You'll not slay me; I've placed a water burden upon you."

Namri drew his crysknife half out of its sheath. "I owe you nothing!"

"But God created Arrakis to train the faithful," Leto said. "I've not only showed you my faith, I've made you conscious of your own existence. Life requires dispute. You've been made to *know*—by me!—that your reality differs from all others; thus, you know you're alive."

"Irreverence is a dangerous game to play with me," Namri said. He held his crysknife half drawn.

"Irreverence is a most necessary ingredient of religion," Leto said. "Not to speak of its importance in philosophy. Irreverence is the only way left to us for testing our universe."

"So you think you understand the universe?" Halleck asked, and he opened a space between himself and Namri.

"Ye-esss," Namri said, and there was death in his voice.

"The universe can be understood only by the wind," Leto said. "There's no mighty seat of reason which dwells within the brain. Creation is discovery. God discovered us in the Void because we moved against a background which He already knew. The wall was blank. Then there was movement."

"You play hide and seek with death," Halleck warned.

"But you are both my friends," Leto said. He faced Namri. "When you offer a candidate as Friend of your Sietch, do you not slay a hawk and an eagle as the offering? And is this not the response: 'God send each man at his end, such hawks, such eagles, and such friends'?"

Namri's hand slid from the knife. The blade slipped back into its sheath. He stared wide-eyed at Leto. Each sietch kept its friendship ritual secret, yet here was a selected part of the rite.

Halleck, though, asked: "Is this place your end?"

"I know what you need to hear from me, Gurney," Leto said, watching the play of hope and suspicion across the ugly face. Leto touched his own breast.

"This child was never a child. My father lives within me, but he is not me. You loved him, and he was a gallant human whose affairs beat upon high shores. His intent was to close down the cycle of wars, but he reckoned without the movement of infinity as expressed by life. That's Rhajia! Namri knows. Its movement can be seen by any mortal. Beware paths which narrow future possibilities. Such paths divert you from infinity into lethal traps."

"What is it I need to hear from you?" Halleck asked.

"He's just word playing," Namri said, but his voice carried deep hesitation, doubts.

"I ally myself with Namri against my father," Leto said. "And my father within allies himself with us' against what was made of him."

"Why?" Halleck demanded.

"Because it's the *amor fati* which I bring to humankind, the act of ultimate self-examination. In this universe, I choose to ally myself against any force which brings humiliation upon humankind. Gurney! Gurney! You were not born and raised in the desert. Your flesh doesn't know the truth of which I speak. But Namri knows. In the open land, one direction is as good as another."

"I still have not heard what I must hear," Halleck snarled.

"He speaks for war and against peace," Namri said.

"No," Leto said. "Nor did my father speak against war. But look what was made of him. Peace has only one meaning in this Imperium. It's the maintenance of a single way of life. You are commanded to be contented. Life must be uniform on all planets as it is in the Imperial Government. The major object of priestly study is to find the correct forms of human behavior. For this they go to the words of Muad'Dib! Tell me, Namri, are you content?"

"No." The words came out flat, spontaneous rejection.

"Then do you blaspheme?"

"Of course not!"

"But you aren't contented. You see, Gurney? Namri proves it to us. Every question, every problem doesn't have a single correct answer. One must permit diversity. A monolith is unstable. Then why do you demand a single correct statement from me? Is that to be the measure of your monstrous judgment?"

"Will you force me to have you slain?" Halleck asked, and there was agony in his voice.

"No, I'll have pity upon you," Leto said. "Send word to my grandmother that I'll cooperate. The Sisterhood may come to regret my cooperation, but an Atreides gives his word."

"A Truthsayer should test that," Namri said. "These Atreides . . ."

"He'll have his chance to say before his grandmother what must be said," Halleck said. He nodded with his head toward the passage.

Namri paused before leaving, glanced at Leto. "I pray we do the right thing in leaving him alive."

"Go, friends," Leto said. "Go and reflect."

As the two men departed, Leto threw himself onto his back, feeling the cold cot against his spine. Movement sent his head spinning over the edge of his spice-burdened consciousness. In that instant he saw the entire planet—every village, every town, every city, the desert places and the planted places. All of the shapes which smashed against his vision bore intimate relationships to a mixture of elements within themselves and without. He saw the structures of Imperial society reflected in physical structures of its planets and their communities. Like a gigantic unfolding within him, he saw this revelation for what it must be: a window into the society's invisible parts. Seeing this, Leto realized that every system had such a window. Even the system of himself and his universe. He began peering into windows, a cosmic voyeur.

This was what his grandmother and the Sisterhood sought! He knew it. His awareness flowed on a new, higher level. He felt the past carried in his cells, in his memories, in the archetypes which haunted his assumptions, in the myths which hemmed him, in his languages and their prehistoric detritus. It was all of the shapes out of his human and nonhuman past, all of the lives which he now commanded, all integrated in him at last. And he felt himself as a thing caught up in the ebb and flow of nucleotides. Against the backdrop of infinity he was a protozoan creature in which birth and death were virtually simultaneous, but he was both infinite and protozoan, a creature of molecular memories.

*We humans are a form of colony organism!* he thought.

They wanted his cooperation. Promising cooperation had won him another reprieve from Namri's knife. By summoning to cooperation, they sought to recognize a healer.

And he thought: *But I'll not bring them social order in the way they expect it!*

A grimace contorted Leto's mouth. He knew he'd not be as unconsciously malevolent as was his father—despotism at one terminal and slavery at the other—but this universe might pray for those "good old days."

His father-within spoke to him then, cautiously probing, unable to demand attention but pleading for audience.

And Leto answered: "No. We will give them complexities to occupy their minds. There are many modes of flight from danger. How will they know I'm dangerous unless they experience me for thousands of years? Yes, father-within, we'll give them question marks."

*There is no guilt or innocence in you. All of that is past. Guilt belabors the dead and I am not the Iron Hammer. You multitude of the dead are merely people who have done certain things, and the memory of those things illuminates my path.*

**—Leto II to His Memory-Lives
After Harq al-Ada**

"It moves of itself!" Farad'n said, and his voice was barely a whisper.

He stood above the Lady Jessica's bed, a brace of guards close behind him. The Lady Jessica had propped herself up in the bed. She was clad in a parasilk gown of shimmering white with a matching band around her copper hair. Farad'n had come bursting in upon her moments before. He wore the grey leotard and his face was sweaty with excitement and the exertions of his dash through the palace corridors.

"What time is it?" Jessica asked.

"Time?" Farad'n appeared puzzled.

One of the guards spoke up: "It is the third hour past midnight, My Lady." The guard glanced fearfully at Farad'n. The young prince had come dashing through the night-lighted corridors, picking up startled guards in his wake.

"But it moves," Farad'n said. He held out his left hand, then his right. "I saw my own hands shrink into chubby fists, and I remembered! They were my hands when I was an infant. I remembered being an infant, but it was . . . a clearer memory. I was reorganizing my old memories!"

"Very good," Jessica said. His excitement was infectious. "And what happened when your hands became old?"

"My . . . mind was . . . sluggish," he said. "I felt an ache in my back. Right here." He touched a place over his left kidney.

"You've learned a most important lesson," Jessica said. "Do you know what that lesson is?"

He dropped his hands to his sides, stared at her. Then: "My mind controls my reality." His eyes glittered, and he repeated it, louder this time: "My mind controls my reality!"

"That is the beginning of *prana-bindu* balance," Jessica said. "It is only the beginning, though."

"What do I do next?" he asked.

"My Lady," the guard who had answered her question ventured now to interrupt. "The hour," he said.

*Aren't their spy posts manned at this hour?* Jessica wondered. She said: "Begone. We have work to do."

"But My Lady," the guard said, and he looked fearfully from Farad'n to Jessica and back.

"You think I'm going to seduce him?" Jessica asked.

The man stiffened.

Farad'n laughed, a joyous outburst. He waved a hand in dismissal. "You heard her. Begone."

The guards looked at each other, but they obeyed.

Farad'n sat on the edge of her bed. "What next?" He shook his head. "I wanted to believe you, yet I did not believe. Then . . . it was as though my mind melted. I was tired. My mind gave up its fighting against you. It happened. Just like that!" He snapped his fingers.

"It was not me that your mind fought against," Jessica said.

"Of course not," he admitted. "I was fighting against myself, all the nonsense I've learned. What next now?"

Jessica smiled. "I confess I didn't expect you to succeed this rapidly. It's been only eight days and . . ."

"I was patient," he said, grinning.

"And you've begun to learn patience, too," she said.

"Begun?"

"You've just crept over the lip of this learning," she said. "Now you're truly an infant. Before . . . you were only a potential, not even born."

The corners of his mouth drew down.

"Don't be so gloomy," she said. "You've done it. That's important. How many can say they were born anew?"

"What comes next?" he insisted.

"You will practice this thing you've learned," she said. "I want you able to do this at will, easily. Later you'll fill a new place in your awareness which this has opened. It will be filled by the ability to test any reality against your own demands."

"Is that all I do now . . . practice the—"

"No. Now you can begin the muscle training. Tell me, can you move the little toe on your left foot without moving any other muscle of your body?"

"My . . ." She saw a distant expression come over his face as he tried to move the toe. He looked down at his foot presently, staring at it. Sweat broke out on his forehead. A deep breath escaped him. "I can't do it."

"Yes you can," she said. "You will learn to do it. You will learn every muscle in your body. You will know these muscles the way you know your hands."

He swallowed hard at the magnitude of this prospect. Then: "What are you doing to me? What is your plan for me?"

"I intend to turn you loose upon the universe," she said. "You will become whatever it is you most deeply desire."

He mulled this for a moment. "Whatever I desire?"

"Yes."

"That's impossible!"

"Unless you learn to control your desires the way you control your reality," she said. And she thought: *There! Let his analysts examine that. They'll advise cautious approval, but Farad'n will move a step closer to realization of what I'm really doing.*

He proved her surmise by saying: "It's one thing to tell a person he'll realize his heart's desire. It's another thing to actually deliver that realization."

"You've come farther than I thought," Jessica said. "Very good. I promise you: if you complete this program of learning, you'll be your own man. Whatever you do, it'll be because that's what you want to do."

*And let a Truthsayer try to pry that apart,* she thought.

He stood up, but the expression he bent upon her was warm, a sense of camaraderie in it. "You know, I believe you. Damned if I know why, but I do. And I won't say a word about the other things I'm thinking."

Jessica watched his retreating back as he let himself out of her bedchamber. She turned off the glowglobes, lay back. This Farad'n was a deep one. He'd as much as told her that he was beginning to see her design, but he was joining her conspiracy of his own volition.

*Wait until he begins to learn his own emotions,* she thought. With that, she composed herself for the return to sleep. The morrow, she knew, would be plagued by casual encounters with palace personnel asking seemingly innocuous questions.

*Humankind periodically goes through a speedup of its affairs, thereby experiencing the race between the renewable vitality of the living and the beckoning vitiation of decadence. In this periodic race, any pause becomes luxury. Only then can one reflect that all is permitted; all is possible.*

**—The Apocrypha of Muad'Dib**

*The touch of sand is important,* Leto told himself.

He could feel the grit beneath him where he sat beneath a brilliant sky. They had force-fed him another heavy dosage of melange, and Leto's mind turned upon itself like a whirlpool. An unanswered question lay deep within the funnel of the whirlpool: *Why do they insist that I say it?* Gurney was stubborn; no doubt of that. And he'd had his orders from his Lady Jessica.

They'd brought him out of the sietch into the daylight for this "lesson." He had the strange sensation that he'd let his body take the short trip from the sietch while his inner being mediated a battle between the Duke Leto I and the old Baron Harkonnen. They'd fought within him, through him, because he would not let them communicate directly. The fight had taught him what had happened to Alia. Poor Alia.

*I was right to fear the spice trip,* he thought.

A welling bitterness toward the Lady Jessica filled him. Her damned gom jabbar! Fight it and win, or die in the attempt. She couldn't put a poisoned needle against his neck, but she could send him into the valley of peril which had claimed her own daughter.

Snuffling sounds intruded upon his awareness. They wavered, growing louder, then softer, louder . . . softer. There was no way for him to determine whether they had current reality or came from the spice.

Leto's body sagged over his folded arms. He felt hot sand through his buttocks. There was a rug directly in front of him, but he sat on open sand. A shadow lay across the rug: Namri. Leto stared into the muddy pattern of the rug, feeling bubbles ripple there. His awareness drifted on its own current through a landscape which stretched out to a horizon of shock-headed greenery.

His skull thrummed with drums. He felt heat, fever. The fever was a pressure of burning which filled his senses, crowding out awareness of flesh until he could only feel the moving shadows of his peril. Namri and the knife. Pressure . . . pressure . . . Leto lay at last suspended between sky and sand, his mind lost to all but the fever. Now he waited for something to happen, sensing that any occurrence would be a first-and-only thing.

Hot-hot pounding sunshine crashed brilliantly around him, without tranquillity, without remedy. *Where is my Golden Path?* Everywhere bugs crawled. Everywhere. *My skin is not my own.* He sent messages along his nerves, waited out the dragging other-person responses.

*Up head,* he told his nerves.

A head which might have been his own crept upward, looked out at patches of blankness in the bright light.

Someone whispered: "He's deep into it now."

No answer.

Burn fire sun building heat on heat.

Slowly, outbending, the current of his awareness took him drifting through a last screen of green blankness and there, across low folding dunes, distant no more than a kilometer beyond the stretched out chalk line of a cliff, *there* lay the green burgeoning future, upflung, flowing into endless green, greenswelling, green-green moving outward endlessly.

In all of that green there was not one great worm.

Riches of wild growth, but nowhere Shai-Hulud.

Leto sensed that he had ventured across old boundaries into a new land which only the imagination had witnessed, and that he looked now directly through the very next veil which a yawning humankind called *Unknown*.

It was bloodthirsty reality.

He felt the red fruit of his life swaying on a limb, fluid slipping away from him, and the fluid was the spice essence flowing through his veins.

Without Shai-Hulud, no more spice.

He had seen a future without the great grey worm-serpent of Dune. He knew this, yet could not tear himself from the trance to rail against such a passage.

Abruptly his awareness plunged back—back, back, away from such a deadly future. His thoughts went into his bowels, becoming primitive, moved only by intense emotions. He found himself unable to focus on any particular aspect of his vision or his surroundings, but there was a voice within him. It spoke an ancient language and he understood it perfectly. The voice was musical and lilting, but its words bludgeoned him.

"It is not the present which influences the future, thou fool, but the future which forms the present. You have it all backward. Since the future is set, an unfolding of events which will assure that future is fixed and inevitable."

The words transfixed him. He felt terror rooted in the heavy matter of his body. By this he knew his body still existed, but the reckless nature and enormous power of his vision left him feeling contaminated, defenseless, unable to signal a muscle and gain its obedience. He knew he was submitting more and more to the onslaught of those collective lives whose memories once had made him believe he was real. Fear filled him. He thought that he might be losing the inner command, falling at last into Abomination.

Leto felt his body twisting in terror.

He had come to depend upon his victory and the newly won benevolent cooperation of those memories. They had turned against him, all of them— even royal Harum whom he'd trusted. He lay shimmering on a surface which had no roots, unable to give any expression to his own life. He tried to concentrate upon a mental picture of himself, was confronted by overlapping frames, each a different age: infant into doddering ancient. He recalled his father's early training: *Let the hands grow young, then old.* But his whole body was immersed now in this lost reality and the entire image progression melted into other faces, the features of those who had given him their memories.

A diamond thunderbolt shattered him.

Leto felt pieces of his awareness drifting apart, yet he retained a sense of himself somewhere between being and nonbeing. Hope quickening, he felt his body breathing. In . . . out. He took in a deep breath: *yin.* He let it out: *yang.*

Somewhere just beyond his grasp lay a place of supreme independence, a victory over all of the confusions inherent in his multitude of lives—no false sense of command, but a true victory. He knew his previous mistake now: he had sought power in the reality of his trance, choosing that rather than face the fears which he and Ghanima had fed in each other.

*Fear defeated Alia!*

But the seeking after power spread another trap, diverting him into fantasy. He saw the illusion. The entire illusion process rotated half a turn and now he knew a center from which he could watch without purpose the flight of his visions, of his inner lives.

Elation flooded him. It made him want to laugh, but he denied himself this luxury, knowing it would bar the doors of memory.

*Ahhhh, my memories,* he thought. *I have seen your illusion. You no longer invent the next moment for me. You merely show me how to create new moments. I'll not lock myself on the old tracks.*

This thought passed through his awareness as though wiping a surface clean and in its wake he felt his entire body, an *einfalle* which reported in most minute detail on every cell, every nerve. He entered a state of intense quiet. In this quiet, he heard voices, knowing they came from a great distance, but he heard them clearly as though they echoed in a chasm.

One of the voices was Halleck's. "Perhaps we gave him too much of it."

Namri answered. "We gave him exactly what she told us to give him."

"Perhaps we should go back out there and have another look at him." Halleck.

"Sabiha is good at such things; she'll call us if anything starts to go wrong." Namri.

"I don't like this business of Sabiha." Halleck.

"She's a necessary ingredient." Namri.

Leto felt bright light outside himself and darkness within, but the darkness was secretive, protective, and warm. The light began to blaze up and he felt that it came from the darkness within, swirling outward like a brilliant cloud. His body became transparent, drawing him upward, yet he retained that *einfalle* contact with every cell and nerve. The multitude of inner lives fell into alignment, nothing tangled or mixed. They became very quiet in duplication of his own inner silence, each memory-life discrete, an entity incorporeal and undivided.

Leto spoke to them then: "I am your spirit. I am the only life you can realize. I am the house of your spirit in the land which is nowhere, the land which is your only remaining home. Without me, the intelligible universe reverts to chaos. Creative and abysmal are inextricably linked in me; only I can mediate between them. Without me, mankind will sink into the mire and vanity of *knowing.* Through me, you and they will find the only way out of chaos: *understanding by living.*"

With this he let go of himself and became himself, his own person compassing the entirety of his past. It was not victory, not defeat, but a new thing to be shared with any inner life he chose. Leto savored this newness, letting it possess every cell, every nerve, giving up what the *einfalle* had presented to him and recovering the totality in the same instant.

After a time, he awoke in white darkness. With a flash of awareness he knew where his flesh was: seated on sand about a kilometer from the cliff wall which marked the northern boundary of the sietch. He knew that sietch now: Jacurutu for certain . . . and Fondak. But it was far different from the myths and legends and the rumors which the smugglers allowed.

A young woman sat on a rug directly in front of him, a bright glowglobe anchored to her left sleeve and drifting just above her head. When Leto looked away from the glowglobe, there were stars. He knew this young woman; she was the one from his vision earlier, the roaster of coffee. She was Namri's niece, as ready with a knife as Namri was. There was the knife in her lap. She wore a simple green robe over a grey stillsuit. *Sabiha,* that was her name. And Namri had his own plans for her.

Sabiha saw the awakening in his eyes, said: "It's almost dawn. You've spent the whole night here."

"And most of a day," he said. "You make good coffee."

This statement puzzled her, but she ignored it with a single-mindedness which spoke of harsh training and explicit instructions for her present behavior.

"It's the hour of assassins," Leto said. "But your knife is no longer needed." He glanced at the crysknife in her lap.

"Namri will be the judge of that," she said.

*Not Halleck, then.* She only confirmed his inner knowledge.

"Shai-Hulud is a great garbage collector and eraser of unwanted evidence," Leto said. "I've used him thus myself."

She rested her hand lightly on the knife handle.

"How much is revealed by where we sit and how we sit," he said. "You sit upon the rug and I upon the sand."

Her hand closed over the knife handle.

Leto yawned, a gaping and stretching which made his jaws ache. "I've had a vision which included you," he said.

Her shoulders relaxed slightly.

"We've been very one-sided about Arrakis," he said. "Barbaric of us. There's a certain momentum in what we've been doing, but now we must undo some of our work. The scales must be brought into better balance."

A puzzled frown touched Sabiha's face.

"My vision," he said. "Unless we restore the dance of life here on Dune, the dragon on the floor of the desert will be no more."

Because he'd used the Old Fremen name for the great worm, she was a moment understanding him. Then: "The worms?"

"We're in a dark passage," he said. "Without spice, the Empire falls apart. The Guild will not move. Planets will slowly lose their clear memories of each other. They'll turn inward upon themselves. Space will become a boundary when the Guild navigators lose their mastery. We'll cling to our dunetops and be ignorant of that which is above us and below us."

"You speak very strangely," she said. "How have you seen *me* in your vision?"

*Trust Fremen superstition!* he thought. He said: "I've become pasigraphic. I'm a living glyph to write out the changes which must come to pass. If I do not write them, you'll encounter such heartache as no human should experience."

"What words are these?" she asked, but her hand remained lightly on the knife.

Leto turned his head toward the cliffs of Jacurutu, seeing the beginning glow which would be Second Moon making its predawn passage behind the rocks. The death-scream of a desert hare shocked its way through him. He saw Sabiha shudder. There came the beating of wings—a predator bird, night creature here. He saw the ember glow of many eyes as they swept past above him, headed for crannies in the cliff.

"I must follow the dictates of my new heart," Leto said. "You look upon me as a mere child, Sabiha, but if—"

"They warned me about you," Sabiha said, and now her shoulders were stiff with readiness.

He heard the fear in her voice, said: "Don't fear me, Sabiha. You've lived eight more years than this flesh of mine. For that, I honor you. But I have untold thousands more years of other lives, far more than you have known. Don't look upon me as a child. I have bridged the many futures and, in one, saw us entwined in love. You and I, Sabiha."

"What are . . . This can't . . ." She broke off in confusion.

"The idea could grow on you," he said. "Now help me back to the sietch, for I've been in far places and am weak with the weariness of my travels. Namri must hear where I have been."

He saw the indecision in her, said: "Am I not the Guest of the Cavern? Namri must learn what I have learned. We have many things to do lest our universe degenerate."

"I don't believe that . . . about the worms," she said.

"Nor about us entwined in love?"

She shook her head. But he could see the thoughts drifting through her mind like windblown feathers. His words both attracted and repelled her. To be consort of power, that certainly carried high allure. Yet there were her uncle's orders. But one day this son of Muad'Dib might rule here on Dune and in the farthest reaches of their universe. She encountered then an extremely Fremen, cavern-hiding aversion to such a future. The consort of Leto would be seen by everyone, would be an object of gossip and speculations. She could have wealth, though, and . . .

"I am the son of Muad'Dib, able to see the future," he said.

Slowly she replaced her knife in its sheath, lifted herself easily from the rug, crossed to his side and helped him to his feet. Leto found himself amused by her actions then: she folded the rug neatly and draped it across her right shoulder.

He saw her measuring the difference in their sizes, reflecting upon his words: *Entwined in love?*

*Size is another thing that changes,* he thought.

She put a hand on his arm then to help him and control him. He stumbled and she spoke sharply: "We're too far from the sietch for *that!*" Meaning the unwanted sound which might attract a worm.

Leto felt that his body had become a dry shell like that abandoned by an insect. He knew this shell: it was one with the society which had been built upon the melange trade and its Religion of the Golden Elixir. It was emptied by its excesses. Muad'Dib's high aims had fallen into wizardry which was enforced by the military arm of Auqaf. Muad'Dib's religion had another name now; it was Shien-san-Shao, an Ixian label which designated the intensity and insanity of those who thought they could bring the universe to paradise at the point of a crysknife. But that too would change as Ix had changed. For they were merely the ninth planet of their sun, and had even forgotten the language which had given them their name.

"The Jihad was a kind of mass insanity," he muttered.

"What?" Sabiha had been concentrating on the problem of making him walk without rhythm, hiding their presence out here on the open sand. She was a moment focusing on his words, then interpreted them as another product of his obvious fatigue. She felt the weakness of him, the way he'd been drained by the trance. It seemed pointless and cruel to her. If he were to be killed as Namri said, then it should be done quickly without all of this byplay. Leto had spoken of a marvelous revelation, though. Perhaps that was what Namri sought. Certainly that must be the motive behind the behavior of this child's own grandmother. Why else would Our Lady of Dune give her sanction to these perilous acts against a child?

*Child?*

Again she reflected upon his words. They were at the cliff base now and she stopped her charge, letting him relax a moment here where it was safer. Looking down at him in the dim starlight, she asked: "How could there be no more worms?"

"Only I can change that," he said. "Have no fear. I can change anything."

"But it's—"

"Some questions have no answers," he said. "I've seen that future, but the contradictions would only confuse you. This is a changing universe and we are the strangest change of all. We resonate to many influences. Our futures need constant updating. Now, there's a barrier which we must remove. This requires that we do brutal things, that we go against our most basic, our dearest wishes. . . . But it must be done."

"What must be done?"

"Have you ever killed a friend?" he asked and, turning, led the way into the gap which sloped upward to the sietch's hidden entrance. He moved as quickly as his trance-fatigue would permit, but she was right behind him, clutching his robe and pulling him to a stop.

"What's this of killing a friend?"

"He'll die anyway," Leto said. "I don't have to do it, but I could prevent it. If I don't prevent it, is that not killing him?"

"Who is this . . . who will die?"

"The alternative keeps me silent," he said. "I might have to give my sister to a monster."

Again he turned away from her, and this time when she pulled at his robe he resisted, refusing to answer her questions. *Best she not know until the time comes,* he thought.

> *Natural selection has been described as an environment selectively screening for those who will have progeny. Where humans are concerned, though, this is an extremely limiting viewpoint. Reproduction by sex tends toward experiment and innovation. It raises many questions, including the ancient one about whether environment is a selective agent after the variation occurs, or whether environment plays a pre-selective role in determining the variations which it screens. Dune did not really answer those questions; it merely raised new questions which Leto and the Sisterhood may attempt to answer over the next five hundred generations.*

> —The Dune Catastrophe
> After Harq al-Ada

The bare brown rocks of the Shield Wall loomed in the distance, visible to Ghanima as the embodiment of that apparition which threatened her future. She stood at the edge of the roof garden atop the Keep, the setting sun at her back. The sun held a deep orange glow from intervening dust clouds, a color as rich as the rim of a worm's mouth. She sighed, thinking: *Alia . . . Alia . . . Is your fate to be my fate?*

The inner lives had grown increasingly clamorous of late. There was something about female conditioning in a Fremen society—perhaps it was a real sexual difference, but whatever— the female was more susceptible to that inner tide. Her grandmother had warned about it as they'd schemed, drawing on the accumulated wisdom of the Bene Gesserit but awakening that wisdom's threats within Ghanima.

"Abomination," the Lady Jessica had said, "our term for the pre-born, has a long history of bitter experiences behind it. The way of it seems to be that the inner lives divide. They split into the benign and the malignant. The benign remain tractable, useful. The malignant appear to unite in one powerful psyche, trying to take over the living flesh and its consciousness. The process is known to take considerable time, but its signs are well known."

"Why did you abandon Alia?" Ghanima asked.

"I fled in terror of what I'd created," Jessica said, her voice low. "I gave up. And my burden now is that . . . perhaps I gave up too soon."

"What do you mean?"

"I cannot explain yet, but . . . maybe . . . no! I'll not give you false hopes.

*Ghafla,* the abominable distraction, has a long history in human mythology. It was called many things, but chiefly it was called *possession.* That's what it seems to be. You lose your way in the malignancy and it takes possession of you."

"Leto . . . feared the spice," Ghanima said, finding that she could talk about him quietly. The terrible price demanded of them!

"And wisely," Jessica had said. She would say no more.

But Ghanima had risked an exploration of her inner memories, peering past an odd blurred veil and futilely expanding on the Bene Gesserit fears. To explain what had befallen Alia did not ease it one bit. The Bene Gesserit accumulation of experience had pointed to a possible way out of the trap, though, and when Ghanima ventured the inner sharing, she first called upon the *Mohalata,* a partnership of the benign which might protect her.

She recalled that sharing as she stood in the sunset glow at the edge of the Keep's roof garden. Immediately she felt the memory-presence of her mother. Chani stood there, an apparition between Ghanima and the distant cliffs.

"Enter here and you will eat the fruit of the Zaqquum, the food of hell!" Chani said. "Bar this door, my daughter; it is your only safety."

The inner clamor lifted itself around the vision and Ghanima fled, sinking her consciousness into the Sisterhood's Credo, reacting out of desperation more than trust. Quickly she recited the Credo, moving her lips, letting her voice rise to a whisper:

*"Religion is the emulation of the adult by the child. Religion is the encystment of past beliefs: mythology, which is guesswork, the hidden assumptions of trust in the universe, those pronouncements which men have made in search of personal power, all of it mingled with shreds of enlightenment. And always the ultimate unspoken commandment is 'Thou shalt not question!' But we question. We break that commandment as a matter of course. The work to which we have set ourselves is the liberating of the imagination, the harnessing of imagination to humankind's deepest sense of creativity."*

Slowly a sense of order returned to Ghanima's thoughts. She felt her body trembling, though, and knew how fragile was this peace she had attained—and that blurring veil remained in her mind.

"Leb Kamai," she whispered. "Heart of my enemy, you shall not be my heart."

And she called up a memory of Farad'n's features, the saturnine young face with its heavy brows and firm mouth.

*Hate will make me strong,* she thought. *In hate, I can resist Alia's fate.*

But the trembling fragility of her position remained, and all she could think about was how much Farad'n resembled his uncle, the late Shaddam IV.

"Here you are!"

It was Irulan coming up from Ghanima's right, striding along the parapet with movements reminiscent of a man. Turning, Ghanima thought: *And she's Shaddam's daughter.*

"Why will you persist in sneaking out alone?" Irulan demanded, stopping in front of Ghanima and towering over her with a scowling face.

Ghanima refrained from saying that she was not alone, that guards had seen her emerge onto the roof. Irulan's anger went to the fact that they were in the open here and that a distant weapon might find them.

"You're not wearing a stillsuit," Ghanima said. "Did you know that in the old days someone caught outside the sietch without a stillsuit was automatically killed. To waste water was to endanger the tribe."

"Water! Water!" Irulan snapped. "I want to know why you endanger yourself this way. Come back inside. You make trouble for all of us."

"What danger is there now?" Ghanima asked. "Stilgar has purged the traitors. Alia's guards are everywhere."

Irulan peered upward at the darkening sky. Stars were already visible against a grey-blue backdrop. She returned her attention to Ghanima. "I won't argue. I was sent to tell you we have word from Farad'n. He accepts, but for some reason he wishes to delay the ceremony."

"How long?"

"We don't know yet. It's being negotiated. But Duncan is being sent home."

"And my grandmother?"

"She chooses to stay on Salusa for the time being."

"Who can blame her?" Ghanima asked.

"That silly fight with Alia!"

"Don't try to gull me, Irulan! That was no silly fight. I've heard the stories."

"The Sisterhood's fears—"

"Are real," Ghanima said. "Well, you've delivered your message. Will you use this opportunity to have another try at dissuading me?"

"I've given up."

"You should know better than to try lying to me," Ghanima said.

"Very well! I'll keep trying to dissuade you. This course is madness." And Irulan wondered why she let Ghanima become so irritating. A Bene Gesserit didn't need to be irritated at anything. She said: "I'm concerned by the extreme danger to you. You know that. Ghani, Ghani . . . you're Paul's daughter. How can you—"

"Because I'm his daughter," Ghanima said. "We Atreides go back to Agamemnon and we know what's in our blood. Never forget that, childless wife of my father. We Atreides have a bloody history and we're not through with the blood."

Distracted, Irulan asked: "Who's Agamemnon?"

"How sparse your vaunted Bene Gesserit education proves itself," Ghanima said. "I keep forgetting that you foreshorten history. But my memories go back to . . ." She broke off; best not to arouse those shades from their fragile sleep.

"Whatever you remember," Irulan said, "you must know how dangerous this course is to—"

"I'll kill him," Ghanima said. "He owes me a life."

"And I'll prevent it if I can."

"We already know this. You won't get the opportunity. Alia is sending you south to one of the new towns until after it's done."

Irulan shook her head in dismay. "Ghani, I took my oath that I'd guard you against any danger. I'll do it with my own life if necessary. If you think I'm going to languish in some brickwalled djedida while you . . ."

"There's always the Huanui," Ghanima said, speaking softly. "We have the deathstill as an alternative. I'm sure you couldn't interfere from there."

Irulan paled, put a hand to her mouth, forgetting for a moment all of her training. It was a measure of how much care she had invested in Ghanima, this almost complete abandonment of everything except animal fear. She spoke out of that shattering emotion, allowing it to tremble on her lips. "Ghani, I don't fear for myself. I'd throw myself into the worm's mouth for you. Yes, I'm what you call me, the childless wife of your father, but you're the child I never had. I beg you . . ." Tears glistened at the corners of her eyes.

Ghanima fought down a tightness in her throat, said: "There is another difference between us. You were never Fremen. I'm nothing else. This is a chasm which divides us. Alia knows. Whatever else she may be, she knows this."

"You can't tell what Alia knows," Irulan said, speaking bitterly. "If I didn't know her for Atreides, I'd swear she has set herself to destroy her own Family."

*And how do you know she's still Atreides?* Ghanima thought, wondering at this blindness in Irulan. This was a Bene Gesserit, and who knew better than they the history of Abomination? She would not let herself even think about it, let alone believe it. Alia must have worked some witchery on this poor woman.

Ghanima said: "I owe you a water debt. For that, I'll guard your life. But your cousin's forfeit. Say no more of that."

Irulan stilled the trembling of her lips, wiped her eyes. "I did love your father," she whispered. "I didn't even know it until he was dead."

"Perhaps he isn't dead," Ghanima said. "This Preacher . . ."

"Ghani! Sometimes I don't understand you. Would Paul attack his own family?"

Ghanima shrugged, looked out at the darkening sky. "He might find amusement in such a—"

"How can you speak so lightly of this—"

"To keep away the dark depths," Ghanima said. "I don't taunt you. The gods know I don't. But I'm not just my father's daughter. I'm every person who's contributed seed to the Atreides. You won't think of Abomination, but I can't think of anything else. I'm the pre-born. I know what's within me."

"That foolish old superstition about—"

"Don't!" Ghanima reached a hand toward Irulan's mouth. "I'm every Bene Gesserit of their damnable breeding program up to and including my grandmother. And I'm very much more." She tore at her left palm, drawing blood with a fingernail. "This is a young body, but its experiences . . . Oh, *gods,* Irulan! My experiences! No!" She put out her hand once more as Irulan moved closer. "I know all of those futures which my father explored. I've the wisdom of so many lifetimes, and all the ignorance, too . . . all the frailties. If you'd help me, Irulan, first learn who I am."

Instinctively Irulan bent and gathered Ghanima into her arms, holding her close, cheek against cheek.

*Don't let me have to kill this woman,* Ghanima thought. *Don't let that happen.* As this thought swept through her, the whole desert passed into night.

*One small bird has called thee*
*From a beak streaked crimson.*
*It cried once over Sietch Tabr*
*And thou went forth unto Funeral Plain.*

**—Lament for Leto II**

Leto awoke to the tinkle of water rings in a woman's hair. He looked to the open doorway of his cell and saw Sabiha sitting there. In the half-immersed awareness of the spice he saw her outlined by all that his vision revealed about her. She was two years past the age when most Fremen women were wed or at least betrothed. Therefore her family was saving her for something . . . or someone. She was nubile . . . obviously. His vision-shrouded eyes saw her as a creature out of humankind's Terranic past: dark hair and pale skin, deep sockets which gave her blue-in-blue eyes a greenish cast. She possessed a small nose and a wide mouth above a sharp chin. And she was a living signal to him that the Bene Gesserit plan was known—or suspected—here in Jacurutu. So they hoped to revive Pharaonic Imperialism through him, did they? Then what was their design to force him into marrying his sister? Surely Sabiha could not prevent that.

His captors knew the plan, though. And how had they learned? They'd not shared its vision. They'd not gone with him where life became a moving membrane in other dimensions. The reflexive and circular subjectivity of the visions which revealed Sabiha were his and his alone.

Again the water rings tinkled in Sabiha's hair and the sound stirred up his visions. He knew where he had been and what he had learned. Nothing could erase that. He was not riding a great Maker palanquin now, the tinkle of water rings among the passengers a rhythm for their passage songs. No . . . . He was here in the cell of Jacurutu, embarked on that most dangerous of all journeys: away from and back to the *Ahl as-sunna wal-jamas*, from the real world of the senses and back to that world.

What was she doing there with the water rings tinkling in her hair? Oh, yes. She was mixing more of the brew which they thought held him captive: food laced with spice essence to keep him half in and half out of the real universe until either he died or his grandmother's plan succeeded. And every time he thought he'd won, they sent him back. The Lady Jessica was right, of course—that old witch! But what a thing to do. The total recall of all those lives within him was of no use at all until he could organize the data and remember it at will. Those lives had been the raw stuff of anarchy. One or all of them could have overwhelmed him. The spice and its peculiar setting here in Jacurutu had been a desperate gamble.

*Now Gurney waits for the sign and I refuse to give it to him. How long will his patience last?*

He stared out at Sabiha. She'd thrown her hood back and revealed the tribal tattoos at her temples. Leto did not recognize the tattoos at first, then remembered where he was. Yes, Jacurutu still lived.

Leto did not know whether to be thankful toward his grandmother or hate her. She wanted him to have conscious-level instincts. But instincts were only racial memories of how to handle crises. His direct memories of those other lives told him far more than that. He had it all organized now, and could see the peril of revealing himself to Gurney. No way of keeping the revelation from Namri. And Namri was another problem.

Sabiha entered the cell with a bowl in her hands. He admired the way the light from outside made rainbow circles at the edges of her hair. Gently she raised his head and began feeding him from the bowl. It was only then he realized how weak he was. He allowed her to feed him while his mind went roving, recalling the session with Gurney and Namri. They believed him! Namri more than Gurney, but even Gurney could not deny what his senses had already reported to him about the planet.

Sabiha wiped his mouth with a hem of her robe.

*Ahhh, Sabiha,* he thought, recalling that other vision which filled his heart with pain. *Many nights have I dreamed beside the open water, hearing the winds pass overhead. Many nights my flesh lay beside the snake's den and I dreamed of Sabiha in the summer heat. I saw her storing spice-bread baked on red-hot sheets of plasteel. I saw the clear water in the qanat, gentle and shining, but a stormwind ran through my heart. She sips coffee and eats. Her teeth shine in the shadows. I see her braiding my water rings into her hair. The amber fragrance of her bosom strikes through to my innermost senses. She torments me and oppresses me by her very existence.*

The pressure of his multi-memories exploded the time-frozen englobement which he had tried to resist. He felt twining bodies, the sounds of sex, rhythms laced in every sensory impression: lips, breathing, moist breaths, tongues. Somewhere in his vision there were helix shapes, coal-colored, and he felt the beat of those shapes as they turned within him. A voice pleaded in his skull: "Please, please, please, please . . ." There was an adult beefswelling in his loins and he felt his mouth open, holding, clinging to the girdershape of ecstasy. Then a sigh, a lingering groundswelling sweetness, a collapse.

Oh, how sweet to let that come into existence!

"Sabiha," he whispered. "Oh, my Sabiha."

When her charge had clearly gone deeply into the trance after his food, Sabiha took the bowl and left, pausing at the doorway to speak to Namri. "He called my name again."

"Go back and stay with him," Namri said. "I must find Halleck and discuss this with him."

Sabiha deposited the bowl beside the doorway and returned to the cell. She sat on the edge of the cot, staring at Leto's shadowed face.

Presently he opened his eyes and put a hand out, touching her cheek. He began to talk to her then, telling her about the vision in which she had lived.

She covered his hand with her own as he spoke. How sweet he was . . . how very swee— She sank onto the cot, cushioned by his hand, unconscious before he pulled the hand away. Leto sat up, feeling the depths of his weakness. The spice and its visions had drained him. He searched through his cells for every spare spark of energy, climbed from the cot without disturbing Sabiha. He had to go, but he knew he'd not get far. Slowly he sealed his stillsuit, drew the robe around him, slipped through the passage to the outer shaft. There were a few people about, busy at their own affairs. They knew him, but he was not their responsibility. Namri and Halleck would know what he was doing; Sabiha could not be far away.

He found the kind of side passage he needed and walked boldly down it.

Behind him Sabiha slept peacefully until Halleck roused her.

She sat up, rubbed her eyes, saw the empty cot, saw her uncle standing behind Halleck, the anger on their faces.

Namri answered the expression on her face: "Yes, he's gone."

"How could you let him escape?" Halleck raged. "How is this possible?"

"He was seen going toward the lower exit," Namri said, his voice oddly calm.

Sabiha cowered in front of them, remembering.

"How?" Halleck demanded.

"I don't know. I don't know."

"It's night and he's weak," Namri said. "He won't get far."

Halleck whirled on him. "You want the boy to die!"

"It wouldn't displease me."

Again Halleck confronted Sabiha. "Tell me what happened."

"He touched my cheek. He kept talking about his vision . . . us together." She looked down at the empty cot. "He made me sleep. He put some magic on me."

Halleck glanced at Namri. "Could he be hiding inside somewhere?"

"Nowhere inside. He'd be found, seen. He was headed for the exit. He's out there."

"Magic," Sabiha muttered.

"No magic," Namri said. "He hypnotized her. Almost did it to me, you remember? Said I was his friend."

"He's very weak," Halleck said.

"Only in his body," Namri said. "He won't go far, though. I disabled the heel pumps of his stillsuit. He'll die with no water if we don't find him."

Halleck almost turned and struck Namri, but held himself in rigid control. Jessica had warned him that Namri might have to kill the lad. Gods below! What a pass they'd come to, Atreides against Atreides. He said: "Is it possible he just wandered away in the spice trance?"

"What difference does it make?" Namri asked. "If he escapes us he must die."

"We'll start searching at first light," Halleck said. "Did he take a Fremkit?"

"There're always a few beside the doorseal," Namri said. "He'd have been a fool not to take one. Somehow he has never struck me as a fool."

"Then send a message to our friends," Halleck said. "Tell them what's happened."

"No messages this night," Namri said. "There's a storm coming. The tribes have been tracking it for three days now. It'll be here by midnight. Already communication's blanked out. The satellites signed off this sector two hours ago."

A deep sigh shook Halleck. The boy would die out there for sure if the sandblast storm caught him. It would eat the flesh from his bones and sliver the bones to fragments. The contrived false death would become real. He slapped a fist into an open palm. The storm could trap them in the sietch. They couldn't even mount a search. And the storm static had already isolated the sietch.

"Distrans," he said, thinking they might imprint a message onto a bat's voice and dispatch it with the alarm.

Namri shook his head. "Bats won't fly in a storm. Come on, man. They're more sensitive than we are. They'll cower in the cliffs until it's past. Best to wait for the satellites to pick us up again. Then we can try to find his remains."

"Not if he took a Fremkit and hid in the sand," Sabiha said.

Cursing under his breath, Halleck whirled away from them, strode out into the sietch.

> *Peace demands solutions, but we never reach living solutions; we only work toward them. A fixed solution is, by definition, a dead solution. The trouble with peace is that it tends to punish mistakes instead of rewarding brilliance.*

> **—The Words of My Father:**
> **an account of Muad'Dib**
> **reconstructed by Harq al-Ada**

"She's training him? She's training Farad'n?"

Alia glared at Duncan Idaho with a deliberate mix of anger and incredulity. The Guild heighliner had swung into orbit around Arrakis at noon local. An hour later the lighter had put Idaho down at Arrakeen, unannounced, but all casual and open. Within minutes a 'thopter had deposited him atop the Keep. Warned of his impending arrival, Alia had greeted him there, coldly formal before her guards, but now they stood in her quarters beneath the north rim. He had just delivered his report, truthfully, precisely, emphasizing each datum in mentat fashion.

"She has taken leave of her senses," Alia said.

He treated the statement as a mentat problem. "All the indicators are that she remains well balanced, sane. I should say her sanity index was—"

"Stop that!" Alia snapped. "What can she be thinking of?"

Idaho, who knew that his own emotional balance depended now upon retreat into mentat coldness, said: "I compute she is thinking of her granddaughter's betrothal." His features remained carefully bland, a mask for the raging grief which threatened to engulf him. There was no Alia here. Alia was dead. For a time he'd maintained a myth-Alia before his senses, someone he'd manu-factured out of his own needs, but a mentat could carry on such self-deception for only a limited time. This creature in human guise was possessed; a demon-psyche drove her. His steely eyes with their myriad facets available at will reproduced upon his vision centers a multiplicity of myth-Alias. But when he combined them into a single image, no Alia remained. Her features moved to other demands. She was a shell within which outrages had been committed.

"Where's Ghanima?" he asked.

She waved the question aside. "I've sent her with Irulan to stay in Stilgar's keeping."

*Neutral territory,* he thought. *There's been another negotiation with rebellious tribes. She's losing ground and doesn't know it . . . or does she? Is there another reason? Has Stilgar gone over to her?*

"The betrothal," Alia mused. "What are conditions in the Corrino House?"

"Salusa swarms with *outrine* relatives, all working upon Farad'n, hoping for a share in his return to power."

"And she's training him in the Bene Gesserit . . ."

"Is it not fitting for Ghanima's husband?"

Alia smiled to herself, thinking of Ghanima's adamant rage. Let Farad'n be trained. Jessica was training a corpse. It would all work out.

"I must consider this at length," she said. "You're very quiet, Duncan."

"I await your questions."

"I see. You know, I was very angry with you. Taking her to Farad'n!"

"You commanded me to make it real."

"I was forced to put out the report that you'd both been taken captive," she said.

"I obeyed your orders."

"You're so literal at times, Duncan. You almost frighten me. But if you hadn't, well . . ."

"The Lady Jessica's out of harm's way," he said. "And for Ghanima's sake we should be grateful that—"

"Exceedingly grateful," she agreed. And she thought: *He's no longer trustworthy. He has that damnable Atreides loyalty. I must make an excuse to send him away . . . and have him eliminated. An accident, of course.*

She touched his cheek.

Idaho forced himself to respond to the caress, taking her hand and kissing it.

"Duncan, Duncan, how sad it is," she said. "But I cannot keep you here with me. Too much is happening and I've so few I can completely trust."

He released her hand, waited.

"I was *forced* to send Ghanima to Tabr," she said. "Things are in deep unrest here. Raiders from the Broken Lands breached the qanats at Kagga Basin and spilled all of their waters into the sands. Arrakeen was on short rations. The Basin's alive with sandtrout yet, reaping the water harvest. They're being dealt with, of course, but we're spread very thin."

He'd already noted how few amazons of Alia's guard were to be seen in the Keep. And he thought: *The Maquis of the Inner Desert will keep on probing her defenses. Doesn't she know that?*

"Tabr is still neutral territory," she said. "Negotiations are continuing there right now. Javid's there with a delegation from the Priesthood. But I'd like you at Tabr to watch them, especially Irulan."

"She *is* Corrino," he agreed.

But he saw in her eyes that she was rejecting him. How transparent this Alia-creature had become!

She waved a hand. "Go now, Duncan, before I soften and keep you here beside me. I've missed you so . . ."

"And I've missed you," he said, allowing all of his grief to flow into his voice.

She stared at him, startled by the sadness. Then: "For my sake, Duncan." And she thought: *Too bad, Duncan.* She said: "Zia will take you to Tabr. We need the 'thopter back here."

*Her pet amazon,* he thought. *I must be careful of that one.*

"I understand," he said, once more taking her hand and kissing it. He stared at the dear flesh which once had been his Alia's. He could not bring himself to look at her face as he left. Someone else stared back at him from her eyes.

As he mounted to the Keep's roofpad, Idaho probed a growing sense of unanswered questions. The meeting with Alia had been extremely trying for the mentat part of him which kept reading data signs. He waited beside the 'thopter with one of the Keep's amazons, stared grimly southward. Imagination took his gaze beyond the Shield Wall to Sietch Tabr. *Why does Zia take me to Tabr? Returning a 'thopter is a menial task. What is the delay? Is Zia getting special instructions?*

Idaho glanced at the watchful guard, mounted to the pilot's position in the 'thopter. He leaned out, said: "Tell Alia I'll send the 'thopter back immediately with one of Stilgar's men."

Before the guard could protest he closed the door and started the 'thopter. He could see her standing there indecisively. Who could question Alia's consort? He had the 'thopter airborne before she could make up her mind what to do.

Now, alone in the 'thopter, he allowed his grief to spend itself in great wracking sobs. Alia was gone. They had parted forever. Tears flowed from his Tleilaxu eyes and he whispered: "Let all the waters of Dune flow into the sand. They will not match my tears."

This was a non-mentat excess, though, and he recognized it as such, forcing himself to sober assessment of present necessities. The 'thopter demanded his attention. The reactions of flying brought him some relief, and he had himself once more in hand.

*Ghanima with Stilgar again. And Irulan.*

Why had Zia been designated to accompany him? He made it a mentat problem and the answer chilled him. *I was to have a fatal accident.*

*This rocky shrine to the skull of a ruler grants no prayers. It has become the*
*grave of lamentations. Only the wind hears the voice of this place. The cries of*
*night creatures and the passing wonder of two moons, all say his day has*
*ended. No more supplicants come. The visitors have gone from the feast. How*
*bare the pathway down this mountain.*

**—Lines at the Shrine of an Atreides Duke**
**Anon.**

The thing had the deceptive appearance of simplicity to Leto: avoiding the vision, do that which has not been seen. He knew the trap in his thought, how the casual threads of a locked future twisted themselves together until they held you fast, but he had a new grip on those threads. Nowhere had he seen himself running from Jacurutu. The thread to Sabiha must be cut first.

He crouched now in the last daylight at the eastern edge of the rock which protected Jacurutu. His Fremkit had produced energy tablets and food. He waited now for strength. To the west lay Lake Azrak, the gypsum plain where once there'd been open water in the days before the worm. Unseen to the east lay the Bene Sherk, a scattering of new settlements encroaching upon the open *bled*. To the south lay the Tanzerouft, the Land of Terror: thirty-eight hundred kilometers of wasteland broken only by patches of grass-locked dunes and windtraps to water them—the work of the ecological transformation remaking the landscape of Arrakis. They were serviced by airborne teams and no one stayed for long.

*I will go south*, he told himself. *Gurney will expect me to do that.* This was not the moment to do the completely unexpected.

It would be dark soon and he could leave this temporary hiding place. He stared at the southern skyline. There was a whistling of dun sky along that horizon, rolling there like smoke, a burning line of undulant dust—a storm. He watched the high center of the storm rising up out of the Great Flat like a questing worm. For a full minute he watched the center, saw that it did not move to the right or the left. The old Fremen saying leaped into his mind: *When the center does not move, you are in its path.*

That storm changed matters.

For a moment he stared back westward, the direction of Tabr, feeling the deceptive grey-tan peace of the desert evening, seeing the white gypsum pan edged by wind-rounded pebbles, the desolate emptiness with its unreal surface of glaring white reflecting dust clouds. Nowhere in any vision had he seen himself surviving the grey serpent of a mother storm or buried too deeply in sand to survive. There was only that vision of rolling in wind . . . but that might come later.

And a storm was out there, winding across many degrees of latitude, whipping its world into submission. It could be risked. There were old stories, always heard from a friend of a friend, that one could lock an exhausted worm on the surface by propping a Maker hook beneath one of its wide rings and, having

immobilized it, ride out a storm in the leeward shadow. There was a line
between audacity and abandoned recklessness which tempted him. That storm
would not come before midnight at the earliest. There was time. How many
threads could be cut here? All, including the final one?

*Gurney will expect me to go south, but not into a storm.*

He stared down to the south, seeking a pathway, saw the fluent ebony
brushstroke of a deep gorge curving through Jacurutu's rock. He saw sand curls
in the bowels of the gorge, chimera sand. It uttered its haughty runnels onto the
plain as though it were water. The gritty taste of thirst whispered in his mouth
as he shouldered his Fremkit and let himself down onto the path which led into
the canyon. It was still light enough that he might be seen, but he knew he was
gambling with time.

As he reached the canyon's lip, the quick night of the central desert fell upon
him. He was left with the parched glissando of moonglow to light his way
toward the Tanzerouft. He felt his heartbeat quicken with all of the fears which
his wealth of memories provided. He sensed that he might be going down
into Huanui-naa, as Fremen fears labeled the greatest storms: the Earth's
Deathstill. But whatever came, it would be visionless. Every step left farther
behind him the spice-induced *dhyana*, that spreading awareness of his
intuitive-creative nature with its unfolding to the motionless chain of causality.
For every hundred steps he took now, there must be at least one step aside,
beyond words and into communion with his newly grasped internal reality.

*One way or another, father, I'm coming to you.*

There were birds invisible in the rocks around him, making themselves
known by small sounds. Fremen-wise, he listened for their echoes to guide his
way where he could not see. Often as he passed crannies he marked the baleful
green of eyes, creatures crouched in hiding because they knew a storm
approached.

He emerged from the gorge onto the desert. Living sand moved and breathed
beneath him, telling of deep actions and latent fumaroles. He looked back and
up to the moon-touched lava caps on Jacurutu's buttes. The whole structure
was metamorphic, mostly pressure-formed. Arrakis still had something to say
in its own future. He planted his thumper to call a worm and, when it began
beating against the sand, took his position to watch and listen. Unconsciously
his right hand went to the Atreides hawk ring concealed in a knotted fold of his
*dishdasha*. Gurney had found it, but had left it. What had he thought, seeing
Paul's ring?

*Father, expect me soon.*

The worm came from the south. It angled in to avoid the rocks, not as large a
worm as he'd hoped, but that could not be remedied. He gauged its passage,
planted his hooks, and went up the scaled side with a quick scrambling as it
swept over the thumper in a swishing dust spray. The worm turned easily under
the pressure of his hooks. The wind of its passage began to whip his robe. He
bent his gaze on the southern stars, dim through dust, and pointed the worm
that way.

*Right into the storm.*

As First Moon rose, Leto gauged the storm height and put off his estimate of its arrival. Not before daylight. It was spreading out, gathering more energy for a great leap. There'd be plenty of work for the ecological transformation teams. It was as though the planet fought them with a conscious fury out here, the fury increasing as the transformation took in more land.

All night he pressed the worm southward, sensing the reserves of its energy in the movements transmitted through his feet. Occasionally he let the beast fall off to the west which it was forever trying to do, moved by the invisible boundaries of its territory or by a deep-seated awareness of the coming storm. Worms buried themselves to escape the sandblast winds, but this one would not sink beneath the desert while Maker hooks held any of its rings open.

At midnight the worm was showing many signs of exhaustion. He moved back along its great ridges and worked the flail, allowing it to slow down but continuing to drive it southward.

The storm arrived just after daybreak. First there was the beady stretched-out immobility of the desert dawn pressing dunes one into another. Next, the advancing dust caused him to seal his face flaps. In the thickening dust the desert became a dun picture without lines. Then sand needles began cutting his cheeks, stinging his lids. He felt the coarse grit on his tongue and knew the moment of decision had come. Should he risk the old stories by immobilizing the almost exhausted worm? He took only a heartbeat to discard this choice, worked his way back to the worm's tail, slacked off his hooks. Barely moving now, the worm began to burrow. But the excesses of the creature's heat-transfer system still churned up a cyclone oven behind him in the quickening storm. Fremen children learned the dangers of this position near the worm's tail with their earliest stories. Worms were oxygen factories; fire burned wildly in their passage, fed by the lavish exhalations from the chemical adaptations to friction within them.

Sand began to whip around his feet. Leto loosed his hooks and leaped wide to avoid the furnace at the tail. Everything depended now on getting beneath the sand where the worm had loosened it.

Grasping the static compaction tool in his left hand, he burrowed into a dune's slipface, knowing the worm was too tired to turn back and swallow him in its great white-orange mouth. As he burrowed with his left hand, his right hand worked the stilltent from his Fremkit and he readied it for inflation. It was all done in less than a minute: he had the tent into a hard-walled sand pocket on the lee face of a dune. He inflated the tent and crawled into it. Before sealing the sphincter, he reached out with the compaction tool, reversed its action. The slipface came sliding down over the tent. Only a few sand grains entered as he sealed the opening.

Now he had to work even more quickly. No sandsnorkel would reach up there to keep him supplied with breathing air. This was a great storm, the kind few survived. It would cover this place with tons of sand. Only the tender bubble of the stilltent with its compacted outer shell would protect him.

Leto stretched flat on his back, folded his hands over his breast and sent himself into a dormancy trance where his lungs would move only once an hour.

In this he committed himself to the unknown. The storm would pass and, if it did not expose his fragile pocket, he might emerge . . . or he might enter the *Madinat as-salam,* the Abode of Peace. Whatever happened, he knew he had to break the threads, one by one, leaving him at last only the Golden Path. It was that, or he could not return to the caliphate of his father's heirs. No more would he live the lie of that *Desposyni,* that terrible caliphate, chanting to the demiurge of his father. No more would he keep silent when a priest mouthed offensive nonsense: *"His crysknife will dissolve demons!"*

With this commitment, Leto's awareness slipped into the web of timeless *dao.*

> There exist obvious higher-order influences in any planetary system. This is often demonstrated by introducing terraform life onto newly discovered planets. In all such cases, the life in similar zones develops striking similarities of adaptive form. This form signifies much more than shape; it connotes a survival organization and a relationship of such organizations. The human quest for this interdependent order and our niche within it represents a profound necessity. The quest can, however, be perverted into a conservative grip on sameness. This has always proved deadly for the entire system.

> **—The Dune Catastrophe**
> **After Harq al-Ada**

"My son didn't really see *the future;* he saw the process of creation and its relationship to the myths in which men sleep," Jessica said. She spoke swiftly but without appearing to rush the matter. She knew the hidden observers would find a way to interrupt as soon as they recognized what she was doing.

Farad'n sat on the floor outlined in a shaft of afternoon sunlight which slanted through the window behind him. Jessica could just see the top of a tree in the courtyard garden when she glanced across from her position standing against the far wall. It was a new Farad'n she saw: more slender, more sinewy. The months of training had worked their inevitable magic on him. His eyes glittered when he stared at her.

"He saw the shapes which existing forces would create unless they were diverted," Jessica said. "Rather than turn against his fellow men, he turned against himself. He refused to accept only that which comforted him because that was moral cowardice."

Farad'n had learned to listen silently testing, probing, holding his questions until he had shaped them into a cutting edge. She had been talking about the Bene Gesserit view of molecular memory expressed as ritual and had, quite naturally, diverged to the Sisterhood's way of analyzing Paul Muad'Dib. Farad'n saw a shadow play in her words and actions, however, a projection of unconscious forms at variance with the surface intent of her statements.

"Of all our observations, this is the most crucial," she'd said. "Life is a mask through which the universe expresses itself. We assume that all of humankind and its supportive life forms represent a *natural* community and that the fate of all life is at stake in the fate of the individual. Thus, when it comes to that ultimate self-examination, the *amor fati*, we stop playing god and revert to teaching. In the crunch, we select individuals and we set them as free as we're able."

He saw now where she had to be going and knowing its effect upon those who watched through the spy eyes, refrained from casting an apprehensive glance at the door. Only a trained eye could have detected his momentary imbalance, but Jessica saw it and smiled. A smile, after all, could mean anything.

"This is a sort of graduation ceremony," she said. "I'm very pleased with you, Farad'n. Will you stand, please."

He obeyed, blocking off her view of the treetop through the window behind him.

Jessica held her arms stiffly at her side, said: "I am charged to say this to you. 'I stand in the sacred human presence. As I do now, so should you stand some day. I pray to your presence that this be so. The future remains uncertain and so it should, for it is the canvas upon which we paint our desires. Thus always the human condition faces a beautifully empty canvas. We possess only this moment in which to dedicate ourselves continuously to the sacred presence which we share and create.' "

As Jessica finished speaking, Tyekanik came through the door on her left, moving with a false casualness which the scowl on his face belied. "My Lord," he said. But it already was too late. Jessica's words and all of the preparation which had gone before had done their work. Farad'n no longer was Corrino. He was now Bene Gesserit.

> *What you of the CHOAM directorate seem unable to understand is that you seldom find real loyalties in commerce. When did you last hear of a clerk giving his life for the company? Perhaps your deficiency rests in the false assumption that you can order men to think and cooperate. This has been a failure of everything from religions to general staffs throughout history. As to religions, I recommend a rereading of Thomas Aquinas. As to you of CHOAM, what nonsense you believe! Men must want to do things out of their own innermost drives. People, not commercial organizations or chains of command, are what make great civilizations work. Every civilization depends upon the quality of the individuals it produces. If you over-organize humans, over-legalize them, suppress their urge to greatness—they cannot work and their civilization collapses.*

> **—A letter to CHOAM**
> **Attributed to The Preacher**

Leto came out of the trance with a softness of transition which did not define one condition as separate from another. One level of awareness simply moved into the other.

He knew where he was. A restoration of energy surged through him, but he sensed another message from the stale deadliness of the oxygen-depleted air within the stilltent. If he refused to move, he knew he would remain caught in the timeless web, the eternal *now* where all events co-existed. This prospect enticed him. He saw Time as a convention shaped by the collective mind of all sentience. Time and Space were categories imposed on the universe by his Mind. He had but to break free of the multiplicity where prescient visions lured him. Bold selection could change provisional futures.

What boldness did this moment require?

The trance state lured him. Leto felt that he had come from the *alam al-mythal* into the universe of reality only to find them identical. He wanted to maintain the Rihani magic of this revelation, but survival demanded decisions of him. His relentless taste for life sent its signals along his nerves.

Abruptly he reached out his right hand to where he had left the sand-compaction tool. He gripped it, rolled onto his stomach, and breached the tent's sphincter. A pool of sand drifted across his hand. Working in darkness, goaded by the stale air, he worked swiftly, tunneling upward at a steep angle. Six times his body lengths he went before he broke out into darkness and clean air. He slipped out onto the moonlit windface of a long curving dune, found himself about a third of the way from the dune's top.

It was Second Moon above him. It moved swiftly across him, departing beyond the dune, and the stars were laid out above him like bright rocks beside a path. Leto searched for the constellation of The Wanderer, found it, and let his gaze follow the outstretched arm to the brilliant glittering of Foum al-Hout, the polar star of the south.

*There's your damned universe for you!* he thought. Seen close up it was a hustling place like the sand all around him, a place of change, of uniqueness piled upon uniqueness. Seen from a distance, only the patterns lay revealed and those patterns tempted one to belief in absolutes.

*In absolutes, we may lose our way.* This made him think of the familiar warning from a Fremen ditty: "*Who loses his way in the Tanzerouft loses his life.*" The patterns could guide and they could trap. One had to remember that patterns change.

He took a deep breath, stirred himself into action. Sliding back down his passage, he collapsed the tent, brought it out and repacked the Fremkit.

A wine glow began to develop along the eastern horizon. He shouldered the pack, climbed to the dunecrest and stood there in the chill predawn air until the rising sun felt warm on his right cheek. He stained his eyepits then to reduce reflection, knowing that he must woo this desert now rather than fight her. When he had put the stain back into the pack he sipped from one of his catchtubes, drew in a sputtering of drops and then air.

Dropping to the sand, he began going over his stillsuit, coming at last to the heel pumps. They had been cut cleverly with a needle knife. He slipped out of the suit and repaired it, but the damage had been done. At least half of his body's water was gone. Were it not for the stilltent's catch . . . He mused on this as he donned the suit, thinking how odd it was that he'd not anticipated this. Here was an obvious danger of visionless future.

Leto squatted on the dunetop then, pressed himself against the loneliness of this place. He let his gaze wander, fishing in the sand for a whistling vent, any irregularity of the dunes which might indicate spice or worm activity. But the storm had stamped its uniformity upon the land. Presently he removed a thumper from the kit, armed it, and sent it rotating to call Shai-Hulud from his depths. He then moved off to wait.

The worm was a long time coming. He heard it before he saw it, turned eastward where the earthshaking susurration made the air tremble, waited for the first glimpse of orange from the mouth rising out of the sand. The worm lifted itself from the depths in a gigantic hissing of dust which obscured its flanks. The curving grey wall swept past Leto and he planted his hooks, went up the side in easy steps. He turned the worm southward in a great curving track as he climbed.

Under his goading hooks, the worm picked up speed. Wind whipped his robe against him. He felt himself to be goaded as the worm was goaded, an intense current of creation in his loins. Each planet has its own period and each life likewise, he reminded himself.

The worm was a type Fremen called a "growler." It frequently dug in its foreplates while the tail was driving. This produced rumbling sounds and caused part of its body to rise clear of the sand in a moving hump. It was a fast worm, though, and when they picked up a following wind the furnace exhalation of his tail sent a hot breeze across him. It was filled with acrid odors carried on the freshet of oxygen.

As the worm sped southward, Leto allowed his mind to run free. He tried to think of this passage as a new ceremony for his life, one which kept him from considering the price he'd have to pay for his Golden Path. Like the Fremen of old, he knew he'd have to adopt many new ceremonies to keep his personality from dividing into its memory parts, to keep the ravening hunters of his soul forever at bay. Contradictory images, never to be unified, must now be encysted in a living tension, a polarizing force which drove him from within.

*Always newness,* he thought. *I must always find the new threads out of my vision.*

In the early afternoon his attention was caught by a protuberance ahead and slightly to the right of his course. Slowly the protuberance became a narrow butte, an upthrust rock precisely where he'd expected it.

*Now Namri . . . Now Sabiha, let us see how your brethren take to my presence,* he thought. This was a most delicate thread ahead of him, dangerous more for its lures than its open threats.

The butte was a long time changing dimensions. And it appeared for a while that it approached him instead of him approaching it.

The worm, tiring now, kept veering left. Leto slid down the immense slope to set his hooks anew and keep the giant on a straight course. A soft sharpness of melange came to his nostrils, the signal of a rich vein. They passed the leprous blotches of violet sand where a spiceblow had erupted and he held the worm firmly until they were well past the vein. The breeze, redolent with the gingery odor of cinnamon, pursued them for a time until Leto rolled the worm onto its new course, headed directly toward the rising butte.

Abruptly colors blinked far out on the southern *bled*: the unwary rainbow flashing of a man-made artifact in that immensity. He brought up his binoculars, focused the oil lenses, and saw in the distance the outbanking wings of a spice-scout glittering in the sunlight. Beneath it a big harvester was shedding its wings like a chrysalis before lumbering off. When Leto lowered the binoculars the harvester dwindled to a speck, and he felt himself overcome by the *hadhdhab*, the immense omnipresence of the desert. It told him how those spice-hunters would see him, a dark object between desert and sky, which was the Fremen symbol for *man*. They'd see him, of course, and they'd be cautious. They'd wait. Fremen were always suspicious of one another in the desert until they recognized the newcomer or saw for certain that he posed no threat. Even within the fine patina of Imperial civilization and its sophisticated rules they remained half-tamed savages, aware always that a crysknife dissolved at the death of its owner.

*That's what can save us*, Leto thought. *That wildness.*

In the distance the spice-scout banked right, then left, a signal to the ground. He imagined the occupants scanning the desert behind him for sign that he might be more than a single rider or a single worm.

Leto rolled the worm to the left, held it until it had reversed its course, dropped down the flank, and leaped clear. The worm, released from his goading, sulked on the surface for a few breaths, then sank its front third and lay there recuperating, a sure sign that it had been ridden too long.

He turned away from the worm; it would stay there now. The scout was circling its crawler, still giving wing signals. They were smuggler-paid renegades for certain, wary of electronic communications. The hunters would be on spice out there. That was the message of the crawler's presence.

The scout circled once more, dipped its wings, came out of the circle and headed directly toward him. He recognized it for a type of light 'thopter his grandfather had introduced on Arrakis. The craft circled once above him, went out along the dune where he stood, and banked to land against the breeze. It came down within ten meters of him, stirring up a scattering of dust. The door on his side cracked enough to emit a single figure in a heavy Fremen robe with a spear symbol at the right breast.

The Fremen approached slowly, giving each of them time to study the other. The man was tall with the total indigo of spice-eyes. The stillsuit mask concealed the lower half of his face and the hood had been drawn down to protect his brows. The movement of the robe revealed a hand beneath it holding a maula pistol.

The man stopped two paces from Leto, looked down at him with a puzzled crinkling around the eyes.

"Good fortune to us all," Leto said.

The man peered all around, scanning the emptiness, then returned his attention to Leto. "What do you here, child?" he demanded. His voice was muffled by the stillsuit mask. "Are you trying to be the cork in a wormhole?"

Again Leto used traditional Fremen formula: "The desert is my home."

"Wenn?" the man demanded. *Which way do you go?*

"I travel south from Jacurutu."

An abrupt laugh erupted from the man. "Well, Batigh! You are the strangest thing I've ever seen in the Tanzerouft."

"I'm not your Little Melon," Leto said, responding to *Batigh*. That was a label with dire overtones. The Little Melon on the desert's edge offered its water to any finder.

"We'll not drink you, Batigh," the man said. "I am Muriz. I am the arifa of this taif." He indicated with a head motion the distant spice-crawler.

Leto noted how the man called himself the Judge of his group and referred to the others as *taif*, a band or company. They were not *ichwan*, not a band of brothers. Paid renegades for sure. Here lay the thread he required.

When Leto remained silent, Muriz asked: "Do you have a name?"

"Batigh will do."

A chuckle shook Muriz. "You've not told me what you do here?"

"I seek the footprints of a worm," Leto said, using the religious phrase which said he was on hajj for his own *umma*, his personal revelation.

"One so young?" Muriz asked. He shook his head. "I don't know what to do with you. You have seen us."

"What have I seen?" Leto asked. "I speak of Jacurutu and you make no response."

"Riddle games," Muriz said. "What is that, then?" He nodded toward the distant butte.

Leto spoke from his vision: "Only Shuloch."

Muriz stiffened and Leto felt his own pulse quicken.

A long silence ensued and Leto could see the man debating and discarding various responses. *Shuloch!* In the quiet story time after a sietch meal, stories of the Shuloch caravanserei were often repeated. Listeners always assumed that Shuloch was a myth, a place for interesting things to happen and only for the sake of the story. Leto recalled a Shuloch story: A waif was found at the desert's edge and brought into the sietch. At first the waif refused to respond to his saviors, then when he spoke no one could understand his words. As days passed he continued unresponsive, refused to dress himself or cooperate in any way. Every time he was left alone he made odd motions with his hands. All the specialists in the sietch were called to study this waif but arrived at no answer. Then a very old woman passed the doorway, saw the moving hands and laughed. "He only imitates his father who rolls the spice-fibers into rope," she explained. "It's the way they still do it at Shuloch. He's just trying to feel less lonely." And the moral: *"In the old ways of Shuloch there is security and a sense of belonging to the golden thread of life."*

As Muriz remained silent, Leto said: "I'm the waif from Shuloch who knows only to move his hands."

In the quick movement of the man's head, Leto saw that Muriz knew the story. Muriz responded slowly, voice low and filled with menace. "Are you human?"

"Human as yourself," Leto said.

"You speak most strangely for a child. I remind you that I am a judge who can respond to the *taqwa*."

*Ah, yes.* Leto thought. In the mouth of such a judge, the *taqwa* carried immediate threat. *Taqwa* was the fear invoked by the presence of a demon, a very real belief among older Fremen. The arifa knew the ways to slay a demon and was always chosen "because he has the wisdom to be ruthless without being cruel, to know when kindness is in fact the way to greater cruelty."

But this thing had come to a point which Leto sought, and he said: "I can submit to the *Mashhad*."

"I'll be the judge of any Spiritual Test," Muriz said. "Do you accept this?"

"Bi-lal kaifa," Leto said. *Without qualification.*

A sly look came over Muriz's face. He said: "I don't know why I permit this. Best you were slain out of hand, but you're a small Batigh and I had a son who is dead. Come, we will go to Shuloch and I'll convene the Isnad for a decision about you."

Leto, noting how the man's every mannerism betrayed deadly decision, wondered how anyone could be fooled by this. He said: "I know Shuloch is the Ahl as-sunna wal-jamas."

"What does a child know of the real world?" Muriz asked, motioning for Leto to precede him to the 'thopter.

Leto obeyed, but listened carefully to the sound of the Fremen's footsteps. "The surest way to keep a secret is to make people believe they already know the answer," Leto said. "People don't ask questions then. It was clever of you who were cast out of Jacurutu. Who'd believe Shuloch, the story-myth place, is real? And how convenient for the smugglers or anyone else who desires access to Dune."

Muriz's footsteps stopped. Leto turned with his back against the 'thopter's side, the wing on his left.

Muriz stood half a pace away with his maula pistol drawn and pointed directly at Leto. "So you're not a child," Muriz said. "A cursed midget come to spy on us! I thought you spoke too wisely for a child, but you spoke too much too soon."

"Not enough," Leto said. "I'm Leto, the child of Paul Muad'Dib. If you slay me, you and your people will sink into the sand. If you spare me, I'll lead you to greatness."

"Don't play games with me, midget," Muriz snarled. "Leto is at the real Jacurutu from whence you say . . ." He broke off. The gun hand dropped slightly as a puzzled frown made his eyes squint.

It was the hesitation Leto had expected. He made every muscle indication of a move to the left which, deflecting his body no more than a millimeter, brought the Fremen's gun swinging wildly against the wing edge. The maula pistol flew from his hand and, before he could recover, Leto was beside him with Muriz's own crysknife pressed against the man's back.

"The tip's poisoned," Leto said. "Tell your friend in the 'thopter that he's to remain exactly where he is without moving at all. Otherwise I'll be forced to kill you."

Muriz, nursing his injured hand, shook his head at the figure in the 'thopter, said: "My companion Behaleth has heard you. He will be as unmoving as the rock."

Knowing he had very little time until the two worked out a plan of action or their friends came to investigate, Leto spoke swiftly: "You need me, Muriz. Without me, the worms and their spice will vanish from Dune." He felt the Fremen stiffen.

"But how do you know of Shuloch?" Muriz asked. "I know they said nothing at Jacurutu."

"So you admit I'm Leto Atreides?"

"Who else could you be? But how do you—"

"Because you are here," Leto said. "Shuloch exists, therefore the rest is utter simplicity. You are the Cast Out who escaped when Jacurutu was destroyed. I saw you signal with your wings, therefore you use no device which could be overheard at a distance. You collect spice, therefore you trade. You could only trade with the smugglers. You are a smuggler, yet you are Fremen. You must be of Shuloch."

"Why did you tempt me to slay you out of hand?"

"Because you would've slain me anyway when we'd returned to Shuloch."

A violent rigidity came over Muriz's body.

"Careful, Muriz," Leto cautioned. "I know about you. It was in your history that you took the water of unwary travelers. By now this would be common ritual with you. How else could you silence the ones who chanced upon you? How else keep your secret? Batigh! You'd seduce me with gentle epithets and kindly words. Why waste any of my water upon the sand? And if I were missed as were many of the others—well, the Tanzerouft got me."

Muriz made the *Horns-of-the-Worm* sign with his right hand to ward off the Rihani which Leto's words called up. And Leto, knowing how older Fremen distrusted mentats or anything which smacked of them by a show of extended logic, suppressed a smile.

"Namri spoke of us at Jacurutu," Muriz said. "I will have his water when—"

"You'll have nothing but empty sand if you continue playing the fool," Leto said. "What will you do, Muriz, when all of Dune has become green grass, trees, and open water?"

"It will never happen!"

"It is happening before your eyes."

Leto heard Muriz's teeth grinding in rage and frustration. Presently the man grated: "How would you prevent this?"

"I know the entire plan of the transformation," Leto said. "I know every weakness in it, every strength. Without me, Shai-Hulud will vanish forever."

A sly note returning to his voice, Muriz asked: "Well, why dispute it here? We're at a standoff. You have your knife. You could kill me, but Behaleth would shoot you."

"Not before I recovered your pistol," Leto said. "Then I'd have your 'thopter. Yes. I can fly it."

A scowl creased Muriz's forehead beneath the hood. "What if you're not who you say?"

"Will my father not identify me?" Leto asked.

"Ahhhh," Muriz said. "There's how you learned, eh? But . . ." He broke off, shook his head. "My own son guides him. He says you two have never . . . How could . . ."

"So you don't believe Muad'Dib reads the future," Leto said.

"Of course we believe! But he says of himself that . . ." Again Muriz broke off.

"And you thought him unaware of your distrust," Leto said. "I came to this exact place in this exact time to meet you, Muriz. I know all about you because I've *seen* you . . . and your son. I know how secure you believe yourselves, how you sneer at Muad'Dib, how you plot to save your little patch of desert. But your little patch of desert is doomed without me, Muriz. Lost forever. It has gone too far here on Dune. My father has almost run out of vision, and you can only turn to me."

"That blind . . ." Muriz stopped, swallowed.

"He'll return soon from Arrakeen," Leto said, "and then we shall see how blind he is. How far have you gone from the old Fremen ways, Muriz?"

"What?"

"He is *Wadquiyas* with you. Your people found him alone in the desert and brought him to Shuloch. What a rich discovery he was! Richer than a spice-vein. *Wadquiyas!* He has lived with you; his water mingled with your tribe's water. He's part of your Spirit River." Leto pressed the knife hard against Muriz's robe. "Careful, Muriz." Leto lifted his left hand, released the Fremen's face flap, dropped it.

Knowing what Leto planned, Muriz said: "Where would you go if you killed us both?"

"Back to Jacurutu."

Leto pressed the fleshy part of his own thumb against Muriz's mouth. "Bite and drink, Muriz. That or die."

Muriz hesitated, then bit viciously into Leto's flesh.

Leto watched the man's throat, saw the swallowing convulsion, withdrew the knife and returned it.

"*Wadquiyas,*" Leto said. "I must offend the tribe before you can take my water."

Muriz nodded.

"Your pistol is over there." Leto gestured with his chin.

"You trust me now?" Muriz asked.

"How else can I live with the Cast Out?"

Again Leto saw the sly look in Muriz's eyes, but this time it was a measuring thing, a weighing of economics. The man turned away with an abruptness which told of secret decisions, recovered his maula pistol and returned to the wing step. "Come," he said. "We tarry too long in a worm's lair."

*The future of prescience cannot always be locked into the rules of the past. The threads of existence tangle according to many unknown laws. Prescient future insists on its own rules. It will not conform to the ordering of the Zensunni nor to the ordering of science. Prescience builds a relative integrity. It demands the work of this instant, always warning that you cannot weave every thread into the fabric of the past.*

**—Kalima: The Words of Muad'Dib**
**The Shuloch Commentary**

Muriz brought the ornithopter in over Shuloch with a practiced ease. Leto, seated beside him, felt the armed presence of Behaleth behind them. Everything went on trust now and the narrow thread of his vision to which he clung. If that failed, *Allahu akbahr*. Sometimes one had to submit to a greater order.

The butte of Shuloch was impressive in this desert. Its unmarked presence here spoke of many bribes and many deaths, of many friends in high places. Leto could see at Shuloch's heart a cliff-walled pan with interfringing blind canyons leading down into it. A thick growth of shadescale and salt bushes lined the lower edges of these canyons with an inner ring of fan palms, indicating the water riches of this place. Crude buildings of greenbush and spice-fiber had been built out from the fan palms. The buildings were green buttons scattered on the sand. There would live the cast out of the Cast Out, those who could go no lower except into death.

Muriz landed in the pan near the base of one of the canyons. A single structure stood on the sand directly ahead of the 'thopter: a thatch of desert vines and bejato leaves, all lined with heat-fused spice-fabric. It was the living replica of the first crude stilltents and it spoke of degradation for some who lived in Shuloch. Leto knew the place would leak moisture and would be full of night-biters from the nearby growth. So this was how his father lived. And poor Sabiha. Here would be her punishment.

At Muriz's order Leto let himself out of the 'thopter, jumped down to the sand, and strode toward the hut. He could see many people working farther toward the canyon among the palms. They looked tattered, poor, and the fact that they barely glanced at him or at the 'thopter said much of the oppression here. Leto could see the rock lip of a qanat beyond the workers, and there was no mistaking the sense of moisture in this air: open water. Passing the hut, Leto saw it was as crude as he'd expected. He pressed on to the qanat, peered down and saw the swirl of predator fish in the dark flow. The workers, avoiding his eyes, went on with clearing sand away from the line of rock openings.

Muriz came up behind Leto, said: "You stand on the boundary between fish and worm. Each of these canyons has its worm. This qanat has been opened and we will remove the fish presently to attract sandtrout."

"Of course," Leto said. "Holding pens. You sell sandtrout and worms off-planet."

"It was Muad'Dib's suggestion!"

"I know. But none of your worms or sandtrout survive for long away from Dune."

"Not yet," Muriz said. "But someday . . ."

"Not in ten thousand years," Leto said. And he turned to watch the turmoil on Muriz's face. Questions flowed there like the water in the qanat. Could this son of Muad'Dib really read the future? Some still believed Muad'Dib had done it, but . . . How could a thing such as this be judged?

Presently Muriz turned away, led them back to the hut. He opened the crude doorseal, motioned for Leto to enter. There was a spice-oil lamp burning against the far wall and a small figure squatted beneath it, back to the door. The burning oil gave off a heavy fragrance of cinnamon.

"They've sent down a new captive to care for Muad'Dib's sietch," Muriz sneered. "If she serves well, she may keep her water for a time." He confronted Leto. "Some think it evil to take such water. Those lace-shirt Fremen now make rubbish heaps in their new towns! Rubbish heaps! When has Dune ever before seen rubbish heaps? When we get such as this one—" He gestured toward the figure by the lamp. "—they're usually half wild with fear, lost to their own kind and never accepted by true Fremen. Do you understand me, Leto-Batigh?"

"I understand you." The crouching figure had not moved.

"You speak of leading us," Muriz said. "Fremen are led by men who've been blooded. What could you lead us in?"

"Kralizec," Leto said, keeping his attention on the crouched figure.

Muriz glared at him, brows contracted over his indigo eyes. Kralizec? That wasn't merely war or revolution; that was the Typhoon Struggle. It was a word from the furthermost Fremen legends: the battle at the end of the universe. Kralizec?

The tall Fremen swallowed convulsively. This sprat was as unpredictable as a city dandy! Muriz turned to the squatting figure. "Woman! Liban wahid!" he commanded. *Bring us the spice-drink!*

She hesitated. "Do as he says, Sabiha," Leto said.

She jumped to her feet, whirling. She stared at him, unable to take her gaze from his face.

"You know this one?" Muriz asked.

"She is Namri's niece. She offended Jacurutu and they have sent her to you."

"Namri? But . . ."

"Liban wahid," Leto said.

She rushed past them, tore herself through the doorseal and they heard the sound of her running feet.

"She will not go far," Muriz said. He touched a finger to the side of his nose. "A kin of Namri, eh. Interesting. What did she do to offend?"

"She allowed me to escape." Leto turned then and followed Sabiha. He found her standing at the edge of the qanat. Leto moved up beside her and looked down at the water. There were birds in the nearby fan palms and he heard their calls, their wings. The workers made scraping sounds as they moved sand. Still he did as Sabiha did, looking down, deep into the water and its reflections. The corners of his eyes saw blue parakeets in the palm fronds. One flew across the qanat and he saw it reflected in a silver swirl of fish, all run together as though birds and predators swam in the same firmament.

Sabiha cleared her throat.

"You hate me," Leto said.

"You shamed me. You shamed me before my people. They held an Isnad and sent me here to lose my water. All because of you!"

Muriz laughed from close behind them. "And now you see, Leto-Batigh, that our Spirit River has many tributaries."

"But my water flows in your veins," Leto said, turning. "That is no tributary. Sabiha is the fate of my vision and I followed her. I fled across the desert to find my future here in Shuloch."

"You and . . ." He pointed at Sabiha, threw his head back in laughter.

"It will not be as either of you might believe," Leto said. "Remember this, Muriz. I have found the footprints of my worm." He felt tears swimming in his eyes then.

"He gives water to the dead," Sabiha whispered.

Even Muriz stared at him in awe. Fremen never cried unless it was the most profound gift of the soul. Almost embarrassed, Muriz closed his mouthseal, pulled his djeballa hood low over his brows.

Leto peered beyond the man, said: "Here in Shuloch they still pray for dew at the desert's edge. Go, Muriz, and pray for Kralizec. I promise you it will come."

> *Fremen speech implies great concision, a precise sense of expression. It is immersed in the illusion of absolutes. Its assumptions are a fertile ground for absolutist religions. Furthermore, Fremen are fond of moralizing. They confront the terrifying instability of all things with institutionalized statements. They say: "We know there is no summa of all attainable knowledge; that is the preserve of God. But whatever men can learn, men can contain." Out of this knife-edged approach to the universe they carve a fantastic belief in signs and omens and in their own destiny. This is an origin of their Kralizec legend: the war at the end of the universe.*

> **—Bene Gesserit Private Reports/folio 800881**

"They have him securely in a safe place," Namri said, smiling across the square stone room at Gurney Halleck. "You may report this to your friends."

"Where is this safe place?" Halleck asked. He didn't like Namri's tone, felt constrained by Jessica's orders. Damn the witch! Her explanations made no sense except the warning about what could happen if Leto failed to master his terrible memories.

"It's a safe place," Namri said. "That's all I'm permitted to tell you."

"How do you know this?"

"I've had a distrans. Sabiha is with him."

"Sabiha! She'll just let him—"

"Not this time."

"Are you going to kill him?"

"That's no longer up to me."

Halleck grimaced. *Distrans*. What was the range of those damned cave bats? He'd often seen them flitting across the desert with hidden messages imprinted upon their squeaking calls. But how far would they go on this hellhole planet?

"I must see him for myself," Halleck said.

"That's not permitted."

Halleck took a deep breath to quiet himself. He had spent two days and two nights waiting for search reports. Now it was another morning and he felt his role dissolving around him, leaving him naked. He had never liked command anyway. Command always waited while others did the interesting and dangerous things.

"Why isn't it permitted?" he asked. The smugglers who'd arranged this safe-sietch had left too many questions unanswered and he wanted no more of the same from Namri.

"Some believe you saw too much when you saw this sietch," Namri said.

Halleck heard the menace, relaxed into the easy stance of the trained fighter, hand near but not on his knife. He longed for a shield, but that had been ruled out by its effect on the worms, its short life in the presence of storm-generated static charges.

"This secrecy isn't part of our agreement," Halleck said.

"If I'd killed him, would that have been part of our agreement?"

Again Halleck felt the jockeying of unseen forces about which the Lady Jessica hadn't warned him. This damned plan of hers! Maybe it was right not to trust the Bene Gesserit. Immediately, he felt disloyal. She'd explained the problem, and he'd come into her plan with the expectation that it, like all plans, would need adjustments later. This wasn't *any* Bene Gesserit; this was Jessica of the Atreides who'd never been other than friend and supporter to him. Without her, he knew he'd have been adrift in a universe more dangerous than the one he now inhabited.

"You can't answer my question," Namri said.

"You were to kill him only if he showed himself to be . . . possessed," Halleck said. "Abomination."

Namri put his fist beside his right ear. "Your Lady knew we had tests for such. Wise of her to leave that judgment in my hands."

Halleck compressed his lips in frustration.

"You heard the Reverend Mother's words to me," Namri said. "We Fremen understand such women but you off-worlders never understand them. Fremen women often send their sons to death."

Halleck spoke past stiff lips. "Are you telling me you've killed him?"

"He lives. He is in a safe place. He'll continue to receive the spice."

"But I'm to escort him back to his grandmother if he survives," Halleck said.

Namri merely shrugged.

Halleck understood that this was all the answer he'd get. Damn! He couldn't go back to Jessica with such unanswered questions! He shook his head.

"Why question what you cannot change?" Namri asked. "You're being well paid."

Halleck scowled at the man. Fremen! They believed all foreigners were influenced primarily by money. But Namri was speaking more than Fremen prejudice. Other forces were at work here and that was obvious to one who'd been trained in observation by a Bene Gesserit. This whole thing had the smell of a feint within a feint within a feint . . .

Shifting to the insultingly familiar form, Halleck said: "The Lady Jessica will be wrathful. She could send cohorts against—"

*"Zanadiq!"* Namri cursed. "You office messenger! You stand outside the *Mohalata!* I take pleasure in possessing your water for the Noble People!"

Halleck rested a hand on his knife, readied his left sleeve where he'd prepared a small surprise for attackers. "I see no water spilled here," he said. "Perhaps you're blinded by your pride."

"You live because I wished you to learn before dying that your Lady Jessica will not send cohorts against anyone. You are not to be lured quietly into the Huanui, off-world scum. I am of the Noble People, and you—"

"And I'm just a servant of the Atreides," Halleck said, voice mild. "We're the scum who lifted the Harkonnen yoke from your smelly neck."

Namri showed white teeth in a grimace. "Your Lady is prisoner on Salusa Secundus. The notes you thought were from her came from her daughter!"

By extreme effort, Halleck managed to keep his voice even. "No matter. Alia will . . ."

Namri drew his crysknife. "What do you know of the Womb of Heaven? I am her servant, you male whore. I do her bidding when I take your water!" And he lunged across the room with foolhardy directness.

Halleck, not allowing himself to be tricked by such seeming clumsiness, flicked up the left arm of his robe, releasing the extra length of heavy fabric he'd had sewn there, letting that take Namri's knife. In the same movement, Halleck swept the fold of cloth over Namri's head, came in under and through the cloth with his own knife aimed directly for the face. He felt the point bite home as Namri's body hit him with a hard surface of metal armor beneath the robe. The Fremen emitted one outraged squeal, jerked backward, and fell. He lay there, blood gushing from his mouth as his eyes glared at Halleck then slowly dulled.

Halleck blew air through his lips. How could that fool Namri have expected anyone to miss the presence of armor beneath a robe? Halleck addressed the corpse as he recovered the trick sleeve, wiped his knife and sheathed it. "How did you think we Atreides *servants* were trained, fool?"

He took a deep breath thinking: *Well, now. Whose feint am I?* There'd been the ring of truth in Namri's words. Jessica a prisoner of the Corrinos and Alia working her own devious schemes. Jessica herself had warned of many contingencies with Alia as enemy, but had not predicted herself as prisoner. He had his orders to obey, though. First there was the necessity of getting away from this place. Luckily one robed Fremen looked much like another. He rolled Namri's body into a corner, threw cushions over it, moved a rug to cover the blood. When it was done, Halleck adjusted the nose and mouth tubes of his stillsuit, brought up the mask as one would in preparing for the desert, pulled the hood of his robe forward and went out into the long passage.

*The innocent move without care*, he thought, setting his pace at an easy saunter. He felt curiously free, as though he'd moved out of danger, not into it.

*I never did like her plan for the boy*, he thought. *And I'll tell her so if I see her. If.* Because if Namri spoke the truth, the most dangerous alternate plan went into effect. Alia wouldn't let him live long if she caught him, but there was always Stilgar—a good Fremen with a good Fremen's superstitions.

Jessica had explained it: "There's a very thin layer of civilized behavior over Stilgar's original nature. And here's how you take that layer off him . . ."

> *The spirit of Muad'Dib is more than words, more than the letter of the Law which arises in his name. Muad'Dib must always be that inner outrage against the complacently powerful, against the charlatans and the dogmatic fanatics. It is that inner outrage which must have its say because Muad'Dib taught us one thing above all others: that humans can endure only in a fraternity of social justice.*

**—The Fedaykin Compact**

Leto sat with his back against the wall of the hut, his attention on Sabiha, watching the threads of his vision unroll. She had prepared the coffee and set it aside. Now she squatted across from him stirring his evening meal. It was a gruel redolent with melange. Her hands moved quickly with the ladle and liquid indigo stained the sides of his bowl. She bent her thin face over the bowl, blending in the concentrate. The crude membrane which made a stilltent of the hut had been patched with lighter material directly behind her, and this formed a grey halo against which her shadow danced in the flickering light of the cooking flame and the single lamp.

That lamp intrigued Leto. These people of Shuloch were profligate with spice-oil: a lamp, not a glowglobe. They kept slave outcasts within their walls in the fashion told by the most ancient Fremen traditions. Yet they employed ornithopters and the latest spice harvesters. They were a crude mixture of ancient and modern.

Sabiha pushed the bowl of gruel toward him, extinguished the cooking flame.

Leto ignored the bowl.

"I will be punished if you do not eat this," she said.

He stared at her, thinking: *If I kill her, that'll shatter one vision. If I tell her Muriz's plans, that'll shatter another vision. If I wait here for my father, this vision-thread will become a mighty rope.*

His mind sorted the threads. Some held a sweetness which haunted him. One future with Sabiha carried alluring reality within his prescient awareness. It threatened to block out all others until he followed it out to its ending agonies.

"Why do you stare at me that way?" she asked.

Still he did not answer.

She pushed the bowl closer to him.

Leto tried to swallow in a dry throat. The impulse to kill Sabiha welled in him. He found himself trembling with it. How easy it would be to shatter one vision and let the wildness run free!

"Muriz commands this," she said, touching the bowl.

Yes, Muriz commanded it. Superstition conquered everything. Muriz wanted a vision cast for him to read. He was an ancient savage asking the witch doctor to throw the ox bones and interpret their sprawl. Muriz had taken his captive's stillsuit "as a simple precaution." There'd been a sly jibe at Namri and Sabiha in that comment. *Only fools let a prisoner escape.*

Muriz had a deep emotional problem, though: the Spirit River. The captive's water flowed in Muriz's veins. Muriz sought a sign that would permit him to hold a threat of death over Leto.

*Like father, like son,* Leto thought.

"The spice will only give you visions," Sabiha said. The long silences made her uneasy. "I've had visions in the orgy many times. They don't mean anything."

*That's it!* he thought, his body locking itself into a stillness which left his skin cold and clammy. The Bene Gesserit training took over his consciousness, a pinpoint illumination which fanned out beyond him to throw the blazoning light of vision upon Sabiha and all of her Cast Out fellows. The ancient Bene Gesserit learning was explicit:

*"Languages build up to reflect specializations in a way of life. Each specialization may be recognized by its words, by its assumptions and sentence structures. Look for stoppages. Specializations represent places where life is being stopped, where the movement is dammed up and frozen."* He saw Sabiha then as a vision-maker in her own right, and every other human carried the same power. Yet she was disdainful of her spice-orgy visions. They caused disquiet and, therefore, must be put aside, forgotten deliberately. Her people prayed to Shai-Hulud because the worm dominated many of their visions. They prayed for dew at the desert's edge because moisture limited their lives. Yet they wallowed in spice wealth and lured sandtrout to open qanats. Sabiha fed him prescient visions with a casual callousness, yet within her words he saw the illuminated signals: she depended upon absolutes, sought finite limits, and all because she couldn't handle the rigors of terrible decisions which touched her own flesh. She clung to her one-eyed vision of the universe, englobing and time-freezing as it might be, because the alternatives terrified her.

In contrast, Leto felt the pure movement of himself. He was a membrane collecting infinite dimensions and, because he saw those dimensions, he could make the terrible decisions.

*As my father did.*

"You must eat this!" Sabiha said, her voice petulant.

Leto saw the whole pattern of the visions now and knew the thread he must follow. *My skin is not my own.* He stood, pulling his robe around him. It felt strange against his flesh with no stillsuit protecting his body. His feet were bare upon the fused spice-fabric of the floor, feeling the sand tracked in there.

"What're you doing?" Sabiha demanded.

"The air is bad in here. I'm going outside."

"You can't escape," she said. "Every canyon has its worm. If you go beyond the qanat, the worms will sense you by your moisture. These captive worms are very alert—not like the ones in the desert at all. Besides—" how gloating her voice became! "—you've no stillsuit."

"Then why do you worry?" he asked, wondering if he might yet provoke a real reaction from her.

"Because you've not eaten."

"And you'll be punished."

"Yes!"

"But I'm already saturated with spice," he said. "Every moment is a vision." He gestured with a bare foot at the bowl. "Pour that onto the sand. Who'll know?"

"They watch," she whispered.

He shook his head, shedding her from his visions, feeling new freedom envelop him. No need to kill this poor pawn. She danced to other music, not even knowing the steps, believing that she might yet share the power which lured the hungry pirates of Shuloch and Jacurutu. Leto went to the doorseal, put a hand upon it.

"When Muriz comes," she said, "he'll be very angry with—"

"Muriz is a merchant of emptiness," Leto said. "My aunt has drained him."

She got to her feet. "I'm going out with you."

And he thought: *She remembers how I escaped her. Now she feels the fragility of her hold upon me. Her visions stir within her.* But she would not listen to those visions. She had but to reflect: How could he outwit a captive worm in its narrow canyon? How could he live in the Tanzerouft without stillsuit or Fremkit?

"I must be alone to consult my visions," he said. "You'll remain here."

"Where will you go?"

"To the qanat."

"The sandtrout come out in swarms at night."

"They won't eat me."

"Sometimes the worm comes down to just beyond the water," she said. "If you cross the qanat . . ." She broke off, trying to edge her words with menace.

"How could I mount a worm without hooks?" he asked, wondering if she still could salvage some bit of her visions.

"Will you eat when you return?" she asked, squatting once more by the bowl, recovering the ladle and stirring the indigo broth.

"Everything in its own time," he said, knowing she'd be unable to detect his delicate use of Voice, the way he insinuated his own desires into her decision-making.

"Muriz will come and see if you've had a vision," she warned.

"I will deal with Muriz in my own way," he said, noting how heavy and slow her movements had become. The pattern of all Fremen lent itself naturally into the way he guided her now. Fremen were people of extraordinary energy at sunrise but a deep and lethargic melancholy often overcame them at nightfall. Already she wanted to sink into sleep and dreams.

Leto let himself out into the night alone.

The sky glittered with stars and he could make out the bulk of surrounding butte against their pattern: He went up under the palms to the qanat.

For a long time Leto squatted at the qanat's edge, listening to the restless hiss of sand within the canyon beyond. A small worm by the sound of it; chosen for that reason, no doubt. A small worm would be easier to transport. He thought about the worm's capture: the hunters would dull it with a water mist, using the traditional Fremen method of taking a worm for the orgy/transformation rite. But this worm would not be killed by immersion. This one would go out on a Guild heighliner to some hopeful buyer whose desert probably would be too moist. Few off-worlders realized the basic desiccation which the sandtrout had maintained on Arrakis. *Had maintained.* Because even here in the Tanzerouft there would be many times more airborne moisture than any worm had ever before known short of its death in a Fremen cistern.

He heard Sabiha stirring in the hut behind him. She was restless, prodded by her own suppressed visions. He wondered how it would be to live outside a vision with her, sharing each moment just as it came, of itself. The thought attracted him far more strongly than had any spice vision. There was a certain cleanliness about facing an unknown future.

*"A kiss in the sietch is worth two in the city."*

The old Fremen maxim said it all. The traditional sietch had held a recognizable wildness mingled with shyness. There were traces of that shyness in the people of Jacurutu/Shuloch, but only traces. This saddened him by revealing what had been lost.

Slowly, so slowly that the knowledge was fully upon him before he recognized its beginnings, Leto grew aware of the soft rustling of many creatures all around him.

*Sandtrout.*

Soon it would be time to shift from one vision to another. He felt the movement of sandtrout as a movement within himself. Fremen had lived with the strange creatures for generations, knowing that if you risked a bit of water as bait, you could lure them into reach. Many a Fremen dying of thirst had risked his last few drops of water in this gamble, knowing that the sweet green syrup teased from a sandtrout might yield a small profit in energy. But the sandtrout were mostly the game of children who caught them for the Huanui. And for play.

Leto shuddered at the thought of what that *play* meant to him now.

He felt one of the creatures slither across his bare foot. It hesitated, then went on, attracted by the greater amount of water in the qanat.

For a moment, though, he'd felt the reality of his terrible decision. *The sandtrout glove.* It was the play of children. If one held a sandtrout in the hand, smoothing it over your skin, it formed a living glove. Traces of blood in the skin's capillaries could be sensed by the creatures, but something mingled with the blood's water repelled them. Sooner or later, the glove would slip off into the sand, there to be lifted into a spice-fiber basket. The spice soothed them until they were dumped into the deathstill.

He could hear sandtrout dropping into the qanat, the swirl of predators eating them. Water softened the sandtrout, made it pliable. Children learned this early. A bit of saliva teased out the sweet syrup. Leto listened to the splashing. This was a migration of sandtrout come up to the open water, but they could not contain a flowing qanat patrolled by predator fish.

Still they came; still they splashed.

Leto groped on the sand with his right hand until his fingers encountered the leathery skin of a sandtrout. It was the large one he had expected. The creature didn't try to evade him, but moved eagerly onto his flesh. He explored its outline with his free hand—roughly diamond-shaped. It had no head, no extremities, no eyes, yet it could find water unerringly. With its fellows it could join body to body, locking one on another by the coarse interlacings of extruded cilia until the whole became one large sack-organism enclosing the water, walling off the "poison" from the giant which the sandtrout would become: Shai-Hulud.

The sandtrout squirmed on his hand, elongating, stretching. As it moved, he felt a counterpart elongating and stretching of the vision he had chosen. *This thread, not that one.* He felt the sandtrout becoming thin, covering more and more of his hand. No sandtrout had ever before encountered a hand such as this one, every cell supersaturated with spice. No other human had ever before lived and reasoned in such a condition. Delicately Leto adjusted his enzyme balance, drawing on the illuminated sureness he'd gained in spice trance. The knowledge from those uncounted lifetimes which blended themselves within him provided the certainty through which he chose the precise adjustments, staving off the death from an overdose which would engulf him if he relaxed his watchfulness for only a heartbeat. And at the same time he blended himself with the sandtrout, feeding on it, feeding it, learning it. His trance vision provided the template and he followed it precisely.

Leto felt the sandtrout grow thin, spreading itself over more and more of his hand, reaching up his arm. He located another, placed it over the first one. Contact ignited a frenzied squirming in the creatures. Their cilia locked and they became a single membrane which enclosed him to the elbow. The sandtrout adjusted to the living glove of childhood play, but thinner and more sensitive as he lured it into the role of a skin symbiote. He reached down with the living glove, felt sand, each grain distinct to his senses. This was no longer sandtrout; it was tougher, stronger. And it would grow stronger and stronger . . . His groping hand encountered another sandtrout which whipped itself into union with the first two and adapted itself to the new role. Leathery softness insinuated itself up his arm to his shoulder.

With a terrible singleness of concentration he achieved the union of this new skin with his body, preventing rejection. No corner of his attention was left to dwell upon the terrifying consequences of what he did here. Only the necessities of his trance vision mattered. Only the Golden Path could come from this ordeal.

Leto shed his robe and lay naked upon the sand, his gloved arm outstretched into the path of migrating sandtrout. He remembered that once he and Ghanima had caught a sandtrout, abraded it against the sand until it contracted into the *child-worm*, a stiff tube, its interior pregnant with the green syrup. One bit gently upon the end and sucked swiftly before the wound was healed, gaining the few drops of sweetness.

They were all over his body now. He could feel the pulse of his blood against the living membrane. One tried to cover his face, but he moved it roughly until it elongated into a thin roll. The thing grew much longer than the child-worm, remaining flexible. Leto bit the end of it, tasted a thin stream of sweetness which continued far longer than any Fremen had ever before experienced. He could feel energy from the sweetness flow through him. A curious excitement suffused his body. He was kept busy for a time rolling the membrane away from his face until he'd built up a stiff ridge circling from jaw to forehead and leaving his ears exposed.

Now the vision must be tested.

He got to his feet, turned to run back toward the hut and, as he moved, found his feet moving too fast for him to balance. He plunged into the sand, rolled and leaped to his feet. The leap took him two meters off the sand and, when he fell back, trying to walk, he again moved too fast.

*Stop!* he commanded himself. He fell into the *prana-bindu* forced relaxation, gathering his senses into the pool of consciousness. This focused the inward ripples of the *constant-now* through which he experienced Time, and he allowed the vision-elation to warm him. The membrane worked precisely as the vision had predicted.

*My skin is not my own.*

But his muscles took some training to live with this amplified movement. When he walked, he fell, rolling. Presently he sat. In the quiet, the ridge below his jaw tried to become a membrane covering his mouth. He spat against it and bit, tasting the sweet syrup. It rolled downward to the pressure of his hand.

Enough time had passed to form the union with his body. Leto stretched flat and turned onto his face. He began to crawl, rasping the membrane against the sand. He could feel the sand distinctly, but nothing abraded his own flesh. With only a few swimming movements he traversed fifty meters of sand. The physical reaction was a friction-induced warming sensation.

The membrane no longer tried to cover his nose and mouth, but now he faced the second major step onto his Golden Path. His exertions had taken him beyond the qanat into the canyon where the trapped worm stayed. He heard it hissing toward him, attracted by his movements.

Leto leaped to his feet, intending to stand and wait, but the amplified movement sent him sprawling twenty meters farther into the canyon. Controlling his reactions with terrible effort, he sat back onto his haunches, straightened. Now the sand began to swell directly in front of him, rising up in a monstrous starlit curve. Sand opened only two body lengths from him. Crystal teeth flashed in the dim light. He saw the yawning mouth-cavern with, far back, the ambient movement of dim flame. The overpowering redolence of the spice swept over him. But the worm had stopped. It remained in front of him as First Moon lifted over the butte. The light reflected off the worm's teeth outlining the faery glow of chemical fires deep within the creature.

So deep was the inbred Fremen fear that Leto found himself torn by a desire to flee. But his vision held him motionless, fascinated by this prolonged moment. No one had ever before stood this close to the mouth of a living worm and survived. Gently Leto moved his right foot, met a sand ridge and, reacting too quickly, was propelled toward the worm's mouth. He came to a stop on his knees.

Still the worm did not move.

It sensed only the sandtrout and would not attack the deep-sand vector of its own kind. The worm would attack another worm in its territory and would come to exposed spice. Only a water barrier stopped it—and sandtrout, encapsulating water, were a water barrier.

Experimentally, Leto moved a hand toward that awesome mouth. The worm drew back a full meter.

Confidence restored, Leto turned away from the worm and began teaching his muscles to live with their new power. Cautiously he walked back toward the qanat. The worm remained motionless behind him. When Leto was beyond the water barrier he leaped with joy, went sailing ten meters across the sand, sprawled, rolled, laughed.

Light flared on the sand as the hut's doorseal was breached. Sabiha stood outlined in the yellow and purple glow of the lamp, staring out at him.

Laughing, Leto ran back across the qanat, stopped in front of the worm, turned and faced her with his arms outstretched.

"Look!" he called. "The worm does my bidding!"

As she stood in frozen shock, he whirled, went racing around the worm and into the canyon. Gaining experience with his new skin, he found he could run with only the lightest flexing of muscles. It was almost effortless. When he put effort into running, he raced over the sand with the wind burning the exposed circle of his face. At the canyon's dead end instead of stopping, he leaped up a full fifteen meters, clawed at the cliff, scrabbled, climbing like an insect, and came out on the crest above the Tanzerouft.

The desert stretched before him, a vast silvery undulance in the moonlight.

Leto's manic exhilaration receded.

He squatted, sensing how light his body felt. Exertion had produced a slick film of perspiration which a stillsuit would have absorbed and routed into the transfer tissue which removed the salts. Even as he relaxed, the film disappeared now, absorbed by the membrane faster than a stillsuit could have done it. Thoughtfully Leto rolled a length of the membrane beneath his lips, pulled it into his mouth, and drank the sweetness.

His mouth was not masked, though. Fremen-wise, he sensed his body's moisture being wasted with every breath. Leto brought a section of the membrane over his mouth, rolled it back when it tried to seal his nostrils, kept at this until the rolled barrier remained in place. In the desert way, he fell into the automatic breathing pattern: in through his nose, out through his mouth. The membrane over his mouth protruded in a small bubble, but remained in place. No moisture collected on his lips and his nostrils remained open. The adaptation proceeded, then.

A 'thopter flew between Leto and the moon, banked, and came in for a spread-wing landing on the butte perhaps a hundred meters to his left. Leto glanced at it, turned, and looked back the way he had come up the canyon. Many lights could be seen down there beyond the qanat, a stirring of a multitude. He heard faint outcries, sensed hysteria in the sounds. Two men approached him from the 'thopter. Moonlight glinted on their weapons.

*The Mashhad,* Leto thought, and it was a sad thought. Here was the great leap onto the Golden Path. He had put on the living, self-repairing stillsuit of a sandtrout membrane, a thing of unmeasurable value on Arrakis . . . until you understood the price. *I am no longer human. The legends about this night will grow and magnify it beyond anything recognizable by the participants. But it will become truth, that legend.*

He peered down from the butte, estimated the desert floor lay two hundred meters below. The moon picked out ledges and cracks on the steep face but no connecting pathway. Leto stood, inhaled a deep breath, glanced back at the approaching men, then stepped to the cliff's edge and launched himself into space. Some thirty meters down his flexed legs encountered a narrow ledge. Amplified muscles absorbed the shock and rebounded in a leap sideways to another ledge, where he caught a narrow outcropping with his hands, dropped twenty meters, leaped to another handhold and once more went down, bouncing, leaping, grasping tiny ledges. He took the final forty meters in one jump, landing in a bent-knee roll which sent him plunging down the slipface of a dune in a shower of sand and dust. At the bottom he scrambled to his feet, launched himself to the next dunecrest in one jump. He could hear hoarse shouts from atop the cliff but ignored them to concentrate on the leaping strides from dunetop to dunetop.

As he grew more accustomed to amplified muscles he found a sensuous joy that he had not anticipated in this distance-gulping movement. It was a ballet on the desert, defiance of the Tanzerouft which no other had ever experienced.

When he judged that the ornithopter's occupants had overcome their shock enough to mount pursuit once more, he dove for the moon-shadowed face of a dune, burrowed into it. The sand was like heavy liquid to his new strength, but the temperature mounted dangerously when he moved too fast. He broke free on the far face of the dune, found that the membrane had covered his nostrils. He removed it, sensed the new skin pulsing over his body in its labor to absorb his perspiration.

Leto fashioned a tube at his mouth, drank the syrup while he peered upward at the starry sky. He estimated he had come fifteen kilometers from Shuloch. Presently a 'thopter drew its pattern across the stars, a great bird shape followed by another and another. He heard the soft swishing of their wings, the whisper of their muted jets.

Sipping at the living tube, he waited. First Moon passed through its track, then Second Moon.

An hour before dawn Leto crept out and up to the dunecrest, examined the sky. No hunters. Now he knew himself to be embarked upon a path of no return. Ahead lay the trap in Time and Space which had been prepared as an unforgettable lesson for himself and all of mankind.

Leto turned northeast and loped another fifty kilometers before burrowing into the sand for the day, leaving only a tiny hole to the surface which he kept open with a sandtrout tube. The membrane was learning how to live with him as he learned how to live with it. He tried not to think of the other things it was doing to his flesh.

*Tomorrow I'll raid Gara Rulen,* he thought. *I'll smash their qanat and loose its water into the sand. Then I'll go on to Windsack, Old Gap, and Harg. In a month the ecological transformation will have been set back a full generation. That'll give us space to develop the new timetable.*

And the wildness of the rebel tribes would be blamed, of course. Some would revive memories of Jacurutu. Alia would have her hands full. As for Ghanima . . . Silently to himself, Leto mouthed the words which would restore her memory. Time for that later . . . if they survived this terrible mixing of threads.

The Golden Path lured him out there on the desert, almost a physical thing which he could see with his open eyes. And he thought how it was: as animals must move across the land, their existence dependent upon that movement, the soul of humankind, blocked for eons, needed a track upon which it could move.

He thought of his father then, telling himself: *"Soon we'll dispute as man to man, and only one vision will emerge."*

> *Limits of survival are set by climate, those long drifts of change which a generation may fail to notice. And it is the extremes of climate which set the pattern. Lonely, finite humans may observe climatic provinces, fluctuations of annual weather and occasionally may observe such things as "This is a colder year than I've ever known." Such things are sensible. But humans are seldom alerted to the shifting average through a great span of years. And it is precisely in this alerting that humans learn how to survive on any planet. They must learn climate.*
>
> **—Arrakis, the Transformation**
> **After Harq al-Ada**

Alia sat cross-legged on her bed, trying to compose herself by reciting the Litany Against Fear, but chuckling derision echoed in her skull to block every effort. She could hear the voice; it controlled her ears, her mind.

"What nonsense is this? What have you to fear?"

The muscles of her calves twitched as her feet tried to make running motions. There was nowhere to run.

She wore only a golden gown of the sheerest Palian silk and it revealed the plumpness which had begun to bulge her body. The Hour of Assassins had just passed; dawn was near. Reports covering the past three months lay before her on the red coverlet. She could hear the humming of the air conditioner and a small breeze stirred the labels on the shigawire spools.

Aides had awakened her fearfully two hours earlier, bringing news of the latest outrage, and Alia had called for the report spools, seeking an intelligible pattern.

She gave up on the Litany.

These attacks had to be the work of rebels. Obviously. More and more of them turned against Muad'Dib's religion.

"And what's wrong with that?" the derisive voice asked within her.

Alia shook her head savagely. Namri had failed her. She'd been a fool to trust such a dangerous double instrument. Her aides whispered that Stilgar was to blame, that he was a secret rebel. And what had become of Halleck? Gone to ground among his smuggler friends? Possibly.

She picked up one of the report spools. *And Muriz!* The man was hysterical. That was the only possible explanation. Otherwise she'd have to believe in miracles. No human, let alone a child (even a child such as Leto) could leap from the butte at Shuloch and survive to flee across the desert in leaps that took him from dunecrest to dunecrest.

Alia felt the coldness of the shigawire under her hand.

Where was Leto, then? Ghanima refused to believe him other than dead. A Truthsayer had confirmed her story: Leto slain by a Laza tiger. Then who was the child reported by Namri and Muriz?

She shuddered.

Forty qanats had been breached, their waters loosed into the sand. The loyal Fremen and even the rebels, superstitious louts, all! Her reports were flooded with stories of mysterious occurrences. Sandtrout leaped into qanats and shattered to become hosts of small replicas. Worms deliberately drowned themselves. Blood dripped from Second Moon and fell to Arrakis, where it stirred up great storms. And the storm frequency *was* increasing!

She thought of Duncan incommunicado at Tabr, fretting under the restraints she'd exacted from Stilgar. He and Irulan talked of little else than the *real* meaning behind these omens. Fools! Even her spies betrayed the influence of these outrageous stories!

Why did Ghanima insist on her story of the Laza tiger?

Alia sighed. Only one of the reports on the shigawire spools reassured her. Farad'n had sent a contingent of his household guard "to help you in your troubles and to prepare the way for the Official Rite of Betrothal." Alia smiled to herself and shared the chuckle which rumbled in her skull. That plan, at least, remained intact. Logical explanations would be found to dispel all of this other superstitious nonsense.

Meanwhile she'd use Farad'n's men to help close down Shuloch and to arrest the known dissidents, especially among the Naibs. She debated moving against Stilgar, but the inner voice cautioned against this.

"Not yet."

"My mother and the Sisterhood still have some plan of their own," Alia whispered. "Why is she training Farad'n?"

"Perhaps he excites her," the Old Baron said.

"Not that cold one."

"You're not thinking of asking Farad'n to return her?"

"I know the dangers in that!"

"Good. Meanwhile, that young aide Zia recently brought in. I believe his name's Agarves—Buer Agarves. If you'd invite him here tonight . . ."

"No!"

"Alia . . ."

"It's almost dawn, you insatiable old fool! There's a Military Council meeting this morning, the Priests will have—"

"Don't trust them, darling Alia."

"Of course not!"

"Very well. Now, this Buer Agarves . . ."

"I said no!"

The Old Baron remained silent within her, but she began to feel a headache. A slow pain crept upward from her left cheek into her skull. Once he'd sent her raging down the corridors with this trick. Now, she resolved to resist him.

"If you persist, I'll take a sedative," she said.

He could see she meant it. The headache began to recede.

"Very well." Petulant. "Another time, then."

"Another time," she agreed.

> *Thou didst divide the sand by thy strength; Thou breakest the heads of the dragons in the desert. Yea, I behold thee as a beast coming up from the dunes; thou hast the two horns of the lamb, but thou speakest as the dragon.*

> **—Revised Orange Catholic Bible**
> **Arran II:4**

It was the immutable prophecy, the threads become rope, a thing Leto now seemed to have known all of his life. He looked out across the evening shadows on the Tanzerouft. One hundred and seventy kilometers due north lay Old Gap, the deep and twisting crevasse through the Shield Wall by which the first Fremen had migrated into the desert.

No doubts remained in Leto. He knew why he stood here alone in the desert, yet filled with a sense that he owned this entire land, that it must do his bidding. He felt the chord which connected him with all of humankind and that profound need for a universe of experiences which made logical sense, a universe of recognizable regularities within its perpetual changes.

*I know this universe.*

The worm which had brought him here had come to the stamping of his foot and, rising up in front of him, had stopped like an obedient beast. He'd leaped atop it and, with only his membrane-amplified hands, had exposed the leading lip of the worm's rings to keep it on the surface. The worm had exhausted itself in the nightlong dash northward. Its silicon-sulfur internal "factory" had worked at capacity, exhaling lavish gusts of oxygen which a following wind had sent in enveloping eddies around Leto. At times the warm gusts had made him dizzy, filled his mind with strange perceptions. The reflexive and circular subjectivity of his visions had turned inward upon his ancestry, forcing him to relive portions of his Terranic past, then comparing those portions with his changing self.

Already he could feel how far he'd drifted from something recognizably human. Seduced by the spice which he gulped from every trace he found, the membrane which covered him no longer was sandtrout, just as he was no longer human. Cilia had crept into his flesh, forming a new creature which would seek its own metamorphosis in the eons ahead.

*You saw this, father, and rejected it,* he thought. *It was a thing too terrible to face.* Leto knew what was believed of his father, and why.

*Muad'Dib died of prescience.*

But Paul Atreides had passed from the universe of reality into the *alam al-mythal* while still alive, fleeing from this thing which his son had dared.

Now there was only The Preacher.

Leto squatted on the sand and kept his attention northward. The worm would come from that direction, and on its back would ride two people: a young Fremen and a blind man.

A flight of pallid bats passed over Leto's head, bending their course southeast. They were random specks in the darkening sky, and a knowledgeable Fremen eye could mark their back-course to learn where shelter lay that way. The Preacher would avoid that shelter, though. His destination was Shuloch, where no wild bats were permitted lest they guide strangers to a secret place.

The worm appeared first as a dark movement between the desert and the northern sky. *Matar,* the rain of sand dropped from high altitudes by a dying stormwind, obscured the view for a few minutes, then it returned clearer and closer.

The cold-line at the base of the dune where Leto crouched began to produce its nightly moisture. He tasted the fragile dampness in his nostrils, adjusted the bubble cap of the membrane over his mouth. There no longer was any need for him to find soaks and sip-wells. From his mother's genes he had that longer, larger Fremen large intestine to take back water from everything which came its way. The living stillsuit grasped and retained every bit of moisture it encountered. And even while he sat here the membrane which touched sand extruded pseudopod-cilia to hunt for bits of energy which it could store.

Leto studied the approaching worm. He knew the youthful guide had seen him by this time, noting the spot atop the dune. The worm rider would discern no principle in this object seen from a distance, but that was a problem Fremen had learned how to handle. Any unknown object was dangerous. The young guide's reactions would be quite predictable, even without the vision.

True to that prediction, the worm's course shifted slightly and aimed directly at Leto. Giant worms were a weapon which Fremen had employed many times. Worms had helped beat Shaddam at Arrakeen. This worm, however, failed to do its rider's bidding. It came to a halt ten meters away and no manner of goading would send it across another grain of sand.

Leto arose, feeling the cilia snap back into the membrane behind him. He freed his mouth and called out: "Achlan, wasachlan!" *Welcome, twice welcome!*

The blind man stood behind his guide atop the worm, one hand on the youth's shoulder. The man held his face high, nose pointed over Leto's head as though trying to sniff out this interruption. Sunset painted orange on his forehead.

"Who is that?" the blind man asked, shaking his guide's shoulder. "Why have we stopped?" His voice was nasal through the stillsuit plugs.

The youth stared fearfully down at Leto, said: "It is only someone alone in the desert. A child by his looks. I tried to send the worm over him, but the worm won't go."

"Why didn't you say?" the blind man demanded.

"I thought it was only someone alone in the desert!" the youth protested. "But it is a demon."

"Spoken like a true son of Jacurutu," Leto said. "And you, sire, you are The Preacher."

"I am that one, yes." And there was fear in The Preacher's voice because, at last, he had met his own past.

"This is no garden," Leto said, "but you are welcome to share this place with me tonight."

"Who are you?" The Preacher demanded. "How have you stopped our worm?" There was an ominous tone of recognition in The Preacher's voice. Now he called up the memories of this alternate vision . . . knowing he could reach an end here.

"It's a demon!" the young guide protested. "We must flee this place or our souls—"

"Silence!" The Preacher roared.

"I am Leto Atreides," Leto said. "Your worm stopped because I commanded it."

The Preacher stood in frozen silence.

"Come, father," Leto said. "Alight and spend the night with me. I'll give you sweet syrup to sip. I see you've Fremkits with food and water jars. We'll share our riches here upon the sand."

"Leto's yet a child," The Preacher protested. "And they say he's dead of Corrino treachery. There's no childhood in your voice."

"You know me, sire," Leto said. "I'm small for my age as you were, but my experience is ancient and my voice has learned."

"What do you here in the Inner Desert?" The Preacher asked.

"Bu ji," Leto said. *Nothing from nothing.* It was the answer of a Zensunni wanderer, one who acted only from a position of rest, without effort and in harmony with his surroundings.

The Preacher shook his guide's shoulder. "Is it a child, truly a child?"

"Aiya," the youth said, keeping a fearful attention on Leto.

A great shuddering sigh shook The Preacher. "No," he said.

"It is a demon in child form," the guide said.

"You will spend the night here," Leto said.

"We will do as he says," The Preacher said. He released his grip on the guide, slipped off the worm's side and slid down a ring to the sand, leaping clear when his feet touched. Turning, he said: "Take the worm off and send it back into the sand. It is tired and will not bother us."

"The worm will not go!" the youth protested.

"It will go," Leto said. "But if you try to flee on it, I'll let it eat you." He moved to one side out of the worm's sensory range, pointed in the direction they had come. "Go that way."

The youth tapped a goad against the ring behind him, wiggled a hook where it held a ring open. Slowly the worm began to slide over the sand, turning as the youth shifted his hook down a side.

The Preacher, following the sound of Leto's voice, clambered up the duneslope and stood two paces away. It was done with a swift sureness which told Leto this would be no easy contest.

Here the visions parted.

Leto said: "Remove your suit mask, father."

The Preacher obeyed, dropping the fold of his hood and withdrawing the mouth cover.

Knowing his own appearance, Leto studied this face, seeing the lines of likeness as though they'd been outlined in light. The lines formed an indefinable reconciliation, a pathway of genes without sharp boundaries, and there was no mistaking them. Those lines came down to Leto from the humming days, from the water-dripping days, from the miracle seas of Caladan. But now they stood at a dividing point on Arrakis as night waited to fold itself into the dunes.

"So, father," Leto said, glancing to the left where he could see the youthful guide trudging back to them from where the wom had been abandoned.

"Mu zein!" The Preacher said, waving his right hand in a cutting gesture. *This is no good!*

"Koolish zein," Leto said, voice soft. *This is all the good we may ever have.* And he added, speaking in Chakobsa, the Atreides battle language: "Here I am; here I remain! We cannot forget that, father."

The Preacher's shoulders sagged. He put both hands to his empty sockets in a long-unused gesture.

"I gave you the sight of my eyes once and took your memories," Leto said. "I know your decisions and I've been to that place where you hid yourself."

"I know." The Preacher lowered his hands. "You will remain?"

"You named me for the man who put that on his coat of arms," Leto said. "J'y suis, j'y reste!"

The Preacher sighed deeply. "How far has it gone, this thing you've done to yourself?"

"My skin is not my own, father."

The Preacher shuddered. "Then I know how you found me here."

"Yes, I fastened my memory to a place my flesh had never known," Leto said. "I need an evening with my father."

"I'm not your father. I'm only a poor copy, a relic." He turned his head toward the sound of the approaching guide. "I no longer go to the visions for my future."

As he spoke, darkness covered the desert. Stars leaped out above them and Leto, too, turned toward the approaching guide. "Wubakh ul kuhar!" Leto called to the youth. *"Greetings!"*

Back came the response: "Subakh un nar!"

Speaking in a hoarse whisper, The Preacher said: "That young Assan Tariq is a dangerous one."

"All of the Cast Out are dangerous," Leto said. "But not to me." He spoke in a low, conversational tone.

"If that's your vision, I will not share it," The Preacher said.

"Perhaps you have no choice," Leto said. "You are the *fil-haquiqa*, The Reality. You are Abu Dhur, Father of the Indefinite Roads of Time."

"I'm no more than bait in a trap," The Preacher said, and his voice was bitter.

"And Alia already has eaten that bait," Leto said. "But I don't like its taste."

"You cannot do this!" The Preacher hissed.

"I've already done it. My skin is not my own."

"Perhaps it's not too late for you to—"

"It is too late." Leto bent his head to one side. He could hear Assan Tariq trudging up the duneslope toward them, coming to the sound of their voices. "Greetings, Assan Tariq of Shuloch," Leto said.

The youth stopped just below Leto on the slope, a dark shadow there in the starlight. There was indecision in the set of his shoulders, the way he tipped his head.

"Yes," Leto said, "I'm the one who escaped from Shuloch."

"When I heard . . ." The Preacher began. And again: "You cannot do this!"

"I am doing it. What matter if you're made blind once more?"

"You think I fear that?" The Preacher asked. "Do you not see the fine guide they have provided for me?"

"I see him." Again Leto faced Tariq. "Didn't you hear me, Assan? I'm the one who escaped from Shuloch."

"You're a demon," the youth quavered.

"Your demon," Leto said. "But you are my demon." And Leto felt the tension grow between himself and his father. It was a shadow play all around them, a projection of unconscious forms. And Leto felt the memories of his father, a form of backward prophecy which sorted visions from the familiar reality of this moment.

Tariq sensed it, this battle of the visions. He slid several paces backward down the slope.

"You cannot control the future," The Preacher whispered, and the sound of his voice was filled with effort as though he lifted a great weight.

Leto felt the dissonance between them then. It was an element of the universe with which his entire life grappled. Either he or his father would be forced to act soon, making a decision by that act, choosing a vision. And his father was right: trying for some ultimate control of the universe, you only built weapons with which the universe eventually defeated you. To choose and manage a vision required you to balance on a single, thin thread—playing God on a high tightwire with cosmic solitude on both sides. Neither contestant could retreat into death-as-surcease-from-paradox. Each knew the visions and the rules. All of the old illusions were dying. And when one contestant moved, the other might countermove. The only real truth that mattered to them now was that which separated them from the vision background. There was no place of safety, only a transitory shifting of relationships, marked out within the limits which they now imposed and bound for inevitable changes. Each of them had only a desperate and lonely courage upon which to rely, but Leto possessed two advantages: he had committed himself upon a path from which there was no turning back, and he had accepted the terrible consequences to himself. His father still hoped there was a way back and had made no final commitment.

"You must not! You must not!" The Preacher rasped.

*He sees my advantage*, Leto thought.

Leto spoke in a conversational tone, masking his own tensions, the balancing effort this other-level contest required. "I have no passionate belief in truth, no faith other than what I create," he said. And he felt then a movement between himself and his father, something with granular characteristics which touched only Leto's own passionately subjective belief in himself. By such belief he knew that he posted the markers of the Golden Path. Someday such markers could tell others how to be human, a strange gift from a creature who no longer would be human on that day. But these markers were always set in place by gamblers. Leto felt them scattered throughout the landscape of his inner lives and, feeling this, poised himself for the ultimate gamble.

Softly he sniffed the air, seeking the signal which both he and his father knew must come. One question remained: Would his father warn the terrified young guide who waited below them?

Presently Leto sensed ozone in his nostrils, the betraying odor of a shield. True to his orders from the Cast Out, young Tariq was trying to kill both of these dangerous Atreides, not knowing the horrors which this would precipitate.

"Don't," The Preacher whispered.

But Leto knew the signal was a true one. He sensed ozone, but there was no tingling in the air around them. Tariq used a pseudo-shield in the desert, a weapon developed exclusively for Arrakis. The Holtzmann Effect would summon a worm while it maddened that worm. Nothing would stop such a worm—not water, not the presence of sandtrout . . . nothing. Yes, the youth had planted the device in the duneslope and was beginning to edge away from the danger zone.

Leto launched himself off the dunetop, hearing his father scream in protest. But the awful impetus of Leto's amplified muscles threw his body like a missile. One outflung hand caught the neck of Tariq's stillsuit, the other slapped around to grip the doomed youth's robe at the waist. There came a single snap as the neck broke. Leto rolled, lifting his body like a finely balanced instrument which dove directly into the sand where the pseudo-shield had been hidden. Fingers found the thing and he had it out of the sand, throwing it in a looping arc far out to the south of them.

Presently there came a great hissing-thrashing din out on the desert where the pseudo-shield had gone. It subsided, and silence returned.

Leto looked up to the top of the dune where his father stood, still defiant, but defeated. That was Paul Muad'Dib up there, blind, angry, near despair as a consequence of his flight from the vision which Leto had accepted. Paul's mind would be reflecting now upon the Zensunni Long Koan: *"In the one act of predicting an accurate future, Muad'Dib introduced an element of development and growth into the very prescience through which he saw human existence. By this, he brought uncertainty onto himself. Seeking the absolute of orderly prediction, he amplified disorder, distorted prediction."*

Returning to the dunetop in a single leap, Leto said: "Now I'm your guide." "Never!"

"Would you go back to Shuloch? Even if they'd welcome you when you arrived without Tariq, where has Shuloch gone now? Do your *eyes* see it?"

Paul confronted his son then, aiming the eyeless sockets at Leto. "Do you really know the universe you have created here?"

Leto heard the particular emphasis. The vision which both of them knew had been set into terrible motion here had required an act of creation at a certain *point* in time. For that moment, the entire sentient universe shared a linear view of time which possessed characteristics of orderly progression. They entered this time as they might step onto a moving vehicle, and they could only leave it the same way.

Against this, Leto held the multi-thread reins, balanced in his own vision-lighted view of time as multilinear and multilooped. He was the sighted man in the universe of the blind. Only he could scatter the orderly rationale because his father no longer held the reins. In Leto's view, a son had altered the past. And a thought as yet undreamed in the farthest future could reflect upon the *now* and move his hand.

Only *his* hand.

Paul knew this because he no longer could see how Leto might manipulate the reins, could only recognize the inhuman consequences which Leto had accepted. And he thought: *Here is the change for which I prayed. Why do I fear it? Because it's the Golden Path!*

"I'm here to give purpose to evolution and, therefore, to give purpose to our lives," Leto said.

"Do you *wish* to live those thousands of years, changing as you now know you will change?"

Leto recognized that his father was not speaking about physical changes. Both of them knew the physical consequences: Leto would adapt and adapt; the skin-which-was-not-his-own would adapt and adapt. The evolutionary thrust of each part would melt into the other and a single transformation would emerge. When metamorphosis came, *if* it came, a thinking creature of awesome dimensions would emerge upon the universe—and that universe would worship him.

No . . . Paul was referring to the inner changes, the thoughts and decisions which would inflict themselves upon the worshipers.

"Those who think you dead," Leto said, "you know what they say about your last words."

"Of course."

*"Now I do what all life must do in the service of life,"* Leto said. "You never said that, but a Priest who thought you could never return and call him a liar put those words into your mouth."

"I'd not call him a liar." Paul took a deep breath. "Those are good last words."

"Would you stay here or return to that hut in the basin of Shuloch?" Leto asked.

"This is your universe now," Paul said.

The words filled with defeat cut through Leto. Paul had tried to guide the last strands of a personal vision, a choice he'd made years before in Sietch Tabr. For that, he'd accepted his role as an instrument of revenge for the Cast Out, the remnants of Jacurutu. They had contaminated him, but he'd accepted this rather than his view of this universe which Leto had chosen.

The sadness in Leto was so great he could not speak for several minutes. When he could manage his voice, Leto said: "So you baited Alia, tempted her and confused her into inaction and the wrong decisions. And now she knows who you are."

"She knows . . . Yes, she knows."

Paul's voice was old then and filled with hidden protests. There was a reserve of defiance in him, though. He said: "I'll take the vision away from you if I can."

"Thousands of peaceful years," Leto said. "That's what I'll give them."

"Dormancy! Stagnation!"

"Of course. And those forms of violence which I permit. It'll be a lesson which humankind will never forget."

"I spit on your lesson!" Paul said. "You think I've not seen a thing similar to what you choose?"

"You saw it," Leto agreed.

"Is your vision any better than mine?"

"Not one whit better. Worse, perhaps," Leto said.

"Then what can I do but resist you?" Paul demanded.

"Kill me, perhaps?"

"I'm not that innocent. I know what you've set in motion. I know about the broken qanats and the unrest."

"And now Assan Tariq will never return to Shuloch. You must go back with me or not at all because this is my vision now."

"I choose not to go back."

*How old his voice sounds,* Leto thought, and the thought was a wrenching pain. He said: "I've the hawk ring of the Atreides concealed in my *dishdasha.* Do you wish me to return it to you?"

"If I'd only died," Paul whispered. "I truly wanted to die when I went into the desert that night, but I knew I could not leave this world. I had to come back and—"

"Restore the legend," Leto said. "I know. And the jackals of Jacurutu were waiting for you that night as you knew they would be. They wanted your visions! You knew that."

"I refused. I never gave them one vision."

"But they contaminated you. They fed you spice essence and plied you with women and dreams. And you *did* have visions."

"Sometimes." How sly his voice sounded.

"Will you take back your hawk ring?" Leto asked.

Paul sat down suddenly on the sand, a dark blotch in the starlight. "No!"

*So he knows the futility of that path,* Leto thought. This revealed much, but not enough. The contest of the visions had moved from its delicate plane of choices down to a gross discarding of alternates. Paul knew he could not win, but he hoped yet to nullify that single vision to which Leto clung.

Presently Paul said: "Yes, I was contaminated by the Jacurutu. But you contaminate yourself."

"That's true," Leto admitted. "I am your son."

"And are you a good Fremen?"

"Yes."

"Will you permit a blind man to go into the desert finally? Will you let me find peace on my own terms?" He pounded the sand beside him.

"No, I'll not permit that," Leto said. "But it's your right to fall upon your knife if you insist upon it."

"And you would have my body!"

"True."

"No!"

*And so he knows that path,* Leto thought. The enshrining of Muad'Dib's body by his son could be contrived as a form of cement for Leto's vision.

"You never told them, did you, father?" Leto asked.

"I never told them."

"But I told them," Leto said. "I told Muriz. Kralizec, the Typhoon Struggle."

Paul's shoulders sagged. "You cannot," he whispered. "You cannot."

"I am a creature of this desert now, father," Leto said. "Would you speak thus to a Coriolis storm?"

"You think me coward for refusing that path," Paul said, his voice husky and trembling. "Oh, I understand you well, son. Augury and haruspication have always been their own torments. But I was never lost in the possible futures because this one is unspeakable!"

"Your Jihad will be a summer picnic on Caladan by comparison," Leto agreed. "I'll take you to Gurney Halleck now."

"Gurney! He serves the Sisterhood through my mother."

And now Leto understood the extent of his father's vision. "No, father. Gurney no longer serves anyone. I know the place to find him and I can take you there. It's time for the new legend to be created."

"I see that I cannot sway· you. Let me touch you, then, for you are my son."

Leto held out his right hand to meet the groping fingers, felt their strength, matched it, and resisted every shift of Paul's arm. "Not even a poisoned knife will harm me now," Leto said. "I'm already a different chemistry."

Tears slipped from the sightless eyes and Paul released his grip, dropped his hand to his side. "If I'd chosen your way, I'd have become the *bicouros* of *shaitan*. What will you become?"

"For a time they'll call me the missionary of *shaitan*, too," Leto said. "Then they'll begin to wonder and, finally, they'll understand. You didn't take your vision far enough, father. Your hands did good things and evil."

"But the evil was known after the event!"

"Which is the way of many great evils," Leto said. "You crossed over only into a part of my vision. Was your strength not enough?"

"You know I couldn't stay there. I could never do an evil act which was known before the act. I'm not Jacurutu." He clambered to his feet. "Do you think me one of those who laugh alone at night?"

"It is sad that you were never really Fremen," Leto said. "We Fremen know how to commission the arifa. Our judges can choose between evils. It's always been that way for us."

"Fremen, is it? Slaves of the fate you helped to make?" Paul stepped toward Leto, reached out in an oddly shy movement, touched Leto's sheathed arm, explored up it to where the membrane exposed an ear, then the cheek and, finally, the mouth. "Ahhhh, that is your own flesh yet," he said. "Where will that flesh take you?" He dropped his hand.

"Into a place where humans may create their futures from instant to instant."

"So you say. An Abomination might say the same."

"I'm not Abomination, though I might've been," Leto said. "I saw how it goes with Alia. A demon lives in her, father. Ghani and I know that demon: it's the Baron, your grandfather."

Paul buried his face in his hands. His shoulders shook for a moment, then he lowered his hands and his mouth was set in a harsh line. "There is a curse upon our House. I prayed that you would throw that ring into the sand, that you'd deny me and run away to make . . . another life. It was there for you."

"At what price?"

After a long silence, Paul said: "The end adjusts the path behind it. Just once

I failed to fight for my principles. Just once. I accepted the Mahdinate. I did it for Chani, but it made me a bad leader."

Leto found he couldn't answer this. The memory of that decision was there within him.

"I cannot lie to you any more than I could lie to myself," Paul said. "I know this. Every man should have such an auditor. I will only ask this one thing: is the Typhoon Struggle necessary?"

"It's that or humans will be extinguished."

Paul heard the truth in Leto's words, spoke in a low voice which acknowledged the greater breadth of his son's vision. "I did not see that among the choices."

"I believe the Sisterhood suspects it," Leto said. "I cannot accept any other explanation of my grandmother's decision."

The night wind blew coldly around them then. It whipped Paul's robe around his legs. He trembled. Seeing this, Leto said: "You've a kit, father. I'll inflate the tent and we can spend this night in comfort."

But Paul could only shake his head, knowing he would have no comfort from this night or any other. Muad'Dib, The Hero, must be destroyed. He'd said it himself. Only The Preacher could go on now.

> *Fremen were the first humans to develop a conscious/unconscious symbology through which to experience the movements and relationships of their planetary system. They were the first people anywhere to express climate in terms of a semi-mathematic language whose written symbols embody (and internalize) the external relationships. The language itself was part of the system it described. Its written form carried the shape of what it described. The intimate local knowledge of what was available to support life was implicit in this development. One can measure the extent of this language/system interaction by the fact that Fremen accepted themselves as foraging and browsing animals.*
>
> **—The Story of Liet-Kynes**
> **by Harq al-Ada**

"Kaveh wahid," Stilgar said. *Bring coffee.* He signaled with a raised hand to an aide who stood at one side near the single door to the austere rock-walled room where he had spent this wakeful night. This was the place where the old Fremen Naib usually took his spartan breakfast, and it was almost breakfast time, but after such a night he did not feel hungry. He stood, stretching his muscles.

Duncan Idaho sat on a low cushion near the door, trying to suppress a yawn. He had just realized that, while they talked, he and Stilgar had gone through an entire night.

"Forgive me, Stil," he said. "I've kept you up all night."

"To stay awake all night adds a day to your life," Stilgar said, accepting the tray with coffee as it was passed in the door. He pushed a low bench in front of Idaho, placed the tray on it and sat across from his guest.

Both men wore the yellow robes of mourning, but Idaho's was a borrowed garment worn because the people of Tabr had resented the Atreides green of his working uniform.

Stilgar poured the dark brew from the fat copper carafe, sipped first, and lifted his cup as a signal to Idaho—the ancient Fremen custom: *"It is safe; I have taken some of it."*

The coffee was Harah's work, done just as Stilgar preferred it: the beans roasted to a rose-brown, ground to a fine powder in a stone mortar while still hot, and boiled immediately; a pinch of melange added.

Idaho inhaled the spice-rich aroma, sipped carefully but noisily. He still did not know if he had convinced Stilgar. His mentat faculties had begun to work sluggishly in the early hours of the morning, all of his computations confronted at last by the inescapable datum supplied in the message from Gurney Halleck.

Alia had known about Leto! She'd known.

And Javid had to be a part of that knowing.

"I must be freed of your restraints," Idaho said at last, taking up the arguments once more.

Stilgar stood his ground. "The agreement of neutrality requires me to make hard judgments. Ghani is safe here. You and Irulan are safe here. But you may not send messages. Receive messages, yes, but you may not send them. I've given my word."

"This is not the treatment usually accorded a guest and an old friend who has shared your dangers," Idaho said, knowing he'd used this argument before.

Stilgar put down his cup, setting it carefully into its place on the tray and keeping his attention on it as he spoke. "We Fremen don't feel guilt for the same things that arouse such feelings in others," he said. He raised his attention to Idaho's face.

*He must be made to take Ghani and flee this place,* Idaho thought. He said: "It was not my intention to raise a storm of guilt."

"I understand that," Stilgar said. "I raise the question to impress upon you our Fremen attitude, because that is what we are dealing with: Fremen. Even Alia thinks Fremen."

"And the Priests?"

"They are another matter," Stilgar said. "They want the people to swallow the grey wind of sin, taking *that* into the everlasting. This is a great blotch by which they seek to know their own piety." He spoke in a level voice, but Idaho heard the bitterness and wondered why that bitterness could not sway Stilgar.

"It's an old, old trick of autocratic rule," Idaho said. "Alia knows it well. Good subjects must feel guilty. The guilt begins as a feeling of failure. The good autocrat provides many opportunities for failure in the populace."

"I've noticed." Stilgar spoke dryly. "But you must forgive me if I mention to you once more that this is your wife of whom you speak. It is the sister of Muad'Dib."

"She's possessed, I tell you!"

"Many say it. She will have to undergo the test one day. Meanwhile there are other considerations more important."

Idaho shook his head sadly. "Everything I've told you can be verified. The communication with Jacurutu was always through Alia's Temple. The plot against the twins had accomplices there. Money for the sale of worms off-planet goes there. All of the strings lead to Alia's office, to the Regency."

Stilgar shook his head, drew in a deep breath. "This is neutral territory. I've given my word."

"Things can't go on this way!" Idaho protested.

"I agree." Stilgar nodded. "Alia's caught inside the circle and every day the circle grows smaller. It's like our old custom of having many wives. This pinpoints male sterility." He bent a questioning gaze on Idaho. "You say she deceives you with other men—'using her sex as a weapon' is the way I believe you've expressed it. Then you have a perfectly legal avenue available to you. Javid's here in Tabr with messages from Alia. You have only to—"

"On your neutral territory?"

"No, but outside in the desert . . . ."

"And if I took that opportunity to escape?"

"You'll not be given such an opportunity."

"Still, I swear to you, Alia's possessed. What do I have to do to convince you of—"

"A difficult thing to prove," Stilgar said. It was the argument he'd used many times during the night.

Idaho recalled Jessica's words, said: "But you've ways of proving it."

"A way, yes," Stilgar said. Again he shook his head. "Painful, irrevocable. That is why I remind you about our attitude toward guilt. We can free ourselves from guilts which might destroy us in everything except the Trial of Possession. For that, the tribunal, which is all of the people, accepts complete responsibility."

"You've done it before, haven't you?"

"I'm sure the Reverend Mother didn't omit our history in her recital," Stilgar said. "You well know we've done it before."

Idaho responded to the irritation in Stilgar's voice. "I wasn't trying to trap you in a falsehood. It's just—"

"It's the long night and the questions without answers," Stilgar said. "And now it's morning."

"I must be allowed to send a message to Jessica," Idaho said.

"That would be a message to Salusa," Stilgar said. "I don't make evening promises. My word is meant to be kept; that is why Tabr's neutral territory. I will hold you in silence. I have pledged this for my entire household."

"Alia must be brought to your Trial!"

"Perhaps. First, we must find out if there are extenuating circumstances. A failure of authority, possibly. Or even bad luck. It could be a case of that natural bad tendency which all humans share, and not possession at all."

"You want to be sure I'm not just the husband wronged, seeking others to execute his revenge," Idaho said.

"The thought has occurred to others, not to me," Stilgar said. He smiled to take the sting out of his words. "We Fremen have our science of tradition, our *hadith*. When we fear a mentat or a Reverend Mother, we revert to the *hadith*. It is said that the only fear we cannot correct is the fear of our own mistakes."

"The Lady Jessica must be told," Idaho said. "Gurney says—"

"That message may not come from Gurney Halleck."

"It comes from no other. We Atreides have our ways of verifying messages. Stil, won't you at least explore some of—"

"Jacurutu is no more," Stilgar said. "It was destroyed many generations ago." He touched Idaho's sleeve. "In any event, I cannot spare the fighting men. These are troubled times, the threat to the qanat . . . you understand?" He sat back. "Now, when Alia—"

"There is no more Alia," Idaho said.

"So you say." Stilgar took another sip of coffee, replaced the cup. "Let it rest there, friend Idaho. Often there's no need to tear off an arm to remove a splinter."

"Then let's talk about Ghanima."

"There's no need. She has my countenance, my bond. No one can harm her here."

*He cannot be that naïve*, Idaho thought.

But Stilgar was rising to indicate that the interview was ended.

Idaho levered himself to his feet, feeling the stiffness in his knees. His calves felt numb. As Idaho stood, an aide entered and stood aside. Javid came into the room behind him. Idaho turned. Stilgar stood four paces away. Without hesitating, Idaho drew his knife in one swift motion and drove its point into the breast of the unsuspecting Javid. The man staggered backward, pulling himself off the knife. He turned, fell onto his face. His legs kicked and he was dead.

"That was to silence the gossip," Idaho said.

The aide stood with drawn knife, undecided how to react. Idaho had already sheathed his own knife, leaving a trace of blood on the edge of his yellow robe.

"You have defiled my honor!" Stilgar cried. "This is neutral—"

"Shut up!" Idaho glared at the shocked Naib. "You wear a collar, Stilgar!"

It was one of the three most deadly insults which could be directed at a Fremen. Stilgar's face went pale.

"You are a servant," Idaho said. "You've sold Fremen for their water."

This was the second most deadly insult, the one which had destroyed the original Jacurutu.

Stilgar ground his teeth, put a hand on his crysknife. The aide stepped back away from the body in the doorway.

Turning his back on the Naib, Idaho stepped into the door, taking the narrow opening beside Javid's body and speaking without turning, delivered the third insult. "You have no immortality, Stilgar. None of your descendants carry your blood!"

"Where do you go now, mentat?" Stilgar called as Idaho continued leaving the room. Stilgar's voice was as cold as a wind from the poles.

"To find Jacurutu," Idaho said, still not turning.

Stilgar drew his knife. "Perhaps I can help you."

Idaho was at the outer lip of the passage now. Without stopping, he said: "If you'd help me with your knife, water-thief, please do it in my back. That's the fitting way for one who wears the collar of a demon."

With two leaping strides Stilgar crossed the room, stepped on Javid's body and caught Idaho in the outer passage. One gnarled hand jerked Idaho around and to a stop. Stilgar confronted Idaho with bared teeth and a drawn knife. Such was his rage that Stilgar did not even see the curious smile on Idaho's face.

"Draw your knife, mentat scum!" Stilgar roared.

Idaho laughed. He cuffed Stilgar sharply—left hand, right hand—two stinging slaps to the head.

With an incoherent screech, Stilgar drove his knife into Idaho's abdomen, striking upward through the diaphragm into the heart.

Idaho sagged onto the blade, grinned up at Stilgar, whose rage dissolved into sudden icy shock.

"Two deaths for the Atreides," Idaho husked. "The second for no better reason than the first." He lurched sideways, collapsed to the stone floor on his face. Blood spread out from his wound.

Stilgar stared down past his dripping knife at the body of Idaho, took a deep, trembling breath. Javid lay dead behind him. And the consort of Alia, the womb of Heaven, lay dead at Stilgar's own hands. It might be argued that a Naib had but protected the honor of his name, avenging the threat to his promised neutrality. But this dead man was Duncan Idaho. No matter the arguments available, no matter the "extenuating circumstances," nothing could erase such an act. Even were Alia to approve privately, she would be forced to respond publicly in revenge. She was, after all, Fremen. To rule Fremen, she could be nothing else, not even to the smallest degree.

Only then did it occur to Stilgar that this situation was precisely what Idaho had intended to buy with his "second death."

Stilgar looked up, saw the shocked face of Harah, his second wife, peering at him in an enclosing throng. Everywhere Stilgar turned there were faces with identical expressions: shock and an understanding of the consequences.

Slowly Stilgar drew himself erect, wiped the blade on his sleeve and sheathed it. Speaking to the faces, his tone casual, he said: "Those who'll go with me should pack at once. Send men to summon worms."

"Where will you go, Stilgar?" Harah asked.

"Into the desert."

"I will go with you," she said.

"Of course you'll go with me. All of my wives will go with me. And Ghanima. Get her, Harah. At once."

"Yes, Stilgar . . . at once." She hesitated. "And Irulan?"

"If she wishes."

"Yes, husband." Still she hesitated. "You take Ghani as hostage?"

"Hostage?" He was genuinely startled by the thought. "Woman . . ." He touched Idaho's body softly with a toe. "If this mentat was right, I'm Ghani's only hope." And he remembered then Leto's warning: *"Beware of Alia. You must take Ghanima and flee."*

*After the Fremen, all Planetologists see life as expressions of energy and look for the overriding relationships. In small pieces, bits and parcels which grow into general understanding, the Fremen racial wisdom is translated into a new certainty. The thing Fremen have as a people, any people can have. They need but develop a sense for energy relationships. They need but observe that energy soaks up the patterns of things and builds with those patterns.*

—The Arrakeen Catastrophe
After Harq al-Ada

It was Tuek's Sietch on the inner lip of False Wall. Halleck stood in the shadow of the rock buttress which shielded the high entrance to the sietch, waiting for those inside to decide whether they would shelter him. He turned his gaze outward to the northern desert and then upward to the grey-blue morning sky. The smugglers here had been astonished to learn that he, an off-worlder, had captured a worm and ridden it. But Halleck had been equally astonished at their reaction. The thing was simple for an agile man who'd seen it done many times.

Halleck returned his attention to the desert, the silver desert of shining rocks and grey-green fields where water had worked its magic. All of this struck him suddenly as an enormously fragile containment of energy, of life—everything threatened by an abrupt shift in the pattern of change.

He knew the source of this reaction. It was the bustling scene on the desert floor below him. Containers of dead sandtrout were being trundled into the sietch for distillation and recovery of their water. There were thousands of the creatures. They had come to an outpouring of water. And it was this outpouring which had set Halleck's mind racing.

Halleck stared downward across the sietch fields and the qanat boundary which no longer flowed with precious water. He had seen the holes in the qanat's stone walls, the rending of the rock liner which had spilled water into the sand. What had made those holes? Some stretched along twenty meters of the qanat's most vulnerable sections, in places where soft sand led outward into water-absorbing depressions. It was those depressions which had swarmed with sandtrout. The children of the sietch were killing them and capturing them.

Repair teams worked on the shattered walls of the qanat. Others carried minims of irrigation water to the most needy plants. The water source in the gigantic cistern beneath Tuek's windtrap had been closed off, preventing the flow into the shattered qanat. The sun-powered pumps had been disconnected. The irrigation water came from dwindling pools at the bottom of the qanat and, laboriously, from the cistern within the sietch.

The metal frame of the doorseal behind Halleck crackled in the growing warmth of the day. As though the sound moved his eyes, Halleck found his gaze drawn to the farthest curve of the qanat, to the place where water had reached most impudently into the desert. The garden-hopeful planners of the sietch had planted a special tree there and it was doomed unless the water flow could be restored soon. Halleck stared at the silly, trailing plumage of a willow tree there shredded by sand and wind. For him, that tree symbolized the new reality for himself and for Arrakis.

*Both of us are alien here.*

They were taking a long time over their decision within the sietch, but they could use good fighting men. Smugglers always needed good men. Halleck had no illusions about them, though. The smugglers of this age were not the smugglers who'd sheltered him so many years ago when he'd fled the dissolution of his Duke's fief. No, these were a new breed, quick to seek profit.

Again he focused on the silly willow. It came to Halleck then that the stormwinds of his new reality might shred these smugglers and all of their friends. It might destroy Stilgar with his fragile neutrality and take with him all of the tribes who remained loyal to Alia. They'd all become colonial peoples. Halleck had seen it happen before, knowing the bitter taste of it on his own homeworld. He saw it clearly, recalling the mannerisms of the city Fremen, the pattern of the suburbs, and the unmistakable ways of the rural sietch which rubbed off even on this smugglers' hideaway. The rural districts were colonies of the urban centers. They'd learned how to wear a padded yoke, led into it by their greed if not their superstitions. Even here, especially here, the people had the attitude of a subject population, not the attitude of free men. They were defensive, concealing, evasive. Any manifestation of authority was subject to resentment—any authority: the Regency's, Stilgar's, their own Council . . .

*I can't trust them,* Halleck thought. He could only use them and nurture their distrust of others. It was sad. Gone was the old give and take of free men. The old ways had been reduced to ritual words, their origins lost to memory.

Alia had done her work well, punishing opposition and rewarding assistance, shifting the Imperial forces in random fashion, concealing the major elements of her Imperial power. The spies! Gods below, the spies she must have!

Halleck could almost see the deadly rhythm of movement and counter-movement by which Alia hoped to keep her opposition off balance.

*If the Fremen remain dormant, she'll win,* he thought.

The doorseal behind him crackled as it was opened. A sietch attendant named Melides emerged. He was a short man with a gourd-like body which dwindled into spindly legs whose ugliness was only accented by a stillsuit.

"You have been accepted," Melides said.

And Halleck heard the sly dissimulation in the man's voice. What that voice revealed told Halleck there was sanctuary here for only a limited time.

*Just until I can steal one of their 'thopters,* he thought.

"My gratitude to your Council," he said. And he thought of Esmar Tuek, for whom this sietch had been named. Esmar, long dead of someone's treachery, would have slit the throat of this Melides on sight.

> *Any path which narrows future possibilities may become a lethal trap.*
> *Humans are not threading their way through a maze; they scan a vast horizon*
> *filled with unique opportunities. The narrowing viewpoint of the maze should*
> *appeal only to creatures with their noses buried in sand. Sexually produced*
> *uniqueness and differences are the life-protection of the species.*

### —The Spacing Guild Handbook

"Why do I not feel grief?" Alia directed the question at the ceiling of her small audience chamber, a room she could cross in ten paces one way and fifteen the other. It had two tall and narrow windows which looked out across the Arrakeen rooftops at the Shield Wall.

It was almost noon. The sun burned down into the pan upon which the city had been built.

Alia lowered her gaze to Buer Agarves, the former Tabrite and now aide to Zia who directed the Temple guards. Agarves had brought the news that Javid and Idaho were dead. A mob of sycophants, aides and guards had come in with him and more crowded the areaway outside, revealing that they already knew Agarves's message.

Bad news traveled fast on Arrakis.

He was a small man, this Agarves, with a round face for a Fremen, almost infantile in its roundness. He was one of the new breed who had gone to water-fatness. Alia saw him as though he had been split into two images: one with a serious face and opaque indigo eyes, a worried expression around the mouth, the other image sensuous and vulnerable, excitingly vulnerable. She especially liked the thickness of his lips.

Although it was not yet noon, Alia felt something in the shocked silence around her that spoke of sunset.

*Idaho should've died at sunset,* she told herself.

"How is it, Buer, that you're the bearer of this news?" she asked, noting the watchful quickness which came into his expression.

Agarves tried to swallow, spoke in a hoarse voice hardly more than a whisper. "I went with Javid, you recall? And when . . . Stilgar sent me to you, he said for me to tell you that I carried his final obedience."

"Final obedience," she echoed. "What'd he mean by that?"

"I don't know, Lady Alia," he pleaded.

"Explain to me again what you saw," she ordered, and she wondered at how cold her skin felt.

"I saw . . ." He bobbed his head nervously, looked at the floor in front of Alia. "I saw the Holy Consort dead upon the floor of the central passage, and

Javid lay dead nearby in a side passage. The women already were preparing them for Huanui."

"And Stilgar summoned you to this scene?"

"That is true, My Lady. Stilgar summoned me. He sent Modibo, the Bent One, his messenger in sietch. Modibo gave me no warning. He merely told me Stilgar wanted me."

He met her eyes with a darting glance, returned his attention once more to the floor in front of her before nodding. "Yes, My Lady. And Javid dead nearby. Stilgar told me . . . told me that the Holy Consort had slain Javid."

"And my husband, you say Stilgar—"

"He said it to me with his own mouth, My Lady. Stilgar said he had done this. He said the Holy Consort provoked him to rage."

"Rage," Alia repeated. "How was that done?"

"He didn't say. No one said. I asked and no one said."

"And that's when you were sent to me with this news?"

"Yes, My Lady."

"Was there nothing you could do?"

Agarves wet his lips with his tongue, then: "Stilgar commanded, My Lady. It was his sietch."

"I see. And you always obeyed Stilgar."

"I always did, My Lady, until he freed me from my bond."

"When you were sent to my service, you mean?"

"I obey only you now, My Lady."

"Is that right? Tell me, Buer, if I commanded you to slay Stilgar, your old Naib, would you do it?"

He met her gaze with a growing firmness. "If you commanded it, My Lady."

"I do command it. Have you any idea where he's gone?"

"Into the desert; that's all I know, My Lady."

"How many men did he take?"

"Perhaps half the effectives."

"And Ghanima and Irulan with him!"

"Yes, My Lady. Those who left are burdened with their women, their children and their baggage. Stilgar gave everyone a choice—go with him or be freed of their bond. Many chose to be freed. They will select a new Naib."

"I'll select their new Naib! And it'll be you, Buer Agarves, on the day you bring me Stilgar's head."

Agarves could accept selection by battle. It was a Fremen way. He said: "As you command, My Lady. What forces may I—"

"See Zia. I can't give you many 'thopters for the search. They're needed elsewhere. But you'll have enough fighting men. Stilgar has defamed his honor. Many will serve with you gladly."

"I'll get about it, then, My Lady."

"Wait!" She studied him a moment, reviewing whom she could send to watch over this vulnerable infant. He would need close watching until he'd proved himself. Zia would know whom to send.

"Am I not dismissed, My Lady?"

"You are not dismissed. I must consult you privately and at length on your plans to take Stilgar." She put a hand to her face. "I'll not grieve until you've exacted my revenge. Give me a few minutes to compose myself." She lowered her hand. "One of my attendants will show you the way." She gave a subtle hand signal to one of her attendants, whispered to Shalus, her new Dame of Chamber: "Have him washed and perfumed before you bring him. He smells of worm."

"Yes, mistress."

Alia turned then, feigning the grief she did not feel, and fled to her private chambers. There, in her bedroom, she slammed the door into its tracks, cursed and stamped her foot.

*Damn that Duncan! Why? Why? Why?*

She sensed a deliberate provocation from Idaho. He'd slain Javid and provoked Stilgar. It said he knew about Javid. The whole thing must be taken as a message from Duncan Idaho, a final gesture.

Again she stamped her foot and again, raging across the bedchamber.

*Damn him! Damn him! Damn him!*

Stilgar gone over to the rebels and Ghanima with him. Irulan, too.

*Damn them all!*

Her stamping foot encountered a painful obstacle, descending onto metal. Pain brought a cry from her and she peered down, finding that she'd bruised her foot on a metal buckle. She snatched it up, stood frozen at the sight of it in her hand. It was an old buckle, one of the silver-and-platinum originals from Caladan awarded originally by the Duke Leto Atreides I to his swordmaster, Duncan Idaho. She'd seen Duncan wear it many times. And he'd discarded it here.

Alia's fingers clutched convulsively on the buckle. Idaho had left it here when . . . when . . .

Tears sprang from her eyes, forced out against the great Fremen conditioning. Her mouth drew down into a frozen grimace and she sensed the old battle begin within her skull, reaching out to her fingertips, to her toes. She felt that she had become two people. One looked upon these fleshly contortions with astonishment. The other sought submission to an enormous pain spreading in her chest. The tears flowed freely from her eyes now, and the Astonished One within her demanded querulously: "Who cries? Who is it that cries? Who is crying now?"

But nothing stopped the tears, and she felt the painfulness which flamed through her breast as it moved her flesh and hurled her onto the bed.

Still something demanded out of that profound astonishment: "Who cries? Who is that . . ."

.

*By these acts Leto II removed himself from the evolutionary succession. He did it with a deliberate cutting action, saying: "To be independent is to be removed." Both twins saw beyond the needs of memory as a measuring process, that is, a way of determining their distance from their human origins. But it was left to Leto II to do the audacious thing, recognizing that a real*

*creation is independent of its creator. He refused to reenact the evolutionary
sequence, saying, "That, too, takes me farther and farther from humanity."
He saw the implications in this: that there can be no truly closed systems in
life.*

**—The Holy Metamorphosis
by Harq al-Ada**

There were birds thriving on the insect life which teemed in the damp sand
beyond the broken qanat: parrots, magpies, jays. This had been a djedida, the
last of the new towns, built on a foundation of exposed basalt. It was abandoned
now. Ghanima, using the morning hours to study the area beyond the original
plantings of the abandoned sietch, detected movement and saw a banded gecko
lizard. There'd been a gila woodpecker earlier, nesting in a mud wall of the
djedida.

She thought of it as a sietch, but it was really a collection of low walls made of
stabilized mud brick surrounded by plantings to hold back the dunes. It lay
within the Tanzerouft, six hundred kilometers south of Sihaya Ridge. Without
human hands to maintain it, the sietch already was beginning to melt back into
the desert, its walls eroded by sandblast winds, its plants dying, its plantation
area cracked by the burning sun.

Yet the sand beyond the shattered qanat remained damp, attesting to the fact
that the squat bulk of the windtrap still functioned.

In the months since their flight from Tabr the fugitives had sampled the
protection of several such places made uninhabitable by the Desert Demon.
Ghanima didn't believe in the Desert Demon, although there was no denying
the visible evidence of the qanat's destruction.

Occasionally they had word from the northern settlements through encounters with rebel spice-hunters. A few 'thopters—some said no more than
six—carried out search flights seeking Stilgar, but Arrakis was large and its
desert was friendly to the fugitives. Reportedly there was a search-and-destroy
force charged with finding Stilgar's band, but the force which was led by the
former Tabrite Buer Agarves had other duties and often returned to Arrakeen.

The rebels said there was little fighting between their men and the troops of
Alia. Random depredations of the Desert Demon made Home Guard duty the
first concern of Alia and the Naibs. Even the smugglers had been hit, but they
were said to be scouring the desert for Stilgar, wanting the price on his head.

Stilgar had brought his band into the djedida just before dark the previous
day, following the unerring moisture sense of his old Fremen nose. He'd
promised they would head south for the palmyries soon, but refused to put a
date on the move. Although he carried a price on his head which once would
have bought a planet, Stilgar seemed the happiest and most carefree of men.

"This is a good place for us," he'd said, pointing out that the windtrap still
functioned. "Our friends have left us some water."

They were a small band now, sixty people in all. The old, the sick, and the
very young had been filtered south into the palmyries, absorbed there by

trusted families. Only the toughest remained, and they had many friends to the north and the south.

Ghanima wondered why Stilgar refused to discuss what was happening to the planet. Couldn't he see it? As qanats were shattered, Fremen pulled back to the nothern and southern lines which once had marked the extent of their holdings. This movement could only signal what must be happening to the Empire. One condition was the mirror of the other.

Ghanima ran a hand under the collar of her stillsuit and resealed it. Despite her worries she felt remarkably free here. The inner lives no longer plagued her, although she sometimes felt their memories inserted into her consciousness. She knew from those memories what this desert had been once, before the work of the ecological transformation. It had been drier, for one thing. That unrepaired windtrap still functioned because it processed moist air.

Many creatures which once had shunned this desert ventured to live here now. Many in the band remarked how the daylight owls proliferated. Even now, Ghanima could see antbirds. They jigged and danced along the insect lines which swarmed in the damp sand at the end of the shattered qanat. Few badgers were to be seen out here, but there were kangaroo mice in uncounted numbers.

Superstitious fear ruled the new Fremen, and Stilgar was no better than the rest. This djedida had been given back to the desert after its qanat had been shattered a fifth time in eleven months. Four times they'd repaired the ravages of the Desert Demon, then they'd no longer had the surplus water to risk another loss.

It was the same all through the djedidas and in many of the old sietches. Eight out of nine new settlements had been abandoned. Many of the old sietch communities were more crowded than they had ever been before. And while the desert entered this new phase, Fremen reverted to their old ways. They saw omens in everything. Were worms increasingly scarce except in the Tanzerouft? It was the judgment of Shai-Hulud! And dead worms had been seen with nothing to say why they died. They went back to desert dust swiftly after death, but those crumbling hulks which Fremen chanced upon filled the observers with terror.

Stilgar's band had encountered such a hulk the previous month and it had taken four days for them to shake off the feeling of evil. The thing had reeked of sour and poisonous putrefaction. Its moldering hulk had been found sitting on top of a giant spiceblow, the spice mostly ruined.

Ghanima turned from observing the qanat and looked back at the djedida. Directly in front of her lay a broken wall which once had protected a *mushtamal*, a small garden annex. She'd explored the place with a firm dependence upon her own curiosity and had found a store of flat, unleavened spicebread in a stone box.

Stilgar had destroyed it, saying: "Fremen would never leave good food behind them."

Ghanima had suspected he was mistaken, but it hadn't been worth the argument or the risk. Fremen were changing. Once they'd moved freely across the *bled*, drawn by natural needs: water, spice, trade. Animal activities had been their alarm clocks. But animals moved to strange new rhythms now while most Fremen huddled close in their old cave-warrens within the shadow of the northern Shield Wall. Spice-hunters in the Tanzerouft were rare, and only Stilgar's band moved in the old ways.

She trusted Stilgar and his fear of Alia. Irulan reinforced his arguments now, reverting to odd Bene Gesserit musings. But on faraway Salusa, Farad'n still lived. Someday there would have to be a reckoning.

Ghanima looked up at the grey-silver morning sky, questing in her mind. Where was help to be found? Where was there someone to listen when she revealed what she saw happening all around them? The Lady Jessica stayed on Salusa, if the reports were to be believed. And Alia was a creature on a pedestal, involved only in being colossal while she drifted farther and farther from reality. Gurney Halleck was nowhere to be found, although he was reported seen everywhere. The Preacher had gone into hiding, his heretical rantings only a fading memory.

And Stilgar.

She looked across the broken wall to where Stilgar was helping repair the cistern. Stilgar reveled in his role as the will-o'-the-desert, the price upon his head growing monthly.

Nothing made sense anymore. Nothing.

Who was this Desert Demon, this creature able to destroy qanats as though they were false idols to be toppled into the sand? Was it a rogue worm? Was it a third force in rebellion—many people? No one believed it was a worm. The water would kill any worm venturing against a qanat. Many Fremen believed the Desert Demon was actually a revolutionary band bent on overthrowing Alia's Mahdinate and restoring Arrakis to its old ways. Those who believed this said it would be a good thing. Get rid of that greedy apostolic succession which did little else than uphold its own mediocrity. Get back to the true religion which Muad'Dib had espoused.

A deep sigh shook Ghanima. *Oh, Leto,* she thought. *I'm almost glad you didn't live to see these days. I'd join you myself, but I've a knife yet unblooded. Alia and Farad'n. Farad'n and Alia. The Old Baron's her demon, and that can't be permitted.*

Harah came out of the djedida, approaching Ghanima with a steady sand-swallowing pace. Harah stopped in front of Ghanima, demanded, "What do you alone out here?"

"This is a strange place, Harah. We should leave."

"Stilgar waits to meet someone here."

"Oh? He didn't tell me that."

"Why should he tell you everything? *Maku?*" Harah slapped the water pouch which bulged the front of Ghanima's robe. "Are you a grown woman to be pregnant?"

"I've been pregnant so many times there's no counting them," Ghanima said. "Don't play those adult-child games with me!"

Harah took a backward step at the venom in Ghanima's voice.

"You're a band of stupids," Ghanima said, waving her hand to encompass the djedida and the activities of Stilgar and his people. "I should never have come with you."

"You'd be dead by now if you hadn't."

"Perhaps. But you don't see what's right in front of your faces! Who is it that Stilgar waits to meet here?"

"Buer Agarves."

Ghanima stared at her.

"He is being brought here secretly by friends from Red Chasm Sietch," Harah explained.

"Alia's little plaything?"

"He is being brought under blindfold."

"Does Stilgar believe that?"

"Buer asked for the parley. He agreed to all of our terms."

"Why wasn't I told about this?"

"Stilgar knew you would argue against it."

"Argue against . . . This is madness!"

Harah scowled. "Don't forget that Buer is . . ."

"He's *Family!*" Ghanima snapped. "He's the grandson of Stilgar's cousin. I know. And the Farad'n whose blood I'll draw one day is as close a relative to me. Do you think that'll stay my knife?"

"We've had a distrans. No one follows his party."

Ghanima spoke in a low voice: "Nothing good will come of this, Harah. We should leave at once."

"Have you read an omen?" Harah asked. "That dead worm we saw! Was that—"

"Stuff that into your womb and give birth to it elsewhere!" Ghanima raged. "I don't like this meeting nor this place. Isn't that enough?"

"I'll tell Stilgar what you—"

"I'll tell him myself!" Ghanima strode past Harah, who made the sign of the worm horns at her back to ward off evil.

But Stilgar only laughed at Ghanima's fears and ordered her to look for sandtrout as though she were one of the children. She fled into one of the djedida's abandoned houses and crouched in a corner to nurse her anger. The emotion passed quickly, though; she felt the stirring of the inner lives and remembered someone saying: "If we can immobilize them, things will go as we plan."

*What an odd thought.*

But she couldn't recall who'd said those words.

*Muad'Dib was disinherited and he spoke for the disinherited of all time. He cried out against that profound injustice which alienates the individual from that which he was taught to believe, from that which seemed to come to him as a right.*

—The Mahdinate, An Analysis
by Harq al-Ada

Gurney Halleck sat on the butte at Shuloch with his baliset beside him on a spice-fiber rug. Below him the enclosed basin swarmed with workers planting crops. The sand ramp up which the Cast Out had lured worms on a spice trail had been blocked off with a new qanat. Plantings moved down the slope to hold it.

It was almost time for the noon meal and Halleck had been on the butte for more than an hour, seeking privacy in which to think. Humans did the labor below him, but everything he saw was the work of melange. Leto's personal estimate was that spice production would fall soon to a stabilized one-tenth of its peak in the Harkonnen years. Stockpiles throughout the empire doubled in value at every new posting. Three hundred and twenty-one liters were said to have bought half of Novebruns Planet from the Metulli Family.

The Cast Out worked like men driven by a devil, and perhaps they were. Before every meal, they faced the Tanzerouft and prayed to Shai-Hulud personified. That was how they saw Leto and, through their eyes, Halleck saw a future where most of humankind shared that view. Halleck wasn't sure he liked the prospect.

Leto had set the pattern when he'd brought Halleck and The Preacher here in Halleck's stolen 'thopter. With his bare hands Leto had breached the Shuloch qanat, hurling large stones more than fifty meters. When the Cast Out had tried to intervene, Leto had decapitated the first to reach him, using no more than a blurred sweep of his arm. He'd hurled others back into their companions and had laughed at their weapons. In a demon-voice he'd roared at them: "Fire will not touch me! Your knives will not harm me! I wear the skin of Shai-Hulud!"

The Cast Out had recognized him then and recalled his escape, leaping from the butte "directly to the desert." They'd prostrated themselves before him and Leto had issued his orders. "I bring you two guests. You will guard them and honor them. You will rebuild your qanat and begin planting an oasis garden. One day I'll make my home here. You will prepare my home. You will sell no more spice, but you will store every bit you collect."

On and on he'd gone with his instructions, and the Cast Out had heard every word, seeing him through fear-glazed eyes, through a terrifying awe.

Here was Shai-Hulud come up from the sand at last!

There'd been no intimation of this metamorphosis when Leto had found Halleck with Ghadhean al-Fali in one of the small rebel sietches at Gare Ruden. With his blind companion, Leto had come up from the desert along the old spice route, traveling by worm through an area where worms were now a rarity. He'd spoken of several detours forced upon him by the presence of moisture in the sand, enough water to poison a worm. They'd arrived shortly after noon and had been brought into the stone-walled common room by guards.

The memory haunted Halleck now.

"So this is The Preacher," he'd said.

Striding around the blind man, studying him, Halleck recalled the stories about him. No stillsuit mask hid the old face in sietch, and the features were there for memory to make its comparisons. Yes, the man did look like the old Duke for whom Leto had been named. Was it a chance likeness?

"You know the stories about this one?" Halleck asked, speaking in an aside to Leto. "That he's your father come back from the desert?"

"I've heard the stories."

Halleck turned to examine the boy. Leto wore an odd stillsuit with rolled edges around his face and ears. A black robe covered it and sandboots sheathed his feet. There was much to be explained about his presence here—how he'd managed to escape once more.

"Why do you bring The Preacher here?" Halleck asked. "In Jacurutu they said he works for them."

"No more. I bring him because Alia wants him dead."

"So ? You think this is a sanctuary?"

"You are his sanctuary."

All this time The Preacher stood near them, listening but giving no sign that he cared which turn their discussion took.

"He has served me well, Gurney," Leto said. "House Atreides has not lost all sense of obligation to those who serve us."

"House Atreides?"

"I am House Atreides."

"You fled Jacurutu before I could complete the testing which your grandmother ordered," Halleck said, his voice cold. "How can you assume—"

"This man's life is to be guarded as though it were your own." Leto spoke as though there were no argument and he met Halleck's stare without flinching.

Jessica had trained Halleck in many of the Bene Gesserit refinements of observation and he'd detected nothing in Leto which spoke of other than calm assurance. Jessica's orders remained, though. "Your grandmother charged me to complete your education and be sure you're not possessed."

"I'm not possessed." Just a flat statement.

"Why did you run away?"

"Namri had orders to kill me no matter what I did. His orders were from Alia."

"Are you a Truthsayer, then?"

"I am." Another flat statement filled with self-assurance.

"And Ghanima as well?"

"No."

The Preacher broke his silence then, turning his blind sockets toward Halleck but pointing at Leto. "You think *you* can test him?"

"Don't interfere when you know nothing of the problem or its consequences," Halleck ordered, not looking at the man.

"Oh, I know its consequences well enough," The Preacher said. "I was tested once by an old woman who thought she knew what she was doing. She didn't know, as it turned out."

Halleck looked at him then. "You're another Truthsayer?"

"Anyone can be a Truthsayer, even you," The Preacher said. "It's a matter of self-honesty about the nature of your own feelings. It requires that you have an inner agreement with truth which allows ready recognition."

"Why do you interfere?" Halleck asked, putting hand to crysknife. Who was this Preacher?

"I'm responsive to these events," The Preacher said. "My mother could put her own blood upon the altar, but I have other motives. And I do see your problem."

"Oh?" Halleck was actually curious now.

"The Lady Jessica ordered you to differentiate between the wolf and the dog, between *ze'eb* and *ke'leb*. By her definition a wolf is someone with power who misuses that power. However, between wolf and dog there is a dawn period when you cannot distinguish between them."

"That's close to the mark," Halleck said, noting how more and more people of the sietch had entered the common room to listen. "How do you know this?"

"Because I know this planet. You don't understand? Think how it is. Beneath the surface there are rocks, dirt, sediment, sand. That's the planet's memory, the picture of its history. It's the same with humans. The dog remembers the wolf. Each universe revolves around a core of *being*, and outward from that core go all of the memories, right out to the surface."

"Very interesting," Halleck said. "How does that help me carry out my orders?"

"Review the picture of your history which is within you. Communicate as animals would communicate."

Halleck shook his head. There was a compelling directness about this Preacher, a quality which he'd recognized many times in the Atreides, and there was more than a little hint that the man was employing the powers of Voice. Halleck felt his heart begin to hammer. Was it possible?

"Jessica wanted an ultimate test, a stress by which the underlying fabric of her grandson exposed itself," The Preacher said. "But the fabric's always there, open to your gaze."

Halleck turned to stare at Leto. The movement came of itself, compelled by irresistible forces.

The Preacher continued as though lecturing an obstinate pupil. "This young person confuses you because he's not a singular being. He's a community. As with any community under stress, any member of that community may assume command. This command isn't always benign, and we get our stories of Abomination. But you've already wounded this community enough, Gurney Halleck. Can't you see that the transformation already has taken place? This youth has achieved an inner cooperation which is enormously powerful, that cannot be subverted. Without eyes I see this. Once I opposed him, but now I do his bidding. He is the Healer."

"Who are you?" Halleck demanded.

"I'm no more than what you see. Don't look at me, look at this person you were ordered to teach and test. He has been formed by crisis. He survived a lethal environment. He is here."

"Who are you?" Halleck insisted.

"I tell you only to look at this Atreides youth! He is the ultimate feedback upon which our species depends. He'll reinsert into the system the results of its past performance. No other human could know that past performance as he knows it. And you consider destroying such a one!"

"I was ordered to test him and I've not—"

"But you have!"

"Is he Abomination?"

A weary laugh shook The Preacher. "You persist in Bene Gesserit nonsense. How they create the myths by which men sleep!"

"Are you Paul Atreides?" Halleck asked.

"Paul Atreides is no more. He tried to stand as a supreme moral symbol while he renounced all moral pretensions. He became a saint without a god, every word a blasphemy. How can you think—"

"Because you speak with his voice."

"Would you test *me*, now? Beware, Gurney Halleck."

Halleck swallowed, forced his attention back to the impassive Leto who still stood calmly observant. "Who's being tested?" The Preacher asked. "Is it, perhaps, that the Lady Jessica tests you, Gurney Halleck?"

Halleck found this thought deeply disturbing, wondering why he let this Preacher's words move him. But it was a deep thing in Atreides servants to obey that autocratic mystique. Jessica, explaining this, had made it even more mysterious. Halleck now felt something changing within himself, a *something* whose edges had only been touched by the Bene Gesserit training Jessica had pressed upon him. Inarticulate fury arose in him. He did not want to change!

"Which of you plays God and to what end?" The Preacher asked. "You cannot rely on reason alone to answer that question."

Slowly, deliberately, Halleck raised his attention from Leto to the blind man. Jessica kept saying he should achieve the balance of *kairits*—"thou shalt-thou shalt not." She called it a discipline without words and phrases, no rules or arguments. It was the sharpened edge of his own internal truth, all-engrossing. Something in the blind man's voice, his tone, his manner, ignited a fury which burned itself into blinding calmness within Halleck.

"Answer my question," The Preacher said.

Halleck felt the words deepen his concentration upon this place, this one moment and its demands. His position in the universe was defined only by his concentration. No doubt remained in him. This was Paul Atreides, not dead, but returned. And this non-child, Leto. Halleck looked once more at Leto, really saw him. He saw the signs of stress around the eyes, the sense of balance in the stance, the passive mouth with its quirking sense of humor. Leto stood out from his background as though at the focus of a blinding light. He had achieved harmony simply by accepting it.

"Tell me, Paul," Halleck said. "Does your mother know?"

The Preacher sighed. "To the Sisterhood, all of it, I am dead. Do not try to revive me."

Still not looking at him, Halleck asked: "But why does she—"

"She does what she must. She makes her own life, thinking she rules many lives. Thus we all play god."

"But you're alive," Halleck whispered, overcome now by his realization, turning at last to stare at this man, younger than himself, but so aged by the desert that he appeared to carry twice Halleck's years.

"What is that?" Paul demanded. "Alive?"

Halleck peered around them at the watching Fremen, their faces caught between doubt and awe.

"My mother never had to learn my lesson." It was Paul's voice! "To be a god can ultimately become boring and degrading. There'd be reason enough for the invention of free will! A god might wish to escape into sleep and be alive only in the unconscious projections of his dream-creatures."

"But you're alive!" Halleck spoke louder now.

Paul ignored the excitement in his old companion's voice, asked: "Would you really have pitted this lad against his sister in the test-Mashdad? What deadly nonsense! Each would have said: 'No! Kill me! Let the other live!' Where would such a test lead? What is it then to be alive, Gurney?"

"That was not the test," Halleck protested. He did not like the way the Fremen pressed closer around them, studying Paul, ignoring Leto.

But Leto intruded now. "Look at the fabric, father."

"Yes . . . yes . . ." Paul held his head high as though sniffing the air. "It's Farad'n, then!"

"How easy it is to follow our thoughts instead of our senses," Leto said.

Halleck had been unable to follow this thought and, about to ask, was interrupted by Leto's hand upon his arm. "Don't ask, Gurney. You might return to suspecting that I'm Abomination. No! Let it happen, Gurney. If you try to force it, you'll only destroy yourself."

But Halleck felt himself overcome by doubts. Jessica had warned him. "*They can be very beguiling, these pre-born. They have tricks you've never even dreamed.*" Halleck shook his head slowly. And Paul! Gods below! Paul alive and in league with this question mark he'd fathered!

The Fremen around them could no longer be held back. They pressed between Halleck and Paul, between Leto and Paul, shoving the two to the background. The air was showered with hoarse questions. "Are you Muad'Dib? Are you truly Muad'Dib? Is it true, what he says? Tell us!"

"You must think of me only as The Preacher," Paul said, pushing against them. "I cannot be Paul Atreides or Muad'Dib, never again. I'm not Chani's mate or Emperor."

Halleck, fearing what might happen if these frustrated questions found no logical answer, was about to act when Leto moved ahead of him. It was there

Halleck first saw an element of the terrible change which had been wrought in Leto. A bull voice roared, "Stand aside!"—and Leto moved forward, thrusting adult Fremen right and left, knocking them down, clubbing them with his hands, wrenching knives from their hands by grasping the blades.

In less than a minute those Fremen still standing were pressed back against the walls in silent consternation. Leto stood beside his father. "When Shai-Hulud speaks, you obey," Leto said.

And when a few of the Fremen had started to argue, Leto had torn a corner of rock from the passage wall beside the room's exit and crumbled it in his bare hands, smiling all the while.

"I will tear your sietch down around your faces," he said.

"The Desert Demon," someone whispered.

"And your qanats," Leto agreed. "I will rip them apart. We have not been here, do you hear me?"

Heads shook from side to side in terrified submission.

"No one here has seen us," Leto said. "One whisper from you and I will return to drive you into the desert without water."

Halleck saw hands being raised in the warding gesture, the sign of the worm.

"We will go now, my father and I, accompanied by our old friend," Leto said. "Make our 'thopter ready."

And Leto had guided them to Shuloch then, explaining enroute that they must move swiftly because "Farad'n will be here on Arrakis very soon. And, as my father has said, then you'll see the real test, Gurney."

Looking down from the Shuloch butte, Halleck asked himself once more, as he asked every day: "What test? What does he mean?"

But Leto was no longer in Shuloch, and Paul refused to answer.

> Church and State, scientific reason and faith, the individual and his community, even progress and tradition—all of these can be reconciled in the teachings of Muad'Dib. He taught us that there exist no intransigent opposites except in the beliefs of men. Anyone can rip aside the veil of Time. You can discover the future in the past or in your own imagination. Doing this, you win back your consciousness in your inner being. You know then that the universe is a coherent whole and you are indivisible from it.

> —The Preacher at Arrakeen
> After Harq al-Ada

Ghanima sat far back outside the circle of light from the spice lamps and watched this Buer Agarves. She didn't like his round face and agitated eyebrows, his way of moving his feet when he spoke, as though his words were a hidden music to which he danced.

*He's not here to parley with Stil,* Ghanima told herself, seeing this confirmed in every word and movement from this man. She moved farther back away from the Council circle.

Every sietch had a room such as this one, but the meeting hall of the abandoned djedida struck Ghanima as a cramped place because it was so low. Sixty people from Stilgar's band plus the nine who'd come with Agarves filled only one end of the hall. Spice-oil lamps reflected against low beams which supported the ceiling. The light cast wavering shadows which danced on the walls, and the pungent smoke filled the place with the smell of cinnamon.

The meeting had started at dusk after the moisture prayers and evening meal. It had been going on for more than an hour now, and Ghanima couldn't fathom the hidden currents in Agarves's performance. His words appeared clear enough, but his motions and eye movements didn't agree.

Agarves was speaking now, responding to a question from one of Stilgar's lieutenants, a niece of Harah's named Rajia. She was a darkly ascetic young woman whose mouth turned down at the corners, giving her an air of perpetual distrust. Ghanima found the expression satisfying in the circumstances.

"Certainly I believe Alia will grant a full and complete pardon to all of you," Agarves said. "I'd not be here with this message otherwise."

Stilgar intervened as Rajia made to speak once more. "I'm not so much worried about our trusting her as I am about whether she trusts you." Stilgar's voice carried growling undertones. He was uncomfortable with this suggestion that he return to his old status.

"It doesn't matter whether she trusts me," Agarves said. "To be candid about it, I don't believe she does. I've been too long searching for you without finding you. But I've always felt she didn't really want you captured. She was—"

"She was the wife of the man I slew," Stilgar said. "I grant you that he asked for it. Might just as well've fallen on his own knife. But this new attitude smells of—"

Agarves danced to his feet, anger plain on his face. "She forgives you! How many times must I say it? She had the Priests make a great show of asking divine guidance from—"

"You've only raised another issue." It was Irulan, leaning forward past Rajia, blonde head set off against Rajia's darkness. "She has convinced you, but she may have other plans."

"The Priesthood has—"

"But there are all of these stories," Irulan said. "That you're more than just a military advisor, that you're her—"

"Enough!" Agarves was beside himself with rage. His hand hovered near his knife. Warring emotions moved just below the surface of his skin, twisting his features. "Believe what you will, but I cannot go on with that woman! She fouls me! She dirties everything she touches! I am used. I am soiled. But I have not lifted my knife against my kin. Now—no more!"

Ghanima, observing this, thought: *That, at least, was truth coming out of him.*

Surprisingly, Stilgar broke into laughter. "Ahhhh, cousin," he said. "Forgive me, but there's truth in anger."

"Then you agree?"

"I've not said that." He raised a hand as Agarves threatened another outburst. "It's not for my sake, Buer, but there are these others." He gestured around him. "They are my responsibility. Let us consider for a moment what reparations Alia offers."

"Reparations? There's no word of reparations. Pardon, but no—"

"Then what does she offer as surety of her word?"

"Sietch Tabr and you as Naib, full autonomy as a neutral. She understands now how—"

"I'll not go back to her entourage or provide her with fighting men," Stilgar warned. "Is that understood?"

Ghanima could hear Stilgar beginning to weaken and thought: *No, Stil! No!*

"No need for that," Agarves said. "Alia wants only Ghanima returned to her and the carrying out of the betrothal promise which she—"

"So now it comes out!" Stilgar said, his brows drawing down. "Ghanima's the price of my pardon. Does she think me—"

"She thinks you sensible," Agarves argued, resuming his seat.

Gleefully, Ghanima thought: *He won't do it. Save your breath. He won't do it.*

As she thought this, Ghanima heard a soft rustling behind and to her left. She started to turn, felt powerful hands grab her. A heavy rag reeking of sleep-drugs covered her face before she could cry out. As consciousness faded, she felt herself being carried toward a door in the hall's darkest reaches. And she thought: *I should have guessed! I should've been prepared!* But the hands that held her were adult and strong. She could not squirm away from them.

Ghanima's last sensory impressions were of cold night air, a glimpse of stars, and a hooded face which looked down at her, then asked: "She wasn't injured, was she?"

The answer was lost as the stars wheeled and streaked across her gaze, losing themselves in a blaze of light which was the inner core of her selfdom.

---

*Muad'Dib gave us a particular kind of knowledge about prophetic insight, about the behavior which surrounds such insight and its influence upon events which are seen to be "on line." (That is, events which are set to occur in a related system which the prophet reveals and interprets.) As has been noted elsewhere, such insight operates as a peculiar trap for the prophet himself. He can become the victim of what he knows—which is a relatively common human failing. The danger is that those who predict real events may overlook the polarizing effect brought about by overindulgence in their own truth. They tend to forget that nothing in a polarized universe can exist without its opposite being present.*

—The Prescient Vision
by Harq al-Ada

Blowing sand hung like fog on the horizon, obscuring the rising sun. The sand was cold in the dune shadows. Leto stood outside the ring of the palmyrie looking into the desert. He smelled dust and the aroma of spiny plants, heard the morning sounds of people and animals. The Fremen maintained no qanat in this place. They had only a bare minimum of hand planting irrigated by the women, who carried water in skin bags. Their windtrap was a fragile thing, easily destroyed by the stormwinds but easily rebuilt. Hardship, the rigors of the spice trade, and adventure were a way of life here. These Fremen still believed heaven was the sound of running water, but they cherished an ancient concept of Freedom which Leto shared.

*Freedom is a lonely state,* he thought.

Leto adjusted the folds of the white robe which covered his living stillsuit. He could feel how the sandtrout membrane had changed him and, as always with this feeling, he was forced to overcome a deep sense of loss. He no longer was completely human. Odd things swam in his blood. Sandtrout cilia had penetrated every organ, adjusting, changing. The sandtrout itself was changing, adapting. But Leto, knowing this, felt himself torn by the old threads of his lost humanity, his life caught in primal anguish with its ancient continuity shattered. He knew the trap of indulging in such emotion, though. He knew it well.

*Let the future happen of itself,* he thought. *The only rule governing creativity is the act of creation itself.*

It was difficult to take his gaze away from the sands, the dunes—the great emptiness. Here at the edge of the sand lay a few rocks, but they led the imagination outward into the winds, the dust, the sparse and lonely plants and animals, dune merging into dune, desert into desert.

Behind him came the sound of a flute playing for the morning prayer, the chant for moisture which now was a subtly altered serenade to the new Shai-Hulud. This knowledge in Leto's mind gave the music a sense of eternal loneliness.

*I could just walk away into that desert,* he thought.

Everything would change then. One direction would be as good as another. He had already learned to live a life free of possessions. He had refined the Fremen mystique to a terrible edge: everything he took with him was necessary, and that was all he took. But he carried nothing except the robe on his back, the Atreides hawk ring hidden in its folds, and the skin-which-was-not-his-own.

It would be easy to walk away from here.

Movement high in the sky caught his attention: the splayed-gap wingtips identified a vulture. The sight filled his chest with aching. Like the wild Fremen, vultures lived in this land because this was where they were born. They knew nothing better. The desert made them what they were.

Another Fremen breed was coming up in the wake of Muad'Dib and Alia, though. They were the reason he could not let himself walk away into the desert as his father had done. Leto recalled Idaho's words from the early days: "These Fremen! They're magnificently alive. I've never met a greedy Fremen."

There were plenty of greedy Fremen now.

A wave of sadness passed over Leto. He was committed to a course which could change all of that, but at a terrible price. And the management of that course became increasingly difficult as they neared the vortex.

Kralizec, the Typhoon Struggle, lay ahead . . . but Kralizec or worse would be the price of a misstep.

Voices sounded behind Leto, then the clear piping sound of a child speaking: "Here he is."

Leto turned.

The Preacher had come out of the palmyrie, led by a child.

*Why do I still think of him as The Preacher?* Leto wondered.

The answer lay there on the clean tablet of Leto's mind: *Because this is no longer Muad'Dib, no longer Paul Atreides.* The desert had made him what he was. The desert and the jackals of Jacurutu with their overdoses of melange and their constant betrayals. The Preacher was old before his time, old not despite the spice but because of it.

"They said you wanted to see me now," The Preacher said, speaking as his child guide stopped.

Leto looked at the child of the palmyrie, a person almost as tall as himself, with awe tempered by an avaricious curiosity. The young eyes glinted darkly above the child-sized stillsuit mask.

Leto waved a hand. "Leave us."

For a moment there was rebellion in the child's shoulders, then the awe and native Fremen respect for privacy took over. The child left them.

"You know Farad'n is here on Arrakis?" Leto asked.

"Gurney told me when he flew me down last night."

And The Preacher thought: *How coldly measured his words are. He's like I was in the old days.*

"I face a difficult choice," Leto said.

"I thought you'd already made all the choices."

"We know *that* trap, father."

The Preacher cleared his throat. The tensions told him how near they were to the shattering crisis. Now Leto would not be relying on pure vision, but on vision management.

"You need my help?" The Preacher asked.

"Yes. I'm returning to Arrakeen and I wish to go as your guide."

"To what end?"

"Would you preach once more in Arrakeen?"

"Perhaps. There are things I've not said to them."

"You will not come back to the desert, father."

"If I go with you?"

"Yes."

"I'll do whatever you decide."

"Have you considered? With Farad'n there, your mother will be with him."

"Undoubtedly."

Once more, The Preacher cleared his throat. It was a betrayal of nervousness which Muad'Dib would never have permitted. This flesh had been too long away from the old regimen of self-discipline, his mind too often betrayed into madness by the Jacurutu. And The Preacher thought that perhaps it wouldn't be wise to return to Arrakeen.

"You don't have to go back with me," Leto said. "But my sister is there and I must return. You could go with Gurney."

"And you'd go to Arrakeen alone?"

"Yes. I must meet Farad'n."

"I will go with you," The Preacher sighed.

And Leto sensed a touch of the old vision madness in The Preacher's manner, wondered: *Has he been playing the prescience game?* No. He'd never go that way again. He knew the trap of a partial commitment. The Preacher's every word confirmed that he had handed over the visions to his son, knowing that everything in this universe had been anticipated.

It was the old polarities which taunted The Preacher now. He had fled from paradox into paradox.

"We'll be leaving in a few minutes, then," Leto said. "Will you tell Gurney?"

"Gurney's not going with us?"

"I want Gurney to survive."

The Preacher opened himself to the tensions then. They were in the air around him, in the ground under his feet, a motile thing which focused onto the non-child who was his son. The blunt scream of his old visions waited in The Preacher's throat.

*This cursed holiness!*

The sandy juice of his fears could not be avoided. He knew what faced them in Arrakeen. They would play a game once more with terrifying and deadly forces which could never bring them peace.

> The child who refuses to travel in the father's harness, this is the symbol of man's most unique capability. *"I do not have to be what my father was. I do not have to obey my father's rules or even believe everything he believed. It is my strength as a human that I can make my own choices of what to believe and what not to believe, of what to be and what not to be."*

> **—Leto Atreides II**
> **The Harq al-Ada Biography**

Pilgrim women were dancing to drum and flute in the Temple plaza, no coverings on their heads, bangles at their necks, their dresses thin and revealing. Their long black hair was thrown straight out, then straggled across their faces as they whirled.

Alia looked down at the scene from her Temple aerie, both attracted and repelled. It was mid-morning, the hour when the aroma of spice-coffee began to waft across the plaza from the vendors beneath the shaded arches. Soon she would have to go out and greet Farad'n, present the formal gifts and supervise his first meeting with Ghanima.

It was all working out according to plan. Ghani would kill him and, in the shattering aftermath, only one person would be prepared to pick up the pieces. The puppets danced when the strings were pulled. Stilgar had killed Agarves just as she'd hoped. And Agarves had led the kidnappers to the djedida without knowing it, a secret signal transmitter hidden in the new boots she'd given him. Now Stilgar and Irulan waited in the Temple dungeons. Perhaps they would die, but there might be other uses for them. There was no harm in waiting.

She noted that town Fremen were watching the pilgrim dancers below her, their eyes intense and unwavering. A basic sexual equality had come out of the desert to persist in Fremen town and city, but social differences between male and female already were making themselves felt. That, too, went according to plan. Divide and weaken. Alia could sense the subtle change in the way the two Fremen watched those off-planet women and their exotic dance.

*Let them watch. Let them fill their minds with ghafla.*

The louvers of Alia's window had been opened and she could feel a sharp increase in the heat which began about sunrise in this season and would peak in mid-afternoon. The temperature on the stone floor of the plaza would be much higher. It would be uncomfortable for those dancers, but still they whirled and bent, swung their arms and their hair in the frenzy of their dedication. They had dedicated their dance to Alia, the Womb of Heaven. An aide had come to whisper this to Alia, sneering at the off-world women and their peculiar ways. The aide had explained that the women were from Ix, where remnants of the forbidden science and technology remained.

Alia sniffed. Those women were as ignorant, as superstitious and backward as the desert Fremen . . . just as that sneering aide had said, trying to curry favor by reporting the dedication of the dance. And neither the aide nor the Ixians even knew Ix was merely a number in a forgotten language.

Laughing lightly to herself, Alia thought: *Let them dance.* The dancing wasted energy which might be put to more destructive uses. And the music was pleasant, a thin wailing played against flat tympani from gourd drums and clapped hands.

Abruptly the music was drowned beneath a roaring of many voices from the plaza's far side. The dancers missed a step, recovered in a brief confusion, but they had lost their sensuous singleness, and even their attention wandered to the far gate of the plaza, where a mob could be seen spreading onto the stones like water rushing through the opened valve of a qanat.

Alia stared at the oncoming wave.

She heard words now, and one above all others: "Preacher! Preacher!"

Then she saw him, striding with the first spread of the wave, one hand on the shoulder of his young guide.

The pilgrim dancers gave up their whirling, retired to the terraced steps below Alia. They were joined by their audience, and Alia sensed awe in the watchers. Her own emotion was fear.

*How dare he!*

She half turned to summon guards, but second thoughts stopped her. The mob already filled the plaza. They could turn ugly if thwarted in their obvious desire to hear the blind visionary.

Alia clenched her fists.

*The Preacher!* Why was Paul doing this? To half the population he was a "desert madman" and, therefore, sacred. Others whispered in the bazaars and shops that it must be Muad'Dib. Why else did the Mahdinate let him speak such angry heresy?

Alia could see refugees among the mob, remnants from the abandoned sietches, their robes in tatters. That would be a dangerous place down there, a place where mistakes could be made.

"Mistress?"

The voice came from behind Alia. She turned, saw Zia standing in the arched doorway to the outer chamber. Armed House Guards were close behind her.

"Yes, Zia?"

"My Lady, Farad'n is out here requesting audience."

"Here? In my chambers?"

"Yes, My Lady."

"Is he alone?"

"Two bodyguards and the Lady Jessica."

Alia put a hand to her throat, remembering her last encounter with her mother. Times had changed, though. New conditions ruled their relationship.

"How impetuous he is," Alia said. "What reason does he give?"

"He has heard about . . ." Zia pointed to the window over the plaza. "He says he was told you have the best vantage."

Alia frowned, "Do you believe this, Zia?"

"No, My Lady. I think he has heard the rumors. He wants to watch your reaction."

"My mother put him up to this!"

"Quite possibly, My Lady."

"Zia, my dear, I want you to carry out a specific set of very important orders for me. Come here."

Zia approached to within a pace. "My Lady?"

"Have Farad'n, his guards, *and* my mother admitted. Then prepare to bring Ghanima. She is to be accoutered as a Fremen bride in every detail—*complete.*"

"With knife, My Lady?"

"With knife."

"My Lady, that's—"

"Ghanima poses no threat to me."

"My Lady, there's reason to believe she fled with Stilgar more to protect him than for any other—"

"Zia!"

"My Lady?"

"Ghanima already has made her plea for Stilgar's life and Stilgar remains alive."

"But she's the heir presumptive!"

"Just carry out my orders. Have Ghanima prepared. While you're seeing to that, send five attendants from the Temple Priesthood out into the plaza. They're to invite The Preacher up here. Have them wait their opportunity and speak to him, nothing more. They are to use no force. I want them to issue a polite invitation. Absolutely no force. And Zia . . ."

"My Lady?" How sullen she sounded.

"The Preacher and Ghanima are to be brought before me simultaneously. They are to enter together upon my signal. Do you understand?"

"I know the plan, My Lady, but—"

"Just do it! Together." And Alia nodded dismissal to the amazon aide. As Zia turned and left, Alia said: "On your way out, send in Farad'n's party, but see that they're preceded by ten of your most trustworthy people."

Zia glanced back but continued leaving the room. "It will be done as you command, My Lady."

Alia turned away to peer out the window. In just a few minutes the *plan* would bear its bloody fruit. And Paul would be here when his daughter delivered the *coup de grace* to his holy pretensions. Alia heard Zia's guard detachment entering. It would be over soon. All over. She looked down with a swelling sense of triumph as The Preacher took his stance on the first step. His youthful guide squatted beside him. Alia saw the yellow robes of Temple Priests waiting on the left, held back by the press of the crowd. They were experienced with crowds, however. They'd find a way to approach their target. The Preacher's voice boomed out over the plaza, and the mob waited upon his words with rapt attention. Let them listen! Soon his words would be made to mean other things than he intended. And there'd be no *Preacher* around to protest.

She heard Farad'n's party enter, Jessica's voice. "Alia?"

Without turning Alia said: "Welcome, Prince Farad'n, mother. Come and enjoy the show." She glanced back then, saw the big Sardaukar, Tyekanik, scowling at her guards who were blocking the way. "But this isn't hospitable," Alia said. "Let them approach." Two of her guards, obviously acting on Zia's orders, came up to her and stood between her and the others. The other guards moved aside. Alia backed to the right side of the window, motioned to it. "This is truly the best vantage point."

Jessica, wearing her traditional black aba robe, glared at Alia, escorted Farad'n to the window, but stood between him and Alia's guards.

"This is very kind of you, Lady Alia," Farad'n said. "I've heard so much about this Preacher."

"And there he is in the flesh," Alia said. She saw that Farad'n wore the dress grey of a Sardaukar commander without decorations. He moved with a lean grace which Alia admired. Perhaps there would be more than idle amusement in this Corrino Prince.

The Preacher's voice boomed into the room over the amplifier pickups beside the window. Alia felt the tremors of it in her bones, began to listen to his words with growing fascination.

"I found myself in the Desert of Zan," The Preacher shouted, "in that waste of howling wilderness. And God commanded me to make that place clean. For we were provoked in the desert, and grieved in the desert, and we were tempted in that wilderness to forsake our ways."

*Desert of Zan*, Alia thought. That was the name given to the place of the first trial of the Zensunni Wanderers from whom the Fremen sprang. But his words! Was he taking credit for the destruction wrought against the sietch strongholds of the loyal tribes?

"Wild beasts lie upon your lands," The Preacher said, his voice booming across the plaza. "Doleful creatures fill your houses. You who fled your homes no longer multiply your days upon the sand. Yea, you who have forsaken our ways, you will die in a fouled nest if you continue on this path. But if you heed my warning, the Lord shall lead you through a land of pits into the Mountains of God. Yea, Shai-Hulud shall lead you."

Soft moans arose from the crowd. The Preacher paused, swinging his eyeless sockets from side to side at the sound. Then he raised his arms, spreading them wide, called out: "O God, my flesh longeth for Thy way in a dry and thirsty land!"

An old woman in front of The Preacher, an obvious refugee by the patched and worn look of her garments, held up her hands to him, pleaded: "Help us, Muad'Dib. Help us!"

In a sudden fearful constriction of her breast, Alia asked herself if that old woman really knew the truth. Alia glanced at her mother, but Jessica remained unmoving, dividing her attention between Alia's guards, Farad'n and the view from the window. Farad'n stood rooted in fascinated attention.

Alia glanced out the window, trying to see her Temple Priests. They were not in view and she suspected they had worked their way around below her near the Temple doors, seeking a direct route down the steps.

The Preacher pointed his right hand over the old woman's head, shouted: "You are the only help remaining! You were rebellious. You brought the dry wind which does not cleanse, nor does it cool. You bear the burden of our desert, and the whirlwind cometh from that place, from that terrible land. I have been in that wilderness. Water runs upon the sand from shattered qanats. Streams cross the ground. Water has fallen from the sky in the Belt of Dune! O my friends, God has commanded me. Make straight in the desert a highway for our Lord, for I am the voice that cometh to thee from the wilderness."

He pointed to the steps beneath his feet, a stiff and quivering finger. "This is no lost djedida which is no more inhabited forever! Here have we eaten the bread of heaven. And here the noise of strangers drives us from our homes! They breed for us a desolation, a land wherein no man dwelleth, nor any man pass thereby."

The crowd stirred uncomfortably, refugees and town Fremen peering about, looking at the pilgrims of the Hajj who stood among them.

*He could start a bloody riot!* Alia thought. *Well, let him. My Priests can grab him in the confusion.*

She saw the five Priests then, a tight knot of yellow robes working down the steps behind The Preacher.

"The waters which we spread upon the desert have become blood," The

Preacher said, waving his arms wide. "Blood upon our land! Behold our desert which could rejoice and blossom; it has lured the stranger and seduced him in our midst. They come for violence! Their faces are closed up as for the last wind of Kralizec! They gather the captivity of the sand. They suck up the abundance of the sand, the treasure hidden in the depths. Behold them as they go forth to their evil work. It is written: 'And I stood upon the sand, and I saw a beast rise up out of that sand, and upon the head of that beast was the name of God!' "

Angry mutterings arose from the crowd. Fists were raised, shaken.

"What is he doing?" Farad'n whispered.

"I wish I knew," Alia said. She put a hand to her breast, feeling the fearful excitement of this moment. The crowd would turn upon the pilgrims if he kept this up!

But The Preacher half turned, aimed his dead sockets toward the Temple and raised a hand to point at the high windows of Alia's aerie. "One blasphemy remains!" he screamed. "Blasphemy! And the name of that blasphemy is Alia!"

Shocked silence gripped the plaza.

Alia stood in unmoving consternation. She knew the mob could not see her, but she felt overcome by a sense of exposure, of vulnerability. The echoes of calming words within her skull competed with the pounding of her heart. She could only stare down at that incredible tableau. The Preacher remained with a hand pointing at her windows.

His words had been too much for the Priests, though. They broke the silence with angry shouts, stormed down the steps, thrusting people aside. As they moved the crowd reacted, breaking like a wave upon the steps, sweeping over the first lines of onlookers, carrying The Preacher before them. He stumbled blindly, separated from his young guide. Then a yellow-clad arm arose from the press of people; a crysknife was brandished in its hand. She saw the knife strike downward, bury itself in The Preacher's chest.

The thunderous clang of the Temple's giant doors being closed broke Alia from her shock. Guards obviously had closed the doors against the mob. But people already were drawing back, making an open space around a crumpled figure on the steps. An eerie quiet fell over the plaza. Alia saw many bodies, but only this one lay by itself.

Then a voice screeched from the mob: "Muad'Dib! They've killed Muad'Dib!"

"Gods below," Alia quavered. "Gods below."

"A little late for that, don't you think?" Jessica asked.

Alia whirled, noting the sudden startled reaction of Farad'n as he saw the rage on her face. "That was Paul they killed!" Alia screamed. "That was your son! When they confirm it, do you know what'll happen?"

Jesica stood rooted for a long moment, thinking that she had just been told something already known to her. Farad'n's hand upon her arm shattered the moment. "My Lady," he said, and there was such compassion in his voice that Jessica thought she might die of it right there. She looked from the cold, glaring anger on Alia's face to the sympathetic misery on Farad'n's features, and thought: *Perhaps I did my job too well.*

There could be no doubting Alia's words. Jessica remembered every intonation of The Preacher's voice, hearing her own tricks in it, the long years of instruction she'd spent there upon a young man meant to be Emperor, but who now lay a shattered mound of bloody rags upon the Temple steps.

*Ghafla blinded me,* Jessica thought.

Alia gestured to one of her aides, called: "Bring Ghanima now."

Jessica forced herself into recognizing these words. *Ghanima? Why Ghanima now?*

The aide had turned toward the outer door, motioning for it to be unbarred, but before a word could be uttered the door bulged. Hinges popped. The bar snapped and the door, a thick plasteel construction meant to withstand terrible energies, toppled into the room. Guards leaped to avoid it, drawing their weapons.

Jessica and Farad'n's bodyguards closed in around the Corrino Prince.

But the opening revealed only two children: Ghanima on the left, clad in her black betrothal robe, and Leto on the right, the grey slickness of a stillsuit beneath a desert-stained white robe.

Alia stared from the fallen door to the children, found she was trembling uncontrollably.

"The family here to greet us," Leto said. "Grandmother." He nodded to Jessica, shifted his attention to the Corrino Prince. "And this must be Prince Farad'n. Welcome to Arrakis, Prince."

Ghanima's eyes appeared empty. She held her right hand on a ceremonial crysknife at her waist, and she appeared to be trying to escape from Leto's grip on her arm. Leto shook her arm and her whole body shook with it.

"Behold me, family," Leto said. "I am Ari, the Lion of the Atreides. And here—" Again he shook Ghanima's arm with that powerful ease which set her whole body jerking. "—here is Aryeh, the Atreides Lioness. We come to set you onto Secher Nbiw, the Golden Path."

Ghanima, absorbing the trigger words, *Secher Nbiw,* felt the locked-away consciousness flow into her mind. It flowed with a linear nicety, the inner awareness of her mother hovering there behind it, a guardian at a gate. And Ghanima knew in that instant that she had conquered the clamorous past. She possessed a gate through which she could peer when she needed that past. The months of self-hypnotic suppression had built for her a safe place from which to manage her own flesh. She started to turn toward Leto with the need to explain this when she became aware of where she stood and with whom.

Leto released her arm.

"Did our plan work?" Ghanima whispered.

"Well enough," Leto said.

Recovering from her shock, Alia shouted at a clump of guards on her left: "Seize them!"

But Leto bent, took the fallen door with one hand, skidded it across the room into the guards. Two were pinned against the wall. The others fell back in terror. That door weighed half a metric ton and this child had thrown it.

Alia, growing aware that the corridor beyond the doorway contained fallen guards, realized that Leto must have dealt with them, that this child had shattered her impregnable door.

Jessica, too, had seen the bodies, seen the awesome power in Leto and had made similar assumptions, but Ghanima's words touched a core of Bene Gesserit discipline which forced Jessica to maintain her composure. This grandchild spoke of a plan.

"What plan?" Jessica asked.

"The Golden Path, our Imperial plan for our Imperium," Leto said. He nodded to Farad'n. "Don't think harshly of me, cousin. I act for you as well. Alia hoped to have Ghanima slay you. I'd rather you lived out your life in some degree of happiness."

Alia screamed at her guards cowering in the passage: "I command you to seize them!"

But the guards refused to enter the room.

"Wait for me here, sister," Leto said. "I have a disagreeable task to perform." He moved across the room toward Alia.

She backed away from him into a corner, crouched and drew her knife. The green jewels of its handle flashed in the light from the window.

Leto merely continued his advance, hands empty, but spread and ready.

Alia lunged with the knife.

Leto leaped almost to the ceiling, struck with his left foot. It caught Alia's head a glancing blow and sent her sprawling with a bloody mark on her forehead. She lost her grip on the knife and it skidded across the floor. Alia scrambled after the knife, but found Leto standing in front of her.

Alia hesitated, called up everything she knew of Bene Gesserit training. She came off the floor, body loose and poised.

Once more Leto advanced upon her.

Alia feinted to the left but her right shoulder came up and her right foot shot out in a toe-pointing kick which could disembowel a man if it struck precisely.

Leto caught the blow on his arm, grabbed the foot, and picked her up by it, swinging her around his head. The speed with which he swung her sent a flapping, hissing sound through the room as her robe beat against her body.

The others ducked away.

Alia screamed and screamed, but still she continued to swing around and around and around. Presently she fell silent.

Slowly Leto reduced the speed of her whirling, dropped her gently to the floor. She lay in a panting bundle.

Leto bent over her. "I could've thrown you through a wall," he said. "Perhaps that would've been best, but we're now at the center of the struggle. You deserve your chance."

Alia's eyes darted wildly from side to side.

"I have conquered those inner lives," Leto said. "Look at Ghani. She, too, can—"

Ghanima interrupted: "Alia, I can show you—"

"No!" The word was wrenched from Alia. Her chest heaved and voices began to pour from her mouth. They were disconnected, cursing, pleading.

"You see! Why didn't you listen?" And again: "Why're you doing this? What's happening?" And another voice: "Stop them! Make them stop!"

Jessica covered her eyes, felt Farad'n's hand steady her.

Still Alia raved: "I'll kill you!" Hideous curses erupted from her. "I'll drink your blood!" The sounds of many languages began to pour from her, all jumbled and confused.

The huddled guards in the outer passage made the sign of the worm, then held clenched fists beside their ears. She was possessed!

Leto stood, shaking his head. He stepped to the window and with three swift blows shattered the supposedly unbreakable crystal-reinforced glass from its frame.

A sly look came over Alia's face. Jessica heard something like her own voice come from that twisting mouth, a parody of Bene Gesserit control. "All of you! Stay where you are!"

Jessica, lowering her hands, found them damp with tears.

Alia rolled to her knees, lurched to her feet.

"Don't you know who I am?" she demanded. It was her old voice, the sweet and lilting voice of the youthful Alia who was no more. "Why're you all looking at me that way?" She turned pleading eyes to Jessica. "Mother, make them stop it."

Jessica could only shake her head from side to side, consumed by ultimate horror. All of the old Bene Gesserit warnings were true. She looked at Leto and Ghani standing side by side near Alia. What did those warnings mean for these poor twins?

"Grandmother," Leto said, and there was pleading in his voice. "Must we have a Trial of Possession?"

"Who are you to speak of trial?" Alia asked, and her voice was that of a querulous man, an autocratic and sensual man far gone in self-indulgence.

Both Leto and Ghanima recognized the voice. The Old Baron Harkonnen. Ghanima heard the same voice begin to echo in her own head, but the inner gate closed and she sensed her mother standing there.

Jessica remained silent.

"Then the decision is mine," Leto said. "And the choice is yours, Alia. Trial of Possession, or . . ." He nodded toward the open window.

"Who're you to give me a choice?" Alia demanded, and it was still the voice of the Old Baron.

"Demon!" Ghanima screamed. "Let her make her own choice!"

"Mother," Alia pleaded in her little-girl tones. "Mother, what're they doing? What do you want me to do? Help me."

"Help yourself," Leto ordered and, for just an instant, he saw the shattered presence of his aunt in her eyes, a glaring hopelessness which peered out at him and was gone. But her body moved, a sticklike, thrusting walk. She wavered, stumbled, veered from her path but returned to it, nearer and nearer the open window.

Now the voice of the Old Baron raged from her lips: "Stop! Stop it, I say! I command you! Stop it! Feel this!" Alia clutched her head, stumbled closer to the window. She had the sill against her thighs then, but the voice still raved. "Don't do this! Stop it and I'll help you. I have a plan. Listen to me. Stop it, I say. Wait!" But Alia pulled her hands away from her head, clutched the broken casement. In one jerking motion, she pulled herself over the sill and was gone. Not even a screech came from her as she fell.

In the room they heard the crowd shout, the sodden thump as Alia struck the steps far below.

Leto looked at Jessica. "We told you to pity her."

Jessica turned and buried her face in Farad'n's tunic.

> *The assumption that a whole system can be made to work better through an assault on its conscious elements betrays a dangerous ignorance. This has often been the ignorant approach of those who call themselves scientists and technologists.*

**—The Butlerian Jihad
by Harq al-Ada**

"He runs at night, cousin," Ghanima said. "He runs. Have you seen him run?"

"No," Farad'n said.

He waited with Ghanima outside the small audience hall of the Keep where Leto had called them to attend. Tyekanik stood at one side, uncomfortable with the Lady Jessica, who appeared withdrawn, as though her mind lived in another place. It was hardly an hour past the morning meal, but already many things had been set moving—a summons to the Guild, messages to CHOAM and the Landsraad.

Farad'n found it difficult to understand these Atreides. The Lady Jessica had warned him, but still the reality of them puzzled him. They still talked of the betrothal, although most political reasons for it seemed to have dissolved. Leto would assume the throne; there appeared little doubt of that. His odd *living skin* would have to be removed, of course . . . but, in time . . .

"He runs to tire himself," Ghanima said. "He's Kralizec embodied. No wind ever ran as he runs. He's a blur atop the dunes. I've seen him. He runs and runs. And when he has exhausted himself at last, he returns and rests his head in my lap. 'Ask our mother within to find a way for me to die,' he pleads."

Farad'n stared at her. In the week since the riot in the plaza, the Keep had moved to strange rhythms, mysterious comings and goings; stories of bitter fighting beyond the Shield Wall came to him through Tyekanik, whose military advice had been asked.

"I don't understand you," Farad'n said. "Find a way for him to die?"

"He asked me to prepare you," Ghanima said. Not for the first time, she was struck by the curious innocence of this Corrino Prince. Was that Jessica's doing, or something born in him?

"For what?"

"He's no longer human," Ghanima said. "Yesterday you asked when he was going to remove the *living skin?* Never. It's part of him now and he's part of it. Leto estimates he has perhaps four thousand years before metamorphosis destroys him."

Farad'n tried to swallow in a dry throat.

"You see why he runs?" Ghanima asked.

"But if he'll live so long and be so—"

"Because the memory of being human is so rich in him. Think of all those lives, cousin. No. You can't imagine what that is because you've no experience of it. But I know. I can imagine his pain. He gives more than anyone ever gave before. Our father walked into the desert to escape it. Alia became Abomination in fear of it. Our grandmother has only the blurred infancy of this condition, yet must use every Bene Gesserit wile to live with it—which is what Reverend Mother training amounts to anyway. But Leto! He's all alone, never to be duplicated."

Farad'n felt stunned by her words. Emperor for four thousand years?

"Jessica knows," Ghanima said, looking across at her grandmother. "He told her last night. He called himself the first truly long-range planner in human history."

"What . . . does he plan?"

"The Golden Path. He'll explain it to you later."

"And he has a role for me in this . . . plan?"

"As my mate," Ghanima said. "He's taking over the Sisterhood's breeding program. I'm sure my grandmother told you about the Bene Gesserit dream for a male Reverend with extraordinary powers. He's—"

"You mean we're just to be—"

"Not *just*." She took his arm, squeezed it with a warm familiarity. "He'll have many very responsible tasks for both of us. When we're not producing children, that is."

"Well, you're a little young yet," Farad'n said, disengaging his arm.

"Don't ever make that mistake again," she said. There was ice in her tone. Jessica came up to them with Tyekanik.

"Tyek tells me the fighting has spread off-planet," Jessica said. "The Central Temple on Biarek is under siege."

Farad'n thought her oddly calm in this statement. He'd reviewed the reports with Tyekanik during the night. A wildfire of rebellion was spreading through the Empire. It would be put down, of course, but Leto would have a sorry Empire to restore.

"Here's Stilgar now," Ghanima said. "They've been waiting for him." And once more she took Farad'n's arm.

The old Fremen Naib had entered by the far door escorted by two former Death Commando companions from the desert days. All were dressed in formal black robes with white piping and yellow headbands for mourning. They approached with steady strides, but Stilgar kept his attention on Jessica. He stopped in front of her, nodded warily.

"You still worry about the death of Duncan Idaho," Jessica said. She didn't like this caution in her old friend.

"Reverend Mother," he said.

*So it's going to be that way!* Jessica thought. *All formal and according to the Fremen code, with blood difficult to expunge.*

She said: "By our view, you but played a part which Duncan assigned you. Not the first time a man has given his live for the Atreides. Why do they do it, Stil? You've been ready for it more than once. Why? Is it that you know how much the Atreides give in return?"

"I'm happy you seek no excuse for revenge," he said. "But these are matters I must discuss with your grandson. These matters may separate us from you forever."

"You mean Tabr will not pay him homage?" Ghanima asked.

"I mean I reserve my judgment." He looked coldly at Ghanima. "I don't like what my Fremen have become," he growled. "We will go back to the old ways. Without you if necessary."

"For a time, perhaps," Ghanima said. "But the desert is dying, Stil. What'll you do when there are no more worms, no more desert?"

"I don't believe it!"

"Within one hundred years," Ghanima said, "there'll be fewer than fifty worms, and those will be sick ones kept in a carefully managed reservation. Their spice will be for the Spacing Guild only, and the price . . ." She shook her head. "I've seen Leto's figures. He's been all over the planet. He knows."

"Is this another trick to keep the Fremen as your vassals?"

"When were you ever my vassal?" Ghanima asked.

Stilgar scowled. No matter what he said or did, these twins always made it his fault!

"Last night he told me about this Golden Path," Stilgar blurted. "I don't like it!"

"That's odd," Ghanima said, glancing at her grandmother. "Most of the Empire will welcome it."

"Destruction of us all," Stilgar muttered.

"But everyone longs for the Golden Age," Ghanima said. "Isn't that so, grandmother?"

"Everyone," Jessica agreed.

"They long for the Pharaonic Empire which Leto will give them," Ghanima said. "They long for a rich peace with abundant harvests, plentiful trade, a leveling of all except the Golden Ruler."

"It'll be the death of the Fremen!" Stilgar protested.

"How can you say that? Will we not need soldiers and brave men to remove the occasional dissatisfaction? Why, Stil, you and Tyek's brave companions will be hard pressed to do the job."

Stilgar looked at the Sardaukar officer and a strange light of understanding passed between them.

"And Leto will control the spice," Jessica reminded them.

"He'll control it absolutely," Ghanima said.

Farad'n, listening with the new awareness which Jessica had taught him, heard a set piece, a prepared performance between Ghanima and her grandmother.

"Peace will endure and endure and endure," Ghanima said. "Memory of war will all but vanish. Leto will lead humankind through that garden for at least four thousand years."

Tyekanik glanced questioningly at Farad'n, cleared his throat.

"Yes, Tyek?" Farad'n said.

"I'd speak privately with you, My Prince."

Farad'n smiled, knowing the question in Tyekanik's military mind, knowing that at least two others present also recognized this question. "I'll not sell the Sardaukar," Farad'n said.

"No need," Ghanima said.

"Do you listen to this child?" Tyekanik demanded. He was outraged. The old Naib there understood the problems being raised by all of this plotting, but nobody else knew a damned thing about the situation!

Ghanima smiled grimly, said: "Tell him, Farad'n."

Farad'n sighed. It was easy to forget the strangeness of this child who was not a child. He could imagine a lifetime married to her, the hidden reservations on every intimacy. It was not a totally pleasant prospect, but he was beginning to recognize its inevitability. Absolute control of dwindling spice supplies! Nothing would move in the universe without the spice.

"Later, Tyek," Farad'n said.

"But—"

"*Later, I said!*" For the first time, he used Voice on Tyekanik, saw the man blink with surprise and remain silent.

A tight smile touched Jessica's mouth.

"He talks of peace and death in the same breath," Stilgar muttered. "Golden Age!"

Ghanima said: "He'll lead humans through the cult of death into the free air of exuberant life! He speaks of death because that's necessary, Stil. It's a tension by which the living know they're alive. When his Empire falls . . . Oh, yes, it'll fall. You think this is Kralizec now, but Kralizec is yet to come. And when it comes, humans will have renewed their memory of what it's like to be alive. The memory will persist as long as there's a single human living. We'll go through the crucible once more, Stil. And we'll come out of it. We always arise from our own ashes. Always."

Farad'n, hearing her words, understood now what she'd meant in telling him about Leto running. *He'll not be human.*

Stilgar was not yet convinced. "No more worms," he growled.

"Oh the worms will come back," Ghanima assured him. "All will be dead within two hundred years, but they'll come back."

"How . . ." Stilgar broke off.

Farad'n felt his mind awash in revelation. He knew what Ghanima would say before she spoke.

"The Guild will barely make it through the lean years, and only then because of its stockpiles and ours," Ghanima said. "But there'll be abundance after Kralizec. The worms will return after my brother goes into the sand."

> As with so many other religions, Muad'Dib's Golden Elixir of Life degenerated into external wizardry. Its mystical signs became mere symbols for deeper psychological processes, and those processes, of course, ran wild. What they needed was a living god, and they didn't have one, a situation which Muad'Dib's son has corrected.
>
> **—Saying attributed to Lu Tung-pin**
> **(Lu, The Guest of the Cavern)**

Leto sat on the Lion Throne to accept the homage of the tribes. Ghanima stood beside him, one step down. The ceremony in the Great Hall went on for hours. Tribe after Fremen tribe passed before him through their delegates and their Naibs. Each group bore gifts fitting for a god of terrifying powers, a god of vengeance who promised them peace.

He'd cowed them into submission the previous week, performing for the assembled arifa of all the tribes. The Judges had seen him walk through a pit of fire, emerging unscathed to demonstrate that his skin bore no marks by asking them to study him closely. He'd ordered them to strike him with knives, and the impenetrable skin had sealed his face while they struck at him to no avail. Acids ran off him with only the lightest mist of smoke. He'd eaten their poisons and laughed at them.

At the end he'd summoned a worm and stood facing them at its mouth. He'd moved from that to the landing field at Arrakeen, where he'd brazenly toppled a Guild frigate by lifting one of its landing fins.

The arifa had reported all of this with a fearful awe, and now the tribal delegates had come to seal their submission.

The vaulted space of the Great Hall with its acoustical dampening systems tended to absorb sharp noises, but a constant rustling of moving feet insinuated itself into the senses, riding on dust and the flint odors brought in from the open.

Jessica, who'd refused to attend, watched from a high spy hole behind the throne. Her attention was caught by Farad'n and the realization that both she and Farad'n had been outmaneuvered. Of course Leto and Ghanima had anticipated the Sisterhood! The twins could consult within themselves a host of Bene Gesserits greater than all now living in the Empire.

She was particularly bitter at the way the Sisterhood's mythology had trapped Alia. *Fear built on fear!* The habits of generations had imprinted the fate of Abomination upon her. Alia had known no hope. Of course she'd succumbed. Her fate made the accomplishment of Leto and Ghanima even more difficult to face. Not one way out of the trap, but two. Ghanima's victory over the inner lives and her insistence that Alia deserved only pity were the bitterest things of all. Hypnotic suppression under stress linked to the wooing of a benign ancestor had saved Ghanima. They might have saved Alia. But without hope, nothing had been attempted until it was too late. Alia's water had been poured upon the sand.

Jessica sighed, shifted her attention to Leto on the throne. A giant canopic jar containing the water of Muad'Dib occupied a place of honor at his right elbow. He'd boasted to Jessica that his father-within laughed at this gesture even while admiring it.

That jar and the boasting had firmed her resolve not to participate in this ritual. As long as she lived, she knew she could never accept Paul speaking through Leto's mouth. She rejoiced that House Atreides had survived, but the things-that-might-have-been were beyond bearing.

Farad'n sat cross-legged beside the jar of Muad'Dib's water. It was the position of the Royal Scribe, an honor newly conferred and newly accepted.

Farad'n felt that he was adjusting nicely to these new realities, although Tyekanik still raged and promised dire consequences. Tyekanik and Stilgar had formed a partnership of distrust which seemed to amuse Leto.

In the hours of the homage ceremony, Farad'n had gone from awe to boredom to awe. They were an endless stream of humanity, these peerless fighting men. Their loyalty renewed to the Atreides on the throne could not be questioned. They stood in submissive terror before him, completely daunted by what the arifa had reported.

At last it drew to a close. The final Naib stood before Leto—Stilgar in the "rearguard position of honor." Instead of panniers heavy with spice, fire jewels, or any of the other costly gifts which lay in mounds around the throne, Stilgar bore a headband of braided spice-fiber. The Atreides Hawk had been worked in gold and green into its design.

Ghanima recognized it and shot a sideways glance at Leto.

Stilgar placed the headband on the second step below the throne, bowed low. "I give you the headband worn by your sister when I took her into the desert to protect her," he said.

Leto suppressed a smile.

"I know you've fallen on hard times, Stilgar," Leto said. "Is there something here you would have in return?" He gestured at the piles of costly gifts.

"No, My Lord."

"I accept your gift then," Leto said. He rocked forward, brought up the hem of Ghanima's robe, ripped a thin strip from it. "In return, I give you this bit of Ghanima's robe, the robe she wore when she was stolen from your desert camp, forcing me to save her."

Stilgar accepted the cloth in a trembling hand. "Do you mock me, My Lord?"

"Mock you? By my name, Stilgar, never would I mock you. I have given you a gift without price. I command you to carry it always next to your heart as a reminder that all humans are prone to error and all leaders are human."

A thin chuckle escaped Stilgar. "What a Naib you would have made!"

"What a Naib I am! Naib of Naibs. Never forget that!"

"As you say, My Lord." Stilgar swallowed, remembering the report of his arifa. And he thought: *Once I thought of slaying him. Now it's too late.* His glance fell on the jar, a graceful opaque gold capped with green. "That is water of my tribe."

"And mine," Leto said. "I command you to read the inscription upon its side. Read it aloud that all may hear it."

Stilgar cast a questioning glance at Ghanima, but she returned it with a lift of her chin, a cold response which sent a chill through him. Were these Atreides imps bent on holding him to answer for his impetuosity and his mistakes?

"Read it," Leto said, pointing.

Slowly Stilgar mounted the steps, bent to look at the jar. Presently he read aloud: "This water is the ultimate essence, a source of outward streaming creativity. Though motionless, this water is the means of all movement."

"What does it mean, My Lord?" Stilgar whispered. He felt awed by the words, touched within himself in a place he could not understand.

"The body of Muad'Dib is a dry shell like that abandoned by an insect," Leto said. "He mastered the inner world while holding the outer in contempt, and this led to catastrophe. He mastered the outer world while excluding the inner world, and this delivered his descendants to the demons. The Golden Elixir will vanish from Dune, yet Muad'Dib's seed goes on, and his water moves our universe."

Stilgar bowed his head. Mystical things always left him in turmoil.

"The beginning and the end are one," Leto said. "You live in air but do not see it. A phase has closed. Out of that closing grows the beginning of its opposite. Thus, we will have Kralizec. Everything returns later in changed form. You have felt thoughts in your head; your descendants will feel thoughts in their bellies. Return to Sietch Tabr, Stilgar. Gurney Halleck will join you there as my advisor in your Council."

"Don't you trust me, My Lord?" Stilgar's voice was low.

"Completely, else I'd not send Gurney to you. He'll begin recruiting the new force we'll need soon. I accept your pledge of fealty, Stilgar. You are dismissed."

Stilgar bowed low, backed off the steps, turned and left the hall. The other Naibs fell into step behind him according to the Fremen principle that "the last shall be first." But some of their queries could be heard on the throne as they departed.

"What were you talking about up there, Stil? What does that mean, those words on Muad'Dib's water?"

Leto spoke to Farad'n. "Did you get all of that, Scribe?"

"Yes, My Lord."

"My grandmother tells me she trained you well in the mnemonic processes of the Bene Gesserit. That's good. I don't want you scribbling beside me."

"As you command, My Lord."

"Come and stand before me," Leto said.

Farad'n obeyed, more than ever thankful for Jessica's training. When you accepted the fact that Leto no longer was human, no longer could think as humans thought, the course of his Golden Path became ever more frightening.

Leto looked up at Farad'n. The guards stood well back out of earshot. Only the counselors of the Inner Presence remained on the floor of the Great Hall, and they stood in subservient groups well beyond the first step. Ghanima had moved closer to rest an arm on the back of the throne.

"You've not yet agreed to give me your Sardaukar," Leto said. "But you will."

"I owe you much, but not that," Farad'n said.

"You think they'd not mate well with my Fremen?"

"As well as those new friends, Stilgar and Tyekanik."

"Yet you refuse?"

"I await your offer."

"Then I must make the offer, knowing you will never repeat it. I pray my grandmother has done her part well, that you are prepared to understand."

"What must I understand?"

"There's always a prevailing mystique in any civilization," Leto said. "It builds itself as a barrier against change, and that always leaves future generations unprepared for the universe's treachery. All mystiques are the same in building these barriers—the religious mystique, the hero-leader mystique, the messiah mystique, the mystique of science/technology, and the mystique of nature itself. We live in an Imperium which such a mystique has shaped, and now that Imperium is falling apart because most people don't distinguish between mystique and their universe. You see, the mystique is like demon possession; it tends to take over the consciousness, becoming all things to the observer."

"I recognize your grandmother's wisdom in these words," Farad'n said.

"Well and good, cousin. She asked me if I were Abomination. I answered in the negative. That was my first treachery. You see, Ghanima escaped this, but I did not. I was forced to balance the inner lives under the pressure of excessive melange. I had to seek the active cooperation of those aroused lives within me. Doing this, I avoided the most malignant and chose a dominant helper thrust upon me by the inner awareness which was my father. I am not, in truth, my father or this helper. Then again, I am not the Second Leto."

"Explain."

"You have an admirable directness," Leto said. "I'm a community dominated by one who was ancient and surpassingly powerful. He fathered a dynasty which endured for three thousand of our years. His name was Harum and, until his line trailed out in the congenital weaknesses and superstitions of a descendant, his subjects lived in a rhythmic sublimity. They moved unconsciously with the changes of the seasons. They bred individuals who tended to be short-lived, superstitious, and easily led by a god-king. Taken as a whole, they were a powerful people. Their survival as a species became habit."

"I don't like the sound of that," Farad'n said.

"Nor do I, really," Leto said. "But it's the universe I'll create."

"Why?"

"It's a lesson I learned on Dune. We kept the presence of death a dominant specter among the living here. By that presence, the dead changed the living. The people of such a society sink down into their bellies. But when the time comes for the opposite, when they arise, they are great and beautiful."

"That doesn't answer my question," Farad'n protested.

"You don't trust me, cousin."

"Nor does your own grandmother."

"And with good reason," Leto said. "But she acquiesces because she must. Bene Gesserits are pragmatists in the end. I share their view of our universe, you know. You wear the marks of that universe. You retain the habits of rule, cataloguing all around you in terms of their possible threat or value."

"I agreed to be your scribe."

"It amused you and flattered your real talent, which is that of historian. You've a definite genius for reading the present in terms of the past. You've anticipated me on several occasions."

"I don't like your veiled insinuations," Farad'n said.

"Good. You come from infinite ambition to your present lowered estate. Didn't my grandmother warn you about infinity? It attracts us like a floodlight in the night, blinding us to the excesses it can inflict upon the finite."

"Bene Gesserit aphorisms!" Farad'n protested.

"But much more precise," Leto said. "The Bene Gesserit believed they could predict the course of evolution. But they overlooked their own changes in the course of that evolution. They assumed they would stand still while their breeding plan evolved. I have no such reflexive blindness. Look carefully at me, Farad'n, for I am no longer human."

"So your sister assures me." Farad'n hesitated. Then: "Abomination?"

"By the Sisterhood's definition, perhaps. Harum is cruel and autocratic. I partake of his cruelty. Mark me well: I have the cruelty of the husbandman, and this human universe is my farm. Fremen once kept tame eagles as pets, but I'll keep a tame Farad'n"

Farad'n's face darkened. "Beware my claws, cousin. I well know my Sardaukar would fall in time before your Fremen. But we'd wound you sorely, and there are jackals waiting to pick off the weak."

"I will use you well, that I promise," Leto said. He leaned forward. "Did you not say I'm no longer human? Believe me, cousin. No children will spring from my loins, for I no longer have loins. And this forces my second treachery."

Farad'n waited in silence, seeing at last the direction of Leto's argument.

"I shall go against every Fremen concept," Leto said. "They will accept because they can do nothing else. I kept you here under the lure of a betrothal, but there will be no betrothal of you and Ghanima. My sister will marry me!"

"But you—"

"Marry, I said. Ghanima must continue the Atreides line. There's also the matter of the Bene Gesserit breeding program, which is now my breeding program."

"I refuse," Farad'n said.

"You refuse to father an Atreides dynasty?"

"What dynasty? You'll occupy the throne for thousands of years."

"And mold your descendants in my image. It will be the most intensive, the most inclusive training program in all of history. We'll be an ecosystem in miniature. You see, whatever system animals choose to survive by must be based on the pattern of interlocking communities, interdependence, working together in the common design which is the system. And this system will produce the most knowledgeable rulers ever seen."

"You put fancy words on a most distasteful—"

"Who will survive Kralizec?" Leto asked. "I promise you, Kralizec will come."

"You're a madman! You will shatter the Empire."

"Of course I will . . . and I'm not a man. But I'll create a new consciousness in all men. I tell you that below the desert of Dune there's a secret place with the greatest treasure of all time. I do not lie. When the last worm dies and the last melange is harvested upon our sands, these deep treasures will spring up throughout our universe. As the power of the spice monopoly fades and the hidden stockpiles make their mark, new powers will appear throughout our realm. It is time humans learned once more to live in their instincts."

Ghanima took her arm from the back of the throne, crossed to Farad'n's side, took his hand.

"As my mother was not wife, you will not be husband," Leto said. "But perhaps there will be love, and that will be enough."

"Each day, each moment brings its change," Ghanima said. "One learns by recognizing the moments."

Farad'n felt the warmth of Ghanima's tiny hand as an insistent presence. He recognized the ebb and flow of Leto's arguments, but not once had Voice been used. It was an appeal to the guts, not to the mind.

"Is this what you offer for my Sardaukar?" he asked.

"Much, much more, cousin. I offer your descendants the Imperium. I offer you peace."

"What will be the outcome of your peace?"

"Its opposite," Leto said, his voice calmly mocking.

Farad'n shook his head. "I find the price for my Sardaukar very high. Must I remain Scribe, the secret father of your royal line?"

"You must."

"Will you try to force me into your habit of peace?"

"I will."

"I'll resist you every day of my life."

"But that's the function I expect of you, cousin. It's why I chose you. I'll make it official. I will give you a new name. From this moment, you'll be called Breaking of the Habit, which in our tongue is Harq al-Ada. Come, cousin, don't be obtuse. My mother taught you well. Give me your Sardaukar."

"Give them," Ghanima echoed. "He'll have them one way or another."

Farad'n heard fear for himself in her voice. Love, then? Leto asked not for reason, but for an intuitive leap. "Take them," Farad'n said.

"Indeed," Leto said. He lifted himself from the throne, a curiously fluid motion as though he kept his terrible powers under most delicate control. Leto stepped down then to Ghanima's level, moved her gently until she faced away from him, turned and placed his back against hers. "Note this, cousin Harq al-Ada. This is the way it will always be with us. We'll stand thus when we are married. Back to back, each looking outward from the other to protect the one thing which we have always been." He turned, looked mockingly at Farad'n, lowered his voice: "Remember that, cousin, when you're face to face with my Ghanima. Remember that when you whisper of love and soft things, when you are most tempted by the habits of my peace and my contentment. Your back will remain exposed."

Turning from them, he strode down the steps into the waiting courtiers, picked them up in his wake like satellites, and left the hall.

Ghanima once more took Farad'n's hand, but her gaze looked beyond the far end of the hall long after Leto had left it. "One of us had to accept the agony," she said, "and he was always the stronger."

# APPENDIX I

# APPENDIX I

## The Ecology of Dune

*Beyond a critical point within a finite space, freedom diminishes as numbers increase. This is as true of humans in the finite space of a planetary ecosystem as it is of gas molecules in a sealed flask. The human question is not how many can possibly survive within the system, but what kind of existence is possible for those who do survive.*

**—Pardot Kynes, First Planetologist of Arrakis**

The effect of Arrakis on the mind of the newcomer usually is that of overpowering barren land. The stranger might think nothing could live or grow in the open here, that this was the true wasteland that had never been fertile and never would be.

To Pardot Kynes, the planet was merely an expression of energy, a machine being driven by its sun. What it needed was reshaping to fit it to man's needs. His mind went directly to the free-moving human population, the Fremen. What a challenge! What a tool they could be! Fremen: an ecological and geological force of almost unlimited potential.

A direct and simple man in many ways, Pardot Kynes. One must evade Harkonnen restrictions? Excellent. Then one marries a Fremen woman. When she gives you a Fremen son, you begin with him, with Liet-Kynes, and the other children, teaching them ecological literacy, creating a new language with symbols that arm the mind to manipulate an entire landscape, its climate, seasonal limits, and finally to break through all ideas of force into the dazzling awareness of *order*.

"There's an internally recognized beauty of motion and balance on any man-healthy planet," Kynes said. "You see in this beauty a dynamic stabilizing effect essential to all life. Its aim is simple: to maintain and produce coordinated patterns of greater and greater diversity. Life improves the closed system's capacity to sustain life. Life—all life—is in the service of life. Necessary nutrients are made available to life *by* life in greater and greater richness as the diversity of life increases. The entire landscape comes alive, filled with relationships and relationships within relationships."

This was Pardot Kynes lecturing to a sietch warren class.

Before the lectures, though, he had to convince the Fremen. To understand how this came about, you must first understand the enormous single-mindedness, the innocence with which he approached any problem. He was not naive, he merely permitted himself no distractions.

He was exploring the Arrakis landscape in a one-man groundcar one hot afternoon when he stumbled onto a deplorably common scene. Six Harkonnen bravos, shielded and fully armed, had trapped three Fremen youths in the open behind the Shield Wall near the village of Windsack. To Kynes, it was a ding-dong battle, more slapstick than real, until he focused on the fact that the Harkonnens intended to kill the Fremen. By this time, one of the youths was down with a severed artery, two of the bravos were down as well, but it was still four armed men against two striplings.

Kynes wasn't brave; he merely had that single-mindedness and caution. The Harkonnens were killing Fremen. They were destroying the tools with which he intended to remake a planet! He triggered his own shield, waded in and had two of the Harkonnens dead with a slip-tip before they knew anyone was behind them. He dodged a sword thrust from one of the others, slit the man's throat with a neat *entrisseur*, and left the lone remaining bravo to the two Fremen youths, turning his full attention to saving the lad on the ground. And save the lad he did . . . while the sixth Harkonnen was being dispatched.

Now here was a pretty kettle of sandtrout! The Fremen didn't know what to make of Kynes. They knew who he was, of course. No man arrived on Arrakis without a full dossier finding its way into the Fremen strongholds. They knew him: he was an Imperial servant.

But he killed Harkonnens!

Adults might have shrugged and, with some regret, sent his shade to join those of the six dead men on the ground. But these Fremen were inexperienced youths and all they could see was that they owed this Imperial servant a mortal obligation.

Kynes wound up two days later in a sietch that looked down on Wind Pass. To him, it was all very natural. He talked to the Fremen about water, about dunes anchored by grass, about palmaries filled with date palms, about open qanats flowing across the desert. He talked and talked and talked.

All around him raged a debate that Kynes never saw. What to do with this madman? He knew the location of a major sietch. What to do? What of his words, this mad talk about a paradise on Arrakis? Just talk. He knows too much. But he killed Harkonnens! What of the water burden? When did we owe the Imperium anything? He killed Harkonnens. Anyone can kill Harkonnens. I have done it myself.

But what of this talk about the flowering of Arrakis?

Very simple: Where is the water for this?

He says it is here! And he *did* save three of ours.

He saved three fools who had put themselves in the way of the Harkonnen fist! And he has seen crysknives!

The necessary decision was known for hours before it was voiced. The tau of a sietch tells its members what they must do; even the most brutal necessity is known. An experienced fighter was sent with a consecrated knife to do the job. Two watermen followed him to get the water from the body. Brutal necessity.

It's doubtful that Kynes even focused on his would-be executioner. He was talking to a group that spread around him at a cautious distance. He walked as he talked: a short circle, gesturing. Open water, Kynes said. Walk in the open without stillsuits. Water for dipping it out of a pond! Portyguls!

The knifeman confronted him.

"Remove yourself," Kynes said, and went on talking about secret windtraps. He brushed past the man. Kynes' back stood open for the ceremonial blow.

What went on in that would-be executioner's mind cannot be known now. Did he finally listen to Kynes and believe? Who knows? But what he did is a matter of record. Uliet was his name, *Older* Liet. Uliet walked three paces and deliberately fell on his own knife, thus "removing" himself. Suicide? Some say Shai-hulud moved him.

Talk about omens!

From that instant, Kynes had but to point, saying "Go there." Entire Fremen tribes went. Men died, women died, children died. But they went.

Kynes returned to his Imperial chores, directing the Biological Testing Stations. And now, Fremen began to appear among the Station personnel. The Fremen looked at each other. They were infiltrating the "system," a possibility they'd never considered. Station tools began finding their way into the sietch warrens—especially cutterays which were used to dig underground catchbasins and hidden windtraps.

Water began collecting in the basins.

It became apparent to the Fremen that Kynes was not a madman totally, just mad enough to be holy. He was one of the umma, the brotherhood of prophets. The shade of Uliet was advanced to the sadus, the throng of heavenly judges.

Kynes—direct, savagely intent Kynes—knew that highly organized research is guaranteed to produce nothing new. He set up small-unit experiments with regular interchange of data for a swift Tansley effect, let each group find its own path. They must accumulate millions of tiny facts. He organized only isolated and rough run-through tests to put their difficulties into perspective.

Core samplings were made throughout the bled. Charts were developed on the long drifts of weather that are called climate. He found that in the wide belt contained by the 70-degree lines, north and south, temperatures for thousands of years hadn't gone outside the 254–332 degrees (absolute) range, and that this belt had long growing seasons where temperatures ranged from 284 to 302 degrees absolute: the "bonanza" range for terraform life . . . once they solved the water problem.

When will we solve it? the Fremen asked. When will we see Arrakis as a paradise?

In the manner of a teacher answering a child who has asked the sum of 2 plus 2, Kynes told them: "From three hundred to five hundred years."

A lesser folk might have howled in dismay. But the Fremen had learned patience from men with whips. It was a bit longer than they had anticipated, but they all could see that the blessed day was coming. They tightened their sashes and went back to work. Somehow, the disappointment made the prospect of paradise more real.

The concern on Arrakis was not with water, but with moisture. Pets were almost unknown, stock animals rare. Some smugglers employed the domesticated desert ass, the kulon, but the water price was high even when the beasts were fitted with modified stillsuits.

Kynes thought of installing reduction plants to recover water from the hydrogen and oxygen locked in native rock, but the energy-cost factor was far too high. The polar caps (disregarding the false sense of water security they gave the pyons) held far too small an amount for his project . . . and he already suspected where the water had to be. There was that consistent increase of moisture at median altitudes, and in certain winds. There was that primary clue in the air balance—23 per cent oxygen, 75.4 per cent nitrogen and .023 per cent carbon dioxide—with the trace gases taking up the rest.

There was a rare native root plant that grew above the 2,500-meter level in the northern temperate zone. A tuber two meters long yielded half a liter of water. And there were the terraform desert plants: the tougher ones showed signs of thriving if planted in depressions lined with dew precipitators.

Then Kynes saw the salt pan.

His 'thopter, flying between stations far out on the bled, was blown off course by a storm. When the storm passed, there was the pan—a giant oval depression some three hundred kilometers on the long axis—a glaring white surprise in the open desert. Kynes landed, tasted the pan's storm-cleaned surface.

Salt.

Now, he was certain.

There'd been open water on Arrakis—once. He began re-examining the evidence of the dry wells where trickles of water had appeared and vanished, never to return.

Kynes set his newly trained Fremen limnologists to work: their chief clue, leathery scraps of matter sometimes found with the spice-mass after a blow. This had been ascribed to a fictional "sandtrout" in Fremen folk stories. As facts grew into evidence, a creature emerged to explain these leathery scraps—a sandswimmer that blocked off water into fertile pockets within the porous lower strata below the 280° (absolute) line.

This "water-stealer" died by the millions in each spice-blow. A five-degree change in temperature could kill it. The few survivors entered a semidormant cyst-hibernation to emerge in six years as small (about three meters long) sandworms. Of these, only a few avoided their larger brothers and the pre-spice water pockets to emerge into maturity as the giant shai-hulud. (Water is poisonous to shai-hulud as the Fremen had long known from drowning the rare "stunted worm" of the Minor Erg to produce the awareness-spectrum narcotic they call Water of Life. The "stunted worm" is a primitive form of shai-hulud that reaches a length of only about nine meters.)

Now they had the circular relationship: little maker to pre-spice mass; little maker to shai-hulud; shai-hulud to scatter the spice upon which fed microscopic creatures called sand plankton, the sand plankton, food for shai-hulud, growing, burrowing, becoming little makers.

Kynes and his people turned their attention from these great relationships and focused now on micro-ecology. First, the climate: the sand surface often reached temperatures of 344° to 350° (absolute). A foot below ground it might be 55° cooler; a foot above ground, 25° cooler. Leaves or black shade could provide another 18° of cooling. Next, the nutrients: sand of Arrakis is mostly a product of worm digestion; dust (the truly omnipresent problem there) is produced by the constant surface creep, the "saltation" movement of sand. Coarse grains are found on the downwind sides of dunes. The windward side is packed smooth and hard. Old dunes are yellow (oxidized), young dunes are the color of the parent rock—usually gray.

Downwind sides of old dunes provided the first plantation areas. The Fremen aimed first for a cycle of poverty grass with peatlike hair cilia to intertwine, mat and fix the dunes by depriving the wind of its big weapon: movable grains.

Adaptive zones were laid out in the deep south far from Harkonnen watchers. The mutated poverty grasses were planted first along the downwind (slipface) of the chosen dunes that stood across the path of the prevailing westerlies. With the downwind face anchored, the windward face grew higher and higher and the grass was moved to keep pace. Giant sifs (long dunes with sinuous crest) of more than 1,500 meters height were produced this way.

When barrier dunes reached sufficient height, the windward faces were planted with tougher sword grasses. Each structure on a base about six times as thick as its height was anchored—"fixed."

Now, they came in with deeper plantings—ephemerals (chenopods, pigweeds, and amaranth to begin), then scotch broom, low lupine, vine eucalyptus (the type adapted for Caladan's northern reaches), dwarf tamarisk, shore pine—then the true desert growths: candelilla, saguaro, and bis-naga, the barrel cactus. Where it would grow, they introduced camel sage, onion grass, gobi feather grass, wild alfalfa, burrow bush, sand verbena, evening primrose, incense bush, smoke tree, creosote bush.

They turned then to the necessary animal life—burrowing creatures to open the soil and aerate it: kit fox, kangaroo mouse, desert hare, sand terrapin . . . and the predators to keep them in check: desert hawk, dwarf owl, eagle and desert owl; and insects to fill the niches these couldn't reach: scorpion, centipede, trapdoor spider, the biting wasp and the wormfly . . . and the desert bat to keep watch on these.

Now came the crucial test: date palms, cotton, melons, coffee, medicinals—more than 200 selected food plant types to test and adapt.

"The thing the ecologically illiterate don't realize about an ecosystem," Kynes said, "is that it's a system. A system! A system maintains a certain fluid stability that can be destroyed by a misstep in just one niche. A system has order, a flowing from point to point. If something dams that flow, order collapses. The untrained might miss that collapse until it was too late. That's why the highest function of ecology is the understanding of consequences."

Had they achieved a system?

Kynes and his people watched and waited. The Fremen now knew what he meant by an open-end prediction to five hundred years.

A report came up from the palmaries:

At the desert edge of the plantings, the sand plankton is being poisoned through interaction with the new forms of life. The reason: protein incompatibility. Poisonous water was forming there which the Arrakis life would not touch. A barren zone surrounded the plantings and even shai-hulud would not invade it.

Kynes went down to the palmaries himself—a twenty-thumper trip (in a palanquin like a wounded man or Reverend Mother because he never became a sandrider). He tested the barren zone (it stank to heaven) and came up with a bonus, a gift from Arrakis.

The addition of sulfur and fixed nitrogen converted the barren zone to a rich plant bed for terraform life. The plantings could be advanced at will!

"Does this change the timing?" the Fremen asked.

Kynes went back to his planetary formulae. Windtrap figures were fairly secure by then. He was generous with his allowances, knowing he couldn't draw neat lines around ecological problems. A certain amount of plant cover had to be set aside to hold dunes in place; a certain amount for foodstuffs (both human and animal); a certain amount to lock moisture in root systems and to feed water out into surrounding parched areas. They'd mapped the roving cold spots on the open bled by this time. These had to be figured into the formulae. Even shai-hulud had a place in the charts. He must never be destroyed, else spice wealth would end. But his inner digestive "factory," with its enormous concentrations of aldehydes and acids, was a giant source of oxygen. A medium worm (about 200 meters long) discharged into the atmosphere as much oxygen as ten square kilometers of green-growing photosynthesis surface.

He had the Guild to consider. The spice bribe to the Guild for preventing weather satellites and other watchers in the skies of Arrakis already had reached major proportions.

Nor could the Fremen be ignored. Especially the Fremen, with their windtraps and irregular landholdings organized around water supply; the Fremen with their new ecological literacy and their dream of cycling vast areas of Arrakis through a prairie phase into forest cover.

From the charts emerged a figure. Kynes reported it. Three per cent. If they could get three per cent of the green plant element on Arrakis involved in forming carbon compounds, they'd have their self-sustaining cycle.

"But how long?" the Fremen demanded.

"Oh, that: about three hundred and fifty years."

So it was true as this umma had said in the beginning: the thing would not come in the lifetime of any man now living, nor in the lifetime of their grandchildren eight times removed, but it would come.

The work continued: building, planting, digging, training the children.

Then Kynes-the-Umma was killed in the cave-in at Plaster Basin.

By this time his son, Liet-Kynes, was nineteen, a full Fremen and sandrider who had killed a hundred Harkonnens. The Imperial appointment for which the elder Kynes already had applied in the name of his son was delivered as a matter of course. The rigid class structure of the faufreluches had its well-ordered purpose here. The son had been trained to follow the father.

The course had been set by this time, the Ecological-Fremen were aimed along their way. Liet-Kynes had only to watch and nudge and spy upon the Harkonnens . . . until the day his planet was afflicted by a Hero.

# APPENDIX II

# APPENDIX II

## *The Religion of Dune*

Before the coming of Muad'Dib, the Fremen of Arrakis practiced a religion whose roots in the Maometh Saari are there for any scholar to see. Many have traced the extensive borrowings from other religions. The most common example is the Hymn to Water, a direct copy from the Orange Catholic Liturgical Manual, calling for rain clouds which Arrakis had never seen. But there are more profound points of accord between the Kitab al-Ibar of the Fremen and the teachings of Bible, Ilm, and Fiqh.

Any comparison of the religious beliefs dominant in the Imperium up to the time of Muad'Dib must start with the major forces which shaped those beliefs:

1. The followers of the Fourteen Sages, whose Book was the Orange Catholic Bible, and whose views are expressed in the Commentaries and other literature produced by the Commission of Ecumenical Translators (C.E.T.);

2. The Bene Gesserit, who privately denied they were a religious order, but who operated behind an almost impenetrable screen of ritual mysticism, and whose training, whose symbolism, organization, and internal teaching methods were almost wholly religious;

3. The agnostic ruling class (including the Guild) for whom religion was a kind of puppet show to amuse the populace and keep it docile, and who believed essentially that all phenomena—even religious phenomena—could be reduced to mechanical explanations;

4. The so-called Ancient Teachings—including those preserved by the Zensunni Wanderers from the first, second, and third Islamic movements; the Navachristianity of Chusuk, the Buddislamic Variants of the types dominant at Lankiveil and Sikun, the Blend Books of the Mahayana Lankavatara, the Zen Hekiganshu of III Delta Pavonis, the Tawrah and Talmudic Zabur surviving on Salusa Secundus, the pervasive Obeah Ritual, the Muadh Quran with its pure Ilm and Fiqh preserved among the pundi rice farmers of Caladan, the Hindu outcroppings found all through the universe in little pockets of insulated pyons, and finally, the Butlerian Jihad.

There *is* a fifth force which shaped religious belief, but its effect is so universal and profound that it deserves to stand alone.

This is, of course, space travel—and in any discussion of religion, it deserves to be written thus:

## SPACE TRAVEL!

Mankind's movement through deep space placed a unique stamp on religion during the one hundred and ten centuries that preceded the Butlerian Jihad. To begin with, early space travel, although widespread, was largely unregulated, slow, and uncertain, and, before the Guild monopoly, was accomplished by a hodgepodge of methods. The first space experiences, poorly communicated and subject to extreme distortion, were a wild inducement to mystical speculation.

Immediately, space gave a different flavor and sense to ideas of Creation. That difference is seen even in the highest religious achievements of the period. All through religion, the feeling of the sacred was touched by anarchy from the outer dark.

It was as though Jupiter in all his descendant forms retreated into the maternal darkness to be superseded by a female immanence filled with ambiguity and with a face of many terrors.

The ancient formulae intertwined, tangled together as they were fitted to the needs of new conquests and new heraldic symbols. It was a time of struggle between beast-demons on the one side and the old prayers and invocations on the other.

There was never a clear decision.

During this period, it was said that Genesis was reinterpreted, permitting God to say:

"Increase and multiply, and fill the *universe*, and subdue it, and rule over all manner of strange beasts and living creatures in the infinite airs, on the infinite earths and beneath them."

It was a time of sorceresses whose powers were real. The measure of them is seen in the fact they never boasted how they grasped the firebrand.

Then came the Butlerian Jihad—two generations of chaos. The god of machine-logic was overthrown among the masses and a new concept was raised:

"Man may not be replaced."

Those two generations of violence were a thalamic pause for all humankind. Men looked at their gods and their rituals and saw that both were filled with that most terrible of all equations: fear over ambition.

Hesitantly, the leaders of religions whose followers had spilled the blood of billions began meeting to exchange views. It was a move encouraged by the Spacing Guild, which was beginning to build its monopoly over all interstellar travel, and by the Bene Gesserit who were banding the sorceresses.

Out of those first ecumenical meetings came two major developments:

1. The realization that all religions had at least one common commandment: "Thou shalt not disfigure the soul."

2. The Commission of Ecumenical Translators.

C.E.T. convened on a neutral island of Old Earth, spawning ground of the mother religions. They met "in the common belief that there exists a Divine Essence in the universe." Every faith with more than a million followers was represented, and they reached a surprisingly immediate agreement on the statement of their common goal:

"We are here to remove a primary weapon from the hands of disputant religions. That weapon—the claim to possession of the one and only revelation."

Jubilation at this "sign of profound accord" proved premature. For more than a standard year, that statement was the only announcement from C.E.T. Men spoke bitterly of the delay. Troubadours composed witty, biting songs about the one hundred and twenty-one "Old Cranks" as the C.E.T. delegates came to be called. (The name arose from a ribald joke which played on the C.E.T. initials and called the delegates "Cranks—Effing-Turners.") One of the songs, "Brown Repose," has undergone periodic revival and is popular today:

"Consider leis,
Brown repose—and
The tragedy
In all of those

Cranks! All those Cranks!
So laze—so laze
Through all your days.
Time has toll'd for
M'Lord Sandwich!"


Occasional rumors leaked out of the C.E.T. sessions. It was said they were comparing texts and, irresponsibly, the texts were named. Such rumors inevitably provoked anti-ecumenism riots and, of course, inspired new witticisms.

Two years passed . . . three years.

The Commissioners, nine of their original number having died and been replaced, paused to observe formal installation of the replacements and announced they were laboring to produce one book, weeding out "all the pathological symptoms" of the religious past.

"We are producing an instrument of Love to be played in all ways," they said.

Many consider it odd that this statement provoked the worst outbreaks of violence against ecumenism. Twenty delegates were recalled by their congregations. One committed suicide by stealing a space frigate and diving it into the sun.

Historians estimate the riots took eighty million lives. That works out to about six thousand for each world then in the Landsraad League. Considering the unrest of the time, this may not be an excessive estimate, although any pretense to real accuracy in the figure must be just that—pretense. Communication between worlds was at one of its lowest ebbs.

The troubadours, quite naturally, had a field day. A popular musical comedy of the period had one of the C.E.T. delegates sitting on a white sand beach beneath a palm tree singing:

"For God, woman and the splendor of love
We dally here sans fears or cares.
Troubadour! Troubadour, sing another melody
For God, woman and the splendor of love!"


Riots and comedy are but symptoms of the times, profoundly revealing. They betray the psychological tone, the deep uncertainties . . . and the striving for something better, plus the fear that nothing would come of it all.

The major dams against anarchy in these times were the embryo Guild, the Bene Gesserit and the Landsraad, which continued its 2,000-year record of meeting in spite of the severest obstacles. The Guild's part appears clear: they gave free transport for all Landsraad and C.E.T business. The Bene Gesserit role is more obscure. Certainly, this is the time in which they consolidated their hold upon the sorceresses, explored the subtle narcotics, developed prana-bindu training and conceived the Missionaria Protectiva, that black arm of superstition. But it is also the period that saw the composing of the Litany against Fear and the assembly of the Azhar Book, that bibliographic marvel that preserves the great secrets of the most ancient faiths.

Ingsley's comment is perhaps the only one possible:

"Those were times of deep paradox."

For almost seven years, then, C.E.T. labored. And as their seventh anniversary approached, they prepared the human universe for a momentous announcement. On that seventh anniversary, they unveiled the Orange Catholic Bible.

"Here is a work with dignity and meaning," they said. "Here is a way to make humanity aware of itself as a total creation of God."

The men of C.E.T. were likened to archeologists of ideas, inspired by God in the grandeur of rediscovery. It was said they had brought to light "the vitality of great ideals overlaid by the deposits of centuries," that they had "sharpened the moral imperatives that come out of a religious conscience."

With the O.C. Bible, C.E.T. presented the Liturgical Manual and the Commentaries—in many respects a more remarkable work, not only because of its brevity (less than half the size of the O.C. Bible), but also because of its candor and blend of self-pity and self-righteousness.

The beginning is an obvious appeal to the agnostic rulers.

"Men, finding no answers to the *sunnah* [the ten thousand religious questions from the Shari-ah] now apply their own reasoning. All men seek to be enlightened. Religion is but the most ancient and honorable way in which men have striven to make sense out of God's universe. Scientists seek the lawfulness of events. It is the task of Religion to fit man into this lawfulness."

In their conclusion, though, the Commentaries set a harsh tone that very likely foretold their fate.

"Much that was called religion has carried an unconscious attitude of hostility toward life. True religion must teach that life is filled with joys pleasing to the eye of God, that knowledge without action is empty. All men must see that the teaching of religion by rules and rote is largely a hoax. The proper teaching is recognized with ease. You can know it without fail because it awakens within you that sensation which tells you this is something you've always known."

There was an odd sense of calm as the presses and shigawire imprinters rolled and the O.C. Bible spread out through the worlds. Some interpreted this as a sign from God, an omen of unity.

But even the C.E.T. delegates betrayed the fiction of that calm as they returned to their respective congregations. Eighteen of them were lynched within two months. Fifty-three recanted within the year.

The O.C. Bible was denounced as a work produced by "the hubris of reason." It was said that its pages were filled with a seductive interest in logic. Revisions that catered to popular bigotry began appearing. These revisions leaned on accepted symbolisms (Cross, Crescent, Feather Rattle, the Twelve Saints, the thin Buddha, and the like) and it soon became apparent that the ancient superstitions and beliefs had *not* been absorbed by the new ecumenism.

Halloway's label for C.E.T.'s seven-year effort—"Galactophasic Determinism"— was snapped up by eager billions who interpreted the initials G.D. as "God-Damned."

C.E.T. Chairman Toure Bomoko, a Ulema of the Zensunnis and one of the fourteen delegates who never recanted ("The Fourteen Sages" of popular history), appeared to admit finally that C.E.T. had erred.

"We shouldn't have tried to create new symbols," he said. "We should've realized we weren't supposed to introduce uncertainties into accepted belief, that we weren't supposed to stir up curiosity about God. We are daily confronted by the terrifying instability of all things human, yet we permit our religions to grow more rigid and controlled, more conforming and oppressive. What is this shadow across the highway of Divine Command? It is a warning that institutions endure, that symbols endure when their meaning is lost, that there is no summa of all attainable knowledge."

The bitter double edge in this "admission" did not escape Bomoko's critics and he was forced soon afterward to flee into exile, his life dependent upon the Guild's pledge of secrecy. He reportedly died on Tupile, honored and beloved, his last words: "Religion must remain an outlet for people who say to themselves, 'I am not the kind of person I want to be.' It must never sink into an assemblage of the self-satisfied."

It is pleasant to think that Bomoko understood the prophecy in his words: "Institutions endure." Ninety generations later, the O.C. Bible and the Commentaries permeated the religious universe.

When Paul-Muad'Dib stood with his right hand on the rock shrine enclosing his father's skull (the right hand of the blessed, not the left hand of the damned) he quoted word for word from "Bomoko's Legacy"—

"You who have defeated us say to yourselves that Babylon is fallen and its works have been overturned. I say to you still that man remains on trial, each man in his own dock. Each man is a little war."

The Fremen said of Muad'Dib that he was like Abu Zide whose frigate defied the Guild and rode one day *there* and back. *There* used in this way translates directly from the Fremen mythology as the land of the ruh-spirit, the alam al-mithal where all limitations are removed.

The parallel between this and the Kwisatz Haderach is readily seen. The Kwisatz Haderach that the Sisterhood sought through its breeding program was interpreted as "The shortening of the way" or "The one who can be two places simultaneously."

But both of these interpretations can be shown to stem directly from the Commentaries: "When law and religious duty are one, your selfdom encloses the universe."

Of himself, Muad'Dib said: "I am a net in the sea of time, free to sweep future and past. I am a moving membrane from whom no possibility can escape."

These thoughts are all one and the same and they harken to 22 Kalima in the O.C. Bible where it says: "Whether a thought is spoken or not it is a real thing and has powers of reality."

It is when we get into Muad'Dib's own commentaries in "The Pillars of the Universe" as interpreted by his holy men, the Qizara Tafwid, that we see his real debt to C.E.T. and Fremen-Zensunni.

Muad'Dib: *"Law and duty are one; so be it. But remember these limitations—Thus are you never fully self-conscious. Thus do you remain immersed in the communal tau. Thus are you always less than an individual."*

O.C. Bible: Identical wording. (61 Revelations.)

Muad'Dib: *"Religion often partakes of the myth of progress that shields us from the terrors of an uncertain future."*

C.E.T. Commentaries: Identical wording. (The Azhar Book traces this statement to the first century religious writer, Neshou; through a paraphrase.)

Muad'Dib: *"If a child, an untrained person, an ignorant person, or an insane person incites trouble, it is the fault of authority for not predicting and preventing that trouble."*

O.C. Bible: "Any sin can be ascribed, at least in part, to a natural bad tendency that is an extenuating circumstance acceptable to God." (The Azhar Book traces this to the ancient Semitic Tawra.)

Muad'Dib: *"Reach forth thy hand and eat what God has provided thee: and when thou art replenished, praise the Lord."*

O.C. Bible: a paraphrase with identical meaning. (The Azhar Book traces this in slightly different form to First Islam.)

Muad'Dib: *"Kindness is the beginning of cruelty."*

Fremen Kitab al-Ibar: "The weight of a kindly God is a fearful thing. Did not God give us the burning sun (Al-Lat)? Did not God give us the Mothers of Moisture (Reverend Mothers)? Did not God give us Shaitan (Iblis, Satan)? From Shaitan did we not get the hurtfulness of speed?"

(This is the source of the Fremen saying: "Speed comes from Shaitan." Consider: for every one hundred calories of heat generated by exercise [speed] the body evaporates about six ounces of perspiration. The Fremen word for perspiration is bakka or tears and, in one pronunciation, translates: "The life essence that Shaitan squeezes from your soul.")

Muad'Dib's arrival is called "religiously timely" by Koneywell, but timing had little to do with it. As Muad'Dib himself said: "I am here; so . . . ."

It is, however, vital to an understanding of Muad'Dib's religious impact that you never lose sight of one fact: the Fremen were a desert people whose entire ancestry was accustomed to hostile landscapes. Mysticism isn't difficult when you survive each second by surmounting open hostility. "You are there—so . . . ."

With such a tradition, suffering is accepted—perhaps as unconscious punishment, but accepted. And it's well to note that Fremen ritual gives almost complete freedom from guilt feelings. This isn't necessarily because their law and religion were identical, making disobedience a sin. It's likely closer to the mark to say they cleansed themselves of guilt easily because their everyday existence required brutal judgments (often deadly) which in a softer land would burden men with unbearable guilt.

This is likely one of the roots of Fremen emphasis on superstition (disregarding the Missionaria Protectiva's ministrations). What matter that whistling sands are an omen? What matter that you must make the sign of the fist when first you see First Moon? A man's flesh is his own and his water belongs to the tribe—and the mystery of life isn't a problem to solve but a reality to experience. Omens help you remember this. And because you are *here*, because you have *the* religion, victory cannot evade you in the end.

As the Bene Gesserit taught for centuries, long before they ran afoul of the Fremen:

"When religion and politics ride the same cart, when that cart is driven by a living holy man (baraka), nothing can stand in their path."

# APPENDIX III

# APPENDIX III

### Report on Bene Gesserit Motives and Purposes

*Here follows an excerpt from the Summa prepared by her own agents at the request of the Lady Jessica immediately after the Arrakis Affair. The candor of this report amplifies its value far beyond the ordinary.*

Because the Bene Gesserit operated for centuries behind the blind of a semi-mystic school while carrying on their selective breeding program among humans, we tend to award them with more status than they appear to deserve. Analysis of their "trial of fact" on the Arrakis Affair betrays the school's profound ignorance of its own role.

It may be argued that the Bene Gesserit could examine only such facts as were available to them and had no direct access to the person of the Prophet Muad'Dib. But the school had surmounted greater obstacles and its error here goes deeper.

The Bene Gesserit program had as its target the breeding of a person they labeled "Kwisatz Haderach," a term signifying "One who can be many places at once." In simpler terms, what they sought was a human with mental powers permitting him to understand and use higher order dimensions.

They were breeding for a super-Mentat, a human computer with some of the prescient abilities found in Guild navigators. Now, attend these facts carefully:

Muad'Dib, born Paul Atreides, was the son of Duke Leto, a man whose bloodline had been watched carefully for more than a thousand years. The Prophet's mother, Lady Jessica, was a natural daughter of the Baron Vladimir Harkonnen and carried gene-markers whose supreme importance to the breeding program was known for almost two thousand years. She was a Bene Gesserit bred and trained, and *should have been a willing tool of the project.*

The Lady Jessica was ordered to produce an Atreides daughter. The plan was to inbreed this daughter with Feyd-Rautha Harkonnen, a nephew of the Baron Vladimir, with the high probability of a Kwisatz Haderach from that union. Instead, for reasons she confesses have never been completely clear to her, the concubine Lady Jessica defied her orders and bore a son.

This alone should have alerted the Bene Gesserit to the possibility that a wild variable had entered their scheme. But there were other far more important indications that they virtually ignored:

1. As a youth, Paul Atreides showed ability to predict the future. He was known to have had prescient visions that were accurate, penetrating, and defied four-dimensional explanation.

2. The Reverend Mother Gaius Helen Mohiam, Bene Gesserit Proctor who tested Paul's humanity when he was fifteen, deposes that he surmounted more agony in the test than any other human of record. Yet she failed to make special note of this in her report!

3. When Family Atreides moved to the planet Arrakis, the Fremen population there hailed the young Paul as a prophet, "the voice from the outer world." The Bene Gesserit were well aware that the rigors of such a planet as Arrakis with its totality of desert landscape, its absolute lack of open water, its emphasis on the most primitive necessities for survival, inevitably produces a high proportion of sensitives. Yet this Fremen reaction and the obvious element of the Arrakeen diet high in spice were glossed over by Bene Gesserit observers.

4. When the Harkonnens and the soldier-fanatics of the Padishah Emperor re-occupied Arrakis, killing Paul's father and most of the Atreides troops, Paul and his mother disappeared. But almost immediately there were reports of a new religious leader among the Fremen, a man called Muad'Dib, who again was hailed as "the voice from the outer world." The reports stated clearly that he was accompanied by a new Reverend Mother of the Sayyadina Rite "who is the woman who bore him." Records available to the Bene Gesserit stated in plain terms that the Fremen legends of the Prophet contained these words: "He shall be born of a Bene Gesserit witch."

(It may be argued here that the Bene Gesserit sent their Missionaria Protectiva onto Arrakis centuries earlier to implant something like this legend as safeguard should any members of the school be trapped there and require sanctuary, and that this legend of "the voice from the outer world" was properly to be ignored because it appeared to be the standard Bene Gesserit ruse. But this would be true only if you granted that the Bene Gesserit were correct in ignoring the other clues about Paul-Muad'Dib.)

5. When the Arrakis Affair boiled up, the Spacing Guild made overtures to the Bene Gesserit. The Guild hinted that its navigators, who use the spice drug on Arrakis to produce the limited prescience necessary for guiding spaceships through the void, were "bothered about the future" or saw "problems on the horizon." This could only mean they saw a nexus, a meeting place of countless delicate decisions, beyond which the path was hidden from the prescient eye. This was a clear indication that some agency was interfering with higher order dimensions!

(A few of the Bene Gesserit had long been aware that the Guild could not interfere directly with the vital spice source because Guild navigators already were dealing in their own inept way with higher order dimensions, at least to the point where they recognized that the slightest misstep they made on Arrakis could be catastrophic. It was a known fact that Guild navigators could predict no way to take control of the spice without producing just such a nexus. The obvious conclusion was that someone of higher order powers *was* taking control of the spice source, yet the Bene Gesserit missed this point entirely!)

In the face of these facts, one is led to the inescapable conclusion that the inefficient Bene Gesserit behavior in this affair was a product of an even higher plan of which they were completely unaware!

# APPENDIX IV

# APPENDIX IV

## The Almanak en-Ashraf
### (Selected Excerpts of the Noble Houses)

**SHADDAM IV (10,134—10,202)**

The Padishah Emperor, 81st of his line (House Corrino) to occupy the Golden Lion Throne, reigned from 10,156 (date his father, Elrood IX, succumbed to chaumurky) until replaced by the 10,196 Regency set up in the name of his eldest daughter, Irulan. His reign is noted chiefly for the Arrakis Revolt, blamed by many historians on Shaddam IV's dalliance with Court functions and the pomp of office. The ranks of Bursegs were doubled in the first sixteen years of his reign. Appropriations for Sardaukar training went down steadily in the final thirty years before the Arrakis Revolt. He had five daughters (Irulan, Chalice, Wensicia, Josifa, and Rugi) and no legal sons. Four of the daughters accompanied him into retirement. His wife, Anirul, a Bene Gesserit of Hidden Rank, died in 10,176.

**LETO ATREIDES (10,140—10,191)**

A distaff cousin of the Corrinos, he is frequently referred to as the Red Duke. House Atreides ruled Caladan as a siridar-fief for twenty generations until pressured into the move to Arrakis. He is known chiefly as the father of Duke Paul Muad'Dib, the Umma Regent. The remains of Duke Leto occupy the "Skull Tomb" on Arrakis. His death is attributed to the treachery of a Suk doctor, and is an act laid to the Siridar Baron, Vladimir Harkonnen.

**LADY JESSICA (Hon. Atreides) (10,154—10,256)**

A natural daughter (Bene Gesserit reference) of the Siridar-Baron Vladimir Harkonnen. Mother of Duke Paul Muad'Dib. She graduated from the Wallach IX B.G. School.

**LADY ALIA ATREIDES (10,191—          )**

Legal daughter of Duke Leto Atreides and his formal concubine, Lady Jessica. Lady Alia was born on Arrakis about eight months after Duke Leto's death. Prenatal exposure to an awareness-spectrum narcotic is the reason generally given for Bene Gesserit references to her as "Accursed One." She is known in popular history as St. Alia or St. Alia-of-the-Knife. (For a detailed history, see *St. Alia, Huntress of a Billion Worlds* by Pander Oulson.)

**VLADIMIR HARKONNEN (10,110—10,193)**

Commonly referred to as Baron Harkonnen, his title is officially Siridar (planetary governor) Baron. Vladimir Harkonnen is the direct-line male descendant of the Bashar Abulurd Harkonnen who was banished for cowardice after the Battle of Corrin. The return of House Harkonnen to power generally is ascribed to adroit manipulation of the whale fur market and later consolidation with melange wealth from Arrakis. The Siridar-Baron died on Arrakis during the Revolt. Title passed briefly to the na-Baron, Feyd-Rautha Harkonnen.

### COUNT HASIMIR FENRING (10,133—10,225)

A distaff cousin of House Corrino, he was a childhood companion of Shaddam IV. (The frequently discredited *Pirate History of Corrino* related the curious story that Fenring was responsible for the chaumurky which disposed of Elrood IX.) All accounts agree that Fenring was the closest friend Shaddam IV possessed. The Imperial chores carried out by Count Fenring included that of Imperial Agent on Arrakis during the Harkonnen regime there and later Siridar-Absentia of Caladan. He joined Shaddam IV in retirement on Salusa Secundus.

### COUNT GLOSSU RABBAN (10,132—10,193)

Glossu Rabban, Count of Lankiveil, was the eldest nephew of Vladimir Harkonnen. Glossu Rabban and Feyd-Rautha Rabban (who took the name Harkonnen when chosen for the Siridar-Baron's household) were legal sons of the Siridir-Baron's youngest demibrother, Abulurd. Abulurd renounced the Harkonnen name and all rights to the title when given the subdistrict governorship of Rabban-Lankiveil. Rabban was a distaff name.

# TERMINOLOGY OF THE IMPERIUM

# TERMINOLOGY OF THE IMPERIUM

In studying the Imperium, Arrakis, and the whole culture which produced Muad'Dib, many unfamiliar terms occur. To increase understanding is a laudable goal, hence the definitions and explanations given below.

**ABA:** loose robe worn by Fremen women; usually black.

**ACH:** left turn: a worm steersman's call.

**ADAB:** the demanding memory that comes upon you of itself.

**AKARSO:** a plant native to Sikun (of 70 Ophiuchi A) characterized by almost oblong leaves. Its green and white stripes indicate the constant multiple condition of parallel active and dormant chlorophyll regions.

**ALAM AL-MITHAL:** the mystical world of similitudes where all physical limitations are removed.

**AL-LAT:** mankind's original sun; by usage: any planet's primary.

**AMPOLIROS:** the legendary "Flying Dutchman" of space.

**AMTAL** or **AMTAL RULE:** a common rule on primitive worlds under which something is tested to determine its limits or defects. Commonly: testing to destruction.

**AQL:** the test of reason. Originally, the "Seven Mystic Questions" beginning: "Who is it that thinks?"

**ARRAKEEN:** first settlement on Arrakis; long-time seat of planetary government.

**ARRAKIS:** the planet known as Dune; third planet of Canopus.

**ASSASSINS' HANDBOOK:** Third-century compilation of poisons commonly used in a War of Assassins. Later expanded to include those deadly devices permitted under the Guild Peace and Great Convention.

**AULIYA:** In the Zensunni Wanderers' religion, the female at the left hand of God; God's handmaiden.

**AUMAS:** poison administered in food. (Specifically: poison in solid food.) In some dialects: Chaumas.

**AYAT:** the signs of life. (*See* Burhan.)


**BAKKA:** in Fremen legend, the weeper who mourns for all mankind.

**BAKLAWA:** a heavy pastry made with date syrup.

**BALISET:** a nine-stringed musical instrument, lineal descendant of the zithra, tuned to the Chusuk scale and played by strumming. Favorite instrument of Imperial troubadours.

**BARADYE PISTOL:** a static-charge dust gun developed on Arrakis for laying down a large dye marker area on sand.

**BARAKA:** a living holy man of magical powers.

**BASHAR** (often Colonel Bashar): an officer of the Sardaukar a fractional point above Colonel in the standardized military classification. Rank created for military ruler of a planetary subdistrict. (Bashar of the Corps is a title reserved strictly for military use.)

**BATTLE LANGUAGE:** any special language of restricted etymology developed for clear-speech communication in warfare.

**BEDWINE:** *see* Ichwan Bedwine.

**BELA TEGEUSE:** fifth planet of Kuentsing: third stopping place of the Zensunni (Fremen) forced migration.

**BENE GESSERIT:** the ancient school of mental and physical training established primarily for female students after the Butlerian Jihad destroyed the so-called "thinking machines" and robots.

**B.G.:** idiomatic for Bene Gesserit except when used with a date. With a date it signifies Before Guild and identifies the Imperial dating system based on the genesis of the Spacing Guild's monopoly.

**BHOTANI JIB:** *see* Chakobsa.

**BI-LA KAIFA:** Amen. (Literally: "Nothing further need be explained.")

**BINDU:** relating to the human nervous system, especially to nerve training. Often expressed as Bindu-nervature. (*See* Prana.)

**BINDU SUSPENSION:** a special form of catalepsis, self-induced.

**BLED:** flat, open desert.

**BOURKA:** insulated mantle worn by Fremen in the open desert.

**BURHAN:** the proofs of life. (Commonly: the ayat and burhan of life. *See* Ayat.)

**BURSEG:** a commanding general of the Sardaukar.

**BUTLERIAN JIHAD:** *see* Jihad, Butlerian (*also* Great Revolt).


**CAID:** Sardaukar officer rank given to a military official whose duties call mostly for dealings with civilians; a military governorship over a full planetary district; above the rank of Bashar but not equal to Burseg.

**CALADAN:** third planet of Delta Pavonis; birthworld of Paul-Muad'Dib.

**CANTO and RESPONDU:** an invocation rite, part of the panoplia propheticus of the Missionaria Protectiva.

**CARRYALL:** a flying wing (commonly "wing"), the aerial workhorse of Arrakis, used to transport large spice mining, hunting, and refining equipment.

**CATCHPOCKET:** any stillsuit pocket where filtered water is caught and stored.

**CHAKOBSA:** the so-called "magnetic language" derived in part from the ancient Bhotani (Bhotani Jib—jib meaning dialect). A collection of ancient dialects modified by needs of secrecy, but chiefly the hunting language of the Bhotani, the hired assassins of the first Wars of Assassins.

**CHAUMAS** (Aumas in some dialects): poison in solid food as distinguished from poison administered in some other way.

**CHAUMURKY** (Musky or Murky in some dialects): poison administered in a drink.

**CHEOPS:** pyramid chess; nine-level chess with double object of putting your queen at the apex and the opponent's king in check.

**CHEREM:** a brotherhood of hate (usually for revenge).

**CHOAM:** acronym for Combine Honnete Ober Advancer Mercantiles—the universal development corporation controlled by the Emperor and Great Houses with the Guild and Bene Gesserit as silent partners.

**CHUSUK:** fourth planet of Theta Shalish; the so-called "Music Planet" noted for the quality of its musical instruments. (*See* Varota.)

**CIELAGO:** any modified *Chiroptera* of Arrakis adapted to carry distrans messages.

**CONE OF SILENCE:** the field of a distorter that limits the carrying power of the voice or any other vibrator by damping the vibrations with an image-vibration 180 degrees out of phase.

**CORIOLIS STORM:** any major sandstorm on Arrakis where winds across the open flatlands are amplified by the planet's own revolutionary motion to reach speeds up to 700 kilometers per hour.

**CORRIN, BATTLE OF:** the space battle from which the Imperial House Corrino took its name. The battle fought near Sigma Draconis in the year 88 B.G. settled the ascendancy of the ruling House from Salusa Secundus.

**COUSINES:** blood relations beyond cousins.

**CRUSHERS:** military space vessels composed of smaller vessels locked together and designed to fall on an enemy position, crushing it.

**CUTTERAY:** short-range version of lasgun used mostly as a cutting tool and surgeon's scalpel.

**CRYSKNIFE:** the sacred knife of the Fremen on Arrakis. It is manufactured in two forms from teeth taken from dead sandworms. The two forms are "fixed" and "unfixed." An unfixed knife requires proximity to a human body's electrical field to prevent disintegration. Fixed knives are treated for storage. All are about 20 centimeters long.

**DAR AL-HIKMAN:** school of religious translation or interpretation.

**DARK THINGS:** idiomatic for the infectious superstitions taught by the Missionaria Protectiva to susceptible civilizations.

**DEATH TRIPOD:** originally, the tripod upon which desert executioners hanged their victims. By usage: the three members of a Cherem sworn to the same revenge.

**DERCH:** right turn, a worm steersman's call.

**DEW COLLECTORS** or **DEW PRECIPITATORS:** not to be confused with dew gatherers. Collectors or precipitators are egg-shaped devices about four centimeters on the long axis. They are made of chromoplastic that turns a reflecting white when subjected to light, and reverts to transparency in darkness. The collector forms a markedly cold surface upon which dawn dew will precipitate. They are used by Fremen to line concave planting depressions where they provide a small but reliable source of water.

**DEW GATHERERS:** workers who reap dew from the plants of Arrakis, using a scythelike dew reaper.

**DEMIBROTHERS:** sons of concubines in the same household and certified as having the same father.

**DICTUM FAMILIA:** that rule of the Great Convention which prohibits the slaying of a royal person or member of a Great House by informal treachery. The rule sets up the formal outline and limits the means of assassination.

**DISTRANS:** a device for producing a temporary neural imprint on the nervous system of *Chiroptera* or birds. The creature's normal cry then carries the message imprint which can be sorted from that carrier wave by another distrans.

**DRUM SAND:** impaction of sand in such a way that any sudden blow against its surface produces a distinct drum sound.

**DOORSEAL:** a portable plastic hermetic seal used for moisture security in Fremen overday cave camps.

**DUMP BOXES:** the general term for any cargo container of irregular shape and equipped with ablation surfaces and suspensor damping system. They are used to dump material from space onto a planet's surface.

**DUNE MEN:** idiomatic for open sand workers, spice hunters and the like on Arrakis. Sandworkers. Spiceworkers.

**DUST CHASM:** any deep crevasse or depression on the desert of Arrakis that has been filled with dust not apparently different from the surrounding surface; a deadly trap because human or animal will sink in it and smother. (*See* Tidal Dust Basin.)

**ECAZ:** fourth planet of Alpha Centauri B; the sculptors' paradise, so called because it is the home of *fogwood*, the plant growth capable of being shaped in situ solely by the power of human thought.

**EGO-LIKENESS:** portraiture reproduced through a shigawire projector that is capable of reproducing subtle movements said to convey the ego essence.

**ELACCA DRUG:** narcotic formed by burning blood-grained elacca wood of Ecaz. Its effect is to remove most of the will to self-preservation. Druggee skin shows a characteristic carrot color. Commonly used to prepare slave gladiators for the ring.

**EL-SAYAL:** the "rain of sand." A fall of dust which has been carried to medium altitude (around 2,000 meters) by a coriolis storm. El-sayals frequently bring moisture to ground level.

**ERG:** an extensive dune area, a sea of sand.

**FAI:** the water tribute, chief specie of tax on Arrakis.

**FANMETAL:** metal formed by the growing of jasmium crystals in duraluminum; noted for extreme tensile strength in relationship to weight. Name derives from its common use in collapsible structures that are opened by "fanning" them out.

**FAUFRELUCHES:** the rigid rule of class distinction enforced by the Imperium. "A place for every man and every man in his place."

**FEDAYKIN:** Fremen death commandos; historically: a group formed and pledged to give their lives to right a wrong.

**FILMBOOK:** any shigawire imprint used in training and carrying a mnemonic pulse.

**FILT-PLUG:** a nose filter unit worn with a stillsuit to capture moisture from the exhaled breath.

**FIQH:** knowledge, religious law; one of the half-legendary origins of the Zensunni Wanderers' religion.

**FIRE, PILLAR OF:** a simple pyrocket for signaling across the open desert.

**FIRST MOON:** the major satellite of Arrakis, first to rise in the night; notable for a distinct human fist pattern on its surface.

**FREE TRADERS:** idiomatic for smugglers.

**FREMEN:** the free tribes of Arrakis, dwellers in the desert, remnants of the Zensunni Wanderers. ("Sand Pirates" according to the Imperial Dictionary.)

**FREMKIT:** desert survival kit of Fremen manufacture.

**FRIGATE:** largest spaceship that can be grounded on a planet and taken off in one piece.

**GALACH:** official language of the Imperium. Hybrid Inglo-Slavic with strong traces of cultural-specialization terms adopted during the long chain of human migrations.

**GAMONT:** third planet of Niushe; noted for its hedonistic culture and exotic sexual practices.

**GARE:** butte.

**GATHERING:** distinguished from Council Gathering. It is a formal convocation of Fremen leaders to witness a combat that determines tribal leadership. (A Council Gathering is an assembly to arrive at decisions involving all the tribes.)

**GEYRAT:** straight ahead; a worm steersman's call.

**GHAFLA:** giving oneself up to gadfly distractions. Thus: a changeable person, one not to be trusted.

**GHANIMA:** something acquired in battle or single combat. Commonly, a memento of combat kept only to stir the memory.

**GIEDI PRIME:** the planet of Ophiuchi B (36), homeworld of House Harkonnen. A median-viable planet with a low active-photosynthesis range.

**GINAZ, HOUSE OF:** one-time allies of Duke Leto Atreides. They were defeated in the War of Assassins with Grumman.

**GIUDICHAR:** a holy truth. (Commonly seen in the expression Giudichar mantene: an original and supporting truth.)

**GLOWGLOBE:** suspensor-buoyed illuminating device, self-powered (usually by melange spice mass; a device of the second stage in spice refining.

**GRABEN:** a long geological ditch formed when the ground sinks because of movements in the underlying crustal layers.

**GREAT CONVENTION:** the universal truce enforced under the power balance maintained by the Guild, the Great Houses, and the Imperium. Its chief rule prohibits the use of atomic weapons against human targets. Each rule of the Great Convention begins: "The forms must be obeyed . . . ."

**GREAT MOTHER:** the horned goddess, the feminine principle of space (commonly: Mother Space), the feminine face of the male-female-neuter trinity accepted as Supreme Being by many religions within the Imperium.

**GREAT REVOLT:** common term for the Butlerian Jihad. (*See* Jihad, Butlerian.)

**GRIDEX PLANE:** a differential-charge separator used to remove sand from the melange spice mass; a device of the second stage in spice refining.

**GRUMMAN:** second planet of Niushe, noted chiefly for the feud of its ruling House (Moritani) with House Ginaz.

**GOM JABBAR:** the high-handed enemy; that specific poison needle tipped with meta-cyanide used by Bene Gesserit Proctors in the death-alternative test of human awareness.

**GUILD:** the Spacing Guild, one leg of the political tripod maintaining the Great Convention. The Guild was the second mental-physical training school (*see* Bene Gesserit) after the Butlerian Jihad. The Guild monopoly on space travel and transport and upon international banking is taken as the beginning point of the Imperial Calendar.

**HAGAL:** the "Jewel Planet" (II Theta Shaowei), mined out in the time of Shaddam I.

**HAIIIII-YOH!:** command to action; worm steersman's call.

**HAJJ:** holy journey.

**HAJR:** desert journey, migration.

**HAJRA:** journey of seeking.

**HAL YAWM:** "Now! At Last!" a Fremen exclamation.

**HARMONTHEP:** Ingsley gives this as the planet name for the sixth stop in the Zensunni migration. It is supposed to have been a no longer existent satellite of Delta Pavonis.

**HARVESTER** or **HARVESTER FACTORY:** a large (often 120 meters by 40 meters) spice mining machine commonly employed on rich, uncontaminated melange blows. (Often called a "crawler" because of buglike body on independent tracks.)

**HEIGHLINER:** major cargo carrier of the Spacing Guild's transportation system.

**HIEREG:** temporary Fremen desert camp on open sand.

**HIGH COUNCIL:** the Landsraad inner circle empowered to act as supreme tribunal in House to House disputes.

**HOLTZMAN EFFECT:** the negative repelling effect of a shield generator.

**HOOKMAN:** Fremen with Maker hooks prepared to catch a sandworm.

**HOUSE:** idiomatic for Ruling Clan of a planet or planetary system.

**HOUSES MAJOR:** holders of planetary fiefs; interplanetary entrepreneurs. (*See* House *above.*)

**HOUSES MINOR:** planet-bound entrepreneur class (Galach: "Richece").

**HUNTER-SEEKER:** a ravening sliver of suspensor-buoyed metal guided as a weapon by a near-by control console; common assassination device.

**IBAD, EYES OF:** characteristic effect of a diet high in melange wherein the whites and pupils of the eyes turn a deep blue (indicative of deep melange addiction).

**IBN QIRTAIBA:** "Thus go the holy words . . . ." Formal beginning to Fremen religious incantation (derived from panoplia propheticus).

**ICHWAN BEDWINE:** the brotherhood of all Fremen on Arrakis.

**IJAZ:** prophecy that by its very nature cannot be denied; immutable prophecy.

**IKHUT-EIGH!:** cry of the water-seller on Arrakis (etymology uncertain). *See* Soo-Soo Sook!

**ILM:** theology; science of religious tradition; one of the half-legendary origins of the Zensunni Wanderers' faith.

**IMPERIAL CONDITIONING:** a development of the Suk Medical Schools: the highest conditioning against taking human life. Initiates are marked by a diamond tattoo on the forehead and are permitted to wear their hair long and bound by a silver Suk ring.

**INKVINE:** a creeping plant native to Giedi Prime and frequently used as a whip in the slave cribs. Victims are marked by beet-colored tattoos that cause residual pain for many years.

**ISTISLAH:** a rule of the general welfare; usually a preface to brutal necessity.

**IX:** *see* Richese.

**JIHAD:** a religious crusade; fanatical crusade.

**JIHAD, BUTLERIAN:** (*see also* Great Revolt)—the crusade against computers, thinking machines, and conscious robots begun in 201 B.G. and concluded in 108 B.G. Its chief commandment remains in the O.C. Bible as "Thou shalt not make a machine in the likeness of a human mind."

**JUBBA CLOAK:** the all-purpose cloak (it can be set to reflect or admit radiant heat, converts to a hammock or shelter) commonly worn over a stillsuit on Arrakis.

**JUDGE OF THE CHANGE:** an official appointed by the Landsraad High Council and the Emperor to monitor a change of fief, a kanly negotiation, or formal battle in a War of Assassins. The Judge's arbitral authority may be challenged only before the High Council with the Emperor present.

**KANLY:** formal feud or vendetta under the rules of the Great Convention carried on according to the strictest limitations. (*See* Judge of the Change.) Originally the rules were designed to protect innocent bystanders.

**KARAMA:** a miracle; an action initiated by the spirit world.

**KHALA:** traditional invocation to still the angry spirits of a place whose name you mention.

**KINDJAL:** double-bladed short sword (or long knife) with about 20 centimeters of slightly curved blade.

**KISWA:** any figure or design from Fremen mythology.

**KITAB AL-IBAR:** the combined survival handbook/religious manual developed by the Fremen on Arrakis.

**KRIMSKELL FIBER** or **KRIMSKELL ROPE:** the "claw fiber" woven from strands of the *hufuf* vine from Ecaz. Knots tied in krimskell will claw tighter and tighter to preset limits when the knot-lines are pulled. (For a more detailed study, *see* Holjance Vohnbrook's "The Strange Vines of Ecaz.")

**KULL WAHAD!:** "I am profoundly stirred!" A sincere exclamation of surprise common in the Imperium. Strict interpretation depends on context. (It is said of Muad'Dib that once he watched a desert hawk chick emerge from its shell and whispered: "Kull wahad!")

**KULON:** wild ass of Terra's Asiatic steppes adapted for Arrakis.

**KWISATZ HADERACH:** "Shortening of the Way." This is the label applied by the Bene Gesserit to the *unknown* for which they sought a genetic solution: a male Bene Gesserit whose organic mental powers would bridge space and time.


**LA, LA, LA:** Fremen cry of grief. (La translates as ultimate denial, a "no" from which you cannot appeal.)

**LASGUN:** continuous-wave laser projector. Its use as a weapon is limited in a field-generator-shield culture because of the explosive pyrotechnics (technically, sub-atomic fusion) created when its beam intersects a shield.

**LEGION, IMPERIAL:** ten brigades (about 30,000 men).

**LIBAN:** Fremen liban is spice water infused with yucca flour. Originally a sour milk drink.

**LISAN AL-GAIB:** "The Voice from the Outer World." In Fremen messianic legends, an off-world prophet. Sometimes translated as "Giver of Water." (*See* Mahdi.)

**LITERJON:** a one-liter container for transporting water on Arrakis; made of high-density, shatterproof plastic with positive seal.

**LITTLE MAKER:** the half-plant-half-animal deep-sand vector of the Arrakis sandworm. The Little Maker's excretions form the pre-spice mass.


**MAHDI:** in the Fremen messianic legend, "The One Who Will Lead Us to Paradise."

**MAKER:** *see* Shai-hulud.

**MAKER HOOKS:** the hooks used for capturing, mounting, and steering a sandworm of Arrakis.

**MANTENE:** underlying wisdom, supporting argument, first principle. (*See* Giudichar.)

**MATING INDEX:** the Bene Gesserit master record of its human breeding program aimed at producing the Kwisatz Haderach.

**MAULA:** slave.

**MAULA PISTOL:** spring-loaded gun for firing poison darts; range about forty meters.

**MELANGE:** the "spice of spices," the crop for which Arrakis is the unique source. The spice, chiefly noted for its geriatric qualities, is mildly addictive when taken in small quantities, severely addictive when imbibed in quantities above two grams daily per seventy kilos of body weight. (*See* Ibad, Water of Life, *and* Pre-Spice Mass.) Muad'Dib claimed the spice as a key to his prophetic powers. Guild navigators make similar claims. Its price on the Imperial market has ranged as high as 620,000 solaris the decagram.

**MENTAT:** that class of Imperial citizens trained for supreme accomplishments of logic. "Human computers."

**METAGLASS:** glass grown as a high-temperature gas infusion in sheets of jasmium quartz. Noted for extreme tensile strength (about 450,000 kilos per square centimeter at two centimeters' thickness) and capacity as a selective radiation filter.

**MIHNA:** the season for testing Fremen youths who wish admittance to manhood.

**MINIMIC FILM:** shigawire of one-micron diameter often used to transmit espionage and counterespionage data.

**MISH-MISH:** apricots.

**MISR:** the historical Zensunni (Fremen) term for themselves: "The People."

**MISSIONARIA PROTECTIVA:** the arm of the Bene Gesserit order charged with sowing infectious superstitions on primitive worlds, thus opening those regions to exploitation by the Bene Gesserit. (*See* Panoplia propheticus.)

**MONITOR:** a ten-section space warcraft mounting heavy armor and shield protection. It is designed to be separated into its component sections for lift-off after planet-fall.

**MUAD'DIB:** the adapted kangaroo mouse of Arrakis, a creature associated in the Fremen earth-spirit mythology with a design visible on the planet's second moon. This creature is admired by Fremen for its ability to survive in the open desert.

**MUDIR NAHYA:** the Fremen name for Beast Rabban (Count Rabban of Lankiveil), the Harkonnen cousin who was siridar governor on Arrakis for many years. The name is often translated as "Demon Ruler."

**MUSHTAMAL:** a small garden annex or garden courtyard.

**MUSKY:** poison in a drink. (*See* Chaumurky.)

**MU ZEIN WALLAH!:** Mu zein literally means "nothing good," and wallah is a reflexive terminal exclamation. In this traditional opening for a Fremen curse against an enemy, Wallah turns the emphasis back upon the words Mu zein, producing the meaning: "Nothing good, never good, good for nothing."

**NA-:** a prefix meaning "nominated" or "next in line." Thus: na-Baron means heir apparent to a barony.

**NAIB:** one who has sworn never to be taken alive by the enemy; traditional oath of a Fremen leader.

**NEZHONI SCARF:** the scarf-pad worn at the forehead beneath the stillsuit hood by married or "associated" Fremen women after birth of a son.

**NOUKKERS:** officers of the Imperial bodyguard who are related to the Emperor by blood. Traditional rank for sons of royal concubines.

**OIL LENS:** hufuf oil held in static tension by an enclosing force field within a viewing tube as part of a magnifying or other light-manipulation system. Because each lens element can be adjusted individually one micron at a time, the oil lens is considered the ultimate in accuracy for manipulating visible light.

**OPAFIRE:** one of the rare opaline jewels of Hagal.

**ORANGE CATHOLIC BIBLE:** the "Accumulated Book," the religious text produced by the Commission of Ecumenical Translators. It contains elements of most ancient religions, including the Maometh Sarri, Mahayana Christianity, Zensunni Catholicism and Buddislamic traditions. Its supreme commandment is considered to be: "Thou shalt not disfigure the soul."

**ORNITHOPTER:** (commonly: 'thopter): any aircraft capable of sustained wing-beat flight in the manner of birds.

**OUT-FREYN:** Galach for "immediately foreign," that is: not of your immediate community, not of the select.

**PALM LOCK:** any lock or seal which may be opened on contact with the palm of the human hand to which it has been keyed.

**PAN:** on Arrakis, any low-lying region or depression created by the subsiding of the underlying basement complex. (On planets with sufficient water, a pan indicates a region once covered by open water. Arrakis is believed to have at least one such area, although this remains open to argument.)

**PANOPLIA PROPHETICUS:** term covering the infectious superstitions used by the Bene Gesserit to exploit primitive regions. (*See* Missionaria Protectiva.)

**PARACOMPASS:** any compass that determines direction by local magnetic anomaly; used where relevant charts are available and where a planet's total magnetic field is unstable or subject to masking by severe magnetic storms.

**PENTASHIELD:** a five-layer shield-generator field suitable for small areas such as doorways or passages (large reinforcing shields become increasingly unstable with each successive layer) and virtually impassable to anyone not wearing a dissembler tuned to the shield codes. (*See* Prudence Door.)

**PLASTEEL:** steel which has been stabilized with stravidium fibers grown into its crystal structure.

**PLENISCENTA:** an exotic green bloom of Ecaz noted for its sweet aroma.

**POLING THE SAND:** the art of placing plastic and fiber poles in the open desert wastes of Arrakis and reading the patterns etched on the poles by sandstorms as a clue to weather prediction.

**PORITRIN:** third planet of Epsilon Alangue, considered by many Zensunni Wanderers as their planet of origin, although clues in their language and mythology show far more ancient planetary roots.

**PORTYGULS:** oranges.

**PRANA:** (Prana-musculature): the body's muscles when considered as units for ultimate training. (*See* Bindu.)

**PRE-SPICE MASS:** the stage of fungusoid wild growth achieved when water is flooded into the excretions of Little Makers. At this stage, the spice of Arrakis forms a characteristic "blow," exchanging the material from deep underground for the matter on the surface above it. This mass, after exposure to sun and air, becomes melange (*See also* Melange *and* Water of Life.)

**PROCES VERBAL:** a semiformal report alleging a crime against the Imperium. Legally: an action falling between a loose verbal allegation and a formal charge of crime.

**PROCTOR SUPERIOR:** a Bene Gesserit Reverend Mother who is also regional director of a B.G. school. (Commonly: Bene Gesserit with the Sight.)

**PRUDENCE DOOR** or **PRUDENCE BARRIER** (idiomatically: pru-door or pru-barrier): any pentashield situated for the escape of selected persons under conditions of pursuit. (*See* Pentashield.)

**PUNDI RICE:** a mutated rice whose grains, high in natural sugar, achieve lengths up to four centimeters; chief export of Caladan.

**PYONS:** planet-bound peasants or laborers, one of the base classes under the Faufreluches. Legally: wards of the planet.

**PYRETIC CONSCIENCE:** so-called "conscience of fire;" that inhibitory level touched by Imperial conditioning. (*See* Imperial conditioning.)

**QANAT:** an open canal for carrying irrigation water under controlled conditions through a desert.

**QIRTAIBA:** *see* Ibn Qirtaiba.

**QUIZARA TAFWID:** Fremen priests (after Muad'Dib).

**RACHAG:** a caffeine-type stimulant from the yellow berries of akarso. (*See* Akarso.)

**RAMADHAN:** ancient religious period marked by fasting and prayer; traditionally, the ninth month of the solar-lunar calendar. Fremen mark the observance according to the ninth meridian-crossing cycle of the first moon.

**RAZZIA:** a semipiratical guerrilla raid.

**RECATHS:** body-function tubes linking the human waste disposal system to the cycling filters of a stillsuit.

**REPKIT:** repair and replacement essentials for a stillsuit.

**RESIDUAL POISON:** an innovation attributed to the Mentat Piter de Vries whereby the body is impregnated with a substance for which repeated antidotes must be administered. Withdrawal of the antidote at any time brings death.

**REVEREND MOTHER:** originally, a proctor of the Bene Gesserit, one who has transformed an "illuminating poison" within her body, raising herself to a higher state of awareness. Title adopted by Fremen for their own religious leaders who accomplished a similar "illumination." (*See also* Bene Gesserit *and* Water of Life.)

**RICHESE:** fourth planet of Eridani A, classed with Ix as supreme in machine culture. Noted for miniaturization. (For a detailed study of how Richese and Ix escaped the more severe effects of the Butlerian Jihad, *see* The Last Jihad by Sumer and Kautman.)

**RIMWALL:** second upper step of the protecting bluffs on the Shield Wall of Arrakis. (*See* Shield Wall.)

**RUH-SPIRIT:** in Fremen belief, that part of the individual which is always rooted in (and capable of sensing) the metaphysical world. (*See* Alam al-Mithal.)

**SADUS:** judges. The Fremen title refers to holy judges, equivalent to saints.

**SALUSA SECUNDUS:** third planet of Gamma Waiping; designated Imperial Prison Planet after removal of the Royal Court to Kaitan. Salusa Secundus is homeworld of House Corrino, and the second stopping point in migrations of the Wandering Zensunni. Fremen tradition says they were slaves on S.S. for nine generations.

**SANDCRAWLER:** general term for machinery designed to operate on the Arrakis surface in hunting and collecting melange.

**SANDMASTER:** general superintendent of spice operations.

**SANDRIDER:** Fremen term for one who is capable of capturing and riding a sandworm.

**SANDSNORK:** breathing device for pumping surface air into a sandcovered stilltent.

**SANDTIDE:** idiomatic for a dust tide: the variation in level within certain dust-filled basins on Arrakis due to gravitational effects of sun and satellites. (*See* Tidal Dust Basin.)

**SANDWALKER:** any Fremen trained to survive in the open desert.

**SANDWORM:** *See* Shai-Hulud.

**SAPHO:** high-energy liquid extracted from barrier roots of Ecaz. Commonly used by Mentats who claim it amplifies mental powers. Users develop deep ruby stains on mouth and lips.

**SARDAUKAR:** the soldier-fanatics of the Padishah Emperor. They were men from an environmental background of such ferocity that it killed six out of thirteen persons before the age of eleven. Their military training emphasized ruthlessness and a near-suicidal disregard for personal safety. They were taught from infancy to use cruelty as a standard weapon, weakening opponents with terror. At the apex of their sway over the affairs of the Universe, their swordsmanship was said to match that of the Ginaz tenth level and their cunning abilities at in-fighting were reputed to approach those of a Bene Gesserit adept. Any one of them was rated a match for any ten ordinary Landsraad military conscripts. By the time of Shaddam IV, while they were still formidable, their strength had been sapped by overconfidence, and the sustaining mystique of their warrior religion had been deeply undermined by cynicism.

**SARFA:** the act of turning away from God.

**SAYYADINA:** feminine acolyte in the Fremen religious hierarchy.

**SCHLAG:** animal native to Tupile once hunted almost to extinction for its thin, tough hide.

**SECOND MOON:** the smaller of the two satellites of Arrakis, noteworthy for the kangaroo mouse figure in its surface markings.

**SELAMLIK:** Imperial audience chamber.

**SEMUTA:** the second narcotic derivative (by crystal extraction) from burned residue of elacca wood. The effect (described as timeless, sustained ecstasy) is elicited by certain atonal vibrations referred to as semuta music.

**SERVOK:** clock-set mechanism to perform simple tasks; one of the limited "automatic" devices permitted after the Butlerian Jihad.

**SHAH-NAMA:** the half-legendary First Book of the Zensunni Wanderers.

**SHAI-HULUD:** Sandworm of Arrakis, the "Old Man of the Desert," "Old Father Eternity," and "Grandfather of the Desert." Significantly, this name, when referred to in a certain tone or written with capital letters, designates the earth deity of Fremen hearth superstitions. Sandworms grow to enormous size (specimens longer than 400 meters have been seen in the deep desert) and live to great age unless slain by one of their fellows or drowned in water, which is poisonous to them. Most of the sand on Arrakis is credited to sandworm action. (*See* Little Maker.)

**SHARI-A:** that part of the panoplia propheticus which sets forth the superstitious ritual. (*See* Missionaria Protectiva.)

**SHADOUT:** well-dipper, a Fremen honorific.

**SHAITAN:** Satan.

**SHIELD, DEFENSIVE:** the protective field produced by a Holtzman generator. This field derives from Phase One of the suspensor-nullification effect. A shield will permit entry only to objects moving at slow speeds (depending on setting, this speed ranges from six to nine centimeters per second) and can be shorted out only by a shire-sized electric field. (*See* Lasgun.)

**SHIELD WALL:** a mountainous geographic feature in the northern reaches of Arrakis which protects a small area from the full force of the planet's coriolis storms.

**SHIGAWIRE:** metallic extrusion of a ground vine (*Narvi narviium*) grown only on Salusa Secundus and III Delta Kaising. It is noted for extreme tensile strength.

**SIETCH:** Fremen: "Place of assembly in time of danger." Because the Fremen lived so long in peril, the term came by general usage to designate any cave warren inhabited by one of their tribal communities.

**SIHAYA:** Fremen: the desert springtime with religious overtones implying the time of fruitfulness and "the paradise to come."

**SINK:** a habitable lowland area on Arrakis surrounded by high ground that protects it from the prevailing storms.

**SINKCHART:** map of the Arrakis surface laid out with reference to the most reliable paracompass routes between places of refuge. (*See* Paracompass.)

**SIRAT:** the passage in the O.C. Bible that describes human life as a journey across a narrow bridge (the Sirat) with "Paradise on my right, Hell on my left, and the Angel of Death behind."

**SLIP-TIP:** any thin, short blade (often poison-tipped) for left-hand use in shield fighting.

**SNOOPER, POISON:** radiation analyzer within the olfactory spectrum and keyed to detect poisonous substances.

**SOLARI:** official monetary unit of the Imperium, its purchasing power set at quatricentennial negotiations between the Guild, the Landsraad, and the Emperor.

**SOLIDO:** the three-dimensional image from a solido projector using 360-degree reference signals imprinted on a shigawire reel. Ixian solido projectors are commonly considered the best.

**SONDAGI:** the fern tulip of Tupali.

**SOO-SOO SOOK!:** water-seller's cry on Arrakis. Sook is a market place. (*See* Ikhut-eigh!)

**SPACING GUILD:** *see* Guild.

**SPICE:** *see* Melange.

**SPICE DRIVER:** any Dune man who controls and directs movable machinery on the desert surface of Arrakis.

**SPICE FACTORY:** *see* Sandcrawler.

**SPOTTER CONTROL:** the light ornithopter in a spice-hunting group charged with control of watch and protection.

**STILLSUIT:** body-enclosing garment invented on Arrakis. Its fabric is a micro-sandwich performing functions of heat dissipation and filter for bodily wastes. Reclaimed moisture is made available by tube from catchpockets.

**STILLTENT:** small sealable enclosure of micro-sandwich fabric designed to reclaim as potable water the ambient moisture discharged within it by the breath of its occupants.

**STUNNER:** slow-pellet projectile weapon throwing a poison- or drug-tipped dart. Effectiveness limited by variations in shield settings and relative motion between target and projectile.

**SUBAKH UL KUHAR:** "Are you well?" a Fremen greeting.

**SUBAKH UN NAR:** "I am well. And you?" traditional reply.

**SUSPENSOR:** secondary (low-drain) phase of a Holtzman field generator. It nullifies gravity within certain limits prescribed by relative mass and energy consumption.

**TAHADDI AL-BURHAN:** an ultimate test from which there can be no appeal (usually because it brings death or destruction).

**TAHADDI CHALLENGE:** Fremen challenge to mortal combat, usually to test some primal issue.

**TAQWA:** literally: "The price of freedom." Something of great value. That which a deity demands of a mortal (and the fear provoked by the demand).

**TAU, THE:** in Fremen terminology, that *oneness* of a sietch community enhanced by spice diet and especially the tau orgy of oneness elicited by drinking the Water of Life.

**TEST-MASHAD:** any test in which honor (defined as spiritual standing) is at stake.

**THUMPER:** short stake with spring-driven clapper at one end. The purpose: to be driven into the sand and set "thumping" to summon shai-hulud. (*See* Maker hooks.)

**TIDAL DUST BASIN:** any of the extensive depressions in the surface of Arrakis which have been filled with dust over the centuries and in which actual dust tides (*see* Sandtides) have been measured.

**TLEILAX:** lone planet of Thalim, noted as renegade training center for Mentats; source of "twisted" Mentats.

**T-P:** idiomatic for telepathy.

**TRAINING:** when applied to Bene Gesserit, this otherwise common term assumes special meaning, referring to that conditioning of nerve and muscle (*see* Bindu *and* Prana) which is carried to the last possible notch permitted by natural function.

**TROOP CARRIER:** any Guild ship designed specifically for transport of troops between planets.

**TRUTHSAYER:** a Reverend Mother qualified to enter truthtrance and detect insincerity or falsehood.

**TRUTHTRANCE:** semihypnotic trance induced by one of several "awareness spectrum" narcotics in which the petit betrayals of deliberate falsehood are apparent to the truthtrance observer (Note: "awareness spectrum" narcotics are frequently fatal except to desensitized individuals capable of transforming the poison-configuration within their own bodies.)

**TUPILE:** so-called "sanctuary planet" (probably several planets) for defeated Houses of the Imperium. Location(s) known only to the Guild and maintained inviolate under the Guild Peace.


**ULEMA:** a Zensunni doctor of theology.

**UMMA:** one of the brotherhood of prophets. (A term of scorn in the Imperium, meaning any "wild" person given to fanatical prediction.)

**UROSHNOR:** one of several sounds empty of general meaning and which Bene Gesserit implant within the psyches of selected victims for purposes of control. The sensitized person, hearing the sound, is temporarily immobilized.

**USUL:** Fremen: "The base of the pillar."


**VAROTA:** famed maker of balisets; a native of Chusuk.

**VERITE:** one of the Ecaz will-destroying narcotics. It renders a person incapable of falsehood.

**VOICE:** that combined training originated by the Bene Gesserit which permits an adept to control others merely by selected tone shadings of the voice.

**WALI:** an untried Fremen youth.

**WALLACH IX:** ninth planet of Laoujin, site of the Mother School of the Bene Gesserit.

**WAR OF ASSASSINS:** the limited form of warfare permitted under the Great Convention and the Guild Peace. The aim is to reduce involvement of innocent bystanders. Rules prescribe formal declarations of intent and restrict permissible weapons.

**WATER BURDEN:** Fremen: a mortal obligation.

**WATERCOUNTERS:** metal rings of different size, each designating a specific amount of water payable out of Fremen stores. Watercounters have profound significance (far beyond the idea of money) especially in birth, death, and courtship ritual.

**WATER DISCIPLINE:** that harsh training which fits the inhabitants of Arrakis for existence there without wasting moisture.

**WATERMAN:** a Fremen consecrated for and charged with the ritual duties surrounding water and the Water of Life.

**WATER OF LIFE:** an "illuminating" poison (*see* Reverend Mother). Specifically, that liquid exhalation of a sandworm (*see* Shai-hulud) produced at the moment of its death from drowning which is changed within the body of a Reverend Mother to become the narcotic used in the sietch tau orgy. An "awareness spectrum" narcotic.

**WATERTUBE:** any tube within a stillsuit or stilltent that carries reclaimed water into a catchpocket or from the catchpocket to the wearer.

**WAY, BENE GESSERIT:** use of the minutiae of observation.

**WEATHER SCANNER:** a person trained in the special methods of predicting weather on Arrakis, including ability to pole the sand and read the wind patterns.

**WEIRDING:** idiomatic: that which partakes of the mystical or of witchcraft.

**WINDTRAP:** a device placed in the path of a prevailing wind and capable of precipitating moisture from the air caught within it, usually by a sharp and distinct drop in temperature within the trap.


**YA HYA CHOUHADA:** "Long live the fighters!" The Fedaykin battle cry. Ya (now) in this cry is augmented by the hya form (the ever-extended now). Chouhada (fighters) carries this added meaning of fighters *against* injustice. There is a distinction in this word that specifies the fighters are not struggling *for* anything, but are consecrated *against* a specific thing—that alone.

**YALI:** a Fremen's personal quarters within the sietch.

**YA! YA! YAWM!:** Fremen chanting cadence used in time of deep ritual significance. Ya carries the root meaning of "Now pay attention!" The yawm form is a modified term calling for urgent immediacy. The chant is usually translated as "Now, hear this!"


**ZENSUNNI:** followers of a schismatic sect that broke away from the teachings of Maometh (the so-called "Third Muhammed") about 1381 B.G. The Zensunni religion is noted chiefly for its emphasis on the mystical and a reversion to "the ways of the fathers." Most scholars name Ali Ben Ohashi as leader of the original schism but there is some evidence that Ohashi may have been merely the male spokesman for his second wife, Nisai.

# CARTOGRAPHIC NOTES FOR MAP

**Basis for latitude:** meridian through Observatory Mountain.
**Baseline for altitude determination:** the Great Bled.
**Polar Sink:** 500 m. below Bled level.


**Carthag:** about 200 km. northeast of Arrakeen.
**Cave of Birds:** in Habbanya Ridge.
**Funeral Plain:** open erg.
**Great Bled:** open, flat desert, as opposed to the erg-dune area. Open desert runs from about 60° north to 70° south. It is mostly sand and rock, with occasional outcroppings of basement complex.
**Great Flat:** an open depression of rock blending into erg. It lies about 100 m. above the Bled. Somewhere in the Flat is the salt pan which Pardot Kynes (father of Liet-Kynes) discovered. There are rock outcroppings rising to 200 m. from Sietch Tabr south to the indicated sietch communities.
**Harg Pass:** the Shrine of Leto's skull overlooks this pass.
**Old Gap:** a crevasse in the Arrakeen Shield Wall down to 2240 m.; blasted out by Paul Muad'Dib.
**Palmaries of the South:** do not appear on this map. They lie at about 40° south latitude.
**Red Chasm:** 1582 m. below Bled level.
**Rimwall West:** a high scarp (4600 m.) rising out of the Arrakeen Shield Wall.
**Wind Pass:** cliff-walled, this opens into the sink villages.
**Wormline:** indicating farthest north points where worms have been recorded. (Moisture, not cold, is determining factor).

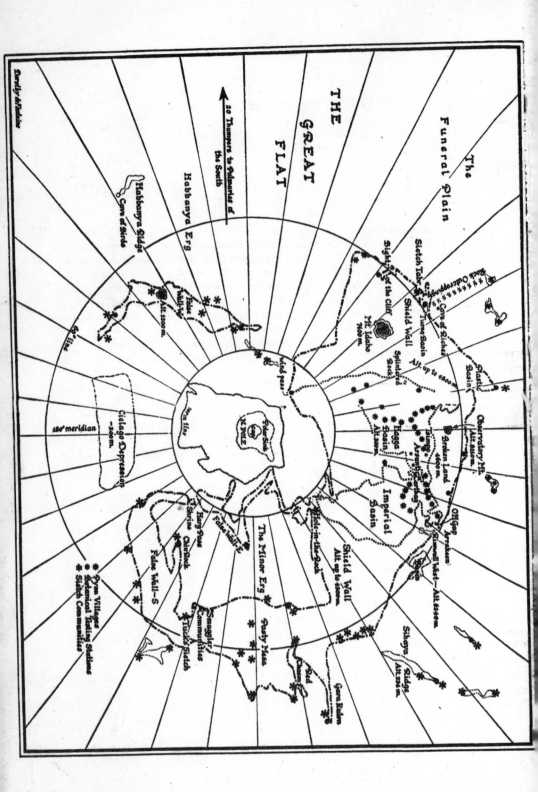